TOM JONES

AN AUTHORITATIVE TEXT

CONTEMPORARY REACTIONS

CRITICISM

W.W. NORTON & COMPANY, INC.
also publishes

THE NORTON ANTHOLOGY OF AMERICAN LITERATURE
edited by Nina Baym et al.

THE NORTON ANTHOLOGY OF ENGLISH LITERATURE
edited by M. H. Abrams et al.

THE NORTON ANTHOLOGY OF LITERATURE BY WOMEN
edited by Sandra M. Gilbert and Susan Gubar

THE NORTON ANTHOLOGY OF MODERN POETRY
edited by Richard Ellmann and Robert O'Clair

THE NORTON ANTHOLOGY OF POETRY
edited by Alexander W. Allison et al.

THE NORTON ANTHOLOGY OF SHORT FICTION
edited by R. V. Cassill

THE NORTON ANTHOLOGY OF WORLD MASTERPIECES
edited by Maynard Mack et al.

THE NORTON FACSIMILE OF
THE FIRST FOLIO OF SHAKESPEARE
prepared by Charlton Hinman

THE NORTON INTRODUCTION TO LITERATURE
edited by Carl E. Bain, Jerome Beaty, and J. Paul Hunter

THE NORTON INTRODUCTION TO THE SHORT NOVEL
edited by Jerome Beaty

THE NORTON READER
edited by Arthur M. Eastman et al.

THE NORTON SAMPLER
edited by Thomas Cooley

A NORTON CRITICAL EDITION

HENRY FIELDING

TOM JONES

AN AUTHORITATIVE TEXT
CONTEMPORARY REACTIONS
CRITICISM

Edited by

SHERIDAN BAKER

THE UNIVERSITY OF MICHIGAN

W · W · NORTON & COMPANY

New York · London

W. W. Norton & Company, Inc., 500 Fifth Avenue, New York, N.Y. 10110

Copyright © 1973 by W. W. Norton & Company, Inc.

Library of Congress Cataloging in Publication Data
Fielding, Henry, 1707–1754.
   Tom Jones: an authoritative text.

   (A Norton critical edition)
   Bibliography: p.
   I. Baker, Sheridan Warner, 1918–   comp.
II. Title.
PZ3.F46To3 [PR3454]   823'.5   72-7320
ISBN 0-393-04359-2
ISBN 0-393-09494-8 pbk.

1 2 3 4 5 6 7 8 9 0

Contents

Preface

Tom Jones, in 1749, was an immediate success. It dropped from sight for a while in the nineteenth century, when Victorian elegance passed it under the table as too coarse for the ladies. But in the 1880's, Fielding's novels began to reappear, in handsome editions. Now the twentieth century has reclaimed *Tom Jones* completely, crowning its recognition in the twentieth-century way, with a motion picture, and certainly one of the best ever made from a novel.

Actually, Fielding is somewhat off the twentieth century's beat. In spite of our many comics, we are not really attuned to comedy, especially to Fielding's amused distancing of life's ups and downs. We are not used to observing life from the outside. We want the inside story, the hidden streams of consciousness. And we are no longer disposed, as George Eliot remarked a century ago, to take time for Fielding's sociability.

Nevertheless, *Tom Jones* prevails. It draws together the forces of its time, just before they diffused in other and soggier directions. It culminates Fielding's new species of comic philosophical realism, evolved through two decades as playwright, essayist, pamphleteer, and, finally, lawyer. It universalizes the contemporary English scene, in part by putting behind it the learning of the ages. It makes the English novel thoroughly literate for the first time. It marries comedy and romance, by the grace of the classics, to produce a peculiarly fresh and ironic wisdom.

Tom Jones is a comic romance, in spite of its epic dimensions. Across the tops of its pages, lest we forget, marches not "The History of Tom Jones" but *"The* HISTORY *of a* FOUNDLING." Our hero is of unknown and mysterious origin. Rendered comic and swathed in lenient irony, this is the quintessential tale of romance, the oldest story in the world—that of an unknown but excellent nobody who becomes somebody at last. Tom Jones is young Mr. Commoner Everyone, representing the mythic mystery of everyone's birth, of everyone's natural nobility (at least in his own dear eyes), of everyone's search for identity.

Not that Tom cares, or thinks of himself. But the reader, true to the ways of romance, vicariously fulfills what may be his deepest psychic need, to find his identity, and with it the dream of recognition, riches, and the beautiful princess. His personal excellence is rewarded, having survived all tests by the world's ogres. And all the while, Fielding's unique comic irony silently tells us that we really cannot have our cake and eat it, that even as we enjoy the dream we know it cannot last.

Readers have responded to the essential powers of *Tom Jones* from the first, and have repeatedly tried to describe its unusual quality. It seems both simple and complex, and it has left some readers baffled, and bored, and angry. The reactions of Fielding's contemporaries, here selected and appended, will convey some sense of this, and the critical essays will suggest how persistently *Tom Jones* has teased us into thought. It has moved the critics to the most fundamental of literary questions—the meaning of plot and characterization, of art and artistry, of comedy, of irony, of style, of how and what literature really means, after all, as it relates its fictions to us.

This present text follows Andrew Millar's fourth and last printing of *Tom Jones* during Fielding's life, dated 1750 but published 11 December 1749. Unfortunately, early scholars backed the slightly shortened and imperfect third edition as definitive (see Textual Appendix, p. 763), and several modern editions have followed suit. But the fourth edition presents the best text, not only in its corrections of many small errors, but in representing Fielding's fullest and final intention. The present edition reproduces the fourth edition in every detail, except that it emends typographical errors (footnoted in the text when significant); modernizes the long eighteenth-century *s*, which looks like an *f* to modern eyes; and deletes the quotation marks that head every line of a long speech in eighteenth-century texts. I have not normalized alternate spellings (*Kitchen* for *Kitchin*, *Pettyfogger* for *Petty-fogger*, for example) since they may reflect Fielding's own inconsistencies.

My annotations, as all must, owe a primary and pervasive debt to Wilbur L. Cross, *The History of Henry Fielding*, 3 vols. (New Haven: Yale University Press, 1918). The first annotated edition, the Shakespeare Head *Tom Jones* (Oxford: Clarendon Press, 1926), which, regrettably, followed the third edition, identified a modest number of quotations and allusions. Virginia M. Bryant added considerably to that number in her unpublished dissertation, "The Literary and Philosophical Background of *Tom Jones*" (University of Cincinnati, 1940). In his Penguin edition (1966), R. P. C. Mutter, independently of Miss Bryant, annotated even more thoroughly. Their work has saved untold hours of searching, but I have managed to correct a few of their details of identification, and to add some discoveries of my own.

SHERIDAN BAKER

The Text of
Tom Jones

THE
HISTORY
OF
TOM JONES,
A
FOUNDLING.

IN FOUR VOLUMES.

By HENRY FIELDING, Esq;

—— *Mores hominum multorum vidit* ——

LONDON:

Printed for A. MILLAR, over-against
Catharine-street in the *Strand.*

M.DCC.L.

Note

The title-page of *Tom Jones,* fourth edition, on the preceding page is re-produced in exact size from the copy owned by the Beinecke Library, Yale University, which copy also provides the text for the present edition. The editor wishes to express his gratitude to the Beinecke Library and its staff for their permission and generous cooperation.

The title-pages of the other three volumes that make up the fourth edi-tion are identical with this, which heads volume one, except that each volume's number—"VOL. II.," for instance—replaces the words "IN FOUR VOLUMES."

Fielding's motto comes from Horace, who is paraphrasing the opening of the *Odyssey* (I. 1–3) in his *Ars Poetica,* 141–42:

> Dic mihi, Musa, virum captae post tempora Trojae
> Qui mores hominum multorum vidit et urbes.

"Tell me, Muse, of the man who, after the times of captured Troy, saw the customs of many men, and their cities" (all translations are the editor's, unless otherwise noted). Fielding, perhaps with a touch of irony, thus casts Tom Jones as something of a young and modern Odysseus, discovering the ways of the world as he wanders to find his proper home.

Horace's couplet is actually a prominent example in William Lily's *Grammar* (1723–24 ed., p. 71), from which Fielding learned his Latin at Eton—it was the standard textbook throughout England for more than three centuries, beginning with its publication in 1527, four years after Lily's death. Many of Fielding's Latin quotations are among Lily's examples, especially those of Partridge, the schoolmaster, which Fielding's readers would recognize with amusement.

To the HONORABLE

George Lyttleton, *Esq;*[1]

One of the Lords Commissioners of the TREASURY.

Sir,

Notwithstanding your constant Refusal, when I have asked Leave to prefix your Name to this Dedication, I must still insist on my Right to desire your Protection of this Work.

To you, Sir, it is owing that this History was ever begun. It was by your Desire that I first thought of such a Composition. So many Years have since past, that you may have, perhaps, forgotten this Circumstance: But your Desires are to me in the Nature of Commands; and the Impression of them is never to be erased from my Memory.

Again, Sir, without your Assistance this History had never been completed. Be not startled at the Assertion. I do not intend to draw on you the Suspicion of being a Romance Writer. I mean no more than that I partly owe to you my Existence during great Part of the Time which I have employed in composing it: another Matter which it may be necessary to remind you of; since there are certain Actions of which you are apt to be extremely forgetful; but of these I hope I shall always have a better Memory than yourself.

Lastly, it is owing to you that the History appears what it now is. If there be in this Work, as some have been pleased to say, a stronger Picture of a truly benevolent Mind than is to be found in any other, who that knows you, and a particular Acquaintance[2] of yours, will doubt whence that Benevolence hath been copied? The World will not, I believe, make me the Compliment of thinking I

1. George, Lord Lyttelton (1709–73), Fielding's classmate at Eton, Member of Parliament, Lord Commissioner of the Treasury (1744–54), minor essayist and poet, supported Fielding with several gifts of money during the writing of *Tom Jones* and prompted Fielding's appointment as Justice of the Peace for Westminster, in London (soon extended to include the county of Middlesex), on 25 Oct. 1748. One of the models for Squire Allworthy. "Lyttelton" was a frequent misspelling of Lyttelton's name, which remains misspelled in all four editions of *Tom Jones*.
2. Ralph Allen, postmaster of Bath, who had made a fortune (about £12,000 a year) by organizing a rural postal service and whose generosity to Fielding began shortly before *Joseph Andrews* appeared in 1742 and continued after Fielding's death in gifts to his family. The principal model for Allworthy.

took it from myself. I care not: This they shall own, that the two Persons from whom I have taken it, that is to say, two of the best and worthiest Men in the World, are strongly and zealously my Friends. I might be contented with this, and yet my Vanity will add a third to the Number; and him one of the greatest and noblest, not only in his Rank, but in every public and private Virtue. But here whilst my Gratitude for the princely Benefactions of the Duke of *Bedford*[3] bursts from my Heart, you must forgive my reminding you, that it was you who first recommended me to the Notice of my Benefactor.

And what are your Objections to the Allowance of the Honour which I have sollicited? Why, you have commended the Book so warmly, that you should be ashamed of reading your Name before the Dedication. Indeed, Sir, if the Book itself doth not make you ashamed of your Commendations, nothing that I can here write will, or ought. I am not to give up my Right to your Protection and Patronage, because you have commended my Book: For though I acknowledge so many Obligations to you, I do not add this to the Number; in which Friendship, I am convinced, hath so little Share: Since that can neither biass your Judgment, nor pervert your Integrity. An Enemy may at any Time obtain your Commendation by only deserving it; and the utmost which the Faults of your Friends can hope for is your Silence; or, perhaps, if too severely accused, your gentle Palliation.

In short, Sir, I suspect, that your Dislike of public Praise is your true Objection to granting my Request. I have observed, that you have, in common with my two other Friends, an Unwillingness to hear the least Mention of your own Virtues; that, as a great Poet says of one of you, (he might justly have said it of all three) you

Do Good by stealth, and blush to find it Fame.[4]

If Men of this Disposition are as careful to shun Applause, as others are to escape Censure, how just must be your Apprehension of your Character falling into my Hands; since what would not a Man have Reason to dread, if attacked by an Author who had received from him Injuries equal to my Obligations to you!

And will not this Dread of Censure increase in Proportion to the

3. At Lyttelton's suggestion, Bedford had arranged for Fielding's commission as Justice of the Peace for the City of Westminster, in central London, and, six months later, had assigned him a lease on "several leasehold messuages and tenements" so that Fielding could qualify as Justice of the Peace for the County of Middlesex. A county magistrate was required to have property worth £100, for which sum the rental value of Fielding's lease was sufficient (Cross II.96–98).

4. Alexander Pope, referring to Ralph Allen, in *Epilogue to the Satires of Horace* 136.

Matter which a Man is conscious of having afforded for it? If his whole Life, for Instance, should have been one continued Subject of Satire, he may well tremble when an incensed Satirist takes him in Hand. Now, Sir, if we apply this to your modest Aversion to Panegyric, how reasonable will your Fears of me appear!

Yet surely you might have gratified my Ambition, from this single Confidence, that I shall always prefer the Indulgence of your Inclinations to the Satisfaction of my own. A very strong Instance of which I shall give you in this Address; in which I am determined to follow the Example of all other Dedicators, and will consider not what my Patron really deserves to have written, but what he will be best pleased to read.

Without further Preface then, I here present you with the Labours of some Years of my Life. What Merit these Labours have is already known to yourself. If, from your favourable Judgment, I have conceived some Esteem for them, it cannot be imputed to Vanity; since I should have agreed as implicitly to your Opinion, had it been given in Favour of any other Man's Production. Negatively, at least, I may be allowed to say, that had I been sensible of any great Demerit in the Work, you are the last Person to whose Protection I would have ventured to recommend it.

From the Name of my Patron, indeed, I hope my Reader will be convinced, at his very Entrance on this Work, that he will find in the whole Course of it nothing prejudicial to the Cause of Religion and Virtue; nothing inconsistent with the strictest Rules of Decency, nor which can offend even the chastest Eye in the Perusal. On the contrary, I declare, that to recommend Goodness and Innocence hath been my sincere Endeavour in this History. This honest Purpose you have been pleased to think I have attained: And to say the Truth, it is likeliest to be attained in Books of this Kind; for an Example is a Kind of Picture, in which Virtue becomes as it were an Object of Sight, and strikes us with an Idea of that Loveliness, which *Plato* asserts there is in her naked Charms.[5]

5. Fielding's imagination has added "naked" to Cicero's misquotation of "a short sentence of Plato, which I have often seen quoted" (*The Champion*, 24 Jan. 1740)—probably in Sidney's *Apology for Poetry*: "if the saying of Plato and Tully be true, that who could see virtue would be wonderfully ravished with the love of her beauty." Plato, however, says: "But we cannot see *Wisdom* with the eyes [as we can Beauty] —how passionately would we have desired her, if she had granted such a clear image of herself to gaze on" (*Phaedrus* 250D; my italics). Cicero paraphrases this "as Plato says," in *De Finibus Bonorum et Malorum* (II.xvi.52— see below, p. 778); but in *De Officiis* (I.v.15) he shifts to *Virtue*, which Sidney, and then Fielding, have picked up: ". . . the very face, as it were, of Virtue herself, which, if the eyes could see, as Plato says, would excite a most wonderful passion for Wisdom." Fielding later equates virtue and wisdom (below, p. 601). See also Battestin's note, below, p. 832.

Besides displaying that Beauty of Virtue which may attract the Admiration of Mankind, I have attempted to engage a stronger Motive to Human Action in her Favour, by convincing Men, that their true Interest directs them to a Pursuit of her. For this Purpose I have shewn, that no Acquisitions of Guilt can compensate the Loss of that solid inward Comfort of Mind, which is the sure Companion of Innocence and Virtue; nor can in the least balance the Evil of that Horror and Anxiety which, in their Room, Guilt introduces into our Bosoms. And again, that as these Acquisitions are in themselves generally worthless, so are the Means to attain them not only base and infamous, but at best incertain, and always full of Danger. Lastly, I have endeavoured strongly to inculcate, that Virtue and Innocence can scarce ever be injured but by Indiscretion; and that it is this alone which often betrays them into the Snares that Deceit and Villainy spread for them. A Moral which I have the more industriously laboured, as the teaching it is, of all others, the likeliest to be attended with Success; since, I believe, it is much easier to make good Men wise, than to make bad Men good.

For these Purposes I have employed all the Wit and Humour of which I am Master in the following History; wherein I have endeavoured to laugh Mankind out of their favourite Follies and Vices. How far I have succeeded in this good Attempt, I shall submit to the candid Reader, with only two Requests: First, That he will not expect to find Perfection in this Work; and Secondly, That he will excuse some Parts of it, if they fall short of that little Merit which I hope may appear in others.

I will detain you, Sir, no longer. Indeed I have run into a Preface, while I professed to write a Dedication. But how can it be otherwise? I dare not praise you; and the only Means I know of to avoid it, when you are in my Thoughts, are either to be entirely silent, or to turn my Thoughts to some other Subject.

Pardon, therefore, what I have said in this Epistle, not only without your Consent, but absolutely against it; and give me at least Leave, in this public Manner, to declare, that I am, with the highest Respect and Gratitude,

SIR,

Your most Obliged,

Obedient Humble Servant,

HENRY FIELDING

Contents of Tom Jones

BOOK I.

Containing as much of the Birth of the Foundling as is necessary or proper to acquaint the Reader with in the Beginning of this History.

BOOK II.

Containing Scenes of matrimonial Felicity in different Degrees of Life; and various other Transactions during the first two Years after the Marriage between Captain Blifil *and Miss* Bridget Allworthy.

BOOK III.

BOOK V.

Containing a Portion of Time, somewhat longer than Half a Year.

BOOK VII.

Containing three Days.

BOOK VIII.

Containing about two Days.

BOOK IX.

Containing twelve Hours.

BOOK X.

In which the History goes forward about Twelve Hours.

BOOK XI.

Containing about three Days.

BOOK XIII.

Containing the Space of Twelve Days.

BOOK XVI.

Containing the Space of Five Days.

BOOK XVII.

Containing three Days.

BOOK XVIII.

Containing about Six Days.

Chapter III.

Chapter IV.

Chapter V.

Chapter VI.

Chapter VII.

Chapter VIII.

Chapter IX.

Chapter X.

Chapter XI.

Chapter XII.

Chapter the last.

The History of a Foundling

BOOK I.

Containing as much of the Birth of the Foundling as is necessary or proper to acquaint the Reader with in the Beginning of this History.

Chapter I.

The Introduction to the Work, or Bill of Fare to the Feast.

An Author ought to consider himself, not as a Gentleman who gives a private or eleemosynary Treat, but rather as one who keeps a public Ordinary, at which all Persons are welcome for their Money. In the former Case, it is well known, that the Entertainer provides what Fare he pleases; and tho' this should be very indifferent, and utterly disagreeable to the Taste of his Company, they must not find any Fault; nay, on the contrary, Good-Breeding forces them outwardly to approve and to commend whatever is set before them. Now the contrary of this happens to the Master of an Ordinary. Men who pay for what they eat, will insist on gratifying their Palates, however nice and whimsical these may prove; and if every Thing is not agreeable to their Taste, will challenge a Right to censure, to abuse, and to d——n their Dinner without Controul.

To prevent therefore giving Offence to their Customers by any such Disappointment, it hath been usual, with the honest and well-meaning Host, to provide a Bill of Fare, which all Persons may peruse at their first Entrance into the House; and, having thence acquainted themselves with the Entertainment which they may expect, may either stay and regale with what is provided for them, or may depart to some other Ordinary better accommodated to their Taste.

As we do not disdain to borrow Wit or Wisdom from any Man who is capable of lending us either, we have condescended to take a Hint from these honest Victuallers, and shall prefix not only a general Bill of Fare to our whole Entertainment, but shall likewise give the Reader particular Bills to every Course which is to be served up in this and the ensuing Volumes.

The Provision then which we have here made is no other than HUMAN NATURE. Nor do I fear that my sensible Reader, though most luxurious in his Taste, will start, cavil, or be offended, because I have named but one Article. The Tortoise, as the Alderman of *Bristol*, well learned in eating, knows by much Experience, besides the delicious *Calipash* and *Calipee*,[1] contains many different kinds of Food; nor can the learned Reader be ignorant, that in *Human Nature*, tho' here collected under one general Name, is such prodigious Variety, that a Cook will have sooner gone through all the several Species of animal and vegetable Food in the World, than an Author will be able to exhaust so extensive a Subject.

An Objection may perhaps be apprehended from the more delicate, that this Dish is too common and vulgar; for what else is the Subject of all the Romances, Novels, Plays and Poems, with which the Stalls abound? Many exquisite Viands might be rejected by the Epicure, if it was a sufficient Cause for his contemning of them as common and vulgar, that something was to be found in the most paultry Alleys under the same Name. In reality, true Nature is as difficult to be met with in Authors, as the *Bayonne* Ham or *Bologna* Sausage is to be found in the Shops.

But the whole, to continue the same Metaphor, consists in the Cookery of the Author; for, as Mr. *Pope* tells us,

> True Wit is Nature to Advantage drest,
> What oft' was thought, but ne'er so well exprest.[2]

The same Animal which hath the Honour to have some Part of his Flesh eaten at the Table of a Duke, may perhaps be degraded in another Part, and some of his Limbs gibbeted, as it were, in the vilest Stall in Town. Where then lies the Difference between the Food of the Nobleman and the Porter, if both are at Dinner on the same Ox or Calf, but in the seasoning, the dressing, the garnishing, and the setting forth? Hence the one provokes and incites the most languid Appetite, and the other turns and palls that which is the sharpest and keenest.

In like manner, the Excellence of the mental Entertainment consists less in the Subject, than in the Author's Skill in well dressing it up. How pleased therefore will the Reader be to find, that we have, in the following Work, adhered closely to one of the highest Principles of the best Cook which the present Age, or perhaps that of *Heliogabalus*,[3] hath produced? This great Man, as is well known to all Lovers of polite eating, begins at first by setting plain Things

---

1. Gelatinous substance near the upper and the lower shells of a turtle, respectively; customary at the annual banquets of the aldermen of Bristol. In all four editions, *Calipash* reads, incorrectly, *Calibash*, probably as Fielding himself mistook the word.

2. *An Essay on Criticism* 297–98.
3. Roman emperor, A.D. 218–22. He was also a priest of the Syrian sun-god whose name he assumed, performing lavish public ceremonies in his honor, for which sumptuousness he had become proverbial in Fielding's time.

before his hungry Guests, rising afterwards by Degrees, as their Stomachs may be supposed to decrease, to the very Quintessence of Sauce and Spices. In like manner, we shall represent Human Nature at first to the keen Appetite of our Reader, in that more plain and simple Manner in which it is found in the Country, and shall hereafter hash and ragoo it with all the high *French* and *Italian* Seasoning of Affectation and Vice which Courts and Cities afford. By these Means, we doubt not but our Reader may be rendered desirous to read on for ever, as the great Person, just above-mentioned, is supposed to have made some Persons eat.

Having premised thus much, we will now detain those, who like our Bill of Fare, no longer from their Diet, and shall proceed directly to serve up the first Course of our History, for their Entertainment.

Chapter II.

A short Description of Squire Allworthy, *and a fuller Account of* Miss Bridget Allworthy *his Sister.*

In that Part of the western Division of this Kingdom, which is commonly called *Somersetshire*, there lately lived (and perhaps lives still) a Gentleman whose Name was Allworthy, and who might well be called the Favourite of both Nature and Fortune; for both of these seem to have contended which should bless and enrich him most. In this Contention, Nature may seem to some to have come off victorious, as she bestowed on him many Gifts; while Fortune had only one Gift in her Power; but in pouring forth this, she was so very profuse, that others perhaps may think this single Endowment to have been more than equivalent to all the various Blessings which he enjoyed from Nature. From the former of these, he derived an agreeable Person, a sound Constitution, a solid Understanding, and a benevolent Heart; by the latter, he was decreed to the Inheritance of one of the largest Estates in the County.

This Gentleman had, in his Youth, married a very worthy and beautiful Woman, of whom he had been extremely fond: By her he had three Children, all of whom died in their Infancy. He had likewise had the Misfortune of burying this beloved Wife herself, about five Years before the Time in which this History chuses to set out. This Loss, however great, he bore like a Man of Sense and Constancy; tho' it must be confest, he would often talk a little whimsically on this Head: For he sometimes said, he looked on himself as still married, and considered his Wife as only gone a little before him a Journey which he should most certainly, sooner or later, take after her; and that he had not the least Doubt of meeting her again, in a Place where he should never part with her more. Sentiments for which his Sense was arraigned by one Part of his Neighbours, his Religion by a second, and his Sincerity by a third.

He now lived, for the most Part, retired in the Country, with one Sister, for whom he had a very tender Affection. This Lady was now somewhat past the Age of 30, an Æra, at which, in the Opinion of the Malicious, the Title of Old Maid may, with no Impropriety, be assumed. She was of that Species of Women, whom you commend rather for good Qualities than Beauty, and who are generally called by their own Sex, very good Sort of Women—as good a Sort of Woman, Madam, as you would wish to know. Indeed she was so far from regretting Want of Beauty, that she never mentioned that Perfection (if it can be called one) without Contempt; and would often thank God she was not as handsome as Miss such a one, whom perhaps Beauty had led into Errors, which she might have otherwise avoided. Miss *Bridget Allworthy* (for that was the Name of this Lady) very rightly conceived the Charms of Person in a Woman to be no better than Snares for herself, as well as for others; and yet so discreet was she in her Conduct, that her Prudence was as much on the Guard, as if she had all the Snares to apprehend which were ever laid for her whole Sex. Indeed, I have observed (tho' it may seem unaccountable to the Reader) that this Guard of Prudence, like the Trained Bands,[1] is always readiest to go on Duty where there is the least Danger. It often basely and cowardly deserts those Paragons for whom the Men are all wishing, sighing, dying, and spreading every Net in their Power; and constantly attends at the Heels of that higher Order of Women, for whom the other Sex have a more distant and awful Respect, and whom (from Despair, I suppose, of Success) they never venture to attack.

Reader, I think proper, before we proceed any farther together, to acquaint thee, that I intend to digress, through this whole History, as often as I see Occasion: Of which I am myself a better Judge than any pitiful Critic whatever. And here I must desire all those Critics to mind their own Business, and not to intermeddle with Affairs, or Works, which no ways concern them: For, till they produce the Authority by which they are constituted Judges, I shall [not][2] plead to their Jurisdiction.

Chapter III.

An odd Accident which befel Mr. Allworthy, at his Return home. The decent Behaviour of Mrs. Deborah Wilkins, with some proper Animadversions on Bastards.

I have told my Reader, in the preceding Chapter, that Mr. *All-*

1. Citizens trained as a military reserve —notoriously inefficient.
2. Either Fielding misspeaks himself, or the printer has inadvertently dropped a "not," an error repeated in all four editions.

worthy inherited a large Fortune; that he had a good Heart, and no Family. Hence, doubtless, it will be concluded by many, that he lived like an honest Man, owed no one a Shilling, took nothing but what was his own, kept a good House, entertained his Neighbours with a hearty Welcome at his Table, and was charitable to the Poor, *i.e.* to those who had rather beg than work, by giving them the Offals from it; that he died immensely rich, and built an Hospital.

And true it is, that he did many of these Things; but, had he done nothing more, I should have left him to have recorded his own Merit on some fair Free-Stone over the Door of that Hospital. Matters of a much more extraordinary Kind are to be the Subject of this History, or I should grossly mispend my Time in writing so voluminous a Work; and you, my sagacious Friend, might, with equal Profit and Pleasure, travel through some Pages, which certain droll Authors have been facetiously pleased to call *The History of England*.[1]

Mr. *Allworthy* had been absent a full Quarter of a Year in *London*, on some very particular Business, though I know not what it was; but judge of its Importance, by its having detained him so long from home, whence he had not been absent a Month at a Time during the Space of many Years. He came to his House very late in the Evening, and after a short Supper with his Sister, retired much fatigued to his Chamber. Here, having spent some Minutes on his Knees, a Custom which he never broke through on any Account, he was preparing to step into Bed, when, upon opening the Cloaths, to his great Surprize, he beheld an Infant, wrapt up in some coarse Linen, in a sweet and profound Sleep, between his Sheets. He stood some Time lost in Astonishment at this Sight; but, as Good-nature had always the Ascendant in his Mind, he soon began to be touched with Sentiments of Compassion for the little Wretch before him. He then rang his Bell, and ordered an elderly Woman Servant to rise immediately and come to him, and in the mean Time was so eager in contemplating the Beauty of Innocence, appearing in those lively Colours with which Infancy and Sleep always display it, that his Thoughts were too much engaged to reflect that he was in his Shirt, when the Matron came in. She had indeed given her Master sufficient Time to dress himself; for out of Respect to him, and Regard to Decency, she had spent many Minutes in adjusting her Hair at the Looking-glass, notwithstanding all the Hurry in which she had been summoned by the Servant, and

1. Laurence Echard and Paul de Rapin both wrote books of this name from opposite political points of view (see *Joseph Andrews* III.i). Rapin and Echard are among Mrs. Western's authorities (below, p. 207). Fielding also ridicules the dullness of John Oldmixon's *The Critical History of England* (1724–26) on p. 161, below. Fielding again ridicules Oldmixon in *The Covent-Garden Journal*, no. 3, 11 Jan. 1752, and parodies his attacks on Echard in no. 17, 29 Jan. 1752. See Pat Rogers, "Fielding's Parody of Oldmixon," *Philological Quarterly*, 49 (1970), 262–66.

tho' her Master, for ought she knew, lay expiring in an Apoplexy or in some other Fit.

It will not be wondered at, that a Creature, who had so strict a Regard to Decency in her own Person, should be shocked at the least Deviation from it in another. She therefore no sooner opened the Door, and saw her Master standing by the Bed-side in his Shirt, with a Candle in his Hand, than she started back in a most terrible Fright, and might perhaps have swooned away, had he not now recollected his being undrest, and put an End to her Terrors, by desiring her to stay without the Door, till he had thrown some Cloaths over his Back, and was become incapable of shocking the pure Eyes of Mrs.[2] *Deborah Wilkins*, who, tho' in the 52d Year of her Age, vowed she had never beheld a Man without his Coat. Sneerers and prophane Wits may perhaps laugh at her first Fright; yet my graver Reader, when he considers the Time of Night, the Summons from her Bed, and the Situation in which she found her Master, will highly justify and applaud her Conduct; unless the Prudence, which must be supposed to attend Maidens at that Period of Life at which Mrs. *Deborah* had arrived, should a little lessen his Admiration.

When Mrs. *Deborah* returned into the Room, and was acquainted by her Master with the finding the little Infant, her Consternation was rather greater than his had been; nor could she refrain from crying out, with great Horror of Accent as well as Look, 'My good Sir! what's to be done?' Mr. *Allworthy* answered, She must take Care of the Child that Evening, and in the Morning he would give Orders to provide it a Nurse. 'Yes, Sir,' says she, 'and I hope your Worship will send out your Warrant to take up the Hussy its Mother (for she must be one of the Neighbourhood) and I should be glad to see her committed to *Bridewel*, and whipt at the Cart's Tail. Indeed such wicked Sluts cannot be too severely punished. I'll warrant 'tis not her first, by her Impudence in laying it to your Worship.' 'In laying it to me! *Deborah*,' answered *Allworthy*, 'I can't think she hath any such Design. I suppose she hath only taken this Method to provide for her Child; and truly I am glad she hath not done worse.' 'I don't know what is worse,' cries *Deborah*, 'than for such wicked Strumpets to lay their Sins at honest Mens Doors; and though your Worship knows your own Innocence, yet the World is censorious; and it hath been many an honest Man's Hap to pass for the Father of Children he never begot; and if your Worship should provide for the Child, it may make the People the apter to believe: Besides, why should your Worship provide for what the Parish is obliged to maintain? For my own Part, if it was an honest Man's Child indeed; but for my own Part, it goes against me to touch these misbegotten Wretches, whom I don't look upon as my fellow Creatures. Faugh, how it stinks! <u>It doth not smell like a Christian.</u> If I might be so bold to give my Advice, I would have it put in a Basket, and sent out and laid at the Church-Warden's Door. It is a good Night, only a little rainy and windy; and if it was well wrapt up, and put in a warm Basket, it is two to one but it lives, till it is found in the Morning. But if it should not, we have discharged our Duty in taking proper Care of it; and it is, perhaps, better for such Creatures to die in a State of Innocence, than to grow up and imitate their Mothers; for nothing better can be expected of them.'

There were some Strokes in this Speech which, perhaps, would have offended Mr. *Allworthy,* had he strictly attended to it; but he had now got one of his Fingers into the Infant's Hand, which, by its gentle Pressure, seeming to implore his Assistance, had certainly out-pleaded the Eloquence of Mrs. *Deborah,* had it been ten times greater than it was. He now gave Mrs. *Deborah* positive Orders to take the Child to her own Bed, and to call up a Maid-servant to provide it Pap, and other Things against it waked. He likewise ordered that proper Cloaths should be procured for it early in the Morning, and that it should be brought to himself as soon as he was stirring.

Such was the Discernment of Mrs. *Wilkins,* and such the Respect she bore her Master, under whom she enjoyed a most excellent Place, that her Scruples gave Way to his peremptory Commands; and she took the Child under her Arms, without any apparent Disgust at the Illegality of its Birth; and declaring it was a sweet little Infant, walked off with it to her own Chamber.

Allworthy here betook himself to those pleasing Slumbers which a Heart that hungers after Goodness is apt to enjoy when thoroughly satisfied: As these are possibly sweeter than what are occasioned by any other hearty Meal, I should take more Pains to display them to the Reader, if I knew any Air to recommend him to for the procuring such an Appetite.

Chapter IV.

The Reader's Neck brought into Danger by a Description; his Escape, and the great Condescension of Miss Bridget Allworthy.

The *Gothic* Stile of Building could produce nothing nobler than Mr. *Allworthy's* House. There was an Air of Grandeur in it, that struck you with Awe, and rival'd the Beauties of the best *Grecian* Architecture; and it was as commodious within, as venerable without.

It stood on the South-east Side of a Hill, but nearer the Bottom than the Top of it, so as to be sheltered from the North-east by a Grove of old Oaks, which rose above it in a gradual Ascent of near half a Mile, and yet high enough to enjoy a most charming Prospect of the Valley beneath.

In the midst of the Grove was a fine Lawn, sloping down towards the House, near the Summit of which rose a plentiful Spring, gushing out of a Rock covered with Firs, and forming a constant Cascade of about thirty Foot, not carried down a regular Flight of Steps, but tumbling in a natural Fall over the broken and mossy Stones, till it came to the Bottom of the Rock; then running off in a pebly Channel, that with many lesser Falls winded along, till it fell into a Lake at the Foot of the Hill, about a Quarter of a Mile below the House on the South-side, and which was seen from every Room in the Front. Out of this Lake, which filled the Center of a beautiful Plain, embellished with Groupes of Beeches and Elms, and fed with Sheep, issued a River, that, for several Miles, was seen to meander through an amazing Variety of Meadows and Woods, till it emptied itself into the Sea; with a large Arm of which, and an Island beyond it, the Prospect was closed.

On the Right of this Valley opened another of less Extent, adorned with several Villages, and terminated by one of the Towers of an old ruined Abbey, grown over with Ivy, and Part of the Front, which remained still entire.

The Left Hand Scene presented the View of a very fine Park, composed of very unequal Ground, and agreeably varied with all the Diversity that Hills, Lawns, Wood, and Water, laid out with admirable Taste, but owing less to Art than to Nature, could give. Beyond this the Country gradually rose into a Ridge of wild Mountains, the Tops of which were above the Clouds.

It was now the Middle of *May*, and the Morning was remarkably serene, when Mr. *Allworthy* walked forth on the Terrace, where the Dawn opened every Minute that lovely Prospect we have before described to his Eye. And now having sent forth Streams of Light, which ascended the blue Firmament before him, as Harbingers preceding his Pomp, in the full Blaze of his Majesty up rose the Sun; than which one Object alone in this lower Creation could be more glorious, and that Mr. *Allworthy* himself presented; a human Being replete with Benevolence, meditating in what Manner he might render himself most acceptable to his Creator, by doing most Good to his Creatures.

Reader, take Care, I have unadvisedly led thee to the Top of as high a Hill as Mr. *Allworthy*'s, and how to get thee down without breaking thy Neck, I do not well know. However, let us e'en venture to slide down together; for Miss *Bridget* rings her Bell, and Mr.

Allworthy is summoned to Breakfast, where I must attend, and, if you please, shall be glad of your Company.

The usual Compliments having past between Mr. *Allworthy* and Miss *Bridget*, and the Tea being poured out, he summoned Mrs. *Wilkins*, and told his Sister he had a Present for her; for which she thanked him, imagining, I suppose, it had been a Gown, or some Ornament for her Person. Indeed, he very often made her such Presents; and she, in Complacence to him, spent much Time in adorning herself. I say, in Complacence to him, because she always exprest the greatest Contempt for Dress, and for those Ladies who made it their Study.

But if such was her Expectation, how was she disappointed, when Mrs. *Wilkins*, according to the Order she had received from her Master, produced the little Infant! Great Surprizes, as hath been observed, are apt to be silent; and so was Miss *Bridget*, 'till her Brother began, and told her the whole Story, which, as the Reader knows it already, we shall not repeat.

Miss *Bridget* had always exprest so great a Regard for what the Ladies are pleased to call Virtue, and had herself maintained such a Severity of Character, that it was expected, especially by *Wilkins*, that she would have vented much Bitterness on this Occasion, and would have voted for sending the Child, as a kind of noxious Animal, immediately out of the House; but, on the contrary, she rather took the good natured Side of the Question, intimated some Compassion for the helpless little Creature, and commended her Brother's Charity in what he had done.

Perhaps the Reader may account for this Behaviour from her Condescension to Mr. *Allworthy*, when we have informed him, that the good Man had ended his Narrative with owning a Resolution to take care of the Child, and to breed him up as his own; for, to acknowledge the Truth, she was always ready to oblige her Brother, and very seldom if ever, contradicted his Sentiments; she would indeed sometimes make a few Observations, as, that Men were headstrong and must have their own Way, and would wish she had been blest with an independent Fortune; but these were always vented in a low Voice, and at the most amounted only to what is called Muttering.

However, what she withheld from the Infant, she bestowed with the utmost Profuseness on the poor unknown Mother, whom she called an impudent Slut, a wanton Hussy, an audacious Harlot, a wicked Jade, a vile Strumpet, with every other Appellation with which the Tongue of Virtue never fails to lash those who bring a Disgrace on the Sex.

A Consultation was now entered into, how to proceed in order to discover the Mother. A Scrutiny was first made into the Characters of the female Servants of the House, who were all acquitted by Mrs. *Wilkins*, and with apparent Merit; for she had collected them herself; and perhaps it would be difficult to find such another Set of Scarecrows.

The next Step was to examine among the Inhabitants of the Parish; and this was referred to Mrs. *Wilkins*, who was to enquire with all imaginable Diligence, and to make her Report in the Afternoon.

Matters being thus settled, Mr. *Allworthy* withdrew to his Study, as was his Custom, and left the Child to his Sister, who, at his Desire, had undertaken the Care of it.

Chapter V.

Containing a few common Matters, with a very uncommon Observation upon them.

When her Master was departed, Mrs. *Deborah* stood silent, expecting her Cue from Miss *Bridget*; for as to what had past before her Master, the prudent Housekeeper by no means relied upon it, as she had often known the Sentiments of the Lady, in her Brother's Absence, to differ greatly from those which she had expressed in his Presence. Miss *Bridget* did not, however, suffer her to continue long in this doubtful Situation; for having looked some Time earnestly at the Child, as it lay asleep in the Lap of Mrs. *Deborah*, the good Lady could not forbear giving it a hearty Kiss, at the same time declaring herself wonderfully pleased with its Beauty and Innocence. Mrs. *Deborah* no sooner observed this, than she fell to squeezing and kissing, with as great Raptures as sometimes inspire the sage Dame of forty and five towards a youthful and vigorous Bridegroom, crying out in a shrill voice, 'O the dear little Creature, the dear, sweet, pretty Creature! Well, I vow, it is as fine a Boy as ever was seen!'

These Exclamations continued, 'till they were interrupted by the Lady, who now proceeded to execute the Commission given her by her Brother, and gave Orders for providing all Necessaries for the Child, appointing a very good Room in the House for his Nursery. Her Orders were indeed so liberal, that, had it been a Child of her own, she could not have exceeded them: But, lest the virtuous Reader may condemn her for shewing too great Regard to a baseborn Infant, to which all Charity is condemned by Law as irreligious, we think proper to observe, that she concluded the Whole with saying, 'Since it was her Brother's Whim to adopt the little Brat, she supposed little Master must be treated with great Tenderness: For her Part, she could not help thinking it was an Encouragement to Vice; but that she knew too much of the Obstinacy of Mankind to oppose any of their ridiculous Humours.'

With Reflections of this Nature she usually, as has been hinted, accompanied every Act of Compliance with her Brother's Inclinations; and surely nothing could more contribute to heighten the Merit of this Compliance, than a Declaration that she knew, at the same Time, the Folly and Unreasonableness of those Inclinations to which she submitted. Tacit Obedience implies no Force upon the Will, and, consequently, may be easily, and without any Pains, preserved; but when a Wife, a Child, a Relation, or a Friend, performs what we desire, with Grumbling and Reluctance, with Expressions of Dislike and Dissatisfaction, the manifest Difficulty which they undergo, must greatly enhance the Obligation.

As this is one of those deep Observations which very few Readers can be supposed capable of making themselves, I have thought proper to lend them my Assistance; but this is a Favour rarely to be expected in the Course of my Work. Indeed I shall seldom or never so indulge him, unless in such Instances as this, where nothing but the Inspiration with which we Writers are gifted, can possibly enable any one to make the Discovery.

Chapter VI.

Mrs. Deborah *is introduced into the Parish, with a Simile. A short Account of* Jenny Jones, *with the Difficulties and Discouragements which may attend young* Women *in the Pursuit of Learning.*

Mrs. *Deborah*, having disposed of the Child according to the Will of her Master, now prepared to visit those Habitations which were supposed to conceal its Mother.

Not otherwise than when a Kite, tremendous Bird, is beheld by the feathered Generation soaring aloft, and hovering over their Heads; the amorous Dove, and every innocent little Bird, spread wide the Alarm, and fly trembling to their Hiding places. He proudly beats the Air, conscious of his Dignity, and meditates intended Mischief.

So when the Approach of Mrs. *Deborah* was proclaimed through the Street, all the Inhabitants ran trembling into their Houses, each Matron dreading lest the Visit should fall to her Lot. She with stately Steps proudly advances over the Field, aloft she bears her tow'ring Head, filled with Conceit of her own Pre-eminence, and Schemes to effect her intended Discovery.

The sagacious Reader will not, from this Simile, imagine these poor People had any Apprehension of the Design with which Mrs. *Wilkins* was now coming towards them; but as the great Beauty of the Simile may possibly sleep these hundred Years, till some future Commentator shall take this Work in hand, I think proper to lend the Reader a little Assistance in this Place.

It is my Intention therefore to signify, that, as it is the Nature of a Kite to devour little Birds, so is it the Nature of such Persons as Mrs. *Wilkins*, to insult and tyrannize over little People. This being indeed the Means which they use to recompense to themselves their extreme Servility and Condescension to their Superiors; for nothing can be more reasonable, than that Slaves and Flatterers should exact the same Taxes on all below them, which they themselves pay to all above them.

Whenever Mrs. *Deborah* had Occasion to exert any extraordinary Condescension to Mrs. *Bridget*, and by that Means had a little sowered her natural Disposition, it was usual with her to walk forth among these People, in order to refine her Temper, by venting, and, as it were, purging off all ill Humours; on which Account, she was by no Means a welcome Visitant: To say the Truth, she was universally dreaded and hated by them all.

On her Arrival in this Place, she went immediately to the Habitation of an elderly Matron; to whom, as this Matron had the good Fortune to resemble herself in the Comeliness of her Person, as well as in her Age, she had generally been more favourable than to any of the rest. To this Woman she imparted what had happened, and the Design upon which she was come thither that Morning. These two began presently to scrutinize the Characters of the several young Girls, who lived in any of those Houses, and at last fixed their strongest Suspicion on one *Jenny Jones*, who they both agreed was the likeliest Person to have committed this Fact.

This *Jenny Jones* was no very comely Girl, either in her Face or Person; but Nature had somewhat compensated the Want of Beauty with what is generally more esteemed by those Ladies, whose Judgment is arrived at Years of perfect Maturity; for she had given her a very uncommon Share of Understanding. This Gift *Jenny* had a good deal improved by Erudition. She had lived several Years a Servant with a Schoolmaster, who discovering a great Quickness of Parts in the Girl, and an extraordinary Desire of learning, (for every leisure Hour she was always found reading in the Books of the Scholars) had the Good-nature, or Folly (just as the Reader pleases to call it,) to instruct her so far, that she obtained a competent Skill in the *Latin* Language, and was, perhaps, as good a Scholar as most of the young Men of Quality of the Age. This Advantage, however, like most others of an extraordinary Kind, was attended with some small Inconveniencies: For as it is not to be wondered at, that a young Woman so well accomplished should have little Relish for the Society of those whom Fortune had made her

Equals, but whom Education had rendered so much her Inferiors; so is it Matter of no greater Astonishment, that this Superiority in *Jenny*, together with that Behaviour which is its certain Consequence, should produce among the rest some little Envy and Ill-will towards her; and these had, perhaps, secretly burnt in the Bosoms of her Neighbours, ever since her Return from her Service.

Their Envy did not, however, display itself openly, till poor *Jenny*, to the Surprize of every Body, and to the Vexation of all the young Women in these Parts, had publickly shone forth on a *Sunday* in a new Silk Gown, with a laced Cap, and other proper Appendages to these.

The Flame, which had before lain in Embryo, now burst forth. *Jenny* had, by her Learning, encreased her own Pride, which none of her Neighbours were kind enough to feed with the Honour she seemed to demand; and now, instead of Respect and Adoration, she gained nothing but Hatred and Abuse by her Finery. The whole Parish declared she could not come honestly by such Things; and Parents, instead of wishing their Daughters the same, felicitated themselves that their Children had them not.

Hence perhaps it was, that the good Woman first mentioned the Name of this poor Girl to Mrs. *Wilkins*; but there was another Circumstance that confirmed the latter in her Suspicion: For *Jenny* had lately been often at Mr. *Allworthy*'s House. She had officiated as Nurse to Miss *Bridget*, in a violent Fit of Illness, and had sat up many Nights with that Lady; besides which, she had been seen there the very Day before Mr. *Allworthy*'s Return, by Mrs. *Wilkins* herself, tho' that sagacious Person had not at first conceived any Suspicion of her on that Account: For, as she herself said, 'She had always esteemed *Jenny* as a very sober Girl, (tho' indeed she knew very little of her) and had rather suspected some of those wanton Trollops, who gave themselves Airs, because, forsooth, they thought themselves handsome.'

Jenny was now summoned to appear in Person before Mrs. *Deborah*, which she immediately did. When Mrs. *Deborah*, putting on the Gravity of a Judge, with somewhat more than his Austerity, began an Oration with the Words 'You audacious Strumpet,' in which she proceeded rather to pass Sentence on the Prisoner than to accuse her.

Tho' Mrs. *Deborah* was fully satisfied of the Guilt of Jenny, from the Reasons above shewn, it is possible Mr. *Allworthy* might have required some stronger Evidence to have convicted her; but she saved her Accusers any such Trouble, by freely confessing the whole Fact with which she was charged.

This Confession, tho' delivered rather in Terms of Contrition, as it appeared, did not at all mollify Mrs. *Deborah*, who now pronounced a second Judgment against her, in more opprobrious Language than before: Nor had it any better Success with the Bye-standers, who were now grown very numerous. Many of them cried out, 'They thought what Madam's Silk Gown would end in;' others spoke sarcastically of her Learning. Not a single Female was present, but found some Means of expressing her Abhorrence of poor *Jenny*; who bore all very patiently, except the Malice of one Woman, who reflected upon her Person, and, tossing up her Nose, said, 'The Man must have a good Stomach, who would give Silk Gowns for such Sort of Trumpery.' *Jenny* replied to this, with a Bitterness which might have surprized a judicious Person, who had observed the Tranquillity with which she bore all the Affronts to her Chastity: But her Patience was, perhaps, tired out; for this is a Virtue which is very apt to be fatigued by Exercise.

Mrs. *Deborah* having succeeded beyond her Hopes in her Enquiry, returned with much Triumph, and, at the appointed Hour, made a faithful Report to Mr. *Allworthy*, who was much surprized at the Relation; for he had heard of the extraordinary Parts and Improvements of this Girl, whom he intended to have given in Marriage, together with a small Living, to a neighbouring Curate. His Concern therefore, on this Occasion, was at least equal to the Satisfaction which appeared in Mrs. *Deborah*, and to many Readers may seem much more reasonable.

Mrs. *Bridget* blessed herself, and said, 'For her Part, she should never hereafter entertain a good Opinion of any Woman.' For *Jenny* before this had the Happiness of being much in her good Graces also.

The prudent Housekeeper was again dispatched to bring the unhappy Culprit before Mr. *Allworthy*, in order, not, as it was hoped by some, and expected by all, to be sent to the House of Correction; but to receive wholesome Admonition and Reproof, which those who relish that Kind of instructive Writing, may peruse in the next Chapter.

Chapter VII.

Containing such grave Matter, that the Reader cannot laugh once through the whole Chapter, unless peradventure he should laugh at the Author.

When *Jenny* appeared, Mr. *Allworthy* took her into his Study, and spoke to her as follows:

'You know, Child, it is in my Power, as a Magistrate, to punish you very rigorously for what you have done; and you will, perhaps, be the more apt to fear I should execute that Power, because you have, in a manner, laid your Sins at my Door.

'But perhaps this is one Reason which hath determined me to act in a milder Manner with you: For, as no private Resentment should ever influence a Magistrate, I will be so far from considering your having deposited the Infant in my House, as an Aggravation of your Offence, that I will suppose, in your Favour, this to have proceeded from a natural Affection to your Child; since you might have some Hopes to see it thus better provided for, than was in the Power of yourself, or its wicked Father, to provide for it. I should indeed have been highly offended with you, had you exposed the little Wretch in the Manner of some inhuman Mothers, who seem no less to have abandoned their Humanity, than to have parted with their Chastity. It is the other Part of your Offence, therefore, upon which I intend to admonish you, I mean the Violation of your Chastity. A Crime, however lightly it may be treated by debauched Persons, very heinous in itself, and very dreadful in its Consequences.

'The heinous Nature of this Offence must be suffiiciently apparent to every Christian, inasmuch as it is committed in Defiance of the Laws of our Religion, and of the express Commands of him who founded that Religion.

'And here its Consequences may well be argued to be dreadful; for what can be more so, than to incur the Divine Displeasure, by the Breach of the Divine Commands; and that in an Instance, against which the highest Vengeance is specifically denounced?

'But these Things, tho' too little, I am afraid, regarded, are so plain, that Mankind, however they may want to be reminded, can never need Information on this Head. A Hint therefore, to awaken your Sense of this Matter, shall suffice; for I would inspire you with Repentance, and not drive you to Desperation.

'There are other Consequences, not indeed so dreadful, or replete with Horror, as this; and yet such as, if attentively considered, must, one would think, deter all, of your Sex at least, from the Commission of this Crime.

'For by it you are rendered infamous, and driven, like Lepers of old, out of Society; at least from the Society of all but wicked and reprobate Persons; for no others will associate with you.

'If you have Fortunes, you are hereby rendered incapable of enjoying them; if you have none, you are disabled from acquiring any, nay almost of procuring your Sustenance; for no Persons of Character will receive you into their Houses. Thus you are often driven by Necessity itself into a State of Shame and Misery, which unavoidably ends in the Destruction of both Body and Soul.

'Can any Pleasure compensate these Evils? Can any Temptation have Sophistry and Delusion strong enough to persuade you to so simple a Bargain? Or can any carnal Appetite so overpower your Reason, or so totally lay it asleep, as to prevent your flying with

Affright and Terror from a Crime which carries such Punishment always with it?

'How base and mean must that Woman be, how void of that Dignity of Mind, and decent Pride, without which we are not worthy the Name of human Creatures, who can bear to level herself with the lowest Animal, and to sacrifice all that is great and noble in her, all her heavenly Part, to an Appetite which she hath in common with the vilest Branch of the Creation! For no Woman sure, will plead the Passion of Love for an Excuse. This would be to own herself the meer Tool and Bubble of the Man. Love, however barbarously we may corrupt and pervert its Meaning, as it is a laudable, is a rational Passion, and can never be violent, but when reciprocal; for though the Scripture bids us love our Enemies, it means not with that fervent Love, which we naturally bear towards our Friends; much less that we should sacrifice to them our Lives; and what ought to be dearer to us, our Innocence. Now in what Light, but that of an Enemy, can a reasonable Woman regard the Man, who solicits her to entail on herself, all the Misery I have described to you, and who would purchase to himself a short, trivial, contemptible Pleasure, so greatly at her Expence! For, by the Laws of Custom, the whole Shame, with all its dreadful Consequences, falls intirely upon her. Can Love, which always seeks the Good of its Object, attempt to betray a Woman into a Bargain where she is so greatly to be the Loser? If such Corrupter, therefore, should have the Impudence to pretend a real Affection for her, ought not the Woman to regard him, not only as an Enemy, but as the worst of all Enemies; a false, designing, treacherous, pretended Friend, who intends not only to debauch her Body, but her Understanding at the same Time?'

Here *Jenny* expressing great Concern, *Allworthy* paused a Moment, and then proceeded: 'I have talked thus to you, Child, not to insult you for what is past, and irrevocable, but to caution and strengthen you for the future. Nor should I have taken this Trouble, but from some Opinion of your good Sense, notwithstanding the dreadful Slip you have made; and from some Hopes of your hearty Repentance, which are founded on the Openness and Sincerity of your Confession. If these do not deceive me, I will take Care to convey you from this Scene of your Shame, where you shall, by being unknown, avoid the Punishment which, as I have said, is allotted to your Crime in this World; and I hope, by Repentance, you will avoid the much heavier Sentence denounced against it in the other. Be a good Girl the rest of your Days, and Want shall be no Motive to your going astray: And believe me, there is more Pleasure, even in this World, in an innocent and virtuous Life, than in one debauched and vicious.

'As to your Child, let no Thoughts concerning it molest you; I will provide for it in a better Manner than you can ever hope. And now Nothing remains, but that you inform me who was the wicked Man that seduced you; for my Anger against him will be much greater than you have experienced on this Occasion.'

Jenny now first lifted her Eyes from the Ground, and with a modest Look, and decent Voice, thus began:

'To know you, Sir, and not love your Goodness, would be an Argument of total Want of Sense or Goodness in any one. In me it would amount to the highest Ingratitude, not to feel in the most sensible Manner, the great Degree of Goodness you have been pleased to exert on this Occasion. As to my Concern for what is past, I know you will spare my Blushes the Repetition. My future Conduct will much better declare my Sentiments, than any Professions I can now make. I beg Leave to assure you, Sir, that I take your Advice much kinder, than your generous Offer with which you concluded it. For, as you are pleased to say, Sir, it is an Instance of your Opinion of my Understanding'—Here her Tears flowing apace, she stopped a few Moments, and then proceeded thus, 'Indeed, Sir, your Kindness overcomes me; but I will endeavour to deserve this good Opinion: For, if I have the Understanding you are so kindly pleased to allow me, such Advice cannot be thrown away upon me. I thank you, Sir, heartily, for your intended Kindness to my poor helpless Child: He is innocent, and, I hope, will live to be grateful for all the Favours you shall shew him. But now, Sir, I must on my Knees intreat you, not to persist in asking me to declare the Father of my Infant. I promise you faithfully, you shall one Day know; but I am under the most solemn Ties and Engagements of Honour, as well as the most religious Vows and Protestations, to conceal his Name at this Time. And I know you too well to think you would desire I should sacrifice either my Honour, or my Religion.'

Mr. *Allworthy*, whom the least Mention of those sacred Words was sufficient to stagger, hesitated a Moment before he replied, and then told her, she had done wrong to enter into such Engagements to a Villain; but since she had, he could not insist on her breaking them. He said, it was not from a Motive of vain Curiosity he had enquired, but in order to punish the Fellow; at least, that he might not ignorantly confer Favours on the Undeserving.

As to these Points, *Jenny* satisfied him by the most solemn Assurances, that the Man was entirely out of his Reach, and was neither subject to his Power, nor in any Probability of becoming an Object of his Goodness.

The Ingenuity of this Behaviour had gained *Jenny* so much Credit with this worthy Man, that he easily believed what she told him: For as she had disdained to excuse herself by a Lie, and had hazarded his farther Displeasure in her present Situation, rather than she would forfeit her Honour, or Integrity, by betraying another, he had but little Apprehension that she would be guilty of Falshood towards himself.

He therefore dismissed her with Assurances, that he would very soon remove her out of the Reach of that Obloquy she had incurred, concluding with some additional Documents, in which he recommended Repentance, saying, 'Consider, Child, there is one still to reconcile yourself to, whose Favour is of much greater Importance to you than mine.'

Chapter VIII.

A *Dialogue between Mesdames* Bridget, *and* Deborah; *containing more Amusement, but less Instruction than the former.*

When Mr. *Allworthy* had retired to his Study with *Jenny Jones,* as hath been seen, Mrs. *Bridget,* with the good House-keeper, had betaken themselves to a Post next adjoining to the said Study; whence, through the Conveyance of a Key-hole, they sucked in at their Ears the instructive Lecture delivered by Mr. *Allworthy,* together with the Answers of *Jenny,* and indeed every other Particular which passed in the last Chapter.

This Hole in her Brother's Study Door was indeed as well known to Mrs. *Bridget,* and had been as frequently applied to by her, as the famous Hole in the Wall was by *Thisbe* of old. This served to many good Purposes. For by such Means Mrs. *Bridget* became often acquainted with her Brother's Inclinations, without giving him the Trouble of repeating them to her. It is true, some Inconveniencies attended this Intercourse, and she had sometimes Reason to cry out with *Thisbe,* in *Shakespear,* 'O wicked, wicked Wall!'[1] For as Mr. *Allworthy* was a Justice of Peace, certain Things occurred in Examinations concerning Bastards, and such like, which are apt to give great Offence to the chaste Ears of Virgins, especially when they approach the Age of Forty, as was the Case of Mrs. *Bridget.* However, she had, on such Occasions, the Advantage of concealing her Blushes from the Eyes of Men; and *De non apparentibus, & non existentibus eadem est ratio.*[2] In *English:* 'When a Woman is not seen to blush, she doth not blush at all.'

Both the good Women kept strict Silence during the whole Scene between Mr. *Allworthy* and the Girl; but as soon as it was ended,

---

1. Fielding misquotes. Pyramus, not Thisbe, says, "Thou wall, O wall, O sweet and lovely wall (V.i.175) and then "O wicked wall, through whom I see no bliss" (181).
2. A rule concerning legal evidence.

"That which does not appear is the same as if it did not exist." Fielding has his bad lawyer misquote this in *Amelia* I.x (1751) and quotes it again in his *Covent-Garden Journal,* no. 2, 7 Jan. 1752.

and that Gentleman out of hearing, Mrs. *Deborah* could not help exclaiming against the Clemency of her Master, and especially against his suffering her to conceal the Father of the Child, which she swore she would have out of her before the Sun set.

At these Words Mrs. *Bridget* discomposed her Features with a Smile; (a Thing very unusual to her.) Not that I would have my Reader imagine, that this was one of those wanton Smiles, which *Homer* would have you conceive came from *Venus*, when he calls her the laughter-loving Goddess;[3] nor was it one of those Smiles, which Lady *Seraphina* shoots from the Stage-Box, and which *Venus* would quit her Immortality to be able to equal. No, this was rather one of those Smiles, which might be supposed to have come from the dimpled Cheeks of the august *Tisiphone*,[4] or from one of the Misses her Sisters.

With such a Smile then, and with a Voice, sweet as the Evening Breeze of *Boreas* in the pleasant Month of *November*, Mrs. *Bridget* gently reproved the Curiosity of Mrs. *Deborah*, a Vice with which it seems the latter was too much tainted, and which the former inveighed against with great Bitterness, adding, 'that among all her Faults, she thanked Heaven, her Enemies could not accuse her of prying into the Affairs of other People.'

She then proceeded to commend the Honour and Spirit with which *Jenny* had acted. She said, she could not help agreeing with her Brother, that there was some Merit in the Sincerity of her Confession, and in her Integrity to her Lover: That she had always thought her a very good Girl, and doubted not but she had been seduced by some Rascal, who had been infinitely more to blame than herself, and very probably had prevailed with her by a Promise of Marriage, or some other treacherous Proceeding.

This Behaviour of Mrs. *Bridget* greatly surprized Mrs. *Deborah*; for this well-bred Woman seldom opened her Lips either to her Master or his Sister, 'till she had first sounded their Inclinations, with which her Sentiments were always strictly consonant. Here, however, she thought she might have launched forth with Safety; and the sagacious Reader will not perhaps accuse her of want of sufficient Forecast in so doing, but will rather admire with what wonderful Celerity she tacked about, when she found herself steering a wrong Course.

'Nay, Madam,' said this able Woman, and truly great Politician, 'I must own I cannot help admiring the Girl's Spirit, as well as your Ladyship. And, as your Ladyship says, if she was deceived by some wicked Man, the poor Wretch is to be pitied. And to be sure, as your Ladyship says, the Girl hath always appeared like a good,

3. *Iliad* III.423 and *Odyssey* VIII.362 refer to "laughter-loving Aphrodite."
4. One of the three Furies of Greek my-
thology, who tortured guilty consciences, and carried out curses on criminals.

honest, plain Girl, and not vain of her Face, forsooth, as some wanton Husseys in the Neighbourhood are.'

'You say true, *Deborah*,' said Mrs. *Bridget*, 'if the Girl had been one of those vain Trollops, of which we have too many in the Parish, I should have condemned my Brother for his Lenity towards her. I saw two Farmers Daughters at Church, the other Day, with bare Necks. I protest they shock'd me. If Wenches will hang out Lures for Fellows, it is no matter what they suffer. I detest such Creatures; and it would be much better for them, that their Faces had been seamed with the Small-Pox; but I must confess, I never saw any of this wanton Behaviour in poor *Jenny*; some artful Villain, I am convinced, hath betrayed, nay perhaps forced her; and I pity the poor Wretch with all my Heart.'

Mrs. *Deborah* approved all these Sentiments, and the Dialogue concluded with a general and bitter Invective against Beauty, and with many compassionate Considerations for all honest, plain Girls, who are deluded by the wicked Arts of deceitful Men.

Chapter IX.

Containing Matters which will surprize the Reader.

Jenny returned home well pleased with the Reception she had met with from Mr. *Allworthy*, whose Indulgence to her she industriously made public; partly perhaps as a Sacrifice to her own Pride, and partly from the more prudent Motive of reconciling her Neighbours to her, and silencing their Clamours.

But though this latter View, if she indeed had it, may appear reasonable enough, yet the Event did not answer her Expectation; for when she was convened before the Justice, and it was universally apprehended, that the House of Correction would have been her Fate; tho' some of the young Women cry'd out, 'it was good enough for her,' and diverted themselves with the Thoughts of her beating Hemp in a Silk Gown; yet there were many others who began to pity her Condition: But when it was known in what manner Mr. *Allworthy* had behaved, the Tide turned against her. One said, 'I'll assure you, Madam hath had good Luck.' A second cry'd, 'See what it is to be a Favourite.' A third, 'Ay, this comes of her Learning.' Every Person made some malicious Comment or other, on the Occasion; and reflected on the Partiality of the Justice.

The Behaviour of these People may appear impolitic and ungrateful to the Reader, who considers the Power, and the Benevolence of Mr. *Allworthy*: But as to his Power, he never used it; and as to his Benevolence, he exerted so much, that he had thereby disobliged all his Neighbours: For it is a Secret well known to great Men, that by conferring an Obligation, they do not always procure a Friend, but are certain of creating many Enemies.

Jenny was, however, by the Care and Goodness of Mr. *Allworthy*, soon removed out of the Reach of Reproach; when Malice, being no longer able to vent its Rage on her, began to seek another Object of its Bitterness, and this was no less than Mr. *Allworthy* himself; for a Whisper soon went abroad, that he himself was the Father of the foundling Child.

This Supposition so well reconciled his Conduct to the general Opinion, that it met with universal Assent; and the Outcry against his Lenity soon began to take another Turn, and was changed into an Invective against his Cruelty to the poor Girl. Very grave and good Women exclaimed against Men who begot Children and then disowned them. Nor were there wanting some, who, after the Departure of *Jenny*, insinuated, that she was spirited away with a Design too black to be mentioned, and who gave frequent Hints, that a legal Inquiry ought to be made into the whole Matter, and that some People should be forced to produce the Girl.

These Calumnies might have probably produced ill Consequences (at the least might have occasioned some Trouble) to a Person of a more doubtful and suspicious Character than Mr. *Allworthy* was blessed with; but in his Case they had no such Effect; and, being heartily despised by him, they served only to afford an innocent Amusement to the good Gossips of the Neighbourhood.

But as we cannot possibly divine what Complexion our Reader may be of, and as it will be some time before he will hear any more of *Jenny*, we think proper to give him a very early Intimation, that Mr. *Allworthy* was, and will hereafter appear to be, absolutely innocent of any criminal Intention whatever. He had indeed committed no other than an Error in Politics, by tempering Justice with Mercy, and by refusing to gratify the good-natured Disposition of the Mob,[1] with an Object for their Compassion to work on in the Person of poor *Jenny*, whom, in order to pity, they desired to have seen sacrificed to Ruin and Infamy by a shameful Correction in a *Bridewell*.

So far from complying with this their Inclination, by which all Hopes of Reformation would have been abolished, and even the Gate shut against her, if her own Inclinations should ever hereafter lead her to chuse the Road of Virtue, Mr. *Allworthy* rather chose to encourage the Girl to return thither by the only possible Means; for too true I am afraid it is, that many Women have become aban-

1. Wherever this Word occurs in our Writings, it intends Persons without Virtue, or Sense, in all stations; and many of the highest Rank are often meant by it [*Fielding's note*].

doned, and have sunk to the last Degree of Vice by being unable to retrieve the first Slip. This will be, I am afraid, always the Case while they remain among their former Acquaintance; it was therefore wisely done by Mr. *Allworthy*, to remove *Jenny* to a Place where she might enjoy the Pleasure of Reputation, after having tasted the ill Consequences of losing it.

To this Place therefore, wherever it was, we will wish her a good Journey, and for the present take Leave of her, and of the little Foundling her Child, having Matters of much higher Importance to communicate to the Reader.

Chapter X.

The Hospitality of Allworthy; *with a short Sketch of the Characters of two Brothers, a Doctor, and a Captain, who were entertained by that Gentleman.*

Neither Mr. *Allworthy*'s House, nor his Heart, were shut against any Part of Mankind, but they were both more particularly open to Men of Merit. To say the Truth, this was the only House in the Kingdom where you was sure to gain a Dinner by deserving it.

Above all others, Men of Genius and Learning shared the principal Place in his Favour; and in these he had much Discernment: For though he had missed the Advantage of a learned Education, yet being blest with vast natural Abilities, he had so well profited by a vigorous, though late Application to Letters, and by much Conversation with Men of Eminence in this Way, that he was himself a very competent Judge in most Kinds of Literature.

It is no Wonder that in an Age when this Kind of Merit is so little in Fashion, and so slenderly provided for, Persons possessed of it should very eagerly flock to a Place where they were sure of being received with great Complaisance; indeed where they might enjoy almost the same Advantages of a liberal Fortune as if they were entitled to it in their own Right; for Mr. *Allworthy* was not one of those generous Persons, who are ready most bountifully to bestow Meat, Drink, and Lodging on Men of Wit and Learning, for which they expect no other Return but Entertainment, Instruction, Flattery, and Subserviency; in a Word, that such Persons should be enrolled in the Number of Domestics, without wearing their Master's Cloaths, or receiving Wages.

On the contrary, every Person in this House was perfect Master of his own Time: And as he might at his Pleasure satisfy all his Appetites within the Restrictions only of Law, Virtue and Religion, so he might, if his Health required, or his Inclination prompted him to Temperance, or even to Abstinence, absent himself from any Meals, or retire from them whenever he was so disposed, without even a Solicitation to the contrary: For indeed, such Solicitations from Superiors always savour very strongly of Commands. But all here were free from such Impertinence, not only those, whose Company is in all other Places esteemed a Favour from their Equality of Fortune, but even those whose indigent Circumstances make such an eleemosynary Abode convenient to them, and who are therefore less welcome to a great Man's Table because they stand in need of it.

Among others of this Kind was Dr. *Blifil*, a Gentleman who had the Misfortune of losing the Advantage of great Talents by the Obstinacy of a Father, who would breed him to a Profession he disliked. In Obedience to this Obstinacy the Doctor had in his Youth been obliged to study Physic, or rather to say he studied it; for in reality Books of this Kind were almost the only ones with which he was unacquainted; and unfortunately for him, the Doctor was Master of almost every other Science but that by which he was to get his Bread; the Consequence of which was, that the Doctor at the age of Forty had no bread to eat.

Such a Person as this was certain to find a Welcome at Mr. *Allworthy*'s Table, to whom Misfortunes were ever a Recommendation when they were derived from the Folly or Villany of others, and not of the unfortunate Person himself. Besides this negative Merit, the Doctor had one positive Recommendation. This was a great Appearance of Religion. Whether his Religion was real, or consisted only in Appearance, I shall not presume to say, as I am not possessed of any Touchstone, which can distinguish the true from the false.

If this Part of his Character pleased Mr. *Allworthy*, it delighted Miss *Bridget*. She engaged him in many religious Controversies; on which Occasions she constantly expressed great Satisfaction in the Doctor's Knowledge, and not much less in the Compliments which he frequently bestowed on her own. To say the Truth, she had read much *English* Divinity, and had puzzled more than one of the neighbouring Curates. Indeed her Conversation was so pure, her Looks so sage, and her whole Deportment so grave and solemn, that she seemed to deserve the Name of Saint equally with her Namesake, or with any other Female in the *Roman* Kalendar.

As Sympathies of all Kinds are apt to beget Love; so Experience teaches us that none have a more direct Tendency this Way than those of a religious Kind between Persons of different Sexes. The Doctor found himself so agreeable to Miss *Bridget*, that he now began to lament an unfortunate Accident which had happened to him about ten Years before; namely, his Marriage with another Woman, who was not only still alive, but what was worse, known to be so by Mr. *Allworthy*. This was a fatal Bar to that Happiness which he otherwise saw sufficient probability of obtaining with this young Lady; for as to criminal Indulgencies, he certainly never thought of them. This was owing either to his Religion, as is most probable, or to the Purity of his Passion, which was fixed on those Things, which Matrimony only, and not criminal Correspondence, could put him in Possession of, or could give him any Title to.

He had not long ruminated on these Matters, before it occurred to his Memory that he had a Brother who was under no such unhappy Incapacity. This Brother he made no doubt would succeed; for he discerned, as he thought, an Inclination to Marriage in the Lady; and the Reader perhaps, when he hears the Brother's Qualifications, will not blame the Confidence which he entertained of his Success.

This Gentleman was about 35 Years of Age. He was of a middle Size, and what is called well built. He had a Scar on his Forehead, which did not so much injure his Beauty, as it denoted his Valour (for he was a half-pay Officer.) He had good Teeth, and something affable, when he pleased, in his Smile; though naturally his Countenance, as well as his Air and Voice, had much of Roughness in it, yet he could at any Time deposite this, and appear all Gentleness and good Humour. He was not ungenteel, nor entirely void of Wit, and in his Youth had abounded in Sprightliness, which, though he had lately put on a more serious Character, he could, when he pleased, resume.

He had, as well as the Doctor, an Academic Education; for his Father had, with the same Paternal Authority we have mentioned before, decreed him for holy Orders; but as the old Gentleman died before he was ordained, he chose the Church Military,[1] and preferred the King's Commission to the Bishop's.

He had purchased the Post of Lieutenant of Dragoons, and afterwards came to be a Captain; but having quarrelled with his Colonel, was by his Interest obliged to sell; from which Time he had entirely rusticated himself, had betaken himself to studying the Scriptures, and was not a little suspected of an Inclination to *Methodism.*

It seemed therefore not unlikely that such a Person should succeed with a Lady of so Saint-like a Disposition, and whose Inclinations were no otherwise engaged than to the married State in gen-

1. Fielding's "Errata" sheet to the first edition, reproduced by Cross (facing II.122), changes this to "Church Militant," as it remains in the second and third editions—certainly a most authoritative change, as Jensen points out (see below, pp. 764–66). The fourth edition, however, changes back to "Church Military." Since the word falls exactly in the same line and place in both third and fourth editions, we may assume that the change appeared as copy marked directly *on* the third-edition pages, which the compositor is obviously following, and that it is not an oversight from using first-edition pages here in preparing copy, as seems to have happened with "Affront" (see below, p. 359). "Church Military" preserves a facetious echo of "Church Militant" but avoids momentarily misleading the reader.

eral; but why the Doctor, who certainly had no great Friendship for his Brother, should for his Sake think of making so ill a Return to the Hospitality of *Allworthy*, is a Matter not so easy to be accounted for.

Is it that some Natures delight in Evil, as others are thought to delight in Virtue? Or is there a Pleasure in being accessary to a Theft when we cannot commit it ourselves? Or lastly, (which Experience seems to make probable) have we a Satisfaction in aggrandizing our Families, even tho' we have not the least Love or Respect for them?

Whether any of these Motives operated on the Doctor we will not determine; but so the Fact was. He sent for his Brother, and easily found Means to introduce him at *Allworthy*'s as a Person who intended only a short Visit to himself.

The Captain had not been in the House a Week, before the Doctor had Reason to felicitate himself on his Discernment. The Captain was indeed as great a Master of the Art of Love as *Ovid*[2] was formerly. He had besides received proper Hints from his Brother, which he failed not to improve to the best Advantage.

Chapter XI.

Containing many Rules, and some Examples, concerning falling in love: Descriptions of Beauty, and other more prudential Inducements to Matrimony.

It hath been observed by wise Men or Women, I forget which, that all Persons are doomed to be in Love once in their Lives. No particular Season is, as I remember, assigned for this; but the Age at which Miss *Bridget* was arrived, seems to me as proper a Period as any to be fixed on for this Purpose: It often indeed happens much earlier; but when it doth not, I have observed, it seldom or never fails about this Time. Moreover, we may remark that at this Season Love is of a more serious and steady Nature than what sometimes shews itself in the younger Parts of Life. The Love of Girls is uncertain, capricious, and so foolish that we cannot always discover what the young Lady would be at; nay, it may almost be doubted, whether she always knows this herself.

Now we are never at a Loss to discern this in Women about Forty; for as such grave, serious and experienced Ladies well know their own Meaning; so it is always very easy for a Man of the least Sagacity to discover it with the utmost Certainty.

Miss *Bridget* is an Example of all these Observations. She had

2. Roman poet (43 B.C.–c. A.D. 18) who wrote three erotic works: *Amores, Ars Amatoria,* and *Remedia Amores.* Field-ing published *Ovid's Art of Love Paraphrased, and Adapted to the Present Times, Book I,* in 1747.

not been many Times in the Captain's Company before she was
seized with this Passion. Nor did she go pining and moping about
the House, like a puny foolish Girl, ignorant of her Distemper: She
felt, she knew, and she enjoyed, the pleasing Sensation, of which, as
she was certain it was not only innocent but laudable, she was neither afraid nor ashamed.

And to say the Truth, there is in all Points, great Difference
between the reasonable Passion which Women at this Age conceive
towards Men, and the idle and childish Liking of a Girl to a Boy,
which is often fixed on the Outside only, and on Things of little
Value and no Duration; as on Cherry Cheeks, small Lily-white
Hands, sloe-black Eyes, flowing Locks, downy Chins, dapper
Shapes, nay sometimes on Charms more worthless than these, and
less the Party's own; such are the outward Ornaments of the
Person, for which Men are beholden to the Taylor, the Laceman,
the Perriwig-maker, the Hatter, and the Milliner, and not to
Nature. Such a Passion Girls may well be ashamed, as they gener-
ally are, to own either to themselves or to others.

The love of Miss *Bridget* was of another Kind. The Captain
owed nothing to any of these Fop-makers in his Dress, nor was his
Person much more beholden to Nature. Both his Dress and Person
were such as, had they appeared in an Assembly, or a Drawing-
room, would have been the Contempt and Ridicule of all the fine
Ladies there. The former of these was indeed neat, but plain,
coarse, ill-fancied, and out of Fashion. As for the latter, we have
expressly described it above. So far was the Skin on his Cheeks from
being Cherry-coloured, that you could not discern what the natural
Colour of his Cheeks was, they being totally overgrown by a black
Beard, which ascended to his Eyes. His Shape and Limbs were
indeed exactly proportioned, but so large, that they denoted the
Strength rather of a Ploughman than any other. His Shoulders were
broad, beyond all Size, and the Calves of his Legs larger than those
of a common Chairman. In short, his whole Person wanted all that
Elegance and Beauty, which is the very reverse of clumsy Strength,
and which so agreeably sets off most of our fine Gentlemen; being
partly owing to the high Blood of their Ancestors, *viz.* Blood made
of rich Sauces and generous Wines, and partly to an early Town
Education.

Tho' Miss *Bridget* was a Woman of the greatest Delicacy of
Taste; yet such were the Charms of the Captain's Conversation,
that she totally overlooked the Defects of his Person. She imagined,
and perhaps very wisely, that she should enjoy more agreeable Minutes with the Captain than with a much prettier Fellow; and fore-
went the Consideration of pleasing her Eyes, in order to procure herself much more solid Satisfaction.

The Captain no sooner perceived the Passion of Miss *Bridget*, in which Discovery he was very quick-sighted, than he faithfully returned it. The Lady, no more than her Lover, was remarkable for Beauty. I would attempt to draw her Picture; but that is done already by a more able Master, Mr. *Hogarth*[1] himself, to whom she sat many Years ago, and hath been lately exhibited by that Gentleman in his Print of a Winter's Morning, of which she was no improper Emblem, and may be seen walking (for walk she doth in the Print) to *Covent-Garden* Church, with a starved Foot-boy behind carrying her Prayer-book.

The Captain likewise very wisely preferred the more solid Enjoyments he expected with this Lady, to the fleeting Charms of Person. He was one of those wise Men, who regard Beauty in the other Sex as a very worthless and superficial Qualification; or, to speak more truly, who rather chuse to possess every Convenience of Life with an ugly Woman, than a handsome one without any of those Conveniencies. And having a very good Appetite, and but little Nicety, he fancied he should play his Part very well at the matrimonial Banquet, without the Sauce of Beauty.

To deal plainly with the Reader, the Captain, ever since his Arrival, at least from the Moment his Brother had proposed the Match to him, long before he had discovered any flattering Symptoms in Miss *Bridget*, had been greatly enamoured; that is to say, of Mr. *Allworthy*'s House and Gardens, and of his Lands, Tenements and Hereditaments; of all which the Captain was so passionately fond, that he would most probably have contracted Marriage with them, had he been obliged to have taken the Witch of *Endor* into the Bargain.

As Mr. *Allworthy* therefore had declared to the Doctor, that he never intended to take a second Wife, as his Sister was his nearest Relation, and as the Doctor had fished out that his Intentions were to make any Child of hers his Heir, which indeed the Law, without his Interposition, would have done for him; the Doctor and his Brother thought it an Act of Benevolence to give Being to a human Creature, who would be so plentifully provided with the most essential Means of Happiness. The whole Thoughts therefore of both the Brothers were how to engage the Affections of this amiable Lady.

But Fortune, who is a tender Parent, and often doth more for her favourite Offspring than either they deserve or wish, had been so industrious for the Captain, that whilst he was laying Schemes to execute his Purpose, the Lady conceived the same Desires with himself, and was on her Side contriving how to give the Captain proper Encouragement, without appearing too forward; for she was a strict

1. William Hogarth (1697–1764), painter and engraver. Fielding refers to Hogarth's work "Morning," from his series *Four Times of Day* (1738).

Observer of all Rules of Decorum. In this, however, she easily succeeded; for as the Captain was always on the Look-out, no Glance,
Gesture, or Word escaped him.

The Satisfaction which the Captain received from the kind
Behaviour of Miss *Bridget*, was not a little abated by his Apprehensions of Mr. *Allworthy*; for, notwithstanding his disinterested Professions, the Captain imagined he would, when he came to act, follow
the Example of the rest of the World, and refuse his Consent to a
Match, so disadvantageous, in point of Interest, to his Sister. From
what Oracle he received this Opinion, I shall leave the Reader to
determine; but, however he came by it, it strangely perplexed him,
how to regulate his Conduct so as at once to convey his Affection to
the Lady, and to conceal it from her Brother. He, at length,
resolved to take all private Opportunities of making his Addresses;
but in the Presence of Mr. *Allworthy* to be as reserved, and as
much upon his Guard, as was possible; and this Conduct was highly
approved by the Brother.

He soon found Means to make his Addresses, in express Terms,
to his Mistress, from whom he received an Answer in the proper
Form, *viz.* the Answer which was first made some thousands of
Years ago, and which hath been handed down by Tradition from
Mother to Daughter ever since. If I was to translate this into *Latin*,
I should render it by these two Words, *Nolo Episcopari*:[2] A Phrase
likewise of immemorial Use on another Occasion.

The Captain, however he came by his Knowledge, perfectly well
understood the Lady; and very soon after repeated his Application,
with more Warmth and Earnestness than before, and was again,
according to due Form, rejected: But as he had increased in the
Eagerness of his Desires, so the Lady, with the same Propriety,
decreased in the Violence of her Refusal.

Not to tire the Reader, by leading him thro' every Scene of this
Courtship, (which, tho', in the Opinion of a certain great Author,
it is the pleasantest Scene of Life to the Actor, is, perhaps, as dull
and tiresome as any whatever to the Audience) the Captain made
his Advances in Form, the Citadel was defended in Form, and at
length, in proper Form, surrendered at Discretion.

During this whole Time, which filled the Space of near a Month,
the Captain preserved great Distance of Behaviour to his Lady, in
the Presence of the Brother; and the more he succeeded with her in
private, the more reserved was he in public. And as for the Lady,
she had no sooner secured her Lover, than she behaved to him

---

2. "I do not wish to be a bishop," the
phrase a candidate traditionally uses on
his nomination, used similarly by William Congreve in *Love for Love* I.i
(1695), a play Fielding knew well.

before Company with the highest Degree of Indifference; so that Mr. *Allworthy* must have had the Insight of the Devil (or perhaps some of his worse Qualities) to have entertained the least Suspicion of what was going forward.

Chapter XII.

Containing what the Reader may, perhaps, expect to find in it.

In all Bargains, whether to fight or to marry, or concerning any other such Business, little previous Ceremony is required, to bring the Matter to an Issue, when both Parties are really in earnest. This was the Case at present, and in less than a Month the Captain and his Lady were Man and Wife.

The great Concern now was to break the Matter to Mr. *Allworthy*; and this was undertaken by the Doctor.

One Day then as *Allworthy* was walking in his Garden, the Doctor came to him, and, with great Gravity of Aspect, and all the Concern which he could possibly affect in his Countenance, said, 'I am come, Sir, to impart an Affair to you of the utmost Consequence; but how shall I mention to you, what it almost distracts me to think of!' He then launched forth into the most bitter Invectives both against Men and Women; accusing the former of having no Attachment but to their Interest, and the latter of being so addicted to vicious Inclinations, that they could never be safely trusted with one of the other Sex. 'Could I,' said he, 'Sir, have suspected, that a Lady of such Prudence, such Judgment, such Learning, should indulge so indiscreet a Passion; or could I have imagined, that my Brother—Why do I call him so? He is no longer a Brother of mine'—

'Indeed but he is,' said *Allworthy*, 'and a Brother of mine too.'— 'Bless me, Sir,' said the Doctor. 'Do you know the shocking Affair?' —'Look'ee, Mr. *Blifil*,' answered the good Man, 'it hath been my constant Maxim in Life, to make the best of all Matters which happen. My Sister, tho' many Years younger than I, is at least old enough to be at the Age of Discretion. Had he imposed on a Child, I should have been more averse to have forgiven him; but a Woman, upwards of thirty, must certainly be supposed to know what will make her most happy. She hath married a Gentleman, tho' perhaps not quite her Equal in Fortune; and if he hath any Perfections in her Eye, which can make up that Deficiency, I see no Reason why I should object to her Choice of her own Happiness; which I, no more than herself, imagine to consist only in immense

Wealth. I might, perhaps, from the many Declarations I have made, of complying with almost any Proposal, have expected to have been consulted on this Occasion; but these Matters are of a very delicate Nature, and the Scruples of Modesty, perhaps, are not to be overcome. As to your Brother, I have really no Anger against him at all. He hath no Obligation to me, nor do I think he was under any Necessity of asking my Consent, since the Woman is, as I have said, *Sui Juris*, and of a proper Age to be entirely answerable only to herself for her Conduct.'

The Doctor accused Mr. *Allworthy* of too great Lenity, repeated his Accusations against his Brother, and declared that he should never more be brought either to see, or to own him for his Relation. He then launched forth into a Panegyric on *Allworthy*'s Goodness; into the highest Encomiums on his Friendship; and concluded by saying, he should never forgive his Brother for having put the Place which he bore in that Friendship to a Hazard.

Allworthy thus answered: 'Had I conceived any Displeasure against your Brother, I should never have carried that Resentment to the Innocent: But, I assure you, I have no such Displeasure. Your Brother appears to me to be a Man of Sense and Honour. I do not disapprove the Taste of my Sister; nor will I doubt but that she is equally the Object of his Inclinations. I have always thought Love the only Foundation of Happiness in a married State; as it can only produce that high and tender Friendship which should always be the Cement of this Union; and, in my Opinion, all those Marriages which are contracted from other Motives, are greatly criminal; they are a Profanation of a most holy Ceremony, and generally end in Disquiet and Misery: For surely we may call it a Profanation, to convert this most sacred Institution into a wicked Sacrifice to Lust or Avarice: And what better can be said of those Matches to which Men are induced merely by the Consideration of a beautiful Person, or a great Fortune!

'To deny that Beauty is an agreeable Object to the Eye, and even worthy some Admiration, would be false and foolish. *Beautiful* is an Epithet often used in Scripture, and always mentioned with Honour. It was my own Fortune to marry a Woman whom the World thought handsome, and I can truly say, I liked her the better on that Account. But, to make this the sole Consideration of Marriage, to lust after it so violently as to overlook all Imperfections for its Sake, or to require it so absolutely as to reject and disdain Religion, Virtue, and Sense, which are Qualities, in their Nature, of much higher Perfection, only because an Elegance of Person is wanting; this is surely inconsistent, either with a wise Man or a good Christian. And it is, perhaps, being too charitable to conclude, that such Persons mean any thing more by their Marriage, than to please their carnal Appetites; for the Satisfaction of which, we are taught, it was not ordained.

'In the next Place, with Respect to Fortune. Worldly Prudence, perhaps, exacts some Consideration on this Head; nor will I absolutely and altogether condemn it. As the World is constituted, the Demands of a married State, and the Care of Posterity, require some little Regard to what we call Circumstances. Yet this Provision is greatly encreased, beyond what is really necessary, by Folly and Vanity, which create abundantly more Wants than Nature. Equipage for the Wife, and large Fortunes for the Children, are by Custom enrolled in the List of Necessaries; and, to procure these, every Thing truly solid and sweet, and virtuous and religious, are neglected and overlooked.

'And this in many Degrees; the last and greatest of which seems scarce distinguishable from Madness. I mean, where Persons of immense Fortunes contract themselves to those who are, and must be, disagreeable to them; to Fools and Knaves, in order to increase an Estate, already larger even than the Demands of their Pleasures. Surely such Persons, if they will not be thought mad, must own, either that they are incapable of tasting the Sweets of the tenderest Friendship, or that they sacrifice the greatest Happiness of which they are capable, to the vain, uncertain, and senseless Laws of vulgar Opinion, which owe as well their Force, as their Foundation, to Folly.'

Here *Allworthy* concluded his Sermon, to which *Blifil* had listened with the profoundest Attention, though it cost him some Pains to prevent now and then a small Discomposure of his Muscles. He now praised every Period of what he had heard, with the Warmth of a young Divine, who hath the Honour to dine with a Bishop the same Day in which his Lordship hath mounted the Pulpit.

Chapter XIII.

Which concludes the first Book; with an Instance of Ingratitude, which, we hope, will appear unnatural.

The Reader, from what hath been said, may imagine, that the Reconciliation (if indeed it could be so called) was only Matter of Form; we shall therefore pass it over, and hasten to what must surely be thought Matter of Substance.

The Doctor had acquainted his Brother with what had past between Mr. *Allworthy* and him; and added, with a Smile, 'I prom-

ise you, I paid you off; nay, I absolutely desired the good Gentleman not to forgive you: For you know, after he had made a Declaration in your Favour, I might, with Safety, venture on such a
Request with a Person of his Temper; and I was willing, as well for
your Sake as for my own, to prevent the least Possibility of a Suspicion.'

Captain *Blifil* took not the least Notice of this, at that Time; but
he afterwards made a very notable Use of it.

One of the Maxims which the Devil, in a late Visit upon Earth,
left to his Disciples, is, when once you are got up, to kick the Stool
from under you. In plain *English*, when you have made your Fortune by the good Offices of a Friend, you are advised to discard him
as soon as you can.

Whether the Captain acted by this Maxim, I will not positively
determine; so far we may confidently say, that his Actions may be
fairly derived from this diabolical Principle; and indeed it is difficult
to assign any other Motive to them: For no sooner was he possessed
of Miss *Bridget*, and reconciled to *Allworthy*, then he began to
shew a Coldness to his Brother, which encreased daily; till at length
it grew into Rudeness, and became very visible to every one.

The Doctor remonstrated to him privately concerning this Behaviour, but could obtain no other Satisfaction than the following
plain Declaration: 'If you dislike any thing in my Brother's House,
Sir, you know you are at Liberty to quit it.' This strange, cruel, and
almost unaccountable Ingratitude in the Captain, absolutely broke
the poor Doctor's Heart: For Ingratitude never so thoroughly
pierces the human Breast, as when it proceeds from those in whose
Behalf we have been guilty of Transgressions. Reflections on great
and good Actions, however they are received or returned by those in
whose Favour they are performed, always administer some Comfort
to us; but what Consolation shall we receive under so biting a
Calamity as the ungrateful Behaviour of our Friend, when our
wounded Conscience at the same time flies in our Face, and
upbraids us with having spotted it in the Service of one so worthless?

Mr. *Allworthy* himself spoke to the Captain in his Brother's
Behalf, and desired to know what Offence the Doctor had committed; when the hard-hearted Villain had the Baseness to say, that he
should never forgive him for the Injury which he had endeavoured
to do him in his Favour; which, he said, he had pumped out of
him, and was such a Cruelty, that it ought not to be forgiven.

Allworthy spoke in very high Terms upon this Declaration,
which, he said, became not a human Creature. He expressed,
indeed, so much Resentment against an unforgiving Temper, that

the Captain at last pretended to be convinced by his Arguments, and outwardly professed to be reconciled.

As for the Bride, she was now in her Honeymoon, and so passionately fond of her new Husband, that he never appeared, to her, to be in the wrong; and his Displeasure against any Person was a sufficient Reason for her Dislike to the same.

The Captain, at Mr. *Allworthy*'s Instance, was outwardly, as we have said, reconciled to his Brother, yet the same Rancour remained in his Heart; and he found so many Opportunities of giving him private Hints of this, that the House at last grew insupportable to the poor Doctor; and he chose rather to submit to any Inconveniencies which he might encounter in the World, than longer to bear these cruel and ungrateful Insults, from a Brother for whom he had done so much.

He once intended to acquaint *Allworthy* with the whole; but he could not bring himself to submit to the Confession, by which he must take to his Share so great a Portion of Guilt. Besides, by how much the worse Man he represented his Brother to be, so much the greater would his own Offence appear to *Allworthy*, and so much the greater, he had Reason to imagine, would be his Resentment.

He feigned, therefore, some Excuse of Business for his Departure, and promised to return soon again; and took Leave of his Brother with so well-dissembled Content, that, as the Captain played his Part to the same Perfection, *Allworthy* remained well satisfied with the Truth of the Reconciliation.

The Doctor went directly to *London*, where he died soon after of a broken Heart; a Distemper which kills many more than is generally imagined, and would have a fair Title to a Place in the Bill of Mortality, did it not differ in one Instance from all other Diseases, *viz*. That no Physician can cure it.

Now, upon the most diligent Enquiry into the former Lives of these two Brothers, I find, besides the cursed and hellish Maxim of Policy above-mentioned, another Reason for the Captain's Conduct: The Captain, besides what we have before said of him, was a Man of great Pride and Fierceness, and had always treated his Brother, who was of a different Complexion, and greatly deficient in both those Qualities, with the utmost Air of Superiority. The Doctor, however, had much the larger Share of Learning, and was by many reputed to have the better Understanding. This the Captain knew, and could not bear; for tho' Envy is, at best, a very malignant Passion, yet is its Bitterness greatly heightened, by mixing with Contempt towards the same Object; and very much afraid I am, that whenever an Obligation is joined to these two, Indignation, and not Gratitude, will be the Product of all three.

BOOK II.

Containing Scenes of matrimonial Felicity in different Degrees of Life; and various other Transactions during the first two Years after the Marriage between Captain Blifil, *and Miss* Bridget Allworthy.

Chapter I.

Shewing what Kind of a History this is; what it is like, and what it is not like.

Tho' we have properly enough entitled this our Work, a History, and not a Life; nor an Apology for a Life,[1] as is more in Fashion; yet we intend in it rather to pursue the Method of those Writers, who profess to disclose the Revolutions of Countries, than to imitate the painful and voluminous Historian, who, to preserve the Regularity of his Series, thinks himself obliged to fill up as much Paper with the Detail of Months and Years in which nothing remarkable happened, as he employs upon those notable Æras when the greatest Scenes have been transacted on the human Stage.

Such Histories as these do, in reality, very much resemble a News-Paper, which consists of just the same Number of Words, whether there be any News in it or not. They may, likewise, be compared to a Stage-Coach, which performs constantly the same Course, empty as well as full. The Writer, indeed, seems to think himself obliged to keep even Pace with Time, whose Amanuensis he is; and, like his Master, travels as slowly through Centuries of monkish Dulness, when the World seems to have been asleep, as through that bright and busy Age so nobly distinguished by the excellent *Latin* Poet.[2]

'*Ad confligendum venientibus undique Pœnis,*
Omnia cum belli trepido concussa tumultu
Horrida contremuere sub altis ætheris auris:
In dubioque fuit sub utrorum regna cadendum
Omnibus humanis esset, terraque marique.'

Of which we wish we could give our Reader a more adequate Translation than that by Mr. *Creech,*

'When dreadful *Carthage* frighted *Rome* with Arms,

---

1. A crack at *An Apology for the Life of Mr. Colley Cibber, Written by Himself* (1740), which Fielding had already ridiculed in *Shamela* (1741) and *Joseph Andrews* (1742).

2. Lucretius, *De Rerum Natura* III.833–37. Fielding quotes from memory: *aetheris auris* should be *aetheris oris; fuit* should be *fuere.* Thomas Creech's translation (1682), III.812–15.

> And all the World was shook with fierce Alarms;
> Whilst undecided yet, which Part should fall,
> Which Nation rise the glorious Lord of all.'

Now it is our Purpose in the ensuing Pages, to pursue a contrary Method. When any extraordinary Scene presents itself, (as we trust will often be the Case) we shall spare no Pains nor Paper to open it at large to our Reader; but if whole Years should pass without producing any Thing worthy his Notice, we shall not be afraid of a Chasm in our History; but shall hasten on to Matters of Consequence, and leave such Periods of Time totally unobserved.

These are indeed to be considered as Blanks in the grand Lottery of Time. We therefore who are the Registers of that Lottery, shall imitate those sagacious Persons who deal in that which is drawn at *Guild-hall*, and who never trouble the Public with the many Blanks they dispose of; but when a great Prize happens to be drawn, the News-Papers are presently filled with it, and the World is sure to be informed at whose Office it was sold: Indeed, commonly two or three different Offices lay claim to the Honour of having disposed of it; by which, I suppose, the Adventurers are given to understand that certain Brokers are in the Secrets of Fortune, and indeed of her Cabinet-Council.

My Reader then is not to be surprised, if, in the Course of this Work, he shall find some Chapters very short, and others altogether as long; some that contain only the Time of a single Day, and others that comprise Years; in a Word, if my History sometimes seems to stand still, and sometimes to fly. For all which I shall not look on myself as accountable to any Court of Critical Jurisdiction whatever: For as I am, in reality, the Founder of a new Province of Writing, so I am at liberty to make what Laws I please therein. And these Laws, my Readers, whom I consider as my Subjects, are bound to believe in and to obey; with which that they may readily and chearfully comply, I do hereby assure them, that I shall principally regard their Ease and Advantage in all such Institutions: For I do not, like a *jure divino* Tyrant, imagine that they are my Slaves, or my Commodity. I am, indeed, set over them for their own Good only, and was created for their Use, and not they for mine. Nor do I doubt, while I make their Interest the great Rule of my Writings, they will unanimously concur in supporting my Dignity, and in rendering me all the Honour I shall deserve or desire.

Chapter II.

Religious Cautions against shewing too much Favour to Bastards;
and a great Discovery made by Mrs. Deborah Wilkins.

Eight Months after the Celebration of the Nuptials between Cap-

tain *Blifil* and Miss *Bridget Allworthy*, a young Lady of great
Beauty, Merit, and Fortune, was Miss *Bridget*, by reason of a
Fright, delivered of a fine Boy. The Child was indeed, to all
Appearance, perfect; but the Midwife discovered, it was born a
Month before its full Time.

Though the Birth of an Heir by his beloved Sister was a Circumstance of great Joy to Mr. *Allworthy*, yet it did not alienate his
Affections from the little Foundling, to whom he had been God-
father, had given his own Name of *Thomas*, and whom he had hitherto seldom failed of visiting, at least once a Day, in his Nursery.

He told his Sister, if she pleased, the new-born Infant should be
bred up together with little *Tommy*, to which she consented, tho'
with some little Reluctance: For she had truly a great Complacence
for her Brother; and hence she had always behaved towards the
Foundling, with rather more Kindness than Ladies of rigid Virtue
can sometimes bring themselves to shew to these Children, who,
however innocent, may be truly called the living Monuments of
Incontinence.

The Captain could not so easily bring himself to bear what he
condemned as a Fault in Mr. *Allworthy*. He gave him frequent
Hints, that to adopt the Fruits of Sin, was to give Countenance to
it. He quoted several Texts, (for he was well read in Scripture)
such as, *He visits the Sins of the Fathers upon the Children*; and,
*the Fathers have eaten sour Grapes, and the Children's Teeth are
set on Edge*, &c. Whence he argued the Legality of punishing the
Crime of the Parent on the Bastard. He said, 'Tho' the Law did not
positively allow the destroying such base-born Children, yet it held
them to be the Children of No-body: That the Church considered
them as the Children of No-body; and that, at the best, they ought
to be brought up to the lowest and vilest Offices of the Commonwealth.'

Mr. *Allworthy* answered to all this, and much more, which the
Captain had urged on this Subject, 'That, however guilty the Parents might be, the Children were certainly innocent: That as to the
Texts he had quoted, the former of them was a particular Denuncia-
tion against the *Jews*, for the Sin of Idolatry, of relinquishing and
hating their heavenly King: And the latter was parabolically spoken,
and rather intended to denote the certain and necessary Consequences of Sin, than any express Judgment against it. But to
represent the Almighty as avenging the Sins of the Guilty on the
Innocent, was indecent, if not blasphemous, as it was to represent
him acting against the first Principles of natural Justice, and against
the original Notions of Right and Wrong, which he himself had
implanted in our Minds; by which we were to judge, not only in all
Matters which were not revealed, but even of the Truth of Revela-

tion itself. He said, he knew many held the same Principles with
the Captain on this Head; but he was himself firmly convinced to
the contrary, and would provide in the same Manner for this poor
Infant, as if a legitimate Child had had the Fortune to have been
found in the same Place.'

While the Captain was taking all Opportunities to press these
and such like Arguments, to remove the little Foundling from Mr.
Allworthy's, of whose Fondness for him he began to be jealous,
Mrs. *Deborah* had made a Discovery, which, in its Event, threatned at least to prove more fatal to poor *Tommy*, than all the Reasonings of the Captain.

Whether the insatiable Curiosity of this good Woman had carried her on to that Business, or whether she did it to confirm herself
in the good Graces of Mrs. *Blifil*, who, notwithstanding her outward Behaviour to the Foundling, frequently abused the Infant in
private, and her Brother too for his Fondness to it, I will not determine; but she had now, as she conceived, fully detected the Father
of the Foundling.

Now, as this was a Discovery of great Consequence, it may be
necessary to trace it from the Fountain-head. We shall therefore
very minutely lay open those previous Matters by which it was produced; and for that Purpose, we shall be obliged to reveal all the
Secrets of a little Family, with which my Reader is at present
entirely unacquainted; and of which the Oeconomy was so rare and
extraordinary, that I fear it will shock the utmost Credulity of many
married Persons.

Chapter III.

*The Description of a domestic Government founded upon Rules
directly contrary to those of* Aristotle.[1]

My Reader may please to remember he hath been informed, that
Jenny Jones had lived some Years with a certain Schoolmaster, who
had, at her earnest Desire, instructed her in *Latin*, in which, to do
Justice to her Genius, she had so improved herself, that she was
become a better Scholar than her Master.

Indeed, tho' this poor Man had undertaken a Profession to which
Learning must be allowed necessary, this was the least of his Commendations. He was one of the best-natured Fellows in the World,
and was, at the same Time, Master of so much Pleasantry and
Humour, that he was reputed the Wit of the Country; and all the
neighbouring Gentlemen were so desirous of his Company, that, as
Denying was not his Talent, he spent much Time at their Houses,

1. *Politica* I.3–13, concerning housekeeping.

which he might, with more Emolument, have spent in his School.

It may be imagined, that a Gentleman so qualified, and so disposed, was in no Danger of becoming formidable to the learned Seminaries of *Eton* or *Westminster*. To speak plainly, his Scholars were divided into two Classes. In the upper of which was a young Gentleman, the Son of a neighbouring Squire, who, at the Age of seventeen, was just entered into his *Syntaxis*;[2] and in the lower was a second Son of the same Gentleman, who, together with seven Parish-boys, was learning to read and write.

The Stipend arising hence would hardly have indulged the Schoolmaster in the Luxuries of Life, had he not added to this Office those of Clerk and Barber, and had not Mr. *Allworthy* added to the whole an Annuity of Ten Pound, which the poor Man received every *Christmas*, and with which he was enabled to chear his Heart during that sacred Festival.

Among his other Treasures, the Pedagogue had a Wife, whom he had married out of Mr. *Allworthy*'s Kitchin for her Fortune, *viz.* Twenty Pound, which she had there amassed.

This Woman was not very amiable in her Person. Whether she sat to my Friend *Hogarth*,[3] or no, I will not determine; but she exactly resembled the young Woman who is pouring out her Mistress's Tea in the third Picture of the Harlot's Progress. She was, besides, a profest Follower of that noble Sect founded by *Xanthippe*[4] of old; by means of which she became more formidable in the School than her Husband; for, to confess the Truth, he was never Master there, or any where else, in her Presence.

Tho' her Countenance did not denote much natural Sweetness of Temper, yet this was, perhaps, somewhat soured by a Circumstance which generally poisons matrimonial Felicity: For Children are rightly called the Pledges of Love; and her Husband, tho' they had been married nine Years, had given her no such Pledges; a Default for which he had no Excuse, either from Age or Health, being not yet thirty Years old, and, what they call, a jolly, brisk, young Man.

Hence arose another Evil, which produced no little Uneasiness to the poor Pedagogue, of whom she maintained so constant a Jealousy, that he durst hardly speak to one Woman in the Parish; for the least Degree of Civility, or even Correspondence with any Female, was sure to bring his Wife upon her Back, and his own.

In order to guard herself against matrimonial Injuries in her own House, as she kept one Maid Servant, she always took Care to chuse her out of that Order of Females, whose Faces are taken as a Kind

2. At seventeen he is only two-thirds through the "Brevissima Institutio," the Latin half of Lily's *Grammar*, which begins on p. 136—still in grammar school. See Partridge's quotations from the same page (*fortuna nunquam* . . .), below, p. 519, and from the following page, below, p. 411.
3. See above, p. 51, and below, p. 104.
4. The wife of Socrates. Legend has made of her the classic shrew.

of Security for their Virtue; of which Number *Jenny Jones*, as the Reader hath been before informed, was one.

As the Face of this young Woman might be called pretty good Security of the before-mentioned Kind, and as her Behaviour had been always extremely modest; which is the certain Consequence of Understanding in Women; she had passed above four Years at Mr. *Partridge*'s, (for that was the Schoolmaster's Name) without creating the least Suspicion in her Mistress. Nay, she had been treated with uncommon Kindness, and her Mistress had permitted Mr. *Partridge* to give her those Instructions, which have been before commemorated.

But it is with Jealousy, as with the Gout. When such Distempers are in the Blood, there is never any Security against their breaking out; and that often on the slightest Occasions, and when least suspected.

Thus it happened to Mrs. *Partridge*, who had submitted four Years to her Husband's teaching this young Woman, and had suffered her often to neglect her Work, in order to pursue her Learning. For passing by one Day, as the Girl was reading, and her Master leaning over her, the Girl, I know not for what Reason, suddenly started up from her Chair: and this was the first Time that Suspicion ever entered into the Head of her Mistress.

This did not, however, at that Time, discover itself, but lay lurking in her Mind, like a concealed Enemy, who waits for a Reinforcement of additional Strength, before he openly declares himself, and proceeds upon hostile Operations: And such additional Strength soon arrived to corroborate her Suspicion; for not long after, the Husband and Wife being at Dinner, the Master said to his Maid, *Da mihi aliquid Potum*:[5] Upon which the poor Girl smiled, perhaps at the Badness of the *Latin*, and when her Mistress cast her Eyes on her, blushed, possibly with a Consciousness of having laughed at her Master. Mrs. *Partridge*, upon this, immediately fell into a Fury, and discharged the Trencher, on which she was eating at the Head of poor *Jenny*, crying out, 'You impudent Whore, do you play Tricks with my Husband before my Face?' and, at the same Instant, rose from her Chair, with a Knife in her Hand, with which, most probably, she would have executed very tragical Vengeance, had not the Girl taken the Advantage of being nearer the Door than her Mistress, and avoided her Fury by running away; for, as to the poor Husband, whether Surprize had rendered him motionless, or Fear (which is full as probable) had restrained him from venturing at any Opposition, he sat staring and trembling in his Chair; nor did he once offer to move or speak, till

5. "Give me some drink." As Mutter notes, *da mihi potum* or *da mihi quod*   *bibam* would be better Latin.

his Wife, returning from the Pursuit of *Jenny*, made some defensive Measures necessary for his own Preservation; and he likewise was obliged to retreat, after the Example of the Maid.

This good Woman was, no more than *Othello*,[6] of a Disposition,

> ——'To make a Life of Jealousy,
> And follow still the Changes of the Moon
> With fresh Suspicions'——

With her, as well as him;

> ——To be once in doubt,
> Was once to be resolved'———

she, therefore ordered *Jenny* immediately to pack up her Alls, and be gone; for that she was determined she should not sleep that Night within her Walls.

Mr. *Partridge* had profited too much by Experience, to interpose in a Matter of this Nature. He therefore had recourse to his usual Receipt of Patience; for, tho' he was not a great Adept in *Latin*, he remembered, and well understood, the Advice contained in these Words:

> —'*Leve fit, quod bene fertur Onus.*'[7]

In *English*,

> 'A Burden becomes lightest, when
> it is well borne.'

Which he had always in his Mouth; and of which, to say the Truth, he had often Occasion to experience the Truth.

Jenny offered to make Protestations of her Innocence; but the Tempest was too strong for her to be heard. She then betook herself to the Business of Packing, for which a small Quantity of brown Paper sufficed; and, having received her small Pittance of Wages, she returned home.

The Schoolmaster and his Consort pass'd their Time unpleasantly enough that Evening; but something or other happened before the next Morning, which a little abated the Fury of Mrs. *Partridge*; and she at length admitted her Husband to make his Excuses. To which she gave the readier Belief, as he had, instead of desiring her to recall *Jenny*, professed a Satisfaction in her being dismissed, saying, She was grown of little Use as a Servant, spending all her Time in Reading, and was become, moreover, very pert and obstinate: For, indeed, she and her Master had lately had frequent Dis-

6. "Think's thou I'ld make a life of jealousy / To follow still the changes of the
moon / With fresh suspicions? No! To
be once in doubt / Is once to be re-
solv'd . . ." (III.iii.177–80).

7. Ovid, *Amores*, I.ii.10. See also *Amelia*
III.x.

putes in Literature; in which, as hath been said, she was become greatly his Superior. This, however, he would by no Means allow; and, as he called her persisting in the Right, Obstinacy, he began to hate her with no small Inveteracy.

Chapter IV.

Containing one of the most bloody Battles, or rather Duels, that were ever recorded in Domestic History.

For the Reasons mentioned in the preceding Chapter, and from some other matrimonial Concessions, well known to most Husbands; and which, like the Secrets of Free Masonry, should be divulged to none who are not Members of that honourable Fraternity, Mrs. *Partridge* was pretty well satisfied, that she had condemned her Husband without Cause, and endeavoured, by Acts of Kindness, to make him Amends for her false Suspicion. Her Passions were, indeed, equally violent, which ever Way they inclined: For, as she could be extremely angry, so could she be altogether as fond.

But tho' these Passions ordinarily succeed each other, and scarce twenty-four Hours ever passed in which the Pedagogue was not, in some Degree, the Object of both; yet, on extraordinary Occasions, when the Passion of Anger had raged very high, the Remission was usually longer, and so was the Case at present; for she continued longer in a State of Affability, after this Fit of Jealousy was ended, than her Husband had ever known before: And, had it not been for some little Exercises, which all the Followers of *Xanthippe* are obliged to perform daily, Mr. *Partridge* would have enjoyed a perfect Serenity of several Months.

Perfect Calms at Sea are always suspected by the experienced Mariner to be the Fore-runners of a Storm: And I know some Persons, who, without being generally the Devotees of Superstition, are apt to apprehend, that great and unusual Peace or Tranquillity, will be attended with its Opposite. For which Reason the Antients used, on such Occasions, to sacrifice to the Goddess *Nemesis*; a Deity who was thought by them to look with an invidious Eye on human Felicity, and to have a peculiar Delight in overturning it.

As we are very far from believing in any such Heathen Goddess, or from encouraging any Superstition, so we wish Mr. *John Fr———*,[1] or some other such Philosopher, would bestir himself a little, in order to find out the real Cause of this sudden Transition,

1. John Freke, *An Essay to Shew the Causes of Electricity, and Why Some Things Are Non-Electricable* (11 Oct. 1746). Cross (II.105) calls Freke's theory a "wild" response to William Watson's experiments (much like Benjamin Franklin's), published in June, 1746. See also below, p. 140.

from good to bad Fortune, which hath been so often remarked, and of which we shall proceed to give an Instance; for it is our Province to relate Facts, and we shall leave Causes to Persons of much higher Genius.

Mankind have always taken great Delight in knowing and descanting on the Actions of others. Hence there have been, in all Ages, and Nations, certain Places set apart for publick Rendezvous, where the Curious might meet, and satisfy their mutual Curiosity. Among these, the Barbers Shops have justly borne the Pre-eminence. Among the *Greeks*, Barbers News was a proverbial Expression; and *Horace*,[2] in one of his Epistles, makes honourable Mention of the *Roman* Barbers in the same Light.

Those of *England* are known to be no wise inferior to their *Greek* or *Roman* Predecessors. You there see foreign Affairs discussed in a Manner little inferior to that with which they are handled in the Coffee-houses; and domestic Occurrences are much more largely and freely treated in the former, than in the latter. But this serves only for the Men. Now, whereas the Females of this Country, especially those of the lower Order, do associate themselves much more than those of other Nations, our Polity would be highly deficient, if they had not some Place set apart likewise for the Indulgence of their Curiosity, seeing they are in this no way inferior to the other half of the Species.

In enjoying, therefore, such Place of Rendezvous, the *British* Fair ought to esteem themselves more happy than any of their foreign Sisters; as I do not remember either to have read in History, or to have seen in my Travels, any thing of the like Kind.

This Place then is no other than the Chandler's Shop; the known Seat of all the News; or, as it is vulgarly called, Gossipping, in every Parish in *England*.

Mrs. *Partridge* being one Day at this Assembly of Females, was asked by one of her Neighbours, if she had heard no News lately of *Jenny Jones*? To which she answered in the negative. Upon this, the other replied, with a Smile, That the Parish was very much obliged to her for having turned *Jenny* away as she did.

Mrs. *Partridge*, whose Jealousy, as the Reader well knows, was long since cured, and who had no other Quarrel to her Maid, answered boldly, She did not know any Obligation the Parish had to her on that Account; for she believed *Jenny* had scarce left her Equal behind her.

'No, truly,' said the Gossip, 'I hope not, tho' I fancy we have Sluts enow too. Then you have not heard, it seems, that she hath been

2. *Satires* I.vii.1–3.

brought to bed of two Bastards; but as they are not born here, my Husband, and the other Overseer, says, we shall not be obliged to keep them.'

'Two Bastards!' answered Mrs. *Partridge* hastily, 'you surprize me. I don't know whether we must keep them; but I am sure they must have been begotten here; for the Wench hath not been nine Months gone away.'

Nothing can be so quick and sudden as the Operations of the Mind, especially when Hope, or Fear, or Jealousy to which the two others are but Journeymen, set it to work. It occurred instantly to her, that *Jenny* had scarce ever been out of her own House, while she lived with her. The leaning over the Chair, the sudden starting up, the Latin, the Smile, and many other Things rushed upon her all at once. The Satisfaction her Husband expressed in the Departure of *Jenny*, appeared now to be only dissembled; again, in the same Instant, to be real; but yet (to confirm her Jealousy) proceeding from Satiety, and a hundred other bad Causes. In a Word, she was convinced of her Husband's Guilt, and immediately left the Assembly in Confusion.

As fair *Grimalkin*, who, though the youngest of the Feline Family, degenerates not in Ferocity from the elder Branches of her House, and though inferior in Strength, is equal in Fierceness to the nobler Tiger himself, when a little Mouse, whom it hath long tormented in Sport, escapes from her Clutches, for a while, frets, scolds, growls, swears; but if the Trunk, or Box, behind which the Mouse lay hid, be again removed, she flies like Lightning on her Prey, and, with envenomed Wrath, bites, scratches, mumbles, and tears the little Animal.

Not with less Fury did Mrs. *Partridge* fly on the poor Pedagogue. Her Tongue, Teeth, and Hands, fell all upon him at once. His Wig was in an Instant torn from his Head, his Shirt from his Back, and from his Face descended five Streams of Blood, denoting the Number of Claws with which Nature had unhappily armed the Enemy.

Mr. *Partridge* acted for some Time on the defensive only; indeed he attempted only to guard his Face with his Hands; but as he found that his Antagonist abated nothing of her Rage, he thought he might, at least, endeavour to disarm her, or rather to confine her Arms; in doing which, her Cap fell off in the Struggle, and her Hair being too short to reach her Shoulders, erected itself on her Head; her Stays likewise, which were laced through one single Hole at the Bottom, burst open; and her Breasts, which were much more redundant than her Hair, hung down below her Middle; her Face was likewise marked with the Blood of her Husband; her Teeth gnashed

with Rage; and Fire, such as sparkles from a Smith's Forge, darted
from her Eyes. So that, altogether, this Amazonian Heroine might
have been an Object of Terror to a much bolder Man than Mr. *Partridge*.

He had, at length, the good Fortune, by getting Possession of her
Arms, to render those Weapons, which she wore at the Ends of her
Fingers, useless; which she no sooner perceived, than the Softness of
her Sex prevailed over her Rage, and she presently dissolved in
Tears, which soon after concluded in a Fit.

That small Share of Sense which Mr. *Partridge* had hitherto preserved through this Scene of Fury, of the Cause of which he was
hitherto ignorant, now utterly abandoned him. He ran instantly
into the Street, hallowing out, that his Wife was in the Agonies of
Death, and beseeching the Neighbours to fly with the utmost Haste
to her Assistance. Several good Women obeyed his Summons, who
entering his House, and applying the usual Remedies on such Occasions, Mrs. *Partridge* was, at length, to the great Joy of her Husband, brought to herself.

As soon as she had a little recollected her Spirits, and somewhat
composed herself with a Cordial, she began to inform the Company
of the manifold Injuries she had received from her Husband; who,
she said, was not contented to injure her in her Bed; but, upon her
upbraiding him with it, had treated her in the cruellest Manner
imaginable; had torn her Cap and Hair from her Head, and her
Stays from her Body, giving her, at the same Time, several Blows,
the Marks of which she should carry to the Grave.

The poor Man, who bore on his Face many and more visible
Marks of the Indignation of his Wife, stood in silent Astonishment
at this Accusation; which the Reader will, I believe, bear Witness
for him, had greatly exceeded the Truth; for indeed he had not
struck her once; and this Silence being interpreted to be a Confession of the Charge, by the whole Court, they all began at once, *una
voce*, to rebuke and revile him, repeating often, that none but a
Coward ever struck a Woman.

Mr. *Partridge* bore all this patiently; but when his Wife appealed
to the Blood on her Face, as an Evidence of his Barbarity, he could
not help laying Claim to his own Blood, for so it really was; as he
thought it very unnatural, that this should rise up (as we are taught
that of a murdered Person often doth) in Vengeance against him.

To this the Women made no other Answer, than that it was Pity
it had not come from his Heart, instead of his Face; all declaring,
that if their Husbands should lift their Hands against them, they
would have their Heart's Bloods out of their Bodies.

After much Admonition for what was past, and much good

Advice to Mr. *Partridge* for his future Behaviour, the Company at length departed, and left the Husband and Wife to a personal Conference together, in which Mr. *Partridge* soon learned the Cause of all his Sufferings.

Chapter V.

Containing much Matter to exercise the Judgment and Reflection of the Reader.

I Believe it is a true Observation, that few Secrets are divulged to one Person only; but certainly, it would be next to a Miracle, that a Fact of this Kind should be known to a whole Parish, and not transpire any farther.

And, indeed, a very few Days had past, before the Country, to use a common Phrase, rung of the Schoolmaster of *Little Badding-ton;* who was said to have beaten his Wife in the most cruel Manner. Nay, in some Places, it was reported he had murdered her; in others, that he had broke her Arms; in others, her Legs; in short, there was scarce an Injury which can be done to a human Creature, but what Mrs. *Partridge* was somewhere or other affirmed to have received from her Husband.

The Cause of this Quarrel was likewise variously reported; for, as some People said that Mrs. *Partridge* had caught her Husband in Bed with his Maid, so many other Reasons, of a very different Kind, went abroad. Nay, some transferred the Guilt to the Wife, and the Jealousy to the Husband.

Mrs. *Wilkins* had long ago heard of this Quarrel; but, as a different Cause from the true one had reached her Ears, she thought proper to conceal it; and the rather, perhaps, as the Blame was universally laid on Mr. *Partridge;* and his Wife, when she was Servant to Mr. *Allworthy,* had in something offended Mrs. *Wilkins,* who was not of a very forgiving Temper.

But Mrs. *Wilkins,* whose Eyes could see Objects at a Distance, and who could very well look forward a few Years into Futurity, had perceived a strong Likelihood of Captain *Blifil's* being hereafter her Master; and, as she plainly discerned, that the Captain bore no great Good-will to the little Foundling, she fancied it would be rendering him an agreeable Service, if she could make any Discoveries that might lessen the Affection which Mr. *Allworthy* seemed to have contracted for this Child, and which gave visible Uneasiness to the Captain; who could not entirely conceal it even before *Allworthy* himself; though his Wife, who acted her Part much better in public, frequently recommended to him her own Example, of conniving at the Folly of her Brother, which, she said, she at least as well perceived, and as much resented as any other possibly could.

Mrs. *Wilkins* having therefore, by Accident, gotten a true Scent of the above Story, though long after it had happened, failed not to satisfy herself thoroughly of all the Particulars; and then acquainted the Captain, that she had at last discovered the true Father of the little Bastard, which she was sorry, she said, to see her Master lose his Reputation in the Country, by taking so much Notice of.

The Captain chid her for the Conclusion of her Speech, as an improper Assurance in judging of her Master's Actions: For if his Honour, or his Understanding, would have suffered the Captain to make an Alliance with Mrs. *Wilkins*, his Pride would by no means have admitted it. And, to say the Truth, there is no Conduct less politic, than to enter into any Confederacy with your Friend's Servants, against their Master. For, by these Means, you afterwards become the Slave of these very Servants; by whom you are constantly liable to be betrayed. And this Consideration, perhaps, it was which prevented Captain *Blifil* from being more explicit with Mrs. *Wilkins*; or from encouraging the Abuse which she had bestowed on *Allworthy*.

But though he declared no Satisfaction to Mrs. *Wilkins* at this Discovery, he enjoyed not a little from it in his own Mind, and resolved to make the best Use of it he was able.

He kept this Matter a long Time concealed within his own Breast, in Hopes that Mr. *Allworthy* might hear it from some other Person; but Mrs. *Wilkins* whether she resented the Captain's behaviour, or whether his Cunning was beyond her, and she feared the Discovery might displease him, never afterwards opened her Lips about the Matter.

I have thought it somewhat strange, upon Reflection, that the House-keeper never acquainted Mrs. *Blifil* with this News, as Women are more inclined to communicate all Pieces of Intelligence to their own Sex, than to ours. The only Way, as it appears to me, of solving this Difficulty, is, by imputing it to that Distance which was now grown between the Lady and the House-keeper: Whether this arose from a Jealousy in Mrs. *Blifil* that *Wilkins* shewed too great a Respect to the Foundling; for while she was endeavouring to ruin the little Infant, in order to ingratiate herself with the Captain, she was every Day more and more commending it before *Allworthy*, as his Fondness for it every Day increased. This, notwithstanding all the Care she took at other Times to express the direct contrary to Mrs. *Blifil*, perhaps offended that delicate Lady, who certainly now hated Mrs. *Wilkins*; and though she did not, or possibly could not, absolutely remove her, from her Place, she found, however, the Means of making her Life very uneasy. This Mrs. *Wilkins*, at length, so resented, that she very openly shewed all

Manner of Respect and Fondness to little *Tommy*, in Opposition to Mrs. *Blifil*.

The Captain, therefore, finding the Story in Danger of perishing, at last took an Opportunity to reveal it himself.

He was one Day engaged with Mr. *Allworthy* in a Discourse on Charity: In which the Captain, with great Learning, proved to Mr. *Allworthy*, that the Word *Charity*, in Scripture, no where means Beneficence or Generosity.

'The Christian Religion, he said,[1] was instituted for much nobler Purposes, than to enforce a Lesson which many Heathen Philosophers had taught us long before, and which, though it might perhaps be called a moral Virtue, savoured but little of that sublime Christian-like Disposition, that vast Elevation of Thought, in Purity approaching to angelic Perfection, to be attained, expressed, and felt only by Grace. Those (he said) came nearer to the Scripture Meaning, who understood by it Candour, or the forming of a benevolent Opinion of our Brethren, and passing a favourable Judgment on their Actions; a Virtue much higher, and more extensive in its Nature, than a pitiful Distribution of Alms, which, though we would never so much prejudice, or even ruin our Families, could never reach many; whereas Charity, in the other and truer Sense, might be extended to all Mankind.'

He said, 'Considering who the Disciples were, it would be absurd to conceive the Doctrine of Generosity, or giving Alms, to have been preached to them. And, as we could not well imagine this Doctrine should be preached by its divine Author to Men who could not practise it, much less shall we think it understood so by those who can practise it, and do not.

'But though, continued he, there is, I am afraid, little Merit in these Benefactions; there would, I must confess, be much Pleasure in them to a good Mind, if it was not abated by one Consideration. I mean, that we are liable to be imposed upon, and to confer our choicest Favours often on the Undeserving, as you must own was your Case in your Bounty to that worthless Fellow *Partridge*: For two or three such Examples must greatly lessen the inward Satisfaction, which a good Man would otherwise find in Generosity; nay, may even make him timorous in bestowing, lest he should be guilty of supporting Vice, and encouraging the Wicked; a Crime of a very black Dye, and for which it will by no means be a sufficient Excuse, that we have not actually intended such an Encouragement; unless we have used the utmost Caution in chusing the Objects of our Beneficence. A Consideration which, I make no Doubt, hath greatly checked the Liberality of many a worthy and pious Man.'

---

1. This mode of punctuation—omitting to set apart *he said* and *she said* by quotation marks—becomes virtually standard for some passages of rapid dialogue in later chapters. See pp. 570–72 for an example.

Mr. *Allworthy* answered, 'He could not dispute with the Captain in the *Greek* Language, and therefore could say nothing as to the true Sense of the Word, which is translated *Charity*; but that he had always thought it was interpreted to consist in Action, and that giving Alms constituted at least one Branch of that Virtue.

'As to the meritorious Part, he said, he readily agreed with the Captain; for where could be the Merit of barely discharging a Duty; which he said, let the Word Charity have what Construction it would, it sufficiently appeared to be from the whole Tenor of the New Testament? And as he thought it an indispensable Duty, enjoined both by the Christian Law, and by the Law of Nature itself; so was it withal so pleasant, that if any Duty could be said to be its own Reward, or to pay us while we are discharging it, it was this.

'To confess the Truth, said he, there is one Degree of Generosity, (of Charity I would have called it) which seems to have some Shew of Merit, and that is, where from a Principle of Benevolence, and Christian Love, we bestow on another what we really want ourselves; where, in order to lessen the Distresses of another, we condescend to share some Part of them by giving what even our own Necessities cannot well spare. This is, I think, meritorious; but to relieve our Brethren only with our Superfluities; to be charitable (I must use the Word) rather at the Expence of our Coffers than ourselves; to save several Families from Misery rather than hang up an extraordinary Picture in our Houses, or gratify any other idle, ridiculous Vanity, this seems to be only being human Creatures. Nay, I will venture to go farther, it is being in some degree Epicures: For what could the greatest Epicure wish rather than to eat with many Mouths instead of one; which I think may be predicated of any one who knows that the Bread of many is owing to his own Largesses?

'As to the Apprehension of bestowing Bounty on such as may hereafter prove unworthy Objects, because many have proved such; surely it can never deter a good Man from Generosity: I do not think a few or many Examples of Ingratitude can justify a Man's hardening his Heart against the Distresses of his Fellow-Creatures; nor do I believe it can ever have such Effect on a truly benevolent Mind. Nothing less than a Persuasion of universal Depravity can lock up the Charity of a good Man; and this Persuasion must lead him, I think, either into Atheism, or Enthusiasm; but surely it is unfair to argue such universal Depravity from a few vicious Individuals; nor was this, I believe, ever done by a Man, who upon searching his own Mind found one certain Exception to the general Rule.' He then concluded by asking 'who that *Partridge* was, whom he had called a worthless Fellow?'

'I mean, said the Captain, *Partridge* the Barber, the Schoolmaster, what do you call him? *Partridge*, the Father of the little Child which you found in your Bed.'

Mr. *Allworthy* exprest great Surprize at this Account, and the Captain as great at his Ignorance of it: For he said, he had known it above a Month, and at length recollected with much Difficulty that he was told it by Mrs. *Wilkins*.

Upon this, *Wilkins* was immediately summoned, who having confirmed what the Captain had said, was by Mr. *Allworthy*, by and with the Captain's Advice, dispatched to *Little Baddington* to inform herself of the Truth of the Fact: For the Captain exprest great Dislike at all hasty Proceedings in criminal Matters, and said he would by no means have Mr. *Allworthy* take any Resolution either to the Prejudice of the Child or its Father, before he was satisfied that the latter was guilty: For tho' he had privately satisfied himself of this from one of *Partridge*'s Neighbours, yet he was too generous to give any such Evidence to Mr. *Allworthy*.

Chapter VI.

The Trial of Partridge, *the Schoolmaster, for Incontinency; The Evidence of his Wife; A short Reflection on the Wisdom of our Law; with other grave Matters, which those will like best who understand them most.*

It may be wondered that a Story so well known, and which had furnished so much Matter of Conversation, should never have been mentioned to Mr. *Allworthy* himself, who was perhaps the only Person in that Country who had never heard of it.

To account in some measure for this to the Reader, I think proper to inform him that there was no one in the Kingdom less interested in opposing that Doctrine concerning the Meaning of the Word Charity, which hath been seen in the preceding Chapter, than our good Man. Indeed, he was equally intitled to this Virtue in either Sense: For as no Man was ever more sensible of the Wants, or more ready to relieve the Distresses of others, so none could be more tender of their Characters, or slower to believe any thing to their Disadvantage.

Scandal, therefore, never found any Access to his Table: For as it hath been long since observed, that you may know a Man by his Companions; so I will venture to say, that by attending to the Conversation at a great Man's Table, you may satisfy yourself of his Religion, his Politics, his Taste, and indeed of his entire Disposition: For tho' a few odd Fellows will utter their own Sentiments in all Places, yet much the greater Part of Mankind have enough of the Courtier to accommodate their Conversation to the Taste and Inclination of their Superiors.

But to return to Mrs. *Wilkins*, who having executed her Commission with great Dispatch, tho' at fifteen Miles Distance, brought back such a Confirmation of the Schoolmaster's Guilt, that Mr. *Allworthy* determined to send for the Criminal, and examine him *viva voce*. Mr. *Partridge*, therefore, was summoned to attend, in order to [make]¹ his Defence (if he could make any) against this Accusation.

At the Time appointed, before Mr. *Allworthy* himself, at *Paradise-Hall*, came as well the said *Partridge*, with *Anne* his Wife, as Mrs. *Wilkins* his Accuser.

And now Mr. *Allworthy* being seated in the Chair of Justice, Mr. *Partridge* was brought before him. Having heard his Accusation from the Mouth of Mrs. *Wilkins*, he pleaded, Not guilty, making many vehement Protestations of his Innocence.

Mrs. *Partridge* was then examined, who, after a modest Apology for being obliged to speak the Truth against her Husband, related all the Circumstances with which the Reader hath already been acquainted; and at last concluded with her Husband's Confession of his Guilt.

Whether she had forgiven him or no, I will not venture to determine: But it is certain, she was an unwilling Witness in this Cause; and it is probable, from certain other Reasons, would never have been brought to depose as she did, had not Mrs. *Wilkins*, with great Art, fished all out of her, at her own House, and had she not indeed made Promises in Mr. *Allworthy*'s Name, that the Punishment of her Husband should not be such as might any wise affect his Family.

Partridge still persisted in asserting his Innocence, tho' he admitted he had made the above-mentioned Confession; which he however endeavoured to account for, by protesting that he was forced into it by the continued Importunity she used, who vowed, that as she was sure of his Guilt, she would never leave tormenting him till he had owned it, and faithfully promised, that in such Case, she would never mention it to him more. Hence, he said, he had been induced falsely to confess himself guilty, tho' he was innocent; and that he believed he should have confest a Murder from the same Motive.

Mrs. *Partridge* could not bear this Imputation with Patience; and having no other Remedy, in the present Place but Tears, she called forth a plentiful Assistance from them, and then addressing herself to Mr. *Allworthy*, she said, (or rather cried) 'May it please your

1. Again, either Fielding or the printer has missed a necessary word, from the first edition onward.

Worship, there never was any poor Woman so injured as I am by
that base Man: For this is not the only Instance of his Falshood to
me. No, may it please your Worship, he hath injured my Bed
many's the good time and often. I could have put up with his
Drunkenness and Neglect of his Business, if he had not broke one
of the sacred *Commandiments*. Besides, if it had been out of Doors
I had not mattered it so much; but with my own Servant, in my
own House, under my own Roof; to defile my own chaste Bed,
which to be sure he hath with his beastly stinking Whores. Yes,
you Villain, you have defiled my own Bed, you have; and then you
have charged me with *bullocking* you into owning the Truth. It is
very likely, an't please your Worship, that I should *bullock* him.—I
have Marks enow about my Body to shew of his Cruelty to me. If
you had been a Man, you Villain, you would have scorned to injure
a Woman in that Manner. But you an't half a Man, you know it.
—Nor have you been half a Husband to me. You need run after
Whores, you need, when I'm sure———And since he provokes me,
I am ready, an't please your Worship, to take my bodily Oath, that
I found them a bed together. What, you have forgot, I suppose,
when you beat me into a Fit, and made the Blood run down my
Forehead, because I only civilly taxed you with your Adultery! but I
can prove it by all my Neighbours. You have almost broke my
Heart, you have, you have.'

Here Mr. *Allworthy* interrupted, and begged her to be pacified,
promising her that she should have Justice; then turning to *Partridge*, who stood aghast, one half of his Wits being hurried away
by Surprize and the other half by Fear, he said, he was sorry to see
there was so wicked a Man in the World. He assured him, that his
prevaricating and lying backward and forward was a great Aggravation of his Guilt: For which, the only Attonement he could make
was by Confession and Repentance. He exhorted him, therefore, to
begin by immediately confessing the Fact, and not to persist in denying what was so plainly proved against him, even by his own Wife.

Here, Reader, I beg your Patience a Moment, while I make a just
Compliment to the great Wisdom and Sagacity of our Law, which
refuses to admit the Evidence of a Wife for or against her Husband. This, says a certain learned Author,[2] who, I believe, was
never quoted before in any but a Law-book, would be the Means of
creating an eternal Dissension between them. It would, indeed, be

2. Sir Edward Coke, *The First Part of
the Institutes of the Laws of England,
Or, A Commentary Upon Littleton, Not
the Name of a Lawyer Only, But the
Law Itself* (London, 1628), sec. 6b—
"Note, it hath been resolved by the Justices, that a Wife cannot be produced either against or for her Husband, *quia*
sunt duae animae in carne una
["because they are two souls in one
flesh"]; and it might be a Cause of implacable Discord and Dissension between
the Husband and the Wife. . . ." Known
as "Coke upon Littleton." See below, p.
94.

the Means of much Perjury, and of much Whipping, Fining, Imprisoning, Transporting, and Hanging.

Partridge stood a while silent, till being bid to speak, he said, he had already spoken the Truth, and appealed to Heaven for his Innocence, and lastly, to the Girl herself, whom he desired his Worship immediately to send for; for he was ignorant, or at least pretended to be so, that she had left that Part of the Country.

Mr. *Allworthy*, whose natural Love of Justice, joined to his Coolness of Temper, made him always a most patient Magistrate in hearing all the Witnesses which an accused Person could produce in his Defence, agreed to defer his final Determination of this Matter, till the Arrival of *Jenny*, for whom he immediately dispatched a Messenger; and then having recommended Peace between *Partridge* and his Wife (tho' he addressed himself chiefly to the wrong Person) he appointed them to attend again the third Day: For he had sent *Jenny* a whole Day's Journey from his own House.

At the appointed Time the Parties all assembled, when the Messenger returning brought word, that *Jenny* was not to be found: For that she had left her Habitation a few Days before, in company with a recruiting Officer.

Mr. *Allworthy* then declared, that the Evidence of such a Slut as she appeared to be, would have deserved no Credit; but he said he could not help thinking that had she been present, and would have declared the Truth, she must have confirmed what so many Circumstances, together with his own Confession, and the Declaration of his Wife, that she had caught her Husband in the Fact, did sufficiently prove. He therefore once more exhorted *Partridge* to confess; but he still avowing his Innocence, Mr. *Allworthy* declared himself satisfied of his Guilt, and that he was too bad a Man to receive any Encouragement from him. He therefore deprived him of his Annuity, and recommended Repentance to him, on account of another World, and Industry to maintain himself and his Wife in this.

There were not, perhaps, many more unhappy Persons, than poor *Partridge*. He had lost the best Part of his Income by the Evidence of his Wife, and yet was daily upbraided by her for having, among other Things, been the Occasion of depriving her of that Benefit: But such was his Fortune, and he was obliged to submit to it.

Tho' I called him, poor *Partridge*, in the last Paragraph, I would have the Reader rather impute that Epithet to the Compassion of my Temper, than conceive it to be any Declaration of his Innocence. Whether he was innocent or not, will perhaps appear hereafter; but if the Historic-Muse hath entrusted me with any Secrets, I will by no means be guilty of discovering them till she shall give me leave.

Here, therefore, the Reader must suspend his Curiosity. Certain it is, that whatever was the Truth of the Case, there was Evidence more than sufficient to convict him before *Allworthy*; indeed much less would have satisfied a Bench of Justices on an Order of Bastardy; and yet notwithstanding the Positiveness of Mrs. *Partridge*, who would have taken the Sacrament upon the Matter, there is a Possibility that the Schoolmaster was entirely innocent: For tho' it appeared clear, on comparing the Time when *Jenny* departed from *Little Baddington*, with that of her Delivery, that she had there conceived this Infant, yet it by no means followed, of Necessity, that *Partridge* must have been its Father: For, to omit other Particulars, there was in the same House a Lad near Eighteen, between whom, and *Jenny*, there had subsisted sufficient Intimacy to found a reasonable Suspicion; and yet, so blind is Jealousy, this Circumstance never once entered into the Head of the enraged Wife.

Whether *Partridge* repented or not, according to Mr. *Allworthy*'s Advice, is not so apparent. Certain it is, that his Wife repented heartily of the Evidence she had given against him; especially when she found Mrs. *Deborah* had deceived her, and refused to make any Application to Mr. *Allworthy* on her Behalf. She had, however, somewhat better Success with Mrs. *Blifil*, who was, as the Reader must have perceived, a much better-tempered Woman; and very kindly undertook to solicit her Brother to restore the Annuity. In which, tho' Good-nature might have some Share, yet a stronger and more natural Motive will appear in the next Chapter.

These Solicitations were nevertheless unsuccessful: For tho' Mr. *Allworthy* did not think, with some late Writers, that Mercy consists only in punishing Offenders; yet he was as far from thinking that it is proper to this excellent Quality to pardon great Criminals wantonly, without any Reason whatever. Any Doubtfulness of the Fact, or any Circumstance of Mitigation was never disregarded; but the Petitions of an Offender, or the Intercessions of others, did not in the least affect him. In a word, he never pardoned, because the Offender himself, or his Friends, were unwilling that he should be punished.

Partridge and his Wife were therefore both obliged to submit to their Fate; which was indeed severe enough: For so far was he from doubling his Industry on the account of his lessened Income, that he did in a manner abandon himself to Despair; and as he was by Nature indolent, that Vice now increased upon him, by which means he lost the little School he had; so that neither his Wife nor himself would have had any Bread to eat, had not the Charity of some good Christian interposed, and provided them with what was just sufficient for their Sustenance.

As this Support was conveyed to them by an unknown Hand,

they imagined, and so, I doubt not, will the Reader, that Mr. *All-worthy* himself was their secret Benefactor; who, though he would not openly encourage Vice, could yet privately relieve the Distresses of the Vicious themselves, when these became too exquisite and disproportionate to their Demerit. In which Light, their Wretchedness appeared now to Fortune herself; for she at length took pity on this miserable Couple, and considerably lessened the wretched State of *Partridge*, by putting a final End to that of his Wife, who soon after caught the Small-Pox, and died.

The Justice which Mr. *Allworthy* had executed on *Partridge*, at first met with universal Approbation; but no sooner had he felt its Consequences, than his Neighbours began to relent, and to compassionate his Case; and presently after, to blame that as Rigour and Severity, which they before called Justice. They now exclaimed against punishing in cold Blood, and sang forth the Praises of Mercy and Forgiveness.

These Cries were considerably increased by the Death of Mrs. *Partridge*, which, tho' owing to the Distemper above mentioned which is no Consequence of Poverty or Distress, many were not ashamed to impute to Mr. *Allworthy*'s Severity, or, as they now termed it, Cruelty.

Partridge, having now lost his Wife, his School, and his Annuity, and the unknown Person having now discontinued the last-mentioned Charity, resolved to change the Scene, and left the Country, where he was in Danger of Starving with the universal Compassion of all his Neighbours.

Chapter VII.

A short Sketch of that Felicity which prudent Couples may extract from Hatred; with a short Apology for those People who over-look Imperfections in their Friends.

Tho' the Captain had effectually demolished poor *Partridge*, yet had he not reaped the Harvest he hoped for, which was to turn the Foundling out of Mr. *Allworthy*'s House.

On the contrary, that Gentleman grew every Day fonder of little *Tommy*, as if he intended to counterbalance his Severity to the Father with extraordinary Fondness and Affection towards the Son.

This a good deal soured the Captain's Temper, as did all the other daily Instances of Mr. *Allworthy*'s Generosity: For he looked on all such Largesses to be Diminutions of his own Wealth.

In this, we have said, he did not agree with his Wife; nor, indeed, in any Thing else: For tho' an Affection placed on the Understanding is, by many wise Persons, thought more durable

than that which is founded on Beauty, yet it happened otherwise in
the present Case. Nay, the Understandings of this Couple were
their principal Bone of Contention, and one great Cause of many
Quarrels, which from time to time arose between them; and which
at last ended, on the Side of the Lady, in a sovereign Contempt for
her Husband; and on the Husband's, in an utter Abhorrence of his
Wife.

As these had both exercised their Talents chiefly in the Study of
Divinity, this was, from their first Acquaintance, the most common
topic of Conversation between them. The Captain, like a well-bred
Man, had, before Marriage, always given up his Opinion to that of
the Lady; and this, not in the clumsy aukward Manner of a conceited Blockhead, who, while he civilly yields to a Superior in an
Argument, is desirous of being still known to think himself in the
Right. The Captain, on the contrary, tho' one of the proudest Fellows in the World, so absolutely yielded the Victory to his Antagonist, that she, who had not the least Doubt of his Sincerity,
retired always from the Dispute, with an Admiration of her own
Understanding, and a Love for his.

But tho' this Complaisance to one whom the Captain thoroughly
despised, was not so uneasy to him, as it would have been, had any
Hopes of Preferment made it necessary to shew the same Submission to a *Hoadley*,[2] or to some other of great Reputation in the Science, yet even this cost him too much to be endured without some
Motive. Matrimony, therefore, having removed all such Motives, he
grew weary of this Condescension, and began to treat the Opinions
of his Wife with that Haughtiness and Insolence, which none but
those who deserve some Contempt themselves can bestow, and
those only who deserve no Contempt can bear.

When the first Torrent of Tenderness was over, and when, in the
Calm and long Interval between the Fits, Reason began to open the
Eyes of the Lady, and she saw this Alteration of Behaviour in the
Captain, who, at length, answered all her Arguments only with *Pish*
and *Pshaw*, she was far from enduring the Indignity with a tame
Submission. Indeed it at first so highly provoked her, that it might
have produced some tragical Event, had it not taken a more harmless Turn, by filling her with the utmost Contempt for her Husband's Understanding, which somewhat qualified her Hatred
towards him; tho' of this likewise she had a pretty moderate Share.

The Captain's Hatred to her was of a purer Kind: For as to any
Imperfections in her Knowledge or Understanding, he no more
despised her for them than for her not being six Feet high. In his

2. Bishop Benjamin Hoadly (1676–
1761), who started a religious controversy in 1717 by minimizing the church's
authority and making sincerity the touchstone of religion. See below, p. 197.

Opinion of the female Sex, he exceeded the Moroseness of *Aristotle*[3] himself: He looked on a Woman as on an Animal of domestic Use, of somewhat higher Consideration than a Cat, since her Offices were of rather more Importance; but the Difference between these two, was, in his Estimation, so small, that, in his Marriage contracted with Mr. *Allworthy*'s Lands and Tenements, it would have been pretty equal which of them he had taken into the Bargain. And yet so tender was his Pride, that it felt the Contempt which his Wife now began to express towards him; and this, added to the Surfeit he had before taken of her Love, created in him a Degree of Disgust and Abhorrence, perhaps, hardly to be exceeded.

One Situation only of the married State is excluded from Pleasure; and that is, a State of Indifference; but as many of my Readers, I hope, know what an exquisite Delight there is in conveying Pleasure to a beloved Object, so some few, I am afraid, may have experienced the Satisfaction of tormenting one we hate. It is, I apprehend, to come at this latter Pleasure, that we see both Sexes often give up that Ease in Marriage, which they might otherwise possess, tho' their Mate was never so disagreeable to them. Hence the Wife often puts on Fits of Love and Jealousy, nay, even denies herself any Pleasure, to disturb and prevent those of her Husband; and he again, in return, puts frequent Restraints on himself, and stays at home in Company which he dislikes, in order to confine his Wife to what she equally detests. Hence too must flow those Tears which a Widow sometimes so plentifully sheds over the Ashes of a Husband, with whom she led a Life of constant Disquiet and Turbulency, and whom now she can never hope to torment any more.

But if ever any Couple enjoyed this Pleasure, it was at present experienced by the Captain and his Lady. It was always a sufficient Reason to either of them to be obstinate in any Opinion, that the other had previously asserted the contrary. If the one proposed any Amusement, the other constantly objected to it: They never loved or hated, commended or abused, the same Person. And for this Reason, as the Captain looked with an evil Eye on the little Foundling, his Wife began now to caress it almost equally with her own Child.

The Reader will be apt to conceive, that this Behaviour between the Husband and Wife did not greatly contribute to Mr. *Allworthy*'s Repose, as it tended so little to that serene Happiness which he had designed for all three, from this Alliance; but the Truth is, tho' he might be a little disappointed in his sanguine Expectations, yet he was far from being acquainted with the whole Matter: For,

3. *Poetics* XV.i—"For a Woman may be Good, and a Servant *may be Good,* tho' the Women *are generally speaking rather* *bad than good,* and the Servants are absolutely naught" (Dacier [London, 1705], p. 250—see note 2, p. 302.)

as the Captain was, from certain obvious Reasons, much on his Guard before him, the Lady was obliged, for fear of her Brother's Displeasure, to pursue the same Conduct. In Fact, it is possible for a third Person to be very intimate, nay even to live long in the same House, with a married Couple, who have any tolerable Discretion, and not even guess at the sour Sentiments which they bear to each other: For tho' the whole Day may be sometimes too short for Hatred, as well as for Love; yet the many Hours which they naturally spend together, apart from all Observers, furnish People, of tolerable Moderation, with such ample Opportunity for the Enjoyment of either Passion, that, if they love, they can support being a few Hours in Company without toying, or if they hate, without spitting in each others Faces.

It is possible, however, that Mr. *Allworthy* saw enough to render him a little uneasy; for we are not always to conclude, that a wise Man is not hurt, because he doth not cry out and lament himself, like those of a childish or effeminate Temper. But indeed it is possible he might see some Faults in the Captain without any Uneasiness at all: For Men of true Wisdom and Goodness are contented to take Persons and Things as they are, without complaining of their Imperfections, or attempting to amend them. They can see a Fault in a Friend, a Relation, or an Acquaintance, without ever mentioning it to the Parties themselves, or to any others; and this often without lessening their Affection. Indeed, unless great Discernment be tempered with this overlooking Disposition, we ought never to contract Friendship but with a Degree of Folly which we can deceive: For I hope my Friends will pardon me, when I declare, I know none of them without a Fault; and I should be sorry if I could imagine, I had any Friend who could not see mine. Forgiveness, of this Kind, we give and demand in Turn. It is an Exercise of Friendship, and perhaps none of the least pleasant. And this Forgiveness we must bestow, without Desire of Amendment. There is, perhaps, no surer Mark of Folly, than an Attempt to correct the natural Infirmities of those we love. The finest Composition of human Nature, as well as the finest China, may have a Flaw in it; and this, I am afraid, in either Case, is equally incurable; though, nevertheless, the Pattern may remain of the highest Value.

Upon the whole then, Mr. *Allworthy* certainly saw some Imperfections in the Captain; but, as this was a very artful Man, and eternally upon his Guard before him, these appeared to him no more than Blemishes in a good Character; which his Goodness made him overlook, and his Wisdom prevented him from discovering to the Captain himself. Very different would have been his Sentiments, had he discovered the whole; which, perhaps, would, in Time, have been the Case, had the Husband and Wife long continued this

Kind of Behaviour to each other; but this kind Fortune took effectual Means to prevent, by forcing the Captain to do that which rendered him again dear to his Wife, and restored all her Tenderness and Affection towards him.

Chapter VIII.

A Receipt to regain the lost Affections of a Wife, *which hath never been known to fail in the most desperate Cases.*

The Captain was made large Amends for the unpleasant Minutes which he passed in the Conversation of his Wife, (and which were as few as he could contrive to make them) by the pleasant Meditations he enjoyed when alone.

These Meditations were entirely employed on Mr. *Allworthy*'s Fortune; for first, he exercised much Thought in calculating, as well as he could, the exact Value of the Whole; which Calculations he often saw Occasion to alter in his own Favour: And secondly, and chiefly, he pleased himself with intended Alterations in the House and Gardens, and in projecting many other Schemes, as well for the Improvement of the Estate, as of the Grandeur of the Place: For this Purpose he applied himself to the Studies of Architecture and Gardening, and read over many Books on both these Subjects; for these Sciences, indeed, employed his whole Time, and formed his only Amusement. He, at last, completed a most excellent Plan; and very sorry we are, that it is not in our Power to present it to our Reader, since even the Luxury of the present Age, I believe, would hardly match it. It had, indeed, in a superlative Degree, the two principal Ingredients which serve to recommend all great and noble Designs of this Nature; for it required an immoderate Expence to execute, and a vast Length of Time to bring it to any Sort of Perfection. The former of these, the immense Wealth of which the Captain supposed Mr. *Allworthy* possessed, and which he thought himself sure of inheriting, promised very effectually to supply; and the latter, the Soundness of his own Constitution, and his Time of Life, which was only what is called Middle Age, removed all Apprehension of his not living to accomplish.

Nothing was wanting to enable him to enter upon the immediate Execution of this Plan, but the Death of Mr. *Allworthy*; in calculating which he had employed much of his own Algebra, besides purchasing every Book extant that treats of the Value of Lives, Reversions, &c. From all which he satisfied himself, that as he had every Day a Chance of this happening, so had he more than an even Chance of its happening within a few Years.

But while the Captain was one Day busied in deep Contemplations of this Kind, one of the most unlucky, as well as unseasonable Accidents, happened to him. The utmost Malice of Fortune could, indeed, have contrived nothing so cruel, so mal-a-propos, so absolutely destructive to all his Schemes. In short, not to keep the Reader in long Suspence, just at the very Instant when his Heart was exulting in Meditations on the Happiness which would accrue to him by Mr. *Allworthy*'s Death, he himself——died of an Apoplexy.

This unfortunately befel the Captain as he was taking his Evening Walk by himself, so that no Body was present to lend him any Assistance, if indeed any Assistance could have preserved him. He took, therefore, Measure of that Proportion of Soil, which was now become adequate to all his future Purposes, and he lay dead on the Ground, a great (tho' not a living) Example of the Truth of that Observation of *Horace*:

> '*Tu secanda marmora*
> *Locas sub ipsum funus: & sepulchri*
> *Immemor, struis domos.*'[1]

Which Sentiment, I shall thus give to the *English* Reader: 'You provide the noblest Materials for Building, when a Pick-ax and a Spade are only necessary; and build Houses of five hundred by a hundred Feet, forgetting that of six by two.'

Chapter IX.

A Proof of the Infallibility of the foregoing Receipt, in the Lamentations of the Widow; with other suitable Decorations of Death, such as Physicians, &c. and an Epitaph in the true Stile.

Mr. *Allworthy*, his Sister, and another Lady, were assembled at the accustomed Hour in the Supper Room, where having waited a considerable Time longer than usual, Mr. *Allworthy* first declared, he began to grow uneasy at the Captain's Stay; (for he was always most punctual at his Meals) and gave Orders that the Bell should be rung without the Doors, and especially towards those Walks which the Captain was wont to use.

All these Summons proving ineffectual, (for the Captain had, by perverse Accident, betaken himself to a new Walk that Evening) Mrs. *Blifil* declared she was seriously frightned. Upon which the other Lady, who was one of her most intimate Acquaintance, and who well knew the true State of her Affections, endeavoured all she could to pacify her; telling her—To be sure she could not help being uneasy; but that she should hope the best. That, perhaps, the

1. *Odes* II.xviii.17–19.

Sweetness of the Evening had inticed the Captain to go farther than his usual Walk; or he might be detained at some Neighbour's. Mrs. *Blifil* answered, No; she was sure some Accident had befallen him; for that he would never stay out without sending her Word, as he must know how uneasy it would make her. The other Lady, having no other Arguments to use, betook herself to the Entreaties usual on such Occasions, and begged her not to frighten herself, for it might be of very ill Consequence to her own Health; and, filling out a very large Glass of Wine, advised, and at last prevailed with, her to drink it.

Mr. *Allworthy* now returned into the Parlour; for he had been himself in Search after the Captain. His Countenance sufficiently shewed the Consternation he was under, which, indeed had a good deal deprived him of Speech; but as Grief operates variously on different Minds, so the same Apprehension which depressed his Voice, elevated that of Mrs. *Blifil*. She now began to bewail herself in very bitter Terms, and Floods of Tears accompanied her Lamentations, which the Lady, her Companion, declared she could not blame; but, at the same Time, dissuaded her from indulging; attempting to moderate the Grief of her Friend, by philosophical Observations on the many Disappointments to which human Life is daily subject, which, she said, was a sufficient Consideration to fortify our Minds against any Accidents, how sudden or terrible soever. She said, her Brother's Example ought to teach her Patience, who, tho' indeed he could not be supposed as much concerned as herself, yet was, doubtless, very uneasy, tho' his Resignation to the Divine Will had restrained his Grief within due Bounds.

'Mention not my Brother,' said Mrs. *Blifil*, 'I alone am the Object of your Pity. What are the Terrors of Friendship to what a Wife feels on these Occasions? O he is lost! Somebody hath murdered him—I shall never see him more'—Here a Torrent of Tears had the same Consequence with what the Suppression had occasioned to Mr. *Allworthy*, and she remained silent.

At this Interval, a Servant came running in, out of Breath, and cried out, 'The Captain was found;' and, before he could proceed farther, he was followed by two more, bearing the dead Body between them.

Here the curious Reader may observe another Diversity in the Operations of Grief: For as Mr. *Allworthy* had been before silent, from the same Cause which had made his Sister vociferous; so did the present Sight, which drew Tears from the Gentleman, put an entire Stop to those of the Lady; who first gave a violent Scream, and presently after fell into a Fit.

The Room was soon full of Servants, some of whom, with the Lady visitant, were employed in Care of the Wife; and others, with

Mr. *Allworthy*, assisted in carrying off the Captain to a warm Bed; where every Method was tried, in order to restore him to Life.

And glad should we be, could we inform the Reader, that both these Bodies had been attended with equal Success; for those who undertook the Care of the Lady, succeeded so well, that after the Fit had continued a decent Time, she again revived, to their great Satisfaction: But as to the Captain, all Experiments of Bleeding, Chafing, Dropping, *&c.* proved ineffectual. Death, that inexorable Judge, had passed Sentence on him, and refused to grant him a Reprieve, though two Doctors who arrived, and were fee'd at one and the same Instant, were his Counsel.

These two Doctors, whom, to avoid any malicious Applications, we shall distinguish by the Names of Dr. Y. and Dr. Z. having felt his Pulse; to wit, Dr. Y. his Right Arm, and Dr. Z. his Left, both agreed that he was absolutely dead; but as to the Distemper, or Cause of his Death, they differed; Dr. Y. holding that he died of an Apoplexy, and Dr. Z. of an Epilepsy.

Hence arose a Dispute between the learned Men, in which each delivered the Reasons of their several Opinions. These were of such equal Force, that they served both to confirm either Doctor in his own Sentiments, and made not the least Impression on his Adversary.

To say the Truth, every Physician, almost, hath his favourite Disease, to which he ascribes all the Victories obtained over human Nature. The Gout, the Rheumatism, the Stone, the Gravel, and the Consumption, have all their several Patrons in the Faculty; and none more than the Nervous Fever, or the Fever on the Spirits. And here we may account for those Disagreements in Opinion, concerning the Cause of a Patient's Death, which sometimes occur between the most learned of the College; and which have greatly surprized that Part of the World who have been ignorant of the Fact we have above asserted.

The Reader may, perhaps, be surprized, that instead of endeavouring to revive the Patient, the learned Gentlemen should fall immediately into a Dispute on the Occasion of his Death; but in reality, all such Experiments had been made before their Arrival: For the Captain was put into a warm Bed, had his Veins scarified, his Forehead chafed, and all Sorts of strong Drops applied to his Lips and Nostrils.

The Physicians, therefore, finding themselves anticipated in every thing they ordered, were at a Loss how to apply that Portion of Time which it is usual and decent to remain for their Fee, and were therefore necessitated to find some Subject or other for Discourse; and what could more naturally present itself than that before-mentioned?

Our Doctors were about to take their Leave, when Mr. *Allworthy*, having given over the Captain, and acquiesced in the Divine Will, began to enquire after his Sister, whom he desired them to visit before their Departure.

This Lady was now recovered of her Fit, and, to use the common Phrase, as well as could be expected for one in her Condition. The Doctors, therefore, all previous Ceremonies being complied with, as this was a new Patient, attended, according to Desire, and laid hold on· each of her Hands, as they had before done on those of the Corpse.

The Case of the Lady was in the other Extreme from that of her Husband; for, as he was past all the Assistance of Physic, so in reality she required none.

There is nothing more unjust than the vulgar Opinion, by which Physicians are misrepresented as Friends to Death. On the contrary, I believe, if the Number of those who recover by Physic could be opposed to that of the Martyrs to it, the former would rather exceed the latter. Nay, some are so cautious on this Head, that, to avoid a Possibility of killing the Patient, they abstain from all Methods of curing, and prescribe nothing but what can neither do Good nor Harm. I have heard some of these, with great Gravity, deliver it as a Maxim, 'That Nature should be left to do her own Work, while the Physician stands by, as it were, to clap her on the Back, and encourage her when she doth well.'

So little then did our Doctors delight in Death, that they discharged the Corpse after a single Fee; but they were not so disgusted with their living Patient; concerning whose Case they immediately agreed, and fell to prescribing with great Diligence.

Whether, as the Lady had, at first, persuaded her Physicians to believe her ill, they had now, in return, persuaded her to believe herself so, I will not determine; but she continued a whole Month with all the Decorations of Sickness. During this Time she was visited by Physicians, attended by Nurses, and received constant Messages from her Acquaintance, to enquire after her Health.

At length, the decent Time for Sickness and immoderate Grief being expired, the Doctors were discharged, and the Lady began to see Company; being altered only from what she was before, by that Colour of Sadness in which she had dressed her Person and Countenance.

The Captain was now interred, and might, perhaps, have already made a large Progress towards Oblivion, had not the Friendship of Mr. *Allworthy* taken Care to preserve his Memory, by the following Epitaph, which was written by a Man of as great Genius as Integrity, and one who perfectly well knew the Captain.

Here lies,
In Expectation of a joyful Rising,
The Body of
Captain J O H N   B L I F I L.
L O N D O N
had the Honour of his Birth,
O X F O R D
of his Education.
His Parts
were an Honour to his Profession
and to his Country:
His Life to his Religion
and human Nature.
He was a dutiful Son,
a tender Husband,
an affectionate Father,
a most kind Brother,
a sincere Friend,
a devout Christian,
and a good Man.
His inconsolable Widow
hath erected this Stone,
The Monument of
His Virtues,
and her Affection.

BOOK III.

*Containing the most memorable Transactions which
passed in the Family of Mr. Allworthy, from the Time
when Tommy Jones arrived at the Age of Fourteen, till
he attained the Age of Nineteen. In this Book the Reader
may pick up some Hints concerning the Education of
Children.*

Chapter I.

Containing little or nothing.

The Reader will be pleased to remember, that, at the Beginning
of the Second Book of this History, we gave him a Hint of our
Intention to pass over several large Periods of Time, in which
nothing happened worthy of being recorded in a Chronicle of this
Kind.

In so doing, we do not only consult our own Dignity and Ease, but the Good and Advantage of the Reader: For besides, that, by these Means, we prevent him from throwing away his Time, in reading either without Pleasure or Emolument, we give him, at all such Seasons, an Opportunity of employing that wonderful Sagacity, of which he is Master, by filling up these vacant Spaces of Time with his own Conjectures; for which Purpose, we have taken Care to qualify him in the preceding Pages.

For Instance, what Reader but knows that Mr. *Allworthy* felt, at first, for the Loss of his Friend, those Emotions of Grief, which, on such Occasions, enter into all Men whose Hearts are not composed of Flint, or their Heads of as solid Materials? Again, what Reader doth not know that Philosophy and Religion, in Time moderated, and at last extinguished this Grief? The former of these, teaching the Folly and Vanity of it, and the latter, correcting it as unlawful; and at the same Time assuaging it, by raising future Hopes and Assurances, which enable a strong and religious Mind to take Leave of a Friend, on his Death-bed, with little less Indifference than if he was preparing for a long Journey; and, indeed, with little less Hope of seeing him again.

Nor can the judicious Reader be at a greater Loss on account of Mrs. *Bridget Blifil*, who, he may be assured, conducted herself through the whole Season in which Grief is to make its Appearance on the Outside of the Body, with the strictest Regard to all the Rules of Custom and Decency, suiting the Alterations of her Countenance to the several Alterations of her Habit: For as this changed from Weeds to Black, from Black to Grey, from Grey to White, so did her Countenance change from Dismal to Sorrowful, from Sorrowful to Sad, and from Sad to Serious, till the Day came in which she was allowed to return to her former Serenity.

We have mentioned these two, as Examples only of the Task which may be imposed on Readers of the lowest Class. Much higher and harder Exercises of Judgment and Penetration may reasonably be expected from the upper Graduates in Criticism. Many notable Discoveries will, I doubt not, be made by such, of the Transactions which happened in the Family of our worthy Man, during all the Years which we have thought proper to pass over: For tho' nothing worthy of a Place in this History occurred within that Period; yet did several Incidents happen, of equal Importance with those reported by the daily and weekly Historians of the Age, in reading which, great Numbers of Persons consume a considerable Part of their Time, very little, I am afraid, to their Emolument. Now, in the Conjectures here proposed, some of the most excellent Faculties of the Mind may be employed to much Advantage, since it is a more useful Capacity to be able to foretel the Actions of Men, in any Circumstance, from their Characters, than to judge of their Characters from their Actions. The former, I own, requires the greater Penetration; but may be accomplished by true Sagacity, with no less Certainty than the latter.

As we are sensible that much the greatest Part of our Readers are very eminently possessed of this Quality, we have left them a Space of twelve Years to exert it in; and shall now bring forth our Heroe, at about fourteen Years of Age, not questioning that many have been long impatient to be introduced to his Acquaintance.

Chapter II.

The Heroe of this great History appears with very bad Omens. A little Tale, of so LOW *a Kind, that some may think it not worth their Notice. A Word or two concerning a Squire, and more relating to a Game-keeper, and a School-master.*

As we determined when we first sat down to write this History, to flatter no Man, but to guide our Pen throughout by the Directions of Truth, we are obliged to bring our Heroe on the Stage in a much more disadvantageous Manner than we could wish; and to declare honestly, even at his first Appearance, that it was the universal Opinion of all Mr. *Allworthy*'s Family, that he was certainly born to be hanged.

Indeed, I am sorry to say, there was too much Reason for this Conjecture. The Lad having, from his earliest Years, discovered a Propensity to many Vices, and especially to one, which hath as direct a Tendency as any other to that Fate, which we have just now observed to have been prophetically denounced against him. He had been already convicted of three Robberies, *viz.* of robbing an Orchard, of stealing a Duck out of a Farmer's Yard, and of picking Master *Blifil*'s Pocket of a Ball.

The Vices of this young Man were, moreover, heightened, by the disadvantageous Light in which they appeared, when opposed to the Virtues of Master *Blifil*, his Companion: A Youth of so different a Cast from little *Jones*, that not only the Family, but all the Neighbourhood, resounded his Praises. He was, indeed, a Lad of a remarkable Disposition; sober, discreet, and pious, beyond his Age; Qualities which gained him the Love of every one who knew him, whilst *Tom Jones* was universally disliked; and many expressed their Wonder, that Mr. *Allworthy* would suffer such a Lad to be educated with his Nephew, lest the Morals of the latter should be corrupted by his Example.

An Incident which happened about this Time, will set the Character of these two Lads more fairly before the discerning Reader, than is in the Power of the longest Dissertation.

Tom Jones, who, bad as he is, must serve for the Heroe of this

History, had only one Friend among all the Servants of the Family; for, as to Mrs. *Wilkins,* she had long since given him up, and was perfectly reconciled to her Mistress. This Friend was the Game-keeper, a Fellow of a loose kind of Disposition, and who was thought not to entertain much stricter Notions concerning the Difference of *meum* and *tuum,* than the young Gentleman himself. And hence, this Friendship gave Occasion to many sarcastical Remarks among the Domestics, most of which were either Proverbs before, or, at least, are become so now; and, indeed, the Wit of them all may be comprised in that short *Latin* Proverb, '*Noscitur a socio,*' which, I think, is thus expressed in *English,* 'You may know him by the company he keeps.'

To say the Truth, some of that atrocious Wickedness in *Jones,* of which we have just mentioned three Examples, might, perhaps, be derived from the Encouragement he had received from this Fellow, who, in two or three Instances, had been what the Law calls an Accessary after the Fact. For the whole Duck, and great Part of the Apples, were converted to the Use of the Game-keeper, and his Family. Tho', as *Jones* alone was discovered, the poor Lad bore not only the whole Smart, but the whole Blame; both which fell again to his Lot, on the following Occasion.

Contiguous to Mr. *Allworthy's* Estate, was the Manor of one of those Gentlemen, who are called *Preservers of the Game.* This Species of Men, from the great Severity with which they revenge the Death of a Hare, or a Partridge, might be thought to cultivate the same Superstition with the Bannians[1] in *India;* many of whom, we are told, dedicate their whole Lives to the Preservation and Protection of certain Animals, was it not that our *English* Bannians, while they preserve them from other Enemies, will most unmercifully slaughter whole Horse-loads themselves, so that they stand clearly acquitted of any such heathenish Superstition.

I have, indeed, a much better Opinion of this Kind of Men than is entertained by some, as I take them to answer the Order of Nature, and the good Purposes for which they were ordained, in a more ample Manner than many others. Now, as *Horace* tells us, that there are a Set of human Beings,

Fruges consumere nati.[2]

'Born to consume the Fruits of the Earth.' So, I make no manner of Doubt but that there are others,

Feras consumere nati.

'Born to consume the Beasts of the Field,' or, as it is commonly

---

1. Banias, members of a vegetarian merchant caste of northwest India. Fielding had alluded to them at length in *The*

Champion, 22 Mar. 1740.
2. *Epistles* I.ii.27.

called, the Game; and none, I believe, will deny, but that those
Squires fulfil this End of their Creation.

Little *Jones* went one Day a shooting with the Game-keeper;
when, happening to spring a Covey of Partridges, near the Border
of that Manor over which Fortune, to fulfil the wise Purposes of
Nature, had planted one of the Game-Consumers, the Birds flew
into it, and were *marked* (as it is called) by the two Sportsmen, in
some Furze Bushes, about two or three hundred Paces beyond Mr.
Allworthy's Dominions.

Mr. *Allworthy* had given the Fellow strict Orders, on Pain of for-
feiting his Place, never to trespass on any of his Neighbours; no
more on those who were less rigid in this Matter, than on the Lord
of this Manor. With regard to others, indeed, these Orders had not
been always very scrupulously kept; but as the Disposition of the
Gentleman with whom the Partridges had taken Sanctuary, was well
known, the Game-keeper had never yet attempted to invade his
Territories. Nor had he done it now, had not the younger Sportsman, who was excessively eager to pursue the flying Game, over-per-
suaded him; but *Jones* being very importunate, the other, who was
himself keen enough after the Sport, yielded to his Persuasions,
entered the Manor, and shot one of the Partridges.

The Gentleman himself was at that Time on Horseback, at a
little Distance from them; and hearing the Gun go off, he immediately made towards the Place, and discovered poor *Tom*: For the
Game-keeper had leapt into the thickest Part of the Furze-brake,
where he had happily concealed himself.

The Gentleman having searched the Lad, and found the Partridge upon him, denounced great Vengeance, swearing he would
acquaint Mr. *Allworthy*. He was as good as his Word; for he rode
immediately to his House, and complained of the Trespass on his
Manor, in as high Terms, and as bitter Language, as if his House
had been broken open, and the most valuable Furniture stole out of
it. He added, that some other Person was in his Company, tho' he
could not discover him: For that two Guns had been discharged
almost in the same Instant. And, says he, "we have found only this
Partridge, but the Lord knows what Mischief they have done."

At his Return home, *Tom* was presently convened before Mr.
Allworthy. He owned the Fact, and alledged no other Excuse but
what was really true, *viz*. that the Covey was originally sprung in
Mr. *Allworthy's* own Manor.

Tom was then interrogated who was with him, which Mr. *Allworthy* declared he was resolved to know, acquainting the Culprit
with the Circumstance of the two Guns, which had been deposed
by the Squire and both his Servants; but Tom stoutly persisted in
asserting that he was alone; yet, to say the Truth, he hesitated **a**

little at first, which would have confirmed Mr. *Allworthy*'s Belief, had what the Squire and his Servants said, wanted any further Confirmation.

The Game-keeper being a suspected Person, was now sent for, and the Question put to him; but he, relying on the Promise which *Tom* had made him, to take all upon himself, very resolutely denied being in Company with the young Gentleman, or indeed having seen him the whole Afternoon.

Mr. *Allworthy* then turned towards *Tom*, with more than usual Anger in his Countenance, and advised him to confess who was with him; repeating, that he was resolved to know. The Lad, however, still maintained his Resolution, and was dismissed with much Wrath by Mr. *Allworthy*, who told him, he should have to the next Morning to consider of it, when he should be questioned by another Person, and in another Manner.

Poor *Jones* spent a very melancholy Night, and the more so, as he was without his usual Companion: For Master *Blifil* was gone abroad on a Visit with his Mother. Fear of the Punishment he was to suffer was on this Occasion his least Evil; his chief Anxiety being, lest his Constancy should fail him, and he should be brought to betray the Game-keeper, whose Ruin he knew must now be the Consequence.

Nor did the Game-keeper pass his Time much better. He had the same Apprehensions with the Youth; for whose Honour he had likewise a much tenderer Regard than for his Skin.

In the Morning, when *Tom* attended the Reverend Mr. *Thwackum*,[3] the Person to whom Mr. *Allworthy* had committed the Instruction of the two Boys, he had the same Questions put to him by that Gentleman, which he had been asked the Evening before, to which he returned the same Answers. The Consequence of this was, so severe a Whipping, that it possibly fell little short of

3. Identified in Sir Richard Colt Hoare, *The History of Wiltshire, Part II, Old and New Sarum or Salisbury*, by Robert Benson and Henry Hatcher (London: John Bowyer Nichols & Son, 1843), p. 602, whose entire paragraph (excerpted in Shakespeare Head ed., 1926) is a basic historical source: "It is well known that Fielding the Novelist married a lady of Salisbury, named Craddock, and was for a time resident in our city. From tradition we learn, That he first occupied the house in the Close, on the south side of St. Ann's Gate. He afterwards removed to that in St. Ann's Street, next to the Friary; and finally established himself in the mansion at the foot of Milford Hill, where he wrote a considerable portion of his Tom Jones. We need not observe that the scene is laid in this neighborhood, and that a few of the incidents are related as happening at Salisbury. Some of the characters also are identified with persons living here at the time. Thwackum is said to have been drawn for Mr. [Richard] Hele, master of the Close School; Square the philosopher for [Thomas] Chubb the Deist; and Dowling the lawyer for a person named [Robert] Stillingfleet, who exercised that profession. The Golden Lion, where the ghost scene was acted, was a well-known inn, at the corner of the Market-place and Winchester Street, where many a merry prank was played, and the person who sustained this part was Doughty [see note 2, p. 229], one of the serjeants at mace [carrying the city's mace at official ceremonies]."

the Torture with which Confessions are in some Countries extorted from Criminals.

Tom bore his Punishment with great Resolution; and tho' his Master asked him between every Stroke, whether he would not confess, he was contented to be flead rather than betray his Friend, or break the Promise he had made.

The Game-keeper was now relieved from his Anxiety, and Mr. *Allworthy* himself began to be concerned at *Tom's* Sufferings: For, besides that Mr. *Thwackum*, being highly enraged that he was not able to make the Boy say what he himself pleased, had carried his Severity much beyond the good Man's Intention, this latter began now to suspect that the Squire had been mistaken; which his extreme Eagerness and Anger seemed to make probable; and as for what the Servants had said in Confirmation of their Master's Account, he laid no great Stress upon that. Now, as Cruelty and Injustice were two Ideas, of which Mr. *Allworthy* could by no Means support the Consciousness a single Moment, he sent for *Tom*, and after many kind and friendly Exhortations, said, 'I am convinced, my dear Child, that my Suspicions have wronged you; I am sorry that you have been so severely punished on this Account.' —And at last gave him a little Horse to make him amends; again repeating his Sorrow for what had past.

Tom's Guilt now flew in his Face more than any Severity could make it. He could more easily bear the Lashes of *Thwackum*, than the Generosity of *Allworthy*. The Tears burst from his Eyes, and he fell upon his Knees, crying, 'Oh! Sir, you are too good to me. Indeed you are. Indeed, I don't deserve it.' And at that very Instant, from the Fullness of his Heart, had almost betrayed the Secret; but the good Genius of the Game-keeper suggested to him what might be the Consequence to the poor Fellow, and this Consideration sealed his Lips.

Thwackum did all he could to dissuade *Allworthy* from shewing any Compassion or Kindness to the Boy, saying, 'He had persisted in an Untruth:' and gave some Hints, that a second Whipping might probably bring the Matter to Light.

But Mr. *Allworthy* absolutely refused to consent to the Experiment. He said, the Boy had suffered enough already, for concealing the Truth, even if he was guilty, seeing that he could have no Motive but a mistaken Point of Honour for so doing.

Honour! cry'd *Thwackum*, with some Warmth, mere Stubborness and Obstinacy! Can Honour teach any one to tell a Lie, or can any Honour exist independent of Religion?

This Discourse happened at Table when Dinner was just ended; and there were present Mr. *Allworthy*, Mr. *Thwackum*, and a third Gentleman who now entered into the Debate, and whom, before we proceed any farther, we shall briefly introduce to our Reader's Acquaintance.

Chapter III.

The Character of Mr. Square *the Philosopher, and of Mr.* Thwackum *the Divine; with a Dispute concerning*————

The Name of this Gentleman who had then resided some time at Mr. *Allworthy's* House, was Mr. *Square.* His natural Parts were not of the first Rate, but he had greatly improved them by a learned Education. He was deeply read in the Antients, and a profest Master of all the Works of *Plato* and *Aristotle*. Upon which great Models he had principally form'd himself, sometimes according with the Opinion of the one, and sometimes with that of the other. In Morals he was a profest *Platonist,* and in Religion he inclined to be an *Aristotelian*.

But tho' he had, as we have said, formed his Morals on the *Platonic* Model, yet he perfectly agreed with the Opinion of *Aristotle*,[1] in considering that great Man rather in the Quality of a Philosopher or a Speculatist, than as a Legislator. This Sentiment he carried a great way; indeed, so far, as to regard all Virtue as Matter of Theory only. This, it is true, he never affirmed, as I have heard, to any one; and yet upon the least Attention to his Conduct, I cannot help thinking, it was his real Opinion, as it will perfectly reconcile some Contradictions, which might otherwise appear in his Character.

This Gentleman and Mr. *Thwackum* scarce ever met without a Disputation; for their Tenets were indeed diametrically opposite to each other. *Square* held human Nature to be the Perfection of all Virtue, and that Vice was a Deviation from our Nature in the same Manner as Deformity of Body is. *Thwackum*, on the contrary, maintained that the human Mind, since the Fall, was nothing but a Sink of Iniquity, till purified and redeemed by Grace. In one Point only they agreed, which was, in all their Discourses on Morality never to mention the Word *Goodness*. The favourite Phrase of the former, was *the natural Beauty of Virtue*; that of the latter, was the *divine Power of Grace*. The former measured all Actions by the *unalterable Rule of Right*, and the *eternal Fitness of Things*; the latter decided all Matters by Authority; but, in doing this, he always used the Scriptures and their Commentators, as the Lawyer doth his *Coke upon Littleton*,[2] where the Comment is of equal Authority with the Text.

1. *Politica* II.v.
2. See above, p. 75. Sir Edward Coke's *Institutes* (1628) provided an English translation, with commentary, of Sir Thomas de Littleton's *Treatise on Tenures* (c. 1480), written in Norman French and laced with Latin legal phrases. Littleton codified English common law concerning property; with Coke's commentary it became the basic legal text and authority.

After this short Introduction, the Reader will be pleased to remember, that the Parson had concluded his Speech with a triumphant Question, to which he had apprehended no Answer; *viz.* Can any Honour exist independent on Religion?

To this *Square* answered, that it was impossible to discourse philosophically concerning Words, till their Meaning was first established; that there were scarce any two Words of a more vague and uncertain Signification, than the two he had mentioned: For that there were almost as many different Opinions concerning Honour, as concerning Religion. 'But, says he, if by Honour you mean the true natural Beauty of Virtue, I will maintain it may exist independent of any Religion whatever. Nay, (added he) you yourself will allow it may exist independent of all but one: So will a *Mahometan*, a *Jew*, and all the Maintainers of all the different Sects in the World.'

Thwackum replied, This was arguing with the usual Malice of all the Enemies to the true Church. He said, he doubted not but that all the Infidels and Hereticks in the World would, if they could, confine Honour to their own absurd Errors, and damnable Deceptions; 'But Honour, says he, is not therefore manifold, because there are many absurd Opinions about it; nor is Religion manifold, because there are various Sects and Heresies in the World. When I mention Religion, I mean the Christian Religion; and not only the Christian Religion, but the Protestant Religion; and not only the Protestant Religion, but the Church of *England*. And when I mention Honour, I mean that Mode of divine Grace which is not only consistent with, but dependent upon, this Religion; and is consistent with, and dependent upon, no other. Now to say that the Honour I here mean, and which was, I thought, all the Honour I could be supposed to mean, will uphold, much less dictate, an Untruth, is to assert an Absurdity too shocking to be conceived.'

'I purposely avoided,' says *Square*, 'drawing a Conclusion which I thought evident from what I have said; but if you perceived it, I am sure you have not attempted to answer it. However, to drop the Article of Religion, I think it is plain, from what you have said, that we have different Ideas of Honour; or why do we not agree in the same Terms of its Explanation? I have asserted, that true Honour and true Virtue are almost synonymous Terms, and they are both founded on the unalterable Rule of Right, and the eternal Fitness of Things; to which an Untruth being absolutely repugnant and contrary, it is certain that true Honour cannot support an Untruth. In this, therefore, I think we are agreed; but that this Honour can be said to be founded on Religion, to which it is antecedent, if by Religion be meant any positive Law——

'I agree,' answered *Thwackum*, with great Warmth, 'with a Man who asserts Honour to be antecedent to Religion!—Mr. *Allworthy*, did I agree——?

He was proceeding, when Mr *Allworthy* interposed, telling them very coldly, they had both mistaken his Meaning; for that he had said nothing of true Honour.—It is possible, however, he would not have easily quieted the Disputants, who were growing equally warm, had not another Matter now fallen out, which put a final End to the Conversation at present.

Chapter IV.

Containing a necessary Apology for the Author; and a childish Incident, which perhaps requires an Apology likewise.

Before I proceed farther, I shall beg Leave to obviate some Misconstructions, into which the Zeal of some few Readers may lead them; for I would not willingly give Offence to any, especially to Men who are warm in the Cause of Virtue or Religion.

I hope, therefore, no Man will, by the grossest Misunderstanding, or Perversion, of my Meaning, misrepresent me, as endeavouring to cast any Ridicule on the greatest Perfections of Human Nature; and which do, indeed, alone purify and enoble the Heart of Man, and raise him above the Brute Creation. This, Reader, I will venture to say, (and by how much the better Man you are yourself, by so much the more will you be inclined to believe me) that I would rather have buried the Sentiments of these two Persons in eternal Oblivion, than have done any Injury to either of these glorious Causes.

On the contrary, it is with a View to their Service that I have taken upon me to record the Lives and Actions of two of their false and pretended Champions. A treacherous Friend is the most dangerous Enemy; and I will say boldly, that both Religion and Virtue have received more real Discredit from Hypocrites, than the wittiest Profligates or Infidels could ever cast upon them: Nay farther, as these two, in their Purity, are rightly called the Bands of civil Society, and are indeed the greatest of Blessings; so when poisoned and corrupted with Fraud, Pretence and Affectation, they have become the worst of civil Curses, and have enabled Men to perpetrate the most cruel Mischiefs to their own Species.

Indeed, I doubt not but this Ridicule will in general be allowed; my chief Apprehension is, as many true and just Sentiments often came from the Mouths of these Persons, lest the whole should be taken together, and I should be conceived to ridicule all alike. Now the Reader will be pleased to consider, that as neither of these Men

were Fools, they could not be supposed to have holden none but
wrong Principles, and to have uttered nothing but Absurdities; what
Injustice, therefore, must I have done to their Characters, had I
selected only what was bad, and how horribly wretched and maimed
must their Arguments have appeared!

Upon the whole, it is not Religion or Virtue, but the Want of
them which is here exposed. Had not *Thwackum* too much
neglected Virtue, and *Square* Religion, in the Composition of their
several Systems; and had not both utterly discarded all natural
Goodness of Heart, they had never been represented as the Objects
of Derision in this History; in which we will now proceed. This
Matter, then, which put an End to the Debate mentioned in the
last Chapter, was no other than a Quarrel between Master *Blifil*
and *Tom Jones*, the Consequence of which had been a bloody Nose
to the former; for though Master *Blifil*, notwithstanding he was the
younger, was in Size above the other's Match, yet *Tom* was much
his Superior at the noble Art of Boxing.

Tom, however, cautiously avoided all Engagements with that
Youth: For besides that *Tommy Jones* was an inoffensive Lad
amidst all his Roguery, and really loved *Blifil*, Mr. *Thwackum* being
always the Second of the latter, would have been sufficient to deter
him.

But well says a certain Author,[1] No Man is wise at all Hours; it
is therefore no Wonder that a Boy is not so. A Difference arising at
Play between the two Lads, Master *Blifil* called *Tom* a *Beggarly
Bastard*. Upon which the latter, who was somewhat passionate in
his Disposition, immediately caused that Phænomenon in the Face
of the former, which we have above remembred.

Master *Blifil* now, with his Blood running from his Nose, and
the Tears galloping after from his Eyes, appeared before his Uncle,
and the tremendous *Thwackum*. In which Court an indictment of
Assault, Battery, and Wounding, was instantly preferred against
Tom; who in his Excuse only pleaded the Provocation, which was
indeed all the Matter that Master *Blifil* had omitted.

It is indeed possible, that this Circumstance might have escaped
his Memory; for, in his Reply, he positively insisted, that he had
made Use of no such Appellation; adding, 'Heaven forbid such
naughty Words should ever come out of his Mouth.'

Tom, though against all Form of Law, rejoined in Affirmance of
the Words. Upon which Master *Blifil* said, 'It is no Wonder. Those
who will tell one Fib, will hardly stick at another. If I had told my

1. Pliny the Younger, quoted in Lily's *Grammar*, p. 158, from *Historiae Naturalis* VII.xli.para.2: "Quid quod nemo mortalium omnibus horis sapit." See also below, pp. 520 and 659.

Master such a wicked Fib as you have done, I should be ashamed to shew my Face.'

'What Fib, Child?' cries *Thwackum* pretty eagerly.

'Why, he told you that Nobody was with him a shooting when he killed the Partridge; but he knows, (here he burst into a Flood of Tears) yes, he knows; for he confessed it to me, that *Black George*[2] the Game-keeper was there. Nay, he said,—Yes you did, —deny it if you can, That you would not have confest the Truth, though Master had cut you to Pieces.'

At this the Fire flashed from *Thwackum's* Eyes; and he cried out in Triumph: 'Oh ho! This is your mistaken Notion of Honour! This is the Boy who was not to be whipped again!' But Mr. *Allworthy*, with a more gentle Aspect, turned towards the Lad, and said, 'Is this true, Child? How came you to persist so obstinately in a Falshood?'

Tom said, 'He scorned a Lie as much as any one; but he thought his Honour engaged him to act as he did; for he had promised the poor Fellow to conceal him; which,' he said, 'he thought himself farther obliged to, as the Game-keeper had begged him not to go into the Gentleman's Manor and had at last gone himself in Compliance with his Persuasions.' He said, 'this was the whole Truth of the Matter, and he would take his Oath of it;' and concluded with very passionately begging Mr. *Allworthy*, 'to have Compassion on the poor Fellow's Family, especially as he himself only had been guilty, and the other had been very difficultly prevailed on to do what he did. Indeed, Sir,' said he, 'it could hardly be called a Lie that I told; for the poor Fellow was entirely innocent of the whole Matter. I should have gone alone after the Birds; nay, I did go at first, and he only followed me to prevent more Mischief. Do, pray Sir, let me be punished; take my little Horse away again; but pray Sir, forgive poor *George*.'

Mr. *Allworthy* hesitated a few Moments, and then dismissed the Boys, advising them to live more friendly and peaceably together.

Chapter V.

The Opinions of the Divine and the Philosopher concerning the two Boys; with some Reasons for their Opinions, and other Matters.

It is probable, that by disclosing this Secret, which had been communicated in the utmost Confidence to him, young *Blifil* pre-

---

2. The first three editions read *"Black Jack"* at this first mention of the game-keeper's name—clearly a slip (probably the compositor's), since Tom soon calls him George, which he remains thereafter. Cross (II.123) takes the fourth edition's "Black George" as unauthorized, mistakenly thinking that Thwackum is speaking, and in scornful irony. Blifil would hardly be speaking in ignorance or irony here.

served his Companion from a good Lashing: For the Offence of the bloody Nose would have been of itself sufficient Cause for *Thwackum* to have proceeded to Correction; but now this was totally absorbed, in the Consideration of the other Matter; and with Regard to this, Mr. *Allworthy* declared privately, he thought the Boy deserved Reward rather than Punishment; so that *Thwackum*'s Hand was withheld by a general Pardon.

Thwackum, whose Meditations were full of Birch, exclaimed against this weak, and, as he said he would venture to call it, wicked Lenity. To remit the Punishment of such Crimes was, he said, to encourage them. He enlarged much on the Correction of Children, and quoted many Texts from *Solomon*, and others; which being to be found in so many other Books, shall not be found here. He then applied himself to the Vice of Lying, on which Head he was altogether as learned as he had been on the other.

Square said, he had been endeavouring to reconcile the Behaviour of *Tom* with his Idea of perfect Virtue; but could not. He owned there was something which at first Sight appeared like Fortitude in the Action; but as Fortitude was a Virtue, and Falshood a Vice, they could by no means agree or unite together. He added, that as this was in some measure to confound Virtue and Vice, it might be worth Mr. *Thwackum*'s Consideration, whether a larger Castigation might not be laid on, upon that Account.

As both these learned Men concurred in censuring *Jones*, so were they no less unanimous in applauding Master *Blifil*. To bring Truth to light, was by the Parson asserted to be the Duty of every religious Man; and by the Philosopher this was declared to be highly conformable with the Rule of Right, and the eternal and unalterable Fitness of Things.

All this, however, weighed very little with Mr. *Allworthy*. He could not be prevailed on to sign the Warrant for the Execution of *Jones*. There was something within his own Breast with which the invincible Fidelity which that Youth had preserved, corresponded much better than it had done with the Religion of *Thwackum*, or with the Virtue of *Square*. He therefore strictly ordered the former of these Gentlemen to abstain from laying violent Hands on *Tom* for what had past. The Pedagogue was obliged to obey those Orders; but not without great Reluctance, and frequent Mutterings, that the Boy would be certainly spoiled.

Towards the Game-keeper the good Man behaved with more Severity. He presently summoned that poor Fellow before him, and after many bitter Remonstrances, paid him his Wages, and dismist him from his Service; for Mr. *Allworthy* rightly observed, that there was a great Difference between being guilty of a Falshood to excuse yourself, and to excuse another. He likewise urged, as the principal Motive to his inflexible Severity against this Man, that he had basely suffered *Tom Jones* to undergo so heavy a Punishment for his Sake, whereas he ought to have prevented it by making the Discovery himself.

When this Story became public, many People differed from *Square* and *Thwackum*, in judging the Conduct of the two Lads on the Occasion. Master *Blifil* was generally called a sneaking Rascal, a poor-spirited Wretch, with other Epithets of the like Kind; whilst *Tom* was honoured with the Appellations of a brave Lad, a jolly Dog, and an honest Fellow. Indeed his Behaviour to *Black George* much ingratiated him with all the Servants; for though that Fellow was before universally disliked, yet he was no sooner turned away than he was as universally pitied; and the Friendship and Gallantry of *Tom Jones* was celebrated by them all with the highest Applause; and they condemned Master *Blifil*, as openly as they durst, without incurring the Danger of offending his Mother. For all this, however, poor *Tom* smarted in the Flesh; for though *Thwackum* had been inhibited to exercise his Arm on the foregoing Account, yet, as the Proverb says, *It is easy to find a Stick*, &c. So was it easy to find a Rod; and, indeed, the not being able to find one was the only thing which could have kept *Thwackum* any long Time from chastising poor *Jones*.

Had the bare Delight in the Sport been the only Inducement to the Pedagogue, it is probable, Master *Blifil* would likewise have had his Share; but though Mr. *Allworthy* had given him frequent Orders to make no Difference between the Lads, yet was *Thwackum* altogether as kind and gentle to this Youth, as he was harsh, nay even barbarous, to the other. To say the Truth, *Blifil* had greatly gained his Master's Affections; partly by the profound Respect he always shewed his Person, but much more by the decent Reverence with which he received his Doctrine; for he had got by Heart, and frequently repeated his Phrases, and maintained all his Master's religious Principles with a Zeal which was surprising in one so young, and which greatly endeared him to the worthy Preceptor.

Tom Jones, on the other hand, was not only deficient in outward Tokens of Respect, often forgetting to pull off his Hat, or to bow at his Master's Approach; but was altogether as unmindful both of his Master's Precepts and Example. He was indeed a thoughtless, giddy Youth, with little Sobriety in his Manners, and less in his Countenance; and would often very impudently and indecently laugh at his Companion for his serious Behaviour.

Mr. *Square* had the same Reason for his Preference of the former Lad; for *Tom Jones* shewed no more Regard to the learned Discourses which this Gentleman would sometimes throw away upon him, than to those of *Thwackum*. He once ventured to make a Jest of the Rule of Right; and at another Time said, He believed there was no Rule in the World capable of making such a Man as his Father, (for so Mr. *Allworthy* suffered himself to be called.)

Master *Blifil*, on the contrary, had Address enough at sixteen to recommend himself at one and the same Time to both these Opposites. With one he was all Religion, with the other he was all Virtue. And when both were present, he was profoundly silent, which both interpreted in his Favour and in their own.

Nor was *Blifil* contented with flattering both these Gentlemen to their Faces; he took frequent Occasions of praising them behind their Backs to *Allworthy*; before whom, when they two were alone, and his Uncle commended any religious or virtuous Sentiment (for many such came constantly from him) he seldom failed to ascribe it to the good Instructions he had received from either *Thwackum* or *Square:* For he knew his Uncle repeated all such Compliments to the Persons for whose Use they were meant; and he found by Experience the great Impressions which they made on the Philosopher, as well as on the Divine: For, to say the Truth, there is no kind of Flattery so irresistible as this, at second Hand.

The young Gentleman, moreover, soon perceived how extremely grateful all those Panegyrics on his Instructors were to Mr. *Allworthy* himself, as they so loudly resounded the Praise of that singular Plan of Education which he had laid down: For this worthy Man having observed the imperfect Institution of our public Schools, and the many Vices which Boys were there liable to learn, had resolved to educate his Nephew, as well as the other Lad, whom he had in a Manner adopted, in his own House; where he thought their Morals would escape all that Danger of being corrupted, to which they would be unavoidably exposed in any public School or University.

Having therefore determined to commit these Boys to the Tuition of a private Tutor, Mr. *Thwackum* was recommended to him for that Office, by a very particular Friend, of whose Understanding Mr. *Allworthy* had a great Opinion, and in whose Integrity he placed much Confidence. This *Thwackum* was Fellow of a College, where he almost entirely resided; and had a great Reputation for Learning, Religion and Sobriety of Manners. And these were doubtless the Qualifications by which Mr. *Allworthy*'s Friend had been induced to recommend him; tho' indeed this Friend had some Obligations to *Thwackum*'s Family, who were the most considerable Persons in a Borough which that Gentleman represented in Parliament.

Thwackum, at his first Arrival, was extremely agreeable to *Allworthy*; and indeed he perfectly answered the Character which had been given of him. Upon longer Acquaintance, however, and more intimate Conversation, this worthy Man saw Infirmities in the

Tutor, which he could have wished him to have been without; tho'
as those seemed greatly over-balanced by his good Qualities, they
did not incline Mr. *Allworthy* to part with him; nor would they
indeed have justified such a Proceeding: For the Reader is greatly
mistaken, if he conceives that *Thwackum* appeared to Mr. *Allworthy* in the same Light as he doth to him in this History; and he is
as much deceived, if he imagines, that the most intimate Acquaintance which he himself could have had with that Divine, would have
informed him of those Things which we, from our Inspiration, are
enabled to open and discover. Of Readers who from such Conceits
as these, condemn the Wisdom or Penetration of Mr. *Allworthy*, I
shall not scruple to say, that they make a very bad and ungrateful
Use of that Knowledge which we have communicated to them.

These apparent Errors in the Doctrine of *Thwackum*, served
greatly to palliate the contrary Errors in that of *Square*, which our
good Man no less saw and condemned. He thought indeed that the
different Exuberancies of these Gentlemen, would correct their different Imperfections; and that from both, especially with his Assistance, the two Lads would derive sufficient Precepts of true Religion
and Virtue. If the Event happened contrary to his Expectations,
this possibly proceeded from some Fault in the Plan itself; which
the Reader hath my Leave to discover, if he can: For we do not
pretend to introduce any infallible characters into this History;
where we hope nothing will be found which hath never yet been
seen in human Nature.

To return therefore; the Reader will not, I think, wonder that the
different Behaviour of the two Lads above commemorated, produced the different Effects, of which he hath already seen some
Instance; and besides this, there was another Reason for the Conduct of the Philosopher and the Pedagogue; but this being Matter
of great Importance, we shall reveal it in the next Chapter.

Chapter VI.

Containing a better Reason still for the before mentioned Opinions.

It is to be known then, that those two learned Personages, who
have lately made a considerable Figure on the Theatre of this History, had from their first Arrival at Mr. *Allworthy*'s House, taken
so great an Affection, the one to his Virtue, the other to his Religion,
that they had meditated the closest Alliance with him.

For this Purpose they had cast their Eyes on that fair Widow,
whom, tho' we have not for some Time made any Mention of her,
the Reader, we trust, hath not forgot. Mrs. *Blifil* was indeed the
Object to which they both aspired.

It may seem remarkable, that of four Persons whom we have commemorated at Mr. *Allworthy*'s House, three of them should fix their Inclinations on a Lady who was never greatly celebrated for her Beauty, and who was, moreover, now a little descended into the Vale of Years; but in reality Bosom Friends, and intimate Acquaintance, have a Kind of natural Propensity to particular Females at the House of a Friend, *viz.* to his Grand-mother, Mother, Sister, Daughter, Aunt, Niece, or Cousin, when they are rich; and to his Wife, Sister, Daughter, Niece, Cousin, Mistress, or Servant Maid, if they should be handsome.

We would not, however, have our Reader imagine, that Persons of such Characters as were supported by *Thwackum* and *Square*, would undertake a Matter of this Kind, which hath been a little censured by some rigid Moralists, before they had thoroughly examined it, and considered whether it was (as *Shakespear* phrases it) 'Stuff o' th' Conscience'[1] or no. *Thwackum* was encouraged to the Undertaking, by reflecting, that to covet your Neighbour's Sister is no where forbidden; and he knew it was a Rule in the Construction of all Laws, that '*Expressum facit cessare Tacitum.*' The Sense of which is, 'When a Law-giver sets down plainly his whole Meaning, we are prevented from making him mean what we please ourselves.' As some Instances of Women, therefore, are mentioned in the Divine Law, which forbids us to covet our Neighbour's Goods, and that of a Sister omitted, he concluded it to be lawful. And as to *Square*, who was in his Person what is called a jolly Fellow, or a Widow's Man, he easily reconciled his Choice to the eternal Fitness of Things.

Now, as both these Gentlemen were industrious in taking every Opportunity of recommending themselves to the Widow, they apprehended one certain Method was, by giving her Son the constant Preference to the other Lad; and, as they conceived the Kindness and Affection which Mr. *Allworthy* shewed the latter, must be highly disagreeable to her, they doubted not but the laying hold on all Occasions to degrade and vilify him, would be highly pleasing to her; who, as she hated the Boy, must love all those who did him any Hurt. In this *Thwackum* had the Advantage; for while *Square* could only scarify the poor Lad's Reputation, he could flea his Skin; and, indeed, he considered every Lash he gave him as a Compliment paid to his Mistress; so that he could, with the utmost Propriety, repeat this old flogging Line, '*Castigo te non quod odio habeam, sed quod* AMEM.[2] I chastize thee not out of Hatred, but out of Love.' And this, indeed, he often had in his Mouth, or rather, according to the old Phrase, never more properly applied, at his Fingers Ends.

1. *Othello* I.ii.2–3.   2. Quoted from Lily, p. 167.

For this Reason principally, the two Gentlemen concurred, as we have seen above, in their Opinion concerning the two Lads; this being, indeed, almost the only Instance of their concurring on any Point: For, beside the Difference of their Principles, they had both long ago strongly suspected each others Design, and hated one another with no little Degree of Inveteracy.

This mutual Animosity was a good deal increased by their alternate Successes: For Mrs. *Blifil* knew what they would be at long before they imagined it; or, indeed, intended she should: For they proceeded with great Caution, lest she should be offended, and acquaint Mr. *Allworthy*. But they had no Reason for any such Fear; she was well enough pleased with a Passion, of which she intended none should have any Fruits but herself. And the only Fruits she designed for herself, were Flattery and Courtship; for which Purpose, she soothed them by Turns and a long Time equally. She was, indeed, rather inclined to favour the Parson's Principles; but *Square*'s Person was more agreeable to her Eye, for he was a comely Man; whereas the Pedagogue did in Countenance very nearly resemble that Gentleman, who, in the Harlot's Progress,[3] is seen correcting the Ladies in *Bridewell*.

Whether Mrs. *Blifil* had been surfeited with the Sweets of Marriage, or disgusted by its Bitters, or from what other Cause it proceeded, I will not determine; but she could never be brought to listen to any second Proposals. However, she at last conversed with *Square* with such a Degree of Intimacy, that malicious Tongues began to whisper Things of her, to which, as well for the Sake of the Lady, as that they were highly disagreeable to the Rule of Right, and the Fitness of Things, we will give no Credit, and therefore shall not blot our Paper with them. The Pedagogue, 'tis certain, whipt on, without getting a Step nearer to his Journey's End.

Indeed he had committed a great Error, and that *Square* discovered much sooner than himself. Mrs. *Blifil* (as, perhaps, the Reader may have formerly guessed) was not over and above pleased with the Behaviour of her Husband; nay, to be honest, she absolutely hated him, till his Death, at last, a little reconciled him to her Affections. It will not be therefore greatly wondered at, if she had not the most violent Regard to the Offspring she had by him. And, in fact, she had so little of this Regard, that in his Infancy she seldom saw her Son, or took any Notice of him; and hence she acquiesced, after a little Reluctance, in all the Favours which Mr. *Allworthy* showered on the Foundling; whom the good Man called his own Boy, and in all Things put on an intire Equality with Master *Blifil*. This Acquiescence in Mrs. *Blifil* was considered by the Neighbours, and by the Family, as a Mark of her Condescen-

3. See above, pp. 51 and 62.

sion to her Brother's Humour, and she was imagined by all others, as well as *Thwackum* and *Square*, to hate the Foundling in her Heart; nay, the more Civility she shewed him, the more they conceived she detested him, and the surer Schemes she was laying for his Ruin: For as they thought it her Interest to hate him, it was very difficult for her to persuade them she did not.

Thwackum was the more confirmed in his Opinion, as she had more than once slily caused him to whip *Tom Jones*, when Mr. *Allworthy*, who was an Enemy to this Exercise, was abroad; whereas she had never given any such Orders concerning young *Blifil*. And this had likewise imposed upon *Square*. In reality, tho' she certainly hated her own Son; of which, however monstrous it appears, I am assured she is not a singular Instance, she appeared, notwithstanding all her outward Compliance, to be in her Heart sufficiently displeased with all the Favour shewn by Mr. *Allworthy* to the Foundling. She frequently complained of this behind her Brother's Back, and very sharply censured him for it, both to *Thwackum* and *Square*; nay, she would throw it in the Teeth of *Allworthy* himself, when a little Quarrel, or Miff, as it is vulgarly called, arose between them.

However, when *Tom* grew up, and gave Tokens of that Gallantry of Temper which greatly recommends Men to Women, this Disinclination which she had discovered to him when a Child, by Degrees abated, and at last she so evidently demonstrated her Affection to him to be much stronger than what she bore her own Son, that it was impossible to mistake her any longer. She was so desirous of often seeing him, and discovered such Satisfaction and Delight in his Company, that before he was eighteen Years old, he was become a Rival to both *Square* and *Thwackum*; and what is worse, the whole Country began to talk as loudly of her Inclination to *Tom*, as they had before done of that which she had shewn to *Square*; on which Account the Philosopher conceived the most implacable Hatred for our poor Heroe.

Chapter VII.

In which the Author himself makes his Appearance on the Stage.

Tho' Mr. *Allworthy* was not of himself hasty to see Things in a disadvantageous Light, and was a Stranger to the public Voice, which seldom reaches to a Brother or a Husband, tho' it rings in the Ears of all the Neighbourhood; yet was this Affection of Mrs. *Blifil* to *Tom*, and the Preference which she too visibly gave him to her own Son, of the utmost Disadvantage to that Youth.

For such was the Compassion which inhabited Mr. *Allworthy's*

Mind, that nothing but the Steel of Justice could ever subdue it. To be unfortunate in any Respect was sufficient, if there was no Demerit to counterpoise it, to turn the Scale of that good Man's Pity, and to engage his Friendship, and his Benefaction.

When therefore he plainly saw Master *Blifil* was absolutely detested (for that he was) by his own Mother, he began, on that Account only, to look with an Eye of Compassion upon him; and what the Effects of Compassion are in good and benevolent Minds, I need not here explain to most of my Readers.

Henceforward, he saw every Appearance of Virtue in the Youth through the magnifying End, and viewed all his Faults with the Glass inverted, so that they became scarce perceptible. And this perhaps the amiable Temper of Pity may make commendable; but the next Step the Weakness of human Nature alone must excuse: For he no sooner perceived that Preference which Mrs. *Blifil* gave to *Tom*, than that poor Youth (however innocent) began to sink in his Affections as he rose in hers. This, it is true, would of itself alone never have been able to eradicate *Jones* from his Bosom; but it was greatly injurious to him, and prepared Mr. *Allworthy*'s Mind for those Impressions, which afterwards produced the mighty Events that will be contained hereafter in this History; and to which, it must be confest, the unfortunate Lad, by his own Wantonness, Wildness, and Want of Caution, too much contributed.

In recording some Instances of these, we shall, if rightly understood, afford a very useful Lesson to those well-disposed Youths, who shall hereafter be our Readers: For they may here find that Goodness of Heart, and Openness of Temper, tho' these may give them great Comfort within, and administer to an honest Pride in their own Minds, will by no Means, alas! do their Business in the World. Prudence and Circumspection are necessary even to the best of Men. They are indeed as it were a Guard to Virtue, without which she can never be safe. It is not enough that your Designs, nay that your Actions, are intrinsically good, you must take Care they shall appear so. If your Inside be never so beautiful, you must preserve a fair Outside also. This must be constantly looked to, or Malice and Envy will take Care to blacken it so, that the Sagacity and Goodness of an *Allworthy* will not be able to see thro' it, and to discern the Beauties within. Let this, my young Readers, be your constant Maxim, That no Man can be good enough to enable him to neglect the Rules of Prudence; nor will Virtue herself look beautiful, unless she be bedecked with the outward Ornaments of Decency and Decorum. And this Precept, my worthy Disciples, if you read with due Attention, you will, I hope, find sufficiently enforced by Examples in the following Pages.

I ask Pardon for this short Appearance, by Way of Chorus, on the Stage. It is in reality for my own Sake, that while I am discovering the Rocks on which Innocence and Goodness often split, I may not be misunderstood to recommend the very Means to my worthy Readers, by which I intend to shew them they will be undone. And this, as I could not prevail on any of my Actors to speak, I myself was obliged to declare.

Chapter VIII.

A childish Incident, in which, however, is seen a good-natured Disposition in Tom Jones.

The Reader may remember, that Mr. *Allworthy* gave *Tom Jones* a little Horse, as a Kind of Smart-money for the Punishment, which he imagined he had suffered innocently.

This Horse *Tom* kept above half a Year, and then rode him to a neighbouring Fair, and sold him.

At his Return, being questioned by *Thwackum*, what he had done with the Money for which the Horse was sold, he frankly declared he would not tell him.

'Oho!' says *Thwackum*, 'you will not! then I will have it out of your Br—h;' that being the Place to which he always applied for Information on every doubtful Occasion.

Tom was now mounted on the Back of a Footman, and every Thing prepared for Execution, when Mr. *Allworthy* entering the Room, gave the Criminal a Reprieve, and took him with him into another Apartment; where being alone with *Tom*, he put the same Question to him which *Thwackum* had before asked him.

Tom answered, He could in Duty refuse him nothing; but as for that tyrannical Rascal, he would never make him any other Answer than with a Cudgel, with which he hoped soon to be able to pay him for all his Barbarities.

Mr. *Allworthy* very severely reprimanded the Lad, for his indecent and disrespectful Expressions concerning his Master; but much more for his avowing an Intention of Revenge. He threatened him with the entire Loss of his Favour, if he ever heard such another Word from his Mouth; for he said, he would never support or befriend a Reprobate. By these and the like Declarations, he extorted some Compunction from *Tom*, in which that Youth was not over sincere: For he really meditated some Return for all the smarting Favours he had received at the Hands of the Pedagogue. He was, however, brought by Mr. *Allworthy* to express a Concern for his Resentment against *Thwackum*; and then the good Man, after some wholesome Admonition, permitted him to proceed, which he did, as follows.

'Indeed, my dear Sir, I love and honour you more than all the

World: I know the great Obligations I have to you, and should detest myself, if I thought my Heart was capable of Ingratitude. Could the little Horse you gave me speak, I am sure he could tell you how fond I was of your Present: For I had more Pleasure in feeding him, than in riding him. Indeed, Sir, it went to my Heart to part with him; nor would I have sold him upon any other Account in the World than what I did. You yourself, Sir, I am convinced, in my Case, would have done the same: For none ever so sensibly felt the Misfortunes of others. What would you feel, dear Sir, if you thought yourself the Occasion of them?—Indeed, Sir, there never was any Misery like theirs.'——'Like whose, Child?' says *Allworthy*: 'What do you mean?' 'Oh, Sir,' answered *Tom*, 'your poor Game-keeper, with all his large Family, ever since your discarding him, have been perishing with all the Miseries of Cold and Hunger. I could not bear to see these poor Wretches naked and starving, and at the same Time know myself to have been the Occasion of all their Sufferings.—I could not bear it, Sir, upon my Soul, I could not.' (Here the Tears run down his Cheeks, and he thus proceeded) 'It was to save them from absolute Destruction, I parted with your dear Present, notwithstanding all the Value I had for it. —I sold the Horse for them, and they have every Farthing of the Money.'

Mr. *Allworthy* now stood silent for some Moments, and before he spoke, the Tears started from his Eyes. He at length dismissed *Tom* with a gentle rebuke, advising him for the future to apply to him in Cases of Distress, rather than to use extraordinary Means of relieving them himself.

This Affair was afterwards the Subject of much Debate between *Thwackum* and *Square*. *Thwackum* held, that this was flying in Mr. *Allworthy's* Face, who had intended to punish the Fellow for his Disobedience. He said, in some Instances, what the World called *Charity* appeared to him to be opposing the Will of the Almighty, which had marked some particular Persons for Destruction; and that this was in like manner acting in Opposition to Mr. *Allworthy*; concluding, as usual, with a hearty Recommendation of Birch.

Square argued strongly, on the other Side, in Opposition perhaps to *Thwackum*, or in Compliance with Mr. *Allworthy*, who seemed very much to approve what *Jones* had done. As to what he urged on this Occasion, as I am convinced most of my Readers will be much abler Advocates for poor *Jones*, it would be impertinent to relate it. Indeed it was not difficult to reconcile to the *Rule of Right*, an Action which it would have been impossible to deduce from the *Rule of Wrong*.

Chapter IX.

Containing an Incident of a more heinous Kind, with the Comments of Thwackum *and* Square.

It hath been observed by some Man of much greater Reputation for Wisdom than myself, that Misfortunes seldom come single.[1] An instance of this may, I believe, be seen in those Gentlemen who have the Misfortune to have any of their Rogueries detected: For here Discovery seldom stops till the Whole is come out. Thus it happened to poor *Tom*; who was no sooner pardoned for selling the Horse, than he was discovered to have some Time before sold a fine Bible which Mr. *Allworthy* gave him, the Money arising from which Sale he had disposed of in the same Manner. This Bible Master *Blifil* had purchased, tho' he had already such another of his own, partly out of Respect for the Book, and partly out of Friendship to *Tom*, being unwilling that the Bible should be sold out of the Family at half Price. He therefore disbursed the said half Price himself; for he was a very prudent Lad, and so careful of his Money, that he had laid up almost every Penny which he had received from Mr. *Allworthy*.

Some People have been noted to be able to read in no Book but their own. On the contrary, from the Time when Master *Blifil* was first possessed of this Bible, he never used any other. Nay, he was seen reading in it much oftner than he had before been in his own. Now, as he frequently asked *Thwackum* to explain difficult Passages to him, that Gentleman unfortunately took notice of *Tom*'s Name, which was written in many Parts of the Book. This brought on an Enquiry, which obliged Master *Blifil* to discover the whole Matter.

Thwackum was resolved, a Crime of this Kind, which he called Sacrilege, should not go unpunished. He therefore proceeded immediately to Castigation; and not contented with that, he acquainted Mr. *Allworthy*, at their next Meeting, with this monstrous Crime, as it appeared to him; inveighing against *Tom* in the most bitter Terms, and likening him to the Buyers and Sellers who were driven out of the Temple.

Square saw this Matter in a very different Light. He said, He could not perceive any higher Crime in selling one Book, than in selling another. That to sell Bibles was strictly lawful by all Laws

1. Shakespeare, *Hamlet* IV.v.78–79: "When sorrows come, they come not single spies / But in battalions" (1602). But as Fielding indicates below, pp. 196 and 223, he had seen this proverbial idea in other authors. Rabelais, *Gargantua and Pantagruel* (1532–64): "As afflictions never come singly" (II.xxxiii.121, LeClercq trans., New York, 1936, 1942). Cervantes, *Don Quixote* (1605): "But, as 'tis a common saying, that Misfortunes seldome come alone" (Modern Library ed., Part I.IV.i.233). Addison, *The Spectator*, no. 7, 8 Mar. 1710: "My dear, misfortunes never come single."

both Divine and Human, and consequently there was no Unfitness in it. He told *Thwackum,* that his great Concern on this Occasion brought to his Mind the Story of a very devout Woman, who out of pure Regard to Religion, stole *Tillotson's* Sermons[2] from a Lady of her Acquaintance.

This Story caused a vast Quantity of Blood to rush into the Parson's Face, which of itself was none of the palest; and he was going to reply with great Warmth and Anger, had not Mrs. *Blifil,* who was present at this Debate, interposed. That Lady declared herself absolutely of Mr. *Square's* Side. She argued, indeed, very learnedly in Support of his Opinion; and concluded with saying, if *Tom* had been guilty of any Fault, she must confess her own Son appeared to be equally culpable; for that she could see no Difference between the Buyer and the Seller; both of whom were alike to be driven out of the Temple.

Mrs. *Blifil* having declared her Opinion put an End to the Debate. *Square's* Triumph would almost have stopt his Words, had he needed them; and *Thwackum,* who for Reasons before-mentioned, durst not venture at disobliging the Lady, was almost choaked with Indignation. As to Mr. *Allworthy,* he said, Since the Boy had been already punished, he would not deliver his Sentiments on the Occasion; and whether he was, or was not angry with the Lad, I must leave to the Reader's own Conjecture.

Soon after this, an Action was brought against the Game-keeper by 'Squire *Western,* (the Gentleman in whose Manor the Partridge was killed) for Depredations of the like Kind. This was a most unfortunate Circumstance for the Fellow, as it not only of itself threatened his Ruin, but actually prevented Mr. *Allworthy* from restoring him to his Favour: For as that Gentleman was walking out one Evening with Master *Blifil* and young *Jones,* the latter slily drew him to the Habitation of *Black George;* where the Family of that poor Wretch, namely, his Wife and Children, were found in all the Misery with which Cold, Hunger, and Nakedness, can affect human Creatures: For as to the Money they had received from *Jones,* former Debts had consumed almost the whole.

Such a Scene as this could not fail of affecting the Heart of Mr. *Allworthy.* He immediately gave the Mother a couple of Guineas, with which he bid her cloath her Children. The poor Woman burst into Tears at this Goodness, and while she was thanking him, could not refrain from expressing her Gratitude to *Tom;* who had, she said, long preserved both her and hers from starving. 'We have not,' says she, 'had a morsel to eat, nor have these poor Children had a Rag to put on, but what his Goodness had bestowed on us.' For indeed, besides the Horse and the Bible, *Tom* had sacrificed a Night-gown and other Things to the Use of this distressed Family.

2. John Tillotson, author of *Sermons* (1682), a Church of England latitudinarian widely admired for his common sense and clarity.

On their Return home *Tom* made use of all his Eloquence to display the Wretchedness of these People, and the Penitence of *Black George* himself; and in this he succeeded so well, that Mr. *Allworthy* said, He thought the Man had suffered enough for what was past; that he would forgive him, and think of some Means of providing for him and his Family.

Jones was so delighted with this News, that tho' it was dark when they returned home, he could not help going back a Mile in a Shower of Rain, to acquaint the poor Woman with the glad Tidings; but, like other hasty Divulgers of News he only brought on himself the Trouble of contradicting it: For the Ill-fortune of *Black George* made use of the very Opportunity of his Friend's Absence to overturn all again.

Chapter X.

In which Master Blifil *and* Jones *appear in different Lights.*

Master *Blifil* fell very short of his Companion in the amiable Quality of Mercy; but he as greatly exceeded him in one of much higher Kind, namely, in Justice: In which he followed both the Precepts and Example of *Thwackum* and *Square*; for tho' they would both make frequent Use of the Word *Mercy*, yet it was plain, that in reality *Square* held it to be inconsistent with the Rule of Right; and *Thwackum* was for doing Justice, and leaving Mercy to Heaven. The two Gentlemen did indeed somewhat differ in Opinion concerning the Objects of this sublime Virtue; by which *Thwackum* would probably have destroyed one half of Mankind, and *Square* the other half.

Master *Blifil* then, though he had kept Silence in the Presence of *Jones*, yet when he had better considered the Matter, could by no Means endure the Thoughts of suffering his Uncle to confer Favours on the Undeserving. He therefore resolved immediately to acquaint him with the Fact which we have above slightly hinted to the Readers. The Truth of which was as follows.

The Game-keeper about a Year after he was dismissed from Mr. *Allworthy*'s Service, and before *Tom*'s selling the Horse, being in Want of Bread, either to fill his own Mouth, or those of his Family, as he passed through a Field belonging to Mr. *Western*, espied a Hare sitting in her Form. This Hare he had basely and barbarously knocked on the Head, against the Laws of the Land,[1] and no less against the Laws of Sportsmen.

The Higler to whom the Hare was sold, being unfortunately taken many Months after with a Quantity of Game upon him, was obliged to make his Peace with the Squire, by becoming Evidence

---

1. The Game Laws, which stipulated that no one whose land yielded less than £100 a year could kill game on it, or anywhere else.

against some Poacher. And now *Black George* was pitched upon by him, as being a Person already obnoxious to Mr. *Western,* and one of no good Fame in the Country. He was, besides, the best Sacrifice the Higler could make, as he had supplied him with no Game since; and by this Means the Witness had an Opportunity of screening his better Customers: For the Squire, being charmed with the Power of punishing *Black George,* whom a single Transgression was sufficient to ruin, made no further Enquiry.

Had this Fact been truly laid before Mr. *Allworthy,* it might probably have done the Game-keeper very little Mischief. But there is no Zeal blinder than that which is inspired with the Love of Justice against Offenders. Master *Blifil* had forgot the Distance of the Time. He varied likewise in the Manner of the Fact: and, by the hasty Addition of the single Letter S, he considerably altered the Story; for he said that *George* had wired Hares. These Alterations might probably have been set right, had not Master *Blifil* unluckily insisted on a Promise of Secrecy from Mr. *Allworthy,* before he revealed the Matter to him; but, by that Means, the poor Game-keeper was condemned, without having any Opportunity to defend himself: For as the Fact of Killing the Hare, and of the Action brought, were certainly true, Mr. *Allworthy* had no Doubt concerning the rest.

Short-lived then was the Joy of these poor People; for Mr. *All-worthy* the next Morning declared he had fresh Reason, without assigning it, for his Anger, and strictly forbad *Tom* to mention *George* any more; though as for his Family, he said, he would endeavour to keep them from starving; but as to the Fellow himself, he would leave him to the Laws, which Nothing could keep him from breaking.

Tom could by no means divine what had incensed Mr. *Allworthy*: For of Master *Blifil* he had not the least Suspicion. However, as his Friendship was to be tired out by no Disappointments, he now determined to try another Method of preserving the poor Game-keeper from Ruin.

Jones was lately grown very intimate with Mr. *Western.* He had so greatly recommended himself to that Gentleman, by leaping over five-barred Gates, and by other Acts of Sportmanship, that the Squire had declared *Tom* would certainly make a great Man, if he had but sufficient Encouragement. He often wished he had himself a Son with such Parts; and one Day very solemnly asserted at a drinking Bout, that *Tom* should hunt a Pack of Hounds for a thousand Pound of his Money, with any Huntsman in the whole Country.

By such kind of Talents he had so ingratiated himself with the Squire, that he was a most welcome Guest at his Table, and a favourite Companion in his Sport: Every Thing which the Squire held most dear, to wit, his Guns, Dogs, and Horses, were now as much at the Command of *Jones*, as if they had been his own. He resolved therefore to make use of this Favour on Behalf of his Friend *Black George*, whom he hoped to introduce into Mr. *Western*'s Family, in the same Capacity in which he had before served Mr. *Allworthy*.

The Reader, if he considers that this Fellow was already obnoxious to Mr. *Western*, and if he considers farther the weighty Business by which that Gentleman's Displeasure had been incurred, will perhaps condemn this as a foolish and desperate Undertaking; but if he should totally condemn young *Jones* on that Account, he will greatly applaud him for strengthening himself with all imaginable Interest on so arduous an Occasion.

For this Purpose then *Tom* applied to Mr. *Western*'s Daughter, a young Lady of about seventeen Years of Age, whom her Father, next after those necessary Implements of Sport just before mentioned, loved and esteemed above all the World. Now, as she had some Influence on the Squire, so *Tom* had some little Influence on her. But this being the intended Heroine of this Work, a Lady with whom we ourselves are greatly in Love, and with whom many of our Readers will probably be in Love too before we part, it is by no Means proper she should make her Appearance in the End of a Book.

BOOK IV.

Containing the Time of a Year.

Chapter I.

Containing five Pages of Paper.

As Truth distinguishes our Writings from those idle Romances which are filled with Monsters, the Productions, not of Nature, but of distempered Brains; and which have been therefore recommended by an eminent Critic[1] to the sole Use of the Pastry-cook: So, on the other hand, we would avoid any Resemblance to that

[handwritten margin note:] Romance — untruthful

---

1. Horace seems the best guess, though Martial actually mentions the cook's using poems to wrap his wares. Horace (*Epistles* II.i.268–70) says: "Cum scriptore meo caspa porrectus operta / Deferar in vicum vendentem tus et odores / Et piper et qui quid chartis amictur ineptis." Pope had used the second line (*Deferar . . .*) prominently on the frontispiece of his *Dunciad* (1729), and had paraphrased the whole poem in his esteemed *First Epistle of the Second Book of Horace* (1737). But the purchases Horace mentions as wrapped up in the "clumsy sheets" of clumsy poets are "frankincense, spices, and pepper." Fielding later used Martial (Lib. 16) as the epigraph for his *Covent-Garden Journal*, no. 6, adding his own translation: "Quam multi tineas pascunt, blattasque disarti / Et redimunt soli carmina docta coci!"—"How many fear the Moth's and Bookworm's Rage / And Pastry-Cooks, sole Buyers in this Age?" Catullus (95.8) probably originates this poetic tradition, describing bad verses as *laxas scombris tunicas*, "loose tunics for mackerels," at the fishmonger's shop.

kind of History which a celebrated Poet[2] seems to think is no less calculated for the Emolument of the Brewer, as the reading it should be always attended with a Tankard of good Ale.

> While—History with her Comrade Ale,
> Sooths the sad Series of her serious Tale.

For as this is the Liquor of modern Historians, nay, perhaps their Muse, if we may believe the Opinion of *Butler*,[3] who attributes Inspiration to Ale, it ought likewise to be the Potation of their Readers, since every Book ought to be read with the same Spirit, and in the same Manner, as it is writ. Thus the famous Author of *Hurlothrumbo*[4] told a learned Bishop, that the Reason his Lordship could not taste the Excellence of his Piece, was, that he did not read it with a Fiddle in his Hand; which Instrument he himself had always had in his own, when he composed it.

That our Work, therefore, might be in no Danger of being likened to the Labours of these Historians, we have taken every Occasion of interspersing through the whole sundry Similies, Descriptions, and other kind of poetical Embellishments. These are, indeed, designed to supply the Place of the said Ale, and to refresh the Mind, whenever those Slumbers which in a long Work are apt to invade the Reader as well as the Writer, shall begin to creep upon him. Without Interruptions of this Kind, the best Narrative of plain Matter of Fact must over-power every Reader; for nothing but the everlasting Watchfulness, which *Homer* has ascribed only to *Jove*[5] himself, can be Proof against a News Paper of many Volumes.

We shall leave to the Reader to determine with what Judgment we have chosen the several Occasions for inserting those ornamental Parts of our Work. Surely it will be allowed that none could be more proper than the present; where we are about to introduce a considerable Character on the Scene; no less, indeed, than the Heroine of this Heroic, Historical, Prosaic Poem. Here, therefore, we have thought proper to prepare the Mind of the Reader for her Reception, by filling it with every pleasing Image, which we can

---

2. Pope, *Dunciad* (1728 version, 205–6): "While happier *Hist'ry* with her comrade *Ale*, / Soothes the sad series of her tedious tale."

3. *Hudibras* I.i.631–58: "We should, as learned Poets use, / Invoke th'assistance of some Muse . . . / Thou, that with Ale, or viler Liquors, / Didst inspire *Withers, Pryn*, and *Vickars* . . . / Assist me but this once, I 'mplore, / And I shall trouble thee no more." See also below, pp. 135 and 303.

4. An extravaganza (1729) by Samuel Johnson (not *the* Samuel Johnson, but

"a half-mad dancing-master from Cheshire"), in which Johnson, as "Lord Flame," played his part on stilts, while playing the violin (Cross I.79).

5. *Iliad* II.1–3: "Both gods and mortal charioteers then slept all night, but sweet sleep did not hold Jupiter." Fielding seems to have in mind Pope's more sweeping paraphrase: "Now pleasing *Sleep* had seal'd each mortal Eye, / Stretch'd in their Tents the *Grecian* Leaders lie, / Th'Immortals slumber'd on their Thrones above; / All, but the ever-wakeful Eyes of *Jove*."

draw from the Face of Nature. And for this Method we plead many
Precedents. First, this is an Art well known to, and much practised
by, our Tragick Poets; who seldom fail to prepare their Audience for
the Reception of their principal Characters.

Thus the Heroe is always introduced with a Flourish of Drums
and Trumpets, in order to rouse a Martial Spirit in the Audience,
and to accommodate their Ears to Bombast and Fustian, which Mr.
Lock's blind Man[6] would not have grossly erred in likening to the
Sound of a Trumpet. Again, when Lovers are coming forth, soft
Music often conducts them on the Stage, either to sooth the Audience with the Softness of the tender Passion, or to lull and prepare
them for that gentle Slumber in which they will most probably be
composed by the ensuing Scene.

And not only the Poets, but the Masters of these Poets, the Managers of Playhouses, seem to be in this Secret; for, besides the aforesaid Kettle Drums, *&c.* which denote the Heroe's Approach, he is
generally ushered on the Stage by a large Troop of half a dozen
Scene-shifters; and how necessary these are imagined to his Appearance, may be concluded from the following Theatrical Story.

King *Pyrrhus*[7] was at Dinner at an Alehouse bordering on the
Theatre, when he was summoned to go on the Stage. The Heroe,
being unwilling to quit his Shoulder of Mutton, and as unwilling to
draw on himself the Indignation of Mr. *Wilks*, (his Brother Man-
ager) for making the Audience wait, had bribed these his Harbingers to be out of the Way. While Mr. *Wilks*, therefore, was thundering out, 'Where are the Carpenters to walk on before King
Pyrrhus,' that Monarch very quietly eat his Mutton, and the Audience, however impatient, were obliged to entertain themselves with
Music in his Absence.

To be plain, I much question whether the Politician, who hath
generally a good Nose, hath not scented out somewhat of the Util-
ity of this Practice. I am convinced that awful Magistrate my Lord
Mayor contracts a good deal of that Reverence which attends him
through the Year, by the several Pageants which precede his Pomp.
Nay, I must confess, that even I myself, who am not remarkably
liable to be captivated with Show, have yielded not a little to the
Impressions of much preceding State. When I have seen a Man
strutting in a Procession, after others whose Business was only to

6. John Locke, *An Essay Concerning
Human Understanding* (1690) III.iv.11
—"A studious blind man . . . bragged
one day that he now understood what
scarlet signified. Upon which his friend
demanding what scarlet was? the blind
man answered, It was like the sound of
a trumpet" (Bryant, p. 143). To illustrate how simple ideas come only from
the senses, Locke recurs to his blind
man a number of times: II.ii, iv, ix;
III.ix; IV.vi. See below, p. 207.
7. Fielding's anecdote concerns Barton
Booth, who was acting Pyrrhus in
Ambrose Philips's tragedy *The Distressed
Mother*, the first night of which was 17
Mar. 1712.

walk before him, I have conceived a higher Notion of his Dignity, than I have felt on seeing him in a common Situation. But there is one Instance which comes exactly up to my Purpose. This is the Custom of sending on a Basket-woman, who is to precede the Pomp at a Coronation, and to strew the Stage with Flowers, before the great Personages begin their Procession. The Antients would certainly have invoked the Goddess *Flora* for this Purpose, and it would have been no Difficulty for their Priests or Politicians to have persuaded the People of the real Presence of the Deity, though a plain Mortal had personated her, and performed her Office. But we have no such Design of imposing on our Reader; and therefore those who object to the Heathen Theology, may, if they please, change our Goddess into the above mentioned Basket-woman. Our Intention, in short, is to introduce our Heroine with the utmost Solemnity in our Power, with an Elevation of Stile, and all other Circumstances proper to raise the Veneration of our Reader. Indeed we would, for certain Causes, advise those of our Male Readers who have any Hearts, to read no farther, were we not well assured, that how amiable soever the Picture of our Heroine will appear, as it is really a Copy from Nature, many of our fair Country-women will be found worthy to satisfy any Passion, and to answer any Idea of Female Perfection, which our Pencil will be able to raise.

And now, without any further Preface, we proceed to our next Chapter.

Chapter II.

A short Hint of what we can do in the Sublime, and a Description of Miss Sophia Western.

Hushed be every ruder Breath. May the Heathen Ruler of the Winds confine in iron Chains the boisterous Limbs of noisy *Boreas*, and the sharp-pointed Nose of bitter, biting *Eurus*. Do thou, sweet *Zephyrus*, rising from thy fragrant Bed, mount the western Sky, and lead on those delicious Gales, the Charms of which call forth the lovely *Flora* from her Chamber, perfumed with pearly Dews, when on the first of *June*, her Birth-day, the blooming Maid, in loose Attire, gently trips it over the verdant Mead, where every Flower rises to do her Homage, 'till the whole Field becomes enamelled, and Colours contend with Sweets which shall ravish her most.

So charming may she now appear; and you the feather'd Choristers of Nature, whose sweetest Notes not even *Handel* can excell, tune your melodious Throats, to celebrate her Appearance. From Love proceeds your Music, and to Love it returns. Awaken therefore that gentle Passion in every Swain: For lo! adorned with all the

Charms in which Nature can array her; bedecked with Beauty, Youth, Sprightliness, Innocence, Modesty, and Tenderness, breath- ~Sophia~ ing Sweetness from her rosy Lips, and darting Brightness from her sparkling Eyes, the lovely *Sophia* comes.

Reader, perhaps thou hast seen the Statue of the *Venus de Medicis*.[1] Perhaps too, thou hast seen the Gallery of Beauties at *Hampton-Court*.[2] Thou may'st remember *each bright* Churchill *of the Galaxy*,[3] and all the Toasts of the *Kit-cat*.[4] Or if their Reign was before thy Times, at least thou hast seen their Daughters, the no less dazling Beauties of the present Age; whose Names, should we here insert, we apprehend they would fill the whole Volume.

Now if thou hast seen all these, be not afraid of the rude Answer which Lord *Rochester*[5] once gave to a Man, who had seen many Things. No. If thou hast seen all these without knowing what Beauty is, thou hast no Eyes; if without feeling its Power, thou hast no Heart.

Yet is it possible, my Friend, that thou mayest have seen all these without being able to form an exact Idea of *Sophia*: For she did not exactly resemble any of them. She was most like the Picture of Lady *Ranelagh*;[6] and I have heard more still to the famous Duchess of *Mazarine*;[7] but most of all, she resembled one whose Image never can depart from my Breast, and whom if thou dost remember, thou hast then, my Friend, an adequate Idea of *Sophia*.

But lest this should not have been thy Fortune, we will endeavour with our utmost Skill to describe this Paragon, though we are sensible that our highest Abilities are very inadequate to the Task.

1. A Greek statue (attributed, probably wrongly, to Cleomenes), found in the seventeenth century in the ruins of the porticus of Octavia in Rome. In Fielding's day, it stood in the Medici Palace in Rome (Mutter). Fielding himself never saw it.
2. Twelve paintings by Kneller of the beauties in the court of William and Mary. Queen Mary hung them in Hampton Court. These "Hampton Court Beauties" rivalled Lely's earlier "Windsor Beauties" (Mutter). Some of both sets may be seen at Hampton Court today.
3. Fielding is chiefly complimenting Sarah Jennings Churchill, widow and Dowager Duchess of John Churchill, First Duke of Marlborough. In 1742, at the age of 82, she had published memoirs defending herself in the old quarrel with Queen Anne, that ended in her dismissal from court in 1710. She had more recently sided with Fielding's friends Chesterfield and Lyttelton against Sir Robert Walpole's government, and Fielding had taken her part against a flood of pamphlets in his *A Full Vindication of*

the Duchess Dowager of Marlborough (1742).
4. The Kit-Cat Club (c. 1703–20) was a social Whig group founded at Christopher Cat's pie-house—his mutton pies were called, after their creator, "kit-cats." The group included Marlborough, Walpole, Vanbrugh, Addison, and Steele.
5. In a poem of sixteen lines entitled "To All Curious Critics and Admirers of Meter," Rochester asks "Have you seen" a series of things—a ship in a storm, a raging bull, a dove, fairies, and so forth —then concludes: "If you have seen all this, then kiss my A—se."
6. Margaret Cecil, Countess of Ranelagh, whose portrait by Kneller was among those at Hampton Court (Mutter).
7. Hortensia, a notorious and wealthy Italian widow (niece of the Cardinal), who came to London in 1675, at the age of twenty-nine, intending to become a mistress of Charles II. Her parties were famous. She died penniless at fifty-three. Cross (II.170) reproduces her portrait by Lely.

Sophia then, the only Daughter of Mr. *Western,* was a middle
sized Woman; but rather inclining to tall. Her Shape was not only
exact, but extremely delicate: and the nice Proportion of her Arms
promised the truest Symmetry in her Limbs. Her Hair, which was
black, was so luxuriant, that it reached her Middle, before she cut it
to comply with the modern Fashion; and it was now curled so
gracefully in her Neck, that few could believe it to be her own. If
Envy could find any Part of the Face which demanded less Commendation than the rest, it might possibly think her Forehead
might have been higher without Prejudice to her. Her Eye-brows
were full, even, and arched beyond the Power of Art to imitate. Her
black Eyes had a Lustre in them, which all her Softness could not
extinguish. Her Nose was exactly regular, and her Mouth, in which
were two Rows of Ivory, exactly answered Sir *John Suckling's*
Description in those Lines,

> *Her Lips were red, and one was thin,*
> *Compar'd to that was next her Chin.*
> *Some Bee had stung it newly.*[8]

Her Cheeks, were of the oval Kind; and in her right she had a
Dimple, which the least Smile discovered. Her Chin had certainly
its Share in forming the Beauty of her Face; but it was difficult to
say it was either large or small, tho' perhaps it was rather of the
former Kind. Her Complexion had rather more of the Lily than of
the Rose; but when Exercise, or Modesty, encreased her natural
Colour, no Vermilion could equal it. Then one might indeed cry
out with the celebrated Dr. *Donne.*

> ——*Her pure and eloquent Blood*
> *Spoke in her Cheeks, and so distinctly wrought,*
> *That one might almost say her Body thought.*[9]

Her Neck was long and finely turned: and here, if I was not
afraid of offending her Delicacy, I might justly say, the highest
Beauties of the famous *Venus de Medicis* were outdone. Here was
Whiteness which no Lilies, Ivory, nor Alabaster could match. The
finest Cambric might indeed be supposed from Envy to cover that
Bosom, which was much whiter than itself.——It was indeed,

> *Nitor splendens Pario marmore purius.*

'A Gloss shining beyond the purest Brightness of *Parian* Marble.'[1]

Such was the Outside of *Sophia;* nor was this beautiful Frame
disgraced by an Inhabitant unworthy of it. Her Mind was every way
equal to her Person; nay, the latter borrowed some Charms from

---

8. Suckling (1609–42), "A Ballad upon
a Wedding" 61–63.
9. John Donne (1572–1631), "The Progress of the Soul: The Second Anniver-
sary" 244–46.
1. Horace, *Odes* I.xix.5–6; *splendens* is
splendentis in the original.

the former: For when she smiled, the Sweetness of her Temper diffused that Glory over her Countenance, which no Regularity of
Features can give. But as there are no Perfections of the Mind
which do not discover themselves, in that perfect Intimacy, to
which we intend to introduce our Reader, with this charming young
Creature; so it is needless to mention them here: Nay, it is a Kind
of tacit Affront to our Reader's Understanding, and may also rob
him of that Pleasure which he will receive in forming his own Judgment of her Character.

It may, however, be proper to say, that whatever mental Accomplishments she had derived from Nature, they were somewhat
improved and cultivated by Art: For she had been educated under
the Care of an Aunt, who was a Lady of great Discretion, and was
thoroughly acquainted with the World, having lived in her Youth
about the Court, whence she had retired some Years since into the
Country. By her Conversation and Instructions, *Sophia* was perfectly well bred, though perhaps she wanted a little of that Ease in
her Behaviour, which is to be acquired only by Habit, and living
within what is called the Polite Circle. But this, to say the Truth, is
often too dearly purchased; and though it hath Charms so inexpressible, that the *French*, perhaps, among other qualities, mean to
express this, when they declare they know not what it is;[2] yet its
Absence is well compensated by Innocence; nor can good Sense,
and a natural Gentility ever stand in need of it.

Chapter III.

*Wherein the History goes back to commemorate a trifling Incident
that happened some Years since; but which, trifling as it was, had
some future Consequences.*

The amiable *Sophia* was now in her eighteenth Year, when she is
introduced into this History. Her Father, as hath been said, was
fonder of her than of any other human Creature. To her, therefore,
Tom Jones applied, in order to engage her Interest on the Behalf of
his Friend the Game-keeper.

But before we proceed to this Business, a short Recapitulation of
some previous Matters may be necessary.

Though the different Tempers of Mr. *Allworthy*, and of Mr.
Western did not admit of a very intimate Correspondence, yet they
lived upon what is called a decent Footing together; by which
Means the young People of both Families had been acquainted
from their Infancy; and as they were all near of the same Age, had
been frequent Play-mates together.

---

2. *Je ne sçais quoi* ("I don't know
what"), a French phrase popular in genteel English society to describe perfection in art and manners.

The Gaiety of *Tom*'s Temper suited better with *Sophia*, than the grave and sober Disposition of Master *Blifil*. And the Preference which she gave the former of these, would often appear so plainly, that a Lad of a more passionate Turn than Master *Blifil* was, might have shewn some Displeasure at it.

As he did not, however, outwardly express any such Disgust, it would be an ill Office in us to pay a Visit to the inmost Recesses of his Mind, as some scandalous People search into the most secret Affairs of their Friends, and often pry into their Closets and Cupboards, only to discover their Poverty and Meanness to the World.

However, as Persons who suspect they have given others Cause of Offence, are apt to conclude they are offended; so *Sophia* imputed an Action of Master *Blifil*, to his Anger, which the superior Sagacity of *Thwackum* and *Square* discerned to have arisen from a much better Principle.

Tom Jones, when very young, had presented *Sophia* with a little Bird, which he had taken from the Nest, had nursed up, and taught to sing.

Of this Bird, *Sophia*, then about thirteen Years old, was so extremely fond, that her chief Business was to feed and tend it, and her chief Pleasure to play with it. By these Means little *Tommy*, for so the Bird was called, was become so tame, that it would feed out of the Hand of its Mistress, would perch upon her Finger, and lie contented in her Bosom, where it seemed almost sensible of its own Happiness; tho' she always kept a small String about its Leg, nor would ever trust it with the Liberty of flying away.

One Day, when Mr. *Allworthy* and his whole Family, dined at Mr. *Western*'s, Master *Blifil*, being in the Garden with little *Sophia*, and observing the extreme Fondness that she shewed for her little Bird, desired her to trust it for a Moment in his Hands. *Sophia* presently complied with the young Gentleman's Request, and after some previous Caution, delivered him her Bird; of which he was no sooner in Possession, than he slipt the String from its Leg, and tossed it into the Air.

The foolish Animal no sooner perceived itself at Liberty, than forgetting all the Favours it had received from *Sophia*, it flew directly from her, and perched on a Bough at some Distance.

Sophia, seeing her Bird gone, screamed out so loud, that *Tom Jones*, who was at a little Distance, immediately ran to her Assistance.

He was no sooner informed of what had happend, than he cursed *Blifil* for a pitiful, malicious Rascal and then immediately stripping off his Coat, he applied himself to climbing the Tree to which the Bird escaped.

Tom had almost recovered his little Name-sake, when the Branch, on which it was perched, and that hung over a Canal, broke, and the poor Lad plumped over Head and Ears into the Water.

Sophia's Concern now changed its Object. And as she apprehended the Boy's Life was in Danger, she screamed ten times louder than before; and indeed Master *Blifil* himself now seconded her with all the Vociferation in his Power.

The Company, who were sitting in a Room next the Garden, were instantly alarmed, and came all forth; but just as they reached the Canal, *Tom*, (for the Water was luckily pretty shallow in that Part) arrived safely on shore.

Thwackum fell violently on poor *Tom*, who stood dropping and shivering before him, when Mr. *Allworthy* desired him to have Patience, and turning to Master *Blifil*, said, Pray Child, what is the Reason of all this Disturbance?

Master *Blifil* answered, 'Indeed, Uncle, I am very sorry for what I have done; I have been unhappily the Occasion of it all. I had Miss *Sophia*'s Bird in my Hand, and thinking the poor Creature languished for Liberty, I own, I could not forbear giving it what it desired: For I always thought there was something very cruel in confining any Thing. It seemed to be against the Law of Nature, by which every Thing hath a Right to Liberty; nay, it is even unchristian; for it is not doing what we would be done by: But if I had imagined Miss *Sophia* would have been so much concerned at it, I am sure I would never have done it; nay, if I had known what would have happened to the Bird itself: For when Master *Jones*, who climbed up that Tree after it, fell into the Water, the Bird took a second Flight, and presently a nasty Hawk carried it away.'

Poor *Sophia*, who now first heard of her little *Tommy*'s Fate; (for her Concern for *Jones* had prevented her perceiving it when it happened,) shed a Shower of Tears. These Mr. *Allworthy* endeavoured to assuage, promising her a much finer Bird: but she declared she would never have another. Her Father chid her for crying so for a foolish Bird; but could not help telling young *Blifil*, if he was a Son of his, his Backside should be well flea'd.

Sophia now returned to her Chamber, the two young Gentlemen were sent home, and the rest of the Company returned to their Bottle; where a Conversation ensued on the Subject of the Bird, so curious, that we think it deserves a Chapter by itself.

Chapter IV.

Containing such very deep and grave Matters, that some Readers, perhaps, may not relish it.

Square had no sooner lighted his Pipe, than addressing himself to *Allworthy*, he thus began: 'Sir, I cannot help congratulating you on your Nephew; who, at an Age when few Lads have any Ideas but of sensible Objects, is arrived at a Capacity of distinguishing Right from Wrong. To confine any thing seems to me against the Law of Nature, by which every thing hath a Right to Liberty. These were his Words; and the Impression they have made on me is never to be eradicated. Can any Man have a higher Notion of the Rule of Right, and the Eternal Fitness of Things? I cannot help promising myself from such a Dawn, that the Meridian of this Youth will be equal to that of either the elder or the younger *Brutus*.'[1]

Here *Thwackum* hastily interrupted, and spilling some of his Wine, and swallowing the rest with great Eagerness, answered, 'From another Expression he made use of, I hope he will resemble much better Men. The Law of Nature is a Jargon of Words, which means nothing. I know not of any such Law, nor of any Right which can be derived from it. To do as we would be done by, is indeed a Christian Motive, as the Boy well expressed himself, and I am glad to find my Instructions have born such good Fruit.'

'If Vanity was a Thing fit, (says *Square*) I might indulge some on the same Occasion; for whence only he can have learnt his Notions of Right or Wrong, I think is pretty apparent. If there be no Law of Nature, there is no Right nor Wrong.'

'How! (says the Parson) Do you then banish Revelation? Am I talking with a Deist or an Atheist?'

'Drink about, (says *Western*) Pox of your Laws of Nature. I don't know what you mean either of you, by Right and Wrong. To take away my Girl's Bird was wrong in my Opinion; and my Neighbour *Allworthy* may do as he pleases; but to encourage Boys in such Practices is to breed them up to the Gallows.'

Allworthy answered, 'That he was sorry for what his Nephew had done; but could not consent to punish him, as he acted rather from a generous than unworthy Motive.' He said, 'If the Boy had stolen the Bird, none would have been more ready to vote for a severe Chastisement than himself; but it was plain that was not his Design:' And, indeed, it was as apparent to him, that he could have no other View but what he had himself avowed. (For as to that malicious Purpose which *Sophia* suspected, it never once entered into the Head of Mr. *Allworthy*). He, at length, concluded with again blaming the Action as inconsiderate, and which he said, was pardonable only in a Child.

---

1. Lucius Junius Brutus, the legendary founder of republican Rome, organized the overthrow of the Tarquins after the rape of Lucrece; Marcus Junius Brutus (85–42 B.C.), centuries later, hoped to restore republican Rome by murdering his friend Julius Caesar. He was thus guilty of "ingratitude," as Fielding goes on to say. The elder Brutus was guilty of "parricide" because he condemned his two sons for plotting against his government and witnessed their execution. The killing of any blood relative was termed parricide by the Romans, and in subsequent usage well into the eighteenth century (Bryant, p. 147).

Square had delivered his Opinion so openly, that if he was now silent, he must submit to have his Judgment censured. He said, therefore, with some Warmth, 'That Mr. *Allworthy* had too much Respect to the dirty Consideration of Property. That in passing our Judgments on great and mighty Actions, all private Regards should be laid aside; for by adhering to those narrow Rules, the younger *Brutus* had been condemned of Ingratitude, and the elder of Parricide.'

'And if they had been hanged too for those Crimes,' cried *Thwackum*, 'they would have had no more than their Deserts. A couple of heathenish Villains! Heaven be praised, we have no *Brutus*'s now-a-days. I wish, Mr. *Square*, you would desist from filling the Minds of my Pupils with such Antichristian Stuff: For the Consequence must be, while they are under my Care, its being well scourged out of them again. There is your Disciple *Tom* almost spoiled already. I overheard him the other Day disputing with Master *Blifil*, That there was no Merit in Faith without Works. I know that is one of your Tenets, and I suppose he had it from you.'

'Don't accuse me of spoiling him,' says *Square*, 'Who taught him to laugh at whatever is virtuous and decent, and fit and right in the Nature of Things? He is your own Scholar, and I disclaim him. No, no, Master *Blifil* is my Boy. Young as he is, that Lad's Notions of moral Rectitude I defy you ever to eradicate.'

Thwackum put on a contemptuous Sneer at this, and replied, 'Ay, ay, I will venture him with you. He is too well grounded for all your philosophical Cant to hurt. No, no, I have taken Care to instil such Principles into him'— *jargon*

'And I have instilled Principles into him too,' cries *Square*, 'What but the sublime Idea of Virtue could inspire a human Mind with the generous Thought of giving Liberty? And I repeat to you again, if it was a fit Thing to be proud, I might claim the Honour of having infused that Idea.'—

'And if Pride was not forbidden,' said *Thwackum*, 'I might boast of having taught him that Duty which he himself assigned as his Motive.'

'So between you both,' says the Squire, 'the young Gentleman hath been taught to rob my Daughter of her Bird. I find I must take Care of my Partridge Mew. I shall have some virtuous religious Man or other set all my Partridges at Liberty.' Then slapping a Gentleman of the Law, who was present, on the [Back, he][2] cried out, 'What say you to this, Mr. Counsellor? Is not this against Law?'

The Lawyer with great Gravity delivered himself as follows:

'If the Case be put of a Partridge, there can be no Doubt but an

---

2. All four editions here carry the obvious typographical error: ". . . Back. He cried out. . . ."

Action would lie: For though this be *Feræ Naturæ*,[3] yet being reclaimed, Property vests; but being the Case of a Singing Bird, though reclaimed, as it is a Thing of base Nature, it must be considered as *nullius in bonis*. In this Case, therefore, I conceive the Plaintiff must be nonsuited;[4] and I should disadvise the bringing any such Action.'

'Well, (says the Squire) if it be *nullus bonus,* let us drink about, and talk a little of the State of the Nation, or some such Discourse that we all understand; for I am sure I don't understand a Word of this. It may be Learning and Sense for aught I know; but you shall never persuade me into it. Pox! you have neither of you mentioned a Word of that poor Lad who deserves to be commended. To venture breaking his Neck to oblige my Girl, was a generous spirited Action: I have Learning enough to see that. D—n me, here's *Tom*'s Health. I shall love the Boy for it the longest Day I have to live.'

Thus was the Debate interrupted; but it would probably have been soon resumed, had not Mr. *Allworthy* presently called for his Coach, and carried off the two Combatants.

Such was the Conclusion of this Adventure of the Bird, and of the Dialogue occasioned by it, which we could not help recounting to our Reader, though it happened some Years before that Stage, or Period of Time, at which our History is now arrived.

---

3. "Wild nature." *Nullius in bonis,* which follows, means "nobody's property." A wild animal is legal property only while in one's possession.

4. Bringing a judgment against a plaintiff who cannot, or will not, prove his charges.

Chapter V.

Containing Matter accommodated to every Taste.

Parva leves capiunt Animos,[1] 'Small things affect light Minds,' was the Sentiment of a great Master of the Passion of Love. And certain it is, that from this Day *Sophia* began to have some little Kindness for *Tom Jones,* and no little Aversion for his Companion.

Many Accidents from time to time improved both these Passions in her Breast; which, without our recounting, the Reader may well conclude, from what we have before hinted of the different Tempers of these Lads, and how much the one suited with her own Inclinations more than the other. To say the Truth, *Sophia,* when very young, discerned that *Tom,* tho' an idle, thoughtless, rattling Rascal, was no-body's Enemy but his own; and that Master *Blifil,* tho' a prudent, discreet, sober, young Gentleman, was, at the same Time, strongly attached to the Interest only of one single Person;

1. Ovid, *Ars Amatoria* I.159.

and who that single Person was, the Reader will be able to divine without any Assistance of ours.

These two Characters are not always received in the World with the different Regard which seems severally due to either; and which one would imagine Mankind, from Self-interest, should shew towards them. But perhaps there may be a political Reason for it: In finding one of a truly benevolent Disposition, Men may very reasonably suppose, they have found a Treasure, and be desirous of keeping it, like all other good Things, to themselves. Hence they may imagine, that to trumpet forth the Praises of such a Person, would, in the vulgar Phrase, be crying *Roast-meat*; and calling in Partakers of what they intend to apply solely to their own Use. If this Reason does not satisfy the Reader, I know no other Means of accounting for the little Respect which I have commonly seen paid to a Character which really does great Honour to Human Nature, and is productive of the highest Good to Society. But it was otherwise with *Sophia*. She honoured *Tom Jones*, and scorned Master *Blifil*, almost as soon as she knew the Meaning of those two Words.

Sophia had been absent upwards of three Years with her Aunt; during all which Time she had seldom seen either of these young Gentlemen. She dined, however, once, together with her Aunt, at Mr. *Allworthy*'s. This was a few Days after the Adventure of the Partridge, before commemorated. *Sophia* heard the whole Story at Table, where she said nothing; nor indeed could her Aunt get many Words from her, as she returned home; but her Maid, when undressing her, happening to say, 'Well, Miss, I suppose you have seen young Master *Blifil* To-day.' She answered with much Passion, 'I hate the Name of Master *Blifil*, as I do whatever is base and treacherous; and I wonder Mr. *Allworthy* would suffer that old barbarous Schoolmaster to punish a poor Boy so cruelly, for what was only the Effect of his Good-nature.' She then recounted the Story to her Maid, and concluded with saying,—'Don't you think he is a Boy of a noble Spirit?'

This young Lady was now returned to her Father; who gave her the Command of his House, and placed her at the upper End of his Table, where *Tom* (who for his great Love of Hunting was become a great Favourite of the Squire) often dined. Young Men of open, generous Dispositions are naturally inclined to Gallantry, which, if they have good Understandings, as was in reality *Tom*'s Case, exerts itself in an obliging, complaisant Behaviour to all Women in general. This greatly distinguished *Tom* from the boisterous Brutality of mere Country Squires on the one Hand; and from the solemn, and somewhat sullen, Deportment of Master *Blifil* on the other: And he began now, at Twenty, to have the Name of a pretty Fellow, among all the Women in the Neighbourhood.

Tom behaved to *Sophia* with no Particularity, unless, perhaps, by shewing her a higher Respect than he paid to any other. This Distinction her Beauty, Fortune, Sense, and amiable Carriage, seemed to demand; but as to Design upon her Person he had none; for which we shall at present suffer the Reader to condemn him of Stupidity; but perhaps we shall be able indifferently well to account for it hereafter.

Sophia, with the highest Degree of Innocence and Modesty, had a remarkable Sprightliness in her Temper. This was so greatly increased whenever she was in Company with *Tom*, that, had he not been very young and thoughtless, he must have observed it; or had not Mr. *Western*'s Thoughts been generally either in the Field, the Stable, or the Dog-kennel, it might have, perhaps, created some Jealousy in him: But so far was the good Gentleman from entertaining any such Suspicions, that he gave *Tom* every Opportunity with his Daughter which any Lover could have wished. And this *Tom* innocently improved to better Advantage, by following only the Dictates of his natural Gallantry and Good-nature, than he might, perhaps, have done, had he had the deepest Designs on the young Lady.

But, indeed, it can occasion little Wonder, that this Matter escaped the Observation of others, since poor *Sophia* herself never remarked it, and her Heart was irretrievably lost before she suspected it was in Danger.

Matters were in this Situation, when *Tom* one Afternoon, finding *Sophia* alone, began, after a short Apology, with a very serious Face, to acquaint her, that he had a Favour to ask of her, which he hoped her Goodness would comply with.

Though neither the young Man's Behaviour, nor indeed his Manner of opening this Business, were such as could give her any just Cause of suspecting he intended to make Love to her; yet, whether Nature whispered something into her Ear, or from what Cause it arose I will not determine, certain it is, some Idea of that Kind must have intruded itself; for her Colour forsook her Cheeks, her Limbs trembled, and her Tongue would have faultered, had *Tom* stopped for an Answer: But he soon relieved her from her Perplexity, by proceeding to inform her of his Request, which was to sollicit her Interest on Behalf of the Game-keeper, whose own Ruin, and that of a large Family, must be, he said, the Consequence of Mr. *Western*'s pursuing his Action against him.

Sophia presently recovered her Confusion, and with a Smile full of Sweetness, said, 'Is this the mighty Favour you asked with so much Gravity? I will do it with all my Heart. I really pity the poor Fellow, and no longer ago than Yesterday sent a small Matter to his Wife.' This small Matter was one of her Gowns, some Linen, and ten Shillings in Money, of which *Tom* had heard, and it had, in reality, put this Sollicitation into his Head.

Our Youth, now emboldened with his Success, resolved to push the Matter farther; and ventured even to beg her Recommendation of him to her Father's Service; protesting that he thought him one of the honestest Fellows in the Country, and extremely well qualified for the Place of a Game-keeper, which luckily then happened to be vacant.

Sophia answered; 'Well, I will undertake this too; but I cannot promise you as much Success as in the former Part, which I assure you I will not quit my Father without obtaining. However, I will do what I can for the poor Fellow; for I sincerely look upon him and his Family as Objects of great Compassion.—And now, Mr. *Jones*, I must ask you a Favour.'—

'A Favour! Madam, (cries *Tom*) if you knew the Pleasure you have given me in the Hopes of receiving a Command from you, you would think by mentioning it you did confer the greatest Favour on me; for by this dear Hand I would sacrifice my Life to oblige you.'

He then snatched her Hand, and eagerly kissed it, which was the first Time his Lips had ever touched her. The Blood, which before had forsaken her Cheeks, now made her sufficient Amends, by rushing all over her Face and Neck with such Violence, that they became all of a scarlet Colour. She now first felt a Sensation to which she had been before a Stranger, and which, when she had Leisure to reflect on it, began to acquaint her with some Secrets, which the Reader, if he does not already guess them, will know in due Time.

Sophia, as soon as she could speak, (which was not instantly) informed him, that the Favour she had to desire of him, was not to lead her Father through so many Dangers in Hunting; for that, from what she had heard, she was terribly frightened every Time they went out together, and expected some Day or other to see her Father brought home with broken Limbs. She therefore begged him, for her sake, to be more cautious; and, as he well knew Mr. *Western* would follow him, not to ride so madly, nor to take those dangerous Leaps for the future.

Tom promised faithfully to obey her Commands; and, after thanking her for her kind Compliance with his Request, took his Leave, and departed highly charmed with his Success.

Poor *Sophia* was charmed too; but in a very different Way. Her Sensations, however, the Reader's Heart (if he or she have any) will better represent than I can, if I had as many Mouths as ever Poet wished for, to eat, I suppose, those many Dainties with which he was so plentifully provided.

It was Mr. *Western's* Custom every Afternoon, as soon as he was drunk, to hear his Daughter play on the Harpsichord: For he was a great Lover of Music, and perhaps, had he lived in Town, might have passed for a Connoisseur; for he always excepted against the finest Compositions of Mr. *Handel.* He never relished any Music but what was light and airy; and indeed his most favourite Tunes, were *Old Sir* Simon *the King,*[2] St. George *he was for* England,[3] *Bobbing* Joan,[4] and some others.

His Daughter, tho' she was a perfect Mistress of Music, and would never willingly have played any but *Handel's,* was so devoted to her Father's Pleasure, that she learnt all those Tunes to oblige him. However, she would now and then endeavour to lead him into her own Taste, and when he required the Repetition of his Ballads, would answer with a 'Nay, dear Sir;' and would often beg him to suffer her to play something else.

This Evening, however, when the Gentleman was retired from his Bottle, she played all his Favourites three Times over, without any Solicitation. This so pleased the good Squire, that he started from his Couch, gave his Daughter a Kiss, and swore her Hand was greatly improved. She took this Opportunity to execute her Promise to *Tom,* in which she succeeded so well, that the Squire declared, If she would give him t'other Bout of old Sir *Simon,* he would give the Game-keeper his Deputation the next Morning. Sir *Simon* was played again and again, till the Charms of the Music soothed Mr. *Western* to sleep. In the Morning *Sophia* did not fail to remind him of his Engagement; and his Attorney was immediately sent for, and ordered to stop any further Proceedings in the Action, and to make out the Deputation.

Tom's Success in this Affair soon began to ring over the Country, and various were the Censures past upon it. Some greatly applauding it as an Act of good Nature; others sneering, and saying, 'No Wonder that one idle Fellow should love another.' Young *Blifil* was greatly enraged at it. He had long hated *Black George* in the same Proportion as *Jones* delighted in him; not from any Offence which he had ever received, but from his great Love to Religion and Virtue: For *Black George* had the Reputation of a loose Kind of a Fellow. *Blifil* therefore represented this as flying in Mr. *Allworthy's*

---

2. Originating c. 1575 and said to refer to Simon Wadlow, tapster at the Devil Tavern (Mutter), this tune gained fresh currency as Air 62 in John Gay's *The Beggar's Opera* (1728); the merry drunkenness and Tory politics of the earlier lyrics, as well as of Gay's, would appeal to Western.
3. A rollicking old ballad cataloguing England's worthies to the refrain: "St. George, he was for *England*, St. *Denis* was for *France*, / Sing *Honi Soit qui mal y pense.*"
4. A bawdy ballad (c. 1650) that became Gay's Air 15 in *Polly* (1729—never acted). Fielding used it as Air 3 in *The Author's Farce* (1730), sparking its popularity in subsequent ballad operas. I am indebted to Harold Gene Moss's "Ballad-opera Songs: A Record of the Ideas Set to Music" (unpublished dissertation, University of Michigan, 1970), and to his personal commentary.

Face; and declared with great Concern, that it was impossible to find any other Motive for doing Good to such a Wretch.

Thwackum and *Square* likewise sung to the same Tune: They were now (especially the latter) become greatly jealous of young *Jones* with the Widow: For he now approached the Age of Twenty, was really a fine young Fellow, and that Lady, by her Encouragements to him, seemed daily more and more to think him so.

Allworthy was not, however, moved with their Malice. He declared himself very well satisfied with what *Jones* had done. He said, the Perseverance and Integrity of his Friendship was highly commendable, and he wished he could see more frequent Instances of that Virtue.

But Fortune, who seldom greatly relishes such Sparks as my Friend *Tom*, perhaps, because they do not pay more ardent Addresses to her, gave now a very different Turn to all his Actions, and shewed them to Mr. *Allworthy* in a Light far less agreeable than that Gentleman's Goodness had hitherto seen them in.

Chapter VI.

An Apology for the Insensibility of Mr. Jones, *to all the Charms of the lovely* Sophia; *in which possibly we may, in a considerable Degree, lower his Character in the Estimation of those Men of Wit and Gallantry, who approve the Heroes in most of our modern Comedies.*

There are two Sorts of People, who, I am afraid, have already conceived some Contempt for my Heroe, on Account of his Behaviour to *Sophia*. The former of these will blame his Prudence in neglecting an Opportunity to possess himself of Mr. *Western's* Fortune; and the latter will no less despise him for his Backwardness to so fine a Girl, who seemed ready to fly into his Arms, if he would open them to receive her.

Now, though I shall not, perhaps, be able absolutely to acquit him of either of these Charges; (for Want of Prudence admits of no Excuse; and what I shall produce against the latter Charge, will, I apprehend, be scarce satisfactory;) yet as Evidence may sometimes be offered in Mitigation, I shall set forth the plain Matter of Fact, and leave the whole to the Reader's Determination.

Mr. *Jones* had Somewhat about him, which, though I think Writers are not thoroughly agreed in its Name, doth certainly inhabit some human Breasts; whose Use is not so properly to distinguish Right from Wrong, as to prompt and incite them to the former, and to restrain and with-hold them from the latter.

This Somewhat may be indeed resembled to the famous Trunk-

maker[1] in the Play-house: For whenever the Person who is possessed of it, doth what is right, no ravished or friendly Spectator is
so eager, or so loud in his Applause; on the contrary, when he doth
wrong, no Critic is so apt to hiss and explode him.

To give a higher Idea of the Principle I mean, as well as one
more familiar to the present Age; it may be considered as sitting on
its Throne in the Mind, like the LORD HIGH CHANCELLOR of this
Kingdom in his Court; where it presides, governs, directs, judges,
acquits and condemns according to Merit and Justice; with a
Knowledge which nothing escapes, a Penetration which nothing can
deceive, and an Integrity which nothing can corrupt.

This active Principle may perhaps be said to constitute the most
essential Barrier between us, and our Neighbours the Brutes; for if
there be some in the human Shape, who are not under any such
Dominion, I chuse rather to consider them as Deserters from us to
our Neighbours; among whom they will have the Fate of Deserters,
and not be placed in the first Rank.

Our Heroe, whether he derived it from *Thwackum* or *Square* I
will not determine, was very strongly under the Guidance of this
Principle: For though he did not always act rightly, yet he never
did otherwise without feeling and suffering for it. It was this which
taught him, that to repay the Civilities and little Friendships of
Hospitality by robbing the House where you have received them, is
to be the basest and meanest of Thieves. He did not think the
Baseness of this Offence lessened by the Height of the Injury committed; on the contrary, if to steal another's Plate deserved Death
and Infamy, it seemed to him difficult to assign a Punishment adequate to the robbing a Man of his whole Fortune, and of his Child
into the Bargain.

This Principle therefore prevented him from any Thought of
making his Fortune by such Means (for this, as I have said, is an
active Principle, and doth not content itself with Knowledge or
Belief only.) Had he been greatly enamoured of *Sophia*, he possibly
might have thought otherwise; but give me Leave to say, there is
great Difference between running away with a Man's Daughter
from the Motive of Love, and doing the same Thing from the
Motive of Theft.

Now though this young Gentleman was not insensible of the
Charms of *Sophia*; tho' he greatly liked her Beauty, and esteemed
all her other Qualifications, she had made, however, no deep
Impression on his Heart: For which, as it renders him liable to the

1. *The Spectator*, no. 235, 29 Nov. 1711,
tells of a man known as "the trunk-
maker in the upper gallery" at the theater (Drury Lane, without a doubt),
who banged on the benches with his
oaken stick as a signal to applaud. Addison wonders whether the title comes
from the sound, like that of a man making trunks, or from the man's real employment in that trade.

Charge of Stupidity, or at least of Want of Taste, we shall now proceed to account.

The Truth then is, his Heart was in the Possession of another
Woman. Here I question not, but the Reader will be surprized at
our long Taciturnity as to this Matter; and quite at a Loss to divine
who this Woman was; since we have hitherto not dropt a Hint of
any one likely to be a Rival to *Sophia*: For as to Mrs. *Blifil*, though
we have been obliged to mention some Suspicions of her Affection
for *Tom*, we have not hitherto given the least Latitude for imagining that he had any for her; and, indeed, I am sorry to say it, but
the Youth of both Sexes are too apt to be deficient in their Gratitude, for that Regard with which Persons more advanced in Years
are sometimes so kind to honour them.

That the Reader may be no longer in Suspence, he will be
pleased to remember, that we have often mentioned the Family of
George Seagrim,[2] (commonly called *Black George*, the Game-
keeper) which consisted at present of a Wife and five Children.

The second of these Children was a Daughter, whose Name was
Molly, and who was esteemed one of the handsomest Girls in the
whole Country.

Congreve[3] well says, *There is in true Beauty something which
vulgar Souls cannot admire;* so can no Dirt or Rags hide this Something from those Souls which are not of the vulgar Stamp.

The Beauty of this Girl made, however, no Impression on *Tom*,
till she grew towards the Age of Sixteen, when *Tom*, who was near
three Years older, began first to cast the Eyes of Affection upon her.
And this Affection he had fixed on the Girl long before he could
bring himself to attempt the Possession of her Person: For tho' his
Constitution urged him greatly to this, his Principles no less forcibly restrained him. To debauch a young Woman, however low her
Condition was, appeared to him a very heinous Crime; and the
Good-will he bore the Father, with the Compassion he had for his
Family, very strongly corroborated all such sober Reflections; so that
he once resolved to get the better of his Inclinations, and he
actually abstained three whole Months without ever going to *Seagrim*'s House, or seeing his Daughter.

Now though *Molly* was, as we have said, generally thought a very
fine Girl, and in reality she was so, yet her Beauty was not of the
most amiable Kind. It had indeed very little of Feminine in it, and
would have become a Man at least as well as a Woman; for, to say

2. Fielding had brought suit against a
Randolph Seagrim for debt, and won the
judgment, in 1742 (Shakespeare Head
ed.; Cross I.376 n.).
3. *The Old Batchelor* (1693) IV.iii—
"There is in true Beauty, as in Courage,
somewhat, which narrow Souls cannot

dare to admire." This play ran no fewer
than six times a season during Fielding's
years as a playwright (1728–37), often in
the same week as Fielding's plays, reaching a peak of fifteen performances in
1741–42, and continuing in popularity for
many years.

the Truth, Youth and florid Health had a very considerable Share in the Composition.

Nor was her Mind more effeminate than her Person. As this was tall and robust, so was that bold and forward. So little had she of Modesty, that *Jones* had more Regard for her Virtue than she herself. And as most probably she liked *Tom* as well as he liked her; so when she perceived his Backwardness, she herself grew proportionably forward; and when she saw he had entirely deserted the House, she found Means of throwing herself in his Way, and behaved in such a Manner, that the Youth must have had very much, or very little of the Heroe, if her Endeavours had proved unsuccessful. In a Word, she soon triumphed over all the virtuous Resolutions of *Jones*: For though she behaved at last with all decent Reluctance, yet I rather chuse to attribute the Triumph to her; since, in Fact, it was her Design which succeeded.

In the Conduct of this Matter, I say, *Molly* so well played her Part, that *Jones* attributed the Conquest entirely to himself, and considered the young Woman as one who had yielded to the violent Attacks of his Passion. He likewise imputed her yielding to the ungovernable Force of her Love towards him; and this the Reader will allow to have been a very natural and probable Supposition, as we have more than once mentioned the uncommon Comeliness of his Person: And indeed he was one of the handsomest young Fellows in the World.

As there are some Minds whose Affections, like Master *Blifil's*, are solely placed on one single Person, whose Interest and Indulgence alone they consider on every Occasion; regarding the Good and Ill of all others as merely indifferent, any farther than as they contribute to the Pleasure or Advantage of that Person: So there is a different Temper of Mind which borrows a Degree of Virtue even from Self-love. Such can never receive any kind of Satisfaction from another, without loving the Creature to whom that Satisfaction is owing, and without making its Well-being in some sort necessary to their own Ease.

Of this latter Species was our Heroe. He considered this poor Girl as one whose Happiness or Misery he had caused to be dependent on himself. Her Beauty was still the Object of Desire, though greater Beauty, or a fresher Object, might have been more so; but the little Abatement which Fruition had occasioned to this, was highly overbalanced by the Considerations of the Affection which she visibly bore him, and of the Situation into which he had brought her. The former of these created Gratitude, the latter Compassion; and both together, with his Desire for her Person, raised in him a Passion, which might, without any great Violence to the

Word, be called *Love*; though, perhaps, it was at first not very judiciously placed.

This then was the true Reason of that Insensibility which he had
shewn to the Charms of *Sophia*, and that Behaviour in her, which
might have been reasonably enough interpreted as an Encouragement to his Addresses: For as he could not think of abandoning his
Molly, poor and destitute as she was, so no more could he entertain
a Notion of betraying such a Creature as *Sophia*. And surely, had he
given the least Encouragement to any Passion for that young Lady,
he must have been absolutely guilty of one or other of those
Crimes; either of which would, in my Opinion, have very justly subjected him to that Fate, which, at his first Introduction into this
History, I mentioned to have been generally predicted as his certain
Destiny.

Chapter VII.

Being the shortest Chapter in this Book.

Her mother first perceived the Alteration in the Shape of *Molly*;
and in order to hide it from her Neighbours, she foolishly clothed
her in that Sack which *Sophia* had sent her. Though indeed that
young Lady had little Apprehension, that the poor Woman would
have been weak enough to let any of her Daughters wear it in that
Form.

Molly was charmed with the first Opportunity she ever had of
shewing her Beauty to Advantage; for though she could very well
bear to contemplate herself in the Glass, even when drest in Rags;
and though she had in that Dress conquered the Heart of *Jones*,
and perhaps of some others; yet she thought the Addition of Finery
would much improve her Charms, and extend her Conquests.

Molly, therefore, having dressed herself out in this Sack, with a
new laced Cap, and some other Ornaments which *Tom* had given
her, repairs to Church with her Fan in her Hand the very next
Sunday. The Great are deceived, if they imagine they have appropriated Ambition and Vanity to themselves. These noble Qualities
flourish as notably in a Country Church, and Church-yard, as in the
Drawing-Room, or in the Closet. Schemes have indeed been laid in
the Vestry, which would hardly disgrace the Conclave. Here is a
Ministry, and here is an Opposition. Here are Plots and Circumven-
tions, Parties and Factions, equal to those which are to be found in
Courts.

Nor are the Women here less practised in the highest Feminine
Arts than their fair Superiors in Quality and Fortune. Here are

Prudes and Coquettes. Here are Dressing and Ogling, Falshood, Envy, Malice, Scandal; in short, every Thing which is common to the most splendid Assembly, or politest Circle. Let those of high Life, therefore, no longer despise the Ignorance of their Inferiors; nor the Vulgar any longer rail at the Vices of their Betters.

Molly had seated herself some time, before she was known by her Neighbours. And then a Whisper ran through the whole Congregation, 'Who is she?' But when she was discovered, such sneering, gigling, tittering, and laughing, ensued among the Women, that Mr. *Allworthy* was obliged to exert his Authority to preserve any Decency among them.

Chapter VIII.

A Battle sung by the Muse in the Homerican Stile, and which none but the classical Reader can taste.

Mr. *Western* had an Estate in this Parish; and as his House stood at little greater Distance from this Church than from his own, he very often came to divine Service here; and both he and the charming *Sophia* happened to be present at this Time.

Sophia was much pleased with the Beauty of the Girl, whom she pitied for her Simplicity, in having dressed herself in that Manner, as she saw the Envy which it had occasioned among her Equals. She no sooner came home, than she sent for the Game-keeper, and ordered him to bring his Daughter to her; saying, She would provide for her in the Family, and might possibly place the Girl about her own Person, when her own Maid, who was now going away, had left her.

Poor *Seagrim* was thunderstruck at this; for he was no Stranger to the Fault in the Shape of his Daughter. He answered, in a stammering Voice, 'That he was afraid *Molly* would be too aukward to wait on her Ladyship, as she had never been at Service.' 'No matter for that,' says *Sophia*, 'she will soon improve. I am pleased with the Girl, and am resolved to try her.'

Black George now repaired to his Wife, on whose prudent Counsel he depended to extricate him out of this Dilemma; but when he came thither, he found his House in some Confusion. So great Envy had this Sack occasioned, that when Mr. *Allworthy* and the other Gentry were gone from Church, the Rage, which had hitherto been confined, burst into an Uproar; and, having vented itself at first in opprobrious Words, Laughs, Hisses, and Gestures, betook itself at last to certain missile Weapons; which though, from their plastic Nature they threatened neither the Loss of Life or of Limb, were however sufficiently dreadful to a well-dressed Lady. *Molly* had

too much Spirit to bear this Treatment tamely. Having therefore—
But hold, as we are diffident of our own Abilities, let us here invite
a superior Power to our Assistance.

Ye Muses then, whoever ye are, who love to sing Battles, and
principally thou, who whilom didst recount the Slaughter in those
Fields where *Hudibrass* and *Trulla*[1] fought, if thou wert not starved
with thy Friend *Butler*, assist me on this great Occasion. All things
are not in the Power of all.

As a vast Herd of Cows in a rich Farmer's Yard, if, while they are
milked, they hear their Calves at a Distance, lamenting the Robbery which is then committing, roar and bellow: So roared forth the
Somersetshire Mob an Hallaloo, made up of almost as many
Squawls, Screams, and other different Sounds, as there were Persons, or indeed Passions, among them: Some were inspired by Rage,
others alarmed by Fear, and others had nothing in their Heads but
the Love of Fun; but chiefly Envy, the Sister of *Satan*, and his constant Companion, rushed among the Crowd, and blew up the Fury
of the Women; who no sooner came up to *Molly*, than they pelted
her with Dirt and Rubbish.

Molly, having endeavoured in vain to make a handsome Retreat,
faced about; and laying hold of ragged *Bess*, who advanced in the
Front of the Enemy, she at one Blow felled her to the Ground. The
whole Army of the Enemy (though near a hundred in Number)
seeing the Fate of their General, gave back many Paces, and retired
behind a new-dug Grave; for the Church-yard was the Field of
Battle, where there was to be a Funeral that very Evening. *Molly*
pursued her Victory, and catching up a Skull which lay on the Side
of the Grave, discharged it with such Fury, that having hit a Taylor
on the Head, the two Skulls sent equally forth a hollow Sound at
their Meeting, and the Taylor took presently measure of his Length
on the Ground, where the Skulls lay side by side, and it was doubtful which was the more valuable of the two. *Molly* then taking a
Thighbone in her Hand, fell in among the flying Ranks, and dealing her Blows with great Liberality on either Side, overthrew the
Carcass of many a mighty Heroe and Heroine.

Recount, O Muse, the Names of those who fell on this fatal Day.
First *Jemmy Tweedle* felt on his hinder Head the direful Bone.
Him the pleasant Banks of sweetly winding *Stour* had nourished,
where he first learnt the vocal Art, with which, wandring up and
down at Wakes and Fairs he cheered the rural Nymphs and Swains,
when upon the Green they interweav'd the sprightly Dance; while

1. Samuel Butler's *Hudibras* I.ii.365–408
and I.iii.769 ff. Hudibras, a quixotic Pu-
ritan knight, fights a crowd watching a
bear-baiting, a sport of which the Puritans disapproved. Trulla, a virago, is one
of his adversaries. Butler was traditionally (and probably erroneously) supposed to have died neglected and
starved. Fielding also mentions Butler
above, p. 114, and below, p. 303.

he himself stood fiddling and jumping to his own Music. How little now avails his Fiddle? He thumps the verdant Floor with his Carcass. Next old *Echepole*, the Sowgelder, received a Blow in his Forehead from our Amazonian Heroine, and immediately fell to the Ground. He was a swinging fat Fellow, and fell with almost as much Noise as a House. His Tobacco-box dropt at the same Time from his Pocket, which *Molly* took up as lawful Spoils. Then *Kate* of the Mill tumbled unfortunately over a Tombstone, which catching hold of her ungartered Stocking, inverted the Order of Nature, and gave her Heels the Superiority to her Head. *Betty Pippin*, with young *Roger* her Lover, fell both to the Ground; where, O perverse Fate! she salutes the Earth, and he the Sky. *Tom Freckle*, the Smith's Son, was the next Victim to her Rage. He was an ingenious Workman, and made excellent Pattins; nay the very Pattin with which he was knocked down, was his own Workmanship. Had he been at the Time singing Psalms in the Church, he would have avoided a broken Head. Miss *Crow*, the Daughter of a Farmer; *John Giddish*, himself a Farmer; *Nan Slouch, Esther Codling, Will Spray, Tom Bennet*; the three Misses *Potter*, whose Father keeps the Sign of the *Red Lion, Betty Chambermaid, Jack Ostler*, and many others of inferior Note, lay rolling among the Graves.

Not that the strenuous Arm of *Molly* reached all these; for many of them in their Flight overthrew each other.

But now Fortune, fearing she had acted out of Character, and had inclined too long to the same Side, especially as it was the right Side, hastily turned about: For now Goody *Brown*,—whom *Zekiel Brown* caressed in his Arms; nor he alone, but half the Parish besides; so famous was she in the Fields of *Venus*, nor indeed less in those of *Mars*. The Trophies of both these, her Husband always bore about on his Head and Face; for if ever human Head did by its Horns display the amorous Glories of a Wife, *Zekiel*'s did; nor did his well-scratched Face less denote her Talents (or rather Talons) of a different Kind.

No longer bore this Amazon the shameful Flight of her Party. She stopt short, and calling aloud to all who fled, spoke as follows: 'Ye *Somersetshire* Men, or rather ye *Somersetshire* Women, are ye not ashamed, thus to fly from a single Woman; but if no other will oppose her, I myself and *Joan Top* here will have the Honour of the Victory.' Having thus said, she flew at *Molly Seagrim*, and easily wrenched the Thigh-bone from her Hand, at the same Time clawing off her Cap from her Head. Then laying hold of the Hair of *Molly*, with her Left Hand, she attacked her so furiously in the Face with the Right, that the Blood soon began to trickle from her Nose. *Molly* was not idle this while. She soon removed the Clout from the Head of Goody *Brown*, and then fastening on her Hair with one Hand, with the other she caused another bloody Stream to issue forth from the Nostrils of the Enemy.

When each of the Combatants had borne off sufficient Spoils of Hair from the Head of her Antagonist, the next Rage was against the Garments. In this Attack they exerted so much Violence, that in a very few Minutes, they were both naked to the middle.

It is lucky for the Women, that the Seat of Fistycuff-War is not the same with them as among Men; but tho' they may seem a little to deviate from their Sex, when they go forth to Battle, yet I have observed they never so far forget, as to assail the Bosoms of each other; where a few Blows would be fatal to most of them. This, I know, some derive from their being of a more bloody Inclination than the Males. On which Account they apply to the Nose, as to the Part whence Blood may most easily be drawn; but this seems a far-fetched, as well as ill-natured Supposition.

Goody *Brown* had great Advantage of *Molly* in this Particular; for the former had indeed no Breasts, her Bosom (if it may be so called) as well in Colour as in many other Properties, exactly resembling an antient Piece of Parchment, upon which any one might have drummed a considerable while, without doing her any great Damage.

Molly, beside her present unhappy Condition, was differently formed in those Parts, and might, perhaps, have tempted the Envy of *Brown* to give her a fatal Blow, had not the lucky Arrival of *Tom Jones* at this Instant put an immediate End to the bloody Scene.

This Accident was luckily owing to Mr. *Square*; for he, Master *Blifil*, and *Jones*, had mounted their Horses, after Church, to take the Air, and had ridden about a Quarter of a Mile, when *Square*, changing his Mind, (not idly, but for a Reason which we shall unfold as soon as we have Leisure) desired the young Gentlemen to ride with him another Way than they had at first purposed. This Motion being compiled with, brought them of Necessity back again to the Church-yard.

Master *Blifil*, who rode first, seeing such a Mob assembled, and two Women in the Posture in which we left the Combatants, stopt his Horse to enquire what was the Matter. A Country Fellow, scratching his Head, answered him; 'I don't know Measter un't I; an't please your Honour, here hath been a Vight, I think, between Goody *Brown* and *Mol Seagrim*.' 'Who, who?' cries *Tom*; but without waiting for an Answer, having discovered the Features of his *Molly* through all the Discomposure in which they now were, he hastily alighted, turned his Horse loose, and leaping over the Wall, ran to her. She now first bursting into Tears, told him how barbarously she had been treated. Upon which, forgetting the Sex of Goody *Brown*, or perhaps not knowing it, in his Rage; for, in real-

ity, she had no feminine Appearance, but a Petticoat, which he
might not observe, he gave her a Lash or two with his Horsewhip;
and then flying at the Mob, who were all accused by *Molly*, he dealt
his Blows so profusely on all Sides, that unless I would again invoke
the Muse, (which the good-natured Reader may think a little too
hard upon her, as she hath so lately been violently sweated) it
would be impossible for me to recount the Horsewhipping of that
Day.

Having scoured the whole Coast of the Enemy, as well as any of
Homer's Heroes ever did, or as *Don Quixote,* or any Knight-Errant
in the World could have done, he returned to *Molly*, whom he
found in a Condition, which must give both me and my Reader
Pain, was it to be described here. *Tom* raved like a Madman, beat
his Breast, tore his Hair, stamped on the Ground, and vowed the
utmost Vengeance on all who had been concerned. He then pulled
off his Coat, and buttoned it round her, put his Hat upon her
Head, wiped the Blood from her Face as well as he could with his
Handkerchief, and called out to the Servant to ride as fast as possible for a Sidesaddle, or a Pillion, that he might carry her safe home.

Master *Blifil* objected to the sending away the Servant, as they
had only one with them; but as *Square* seconded the Order of
Jones, he was obliged to comply.

The Servant returned in a very short Time with the Pillion, and
Molly, having collected her Rags as well as she could, was placed
behind him. In which Manner she was carried home, *Square, Blifil,*
and *Jones* attending.

Here *Jones*, having received his Coat, given her a sly Kiss, and
whispered her, that he would return in the Evening, quitted his
Molly, and rode on after his Companions.

Chapter IX.

Containing Matter of no very peaceable Colour.

Molly had no sooner apparelled herself in her accustomed Rags,
than her Sisters began to fall violently upon her; particularly her
eldest Sister, who told her she was well-enough served. 'How had
she the Assurance to wear a Gown which young Madam *Western*
had given to Mother! If one of us was to wear it, I think,' says she,
'I myself have the best Right; but I warrant you think it belongs to
your Beauty. I suppose you think yourself more handsomer than
any of us.' 'Hand her down the Bit of Glass from over the Cup-
board,' cries another; 'I'd wash the Blood from my Face before I
tauked of my Beauty.' 'You'd better have minded what the Parson
says,' cries the eldest, 'and not a harkened after Men Voke.'
'Indeed, Child, and so she had,' says the Mother sobbing, 'she hath

brought a Disgrace upon us all. She's the vurst of the Vamily that ever was a Whore.' 'You need not upbraid me with that, Mother,' cries *Molly*; 'you yourself was brought-to-bed of Sister there, within a Week after you was married.' 'Yes, Hussy,' answered the enraged Mother, 'so I was, and what was the mighty Matter of that? I was made an honest Woman then; and if you was to be made an honest Woman, I should not be angry; but you must have to doing with a Gentleman, you nasty Slut; you will have a Bastard, Hussy, you will; and that I defy anyone to say of me.'

In this Situation *Black George* found his Family, when he came home for the Purpose before-mentioned. As his Wife and three Daughters were all of them talking together, and most of them crying, it was some Time before he could get an Opportunity of being heard; but as soon as such an Interval occurred, he acquainted the Company with what *Sophia* had said to him.

Goody *Seagrim* then began to revile her Daughter afresh. 'Here,' says she, 'you have brought us into a fine Quandary indeed. What will Madam say to that big Belly? Oh that ever I should live to see this Day!'

Molly answered with great Spirit, 'And what is this mighty Place which you have got for me, Father?' (for he had not well understood the Phrase used by *Sophia* of being about her Person) 'I suppose it is to be under the Cook; but I shan't wash Dishes for any Body. My Gentleman will provide better for me. See what he hath given me this Afternoon: He hath promised I shall never want Money; and you shan't want Money neither, Mother, if you will hold your Tongue, and know when you are well.' And so saying, she pulled out several Guineas, and gave her Mother one of them.

The good Woman no sooner felt the Gold within her Palm, than her Temper began (such is the Efficacy of that *Panacea*) to be mollified. 'Why, Husband,' says she, 'would any but such a Blockhead as you not have enquired what Place this was before he had accepted it? Perhaps, as *Molly* says, it may be in the Kitchin; and truly I don't care my Daughter should be a Scullion Wench: For poor as I am, I am a Gentlewoman. And thof I was obliged, as my Father, who was a Clergyman, died worse than Nothing, and so could not give me a Shilling of *Potion*, to undervalue myself, by marrying a poor Man; yet I would have you to know, I have a Spirit above all *them* Things. Marry come up! it would better become Madam *Western* to look at home, and remember who her own Grandfather was. Some of my Family, for ought I know, might ride in their Coaches, when the Grandfathers of some Voke walked a-voot. I warrant she fancies she did a mighty Matter, when she sent us that old *Gownd*; some of my Family would not have picked up such Rags in the Street; but poor People are always trampled upon. —The Parish need not have been in such a Fluster with *Molly*.—

You might have told them, Child, your Grandmother wore better Things new out of the Shop.'

'Well, but consider,' cried *George*, 'What Answer shall I make to Madam?' 'I don't know what Answer,' says she, 'You are always bringing your Family into one Quandary or other. Do you remember when you shot the Partridge, the Occasion of all our Misfortunes? Did not I advise you never to go into Squire *Western's* Manor? Did not I tell you many a good Year ago what would come of it? But you would have your own headstrong Ways; yes, you would, you Villain'—

Black George was, in the main, a peaceable Kind of Fellow, and nothing *choleric, nor rash*; yet did he bear about him something of what the Antients called the *Irascible*, and which his Wife, if she had been endowed with much *Wisdom, would have feared*.[1] He had long experienced, that when the Storm grew very high, Arguments were but Wind, which served rather to increase than to abate it. He was therefore seldom unprovided with a small Switch, a Remedy of wonderful Force, as he had often essayed, and which the Word Villain served as a Hint for his applying.

No sooner, therefore, had this Symptom appeared, than he had immediate Recourse to the said Remedy, which though, as it is usual in all very efficacious Medicines, it at first seemed to heighten and inflame the Disease, soon produced a total Calm, and restored the Patient to perfect Ease and Tranquillity.

This is, however, a Kind of Horse-medicine, which requires a very robust Constitution to digest, and is therefore proper only for the Vulgar, unless in one single Instance, *viz.* where Superiority of Birth breaks out; in which Case, we should not think it very improperly applied by any Husband whatever, if the Application was not in itself so base, that, like certain Applications of the physical Kind which need not be mentioned, it so much degrades and contaminates the Hand employed in it, that no Gentleman should endure the Thought of any Thing so low and detestable.

The whole Family were soon reduced to a State of perfect Quiet: For the Virtue of this Medicine, like that of Electricity, is often communicated through one Person to many others, who are not touched by the Instrument. To say the Truth, as they both operate by Friction, it may be doubted whether there is not something analogous between them, of which Mr. *Freke*[2] would do well to enquire, before he publishes the next Edition of his Book.

A Council was now called, in which, after many Debates, *Molly* still persisting that she would not go to Service, it was at length resolved, that Goody *Seagrim* herself should wait on Miss *Western*,

---

1. Fielding is humorously echoing Hamlet's warning to Laertes as they grapple in Ophelia's grave: "For, though I am not splenitive and rash, / Yet have I in me something dangerous, / Which let thy wisdom fear" (V.i.284–86).
2. See above, p. 65.

and endeavour to procure the Place for her eldest Daughter, who declared great Readiness to accept it: But Fortune, who seems to have been an Enemy of this little Family, afterwards put a Stop to her Promotion.

Chapter X.

A Story told by Mr. Supple, the Curate. The Penetration of Squire Western. His great Love for his Daughter, and the Return to it made by her.

The next morning *Tom Jones* hunted with Mr. *Western*, and was at his Return invited by that Gentleman to Dinner.

The lovely *Sophia* shone forth that Day with more Gaiety and Sprightliness than usual. Her Battery was certainly levelled at our Heroe; tho', I believe, she herself scarce yet knew her own Intention; but if she had any Design of charming him, she now succeeded.

Mr. *Supple*, the Curate of Mr. *Allworthy*'s Parish, made one of the Company. He was a good-natured worthy Man; but chiefly remarkable for his great taciturnity at Table, tho' his Mouth was never shut at it. In short, he had one of the best Appetites in the World. However, the Cloth was no sooner taken away, than he always made sufficient Amends for his Silence: For he was a very hearty Fellow; and his Conversation was often entertaining, never offensive.

At his first Arrival, which was immediately before the Entrance of the Roast-beef, he had given an Intimation that he had brought some News with him, and was beginning to tell, that he came that Moment from Mr. *Allworthy*'s, when the Sight of the Roast-beef struck him dumb, permitting him only to say Grace, and to declare, He must pay his Respect to the Baronet: For so he called the Sirloin.

When Dinner was over, being reminded by *Sophia* of his News, he began as follows, 'I believe, Lady, your Ladyship observed a young Woman at Church Yesterday at Even-song, who was drest in one of your outlandish Garments; I think I have seen your Ladyship in such a one. However, in the Country, such Dresses are

Rara avis in Terris, nigroque simillima Cygno,[1]

That is, Madam, as much as to say,

A rare Bird upon the Earth, and very like a black Swan.

'The Verse is in *Juvenal*: But to return to what I was relating. I was saying such Garments are rare Sights in the Country; and

1. Juvenal, *Satires* VI.165. Quoted in Lily, p. 138. See also below, p. 307.

perchance too, it was thought the more rare, Respect being had to the Person who wore it, who, they tell me, is the Daughter of *Black George,* your Worship's Game-keeper, whose Sufferings I should have opined, might have taught him more Wit, than to dress forth his Wenches in such gaudy Apparel. She created so much Confusion in the Congregation, that if Squire *Allworthy* had not silenced it, it would have interrupted the Service: For I was once about to stop in the Middle of the first Lesson. Howbeit, nevertheless, after Prayer was over, and I was departed home, this occasioned a Battle in the Church-yard, where, amongst other Mischief, the Head of a travelling Fidler was very much broken. This Morning the Fidler came to Squire *Allworthy* for a Warrant, and the Wench was brought before him. The Squire was inclined to have compounded Matters; when, lo! on a sudden, the Wench appeared (I ask your Ladyship's Pardon) to be, as it were, at the Eve of bringing forth a Bastard. The Squire demanded of her who was the Father? But she pertinaciously refused to make any Response. So that he was about to make her Mittimus to *Bridewel,* when I departed.'

'And is a Wench having a Bastard all your News, Doctor?' cries *Western,* 'I thought it might have been some public Matter, something about the Nation.'

'I am afraid it is too common, indeed,' answered the Parson, 'but I thought the whole Story all together deserved commemorating. As to national Matters, your Worship knows them best. My Concerns extend no farther than my own Parish.'

'Why, ay,' says the Squire, 'I believe I do know a little of that Matter, as you say; but come, *Tommy,* drink about, the Bottle stands with you.'

Tom begged to be excused, for that he had particular Business; and getting up from Table, escaped the Clutches of the Squire, who was rising to stop him, and went off with very little Ceremony.

The Squire gave him a good Curse at his Departure; and then turning to the Parson, he cried out, 'I smoke it: I smoke it. *Tom* is certainly the Father of this Bastard. 'Zooks, Parson, you remember how he recommended the Veather o'her to me.—D—n un, what a sly B—ch 'tis. Ay, ay, as sure as Two-pence, *Tom* is the Veather of the Bastard.'[2]

'I should be very sorry for that,' says the Parson.

'Why sorry,' cries the Squire, 'Where is the mighty Matter o't? What, I suppose, dost pretend that thee hast never got a Bastard? Pox! more good Luck's thine: For I warrant hast a done *therefore*[3]

2. This is the first display of Western's west-country dialect, a direct descendant of West Saxon, the language of King Alfred. Western's characteristic *un* for *him* remains in rural speech from *hine* (pronounced "hinna"), the West Saxon objective form eventually displaced by *him,* the old dative, in the dialects around London. Western's *un* is thus older and, in a sense, more valid than *him.*

3. The parson (says Western) has said more than one "therefore I pronounce you man and wife" to marry off his pregnant mistresses to unsuspecting youths in his parish.

many's the good Time and often.' 'Your Worship is pleased to be jocular,' answered the Parson, 'but I do not only animadvert on the Sinfulness of the Action, though that surely is to be greatly deprecated; but I fear his Unrighteousness may injure him with Mr. *Allworthy*. And truly I must say, though he hath the Character of being a little wild, I never saw any Harm in the young Man; nor can I say I have heard any, save what your Worship now mentions. I wish, indeed, he was a little more regular in his Responses at Church; but altogether he seems

Ingenui vultus puer ingenuique pudoris.[4]

That is a classical Line, young Lady, and being rendered into *English*, is, "A Lad of an ingenuous Countenance, and of an ingenuous Modesty:" For this was a Virtue in great Repute both among the *Latins* and *Greeks*. I must say the young Gentleman (for so I think I may call him, notwithstanding his Birth) appears to me a very modest civil Lad, and I should be sorry that he should do himself any Injury in Squire *Allworthy*'s Opinion.'

'Poogh!' says the Squire, 'Injury with *Allworthy*! Why *Allworthy* loves a Wench himself. Doth not all the Country know whose Son *Tom* is? You must talk to another Person in that Manner. I remember *Allworthy* at College.'

'I thought,' said the Parson, 'he had never been at the University.'

'Yes, yes, he was,' says the Squire, 'and many a Wench have we two had together. As arrant a Whoremaster as any within five Miles o'un. No, no. It will do'n no Harm with he, assure yourself; nor with any Body else. Ask *Sophy* there—You have not the worse Opinion of a young Fellow for getting a Bastard, have you, Girl? No, no, the Women will like un the better for't.'

This was a cruel Question to poor *Sophia*. She had observed *Tom*'s Colour change at the Parson's Story; and that, with his hasty and abrupt Departure, gave her sufficient Reason to think her Father's Suspicion not groundless. Her Heart now, at once, discovered the great Secret to her, which it had been so long disclosing by little and little; and she found herself highly interested in this Matter. In such a Situation, her Father's malapert Question rushing suddenly upon her, produced some Symptoms which might have alarmed a suspicious Heart; but to do the Squire Justice, that was not his Fault. When she rose therefore from her Chair, and told him, a Hint from him was always sufficient to make her withdraw, he suffered her to leave the Room; and then with great Gravity of Countenance remarked, 'That it was better to see a Daughter over-modest, than over-forward:' A Sentiment which was highly applauded by the Parson.

4. Juvenal, *Satires* XI.154.

There now ensued between the Squire and the Parson, a most excellent political Discourse, framed out of News-papers, and political Pamphlets; in which they made a Libation of four Bottles of Wine to the Good of their Country; and then, the Squire being fast asleep, the Parson lighted his Pipe, mounted his Horse, and rode home.

When the Squire had finished his Half-hour's Nap, he summoned his Daughter to her Harpsichord; but she begged to be excused that Evening, on Account of a violent Head-ach. This Remission was presently granted: For indeed she seldom had Occasion to ask him twice, as he loved her with such ardent Affection, that by gratifying her, he commonly conveyed the highest Gratification to himself. She was really what he frequently called her, his little Darling; and she well deserved to be so: For she returned all his Affection in the most ample Manner. She had preserved the most inviolable Duty to him in all Things; and this her Love made not only easy, but so delightful, that when one of her Companions laughed at her, for placing so much Merit in such scrupulous Obedience, as that young Lady called it, *Sophia* answered, 'You mistake me, Madam, if you think I value myself upon this Account: For besides that I am barely discharging my Duty, I am likewise pleasing myself. I can truly say, I have no Delight equal to that of contributing to my Father's Happiness; and if I value myself, my Dear, it is on having this Power, and not on executing it.'

This was a Satisfaction, however, which poor *Sophia* was incapable of tasting this Evening. She therefore not only desired to be excused from her Attendance at the Harpsichord, but likewise begged that he would suffer her to absent herself from Supper. To this Request likewise the Squire agreed, though not without some Reluctance; for he scarce ever permitted her to be out of his Sight, unless when he was engaged with his Horses, Dogs, or Bottle. Nevertheless he yielded to the Desire of his Daughter, though the poor Man was, at the same Time, obliged to avoid his own Company, (if I may so express myself) by sending for a neighbouring Farmer to sit with him.

Chapter XI.

The narrow Escape of Molly Seagrim, *with some Observations for which we have been forced to dive pretty deep into Nature.*

Tom Jones had ridden one of Mr. *Western*'s Horses that Morning in the Chace; so that having no Horse of his own in the Squire's Stable, he was obliged to go Home on Foot: This he did so expeditiously, that he ran upwards of three Miles within the half Hour.

Just as he arrived at Mr. *Allworthy's* outward Gate, he met the Constable and Company, with *Molly* in their Possession, whom they were conducting to that House where the inferior Sort of People may learn one good Lesson, *viz.* Respect and Deference to their Superiors: Since it must shew them the wide Distinction Fortune intends between those Persons who are to be corrected for their Faults, and those who are not; which Lesson, if they do not learn, I am afraid, they very rarely learn any other good Lesson, or improve their Morals, at the House of Correction.

A Lawyer may, perhaps, think Mr. *Allworthy* exceeded his Authority a little in this Instance. And, to say the Truth, I question, as here was no regular Information before him, whether his Conduct was strictly regular. However, as his Intention was truly upright, he ought to be excused in *Foro Conscientiæ*;[1] since so many arbitrary Acts are daily committed by Magistrates, who have not this Excuse to plead for themselves.

Tom was no sooner informed by the Constable, whither they were proceeding, (indeed he pretty well guessed it of himself) than he caught *Molly* in his Arms, and embracing her tenderly before them all, swore he would murder the first Man who offered to lay hold of her. He bid her dry her Eyes, and be comforted; for wherever she went he would accompany her. Then turning to the Constable, who stood trembling with his Hat off, he desired him, in a very mild Voice, to return with him for a Moment only to his Father, (so he now called *Allworthy*) for he durst, he said, be assured, that when he had alledged what he had to say in her Favour, the Girl would be discharged.

The Constable, who, I make no Doubt, would have surrendered his Prisoner, had *Tom* demanded her, very readily consented to this Request. So back they all went into Mr. *Allworthy's* Hall, where *Tom* desired them to stay till his Return, and then went himself in Pursuit of the good Man. As soon as he was found, *Tom* threw himself at his Feet, and having begged a patient Hearing, confessed himself to be the Father of the Child, of which *Molly* was then big. He entreated him to have Compassion on the poor Girl, and to consider, if there was any Guilt in the Case, it lay principally at his Door.

'If there is any Guilt in the Case!' answered *Allworthy* warmly, 'Are you then so profligate and abandoned a Libertine, to doubt whether the breaking the Laws of God and Man, the corrupting and ruining a poor Girl, be Guilt? I own, indeed, it doth lie principally upon you, and so heavy it is, that you ought to expect it should crush you.'

'Whatever may be my Fate,' says *Tom*, 'let me succeed in my

1. "In the forum of conscience."

Intercessions for the poor Girl. I confess I have corrupted her; but whether she shall be ruined, depends on you. For Heaven's Sake, Sir, revoke your Warrant, and do not send her to a place which must unavoidably prove her Destruction.'

Allworthy bid him immediately call a Servant. *Tom* answered, There was no Occasion; for he had luckily met them at the Gate, and relying upon his Goodness, had brought them all back into his Hall, where they now waited his final Resolution, which, upon his Knees, he besought him might be in favour of the Girl; that she might be permitted to go home to her Parents, and not be exposed to a greater Degree of Shame and Scorn than must necessarily fall upon her. 'I know,' said he, 'that is too much. I know I am the wicked Occasion of it. I will endeavour to make Amends, if possible; and if you shall have hereafter the Goodness to forgive me, I hope I shall deserve it.'

Allworthy hesitated some Time, and at last said, 'Well, I will discharge my Mittimus.—You may send the Constable to me.' He was instantly called, discharged, and so was the Girl.

It will be believed, that Mr. *Allworthy* failed not to read *Tom* a very severe Lecture on this Occasion; but it is unnecessary to insert it here, as we have faithfully transcribed what he said to *Jenny Jones* in the first Book, most of which may be applied to the Men, equally with the Women. So sensible an Effect had these Reproofs on the young Man, who was no hardened Sinner, that he retired to his own Room, where he passed the Evening alone, in much melancholy Contemplation.

Allworthy was sufficiently offended by this Transgression of *Jones*; for, notwithstanding the Assertions of Mr. *Western*, it is certain, this worthy Man had never indulged himself in any loose Pleasures with Women, and greatly condemned the Vice of Incontinence in others. Indeed, there is much Reason to imagine, that there was not the least Truth in what Mr. *Western* affirmed, especially as he laid the Scene of those Impurities at the University, where Mr. *Allworthy* had never been. In fact, the good Squire was a little too apt to indulge that Kind of Pleasantry which is generally called *Rhodomontade*; but which may, with as much Propriety, be expressed by a much shorter Word; and, perhaps, we too often supply the Use of this little Monosyllable by others; since very much of what frequently passes in the World for Wit and Humour, should, in the strictest Purity of Language, receive that short Appellation, which, in Conformity to the well-bred Laws of Custom, I here suppress.

But whatever Detestation Mr. *Allworthy* had to this or to any other Vice, he was not so blinded by it, but that he could discern any Virtue in the guilty Person, as clearly, indeed, as if there had been no Mixture of Vice in the same Character. While he was angry, therefore, with the Incontinence of *Jones*, he was no less pleased with the Honour and Honesty of his Self-accusation. He began now to form in his Mind the same Opinion of this young Fellow, which, we hope, our Reader may have conceived. And in balancing his Faults with his Perfections, the latter seemed rather to preponderate.

It was to no Purpose, therefore, that *Thwackum*, who was immediately charged by Mr. *Blifil* with the Story, unbended all his Rancour against poor *Tom*. *Allworthy* gave a patient Hearing to their Invectives, and then answered coldly; 'That young Men of *Tom's* Complexion were too generally addicted to this Vice; but he believed That Youth was sincerely affected with what he had said to him on the Occasion, and he hoped he would not transgress again.' So that, as the Days of Whipping were at an End, the Tutor had no other Vent but his own Mouth for his Gall, the usual poor Resource of impotent Revenge.

But *Square*, who was a less violent, was a much more artful Man; and as he hated *Jones* more, perhaps, than *Thwackum* himself did, so he contrived to do him more Mischief in the Mind of Mr. *Allworthy*.

The Reader must remember the several little Incidents of the Partridge, the Horse, and the Bible, which were recounted in the second Book. By all which *Jones* had rather improved than injured the Affection which Mr. *Allworthy* was inclined to entertain for him. The same, I believe, must have happened to him with every other Person who hath any Idea of Friendship, Generosity, and Greatness of Spirit; that is to say, who hath any Traces of Goodness in his Mind.

Square himself was not unacquainted with the true Impression which those several Instances of Goodness had made on the excellent Heart of *Allworthy*; for the Philosopher very well knew what Virtue was, though he was not always, perhaps, steady in its Pursuit: But as for *Thwackum*, from what Reason I will not determine, no such Thoughts ever entered into his Head: He saw *Jones* in a bad Light, and he imagined *Allworthy* saw him in the same, but that he was resolved, from Pride and Stubbornness of Spirit, not to give up the Boy whom he had once cherished; since, by so doing, he must tacitly acknowledge, that his former Opinion of him had been wrong.

Square therefore embraced this Opportunity of injuring *Jones* in the tenderest Part, by giving a very bad Turn to all these beforementioned Occurrences. 'I am sorry, Sir,' said he, 'to own I have been deceived as well as yourself. I could not, I confess, help being pleased with what I ascribed to the Motive of Friendship, though it was carried to an Excess, and all Excess is faulty and vicious; but in this I made Allowance for Youth. Little did I suspect that the Sacrifice of Truth, which we both imagined to have been made to Friendship, was, in reality, a Prostitution of it to a depraved and debauched Appetite. You now plainly see whence all the seeming Generosity of this young Man to the Family of the Game-keeper proceeded. He supported the Father, in order to corrupt the Daughter, and preserved the Family from starving, to bring one of them to Shame and Ruin. This is Friendship! this is Generosity! As Sir *Richard Steele*[2] says, "Gluttons, who give high Prices for Delicacies, are very worthy to be called generous." In short, I am resolved, from this Instance, never to give Way to the Weakness of human Nature more, nor to think any thing Virtue which doth not exactly quadrate with the unerring Rule of Right.'

The Goodness of *Allworthy* had prevented those Considerations from occurring to himself; yet were they too plausible to be absolutely and hastily rejected, when laid before his Eyes by another. Indeed what *Square* had said sunk very deeply into his Mind, and the Uneasiness which it there created, was very visible to the other; though the good Man would not acknowledge this, but made a very slight Answer, and forcibly drove off the Discourse to some other Subject. It was well, perhaps, for poor *Tom*, that no such Suggestions had been made before he was pardoned; for they certainly stamped in the Mind of *Allworthy* the first bad Impression concerning *Jones*.

Chapter XII.

Containing much clearer Matters, but which flowed from the same Fountain with those in the preceding Chapter.

The Reader will be pleased, I believe, to return with me to *Sophia*. She passed the Night, after we saw her last, in no very agreeable Manner. Sleep befriended her but little, and Dreams less. In the Morning, when Mrs. *Honour* her Maid attended her, at the usual Hour, she was found already up and drest.

Persons who live two or three Miles Distance in the Country are considered as next Door Neighbours, and Transactions at the one House fly with incredible Celerity to the other. Mrs. *Honour*, therefore, had heard the whole Story of *Molly*'s Shame; which she, being of a very communicative Temper, had no sooner entered the Apartment of her Mistress, than she began to relate in the following Manner:

'La Ma'am, what doth your La'ship think? the Girl that your

2. *The Conscious Lovers* (1722) V.iii "Bounty! When Gluttons give high Prices for Delicates, they are prodigious bountiful."

La'ship saw at Church on *Sunday*, whom you thought so handsome; though you would not have thought her so handsome neither, if you had seen her nearer; but to be sure she hath been carried before the Justice for being big with Child. She seemed to me to look like a confident Slut; and to be sure she hath laid the Child to young Mr. *Jones*. And all the Parish says Mr. *Allworthy* is so angry with young Mr. *Jones*, that he won't see him. To be sure, one can't help pitying the poor young Man, and yet he doth not deserve much Pity neither, for demeaning himself with such Kind of Trumpery. Yet he is so pretty a Gentleman, I should be sorry to have him turned out of Doors. I dares to swear the Wench was as willing as he; for she was always a forward Kind of Body. And when Wenches are so coming, young Men are not so much to be blamed neither; for to be sure they do no more than what is natural. Indeed it is beneath them to meddle with such dirty Draggle-tails; and whatever happens to them, it is good enough for them. And yet to be sure the vile Baggages are most in Fault. I wishes, with all my Heart, they were well to be whipped at the Cart's Tail; for it is Pity they should be the Ruin of a pretty young Gentleman; and no body can deny but that Mr. *Jones* is one of the most handsomest young Men that ever——

She was running on thus, when *Sophia*, with a more peevish Voice than she had ever spoken to her in before, cried, 'Prithee why do'st thou trouble me with all this Stuff? What Concern have I in what Mr. *Jones* doth? I suppose you are all alike. And you seem to me to be angry it was not your own Case.'

'I, Ma'am!' answered Mrs. *Honour*, 'I am sorry your Ladyship should have such an Opinion of me. I am sure no-body can say any such thing of me. All the young Fellows in the World may go to the *Divil*, for me. Because I said he was a handsome Man! Every body says it as well as I—To be sure, I never thought as it was any Harm to say a young Man was handsome; but to be sure I shall never think him so any more now; for handsome is that handsome does. A Beggar Wench!——

'Stop thy Torrent of Impertinence,' cries *Sophia*, 'and see whether my Father wants me at Breakfast.'

Mrs. *Honour* then flung out of the Room muttering much to her-self——of which—'Marry come up, I assure you,' was all that could be plainly distinguished.

Whether Mrs. *Honour* really deserved that Suspicion, of which her Mistress gave her a Hint, is a Matter which we cannot indulge our Reader's Curiosity by resolving. We will however make him Amends, in disclosing what passed in the Mind of *Sophia*.

The Reader will be pleased to recollect, that a secret Affection for Mr. *Jones* had insensibly stolen into the Bosom of this young

Lady. That it had there grown to a pretty great Height before she herself had discovered it. When she first began to perceive its Symptoms, the Sensations were so sweet and pleasing, that she had not Resolution sufficient to check or repel them; and thus she went on cherishing a Passion of which she never once considered the Consequences.

This Incident relating to *Molly* first opened her Eyes. She now first perceived the Weakness of which she had been guilty; and though it caused the utmost Perturbation in her Mind, yet it had the Effect of other nauseous Physic, and for the Time expelled her Distemper. Its Operation indeed was most wonderfully quick; and in the short Interval, while her Maid was absent, so entirely removed all Symptoms, that when Mrs. *Honour* returned with a Summons from her Father, she was become perfectly easy, and had brought herself to a thorough Indifference for Mr. *Jones*.

The Diseases of the Mind do in almost every Particular imitate those of the Body. For which Reason, we hope, That learned Faculty, for whom we have so profound a Respect, will pardon us the violent Hands we have been necessitated to lay on several Words and Phrases, which of Right belong to them, and without which our Descriptions must have been often unintelligible.

Now there is no one Circumstance in which the Distempers of the Mind bear a more exact Analogy to those which are called Bodily, than that Aptness which both have to a Relapse. This is plain, in the violent Diseases of Ambition and Avarice. I have known Ambition, when cured at Court by frequent Disappointments, (which are the only Physic for it,) to break out again in a Contest for Foreman of the Grand Jury at an Assizes; and have heard of a Man who had so far conquered Avarice, as to give away many a Sixpence, that comforted himself, at last, on his Death-bed, by making a crafty and advantageous Bargain concerning his ensuing Funeral, with an Undertaker who had married his only Child.

In the Affair of Love, which out of strict Conformity with the Stoic Philosophy, we shall here treat as a Disease, this Proneness to relapse is no less conspicuous. Thus it happened to poor *Sophia*; upon whom, the very next Time she saw young *Jones*, all the former Symptoms returned, and from that Time cold and hot Fits alternately seized her Heart.

The Situation of this young Lady was now very different from what it had ever been before. That Passion, which had formerly been so exquisitely delicious, became now a Scorpion in her Bosom. She resisted it therefore with her utmost Force, and summoned every Argument her Reason (which was surprisingly strong for her Age) could suggest, to subdue and expel it. In this she so far succeeded, that she began to hope from Time and Absence a perfect Cure. She resolved therefore to avoid *Tom Jones* as much as possible; for which Purpose she began to conceive a Design of visiting her Aunt, to which she made no Doubt of obtaining her Father's Consent.

But Fortune, who had other Designs in her Head, put an immediate Stop to any such Proceedings, by introducing an Accident, which will be related in the next Chapter.

Chapter XIII.

A dreadful Accident which befel Sophia. *The gallant Behaviour of* Jones, *and the more dreadful Consequence of that Behaviour to the young Lady; with a short Digression in Favour of the Female Sex.*

Mr. *Western* grew every Day fonder and fonder of *Sophia,* insomuch that his beloved Dogs themselves almost gave Place to her in his Affections; but as he could not prevail on himself to abandon these, he contrived very cunningly to enjoy their Company, together with that of his Daughter, by insisting on her riding a hunting with him.

Sophia, to whom her Father's Word was a Law, readily complied with his Desires, though she had not the least Delight in a Sport, which was of too rough and masculine a Nature to suit with her Disposition. She had, however, another Motive, beside her Obedience, to accompany the old Gentleman in the Chace; for by her Presence she hoped in some Measure to restrain his Impetuosity, and to prevent him from so frequently exposing his Neck to the utmost Hazard.

The strongest Objection was that which would have formerly been an Inducement to her, namely, the frequent meeting with young *Jones,* whom she had determined to avoid; but as the End of the hunting Season now approached, she hoped, by a short Absence with her Aunt, to reason herself entirely out of her unfortunate Passion; and had not any Doubt of being able to meet him in the Field the subsequent Season without the least Danger.

On the second Day of her Hunting, as she was returning from the Chace, and was arrived within a little Distance from Mr. *Western*'s House, her Horse, whose mettlesome Spirit required a better Rider, fell suddenly to prancing and capering, in such a Manner, that she was in the most imminent Peril of falling. *Tom Jones,* who was at a little Distance behind, saw this, and immediately galloped up to her Assistance. As soon as he came up, he leapt from his own Horse, and caught hold of her's by the Bridle. The unruly Beast presently reared himself an End[1] on his hind Legs, and threw his lovely Burthen from his Back, and *Jones* caught her in his Arms.

She was so affected with the Fright, that she was not immediately able to satisfy *Jones,* who was very sollicitous to know whether

---

1. Idiomatic for "on end." See p. 708.

she had received any Hurt. She soon after, however, recovered her Spirits, assured him she was safe, and thanked him for the Care he had taken of her. *Jones* answered, 'If I have preserved you, Madam, I am sufficiently repaid; for I promise you, I would have secured you from the least Harm, at the Expence of a much greater Misfortune to myself, than I have suffered on this Occasion.'

'What Misfortune,' replied *Sophia,* eagerly, 'I hope you have come to no Mischief?'

'Be not concerned, Madam,' answered *Jones,* 'Heaven be praised, you have escaped so well, considering the Danger you was in. If I have broke my Arm, I consider it as a Trifle, in Comparison of what I feared upon your Account.'

Sophia then screamed out, 'Broke your Arm! Heaven forbid.'

'I am afraid I have, Madam,' says *Jones,* 'but I beg you will suffer me first to take Care of you. I have a Right-hand yet at your Service, to help you into the next Field, whence we have but a very little Walk to your Father's House.'

Sophia seeing his Left Arm dangling by his Side, while he was using the other to lead her, no longer doubted of the Truth. She now grew much paler than her Fears for herself had made her before. All her Limbs were seized with a Trembling, insomuch that *Jones* could scarce support her; and as her Thoughts were in no less Agitation, she could not refrain from giving *Jones* a Look so full of Tenderness, that it almost argued a stronger Sensation in her Mind, than even Gratitude and Pity united can raise in the gentlest female Bosom, without the Assistance of a third more powerful Passion.

Mr. *Western,* who was advanced at some Distance when this Accident happened, was now returned, as were the rest of the Horse-men. *Sophia* immediately acquainted them with what had befallen *Jones,* and begged them to take Care of him. Upon which, *Western,* who had been much alarmed by meeting his Daughter's Horse without its Rider, and was now overjoyed to find her unhurt, cried out, 'I am glad it is no worse, if *Tom* hath broken his Arm, we will get a Joiner to mend un again.'

The Squire alighted from his Horse, and proceeded to his House on foot, with his Daughter and *Jones.* An impartial Spectator, who had met them on the Way, would, on viewing their several Countenances, have concluded *Sophia* alone to have been the Object of Compassion: For as to *Jones,* he exulted in having probably saved the Life of the young Lady, at the Price only of a broken Bone; and Mr. *Western,* though he was not unconcerned at the Accident which had befallen *Jones,* was, however, delighted in a much higher Degree with the fortunate Escape of his Daughter.

The Generosity of *Sophia*'s Temper construed this Behaviour of *Jones* into great Bravery; and it made a deep Impression on her Heart: For certain it is, that there is no one Quality which so gener-

ally recommends Men to Women as this; proceeding, if we
the common Opinion, from that natural Timidity of the Sex;
is, says Mr. *Osborne*,[1] so great, that a Woman is the most cow,
of all the Creatures God ever made.' A Sentiment more remarkₑ
for its Bluntness than for its Truth. *Aristotle*, in his Politics, do
them, I believe, more Justice, when he says, 'The Modesty and Foₑ
titude of Men differ from those Virtues in Women; for the Fortitude which becomes a Woman, would be Cowardice in a Man; and
the Modesty which becomes a Man, would be Pertness in a
Woman.' Nor is there, perhaps, more of Truth in the Opinion of
those who derive the Partiality which Women are inclined to shew
to the Brave, from this Excess of their Fear. Mr. *Bayle*[2] (I think, in
his article of *Helen*) imputes this, and with greater Probability, to
their violent Love of Glory; for the Truth of which, we have the
Authority of him, who, of all others, saw farthest into human
Nature; and who introduces the Heroine of his Odyssey, the great
Pattern of matrimonial Love and Constancy, assigning the Glory of
her Husband as the only Source of her Affection towards him.[3]

However this be, certain it is that the Accident operated very
strongly on *Sophia*; and, indeed, after much Enquiry into the
Matter, I am inclined to believe, that at this very Time, the charm-
ing *Sophia* made no less Impression on the Heart of *Jones*; to say
Truth, he had for some Time become sensible of the irresistible
Power of her Charms.

Chapter XIV.

*The Arrival of a Surgeon. His Operations, and a long Dialogue
between* Sophia *and her Maid.*

When they arrived in Mr. *Western*'s Hall, *Sophia*, who had totter'd along with much Difficulty, sunk down in a Chair; but by the
Assistance of Hartshorn and Water, she was prevented from fainting

1. Francis Osborne, *Advice to a Son, or, Direction for Your Better Conduct* (1656) II.22. Fielding overstates Osborne's "*It remaining equally rare,* to find a *starched and Complemental Man* wise, *as a woman* Valiant." Aristotle's *Politica* I.13: "... the courage and justice of a man and a woman, are not, as Socrates maintained, the same; the courage of a man is shown in commanding, of a woman in obeying" (Jowett trans.; quoted in Bryant, p. 150).
2. Pierre Bayle, *Dictionaire Historique et Critique* (1695–97, 1702), translated in numerous editions as *Historical and Critical Dictionary*, beginning 1702. A pioneering and popular encyclopedia of biography, religion, and legend. Fielding recalls the article on Henry IV, not on Helen.

3. The *English* Reader will not find this in the Poem: For the Sentiment is entirely left out in the Translation [*Fielding's note*]. *Odyssey* I.343–44: Penelope has asked a minstrel not to sing of Troy and her lost husband Odysseus, since those songs always "waste her heart in her breast," as she longs for "such a head, always remembering the man whose glory [fame] is spread through Hellas and the midst of Argos." She does not say that she loves him *because* of his glory, nor does Pope's translation (to which Fielding surely alludes) omit the idea: "[a man] / To sorrow sacred, and secure to fame: / My bleeding bosom sickens to the sound, / And ev'ry piercing note inflicts a wound" (I.437–40).

ell recovered her Spirits, when the Surgeon,

es, appeared. Mr. *Western*, who imputed

ghter to her Fall, advised her to be pres-

revention. In this Opinion he was sec-

who gave so many Reasons for bleeding, and

ses where Persons had miscarried for want of it,

became very importunate, and indeed insisted

that his Daughter should be blooded.

soon yielded to the Commands of her Father, though

ely contrary to her own Inclinations: For she suspected, I

believe, less Danger from the Fright, than either the Squire or the

Surgeon. She then stretched out her beautiful Arm, and the Opera-

tor began to prepare for his Work.

While the Servants were busied in providing Materials; the Surgeon, who imputed the Backwardness which had appeared in *Sophia* to her Fears, began to comfort her with Assurances that there was not the least Danger; for no Accident, he said, could ever happen in Bleeding, but from the monstrous Ignorance of Pretenders to Surgery, which he pretty plainly insinuated was not at present to be apprehended. *Sophia* declared she was not under the least Apprehension; adding, if you open an Artery, I promise you I'll forgive you; 'Will you,' cries *Western*, 'D—n me, if I will; if he does thee the least Mischief, d—n me, if I don't ha' the Heart's Blood o'un out.' The Surgeon assented to bleed her upon these Conditions, and then proceeded to his Operation, which he performed with as much Dexterity as he had promised; and with as much Quickness: For he took but little Blood from her, saying, it was much safer to bleed again and again, than to take away too much at once.

Sophia, when her Arm was bound up, retired: For she was not willing (nor was it, perhaps, strictly decent) to be present at the Operation on *Jones*. Indeed one Objection which she had to Bleeding, (tho' she did not make it) was the Delay which it would occasion to setting the broken Bone. For *Western*, when *Sophia* was concerned, had no Consideration, but for her; and as for *Jones* himself, he 'sat like Patience on a Monument smiling at Grief.'[1] To say the Truth, when he saw the Blood springing from the lovely Arm of *Sophia*, he scarce thought of what had happened to himself.

The Surgeon now ordered his Patient to be stript to his Shirt, and then entirely baring the Arm, he began to stretch and examine it, in such a Manner, that the Tortures he put him to, caused *Jones* to make several wry Faces, which the Surgeon observing, greatly wondered at, crying, 'What is the Matter, Sir? I am sure it is

1. Shakespeare, *Twelfth Night* II.iv.117–18.

impossible I should hurt you.' And then holding forth the
Arm, he began a long and very learned Lecture of Anaton
which simple and double Fractures were most accurately consid\
and the several Ways in which *Jones* might have broken his A
were discussed, with proper Annotations, shewing how many \
these would have been better, and how many worse than the present Case.

Having at length finish'd his laboured Harangue, with which the
Audience, tho' it had greatly raised their Attention and Admiration,
were not much edified, as they really understood not a single Syllable of all he had said, he proceeded to Business, which he was more
expeditious in finishing, then he had been in beginning.

Jones was then ordered into a Bed, which Mr. *Western* compelled him to accept at his own House, and Sentence of Water-
Gruel was passed upon him.

Among the good Company which had attended in the Hall
during the Bone-setting, Mrs. *Honour* was one; who being summoned to her Mistress as soon as it was over, and asked by her how
the young Gentleman did, presently launched into extravagant
Praises on the *Magnimity*, as she called it, of his Behaviour, which,
she said, 'was so charming in so pretty a Creature.' She then burst
forth into much warmer Encomiums on the Beauty of his Person;
enumerating many Particulars, and ending with the Whiteness of
his Skin.

This Discourse had an Effect on *Sophia*'s Countenance, which
would not perhaps have escaped the Observance of the sagacious
Waiting-woman, had she once looked her Mistress in the Face, all
the Time she was speaking; but as a Looking-glass, which was most
commodiously placed opposite to her, gave her an Opportunity of
surveying those Features, in which, of all others, she took most
Delight; so she had not once removed her Eyes from that amiable
Object during her whole Speech.

Mrs. *Honour* was so intirely wrapped up in the Subject on which
she exercised her Tongue, and the Object before her Eyes, that she
gave her Mistress Time to conquer her Confusion; which having
done, she smiled on her Maid, and told her, 'She was certainly in
Love with this young Fellow.' 'I in Love, Madam!' answers she,
'upon my Word, Ma'am, I assure you, Ma'am, upon my Soul, Ma'am
I am not.' 'Why if you was,' cries her Mistress, 'I see no Reason that
you should be ashamed of it; for he is certainly a pretty Fellow'—
'Yes, Ma'am,' answered the other, 'That he is, the most handsomest
Man I ever saw in my Life. Yes, to be sure, that he is, and, as your
Ladyship says, I don't know why I should be ashamed of loving him,
though he is my Betters. To be sure gentle Folks are but Flesh and
Blood no more than us Servants. Besides, as for Mr. *Jones*, thof

...made a Gentleman of him, he was not so
...For thof I am a poor Body, I am an honest
...her and Mother were married, which is
...an say, as high as they hold their Heads.
...re you, my dirty Cousin! thof his Skin be so
...e, it is the most whitest that ever was seen, I am
...ell as he, and nobody can say that I am base born,
...her was a Clergyman,[2] and would have been very angry,
...e, to have thought any of his Family should have taken up
...*Molly Seagrim*'s dirty Leavings.'

Perhaps *Sophia* might have suffered her Maid to run on in this
Manner, from wanting sufficient Spirits to stop her Tongue, which
the Reader may probably conjecture was no very easy Task: For, certainly there were some Passages in her Speech, which were far from
being agreeable to the Lady. However, she now checked the Torrent, as there seemed no End of its Flowing. 'I wonder,' says she, 'at
your Assurance in daring to talk thus of one of my Father's Friends.
As to the Wench, I order you never to mention her Name to me.
And, with Regard to the young Gentleman's Birth, those who can
say nothing more to his Disadvantage, may as well be silent on that
Head, as I desire you will be for the future.'

'I am sorry, I have offended your Ladyship,' answered Mrs.
Honour, 'I am sure I hate *Molly Seagrim* as much as your Ladyship
can, and as for abusing Squire *Jones*, I can call all the Servants in
the House to witness, that whenever any Talk hath been about Bastards, I have always taken his Part: For which of you,' says I to
the Footmen, 'would not be a Bastard, if he could, to be made a
Gentleman of? and,' says I, 'I am sure he is a very fine Gentleman;
and he hath one of the whitest Hands in the World: For to be sure
so he hath; and,' says I, 'one of the sweetest temperedest, best
naturedest Men in the World he is,' and says I, 'all the Servants and
Neighbours all round the Country loves him. And, to be sure, I
could tell your Ladyship something, but that I am afraid it would
offend you.'—'What could you tell me, *Honour*?' says *Sophia*. 'Nay,
Ma'am, to be sure he meant nothing by it, therefore I would not
have your Ladyship be offended.'—'Prithee tell me,' says *Sophia*,—'I
will know it this Instant.' 'Why, Ma'am,' answered Mrs. *Honour*,
'he came into the Room, one Day last Week when I was at Work,
and there lay your Ladyship's Muff on a Chair, and to be sure he
put his Hands into it, that very Muff your Ladyship gave me but
yesterday; 'La,' says I, 'Mr. *Jones*, you will stretch my Lady's Muff
and spoil it; but he still kept his Hands in it, and then he kissed it

2. This is the second Person of low Condition whom we have recorded in this
History, to have sprung from the Clergy.
It is to be hoped such Instances will, in
future Ages, when some Provision is
made for the Families of the inferior
Clergy, appear stranger than they can be
thought at present [*Fielding's note*].

—to be sure, I hardly ever saw such a Kiss in my Life as he
—'I suppose he did not know it was mine,' replied *Sophia*.
Ladyship shall hear, Ma'am. He kissed it again and again, and
it was the prettiest Muff in the World. 'La! Sir,' says I, 'you
seen it a hundred Times.'—'Yes, Mrs. *Honour*,' cry'd he; 'but w
can see any thing beautiful in the Presence of your Lady but he
self:' Nay, that's not all neither, but I hope your Ladyship won't be
offended, for to be sure he meant nothing: One Day as your Ladyship was playing on the Harpsichord to my Master, Mr. *Jones* was
sitting in the next Room, and methought he looked melancholy.
'La!' says I, 'Mr. *Jones*, what's the Matter! A Penny for your
Thoughts,' says I; 'Why, Hussy,' says he, starting up from a Dream,
'what can I be thinking of, when that Angel your Mistress is
playing?' And then squeezing me by the Hand—'Oh! Mrs. *Honour*,'
says he, 'how happy will that Man be!'—and then he sighed; upon
my Troth, his Breath is as sweet as a Nosegay—but to be sure he
meant no Harm by it. So I hope your Ladyship will not mention a
Word: For he gave me a Crown never to mention it, and made me
swear upon a Book, but I believe, indeed, it was not the Bible.'

Till something of a more beautiful Red than Vermilion be found
out, I shall say nothing of *Sophia*'s Colour on this Occasion. '*Ho*—
nour,' says she, 'I—if you will not mention this any more to me,—
nor to any Body else, I will not betray you—I mean I will not be
angry; but I am afraid of your Tongue. Why, my Girl, will you give
it such Liberties?' 'Nay, Ma'am,' answered she, 'to be sure, I would
sooner cut out my Tongue than offend your Ladyship—to be sure, I
shall never mention a Word that your Ladyship would not have me.'
'—Why I would not have you mention this any more,' said *Sophia*,
'for it may come to my Father's Ears, and he would be angry with
Mr. *Jones*, tho' I really believe, as you say, he meant nothing. I
should be very angry myself if I imagined'—'Nay, Ma'am,' says
Honour, 'I protest I believe he meant nothing. I thought he talked
as if he was out of his Senses; nay, he said he believed he was beside
himself when he had spoken the Words. 'Ay, Sir,' says I, 'I believe
so too.' 'Yes,' says he, '*Honour*,—but I ask your Ladyship's Pardon;
I could tear my Tongue out for offending you.' 'Go on,' says
Sophia, 'you may mention any thing you have not told me before.'
'Yes, *Honour*,' says he, (this was some time afterwards when he gave
me the Crown) 'I am neither such a Coxcomb, or such a Villain
as to think of her, in any other *Delight*, but as my Goddess; as such
I will always worship and adore her while I have Breath. This was
all, Ma'am, I will be sworn, to the best of my Remembrance; I was
in a Passion with him myself, till I found he meant no Harm.'
'Indeed, *Honour*,' says *Sophia*, 'I believe you have a real Affection
for me; I was provoked the other Day when I gave you Warning;

157

to stay with me, you shall.' 'To be sure,
nour, 'I shall never desire to part with
almost cried my Eyes out when you
be very ungrateful in me, to desire to
ause as why, I should never get so good a
re I would live and die with your Ladyship—
ones said, happy is the Man——

Dinner-bell interrupted a Conversation which had
such an Effect on *Sophia*, that she was, perhaps, more
d to her bleeding in the Morning, than she, at the time, had
pprehended she should be. As to the present Situation of her
Mind, I shall adhere to a Rule of *Horace*,[3] by not attempting to
describe it, from Despair of Success. Most of my Readers will suggest it easily to themselves; and the few who cannot, would not
understand the Picture, or at least would deny it to be natural, if
ever so well drawn.

BOOK V⚹

*Containing a Portion of Time, somewhat longer than
Half a Year.*

Chapter I.⚹ *critique of critics*

Of THE SERIOUS *in Writing, and for what Purpose it is intro-
duced.*

*defending New Lit.
Form?*

Peradventure there may be no Parts in this prodigious Work
which will give the Reader less Pleasure in the perusing, than those
which have given the Author the greatest Pains in composing.
Among these, probably, may be reckoned those initial Essays which
we have prefixed to the historical Matter contained in every Book;
and which we have determined to be essentially necessary to this
Kind of Writing, of which we have set ourselves at the Head.

For this our Determination we do not hold ourselves strictly
bound to assign any Reason; it being abundantly sufficient that we
have laid it down as a Rule necessary to be observed in all prosai-
comi-epic Writing. Who ever demanded the Reasons of that nice
Unity of Time or Place which is now established to be so essential
to dramatic Poetry? What Critic hath been ever asked, Why a Play
may not contain two Days as well as one? Or why the Audience
(provided they travel, like Electors, without any Expence) may not
be wafted Fifty Miles as well as Five? Hath any Commentator well

3. *Ars Poetica* 149–50.

frustration with limitations on form

accounted for the Limitation which an antient Critic[1] hath set to the Drama, which he will have contain neither more nor less than five acts? Or hath any one living attempted to explain, what the modern Judges of our Theatres mean by that Word *low*; by which they have happily succeeded in banishing all Humour from the Stage, and have made the Theatre as dull as a Drawing-room? Upon all these Occasions, the World seems to have embraced a Maxim of our Law, *viz. Cuicunque in Arte sua perito credendum est:*[2] For it seems, perhaps, difficult to conceive that any one should have had enough of Impudence, to lay down dogmatical Rules in any Art or Science without the least Foundation. In such Cases, therefore, we are apt to conclude, there are sound and good Reasons at the Bottom, though we are unfortunately not able to see so far.

Now, in reality, the World have paid too great a Compliment to Critics, and have imagined them Men of much greater Profundity than they really are. From this Complaisance, the Critics have been emboldened to assume a Dictatorial Power, and have so far succeeded, that they are now become the Masters, and have the Assurance to give Laws to those Authors, from whose Predecessors they originally received them.

The Critic, rightly considered, is no more than the Clerk, whose Office it is to transcribe the Rules and Laws laid down by those great Judges, whose vast Strength of Genius hath placed them in the Light of Legislators, in the several Sciences over which they presided. This Office was all which the Critics of old aspired to, nor did they ever dare to advance a Sentence, without supporting it by the Authority of the Judge from whence it was borrowed.

But in Process of Time, and in Ages of Ignorance, the Clerk began to invade the Power, and assume the Dignity of his Master. The Laws of Writing were no longer founded on the Practice of the Author, but on the Dictates of the Critic. The Clerk became the Legislator, and those very peremptorily gave Laws, whose Business it was, at first, only to transcribe them.

Hence arose an obvious, and, perhaps, an unavoidable Error: For these Critics being Men of shallow Capacities, very easily mistook mere Form for Substance. They acted as a Judge would, who should adhere to the lifeless Letter of Law, and reject the Spirit. Little Circumstances which were, perhaps, accidental in a great Author, were, by these Critics, considered to constitute his chief Merit, and transmitted as Essentials to be observed by all his Successors. To these Encroachments, Time and Ignorance, the two great Supporters of Imposture, gave Authority; and thus, many Rules for good Writing have been established, which have not the least Foundation in Truth or Nature; and which commonly serve for no other Purpose

1. Horace, *Ars Poetica* 189.
2. "Anyone expert in his profession must be believed."

than to curb and restrain Genius, in the same Manner as it would have restrained the Dancing-master, had the many excellent Treatises on that Art laid it down as an essential Rule, that every Man must dance in Chains.

To avoid, therefore, all Imputation of laying down a Rule for Posterity, founded only on the Authority of *ipse dixit*; for which, to say the Truth, we have not the profoundest Veneration, we shall here waive the Privilege above contended for, and proceed to lay before the Reader the Reasons which have induced us to intersperse these several digressive Essays, in the Course of this Work.

And here we shall of Necessity be led to open a new Vein of Knowledge, which, if it hath been discovered, hath not, to our Remembrance, been wrought on by any antient or modern Writer. This Vein is no other than that of Contrast, which runs through all the Works of the Creation, and may, probably, have a large Share in constituting in us the Idea of all Beauty, as well natural as artificial: For what demonstrates the Beauty and Excellence of any Thing, but its Reverse? Thus the Beauty of Day, and that of Summer, is set off by the Horrors of Night and Winter. And, I believe, if it was possible for a Man to have seen only the two former, he would have a very imperfect Idea of their Beauty.

But to avoid too serious an Air: Can it be doubted, but that the finest Woman in the World would lose all Benefit of her Charms, in the Eye of a Man who had never seen one of another Cast? The Ladies themselves seem so sensible of this, that they are all industrious to procure Foils; nay, they will become Foils to themselves: For I have observed (at *Bath* particularly) that they endeavour to appear as ugly as possible in the Morning, in order to set off that Beauty which they intend to shew you in the Evening.

Most Artists have this Secret in Practice, tho' some, perhaps, have not much studied the Theory. The Jeweller knows that the finest Brilliant requires a Foil; and the Painter, by the Contrast of his Figures, often acquires great Applause.

A great Genius among us will illustrate this Matter fully. I cannot, indeed, range him under any general Head of common Artists, as he hath a Title to be placed among those

> *Inventas qui vitam excoluere per Artes.*[3]
>
> Who by invented Arts have Life improv'd.

I mean here the Inventor of that most exquisite Entertainment, called the *English* Pantomime.[4]

---

3. *Aeneid* VI.663. Fielding omits an *aut* ("or") after *Inventas*, to suit his context.
4. John Rich, who opened a new theater in Lincoln's Inn Fields in 1716 and, acting under the name of John Lun, introduced pantomime to compete successfully with the established Theater Royal in Drury Lane. He opened Covent Garden Theater in 1733. See also below, p. 751.

This Entertainment consisted of two Parts, which the Inventor distinguished by the Names of *the Serious* and *the Comic*. The Serious exhibited a certain Number of Heathen Gods and Heroes, who were certainly the worst and dullest Company into which an Audience was ever introduced; and (which was a Secret known to few) were actually intended so to be, in order to contrast the *Comic* Part of the Entertainment, and to display the Tricks of Harlequin to the better Advantage.

This was, perhaps, no very civil Use of such Personages; but the Contrivance was, nevertheless, ingenious enough, and had its Effect. And this will now plainly appear, if instead of *Serious* and *Comic*, we supply the Words *Duller* and *Dullest*; for the *Comic* was certainly duller than any Thing before shewn on the Stage, and could be set off only by that superlative Degree of Dulness, whch composed the Serious. So intolerably serious, indeed, were these Gods and Heroes, that Harlequin (though the *English* Gentleman of that Name is not at all related to the *French* Family, for he is of a much more serious Disposition) was always welcome on the Stage, as he relieved the Audience from worse Company.

Judicious Writers have always practised this Art of Contrast, with great Success. I have been surprized that *Horace* should cavil at this Art in *Homer*; but indeed he contradicts himself in the very next Line.

> *Indignor quandoque bonus dormitat* Homerus,
> *Verùm Opere in longo fas et obrepere Somnum.*[5]

I grieve if e'er great *Homer* chance to sleep,
Yet Slumbers on long Works have right to creep.

For we are not here to understand, as, perhaps, some have, that an Author actually falls asleep while he is writing. It is true that Readers are too apt to be so overtaken; but if the Work was as long as any of *Oldmixon*,[6] the Author himself is too well entertained to be subject to the least Drowsiness. He is, as Mr *Pope* observes,

> *Sleepless himself, to give his Readers Sleep.*[7]

To say the Truth, these soporific Parts are so many Scenes of *Serious* artfully interwoven, in order to contrast and set off the rest; and this is the true Meaning of a late facetious Writer,[8] who told the Public, that whenever he was dull, they might be assured there was a Design in it.

5. *Ars Poetica* 359–60. The translation may be Fielding's own—at least it is not Creech's nor Francis's, the most admired of the period, whom Fielding quotes elsewhere.
6. See above, p. 29.
7. *Dunciad* I.93–94—"While pensive

Poets painful vigils keep, / Sleepless themselves to give their readers sleep."
8. Sir Richard Steele, *The Tatler*, no. 38 (Shakespeare Head ed.). Fielding again refers to this in *The Covent-Garden Journal*, no. 1 (Jensen ed., I.135).

In this Light then, or rather in this Darkness, I would have the Reader to consider these initial Essays. And after this Warning, if he shall be of Opinion, that he can find enough of Serious in other Parts of this History, he may pass over these, in which we profess to be laboriously dull, and begin the following Books, at the second Chapter.

Chapter II.

In which Mr. Jones *receives many friendly Visits during his Confinement; with some fine Touches of the Passion of Love, scarce visible to the naked Eye.*

Tom Jones had many Visitors during his Confinement, though some, perhaps, were not very agreeable to him. Mr. *Allworthy* saw him almost every Day; but though he pitied *Tom*'s Sufferings, and greatly approved the gallant Behaviour which had occasioned them; yet he thought this was a favourable Opportunity to bring him to a sober Sense of his indiscreet Conduct; and that wholesome Advice for that Purpose could never be applied at a more proper Season than at the present; when the Mind was softened by Pain and Sickness, and alarmed by Danger; and when its Attention was unembaɪ assed with those turbulent Passions, which engage us in the Pursuit of Pleasure.

At all Seasons, therefore, when the good Man was alone with the Youth, especially when the latter was totally at Ease, he took Occasion to remind him of his former Miscarriages, but in the mildest and tenderest Manner, and only in order to introduce the Caution, which he prescribed for his future Behaviour; 'on which alone,' he assured him, 'would depend his own Felicity, and the Kindness which he might yet promise himself to receive at the Hands of his Father by Adoption, unless he should hereafter forfeit his good Opinion: For as to what had past,' he said, 'it should be all forgiven and forgotten. He, therefore, advised him to make a good Use of this Accident, that so in the End it might prove a Visitation for his own Good.'

Thwackum was likewise pretty assiduous in his Visits; and he too considered a Sick-bed to be a convenient Scene for Lectures. His Stile, however, was more severe than Mr. *Allworthy*'s: He told his Pupil, 'that he ought to look on his broken Limb as a Judgment from Heaven on his Sins. That it would become him to be daily on his Knees, pouring forth Thanksgivings that he had broken his Arm only, and not his Neck; which latter,' he said, 'was very probably reserved for some future Occasion, and that, perhaps, not very remote. For his Part,' he said, 'he had often wondered some Judgment had not overtaken him before; but it might be perceived by this, that Divine Punishments, though slow, are always sure.' Hence likewise he advised him, 'to foresee, with equal Certainty, the greater Evils which were yet behind, and which were as sure as this, of overtaking him in his State of Reprobacy. These are,' said he, 'to be averted only by such a thorough and sincere Repentance, as is not to be expected or hoped for, from one so abandoned in his Youth, and whose Mind, I am afraid, is totally corrupted. It is my Duty, however, to exhort you to this Repentance, though I too well know all Exhortations will be vain and fruitless. But *liberavi Animam meam*.[1] I can accuse my own Conscience of no Neglect; tho' it is at the same Time, with the utmost Concern, I see you travelling on to certain Misery in this World, and to as certain Damnation in the next.'

Square talked in a very different Strain; he said, 'Such Accidents as a broken Bone were below the Consideration of a wise Man. That it was abundantly sufficient to reconcile the Mind to any of these mischances, to reflect that they are liable to befal the wisest of Mankind, and are undoubtedly for the Good of the Whole.' He said, 'it was a mere Abuse of Words, to call those Things Evils, in which there was no moral Unfitness: That Pain, which was the worst Consequence of such Accidents, was the most contemptible Thing in the World;' with more of the like Sentences, extracted out of the Second Book of *Tully's* Tusculan *Questions*, and from the great Lord *Shaftesbury*.[2] In pronouncing these he was one Day so eager, that he unfortunately bit his Tongue; and in such a Manner, that it not only put an End to his Discourse, but created much Emotion in him, and caused him to mutter an Oath or two; but what was worst of all, this Accident gave *Thwackum*, who was present, and who held all such Doctrine to be heathenish and atheistical, an Opportunity to clap a Judgment on his Back. Now this was done with so malicious a Sneer, that it totally unhinged (if I may so say) the Temper of the Philosopher, which the Bite of his Tongue had somewhat ruffled; and as he was disabled from venting his Wrath at his Lips, he had possibly found a more violent Method of revenging himself, had not the Surgeon, who was then luckily in the Room, contrary to his own Interest, interposed, and preserved the Peace.

Mr. *Blifil* visited his Friend *Jones* but seldom, and never alone.

1. "I have freed my soul." Bernard of Clairvaux (1091–1153), *Epistle 371* (Mutter).
2. Marcus Tullius ("Tully") Cicero, *Tusculan Disputations*, Stoic in viewpoint. Book II deals with the endurance of pain, arguing that pain is not an evil. Anthony Ashley Cooper, 3rd Earl of Shaftsbury, *Characteristics of Men, Manners, Opinions, and Times*, 3 vols. (1711, rev. 1713). Fielding probably has in mind "An Inquiry Concerning Virtue" (in Vol. II), which develops the proposition that "every thing ... exists ... *for the best*" and that "there is no such thing as real ILL in the Universe" (p. 9).

This worthy young Man, however, professed much Regard for him, and as great Concern at his Misfortune; but cautiously avoided any Intimacy, lest, as he frequently hinted, it might contaminate the Sobriety of his own Character: For which Purpose, he had constantly in his Mouth that Proverb in which *Solomon* speaks against evil Communication.[3] Not that he was so bitter as *Thwackum*; for he always expressed some Hopes of *Tom*'s Reformation; 'which,' he said, 'the unparallelled Goodness shewn by his Uncle on this Occasion, must certainly effect in one not absolutely abandoned:' But concluded, 'if Mr. *Jones* ever offends hereafter, I shall not be able to say a syllable in his Favour.'

As to Squire *Western*, he was seldom out of the Sick-Room; unless when he was engaged either in the Field, or over his Bottle. Nay, he would sometimes retire hither to take his Beer, and it was not without Difficulty, that he was prevented from forcing *Jones* to take his Beer too. For no Quack ever held his Nostrum to be a more general *Panacea*, then he did this; which, he said, had more Virtue in it than was in all the Physic in an Apothecary's Shop. He was, however, by much Entreaty, prevailed on to forbear the Application of this Medicine; but from serenading his Patient every Hunting Morning with the Horn under his Window, it was impossible to withhold him; nor did he ever lay aside that Hallow, with which he entered into all Companies, when he visited *Jones* without any Regard to the sick Person's being at that Time either awake or asleep.

This boisterous Behaviour, as it meant no Harm, so happily it effected none, and was abundantly compensated to *Jones*, as soon as he was able to sit up, by the Company of *Sophia*, whom the Squire then brought to visit him; nor was it, indeed, long before *Jones* was able to attend her to the Harpsichord, where she would kindly condescend, for Hours together, to charm him with the most delicious Music, unless when the Squire thought proper to interrupt her, by insisting on *Old Sir* Simon, or some other of his favourite Pieces.

Notwithstanding the nicest Guard which *Sophia* endeavoured to set on her Behaviour, she could not avoid letting some Appearances now and then slip forth: For Love may again be likened to a Disease in this, that when it is denied a Vent in one Part, it will certainly break out in another. What her Lips therefore concealed, her Eyes, her Blushes, and many little involuntary Actions, betrayed.

One Day when *Sophia* was playing on the Harpsichord, and *Jones* was attending, the Squire came into the Room, crying,

3. Solomon speaks a good deal against bad companions (Proverbs i.10 ff., iv.14–17, v.3 ff., and esp. 20 ff., vii.5 ff.), but Fielding is remembering St. Paul (I Corinthians xv.33): "Be not deceived: evil communications corrupt good manners."

'There, *Tom*, I have had a Battle for thee below Stairs with thick Parson *Thwackum.*—He hath been a telling *Allworthy*, before my Face, that the broken Bone was a Judgment upon thee. D—n it, says I, how can that be? Did not he come by it in Defence of a young Woman? A Judgment indeed! Pox, if he never doth any Thing worse, he will go to Heaven sooner than all the Parsons in the Country. He hath more Reason to glory in it, than to be ashamed of it.' 'Indeed, Sir,' says *Jones*, 'I have no Reason for either; but if it preserved Miss *Western*, I shall always think it the happiest Accident of my Life.'—'And to gu,' said the Squire, 'to zet *Allworthy* against thee vor it.—D—n 'un, if the Parson had unt had his Petticuoats on, I should have lent un o Flick; for I love thee dearly, my Boy, and d—n me if there is any Thing in my Power which I won't do for thee. Sha't take thy choice of all the Horses in my Stable to-morrow Morning, except only the *Chevalier* and Miss *Slouch.*' *Jones* thanked him, but declined accepting the Offer.— 'Nay,' added the Squire, 'shat ha thee the Sorrel mare that *Sophy* rode. She cost me fifty Guineas, and comes six Years old this Grass.' 'If she had cost me a thousand,' cries *Jones* passionately, 'I would have given her to the Dogs.' 'Pooh! pooh!' answered *Western*, 'What because she broke thy Arm. Shouldst forget and forgive. I thought hadst been more a Man than to bear Malice against a dumb Creature.'—Here *Sophia* interposed, and put an End to the Conversation, by desiring her Father's Leave to play to him; a Request which he never refused.

The Countenance of *Sophia* had undergone more than one Change during the foregoing Speeches; and probably she imputed the passionate Resentment, which *Jones* had expressed against the Mare, to a different Motive from that from which her Father had derived it. Her Spirits were at this Time in a visible Flutter; and she played so intolerably ill, that had not *Western* soon fallen asleep, he must have remarked it. *Jones*, however, who was sufficiently awake, and was not without an Ear, any more than without Eyes, made some Observations; which being joined to all which the Reader may remember to have passed formerly, gave him pretty strong Assurances, when he came to reflect on the Whole, that all was not well in the tender Bosom of *Sophia*. An Opinion which many young Gentlemen will, I doubt not, extremely wonder at his not having been well confirmed in long ago. To confess the Truth, he had rather too much Diffidence in himself, and was not forward enough in seeing the Advances of a young Lady; a Misfortune which can be cured only by that early Town Education, which is at present so generally in Fashion.

When these Thoughts had fully taken Possession of *Jones*, they occasioned a Perturbation in his Mind, which, in a Constitution

less pure and firm than his, might have been, at such a Season,
attended with very dangerous Consequences. He was truly sensible
of the great Worth of *Sophia*. He extremely liked her Person, no
less admired her Accomplishments, and tenderly loved her Goodness. In reality, as he had never once entertained any Thought of
possessing her, nor had ever given the least voluntary Indulgence to
his Inclinations, he had a much stronger Passion for her than he
himself was acquainted with. His Heart now brought forth the full
Secret, at the same Time that it assured him the adorable Object
returned his Affection.

Chapter III.

Which all who have no Heart, will think to contain much ado about Nothing.

The Reader will perhaps imagine, the Sensations which now
arose in *Jones* to have been so sweet and delicious, that they would
rather tend to produce a chearful Serenity in the Mind, than any of
those dangerous Effects which we have mentioned; but in Fact,
Sensations of this Kind, however delicious, are, at their first Recognition, of a very tumultuous Nature, and have very little of the
Opiate in them. They were, moreover, in the present Case, embit-
tered with certain Circumstances, which being mixed with sweeter
Ingredients, tended altogether to compose a Draught that might be
termed *Bittersweet*; than which, as nothing can be more disagreeable to the Palate, so nothing, in the metaphorical Sense, can be so
injurious to the Mind.

For first, though he had sufficient Foundation to flatter himself
in what he had observed in *Sophia*, he was not yet free from Doubt
of misconstruing Compassion, or, at best, Esteem, into a warmer
Regard. He was far from a sanguine Assurance that *Sophia* had any
such Affection towards him, as might promise his Inclinations that
Harvest, which, if they were encouraged and nursed, they would
finally grow up to require. Besides, if he could hope to find no Bar
to his Happiness from the Daughter, he thought himself certain of
meeting an effectual Bar in the Father; who, though he was a
Country Squire in his Diversions, was perfectly a Man of the World
in whatever regarded his Fortune; had the most violent Affection
for his only Daughter, and had often signified, in his Cups, the
Pleasure he proposed in seeing her married to one of the richest
Men in the County. *Jones* was not so vain and senseless a Coxcomb
as to expect, from any Regard which *Western* had professed for
him, that he would ever be induced to lay aside these Views of
advancing his Daughter. He well knew, that Fortune is generally

the principal, if not the sole Consideration, which operates on the best of Parents in these Matters: For Friendship makes us warmly espouse the Interest of others; but it is very cold to the Gratification of their Passions. Indeed, to feel the Happiness which may result from this, it is necessary we should possess the Passion ourselves. As he had therefore no Hopes of obtaining her Father's Consent; so he thought to endeavour to succeed without it, and by such Means to frustrate the great Point of Mr. *Western*'s Life, was to make a very ill Use of his Hospitality, and a very ungrateful Return to the many little Favours received (however roughly) at his Hands. If he saw such a Consequence with Horror and Disdain, how much more was he shocked with what regarded Mr. *Allworthy*; to whom, as he had more than filial Obligations, so had he for him more than filial Piety? He knew the Nature of that good Man to be so averse to any Baseness or Treachery, that the least Attempt of such a Kind would make the Sight of the guilty Person for ever odious to his Eyes, and his Name a detestable Sound in his Ears. The Appearance of such unsurmountable Difficulties was sufficient to have inspired him with Despair, however ardent his Wishes had been; but even these were controlled by Compassion for another Woman. The Idea of lovely *Molly* now intruded itself before him. He had sworn eternal Constancy in her Arms, and she had as often vowed never to outlive his deserting her. He now saw her in all the most shocking Postures of Death; nay, he considered all the Miseries of Prostitution to which she would be liable, and of which he would be doubly the Occasion; first by seducing, and then by deserting her; for he well knew the Hatred which all her Neighbours, and even her own Sisters, bore her, and how ready they would all be to tear her to Pieces. Indeed he had exposed her to more Envy than Shame, or rather to the latter by Means of the former: For many Women abused her for being a Whore, while they envied her her Lover and her Finery, and would have been themselves glad to have purchased these at the same Rate. The Ruin, therefore, of the poor Girl must, he foresaw, unavoidably attend his deserting her; and this Thought stung him to the Soul. Poverty and Distress seemed to him to give none a Right of aggravating those Misfortunes. The Meanness of her Condition did not represent her Misery as of little Consequence in his Eyes, nor did it appear to justify, or even to palliate, his Guilt, in bringing that Misery upon her. But why do I mention Justification? His own Heart would not suffer him to destroy a human Creature, who, he thought, loved him, and had to that Love sacrificed her Innocence. His own good Heart pleaded her Cause; not as a cold venal Advocate; but as one interested in the Event, and which must itself deeply share in all the Agonies its Owner brought on another.

When this powerful Advocate had sufficiently raised the Pity of *Jones*, by painting poor *Molly* in all the Circumstances of Wretchedness; it artfully called in the Assistance of another Passion, and represented the Girl in all the amiable Colours of Youth, Health, and Beauty; as one greatly the Object of Desire, and much more so, at least to a good Mind, from being, at the same time, the Object of Compassion.

Amidst these Thoughts, poor *Jones* passed a long sleepless Night, and in the Morning the Result of the whole was to abide by *Molly*, and to think no more of *Sophia*.

In this virtuous Resolution he continued all the next Day till the Evening, cherishing the Idea of *Molly*, and driving *Sophia* from his Thoughts; but in the fatal Evening, a very trifling Accident set all his Passions again on float, and worked so total a Change in his Mind, that we think it decent to communicate it in a fresh Chapter.

Chapter IV.

A little Chapter, in which is contained a little Incident.

Among other Visitants, who paid their Compliments to the young Gentleman in his Confinement, Mrs. *Honour* was one. The Reader, perhaps, when he reflects on some Expressions which have formerly dropt from her, may conceive that she herself had a very particular Affection for Mr. *Jones*; but, in reality, it was no such thing. *Tom* was a handsome young Fellow; and for that Species of Men Mrs. *Honour* had some Regard; but this was perfectly indiscriminate: For having been crossed in the Love which she bore a certain Nobleman's Footman, who had basely deserted her after a Promise of Marriage, she had so securely kept together the broken Remains of her Heart, that no Man had ever since been able to possess himself of any single Fragment. She viewed all handsome Men with that equal Regard and Benevolence, which a sober and virtuous Mind bears to all the Good.—She might, indeed, be called a Lover of Men, as *Socrates* was a Lover of Mankind, preferring one to another for corporeal, as he for mental Qualifications; but never carrying this Preference so far as to cause any Perturbation in the philosophical Serenity of her Temper.

The Day after Mr. *Jones* had that Conflict with himself, which we have seen in the preceding Chapter, Mrs. *Honour* came into his Room, and finding him alone, began in the following Manner: 'La, Sir, where do you think I have been? I warrants you, you would not guess in fifty Years; but if you did guess, to be sure, I must not tell you neither.' 'Nay, if it be something which you must not tell me,' said *Jones*, 'I shall have the Curiosity to enquire, and I know

you will not be so barbarous to refuse me.' 'I don't know,' cries she,
'why I should refuse you neither, for that Matter; for to be sure you
won't mention it any more. And for that Matter, if you knew where
I have been, unless you knew what I have been about, it would not
signify much. Nay, I don't see why it should be kept a Secret, for
my Part; for to be sure she is the best Lady in the World.' Upon
this, *Jones* began to beg earnestly to be let into this Secret, and
faithfully promised not to divulge it. She then proceeded thus:
'Why you must know, Sir, my young Lady sent me to enquire after
Molly Seagrim, and to see whether the Wench wanted any thing;
to be sure, I did not care to go, methinks; but Servants must do
what they are ordered.——How could you undervalue yourself so,
Mr. *Jones*?——So my Lady bid me go, and carry her some Linen,
and other things.——She is too good. If such forward Sluts were
sent to *Bridewell*, it would be better for them. I told my Lady,
says I, Madam, Your La'ship is encouraging Idleness——' 'And was
my *Sophia* so good?' says *Jones*.—My *Sophia*! I assure you, marry
come up,' answered *Honour*. 'And yet if you knew all,—Indeed, if I
was as Mr. *Jones*, I should look a little higher than such Trumpery
as *Molly Seagrim*.' 'What do you mean by these Words,' replied
Jones, 'If I knew all?' 'I mean what I mean,' says *Honour*.
'Don't you remember putting your Hands in my Lady's Muff
once? I vow I could almost find in my Heart to tell, if I was certain
my Lady would never come to the Hearing on't.—*Jones* then made
several solemn Protestations. And *Honour* proceeded,—'then to be
sure, my Lady gave me that Muff; and afterwards, upon hearing
what you had done—— 'Then you told her what I had done!' interrupted *Jones*. 'If I did, Sir,' answered she, 'you need not be angry
with me. Many's the Man would have given his Head to have had
my Lady told, if they had known——for, to be sure, the biggest
Lord in the Land might be proud—but, I protest, I have a great
Mind not to tell you.' *Jones* fell to Entreaties, and soon prevailed
on her to go on thus. 'You must know then, Sir, that my Lady had
given this Muff to me; but about a Day or two after I had told her
the Story, she quarrels with her new Muff, and to be sure it is the
prettiest that ever was seen. *Honour*, says she,——this is an odious
Muff; it is too big for me,——I can't wear it——till I can get
another, you must let me have my old one again, and you may have
this in the room on't—for she's a good Lady, and scorns to give a
Thing and take a Thing, I promise you that. So to be sure I fetched
it her back again, and, I believe, she hath worn it upon her Arm
almost ever since, and I warrants hath given it many a Kiss when
nobody hath seen her.'

Here the Conversation was interrupted by Mr. *Western* himself,
who came to summon *Jones* to the Harpsichord; whither the poor

young Fellow went all pale and trembling. This *Western* observ'd, but, on seeing Mrs. *Honour*, imputed it to a wrong Cause; and having given *Jones* a hearty Curse between Jest and Earnest, he bid him beat abroad, and not poach up the Game in his Warren.

Sophia looked this Evening with more than usual Beauty, and we may believe it was no small Addition to her Charms, in the Eye of Mr. *Jones*, that she now happened to have on her Right Arm this very Muff.

She was playing one of her Father's favourite Tunes, and he was leaning on her Chair, when the Muff fell over her Fingers, and put her out. This so disconcerted the Squire, that he snatched the Muff from her, and with a hearty Curse threw it into the Fire. *Sophia* instantly started up, and with the utmost Eagerness recovered it from the Flames.

Though this Incident will probably appear of little Consequence to many of our Readers; yet, trifling as it was, it had so violent an Effect on poor *Jones*, that we thought it our Duty, to relate it. In reality, there are many little Circumstances too often omitted by injudicious Historians, from which Events of the utmost Importance arise. The World may indeed be considered as a vast Machine, in which the great Wheels are originally set in Motion by those which are very minute, and almost imperceptible to any but the strongest Eyes.

Thus, not all the Charms of the incomparable *Sophia*; not all the dazzling Brightness, and languishing Softness of her Eyes; the Harmony of her Voice, and of her Person; not all her Wit, good Humour, Greatness of Mind, or Sweetness of Disposition, had been able so absolutely to conquer and enslave the Heart of poor *Jones*, as this little Incident of the Muff. Thus the Poet sweetly sings of *Troy*.

> ———*Captique dolis lachrymisque coacti*
> *Quos neque Tydides, nec Larissæus Achilles,*
> *Non anni domuere decem, non mille Carinæ*[1]

> What *Diomede*, or *Thetis'* greater Son,
> A thousand Ships, nor ten Years Siege had done,
> False Tears, and fawning Words, the City won.

The Citadel of *Jones* was now taken by Surprize. All those Considerations of Honour and Prudence, which our Heroe had lately with so much military Wisdom placed as Guards over the Avenues of his Heart, ran away from their Posts, and the God of Love marched in in Triumph.

---

1. *Aeneid* II.196–98; *coacti* reads *coactis*. The translation is Dryden's (1697), II.261–63.

Chapter V.

A very long Chapter, containing a very great Incident.

But though this victorious Deity easily expelled his avowed Enemies from the Heart of *Jones*, he found it more difficult to supplant
the Garrison which he himself had placed there. To lay aside all
Allegory, the Concern for what must become of poor *Molly*, greatly
disturbed and perplexed the Mind of the worthy Youth. The superior Merit of *Sophia* totally eclipsed, or rather extinguished all the
Beauties of the poor Girl; but Compassion instead of Contempt
succeeded to Love. He was convinced the Girl had placed all her
Affections, and all her Prospect of future Happiness in him only.
For this he had, he knew, given sufficient Occasion, by the utmost
Profusion of Tenderness towards her: A Tenderness which he had
taken every Means to persuade her he would always maintain. She,
on her Side, had assured him of her firm Belief in his Promise, and
had with the most solemn Vows declared, that on his fulfilling, or
breaking these Promises, it depended, whether she should be the
happiest or most miserable of Womankind. And to be the Author
of this highest Degree of Misery to a human Being, was a Thought
on which he could not bear to ruminate a single Moment. He considered this poor Girl as having sacrificed to him everything in her
little Power; as having been at her own Expence the Object of his
Pleasure; as sighing and languishing for him even at that very
Instant. Shall then, says he, my Recovery, for which she hath so
ardently wished; shall my Presence which she hath so eagerly
expected, instead of giving her that Joy with which she hath flattered herself, cast her at once down into Misery and Despair? Can I
be such a Villain? Here, when the Genius of poor *Molly* seem'd
triumphant, the Love of *Sophia* towards him, which now appeared
no longer dubious, rushed upon his Mind, and bore away every
Obstacle before it.

At length it occurred to him, that he might possibly be able to
make *Molly* amends another Way; namely, by giving her a Sum of
Money. This, nevertheless, he almost despaired of her accepting,
when he recollected the frequent and vehement Assurances he had
received from her, that the World put in Balance with him would
make her no Amends for his Loss. However, her extreme Poverty,
and chiefly her egregious Vanity (somewhat of which hath been
already hinted to the Reader,) gave him some little Hope, that
notwithstanding all her avowed Tenderness, she might in time be
brought to content herself with a Fortune superior to her Expecta-

tion, and which might indulge her Vanity, by setting her above all her Equals. He resolved therefore, to take the first Opportunity of making a Proposal of this kind.

One Day accordingly, when his Arm was so well recovered, that he could walk easily with it slung in a Sash, he stole forth, at a Season when the Squire was engaged in his Field Exercises, and visited his Fair-one. Her Mother and Sisters, whom he found taking their Tea, inform'd him first that *Molly* was not at home; but afterwards, the eldest Sister acquainted him with a malicious Smile, that she was above Stairs a-bed. *Tom* had no Objection to this Situation of his Mistress, and immediately ascended the Ladder which led towards her Bedchamber; but when he came to the Top, he, to his great Surprize, found the Door fast; nor could he for some time obtain any Answer from within; for *Molly*, as she herself afterwards informed him, was fast asleep.

The Extremes of Grief and Joy have been remarked to produce very similar Effects; and when either of these rushes on us by Surprize, it is apt to create such a total Perturbation and Confusion, that we are often thereby deprived of the Use of all our Faculties. It cannot therefore be wondered at, that the unexpected Sight of Mr. *Jones* should so strongly operate on the Mind of *Molly*, and should overwhelm her with such Confusion, that for some Minutes she was unable to express the great Raptures, with which the Reader will suppose she was affected on this Occasion. As for *Jones*, he was so entirely possessed, and as it were enchanted by the Presence of his beloved Object, that he for a while forgot *Sophia*, and consequently the principal Purpose of his Visit.

This, however, soon recurred to his Memory; and after the first Transports of their Meeting were over, he found Means by Degrees to introduce a Discourse on the fatal Consequences which must attend their Amour, if Mr. *Allworthy*, who had strictly forbidden him ever seeing her more, should discover that he still carried on this Commerce. Such a Discovery, which his Enemies gave him reason to think would be unavoidable, must, he said, end in his Ruin, and consequently in hers. Since, therefore, their hard Fates had determined that they must separate, he advised her to bear it with Resolution, and swore he would never omit any Opportunity through the Course of his Life, of shewing her the Sincerity of his Affection, by providing for her in a manner beyond her utmost Expectation, or even beyond her Wishes, if ever that should be in his Power; concluding at last, that she might soon find some Man who would marry her, and who would make her much happier than she could be by leading a disreputable Life with him.

Molly remained a few Moments in Silence, and then bursting into a Flood of Tears, she began to upbraid him in the following Words: 'And this is your Love for me, to forsake me in this manner, now you have ruined me? How often, when I have told you that all Men are false and Perjury alike, and grow tired of us as soon as ever they have had their wicked Wills of us, how often have you sworn you would never forsake me? And can you be such a per-jury Man after all? What signifies all the Riches in the World to me without you, now you have gained my Heart, so you have—you have—? Why do you mention another Man to me? I can never love any other Man as long as I live. All other Men are nothing to me. If the greatest Squire in all the Country would come a suiting to me to-morrow, I would not give my Company to him. No, I shall always hate and despise the whole Sex for your sake'——

She was proceeding thus, when an Accident put a stop to her Tongue, before it had run out half its Career. The Room, or rather Garret, in which *Molly* lay, being up one Pair of Stairs, that is to say, at the Top of the House, was of a sloping Figure, resembling the great *Delta* of the *Greeks*. The *English* Reader may, perhaps, form a better Idea of it, by being told, that it was impossible to stand upright any where but in the Middle. Now, as this Room wanted the Conveniency of a Closet, *Molly* had, to supply that Defect, nailed up an old Rug against the Rafters of the House, which enclosed a little Hole where her best Apparel, such as the Remains of that Sack which we have formerly mention'd, some Caps, and other things with which she had lately provided herself, were hung up and secured from the Dust.

This inclosed Place exactly fronted the Foot of the Bed, to which, indeed, the Rug hung so near, that it served, in a manner, to supply the Want of Curtains. Now, whether *Molly* in the Agonies of her Rage, pushed this Rug with her Feet; or, *Jones* might touch it; or whether the Pin or Nail gave way of its own accord, I am not certain; but as *Molly* pronounced those last Words, which are recorded above, the wicked Rug got loose from its Fastning, and discovered every thing hid behind it; where among other female Utensils appeared—(with Shame I write it, and with Sorrow will it be read)——the Philosopher *Square*, in a Posture (for the Place would not near admit his standing upright) as ridiculous as can pos-sibly be conceived.

The Posture, indeed, in which he stood, was not greatly unlike that of a Soldier who is tyed Neck and Heels; or rather resembling the Attitude in which we often see Fellows in the public Streets of *London*, who are not suffering but deserving Punishment by so standing. He had a Night-cap belonging to *Molly* on his Head, and his two large Eyes, the Moment the Rug fell, stared directly at *Jones*; so that when the Idea of Philosophy was added to the Figure now discovered, it would have been very difficult for any Spectator to have refrained from immoderate Laughter.

I question not but the Surprize of the Reader will be here equal to that of *Jones*; as the Suspicions which must arise from the Appearance of this wise and grave Man in such a Place, may seem so inconsistent with that Character, which he hath, doubtless, maintain'd hitherto, in the Opinion of every one.

But to confess the Truth, this Inconsistency is rather imaginary than real. Philosophers are composed of Flesh and Blood as well as other human Creatures; and however sublimated and refined the Theory of these may be, a little practical Frailty is as incident to them as to other Mortals. It is indeed, in Theory only and not in Practice, as we have before hinted, that consists the Difference: For though such great Beings think much better and more wisely, they always act exactly like other Men. They know very well how to subdue all Appetites and Passions, and to despise both Pain and Pleasure; and this Knowledge affords much delightful Contemplation, and is easily acquired; but the Practice would be vexatious and troublesome; and, therefore, the same Wisdom which teaches them to know this, teaches them to avoid carrying it into Execution.

Mr. *Square* happened to be at Church, on that *Sunday*, when, as the Reader may be pleased to remember, the Appearance of *Molly* in her Sack had caused all that Disturbance. Here he first observed her, and was so pleased with her Beauty, that he prevailed with the young Gentlemen to change their intended Ride that Evening, that he might pass by the Habitation of *Molly*, and, by that means, might obtain a second Chance of seeing her. This Reason, however, as he did not at that Time mention to any, so neither did we think proper to communicate it then to the Reader.

Among other Particulars which constituted the Unfitness of Things in Mr. *Square*'s Opinion, Danger and Difficulty were two. The Difficulty, therefore, which he apprehended there might be in corrupting this young Wench, and the Danger which would accrue to his Character on the Discovery, were such strong Dissuasives, that it is probable, he at first intended to have contented himself with the pleasing Ideas which the Sight of Beauty furnishes us with. These the gravest Men, after a full Meal of serious Meditation, often allow themselves by way of Dessert: For which Purpose, certain Books and Pictures find their way into the most private Recesses of their Study, and a certain liquorish Part of natural Philosophy is often the principal Subject of their Conversation.

But when the Philosopher heard a Day or two afterwards, that the Fortress of Virtue had already been subdued, he began to give a larger Scope to his Desires. His Appetite was not of that squeamish kind which cannot feed on a Dainty because another hath tasted it. In short, he liked the Girl the better for the Want of that Chastity, which, if she had possessed it, must have been a Bar to his Pleasures; he pursued, and obtained her.

The Reader will be mistaken, if he thinks *Molly* gave *Square* the Preference to her younger Lover: On the contrary, had she been confined to the Choice of one only, *Tom Jones* would, undoubtedly, have been, of the two, the victorious Person. Nor was it solely the Consideration that two are better than one (tho' this had its proper Weight) to which Mr. *Square* owed his Success; the Absence of *Jones* during his Confinement was an unlucky Circumstance; and in that Interval, some well chosen Presents from the Philosopher so softened and unguarded the Girl's Heart, that a favourable Opportunity became irresistible, and *Square* triumphed over the poor Remains of Virtue which subsisted in the Bosom of *Molly*.

It was now about a Fortnight since this Conquest, when *Jones* paid the abovementioned Visit to his Mistress, at a time when she and *Square* were in Bed together. This was the true Reason why the Mother denied her as we have seen; for as the old Woman shared in the Profits arising from the Iniquity of her Daughter, she encouraged and protected her in it to the utmost of her Power; but such was the Envy and Hatred which the eldest Sister bore towards *Molly*, that, notwithstanding she had some Part of the Booty, she would willingly have parted with this to ruin her Sister and spoil her Trade. Hence she had acquainted *Jones* with her being above Stairs in Bed, in hopes that he might have caught her in *Square*'s Arms. This, however, *Molly* found means to prevent, as the Door was fastened; which gave her an Opportunity of conveying her Lover behind that Rug or Blanket where he now was unhappily discovered.

Square no sooner made his Appearance than *Molly* flung herself back in her Bed, cried out she was undone, and abandoned herself to Despair. This poor Girl, who was yet but a Novice in her Business, had not arrived to that Perfection of Assurance which helps off a Town Lady in any Extremity; and either prompts her with an Excuse, or else inspires her to brazen out the Matter with her Husband; who from Love of Quiet, or out of Fear of his Reputation, and sometimes, perhaps, from Fear of the Gallant, who, like Mr. *Constant*[1] in the Play, wears a Sword, is glad to shut his Eyes, and contented to put his Horns in his Pocket. *Molly*, on the contrary, was silenced by this Evidence, and very fairly gave up a Cause which she had hitherto maintained with so many Tears, and with such solemn and vehement Protestations of the purest Love and Constancy.

As to the Gentleman behind the Arras, he was not in much less Consternation. He stood for a while motionless, and seemed equally

---

1. In Vanbrugh's *The Provoked Wife* (1697) V.vi, Constant, discovered in a   closet by a jealous husband, offers a duel and wins the confrontation.

at a loss what to say, or whither to direct his Eyes. *Jones*, though perhaps the most astonished of the three, first found his Tongue; and, being immediately recovered from those uneasy Sensations, which *Molly* by her Upbraidings had occasioned, he burst into a loud Laughter, and then saluting Mr. *Square*, advanced to take him by the Hand, and to relieve him from his Place of Confinement.

Square, being now arrived in the Middle of the Room, in which Part only he could stand upright, looked at *Jones* with a very grave Countenance, and said to him, 'Well, Sir, I see you enjoy this mighty Discovery, and, I dare swear, taste great Delight in the Thoughts of exposing me; but if you will consider the Matter fairly, you will find you are yourself only to blame. I am not guilty of corrupting Innocence. I have done nothing for which that Part of the World which judges of Matters by the Rule of Right, will condemn me. Fitness is governed by the Nature of Things, and not by Customs, Forms, or municipal Laws. Nothing is, indeed, unfit which is not unnatural.' 'Well reasoned, old Boy,' answered *Jones*; 'but why dost thou think that I should desire to expose thee? I promise thee, I was never better pleased with thee in my Life; and unless thou hast a mind to discover it thyself, this Affair may remain a profound Secret for me.' 'Nay, Mr. *Jones*,' replied *Square*, 'I would not be thought to undervalue Reputation. Good Fame is a Species of the KALON,[2] and it is by no means fitting to neglect it. Besides, to murder one's own Reputation is a kind of Suicide, a detestable and odious Vice. If you think proper, therefore, to conceal any Infirmity of mine; (for such I may have, since no Man is perfectly perfect;) I promise you I will not betray myself. Things may be fitting to be done, which are not fitting to be boasted of; for by the perverse Judgment of the World, That often becomes the Subject of Censure, which is, in Truth, not only innocent but laudable.' 'Right!' cries *Jones*, 'what can be more innocent than the Indulgence of a natural Appetite? or what more laudable than the Propagation of our Species?' 'To be serious with you,' answered *Square*, 'I profess they always appeared so to me.' 'And yet,' said *Jones*, 'you was of a different Opinion, when my Affair with this Girl was first discovered.' 'Why, I must confess,' says *Square*, 'as the Matter was misrepresented to me by that Parson *Thwackum*, I might condemn the Corruption of Innocence: It was that, Sir, it was that—and that—: For you must know, Mr. *Jones*, in the Consideration of Fitness, very minute Circumstances, Sir, very minute Circumstances cause great Alteration.'——'Well,' cries *Jones*, 'be that as it will, it shall be your own Fault, as I have promised you, if you ever hear any more of this Adventure. Behave kindly to the Girl, and I will never open my Lips concerning the Matter to any one. And, *Molly*, do

2. "The Beautiful" (Greek).

you be faithful to your Friend, and I will not only forgive your Infidelity to me, but will do you all the Service I can.' So saying, he took a hasty Leave, and slipping down the Ladder retired with much Expedition.

Square was rejoyced to find this Adventure was likely to have no worse Conclusion; and as for *Molly*, being recovered from her Confusion, she began at first to upbraid *Square* with having been the Occasion of her Loss of *Jones*; but that Gentleman soon found the Means of mitigating her Anger, partly by Caresses, and partly by a small Nostrum from his Purse, of wonderful and approved Efficacy in purging off the ill Humours of the Mind, and in restoring it to a good Temper.

She then poured forth a vast Profusion of Tenderness towards her new Lover; turned all she had said to *Jones*, and *Jones* himself into Ridicule, and vowed, tho' he once had the Possession of her Person, that none but *Square* had ever been Master of her Heart.

Chapter VI.

By comparing which with the former, the Reader may possibly correct some Abuse which he hath formerly been guilty of in the Application of the Word Love.

The Infidelity of *Molly*, which *Jones* had now discovered, would, perhaps, have vindicated a much greater Degree of Resentment than he expressed on the Occasion; and if he had abandoned her directly from that Moment, very few, I believe, would have blamed him.

Certain, however, it is, that he saw her in the Light of Compassion; and tho' his Love to her was not of that Kind which could give him any great Uneasiness at her Inconstancy; yet was he not a little shocked on reflecting that he had himself originally corrupted her Innocence; for to this Corruption he imputed all the Vice, into which she appeared now so likely to plunge herself.

This Consideration gave him no little Uneasiness, till *Betty*, the elder Sister, was so kind some time afterwards entirely to cure him by a Hint, that one *Will Barnes*, and not himself, had been the first Seducer of *Molly*; and that the little Child, which he had hitherto so certainly concluded to be his own, might very probably have an equal Title, at least, to claim *Barnes* for its Father.

Jones eagerly pursued this Scent when he had first received it; and in a very short Time was sufficiently assured that the Girl had told him Truth, not only by the Confession of the Fellow, but, at last, by that of *Molly* herself.

This *Will Barnes* was a Country Gallant, and had acquired as many Trophies of this Kind as any Ensign or Attorney's Clerk in the Kingdom. He had, indeed, reduced several Women to a State of utter Profligacy, had broke the Hearts of some, and had the Honour of occasioning the violent Death of one poor Girl, who had either drowned herself, or, what was rather more probable, had been drowned by him.

Among other of his Conquests, this Fellow had triumphed over the Heart of *Betty Seagrim.* He had made Love to her long before *Molly* was grown to be a fit Object of that Pastime; but had afterwards deserted her, and applied to her Sister, with whom he had almost immediate Success. Now *Will* had, in reality, the sole Possession of *Molly's* Affection, while *Jones* and *Square* were almost equally Sacrifices to her Interest, and to her Pride.

Hence had grown that implacable Hatred which we have before seen raging in the Mind of *Betty*; though we did not think it necessary to assign this Cause sooner, as Envy itself alone was adequate to all the Effects we have mentioned.

Jones was become perfectly easy by Possession of this Secret with regard to *Molly*; but as to *Sophia*, he was far from being in a State of Tranquillity; nay, indeed, he was under the most violent Perturbation: His Heart was now, if I may use the Metaphor, entirely evacuated, and *Sophia* took absolute Possession of it. He loved her with an unbounded Passion, and plainly saw the tender Sentiments she had for him; yet could not this Assurance lessen his Despair of obtaining the Consent of her Father, nor the Horrors which attended his Pursuit of her by any base or treacherous Method.

The Injury which he must thus do to Mr. *Western,* and the Concern which would accrue to Mr. *Allworthy,* were Circumstances that tormented him all Day, and haunted him on his Pillow at Night. His Life was a constant Struggle between Honour and Inclination, which alternately triumphed over each other in his Mind. He often resolved, in the Absence of *Sophia,* to leave her Father's House, and to see her no more; and as often, in her Presence, forgot all those Resolutions, and determined to pursue her at the Hazard of his Life, and at the Forfeiture of what was much dearer to him.

This Conflict began soon to produce very strong and visible Effects: For he lost all his usual Sprightliness and Gaiety of Temper, and became not only melancholy when alone, but dejected and absent in Company; nay, if ever he put on a forced Mirth, to comply with Mr. *Western's* Humour, the Constraint appeared so plain, that he seemed to have been giving the strongest Evidence of what he endeavoured to conceal by such Ostentation.

It may, perhaps, be a Question, whether the Art which he used to conceal his Passion, or the Means which honest Nature employed to reveal it, betrayed him most: For while Art made him more than ever reserved to *Sophia*, and forbad him to address any of his Discourse to her; nay, to avoid meeting her Eyes, with the utmost Caution; Nature was no less busy in counterplotting him. Hence, at the Approach of the young Lady, he grew pale; and if this was sudden, started. If his Eyes accidentally met hers, the Blood rushed into his Cheeks, and his Countenance became all over Scarlet. If common Civility ever obliged him to speak to her, as to drink her Health at Table, his Tongue was sure to faulter. If he touched her, his Hand, nay his whole Frame trembled. And if any Discourse tended, however remotely, to raise the Idea of Love, an involuntary Sigh seldom failed to steal from his Bosom. Most of which Accidents Nature was wonderfully industrious to throw daily in his Way.

All these Symptoms escaped the Notice of the Squire; but not so of *Sophia*. She soon perceived these Agitations of Mind in *Jones*, and was at no Loss to discover the Cause; for indeed she recognized it in her own Breast. And this Recognition is, I suppose, that Sympathy which hath been so often noted in Lovers, and which will sufficiently account for her being so much quicker-sighted than her Father.

But, to say the Truth, there is a more simple and plain Method of accounting for that prodigious Superiority of Penetration which we must observe in some Men over the rest of the human Species, and one which will serve not only in the Case of Lovers, but of all others. From whence is it that the Knave is generally so quicksighted to those Symptoms and Operations of Knavery which often dupe an honest Man of a much better Understanding? There surely is no general Sympathy among Knaves, nor have they, like Free-Masons, any common Sign of Communication. In reality, it is only because they have the same thing in their Heads, and their Thoughts are turned the same Way. Thus, that *Sophia* saw, and that *Western* did not see the plain Symptoms of Love in *Jones* can be no Wonder, when we consider that the Idea of Love never entered into the Head of the Father, whereas the Daughter, at present, thought of nothing else.

When *Sophia* was well satisfied of the violent Passion which tormented poor *Jones*, and no less certain that she herself was its Object, she had not the least Difficulty in discovering the true Cause of his present Behaviour. This highly endeared him to her, and raised in her Mind two of the best Affections which any Lover can wish to raise in a Mistress. These were Esteem and Pity; for sure the most outrageously rigid among her Sex will excuse her pitying a Man, whom she saw miserable on her own Account; nor can they blame her for esteeming one who visibly, from the most honourable Motives endeavoured to smother a Flame in his own

Bosom, which, like the famous *Spartan* Theft,[1] was preying upon and consuming his very Vitals. Thus his Backwardness, his Shunning her, his Coldness and his Silence, were the forwardest, the most diligent, the warmest, and most eloquent Advocates; and wrought so violently on her sensible and tender Heart, that she soon felt for him all those gentle Sensations which are consistent with a virtuous and elevated female Mind—In short, all which Esteem, Gratitude and Pity, can inspire in such, towards an agreeable Man—Indeed, all which the nicest Delicacy can allow.—In a Word,—she was in Love with him to Distraction.

One Day, this young Couple accidentally met in the Garden, at the End of two Walks, which were both bounded by that Canal in which *Jones* had formerly risqued drowning to retrieve the little Bird that *Sophia* had there lost.

This Place had been of late much frequented by *Sophia*. Here she used to ruminate, with a Mixture of Pain and Pleasure, on an Incident, which, however trifling in itself, had possibly sown the first Seeds of that Affection which was now arrived to such Maturity in her Heart.

Here then this young Couple met. They were almost close together before either of them knew anything of the other's Approach. A Bystander would have discovered sufficient Marks of Confusion in the Countenance of each; but they felt too much themselves to make any Observation. As soon as *Jones* had a little recovered his first Surprize, he accosted the young Lady with some of the ordinary Forms of Salutation, which she in the same Manner returned, and their Conversation began, as usual, on the delicious Beauty of the Morning. Hence they past to the Beauty of the Place, on which *Jones* launched forth very high Encomiums. When they came to the Tree whence he had formerly tumbled into the Canal, *Sophia* could not help reminding him of that Accident, and said, 'I fancy, Mr. *Jones*, you have some little Shuddering when you see that Water.' 'I assure you, Madam,' answered *Jones*, 'the Concern you felt at the Loss of your little Bird, will always appear to me the highest Circumstance in that Adventure. Poor little *Tommy*, there is the Branch he stood upon. How could the little Wretch have the Folly to fly away from that State of Happiness in which I had the Honour to place him? His Fate was a just Punishment for his Ingratitude.' 'Upon my Word, Mr. *Jones*,' said she, 'your Gallantry very narrowly escaped as severe a Fate. Sure, the Remembrance must affect you.' 'Indeed, Madam,' answered he, 'if I have any

1. Plutarch, "Life of Lycurgus" XVIII —"The boys make such a serious matter of their stealing, that one of them, as the story goes, who was carrying concealed under his cloak a young fox which he had stolen, suffered the animal to tear out his bowels with its teeth and claws, and died rather than have his theft detected" (Perrin trans., I.261–63; quoted in Bryant, p. 153).

Reason to reflect with Sorrow on it, it is, perhaps, that the Water
had not been a little deeper, by which I might have escaped many
bitter Heart-achs, that Fortune seems to have in Store for me.' 'Fie,
Mr. *Jones*,' replied *Sophia*, 'I am sure you cannot be in Earnest
now. This affected Contempt of Life is only an Excess of your
Complaisance to me. You would endeavour to lessen the Obligation
of having twice ventured it for my Sake. Beware the third Time.'—
She spoke these last Words with a Smile and a Softness inexpressible. *Jones* answered with a Sigh, 'He feared it was already too late
for Caution;'—and then looking tenderly and stedfastly on her, he
cry'd, 'Oh! Miss *Western*,—Can you desire me to live? Can you
wish me so ill?'—*Sophia* looking down on the Ground, answered
with some Hesitation, 'Indeed, Mr. *Jones*, I do not wish you ill.'—
'Oh! I know too well that heavenly Temper,' cries *Jones*, 'that
divine Goodness which is beyond every other Charm.' 'Nay, now,'
answered she, 'I understand you not.—I can stay no longer,—I,—' 'I
would not be understood,' cries he, 'nay I can't be understood. I
know not what I say. Meeting you here so unexpectedly—I have
been unguarded—for Heaven's Sake pardon me, if I have said any
Thing to offend you—I did not mean it—indeed, I would rather
have died—nay, the very Thought would kill me.' 'You surprize
me,' answered she,—'How can you possibly think you have offended
me?' 'Fear, Madam,' says he, 'easily runs into Madness; and there is
no Degree of Fear like that which I feel of offending you. How can
I speak then? Nay don't look angrily at me, one Frown will destroy
me.—I mean nothing—Blame my Eyes, or blame those Beauties—
What am I saying? Pardon me if I have said too much. My Heart
overflowed. I have struggled with my Love to the utmost, and have
endeavoured to conceal a Fever which preys on my Vitals, and will,
I hope, soon make it impossible for me ever to offend you more.'

   Mr. *Jones* now fell a trembling as if he had been shaken with the
Fit of an Ague. *Sophia*, who was in a Situation not very different
from his, answered in these words: 'Mr. *Jones*, I will not affect to
misunderstand you; indeed I understand you too well; but for Heav-
en's Sake, if you have any Affection for me, let me make the best of
my way into the House. I wish I may be able to support myself
thither.'

   Jones, who was hardly able to support himself, offered her his
Arm, which she condescended to accept, but begged he would not
mention a Word more to her of this Nature at present. He promised he would not, insisting only on her Forgiveness of what Love,
without the Leave of his Will, had forced from him: This, she told
him, he knew how to obtain, by his future Behaviour; and thus this
young Pair tottered and trembled along, the Lover not once daring
to squeeze the Hand of his Mistress, tho' it was lock'd in his.

Sophia immediately retired to her Chamber, where Mrs. *Honour* and the Hartshorn were summoned to her Assistance. As to poor *Jones*, the only Relief to his distempered Mind was an unwelcome Piece of News, which, as it opens a Scene of different Nature from those in which the Reader hath lately been conversant, will be communicated to him in the next Chapter.

Chapter VII.

In which Mr. Allworthy *appears on a Sick-Bed.*

Mr. *Western* was become so fond of *Jones*, that he was unwilling to part with him, tho' his Arm had been long since cured; and *Jones*, either from the Love of Sport, or from some other Reason, was easily persuaded to continue at his House, which he did sometimes for a Fortnight together without paying a single Visit at Mr. *Allworthy*'s; nay, without ever hearing from thence.

Mr. *Allworthy* had been for some Days indisposed with a Cold, which had been attended with a little Fever. This he had, however, neglected, as it was usual with him to do all Manner of Disorders which did not confine him to his Bed, or prevent his several Faculties from performing their ordinary Functions. A Conduct which we would by no means be thought to approve or recommend to Imitation: For surely the Gentlemen of the *Æsculapian* Art are in the Right in advising, that the Moment the Disease is entered at one Door, the Physician should be introduced at the other; what else is meant by that old Adage: *Venienti occurrite Morbo?*[1] "Oppose a Distemper at its first Approach." Thus the Doctor and the Disease meet in fair and equal Conflict; whereas, by giving Time to the latter, we often suffer him to fortify and entrench himself, like a *French* Army; so that the learned Gentleman finds it very difficult, and sometimes impossible to come at the Enemy. Nay sometimes by gaining Time, the Disease applies to the *French* military Politics, and corrupts Nature over to his Side, and then all the Powers of Physic must arrive too late. Agreeable to these Observations was, I remember, the Complaint of the great Doctor *Misaubin*,[2] who used very pathetically to lament the late Applications which were made to his Skill: Saying, 'Bygar, me believe my Pation take me for de Undertaker: For dey never send for me till de Physicion have kill dem.'

Mr. *Allworthy*'s Distemper, by Means of this Neglect, gained

1. Persius, *Satires* III.64, quoted in Lily, p. 150.
2. John Misaubin, a French doctor practicing in London, widely ridiculed for his broken English. Fielding had dedicated his play *The Mock Doctor* (1732), with ambiguous irony, "To Dr. John Misaubin," going on to praise, ironically, Misaubin's "Little Pill," which was supposed to cure venereal disease; Hogarth had caricatured him in *The Harlot's Progress* of the same year. See also below, p. 527.

such Ground, that, when the Increase of his Fever obliged him to send for Assistance, the Doctor at his first Arrival shook his Head, wished he had been sent for sooner, and intimated that he thought him in very imminent Danger. Mr. *Allworthy*, who had settled all his Affairs in this World, and was as well prepared as it is possible for human Nature to be, for the other, received this Information with the utmost Calmness and Unconcern. He could, indeed, whenever he laid himself down to Rest, say with *Cato*[3] in the tragical Poem,

> ————Let *Guilt* or *Fear*
> *Disturb Man's Rest*, Cato *knows neither of them;*
> *Indifferent in his Choice, to sleep or die.*

In Reality he could say this with ten times more Reason and Confidence than *Cato*, or any other proud Fellow among the antient or modern Heroes: For he was not only devoid of Fear; but might be considered as a faithful Labourer, when at the End of Harvest he is summoned to receive his Reward at the Hands of a bountiful Master.

The good Man gave immediate Orders for all his Family to be summoned round him. None of these were then abroad, but Mrs. *Blifil*, who had been some Time in *London*, and Mr. *Jones*, whom the Reader had just parted from at Mr. *Western's*, and who received this Summons just as *Sophia* had left him.

The News of Mr. *Allworthy's* Danger (for the Servant told him he was dying) drove all Thoughts of Love out of his Head. He hurried instantly into the Chariot which was sent for him, and ordered the Coachman to drive with all imaginable Haste; nor did the Idea of *Sophia*, I believe, once occur to him on the Way.

And now, the whole Family, namely, Mr. *Blifil*, Mr. *Jones*, Mr. *Thwackum*, Mr. *Square*, and some of the Servants (for such were Mr. *Allworthy's* Orders) being all assembled round his Bed, the good Man sat up in it, and was beginning to speak, when *Blifil* fell to blubbering; and began to express very loud and bitter Lamentations. Upon this Mr. *Allworthy* shook him by the Hand, and said, 'Do not sorrow thus, my dear Nephew, at the most ordinary of all human Occurrences. When Misfortunes befal our Friends we are justly grieved: For those are Accidents which might often have been avoided, and which may seem to render the Lot of one Man more peculiarly unhappy than that of others; but Death is certainly unavoidable, and is that common Lot, in which alone the Fortunes of all Men agree; nor is the Time when this happens to us very material. If the wisest of Men hath compared Life to a Span, surely we may be allowed to consider it as a Day. It is my Fate to leave it in the Evening; but those who are taken away earlier, have only lost a few

---

3. Addison's tragedy, *Cato* (1713), V.i.38–40; "of them" reads "of 'em."

Hours, at the best little worth lamenting, and much oftener Hours of Labour and Fatigue, of Pain and Sorrow. One of the *Roman* Poets,[4] I remember, likens our leaving Life to our Departure from a Feast. A Thought which hath often occurred to me, when I have seen Men struggling to protract an Entertainment, and to enjoy the Company of their Friends a few Moments longer. Alas! how short is the most protracted of such Enjoyments! How immaterial the Difference between him who retires the soonest, and him who stays the latest! This is seeing Life in the best View, and this Unwillingness to quit our Friends is the most amiable Motive, from which we can derive the Fear of Death; and yet the longest Enjoyment which we can hope for of this Kind, is of so trivial a Duration, that it is to a wise Man truly contemptible. Few Men, I own, think in this Manner: For, indeed, few Men think of Death 'till they are in its Jaws. However gigantic and terrible an Object this may appear when it approaches them, they are nevertheless incapable of seeing it at any Distance; nay, tho' they have been ever so much alarmed and frightned when they have apprehended themselves in Danger of dying, they were no sooner cleared from this Apprehension than even the Fears of it are erased from their Minds. But alas! he who escapes from Death is not pardoned, he is only reprieved, and reprieved to a short Day.

'Grieve, therefore, no more, my dear Child, on this Occasion; an Event which may happen every Hour, which every Element, nay almost every Particle of Matter that surrounds us is capable of producing, and which must and will most unavoidably reach us all at last, ought neither to occasion our Surprize, nor our Lamentation.

'My Physician having acquainted me (which I take very kindly of him) that I am in Danger of leaving you all very shortly, I have determined to say a few Words to you at this our Parting, before my Distemper, which I find grows very fast upon me, puts it out of my Power.

'But I shall waste my Strength too much.—I intended to speak concerning my Will, which tho' I have settled long ago, I think proper to mention such Heads of it as concern any of you, that I may have the Comfort of perceiving you are all satisfied with the Provision I have there made for you.

'Nephew *Blifil*, I leave you the Heir to my whole Estate, except only 500*l.* a Year which is to revert to you after the Death of your Mother, and except one other Estate of 500*l.* a Year, and the Sum of 6000*l.* which I have bestowed in the following Manner.

'The Estate of 500*l.* a Year I have given to you Mr. *Jones*. And as I know the Inconvenience which attends the Want of ready Money, I have added 1000*l.* in Specie. In this I know not whether I

4. Horace, *Satires* I.i.118–19.

have exceeded or fallen short of your Expectation. Perhaps you will think I have given you too little, and the World will be as ready to condemn me for giving you too much; but the latter Censure I despise, and as to the former, unless you should entertain that common Error, which I have often heard in my Life pleaded as an Excuse for a total Want of Charity; namely, that instead of raising Gratitude by voluntary Acts of Bounty, we are apt to raise Demands, which of all others are the most boundless and most difficult to satisfy.—Pardon me the bare Mention of this, I will not suspect any such Thing.'

Jones flung himself at his Benefactor's Feet, and taking eagerly hold of his Hand, assured him, his Goodness to him, both now, and all other Times, had so infinitely exceeded not only his Merit, but his Hopes, that no Words could express his Sense of it. 'And I assure you, Sir,' said he, 'your present Generosity hath left me no other Concern than for the present melancholy Occasion—Oh, my Friend! my Father!' Here his Words choaked him, and he turned away to hide a Tear which was starting from his Eyes.

Allworthy then gently squeezed his Hand, and proceeded thus. 'I am convinced, my Child, that you have much Goodness, Generosity, and Honour in your Temper; if you will add Prudence and Religion to these, you must be happy: For the three former Qualities, I admit, make you worthy of Happiness, but they are the latter only which will put you in Possession of it.

'One thousand Pound I have given to you, Mr. *Thwackum*; a Sum, I am convinced, which greatly exceeds your Desires, as well as your Wants. However, you will receive it as a Memorial of my Friendship; and whatever Superfluities may redound to you, that Piety which you so rigidly maintain, will instruct you how to dispose of them.

'A like Sum, Mr. *Square*, I have bequeathed to you. This, I hope, will enable you to pursue your Profession with better Success than hitherto. I have often observed with Concern, that Distress is more apt to excite Contempt than Commiseration, especially among Men of Business, with whom Poverty is understood to indicate Want of Ability. But the little I have been able to leave you, will extricate you from those Difficulties with which you have formerly struggled; and then I doubt not but you will meet with sufficient Prosperity to supply what a Man of your philosophical Temper will require.

'I find myself growing faint, so I shall refer you to my Will for my Disposition of the Residue. My Servants will there find some Tokens to remember me by; and there are a few Charities which, I trust, my Executors will see faithfully performed. Bless you all. I am setting out a little before you——

Here a Footman came hastily into the Room, and said there was an Attorney from *Salisbury*,[5] who had a particular Message, which he said he must communicate to Mr. *Allworthy* himself: That he seemed in a violent Hurry, and protested he had so much Business to do, that if he could cut himself into four Quarters, all would not be sufficient.

'Go, Child,' said *Allworthy* to *Blifil*, 'see what the Gentleman wants. I am not able to do any business now, nor can he have any with me, in which you are not at present more concerned than myself. Besides I really am—I am incapable of seeing any one at present, or of any longer Attention.' He then saluted them ·[all, saying, Perhaps he should be able to see them][6] again, but he should be now glad to compose himself a little, finding that he had too much exhausted his Spirits in Discourse.

Some of the Company shed Tears at their Parting; and even the Philosopher *Square* wiped his Eyes, *albeit unused to the melting Mood.* As to Mrs. *Wilkins,* she dropt her Pearls as fast *as the* Arabian *Trees their medicinal Gums;*[7] for this was a Ceremonial which that Gentlewoman never omitted on a proper Occasion.

After this Mr. *Allworthy* again laid himself down on his Pillow, and endeavoured to compose himself to Rest.

Chapter VIII.

Containing Matter rather natural than pleasing.

Besides Grief for her Master, there was another Source for that briny Stream which so plentifully rose above the two mountainous Cheek-Bones of the House-keeper. She was no sooner retired, than she began to mutter to herself in the following pleasant Strain. 'Sure Master might have made some Difference, methinks, between me and the other Servants. I suppose he hath left me Mourning; but, i-fackins! if that be all, the Devil shall wear it for him for me. I'd have his Worship know I am no Beggar. I have saved five hundred Pound in his Service, and after all to be used in this Manner. —It is a fine Encouragement to Servants to be honest; and to be sure, if I have taken a little Something now and then, others have taken ten times as much; and now we are all put in a Lump together. If so be that it be so, the Legacy may go to the Devil with him that gave it. No, I won't give it up neither, because that will please some

5. See note, p. 92.
6. Jensen (see Textual Appendix, below, pp. 763–66) points out this typographical error. The fourth edition skips a full line, restored here from the third edition, a reading identical in the first edition, except for its capital *P.*
7. From Othello's famous closing descrip-

tion of himself: ". . . of one whose hand/ (Like the base Indian) threw a pearl away/ Richer than all his tribe; of one whose subdu'd eyes,/ Albeit unused to the melting mood,/ Drop tears as fast as the Arabian trees/ Their med'cinable gum . . ." (V.ii.346–51).

Folks. No, I'll buy the gayest Gown I can get, and dance over the old Curmudgeon's Grave in it. This is my Reward for taking his Part so often, when all the Country have cried Shame of him, for breeding up his Bastard in that Manner: But he is going now where he must pay for all. It would have become him better to have repented of his Sins on his Death bed, than to glory in them, and give away his Estate out of his own Family to a mis-begotten Child. Found in his Bed, forsooth! A pretty Story! Ay, ay, those that hide know where to find. Lord forgive him, I warrant he hath many more Bastards to answer for, if the Truth was known. One Comfort is, they will all be known where he is a going now. "The Servants will find some Token to remember me by." Those were the very Words; I shall never forget them, if I was to live a thousand Years. Ay, ay, I shall remember you for huddling me among the Servants. One would have thought he might have mentioned my Name as well as that of *Square*; but he is a Gentleman forsooth, though he had not Clothes on his Back when he came hither first. Marry come up with such Gentlemen! though he hath lived here this many Years, I don't believe there is *arrow* a Servant in the House ever saw the Colour of his Money. The Devil shall wait upon such a Gentleman for me.' Much more of the like Kind she muttered to herself; but this Taste shall suffice to the Reader.

Neither *Thwackum* nor *Square* were much better satisfied with their Legacies. Though they breathed not their Resentment so loud, yet from the Discontent-which appeared in their Countenances, as well as from the following Dialogue, we collect that no great Pleasure reigned in their Minds.

About an Hour after they had left the sick Room, *Square* met *Thwackum* in the Hall, and accosted him thus, 'Well, Sir, have you heard any News of your Friend since we parted from him?' 'If you mean Mr. *Allworthy*,' answered *Thwackum*, 'I think you might rather give him the Appellation of your Friend: For he seems to me to have deserved that Title.' 'The Title is as good on your Side,' replied *Square*, 'for his Bounty, such as it is, hath been equal to both.' 'I should not have mentioned it first,' cries *Thwackum*, 'but since you begin, I must inform you I am of a different Opinion. There is a wide Distinction between voluntary Favours and Rewards. The Duty I have done in his Family, and the Care I have taken in the Education of his two Boys, are Services for which some Men might have expected a greater Return. I would not have you imagine I am therefore dissatisfied; For St. *Paul* hath taught me to be content with the little I have. Had the Modicum been less, I should have known my Duty. But though the Scripture obliges me to remain contented, it doth not enjoin me to shut my Eyes to my own Merit, nor restrain me from seeing, when I am injured by an unjust Comparison.' 'Since you provoke me,' returned *Square*, 'that Injury is done to me: Nor did I ever imagine Mr. *Allworthy* had held my Friendship so light, as to put me in Balance with one who received his Wages: I know to what it is owing; it proceeds from those narrow Principles which you have been so long endeavouring to infuse into him, in Contempt of every Thing which is great and noble. The Beauty and Loveliness of Friendship is too strong for dim Eyes, nor can it be perceived by any other Medium, than that unerring Rule of Right, which you have so often endeavoured to ridicule, that you have perverted your Friend's Understanding.' 'I wish,' cries *Thwackum*, in a Rage, 'I wish for the Sake of his Soul, your damnable Doctrines have not perverted his Faith. It is to this I impute his present Behaviour so unbecoming a Christian. Who but an Atheist could think of leaving the World without having first made up his Account? Without confessing his Sins, and receiving that Absolution which he knew he had one in the House duly authorised to give him? He will feel the Want of these Necessaries when it is too late. When he is arrived at that Place where there is Wailing and Gnashing of Teeth; it is then he will find in what mighty Stead that Heathen Goddess, that Virtue, which you and all other Deists of the Age adore, will stand him. He will then summon his Priest when there is none to be found, and will lament the Want of that Absolution, without which no Sinner can be safe.' 'If it be so material,' says *Square*, 'Why don't you present it him of your own Accord?' 'It hath no Virtue,' cries *Thwackum*, 'but to those who have sufficient Grace to require it. But why do I talk thus to a Heathen and an Unbeliever? It is you that taught him this Lesson, for which you have been well rewarded in this World, as I doubt not your Disciple will soon be in the other.' 'I know not what you mean by Reward,' said *Square*, 'but if you hint at that pitiful Memorial of our Friendship, which he hath thought fit to bequeath me, I despise it; and nothing but the unfortunate Situation of my Circumstances should prevail on me to accept it.'

The Physician now arrived, and began to enquire of the two Disputants, *How we all did above Stairs?* 'In a miserable Way,' answered *Thwackum*. 'It is no more than I expected,' cries the Doctor: 'But pray what Symptoms have appeared since I left you?' 'No good ones, I am afraid,' replied *Thwackum*, 'after what past at our Departure, I think there were little Hopes.' The bodily Physician, perhaps, misunderstood the Curer of Souls, and before they came to an Explanation, Mr. *Blifil* came to them with a most melancholy Countenance, and acquainted them, that he brought sad News: For that his Mother was dead at *Salisbury*. That she had been seized on the Road home with the Gout in her Head and Stomach, which had carried her off in a few Hours. 'Good-lack-a-day,' says the Doctor, 'One cannot answer for Events; but I wish I had been at Hand to have been called in. The Gout is a Distemper which it is difficult to treat; yet I have been remarkably successful in it.' *Thwackum* and *Square* both condoled with Mr. *Blifil* for the Loss of his Mother, which the one advised him to bear like a Man, and the other like a Christian. The young Gentleman said, He knew very well we were all mortal, and he would endeavour to submit to his Loss as well as he could. That he could not, however, help complaining a little against the peculiar Severity of his Fate, which brought the News of so great a Calamity to him by Surprize, and that at a Time when he hourly expected the severest Blow he was capable of feeling from the Malice of Fortune. He said, the present Occasion would put to the Test those excellent Rudiments which he had learnt from Mr. *Thwackum* and Mr. *Square*, and it would be entirely owing to them, if he was enabled to survive such Misfortunes.

It was now debated whether Mr. *Allworthy* should be informed of the Death of his Sister: This the Doctor violently opposed; in which, I believe, the whole College would agree with him: But Mr. *Blifil* said, he had received such positive and repeated Orders from his Uncle, never to keep any Secret from him, for Fear of the Disquietude which it might give him, that he durst not think of Disobedience, whatever might be the Consequence. He said, for his Part, considering the religious and philosophic Temper of his Uncle, he could not agree with the Doctor in his Apprehensions. He was therefore resolved to communicate it to him: For if his Uncle recovered (as he heartily prayed he might) he knew he would never forgive an Endeavour to keep a Secret of this Kind from him.

The Physician was forced to submit to these Resolutions, which the two other learned Gentlemen very highly commended. So together moved Mr. *Blifil* and the Doctor towards the Sick-Room; where the Physician first entered, and approached the Bed, in order to feel his Patient's Pulse, which he had no sooner done, than he declared he was much better; that the last Application had succeeded to a Miracle, and had brought the Fever to intermit: So that, he said, there appeared now to be as little Danger as he had before apprehended there were Hopes.

To say the Truth, Mr. *Allworthy*'s Situation had never been so bad, as the great Caution of the Doctor had represented it: But as a wise General never despises his Enemy, however inferior that Enemy's Force may be, so neither doth a wise Physician ever despise a Distemper, however inconsiderable. As the former preserves the same strict Discipline, places the same Guards, and employs the same Scouts, though the Enemy be never so weak; so the latter maintains the same Gravity of Countenance, and shakes his Head with the same significant Air, let the Distemper be never so trifling. And both, among many other good ones, may assign this solid Reason for their Conduct, that by these Means the greater Glory redounds to them if they gain the Victory, and the less Disgrace, if by any unlucky Accident they should happen to be conquered.

Mr. *Allworthy* had no sooner lifted up his Eyes, and thanked Heaven for these Hopes of his Recovery, than Mr. *Blifil* drew near, with a very dejected Aspect, and having applied his Handkerchief to his Eye, either to wipe away his Tears, or, to do, as *Ovid*[1] somewhere expresses himself on another Occasion.

Si nullus erit, tamen excute nullum.

'If there be none, then wipe away that none.'

he communicated to his Uncle what the Reader hath been just before acquainted with.

Allworthy received the News with Concern, with Patience, and with Resignation. He dropt a tender Tear, then composed his Countenance, and at last cried, 'The Lord's Will be done in every Thing.'

He now enquired for the Messenger; but *Blifil* told him, it had been impossible to detain him a Moment; for he appeared by the great Hurry he was in to have some Business of Importance on his Hands: That he complained of being hurried, and driven and torn out of his Life, and repeated many Times, that if he could divide himself into four Quarters, he knew how to dispose of every one.

Allworthy then desired *Blifil* to take Care of the Funeral. He said, he would have his Sister deposited in his own Chapel; and as to the Particulars, he left them to his own Discretion, only mentioning the Person whom he would have employed on this Occasion.

1. *Ars Amatoria* I.151. Fielding omits *pulvis* ("dust") after *erit*.

Chapter IX.

Which, among other Things, may serve as a Comment on that Saying of Æschines,[1] THAT DRUNKENNESS SHEWS THE MIND OF A MAN, AS A MIRROUR REFLECTS HIS PERSON.

The Reader may, perhaps, wonder at hearing nothing of Mr. *Jones* in the last Chapter. In fact, his Behaviour was so different from that of the Persons there mentioned, that we chose not to confound his Name with theirs.

1. Source unknown. Not in Aeschines's orations; not listed in William R. Fraser, *Metaphors in Aeschines the Orator* (Baltimore, 1897).

When the good Man had ended his Speech, *Jones* was the last who deserted the Room. Thence he retired to his own Apartment, to give Vent to his Concern; but the Restlessness of his Mind would not suffer him to remain long there; he slipped softly, therefore, to *Allworthy*'s Chamber Door, where he listened a considerable Time without hearing any Kind of Motion within, unless a violent Snoring, which at last his Fears misrepresented as Groans. This so alarmed him, that he could not forbear entering the Room; where he found the good Man in the Bed, in a sweet composed Sleep, and his Nurse snoring in the above-mentioned hearty Manner, at the Bed's Feet. He immediately took the only Method of silencing this Thorough-Bass, whose Music he feared might disturb Mr. *Allworthy*; and then sitting down by the Nurse, he remained motionless till *Blifil* and the Doctor came in together, and waked the sick Man, in order that the Doctor might feel his Pulse, and that the other might communicate to him that Piece of News, which, had *Jones* been apprized of it, would have had great Difficulty of finding its Way to Mr. *Allworthy*'s Ear at such a Season.

When he first heard *Blifil* tell his Uncle this Story, *Jones* could hardly contain the Wrath which kindled in him at the other's Indiscretion, especially as the Doctor shook his Head, and declared his Unwillingness to have the Matter mentioned to his Patient. But as his Passion did not so far deprive him of all Use of his Understanding, as to hide from him the Consequences which any violent Expression towards *Blifil* might have on the Sick, this Apprehension stilled his Rage, at the present; and he grew afterwards so satisfied with finding that this News had, in Fact, produced no Mischief, that he suffered his Anger to die in his own Bosom, without ever mentioning it to *Blifil*.

The Physician dined that Day at Mr. *Allworthy*'s; and having after Dinner visited his Patient, he returned to the Company, and told them, that he had now the Satisfaction to say, with Assurance, that his Patient was out of all Danger: That he had brought his Fever to a perfect Intermission, and doubted not by throwing in the Bark to prevent its Return.

This Account so pleased *Jones*, and threw him into such immoderate Excess of Rapture, that he might be truly said to be drunk with Joy. An Intoxication which greatly forwards the Effects of Wine; and as he was very free too with the Bottle on this Occasion, (for he drank many Bumpers to the Doctor's Health, as well as to other Toasts) he became very soon literally drunk.

Jones had naturally violent animal Spirits: These being set on float, and augmented by the Spirit of Wine, produced most extravagant Effects. He kissed the Doctor, and embraced him with the most passionate Endearments; swearing that, next to Mr. *Allworthy* himself, he loved him of all Men living. 'Doctor,' added he, 'you deserve a Statue to be erected to you at the public Expence, for having preserved a Man, who is not only the Darling of all good Men who know him, but a Blessing to Society, the Glory of his Country, and an Honour to Human Nature. D——n me if I don't love him better than my own Soul.'

'More Shame for you,' cries *Thwackum*. 'Though I think you have Reason to love him, for he hath provided very well for you. And, perhaps, it might have been better for some Folks, that he had not lived to see just Reason of revoking his Gift.'

Jones now, looking on *Thwackum* with inconceivable Disdain, answered, 'And doth thy mean Soul imagine, that any such Considerations could weigh with me? No, let the Earth open and swallow her own Dirt (if I had Millions of Acres I would say it) rather than swallow up my dear glorious Friend.'

> *Quis Desiderio sit Pudor aut modus*
> *Tam chari Capitis?*[2]

The Doctor now interposed, and prevented the Effects of a Wrath which was kindling between *Jones* and *Thwackum*; after which the former gave a Loose to Mirth, sang two or three amorous Songs, and fell into every frantic Disorder which unbridled Joy is apt to inspire; but so far was he from any Disposition to quarrel, that he was ten times better humoured, if possible, than when he was sober.

To say Truth, Nothing is more erroneous than the common Observation, That Men who are ill-natured and quarrelsome when they are drunk, are very worthy Persons when they are sober: For Drink, in reality, doth not reverse Nature, or create Passions in Men which did not exist in them before. It takes away the Guard of Reason, and consequently forces us to produce those Symptoms which many, when sober, have Art enough to conceal. It heightens and inflames our Passions, (generally indeed that Passion which is uppermost in our Mind) so that the angry Temper, the amorous, the generous, the good-humoured, the avaricious, and all other Dispositions of Men, are in their Cups heightened and exposed.

And yet as no Nation produces so many drunken Quarrels, especially among the lower People, as *England;* (for, indeed, with them, to drink and to fight together, are almost synonymous Terms) I would not, methinks, have it thence concluded, that the *English* are the worst-natured People alive. Perhaps the Love of Glory only is at the Bottom of this; so that the fair Conclusion seems to be, that

---

2. Horace, *Odes* I.xxiv.1–2. ['What Modesty or Measure can set Bounds to our Desire of so dear a friend!' The Word *Desiderium* here cannot be easily trans- lated. It includes our Desire of enjoying our Friend again, and the Grief which attends that Desire.—*Fielding's note.*]

our Countrymen have more of that Love, and more of Bravery, than any other Plebeians. And this the rather, as there is seldom any Thing ungenerous, unfair, or ill-natured, exercised on those Occasions: Nay, it is common for the Combatants to express Good-will for each other, even at the Time of the Conflict; and as their drunken Mirth generally ends in a Battle, so do most of their Battles end in Friendship.

But to return to our History. Though *Jones* had shewn no Design of giving Offence, yet Mr. *Blifil* was highly offended at a Behaviour which was so inconsistent with the sober and prudent Reserve of his own Temper. He bore it too with the greater Impatience, as it appeared to him very indecent at this Season; 'When,' as he said, 'The House was a House of Mourning, on the Account of his dear Mother; and if it had pleased Heaven to give him some Prospect of Mr. *Allworthy*'s Recovery, it would become them better to express the Exultations of their Hearts in Thanksgiving, than in Drunkenness and Riots; which were properer Methods to encrease the Divine Wrath, than to avert it. *Thwackum*, who had swallowed more Liquor than *Jones*, but without any ill Effect on his Brain, seconded the pious Harangue of *Blifil*: But *Square*, for Reasons which the Reader may probably guess, was totally silent.

Wine had not so totally overpowered *Jones*, as to prevent his recollecting Mr. *Blifil*'s Loss, the Moment it was mentioned. As no Person, therefore, was more ready to confess and condemn his own Errors, he offered to shake Mr. *Blifil* by the Hand, and begged his Pardon, saying, 'His excessive Joy for Mr. *Allworthy*'s Recovery had driven every other Thought out of his Mind.'

Blifil scornfully rejected his Hand; and, with much Indignation, answered, 'It was little to be wondered at, if tragical Spectacles made no Impression on the Blind; but, for his Part, he had the Misfortune to know who his Parents were, and consequently must be affected with their Loss.'

Jones, who, notwithstanding his good Humour, had some Mixture of the irascible in his Constitution, leaped hastily from his Chair, and catching hold of *Blifil*'s Collar, cried out, 'D—n you for a Rascal, do you insult me with the Misfortune of my Birth?' He accompanied these Words with such rough Actions, that they soon got the better of Mr. *Blifil*'s peaceful Temper; and a Scuffle immediately ensued, which might have produced Mischief, had it not been prevented by the Interposition of *Thwackum* and the Physician; for the Philosophy of *Square* rendered him superior to all Emotions, and he very calmly smoaked his Pipe, as was his Custom in all Broils, unless when he apprehended some Danger of having it broke in his Mouth.

The Combatants being now prevented from executing present

Vengeance on each other, betook themselves to the common Resources of disappointed Rage, and vented their Wrath in Threats and Defiance. In this Kind of Conflict, Fortune, which in the personal Attack, seemed to incline to *Jones*, was now altogether as favourable to his Enemy.

A Truce, nevertheless, was at length agreed on, by the Mediation of the neutral Parties, and the whole Company again sat down at the Table; where *Jones* being prevailed on to ask Pardon, and *Blifil* to give it, Peace was restored, and every Thing seemed in *Statu quo*.

But though the Quarrel was, in all Appearance, perfectly reconciled, the Good-humour which had been interrupted by it, was by no Means restored. All Merriment was now at an End, and the subsequent Discourse consisted only of grave Relations of Matters of Fact, and of as grave Observations upon them. A Species of Conversation, in which, though there is much of Dignity and Instruction, there is but little Entertainment. As we presume, therefore, to convey only this last to the Reader, we shall pass by whatever was said, till the rest of the Company having, by Degrees, dropped off, left only *Square* and the Physician together; at which Time the Conversation was a little heightened by some Comments on what had happened between the two young Gentlemen; both of whom the Doctor declared to be no better than Scoundrels; to which Appellation the Philosopher, very sagaciously shaking his Head, agreed.

Chapter X.

Shewing the Truth of many Observations of Ovid, *and of other more grave Writers, who have proved, beyond Contradiction, that Wine is often the Fore-runner of Incontinency.*

Jones retired from the Company, in which we have seen him engaged, into the Fields, where he intended to cool himself by a Walk in the open Air, before he attended Mr. *Allworthy*. There, whilst he renewed those Meditations on his dear *Sophia*, which the dangerous Illness of his Friend and Benefactor had for some time interrupted, an Accident happened, which with Sorrow we relate, and with Sorrow, doubtless, will it be read; however, that historic Truth to which we profess so inviolable an Attachment, obliges us to communicate it to Posterity.

It was now a pleasant Evening in the latter End of *June*, when our Heroe was walking in a most delicious Grove, where the gentle Breezes fanning the Leaves, together with the sweet Trilling of a murmuring Stream, and the melodious Notes of Nightingales, formed all together the most enchanting Harmony. In this Scene, so sweetly accommodated to Love, he meditated on his dear *Sophia*. While his wanton Fancy roved unbounded over all her Beauties, and his lively Imagination painted the charming Maid in various ravishing Forms, his warm Heart melted with Tenderness, and at length throwing himself on the Ground, by the Side of a gently murmuring Brook, he broke forth into the following Ejaculation.

'O *Sophia*, would Heaven give thee to my Arms, how blest would be my Condition! Curst be that Fortune which sets a Distance between us. Was I but possessed of thee, one only Suit of Rags thy whole Estate, is there a Man on Earth whom I would envy! How contemptible would the brightest *Circassian* Beauty,[1] drest in all the Jewels of the *Indies*, appear to my Eyes! But why do I mention another Woman? Could I think my Eyes capable of looking at any other with Tenderness, these Hands should tear them from my Head. No, my *Sophia*, if cruel Fortune separates us for ever, my Soul shall doat on thee alone. The chastest Constancy will I ever preserve to thy Image. Though I should never have Possession of thy charming Person, still shalt thou alone have Possession of my Thoughts, my Love, my Soul. Oh! my fond heart is so wrapt in that tender Bosom, that the brightest Beauties would for me have no Charms, nor would a Hermit be colder in their Embraces. *Sophia*, *Sophia* alone shall be mine. What Raptures are in that Name! I will engrave it on every Tree.'

At these Words he started up, and beheld—not his *Sophia*—no, nor a *Circassian* Maid richly and elegantly attired for the Grand Signior's Seraglio. No; without a Gown, in a Shift that was somewhat of the coarsest, and none of the cleanest, bedewed likewise with some odoriferous Effluvia, the Produce of the Day's Labour, with a Pitchfork in her Hand, *Molly Seagrim* approached. Our Heroe had his Penknife in his Hand, which he had drawn for the before-mentioned Purpose of carving on the Bark; when the Girl coming near him, cry'd out with a Smile, 'You don't intend to kill me, Squire, I hope!' 'Why should you think I would kill you?' answered *Jones*. 'Nay,' replied she, 'after your cruel Usage of me when I saw you last, killing me would, perhaps, be too great Kindness for me to expect.'

Here ensued a Parly, which, as I do not think myself obliged to relate it, I shall omit. It is sufficient that it lasted a full Quarter of an Hour, at the Conclusion of which they retired into the thickest Part of the Grove.

Some of my Readers may be inclined to think this Event unnatu-

1. The Circassians, of the northwestern Caucasus, near the Black Sea, were noted for their fierce independence, their constant warfare against Russia, their beauty of feature, their hospitality, and their habit of selling their beautiful daughters, who seemed quite willing, to Turkish dealers for the harems of Eastern kings. See below, p. 425.

ral. However, the Fact is true; and, perhaps, may be sufficiently
accounted for, by suggesting, that *Jones* probably thought one
Woman better than none, and *Molly* as probably imagined two
Men to be better than one. Besides the before-mentioned Motive
assigned to the present Behaviour of *Jones*, the Reader will be likewise pleased to recollect in his Favour, that he was not at this Time
perfect Master of that wonderful Power of Reason, which so well
enabled grave and wise Men to subdue their unruly Passions and to
decline any of these prohibited Amusements. Wine now had totally
subdued this Power in *Jones*. He was, indeed, in a Condition, in
which if Reason had interposed, though only to advise, she might
have received the Answer which one *Cleostratus*[2] gave many Years
ago to a silly Fellow, who asked him, if he was not ashamed to be
drunk? 'Are not you,' said *Cleostratus*, 'ashamed to admonish a
drunken Man?'——To say the Truth, in a Court of Justice, Drunkenness must not be an Excuse, yet in a Court of Conscience it is
greatly so; and therefore *Aristotle*,[3] who commends the Laws of *Pit-
tacus*, by which drunken Men received double Punishment for their
Crimes, allows there is more of Policy than Justice in that Law. Now,
if there are any Transgressions pardonable from Drunkenness, they
are certainly such as Mr. *Jones* was at present guilty of; on which
Head I could pour forth a vast Profusion of Learning, if I imagined
it would either entertain my Reader, or teach him any Thing more
than he knows already. For his Sake, therefore, I shall keep my
Learning to myself, and return to my History.

It hath been observed, that Fortune[4] seldom doth Things by
Halves. To say Truth, there is no End to her Freaks whenever she is
disposed to gratify or displease. No sooner had our Heroe retired
with his *Dido*, but

> *Speluncam* Blifil, *Dux & Divinus eandem*
> *Deveniunt.*——[5]

the Parson and the young Squire, who were taking a serious Walk,
arrived at the Stile which leads into the Grove, and the latter
caught a View of the Lovers, just as they were sinking out of Sight.

Blifil knew *Jones* very well, though he was at above a hundred
Yards Distance, and he was as positive to the Sex of his Companion, though not to the individual Person. He started, blessed himself, and uttered a very solemn Ejaculation.

2. Bryant (pp. 154–55), successful neither in finding the source, nor in identifying the person, offers two Cleostratuses
for further research—(1) the astronomer
who devised the signs of the zodiac, c.
500 B.C., (Theophrastus, *De Signis Pluvi-
arum*, Baid ed., 1541, p. 239, and Pliny,
Historiae Naturalis II.8); (2) the Argive
ambassador mentioned in Xenophon's
History of Greece I.iii.13.

3. *Politica* II.12.
4. See above, p. 109.
5. "Blifil and the divine leader [i.e.,
Thwackum] arrived at the same grotto."
Fielding paraphrases *Aeneid* IV.165–66,
in proper meter: "Speluncam Dido dux
et Troianus eandam / Deveniunt . . ."—
"Dido and the Trojan leader arrived at
the same grotto."

Thwackum expressed some Surprize at these sudden Emotions, and asked the Reason of them. To which *Blifil* answered, 'He was certain he had seen a Fellow and Wench retire together among the Bushes, which he doubted not was with some wicked Purpose.' As to the Name of *Jones* he thought proper to conceal it, and why he did so must be left to the Judgment of the sagacious Reader: For we never chuse to assign Motives to the Actions of Men, when there is any Possibility of our being mistaken.

The Parson, who was not only strictly chaste in his own Person, but a great Enemy to the opposite Vice in all others, fired at this Information. He desired Mr. *Blifil* to conduct him immediately to the Place, which as he approached, he breathed forth Vengeance mixed with Lamentations; nor did he refrain from casting some oblique Reflections on Mr. *Allworthy*; insinuating that the Wickedness of the Country was principally owing to the Encouragement he had given to Vice, by having exerted such kindness to a Bastard, and by having mitigated that just and wholesome Rigour of the Law, which allots a very severe Punishment to loose Wenches.

The Way, through which our Hunters were to pass in Pursuit of their Game, was so beset with Briars, that it greatly obstructed their Walk, and caused, besides, such a Rustling, that *Jones* had sufficient Warning of their Arrival, before they could surprize him; nay, indeed, so incapable was *Thwackum* of concealing his Indignation, and such Vengeance did he mutter forth every Step he took, that this alone must have abundantly satisfied *Jones*, that he was (to use the Language of Sportsmen) *found sitting.*

Chapter XI.

In which a Simile in Mr. Pope's Period of a Mile,[1] introduces as bloody a Battle as can possibly be fought without the Assistance of Steel or cold Iron.

As in the Season of RUTTING (an uncouth Phrase, by which the Vulgar denote that gentle Dalliance, which, in the well-wooded[2] Forest of *Hampshire*, passes between Lovers of the Ferine Kind) if while the lofty crested Stag meditates the amorous Sport, a Couple of Puppies, or any other Beasts of hostile Note, should wander so near the Temple of *Venus Ferina*,[3] that the fair Hind should shrink from the Place, touched with that Somewhat, either of Fear

1. *Satires of Dr. Donne Versified* IV.72–73. A certain pedant asks Pope what writers he esteems. Pope answers, "... *'Swift,* for closer Style / And 'Hoïadlly for a Period of a Mile.'" He is poking fun at Bishop Benjamin Hoadly's mile-long sentences. See above, p. 79.

2. This is an ambiguous Phrase, and may mean either a Forest well cloathed with Wood, or well stript of it [*Fielding's* note].
3. Fielding invents a Goddess of Love for wild animals ("lovers of the ferine kind").

or Frolic, of Nicety or Skittishness, with which Nature hath
bedecked all Females, or hath, at least, instructed them how to put
it on; lest, through the Indelicacy of Males, the *Samian* Mysteries[4]
should be pryed into by unhallowed Eyes: For at the Celebration of
these Rites, the female Priestess cries out with her in *Virgil,* (who
was then, probably, hard at Work on such Celebration)

—*Procul, O procul este, profani;*
Proclamat Vates, totoque absistite Luco.[5]

—Far hence be Souls prophane,
The Sibyl cry'd, and from the Grove abstain.
DRYDEN.

If, I say, while these sacred Rites, which are in common to
Genus omne Animantium,[6] are in Agitation between the Stag and
his Mistress, any hostile Beasts should venture too near, on the first
Hint given by the frighted Hind, fierce and tremendous rushes forth
the Stag to the Entrance of the Thicket; there stands he Centinel
over his Love, stamps the Ground with his Foot, and with his Horns
brandished aloft in Air, proudly provokes the apprehended Foe to
Combat.

Thus, and more terrible, when he perceived the Enemy's
Approach, leaped forth our Heroe. Many a Step advanced he forwards, in order to conceal the trembling Hind, and, if possible, to
secure her Retreat. And now *Thwackum* having first darted some
livid Lightning from his fiery Eyes, began to thunder forth, 'Fie
upon it! Fie upon it! Mr. *Jones.* Is it possible you should be the
Person!' 'You see,' answered *Jones,* 'it is possible I should be here.'
'And who,' said *Thwackum,* 'is that wicked Slut with you?' 'If I
have any wicked Slut with me,' cries *Jones,* 'it is possible I shall not
let you know who she is.' 'I command you to tell me immediately,'
says *Thwackum,* 'and I would not have you imagine, young Man,
that your Age, though it hath somewhat abridged the Purpose of
Tuition, hath totally taken away the Authority of the Master. The
Relation of the Master and Scholar is indelible, as, indeed, all other
Relations are: For they all derive their Original from Heaven. I
would have you think yourself, therefore, as much obliged to obey
me now, as when I taught you your first Rudiments.' 'I believe you
would,' cries *Jones,* 'but that will not happen, unless you had the
same Birchen Argument to convince me.' 'Then I must tell you

4. The island of Samos, the most important center for the worship of Hera, the
goddess of marriage, sanctioned sexual
intercourse by betrothed couples, similar
to that of Zeus and Hera before marriage.
5. *Aeneid* VI.258–59. Fielding's *Procla-*

mat reads *Conclamat.* The Cumaean
Sibyl is using a formula common to religious mysteries to warn Aeneas's soldiers
that they may not follow him on his
visit to his dead father in the underworld.
6. "Every kind of living creature."

plainly,' said *Thwackum*, 'I am resolved to discover the wicked Wretch.' 'And I must tell you plainly,' returned *Jones*, 'I am resolved you shall not.' *Thwackum* then offered to advance, and *Jones* laid hold of his Arms; which Mr. *Blifil* endeavoured to rescue, declaring 'he would not see his old Master insulted.'

Jones now finding himself engaged with two, thought it necessary to rid himself of one of his Antagonists as soon as possible. He, therefore, applied to the weakest first; and letting the Parson go, he directed a Blow at the young Squire's Breast, which luckily taking place, reduced him to measure his Length on the Ground.

Thwackum was so intent on the Discovery, that the Moment he found himself at Liberty, he stept forward directly into the Fern, without any great Consideration of what might, in the mean time, befal his Friend; but he had advanced a very few Paces into the Thicket, before *Jones* having defeated *Blifil*, overtook the Parson, and dragged him backward by the Skirt of his Coat.

This Parson had been a Champion in his Youth, and had won much Honour by his Fist, both at School and at the University. He had now, indeed, for a great Number of Years, declined the Practice of that noble Art; yet was his Courage full as strong as his Faith, and his Body no less strong than either. He was moreover, as the Reader may, perhaps, have conceived, somewhat irascible in his Nature. When he looked back, therefore, and saw his Friend stretched out on the Ground, and found himself at the same time so roughly handled by one who had formerly been only passive in all Conflicts between them, (a Circumstance which highly aggravated the whole) his Patience at length gave way; he threw himself into a Posture of Offence, and collecting all his Force, attacked *Jones* in the Front, with as much Impetuosity as he had formerly attacked him in the Rear.

Our Heroe received the Enemy's Attack with the most undaunted Intrepidity, and his Bosom resounded with the Blow. This he presently returned with no less Violence, aiming likewise at the Parson's Breast; but he dextrously drove down the Fist of *Jones*, so that it reached only his Belly, where two Pounds of Beef and as many of Pudding were then deposited, and whence consequently no hollow Sound could proceed. Many lusty Blows, much more pleasant as well as easy to have seen, than to read or describe, were given on both Sides; at last a violent Fall in which *Jones* had thrown his Knees into *Thwackum*'s Breast, so weakened the latter, that Victory had been no longer dubious, had not *Blifil*, who had now recovered his Strength, again renewed the Fight, and, by engaging with *Jones*, given the Parson a Moment's time to shake his Ears, and to regain his Breath.

And now both together attacked our Heroe, whose Blows did not retain that Force with which they had fallen at first; so weakened was he by his Combat with *Thwackum*: For though the Pedagogue chose rather to play *Solos* on the human Instrument, and had been lately used to those only, yet he still retained enough of his antient Knowledge to perform his Part very well in a *Duet*.

The Victory, according to modern Custom, was like to be decided by Numbers, when, on a sudden, a fourth Pair of Fists appeared in the Battle, and immediately paid their Compliments to the Parson; and the Owner of them, at the same time, crying out, 'Are not you ashamed and be d—nd to you, to fall two of you upon one?'

The Battle, which was of the kind, that for Distinction's sake is called Royal, now raged with the utmost Violence during a few Minutes; till *Blifil* being a second time laid sprawling by *Jones*, *Thwackum* condescended to apply for Quarter to his new Antagonist, who was now found to be Mr. *Western* himself: For in the Heat of the Action none of the Combatants had recognized him.

In fact, that honest Squire, happening in his Afternoon's Walk with some Company, to pass through the Field where the bloody Battle was fought, and having concluded from seeing three Men engaged, that two of them must be on a Side, he hastened from his Companions, and with more Gallantry than Policy, espoused the Cause of the weaker Party. By which generous Proceeding, he very probably prevented Mr. *Jones* from becoming a Victim to the Wrath of *Thwackum*, and to the pious Friendship which *Blifil* bore his old Master: For besides the Disadvantage of such Odds, *Jones* had not yet sufficiently recovered the former Strength of his broken Arm. This Reinforcement, however, soon put an End to the Action, and *Jones* with his Ally obtained the Victory.

Chapter XII.

In which is seen a more moving Spectacle, than all the Blood in the Bodies of Thwackum *and* Blifil *and of Twenty other such, is capable of producing.*

The rest of Mr. *Western*'s Company were now come up, being just at the Instant when the Action was over. These were the honest Clergyman, whom we have formerly seen at Mr. *Western*'s Table, Mrs. *Western* the Aunt of *Sophia*; and lastly, the lovely *Sophia* herself.

At this time, the following was the Aspect of the bloody Field. In one Place, lay on the Ground, all pale and almost breathless, the vanquished *Blifil*. Near him stood the Conqueror *Jones*, almost covered with Blood, part of which was naturally his own, and Part had been lately the Property of the Reverend Mr. *Thwackum*. In a third Place stood the said *Thwackum*, like King *Porus*,[1] sullenly submitting to the Conqueror. The last Figure in the Piece was *Western the Great*, most gloriously forbearing the vanquished Foe.

Blifil, in whom there was little Sign of Life, was at first the principal Object of the Concern of every one, and particularly of Mrs. *Western*, who had drawn from her Pocket a Bottle of Hartshorn, and was herself about to apply it to his Nostrils; when on a sudden the Attention of the whole Company was diverted from poor *Blifil*, whose Spirit, if it had any such Design, might have now taken an Opportunity of stealing off to the other World, without any Ceremony.

For now a more melancholy and a more lovely Object lay motionless before them. This was no other than the charming *Sophia* herself, who, from the Sight of Blood, or from Fear for her Father, or from some other Reason, had fallen down in a Swoon, before any one could get to her Assistance.

Mrs. *Western* first saw her, and screamed. Immediately two or three Voices cried out, 'Miss *Western* is dead.' Hartshorn, Water, every Remedy was called for, almost at one and the same Instant.

The Reader may remember, that in our Description of this Grove we mentioned a murmuring Brook, which Brook did not come there, as such gentle Streams flow through vulgar Romances, with no other Purpose than to murmur. No; Fortune had decreed to enoble this little Brook with a higher Honour than any of those which wash the Plains of *Arcadia*, ever deserved.

Jones was rubbing *Blifil*'s Temples: For he began to fear he had given him a Blow too much, when the Words, Miss *Western* and *Dead*, rushed at once on his Ear. He started up, left *Blifil* to his Fate, and flew to *Sophia*, whom, while all the rest were running against each other backward and forward looking for Water in the dry Paths, he caught up in his Arms, and then ran away with her over the Field to the Rivulet above mentioned; where, plunging himself into the Water, he contrived to besprinkle her Face, Head, and Neck very plentifully.

Happy was it for *Sophia*, that the same Confusion which prevented her other Friends from serving her, prevented them likewise from obstructing *Jones*. He had carried her half ways before they knew what he was doing, and he had actually restored her to Life before they reached the Water-side: She stretched out her Arms, opened her Eyes, and cried, 'Oh, Heavens!' just as her Father, Aunt, and the Parson came up.

---

1. An Indian king, nearly seven feet tall, who so well resisted Alexander's invasion of his country that Alexander let him keep his kingdom, increased his territo-ries, and made him a satrap. Fielding may have had a current opera in mind (see the essay by Frederick W. Hilles, below, p. 928).

Jones, who had hitherto held this lovely Burthen in his Arms, now relinquished his Hold; but gave her at the same Instant a tender Caress, which, had her Senses been then perfectly restored, could not have escaped her Observation. As she expressed, therefore, no Displeasure at this Freedom, we suppose she was not sufficiently recovered from her Swoon at the Time.

This tragical Scene was now converted into a sudden Scene of Joy. In this, our Heroe was, most certainly, the principal Character: For as he probably felt more ecstatic Delight in having saved *Sophia,* than she herself received from being saved; so neither were the Congratulations paid to her equal to what were conferred on *Jones,* especially by Mr. *Western* himself, who, after having once or twice embraced his Daughter, fell to hugging and kissing *Jones.* He called him the Preserver of *Sophia,* and declared there was nothing, except her, or his Estate, which he would not give him; but upon Recollection, he afterwards excepted his Fox-hounds, the *Chevalier,* and Miss *Slouch* (for so he called his favourite Mare.)

All Fears for *Sophia* being now removed, *Jones* became the Object of the Squire's Consideration. 'Come, my Lad,' says *Western,* 'D'off thy *Quoat* and wash thy *Feace*: For *att* in a devilish Pickle, I promise thee. Come, come, wash thyself, and *shat* go *Huome* with me; and *we'l zee* to *vind* thee another *Quoat.*'

Jones immediately complied, threw off his Coat, went down to the Water, and washed both his Face and Bosom: For the latter was as much exposed, and as bloody as the former: But tho' the Water could clear off the Blood, it could not remove the black and blue Marks which *Thwackum* had imprinted on both his Face and Breast, and which, being discerned by *Sophia,* drew from her a Sigh, and a Look full of inexpressible Tenderness.

Jones received this full in his Eyes, and it had infinitely a stronger Effect on him than all the Contusions which he had received before. An Effect, however, widely different; for so soft and balmy was it, that, had all his former Blows been Stabs, it would for some Minutes have prevented his feeling their Smart.

The Company now moved backwards, and soon arrived where *Thwackum* had got Mr. *Blifil* again on his Legs. Here we cannot suppress a pious Wish, that all Quarrels were to be decided by those Weapons only, with which Nature, knowing what is proper for us, hath supplied us; and that cold Iron was to be used in digging no Bowels, but those of the Earth. Then would War, the Pasttime of Monarchs, be almost inoffensive, and Battles between great Armies might be fought at the particular Desire of several Ladies of Quality; who, together with the Kings themselves, might be actual Spectators of the Conflict. Then might the Field be this Moment well strewed with human Carcasses, and the next, the dead Men, or infinitely the greatest Part of them, might get up, like Mr. *Bayes's*

Troops,[2] and march off either at the Sound of a Drum or Fiddle, as should be previously agreed on.

I would avoid, if possible, treating this Matter ludicrously, lest grave Men and Politicians, whom I know to be offended at a Jest, may cry Pish at it; but, in reality, might not a Battle be as well decided by the greater Number of broken Heads, bloody Noses, and black Eyes, as by the greater Heaps of mangled and murdered human Bodies? Might not Towns be contended for in the same manner? Indeed, this may be thought too detrimental a Scheme to the *French* Interest, since they would thus lose the Advantage they have over other Nations, in the Superiority of their Engineers: But when I consider the Gallantry and Generosity of that People, I am persuaded they would never decline putting themselves upon a Par with their Adversary; or, as the Phrase is, *making themselves his Match*.

But such Reformations are rather to be wished than hoped for: I shall content myself, therefore, with this short Hint, and return to my Narrative.

Western began now to enquire into the original Rise of this Quarrel. To which neither *Blifil* nor *Jones* gave any Answer; but *Thwackum* said surlily, 'I believe, the Cause is not far off; if you beat the Bushes well, you may find her.' 'Find her!' replied *Western*, 'what, have you been fighting for a Wench?' 'Ask the Gentleman in his Wastecoat there,' said *Thwackum*, 'he best knows.' 'Nay, then,' cries *Western*, 'it is a Wench certainly—Ay, *Tom, Tom*; thou art a liquorish[3] Dog———but come, Gentlemen, be all Friends, and go home with me, and make final Peace over a Bottle.' 'I ask your Pardon, Sir,' says *Thwackum*, 'it is no such slight Matter for a Man of my Character to be thus injuriously treated, and buffeted by a Boy; only because I would have done my Duty, in endeavouring to detect and bring to Justice a wanton Harlot; but, indeed, the principal Fault lies in Mr. *Allworthy* and yourself: For, if you put the Laws in Execution, as you ought to do, you will soon rid the Country of these Vermin.'

'I would as soon rid the Country of Foxes,' cries *Western*. 'I think we ought to encourage the recruiting those Numbers which we are every Day losing in the War: But where is she?———Prithee, *Tom*, shew me.' He then began to beat about, in the same Language, and in the same Manner, as if he had been beating for a Hare, and at last cried out, 'Soho! Puss is not far off. Here's her Form, upon my Soul; I believe I may cry *stole away*.' And indeed so he might, for he had now discovered the Place whence the poor

2. In *The Rehearsal* (1671) by Buckingham *et al.*, Mr. Bayes, a caricature of Poet Laureate John Dryden, stops the music and announces, after his soldiers onstage have all killed each other, "Now here's an odd surprise: all these dead men you see shall rise up presently, at a certain Note that I have made, in *Effaut flat*, and fall a dancing" (II.v.).
3. A variant of "lecherous."

Girl had, at the Beginning of the Fray, *stolen away*, upon as many Feet as a Hare generally uses in travelling.

Sophia now desired her Father to return home; saying, she found herself very faint, and apprehended a Relapse. The Squire immediately complied with his Daughter's Request, (for he was the fondest of Parents.) He earnestly endeavoured to prevail with the whole Company to go and sup with him; but *Blifil* and *Thwackum* absolutely refused; the former saying, There were more Reasons than he could then mention, why he must decline this Honour; and the latter declaring (perhaps rightly) that it was not proper for a Person of his Function to be seen at any Place in his present Condition.

Jones was incapable of refusing the Pleasure of being with his *Sophia*. So on he marched with Squire *Western* and his Ladies, the Parson bringing up the Rear. This had, indeed, offered to tarry with his Brother *Thwackum*, professing his Regard for the Cloth would not permit him to depart; but *Thwackum* would not accept the Favour, and, with no great Civility, pushed him after Mr. *Western*.

Thus ended this bloody Fray; and thus shall end the fifth Book of this History.

BOOK VI.

Containing about three Weeks.

Chapter I.

Of Love.

In our last Book we have been obliged to deal pretty much with the Passion of Love; and, in our succeeding Book, shall be forced to handle this Subject still more largely. It may not, therefore, in this Place, be improper to apply ourselves to the Examination of that modern Doctrine, by which certain Philosophers, among many other wonderful Discoveries, pretend to have found out, that there is no such Passion in the human Breast.

Whether these Philosophers be the same with that surprising Sect, who are honourably mentioned by the late Dr. *Swift*;[1] as having, by

1. *An Argument Against Abolishing Christianity* (1710)—'For it is confidently reported, that two young Gentlemen of real Hopes, bright Wit, and profound Judgment, who, upon a thorough Examination of Causes and Effects, and by the mere Force of natural Abilities, without the least Tincture of Learning, have made a Discovery, that there was no God, and generously communicating their Thoughts for the Good of the Public, were some Time ago, by an unparallel'd Severity, and upon I know not what obsolete Law, Broke for Blasphemy.'

the mere Force of Genius alone, without the least Assistance of any Kind of Learning, or even Reading, discovered that profound and invaluable Secret, That there is no God: or whether they are not rather the same with those who, some Years since, very much alarmed the World, by shewing that there were no such Things as Virtue or Goodness really existing in Human Nature, and who deduced our best Actions from Pride, I will not here presume to determine. In reality, I am inclined to suspect, that all these several Finders of Truth are the very identical Men, who are by others called the *Finders of Gold.*[2] The Method used in both these Searches after Truth and after Gold, being indeed one and the same; *viz.* the searching, rummaging, and examining into a nasty Place; indeed, in the former Instances, into the nastiest of all Places, A BAD MIND.

But though, in this Particular, and perhaps in their Success, the Truth-finder, and the Gold-finder, may very properly be compared together; yet in Modesty, surely, there can be no Comparison between the two; for who ever heard of a Gold-finder that had the Impudence or Folly to assert, from the ill Success of his Search, that there was no such thing as Gold in the World? Whereas the Truth-finder, having raked out that *Jakes*, his own Mind, and being there capable of tracing no Ray of Divinity, nor any thing virtuous, or good, or lovely, or loving, very fairly, honestly, and logically concludes, that no such things exist in the whole Creation.

To avoid, however, all Contention, if possible, with these Philosophers, if they will be called so; and to shew our own Disposition to accommodate Matters peaceably between us, we shall here make them some Concessions, which may possibly put an End to the Dispute.

First, we will grant that many Minds, and perhaps those of the Philosophers, are entirely free from the least Traces of such a Passion.

Secondly, That what is commonly called Love, namely, the Desire of satisfying a voracious Appetite with a certain Quantity of delicate white human Flesh, is by no means that Passion for which I here contend. This is indeed more properly Hunger; and as no Glutton is ashamed to apply the Word Love to his Appetite, and to say he LOVES such and such Dishes; so may the Lover of this Kind, with equal Propriety say, he HUNGERS after such and such Women.

Thirdly, I will grant, which I believe will be a most acceptable Concession, that this Love for which I am an Advocate, though it satisfies itself in a much more delicate Manner, doth nevertheless seek its own Satisfaction as much as the grossest of all our Appetites.

2. A euphemism for the cleaners of privies (Mutter).

And, Lastly, That this Love, when it operates towards one of a different Sex, is very apt, towards its complete Gratification, to call in the Aid of that Hunger which I have mentioned above; and which it is so far from abating, that it heightens all its Delights to a Degree scarce imaginable by those who have never been susceptible of any other Emotions, than what have proceeded from Appetite alone.

In return to all these Concessions, I desire of the Philosophers to grant, that there is in some (I believe in many) human Breasts, a kind and benevolent Disposition, which is gratified by contributing to the Happiness of others. That in this Gratification alone, as in Friendship, in parental and filial Affection, as indeed in general Philanthrophy, there is a great and exquisite Delight. That if we will not call such Disposition Love, we have no Name for it. That though the Pleasures arising from such pure Love may be heightened and sweetened by the Assistance of amorous Desires, yet the former can subsist alone, nor are they destroyed by the Intervention of the latter. Lastly, That Esteem and Gratitude are the proper Motives to Love, as Youth and Beauty are to Desire; and therefore though such Desire may naturally cease, when Age or Sickness overtakes its Object; yet these can have no Effect on Love, nor ever shake or remove from a good Mind, that Sensation or Passion which hath Gratitude and Esteem for its Basis.

To deny the Existence of a Passion of which we often see manifest Instances, seems to be very strange and absurd; and can indeed proceed only from that Self-Admonition which we have mentioned above: But how unfair is this? Doth the Man who recognizes in his own Heart no Traces of Avarice or Ambition, conclude therefore that there are no such Passions in Human Nature? Why will we not modestly observe the same Rule in judging of the Good, as well as the Evil of others? Or why, in any Case, will we, as *Shakespear*[3] phrases it, 'put the World in our own Person?'

Predominant Vanity is, I am afraid, too much concerned here. This is one Instance of that Adulation which we bestow on our own Minds, and this almost universally. For there is scarce any Man, how much soever he may despise the Character of a Flatterer, but will condescend in the meanest Manner to flatter himself.

To those, therefore, I apply for the Truth of the above Observations, whose own Minds can bear Testimony to what I have advanced.

Examine your Heart, my good Reader, and resolve whether you do believe these Matters with me. If you do, you may now proceed to their Exemplification in the following Pages; if you do not, you

3. *Much Ado about Nothing* II.i.215–16 —"It is the base (though bitter) disposi-   tion of Beatrice that puts the world into her person. . . ."

have, I assure you, already read more than you have understood;
and it would be wiser to pursue your Business, or your Pleasures
(such as they are) than to throw away any more of your Time in
reading what you can neither taste nor comprehend. To treat of the
Effects of Love to you, must be as absurd as to discourse on Colours
to a Man born blind; since possibly your Idea of Love may be as
absurd as that which we are told such blind Man once entertained
of the Colour Scarlet: that Colour seemed to him to be very much
like the Sound of a Trumpet; and Love probably may, in your
Opinion, very greatly resemble a Dish of Soup, or a Sir-loin of
Roast-beef.

Chapter II.

*The Character of Mrs. Western. Her great Learning and Knowl-
edge of the World, and an Instance of the deep Penetration which
she derived from those Advantages.*

The Reader hath seen Mr. Western, his Sister and Daughter,
with young *Jones*, and the Parson, going together to Mr. Western's
House, where the greater Part of the Company spent the Evening
with much Joy and Festivity. *Sophia* was indeed the only grave
Person: For as to *Jones*, though Love had now gotten entire Possession of his Heart, yet the pleasing Reflection on Mr. *Allworthy*'s
Recovery, and the Presence of his Mistress, joined to some tender
Looks which she now and then could not refrain from giving him,
so elevated our Heroe, that he joined the Mirth of the other three,
who were perhaps as good-humoured People as any in the World.

Sophia retained the same Gravity of Countenance the next
Morning at Breakfast; whence she retired likewise earlier than usual,
leaving her Father and Aunt together. The Squire took no Notice of
this Change in his Daughter's Disposition. To say the Truth,
though he was somewhat of a Politician, and had been twice a Candidate in the Country Interest at an Election, he was a Man of no
great Observation. His Sister was a Lady of a different Turn. She
had lived about the Court, and had seen the World. Hence she had
acquired all that Knowledge which the said World usually communicates; and was a perfect Mistress of Manners, Customs, Ceremonies, and Fashions; nor did her Erudition stop here. She had considerably improved her Mind by Study; she had not only read all the
modern Plays, Operas, Oratorios, Poems and Romances; in all
which she was a Critic; but had gone thro' *Rapin*'s[1] History of
England, Eachard's Roman History, and many *French Memoires*

1. See above, p. 29. Laurence Echard   *Roman History* in 1718.
(the accepted spelling) published his

pour servir à l' Histoire; to these she had added most of the political Pamphlets and Journals, published within the last twenty Years. From which she had attained a very competent Skill in Politics, and could discourse very learnedly on the Affairs of *Europe*. She was moreover excellently well skilled in the Doctrine of Amour, and knew better than any Body who and who were together: A Knowledge which she the more easily attained, as her Pursuit of it was never diverted by any Affairs of her own; for either she had no Inclinations, or they had never been sollicited; which last is indeed very probable: For her masculine Person, which was near six Foot high, added to her Manner and Learning, possibly prevented the other Sex from regarding her, notwithstanding her Petticoats, in the Light of a Woman. However, as she had considered the Matter scientifically, she perfectly well knew, though she had never practised them, all the Arts which fine Ladies use when they desire to give Encouragement, or to conceal Liking, with all the long Appendage of Smiles, Ogles, Glances, &c. as they are at present practised in the Beau-monde. To sum the whole, no Species of Disguise or Affectation had escaped her Notice; but as to the plain simple Workings of honest Nature, as she had never seen any such, she could know but little of them.

By means of this wonderful Sagacity, Mrs. *Western* had now, as she thought, made a Discovery of something in the Mind of *Sophia*. The first Hint of this she took from the Behaviour of the young Lady in the Field of Battle; and the Suspicion which she then conceived, was greatly corroborated by some Observations which she had made that Evening and the next Morning. However, being greatly cautious to avoid being found in a Mistake, she carried the Secret a whole Fortnight in her Bosom, giving only some oblique Hints, by Simperings, Winks, Nods, and now and then dropping an obscure Word, which indeed sufficiently alarmed *Sophia*, but did not at all affect her Brother.

Being at length, however, thoroughly satisfied of the Truth of her Observation, she took an Opportunity, one Morning, when she was alone with her Brother, to interrupt one of his Whistles in the following Manner:

'Pray, Brother, have you not observed something very extraordinary in my Niece lately?' 'No, not I,' answered *Western*; 'Is any thing the Matter with the Girl?' 'I think there is,' replies she, 'and something of much Consequence too.' 'Why she doth not complain of any thing,' cries *Western*, 'and she hath had the Small Pox.' 'Brother,' returned she, 'Girls are liable to other Distempers besides the Small Pox, and sometimes possibly to much worse.' Here *Western* interrupted her with much Earnestness, and begged her, if any thing ailed his Daughter, to acquaint him immediately, adding, 'she

knew he loved her more than his own Soul, and that he would send
to the World's End for the best Physician to her.' 'Nay, nay,'
answered she, smiling, 'the Distemper is not so terrible; but I
believe, Brother, you are convinced I know the World, and I promise you I was never more deceived in my Life, if my Niece be not
most desperately in Love.' 'How! in Love,' cries *Western*, in a Passion, 'in Love without acquainting me! I'll disinherit her, I'll turn
her out of Doors, stark naked, without a Farthing. Is all my kindness vor 'ur, and vondness o'ur come to this, to fall in Love without
asking me Leave!' 'But you will not,' answered Mrs. *Western*, 'turn
this Daughter, whom you love better than your own Soul, out of
Doors, before you know whether you shall approve her Choice. Suppose she should have fixed on the very Person whom you yourself
would wish, I hope you would not be angry then.' 'No, no,' cries
Western, 'that would make a Difference. If she marries the Man I
would ha' her, she may love whom she pleases, I shan't trouble my
Head about that.' 'That is spoken,' answered the Sister, 'like a sensible Man, but I believe the very Person she hath chosen, would be
the very Person you would chuse for her. I will disclaim all Knowledge of the World if it is not so; and I believe, Brother, you will
allow I have some.' 'Why lookee, Sister,' said *Western*, 'I do believe
you have as much as any Woman; and to be sure those are
Women's Matters. You know I don't love to hear you talk about
Politics, they belong to us, and Petticoats should not meddle: But
come, who is the Man?' 'Marry!' said she, 'you may find him out
yourself, if you please. You who are so great a Politician, can be at
no great Loss. The Judgment which can penetrate into the Cabinets
of Princes, and discover the secret Springs which move the great
State Wheels in all the political Machines of *Europe*, must surely,
with very little Difficulty find out what passes in the rude unin-
formed Mind of a Girl.' 'Sister,' cries the Squire, 'I have often
warned you not to talk the Court Gibberish to me. I tell you, I
don't understand the Lingo; but I can read a Journal, or the
London Evening-Post.[2] Perhaps indeed, there may be now and tan
a Verse which I can't make much of, because half the Letters are
left out; yet I know very well what is meant by that, and that our
Affairs don't go so well as they should do, because of Bribery and
Corruption.' 'I pity your Country Ignorance from my Heart,' cries
the Lady. 'Do you?' answered *Western*, 'and I pity your Town
Learning; I had rather be any thing than a Courtier, and a Presbyterian, and a *Hanoverian* too, as some People, I believe, are.' 'If you
mean me,' answered she, 'you know I am a Woman, Brother; and it

2. A Tory newspaper, critical of the
Whig government. As he was writing
Tom Jones, Fielding was also battling
with *The London Evening-Post*, and others, in his weekly newspaper, *The Jacobite's Journal* (5 Dec. 1747 to 5 Nov.
1748).

signifies nothing what I am. Besides——'I do know you are a Woman,' cries the Squire, 'and its well for thee, that art one; if hadst been a Man, I promise thee I had lent thee a *Flick* long ago.' 'Ay there,' said she, 'In that *Flick* lies all your fancied Superiority. Your Bodies, and not your Brains, are stronger than ours. Believe me, it is well for you that you are able to beat us; or, such is the Superiority of our Understanding, we should make all of you what the brave, and wise, and witty, and polite are already,—our Slaves.' 'I am glad I know your Mind,' answered the Squire, 'but we'll talk more of this Matter another Time. At present, do tell me what Man is it you mean about my Daughter.' 'Hold a Moment,' said she, 'while I digest that sovereign Contempt I have for your Sex; or else I ought to be angry too with you. There——I have made a Shift to gulp it down. And now, good politic Sir, what think you of Mr. *Blifil*? Did she not faint away on seeing him lie breathless on the Ground? Did she not, after he was recovered, turn pale again the Moment we came up to that Part of the Field where he stood? And pray what else should be the Occasion of all her Melancholy that Night at Supper, the next Morning, and indeed ever since?' 'Fore *George!*' cries the Squire, 'now you mind me on't, I remember it all. It is certainly so, and I am glad on't, with all my Heart. I knew *Sophy* was a good Girl, and would not fall in Love to make me angry. I was never more rejoiced in my Life: For nothing can lie so handy together as our two Estates. I had this Matter in my Head some Time ago; for certainly the two Estates are in a Manner joined together in Matrimony already, and it would be a thousand Pities to part them. It is true indeed, there be larger Estates in the Kingdom, but not in this County, and I had rather bate something, than marry my Daughter among Strangers and Foreigners. Besides most o'zuch great Estates be in the Hands of Lords, and I heate the very Name of *themmun*. Well but, Sister, what would you advise me to do: For I tell you Women know these Matters better than we do?' 'O your humble Servant, Sir,' answered the Lady, 'we are obliged to you for allowing us a Capacity in any Thing. Since you are pleased then, most politic Sir, to ask my Advice, I think you may propose the Match to *Allworthy* yourself. There is no Indecorum in the Proposal's coming from the Parent of either Side.' King *Alcinous*, in Mr. *Pope*'s Odyssey,[3] offers his Daughter to *Ulysses*. I need not caution so politic a Person not to say that your Daughter is in Love; that would indeed be against all Rules.' 'Well,' said the Squire, 'I will propose it; but I shall certainly lend un a *Flick*, if he should refuse me.' 'Fear not,' cries Mrs. *Western*, 'the Match is too advantageous to be refused.' 'I don't know that,' answered the Squire, '*Allworthy* is a queer B—ch, and

3. VII.398–402.

Money hath no Effect o'un.' 'Brother,' said the Lady, 'your Politics astonish me. Are you really to be imposed on by Professions? Do you think Mr. *Allworthy* hath more Contempt for Money than other Men, because he professes more? Such Credulity would better become one of us weak Women, than that wise Sex which Heaven hath formed for Politicians. Indeed, Brother, you would make a fine Plenipo to negotiate with the *French*. They would soon persuade you, that they take Towns out of mere defensive Principles.' 'Sister,' answered the Squire, with much Scorn, 'let your Friends at Court answer for the Towns taken; as you are a Woman, I shall lay no Blame upon you: For I suppose they are wiser than to trust Women with Secrets.' He accompanied this with so sarcastical a Laugh, that Mrs. *Western* could bear no longer. She had been all this Time fretted in a tender Part (for she was indeed very deeply skilled in these Matters, and very violent in them) and therefore burst forth in a Rage, declared her Brother to be both a Clown and a Blockhead, and that she would stay no longer in his House.

The Squire, tho' perhaps he had never read *Machiavel*, was, however, in many Points, a perfect Politician. He strongly held all those wise Tenets, which are so well inculcated in that Politico-Peripatetic School of *Exchange-Alley*.[4] He knew the just Value and only Use of Money, *viz.* to lay it up. He was likewise well skilled in the exact Value of Reversions, Expectations, *&c.* and had often considered the Amount of his Sister's Fortune, and the Chance which he or his Posterity had of inheriting it. This he was infinitely too wise to sacrifice to a trifling Resentment. When he found, therefore, he had carried Matters too far, he began to think of reconciling them; which was no very difficult Task, as the Lady had great Affection for her Brother, and still greater for her Niece; and tho' too susceptible of an Affront offered to her Skill in Politics, on which she much valued herself, was a Woman of a very extraordinary good and sweet Disposition.

Having first, therefore, laid violent Hands on the Horses, for whose Escape from the Stable no Place but the Window was left open; he next applied himself to his Sister, softened and soothed her, by unsaying all he had said, and by Assertions directly contrary to those which had incensed her. Lastly, he summoned the Eloquence of *Sophia* to his Assistance, who, besides a most graceful and winning Address, had the Advantage of being heard with great Favour and Partiality by her Aunt.

The Result of the Whole was a kind Smile from Mrs. *Western*,

---

4. Fielding invents a name for pounds-and-pence philosophy: London's Exchange Alley represents the universal marketplace; "Politico" represents the political interest therein; 'Peripatetic" was Aristotle's practical school of philosophy, so called from his habit of walking up and down in the Lyceum Garden in Athens while teaching.

who said, 'Brother, you are absolutely a perfect *Croat*;[5] but as those
have their use in the Army of the Empress Queen, so you likewise
have some Good in you. I will therefore once more sign a Treaty of
Peace with you, and see that you do not infringe it on your Side; at
least, as you are so excellent a Politician, I may expect you will keep
your Leagues, like the *French*, till your Interest calls upon you to
break them.'

Chapter III.

Containing two Defiances to the Critics.

The Squire having settled Matters with his Sister, as we have
seen in the last Chapter, was so greatly impatient to communicate
the Proposal to *Allworthy*, that Mrs. *Western* had the utmost
Difficulty to prevent him from visiting that Gentleman in his Sickness, for this Purpose.

Mr. *Allworthy* had been engaged to dine with Mr. *Western* at the
Time when he was taken ill. He was, therefore, no sooner discharged out of the Custody of Physic, but he thought (as was usual
with him on all Occasions, both the highest and the lowest) of fulfilling his Engagement.

In the Interval between the Time of the Dialogue in the last
Chapter, and this Day of public Entertainment, *Sophia* had, from
certain obscure Hints thrown out by her Aunt, collected some
Apprehension that the sagacious Lady suspected her Passion for
Jones. She now resolved to take this Opportunity of wiping out all
such Suspicion, and for that Purpose put an entire Constraint on
her Behaviour.

First she endeavoured to conceal a throbbing melancholy Heart
with the utmost Sprightliness in her Countenance, and the highest
Gaiety in her Manner. Secondly, she addressed her whole Discourse
to Mr. *Blifil*, and took not the least Notice of poor *Jones* the whole
Day.

The Squire was so delighted with this Conduct of his Daughter,
that he scarce eat any Dinner, and spent almost his whole Time in
watching Opportunities of conveying Signs of his Approbation by
Winks and Nods to his Sister; who was not at first altogether so
pleased with what she saw as was her Brother.

In short, *Sophia* so greatly overacted her Part, that her Aunt was
at first staggered, and began to suspect some Affectation in her
Niece; but as she was herself a Woman of great Art, so she soon
attributed this to extreme Art in *Sophia*. She remembered the many

5. Maria Theresa of Austria used Croa-
tian troops in the War of the Spanish   Succession (1701–14); they were reput-
edly fierce and barbaric.

Hints she had given her Niece concerning her being in Love, and
imagined the young Lady had taken this Way to rally her out of her
Opinion, by an overacted Civility; a Notion that was greatly corroborated by the excessive Gaiety with which the whole was accompanied. We cannot here avoid remarking that this Conjecture would
have been better founded, had *Sophia* lived ten Years in the Air of
Grosvenor-square, where young Ladies do learn a wonderful Knack
of rallying and playing with that Passion, which is a mighty serious
Thing, in Woods and Groves an hundred Miles distant from
London.

To say the Truth, in discovering the Deceit of others, it matters
much that our own Art be wound up, if I may use the Expression,
in the same Key with theirs: For very artful Men sometimes mis-
carry by fancying others wiser, or in other Words, greater Knaves
than they really are. As this Observation is pretty deep, I will illustrate it by the following short Story. Three Countrymen were pursuing a *Wiltshire* Thief through *Brentford*. The simplest of them
seeing the *Wiltshire House* written under a Sign, advised his Companions to enter it, for there most probably they would find their
Countryman. The second, who was wiser, laughed at this Simplicity; but the third, who was wiser still, answered, 'Let us go in, however, for he may think we should not suspect him of going amongst
his own Countrymen.' They accordingly went in and searched the
House, and by that Means missed overtaking the Thief, who was,
at that Time, but a little Way before them; and who, as they all
knew, but had never once reflected, could not read.

The Reader will pardon a Digression in which so invaluable a
Secret is communicated, since every Gamester will agree how necessary it is to know exactly the Play of another, in order to counter-
mine him. This will, moreover, afford a Reason why the wiser Man,
as is often seen, is the Bubble of the weaker, and why many simple
and innocent Characters are so generally misunderstood and misrepresented; but what is most material, this will account for the Deceit
which *Sophia* put on her politic Aunt.

Dinner being ended, and the Company retired into the Garden,
Mr. *Western*, who was thoroughly convinced of the Certainty of
what his Sister had told him, took Mr. *Allworthy* aside, and very
bluntly proposed a Match between *Sophia* and young Mr. *Blifil*.

Mr. *Allworthy* was not one of those Men, whose Hearts flutter at
any unexpected and sudden Tidings of worldly Profit. His Mind
was, indeed, tempered with that Philosophy which becomes a Man
and a Christian. He affected no absolute Superiority to all Pleasure
and Pain, to all Joy and Grief; but was not at the same time to be
discomposed and ruffled by every accidental Blast; by every Smile or
Frown of Fortune. He received, therefore, Mr. *Western*'s Proposal

without any visible Emotion, or without any Alteration of Countenance. He said, the Alliance was such as he sincerely wished, then launched forth into a very just Encomium on the young Lady's Merit; acknowledged the Offer to be advantageous in Point of Fortune; and after thanking Mr. *Western* for the good Opinion he had profess'd of his Nephew, concluded, that if the young People liked each other, he should be very desirous to complete the Affair.

Western was a little disappointed at Mr. *Allworthy*'s Answer; which was not so warm as he expected. He treated the Doubt whether the young People might like one another with great Contempt; saying, 'That Parents were the best Judges of proper Matches for their Children; that, for his Part, he should insist on the most resigned Obedience from his Daughter; and if any young Fellow could refuse such a Bedfellow, he was his humble Servant, and hoped there was no Harm done.'

Allworthy endeavoured to soften this Resentment by many Elogiums on *Sophia*; declaring, he had no Doubt but that Mr. *Blifil* would very gladly receive the Offer; but all was ineffectual, he could obtain no other Answer from the Squire but—'I say no more—I humbly hope there's no Harm done—that's all.' Which Words he repeated at least a hundred Times before they parted.

Allworthy was too well acquainted with his Neighbour to be offended at this Behaviour; and tho' he was so averse to the Rigour which some Parents exercise on their Children in the Article of Marriage, that he had resolved never to force his Nephew's Inclinations, he was neverthless much pleased with the Prospect of this Union: For the whole Country resounded the Praises of *Sophia*, and he had himself greatly admired the uncommon Endowments of both her Mind and Person. To which, I believe we may add, the Consideration of her vast Fortune, which, tho' he was too sober to be intoxicated with it, he was too sensible to despise.

And here, in Defiance of all the barking Critics in the World, I must and will introduce a Digression concerning true Wisdom, of which Mr. *Allworthy* was in Reality as great a Pattern as he was of Goodness.

True Wisdom then, notwithstanding all which Mr. *Hogarth*'s poor Poet[1] may have writ against Riches, and in Spite of all which any rich, well-fed Divine may have preached against Pleasure, consists not in the Contempt of either of these. A Man may have as much Wisdom in the Possession of an affluent Fortune, as any Beggar in the Streets; or may enjoy a handsome Wife or a hearty Friend, and still remain as wise as any sour Popish Recluse, who buries all his social Faculties, and starves his Belly while he well lashes his Back.

1. *The Distrest Poet* (1736).

To say Truth, the wisest Man is the likeliest to possess all worldly Blessings in an eminent Degree: For as that Moderation which Wisdom prescribes is the surest Way to useful Wealth; so can it alone qualify us to taste many Pleasures. The wise Man gratifies every Appetite and every Passion, while the Fool sacrifices all the rest to pall and satiate one.

It may be objected, That very wise Men have been notoriously avaricious. I answer, Not wise in that Instance. It may likewise be said, That the wisest Men have been, in their Youth, immoderately fond of Pleasure. I answer, they were not wise then.

Wisdom, in short, whose Lessons have been represented as so hard to learn by those who never were at her School, only teaches us to extend a simple Maxim universally known and followed even in the lowest Life, a little farther than that Life carries it. And this is not to buy at too dear a Price.

Now, whoever takes this Maxim abroad with him into the grand Market of the World, and constantly applies it to Honours, to Riches, to Pleasures, and to every other Commodity which that Market affords, is, I will venture to affirm, a wise Man; and must be so acknowledged in the worldly sense of the Word: For he makes the best of Bargains; since in Reality he purchases every Thing at the Price only of a little Trouble, and carries home all the good Things I have mentioned, while he keeps his Health, his Innocence, and his Reputation, the common Prices which are paid for them by others, entire and to himself.

From this Moderation, likewise, he learns two other Lessons, which complete his Character. First, never to be intoxicated when he hath made the best Bargain, nor dejected when the Market is empty, or when its Commodities are too dear for his Purchase.

But I must remember on what Subject I am writing, and not trespass too far on the Patience of a good-natured Critic. Here therefore I put an End to the Chapter.

Chapter IV.

Containing sundry curious Matters.

As soon as Mr. *Allworthy* returned home, he took Mr. *Blifil* apart, and after some Preface, communicated to him the Proposal which had been made by Mr. *Western*, and, at the same Time, informed him how agreeable this Match would be to himself.

The Charms of *Sophia* had not made the least Impression on *Blifil*; not that his Heart was pre-engaged; neither was he totally insensible of Beauty, or had any Aversion to Women; but his Appetites were, by Nature, so moderate, that he was able, by Philosophy or by Study, or by some other Method, easily to subdue them; and as to that Passion which we have treated of in the first Chapter of this Book, he had not the least Tincture of it in his whole Composition.

But tho' he was so entirely free from that mixed Passion, of which we there treated, and of which the Virtues and Beauty of *Sophia* formed so notable an Object; yet was he altogether as well furnished with some other Passions, that promised themselves very full Gratification in the young Lady's Fortune. Such were Avarice and Ambition, which divided the Dominion of his Mind between them. He had more than once considered the Possession of this Fortune as a very desirable Thing, and had entertained some distant Views concerning it: But his own Youth and that of the young Lady, and indeed principally a Reflection that Mr. *Western* might marry again, and have more Children, had restrained him from too hasty or eager a Pursuit.

This last and most material Objection was now in great Measure removed, as the Proposal came from Mr. *Western* himself. *Blifil*, therefore, after a very short Hesitation, answered Mr. *Allworthy*, that Matrimony was a Subject on which he had not yet thought: But that he was so sensible of his friendly and fatherly Care, that he should in all Things submit himself to his Pleasure.

Allworthy was naturally a Man of Spirit, and his present Gravity arose from true Wisdom and Philosophy, not from any original Phlegm in his Disposition: For he had possessed much Fire in his Youth, and had married a beautiful Woman for Love. He was not, therefore, greatly pleased with this cold Answer of his Nephew; nor could he help launching forth into the Praises of *Sophia*, and expressing some Wonder that the Heart of a young Man could be impregnable to the Force of such Charms, unless it was guarded by some prior Affection.

Blifil assured him he had no such Guard; and then proceeded to discourse so wisely and religiously on Love and Marriage, that he would have stopt the Mouth of a Parent much less devoutly inclined than was his Uncle. In the End, the good Man was satisfied, that his Nephew, far from having any Objections to *Sophia*, had that Esteem for her, which in sober and virtuous Minds is the sure Foundation of Friendship and Love. And as he doubted not but the Lover would, in a little Time, become altogether as agreeable to his Mistress, he foresaw great Happiness arising to all Parties by so proper and desirable an Union. With Mr. *Blifil*'s Consent, therefore, he wrote the next Morning to Mr. *Western*, acquainting him that his Nephew had very thankfully and gladly received the Proposal, and would be ready to wait on the young Lady, whenever she should be pleased to accept his Visit.

Western was much pleased with this Letter, and immediately returned an Answer; in which, without having mentioned a Word to his Daughter, he appointed that very Afternoon for opening the Scene of Courtship.

As soon as he had dispatched this Messenger, he went in Quest of his Sister, whom he found reading and expounding the Gazette[1] to Parson *Supple*. To this Exposition he was obliged to attend near a Quarter of an Hour, tho' with great Violence to his natural Impetuosity, before he was suffered to speak. At length, however, he found an Opportunity of acquainting the Lady, that he had Business of great Consequence to impart to her; to which she answered, 'Brother, I am entirely at your Service. Things look so well in the North that I was never in a better Humour.'

The Parson then withdrawing, *Western* acquainted her with all which had passed, and desired her to communicate the Affair to *Sophia*, which she readily and chearfully undertook; tho' perhaps her Brother was a little obliged to that agreeable Northern Aspect which had so delighted her, that he heard no Comment on his Proceedings: for they were certainly somewhat too hasty and violent.

1. *The London Gazette*, an official government newspaper, and the oldest surviving newspaper in England (founded 1665), specializing in foreign news, from a wide network of foreign correspondents.

Chapter V.

In which is related what passed between Sophia *and her Aunt*.

Sophia was in her Chamber reading, when her Aunt came in. The Moment she saw Mrs. *Western*, she shut the Book with so much Eagerness, that the good Lady could not forbear asking her, What Book that was which she seemed so much afraid of shewing? 'Upon my Word, Madam,' answered *Sophia*, 'it is a Book which I am neither ashamed nor afraid to own I have read. It is the production of a young Lady of Fashion,[1] whose good Understanding, I think, doth Honour to her Sex and whose good Heart is an Honour to Human Nature.' Mrs. *Western* then took up the Book, and immediately after threw it down saying—'Yes, the Author is of a very good Family; but she is not much among People one knows. I have never read it; for the best Judges say, there is not much in it.' 'I dare not, Madam, set up my own Opinion,' says *Sophia*, 'against the best Judges, but there appears to me a great deal of human Nature

1. Fielding's sister Sarah, to whose novel *David Simple* (1744) Fielding had contributed a Preface for the second edition (also 1744). For the sequel, *Familiar Letters between the Principal Characters in David Simple* (1747), Fielding had again written the Preface, and had contributed Letters XL–XLIV.

in it; and in many Parts, so much true Tenderness and Delicacy, that it hath cost me many a Tear.' 'Ay, and do you love to cry then?' says the Aunt. 'I love a tender Sensation,' answered the Niece, 'and would pay the Price of a Tear for it at any Time.' 'Well, but shew me,' said the Aunt, 'what was you reading when I came in; there was something very tender in that, I believe, and very loving too. You blush, my dear *Sophia*. Ah! Child, you should read Books, which would teach you a little Hypocrisy, which would instruct you how to hide your Thoughts a little better.' 'I hope, Madam,' answered *Sophia*, 'I have no Thoughts which I ought to be ashamed of discovering.' 'Ashamed! no,' cries the Aunt, 'I don't think you have any Thoughts which you ought to be ashamed of; and yet, Child, you blushed just now when I mentioned the Word *Loving*. Dear *Sophy*, be assured you have not one Thought which I am not well acquainted with; as well, Child, as the *French* are with our Motions, long before we put them in Execution. Did you think, Child, because you have been able to impose upon your Father, that you could impose upon me? Do you imagine I did not know the Reason of your over-acting all that Friendship for Mr. *Blifil* yesterday? I have seen a little too much of the World, to be so deceived. Nay, nay, do not blush again. I tell you it is a Passion you need not be ashamed of.—It is a Passion I myself approve, and have already brought your Father into the Approbation of it. Indeed, I solely consider your Inclination; for I would always have that gratified, if possible, though one may sacrifice higher prospects. Come, I have News which will delight your very Soul. Make me your Confident, and I will undertake you shall be happy to the very Extent of your Wishes.' 'La, Madam,' says *Sophia*, looking more foolishly than ever she did in her Life, 'I know not what to say—Why, Madam, should you suspect?'—'Nay, no Dishonesty,' returned Mrs. *Western*. 'Consider, you are speaking to one of your own Sex, to an Aunt, and I hope you are convinced you speak to a Friend. Consider, you are only revealing to me what I know already, and what I plainly saw yesterday through that most artful of all Disguises, which you had put on, and which must have deceived any one who had not perfectly known the World. Lastly, consider it is a Passion which I highly approve.' 'La, Madam,' says *Sophia*, 'you come upon one so unawares, and on a sudden. To be sure, Madam, I am not blind—and certainly, if it be a Fault to see all human Perfections assembled together—But is it possible my Father and you, Madam, can see with my Eyes?' 'I tell you,' answered the Aunt, 'we do entirely approve; and this very afternoon your Father hath appointed for you to receive your Lover.' 'My Father, this Afternoon!' cries *Sophia*, with the Blood starting from her Face.—'Yes, Child,' said the Aunt, 'this Afternoon. You know the Impetuosity of my Brother's Temper. I acquainted him with the Passion which I first discovered in you that Evening when you fainted away in the Field. I saw it in your Fainting. I saw it immediately upon your Recovery. I saw it that Evening at Supper, and the next Morning at Breakfast: (you know, Child, I have seen the World). Well, I no sooner acquainted my Brother, but he immediately wanted to propose it to *Allworthy*. He proposed it Yesterday, *Allworthy* consented, (as to be sure he must with Joy) and this Afternoon, I tell you, you are to put on all your best Airs.' 'This afternoon!' cries *Sophia*. 'Dear Aunt, you frighten me out of my Senses.' 'O, my Dear,' said the Aunt, 'you will soon come to yourself again; for he is a charming young Fellow, that's the Truth on't.' 'Nay, I will own,' says *Sophia*, 'I know none with such Perfections. So brave, and yet so gentle; so witty, yet so inoffensive; so humane, so civil, so genteel, so handsome! What signifies his being base born, when compared with such Qualifications as these?' 'Base born! what do you mean?' said the Aunt, 'Mr. *Blifil* base born!' *Sophia* turned instantly pale at this Name, and faintly repeated it. Upon which the Aunt cried, 'Mr. *Blifil*, ay Mr. *Blifil*, of whom else have we been talking?' 'Good Heavens,' answered *Sophia*, ready to sink, 'of Mr. *Jones*, I thought; I am sure I know no other who deserves—' 'I protest,' cries the Aunt, 'you frighten me in your Turn. Is it Mr. *Jones*, and not Mr. *Blifil*, who is the Object of your Affection?' 'Mr. *Blifil*!' repeated *Sophia*. 'Sure it is impossible you can be in earnest; if you are, I am the most miserable Woman alive.' Mrs. *Western* now stood a few Moments silent, while Sparks of fiery Rage flashed from her Eyes. At length, collecting all her Force of Voice, she thundered forth in the following articulate Sounds:

'And is it possible you can think of disgracing your Family by allying yourself to a Bastard? Can the Blood of the *Westerns* submit to such Contamination! If you have not Sense sufficient to restrain such monstrous Inclinations, I thought the Pride of our Family would have prevented you from giving the least Encouragement to so base an Affection; much less did I imagine you would ever have had the Assurance to own it to my Face.'

'Madam,' answered *Sophia*, trembling, 'what I have said you have extorted from me. I do not remember to have ever mentioned the Name of Mr. *Jones*, with Approbation, to any one before; nor should I now, had I not conceived he had your Approbation. Whatever were my Thoughts of that poor unhappy young Man, I intended to have carried them with me to my Grave—To that Grave where only now, I find, I am to seek Repose.'—Here she sunk down in her Chair, drowned in her Tears, and, in all the moving Silence of unutterable Grief, presented a Spectacle which must have affected almost the hardest Heart.

All this tender Sorrow, however, raised no Compassion in her Aunt. On the contrary, she now fell into the most violent Rage— 'And I would rather,' she cried, in a most vehement Voice, 'follow you to your Grave, than I would see you disgrace yourself and your Family by such a Match. O Heavens! could I have ever suspected that I should live to hear a Niece of mine declare a Passion for such a Fellow? You are the first—yes, Miss *Western*, you are the first of your Name who ever entertained so grovelling a Thought. A Family so noted for the Prudence of its Women'—Here she run on a full Quarter of an Hour, till having exhausted her Breath rather than her Rage, she concluded with threatning to go immediately and acquaint her Brother.

Sophia then threw herself at her Feet, and laying hold of her Hands, 'begged her, with Tears, to conceal what she had drawn from her; urging the Violence of her Father's Temper, and protesting that no Inclinations of hers should ever prevail with her to do any thing which might offend him.'

Mrs. *Western* stood a Moment looking at her, and then having recollected herself, said, that 'on one Consideration only she would keep the Secret from her Brother; and this was, that *Sophia* should promise to entertain Mr. *Blifil* that very Afternoon as her Lover, and to regard him as the Person who was to be her Husband.'

Poor *Sophia* was too much in her Aunt's Power to deny her any thing positively; she was obliged to promise that she would see Mr. *Blifil*, and be as civil to him as possible; but begged her Aunt that the Match might not be hurried on. She said, 'Mr. *Blifil* was by no means agreeable to her, and she hoped her Father would be prevailed on not to make her the most wretched of Women.'

Mrs. *Western* assured her, 'that the Match was entirely agreed upon, and that nothing could or should prevent it.' 'I must own,' said she, 'I looked on it as on a Matter of Indifference; nay, perhaps, had some Scruples about it before, which were actually got over by my thinking it highly agreeable to your own Inclinations; but now I regard it as the most eligible thing in the World; nor shall there be, if I can prevent it, a Moment of Time lost on the Occasion.'

Sophia replied, 'Delay at least, Madam, I may expect from both your Goodness and my Father's. Surely you will give me Time to endeavour to get the better of so strong a Disinclination as I have at present to this Person.'

The Aunt answered, 'She knew too much of the World to be so deceived; that as she was sensible another Man had her Affections, she should persuade Mr. *Western* to hasten the Match as much as possible. It would be bad Politics indeed,' added she, 'to protract a Siege when the Enemy's Army is at Hand, and in Danger of relieving it. No, no, *Sophy*,' said she, 'as I am convinced you have a violent Passion, which you can never satisfy with Honour, I will do all I can to put your Honour out of the Care of your Family: For when you are married, those Matters will belong only to the Consideration of your Husband. I hope, Child, you will always have Prudence enough to act as becomes you; but if you should not, Marriage hath saved many a Woman from Ruin.'

Sophia well understood what her Aunt meant; but did not think proper to make her an Answer. However, she took a Resolution to see Mr. *Blifil*, and to behave to him as civilly as she could: For on that Condition only she obtained a Promise from her Aunt to keep secret the Liking which her ill Fortune, rather than any Scheme of Mrs. *Western*, had unhappily drawn from her.

Chapter VI.

Containing a Dialogue between Sophia *and Mrs.* Honour, *which may a little relieve those tender Affections which the foregoing Scene may have raised in the Mind of a good-natured Reader.*

Mrs. *Western* having obtained that Promise from her Niece which we have seen in the last Chapter, withdrew; and presently after arrived Mrs. *Honour*. She was at Work in a neighbouring Apartment, and had been summoned to the Key-hole by some Vociferation in the preceding Dialogue, where she had continued during the remaining Part of it. At her Entry into the Room, she found *Sophia* standing motionless, with the Tears trickling from her Eyes. Upon which she immediately ordered a proper Quantity of Tears into her own Eyes, and then began, 'O Gemini, my dear Lady, what is the Matter?' 'Nothing,' cries *Sophia*. 'Nothing! O dear Madam,' answers Mrs. *Honour*, 'you must not tell me that, when your Ladyship is in this Taking, and when there hath been such a *Preamble* between your Ladyship and Madam *Western*.' 'Don't teaze me,' cries *Sophia*, 'I tell you nothing is the Matter.—Good Heavens! Why was I born!'—'Nay, Madam,' says Mrs. *Honour*, 'you shall never persuade me, that your La'ship can lament yourself so for nothing. To be sure, I am but a Servant; but to be sure I have been always faithful to your Ladyship, and to be sure I would serve your La'ship with my Life.' 'My dear *Honour*,' says *Sophia*, ' 'tis not in thy Power to be of any Service to me. I am irretrievably undone.' 'Heaven forbid,' answered the Waiting-woman; 'but if I can't be of any service to you, pray tell me, Madam, it will be some Comfort to me to know: Pray dear Ma'am, tell me what's the Matter.' 'My Father,' cries *Sophia*, 'is going to marry me to a Man

I both despise and hate.' 'O, dear Ma'am,' answered the other, 'who is this wicked Man? For to be sure he is very bad, or your La'ship would not despise him.' 'His Name is Poison to my Tongue,' replied *Sophia*, 'thou wilt know it too soon.' Indeed, to confess the Truth, she knew it already, and therefore was not very inquisitive as to that Point. She then proceeded thus: 'I don't pretend to give your La'ship Advice, *whereof* your La'ship knows much better than I can pretend to, being but a Servant; but, i-fackins! no Father in *England* should marry me against my Consent. And to be sure, the Squire is so good, that if he did but know your La'ship despises and hates the young Man, to be sure he would not desire you to marry him. And if your La'ship would but give me Leave to tell my Master so—To be sure, it would be more properer to come from your own Mouth; but as your La'ship doth not care to foul your Tongue with his nasty Name.' 'You are mistaken, *Honour*,' says *Sophia*, 'my Father was determined before he ever thought fit to mention it to me.' 'More Shame for him,' cries *Honour*, 'you are to go to Bed to him, and not Master. And thof a Man may be a very proper Man, yet every Woman mayn't think him handsome alike. I am sure my Master would never act in this Manner of his own Head. I wish some People would trouble themselves only with what belongs to them; they would not, I believe, like to be served so, if it was their own Case: For tho' I am a Maid, I can easily believe as how all Men are not equally agreeable. And what signifies your La'ship having so great a Fortune, if you can't please yourself with the Man you think most handsomest? Well, I say nothing, but to be sure it is Pity some Folks had not been better born; nay, as for that Matter, I should not mind it myself: But then there is not so much Money, and what of that? your La'ship hath Money enough for both; and where can your La'ship bestow your Fortune better? For to be sure every one must allow, that he is the most handsomest, charmingest, finest, tallest, properest Man in the World.' 'What do you mean by running on in this Manner to me?' cries *Sophia*, with a very grave Countenance. 'Have I ever given any Encouragement for these Liberties?' 'Nay Ma'am, I ask Pardon; I meant no Harm,' answered she; 'but to be sure the poor Gentleman hath run in my Head ever since I saw him this Morning.—To be sure, if your Ladyship had but seen him just now, you must have pitied him. Poor Gentleman! I wishes some Misfortune hath not happened to him: For he hath been walking about with his Arms a-cross, and looking so melancholy all this Morning; I vow and protest it made me almost cry to see him.' 'To see whom?' says *Sophia*. 'Poor Mr. *Jones*,' answered *Honour*. 'See him! Why, where did you see him?' cries *Sophia*. 'By the Canal, Ma'am,' says *Honour*. 'There he hath been walking all this Morning, and at last there he laid himself down; I believe he lies there still. To be sure, if it hath not

been for my Modesty, being a Maid as I am, I should have gone
and spoke to him. Do, Ma'am, let me go and see, only for a Fancy,
whether he is there still.' 'Pugh!' says *Sophia*, 'There! no, no, what
should he do there? He is gone before this Time to be sure. Besides,
why—what—why should you go to see?—Besides, I want you for
something else. Go, fetch me my Hat and Gloves. I shall walk with
my Aunt in the Grove before Dinner.' *Honour* did immediately as
she was bid, and *Sophia* put her Hat on; when looking in the Glass,
she fancied the Ribbon with which her Hat was tied, did not
become her, and so sent her Maid back again for a Ribbon of a different Colour; and then giving Mrs. *Honour* repeated Charges not
to leave her Work on any Account, as she said it was in violent
Haste, and must be finished that very Day; she muttered something
more about going to the Grove, and then sallied out the contrary
Way, and walked as fast as her tender trembling Limbs could carry
her, directly towards the Canal.

Jones had been there, as Mrs. *Honour* had told her: He had
indeed spent two Hours there that Morning in melancholy Contemplation on his *Sophia*, and had gone out from the Garden at one
Door, the Moment she entered it at another. So that those unlucky
Minutes which had been spent in changing the Ribbons, had prevented the Lovers from meeting at this Time. A most unfortunate
Accident, from which my fair Readers will not fail to draw a very
wholesom Lesson. And here I strictly forbid all Male Critics to
intermeddle with a Circumstance, which I have recounted only for
the sake of the Ladies, and upon which they only are at Liberty to
comment.

Chapter VII.

*A Picture of formal Courtship in Miniature, as it always ought to
be drawn, and a Scene of a tenderer Kind, painted at full Length.*

It was well-remarked by one, (and perhaps by more) that Misfortunes do not come single.[1] This wise Maxim was now verified by
Sophia, who was not only disappointed of seeing the Man she
loved; but had the Vexation of being obliged to dress herself out, in
order to receive a Visit from the Man she hated.

That Afternoon, Mr. *Western*, for the first Time, acquainted his
Daughter with his Intention; telling her, he knew very well that she
had heard it before from her Aunt. *Sophia* looked very grave upon
this, nor could she prevent a few Pearls from stealing into her Eyes.
'Come, come,' says *Western*, 'none of your Maidenish Airs; I know
all; I assure you, Sister hath told me all.'

'Is it possible,' says *Sophia*, 'that my Aunt can have betrayed me

1. See above, p. 109.

already?' 'Ay, ay,' says *Western,* 'betrayed you! ay. Why, you
betrayed yourself Yesterday at Dinner. You shewed your Fancy very
plainly, I think. But you young Girls never know what you would
be at. So you cry because I am going to marry you to the Man you
are in Love with! Your Mother, I remember, whimpered and
whined just in the same Manner; but it was all over within twenty-
four Hours after we were married: Mr. *Blifil* is a brisk young Man,
and will soon put an End to your Squeamishness. Come, chear up,
chear up, I expect un every Minute.'

Sophia was now convinced that her Aunt had behaved honourably to her; and she determined to go through that disagreeable Afternoon with as much Resolution as possible, and without giving the
least Suspicion in the World to her Father.

Mr. *Blifil* soon arrived; and Mr. *Western* soon after withdrawing,
left the young Couple together.

Here a long Silence of near a Quarter of an Hour ensued: For
the Gentleman who was to begin the Conversation had all that
unbecoming Modesty which consists in Bashfulness. He often
attempted to speak, and as often suppressed his Words just at the
very Point of Utterance. At last out they broke in a Torrent of far-
fetched and high-strained Compliments, which were answered on
her Side, by downcast Looks, half Bows and civil Monosyllables.
Blifil from his Inexperience in the Ways of Women, and from his
Conceit of himself, took this Behaviour for a modest Assent to his
Courtship; and when to shorten a Scene which she could no longer
support, *Sophia* rose up and left the Room, he imputed that too,
merely to Bashfulness, and comforted himself, that he should soon
have enough of her Company.

He was indeed perfectly well satisfied with his Prospect of Success: For as to that entire and absolute Posession of the Heart of
his Mistress, which romantic Lovers require, the very Idea of it
never entered his Head. Her Fortune and her Person were the sole
Objects of his Wishes, of which he made no Doubt soon to obtain
the absolute Property; as Mr. *Western's* Mind was so earnestly bent
on the Match; and as he well knew the strict Obedience which
Sophia was always ready to pay to her Father's Will, and the greater
still which her Father would exact, if there was Occasion. This
Authority, therefore, together with the Charms which he fancied in
his own Person and Conversation, could not fail, he thought, of
succeeding with a young Lady, whose Inclinations, were, he
doubted not, entirely disengaged.

Of *Jones* he certainly had not even the least Jealousy; and I have
often thought it wonderful that he had not. Perhaps he imagined
the Character which *Jones* bore all over the Country, (how justly
let the Reader determine) of being one of the wildest Fellows in

England, might render him odious to a Lady of the most exemplary Modesty. Perhaps his Suspicions might be laid asleep by the Behaviour of *Sophia*, and of *Jones* himself, when they were all in Company together. Lastly, and indeed principally, he was well assured there was not another Self in the Case. He fancied that he knew *Jones* to the Bottom, and had in reality a great Contempt for his Understanding, for not being more attached to his own Interest. He had no Apprehension that *Jones* was in Love with *Sophia*; and as for any lucrative Motives, he imagined they would sway very little with so silly a Fellow. *Blifil*, moreover, thought the Affair of *Molly Seagrim* still went on, and indeed believed it would end in Marriage: For *Jones* really loved him from his Childhood, and had kept no Secret from him, till his Behaviour on the Sickness of Mr. *Allworthy* had entirely alienated his Heart; and it was by Means of the Quarrel which had ensued on this Occasion, and which was not yet reconciled, that Mr. *Blifil* knew nothing of the Alteration which had happened in the Affection which *Jones* had formerly borne towards *Molly*.

From these Reasons, therefore, Mr. *Blifil* saw no Bar to his Success with *Sophia*. He concluded, her Behaviour was like that of all other young Ladies on a first Visit from a Lover, and it had indeed entirely answered his Expectations.

Mr. *Western* took Care to way-lay the Lover at his Exit from his Mistress. He found him so elevated with his Success, so enamoured with his Daughter, and so satisfied with her Reception of him, that the old Gentleman began to caper and dance about his Hall, and by many other antic Actions, to express the Extravagance of his Joy: For he had not the least Command over any of his Passions: and that which had at any Time the Ascendant in his Mind, hurried him to the wildest Excesses.

As soon as *Blifil* was departed, which was not till after many hearty Kisses and Embraces bestowed on him by *Western*, the good Squire went instantly in quest of his Daughter, whom he no sooner found than he poured forth the most extravagant Raptures, bidding her chuse what Clothes and Jewels she pleased; and declaring that he had no other Use for Fortune but to make her happy. He then caressed her again and again with the utmost Profusion of Fondness, called her by the most endearing Names, and protested she was his only Joy on Earth.

Sophia perceiving her Father in this Fit of Affection, which she did not absolutely know the Reason of (for Fits of Fondness were not unusual to him, tho' this was rather more violent than ordinary) thought she should never have a better Opportunity of disclosing herself than at present; as far at least, as regarded Mr. *Blifil*; and she too well foresaw the Necessity which she should soon be

under of coming to a full Explanation. After having thanked the
Squire, therefore for all his Professions of Kindness, she added, with
a Look full of inexpressible Softness, 'And is it possible my Papa
can be so good to place all his Joy in his *Sophy*'s Happiness?' which
Western having confirmed by a great Oath and a Kiss; she then laid
hold of his Hand, and falling on her Knees, after many warm and
passionate Declarations of Affection and Duty, she begged him, 'not
to make her the most miserable Creature on Earth, by forcing her
to marry a Man whom she detested. This I entreat of you, dear Sir,'
said she, 'for your Sake, as well as my own, since you are so very
kind to tell me your Happiness depends on mine.' 'How! what!'
says *Western*, staring wildly. 'O Sir,' continued she, 'not only your
poor *Sophy*'s Happiness, her very Life, her Being depends upon
your granting her Request. I cannot live with Mr. *Blifil*. To force
me into this Marriage, would be killing me.' 'You can't live with
Mr. *Blifil*!' says *Western*. 'No, upon my Soul I can't,' answered
Sophia. 'Then die and be d—ned,' cries he, spurning her from him.
'Oh! Sir,' cries *Sophia*, catching hold of the Skirt of his Coat, 'take
Pity on me, I beseech you. Don't look, and say such cruel—Can
you be unmoved while you see your *Sophy* in this dreadful Condition? Can the best of Fathers break my Heart? Will he kill me by
the most painful, cruel, lingering Death?' 'Pooh! Pooh!' cries the
Squire, 'all Stuff and Nonsense, all maidenish Tricks. Kill you
indeed! Will Marriage kill you?'—'Oh! Sir,' answered *Sophia*, 'such
a Marriage is worse than Death—He is not even indifferent, I hate
and detest him.'—'If you detest un never so much,' cries *Western*,
'you shall ha' un.' This he bound by an Oath too shocking to
repeat, and after many violent Asseverations, concluded in these
Words: 'I am resolved upon the Match, and unless you consent to
it, I will not give you a Groat, not a single Farthing; no, tho' I saw
you expiring with Famine in the Street, I would not relieve you
with a Morsel of Bread. This is my fixed Resolution, and so I leave
you to consider on it.' He then broke from her with such Violence,
that her Face dashed against the Floor, and he burst directly out of
the Room, leaving poor *Sophia* prostrate on the Ground.

When *Western* came into the Hall, he there found *Jones*; who
seeing his Friend looking wild, pale, and almost breathless, could not
forbear enquiring the Reason of all these melancholy Appearances.
Upon which the Squire immediately acquainted him with the
whole Matter, concluding with bitter Denunciations against *Sophia*,
and very pathetic Lamentations of the Misery of all Fathers who
are so unfortunate to have Daughters.

Jones, to whom all the Resolutions which had been taken in
Favour of *Blifil* were yet a Secret, was at first almost struck dead
with this Relation; but recovering his Spirits a little, mere Despair,
as he afterwards said, inspired him to mention a Matter to Mr.

Western, which seemed to require more Impudence than a human Forehead was ever gifted with. He desired Leave to go to *Sophia*, that he might endeavour to obtain her Concurrence with her Father's Inclinations.

If the Squire had been as quick-sighted, as he was remarkable for the contrary, Passion might at present very well have blinded him. He thanked *Jones* for offering to undertake the Office, and said, 'Go, go, prithee, try what canst do;' and then swore many execrable Oaths that he would turn her out of Doors unless she consented to the Match.

Chapter VIII.

The Meeting between Jones *and* Sophia.

Jones departed instantly in Quest of *Sophia*, whom he found just risen from the Ground where her Father had left her, with the Tears trickling from her Eyes, and the Blood running from her Lips. He presently ran to her, and with a Voice full at once of Tenderness and Terrour, cried, 'O my *Sophia*, what means this dreadful Sight!—She looked softly at him for a Moment before she spoke, and then said, 'Mr. *Jones*, for Heaven's Sake, how came you here? —Leave me, I beseech you, this Moment.' 'Do not,' says he, 'impose so harsh a Command upon me—my Heart bleeds faster than those Lips. O *Sophia*, how easily could I drain my Veins to preserve one Drop of that dear Blood.' 'I have too many Obligations to you already,' answered she, 'for sure you meant them such.' —Here she looked at him tenderly almost a Minute, and then bursting into an Agony, cried,—'O Mr. *Jones*,—why did you save my Life?—my Death would have been happier for us both.'—'Happier for us both!' cried he, 'Could Racks or Wheels kill me so painfully as *Sophia*'s!—I cannot bear the dreadful Sound—Do I live but for her?'—Both his Voice and Look were full of inexpressible Tenderness when he spoke these Words, and at the same Time he laid gently hold on her Hand, which she did not withdraw from him; to say the Truth, she hardly knew what she did or suffered. A few Moments now passed in Silence between these Lovers, while his Eyes were eagerly fixed on *Sophia*, and hers declining towards the Ground; at last she recovered Strength enough to desire him again to leave her; for that her certain Ruin would be the Consequence of their being found together; adding,—'O Mr. *Jones*, you know not, you know not what hath passed this cruel Afternoon.' 'I know all, my *Sophia*,' answered he; 'your cruel Father hath told me all, and he himself hath sent me hither to you.' 'My Father sent you to me!' replied she, 'sure you dream.' 'Would to Heaven,' cries he, 'it was but a Dream. O *Sophia*, your Father hath sent me to you, to be an

Advocate for my odious Rival, to solicite you in his Favour—I took any Means to get Access to you—O speak to me, *Sophia*, comfort my bleeding Heart. Sure no one ever loved, ever doated like me. Do not unkindly withhold this dear, this soft, this gentle Hand—One Moment, perhaps, tears you for ever from me—Nothing less than this cruel Occasion could, I believe, have ever conquered the Respect and Awe, with which you have inspired me.' She stood a Moment silent and covered with Confusion, then lifting up her Eyes gently towards him, she cried, 'What would Mr. *Jones* have me say?' 'O do but promise,' cries he, 'that you never will give your-self to *Blifil*.' 'Name not,' answered she, 'the detested Sound. Be assured I never will give him what is in my Power to with-hold from him.' 'Now then,' cries he, 'while you are so perfectly kind, go a little farther, and add that I may hope.'—'Alas,' says she, 'Mr. *Jones*, whither will you drive me? What Hope have I to bestow? You know my Father's Intentions.'—'But I know,' answered he, 'your Compliance with them cannot be compelled.' 'What,' says she, 'must be the dreadful Consequence of my Disobedience? My own Ruin is my least Concern. I cannot bear the Thoughts of being the Cause of my Father's Misery.' 'He is himself the Cause,' cries *Jones*, 'by exacting a Power over you which Nature hath not given him. Think on the Misery which I am to suffer, if I am to lose you, and see on which Side Pity will turn the Balance.' 'Think of it!' replied she, 'can you imagine I do not feel the Ruin which I must bring on you, should I comply with your Desire—It is that Thought which gives me Resolution to bid you fly from me for ever, and avoid your own Destruction.' 'I fear no Destruction,' cries he, 'but the Loss of *Sophia*; if you would save me from the most bitter Agonies, recall that cruel Sentence—Indeed, I can never part with you, indeed I cannot.'

The Lovers now stood both silent and trembling, *Sophia* being unable to withdraw her Hand from *Jones*, and he almost as unable to hold it; when the Scene, which I believe some of my Readers will think had lasted long enough, was interrupted by one of so different a Nature, that we shall reserve the Relation of it for a different Chapter.

Chapter IX.

Being of a much more tempestuous Kind than the former.

Before we proceed with what now happened to our Lovers, it may be proper to recount what had past in the Hall, during their tender Interview.

Soon after *Jones* had left Mr. *Western* in the Manner above-mentioned, his Sister came to him; and was presently informed of all that had past between her Brother and *Sophia*, relating to *Blifil*.

This Behaviour of her Niece, the good Lady construed to be an absolute Breach of the Condition, on which she had engaged to keep her Love for Mr. *Jones* a Secret. She considered herself, therefore, at full Liberty to reveal all she knew to the Squire, which she immediately did in the most explicit Terms, and without any Ceremony or Preface.

The Idea of a Marriage between *Jones* and his Daughter, had never once entered into the Squire's Head, either in the warmest Minutes of his Affection towards that young Man, or from Suspicion, or on any other Occasion. He did indeed consider a Parity of Fortune and Circumstances, to be physically as necessary an Ingredient in Marriage, as Difference of Sexes, or any other Essential; and had no more Apprehension of his Daughter's falling in Love with a poor Man, than with any Animal of a different Species.

He became, therefore, like one Thunderstruck at his Sister's Relation. He was, at first, incapable of making any Answer, having been almost deprived of his Breath by the Violence of the Surprize. This, however, soon returned, and, as is usual in other Cases after an Intermission, with redoubled Force and Fury.

The first Use he made of the Power of Speech, after his Recovery from the sudden Effects of his Astonishment, was to discharge a round Volley of Oaths and Imprecations. After which he proceeded hastily to the Apartment, where he expected to find the Lovers, and murmured, or indeed, rather roared forth Intentions of Revenge every Step he went.

As when two Doves, or two Wood-pigeons, or as when *Strephon* and *Phyllis*[1] (for that comes nearest to the mark) are retired into some pleasant solitary Grove, to enjoy the delightful Conversation of Love; that bashful Boy who cannot speak in Public, and is never a good Companion to more than two at a Time. Here while every Object is serene, should hoarse Thunder burst suddenly through the shattered Clouds, and rumbling roll along the Sky, the frightened Maid starts from the mossy Bank or verdant Turf; the pale Livery of Death succeeds the red Regimentals in which Love had before drest her Cheeks; Fear shakes her whole Frame, and her Lover scarce supports her trembling, tottering Limbs.

Or as when the two Gentlemen, Strangers to the wonderous Wit of the Place, are cracking a Bottle together at some Inn or Tavern at *Salisbury*, if the great *Dowdy*[2] who acts the Part of a Madman, as well as some of his Setters-on do that of a Fool, should rattle his

1. Traditional names for lovers in romances, Strephon from Sidney's *Arcadia*, Phyllis from Virgil's *Eclogues*.
2. *The Salisbury Journal*, 18 Jan. 1762, reports that Daniel Pearce, serjeant at mace, used to frighten strangers at The Three Lions inn (afterwards "The Three Golden Lions"), in Salisbury, by walking the galleries as a ghost. (Cross II.167—who finds no Dowdy or Doughty as a Salisbury official in Fielding's time, and notes that Fielding's Dowdy acts the madman, not the ghost). See note above, p. 92.

Chains, and dreadfully hum forth the grumbling Catch along the Gallery; the frighted Strangers stand aghast, scared at the horrid Sound, they seek some Place of Shelter from the approaching Danger, and if the well-barred Windows did admit their Exit, would venture their Necks to escape the threatning Fury now coming upon them.

So trembled poor *Sophia*, so turned she pale at the Noise of her Father, who in a Voice most dreadful to hear, came on swearing, cursing and vowing the Destruction of *Jones*. To say the Truth, I believe the Youth himself would, from some prudent Considerations, have preferred another Place of Abode at this Time, had his Terror on *Sophia*'s Account given him Liberty to reflect a Moment on what any otherways concerned himself, than as his Love made him partake whatever affected her.

And now the Squire having burst open the Door, beheld an Object which instantly suspended all his Fury against *Jones*; this was the ghastly Appearance of *Sophia*, who had fainted away in her Lover's Arms. This tragical Sight Mr. *Western* no sooner beheld, than all his Rage forsook him, he roared for Help with his utmost Violence; ran first to his Daughter, then back to the Door, calling for Water, and then back again to *Sophia*, never considering in whose Arms she then was, nor perhaps once recollecting that there was such a Person in the World as *Jones*: For, indeed, I believe, the present Circumstances of his Daughter were now the sole Consideration which employed his Thoughts.

Mrs. *Western* and a great Number of Servants soon came to the Assistance of *Sophia* with Water, Cordials, and every Thing necessary on those Occasions. These were applied with such Success, that *Sophia* in a very few Minutes began to recover, and all the Symptoms of life to return. Upon which she was presently led off by her own Maid and Mrs. *Western*; nor did that good Lady depart without leaving some wholesome Admonitions with her Brother, on the dreadful Effects of his Passion, or, as she pleased to call it, Madness.

The Squire, perhaps, did not understand this good Advice, as it was delivered in obscure Hints, Shrugs, and Notes of Admiration; at least, if he did understand it, he profited very little by it: For no sooner was he cured of his immediate Fears for his Daughter, than he relapsed into his former Frenzy, which must have produced an immediate Battle with *Jones*, had not Parson *Supple*, who was a very strong Man, been present, and by mere Force restrained the Squire from Acts of Hostility.

The Moment *Sophia* was departed, *Jones* advanced in a very suppliant Manner to Mr. *Western*, whom the Parson held in his Arms, and begged him to be pacified; for that, while he continued in such a Passion, it would be impossible to give him any Satisfaction.

'I wull have Satisfaction o'thee,' answered the Squire, 'so doff thy clothes. At *unt* half a Man, and I'll lick thee as well as wast ever licked in thy Life.' He then bespattered the Youth with Abundance of that Language, which passes between Country Gentlemen who embrace opposite Sides of the Question; with frequent Applications to him to salute that Part which is generally introduced into all Controversies, that arise among the lower Orders of the *English* Gentry, at Horse-races, Cock-matches, and other public Places. Allusions to this Part are likewise often made for the Sake of the Jest. And here, I believe, the Wit is generally misunderstood. In Reality, it lies in desiring another to kiss your A— for having just before threatned to kick his: For I have observed very accurately, that no one ever desires you to kick that which belongs to himself, nor offers to kiss this Part in another.

It may likewise seem surprizing, that in the many thousand kind Invitations of this Sort, which every one who hath conversed with Country Gentlemen must have heard, no one, I believe, hath ever seen a single Instance where the Desire hath been complied with. A great Instance of their Want of Politeness: For in Town, nothing can be more common than for the finest Gentlemen to perform this Ceremony every Day to their Superiors, without having that Favour once requested of them.

To all such Wit, *Jones* very calmly answered, 'Sir, this Usage may, perhaps, cancel every other Obligation you have conferred on me; but there is one you can never cancel; nor will I be provoked by your Abuse, to lift my Hand against the Father of *Sophia*.'

At these Words the Squire grew still more outrageous than before; so that the Parson begged *Jones* to retire, saying, 'You behold, Sir, how he waxeth wroth at your Abode here; therefore let me pray you not to tarry any longer. His Anger is too much kindled for you to commune with him at present. You had better, therefore, conclude your Visit, and refer what Matters you have to urge in your Behalf to some other Opportunity.'

Jones accepted this Advice with Thanks, and immediately departed. The Squire now regained the Liberty of his Hands, and so much Temper as to express some Satisfaction in the Restraint which had been laid upon him; declaring that he should certainly have beat his Brains out; and adding, 'It would have vexed one confoundedly to have been hanged for such a Rascal.'

The Parson now began to triumph in the Success of his Peace-making Endeavours, and proceeded to read a Lecture against Anger, which might perhaps rather have tended to raise than to quiet that Passion in some hasty Minds. This Lecture he enriched with many valuable Quotations from the Antients, particularly from *Seneca*;[3] who hath, indeed, so well handled this Passion, that none but a

---

3. *Dialogorum* III, "Ad Novatum" ("De Ira").

very angry Man can read him without great Pleasure and Profit.
The Doctor concluded this Harangue with the famous Story of
Alexander and *Clitus*;[4] but as I find that entered in my Common-
Place under Title *Drunkenness*, I shall not insert it here.

The Squire took no Notice of this Story, nor perhaps of any
Thing he said: For he interrupted him before he had finished, by
calling for a Tankard of Beer; observing (which is perhaps as true
as any Observation on this Fever of the Mind) *that Anger makes a
Man dry.*

No sooner had the Squire swallowed a large Draught than he
renewed the Discourse on *Jones*, and declared a Resolution of going
the next Morning early to acquaint Mr. *Allworthy*. His Friend
would have dissuaded him from this, from the mere Motive of
Good-nature; but his Dissuasion had no other Effect than to produce a large Volley of Oaths and Curses, which greatly shocked the
pious Ears of *Supple*; but he did not dare to remonstrate against a
Privilege, which the Squire claimed as a free-born *Englishman*. To
say Truth, the Parson submitted to please his Palate at the Squire's
Table, at the Expence of suffering now and then this Violence to
his Ears. He contented himself with thinking he did not promote
this evil Practice, and that the Squire would not swear an Oath the
less, if he never entered within his Gates. However, tho' he was not
guilty of ill Manners by rebuking a Gentleman in his own House,
he paid him off obliquely in the Pulpit; which had not, indeed, the
good Effect of working a Reformation in the Squire himself; yet it
so far operated on his Conscience, that he put the Laws very
severely in Execution against others, and the Magistrate was the
only Person in the Parish who could swear with Impunity.

Chapter X.

In which Mr. Western *visits Mr.* Allworthy.

Mr. *Allworthy* was now retired from Breakfast with his Nephew,
well satisfied with the Report of the young Gentleman's successful
Visit to *Sophia*, (for he greatly desired the Match, more on
Account of the young Lady's Character than of her Riches) when
Mr. *Western* broke abruptly in upon them, and without any Cere-
mony began as follows.

'There, you have done a fine Piece of Work truly. You have
brought up your Bastard to a fine Purpose; not that I believe you
have had any Hand in it neither, that is, as a Man may say,
designedly; but there is a fine Kettle of Fish made on't up at our

4. At a drunken banquet, Alexander, to
his lasting grief, killed Clitus, his friend
and general who had once saved his life,
with a javelin, for maintaining that
Philip, Alexander's father, was a greater
warrior than he.

House.' 'What can be the matter, Mr. *Western?*' said *Allworthy.* 'O Matter *enow* of all Conscience; my Daughter hath fallen in Love with your Bastard, that's all; but I won't *ge* her a *Hapenny*, not the Twentieth Part of a Brass *Varden.* I always thought what would come o' breeding up a Bastard like a Gentleman, and letting *un* come about to *Vok's* Houses. Its well *vor un* I could not get at *un*, I'd *a licked un*, I'd a spoil'd his Caterwauling, I'd a taught the Son of a Whore to meddle with Meat for his Master. He shan't ever have a Morsel of Meat of mine, or a *Varden* to buy it: If she will *ha un*, one Smock shall be her Portion. I'll sooner *ge* my *Esteate* to the *zinking* Fund,[1] that it may be sent to *Hannover* to corrupt our Nation with.' 'I am heartily sorry,' cries *Allworthy.* 'Pox o' your Sorrow,' says *Western*, 'it will do me Abundance of Good, when I have lost my only Child, my poor *Sophy*, that was the Joy of my Heart, and all the Hope and Comfort of my Age; but I am resolved I will turn her out o' Doors; she shall beg and starve, and rot in the Streets. Not one *Hapenny*, not a *Hapenny* shall she ever *hae* o' mine. The Son of Bitch was always good at finding a Hare sitting; an be rotted to'n, I little thought what Puss he was looking after; but it shall be the worst he ever *vound* in his Life. She shall be no better than Carrion; the Skin o'er is all he shall *ha*, and *zu* you may tell *un.*' 'I am in Amazement,' cries *Allworthy*, 'at what you tell me, after what passed between my Nephew and the young Lady no longer ago than Yesterday.' 'Yes, Sir,' answered *Western*, 'it was after what passed between your Nephew and she that the whole Matter came out. Mr. *Blifil* there was no sooner gone than the Son of a Whore came lurching about the House. Little did I think, when I used to love him for a Sportsman, that he was all the while a poaching after my Daughter.' 'Why, truly,' says *Allworthy*, 'I could wish you had not given him so many Opportunities with her; and you will do me the Justice to acknowledge, that I have always been averse to his staying so much at your House, tho' I own I had no Suspicion of this Kind.' 'Why, Zounds!' cries *Western*, 'who could have thought it? What the Devil had she to do wi'n? He did not come there a courting to her; he came there a hunting with me.' 'But was it possible,' says *Allworthy*, 'that you should never discern any Symptoms of Love between them, when you have seen them so often together?' 'Never in my Life, as I hope to be saved,' cries *Western*. 'I never so much as zeed him kiss her in all my Life; and so far from courting her, he used rather to be more silent when she was in Company than at any other Time: And as for the Girl, she was always less civil to'n than to any young Man that came to the

---

1. In 1716, the British government established a sinking fund to reduce the national debt (Act 3 George I. c.7). In the early 1740's, resentment over paying English money to George II's German mistresses and army in Hanover, his hereditary German principality, broke into hot Parliamentary debate.

House. As to that Matter, I am not more easy to be deceived than another; I would not have you think I am, Neighbour.' *Allworthy* could scarce refrain Laughter at this: but he resolved to do a Violence to himself: For he perfectly well knew Mankind, and had too much good Breeding and good Nature to offend the Squire in his present Circumstances. He then asked *Western* what he would have him do upon this Occasion. To which the other answered, 'That he would have him keep the Rascal away from his House, and that he would go and lock up the Wench: For he was resolved to make her marry Mr. *Blifil* in Spite of her Teeth.' He then shook *Blifil* by the Hand, and swore he would have no other Son-in-law. Presently after which he took his Leave, saying, his House was in such Disorder, that it was necessary for him to make haste home, to take care his Daughter did not give him the Slip; and as for *Jones*, he swore, if he caught him at his House, he would qualify him to run for the Gelding's Plate.

When *Allworthy* and *Blifil* were again left together, a long Silence ensued between them; all which Interval the young Gentleman filled up with Sighs, which proceeded partly from Disappointment, but more from Hatred: For the Success of *Jones* was much more grievous to him than the Loss of *Sophia*.

At length his Uncle asked him what he was determined to do, and he answered in the following words. 'Alas, Sir, can it be a Question what Step a Lover will take, when Reason and Passion point different Ways? I am afraid it is too certain he will, in that Dilemma, always follow the latter. Reason dictates to me, to quit all Thoughts of a Woman who places her Affections on another; my Passion bids me hope she may, in Time, change her Inclinations in my Favour. Here, however, I conceive an Objection may be raised, which, if it could not fully be answered, would totally deter me from any further Pursuit. I mean the Injustice of endeavouring to supplant another, in a Heart, of which he seems already in Possession; but the determined Resolution of Mr. *Western* shews, that in this Case I shall, by so doing, promote the Happiness of every Party; not only that of the Parent, who will thus be preserved from the highest Degree of Misery, but of both the others, who must be undone by this Match. The Lady, I am sure, will be undone in every Sense: For, besides the Loss of most Part of her own Fortune, she will be not only married to a Beggar, but the little Fortune which her Father cannot with-hold from her, will be squandered on that Wench, with whom I know he yet converses—Nay, that is a Trifle: For I know him to be one of the worst Men in the World: For had my dear Uncle known what I have hitherto endeavoured to conceal, he must have long since abandoned so profligate a Wretch.' 'How,' said *Allworthy*, 'hath he done any Thing worse than

I already know? Tell me, I beseech you.' 'No,' replied *Blifil*, 'it is
now past, and perhaps he may have repented of it.' 'I command
you, on your Duty,' said *Allworthy*, 'to tell me what you mean.'
'You know, Sir,' says *Blifil*, 'I never disobeyed you; but I am sorry I
mentioned it, since it may now look like Revenge, whereas, I thank
Heaven, no such Motive ever entered my Heart; and if you oblige
me to discover it, I must be his Petitioner to you for your Forgiveness.' 'I will have no Conditions,' answered *Allworthy*, 'I think I
have shewn Tenderness enough towards him, and more perhaps
than you ought to thank me for.' 'More, indeed, I fear than he
deserved,' cries *Blifil*; 'for in the very Day of your utmost Danger,
when myself and all the Family were in Tears, he filled the House
with Riot and Debauchery. He drank and sung and roared; and
when I gave him a gentle Hint of the Indecency of his Actions, he
fell into a violent Passion, swore many Oaths, called me Rascal, and
struck me.' 'How!' cries *Allworthy*, 'did he dare to strike you?' 'I am
sure,' cries *Blifil*, 'I have forgiven him that long ago. I wish I could
so easily forget his Ingratitude to the best of Benefactors; and yet,
even that I hope you will forgive him, since he must have certainly
been possessed with the Devil: For that very Evening, as Mr.
Thwackum and myself were taking the Air in the Fields, and exulting in the good Symptoms which then first began to discover themselves, we unluckily saw him engaged with a Wench in a Manner
not fit to be mentioned. Mr. *Thwackum*, with more Boldness than
Prudence, advanced to rebuke him, when (I am sorry to say it) he
fell upon the worthy Man, and beat him so outrageously, that I
wish he may have yet recovered the Bruises. Nor was I without my
Share of the Effects of his Malice, while I endeavoured to protect
my Tutor: But that I have long forgiven; nay, I prevailed with Mr.
Thwackum to forgive him too, and not to inform you of a Secret
which I feared might be fatal to him. And now, Sir, since I have
unadvisedly dropped a Hint of this Matter, and your Commands
have obliged me to discover the Whole, let me intercede with you
for him.' 'O Child,' said *Allworthy*, 'I know not whether I should
blame or applaud your Goodness, in concealing such Villainy a
Moment: But where is Mr. *Thwackum*? Not that I want any Confirmation of what you say; but I will examine all the Evidence of
this Matter, to justify to the World the Example I am resolved to
make of such a Monster.'

Thwackum was now sent for, and presently appeared. He corroborated every Circumstance which the other had deposed; nay, he
produced the Record upon his Breast, where the Handwriting of
Mr. *Jones* remained very legible in Black and Blue. He concluded
with declaring to Mr. *Allworthy*, that he should have long since
informed him of this Matter, had not Mr. *Blifil*, by the most ear-

nest Interpositions, prevented him. 'He is,' says he, 'an excellent Youth; though such Forgiveness of Enemies is carrying the Matter too far.'

In Reality, *Blifil* had taken some Pains to prevail with the Parson, and to prevent the Discovery at that Time; for which he had many Reasons. He knew that the Minds of Men are apt to be softened and relaxed from their usual Severity by Sickness. Besides, he imagined that if the Story was told when the Fact was so recent, and the Physician about the House, who might have unravelled the real Truth, he should never be able to give it the malicious Turn which he intended. Again, he resolved to hoard up this Business, till the Indiscretion of *Jones* should afford some additional Complaints; for he thought the joint Weight of many Facts falling upon him together, would be the most likely to crush him; and he watched therefore some such Opportunity as that with which Fortune had now kindly presented him. Lastly, by prevailing with *Thwackum* to conceal the Matter for a Time, he knew he should confirm an Opinion of his Friendship to *Jones*, which he had greatly laboured to establish in Mr. *Allworthy*.

Chapter XI.

A short Chapter; but which contains sufficient Matter to affect the good-natured Reader.

It was Mr. *Allworthy*'s Custom never to punish any one, not even to turn away a Servant, in a Passion. He resolved, therefore, to delay passing Sentence on *Jones* till the Afternoon.

The poor young Man attended at Dinner, as usual; but his Heart was too much loaded to suffer him to eat. His Grief too was a good deal aggravated by the unkind Looks of Mr. *Allworthy*; whence he concluded that *Western* had discovered the whole Affair between him and *Sophia*: But as to Mr. *Blifil*'s Story, he had not the least Apprehension; for of much the greater Part he was entirely innocent; and for the Residue, as he had forgiven and forgotten it himself, so he suspected no Remembrance on the other Side. When Dinner was over, and the Servants departed, Mr. *Allworthy* began to harangue. He set forth, in a long Speech, the many Iniquities of which *Jones* had been guilty, particularly those which this Day had brought to Light; and concluded by telling him, 'That unless he could clear himself of the Charge, he was resolved to banish him his Sight for ever.'

Many Disadvantages attended poor *Jones* in making his Defence; nay, indeed, he hardly knew his Accusation: For as Mr. *Allworthy*, in recounting the Drunkenness, &c. while he lay ill, out of Modesty sunk every thing that related particularly to himself, which indeed principally constituted the Crime; *Jones* could not deny the Charge. His Heart was, besides, almost broken already; and his Spirits were so sunk, that he could say nothing for himself; but acknowledged the Whole, and, like a Criminal in Despair, threw himself upon Mercy; concluding, 'That tho' he must own himself guilty of many Follies and Inadvertencies, he hoped he had done nothing to deserve what would be to him the greatest Punishment in the World.'

Allworthy answered, 'That he had forgiven him too often already, in Compassion to his Youth, and in Hopes of his Amendment: That he now found he was an abandoned Reprobate, and such as it would be criminal in any one to support and encourage. Nay,' said Mr. *Allworthy* to him, 'your audacious Attempt to steal away the young Lady calls upon me to justify my own Character in punishing you. The World, who have already censured the Regard I have shewn for you, may think, with some Colour at least of Justice, that I connive at so base and barbarous an Action. An Action of which you must have known my Abhorrence; and which, had you had any Concern for my Ease and Honour, as well as for my Friendship, you would never have thought of undertaking. Fie upon it, young Man! indeed there is scarce any Punishment equal to your Crimes, and I can scarce think myself justifiable in what I am now going to bestow on you. However, as I have educated you like a Child of my own, I will not turn you naked into the World. When you open this Paper, therefore, you will find something which may enable you, with Industry, to get an honest Livelihood; but if you employ it to worse Purposes, I shall not think myself obliged to supply you farther, being resolved, from this Day forward, to converse no more with you on any Account. I cannot avoid saying, There is no Part of your Conduct which I resent more than your ill Treatment of that good young Man (meaning *Blifil*) who hath behaved with so much Tenderness and Honour towards you.'

These last Words were a Dose almost too bitter to be swallowed. A Flood of Tears now gushed from the Eyes of *Jones,* and every Faculty of Speech and Motion seemed to have deserted him. It was some Time before he was able to obey *Allworthy*'s peremptory Commands of departing; which he at length did, having first kissed his Hands with a Passion difficult to be affected, and as difficult to be described.

The Reader must be very weak, if, when he considers the Light in which *Jones* then appeared to Mr. *Allworthy*, he should blame the Rigour of his Sentence. And yet all the Neighbourhood, either from this Weakness, or from some worse Motive, condemned this Justice and Severity as the highest Cruelty. Nay, the very Persons who had before censured the good Man for the Kindness and Tenderness shewn to a Bastard (his own, according to the general Opinion) now cried out as loudly against turning his own Child out of Doors. The Women especially were unanimous in taking the Part of *Jones*, and raised more Stories on the Occasion than I have Room, in this Chapter, to set down.

One Thing must not be omitted, that in their Censures on this Occasion, none ever mentioned the Sum contained in the Paper which *Allworthy* gave *Jones*, which was no less than Five hundred Pounds; but all agreed that he was sent away Pennyless, and some said, naked from the House of his inhuman Father.

Chapter XII.

Containing Love-Letters, &c.

Jones was commanded to leave the House immediately, and told, that his Clothes and every Thing else should be sent to him whithersoever he should order them.

He accordingly set out, and walked above a Mile, not regarding, and indeed scarce knowing whither he went. At length a little Brook obstructing his Passage, he threw himself down by the Side of it; nor could he help muttering, with some little Indignation, 'Sure my Father will not deny me this Place to rest in?'

Here he presently fell into the most violent Agonies, tearing his Hair from his Head, and using most other Actions which generally accompany Fits of Madness, Rage, and Despair.

When he had in this Manner vented the first Emotions of Passion, he began to come a little to himself. His Grief now took another Turn, and discharged itself in a gentler Way, till he became at last cool enough to reason with his Passion, and to consider what Steps were proper to be taken in his deplorable Condition.

And now the great Doubt was, how to act with regard to *Sophia*. The Thoughts of leaving her, almost rent his Heart asunder; but the Consideration of reducing her to Ruin and Beggary still racked him, if possible, more; and if the violent Desire of possessing her Person could have induced him to listen one Moment to this Alternative, still he was by no means certain of her Resolution to indulge his Wishes at so high an Expence. The Resentment of Mr. *Allworthy*, and the Injury he must do to his Quiet, argued strongly against this latter; and lastly, the apparent Impossibility of his Success, even if he would sacrifice all these Considerations to it, came to his Assistance; and thus Honour at last, backed with Despair, with Gratitude to his Benefactor, and with real Love to his Mistress, got the better of burning Desire, and he resolved rather to quit *Sophia* than to pursue her to her Ruin.

It is difficult for any who have not felt it, to conceive the glowing

Warmth which filled his Breast on the first Contemplation of this
Victory over his Passion. Pride flattered him so agreeably, that his
Mind perhaps enjoyed perfect Happiness; but this was only mo-
mentary; *Sophia* soon returned to his Imagination, and allayed the
Joy of his Triumph with no less bitter Pangs than a good-natured
General must feel when he surveys the bleeding Heaps, at the Price
of whose Blood he hath purchased his Laurels; for thousands of
tender Ideas lay murdered before our Conqueror.

Being resolved, however, to pursue the Paths of this Giant
Honour, as the gigantic Poet *Lee*[1] calls it, he determined to write a
farewell Letter to *Sophia*; and accordingly proceeded to a House not
far off, where, being furnished with proper Materials, he wrote as
follows.

MADAM,

'When you reflect on the Situation in which I write, I am sure
your Good-nature will pardon any Inconsistency or Absurdity which
my Letter contains; for every thing here flows from a Heart so full,
that no Language can express its Dictates.

'I have resolved, Madam, to obey your Commands, in flying for
ever from your dear, your lovely Sight. Cruel indeed those Commands are; but it is a Cruelty which proceeds from Fortune, not
from my *Sophia*. Fortune hath made it necessary, necessary to your
Preservation, to forget there ever was such a Wretch as I am.

'Believe me, I would not hint all my Sufferings to you, if I imagined they could possibly escape your Ears. I know the Goodness and
Tenderness of your Heart, and would avoid giving you any of those
Pains which you always feel for the Miserable. O let nothing, which
you shall hear of my hard Fortune, cause a Moment's Concern; for
after the Loss of you, every Thing is to me a Trifle.

'O *Sophia!* it is hard to leave you; it is harder still to desire you
to forget me; yet the sincerest Love obliges me to both. Pardon my
conceiving that any Remembrance of me can give you Disquiet; but
if I am so gloriously wretched, sacrifice me every Way to your
Relief. Think I never loved you; or think truly how little I deserve
you; and learn to scorn me for a Presumption which can never be
too severely punished.—I am unable to say more.——May Guardian Angels protect you for ever.'

He was now searching his Pockets for his Wax, but found none,
nor indeed any thing else, therein; for in Truth he had, in his fran-

1. Nathaniel Lee, *Theodosius* (1680),
II.i.340: "And I am dar'd with this Gi-
gantick honour." Fielding parodies several of Lee's grandiose plays, though not
Theodosius, in *Tom Thumb* (1730,
1731). But in *Joseph Andrews* (III.x),
an actor quotes twelve lines that come
earlier in this same scene, and with
small inaccuracies suggesting that Fielding (or his actor) is quoting from memory, as here in *Tom Jones*.

tic Disposition, tossed every thing from him, and, amongst the rest, his Pocket-book, which he had received from Mr. *Allworthy*, which he had never opened, and which now first occurred to his Memory.

The House supplied him with a Wafer for his present Purpose, with which having sealed his Letter, he returned hastily towards the Brook Side, in order to search for the Things which he had there lost. In his Way he met his old Friend *Black George*, who heartily condoled with him on his Misfortune; for this had already reached his Ears, and indeed those of all the Neighbourhood.

Jones acquainted the Game-keeper with his Loss, and he as readily went back with him to the Brook, where they searched every Tuft of Grass in the Meadow, as well where *Jones* had not been, as where he had been; but all to no Purpose, for they found nothing: For indeed, though the Things were then in the Meadow, they omitted to search the only Place where they were deposited; to wit, in the Pockets of the said *George*; for he had just before found them, and being luckily apprized of their Value, had very carefully put them up for his own Use.

The Game-keeper having exerted as much Diligence in Quest of the lost Goods, as if he had hoped to find them, desired Mr. *Jones* to recollect if he had been in no other Place; 'For sure,' said he, 'if you had lost them here so lately, the Things must have been here still; for this is a very unlikely Place for any one to pass by;' and indeed it was by great Accident that he himself had passed through that Field, in order to lay Wires for Hares, with which he was to supply a Poulterer at *Bath* the next Morning.

Jones now gave over all Hopes of recovering his Loss, and almost all Thoughts concerning it, and turning to *Black George*, asked him earnestly, If he would do him the greatest Favour in the World?

George answered, with some Hesitation, 'Sir, you know you may command me whatever is in my Power, and I heartily wish it was in my Power to do you any Service.' In fact, the Question staggered him; for he had, by selling Game, amassed a pretty good Sum of Money in Mr. *Western's* Service, and was afraid that *Jones* wanted to borrow some small Matter of him; but he was presently relieved from his Anxiety, by being desired to convey a Letter to *Sophia*, which with great Pleasure he promised to do. And indeed, I believe there are few Favours which he would not have gladly conferred on Mr. *Jones*; for he bore as much Gratitude towards him as he could, and was as honest as Men who love Money better than any other Thing in the Universe, generally are.

Mrs. *Honour* was agreed by both to be the proper Means by which this Letter should pass to *Sophia*. They then separated; the Game-keeper returned home to Mr. *Western's*, and *Jones* walked to an Alehouse at half a Mile's Distance, to wait for his Messenger's Return.

George no sooner came home to his Master's House, than he met with Mrs. *Honour*; to whom, having first sounded her with a few previous Questions, he delivered the Letter for her Mistress, and received at the same Time another from her for Mr. *Jones*; which *Honour* told him she had carried all that Day in her Bosom, and began to despair of finding any Means of delivering it.

The Game-keeper returned hastily and joyfully to *Jones*, who having received *Sophia*'s Letter from him instantly withdrew, and eagerly breaking it open read as follows:

Sir,

'It is impossible to express what I have felt since I saw you. Your submitting, on my Account, to such cruel Insults from my Father, lays me under an Obligation I shall ever own. As you know his Temper, I beg you will, for my Sake, avoid him. I wish I had any Comfort to send you; but believe this, that nothing but the last Violence shall ever give my Hand or Heart where you would be sorry to see them bestowed.'

Jones read this Letter a hundred Times over, and kissed it a hundred Times as often. His Passion now brought all tender Desires back into his Mind. He repented that he had writ to *Sophia* in the Manner we have seen above; but he repented more that he had made use of the Interval of his Messenger's Absence to write and dispatch a Letter to Mr. *Allworthy*, in which he had faithfully promised and bound himself to quit all Thoughts of his Love. However, when his cool Reflections returned, he plainly perceived that his Case was neither mended nor altered by *Sophia*'s Billet, unless to give him some little Glimpse of Hope from her Constancy, of some favourable Accident hereafter. He therefore resumed his Resolution, and taking leave of *Black George*, set forward to a Town about five Miles distant, whither he had desired Mr. *Allworthy*, unless he pleased to revoke his Sentence, to send his Things after him.

Chapter XIII.

The Behaviour of Sophia *on the present Occasion; which none of her Sex will blame, who are capable of behaving in the same Manner. And the Discussion of a knotty Point in the Court of Conscience.*

Sophia had passed the last twenty-four Hours in no very desirable Manner. During a large Part of them she had been entertained by her Aunt, with Lectures of Prudence, recommending to her the Example of the polite World, where Love (so the good Lady said) is at present entirely laughed at, and where Women consider Matrimony, as Men do Offices of public Trust, only as the Means of making their Fortunes, and of advancing themselves in the World. In commenting on which Text Mrs. *Western* had displayed her Eloquence during several Hours.

These sagacious Lectures, though little suited either to the Taste or Inclination of *Sophia*, were, however, less irksome to her than her own Thoughts, that formed the Entertainment of the Night, during which she never once closed her Eyes.

But though she could neither sleep nor rest in her Bed; yet, having no Avocation from it, she was found there by her Father at his Return from *Allworthy*'s, which was not till past Ten o'Clock in the Morning. He went directly up to her Apartment, opened the Door, and seeing she was not up—cried—'Oh! you are safe then, and I am resolved to keep you so.' He then locked the Door, and delivered the Key to *Honour*, having first given her the strictest Charge, with great Promises of Rewards for her Fidelity, and most dreadful Menaces of Punishment, in case she should betray her Trust.

Honour's Orders were not to suffer her Mistress to come out of her Room without the Authority of the Squire himself, and to admit none to her but him and her Aunt; but she was herself to attend her with whatever *Sophia* pleased, except only Pen, Ink, and Paper, of which she was forbidden the Use.

The Squire ordered his Daughter to dress herself and attend him at Dinner; which she obeyed; and having sat the usual Time, was again conducted to her Prison.

In the Evening, the Goaler[1] *Honour* brought her the Letter which she received from the Game-keeper. *Sophia* read it very attentively twice or thrice over, and then threw herself upon the Bed, and burst into a Flood of Tears. Mrs. *Honour* expressed great Astonishment at this Behaviour in her Mistress; nor could she forbear very eagerly begging to know the Cause of this Passion. *Sophia* made her no Answer for some Time, and then starting suddenly up caught her Maid by the Hand, and cried, 'O *Honour*! I am undone.' 'Marry forbid,' cries *Honour*, 'I wish the Letter had been burnt before I had brought it to your La'ship. I'm sure I thought it would have comforted your La'ship, or I would have seen it at the Devil before I would have touch'd it.' '*Honour*,' says *Sophia*, 'you are a good Girl, and it is vain to attempt concealing longer my Weakness from you; I have thrown away my Heart on a Man who hath forsaken me.' 'And is Mr. *Jones*,' answered the Maid, 'such a Perfidy Man?' 'He hath taken his Leave of me,' says *Sophia*, 'for ever in that Letter. Nay, he hath desired me to forget him. Could he have

---

1. A widespread eighteenth-century misspelling of *gaoler* ("jailer").

desired that, if he had loved me? Could he have borne such a Thought? Could he have written such a Word?' 'No certainly, Ma'am,' cries Honour, 'and to be sure, if the best Man in *England* was to desire me to forget him, I'd take him at his Word. Marry come up! I am sure your La'ship hath done him too much Honour ever to think on him. A young Lady who may take her Choice of all the young Men in the Country.—And to be sure, if I may be so presumptuous as to offer my poor Opinion, there is young Mr. *Blifil*, who besides that he is come of honest Parents, and will be one of the greatest Squires all hereabouts, he is to be sure, in my poor Opinion, a more handsomer, and a more politer Man by half; and besides, he is a young Gentleman of a sober Character, and who may defy any of the Neighbours to say black is his Eye: He follows no dirty Trollops, nor can any Bastards be laid at his Door. Forget him indeed! I thank Heaven I myself am not so much at my last Prayers, as to suffer any Man to bid me forget him twice. If the best He that wears a Head was for to go for to offer to say such an affronting Word to me, I would never give him my Company afterwards, if there was another young Man in the Kingdom. And as I was a saying, to be sure, there is young Mr. *Blifil*'—'Name not his detested Name,' cries *Sophia*. 'Nay, Ma'am,' says Honour, 'If your La'ship doth not like him, there be more jolly handsome young Men that would court your La'ship, if they had but the least Encouragement. I don't believe there is arrow young Gentleman in this Country, or in the next to it, that if your La'ship was but to look as if you had a Mind to him, would not come about to make his Offers directly.' 'What a Wretch dost thou imagine me,' cries *Sophia*, 'by affronting my Ears with such Stuff! I detest all Mankind.' 'Nay, to be sure, Ma'am,' answered Honour, 'your La'ship hath had enough to give you a Surfeit of them. To be used ill by such a poor beggarly bastardly Fellow.' 'Hold your blasphemous Tongue,' cries *Sophia*, 'how dare you mention his Name with Disrespect before me? He use me ill? No, his poor bleeding Heart suffered more when he writ the cruel Words, than mine from reading them. O! he is all heroic Virtue, and angelic Goodness. I am ashamed of the Weakness of my own Passion, for blaming what I ought to admire.—O Honour! it is my Good only which he consults. To my Interest he sacrifices both himself and me———— The Apprehension of ruining me hath driven him to Despair.' 'I am very glad,' says Honour, 'to hear your La'ship takes that into your Consideration: for to be sure, it must be nothing less than Ruin, to give your Mind to one that is turned out of Doors, and is not worth a Farthing in the World.' 'Turned out of Doors!' cries *Sophia* hastily, 'how! what dost thou mean?' 'Why, to be sure, Ma'am, my Master no sooner told Squire *Allworthy* about Mr. *Jones* having offered to make Love to your Ladyship, than the Squire stripped him stark naked, and turned him out of Doors.' 'Ha!' says *Sophia*, 'I have been the cursed, wretched Cause of his Destruction?—Turn'd naked out of Doors! Here, *Honour*, take all the Money I have; take the Rings from my Fingers.—Here my Watch, carry him all.—Go, find him immediately.' 'For Heaven's Sake, Ma'am,' answered Mrs. *Honour*, 'do but consider, if my Master should miss any of these Things, I should be made to answer for them. Therefore let me beg your Ladyship not to part with your Watch and Jewels. Besides the Money, I think, is enough of all Conscience; and as for that, my Master can never know any thing of the Matter.' 'Here then,' cries *Sophia*, "take every Farthing I am worth, find him out immediately and give it him. Go, go, lose not a Moment.'

Mrs. *Honour* departed according to Orders, and finding *Black George* below Stairs, delivered him the Purse which contained Sixteen Guineas, being indeed the whole Stock of *Sophia*: For tho' her Father was very liberal to her, she was much too generous herself to be rich.

Black George having received the Purse, set forward towards the Alehouse; but in the Way a Thought occurred to him, whether he should not detain this Money likewise. His Conscience, however, immediately started at this Suggestion, and began to upbraid him with Ingratitude to his Benefactor. To this his Avarice answered, 'That his Conscience should have considered the Matter before, when he deprived poor *Jones* of his 500*l.* That having quietly acquiesced in what was of so much greater Importance, it was absurd, if not downright Hypocrisy, to affect any Qualms at this Trifle.' In return to which, Conscience, like a good Lawyer, attempted to distinguish between an absolute Breach of Trust, as here where the Goods were delivered, and a bare Concealment of what was found, as in the former Case. Avarice presently treated this with Ridicule, called it a Distinction without a Difference, and absolutely insisted, that when once all Pretensions of Honour and Virtue were given up in any one Instance, that there was no Precedent for resorting to them upon a second Occasion. In short, poor Conscience had certainly been defeated in the Argument, had not Fear stept in to her Assistance, and very strenuously urged, that the real Distinction between the two Actions, did not lie in the different Degrees of Honour, but of Safety: For that the secreting the 500*l.* was a Matter of very little Hazard; whereas the detaining the Sixteen Guineas was liable to the utmost Danger of Discovery.

By this friendly Aid of Fear, Conscience obtained a compleat Victory in the Mind of *Black George*, and, after making him a few Compliments on his Honesty, forced him to deliver the Money to *Jones*.

Chapter XIV.

A *short Chapter, containing a short Dialogue between* Squire *West-ern and his Sister.*

Mrs. *Western* had been engaged abroad all that Day. The Squire met her at her Return home; and when she enquired after *Sophia,* he acquainted her that he had secured her safe enough. 'She is locked up in Chamber,' cries he, 'and *Honour* keeps the Key.' As his Looks were full of prodigious Wisdom and Sagacity when he gave his Sister this Information, it is probable he expected much Applause from her for what he had done; but how was he disappointed! when with a most disdainful Aspect, she cried, 'Sure, Brother, you are the weakest of all Men. Why will you not confide in me for the Management of my Niece? Why will you interpose? You have now undone all that I have been spending my Breath in order to bring about. While I have been endeavouring to fill her Mind with Maxims of Prudence, you have been provoking her to reject them. *English* Women, Brother, I thank Heaven, are no Slaves. We are not to be locked up like the *Spanish* and *Italian* Wives. We have as good a Right to Liberty as yourselves. We are to be convinced by Reason and Persuasion only, and not governed by Force. I have seen the World, Brother, and know what Arguments to make Use of; and if your Folly had not prevented me, should have prevailed with her to form her Conduct by those Rules of Prudence and Discretion which I formerly taught her.' 'To be sure,' said the Squire, 'I am always in the Wrong.' 'Brother,' answered the Lady, 'you are not in the Wrong, unless when you meddle with Matters beyond your Knowledge. You must agree, that I have seen most of the World? and happy had it been for my Niece, if she had not been taken from under my Care. It is by living at home with you that she hath learnt romantic Notions of Love and Nonsense.' 'You don't imagine, I hope,' cries the Squire, 'that I have taught her any such Things.' 'Your Ignorance, Brother,' returned she, 'as the great *Milton* says, almost subdues my Patience.'[1] 'D——n *Milton*,' answered the Squire, 'if he had the Impudence to say so to my Face, I'd lend him a Douse, thof he was never so great a Man. Patience! an you come to that, Sister, I have more Occasion of Patience, to be used like an overgrown School-boy; as I am by you. Do you think no one hath any Understanding, unless he hath been about at Court? Pox! the World is come to a fine Pass indeed, if we are all Fools, except a Parcel of Roundheads

---

1. The Reader may perhaps subdue his own Patience, if he searches for this in *Milton* [*Fielding's note*]. See below, pp. 252, 425, and 688.

and *Hannover* Rats.[2] Pox! I hope the Times are a coming that we shall make Fools of them, and every Man shall enjoy his own. That's all, Sister, and every Man shall enjoy his own. I hope to *zee* it, Sister, before the *Hannover* Rats have eat up all our Corn, and left us nothing but Turneps to feed upon.' 'I protest, Brother,' cries she, 'you are now got beyond my Understanding. Your Jargon of Turneps and *Hannover* Rats, is to me perfectly unintelligible.' 'I believe,' cries he, 'you don't care to hear o'em; but the Country Interest may succeed one Day or other for all that.' 'I wish,' answered the Lady, 'you would think a little of your Daughter's Interest: For believe me, she is in greater Danger than the Nation.' 'Just now,' said he, 'you chid me for thinking on her, and would ha' her left to you.' 'And if you will promise to interpose no more,' answered she, 'I will out of my Regard to my Niece, undertake the Charge.' 'Well, do then,' said the Squire, 'for you know I always agreed, that Women are the properest to manage Women.'

Mrs. *Western* then departed, muttering something with an Air of Disdain, concerning Women and Management of the Nation. She immediately repaired to *Sophia*'s Apartment, who was now, after a Day's Confinement, released again from her Captivity.

BOOK VII.

Containing three Days.

Chapter I.

A Comparison between the World and the Stage.

The World hath been often compared to the Theatre; and many grave Writers, as well as the Poets, have considered human Life as a great Drama, resembling, in almost every Particular, those scenical Representations, which *Thespis* is first reported to have invented, and which have been since received with so much Approbation and Delight in all polite Countries.

This Thought hath been carried so far, and is become so general, that some Words proper to the Theatre, and which were, at first, metaphorically applied to the World, are now indiscriminately and literally spoken of both: Thus Stage and Scene are by common Use grown as familiar to us, when we speak of Life in general, as when

2. The Puritans, or Roundheads (so called for their close-cropped hair) overthrew and beheaded Charles I, a Stuart, in 1649; when George I, Elector of Hanover, succeeded Queen Anne in 1714, the Stuart line was again supplanted. Most country-dwellers, like Western, favored the Stuarts, especially Bonnie Prince Charlie, then invading England to regain the throne for the Stuarts.

we confine ourselves to dramatic Performances; and when Transactions behind the Curtain, are mentioned, *St. James's*[1] is more likely to occur to our Thoughts than *Drury Lane.*

It may seem easy enough to account for all this, by reflecting that the theatrical Stage is nothing more than a Representation, or, as *Aristotle*[2] calls it, an Imitation of what really exists; and hence, perhaps, we might fairly pay a very high Compliment to those, who by their Writings or Actions have been so capable of imitating Life, as to have their Pictures in a Manner confounded with, or mistaken for the Originals.

But, in Reality, we are not so fond of paying Compliments to these People, whom we use as Children frequently do the Instruments of their Amusement; and have much more Pleasure in hissing and buffeting them, than in admiring their Excellence. There are many other Reasons which have induced us to see this Analogy between the World and the Stage.

Some have considered the larger Part of Mankind in the Light of Actors, as personating Characters no more their own, and to which, in Fact, they have no better Title, than the Player hath to be in Earnest thought the King or Emperor whom he represents. Thus the Hypocrite may be said to be a Player;[3] and indeed the *Greeks* called them both by one and the same Name.

The Brevity of Life hath likewise given Occasion to this Comparison. So the immortal *Shakespear.*

> ———*Life's a poor Player,*
> *That struts and frets his Hour upon the Stage,*
> *And then is heard no more.*[4]

For which hackneyed Quotation, I will make the Reader Amends by a very noble one, which few, I believe, have read. It is taken from a Poem called the DEITY,[5] published about nine Years ago, and long since buried in Oblivion. A Proof that good Books no more than good Men do always survive the bad.

> *From thee*[6] *all human Actions take their Springs,*
> *The Rise of Empires and the Fall of Kings!*
> *See the* VAST THEATRE OF TIME *display'd,*
> *While o'er the Scene succeeding Heroes tread!*
> *With Pomp the shining Images succeed,*
> *What Leaders Triumph, and what Monarchs bleed!*

1. St. James's Palace was the royal residence; Drury Lane, the royal theater. The curtains, presumably, are those of either a bed or a courtroom; the transactions, either sexual or political.
2. That the playwright imitates life is the central idea of the *Poetics.*
3. The Greek word for acting on the stage was *hypokrisis,* whence the transferred meaning of acting a part in life.
4. *Macbeth* V.v.24–26. The full first line reads, "Life's but a walking shadow, a poor player." Fielding wrote "storms and struts" in the first edition, then corrected his error when he revised for the fourth edition.
5. By Samuel Boyse, 1739.
6. The DEITY [*Fielding's note*].

Perform the Parts thy Providence assign'd,
Their Pride, their Passions to thy Ends inclin'd:
A while they glitter in the Face of Day,
Then at thy Nod the Phantoms pass away;
No Traces left of all the busy Scene,
But that Remembrance joys—THE THINGS HAVE BEEN!

In all these, however, and in every other Similitude of Life to the
Theatre, the Resemblance hath been always taken from the Stage
only. None, as I remember, have at all considered the Audience at
this great Drama.

But as Nature often exhibits some of her best Performances to a
very full House; so will the Behaviour of her Spectators no less
admit the above mentioned Comparison than that of her Actors.
In this vast Theatre of Time are seated the Friend and the Critic;
here are Claps and Shouts, Hisses and Groans; in short, every Thing
which was ever seen or heard at the Theatre-Royal.

Let us examine this in one Example: For Instance, in the Behaviour of the great Audience on that Scene which Nature was pleased
to exhibit in the 12th Chapter of the preceding Book, where she
introduced *Black George* running away with the 500*l.* from his
Friend and Benefactor.

Those who sat in the World's upper Gallery, treated that Inci-
dent, I am well convinced, with their usual Vociferation; and every
Term of scurrilous Reproach was most probably vented on that
Occasion.

If we had descended to the next Order of Spectators, we should
have found an equal Degree of Abhorrence, tho' less of Noise and
Scurrility; yet here the good Women gave *Black George* to the Devil,
and many of them expected every Minute that the cloven footed
Gentleman would fetch his own.

The Pit, as usual, was no doubt divided: Those who delight in
heroic Virtue and perfect Character, objected to the producing such
Instances of Villainy, without punishing them very severely for the
Sake of Example. Some of the Author's Friends cry'd—'Look'e,
Gentlemen, the Man is a Villain; but it is Nature for all that.' And
all the young Critics of the Age, the Clerks, Apprentices, &c. called
it low, and fell a groaning.

As for the Boxes, they behaved with their accustomed Politeness.
Most of them were attending to something else. Some of those few
who regarded the Scene at all, declared he was a bad Kind of Man;
while others refused to give their Opinion, 'till they had heard that
of the best Judges.

Now we, who are admitted behind the Scenes of this great Theatre of Nature, (and no Author ought to write any Thing besides
Dictionaries and Spelling Books who hath not this Privilege) can
censure the Action, without conceiving any absolute Detestation of

the Person, whom perhaps Nature may not have designed to act an
ill Part in all her Dramas: For in this Instance, Life most exactly
resembles the Stage, since it is often the same Person who represents the Villain and the Heroe; and he who engages your Admiration To-day, will probably attract your Contempt To-morrow. As
Garrick, whom I regard in Tragedy to be the greatest Genius the
World hath ever produced, sometimes condescends to play the
Fool; so did *Scipio* the Great and *Lælius* the Wise,[7] according to
Horace, many Years ago: nay, *Cicero* reports them to have been
'incredibly childish.'——These, it is true, played the Fool, like my
Friend *Garrick*, in Jest only; but several eminent Characters have,
in numberless Instances of their Lives, played the Fool egregiously
in Earnest; so far as to render it a matter of some Doubt, whether
their Wisdom or Folly was predominant; or whether they were
better intitled to the Applause or Censure, the Admiration or Contempt, the Love or Hatred of Mankind.

Those Persons, indeed, who have passed any Time behind the
Scenes of this Great Theatre, and are thoroughly acquainted not
only with the several Disguises which are there put on, but also
with the fantastic and capricious Behaviour of the Passions, who are
the Managers and Directors of this Theatre, (for as to Reason the
Patentee, he is known to be a very idle Fellow, and seldom to exert
himself) may most probably have learned to understand the famous
Nil admirari of *Horace*,[8] or in the *English* Phrase, *To stare at nothing*.

A single bad act no more constitutes a Villain in Life, than a
single bad Part on the Stage. The Passions, like the Managers of a
Playhouse, often force Men upon Parts, without consulting their
Judgment, and sometimes without any Regard to their Talents.
Thus the Man, as well as the Player, may condemn what he himself
acts; nay, it is common to see Vice sit as awkwardly on some Men,
as the Character of *Iago* would on the honest Face of Mr. *William
Mills*.[9]

Upon the whole, then, the Man of Candour and of true Understanding is never hasty to condemn. He can censure an Imperfection, or even a Vice, without Rage against the guilty Party. In a
Word, they are the same Folly, the same Childishness, the same Ill-
breeding, and the same Ill-nature, which raise all the Clamours and

---

7. Famous friends. Horace, *Satires*
II.i.71–74. Cicero's words are *incredibili-
ter repuerascere* (*De Oratore* II.6.22).

8. *Epistles* I.vi.1: "Nil admirari prope
res est una, Numici, / Solaque quae pos-
sit facere et servare beatum." ("Don't
be amazed, Numicius, that one thing almost by itself can make and preserve
happiness [i.e., indifference to material
possessions and losses].")

9. An actor of whom Fielding speaks

with affection. Fielding again calls him
"Honest Billy Mills" in *The Jacobite's
Journal*, 23 Apr. 1748, in an appeal for
a benefit night for him at the theater. In
Joseph Andrews (I.viii), Fielding commends Mills's ability to rise, as a ghost,
through a trap door, "with a Face all
pale with Powder, and a Shirt all bloody
with Ribbons." His most famous role
was as Banquo (and ghost) in *Macbeth*.
He died in 1750.

Uproars both in Life and on the Stage. The worst of Men generally have the Words *Rogue* and *Villain* most in their Mouths, as the lowest of all Wretches are the aptest to cry out *low* in the Pit.

Chapter II.

Containing a Conversation which Mr. Jones had with himself.

Jones received his Effects from Mr. *Allworthy*'s early in the Morning, with the following Answer to his Letter.

SIR,

'I Am commanded by my Uncle to acquaint you, that as he did not proceed to those Measures he had taken with you, without the greatest Deliberation, and after the fullest Evidence of your Unworthiness, so will it be always out of your Power to cause the least Alteration in his Resolution. He expresses great Surprize at your Presumption in saying, you have resigned all Pretensions to a young Lady, to whom it is impossible you should ever have had any, her Birth and Fortune having made her so infinitely your Superior. Lastly, I am commanded to tell you, that the only Instance of your Compliance with my Uncle's Inclinations, which he requires, is, your immediately quitting this Country. I cannot conclude this without offering you my Advice, as a Christian, that you would seriously think of amending your Life: That you may be assisted with Grace so to do, will be always the Prayer of

Your humble Servant,

W. BLIFIL.

Many contending Passions were raised in our Heroe's Mind by this Letter; but the Tender prevailed at last over the Indignant and Irascible, and a Flood of Tears came seasonably to his Assistance, and possibly prevented his Misfortunes from either turning his Head, or bursting his Heart.

He grew, however, soon ashamed of indulging this Remedy; and starting up, he cried, 'Well then, I will give Mr. *Allworthy* the only Instance he requires of my Obedience. I will go this Moment—but whither?—why let Fortune direct; since there is no other who thinks it of any Consequence what becomes of this wretched Person, it shall be a Matter of equal Indifference to myself. Shall I alone regard what no other?——Ha! have I not Reason to think there is another?—One whose Value is above that of the whole World!—I may, I must imagine my *Sophia* is not indifferent to what becomes of me. Shall I then leave this only Friend—And such a Friend? Shall I not stay with her?—Where? How can I stay with her? Have I any Hopes of ever seeing her, tho' she was as desirous as myself, without exposing her to the Wrath of her Father? And to what Purpose? Can I think of soliciting such a Creature to consent to her own Ruin? Shall I indulge any Passion of mine at such a Price?—Shall I lurk about this Country like a Thief, with such Intentions?—No, I disdain, I detest the Thought. Farewel, *Sophia*; farewel most lovely, most beloved—' Here Passion stopped his Mouth, and found a Vent at his Eyes.

And now, having taken a Resolution to leave the Country, he began to debate with himself whither he should go. *The World*, as *Milton*[1] phrases it, *lay all before him*; and *Jones*, no more than *Adam*, had any Man to whom he might resort for Comfort or Assistance. All his Acquaintance were the Acquaintance of Mr. *All-worthy*, and he had no Reason to expect any Countenance from them, as that Gentleman had withdrawn his Favour from him. Men of great and good Characters should indeed be very cautious how they discard their Dependents; for the Consequence to the unhappy Sufferer is being discarded by all others.

What Course of Life to pursue, or to what Business to apply himself, was a second Consideration; and here the Prospect was all a melancholy Void. Every Profession, and every Trade, required Length of Time, and what was worse, Money; for Matters are so constituted that 'Nothing out of Nothing' is not a truer Maxim in Physics than in Politics; and every Man who is greatly destitute of Money, is on that Account entirely excluded from all Means of acquiring it.

At last the Ocean, that hospitable Friend to the Wretched, opened her capacious Arms to receive him; and he instantly resolved to accept her kind Invitation. To express myself less figuratively, he determined to go to Sea.

This Thought indeed no sooner suggested itself, than he eagerly embraced it; and having presently hired Horses, he set out for *Bristol* to put it in Execution.

But before we attend him on this Expedition, we shall resort a while to Mr. *Western's*, and see what farther happened to the charming *Sophia*.

Chapter III.

Containing several Dialogues.

The Morning in which Mr. *Jones* departed, Mrs. *Western* summoned *Sophia* into her Apartment, and having first acquainted her that she had obtained her Liberty of her Father, she proceeded to read her a long Lecture on the Subject of Matrimony; which she

1. The conclusion of *Paradise Lost*, as Adam and Eve, expelled, leave Paradise: "The World was all before them ..."   (XII.646). Jones has been expelled from Paradise Hall, Allworthy's estate.

treated not as a romantic Scheme of Happiness arising from Love, as it hath been described by the Poets; nor did she mention any of those Purposes for which we are taught by Divines to regard it as instituted by sacred Authority; she considered it rather as a Fund in which prudent Women deposite their Fortunes to the best Advantage, in order to receive a larger Interest for them than they could have elsewhere.

When Mrs. *Western* had finished, *Sophia* answered, 'That she was very incapable of arguing with a Lady of her Aunt's superior Knowledge and Experience, especially on a Subject which she had so very little considered, as this of Matrimony.'

'Argue with me, Child!' replied the other, 'I do not indeed expect it. I should have seen the World to very little Purpose truly, if I am to argue with one of your Years. I have taken this Trouble, in order to instruct you. The antient Philosophers, such as *Socrates, Alcibiades,* and others, did not use to argue with their Scholars. You are to consider me, Child, as *Socrates,* not asking your Opinion, but only informing you of mine.' From which last Words the Reader may possibly imagine, that this Lady had read no more of the Philosophy of *Socrates,* than she had of that of *Alcibiades*; and indeed we cannot resolve his Curiosity as to this Point.[1]

'Madam,' cries *Sophia,* 'I have never presumed to controvert any Opinion of yours; and this Subject, as I said, I have never yet thought of, and perhaps never may.'

'Indeed *Sophy,*' replied the Aunt, 'this Dissimulation with me is very foolish. The *French* shall as soon persuade me, that they take foreign Towns in Defence only of their own Country, as you can impose on me to believe you have never yet thought seriously of Matrimony. How can you, Child, affect to deny that you have considered of contracting an Alliance, when you so well know I am acquainted with the Party with whom you desire to contract it? An Alliance as unnatural, and contrary to your Interest, as a separate League with the *French* would be to the Interest of the *Dutch!* But however, if you have not hitherto considered of this Matter, I promise you it is now high Time; for my Brother is resolved immediately to conclude the Treaty with Mr. *Blifil*; and indeed I am a sort of Guarantee in the Affair, and have promised your Concurrence.'

'Indeed, Madam,' cries *Sophia,* 'this is the only Instance in which I must disobey both yourself and my Father. For this is a Match which requires very little Consideration in me to refuse.'

'If I was not as great a Philosopher as *Socrates* himself,' returned Mrs. *Western,* 'you would overcome my Patience. What Objection can you have to the young Gentleman?'

1. Aristotle asked his students questions, rather than "informing" them. Alcibiades was a famous general and no philosopher, though an intimate friend of Aristotle. Mrs. Western also blunders on pp. 245, 425, and 688.

'A Very solid Objection, in my Opinion,' says *Sophia*,—'I hate him.'

'Will you never learn a proper Use of Words?' answered the Aunt. 'Indeed, Child, you should consult *Bailey's Dictionary*.[2] It is impossible you should hate a Man from whom you have received no Injury. By Hatred, therefore, you mean no more than Dislike, which is no sufficient Objection against your marrying of him. I have known many Couples, who have entirely disliked each other, lead very comfortable, genteel Lives. Believe me, Child, I know these Things better than you. You will allow me, I think, to have seen the World, in which I have not an Acquaintance who would not rather be thought to dislike her Husband, than to like him. The contrary is such out-of-Fashion romantic Nonsense, that the very Imagination of it is shocking.'

'Indeed, Madam,' replied *Sophia*, 'I shall never marry a Man I dislike. If I promise my Father never to consent to any Marriage contrary to his Inclinations, I think I may hope he will never force me into that State contrary to my own.'

'Inclinations!' cries the Aunt, with some Warmth. 'Inclinations! I am astonished at your Assurance. A young Woman of your Age, and unmarried, to talk of Inclinations!

'But whatever your Inclinations may be, my Brother is resolved; nay, since you talk of Inclinations, I shall advise him to hasten the Treaty. Inclinations!'

Sophia then flung herself upon her Knees, and Tears began to trickle from her shining Eyes. She entreated her Aunt 'to have Mercy upon her, and not to resent so cruelly her Unwillingness to make herself miserable; often urging, that she alone was concerned, and that her Happiness only was at Stake.'

As a Bailiff, when well authorised by his Writ, having possessed himself of the Person of some unhappy Debtor, views all his Tears without Concern: In vain the wretched Captive attempts to raise Compassion; in vain the tender Wife bereft of her Companion, the little prattling Boy, or frighted Girl, are mentioned as Inducements to Reluctance. The noble Bumtrap,[3] blind and deaf to every Circumstance of Distress, greatly rises above all the Motives to Humanity, and into the Hands of the Goaler resolves to deliver his miserable Prey.

Not less blind to the Tears, or less deaf to every Entreaty of *Sophia* was the politic Aunt, nor less determined was she to deliver over the trembling Maid into the Arms of the Goaler *Blifil*. She answered with great Impetuosity, 'So far, Madam, from your being

2. Nathaniel Bailey (d. 1742), *Dictionarium Britannicum: A more compleat universal etymological English dictionary than any extant* (1721, dated 1730)—the basis for Samuel Johnson's *Dictionary* of 1755.
3. A bailiff, who trapped debtors.

concerned alone, your Concern is the least, or surely the least important. It is the Honour of your Family which is concerned in this Alliance; you are only the Instrument. Do you conceive, Mistress, that in an Intermarriage between Kingdoms, as when a Daughter of *France* is married into *Spain*, the Princess herself is alone considered in the Match? No, it is a Match between two Kingdoms, rather than between two Persons. The same happens in great Families, such as ours. The Alliance between the Families is the principal Matter. You ought to have a greater Regard for the Honour of your Family, than for your own Person; and if the Example of a Princess cannot inspire you with these noble Thoughts, you cannot surely complain at being used no worse than all Princesses are used.'

'I hope, Madam,' cries *Sophia*, with a little Elevation of Voice, 'I shall never do any Thing to dishonour my Family; but as for Mr. *Blifil*, whatever may be the Consequence, I am resolved against him, and no Force shall prevail in his Favour.'

Western, who had been within hearing during the greater Part of the preceding Dialogue, had now exhausted all his Patience; he therefore entered the Room in a violent Passion, crying, 'D—n me then if *shatunt* ha'un, d—n me if *shatunt*, that's all—that's all——D—n me if *shatunt*.'

Mrs. *Western* had collected a sufficient Quantity of Wrath for the Use of *Sophia*; but she now transferred it all to the Squire. 'Brother,' said she, 'it is astonishing that you will interfere in a Matter which you had totally left to my Negotiation. Regard to my Family hath made me take upon myself to be the mediating Power, in order to rectify those Mistakes in Policy which you have committed in your Daughter's Education. For, Brother, it is you; it is your preposterous Conduct which hath eradicated all the Seeds that I had formerly sown in her tender Mind.—It is you yourself who have taught her Disobedience.'——'Blood!' cries the Squire, foaming at the Mouth, 'you are enough to conquer the Patience of the Devil! Have I ever taught my Daughter Disobedience?—Here she stands; Speak honestly, Girl, did ever I bid you be disobedient to me? Have not I done every Thing to humour, and to gratify you, and to make you obedient to me? And very obedient to me she was when a little Child, before you took her in Hand and spoiled her, by filling her Head with a Pack of Court Notions.—Why—why—why—did not I over-hear you telling her she must behave like a Princess? You have made a Whig of the Girl; and how should her Father, or any body else, expect any Obedience from her?' 'Brother,' answered Mrs. *Western*, with an Air of great Disdain, 'I cannot express the Contempt I have for your Politics of all Kinds; but I will appeal likewise to the young Lady herself, whether I have

ever taught her any Principles of Disobedience. On the contrary,
Niece, have I not endeavoured to inspire you with a true Idea of
the several Relations in which a human Creature stands in Society?
Have I not taken infinite Pains to shew you, that the Law of
Nature hath enjoined a Duty on Children to their Parents? Have I
not told you what *Plato*[4] says on that Subject?—A Subject on
which you was so notoriously ignorant when you came first under
my Care, that I verily believe you did not know the Relation
between a Daughter and a Father.' ' 'Tis a Lie,' answered *Western*.
'The Girl is no such Fool, as to live to eleven Years old without
knowing that she was her Father's Relation.' 'O more than *Gothic*
Ignorance,' answered the Lady.——'And as for your Manners,
Brother, I must tell you, they deserve a Cane.' 'Why then you may
gi'it me, if you think you are able,' cries the Squire; 'nay, I suppose your Niece there will be ready enough to help you.' 'Brother,'
said Mrs. *Western*, 'tho' I despise you beyond Expression, yet I
shall endure your Insolence no longer; so I desire my Coach may be
got ready immediately, for I am resolved to leave your House this
very Morning.' 'And a good Riddance too,' answered he; 'I can bear
your Insolence no longer, an you come to that. Blood! it is almost
enough of itself, to make my Daughter undervalue my Sense, when
she hears you telling me every Minute you despise me.' 'It is impossible, it is impossible,' cries the Aunt, 'no one can undervalue such a
Boor.' 'Boar,' answered the Squire, 'I am no Boar; no, nor Ass; no,
nor Rat neither, Madam. Remember that—I am no Rat. I am a
true *Englishman*, and not of your *Hanover* Breed, that have eat up
the Nation.' 'Thou art one of those wise Men,' cries she, 'whose
nonsensical Principles have undone the Nation; by weakening the
Hands of our Government at home, and by discouraging our
Friends, and encouraging our Enemies abroad.' 'Ho! are you come
back to your Politics,' cries the Squire, 'as for those I despise them
as much as I do a F—t.' Which last Word he accompanied and
graced with the very Action, which, of all others, was the most
proper to it. And whether it was this Word, or the Contempt
exprest for her Politics, which most affected Mrs. *Western*, I will
not determine; but she flew into the most violent Rage, uttered
Phrases improper to be here related, and instantly burst out of the
House. Nor did her Brother or her Niece think proper either to stop
or to follow her: For the one was so much possessed by Concern,
and the other by Anger, that they were rendered almost motionless.

The Squire, however, sent after his Sister the same Holla which
attends the Departure of a Hare, when she is first started before the
Hounds. He was indeed a great Master of his Kind of Vociferation,
and had a Holla proper for most Occasions in Life.

4. *Laws* IV, on the duty of children to parents (Bryant, p. 163).

Women who, like Mrs. *Western*, know the World, and have applied themselves to Philosophy and Politics, would have immediately availed themselves of the present Disposition of Mr. *Western*'s Mind; by throwing in a few artful Compliments to his Understanding at the Expence of his absent Adversary; but poor *Sophia* was all Simplicity. By which Word we do not intend to insinuate to the Reader, that she was silly, which is generally understood as a synonimous Term with simple: For she was indeed a most sensible Girl, and her Understanding was of the first Rate; but she wanted all that useful Art which Females convert to so many good Purposes in Life, and which, as it rather arises from the Heart, than from the Head, is often the Property of the silliest of Women.

Chapter IV.

A Picture of a Country Gentlewoman taken from the Life.

Mr. *Western* having finished his Holla, and taken a little Breath, began to lament, in very pathetic Terms, the unfortunate Condition of Men, who are, says he, always *whipt in* by the Humours of some d—nd B—— or other. I think I was *hard run* enough by your Mother for one Man; but after giving her a *Dodge*, here's another B—— follows me upon the *Foil*; but curse my Jacket if I will be *run down* in this Manner by any o'um.

Sophia never had a single Dispute with her Father, till this unlucky Affair of *Blifil*, on any Account, except in Defence of her Mother, whom she had loved most tenderly, though she lost her in the eleventh Year of her Age. The Squire, to whom that poor Woman had been a faithful upper Servant all the Time of their Marriage, had returned that Behaviour, by making what the World calls a good Husband. He very seldom swore at her (perhaps not above once a Week) and never beat her: She had not the least Occasion for Jealousy, and was perfect Mistress of her Time; for she was never interrupted by her Husband, who was engaged all the Morning in his Field Exercises, and all the Evening with Bottle Companions. She scarce indeed ever saw him but at Meals; where she had the Pleasure of carving those Dishes which she had before attended at the Dressing. From these Meals she retired about five Minutes after the other Servants, having only stayed to drink the King over the Water.[1] Such were, it seems, Mr. *Western*'s Orders: For it was a Maxim with him, that Women should come in with the first Dish, and go out after the first Glass.

---

1. A toast to James II, the Stuart (and Catholic) king forced into exile in France in 1688, hence "The Old Pretender" to the throne and the grandfather of "The Young Pretender," Prince Charles Edward, whose invasion of England in 1745 furnishes the historical setting for *Tom Jones.*

Obedience to these Orders was perhaps no difficult Task: For the Conversation (if it may be called so) was seldom such as could entertain a Lady. It consisted chiefly of Hallowing, Singing, Relations of sporting Adventures, B—d—y,[2] and Abuse of Women and of the Government.

These, however, were the only Seasons when Mr. *Western* saw his Wife: For when he repaired to her Bed, he was generally so drunk that he could not see; and in the sporting Season he always rose from her before it was light. Thus was she perfect Mistress of her Time; and had besides a Coach and four usually at her Command; tho' unhappily indeed the Badness of the Neighbourhood, and of the Roads, made this of little Use: For none who had set much Value on their Necks would have passed through the one, or who had set any Value on their Hours, would have visited the other. Now to deal honestly with the Reader, she did not make all the Return expected to so much Indulgence: For she had been married against her Will, by a fond Father, the Match having been rather advantageous on her Side: For the Squire's Estate was upwards of 3000*l.* a Year, and her Fortune no more than a bare 8000*l.* Hence perhaps she had contracted a little Gloominess of Temper: For she was rather a good Servant than a good Wife; nor had she always the Gratitude to return the extraordinary Degree of roaring Mirth, with which the Squire received her, even with a good humoured Smile. She would, moreover, sometimes interfere with Matters which did not concern her, as the violent Drinking of her Husband, which in the gentlest Terms she would take some of the few Opportunities he gave her of remonstrating against. And once in her Life she very earnestly entreated him to carry her for two Months to *London,* which he peremptorily denied; nay, was angry with his Wife for the Request ever after, being well assured, that all the Husbands in *London* are Cuckolds.

For this last, and many other good Reasons, *Western* at length heartily hated his Wife; and as he never concealed this Hatred before her Death, so he never forgot it afterwards; but when any Thing in the least soured him, as a bad scenting Day, or a Distemper among his Hounds, or any other such Misfortune, he constantly vented his Spleen by Invectives against the Deceased; saying,—'If my Wife was alive now, she would be glad of this.'

These Invectives he was especially desirous of throwing forth before *Sophia:* For as he loved her more than he did any other, so he was really jealous that she had loved her Mother better than him. And this Jealousy *Sophia* seldom failed of heightening on these Occasions: For he was not contented with violating her Ears with the Abuse of her Mother; but endeavoured to force an explicit

2. "Bawdry."

Approbation of all this Abuse, with which Desire he never could prevail upon her by any Promise or Threats to comply.

Hence some of my Readers will, perhaps, wonder that the Squire had not hated *Sophia* as much as he had hated her Mother; but I must inform them, that Hatred is not the Effect of Love, even through the Medium of Jealousy. It is, indeed, very possible for jealous Persons to kill the Objects of their Jealousy, but not to hate them. Which Sentiment being a pretty hard Morsel, and bearing something of the Air of a Paradox, we shall leave the Reader to chew the Cud upon it to the End of the Chapter.

Chapter V.

The generous Behaviour of Sophia *towards her Aunt.*

Sophia kept Silence during the foregoing Speech of her Father, nor did she once answer otherwise than with a Sigh; but as he understood none of the Language, or, as he called it, Lingo, of the Eyes, so he was not satisfied without some further Approbation of his Sentiments; which he now demanded of his Daughter; telling her, in the usual Way 'he expected she was ready to take the Part of every Body against him, as she had always done that of the B—— her Mother.' *Sophia* remaining still silent, he cry'd out, 'What art dumb? why dost unt speak. Was not thy Mother a D—d B—— to me? Answer me that. What, I suppose, you despise your Father too, and don't think him good enough to speak to?'

'For Heaven's Sake, Sir,' answered *Sophia,* 'do not give so cruel a Turn to my Silence. I am sure I would sooner die than be guilty of any Disrespect towards you; but how can I venture to speak, when every Word must either offend my dear Papa, or convict me of the blackest Ingratitude as well as Impiety to the Memory of the best of Mothers: For such, I am certain my Mamma was always to me?'

'And your Aunt, I suppose, is the best of Sisters too!' replied the Squire. 'Will you be so kind as to allow that she is a B——? I may fairly insist upon that, I think.'

'Indeed, Sir,' says *Sophia,* 'I have great Obligations to my Aunt. She hath been a second Mother to me.'

'And a second Wife to me too,' returned *Western;* 'so you will take her Part too! You won't confess that she hath acted the Part of the vilest Sister in the World?'

'Upon my Word, Sir,' cries *Sophia,* 'I must belie my Heart wickedly if I did. I know my Aunt and you differ very much in your Ways of thinking; but I have heard her a thousand Times express the greatest Affection for you; and I am convinced, so far from her being the worst Sister in the World, there are very few who love a Brother better.'

'The *English* of all which is,' answered the Squire, 'that I am in the wrong. Ay, certainly. Ay, to be sure the Woman is in the Right, and the Man in the Wrong always.'

'Pardon me, Sir,' cries *Sophia*, 'I do not say so.'

'What don't you say?' answered the Father, 'you have the Impudence to say she's in the right; doth it not follow then of Course that I am in the wrong? And perhaps I am in the wrong to suffer such a Presbyterian *Hannoverian* B—— to come into my House. She may 'dite me of a Plot for any Thing I know, and give my Estate to the Government.'

'So far, Sir, from injuring you or your Estate,' says *Sophia*, 'if my Aunt had died Yesterday, I am convinced she would have left you her whole Fortune.'

Whether *Sophia* intended it or no, I shall not presume to assert; but certain it is, these last Words penetrated very deep into the Ears of her Father, and produced a much more sensible Effect than all she had said before. He received the Sound with much the same Action as a Man receives a Bullet in his Head. He started, staggered and turned pale. After which he remained silent above a Minute, and then began in the following hesitating Manner. 'Yesterday! she would have left me her Estate Yesterday! would she? Why Yesterday of all the Days in the Year? I suppose if she dies To-morrow she will leave it to somebody else, and perhaps out of the Vamily:' 'My Aunt, Sir,' cries *Sophia*, 'hath very violent Passions, and I can't answer what she may do under their Influence.'

'You can't!' returned the Father, 'and pray who hath been the Occasion of putting her into those violent Passions? Nay, who hath actually put her into them? Was not you and she hard at it before I came into the Room? Besides, was not all our Quarrel about you? I have not quarrelled with Sister this many Years but upon your Account; and now you would throw the whole Blame upon me, as thof I should be the Occasion of her leaving the Esteate out o' the Vamily. I could have expected no better indeed, this is like the Return you make to all the rest of my Fondness.'

'I beeseech you then,' cries *Sophia*, 'upon my Knees I beseech you, if I have been the unhappy Occasion of this Difference, that you will endeavour to make it up with my Aunt, and not suffer her to leave your House in this violent Rage of Anger: She is a very good-natured Woman, and a few civil Words will satisfy her—Let me intreat you, Sir.'

'So I must go and ask Pardon for your Fault, must I?' answered *Western*. 'You have lost the Hare, and I must draw every Way to find her again? Indeed if I was certain'—Here he stopt, and *Sophia* throwing in more Entreaties, at length prevailed upon him; so that after venting two or three bitter sarcastical Expressions against his Daughter, he departed as fast as he could to recover his Sister, before her Equipage could be gotten ready.

Sophia then returned to her Chamber of Mourning, where she indulged herself (if the Phrase may be allowed me) in all the Luxury of tender Grief. She read over more than once the Letter which she had received from *Jones*; her Muff too was used on this Occasion; and she bathed both these, as well as herself, with her Tears. In this Situation, the friendly Mrs. *Honour* exerted her utmost Abilities to comfort her afflicted Mistress. She ran over the Names of many young Gentlemen; and having greatly commended their Parts and Persons, assured *Sophia* that she might take her Choice of any. These Methods must have certainly been used with some Success in Disorders of the like Kind, or so skilful a Practitioner as Mrs. *Honour* would never have ventured to apply them; nay, I have heard that the College of Chambermaids hold them to be as sovereign Remedies as any in the female Dispensary; but whether it was that *Sophia*'s Disease differed, inwardly, from those Cases with which it agreed in external Symptoms, I will not assert; but, in Fact, the good Waiting-woman did more Harm than Good, and at last so incensed her Mistress (which was no easy Matter) that with an angry Voice she dismissed her from her Presence.

Chapter VI.

Containing great Variety of Matter.

The Squire overtook his Sister just as she was stepping into the Coach, and partly by Force and partly by Solicitations, prevailed upon her to order her Horses back into their Quarters. He succeeded in this Attempt without much Difficulty: For the Lady was, as we have already hinted, of a most placable Disposition, and greatly loved her Brother, tho' she despised his Parts, or rather his little Knowledge of the World.

Poor *Sophia*, who had first set on Foot this Reconciliation, was now made the Sacrifice to it. They both concurred in their Censures on her Conduct; jointly declared War against her; and directly proceeded to Counsel, how to carry it on in the most vigorous Manner. For this Purpose, Mrs. *Western* proposed not only an immediate Conclusion of the Treaty with *Allworthy*; but as immediately to carry it into Execution; saying, 'That there was no other Way to succeed with her Niece but by violent Methods, which she was convinced *Sophia* had not sufficient Resolution to resist. By violent,' says she, 'I mean rather, hasty Measures: For as to Confinement or absolute Force, no such Things must or can be attempted. Our Plan must be concerted for a Surprize, and not for a Storm.'

These Matters were resolved on, when Mr. *Blifil* came to pay a Visit to his Mistress. The Squire no sooner heard of his Arrival, than he stept aside, by his Sister's Advice, to give his Daughter Orders for the proper Reception of her Lover; which he did with the most bitter Execrations and Denunciations of Judgment on her Refusal.

The Impetuosity of the Squire bore down all before him; and *Sophia*, as her Aunt very wisely foresaw, was not able to resist him. She agreed, therefore, to see *Blifil*, tho' she had scarce Spirits or Strength sufficient to utter her Assent. Indeed, to give a peremptory Denial to a Father whom she so tenderly loved, was no easy Task. Had this Circumstance been out of the Case, much less Resolution than what she was really Mistress of, would, perhaps, have served her; but it is no unusual Thing to ascribe those Actions entirely to Fear, which are in a great Measure produced by Love.

In Pursuance, therefore, of her Father's peremptory Command, *Sophia* now admitted Mr. *Blifil*'s Visit. Scenes, like this, when painted at large, afford, as we have observed, very little Entertainment to the Reader. Here, therefore, we shall strictly adhere to a Rule of *Horace*;[1] by which Writers are directed to pass over all those Matters, which they despair of placing in a shining Light. A Rule, we conceive, of excellent Use as well to the Historian as to the Poet; and which, if followed, must, at least, have this good Effect, that many a great Evil (for so all great Books are called) would thus be reduced to a small one.

It is possible the great Art used by *Blifil* at this Interview would have prevailed on *Sophia* to have made another Man in his Circumstances her Confident, and to have revealed the whole Secret of her Heart to him; but she had contracted so ill an Opinion of this young Gentleman, that she was resolved to place no Confidence in him: For Simplicity, when set on its Guard, is often a Match for Cunning. Her Behaviour to him, therefore, was entirely forced, and indeed such as is generally prescribed to Virgins upon the second formal Visit from one who is appointed for their Husband.

But tho' *Blifil* declared himself to the Squire perfectly satisfied with his Reception; yet that Gentleman, who in Company with his Sister had overheard all, was not so well pleased. He resolved, in Pursuance of the Advice of the sage Lady, to push Matters as forward as possible; and addressing himself to his intended Son-in-Law in the hunting Phrase, he cry'd after a loud Holla, 'Follow her, Boy, follow her; run in, run in, that's it, Honeys. Dead, dead, dead.— Never be bashful, nor stand shall I, shall I?—*Allworthy* and I can

1. *Ars Poetica* 149–50.

finish all Matters between us this Afternoon, and let us ha' the Wedding To-morrow.'

Blifil having conveyed the utmost Satisfaction into his Countenance, answered; 'As there is nothing, Sir, in this World, which I so eagerly desire as an Alliance with your Family, except my Union with the most amiable and deserving *Sophia*, you may easily imagine how impatient I must be to see myself in Possession of my two highest Wishes. If I have not therefore importuned you on this Head, you will impute it only to my Fear of offending the Lady, by endeavouring to hurry on so blessed an Event, faster than a strict Compliance with all the Rules of Decency and Decorum will permit. But if by your Interest, Sir, she might be induced to dispense with any Formalities'—

'Formalities! with a Pox!' answered the Squire, 'Pooh, all Stuff and Nonsense. I tell thee, she shall ha' thee To-Morrow; you will know the World better hereafter, when you come to my Age. Women never gi' their Consent, Man, if they can help it, 'tis not the Fashion. If I had staid for her Mother's Consent, I might have been a Batchelor to this Day——To her, to her, co to her, that's it, you jolly Dog. I tell thee shat ha' her To-morrow Morning.'

Blifil suffered himself to be overpowered by the forcible Rhetoric of the Squire; and it being agreed that *Western* should close with *Allworthy* that very Afternoon, the Lover departed home, having first earnestly begged that no Violence might be offered to the Lady by this Haste, in the same Manner as a Popish Inquisitor begs the Lay Power to do no Violence to the Heretic, delivered over to it, and against whom the Church hath passed Sentence.

And to say the Truth, *Blifil* had passed Sentence against *Sophia*; for however pleased he had declared himself to *Western*, with his Reception, he was by no means satisfied, unless it was that he was convinced of the Hatred and Scorn of his Mistress; and this had produced no less reciprocal Hatred and Scorn in him. It may, perhaps, be asked, Why then did he not put an immediate End to all further Courtship? I answer, for that very Reason, as well as for several others equally good, which we shall now proceed to open to the Reader.

Tho' Mr. *Blifil* was not of the Complexion of *Jones*, nor ready to eat every Woman he saw; yet he was far from being destitute of that Appetite which is said to be the common Property of all Animals. With this, he had likewise that distinguishing Taste, which serves to direct Men in their Choice of the Object, or Food of their several Appetites; and this taught him to consider *Sophia* as a most delicious Morsel, indeed to regard her with the same Desires which an Ortolan[2] inspires into the Soul of an Epicure. Now the Agonies

2. A small bird, about the size of a sparrow; a choice food.

which affected the Mind of *Sophia* rather augmented than impaired her Beauty; for her Tears added Brightness to her Eyes, and her Breasts rose higher with her Sighs. Indeed no one hath seen Beauty in its highest Lustre, who hath never seen it in Distress. *Blifil* therefore looked on this human Ortolan with greater Desire than when he viewed her last; nor was his Desire at all lessened by the Aversion which he discovered in her to himself. On the contrary, this served rather to heighten the Pleasure he proposed in rifling her Charms, as it added Triumph to Lust: nay, he had some further Views, from obtaining the absolute Possession of her Person, which we detest too much even to mention; and Revenge itself was not without its Share in the Gratifications which he promised himself. The rivalling poor *Jones*, and supplanting him in her Affections, added another Spur to his Pursuit, and promised another additional Rapture to his Enjoyment.

Besides all these Views, which to some scrupulous Persons may seem to savour too much of Malevolence, he had one Prospect, which few Readers will regard with any great Abhorrence. And this was the Estate of Mr. *Western*; which was all to be settled on his Daughter and her Issue, for so extravagant was the Affection of that fond Parent, that provided his Child would but consent to be miserable with the Husband he chose, he cared not at what Price he purchased him.

For these Reasons Mr. *Blifil* was so desirous of the Match, that he intended to deceive *Sophia*, by pretending Love to her; and to deceive her Father and his own Uncle, by pretending he was beloved by her. In doing this, he availed himself of the Piety of *Thwackum*, who held, that if the End proposed was religious (as surely Matrimony is) it mattered not how wicked were the Means. As, to other Occasions he used to apply the Philosophy of *Square*, which taught, that the End was immaterial, so that the Means were fair and consistent with moral Rectitude. To say Truth, there were few Occurrences in Life on which he could not draw Advantage from the Precepts of one or other of those great Masters.

Little Deceit was indeed necessary to be practiced on Mr. *Western*; who thought the Inclinations of his Daughter of as little Consequence, as *Blifil* himself conceived them to be; but as the Sentiments of Mr. *Allworthy* were of a very different Kind, so it was absolutely necessary to impose on him. In this, however, *Blifil* was so well assisted by *Western* that he succeeded without Difficulty: For as Mr. *Allworthy* had been assured by her Father, that *Sophia* had a proper Affection for *Blifil*, and that all which he had suspected concerning *Jones*, was entirely false, *Blifil* had nothing more to do, than to confirm these Assertions; which he did with such Equivocations, that he preserved a Salvo for his Conscience; and had the Satisfac-

tion of conveying a Lie to his Uncle, without the Guilt of telling
one. When he was examined touching the Inclinations of *Sophia*,
by *Allworthy*, who said, 'he would, on no Account, be accessary to
forcing a young Lady into a Marriage contrary to her own Will,' he
answered, 'That the real Sentiments of young Ladies were very
difficult to be understood; that her Behaviour to him was full as forward as he wished it, and that if he could believe her Father, she
had all the Affection for him which any Lover could desire. As for
Jones,' said he, 'whom I am loth to call Villain, tho' his Behaviour
to you, Sir, sufficiently justifies the Appellation, his own Vanity, or
perhaps some wicked Views, might make him boast of a Falshood;
for if there had been any reality in Miss *Western*'s Love to him, the
Greatness of her Fortune would never have suffered him to desert
her, as you are well informed he hath. Lastly, Sir, I promise you I
would not myself, for any Consideration, no not for the whole
World, consent to marry this young Lady, if I was not persuaded
she had all the Passion for me which I desire she should have.'

This excellent Method of conveying a Falshood with the Heart
only, without making the Tongue guilty of an Untruth, by the
Means of Equivocation and Imposture, hath quieted the Conscience of many a notable Deceiver; and yet when we consider that
it is Omniscience on which these endeavour to impose, it may possibly seem capable of affording only a very superficial Comfort; and
that this artful and refined Distinction between communicating a
Lie, and telling one, is hardly worth the Pains it costs them.

Allworthy was pretty well satisfied with what Mr. *Western* and
Mr. *Blifil* told him; and the Treaty was now, at the End of two
Days, concluded. Nothing then remained previous to the Office of
the Priest, but the Office of the Lawyers, which threatned to take
up so much Time, that *Western* offered to bind himself by all
Manner of Covenants, rather than defer the Happiness of the
young Couple. Indeed he was so very earnest and pressing, that an
indifferent Person might have concluded he was more a Principal in
this Match than he really was: But this Eagerness was natural to
him on all Occasions; and he conducted every Scheme he undertook
in such a Manner, as if the Success of that alone was sufficient to
constitute the whole Happiness of his Life.

The joint Importunities of both Father and Son-in-law would
probably have prevailed on Mr. *Allworthy*, who brooked but ill any
Delay of giving Happiness to others, had not *Sophia* herself prevented it, and taken Measures to put a final End to the whole
Treaty, and to rob both Church and Law of those Taxes which
these wise Bodies have thought proper to receive from the Propagation of the human Species in a lawful Manner. Of which in the
next Chapter.

Chapter VII.

A *Strange Resolution of* Sophia, *and a more strange Stratagem of*
Mrs. Honour.

Tho' Mrs. *Honour* was principally attached to her own Interest,
she was not without some little Attachment to *Sophia*. To say
Truth, it was very difficult for any one to know that young Lady
without loving her. She no sooner, therefore, heard a Piece of News,
which she imagined to be of great Importance to her Mistress, than
quite forgetting the Anger which she had conceived two Days
before, at her unpleasant Dismission from *Sophia*'s Presence, she
ran hastily to inform her of the News.

The Beginning of her Discourse was as abrupt as her Entrance
into the Room. 'O dear Ma'am,' says she, 'what doth your La'ship
think? To be sure, I am frightened out of my Wits; and yet I
thought it my Duty to tell your La'ship, tho' perhaps it may make
you angry, for we Servants don't always know what will make our
Ladies angry; for to be sure, every thing is always laid to the Charge
of a Servant. When our Ladies are out of Humour, to be sure, we
must be scolded; and to be sure I should not wonder if your La'ship
should be out of Humour; nay, it must surprize you certainly, ay,
and shock you too.'—'Good *Honour!* let me know it without any
longer Preface,' says *Sophia*; 'there are few Things, I promise you,
which will surprize, and fewer which will shock me.' 'Dear Ma'am,'
answered *Honour*, 'to be sure, I overheard my Master talking to
Parson *Supple* about getting a Licence this very Afternoon; and to
be sure I heard him say your La'ship should be married To-morrow
Morning.' *Sophia* turned pale at these Words, and repeated eagerly,
'To-morrow Morning!'—'Yes, Madam,' replied the trusty Waiting-
Woman, 'I will take my Oath I heard my Master say so.' '*Honour*,'
says *Sophia*, 'you have both surprized and shocked me to such a
Degree, that I have scarce any Breath or Spirits left. What is to be
done in my dreadful Situation?' 'I wish I was able to advise your
La'ship,' says she. 'Do, advise me,' cries *Sophia*, 'pray, dear *Honour*
advise me. Think what you would attempt if it was your own Case.'
'Indeed, Ma'am,' cries *Honour*, 'I wish your La'ship and I could
change Situations; that is, I mean, without hurting your La'ship; for
to be sure I don't wish you so bad as to be a Servant; but because
that if so be it was my Case, I should find no Manner of Difficulty
in it; for in my poor Opinion, young Squire *Blifil* is a charming,
sweet, handsome Man.'—'Don't mention such Stuff,' cries *Sophia*.
—'Such Stuff,' repeated *Honour*, 'Why there—Well, to be sure
what's one Man's Meat is another Man's Poison, and the same is

altogether as true of Women.' 'Honour,' says *Sophia*, 'rather than submit to be the Wife of that contemptible Wretch, I would plunge a Dagger into my Heart.' 'O lud, Ma'am,' answered the other, 'I am sure you frighten me out of my Wits now. Let me beseech your La'ship not to suffer such wicked Thoughts to come into your Head. O lud, to be sure I tremble every Inch of me. Dear Ma'am, consider—that to be denied Christian burial, and to have your Corpse buried in the Highway, and a Stake drove through you, as Farmer *Halfpenny* was served at *Ox-Cross*, and, to be sure, his Ghost hath walked there ever since; for several People have seen him. To be sure it can be nothing but the Devil which can put such wicked Thoughts into the Head of any body; for certainly it is less wicked to hurt all the World than one's own dear Self, and so I have heard said by more Parsons than one. If your La'ship hath such a violent Aversion, and hates the young Gentleman so very bad, that you can't bear to think of going into Bed to him; for to be sure there may be such Antipathies in Nature, and one had liev- erer touch a Toad than the Flesh of some People.————

Sophia had been too much wrapt in Contemplation to pay any great Attention to the Foregoing excellent Discourse of her Maid; interrupting her therefore, without making any Answer to it, she said, 'Honour, I am come to a Resolution. I am determined to leave my Father's House this very Night; and if you have the Friendship for me which you have often professed, you will keep me Com- pany.' 'That I will, Ma'am, to the World's End,' answered *Honour*; 'but I beg your La'ship to consider the Consequence, before you undertake any rash Action. Where can your La'ship possibly go?' 'There is,' replied *Sophia*, 'a Lady of Quality in *London*, a Relation of mine, who spent several Months with my Aunt in the Country; during all which Time she treated me with great Kindness, and expressed so much Pleasure in my Company, that she earnestly desired my Aunt to suffer me to go with her to *London*. As she is a Woman of very great Note, I shall easily find her out, and I make no Doubt of being very well and kindly received by her.' 'I would not have your La'ship too confident of that,' cries *Honour*; 'for the first Lady I lived with used to invite People very earnestly to her House; but if she heard afterwards they were coming, she used to get out of the Way. Besides, tho' this Lady would be very glad to see your La'ship, as to be sure any body would be glad to see your La'ship; yet when she hears your La'ship is run away from my Mas- ter'—'You are mistaken, *Honour*,' says *Sophia*, 'she looks upon the Authority of a Father in a much lower Light than I do; for she pressed me violently to go to *London* with her, and when I refused to go without my Father's Consent, she laughed me to Scorn, called me silly Country Girl, and said I should make a pure loving Wife, since I could be so dutiful a Daughter. So I have no Doubt but she will both receive me, and protect me too, till my Father, finding me out of his Power, can be brought to some Reason.'

'Well but, Ma'am,' answered *Honour*, 'how doth your La'ship think of making your Escape? Where will you get any Horses or Conveyance? For as for your own Horse, as all the Servants know a little how Matters stand between my Master and your La'ship, *Robin* will be hanged before he will suffer it to go out of the Stable without my Master's express Orders.' 'I intend to escape,' said *Sophia*, 'by walking out of the Doors when they are open. I thank Heaven my Legs are very able to carry me. They have supported me many a long Evening, after a Fiddle, with no very agreeable Partner; and surely they will assist me in running from so detestable a Partner for Life.' 'O Heaven, Ma'am, doth your La'ship know what you are saying?' cries *Honour*, 'would you think of walking about the Country by Night and alone?' 'Not alone,' answered the Lady, 'you have promised to bear me Company.' 'Yes, to be sure,' cries *Honour*, 'I will follow your La'ship through the World; but your La'ship had almost as good be alone; for I shall not be able to defend you, if any Robbers, or other Villains, should meet with you. Nay, I should be in as horrible a Fright as your La'ship; for to be certain, they would ravish us both. Besides, Ma'am, consider how cold the Nights are now; we shall be frozen to Death.' 'A good brisk Pace,' answered *Sophia*, 'will preserve us from the Cold; and if you cannot defend me from a Villain, *Honour*, I will defend you; for I will take a Pistol with me. There are two always charged in the Hall.' 'Dear Ma'am, you frighten me more and more,' cries *Honour*, 'sure your La'ship would not venture to fire it off! I had rather run any Chance, than your La'ship should do that.' 'Why so?' says *Sophia*, smiling; 'would not you, *Honour*, fire a Pistol at any one who should attack your Virtue?' 'To be sure, Ma'am,' cries *Honour*, 'one's Virtue is a dear Thing, especially to us poor Servants; for it is our Livelihood, as a Body may say; yet I mortally hate Fire-arms; for so many Accidents happen by them.' 'Well, well,' says *Sophia*, 'I believe I may ensure your Virtue at a very cheap Rate, without carrying any Arms with us; for I intend to take Horses at the very first Town we come to, and we shall hardly be attacked in our Way thither. Look'ee, *Honour*, I am resolved to go, and if you will attend me, I promise you I will reward you to the very utmost of my Power.'

This last Argument had a stronger Effect on *Honour* than all the preceding. And since she saw her Mistress so determined, she desisted from any further Dissuasions. They then entered into a Debate on Ways and Means of executing their Project. Here a very stubborn Difficulty occurred, and this was the Removal of their

Effects, which was much more easily got over by the Mistress than
by the Maid: For when a Lady hath once taken a Resolution to run
to a Lover, or to run from him, all Obstacles are considered as Trifles. But *Honour* was inspired by no such Motive; she had no Raptures to expect, nor any Terrors to shun; and besides the real Value
of her Clothes, in which consisted a great Part of her Fortune, she
had a capricious Fondness for several Gowns, and other Things;
either because they became her, or because they were given her by
such a particular Person; because she had bought them lately, or
because she had had them long; or for some other Reasons equally
good; so that she could not endure the Thoughts of leaving the
poor Things behind her exposed to the Mercy of *Western*, who, she
doubted not, would in his Rage make them suffer Martyrdom.

The ingenious Mrs. *Honour* having applied all her Oratory to dissuade her Mistress from her Purpose, when she found her positively
determined, at last started the following Expedient to remove her
Clothes, *viz.* to get herself turned out of Doors that very evening.
Sophia highly approved this Method, but doubted how it might be
brought about. 'Oh! Ma'am,' cries *Honour*, 'your La'ship may trust
that to me; we Servants very well know how to obtain this Favour of
our Masters and Mistresses; tho' some times indeed, where they owe
us more Wages than they can readily pay, they will put up with all
our Affronts, and will hardly take any Warning we can give them;
but the Squire is none of those; and since your La'ship is resolved
upon setting out To-night, I warrant I get discharged this Afternoon.' It was then resolved that she should pack up some Linen,
and a Night-gown for *Sophia*, with her own Things; and as for all
her other Clothes, the young Lady abandoned them with no more
Remorse than the Sailor feels when he throws over the Goods of
others, in order to save his own Life.

Chapter VIII.

Containing Scenes of Altercation, of no very uncommon Kind.

Mrs. *Honour* had scarce sooner parted from her young Lady,
than something (for I would not, like the old Woman in *Quivedo*,[1]
injure the Devil by any false Accusation, and possibly he might
have no Hand in it) but something, I say, suggested itself to her,
that by sacrificing *Sophia* and all her Secrets to Mr. *Western*, she
might probably make her Fortune. Many Considerations urged this

1. Francisco Gómez de Quevedo y Ville-
gas (1580–1645), Spanish satirist and
picaresque writer. I can find no reference to injuring the devil by a false accusation, either in Sir Roger L'Estrange's
1667 translation of Quevedo's *Sueños*
(the *Visions*), which are imaginary visits
to Hell and the Last Judgment, with numerous devils, nor in Quevedo's *Comical Works* (trans. 1707, 1709, 1742), in
which a few appropriate old ladies, and
more references to the devil, appear.

Discovery. The fair Prospect of a handsome Reward for so great and acceptable a Service to the Squire, tempted her Avarice; and again, the Danger of the Enterprize she had undertaken; the Uncertainty of its Success; Night, Cold, Robbers, Ravishers, all alarmed her Fears. So forcibly did all these operate upon her, that she was almost determined to go directly to the Squire, and to lay open the whole Affair. She was, however, too upright a Judge to decree on one Side, before she had heard the other. And here, first, a Journey to *London* appeared very strongly in Support of *Sophia*. She eagerly longed to see a Place in which she fancied Charms short only of those which a raptured Saint imagines in Heaven. In the next Place, as she knew *Sophia* to have much more Generosity than her Master; so her Fidelity promised her a greater Reward than she could gain by Treachery. She then cross examined all the Articles which had raised her Fears on the other Side, and found, on fairly sifting the Matter, that there was very little in them. And now both Scales being reduced to a pretty even Balance, her Love to her Mistress being thrown into the Scale of her Integrity, made that rather preponderate, when a Circumstance struck upon her Imagination, which might have had a dangerous Effect, had its whole Weight been fairly put into the other Scale. This was the Length of Time which must intervene, before *Sophia* would be able to fulfil her Promises; for tho' she was intitled to her Mother's Fortune, at the Death of her Father, and to the Sum of 3000*l.* left her by an Uncle when she came of Age; yet these were distant Days, and many Accidents might prevent the intended Generosity of the young Lady; whereas the Rewards she might expect from Mr. *Western*, were immediate. But while she was pursuing this Thought, the good Genius of *Sophia*, or that which presided over the Integrity of Mrs. *Honour*, or perhaps mere Chance, sent an Accident in her Way, which at once preserved her Fidelity, and even facilitated the intended Business.

Mrs. *Western*'s Maid claimed great Superiority over Mrs. *Honour*, on several Accounts. First, her Birth was higher: For her great Grandmother by the Mother's Side was a Cousin, not far removed, to an *Irish* Peer. Secondly, her Wages were greater. And lastly, she had been at *London*, and had of Consequence seen more of the World. She had always behaved, therefore, to Mrs. *Honour* with that Reserve, and had always exacted of her those Marks of Distinction, which every Order of Females preserves and requires in Conversation with those of an inferior Order. Now as *Honour* did not at all Times agree with this Doctrine, but would frequently break in upon the Respect which the other demanded, Mrs. *Western*'s Maid was not at all pleased with her Company: Indeed, she earnestly longed to return home to the House of her Mistress,

where she domineered at Will over all the other Servants. She had
been greatly, therefore, disappointed in the Morning when Mrs.
Western had changed her Mind on the very Point of Departure,
and had been in what is vulgarly called, a glouting Humour ever
since.

In this Humour, which was none of the sweetest, she came into
the Room where *Honour* was debating with herself, in the Manner
we have above related. *Honour* no sooner saw her, than she
addressed her in the following obliging Phrase. 'Soh! Madam, I find
we are to have the Pleasure of your Company longer, which I was
afraid the Quarrel between my Master and your Lady would have
robbed us of.' 'I don't know, Madam,' answered the other, 'who
you mean by We and Us. I assure you I do not look on any of the
Servants in this House to be proper Company for me. I am Company, I hope, for their Betters every Day in the Week. I do not
speak on your Account Mrs. *Honour*; for you are a civilized young
Woman; and when you have seen a little more of the World, I
should not be ashamed to walk with you in *St. James's* Park. 'Hoity!
toity!' cries *Honour*, 'Madam is in her Airs, I protest. Mrs. *Honour*,
forsooth! sure, Madam, you might call me by my Sir-name; for tho'
my Lady calls me *Honour*, I have a Sir-name as well as other Folks.
Ashamed to walk with me, quotha! Marry, as good as yourself, I
hope.' 'Since you make such a Return to my Civility,' said the
other, 'I must acquaint you, Mrs. *Honour*, that you are not so good
as me. In the Country indeed one is obliged to take up with all
kind of Trumpery; but in Town I visit none but the Women of
Women of Quality. Indeed, Mrs. *Honour*, there is some Difference,
I hope, between you and me.' 'I hope so too,' answered *Honour*,
'there is some Difference in our Ages, and—I think in our Persons.'
Upon speaking which last Words, she strutted by Mrs. *Western's*
Maid with the most provoking Air of Contempt; turning up her
Nose, tossing her Head, and violently brushing the Hoop of her
Competitor with her own. The other Lady put on one of her most
malicious Sneers, and said, 'Creature! you are below my Anger; and
it is beneath me to give ill Words to such an audacious saucy Trollop; but, Hussy, I must tell you, your Breeding shews the Meanness
of your Birth as well as of your Education; and both very properly
qualify you to be the mean serving Woman of a Country Girl.'
'Don't abuse my Lady,' cries *Honour*, 'I won't take that of you;
she's as much better than yours as she is younger, and ten thousand Times more handsomer.'

Here ill Luck, or rather good Luck, sent Mrs. *Western* to see her
Maid in Tears, which began to flow plentifully at her Approach;
and of which being asked the Reason by her Mistress, she presently
acquainted her, that her Tears were occasioned by the rude Treat-

ment of that Creature there, meaning *Honour.* 'And, Madam,' continued she, 'I could have despised all she said to me; but she hath had the Audacity to affront your Ladyship, and to call you ugly—Yes, Madam, she called you ugly old Cat, to my Face. I could not bear to hear your Ladyship called ugly.'—'Why do you repeat her Impudence so often?' said Mrs. *Western.* And then turning to Mrs. *Honour,* she asked her, 'how she had the Assurance to mention her Name with Disrespect?' 'Disrespect, Madam!' answered *Honour,* 'I never mentioned your Name at all; I said somebody was not as handsome as my Mistress, and to be sure you know that as well as I.' 'Hussy,' replied the Lady, 'I will make such a saucy Trollop as yourself, know that I am not a proper Subject of your Discourse. And if my Brother doth not discharge you this Moment, I will never sleep in his House again. I will find him out and have you discharged this Moment.' 'Discharged!' cries *Honour,* 'and suppose I am; there are more Places in the World than one. Thank Heaven, good Servants need not want Places; and if you turn away all who do not think you handsome, you will want Servants very soon; let me tell you that.'

Mrs. *Western* spoke, or rather thundered, in Answer; but as she was hardly articulate, we cannot be very certain of the identical Words: We shall, therefore, omit inserting a Speech, which, at best, would not greatly redound to her Honour. She then departed in Search of her Brother, with a Countenance so full of Rage, that she resembled one of the Furies rather than a human Creature.

The two Chambermaids being again left alone, began a second Bout at Altercation, which soon produced a Combat of a more active Kind. In this the Victory belonged to the Lady of inferior Rank, but not without some Loss of Blood, of Hair, and of Lawn and Muslin.

Chapter IX.

The wise Demeanour of Mr. Western *in the Character of a Magistrate. A Hint to Justices of Peace, concerning the necessary Qualifications of a Clerk; with extraordinary Instances of paternal Madness, and filial Affection.*

Logicians sometimes prove too much by an Argument, and Politicians often over-reach themselves in a Scheme. Thus had it like to have happened to Mrs. *Honour,* who instead of recovering the rest of her Clothes, had like to have stopped even those she had on her Back from escaping: For the Squire no sooner heard of her having abused his Sister, than he swore twenty Oaths he would send her to *Bridewell.*

Mrs. *Western* was a very good-natured Woman, and ordinarily of a forgiving Temper. She had lately remitted the Trespass of a Stage-coachman, who had overturned her Post-chaise into a Ditch; nay, she had even broken the Law in refusing to prosecute a High-wayman who had robbed her, not only of a Sum of Money, but of her Ear-rings; at the same time d—ning her, and saying, 'such handsome B—s as you, don't want Jewels to set them off, and be d—ned to you.' But now, so uncertain are our Tempers, and so much do we at different Times differ from ourselves, she would hear of no Mitigation; nor could all the affected Penitence of *Honour*, nor all the Entreaties of *Sophia* for her own Servant, prevail with her to desist from earnestly desiring her Brother to execute Justice-ship (for it was indeed a Syllable more than Justice) on the Wench.

But luckily the Clerk had a Qualification, which no Clerk to a Justice of Peace ought ever to be without, namely, some Under-standing in the Law of this Realm. He therefore whispered in the Ear of the Justice, that he would exceed his Authority by commit-ting the Girl to *Bridewell*, as there had been no Attempt to break the Peace; 'for I am afraid, Sir,' says he, 'you cannot legally commit any one to *Bridewell* only for Ill-breeding.'

In Matters of high Importance, particularly in Cases relating to the Game, the Justice was not always attentive to these Admoni-tions of his Clerk: For, indeed, in executing the Laws under that Head, many Justices of Peace suppose they have a large discretion-ary Power. By Virtue of which, under the Notion of searching for, and taking away Engines for the Destruction of the Game, they often commit Trespasses, and sometimes Felony at their Pleasure.

But this Offence was not of quite so high a Nature, nor so dan-gerous to the Society. Here, therefore, the Justice behaved with some Attention to the Advice of his Clerk: For, in Fact, he had already had two Informations exhibited against him in the King's-Bench, and had no Curiosity to try a third.

The Squire, therefore, putting on a most wise and significant Countenance, after a Preface of several Hum's and Ha's, told his Sister, that upon more mature Deliberation, he was of Opinion that 'as there was no breaking up of the Peace, such as the Law,' says he, 'calls breaking open a Door, or breaking a Hedge, or breaking a Head; or any such Sort of Breaking; the Matter did not amount to a felonious Kind of a Thing, nor Trespasses nor Damages, and, therefore, there was no Punishment in the Law for it.'

Mrs. *Western* said, 'she knew the Law much better; that she had known Servants very severely punished for affronting their Masters;' and then named a certain Justice of the Peace in *London*, 'who,' she said, 'would commit a Servant to *Bridewell*, at any Time when a Master or Mistress desired it.'

'Like enough,' cries the Squire, 'it may be so in *London*; but the
Law is different in the Country.' Here followed a very learned Dispute between the Brother and Sister concerning the Law, which we
would insert, if we imagined many of our Readers could understand
it. This was, however, at length referred by both Parties to the
Clerk, who decided it in Favour of the Magistrate; and Mrs. *Western* was, in the End, obliged to content herself with the Satisfaction
of having *Honour* turned away; to which *Sophia* herself very readily
and chearfully consented.

Thus Fortune, after having diverted herself, according to Custom, with two or three Frolicks, at last disposed all Matters to
the Advantage of our Heroine; who, indeed succeeded admirably
well in her Deceit, considering it was the first she had ever practised. And, to say the Truth, I have often concluded, that the
honest Part of Mankind would be much too hard for the knavish, if
they could bring themselves to incur the Guilt, or thought it worth
their while to take the Trouble.

Honour acted her Part to the utmost Perfection. She no sooner
saw herself secure from all Danger of *Bridewell*, a Word which had
raised most horrible Ideas in her Mind, than she resumed those Airs
which her Terrors before had a little abated; and laid down her
Place, with as much Affectation of Content, and indeed of Contempt, as was ever practised at the Resignation of Places of much
greater Importance. If the Reader pleases, therefore, we chuse
rather to say she resigned—which hath, indeed, been always held a
synonymous Expression with being turned out, or turned away.

Mr. *Western* ordered her to be very expeditious in packing: For
his Sister declared she would not sleep another Night under the
same Roof with so impudent a Slut. To work therefore she went,
and that so earnestly, that every Thing was ready early in the Evening; when having received her Wages, away packed she Bag and
Baggage, to the great Satisfaction of every one, but of none more
than of *Sophia*; who, having appointed her Maid to meet her at a
certain Place not far from the House, exactly at the dreadful and
ghostly Hour of Twelve, began to prepare for her own Departure.

But first she was obliged to give two painful Audiences, the one
to her Aunt, and the other to her Father. In these Mrs. *Western*
herself began to talk to her in a more peremptory Stile than before;
but her Father treated her in so violent and outrageous a Manner,
that he frightened her into an affected Compliance with his Will,
which so highly pleased the good Squire, that he changed his
Frowns into Smiles, and his Menaces into Promises; he vowed his
whole Soul was wrapped in hers, that her Consent (for so he construed the Words, *You know, Sir, I must not, nor can refuse to
obey any absolute Command of yours,*) had made him the happiest

of Mankind. He then gave her a large Bank-bill to dispose of in any Trinkets she pleased, and kissed and embraced her in the fondest Manner, while Tears of Joy trickled from those Eyes, which a few Moments before had darted Fire and Rage against the dear Object of all his Affection.

Instances of this Behaviour in Parents are so common, that the Reader, I doubt not, will be very little astonish'd at the whole Conduct of Mr. *Western*. If he should, I own I am not able to account for it; since that he loved his Daughter most tenderly, is, I think, beyond Dispute. So indeed have many others, who have rendered their Children most compleatly miserable by the same Conduct; which, tho' it is almost universal in Parents, hath always appeared to me to be the most unaccountable of all the Absurdities, which ever entered into the Brain of *that strange prodigious Creature Man*.[1]

The latter Part of Mr. *Western*'s Behaviour had so strong an Effect on the tender Heart of *Sophia*, that it suggested a Thought to her, which not all the Sophistry of her politic Aunt, nor all the Menaces of her Father had ever once brought into her Head. She reverenced her Father so piously, and loved him so passionately, that she had scarce ever felt more pleasing Sensations, than what arose from the Share she frequently had of contributing to his Amusement; and sometimes, perhaps, to higher Gratifications; for he never could contain the Delight of hearing her commended, which he had the Satisfaction of hearing almost every Day of her Life. The Idea, therefore, of the immense Happiness she should convey to her Father by her Consent to this Match, made a strong Impression on her Mind. Again, the extreme Piety of such an Act of Obedience worked very forcibly, as she had a very deep Sense of Religion. Lastly, when she reflected how much she herself was to suffer, being indeed to become little less than a Sacrifice, or a Martyr, to filial Love and Duty, she felt an agreeable Tickling in a certain little Passion, which tho' it bears no immediate Affinity either to Religion or Virtue, is often so kind as to lend great Assistance in executing the Purposes of both.

Sophia was charmed with the Contemplation of so heroic an Action, and began to compliment herself with much premature Flattery, when *Cupid*, who lay hid in her Muff, suddenly crept out, and, like *Punchinello* in a Puppet-shew, kicked all out before him. In Truth (for we scorn to deceive our Reader, or to vindicate the Character of our Heroine, by ascribing her Actions to supernatural Impulse) the Thoughts of her beloved *Jones*, and some Hopes (however distant) in which he was very particularly concerned, immediately destroyed all which filial Love, Piety and Pride had, with their joint Endeavours, been labouring to bring about.

1. The opening of Rochester's *Satyr Against Mankind* (1679).

But before we proceed any farther with *Sophia*, we must now look back to Mr. *Jones*.

Chapter X.

Containing several Matters, natural enough, perhaps, but Low.

The Reader will be pleased to remember, that we left Mr. *Jones* in the Beginning of this Book, on his Road to *Bristol*; being determined to seek his Fortune at Sea; or rather, indeed, to fly away from his Fortune on Shore.

It happened, (a Thing not very unusual) that the Guide who undertook to conduct him on his Way, was unluckily unacquainted with the Road; so that having missed his right Track, and being ashamed to ask Information, he rambled about backwards and forwards till Night came on, and it began to grow dark. *Jones* suspecting what had happened, acquainted the Guide with his Apprehensions; but he insisted on it, that they were in the right Road, and added, it would be very strange if he should not know the Road to *Bristol*; tho', in Reality, it would have been much stranger if he had known it, having never past through it in his Life before.

Jones had not such implicit Faith in his Guide, but that on their Arrival at a Village he enquired of the first Fellow he saw, whether they were in the Road to *Bristol*. 'Whence did you come?' cries the Fellow. 'No Matter,' says *Jones*, a little hastily, 'I want to know if this be the Road to *Bristol*.' 'The Road to *Bristol*!' cries the Fellow, scratching his Head, 'Why, Master, I believe you will hardly get to *Bristol* this Way To-night.' 'Prithee, Friend, then,' answered *Jones*, 'do tell us which is the Way.'—'Why, Measter,' cries the Fellow, 'you must be come out of your Road the Lord knows whither: For thick Way goeth to *Glocester*.' 'Well, and which Way goes to *Bristol*?' said *Jones*. 'Why, you be going away from *Bristol*,' answered the Fellow—'Then,' said *Jones*, 'we must go back again.' 'Ay, you must,' said the Fellow. 'Well, and when we come back to the Top of the Hill, which Way must we take?' 'Why you must keep the strait Road.' 'But I remember there are two Roads, one to the Right and the other to the Left.' 'Why you must keep the right-hand Road, and then gu strait vorwards; only remember to turn first to your Right, and then to your Left agai.., and then to your Right; and that brings you to the Squire's, and then you must keep strait vorwards, and turn to the Left.'

Another Fellow now came up, and asked which Way the Gentlemen were going?—of which being informed by *Jones*, he first scratched his Head, and then leaning upon a Pole he had in his Hand, began to tell him, 'That he must keep the Right-hand Road for about a Mile, or a Mile and half or such a Matter, and then he must turn short to the Left, which would bring him round by Measter *Jin Bearnes*'s.' 'But which is Mr. *John Bearnes*'s? says *Jones*. 'O Lord,' cries the Fellow, 'why don't you know Measter *Jin Bearnes*? Whence then did you come?'

These two Fellows had almost conquered the Patience of *Jones*, when a plain well-looking Man (who was indeed a Quaker) accosted him thus: 'Friend, I perceive thou hast lost thy Way; and if thou wilt take my Advice, thou wilt not attempt to find it To-night. It is almost dark, and the Road is difficult to hit; besides there have been several Robberies committed lately between this and *Bristol*. Here is a very creditable good House just by, where thou may'st find good Entertainment for thyself and thy Cattle till Morning.' *Jones*, after a little Persuasion, agreed to stay in this Place 'till the Morning, and was conducted by his Friend to the Public-House.

The Landlord, who was a very civil Fellow, told *Jones*, 'he hoped he would excuse the Badness of his Accommodation: For that his Wife was gone from home, and had locked up almost every Thing, and carried the Keys along with her.' Indeed, the Fact was, that a favourite Daughter of hers was just married, and gone, that Morning, home with her Husband; and that she and her Mother together, had almost stript the poor Man of all his Goods, as well as Money: For tho' he had several Children, this Daughter only, who was the Mother's Favourite, was the Object of her Consideration; and to the Humour of this one Child she would, with Pleasure have sacrificed all the rest, and her Husband into the Bargain.

Tho' *Jones* was very unfit for any Kind of Company, and would have preferred being alone; yet he could not resist the Importunities of the honest Quaker; who was the more desirous of sitting with him, from having remarked the Melancholy which appeared both in his Countenance and Behaviour; and which the poor Quaker thought his Conversation might in some Measure relieve.

After they had past some Time together, in such a Manner that my honest Friend might have thought himself at one of his Silent-Meetings, the Quaker began to be moved by some Spirit or other, probably that of Curiosity; and said, 'Friend, I perceive some sad Disaster hath befallen thee; but, pray be of Comfort. Perhaps thou hast lost a Friend. If so, thou must consider we are all mortal. And why shouldst thou grieve, when thou knowest thy Grief will do thy Friend no Good? We are all born to Affliction. I myself have my Sorrows as well as thee, and most probably greater Sorrows. Tho' I have a clear Estate of 100*l.* a Year, which is as much as I want, and I have a Conscience, I thank the Lord, void of Offence. My Constitution is sound and strong, and there is no Man can demand a Debt of me, nor accuse me of an Injury—yet, Friend, I should be concerned to think thee as miserable as myself.'

Here the Quaker ended with a deep Sigh; and *Jones* presently answered, 'I am very sorry, Sir, for your Unhappiness, whatever is the Occasion of it.' 'Ah! Friend,' replied the Quaker, 'one only Daughter is the Occasion. One who was my greatest Delight upon Earth, and who within this Week is run away from me, and is married against my Consent. I had provided her a proper Match, a sober Man, and one of Substance; but she, forsooth, would chuse for herself, and away she is gone with a young Fellow not worth a Groat. If she had been dead, as I suppose thy Friend is, I should have been happy!' 'That is very strange, Sir,' said *Jones*. 'Why, would it not be better for her to be dead, than to be a Beggar?' replied the Quaker: 'For, as I told you, the Fellow is not worth a Groat; and surely she cannot expect that I shall ever give her a Shilling. No, as she hath married for Love, let her live on Love if she can; let her carry her Love to Market, and see whether any one will change it into Silver, or even into Half-pence.' 'You know your own Concerns best, Sir,' said *Jones*. 'It must have been,' continued the Quaker, 'a long premeditated Scheme to cheat me: For they have known one another from their Infancy; and I always preached to her against Love—and told her a thousand Times over it was all Folly and Wickedness. Nay, the cunning Slut pretended to hearken to me, and to despise all wantonness of the Flesh; and yet, at last, broke out at a Window two Pair of Stairs: For I began, indeed, a little to suspect her, and had locked her up carefully, intending the very next Morning to have married her up to my Liking. But she disappointed me within a few Hours, and escaped away to the Lover of her own chusing, who lost no Time: For they were married and bedded, and all within an Hour.

'But it shall be the worst Hour's Work for them both that ever they did; for they may starve, or beg, or steal together for me. I will never give either of them a Farthing.' Here *Jones* starting up, cry'd, 'I really must be excused; I wish you would leave me.' 'Come, come, Friend,' said the Quaker, 'don't give Way to Concern. You see there are other People miserable, besides yourself.' 'I see there are Madmen and Fools and Villains in the World,' cries *Jones*— 'But let me give you a Piece of Advice; send for your Daughter and Son-in-law home, and don't be yourself the only Cause of Misery to one you pretend to love.' 'Send for her and her Husband home!' cries the Quaker loudly. 'I would sooner send for the two greatest Enemies I have in the World!' 'Well, go home yourself, or where you please,' said Jones: 'For I will sit no longer in such Company.'— 'Nay, Friend,' answered the Quaker, 'I scorn to impose my Company on any one.' He then offered to pull Money from his Pocket, but *Jones* pushed him with some Violence out of the Room.

The Subject of the Quaker's Discourse had so deeply affected *Jones*, that he stared very wildly all the Time he was speaking. This the Quaker had observed, and this; added to the rest of his Behaviour, inspired honest *Broadbrim* with a Conceit, that his Companion was, in Reality, out of his Senses. Instead of resenting the Affront, therefore, the Quaker was moved with Compassion for his unhappy Circumstances; and having communicated his Opinion to the Landlord, he desired him to take great Care of his Guest, and to treat him with the highest Civility.

'Indeed,' says the Landlord, 'I shall use no such Civility towards him: For it seems, for all his laced Waste-coat there, he is no more a Gentleman than myself; but a poor Parish Bastard bred up at a great Squire's about 30 Miles off and now turned out of Doors, (not for any Good to be sure.) I shall get him out of my House as soon as possible. If I do lose my Reckoning, the first Loss is always the best. It is not above a Year ago that I lost a Silver-spoon.'

'What dost thou talk of a Parish Bastard, *Robin?*' answered the Quaker. 'Thou must certainly be mistaken in thy Man.'

'Not at all,' replied *Robin*, 'the Guide, who knows him very well, told it me.' For, indeed, the Guide had no sooner taken his Place at the Kitchin-Fire, than he acquainted the whole Company with all he knew, or had ever heard concerning *Jones*.

The Quaker was no sooner assured by this Fellow of the Birth and low Fortune of *Jones*, than all Compassion for him vanished; and the honest, plain Man went home fired with no less Indignation than a Duke would have felt at receiving an Affront from such a Person.

The Landlord himself conceived an equal Disdain for his Guest; so that when *Jones* rung the Bell in order to retire to Bed, he was acquainted that he could have no Bed there. Besides Disdain of the mean Condition of his Guest, *Robin* entertained violent Suspicion of his Intentions, which were, he supposed, to watch some favourable Opportunity of robbing the House. In reality, he might have been very well eased of these Apprehensions by the prudent Precautions of his Wife and Daughter, who had already removed every thing which was not fixed to the Freehold; but he was by Nature suspicious, and had been more particularly so since the Loss of his Spoon. In short, the Dread of being robbed totally absorbed the comfortable Consideration that he had nothing to lose.

Jones being assured that he could have no Bed, very contentedly betook himself to a great Chair made with Rushes, when Sleep, which had lately shunned his Company in much better Apartments, generously paid him a Visit in his humble Cell.

As for the Landlord, he was prevented by his Fears from retiring to rest. He returned therefore to the Kitchin-Fire, whence he could survey the only Door which opened into the Parlour, or rather Hole, where *Jones* was seated; and as for the Window to that Room, it was impossible for any Creature larger than a Cat to have made his Escape through it.

Chapter XI.

The Adventure of a Company of Soldiers.

The Landlord having taken his Seat directly opposite to the Door of the Parlour, determined to keep Guard there the whole Night. The Guide and another Fellow remained long on Duty with him, tho' they neither knew his Suspicions, nor had any of their own. The true Cause of their watching did indeed, at length, put an End to it; for this was no other than the Strength and Goodness of the Beer, of which having tippled a very large Quantity, they grew at first very noisy and vociferous, and afterwards fell both asleep.

But it was not in the Power of Liquor to compose the Fears of *Robin*. He continued still waking in his Chair, with his Eyes fixed stedfastly on the Door which led into the Apartment of Mr. *Jones,* till a violent Thundering at his outward Gate called him from his Seat, and obliged him to open it; which he had no sooner done, than his Kitchin was immediately full of Gentlemen in red Coats, who all rushed upon him in as tumultuous a Manner, as if they intended to take his little Castle by Storm.

The Landlord was now forced from his Post to furnish his numerous Guests with Beer, which they called for with great Eagerness; and upon his second or third Return from the Cellar, he saw Mr. *Jones* standing before the Fire in the midst of the Soldiers; for it may easily be believed, that the Arrival of so much good Company should put an End to any Sleep, unless that from which we are to be awakened only by the last Trumpet.

The Company having now pretty well satisfied their Thirst, nothing remained but to pay the Reckoning, a Circumstance often productive of much Mischief and Discontent among the inferior Rank of Gentry; who are apt to find great Difficulty in assessing the Sum, with exact Regard to distributive Justice, which directs, that every Man shall pay according to the Quantity which he drinks. This Difficulty occurred upon the present Occasion; and it was the greater, as some Gentlemen had, in their extreme Hurry, marched off, after their first Draught, and had entirely forgot to contribute any thing towards the said Reckoning.

A violent Dispute now arose, in which every Word may be said to have been deposed upon Oath; for the Oaths were at least equal to all the other Words spoken. In this Controversy, the whole Company spoke together, and every Man seemed wholly bent to extenuate the Sum which fell to his Share; so that the most probable Conclusion which could be foreseen, was, that a large Portion of the Reckoning would fall to the Landlord's Share to pay, or (what is much the same thing) would remain unpaid.

All this while Mr. *Jones* was engaged in Conversation with the Serjeant; for that Officer was entirely unconcerned in the present Dispute, being privileged, by immemorial Custom, from all Contribution.

The Dispute now grew so very warm, that it seemed to draw towards a military Decision, when *Jones* stepping forward, silenced all their Clamours at once, by declaring that he would pay the whole Reckoning, which indeed amounted to no more than three Shillings and Four-pence.

This Declaration procured *Jones* the Thanks and Applause of the whole Company. The Terms honourable, noble, and worthy Gentleman, resounded through the Room; nay, my Landlord himself began to have a better Opinion of him, and almost to disbelieve the Account which the Guide had given.

The Serjeant had informed Mr. *Jones*, that they were marching against the Rebels, and expected to be commanded by the glorious Duke of *Cumberland*. By which the Reader may perceive (a Circumstance which we have not thought necessary to communicate before) that this was the very Time when the late Rebellion[1] was at the highest; and indeed the Banditti were now marched into *England*, intending, as it was thought, to fight the King's Forces, and to attempt pushing forward to the Metropolis.

Jones had some Heroic Ingredients in his Composition, and was a hearty Well-wisher to the glorious Cause of Liberty, and of the Protestant Religion. It is no Wonder, therefore, that in Circumstances which would have warranted a much more romantic and wild Undertaking, it should occur to him to serve as a Volunteer in this Expedition.

Our commanding Officer had said all in his Power to encourage and promote this good Disposition, from the first Moment he had been acquainted with it. He now proclaimed the noble Resolution aloud, which was received with great Pleasure by the whole Company, who all cried out, 'God bless King *George*, and your Honour;' and then added, with many Oaths, 'We will stand by you both to the last Drops of our Blood.'

The Gentleman, who had been all Night tippling at the Alehouse, was prevailed on by some Arguments which a Corporal had put into his Hand, to undertake the same Expedition. And now the Portmanteau belonging to Mr. *Jones* being put up in the Baggagecart, the Forces were about to move forwards; when the Guide, step-

---

1. The Jacobite Rebellion of 1745, in which Prince Charles Edward Stuart,   grandson of deposed James II, attempted to retake the throne of England.

ping up to Jones, said, 'Sir, I hope you will consider that the Horses have been kept out all Night, and we have travelled a great ways out of our Way.' *Jones* was surprized at the Impudence of this Demand, and acquainted the Soldiers with the Merits of his Cause, who were all unanimous in condemning the Guide for his Endeavours to put upon a Gentleman. Some said, he ought to be tied Neck and Heels; others, that he deserved to run the Gantlope; and the Serjeant shook his Cane at him, and wished he had him under his Command, swearing heartily he would make an Example of him.

Jones contented himself, however, with a negative Punishment, and walked off with his new Comrades, leaving the Guide to the poor Revenge of cursing and reviling him, in which latter the Landlord joined, saying, 'Ay, ay, he is a pure one, I warrant you. A pretty Gentleman, indeed, to go for a Soldier. He shall wear a laced Wastecoat truly. It is an old Proverb and a true one, all is not Gold that glisters. I am glad my House is well rid of him.'

All that Day the Serjeant and the young Soldier marched together; and the former, who was an arch Fellow, told the latter many entertaining Stories of his Campaigns, tho' in Reality he had never made any; for he was but lately come into the Service, and had, by his own Dexterity, so well ingratiated himself with his Officers, that he had promoted himself to a Halberd, chiefly indeed by his Merit in recruiting, in which he was most excellently well skilled.

Much Mirth and Festivity passed among the Soldiers during their March. In which the many Occurrences that had passed at their last Quarters were remembered, and every one, with great Freedom, made what Jokes he pleased on his Officers, some of which were of the coarser Kind, and very near bordering on Scandal. This brought to our Heroe's Mind the Custom which he had read of among the *Greeks* and *Romans*, of indulging, on certain Festivals and solemn Occasions, the Liberty to Slaves, of using an uncontrouled Freedom of Speech towards their Masters.

Our little Army, which consisted of two Companies of Foot, were now arrived at the Place where they were to halt that Evening. The Serjeant then acquainted his Lieutenant, who was the commanding Officer, that they had picked up two Fellows in that Day's March; one of which, he said, was as fine a Man as ever he saw (meaning the Tippler) for that he was near six Feet, well-proportioned, and strongly limbed; and the other, (meaning *Jones*,) would do well enough for the rear Rank.

The new Soldiers were now produced before the Officer, who having examined the six Foot Man, he being first produced, came next to survey *Jones*: at the first Sight of whom, the Lieutenant could not help shewing some Surprize; for, besides that he was very well dressed, and was naturally genteel, he had a remarkable Air of Dignity in his Look, which is rarely seen among the Vulgar, and is indeed not inseparably annexed to the Features of their Superiors.

'Sir,' said the Lieutenant, 'my Serjeant informed me, that you are desirous of enlisting in the Company I have at present under my Command; if so, Sir, we shall very gladly receive a Gentleman who promises to do much Honour to the Company, by bearing Arms in it.'

Jones answered: 'That he had not mentioned any thing of enlisting himself; that he was most zealously attached to the glorious Cause for which they were going to fight, and was very desirous of serving as a Volunteer;' concluding with some Compliments to the Lieutenant, and expressing the great Satisfaction he should have in being under his Command.

The Lieutenant returned his Civility, commended his Resolution, shook him by the Hand, and invited him to dine with himself and the rest of the Officers.

Chapter XII.

The Adventure of a Company of Officers.

The Lieutenant, whom we mentioned in the preceding Chapter, and who commanded this Party, was now near sixty Years of Age. He had entered very young into the Army, and had served in the Capacity of an Ensign at the Battle of *Tannieres;*[1] here he had received two Wounds, and had so well distinguished himself, that he was by the Duke of *Marlborough* advanced to be a Lieutenant, immediately after that Battle.

In this Commission he had continued ever since, *viz.* near forty Years; during which Time he had seen vast Numbers preferred over his Head, and had now the Mortification to be commanded by Boys, whose Fathers were at Nurse when he first entered into the Service.

Nor was this ill Success in his Profession solely owing to his having no Friends among the Men in Power. He had the Misfortune to incur the Displeasure of his Colonel, who for many Years continued in the Command of this Regiment. Nor did he owe the implacable Ill-will which this Man bore him, to any Neglect or Deficiency as an Officer, nor indeed to any Fault in himself; but solely to the Indiscretion of his Wife, who was a very beautiful Woman, and who, tho' she was remarkably fond of her Husband,

1. Bryant suggests (p. 165) that Fielding means Tavieres, a village where Marlborough, toward the end of May, 1706, tricked the French by his maneuvers and badly defeated them; Mutter suggests the wood of Taisnières, featuring in the battle of Malplaquet, where Marlborough defeated the French on 11 Sept. 1709.

would not purchase his Preferment at the Expence of certain Favours which the Colonel required of her.

The poor Lieutenant was more peculiarly unhappy in this, that while he felt the Effects of the Enmity of his Colonel, he neither knew, nor suspected, that he really bore him any; for he could not suspect an Ill-will for which he was not conscious of giving any Cause; and his Wife, fearing what her Husband's nice Regard to his Honour might have occasioned, contented herself with preserving her Virtue, without enjoying the Triumphs of her Conquest.

This unfortunate Officer (for so I think he may be called) had many good Qualities, besides his Merit in his Profession; for he was a religious, honest, good-natured Man; and had behaved so well in his Command, that he was highly esteemed and beloved, not only by the Soldiers of his own Company, but by the whole Regiment.

The other Officers who marched with him were a *French* Lieutenant, who had been long enough out of *France* to forget his own Language, but not long enough in *England* to learn ours, so that he really spoke no Language at all, and could barely make himself understood, on the most ordinary Occasions. There were likewise two Ensigns, both very young Fellows; one of whom had been bred under an Attorney, and the other was Son to the Wife of a Nobleman's Butler.

As soon as Dinner was ended, *Jones* informed the Company of the Merriment which had passed among the Soldiers upon their March; 'and yet,' says he, 'notwithstanding all their Vociferation, I dare swear they will behave more like *Grecians* than *Trojans* when they come to the Enemy.' '*Grecians* and *Trojans!*' says one of the Ensigns, 'who the Devil are they? I have heard of all the Troops in *Europe*, but never of any such as these.'

'Don't pretend to more Ignorance than you have, Mr. *Northerton*,' said the worthy Lieutenant, 'I suppose you have heard of the *Greeks* and *Trojans*, tho', perhaps, you never read *Pope's Homer*;[2] who, I remember, now the Gentleman mentions it, compares the March of the *Trojans* to the Cackling of Geese, and greatly commends the Silence of the *Grecians*. And upon my Honour, there is great Justice in the Cadet's Observation.'

'Begar, me remember dem ver well,' said the *French* Lieutenant, 'me ave read dem at School in dans Madam *Daciere*,[3] des *Greek*, des *Trojan*, dey fight for von Woman—ouy, ouy, me ave read all dat.'

'D—n *Homo* with all my Heart,' says *Northerton*, 'I have the

2. III.7–13. Pope, and Homer, compare the Trojans, as noisy as cranes flying south to attack pygmies, to the silent Greeks.
3. Anne Lefèvre Dacier's French prose translation of the *Iliad*, 1699 (she trans-lated the *Odyssey* in 1708). Mme. Dacier, daughter of one distinguished French classicist and wife of another, made Homer generally available to the French, in translation, for the first time. See below, p. 302.

Marks of him in my A— yet. There's *Thomas* of our Regiment, always carries a *Homo* in his Pocket: D—n me if ever I come at it, if I don't burn it. And there's *Corderius*,[4] another d—n'd Son of a Whore that hath got me many a Flogging.'

'Then you have been at School, Mr. *Northerton?*' said the Lieutenant.

'Ay d—n me, have I,' answered he, 'the Devil take my Father for sending me thither. The old Put wanted to make a Parson of me, but d—n me, thinks I to myself, I'll nick you there, old Cull: The Devil a Smack of your Nonsense, shall you ever get into me. There's *Jemmy Oliver* of our Regiment, he narrowly escaped being a Pimp too; and that would have been a thousand Pities: For d—n me if he is not one of the prettiest Fellows in the whole World; but he went farther than I with the old Cull: For *Jimmey* can neither write nor read.'

'You give your Friend a very good Character,' said the Lieutenant, 'and a very deserved one, I dare say; but prithee, *Northerton*, leave off that foolish as well as wicked Custom of swearing: For you are deceived, I promise you, if you think there is Wit or Politeness in it. I wish too, you would take my Advice, and desist from abusing the Clergy. Scandalous Names and Reflections cast on any Body of Men, must be always unjustifiable; but especially so, when thrown on so sacred a Function: For to abuse the Body is to abuse the Function itself; and I leave to you to judge how inconsistent such Behaviour is in Men, who are going to fight in Defence of the Protestant Religion.'

Mr. *Adderly*, which was the Name of the other Ensign, had sat hitherto kicking his Heels and humming a Tune, without seeming to listen to the Discourse; he now answered. 'O *Monsieur, on ne parle pas de la Religion dans la Guerre.*'[5] 'Well said, Jack,' cries *Northerton*, 'if la Religion was the only Matter, the Parsons should fight their own Battles for me.'

'I don't know, Gentlemen,' says *Jones*, what may be your Opinion; but I think no Man can engage in a nobler Cause than that of his Religion; and I have observed in the little I have read of History, that no Soldiers have fought so bravely, as those who have been inspired with a religious Zeal: For my own Part, tho' I love my King and Country, I hope, as well as any Man in it; yet the Protestant Interest is no small Motive to my becoming a Volunteer in the Cause.'

Northerton now winked on *Adderly*, and whispered to him slily, 'Smoke the Prig, *Adderly*, smoke him.' Then turning to *Jones*, said

4. Mathurin Cordier (c. 1480–1564), French teacher, and author of Latin textbooks for children. His *Colloquia* was a standard text throughout Europe for three centuries.
5. "Oh, sir, one doesn't speak of religion during war."

to him, 'I am very glad, Sir, you have chosen our Regiment to be a
Volunteer in: For if our Parson should at any Time take a Cup too
much, I find you can supply his Place. I presume, Sir, you have
been at the University; may I crave the Favour to know what College?'

'Sir,' answered *Jones*, 'so far from having been at the University,
I have even had the Advantage of yourself: For I was never at
School.'

'I presumed,' cries the Ensign, 'only upon the Information of
your great Learning—' 'Oh! Sir,' answered *Jones*, 'it is as possible
for a Man to know something without having been at School; as it
is to have been at School and to know nothing.'

'Well said, young Volunteer,' cries the Lieutenant, 'upon my
Word, *Northerton*, you had better let him alone; for he will be too
hard for you.'

Northerton did not very well relish the Sarcasm of *Jones*; but he
thought the Provocation was scarce sufficient to justify a Blow, or a
Rascal, or Scoundrel, which were the only Repartees that suggested
themselves. He was, therefore, silent at present; but resolved to take
the first Opportunity of returning the Jest by Abuse.

It now came to the Turn of Mr. *Jones* to give a Toast, as it is
called; who could not refrain from mentioning his dear *Sophia*.
This he did the more readily, as he imagined it utterly impossible,
that any one present should guess the Person he meant.

But the Lieutenant, who was the Toast-master, was not contented with *Sophia* only. He said, he must have her Sir-name; upon
which *Jones* hesitated a little, and presently afternamed Miss
Sophia Western. Ensign *Northerton* declared, he would not drink
her Health in the same Round with his own Toast, unless somebody would vouch for her. 'I knew one *Sophy Western*,' says he,
'that was lain-with by half the young Fellows at *Bath*; and, perhaps,
this is the same Woman.' *Jones* very solemnly assured him of the
contrary; asserting that the young Lady he named was one of great
Fashion and Fortune. 'Ay, ay,' says the Ensign, 'and so she is; d—n
me, it is the same Woman; and I'll hold half a Dozen of *Burgundy*,
Tom French of our Regiment brings her into Company with us at
any Tavern in *Bridges-street*.' He then proceeded to describe her
Person exactly, (for he had seen her with her Aunt) and concluded
with saying, 'That her Father had a great Estate in *Somersetshire*.'

The Tenderness of Lovers can ill brook the least jesting with the
Names of their Mistresses. However, *Jones*, tho' he had enough of
the Lover and of the Heroe too in his Disposition, did not resent
these Slanders as hastily as, perhaps, he ought to have done. To say
the Truth, having seen but little of this Kind of Wit, he did not
readily understand it, and for a long Time imagined Mr. *Norther-*

ton had really mistaken his Charmer for some other. But now turning to the Ensign with a stern Aspect, he said, 'Pray, Sir, Chuse
some other Subject for your Wit: For I promise you I will bear no
jesting with this Lady's Character.' 'Jesting,' cries the other, 'd—n
me if ever I was more in Earnest in my Life. *Tom French* of our
Regiment had both her and her Aunt at *Bath*.' 'Then I must tell
you in Earnest,' cries *Jones*, 'that you are one of the most impudent
Rascals upon Earth.'

He had no sooner spoken these Words, than the Ensign, together
with a Volley of Curses, discharged a Bottle full at the Head of
Jones, which hitting him a little above the right Temple, brought
him instantly to the Ground.

The Conqueror perceiving the Enemy to lie motionless before
him, and Blood beginning to flow pretty plentifully from his
Wound, began now to think of quitting the Field of Battle, where
no more Honour was to be gotten; but the Lieutenant interposed,
by stepping before the Door, and thus cut off his Retreat.

Northerton was very importunate with the Lieutenant for his
Liberty; urging the ill Consequences of his Stay, asking him, what he
could have done less! 'Zounds!' says he, 'I was but in Jest with the
Fellow. I never heard any Harm of Miss *Western* in my Life.'
'Have not you?' said the Lieutenant, 'then you richly deserve to be
hanged, as well for making such Jests, as for using such a Weapon.
You are my Prisoner, Sir; nor shall you stir from hence, till a proper
Guard comes to secure you.'

Such an Ascendant had our Lieutenant over this Ensign, that all
that Fervency of Courage which had levelled our poor Heroe with
the Floor, would scarce have animated the said Ensign to have
drawn his Sword against the Lieutenant, had he then one dangling
at his Side; but all the Swords being hung up in the Room, were, at
the very Beginning of the Fray, secured by the *French* Officer. So
that Mr. *Northerton* was obliged to attend the final Issue of this
Affair.

The *French* Gentleman and Mr. *Adderly*, at the Desire of their
Commanding-Officer, had raised up the Body of *Jones*; but as they
could perceive but little (if any) Sign of Life in him, they again
let him fall. *Adderly* damning him for having blooded his Waste-
coat; and the *Frenchman* declaring, 'Begar me no tush de Englise-
man de mort me ave heard de Englise Ley, Law, what you call,
hang up de Man dat tush him last.'

When the good Lieutenant applied himself to the Door, he
applied himself likewise to the Bell; and the Drawer immediately
attending, he dispatched him for a File of Musquetteers and a Surgeon. These Commands, together with the Drawer's Report of what
he had himself seen, not only produced the Soldiers, but presently

drew up the Landlord of the House, his Wife and Servants, and, indeed, every one else, who happened, at that Time, to be in the Inn.

To describe every Particular, and to relate the whole Conversation of the ensuing Scene, is not within my Power, unless I had forty Pens, and could, at once, write with them all together, as the Company now spoke. The Reader must, therefore, content himself with the most remarkable Incidents, and perhaps he may very well excuse the rest.

The first Thing done was securing the Body of *Northerton*, who being delivered into the Custody of six Men with a Corporal at their Head, was by them conducted from a Place which he was very willing to leave, but it was unluckily to a Place whither he was very unwilling to go. To say the Truth, so whimsical are the Desires of Ambition, the very Moment this Youth had attained the above-mentioned Honour, he would have been well contented to have retired to some Corner of the World, where the Fame of it should never have reached his Ears.

It surprizes us, and so, perhaps, it may the Reader, that the Lieutenant, a worthy and good Man, should have applied his chief Care, rather to secure the Offender, than to preserve the Life of the wounded Person. We mention this Observation, not with any View of pretending to account for so odd a Behaviour, but lest some Critic should hereafter plume himself on discovering it. We would have these Gentlemen know we can see what is odd in Characters as well as themselves, but it is our Business to relate Facts as they are; which when we have done, it is the Part of the learned and sagacious Reader to consult that original Book of Nature, whence every Passage in our Work is transcribed, tho' we quote not always the particular Page for its Authority.

The Company which now arrived were of a different Disposition. They suspended their Curiosity concerning the Person of the Ensign, till they should see him hereafter in a more engaging Attitude. At present, their whole Concern and Attention were employed about the bloody Object on the Floor; which being placed upright in a Chair, soon began to discover some Symptoms of Life and Motion. These were no sooner perceived by the Company (for *Jones* was, at first, generally concluded to be dead) than they all fell at once to prescribing for him: (For as none of the physical Order was present, every one there took that Office upon him.)

Bleeding was the unanimous Voice of the whole Room; but unluckily there was no Operator at hand: Every one then cry'd, 'Call the Barber;' but none stirred a Step. Several Cordials were likewise prescribed in the same ineffective Manner; till the Landlord ordered up a Tankard of strong Beer, with a Toast, which he said was the best Cordial in *England*.

The Person principally assistant on this Occasion, indeed the only one who did any Service, or seemed likely to do any, was the Landlady. She cut off some of her Hair, and applied it to the Wound to stop the Blood: She fell to chafing the Youth's Temples with her Hand; and having exprest great Contempt for her Husband's Prescription of Beer, she dispatched one of her Maids to her own Closet for a Bottle of Brandy, of which, as soon as it was brought, she prevailed upon *Jones*, who was just returned to his Senses, to drink a very large and plentiful Draught.

Soon afterwards arrived the Surgeon, who having viewed the Wound, having shaken his Head, and blamed every Thing which was done, ordered his Patient instantly to Bed; in which Place, we think proper to leave him some Time, to his Repose, and shall here, therefore, put an End to this Chapter.

Chapter XIII.

Containing the great Address of the Landlady; the great Learning of a Surgeon, and the solid Skill in Casuistry of the worthy Lieutenant.

When the wounded Man was carried to his Bed, and the House began again to clear up from the Hurry which this Accident had occasioned; the Landlady thus addressed the commanding Officer. 'I am afraid, Sir,' said she, 'this young Man did not behave himself as well as he should do to your Honours; and if he had been killed, I suppose he had but his *Desarts*; to be sure, when Gentlemen admit inferior *Parsons* into their Company, they *oft* to keep their Distance; but, as my first Husband used to say, few of em know how to do it. For my own Part, I am sure, I should not have suffered any Fellows to *include* themselves into Gentlemen's Company: but I *thoft* he had been an Officer himself, till the Serjeant told me he was but a Recruit.'

'Landlady,' answered the Lieutenant, 'you mistake the whole Matter. The young Man behaved himself extremely well, and is, I believe, a much better Gentleman than the Ensign, who abused him. If the young Fellow dies, the Man who struck him will have most Reason to be sorry for it: For the Regiment will get rid of a very troublesome Fellow, who is a Scandal to the Army; and if he escapes from the Hands of Justice, blame me, Madam, that's all.'

'Ay! Ay! good Lack-a-day!' said the Landlady, 'who could have *thoft* it? Ay, ay, ay, I am satisfied your Honour will see Justice done; and to be sure it *oft* to be to every one. Gentlemen *oft* not to kill poor Folks without answering for it. A poor Man hath a Soul to be saved as well as his Betters.'

'Indeed, Madam,' said the Lieutenant, 'you do the Volunteer wrong; I dare swear he is more of a Gentleman than the Officer.'

'Ay,' cries the Landlady, 'why look you there now: Well, my first Husband was a wise Man; he used to say, you can't always know the Inside by the Outside. Nay, that might have been well enough too: For I never *saw'd* him till he was all over Blood. Who would have *thoft* it! mayhap, some young Gentleman crossed in Love. Good Lack-a-day! if he should die, what a Concern it will be to his Parents! Why sure the Devil must possess the wicked Wretch to do such an Act. To be sure, he is a Scandal to the Army, as your Honour says: For most of the Gentlemen of the Army that ever I saw, are quite different Sort of People, and look as if they would scorn to spill any Christian Blood as much as any Men, I mean, that is, in a civil Way, as my first Husband used to say. To be sure, when they come into the Wars, there must be Bloodshed; but that they are not to be blamed for. The more of our Enemies they kill there, the better; and I wish with all my Heart, they could kill every Mother's Son of them.'

'O fie! Madam,' said the Lieutenant smiling, 'ALL is rather too bloody-minded a Wish.'

'Not at all, Sir,' answered she, 'I am not at all bloody-minded, only to our Enemies, and there is no Harm in that. To be sure it is natural for us to wish our Enemies dead, that the Wars may be at an End, and our Taxes be lowered: For it is a dreadful Thing to pay as we do. Why now there is above forty Shillings for Window-lights,[1] and yet we have stopt up all we could; we have almost blinded the House I am sure: Says I to the Exciseman, says I, I think you *oft* to favour us, I am sure we are very good Friends to the Government; and so we are for *sartain*: For we pay a Mint of Money to 'um. And yet I often think to myself, the Government doth not imagine itself more obliged to us, than to those that don't pay 'um a Farthing. Ay, ay; it is the Way of the World.'

She was proceeding in this Manner, when the Surgeon entered the Room. The Lieutenant immediately asked how his Patient did? But he resolved him only by saying, 'Better, I believe, than he would have been by this Time, if I had not been called; and even as it is, perhaps it would have been lucky if I could have been called sooner.' 'I hope, Sir,' said the Lieutenant, 'the Skull is not fractured.' 'Hum,' cries the Surgeon, 'Fractures are not always the most dangerous Symptoms. Contusions and Lacerations are often

---

1. The tax on windows had recently (1747) been increased to 6d. a window for 10 to 14 windows, 9d. for 15 to 19, 1s. for more than 20. The inn has over 40 windows, even after the landlady has closed off all she possibly could to cut down her taxes (Mutter).

attended with worse Phænomena, and with more fatal Consequences than Fractures. People who know nothing of the Matter
conclude, if the Skull is not fractured, all is well; whereas, I had
rather see a Man's Skull broken all to Pieces, than some Contusions
I have met with.' 'I hope,' says the Lieutenant, 'there are no such
Symptoms here.' 'Symptoms,' answered the Surgeon, 'are not always
regular nor constant. I have known very unfavourable Symptoms in
the Morning change to favourable ones at Noon, and return to
unfavourable again at Night. Of Wounds, indeed, it is rightly and
truly said, *Nemo repente fuit turpissimus*.[2] I was once, I remember,
called to a Patient, who had received a violent Contusion in his
Tibia, by which the exterior Cutis was lacerated, so that there was a
profuse sanguinary Discharge; and the interior Membranes were so
divellicated, that the Os or Bone very plainly appeared through the
Aperture of the Vulnus or Wound. Some febrile Symptoms intervening at the same Time, (for the Pulse was exuberant and indicated much Phlebotomy) I apprehended an immediate Mortification. To prevent which I presently made a large Orifice in the Vein
of the left Arm, whence I drew twenty Ounces of Blood; which I
expected to have found extremely sizy and glutinous, or indeed
coagulated, as it is in pleuretic Complaints; but, to my Surprize, it
appeared rosy and florid, and its Consistency differed little from the
Blood of those in perfect Health. I then applied a Fomentation to
the Part, which highly answered the Intention, and after three or
four Times dressing, the Wound began to discharge a thick Pus or
Matter, by which Means the Cohesion————but perhaps I do not
make myself perfectly well understood.' 'No really,' answered the
Lieutenant, 'I cannot say I understand a Syllable.' 'Well, Sir,' said
the Surgeon, 'then I shall not tire your Patience; in short, within six
Weeks, my Patient was able to walk upon his Legs, as perfectly as
he could have done before he received the Contusion.' 'I wish, Sir,'
said the Lieutenant, 'you would be so kind only to inform me,
whether the Wound this young Gentleman hath had the Misfortune to receive is likely to prove mortal?' 'Sir,' answered the Surgeon, 'to say whether a Wound will prove mortal or not at first
Dressing, would be very weak and foolish Presumption: We are all
mortal, and Symptoms often occur in a Cure which the greatest of
our Profession could never forsee.—'But do you think him in
Danger?' says the other. 'In Danger! ay, surely,' cries the Doctor,
'who is there among us, who in the most perfect Health can be said
not to be in Danger? Can a Man, therefore, with so bad a Wound
as this be said to be out of Danger? All I can say at present is, that it
is well I was called as I was, and perhaps it would have been better
if I had been called sooner. I will see him again early in the Morn-

2. "No one was most wicked all of a sudden"; Juvenal, *Satires* II.83.

ing, and in the mean Time let him be kept extremely quiet, and
drink liberally of Water-Gruel.' 'Won't you allow him Sack-whey,'
said the Landlady? 'Ay, ay, Sack-whey,' cries the Doctor, 'if you
will, provided it be very small.' 'And a little Chicken-broth too,'
added she?—'Yes, yes, Chicken-broth,' said the Doctor, 'is very
good.' 'Mayn't I make him some Jellies too,' said the Landlady?
'Ay, ay,' answered the Doctor, 'Jellies are very good for Wounds, for
they promote Cohesion.' And, indeed, it was lucky she had not
named Soop or high Sauces, for the Doctor would have complied,
rather than have lost the Custom of the House.

The Doctor was no sooner gone, than the Landlady began to
trumpet forth his Fame to the Lieutenant, who had not, from their
short Acquaintance, conceived quite so favourable an Opinion of
his physical Abilities as the good Woman, and all the Neighbourhood, entertained; (and perhaps very rightly) for tho' I am afraid
the Doctor was a little of a Coxcomb, he might be nevertheless very
much of a Surgeon.

The Lieutenant having collected from the learned Discourse of
the Surgeon, that Mr. *Jones* was in great Danger, gave Orders for
keeping Mr. *Northerton* under a very strict Guard, designing in the
Morning to attend him to a Justice of Peace, and to commit the
conducting the Troops to *Gloucester* to the *French* Lieutenant,
who, tho' he could neither read, write, nor speak any Language, was,
however, a good Officer.

In the Evening our Commander sent a Message to Mr. *Jones*,
that if a Visit would not be troublesome he would wait on him.
This Civility was very kindly and thankfully received by *Jones*, and
the Lieutenant accordingly went up to his Room, where he found
the wounded Man much better than he expected; nay, *Jones*
assured his Friend, that if he had not received express Orders to the
contrary from the Surgeon, he should have got up long ago: For he
appeared to himself to be as well as ever, and felt no other Inconvenience from his Wound but an extreme Soreness on that Side of
his Head.

'I should be very glad,' quoth the Lieutenant, 'if you was as well
as you fancy yourself: For then you could be able to do yourself Justice immediately; for when a Matter can't be made up, as in a Case
of a Blow, the sooner you take him out the better; but I am afraid
you think yourself better than you are, and he would have too
much Advantage over you.'

'I'll try, however,' answered *Jones*, 'if you please, and will be so
kind to lend me a Sword: For I have none here of my own.'

'My Sword is heartily at your Service, my dear Boy,' cries the
Lieutenant, kissing him, 'you are a brave Lad, and I love your Spirit;
but I fear your Strength: For such a Blow, and so much Loss of

Blood, must have very much weakened you; and tho' you feel no
Want of Strength in your Bed, yet you most probably would after a
Thrust or two. I can't consent to your taking him out To-night; but
I hope you will be able to come up with us before we get many
Days March Advance; and I give you my Honour you shall have
Satisfaction, or the Man who hath injured you shan't stay in our
Regiment.'

'I wish,' said *Jones*, 'it was possible to decide this Matter To-
night: Now you have mentioned it to me, I shall not be able to
rest.'

'O never think of it,' returned the other, 'a few Days will make
no Difference. The Wounds of Honour are not like those in your
Body. They suffer nothing by the Delay of Cure. It will be altogether as well for you, to receive Satisfaction a Week hence as now.'

'But suppose,' says *Jones*, 'I should grow worse, and die of the
Consequences of my present Wound.'

'Then your Honour,' answered the Lieutenant, 'will require no
Reparation at all. I myself will do Justice to your Character, and
testify to the World your Intention to have acted properly if you
had recovered.'

'Still,' replied *Jones*, 'I am concerned at the Delay. I am almost
afraid to mention it to you who are a Soldier; but tho' I have been
a very wild young Fellow, still in my most serious Moments and at
the Bottom, I am really a Christian.'

'So am I too, I assure you,' said the Officer: 'And so zealous a
one, that I was pleased with you at Dinner for taking up the Cause
of your Religion; and I am a little offended with you now young
Gentleman, that you should express a Fear of declaring your Faith
before any one.'

'But how terrible must it be,' cries *Jones*, to any one who is really
a Christian, to cherish Malice in his Breast, in Opposition to the
Command of him who hath expressly forbid it? How can I bear to
do this on a sick Bed? Or how shall I make up my Account, with
such an Article as this in my Bosom against me?'

'Why I believe there is such a Command,' cries the Lieutenant;
'but a Man of Honour can't keep it. And you must be a Man of
Honour, if you will be in the Army. I remember I once put the
Case to our Chaplain over a Bowl of Punch, and he confessed there
was much Difficulty in it; but he said, he hoped there might be a
Latitude granted to Soldiers in this one Instance; and to be sure it
is our Duty to hope so: For who would bear to live without his
Honour? No, no, my dear Boy, be a good Christian as long as you
live; but be a Man of Honour too, and never put up an Affront; not
all the Books, nor all the Parsons in the World, shall ever persuade
me to that. I love my Religion very well, but I love my Honour

more. There must be some Mistake in the wording the Text, or in the Translation, or in the understanding it, or somewhere or other. But however that be, a Man must run the Risque; for he must preserve his Honour. So compose yourself To-night, and I promise you, you shall have an Opportunity of doing yourself Justice.' Here he gave *Jones* a hearty Buss, shook him by the Hand, and took his Leave.

But tho' the Lieutenant's Reasoning was very satisfactory to himself, it was not entirely so to his Friend. *Jones* therefore having revolved this Matter much in his Thoughts, at last came to a Resolution, which the Reader will find in the next Chapter.

Chapter XIV.

A most dreadful Chapter indeed; and which few Readers ought to venture upon in an Evening, especially when alone.

Jones swallowed a large Mess of Chicken, or rather Cock, Broth, with a very good Appetite, as indeed he would have done the Cock it was made of, with a Pound of Bacon into the Bargain; and now, finding in himself no Deficiency of either Health or Spirit, he resolved to get up and seek his Enemy.

But first he sent for the Serjeant, who was his first Acquaintance among these military Gentlemen. Unluckily that worthy Officer having, in a literal Sense, taken his Fill of Liquor, had been some Time retired to his Bolster, where he was snoring so loud, that it was not easy to convey a Noise in at his Ears capable of drowning that which issued from his Nostrils.

However, as *Jones* persisted in his Desire of seeing him, a vociferous Drawer at length found Means to disturb his Slumbers, and to acquaint him with the Message. Of which the Serjeant was no sooner made sensible, than he arose from his Bed, and having his Clothes already on, immediately attended. *Jones* did not think fit to acquaint the Serjeant with his Design, tho' he might have done it with great Safety; for the Halberdier was himself a Man of Honour, and had killed his Man. He would therefore have faithfully kept this Secret, or indeed any other which no Reward was published for discovering. But as *Jones* knew not those Virtues in so short an Acquaintance, his Caution was perhaps prudent and commendable enough.

He began therefore by acquainting the Serjeant, that as he was now entered into the Army, he was ashamed of being without what was perhaps the most necessary Implement of a Soldier, namely, a Sword; adding, that he should be infinitely obliged to him, if he could procure one. 'For which,' says he, 'I will give you any reasonable Price; nor do I insist upon its being Silver-hilted, only a good Blade, and such as may become a Soldier's Thigh.'

The Serjeant, who well knew what had happened, and had heard that *Jones* was in a very dangerous Condition, immediately concluded, from such a Message, at such a Time of Night, and from a Man in such a Situation, that he was light-headed. Now as he had his Wit (to use that Word in its common Signification) always ready, he bethought himself of making his Advantage of this Humour in the sick Man. 'Sir,' says he, 'I believe I can fit you. I have a most excellent Piece of Stuff by me. It is not indeed Silver-hilted, which, as you say, doth not become a Soldier; but the Handle is decent enough, and the Blade one of the best in *Europe*. ——It is a Blade that—a Blade that—In short, I will fetch it you this Instant, and you shall see it and handle it—I am glad to see your Honour so well with all my Heart.'

Being instantly returned with the Sword, he delivered it to *Jones*, who took it and drew it; and then told the Serjeant it would do very well, and bid him name his Price.

The Serjeant now began to harangue in Praise of his Goods. He said (nay he swore very heartily) 'that the Blade was taken from a *French* Officer of very high Rank, at the Battle of *Dettingen*.[1] I took it myself,' says he, 'from his Side, after I had knocked him o' the Head. The Hilt was a golden one. That I sold to one of our fine Gentlemen; for there are some of them, an't please your Honour, who value the Hilt of a Sword more than the Blade.'

Here the other stopped him, and begged him to name a Price. The Serjeant, who thought *Jones* absolutely out of his Senses, and very near his End, was afraid, lest he should injure his Family by asking too little.—However, after a Moment's Hesitation, he contented himself with naming twenty Guineas, and swore he would not sell it for less to his own Brother.

'Twenty Guineas!' says *Jones*, in the utmost Surprize, 'sure you think I am mad, or that I never saw a Sword in my Life. Twenty Guineas, indeed! I did not imagine you would endeavour to impose upon me.—Here, take the Sword—No, now I think on't, I will keep it myself, and shew it your Officer in the Morning, acquainting him, at the same Time, what a Price you asked me for it.'

The Serjeant, as we have said, had always his Wit (*in sensu prædicto*)[2] about him, and now plainly saw that *Jones* was not in the Condition he had apprehended him to be; he now, therefore, counterfeited as great Surprize as the other had shewn, and said, 'I am certain, Sir, I have not asked you so much out of the way.

---

1. War of the Austrian Succession. Austria, England, Holland, and others, against Prussia, France, Spain, Bavaria, and others. English forces, under George II, forced their way out of a box at Dettingen (27 June 1743), badly damaging the French.
2. "In the aforesaid sense."

Besides, you are to consider, it is the only Sword I have, and I must run the Risque of my Officer's Displeasure, by going without one myself. And truly, putting all this together, I don't think twenty Shillings was so much out of the Way.'

'Twenty Shillings!' cried *Jones*, 'why you just now asked me twenty Guineas.' 'How!' cries the Serjeant—'Sure your Honour must have mistaken me; or else I mistook myself—and indeed I am but half awake——Twenty Guineas indeed! no wonder your Honour flew into such a Passion. I say twenty Guineas too—No, no, I meant twenty Shillings, I assure you. And when your Honour comes to consider every Thing, I hope you will not think that so extravagant a Price. It is indeed true, you may buy a Weapon which looks as well for less Money. But—

Here *Jones* interrupted him, saying, 'I will be so far from making any Words with you, that I will give you a Shilling more than your Demand.' He then gave him a Guinea, bid him return to his Bed, and wished him a good March; adding, he hoped to overtake them before the Division reached *Worcester*.

The Serjeant very civilly took his Leave, fully satisfied with his Merchandize, and not a little pleased with his dextrous Recovery from that false Step into which his Opinion of the sick Man's Light-headedness had betrayed him.

As soon as the Serjeant was departed, *Jones* rose from his Bed, and dressed himself entirely, putting on even his Coat, which, as its Colour was white, shewed very visibly the Streams of Blood which had flowed down it; and now, having grasped his new-purchased Sword in his Hand, he was going to issue forth, when the Thought of what he was about to undertake laid suddenly hold of him, and he began to reflect that in a few Minutes he might possibly deprive a human Being of Life, or might lose his own. 'Very well,' said he, 'and in what Cause do I venture my Life? Why, in that of my Honour. And who is this human Being? A Rascal who hath injured and insulted me without Provocation. But is not Revenge forbidden by Heaven?—Yes, but it is enjoined by the World. Well, but shall I obey the World in Opposition to the express Commands of Heaven? Shall I incur the divine Displeasure rather than be called— Ha—Coward—Scoundrel?—I'll think no more; I am resolved, and must fight him.'

The Clock had now struck Twelve, and every one in the House were in their Beds, except the Centinel who stood to guard *North-erton*, when *Jones* softly opening his Door, issued forth in Pursuit of his Enemy, of whose Place of Confinement he had received a perfect Description from the Drawer. It is not easy to conceive a much more tremendous Figure than he now exhibited. He had on, as we have said, a light-coloured Coat, covered with Streams of

Blood. His Face, which missed that very Blood, as well as twenty
Ounces more drawn from him by the Surgeon, was pallid. Round
his Head was a Quantity of Bandage, not unlike a Turban. In the
right Hand he carried a Sword, and in the left a Candle. So that
the bloody *Banquo* was not worthy to be compared to him. In Fact,
I believe a more dreadful Apparition was never raised in a Church-
yard, nor in the Imagination of any good People met in a Winter
Evening over a Christmas Fire in *Somersetshire*.

When the Centinel first saw our Heroe approach, his Hair began
gently to lift up his Grenadier Cap; and in the same Instant his
Knees fell to Blows with each other. Presently his whole Body was
seized with worse than an Ague Fit. He then fired his Piece, and
fell flat on his Face.

Whether Fear or Courage was the Occasion of his Firing, or
whether he took Aim at the Object of his Terror, I cannot say. If
he did, however, he had the good Fortune to miss his Man.

Jones seeing the Fellow fall, guessed the Cause of his Fright, at
which he could not forbear smiling, not in the least reflecting on
the Danger from which he had just escaped. He then passed by the
Fellow, who still continued in the Posture in which he fell, and
entered the Room where *Northerton*, as he had heard, was confined. Here, in a solitary Situation, he found—an empty Quart-Pot
standing on the Table, on which some Beer being spilt, it looked as
if the Room had lately been inhabited; but at present it was
entirely vacant.

Jones then apprehended it might lead to some other Apartment;
but, upon searching all round it, he could perceive no other Door
than that at which he entered, and where the Centinel had been
posted. He then proceeded to call *Northerton* several Times by his
Name; but no one answered; nor did this serve to any other Purpose
than to confirm the Centinel in his Terrors, who was now convinced that the Volunteer was dead of his Wounds, and that his
Ghost was come in Search of the Murtherer: He now lay in all the
Agonies of Horror; and I wish, with all my Heart, some of those
Actors, who are hereafter to represent a Man frighted out of his
Wits, had seen him, that they might be taught to copy Nature,
instead of performing several antic Tricks and Gestures, for the
Entertainment and Applause of the Galleries.

Perceiving the Bird was flown, at least despairing to find him,
and rightly apprehending that the Report of the Firelock would
alarm the whole House, our Heroe now blew out his Candle, and
gently stole back again to his Chamber, and to his Bed: Whither
he would not have been able to have gotten undiscovered, had any
other Person been on the same Stair-case, save only one Gentleman
who was confined to his Bed by the Gout; for before he could reach

the Door to his Chamber, the Hall where the Centinel had been posted, was half full of People, some in their Shirts, and others not half drest, all very earnestly enquiring of each other, what was the Matter?

The Soldier was now found lying in the same Place and Posture in which we just now left him. Several immediately applied themselves to raise him, and some concluded him dead: But they presently saw their Mistake; for he not only struggled with those who laid their Hands on him, but fell a roaring like a Bull. In reality, he imagined so many Spirits or Devils were handling him; for his Imagination being possessed with the Horror of an Apparition, converted every Object he saw or felt, into nothing but Ghosts and Spectres.

At length he was overpowered by Numbers, and got upon his Legs; when Candles being brought, and seeing two or three of his Comrades present, he came a little to himself; but when they asked him what was the Matter? he answered, 'I am a dead Man, that's all, I am a dead Man. I can't recover it. I have seen him.' 'What hast thou seen, *Jack?*' says one of the Soldiers. 'Why, I have seen the young Volunteer that was killed Yesterday.' He then imprecated the most heavy Curses on himself, if he had not seen the Volunteer, all over Blood, vomiting Fire out of his Mouth and Nostrils, pass by him into the Chamber where Ensign *Northerton* was, and then seizing the Ensign by the Throat, fly away with him in a Clap of Thunder.

This Relation met with a gracious Reception from the Audience. All the Women present believed it firmly, and prayed Heaven to defend them from Murther. Amongst the Men too, many had Faith in the Story; but others turned it into Derision and Ridicule; and a Serjeant who was present, answered very coolly: 'Young Man, you will hear more of this for going to sleep, and dreaming on your Post.'

The Soldier replied, 'You may punish me if you please; but I was as broad awake as I am now; and the Devil carry me away, as he hath the Ensign, if I did not see the dead Man, as I tell you, with Eyes as big and as fiery as two large Flambeaux.'

The Commander of the Forces, and the Commander of the House, were now both arrived: For the former being awake at the Time, and hearing the Centinel fire his Piece, thought it his Duty to rise immediately, tho' he had no great Apprehensions of any Mischief; whereas the Apprehensions of the latter were much greater, lest her Spoons and Tankards should be upon the March, without having received any such Orders from her.

Our poor Centinel, to whom the Sight of this Officer was not much more welcome than the Apparition, as he thought it, which he had seen before, again related the dreadful Story, and with many

Additions of Blood and Fire: But he had the Misfortune to gain no
Credit with either of the last-mentioned Persons; for the Officer,
tho' a very religious Man, was free from all Terrors of this Kind;
besides, having so lately left *Jones* in the Condition we have seen,
he had no Suspicion of his being dead. As for the Landlady, tho'
not over religious, she had no kind of Aversion to the Doctrine of
Spirits; but there was a Circumstance in the Tale which she well
knew to be false, as we shall inform the Reader presently.

But whether *Northerton* was carried away in Thunder or Fire, or
in whatever other Manner he was gone; it was now certain, that his
Body was no longer in Custody. Upon this Occasion, the Lieutenant
formed a Conclusion not very different from what the Serjeant is
just mentioned to have made before, and immediately ordered the
Centinel to be taken Prisoner. So that, by a strange Reverse of Fortune, (tho' not very uncommon in a military Life) the Guard
became the guarded.

Chapter XV.

The Conclusion of the foregoing Adventure.

Besides the Suspicion of Sleep, the Lieutenant harboured
another, and worse Doubt against the poor Centinel, and this was
that of Treachery: For as he believed not one Syllable of the Apparition, so he imagined the whole to be an Invention, formed only to
impose upon him, and that the Fellow had, in Reality, been bribed
by *Northerton* to let him escape. And this he imagined the rather,
as the Fright appeared to him the more unnatural in one who had
the Character of as brave and bold a Man as any in the Regiment,
having been in several Actions, having received several Wounds,
and, in a Word, having behaved himself always like a good and valiant Soldier.

That the Reader, therefore, may not conceive the least ill Opinion of such a Person, we shall not delay a Moment in rescuing his
Character from the Imputation of this Guilt.

Mr. *Northerton* then, as we have before observed, was fully satisfied with the Glory which he had obtained from this Action. He
had, perhaps, seen, or heard, or guessed, that Envy is apt to attend
Fame. Not that I would here insinuate, that he was heathenishly
inclined to believe in, or to worship, the Goddess *Nemesis*; for, in
Fact, I am convinced he never heard of her Name. He was, besides,
of an active Disposition, and had a great Antipathy to those close
Winter Quarters in the Castle of *Gloucester*, for which a Justice of
Peace might possibly give him a Billet. Nor was he moreover free
from some uneasy Meditations on a certain wooden Edifice, which I

forbear to name, in Conformity to the Opinion of Mankind, who, I think, rather ought to honour than to be ashamed of this Building, as it is, or at least might be made, of more Benefit to Society than almost any other public Erection. In a Word, to hint at no more Reasons for his Conduct, Mr. *Northerton* was desirous of departing that Evening, and nothing remained for him but to contrive the *Quomodo*,[1] which appeared to be a Matter of some Difficulty.

Now this young Gentleman, tho' somewhat crooked in his Morals, was perfectly strait in his Person, which was extremely strong and well made. His Face too was accounted handsome by the Generality of Women, for it was broad and ruddy, with tolerably good Teeth. Such Charms did not fail making an Impression on my Landlady, who had no little Relish for this kind of Beauty. She had, indeed, a real Compassion for the young Man; and hearing from the Surgeon that Affairs were like to go ill with the Volunteer, she suspected they might hereafter wear no benign Aspect with the Ensign. Having obtained, therefore, Leave to make him a Visit, and finding him in a very melancholy Mood, which she considerably heightened, by telling him there were scarce any Hopes of the Volunteer's Life, she proceeded to throw forth some Hints, which the other readily and eagerly taking up, they soon came to a right Understanding; and it was at length agreed, that the Ensign should, at a certain Signal, ascend the Chimney, which communicating very soon with that of the Kitchin, he might there again let himself down; for which she would give him an Opportunity, by keeping the Coast clear.

But lest our Readers, of a different Complexion, should take this Occasion of too hastily condemning all Compassion as a Folly, and pernicious to Society, we think proper to mention another Particular, which might possibly have some little Share in this Action. The Ensign happened to be at this Time possessed of the Sum of fifty Pounds, which did indeed belong to the whole Company: For the Captain having quarreled with his Lieutenant, had entrusted the Payment of his Company to the Ensign. This Money, however, he thought proper to deposite in my Landlady's Hand, possibly by way of Bail or Security that he would hereafter appear and answer to the Charge against him; but whatever were the Conditions, certain it is, that she had the Money, and the Ensign his Liberty.

The Reader may, perhaps, expect, from the compassionate Temper of this good Woman, that when she saw the poor Centinel taken Prisoner for a Fact of which she knew him innocent, she should immediately have interposed in his Behalf; but whether it was that she had already exhausted all her Compassion in the above-mentioned Instance, or that the Features of this Fellow, tho'

1. "The means" (Latin for "by what means").

not very different from those of the Ensign, could not raise it, I will
not determine; but far from being an Advocate for the present Prisoner, she urged his Guilt to his Officer, declaring with uplifted
Eyes and Hands, that she would not have had any Concern in the
Escape of a Murderer for all the World.

Every thing was now once more quiet; and most of the Company
returned again to their Beds; but the Landlady, either from the natural Activity of her Disposition, or from her Fear for her Plate,
having no Propensity to sleep, prevailed with the Officers, as they
were to march within little more than an Hour, to spend that Time
with her over a Bowl of Punch.

Jones had lain awake all this while, and had heard great Part of
the Hurry and Bustle that had passed, of which he had now some
Curiosity to know the Particulars. He therefore applied to his Bell,
which he rung at least twenty Times without any Effect; for my
Landlady was in such high Mirth with her Company, that no Clap-
per could be heard there but her own, and the Drawer and Chambermaid, who were sitting together in the Kitchin (for neither durst
he sit up, nor she lie in Bed alone) the more they heard the Bell
ring, the more they were frightened, and, as it were, nailed down in
their Places.

At last, at a lucky Interval of Chat, the Sound reached the Ears
of our good Landlady, who presently sent forth her Summons, which
both her Servants instantly obeyed. '*Joo*,' says the Mistress, 'don't
you hear the Gentleman's Bell ring? why don't you go up?' 'It is
not my Business,' answered the Drawer, 'to wait upon the Chambers. It is *Betty* Chambermaid's!' 'If you come to that,' answered
the Maid, 'it is not my Business to wait upon Gentlemen. I have
done it, indeed, sometimes; but the Devil fetch me if ever I do
again, since you make your Preambles about it.' The Bell still ringing violently, their Mistress fell into a Passion, and swore, if the
Drawer did not go up immediately, she would turn him away that
very Morning. 'If you do, Madam,' says he, 'I can't help it. I won't
do another Servant's Business.' She then applied herself to the
Maid, and endeavoured to prevail by gentle Means; but all in vain,
Betty was as inflexible as *Joo*. Both insisted it was not their Business,
and they would not do it.

The Lieutenant then fell a laughing, and said, 'Come, I will put
an End to this Contention;' and then turning to the Servants, commended them for their Resolution, in not giving up the Point; but
added, he was sure, if one would consent to go, the other would. To
which Proposal they both agreed in an Instant, and accordingly went
up very lovingly and close together. When they were gone, the
Lieutenant appeased the Wrath of the Landlady, by satisfying her
why they were both so unwilling to go alone.

They returned soon after, and acquainted their Mistress, that the sick Gentleman was so far from being dead, that he spoke as heartily as if he was well; and that he gave his Service to the Captain, and should be very glad of the Favour of seeing him before he marched.

The good Lieutenant immediately complied with his Desires, and sitting down by his Bedside, acquainted him with the Scene which had happened below, concluding with his Intentions to make an Example of the Centinel.

Upon this, *Jones* related to him the whole Truth, and earnestly begged him not to punish the poor Soldier, 'who, I am confident,' says he, 'is as innocent of the Ensign's Escape, as he is of forging any Lie, or of endeavouring to impose on you.'

The Lieutenant hesitated a few Moments, and then answered: 'Why, as you have cleared the Fellow of one Part of the Charge, so it will be impossible to prove the other; because he was not the only Centinel. But I have a good mind to punish the Rascal for being a Coward. Yet who knows what Effect the Terror of such an Apprehension may have? and to say the Truth, he hath always behaved well against an Enemy. Come, it is a good Thing to see any Sign of Religion in these Fellows; so I promise you he shall be set at Liberty when we march. But hark, the General[2] beats. My dear Boy, give me another Buss. Don't discompose nor hurry yourself; but remember the Christian Doctrine of Patience, and I warrant you will soon be able to do yourself Justice, and to take an honourable Revenge on the Fellow who hath injured you.' The Lieutenant then departed, and *Jones* endeavoured to compose himself to Rest.

BOOK VIII.

Containing above two Days.

Chapter I.

A *wonderful long Chapter concerning the Marvellous; being much the longest of all our introductory Chapters.*

As we are now entering upon a Book, in which the Course of our History will oblige us to relate some Matters of a more strange and surprizing Kind than any which have hitherto occurred, it may not be amiss in the prolegomenous, or introductory Chapter, to say something of that Species of Writing which is called the Marvellous. To this we shall, as well for the Sake of ourselves, as of others,

2. The drum call for general muster.

endeavour to set some certain Bounds; and indeed nothing can be more necessary, as Critics[1] of different Complexions are here apt to run into very different Extremes; for while some are, with M. *Dacier*,[2] ready to allow, that the same Thing which is impossible may be yet probable,[3] others have so little Historic or Poetic Faith, that they believe nothing to be either possible or probable, the like to which hath not occurred to their own Observation.

First then, I think, it may very reasonably be required of every Writer, that he keeps within the Bounds of Possibility; and still remembers that what it is not possible for Man to perform, it is scarce possible for Man to believe he did perform. This Conviction, perhaps, gave Birth to many Stories of the antient Heathen Deities (for most of them are of poetical Original.) The Poet, being desirous to indulge a wanton and extravagant Imagination, took Refuge in that Power, of the Extent of which his Readers were no Judges, or rather which they imagined to be infinite, and consequently they could not be shocked at any Prodigies related of it. This hath been strongly urged in Defence of *Homer*'s Miracles; and it is, perhaps, a Defence; not, as Mr. *Pope* would have it, because *Ulysses* told a Set of foolish Lies to the *Phæacians*,[4] who were a very dull Nation; but because the Poet himself wrote to Heathens, to whom poetical Fables were Articles of Faith. For my own Part, I must confess, so compassionate is my Temper, I wish *Polypheme*[5] had confined himself to his Milk Diet, and preserved his Eye; nor could *Ulysses* be much more concerned than myself, when his Companions were turned into Swine by *Circe*, who shewed, I think, afterwards, too much Regard for Man's Flesh to be supposed capable of converting

---

1. By this Word here, and in most other Parts of our Work, we mean every Reader in the World [*Fielding's note*].

2. André Dacier (1661–1722), renowned French classicist and translator, especially of Aristotle's *Poetics* (*La poetique d'Aristote*, 1692), and husband of Mme. Dacier, recently mentioned (above, p. 283). In the English translation of Dacier, Aristotle's famous passage reads: "The Poet ought rather to chuse Impossibilities, provided they have a Resemblence to the Truth, than the Possible, which are Incredible with all their Possibility" (*Aristotle's Art of Poetry*, London, 1705, XXV.ix.407). Dacier's comments are: "The *Ilias, Odysses*, and *Aeneis*, are full of things that are humanly speaking Impossible, and yet they continue to be Probable. . . ," with a long paragraph of continuing explanation (p. 427). Reference to his not being an Irishman is to the so-called "Irish bull," or blunder; see next note (Bryant, p. 167).

3. It is happy for M. Dacier that he was not an *Irishman* [*Fielding's note*].

4. William Broome's preface to Pope's *Odyssey* (of which Broome supplied

about a third of the translation and annotation) is "Extracted from BOSSU" (*Traité du Poëme Epique*, Paris, 1675). The preface remarks that the Phaeacians, being remote islanders, were fascinated with Odysseus's accounts of war and courage because their talents lay only in "singing and dancing, and whatsoever was charming in a quiet life" (sec. V), and that Homer, by their "Simplicity and Ignorance," has made the telling of the tales seem "humanly probable" (sec. VII). Fielding seems rather to be recalling Dacier's similar commentary on probability, mentioned above (no doubt also derived from Bossu): Homer brings "into Humane Probability those things which are not so"; the Phaeacians were "a Foolish, Simple, and Credulous People, very Idle, and loved dearly to hear such stories" (p. 427).

5. Polyphemus, the Cyclops, trapped Odysseus (Ulysses) and his men in his cave, eating a man a day until they blinded his single eye and escaped (*Odyssey* IX.106ff.). Circe, the enchantress, similarly captured them, turning the men into swine (*Odyssey* X.210ff.).

it into Bacon. I wish, likewise, with all my Heart, that *Homer* could have known the Rule prescribed by *Horace*,[6] to introduce supernatural Agents as seldom as possible. We should not then have seen his Gods coming on trivial Errands, and often behaving themselves so as not only to forfeit all Title to Respect, but to become the Objects of Scorn and Derision. A Conduct which must have shocked the Credulity of a pious and sagacious Heathen; and which could never have been defended, unless by agreeing with a Supposition to which I have been sometimes almost inclined, that this most glorious Poet, as he certainly was, had an Intent to burlesque the superstitious Faith of his own Age and Country.

But I have rested too long on a Doctrine which can be of no Use to a Christian Writer: For as he cannot introduce into his Works any of that heavenly Host which make a Part of his Creed; so is it horrid Puerility to search the Heathen Theology for any of those Deities who have been long since dethroned from their Immortality. Lord *Shaftesbury*[7] observes, that nothing is more cold than the Invocation of a Muse by a Modern; he might have added that nothing can be more absurd. A Modern may with much more Elegance invoke a Ballad, as some have thought *Homer* did, or a Mug of Ale with the Author of *Hudibras*;[8] which latter may perhaps have inspired much more Poetry as well as Prose, than all the Liquors of *Hippocrene* or *Helicon*.[9]

The only supernatural Agents which can in any Manner be allowed to us Moderns, are Ghosts; but of these I would advise an Author to be extremely sparing. These are indeed like Arsenic, and other dangerous Drugs in Physic, to be used with the utmost Caution; nor would I advise the Introduction of them at all in those Works, or by those Authors to which, or to whom a Horse-Laugh in the Reader would be any great Prejudice or Mortification.

As for Elves and Fairies, and other such Mummery, I purposely omit the Mention of them, as I should be very unwilling to confine within any Bounds those surprizing Imaginations, for whose vast Capacity the Limits of human Nature are too narrow; whose Works are to be considered as a new Creation; and who have consequently just Right to do what they will with their own.

Man therefore is the highest Subject (unless on very extraordinary Occasions indeed) which presents itself to the Pen of our Historian, or of our Poet; and in relating his Actions, great Care is to be taken, that we do not exceed the Capacity of the Agent we describe.

6. *Ars Poetica* 191–92.
7. Anthony Ashley Cooper, Third Earl of Shaftesbury (1671–1713), "A Letter Concerning Enthusiasm," sec. I, par. 2, in his *Characteristics of Men, Manners, Opinions, Times* (1711, rev. 1713), the central formulation of the benevolistic theory that man was instinctively good. See below, p. 564.
8. See above, pp. 114 and 135.
9. Hippocrene was the spring sacred to the Muses on Mount Helicon (southwestern Boeotia), the Muses' home. Drinking from it brought inspiration.

Nor is Possibility alone sufficient to justify us, we must keep likewise within the Rules of Probability. It is, I think, the Opinion of *Aristotle;*[1] or if not, it is the Opinion of some wise Man, whose Authority will be as weighty, when it is as old; 'that it is no Excuse for a Poet who relates what is incredible, that the thing related is really Matter of Fact.' This may perhaps be allowed true with regard to Poetry, but it may be thought impracticable to extend it to the Historian: For he is obliged to record Matters as he finds them; though they may be of so extraordinary a Nature, as will require no small Degree of historical Faith to swallow them. Such was the successless Armament of *Xerxes,* described by *Herodotus,*[2] or the successful Expedition of *Alexander* related by *Arrian.*[3] Such of later Years was the Victory of *Agincourt*[4] obtained by *Harry* the Fifth, or that of *Narva* won by *Charles* the Twelfth of *Sweden.* All which Instances, the more we reflect on them, appear still the more astonishing.

Such Facts, however, as they occur in the Thread of the Story; nay, indeed, as they constitute the essential Parts of it, the Historian is not only justifiable in recording as they really happened; but indeed would be unpardonable, should he omit or alter them. But there are other Facts not of such Consequence nor so necessary, which tho' ever so well attested, may nevertheless be sacrificed to Oblivion in Complaisance to the Scepticism of a Reader. Such is that memorable Story of the Ghost of *George Villiers,*[5] which might with more Propriety have been made a Present of to Dr. *Drelincourt,*[6] to have kept the Ghost of Mrs. *Veale* Company, at the Head of his Discourse upon Death, than have been introduced into so solemn a Work as the History of the Rebellion.

To say the Truth, if the Historian will confine himself to what really happened, and utterly reject any Circumstance, which, tho' never so well attested, he must be well assured is false, he will sometimes fall into the Marvellous, but never into the Incredible. He will often raise the Wonder and Surprize of his Reader, but never

---

1. Fielding seems to paraphrase loosely the argument he has just poked fun at above, p. 302. Aristotle does not say that a writer shouldn't excuse his incredibilities because they really happened. He simply says he shouldn't choose them, and that probable impossibilities are better. His final statement on the subject (1461b.10–15) actually says that a writer may, in a pinch, excuse his improbabilities exactly on the grounds of fact, because there is indeed a probability that some improbable things happen.
2. *History* VII.21–IX.107. Xerxes (519–c. 464 B.C.) was the Persian invader of Greece, ultimately defeated.
3. Arrian (born about A.D. 96) wrote the *Anabasis of Alexander,* a history of Alexander's triumphs.
4. In these battles, Henry V against the French (25 Oct. 1415) and Charles XII against the Russians (17 Nov. 1700) annihilated vastly superior forces.
5. In Edward Hyde, Earl of Clarendon's *History of the Rebellion and Civil Wars in England* (1702-4) I.89–91. The ghost of Villiers, First Duke of Buckingham, appeared to his son, predicting his death unless he could overcome the ill will of the people. Buckingham, a popular favorite of both James I and Charles I, fell from popularity during Charles's struggles with Parliament and was stabbed to death 23 Aug. 1628.
6. Daniel Defoe's account of how the ghost of Mrs. Veale paid a visit to her friend was prefixed to the fourth edition (1716) of the English translation of Charles Drelincourt's *Christian's Defense Against the Fears of Death* (1651).

that incredulous Hatred mentioned by *Horace*.[7] It is by falling into
Fiction therefore, that we generally offend against this Rule, of
deserting Probability, which the Historian seldom if ever quits, till
he forsakes his Character, and commences a Writer of Romance. In
this, however, those Historians who relate publick Transactions have
the Advantage of us who confine ourselves to Scenes of private Life.
The Credit of the former is by common Notoriety supported for a
long Time; and publick Records, with the concurrent Testimony of
many Authors, bear Evidence to their Truth in future Ages. Thus a
Trajan and an *Antoninus*, a *Nero* and a *Caligula*, have all met with
the Belief of Posterity; and no one doubts but that Men so very
good, and so very bad, were once the Masters of Mankind.

But we who deal in private Character, who search into the most
retired Recesses, and draw forth Examples of Virtue and Vice, from
Holes and Corners of the World, are in a more dangerous Situation. As we have no publick Notoriety, no concurrent Testimony,
no Records to support and corroborate what we deliver, it becomes
us to keep within the Limits not only of Possibility, but of Probability too; and this more especially in painting what is greatly good
and amiable. Knavery and Folly, though never so exorbitant, will
more easily meet with Assent; for Ill-nature adds great Support and
Strength to Faith.

Thus we may, perhaps, with little Danger, relate the History of
Fisher;[8] who having long owed his Bread to the Generosity of Mr.
Derby, and having one Morning received a considerable Bounty
from his Hands, yet in order to possess himself of what remained in

7. Horace says he hates things that make him incredulous, such as Medea's murdering her children, Atreus's cooking human organs, Procne's turning into a bird, and Cadmus's turning into a snake (*Ars Poetica* 185–88).

8. On Monday night, 10 April 1727, Henry Fisher, a sometime lawyer's clerk and billiard player in debt, shot and killed his friend Widdrington Darby, Jr., in the darkened office, in the Inner Temple, of Sir George Cooke, lawyer, to whom Darby was clerk. Darby had entertained some gentlemen at dinner in his rooms behind the office, and had let his guests and servant out the street door. Fisher, who had evidently entered the office and hidden under a desk shortly before the party broke up, shot Darby as he returned to his rooms, directly in the left temple, the bullet reaching the right temporal bone opposite. He robbed Darby of £1,400 and other valuables. He was arrested on 30 April 1727, and indicted on 15 May to be tried at Old Bailey on Thursday, 18 May. But on Wednesday night, 17 May 1727, Fisher escaped from Newgate Prison, never to appear on either the Calendar of Indictments or in the Gaol Delivery Books for Old Bailey (Middlesex Records Office, Dartmouth St., London), at least up to the publication of *Tom Jones* (28 February 1749). Fielding is spelling "Darby" by ear, and his other slight inaccuracies also suggest that he did not see the papers. He probably arrived in London that summer or fall (cf. Cross I.55). *Hamlet* played only on the Saturday after the murder (15 April 1727), with Barton Booth as the ghost, speaking of "murther most foul." See Sir William Musgrave, *Obituary Prior to 1800*, Publication of the Harleian Soc., vol. 45 (London, 1900), II.140; Abel Boyer, *The Political State of Great Britain*, 33 (1727), 530–32; *The Daily Journal*, 12, 13 April, 1, 8, 16 May 1727; *The Daily Post*, 12, 13 April, 1, 8, 18 May 1727; *The Daily Post*, 12, 13 April, 1, 8, 18 May 1727; *The Lives of the Most Remarkable Criminals*, anonymous (London, John Osborn, 1735), II.393–99; modern reprint, ed. Arthur L. Hayward (London: Routledge, 1927), pp. 417–20. These last two mispell Darby's name as "Widdington."

Fielding loosely translates from Suetonius's *Lives of the Twelve Caesars* XXXIV, probably from memory.

his Friend's Scrutore, concealed himself in a publick Office of the Temple, through which there was a Passage into Mr. *Derby's* Chambers. Here he overheard Mr. *Derby* for many Hours solacing himself at an Entertainment which he that Evening gave his Friends, and to which *Fisher* had been invited. During all this Time, no tender, no grateful Reflections arose to restrain his Purpose; but when the poor Gentleman had let his Company out through the Office, *Fisher* came suddenly from his lurking Place, and walking softly behind his Friend into his Chamber, discharged a Pistol-Ball into his Head. This may be believed, when the Bones of *Fisher* are as rotten as his Heart. Nay, perhaps, it will be credited that the Villain went two Days afterwards with some young Ladies to the Play of *Hamlet*; and with an unaltered Countenance heard one of the Ladies, who little suspected how near she was to the Person, cry out, 'Good God! if the Man that murdered Mr. *Derby* was now present!' Manifesting in this a more seared and callous Conscience than even *Nero* himself; of whom we are told by *Suetonius*, 'that the Consciousness of his Guilt, after the Death of his Mother, became immediately intolerable, and so continued; nor could all the Congratulations of the Soldiers, of the Senate, and the People, allay the Horrors of his Conscience.'

But now, on the other Hand, should I tell my Reader, that I had known a Man whose penetrating Genius[9] had enabled him to raise a large Fortune in a Way where no Beginning was chaulked out to him: That he had done this with the most perfect Preservation of his Integrity, and not only without the least Injustice or Injury to any one individual Person, but with the highest Advantage to Trade, and a vast Increase of the public Revenue: That he had expended one Part of the Income of this Fortune in discovering a Taste superior to most, by Works where the highest Dignity was united with the purest Simplicity, and another Part in displaying a Degree of Goodness superior to all Men, by Acts of Charity to Objects whose only Recommendations were their Merits, or their Wants: That he was most industrious in searching after Merit in Distress, most eager to relieve it, and then as careful (perhaps too careful) to conceal what he had done: That his House, his Furniture, his Gardens, his Table, his private Hospitality, and his public Beneficence, all denoted the Mind from which they flowed, and were all intrinsically rich and noble, without Tinsel, or external Ostentation: That he filled every Relation in Life with the most adequate Virtue: That he was most piously religious to his Creator, most zealously loyal to his Sovereign; a most tender Husband to his Wife, a kind Relation, a munificent Patron, a warm and firm Friend, a knowing and a chearful Companion, indulgent to his Servants, hospitable to his Neighbours, charitable to the Poor, and be-

9. **Evidently Ralph Allen. See Dedication, above, p. 5.**

nevolent to all Mankind. Should I add to these the Epithets of wise, brave, elegant, and indeed every other amiable Epithet in our Language, I might surely say,

> —*Quis credet? nemo Hercule! nemo;*
> *Vel duo, vel nemo.*[1]

And yet I know a Man who is all I have here described. But a single Instance (and I really know not such another) is not sufficient to justify us, while we are writing to thousands who never heard of the Person, nor of any thing like him. Such *Raræ Aves*[2] should be remitted to the Epitaph-Writer, or to some Poet, who may condescend to hitch him in a Distich,[3] or to slide him into a Rhime with an Air of Carelessness and Neglect, without giving any Offence to the Reader.

In the last Place, the Actions should be such as may not only be within the Compass of human Agency, and which human Agents may probably be supposed to do; but they should be likely for the very Actors and Characters themselves to have performed: For what may be only wonderful and surprizing in one Man, may become improbable, or indeed impossible, when related of another.

This last Requisite is what the dramatic Critics call Conservation of Character;[4] and it requires a very extraordinary Degree of Judgment, and a most exact Knowledge of human Nature.

It is admirably remarked by a most excellent Writer, That Zeal can no more hurry a Man to act in direct Opposition to itself, than a rapid Stream can carry a Boat against its own Current. I will venture to say, that for a Man to act in direct Contradiction to the Dictates of his Nature, is, if not impossible, as improbable and as miraculous as any Thing which can well be conceived. Should the best Parts of the Story of *M. Antoninus* be ascribed to *Nero*, or should the worst Incidents of *Nero*'s Life be imputed to *Antoninus*, what would be more shocking to Belief than either Instance? whereas both these being related of their proper Agent, constitute the Truly Marvellous.

Our modern Authors of Comedy have fallen almost universally into the Error here hinted at: Their Heroes generally are notorious Rogues, and their Heroines abandoned Jades, during the first four Acts; but in the fifth, the former become very worthy Gentlemen, and the latter, Women of Virtue and Discretion: Nor is the Writer often so kind as to give himself the least Trouble, to reconcile or

---

1. "Who will believe it? No one, by Hercules, no one. Perhaps two, perhaps no one." Persius, *Satires* I.ii, altered to suit Fielding's context. He substitutes *credet* for *leget*, "read" (Mutter).
2. See above, p. 141.
3. Two lines of poetry, a couplet.
4. John Coolidge, in "Fielding and the 'Conservation of Character,'" *Modern Philology*, 57 (1960), identifies Horace's *Ars Poetica* as the most concise statement of this classical precept, 119–27, ending: "si ... audes / personam formare novam, servetur ad imum, / qualis ab incepto processerit, et sibi constet"— "if you dare create a new character, conserve him to the end as he has first appeared, remaining constantly himself."

account for this monstrous Change and Incongruity. There is, indeed, no other Reason to be assigned for it, than because the Play is drawing to a Conclusion; as if it was no less natural in a Rogue to repent in the last Act of a Play, than in the last of his Life; which we perceive to be generally the Case at *Tyburn*,[5] a Place which might, indeed, close the Scene of some Comedies with much Propriety, as the Heroes in these are most commonly eminent for those very Talents which not only bring Men to the Gallows, but enable them to make an heroic Figure when they are there.

Within these few Restrictions, I think, every Writer may be permitted to deal as much in the Wonderful as he pleases; nay, if he thus keeps within the Rules of Credibility, the more he can surprise the Reader, the more he will engage his Attention, and the more he will charm him. As a Genius of the highest Rank observes in his 5th Chapter of the *Bathos*,[6] 'The great Art of all Poetry is to mix Truth with Fiction; in order to join the Credible with the Surprizing.'

For tho' every good Author will confine himself within the Bounds of Probability, it is by no means necessary that his Characters, or his Incidents, should be trite, common, or vulgar; such as happen in every Street, or in every House, or which may be met with in the home Articles of a News-Paper. Nor must he be inhibited from shewing many Persons and Things, which may possibly have never fallen within the Knowledge of great Part of his Readers. If the Writer strictly observes the Rules abovementioned, he hath discharged his Part; and is then intitled to some Faith from his Reader, who is indeed guilty of critical Infidelity if he disbelieves him. For want of a Portion of such Faith, I remember the Character of a young Lady of Quality,[7] which was condemned on the Stage for being unnatural, by the unanimous Voice of a very large Assembly of Clerks and Apprentices; tho' it had the previous Suffrages of many Ladies of the first Rank; one of whom, very eminent for her Understanding, declared it was the Picture of half the young People of her Acquaintance.

Chapter II.

In which the Landlady pays a Visit to Mr. Jones.

When *Jones* had taken Leave of his Friend the Lieutenant, he endeavoured to close his Eyes, but all in vain; his Spirits were too

5. Where criminals were hanged, northeast corner of Hyde Park, where the Marble Arch now stands.
6. Pope's *Peri Bathous, or The Art of Sinking in Poetry* by "Martinus Scriblerus." Correctly quoted except for the begining: "And since the great art of poetry . . ." (Elwin and Courthope ed., vol.

X, ch. V, pp. 354–55).
7. Lady Charlotte in Fielding's play *The Modern Husband*, hissed on its opening night, 14 Feb. 1732. Fielding had had his cousin Lady Mary Wortley Montagu read and comment on it beforehand; presumably he is quoting her (Cross I.118–20).

lively and wakeful to be lulled to Sleep. So having amused, or rather tormented himself with the Thoughts of his *Sophia*, till it was open Daylight, he called for some Tea; upon which Occasion my Landlady herself vouchsafed to pay him a Visit.

This was indeed the first Time she had seen him, or at least had taken any Notice of him; but as the Lieutenant had assured her that he was certainly some young Gentleman of Fashion, she now determined to shew him all the Respect in her Power: for, to speak truly, this was one of those Houses where Gentlemen, to use the Language of Advertisements, meet with civil Treatment for their Money.

She had no sooner begun to make his Tea, than she likewise began to discourse. 'La! Sir,' said she, 'I think it is great Pity that such a pretty young Gentleman should undervalue himself so, as to go about with these Soldier Fellows. They call themselves Gentlemen, I warrant you; but, as my first Husband used to say, they should remember it is we that pay them. And to be sure it is very hard upon us to be obliged to pay them, and to keep 'em too as we Publicans are. I had twenty of 'um last Night besides Officers; nay, for matter o' that, I had rather have the Soldiers than Officers: For nothing is ever good enough for those Sparks; and I am sure, if you was to see the Bills; La, Sir, it is nothing. I have had less Trouble, I warrant you, with a good Squire's Family, where we take forty or fifty Shillings of a Night, besides Horses. And yet I warrants me, there is *narrow* a one of all those Officer Fellows, but looks upon himself to be as good as *arrow* a Squire of 500*l.* a Year. To be sure it doth me Good to hear their Men run about after um, crying your Honour, and your Honour. Marry come up with such Honour, and an Ordinary at a Shilling a Head. Then there's such Swearing among 'um, to be sure, it frightens me out o' my Wits; I thinks nothing can ever prosper with such wicked People. And here one of 'um has used you in so barbarous a Manner. I thought indeed how well the rest would secure him; they all hang together; for if you had been in Danger of Death, which I am glad to see you are not, it would have been all as one to such wicked People. They would have let the Murderer go. Laud have Mercy upon 'um; I would not have such a Sin to answer for, for the whole World. But tho' you are likely, with the Blessing, to recover, there is Laa for him yet; and if you will employ Lawyer *Small*, I darest be sworn he'll make the Fellow fly the Country for him; tho' perhaps he'll have fled the Country before; for it is here To-day and gone To-morrow with such Chaps. I hope, however, you will learn more Wit for the future, and return back to your Friends: I warrant they are all miserable for your Loss; and if they was but to know what had happened. La, my seeming! I would not for the World they should. Come, come, we know very well what all the Matter is; but if one won't, another will; so pretty a Gentleman need never want a Lady. I am sure, if I was as you, I would see the finest She that ever wore a Head hanged, before I would go for a Soldier for her.—Nay, don't blush so (for indeed he did to a violent Degree;) why, you thought, Sir, I knew nothing of the Matter, I warrant you, about Madam *Sophia*.' 'How,' says *Jones*, starting up, 'do you know my *Sophia?*' 'Do I! ay marry,' cries the Landlady, 'many's the Time hath she lain in this House.' 'With her Aunt, I suppose,' says *Jones*.— 'Why there it is now,' cries the Landlady. 'Ay, ay, ay, I know the old Lady very well. And a sweet young Creature is Madam *Sophia*, that's the Truth on't.' 'A Sweet Creature!' cries *Jones*, 'O Heavens!

> *Angels are painted fair to look like her.*
> *There's in her all that we believe of Heaven,*
> *Amazing Brightness, Purity and Truth,*
> *Eternal Joy, and everlasting Love.*[1]

'And could I ever have imagined that you had known my *Sophia!*' 'I wish,' says the Landlady, 'you knew half so much of her. What would you have given to have sat by her Bed-side? What a delicious Neck she hath! Her lovely Limbs have stretched them-selves in that very Bed you now lie in.' 'Here!' cries *Jones*, 'hath *Sophia* ever laid here?'—'Ay, ay, here: there; in that very Bed,' says the Landlady, 'where I wish you had her this Moment; and she may wish so too for any Thing I know to the contrary: For she hath mentioned your Name to me.'—'Ha,' cries he, 'did she ever men-tion her poor *Jones?*—You flatter me now; I can never believe so much.' 'Why then,' answered she, 'as I hope to be saved, and may the Devil fetch me, if I speak a Syllable more than the Truth. I have heard her mention Mr. *Jones*; but in a civil and modest Way, I confess; yet I could perceive she thought a great deal more than she said.' 'O my dear Woman,' cries *Jones*, 'her Thoughts of me I shall never be worthy of. O she is all Gentleness, Kindness, Goodness. Why was such a Rascal as I born, ever to give her soft Bosom a Moment's Uneasiness? Why am I cursed? I, who would undergo all the Plagues and Miseries which any Dæmon ever invented for Mankind, to procure her any Good; nay, Torture itself could not be Misery to me, did I but know that she was happy.' 'Why, look you there now,' says the Landlady, 'I told her you was a constant Lovier.' 'But pray, Madam, tell me when or where you knew any thing of me; for I never was here before, nor do I remem-ber ever to have seen you.' 'Nor is it possible you should,' answered she; 'for you was a little Thing when I had you in my Lap at the Squire's.'—'How the Squire's,' says *Jones*, 'what, do you know that

---

1. Thomas Otway, *Venice Preserved*   "her" for Otway's "you" (Bryant, p. (1682) I.i.337–40. Fielding substitutes   171).

great and good Mr. *Allworthy* then?' 'Yes, marry do I,' says she; 'Who in the Country doth not?'—'The Fame of his Goodness indeed,' answered *Jones,* 'must have extended farther than this; but Heaven only can know him, can know that Benevolence which it copied from itself, and sent upon Earth as its own Pattern. Mankind are as ignorant of such divine Goodness, as they are unworthy of it; but none so unworthy of it as myself. I who was raised by him to such a Height; taken in, as you must well know, a poor base-born Child, adopted by him, and treated as his own Son, to dare by my Follies to disoblige him, to draw his Vengeance upon me. Yes, I deserve it all: For I will never be so ungrateful as ever to think he hath done an Act of Injustice by me. No, I deserve to be turned out of Doors, as I am. And now, Madam, says he, I believe you will not blame me for turning Soldier, especially with such a Fortune as this in my Pocket.' At which Words he shook a Purse, which had but very little in it, and which still appeared to the Landlady to have less.

My good Landlady was (according to vulgar Phrase) struck all of a Heap by this Relation. She answered coldly, 'That to be sure People were the best Judges what was most proper for their Circumstances.—But hark,' says she, 'I think I hear somebody call. Coming! coming! the Devil's in all our Volk, nobody hath any Ears. I must go down Stairs; if you want any more Breakfast, the Maid will come up. Coming!' At which Words, without taking any Leave, she flung out of the Room: For the lower Sort of People are very tenacious of Respect; and tho' they are contented to give this *gratis* to Persons of Quality, yet they never confer it on those of their own Order without taking care to be well paid for their Pains.

Chapter III.

In which the Surgeon makes his second Appearance.

Before we proceed any farther, that the Reader may not be mistaken in imagining the Landlady knew more than she did, nor surprized that she knew so much, it may be necessary to inform him, that the Lieutenant had acquainted her that the Name of *Sophia* had been the Occasion of the Quarrel; and as for the rest of her Knowledge, the sagacious Reader will observe how she came by it in the preceding Scene. Great Curiosity was indeed mixed with her Virtues; and she never willingly suffered any one to depart from her House without enquiring as much as possible into their Names, Families and Fortunes.

She was no sooner gone than *Jones,* instead of animadverting on

her Behaviour, reflected that he was in the same Bed, which he was
informed had held his dear *Sophia*. This occasioned a thousand
fond and tender Thoughts, which we would dwell longer upon, did
we not consider that such kind of Lovers will make a very inconsiderable Part of our Readers.

In this Situation the Surgeon found him, when he came to dress
his Wound. The Doctor, perceiving, upon Examination, that his
Pulse was disordered, and hearing that he had not slept, declared
that he was in great Danger: For he apprehended a Fever was
coming on; which he would have prevented by Bleeding, but *Jones*
would not submit, declaring he would lose no more Blood; and
'Doctor,' says he, 'if you will be so kind only to dress my Head, I
have no doubt of being well in a Day or two.'

'I wish,' answered the Surgeon, 'I could assure your being well in
a Month or two. Well, indeed! No, no, People are not so soon well
of such Contusions; but, Sir, I am not at this Time of Day to be
instructed in my Operations by a Patient, and I insist on making a
Revulsion before I dress you.'

Jones persisted obstinately in his Refusal, and the Doctor at last
yielded; telling him at the same Time, that he would not be answerable for the ill Consequence, and hoped he would do him the Justice to acknowledge that he had given him a contrary Advice; which
the Patient promised he would.

The Doctor retired into the Kitchin, where, addressing himself
to the Landlady, he complained bitterly of the undutiful Behaviour
of his Patient, who would not be blooded, though he was in a
Fever.

'It is an eating Fever then,' says the Landlady: 'For he hath
devoured two swinging buttered Toasts this Morning for Breakfast.'

'Very likely,' says the Doctor; 'I have known People eat in a
Fever; and it is very easily accounted for; because the Acidity occasioned by the febrile Matter, may stimulate the Nerves of the Dia-
phragm, and thereby occasion a Craving, which will not be easily
distinguishable from a natural Appetite; but the Aliment will not be
concreted, nor assimilated into Chyle, and so will corrode the vascu-
lar Orifices, and thus will aggravate the febrific Symptoms. Indeed I
think the Gentleman in a very dangerous Way, and, if he is not
blooded, I am afraid will die.'

'Every Man must die some Time or other,' answered the good
Woman; 'it is no Business of mine. I hope, Doctor, you would not
have me hold him while you bleed him.——But, harkee, a Word in
your Ear; I would advise you before you proceed too far, to take
care who is to be your Paymaster.'

'Paymaster!' said the Doctor, staring, 'why, I've a Gentleman
under my Hands, have I not?'

'I imagined so as well as you,' said the Landlady; 'but as my first Husband used to say, every Thing is not what it looks to be. He is an arrant Scrub, I assure you. However, take no Notice that I mentioned any thing to you of the Matter; but I think People in Business *oft* always to let one another know such Things.'

'And have I suffered such a Fellow as this,' cries the Doctor, in a Passion, 'to instruct me? Shall I hear my Practice insulted by one who will not pay me! I am glad I have made this Discovery in Time. I will see now whether he will be blooded or no.' He then immediately went up Stairs, and flinging open the Door of the Chamber with much Violence, awaked poor *Jones* from a very sound Nap, into which he was fallen, and what was still worse, from a delicious Dream concerning *Sophia*.

'Will you be blooded or no?' cries the Doctor, in a Rage. 'I have told you my Resolution already,' answered *Jones*, 'and I wish with all my Heart you had taken my Answer: For you have awaked me out of the sweetest Sleep which I ever had in my Life.'

'Ay, ay,' cries the Doctor, 'many a Man hath dosed away his Life. Sleep is not always good, no more than Food; but remember I demand of you for the last Time, will you be blooded?' 'I answer you for the last Time,' said *Jones*, 'I will not.' 'Then I wash my Hands of you,' cries the Doctor; 'and I desire you to pay me for the Trouble I have had already. Two Journeys at 5 *s.* each, two Dressings at 5 *s.* more, and half a Crown for Phlebotomy.' 'I hope,' said *Jones*, 'you don't intend to leave me in this Condition.' 'Indeed but I shall,' said the other. 'Then,' said *Jones*, 'you have used me rascally, and I will not pay you a Farthing.' 'Very well,' cries the Doctor, 'the first Loss is the best. What a Pox did my Landlady mean by sending for me to such Vagabonds?' At which Words he flung out of the Room, and his Patient turning himself about soon recovered his Sleep; but his Dream was unfortunately gone.

Chapter IV.

In which is introduced one of the pleasantest Barbers that was ever recorded in History, the Barber of Bagdad, *or he in* Don Quixote[1] *not excepted.*

The Clock had now struck Five, when *Jones* awaked from a Nap of seven Hours, so much refreshed, and in such perfect Health and Spirits, that he resolved to get up and dress himself: for which Purpose he unlocked his Portmanteau, and took out clean Linen, and a

1. A mighty talker, storyteller, and universal genius in "The History of the Little Hunchback," in the *Arabian Nights*, and probably Cervantes's barber who helps the curate go through Don Quixote's library of romances. Another barber, riding along with his brass basin on his head, becomes in Don Quixote's eyes a knight wearing Mambrino's famous golden helmet (pt. I, bk. III, vii).

Suit of Cloaths; but first he slipt on a Frock, and went down into the Kitchin to bespeak something that might pacify certain Tumults he found rising within his Stomach.

Meeting the Landlady he accosted her with great Civility, and asked 'what he could have for Dinner.' 'For Dinner!' says she, 'it is an odd Time a Day to think about Dinner. There is nothing drest in the House, and the Fire is almost out.' 'Well but,' says he, 'I must have something to eat, and it is almost indifferent to me what: For to tell you the Truth, I was never more hungry in my Life.' 'Then,' says she, 'I believe there is a Piece of cold Buttock and Carrot, which will fit you.'—'Nothing better,' answered *Jones*, 'but I should be obliged to you, if you would let it be fried.' To which the Landlady consented, and said smiling, 'she was glad to see him so well recovered:' For the Sweetness of our Heroe's Temper was almost irresistible; besides, she was really no ill-humoured Woman at the Bottom; but she loved Money so much, that she hated every Thing which had the Semblance of Poverty.

Jones now returned in order to dress himself, while his Dinner was preparing, and was, according to his Orders, attended by the Barber.

This Barber who went by the Name of little *Benjamin*, was a Fellow of great Oddity and Humour, which had frequently led him into small Inconveniencies, such as Slaps in the Face, Kicks in the Breech, broken Bones, &c. For every one doth not understand a Jest; and those who do, are often displeased with being themselves the Subjects of it. This Vice was, however, incurable in him; and though he had often smarted for it, yet if ever he conceived a Joke, he was certain to be delivered of it, without the least Respect of Persons, Time or Place.

He had a great many other Particularities in his Character, which I shall not mention, as the Reader will himself very easily perceive them, on his farther Acquaintance with this extraordinary Person.

Jones being impatient to be drest, for a Reason which may easily be imagined, thought the Shaver was very tedious in preparing his Suds, and begged him to make haste; to which the other answered, with much Gravity: For he never discomposed his Muscles on any Account. '*Festina lenté*[2] is a Proverb which I learnt long before I ever touched a Razor.' 'I find, Friend, you are a Scholar,' replied Jones. 'A poor one,' said the Barber, '*non omnia possumus omnes*.'[3] 'Again!' said *Jones*; 'I fancy you are good at capping Verses.' 'Excuse me, Sir,' said the Barber, '*non tanto me dignor honore*.'[4] And then proceeding to his Operation, 'Sir,' said he, 'since I have

2. "Hasten slowly," a favorite saying of Augustus's (Suetonius, *The Twelve Caesars* XXV).
3. "We all can't do all things." Virgil, *Eclogues* VIII.63. See also Fielding's *Champion*, 14 Feb. 1740; *Joseph Andrews* II.viii; and below, p. 413.
4. "I don't think myself worthy of so much honor." Probably for *haud equidem tali me dignor honore*. Virgil, *Aeneid* I.335 (Mutter).

dealt in Suds, I could never discover more than two Reasons for
shaving, the one is to get a Beard, and the other to get rid of one. I
conjecture, Sir, it may not be long since you shaved, from the
former of these Motives. Upon my Word you have had good Success; for one may say of your Beard, that it is *Tondenti gravior*.'5 'I
conjecture,' says *Jones*, 'that thou art a very comical Fellow.' 'You
mistake me widely, Sir,' said the Barber, 'I am too much addicted
to the Study of Philosophy, *Hinc illæ Lacrymæ*,6 Sir, that's my Misfortune. Too much Learning hath been my Ruin.' 'Indeed,' says
Jones, 'I confess, Friend, you have more Learning than generally
belongs to your Trade; but I can't see how it can have injured you.'
'Alas, Sir,' answered the Shaver, 'my Father disinherited me for it.
He was a Dancing-Master; and because I could read, before I could
dance, he took an Aversion to me, and left every Farthing among
his other Children.——Will you please to have your Temples—
O la! I ask your Pardon, I fancy there is *Hiatus in manuscriptis*.7 I
heard you was going to the Wars: but I find it was a Mistake.'
'Why do you conclude so?' says *Jones*. 'Sure, Sir,' answered the
Barber, 'you are too wise a Man to carry a broken Head thither; for
that would be carrying Coals to *Newcastle*.'

'Upon my Word,' cries *Jones*, 'thou art a very odd Fellow, and I
like thy Humour extremely; I shall be very glad if thou wilt come to
me after Dinner, and drink a Glass with me; I long to be better
acquainted with thee.'

'O dear Sir,' said the Barber, 'I can do you twenty Times as great
a Favour, if you will accept of it.' 'What is that, my Friend?' cries
Jones. 'Why I will drink a Bottle with you, if you please; For I
dearly love Good-nature; and as you have found me out to be a
comical Fellow, so I have no Skill in Physiognomy, if you are not
one of the best-natured Gentlemen in the Universe.' *Jones* now
walked down Stairs neatly drest, and perhaps the fair *Adonis* was
not a lovelier Figure; and yet he had no Charms for my Landlady:
For as that good Woman did not resemble *Venus* at all in her
Person, so neither did she in her Taste. Happy had it been for
Nanny the Chambermaid, if she had seen with the Eyes of her Mistress; for that poor Girl fell so violently in love with *Jones* in five
Minutes, that her Passion afterwards cost her many a Sigh. This
*Nancy*8 was extremely pretty, and altogether as coy; for she had
refused a Drawer, and one or two young Farmers in the Neighbour-
hood, but the bright Eyes of our Heroe thawed all her Ice in a
Moment.

When *Jones* returned to the Kitchin, his Cloth was not yet laid;

<hr/>

5. "Heavier for the shaver."
6. "Hence those tears." Terence, *Andria*
(166 B.C.) 126. The quotation became
proverbial. Cicero uses it a century later
(*Pro Caelio* XXV.61), then Horace

(*Epistles* I.xix.41) fifty years after that.
See below, p. 462.
7. "A gap in the manuscripts."
8. *Nanny* was a nickname for *Nancy*; see
below, p. 541.

nor indeed was there any Occasion it should, his Dinner remaining in *Statu quo*, as did the Fire which was to dress it. This Disappointment might have put many a philosophical Temper into a Passion; but it had no such Effect on *Jones*. He only gave the Landlady a gentle Rebuke, saying, 'Since it was so difficult to get it heated, he would eat the Beef cold.' But now the good Woman, whether moved by Compassion, or by Shame, or by whatever other Motive, I cannot tell, first gave her Servants a round Scold for disobeying the Orders which she had never given, and then bidding the Drawer lay a Napkin in the Sun, she set about the Matter in good earnest, and soon accomplished it.

This Sun, into which *Jones* was now conducted, was truly named as *Lucus a non lucendo*;[9] for it was an Apartment into which the Sun had scarce ever looked. It was indeed the worst Room in the House; and happy was it for *Jones* that it was so. However, he was now too hungry to find any Fault; but having once satisfied his Appetite, he ordered the Drawer to carry a Bottle of Wine into a better Room, and expressed some Resentment at having been shewn into a Dungeon.

The Drawer having obeyed his Commands, he was, after some Time, attended by the Barber; who would not indeed have suffered him to wait so long for his Company, had he not been listening in the Kitchin to the Landlady, who was entertaining a Circle that she had gathered round her with the History of poor *Jones*, Part of which she had extracted from his own Lips, and the other Part was her own ingenious Composition; 'for she said he was a poor Parish Boy, taken into the House of Squire *Allworthy*, where he was bred up as an Apprentice, and now turned out of Doors for his Misdeeds, particularly for making Love to his young Mistress, and probably for robbing the House; for how else should he come by the little Money he hath; And this,' says she, 'is your Gentleman, forsooth.' 'A Servant of Squire *Allworthy*!' says the Barber, 'what's his Name?'—'Why he told me his Name was *Jones*,' says she, 'perhaps he goes by a wrong Name. Nay, and he told me too, that the Squire had maintained him as his own Son, *thof* he had quarrelled with him now.' 'And if his Name be *Jones*, he told you the Truth,' said the Barber; 'for I have Relations who live in that Country, nay, and some People say he is his Son.' 'Why doth he not go by the Name of his Father?' 'I can't tell that,' said the Barber, 'many People's Sons don't go by the Name of their Father.' 'Nay,' said the Landlady, 'if I thought he was a Gentleman's Son, *thof* he was a Bye Blow, I should behave to him in anotherguess Manner; for many of

---

9. "A grove [so called] because it has no light." An ancient joke at the accidental similarity between the words *lucus* ("[shady] grove") and *lucendo* ("to be lit up"), which really mean contradictory things, quoted by Quintilian, *De Institutione Oratoria* I.vi.34, as a serious etymology.

these Bye Blows come to be great Men, and, as my poor first Husband used to say, Never affront any Customer that's a Gentleman.'

Chapter V.

A *Dialogue between Mr.* Jones *and the Barber.*

This Conversation passed partly while *Jones* was at Dinner in his Dungeon, and partly while he was expecting the Barber in the Parlour. And, as soon as it was ended, Mr. *Benjamin*, as we have said, attended him, and was very kindly desired to sit down. *Jones* then filling out a Glass of Wine, drank his Health by the Appellation of *Doctissime Tonsorum.*[1] *Ago tibi Gratias, Domine,*[2] said the Barber; and then looking very steadfastly at *Jones*, he said, with great Gravity, and with a seeming Surprize, as if he had recollected a Face he had seen before, 'Sir, may I crave the Favour to know if your Name is not *Jones?*' To which the other answered, that it was. '*Proh Deûm atque Hominum Fidem,*'[3] says the Barber, 'how strangely Things come to pass! Mr. *Jones* I am your most obedient Servant. I find you do not know me, which indeed is no Wonder, since you never saw me but once, and then you was very young. Pray, Sir, how doth the good Squire *Allworthy?* How doth *Ille optimus omnium Patronus?*'[4] 'I find,' said *Jones*, 'you do indeed know me; but I have not the like Happiness of recollecting you.'—'I do not wonder at that,' cries *Benjamin*; 'but I am surprized I did not know you sooner, for you are not in the least altered. And pray, Sir, may I without Offence enquire whither you are travelling this Way?' 'Fill the Glass, Mr. Barber,' said *Jones*, 'and ask no more Questions.' 'Nay, Sir,' answered *Benjamin*, 'I would not be troublesome; and I hope you don't think me a Man of an impertinent Curiosity, for that is a Vice which no-body can lay to my Charge; but I ask Pardon, for when a Gentleman of your Figure travels without his Servants, we may suppose him to be, as we say, in *Casu incognito*, and perhaps I ought not to have mentioned your Name.' 'I own,' says *Jones*, 'I did not expect to have been so well known in this Country as I find I am, yet, for particular Reasons, I shall be obliged to you if you will not mention my Name to any other Person, till I am gone from hence.' '*Pauca Verba,*'[5] answered the Barber; 'and I wish no others here knew you but myself; for some People have Tongues; but I promise you I can keep a Secret. My Enemies will allow me that Virtue.' 'And yet that is not the Characteristic of your Profession, Mr. Barber,' answered *Jones*. 'Alas,

---

1. "O most learned of barbers."
2. "I give you thanks, my lord."
3. "Oh, the faith of gods and men!" Terence, *Andria* I.v.2 and *Heautontimorumenos* I.i.9; Cicero, *Tusculan Disputa-*

tions V.xvi.48; Fielding, *Champion,* 19 Apr. 1740.
4. "That best of all patrons."
5. "Few words."

Sir,' replied *Benjamin*, '*Non si male nunc & olim sic erit.*[6] I was not born nor bred a Barber, I assure you. I have spent most of my Time among Gentlemen, and tho' I say it, I understand something of Gentility. And if you had thought me as worthy of your Confidence as you have some other People, I should have shewn you I could have kept a Secret better. I should not have degraded your Name in a public Kitchin; for indeed, Sir, some People have not used you well; for besides making a public Proclamation of what you told them of a Quarrel between yourself and Squire *Allworthy*, they added Lies of their own, Things which I knew to be Lies.' 'You surprize me greatly,' cries Jones. 'Upon my Word, Sir,' answered *Benjamin*, 'I tell the Truth, and I need not tell you my Landlady was the Person. I am sure it moved me to hear the Story, and I hope it is all false; for I have a great Respect for you, I do assure you I have, and have had, ever since the Good-nature you shewed to *Black George*, which was talked of all over the Country, and I received more than one Letter about it. Indeed it made you beloved by every body. You will pardon me, therefore; for it was real Concern at what I heard made me ask many Questions; for I have no impertinent Curiosity about me; but I love Good-nature, and thence became *Amoris abundantia ergo Te.*'[7]

Every Profession of Friendship easily gains Credit with the Miserable; it is no wonder, therefore, if *Jones*, who, besides his being miserable, was extremely open-hearted, very readily believed all the Professions of *Benjamin*, and received him into his Bosom. The Scraps of *Latin*, some of which *Benjamin* applied properly enough, tho' it did not savour of profound Literature, seemed yet to indicate something superior to a common Barber, and so indeed did his whole Behaviour. *Jones* therefore believed the Truth of what he had said, as to his Original and Education, and at length, after much Entreaty, he said, 'Since you have heard, my Friend, so much of my Affairs, and seem so desirous to know the Truth, if you will have Patience to hear it, I will inform you of the whole.' 'Patience,' cries *Benjamin*, 'that I will, if the Chapter was never so long, and I am very much obliged to you for the Honour you do me.'

Jones now began, and related the whole History, forgetting only a Circumstance or two, namely, every Thing which passed on that Day in which he had fought with *Thwackum*, and ended with his Resolution to go to Sea, till the Rebellion in the North had made him change his Purpose, and had brought him to the Place where he then was.

Little *Benjamin*, who had been all Attention, never once interrupted the Narrative; but when it was ended, he could not help

6. "No, and if it goes badly now, it will be [better] after this." Horace, *Odes* II.x.17–18.

7. "An abundance of love for you." Cicero, *Epistolae ad Familiares* I.ix.1, and elsewhere.

observing, that there must be surely something more invented by his Enemies, and told Mr. *Allworthy* against him, or so good a Man would never have dismissed one he had loved so tenderly, in such a Manner. To which *Jones* answered, 'He doubted not but such villanous Arts had been made use of to destroy him.'

And surely it was scarce possible for any one to have avoided making the same Remark with the Barber; who had not, indeed, heard from *Jones*, one single Circumstance upon which he was condemned; for his Actions were not now placed in those injurious Lights, in which they had been misrepresented to *Allworthy*: Nor could he mention those many false Accusations which had been from time to time preferred against him to *Allworthy*; for with none of these he was himself acquainted. He had likewise, as we have observed, omitted many material Facts in his present Relation. Upon the whole, indeed, every thing now appeared in such favourable Colours to *Jones*, that Malice itself would have found it no easy Matter to fix any Blame upon him.

Not that *Jones* desired to conceal or to disguise the Truth; nay, he would have been more unwilling to have suffered any Censure to fall on Mr. *Allworthy* for punishing him, than on his own Actions for deserving it, but, in Reality, so it happened, and so it always will happen: For let a Man be never so honest, the Account of his own Conduct will, in Spite of himself, be so very favourable, that his Vices will come purified through his Lips, and, like foul Liquors well strained, will leave all their Foulness behind. For tho' the Facts themselves may appear, yet so different will be the Motives, Circumstances, and Consequences, when a Man tells his own Story, and when his Enemy tells it, that we scarce can recognize the Facts to be one and the same.

Tho' the Barber had drank down this Story with greedy Ears, he was not yet satisfied. There was a Circumstance behind, which his Curiosity, cold as it was, most eagerly longed for. *Jones* had mentioned the Fact of his Amour, and of his being the Rival of *Blifil*, but had cautiously concealed the Name of the young Lady. The Barber therefore, after some Hesitation, and many Hums and Ha's, at last begged Leave to crave the Name of the Lady, who appeared to be the principal Cause of all this Mischief. *Jones* paused a Moment, and then said, 'Since I have trusted you with so much, and since, I am afraid, her Name is become too publick already on this Occasion, I will not conceal it from you. Her Name is *Sophia Western.*'

'*Proh Deum atque Hominum Fidem!* Squire *Western* hath a Daughter grown a Woman!' 'Ay, and such a Woman,' cries *Jones*, 'that the World cannot match. No Eye ever saw any thing so beautiful; but that is her least Excellence. Such Sense! such Goodness!

O I could praise her for ever, and yet should omit half her Virtues.'
'Mr. *Western* a Daughter grown up!' cries the Barber, 'I remember
the Father a Boy; well, *Tempus edax Rerum*.'[8]

The Wine being now at an End, the Barber pressed very eagerly
to be his Bottle; but *Jones* absolutely refused, saying, 'He had
already drank more than he ought; and that he now chose to retire
to his Room, where he wished he could procure himself a Book.' 'A
Book!' cries *Benjamin*, 'what Book would you have? *Latin* or *English*? I have some curious Books in both Languages. Such as *Erasmi
Colloquia*,[9] *Ovid de Tristibus*,[1] *Gradus ad Parnassum*;[2] and in
English I have several of the best Books, tho' some of them are a
little torn; but I have a great Part of *Stowe*'s Chronicle;[3] the sixth
Volume of *Pope*'s *Homer*;[4] the third Volume of the Spectator;[5] the
second Volume of *Echard*'s *Roman* History;[6] the Craftsman;[7] *Rob-
inson Crusoe*; *Thomas a Kempis*,[8] and two Volumes of *Tom
Brown*'s Works.'[9]

'Those last,' cries *Jones*, 'are Books I never saw, so if you please
to lend me one of those Volumes.' The Barber assured him he
would be highly entertained; for he looked upon the Author to have
been one of the greatest Wits that ever the Nation produced. He
then stepp'd to his House, which was hard by, and immediately
returned; after which, the Barber having received very strict Injunctions of Secrecy from *Jones*, and having sworn inviolably to main-

8. "Time, gluttonous of things." Ovid, *Metamorphoses* XV.234, quoted in Lily, p. 141. See below, p. 358.

9. Erasmus's *Familiarum Colloquiarum Formulae* L(London, 1519), dialogues written first for Erasmus's pupils as models for polite Latin phrases of ad-dress, then expanded to cover many cur-rent topics. Widely used as a school text, from which Shakespeare acquired some phrases echoed in his plays.

1. Ovid's *Tristia* tells of his sufferings as an exile banished from Rome by Augus-tus for some unknown scandal.

2. "A Step to Parnassus"—any Latin, or Greek, dictionary with long and short vowels marked to help pupils write Latin, or Greek, verse, also including fa-mous poetical expressions and quota-tions, for the same purpose. The first was compiled by Paul Aler in 1702.

3. Fielding misspells the name of John Stow (1525?–1605), indefatigable Elizabe-than historian and antiquarian, author and editor of several *Chronicles*. This one is probably *The Chronicle of Eng-land* (1580).

4. Since Pope's *Odyssey* appeared in five volumes (1725–26), this is the sixth and last volume of his *Iliad* (1715–20), con-taining Books XXI–XXIV, which re-count Achilles's furious re-entry into bat-tle, and the funerals of Patroclus and

Hector.

5. Editions, beginning in 1715, usually ran to eight volumes.

6. The 1699 publication was in two vol-umes, the 1705 edition in five volumes. See above, pp. 29 and 207.

7. An anti-Walpole newspaper, founded in Dec. 1726, running for ten years, and now (in 1745) defunct for almost an-other ten, and also passé, because Wal-pole (the crafty "craftsman") had fallen from power in 1742. Swift, Arbuthnot, and perhaps Pope had contributed to it, and it was on Fielding's side of the po-litical fence.

8. Author of *Imitatio Christi* ("The Imi-tation of Christ"), c. 1424–27, a simple and powerful book of devotion that has been translated into more languages than any other book except the Bible.

9. Brown (1663–1704) was a satirist and translator most noted for his *Amuse-ments Serious and Comical* (1700), sketches of London life. His *Wcrks* (1707) contained three volumes, but later editions came in four and five. Fielding's *Joseph Andrews* had drawn some of its manner and ideas from Tom Brown's translation of Scarron's *Roman Comique*, which was eventually included in the later editions of Brown's *Works*.

tain it, they separated; the Barber went home, and *Jones* retired to his Chamber.

Chapter VI.

In which more of the Talents of Mr. Benjamin *will appear, as well as who this extraordinary Person was.*

In the Morning *Jones* grew a little uneasy at the Desertion of his Surgeon, as he apprehended some Inconvenience, or even Danger, might attend the not dressing his Wound; he enquired therefore of the Drawer what other Surgeons were to be met with in that Neighbourhood. The Drawer told him there was one not far off; but he had known him often refuse to be concerned after another had been sent for before him; 'but, Sir,' says he, 'if you will take my Advice, there is not a Man in the Kingdom can do your Business better than the Barber who was with you last Night. We look upon him to be one of the ablest Men at a Cut in all this Neighbourhood. For tho' he hath not been here above three Months, he hath done several great Cures.'

The Drawer was presently dispatched for little *Benjamin*, who being acquainted in what Capacity he was wanted, prepared himself accordingly, and attended; but with so different an Air and Aspect from that which he wore when his Bason was under his Arm, that he could scarce be known to be the same Person.

'So, Tonsor,' says *Jones*, 'I find you have more Trades than one; how came you not to inform me of this last Night?' 'A Surgeon,' answered *Benjamin*, with great Gravity, 'is a Profession, not a Trade. The Reason why I did not acquaint you last Night that I professed this Art, was that I then concluded you was under the Hands of another Gentleman, and I never love to interfere with my Brethren in their Business. *Ars omnibus communis*.[1] But now, Sir, if you please, I will inspect your Head, and when I see into your Skull, I will give my Opinion of your Case.'

Jones had no great Faith in this new Professor; however he suffered him to open the Bandage, and to look at his Wound, which as soon as he had done, *Benjamin* began to groan and shake his Head violently. Upon which *Jones*, in a peevish Manner, bid him not play the Fool, but tell him in what Condition he found him. 'Shall I answer you as a Surgeon, or a Friend?' said *Benjamin*. 'As a Friend, and seriously,' said *Jones*. 'Why then upon my Soul,' cries *Benjamin*, 'it would require a great deal of Art to keep you from being well after a very few Dressings; and if you will suffer me to

---

1. "The art [of healing] is common to all [practitioners]" (Mutter). Partridge is paraphrasing "Mors omnibus commu- nis" ("Death is common to all"), which he quotes later (p. 481), from Lily's *Grammar*, p. 143.

apply some Salve of mine, I will answer for the Success.' *Jones* gave
his Consent, and the Plaister was applied accordingly.

'There, Sir,' cries *Benjamin*, 'now I will, if you please, resume
my former Self; but a Man is obliged to keep up some Dignity in
his Countenance whilst he is performing these Operations, or the
World will not submit to be handled by him. You can't imagine,
Sir, of how much Consequence a grave Aspect is to a grave Character. A Barber may make you laugh, but a Surgeon ought rather to
make you cry.'

'Mr. *Barber*, or Mr. *Surgeon*, or Mr. *Barber-Surgeon*,' said *Jones*.
—'O dear Sir,' answered *Benjamin*, interrupting him, '*Infandum*,
Regina, jubes renovare Dolorem.[2] You recal to my Mind that cruel
Separation of the united Fraternities,[3] so much to the Prejudice of
both Bodies, as all Separations must be, according to the old Adage,
V*is unita fortior*;[4] which to be sure there are not wanting some of
one or of the other Fraternity who are able to construe. What a
Blow was this to me who unite both in my own Person.'—'Well, by
whatever Name you please to be called,' continued *Jones*, 'you certainly are one of the oddest, most comical Fellows I ever met with,
and must have something very surprizing in your Story, which you
must confess I have a Right to hear.' 'I do confess it,' answered
Benjamin, 'and will very readily acquaint you with it, when you have
sufficient Leisure; for I promise you it will require a good deal of
Time.' *Jones* told him, He could never be more at Leisure than at
present. 'Well then,' said *Benjamin*, 'I will obey you; but first I will
fasten the Door, that none may interrupt us.' He did so, and then
advancing with a solemn Air to *Jones*, said; 'I must begin by telling
you, Sir, that you yourself have been the greatest Enemy I ever
had.' *Jones* was a little startled at this sudden Declaration. 'I your
Enemy, Sir!' says he, with much Amazement; and some Sternness in
his Look. 'Nay, be not angry,' said *Benjamin*, 'for I promise you I
am not. You are perfectly innocent of having intended me any
Wrong; for you was then an Infant; but I shall, I believe, unriddle
all this the Moment I mention my Name. Did you never hear, Sir,
of one *Partridge*, who had the Honour of being reputed your
Father, and the Misfortune of being ruined by that Honour?' 'I
have indeed heard of that *Partridge*,' says *Jones*, 'and have always
believed myself to be his Son.' 'Well, Sir,' answered *Benjamin*, 'I am
that *Partridge*; but I here absolve you from all filial Duty; for I do

2. "You order [me], O queen, to renew
unspeakable sorrow" (*Aeneid* II.3). See
below, pp. 333, 481, 576.
3. The barbers and the surgeons. Henry
VIII had united barbers and surgeons
into one company, but specified that barbers be limited to bloodletting and ex-
tracting teeth (the traditional barber's

pole of spiraled red and white signifies a
bandage around an arm for bloodletting). In 1745, the very year in which
Partridge is speaking, barber-surgeons
were again separated into two distinct
corporations by the Act of 18 George
II.c.15.
4. "United power is stronger."

assure you, you are no Son of mine.' 'How!' replied *Jones*, 'and is it possible that a false Suspicion should have drawn all the ill Consequences upon you, with which I am too well acquainted?' 'It is possible,' cries *Benjamin*, 'for it is so; but tho' it is natural enough for Men to hate even the innocent Causes of their Sufferings, yet I am of a different Temper. I have loved you ever since I heard of your Behaviour to *Black George*, as I told you; and I am convinced, from this extraordinary Meeting, that you are born to make me Amends for all I have suffered on that Account. Besides, I dreamt, the Night before I saw you, that I stumbled over a Stool without hurting myself; which plainly shewed me something good was towards me; and last Night I dreamt again, that I rode behind you on a milk-white Mare, which is a very excellent Dream, and betokens much good Fortune, which I am resolved to pursue, unless you have the Cruelty to deny me.'

'I should be very glad, Mr. *Partridge*,' answered *Jones*, 'to have it in my Power to make you Amends for your Sufferings on my Account, tho' at present I see no Likelihood of it; however, I assure you I will deny you nothing which is in my Power to grant.'

'It is in your Power sure enough,' replied *Benjamin*; 'for I desire nothing more than Leave to attend you in this Expedition. Nay, I have so entirely set my Heart upon it, that if you should refuse me, you will kill both a Barber and a Surgeon in one Breath.'

Jones answered smiling, That he should be very sorry to be the Occasion of so much Mischief to the Public. He then advanced many prudential Reasons, in order to dissuade *Benjamin* (whom we shall hereafter call *Partridge*) from his Purpose; but all were in vain. *Partridge* relied strongly on his Dream of the milk-white Mare. 'Besides, Sir,' says he, 'I promise you, I have as good an Inclination to the Cause as any Man can possibly have; and go I will, whether you admit me to go in your Company or not.

Jones, who was as much pleased with *Partridge*, as *Partridge* could be with him, and who had not consulted his own Inclination, but the Good of the other in desiring him to stay behind, when he found his Friend so resolute, at last gave his Consent; but then recollecting himself, he said, 'Perhaps, Mr. *Partridge*, you think I shall be able to support you, but I really am not;' and then taking out his Purse, he told out nine Guineas, which he declared were his whole Fortune.

Partridge answered, 'That his Dependance was only on his future Favour: For he was thoroughly convinced he would shortly have enough in his Power. At present, Sir,' said he, 'I believe I am rather the richer Man of the two; but all I have is at your Service, and at your Disposal. I insist upon your taking the whole, and I beg only to attend you in the Quality of your Servant, *Nil desperandum est*

Teucro duce & auspice Teucro;[5] but to this generous Proposal concerning the Money, *Jones* would by no means submit.

It was resolved to set out the next Morning, when a Difficulty arose concerning the Baggage; for the Portmanteau of Mr. *Jones* was too large to be carried without a Horse.

'If I may presume to give my Advice,' says *Partridge*, 'this Portmanteau, with every Thing in it, except a few Shirts, should be left behind. Those I shall be easily able to carry for you, and the rest of your Clothes will remain very safely locked up in my House.'

This Method was no sooner proposed than agreed to, and then the Barber departed, in order to prepare every thing for his intended Expedition.

Chapter VII.

Containing better Reasons, than any which have yet appeared for the Conduct of Partridge; *an Apology for the Weakness of* Jones; *and some farther Anecdotes concerning my Landlady.*

Through Partridge was one of the most superstitious of Men, he would hardly, perhaps, have desired to accompany *Jones* on his Expedition merely from the Omens of the Joint-stool, and white Mare, if his Prospect had been no better than to have shared the Plunder gained in the Field of Battle. In Fact, when *Partridge* came to ruminate on the Relation he had heard from *Jones*, he could not reconcile to himself, that Mr. *Allworthy* should turn his Son (for so he most firmly believed him to be) out of Doors, for any Reason which he had heard assigned. He concluded therefore, that the whole was a Fiction, and that *Jones*, of whom he had often from his Correspondents heard the wildest Character, had in reality run away from his Father. It came into his Head, therefore, that if he could prevail with the young Gentleman to return back to his Father, he should by that Means render a Service to *Allworthy*, which would obliterate all his former Anger; nay, indeed, he conceived that very Anger was counterfeited, and that *Allworthy* had sacrificed him to his own Reputation. And this Suspicion, indeed, he well accounted for, from the tender Behaviour of that excellent Man to the Foundling Child; from his great Severity to *Partridge*, who knowing himself to be innocent, could not conceive that any

5. "Never despair, with Teucer as leader and Teucer as protector" (Horace, *Odes* I.vi.27). Teucer and his half-brother Ajax were put in each other's care by their father when they set out for the Trojan War: both were to return, or neither. Ajax killed himself for shame after he had run amok, killing the cattle in the Greek camp when driven mad by Athena. Teucer's father refused to receive him when he returned, so he spoke these words of encouragement to his men as they set out to find a new home. Fielding had probably memorized this line as a boy in Lily's Christianized example: "Nil desperandum, Christo duce & auspice Christo" (*Grammar*, p. 155).

other should think him guilty; lastly, from the Allowance which he
had privately received long after the Annuity had been publickly
taken from him; and which he looked upon as a kind of Smart-
money, or rather by way of Atonement for Injustice: For it is very
uncommon, I believe, for Men to ascribe the Benefactions they
receive to pure Charity, when they can possibly impute them to any
other Motive. If he could by any Means, therefore, persuade the
young Gentleman to return home, he doubted not but that he
should again be received into the Favour of *Allworthy*, and well
rewarded for his Pains; nay, and should be again restored to his
native Country; a Restoration which *Ulysses* himself never wished
more heartily than poor *Partridge*.

As for *Jones*, he was well satisfied with the Truth of what the
other had asserted, and believed that *Partridge* had no other Inducements but Love to him, and Zeal for the Cause. A blameable Want
of Caution and Diffidence in the Veracity of others, in which he
was highly worthy of Censure. To say the Truth, there are but two
Ways by which Men become possessed of this excellent Quality.
The one is from long Experience, and the other is from Nature;
which last, I presume, is often meant by Genius, or great natural
Parts; and it is infinitely the better of the two, not only as we are
Masters of it much earlier in Life, but as it is much more infallible
and conclusive: For a Man who hath been imposed on by ever so
many, may still hope to find others more honest; whereas he who
receives certain necessary Admonitions from within, that this is
impossible, must have very little Understanding indeed, if he ever
renders himself liable to be once deceived. As *Jones* had not this
Gift from Nature, he was too young to have gained it by Experience; for at the diffident Wisdom which is to be acquired this Way,
we seldom arrive till very late in Life; which is perhaps the Reason
why some old Men are apt to despise the Understandings of all
those who are a little younger than themselves.

Jones spent most Part of the Day in the Company of a new
Acquaintance. This was no other than the Landlord of the House,
or rather the Husband of the Landlady. He had but lately made his
Descent down Stairs, after a long Fit of the Gout, in which Distemper he was generally confined to his Room during one half of the
Year; and during the rest, he walked about the House, smoked his
Pipe, and drank his Bottle with his Friends, without concerning
himself in the least with any Kind of Business. He had been bred,
as they call it, a Gentleman, that is, bred up to do nothing, and had
spent a very small Fortune, which he inherited from an industrious
Farmer his Uncle, in Hunting, Horse-racing, and Cock-fighting, and
had been married by my Landlady for certain Purposes, which he
had long since desisted from answering: For which she hated him

heartily. But as he was a surly Kind of Fellow, so she contented herself with frequently upbraiding him by disadvantageous Comparisons with her first Husband, whose Praise she had eternally in her Mouth; and as she was for the most part Mistress of the Profit, so she was satisfied to take upon herself the Care and Government of the Family, and after a long successless Struggle, to suffer her Husband to be Master of himself.

In the Evening, when *Jones* retired to his Room, a small Dispute arose between this fond Couple concerning him, 'What,' says the Wife, 'you have been tippling with the Gentleman! I see.' 'Yes,' answered the Husband, 'we have cracked a Bottle together, and a very Gentleman-like Man he is, and hath a very pretty Notion of Horse-flesh. Indeed he is young, and hath not seen much of the World: For I believe he hath been at very few Horse-races.' 'O ho! he is one of your Order, is he?' replies the Landlady; 'he must be a Gentleman to be sure, if he is a Horse-racer. The Devil fetch such Gentry; I am sure I wish I had never seen any of them. I have Reason to love Horse-racers truly.' 'That you have,' says the Husband; 'for I was one, you know.' 'Yes,' answered she, 'you are a pure one indeed. As my first Husband used to say, I may put all the good I have ever got by you in my Eyes, and see never the worse.' 'D—n your first Husband,' cries he.—'Don't D—n a better Man than yourself,' answered the Wife; 'if he had been alive, you durst not have done it.' 'Then you think,' says he, 'I have not so much Courage as yourself: For you have D—n'd him often in my Hearing.' 'If I did,' says she, 'I have repented of it many's the good Time and oft. And if he was so good to forgive me a Word spoken in Haste, or so, it doth not become such a one as you to *twitter* me. He was a Husband to me, he was; and if ever I did make use of an ill Word or so in a Passion, I never called him Rascal; I should have told a Lie, if I had called him Rascal.' Much more she said, but not in his Hearing: For having lighted his Pipe, he staggered off as fast as he could. We shall therefore transcribe no more of her Speech, as it approached still nearer and nearer to a Subject too indelicate to find any Place in this History.

Early in the Morning *Partridge* appeared at the Bedside of *Jones*, ready equipped for the Journey, with his Knapsack at his Back. This was his own Workmanship; for besides his other Trades, he was no indifferent Taylor. He had already put up his whole Stock of Linen in it, consisting of four Shirts, to which he now added eight for Mr. *Jones*; and then packing up the Portmanteau, he was departing with it towards his own House, but was stopt in his Way by the Landlady, who refused to suffer any Removals till after the Payment of the Reckoning.

The Landlady was, as we have said, absolute Governess in these

Regions; it was therefore necessary to comply with her Rules; so the Bill was presently writ out, which amounted to a much larger Sum than might have been expected, from the Entertainment which *Jones* had met with. But here we are obliged to disclose some Maxims, which Publicans hold to be the grand Mysteries of their Trade. The first is, if they have any Thing good in their House (which indeed very seldom happens) to produce it only to Persons who travel with great Equipages. 2dly, To charge the same for the very worst Provisions, as if they were the best. And, lastly, if any of their Guests call but for little, to make them pay a double Price for every Thing they have; so that the Amount by the Head may be much the same.

The Bill being made and discharged, *Jones* set forward with *Partridge*, carrying his Knapsack; nor did the Landlady condescend to wish him a good Journey: for this was, it seems, an Inn frequented by People of Fashion; and I know not whence it is, but all those who get their Livelihood by People of Fashion, contract as much Insolence to the rest of Mankind, as if they really belonged to that Rank themselves.

Chapter VIII.

Jones arrives at Gloucester, *and goes to the* Bell; *the Character of that House, and of a Petty-fogger, which he there meets with.*

Mr. *Jones*, and *Partridge*, or *Little Benjamin* (which Epithet of *Little* was perhaps given him ironically, he being in reality near six Feet high) having left their last Quarters in the Manner before described, travelled on to *Gloucester*, without meeting any Adventure worth relating.

Being arrived here, they chose for their House of Entertainment the Sign of the *Bell*, an excellent House indeed, and which I do most seriously recommend to every Reader who shall visit this ancient City. The Master of it is Brother to the great Preacher *Whitefield*;[1] but is absolutely untainted with the pernicious Principles of Methodism, or of any other heretical Sect. He is indeed a very honest plain Man, and, in my Opinion, not likely to create any Disturbance either in Church or State. His Wife hath, I believe, had much Pretension to Beauty, and is still a very fine Woman. Her Person and Deportment might have made a shining Figure in the politest Assemblies; but tho' she must be conscious of this, and many other Perfections, she seems perfectly contented with, and

1. George Whitefield (1714–70), a vigorous young Methodist evangelist whose Calvinistic ideas led him to break with Charles Wesley's Methodist Society.

Whitefield was born at the Bell, his father's inn, now (at the time of the story) being run by his brother and sister-in-law.

resigned to that State of Life to which she is called; and this Resignation is entirely owing to the Prudence and Wisdom of her Temper: For she is at present as free from any methodistical Notions as her Husband. I say at present: For she freely confesses that her Brother's Documents made at first some Impression upon her, and that she had put herself to the Expence of a long Hood, in order to attend the extraordinary Emotions of the Spirit; but having found, during an Experiment of three Weeks, no Emotions, she says, worth a Farthing, she very wisely laid by her Hood, and abandoned the Sect. To be concise, she is a very friendly, good natured Woman; and so industrious to oblige, that the Guests must be of a very morose Disposition who are not extremely well satisfied in her House.

Mrs. *Whitefield* happened to be in the Yard when *Jones* and his Attendant marched in. Her Sagacity soon discovered in the Air of our Heroe something which distinguished him from the Vulgar. She ordered her Servants, therefore, immediately to shew him into a Room, and presently afterwards invited him to Dinner with herself; which Invitation he very thankfully accepted: For indeed much less agreeable Company than that of Mrs. *Whitefield*, and a much worse Entertainment than she had provided, would have been welcome, after so long fasting, and so long a Walk.

Besides Mr. *Jones* and the good Governess of the Mansion, there sat down at Table an Attorney of *Salisbury*, indeed the very same who had brought the News of Mrs. *Blifil*'s Death to Mr. *Allworthy*, and whose Name, which, I think, we did not before mention, was *Dowling*: There was likewise present another Person, who stiled himself a Lawyer, and who lived somewhere near *Lindlinch* in *Somersetshire*. This Fellow, I say, stiled himself a Lawyer, but was indeed a most vile Petty-fogger, without Sense or Knowledge of any Kind; one of those who may be termed Train-bearers to the Law; a Sort of Supernumeraries in the Profession, who are the Hackneys of Attornies, and will ride more Miles for half a Crown than a Post-boy.

During the Time of Dinner, the *Somersetshire* Lawyer recollected the Face of *Jones*, which he had seen at Mr. *Allworthy*'s: For he had often visited in that Gentleman's Kitchin. He therefore took Occasion to enquire after the good Family there, with that Familiarity which would have become an intimate Friend or Acquaintance of Mr. *Allworthy*; and indeed he did all in his Power to insinuate himself to be such, though he had never had the Honour of speaking to any Person in that Family higher than the Butler. *Jones* answered all his Questions with much Civility, though he never remembered to have seen the Petty-fogger before, and though he concluded from the outward Appearance and Behaviour of the

Man, that he usurped a Freedom with his Betters, to which he was
by no means intitled.

As the Conversation of Fellows of this Kind, is of all others the
most detestable to Men of any Sense, the Cloth was no sooner
removed than Mr. *Jones* withdrew, and a little barbarously left poor
Mrs. *Whitefield* to do a Pennance, which I have often heard Mr.
Timothy Harris,[2] and other Publicans of good Taste, lament, as the
severest Lot annexed to their Calling, namely, that of being obliged
to keep Company with their Guests.

Jones had no sooner quitted the Room, than the Petty-fogger, in
a whispering Tone, asked Mrs. *Whitefield*, 'if she knew who that
fine Spark was?' She answered, 'she had never seen the Gentleman
before.' 'The Gentleman, indeed!' replied the Petty-fogger; 'a pretty
Gentleman truly! Why, he's the Bastard of a Fellow who was
hanged for Horse-stealing. He was dropt at Squire *Allworthy*'s
Door, where one of the Servants found him in a Box so full of
Rain-water, that he would certainly have been drowned, had he not
been reserved for another Fate.' 'Ay, ay, you need not mention it, I
protest; we understand what that Fate is very well,' cries *Dowling*,
with a most facetious Grin. 'Well,' continued the other, 'the Squire
ordered him to be taken in: For he is a timbersome Man every
Body knows, and was afraid of drawing himself into a Scrape; and
there the Bastard was bred up, and fed and cloathified all to the
World like any Gentleman; and there he got one of the Servant
Maids with Child, and persuaded her to swear it to the Squire himself; and afterwards he broke the Arm of one Mr. *Thwackum* a Clergyman, only because he reprimanded him for following Whores; and
afterwards he snapt a Pistol at Mr. *Blifil* behind his Back; and once
when Squire *Allworthy* was sick, he got a Drum, and beat it all
over the House, to prevent him from sleeping: And twenty other
Pranks he hath played; for all which, about four or five Days ago,
just before I left the Country, the Squire strip'd him stark naked,
and turned him out of Doors.'

'And very justly too, I protest,' cries *Dowling*; 'I would turn my
own Son out of Doors, if he was guilty of half as much. And pray
what is the Name of this pretty Gentleman?'

'The Name o'un!' answered Petty-fogger, 'why, he is called
Thomas Jones.'

'*Jones*!' answered *Dowling*, a little eagerly, 'what, Mr. *Jones* that
lived at Mr. *Allworthy*'s! was that the Gentleman that dined with
us?' 'The very same,' said the other. 'I have heard of the Gentleman,' cries *Dowling*, 'often; but I never heard any ill Character of
him.' 'And I am sure,' says Mrs. *Whitefield*, 'if half what this Gen-

2. Keeper of The Red Lion inn at   in *Joseph Andrews* I.xi. Identified by
Egham, Surrey, who died 1748, described   Battestin (Wesleyan ed., p. 50).

tleman hath said be true, Mr. *Jones* hath the most deceitful Countenance I ever saw; for sure his Looks promise something very different; and I must say, for the little I have seen of him, he is as civil a
well-bred Man as you would wish to converse with.'

Pettyfogger calling to mind that he had not been sworn, as he
usually was, before he gave his Evidence, now bound what he had
declared with so many Oaths and Imprecations, that the Landlady's
Ears were shocked, and she put a Stop to his swearing, by assuring
him of her Belief. Upon which he said, 'I hope, Madam, you imagine I would scorn to tell such Things of any Man, unless I knew
them to be true. What Interest have I in taking away the Reputation of a Man who never injured me? I promise you every Syllable
of what I have said is Fact, and the whole Country knows it.'

As Mrs. *Whitefield* had no Reason to suspect that the Pettyfogger had any Motive or Temptation to abuse *Jones*, the Reader
cannot blame her for believing what he so confidently affirmed with
many Oaths. She accordingly gave up her Skill in Physiognomy, and
henceforwards conceived so ill an Opinion of her Guest, that she
heartily wished him out of her House.

This Dislike was now farther increased by a Report which Mr.
Whitefield made from the Kitchin, where *Partridge* had informed
the Company, 'That tho' he carried the Knapsack, and contented
himself with staying among Servants, while *Tom Jones* (as he called
him) was regaling in the Parlour, he was not his Servant, but only a
Friend and Companion, and as good a Gentleman as Mr. *Jones*
himself.'

Dowling sat all this while silent, biting his Fingers, making Faces,
grinning, and looking wonderfully arch; at last he opened his Lips,
and protested that the Gentleman looked like another Sort of Man.
He then called for his Bill with the utmost Haste, declared he must
be at *Hereford* that Evening, lamented his great Hurry of Business,
and wished he could divide himself into twenty Pieces, in order to
be at once in twenty Places.

The Pettyfogger now likewise departed, and then *Jones* desired
the Favour of Mrs. *Whitefield*'s Company to drink Tea with him;
but she refused, and with a Manner so different from that with
which she had received him at Dinner, that it a little surprized him.
And now he soon perceived her Behaviour totally changed; for
instead of that natural Affability which we have before celebrated,
she wore a constrained Severity on her Countenance, which was so
disagreeable to Mr. *Jones* that he resolved, however late, to quit the
House that Evening.

He did indeed account somewhat unfairly for this sudden
Change; for besides some hard and unjust Surmises concerning
female Fickleness and Mutability, he began to suspect that he owed

this Want of Civility to his Want of Horses; a Sort of Animals which, as they dirty no Sheets, are thought, in Inns, to pay better for their Beds than their Riders, and are therefore considered as the more desirable Company; but Mrs. *Whitefield*, to do her Justice, had a much more liberal Way of thinking. She was perfectly well-bred, and could be very civil to a Gentleman, tho' he walked on Foot: In Reality, she looked on our Heroe as a sorry Scoundrel, and therefore treated him as such, for which not even *Jones* himself, had he known as much as the Reader, could have blamed her; nay, on the contrary, he must have approved her Conduct, and have esteemed her the more for the Disrespect shewn towards himself. This is indeed a most aggravating Circumstance which attends depriving Men unjustly of their Reputation; for a Man who is conscious of having an ill Character, cannot justly be angry with those who neglect and slight him; but ought rather to despise such as affect his Conversation, unless where a perfect Intimacy must have convinced them that their Friend's Character hath been falsely and injuriously aspersed.

This was not, however, the Case of *Jones*; for as he was a perfect Stranger to the Truth, so he was with good Reason offended at the Treatment he received. He therefore paid his Reckoning and departed, highly against the Will of Mr. *Partridge*, who having remonstrated much against it to no Purpose, at last condescended to take up his Knapsack, and to attend his Friend.

Chapter IX.

Containing several Dialogues between Jones *and* Partridge, *concerning Love, Cold, Hunger, and other Matters; with the lucky and narrow Escape of* Partridge, *as he was on the very Brink of making a fatal Discovery to his Friend.*

The Shadows began now to descend larger from the high Mountains: The feather'd Creation had betaken themselves to their Rest. Now the highest Order of Mortals were sitting down to their Dinners, and the lowest Order to their Suppers. In a Word, the Clock struck five just as Mr. *Jones* took his Leave of *Gloucester*; an Hour at which (as it was now Midwinter) the dirty Fingers of Night would have drawn her sable Curtain over the Universe, had not the Moon forbid her, who now, with a Face as broad and as red as those of some jolly Mortals, who, like her, turn Night into Day, began to rise from her Bed, where she had slumbred away the Day, in order to sit up all Night. *Jones* had not travelled far before he paid his Compliments to that beautiful Planet, and turning to his Companion, asked him, If he had ever beheld so delicious an Evening. *Partridge* making no ready Answer to his Question, he proceeded to comment on the Beauty of the Moon, and repeated some Passages from *Milton*,[1] who hath certainly excelled all other Poets in his Description of the heavenly Luminaries. He then told *Partridge* the Story from the *Spectator*,[2] of two Lovers who had agreed to entertain themselves when they were at a great Distance from each other by repairing, at a certain fixed Hour, to look at the Moon; thus pleasing themselves with the Thought that they were both employed in contemplating the same Object at the same Time. 'Those Lovers,' added he, 'must have had Souls truly capable of feeling all the Tenderness of the sublimest of all human Passions.' 'Very probably,' cries *Partridge;* 'but I envy them more, if they had Bodies incapable of feeling Cold; for I am almost frozen to Death, and am very much afraid I shall lose a Piece of my Nose before we get to another House of Entertainment. Nay, truly, we may well expect some Judgment should happen to us for our Folly in running away so by Night from one of the most excellent Inns I ever set my Foot into. I am sure I never saw more good Things in my Life, and the greatest Lord in the Land cannot live better in his own House than he may there. And to forsake such a House, and go a rambling about the Country, the Lord knows whither, *per devia rura viarum*,[3] I say nothing for my Part; but some People might not have Charity enough to conclude we were in our sober Senses.' 'Fie upon it, Mr. Partridge,' says *Jones*, 'have a better Heart: Consider you are going to face an Enemy; and are you afraid of facing a little Cold? I wish, indeed, we had a Guide to advise which of these Roads we should take.' 'May I be so bold,' says *Partridge*, 'to offer my Advice: *Interdum Stultus opportuna loquitur*.'[4] 'Why, which of them,' cries *Jones*, 'would you recommend?' 'Truly neither of them,' answered *Partridge*. 'The only Road we can be certain of finding, is the Road we came. A good hearty Pace will bring us back to *Gloucester* in an Hour; but if we go forward, the Lord *Harry* knows when we shall arrive at any Place; for I see at least fifty Miles before me, and no House in all the Way.' 'You see, indeed, a very fair Prospect,' says *Jones*, 'which receives great additional Beauty from the extreme Lustre of the Moon. However, I will keep the Left-hand Track, as that seems to lead directly to those Hills, which we were informed lie not far from *Worcester*. And here, if you are inclined to quit me, you may, and return back again; but for my Part, I am resolved to go forward.'

1. Perhaps *Paradise Lost* IV.606–9, 645–49, 654–68, or *Il Penseroso* 67–72.
2. No. 241, a tale recalled from "one of Scudery's Romances" in which the lovers agree to think of each other at a particular "half hour in a day." The moonlight is Fielding's.
3. "By roads through remote lands." Perhaps a jumbled remembrance of Ovid's *Metamorphoses* I.676 and Lucan (Mutter).
4. "Sometimes a fool says apt things." The usual proverb is "Interdum stultus bene loquitur."

'It is unkind in you, Sir,' says *Partridge*, 'to suspect me of any such Intention. What I have advised hath been as much on your Account as on my own; but since you are determined to go on, I am as much determined to follow. *I præ, sequar te.*'[5]

They now travelled some Miles without speaking to each other, during which Suspence of Discourse *Jones* often sighed, and *Benjamin* groaned as bitterly, tho' from a very different Reason. At length *Jones* made a full Stop, and turning about, cries, 'Who knows, *Partridge*, but the loveliest Creature in the Universe may have her Eyes now fixed on that very Moon which I behold at this Instant!' 'Very likely, Sir,' answered *Partridge*; 'and if my Eyes were fixed on a good Surloin of roast Beef, the Devil might take the Moon and her Horns into the Bargain.' 'Did ever *Tramontane*[6] make such an Answer?' cries *Jones*. 'Prithee, *Partridge*, wast thou ever susceptible of Love in thy Life, or hath Time worn away all the Traces of it from thy Memory?' 'Alack-a-day,' cries *Partridge*, 'well would it have been for me if I had never known what Love was. *Infandum Regina jubes renovare Dolorem.*[7] I am sure I have tasted all the Tenderness and Sublimities, and Bitternesses of the Passion.' 'Was your Mistress unkind then?' says *Jones*. 'Very unkind indeed, Sir,' answered *Partridge*; 'for she married me, and made one of the most confounded Wives in the World. However, Heaven be praised, she's gone; and if I believed she was in the Moon, according to a Book I once read, which teaches that to be the Receptacle of departed Spirits, I would never look at it for fear of seeing her: But I wish, Sir, that the Moon was a Looking-glass for your Sake, and that Miss *Sophia Western* was now placed before it.' 'My dear *Partridge*,' cries *Jones*, 'what a Thought was there! A Thought which I am certain could never have entered into any Mind but that of a Lover. O *Partridge*, could I hope once again to see that Face; but, alas! all those golden Dreams are vanished for ever, and my only Refuge from future Misery is to forget the Object of all my former Happiness.' 'And do you really despair of ever seeing Miss *Western* again?' answered *Partridge*: 'If you will follow my Advice, I will engage you shall not only see her, but have her in your Arms.' 'Ha! do not awaken a Thought of that Nature,' cries *Jones*. 'I have struggled sufficiently to conquer all such Wishes already.' 'Nay,' answered *Partridge*, 'if you do not wish to have your Mistress in your Arms, you are a most extraordinary Lover indeed.' 'Well, well,' says *Jones*, 'let us avoid this Subject; but pray what is your Advice?' 'To give it you in the military Phrase then,' says *Partridge*, 'as we are Soldiers; 'To the Right about.' 'Let us return the Way we came;

5. "Go ahead, I'll follow you." Terence, *Andria* I.i.144; same in *Eunuchus* V.ii.69.
6. A barbarian, from "across the moun-
tains," or Alps—a word reflecting the Roman view of Gaul.
7. See above, p. 322.

we may yet reach *Gloucester* To-night, tho' late; whereas if we proceed, we are likely, for ought I see, to ramble about for ever without
coming either to House or Home.' 'I have already told you my Resolution is to go on,' answered *Jones;* 'but I would have you go back.
I am obliged to you for your Company hither; and I beg you to
accept a Guinea as a small Instance of my Gratitude. Nay, it would
be cruel in me to suffer you to go any farther; for, to deal plainly
with you, my chief End and Desire is a glorious Death in the Service of my King and Country.' 'As for your Money,' replied *Partridge,* 'I beg, Sir, you will put it up; I will receive none of you at
this Time; for at present I am, I believe, the richer Man of the two.
And as your Resolution is to go on, so mine is to follow you if you
do. Nay, now my Presence appears absolutely necessary to take care
of you, since your Intentions are so desperate; for I promise you my
Views are much more prudent: As you are resolved to fall in Battle
if you can, so I am resolved as firmly to come to no Hurt if I can
help it. And indeed I have the Comfort to think there will be but
little Danger; for a popish Priest told me the other Day, the Business would soon be over, and he believed without a Battle.' 'A
popish Priest,' cries *Jones,* 'I have heard, is not always to be
believed when he speaks in Behalf of his Religion.' 'Yes, but so far,'
answered the other, 'from speaking in Behalf of his Religion, he
assured me, the Catholicks did not expect to be any Gainers by the
Change; for that Prince *Charles* was as good a Protestant as any in
England; and that nothing but Regard to Right made him and the
rest of the popish Party to be *Jacobites.*' 'I believe him to be as
much a Protestant as I believe he hath any Right,' says *Jones,* 'and
I make no Doubt of our Success, but not without a Battle. So that
I am not so sanguine as your Friend the popish Priest.' 'Nay, to be
sure, Sir,' answered *Partridge,* 'all the Prophecies I have ever read,
speak of a great deal of Blood to be spilt in the Quarrel, and the
Miller with three Thumbs, who is now alive, is to hold the Horses
of three Kings, up to his Knees in Blood. Lord have Mercy upon us
all, and send better Times!' 'With what Stuff and Nonsense hast
thou filled thy Head,' answered *Jones.* 'This too, I suppose, comes
from the popish Priest. Monsters and Prodigies are the proper Arguments to support monstrous and absurd Doctrines. The Cause of
King *George* is the Cause of Liberty and true Religion. In other
Words, it is the Cause of common Sense, my Boy, and I warrant
you will succeed, tho' *Briareus*[8] himself was to rise again with his
hundred Thumbs, and to turn Miller.' *Partridge* made no Reply to
this. He was indeed cast into the utmost Confusion by this Declaration of *Jones.* For to inform the Reader of a Secret, which we had

---

8. A giant, with a hundred arms and fifty heads, who helped Zeus defeat the Titans.

no proper Opportunity of revealing before, *Partridge* was in Truth a *Jacobite*, and had concluded that *Jones* was of the same Party, and was now proceeding to join the Rebels. An Opinion which was not without Foundation. For the tall long-sided Dame,[9] mentioned by *Hudibras*; that many-eyed, many-tongued, many-mouthed, many-eared Monster of *Virgil*, had related the Story of the Quarrel between *Jones* and the Officer, with her usual Regard to Truth. She had indeed changed the Name of *Sophia* into that of the Pretender, and had reported, that drinking his Health was the Cause for which *Jones* was knocked down. This *Partridge* had heard, and most firmly believed. 'Tis no Wonder, therefore, that he had thence entertained the above-mentioned Opinion of *Jones*; and which he had almost discovered to him before he found out his own Mistake. And at this the Reader will be the less inclined to wonder, if he pleases to recollect the doubtful Phrase in which *Jones* first communicated his Resolution to Mr. *Partridge*; and, indeed, had the Words been less ambiguous, *Partridge* might very well have construed them as he did; being persuaded, as he was, that the whole Nation were of the same Inclination in their Hearts: Nor did it stagger him that *Jones* had travelled in the Company of Soldiers; for he had the same Opinion of the Army which he had of the rest of the People.

But however well affected he might be to *James* or *Charles*, he was still much more attached to little *Benjamin* than to either; for which Reason he no sooner discovered the Principles of his Fellow-traveller, than he thought proper to conceal, and outwardly to give up his own to the Man on whom he depended for the making his Fortune, since he by no means believed the Affairs of *Jones* to be so desperate as they really were with Mr. *Allworthy*; for as he had kept a constant Correspondence with some of his Neighbours since he left that Country, he had heard much, indeed more than was true, of the great Affection Mr. *Allworthy* bore this young Man, who, as *Partridge* had been instructed, was to be that Gentleman's Heir, and whom, as we have said, he did not in the least doubt to be his Son.

He imagined, therefore, that whatever Quarrel was between them, it would be certainly made up at the Return of Mr. *Jones*; an Event from which he promised great Advantages, if he could take this Opportunity of ingratiating himself with that young Gentleman; and if he could by any Means be instrumental in procuring his Return, he doubted not, as we have before said, but it would as highly advance him in the Favour of Mr. *Allworthy*.

9. *Hudibras* II.i.45–46—"There is a Tall Long-sided Dame, / (But wondrous light) ycleped *Fame*." Butler bases his description on Virgil's picture of the goddess Fame, which Fielding then goes on to paraphrase (*Aeneid* IV.173 ff., esp. 181–84).

We have already observed, that he was a very good-natured Fellow, and he hath himself declared the violent Attachment he had to the Person and Character of *Jones*; but possibly the Views which I have just before mentioned, might likewise have some little Share in prompting him to undertake this Expedition, at least in urging him to continue it, after he had discovered, that his Master and himself, like some prudent Fathers and Sons, tho' they travelled together in great Friendship, had embraced opposite Parties. I am led into this Conjecture, by having remarked, that tho' Love, Friendship, Esteem, and such like, have very powerful Operations in the human Mind; Interest, however, is an Ingredient seldom omitted by wise Men, when they would work others to their own Purposes. This is indeed a most excellent Medicine, and like *Ward*'s Pill,[1] flies at once to the particular Part of the Body on which you desire to operate, whether it be the Tongue, the Hand, or any other Member, where it scarce ever fails of immediately producing the desired Effect.

Chapter X.

In which our Travellers meet with a very extraordinary Adventure.

Just as *Jones* and his Friend came to the End of their Dialogue in the preceding Chapter, they arrived at the Bottom of a very steep Hill. Here *Jones* stopt short, and directing his Eyes upwards, stood for a while silent. At length he called to his Companion, and said, '*Partridge*, I wish I was at the Top of this Hill; it must certainly afford a most charming Prospect, especially by this Light: For the solemn Gloom which the Moon casts on all Objects, is beyond Expression beautiful, especially to an Imagination which is desirous of cultivating melancholy Ideas.' 'Very probably,' answered *Partridge*; 'but if the Top of the Hill be properest to produce melancholy Thoughts, I suppose the Bottom is the likeliest to produce merry ones, and these I take to be much the better of the two. I protest you have made my Blood run cold with the very mentioning the Top of that Mountain; which seems to me to be one of the highest in the World. No, no, if we look for any thing, let it be for a Place under Ground, to screen ourselves from the Frost.'—'Do so,' said *Jones*, 'let it be but within Hearing of this Place, and I will hallow to you at my Return back.' 'Surely, Sir, you are not mad,' said *Partridge*. 'Indeed I am,' answered *Jones*, 'if ascending this Hill

1. Dr. Joshua Ward (1685–1761), a quack who nevertheless had considerable success, including the patronage of George II. He was known as "Spot Ward" both because his pill was supposed to hit the affected spot and because of a red birthmark on his left cheek. He treated Fielding (who commends Ward's wisdom and kindness in his *Journal of a Voyage to Lisbon*, Introduction) in his last illness, until Fielding tried another doctor (Cross III.14–16).

be Madness: But as you complain so much of the Cold already, I would have you stay below. I will certainly return to you within an Hour.' 'Pardon me, Sir,' cries *Partridge*, 'I have determined to follow you where-ever you go.' Indeed he was now afraid to stay behind; for tho' he was Coward enough in all Respects, yet his chief Fear was that of Ghosts, with which the present Time of Night, and the Wildness of the Place extremely well suited.

At this Instant *Partridge* espied a glimmering Light through some Trees, which seemed very near to them. He immediately cried out in a Rapture, 'Oh, Sir! Heaven hath at last heard my Prayers, and hath brought us to a House; perhaps it may be an Inn. Let me beseech you, Sir, if you have any Compassion either for me or your-self, do not despise the Goodness of Providence, but let us go directly to yon Light. Whether it be a Public-house or no, I am sure if they be Christians that dwell there, they will not refuse a little House-room to Persons in our miserable Condition.' *Jones* at length yielded to the earnest Supplications of *Partridge*, and both together made directly towards the Place whence the Light issued.

They soon arrived at the Door of this House or Cottage: For it might be called either, without much Impropriety. Here *Jones* knocked several Times without receiving any Answer from within; at which *Partridge*, whose Head was full of nothing but of Ghosts, Devils, Witches, and such like, began to tremble, crying, 'Lord have Mercy upon us, sure the People must be all dead. I can see no Light neither now, and yet I am certain I saw a Candle burning but a Moment before.—Well! I have heard of such Things.'—'What hast thou heard of,' said *Jones*. 'The People are either fast asleep, or probably as this is a lonely Place, are afraid to open their Door.' He then began to vociferate pretty loudly, and at last an old Woman opening an upper Casement, asked 'who they were, and what they wanted?' *Jones* answered, 'they were Travellers who had lost their Way, and having seen a Light in the Window, had been led thither in Hopes of finding some Fire to warm themselves.' 'Whoever you are,' cries the Woman, 'you have no Business here; nor shall I open the Door to any body at this Time of Night.' *Partridge*, whom the Sound of a human Voice had recovered from his Fright, fell to the most earnest Supplications to be admitted for a few Minutes to the Fire, saying, 'he was almost dead with the Cold,' to which Fear had indeed contributed equally with the Frost. He assured her, that the Gentleman who spoke to her, was one of the greatest Squires in the Country, and made use of every Argument save one, which *Jones* afterwards effectually added, and this was the Promise of Half a Crown. A Bribe too great to be resisted by such a Person, especially as the genteel Appearance of *Jones*, which the Light of the Moon plainly discovered to her, together with his affable Behaviour, had entirely subdued those Apprehensions of Thieves which she had at first conceived. She agreed, therefore, at last to let them in, where *Partridge*, to his infinite Joy, found a good Fire ready for his Reception.

The poor Fellow, however, had no sooner warmed himself, than those Thoughts which were always uppermost in his Mind, began a little to disturb his Brain. There was no Article of his Creed in which he had a stronger Faith, than he had in Witchcraft, nor can the Reader conceive a Figure more adapted to inspire this Idea, than the old Woman who now stood before him. She answered exactly to that Picture drawn by *Otway* in his *Orphan*.[1] Indeed if this Woman had lived in the Reign of *James* the First, her Appearance alone would have hanged her, almost without any Evidence.

Many Circumstances likewise conspired to confirm *Partridge* in his Opinion. Her living, as he then imagined, by herself in so lonely a Place; and in a House, the Outside of which seemed much too good for her; but its Inside was furnished in the most neat and elegant Manner. To say the Truth, *Jones* himself was not a little surprized at what he saw: For, besides the extraordinary Neatness of the Room, it was adorned with a great Number of Nicknacks, and Curiosities, which might have engaged the Attention of a Virtuoso.

While *Jones* was admiring these Things, and *Partridge* sat trembling with the firm Belief that he was in the House of a Witch, the old Woman said, 'I hope, Gentlemen, you will make what Haste you can; for I expect my Master presently, and I would not for double the Money he should find you here.' 'Then you have a Master,' cried *Jones*; 'indeed you will excuse me, good Woman, but I was surprized to see all those fine Things in your House.' 'Ah, Sir!' said she, 'if the twentieth Part of these Things were mine, I should think myself a rich Woman; but pray, Sir, do not stay much longer: For I look for him in every Minute.'—'Why sure he would not be angry with you,' said *Jones*, 'for doing a common Act of Charity.' 'Alack-a-day, Sir,' said she, 'he is a strange Man, not at all like other People. He keeps no Company with any Body, and seldom walks out but by Night, for he doth not care to be seen; and all the Country People are as much afraid of meeting him; for his Dress is enough to frighten those who are not used to it. They call him, *The Man of the Hill* (for there he walks by Night) and the Country People are not, I believe, more afraid of the Devil himself. He would be terribly angry if he found you here.' 'Pray, Sir,' says *Partridge*, 'don't let us offend the Gentleman, I am ready to walk, and was never warmer in my Life.—Do, pray Sir, let us go—here are Pistols over the Chimney; who knows whether they be charged

1. *The Orphan* (1680) II.i.246–56. The passage had been quoted in *The Spectator*, no. 117 (Mutter). See below, p. 449.

James I wrote *Daemonologie* (1599), a treatise against witchcraft, and was notoriously hard on witches.

or no, or what he may do with them?' 'Fear nothing, *Partridge*,'
cries *Jones*, 'I will secure thee from Danger.'—'Nay, for Matter o'
that, he never doth any Mischief,' said the Woman; 'but to be sure
it is necessary he should keep some Arms for his own Safety; for his
House hath been beset more than once, and it is not many Nights
ago, that we thought we heard Thieves about it: For my own Part,
I have often wondered that he is not murdered by some Villain or
other, as he walks out by himself at such Hours; but then, as I said,
the People are afraid of him, and besides they think, I suppose, he
hath nothing about him worth taking.' 'I should imagine, by this
Collection of Rarities,' cries *Jones*, 'that your Master had been a
Traveller.' 'Yes, Sir,' answered she, 'he hath been a very great one;
there be few Gentlemen that know more of all Matters than he; I
fancy he hath been crost in Love, or whatever it is, I know not, but
I have lived with him above these thirty Years, and in all that Time
he hath hardly spoke to six living People.' She then again solicited
their Departure, in which she was backed by *Partridge*; but *Jones*
purposely protracted the Time: For his Curiosity was greatly raised
to see this extraordinary Person. Tho' the old Woman, therefore,
concluded every one of her Answers with desiring him to be gone,
and *Partridge* proceeded so far as to pull him by the Sleeve, he still
continued to invent new Questions, till the old Woman with an
affrighted Countenance, declared she heard her Master's Signal; and
at the same Instant more than one Voice was heard without the
Door, crying, 'D—n your Blood, shew us your Money this Instant.
Your Money, you Villain, or we will blow your Brains about your
Ears.'

'O, good Heaven!' cries the old Woman, 'some Villains, to be
sure, have attacked my Master. O la! what shall I do? what shall I
do?' 'How,' cries *Jones*, 'how—Are these Pistols loaded?' 'O, good
Sir, there is nothing in them, indeed—O, pray don't murder us,
Gentlemen,' (for in Reality she now had the same Opinion of those
within, as she had of those without.) *Jones* made her no Answer;
but snatching an old Broad-sword which hung in the Room, he
instantly sallied out, where he found the old Gentleman struggling
with two Ruffians, and begging for Mercy. *Jones* asked no Questions, but fell so briskly to work with his Broad-sword, that the Fellows immediately quitted their Hold; and, without offering to attack
our Heroe, betook themselves to their Heels, and made their
Escape; for he did not attempt to pursue them, being contented
with having delivered the old Gentleman; and indeed he concluded
he had pretty well done their Business: For both of them, as they
ran off, cried out with bitter Oaths, that they were dead Men.

Jones presently ran to lift up the old Gentleman, who had been
thrown down in the Scuffle, expressing at the same Time great Con-

cern, lest he should have received any Harm from the Villains. The old Man stared a Moment at *Jones*, and then cried,—'No, Sir, no, I have very little Harm, I thank you. Lord have Mercy upon me.' 'I see, Sir,' said *Jones*, 'you are not free from Apprehensions even of those who have had the Happiness to be your Deliverers; nor can I blame any Suspicions which you may have; but indeed, you have no real Occasion for any; here are none but your Friends present. Having mist our Way this cold Night, we took the Liberty of warming ourselves at your Fire, whence we were just departing when we heard you call for Assistance, which I must say, Providence alone seems to have sent you.'—'Providence indeed,' cries the old Gentleman, 'if it be so.'—'So it is, I assure you,' cries *Jones*, 'here is your own Sword, Sir. I have used it in your Defence, and I now return it into your own Hand.' The old Man having received the Sword, which was stained with the Blood of his Enemies, looked stedfastly at *Jones* during some Moments, and then with a Sigh, cried out, 'You will pardon me, young Gentleman, I was not always of a suspicious Temper, nor am I a Friend to Ingratitude.' 'Be thankful then,' cries *Jones*, 'to that Providence to which you owe your Deliverance; as to my Part, I have only discharged the common Duties of Humanity, and what I would have done for any Fellow Creature in your Situation.' 'Let me look at you a little longer,' cries the old Gentleman—'You are a human Creature then? —Well, perhaps you are. Come, pray walk into my little Hutt. You have been my Deliverer indeed.'

The old Woman was distracted between the Fears which she had of her Master, and for him; and *Partridge* was, if possible, in a greater Fright. The former of these, however, when she heard her Master speak kindly to *Jones*, and perceived what had happened, came again to herself; but *Partridge* no sooner saw the Gentleman, than the Strangeness of his Dress infused greater Terrors into that poor Fellow, than he had before felt either from the strange Description which he had heard, or from the Uproar which had happened at the Door.

To say the Truth, it was an Appearance which might have affected a more constant Mind than that of Mr. *Partridge*. This Person was of the tallest Size, with a long Beard as white as Snow. His Body was cloathed with the Skin of an Ass, made something into the Form of a Coat. He wore likewise Boots on his Legs, and a Cap on his Head, both composed of the Skin of some other Animals.

As soon as the old Gentleman came into his House, the old Woman began her Congratulations on his happy Escape from the Ruffians. 'Yes,' cried he, 'I have escaped indeed, Thanks to my Preserver.' 'O the Blessing on him,' answered she, 'he is a good Gentleman, I warrant him. I was afraid your Worship would have been angry with me for letting him in; and to be certain I should not have done it, had not I seen by the Moon-light, that he was a Gentleman, and almost frozen to Death. And to be certain it must have been some good Angel that sent him hither, and tempted me to do it.'

'I am afraid, Sir,' said the old Gentleman to *Jones*, 'that I have nothing in this House which you can either eat or drink, unless you will accept a Dram of Brandy; of which I can give you some most excellent, and which I have had by me these thirty Years.' *Jones* declined this Offer in a very civil and proper Speech, and then the other asked him 'Whither he was travelling when he mist his Way; saying, I must own myself surprized to see such a Person as you appear to be journeying on Foot at this Time of Night. I suppose, Sir, you are a Gentleman of these Parts: for you do not look like one who is used to travel far without Horses.'

'Appearances,' cried *Jones*, 'are often deceitful; Men sometimes look like what they are not. I assure you, I am not of this Country, and whither I am travelling, in Reality I scarce know myself.'

'Whoever you are, or whithersoever you are going,' answered the old Man, 'I have Obligations to you which I can never return.'

'I once more,' replied *Jones*, 'affirm, that you have none: For there can be no Merit in having hazarded that in your Service on which I set no Value. And nothing is so contemptible in my Eyes as Life.'

'I am sorry, young Gentleman,' answered the Stranger, 'that you have any Reason to be so unhappy at your Years.'

'Indeed I am, Sir,' answered *Jones*, 'the most unhappy of Mankind.'—'Perhaps you have had a Friend, or a Mistress,' replied the other. 'How could you,' cries *Jones*, 'mention two Words sufficient to drive me to Distraction.' 'Either of them are enough to drive any Man to Distraction,' answered the old Man. 'I enquire no farther, Sir. Perhaps my Curiosity hath led me too far already.'

'Indeed, Sir,' cries *Jones*, 'I cannot censure a Passion, which I feel at this Instant in the highest Degree. You will pardon me, when I assure you, that every Thing which I have seen or heard since I first entered this House, hath conspired to raise the greatest Curiosity in me. Something very extraordinary must have determined you to this Course of Life, and I have reason to fear your own History is not without Misfortunes.'

Here the old Gentleman again sighed, and remained silent for some Minutes; at last, looking earnestly on *Jones*, he said, 'I have read that a good Countenance is a Letter of Recommendation; if so, none ever can be more strongly recommended than yourself. If I did not feel some Yearnings towards you from another Consideration, I must be the most ungrateful Monster upon Earth; and I am really concerned it is no otherwise in my Power, than by Words, to convince you of my Gratitude.'

Jones after a Moment's Hesitation, answered, 'That it was in his Power by Words to gratify him extremely. I have confest a Curiosity,' said he, 'Sir; need I say how much obliged I should be to you, if you would condescend to gratify it? Will you suffer me therefore to beg, unless any Consideration restrains you, that you would be pleased to acquaint me what Motives have induced you thus to withdraw from the Society of Mankind, and to betake yourself to a Course of Life to which it sufficiently appears you were not born?'

'I scarce think myself at Liberty to refuse you any thing after what hath happened,' replied the old Man, 'If you desire therefore to hear the Story of an unhappy Man, I will relate it to you. Indeed you judge rightly, in thinking there is commonly something extraordinary in the Fortunes of those who fly from Society: For however it may seem a Paradox, or even a Contradiction, certain it is that great Philanthropy chiefly inclines us to avoid and detest Mankind; not on Account so much of their private and selfish Vices, but for those of a relative Kind; such as Envy, Malice, Treachery, Cruelty, with every other Species of Malevolence. These are the Vices which true Philanthropy abhors, and which rather than see and converse with, she avoids Society itself. However, without a Compliment to you, you do not appear to me one of those whom I should shun or detest; nay, I must say, in what little hath dropt from you, there appears some Parity in our Fortunes; I hope however yours will conclude more successfully.'

Here some Compliments passed between our Heroe and his Host, and then the latter was going to begin his History, when *Partridge* interrupted him. His Apprehensions had now pretty well left him; but some Effects of his Terrors remained; he therefore reminded the Gentleman of that excellent Brandy which he had mentioned. This was presently brought, and *Partridge* swallowed a large Bumper.

The Gentleman then, without any farther Preface, began as you may read in the next Chapter.

Chapter XI.

In which the Man of the Hill begins to relate his History.

'I was born in a Village of *Somersetshire*, called *Mark*, in the Year 1657; my Father was one of those whom they call Gentlemen Farmers. He had a little Estate of about 300*l*. a Year of his own, and rented another Estate of near the same Value. He was prudent and industrious, and so good a Husbandman, that he might have led a very easy and comfortable Life, had not an arrant Vixen of a Wife soured his domestic Quiet. But tho' this Circumstance perhaps made him miserable, it did not make him poor: For he confined her almost entirely at Home, and rather chose to bear eternal upbraidings in his own House, than to injure his Fortune by indulging her in the Extravagancies she desired abroad.

'By this *Xanthippe*' (so was the Wife of *Socrates* called, said *Partridge*) 'By this *Xanthippe* he had two Sons, of which I was the younger. He designed to give us both good Education; but my elder Brother, who, unhappily for him, was the Favourite of my Mother, utterly neglected his Learning; insomuch that after having been five or six Years at School with little or no Improvement, my Father being told by his Master, that it would be to no Purpose to keep him longer there, at last complied with my Mother in taking him home from the Hands of that Tyrant, as she called his Master; though indeed he gave the Lad much less Correction than his Idleness deserved, but much more, it seems, than the young Gentleman liked, who constantly complained to his Mother of his severe Treatment, and she as constantly gave him a Hearing.'

'Yes, yes,' cries *Partridge*, 'I have seen such Mothers; I have been abused myself by them, and very unjustly; such Parents deserve Correction as much as their Children.'

Jones chid the Pedagogue for his Interruption, and then the Stranger proceeded. 'My Brother now, at the Age of fifteen, bid adieu to all Learning, and to every thing else but to his Dog and Gun, with which latter he became so expert, that, though perhaps you may think it incredible, he could not only hit a standing Mark with great Certainty, but hath actually shot a Crow as it was flying in the Air. He was likewise excellent at finding a Hare sitting, and was soon reputed one of the best Sportsmen in the Country. A Reputation which both he and his Mother enjoyed as much as if he had been thought the finest Scholar.

'The Situation of my Brother made me at first think my Lot the harder, in being continued at School; but I soon changed my Opinion; for as I advanced pretty fast in Learning, my Labours became easy, and my Exercise so delightful, that Holidays were my most unpleasant Time: For my Mother, who never loved me, now apprehending that I had the greater Share of my Father's Affection, and finding, or at least thinking, that I was more taken Notice of by some Gentlemen of Learning, and particularly by the Parson of the Parish, than my Brother, she now hated my Sight, and made Home so disagreeable to me, that what is called by Schoolboys Black Monday, was to me the whitest in the whole Year.

'Having, at length, gone through the School at *Taunton*, I was thence removed to *Exeter* College in *Oxford,* where I remained four Years; at the End of which an Accident took me off entirely from my Studies; and hence I may truly date the Rise of all which happened to me afterwards in Life.

'There was at the same College with myself one Sir *George Gresham,* a young Fellow who was intitled to a very considerable Fortune; which he was not, by the Will of his Father, to come into full Possession of, till he arrived at the Age of Twenty-five. However, the Liberality of his Guardians gave him little Cause to regret the abundant Caution of his Father: For they allowed him Five hundred Pound a Year while he remained at the University, where he kept his Horses and his Whore, and lived as wicked and as profligate a Life, as he could have done, had he been never so entirely Master of his Fortune; for besides the Five hundred a Year which he received from his Guardians, he found Means to spend a Thousand more. He was above the Age of Twenty-one, and had no Difficulty in gaining what Credit he pleased.

'This young Fellow, among many other tolerable bad Qualities, had one very diabolical. He had a great Delight in destroying and ruining the Youth of inferior Fortune, by drawing them into Expences which they could not afford so well as himself; and the better, and worthier, and soberer, any young Man was, the greater Pleasure and Triumph had he in his Destruction. Thus acting the Character which is recorded of the Devil, and going about seeking whom he might devour.

'It was my Misfortune to fall into an Acquaintance and Intimacy with this Gentleman. My Reputation of Diligence in my Studies made me a desirable Object of his mischievous Intention; and my own Inclination made it sufficiently easy for him to effect his Purpose; for tho' I had applied myself with much Industry to Books, in which I took great Delight, there were other Pleasures in which I was capable of taking much greater; for I was high-mettled, had a violent Flow of animal Spirits, was a little ambitious, and extremely amorous.

'I had not long contracted an Intimacy with Sir *George,* before I became a Partaker of all his Pleasures; and when I was once entered on that Scene, neither my Inclination, nor my Spirit, would suffer me to play an Under-Part. I was second to none of the Company in any Acts of Debauchery; nay, I soon distinguished myself so notably in all Riots and Disorders, that my Name generally stood first in the Roll of Delinquents; and instead of being lamented as the unfortunate Pupil of Sir *George,* I was now accused as the Person who had misled and debauched that hopeful young Gentleman; for tho' he was the Ring-leader and Promoter of all the Mischief, he was never so considered. I fell at last under the Censure of the Vice-Chancellor, and very narrowly escaped Expulsion.

'You will easily believe, Sir, that such a Life as I am now describing must be incompatible with my further Progress in Learning; and that in Proportion as I addicted myself more and more to loose Pleasure, I must grow more and more remiss in Application to my Studies. This was truly the Consequence; but this was not all. My Expences now greatly exceeded not only my former Income, but those Additions which I extorted from my poor generous Father, on Pretences of Sums being necessary for preparing for my approaching Degree of Batchelor of Arts. These Demands, however, grew at last so frequent and exorbitant, that my Father, by slow Degrees, opened his Ears to the Accounts which he received from many Quarters of my present Behaviour, and which my Mother failed not to echo very faithfully and loudly; adding, "Ay, this is the fine Gentleman, the Scholar who doth so much Honour to his Family, and is to be the Making of it. I thought what all this Learning would come to. He is to be the Ruin of us all, I find, after his elder Brother hath been denied Necessaries for his Sake, to perfect his Education forsooth, for which he was to pay us such Interest: I thought what the Interest would come to;" with much more of the same Kind; but I have, I believe satisfied you with this Taste.

'My Father, therefore, began now to return Remonstrances, instead of Money, to my Demands, which brought my Affairs perhaps a little sooner to a Crisis; but had he remitted me his whole Income, you will imagine it could have sufficed a very short Time to support one who kept Pace with the Expences of Sir *George Gresham.*

'It is more than possible, that the Distress I was now in for Money, and the Impracticability of going on in this Manner, might have restored me at once to my Senses, and to my Studies, had I opened my Eyes, before I became involved in Debts, from which I saw no Hopes of ever extricating myself. This was indeed the great Art of Sir *George,* and by which he accomplished the Ruin of many, whom he afterwards laughed at as Fools and Coxcombs, for vying, as he called it, with a Man of his Fortune. To bring this about, he would now and then advance a little Money himself, in order to support the Credit of the unfortunate Youth with other People; till, by Means of that very Credit, he was irretrievably undone.

'My Mind being, by these Means, grown as desperate as my Fortune, there was scarce a Wickedness which I did not meditate, in order for my Relief. Self-murder itself became the Subject of my serious Deliberation; and I had certainly resolved on it, had not a more shameful, tho' perhaps less sinful, Thought expelled it from my Head.' Here he hesitated a Moment, and then cried out, 'I protest, so many Years have not washed away the Shame of this Act, and I shall blush while I relate it.' *Jones* desired him to pass over any Thing that might give him Pain in the Relation; but *Partridge* eagerly cried out, 'O pray, Sir, let us hear this; I had rather hear this than all the rest: As I hope to be saved, I will never mention a Word of it.' *Jones* was going to rebuke him, but the Stranger prevented it by proceeding thus. 'I had a Chum, a very prudent, frugal young Lad, who, tho' he had no very large Allowance, had by his Parsimony heaped up upwards of forty Guineas, which I knew he kept in his Escritore. I took therefore an Opportunity of purloining his Key from his Breeches Pocket while he was asleep, and thus made myself Master of all his Riches. After which I again conveyed his Key into his Pocket, and counterfeiting Sleep, tho' I never once closed my Eyes, lay in Bed till after he arose and went to Prayers, an Exercise to which I had long been unaccustomed.

'Timorous Thieves, by extreme Caution, often subject themselves to Discoveries, which those of a bolder Kind escape. Thus it happened to me; for had I boldly broke open his Escritore, I had, perhaps, escaped even his Suspicion; but as it was plain that the Person who robbed him had possessed himself of his Key, he had no doubt, when he first missed his Money, but that his Chum was certainly the Thief. Now as he was of a fearful Disposition, and much my Inferior in Strength, and, I believe, in Courage, he did not dare to confront me with my Guilt, for fear of worse bodily Consequences which might happen to him. He repaired therefore immediately to the Vice-Chancellor, and, upon swearing to the Robbery, and to the Circumstances of it, very easily obtained a Warrant against one who had now so bad a Character through the whole University.

'Luckily for me I lay out of the College the next Evening; for that Day I attended a young Lady in a Chaise to *Whitney*, where we staid all Night; and in our Return the next Morning to *Oxford*, I met one of my Cronies, who acquainted me with sufficient News concerning myself to make me turn my Horse another Way.'

'Pray, Sir, did he mention any thing of the Warrant?' said *Partridge*. But *Jones* begged the Gentleman to proceed without regarding any impertinent Questions; which he did as follows.

'Having now abandoned all Thoughts of returning to *Oxford*, the next Thing which offered itself was a Journey to *London*. I imparted this Intention to my female Companion, who at first remonstrated against it; but upon producing my Wealth, she immediately consented. We then struck across the Country into the great *Cirencester* Road, and made such Haste, that we spent the next Evening (save one) in *London*.

'When you consider the Place where I now was, and the Company with whom I was, you will, I fancy, conceive that a very short Time brought me to an End of that Sum of which I had so iniquitously possessed myself.

'I was now reduced to a much higher Degree of Distress than before; the Necessaries of Life began to be numbred among my Wants; and what made my Case still the more grievous, was, that my Paramour, of whom I was now grown immoderately fond, shared the same Distresses with myself. To see a Woman you love in Distress; to be unable to relieve her, and at the same Time to reflect that you have brought her into this Situation, is, perhaps, a Curse of which no Imagination can represent the Horrors to those who have not felt it.' 'I believe it from my Soul,' cries *Jones*; 'and I pity you from the Bottom of my Heart.' He then took two or three disorderly Turns about the Room, and at last begged Pardon, and flung himself into his Chair, crying, 'I thank Heaven I have escaped that.'

'This Circumstance,' continued the Gentleman, 'so severely aggravated the Horrors of my present Situation, that they became absolutely intolerable. I could with less Pain endure the raging of my own natural unsatisfied Appetites, even Hunger or Thirst, than I could submit to leave ungratified the most whimsical Desires of a Woman, on whom I so extravagantly doated, that tho' I knew she had been the Mistress of half my Acquaintance, I firmly intended to marry her. But the good Creature was unwilling to consent to an Action which the World might think so much to my Disadvantage. And as, possibly, she compassionated the daily Anxieties which she must have perceived me suffer on her Account, she resolved to put an End to my Distress. She soon, indeed, found Means to relieve me from my troublesome and perplexed Situation: For while I was distracted with various Inventions to supply her with Pleasures, she very kindly—betrayed me to one of her former Lovers at *Oxford*, by whose Care and Diligence I was immediately apprehended and committed to Goal.

'Here I first began seriously to reflect on the Miscarriages of my former Life; on the Errors I had been guilty of; on the Misfortunes which I had brought on myself; and on the Grief which I must have occasioned to one of the best of Fathers. When I added to all these the Perfidy of my Mistress, such was the Horror of my Mind, that Life, instead of being longer desirable, grew the Object of my Abhorrence; and I could have gladly embraced Death, as my dearest Friend, if it had offered itself to my Choice unattended by Shame.

'The Time of the Assizes soon came, and I was removed by *Habeas Corpus* to *Oxford*, where I expected certain Conviction and Condemnation; but, to my great Surprize, none appeared against me, and I was, at the End of the Sessions, discharged for Want of Prosecution. In short, my Chum had left *Oxford*, and whether from Indolence, or from what other Motive, I am ignorant, had declined concerning himself any farther in the Affair.

'Perhaps,' cries *Partridge*, 'he did not care to have your Blood upon his Hands, and he was in the Right on't. If any Person was to be hanged upon my Evidence, I should never be able to lie alone afterwards, for fear of seeing his Ghost.'

'I shall shortly doubt, *Partridge*,' says *Jones*, 'whether thou art more brave or wise.' 'You may laugh at me, Sir, if you please,' answered *Partridge*; 'but if you will hear a very short Story which I can tell, and which is most certainly true, perhaps you may change your Opinion. In the Parish where I was born——' Here *Jones* would have silenced him; but the Stranger interceded that he might be permitted to tell his Story, and in the mean Time promised to recollect the Remainder of his own.

Partridge then proceeded thus. 'In the Parish where I was born, there lived a Farmer whose Name was *Bridle*, and he had a Son named *Francis*, a good hopeful young Fellow: I was at the Grammar-School with him, where I remember he was got into *Ovid*'s *Epistles*, and he could construe you three Lines together sometimes without looking into a Dictionary. Besides all this, he was a very good Lad, never missed Church o' *Sundays*, and was reckoned one of the best Psalm-singers in the whole Parish. He would indeed now and then take a Cup too much and that was the only Fault he had.' —'Well, but come to the Ghost,' cries *Jones*. 'Never fear, Sir, I shall come to him soon enough,' answered *Partridge*. 'You must know then, that Farmer *Bridle* lost a Mare, a sorrel one to the best of my Remembrance; and so it fell out, that this young *Francis* shortly afterward being at a Fair at *Hindon*, and as I think it was on—I can't remember the Day; and being as he was, what should he happen to meet, but a Man upon his Father's Mare. *Frank* called out presently, Stop Thief; and it being in the Middle of the Fair, it was impossible, you know, for the Man to make his Escape. So they apprehended him, and carried him before the Justice; I remember it was Justice *Willoughby* of *Noyle*,[1] a very worthy good Gentleman, and he committed him to Prison, and bound *Frank* in a Recognizance, I think they call it, a hard Word compounded of *re* and *cognosco*; but it differs in its Meaning from the Use of the Simple, as many other Compounds do. Well, at last, down came my Lord Justice *Page*[2] to hold the Assizes, and so the Fellow was had up, and *Frank* was had up for a Witness. To be sure I shall never forget the Face of the Judge, when he began to ask him what he had to say against the Prisoner. He made poor *Frank* tremble and shake in his Shoes. Well, you Fellow, says my Lord, what have you to say? Don't stand humming and hawing, but speak out; but however he

---

1. Presumably Richard Willoughby of West Knoyle, Wiltshire, ten miles or so to the north of Fielding's boyhood home at East Stour, Dorset, who subscribed to Fielding's *Miscellanies* (Cross II.174).
2. Sir Francis Page (d. 1741), presided at the summer Assizes on the Western Circuit in 1737–39. Partridge recounts an actual incident, which happened before Fielding's days as a lawyer (J. Paul de Castro, *Notes & Queries*, 11 ser., X [26 Sept. 1914], 253; Cross II.3)'.

soon turned altogether as civil to *Frank*, and began to thunder at
the Fellow; and when he asked him, if he had any Thing to say for
himself, the Fellow said he had found the Horse. Ay! answered the
Judge, thou art a lucky Fellow; I have travelled the Circuit these
forty Years, and never found a Horse in my Life; but I'll tell thee
what, Friend, thou wast more lucky than thou didst know of: For
thou didst not only find a Horse, but a Halter too, I promise thee.
To be sure I shall never forget the Word. Upon which every Body
fell a laughing, as how could they help it? Nay, and twenty other
Jests he made, which I can't remember now. There was something
about his Skill in Horse-Flesh, which made all the Folks laugh. To
be certain the Judge must have been a very brave Man, as well as a
Man of much Learning. It is indeed charming Sport to hear Trials
upon Life and Death. One Thing I own I thought a little hard, that
the Prisoner's Counsel was not suffered to speak for him, though he
desired only to be heard one very short Word; but my Lord would
not hearken to him, though he suffered a Counsellor to talk against
him for above half an Hour. I thought it hard, I own, that there
should be so many of them; my Lord, and the Court, and the Jury,
and the Counsellors, and the Witnesses all upon one poor Man,
and he too in Chains. Well, the Fellow was hanged, as to be sure it
cou'd be no otherwise, and poor *Frank* could never be easy about it.
He never was in the Dark alone, but he fancied he saw the Fellow's
Spirit.' 'Well, and is this thy Story?' cries *Jones*. 'No, no,' answered
Partridge; 'O Lord have Mercy upon me.—I am just now coming to
the Matter; for one Night, coming from the Alehouse in a long
narrow dark Lane, there he ran directly up against him, and the
Spirit was all in White, and fell upon *Frank*; and *Frank*, who is a
sturdy Lad, fell upon the Spirit again, and there they had a Tussel
together, and poor *Frank* was dreadfully beat: Indeed he made a
Shift at last to crawl home; but what with the Beating, and what
with the Fright, he lay ill above a Fortnight; and all this is most
certainly true, and the whole Parish will bear Witness to it.'

The Stranger smiled at this Story, and *Jones* burst into a loud Fit
of Laughter, upon which *Partridge* cried, 'Ay, you may laugh, Sir,
and so did some others, particularly a Squire, who is thought to be
no better than an Atheist; who forsooth, because there was a Calf
with a white Face found dead in the same Lane the next Morning,
would fain have it, that the Battle was between *Frank* and that, as
if a Calf would set upon a Man. Besides, *Frank* told me he knew it
to be a Spirit, and could swear to him in any Court in Christen-
dom, and he had not drank above a Quart or two, or such a Matter
of Liquor at the Time. Lud have Mercy upon us, and keep us all
from dipping our Hands in Blood, I say.'

'Well, Sir,' said *Jones* to the Stranger, 'Mr. *Partridge* hath finished his Story, and I hope will give you no future Interruption, if you will be so kind to proceed.' He then resumed his Narration; but as he hath taken Breath for a while, we think proper to give it to our Reader, and shall therefore put an End to this Chapter.

Chapter XII.

In which the Man of the Hill continues his History.

'I had now regained my Liberty,' said the Stranger, 'but I had lost my Reputation; for there is a wide Difference between the Case of a Man who is barely acquitted of a Crime in a Court of Justice, and of him who is acquitted in his own Heart, and in the Opinion of the People. I was conscious of my Guilt, and ashamed to look any one in the Face, so resolved to leave *Oxford* the next Morning, before the Day-light discovered me to the Eyes of any Beholders.

'When I had got clear of the City, it first entered into my Head to return Home to my Father, and endeavour to obtain his Forgiveness; but as I had no Reason to doubt his Knowledge of all which had past, and as I was well assured of his great Aversion to all Acts of Dishonesty, I could entertain no Hopes of being received by him, especially since I was too certain of all the good Offices in the Power of my Mother: Nay, had my Father's Pardon been as sure, as I conceived his Resentment to be, I yet question whether I could have had the Assurance to behold him, or whether I could, upon any Terms, have submitted to live and converse with those, who, I was convinced, knew me to have been guilty of so base an Action.

'I hastened therefore back to *London*, the best Retirement of either Grief or Shame, unless for Persons of a very public Character; for here you have the Advantage of Solitude without its Disadvantage, since you may be alone and in Company at the same Time; and while you walk or sit unobserved, Noise, Hurry, and a constant Succession of Objects, entertain the Mind, and prevent the Spirits from preying on themselves, or rather on Grief or Shame, which are the most unwholesome Diet in the World; and on which (though there are many who never taste either but in public) there are some who can feed very plentifully, and very fatally when alone.

'But as there is scarce any human Good without its concomitant Evil, so there are People who find an Inconvenience in this unobserving Temper of Mankind; I mean Persons who have no Money; for as you are not put out of Countenance, so neither are you cloathed or fed by those who do not know you. And a Man may be as easily starved in *Leadenhall* Market as in the Deserts of *Arabia*.

'It was at present my Fortune to be destitute of that great Evil, as it is apprehended to be by several Writers, who I suppose were

overburdened with it, namely, Money.' 'With Submission, Sir,' said
Partridge, 'I do not remember any Writers who have called it
Malorum; but *Irritamenta Malorum. Effodiuntur opes irritamenta
Malorum.*'[1] 'Well, Sir,' continued the Stranger, 'whether it be an
Evil, or only the Cause of Evil, I was entirely void of it, and at the
same Time of Friends, and as I thought of Acquaintance; when one
Evening as I was passing through the *Inner Temple*, very hungry,
and very miserable, I heard a Voice on a sudden haling me with
great Familiarity by my Christian Name; and upon my turning
about, I presently recollected the Person who so saluted me, to
have been my Fellow Collegiate; one who had left the University
above a Year, and long before any of my Misfortunes had befallen
me. This Gentleman, whose Name, was *Watson*, shook me heartily
by the Hand, and expressing great Joy at meeting me, proposed our
immediately drinking a Bottle together. I first declined the Proposal, and pretended Business; but as he was very earnest and
pressing, Hunger at last overcame my Pride, and I fairly confessed
to him I had no Money in my Pocket; yet not without framing a
Lie for an Excuse, and imputing it to my having changed my
Breeches that Morning. Mr. *Watson* answered, "I thought, *Jack*,
you and I had been too old Acquaintance for you to mention such a
Matter." He then took me by the Arm, and was pulling me along;
but I gave him very little Trouble, for my own Inclinations pulled
me much stronger than he could do.

'We then went into the Friars, which you know is the Scene of
all Mirth and Jollity. Here when we arrived at the Tavern, Mr.
Watson applied himself to the Drawer only, without taking the
least Notice of the Cook; for he had no Suspicion but that I had
dined long since. However, as the Case was really otherwise, I
forged another Falshood, and told my Companion, I had been at
the further End of the City on Business of Consequence, and had
snapt up a Mutton Chop in Haste; so that I was again hungry and
wished he would add a Beef Steak to his Bottle.' 'Some People,'
cries *Partridge*, 'ought to have good Memories, or did you find just
Money enough in your Breeches to pay for the Mutton Chop?'
'Your Observation is right,' answered the Stranger, 'and I believe
such Blunders are inseparable from all dealing in Untruth.—But to
proceed—I began now to feel myself extremely happy. The Meat
and Wine soon revived my Spirits to a high Pitch, and I enjoyed
much Pleasure in the Conversation of my old Acquaintance, the
rather, as I thought him entirely ignorant of what had happened at
the University since his leaving it.

'But he did not suffer me to remain long in this agreeable Delusion, for taking a Bumper in one Hand, and holding me by the

1. "Riches are dug up, the provokers of evils" (Ovid, *Metamorphoses* I.140).

other, "Here, my Boy," cries he, "here's wishing you Joy of your being so honourably acquitted of that Affair laid to your Charge." 'I was Thunderstruck with Confusion at those Words, which *Watson* observing, proceeded thus——"Nay, never be ashamed, Man; thou hast been acquitted, and no one now dares call thee guilty; but prithee do tell me, who am thy Friend, I hope thou didst really rob him; for rat me if it was not a meritorious Action to strip such a sneaking pitiful Rascal, and instead of the Two hundred Guineas, I wish you had taken as many thousand. Come, come, my Boy, don't be shy of confessing to me, you are not now brought before one of the Pimps. D——n me, if I don't honour you for it; for, as I hope for Salvation, I would have made no manner of Scruple of doing the same Thing."

'This Declaration a little relieved my Abashment, and as Wine had now some what opened my Heart, I very freely acknowledged the Robbery, but acquainted him that he had been misinformed as to the Sum taken, which was little more than a fifth Part of what he had mentioned.'

"I am sorry for it with all my Heart," quoth he, "and I wish thee better Success another Time. Tho' if you will take my Advice, you shall have no Occasion to run any Such Risque. Here," said he, (taking some Dice out of his Pocket) "here's the Stuff. Here are the implements; here are the little Doctors which cure the Distempers of the Purse. Follow but my Counsel, and I will shew you a Way to empty the Pocket of a *Queer Cull* without any Danger of the *Nubbing Cheat*."

'*Nubbing Cheat*,' cries *Partridge*, 'Pray, Sir, what is that?'

'Why that, Sir,' says the Stranger, 'is a Cant Phrase for the Gallows; for as Gamesters differ little from Highwaymen in their Morals, so do they very much resemble them in their Language.

'We had now each drank our Bottle, when Mr. *Watson* said, the Board was sitting, and that he must attend, earnestly pressing me, at the same Time, to go with him and try my Fortune. I answered, he knew that was at present out of my Power, as I had informed him of the Emptiness of my Pocket. To say the Truth, I doubted not, from his many strong Expressions of Friendship, but that he would offer to lend me a small Sum for that Purpose; but he answered, "Never mind that, Man, e'en boldly run a Levant;" (*Partridge* was going to enquire the Meaning of that Word; but *Jones* stopped his Mouth;) "but be circumspect as to the Man. I will tip you the proper Person, which may be necessary, as you do not know the Town, nor can distinguish a Rum Cull from a Queer one."

'The Bill was now brought, when *Watson* paid his Share, and was departing. I reminded him, not without blushing, of my having no Money. He answered, "That signifies nothing, score it behind the Door, or make a bold Brush, and take no Notice—Or—stay," says he, "I will go down Stairs first, and then do you take up my Money, and score the whole Reckoning at the Bar, and I will wait for you at the Corner." 'I expressed some Dislike at this, and hinted my Expectations that he would have deposited the whole; but he swore he had not another Sixpence in his Pocket.

'He then went down, and I was prevailed on to take up the Money and follow him, which I did close enough to hear him tell the Drawer the Reckoning was upon the Table. The Drawer passed by me up Stairs; but I made such Haste into the Street, that I heard nothing of his Disappointment, nor did I mention a Syllable at the Bar, according to my Instructions.

'We now went directly to the Gaming Table, where Mr. *Watson* to my Surprize, pulled out a large Sum of Money, and placed it before him, as did many others; all of them, no doubt, considering their own Heaps as so many decoy Birds, which were to entice and draw over the Heaps of their Neighbours.

'Here it would be tedious to relate all the Freaks which Fortune, or rather the Dice, played in this her Temple. Mountains of Gold were in a few Moments reduced to nothing at one Part of the Table, and rose as suddenly in another. The rich grew in a Moment poor, and the Poor as suddenly became rich; so that it seemed a Philosopher could no where have so well instructed his Pupils in the Contempt of Riches, at least he could no where have better inculcated the Incertainty of their Duration.

'For my own Part, after having considerably improved my small Estate, I at last entirely demolished it. Mr. *Watson* too, after much Variety of Luck, rose from the Table in some Heat, and declared he had lost a cool Hundred, and would play no longer. Then coming up to me, he asked me to return with him to the Tavern; but I positively refused, saying, I would not bring myself a second Time into such a Dilemma, and especially as he had lost all his Money, and was now in my own Condition.' "Pooh," says he, "I have just borrowed a couple of Guineas of a Friend; and one of them is at your Service." He immediately put one of them into my Hand, and I no longer resisted his Inclination.

'I was at first a little shocked at returning to the same House whence we had departed in so unhandsome a Manner; but when the Drawer, with very civil Address, told us, "he believed we had forgot to pay our Reckoning," I became perfectly easy, and very readily gave him a Guinea, bid him pay himself, and acquiesced in the unjust Charge which had been laid on my Memory.

'Mr. *Watson* now bespoke the most extravagant Supper he could well think of, and tho' he had contented himself with simple Claret before, nothing now but the most precious Burgundy would serve his Purpose.

'Our Company was soon encreased by the Addition of several

Gentlemen from the Gaming Table; most of whom, as I afterwards found, came not to the Tavern to drink, but in the Way of Business: for the true Gamesters pretended to be ill, and refused their Glass, while they plied heartily two young Fellows, who were to be afterwards pillaged, as indeed they were without Mercy. Of this Plunder I had the good Fortune to be a Sharer, tho' I was not yet let into the Secret.

'There was one remarkable Accident attended this Tavern Play; for the Money, by Degrees, totally disappeared, so that tho' at the Beginning the Table was half covered with Gold, yet before the Play ended, which it did not till the next Day, being *Sunday*, at Noon, there was scarce a single Guinea to be seen on the Table; and this was the stranger, as every Person present except myself declared he had lost; and what was become of the Money, unless the Devil himself carried it away, is difficult to determine.'

'Most certainly he did,' says *Partridge*, 'for evil Spirits can carry away any thing without being seen, tho' there were never so many Folk in the Room; and I should not have been surprized if he had carried away all the Company of a set of wicked Wretches, who were at play in Sermon-time. And I could tell you a true Story, if I would, where the Devil took a Man out of Bed from another Man's Wife, and carried him away through the Key-hole of the Door. I've seen the very House where it was done, and no Body hath lived in it these thirty Years.'

Tho' *Jones* was a little offended by the Impertinence of *Partridge*, he could not however avoid smiling at his Simplicity. The Stranger did the same, and then proceeded with his Story, as will be seen in the next Chapter.

Chapter XIII.

In which the foregoing Story is farther continued.

'My Fellow Collegiate had now entered me in a new Scene of Life. I soon became acquainted with the whole Fraternity of Sharpers, and was let into their Secrets. I mean into the Knowledge of those gross Cheats which are proper to impose upon the raw and unexperienced: For there are some Tricks of a finer Kind, which are known only to a few of the Gang, who are at the Head of their Profession; a Degree of Honour beyond my Expectation; for Drink, to which I was immoderately addicted, and the natural Warmth of my Passions, prevented me from arriving at any great Success in an Art, which requires as much Coolness as the most austere School of Philosophy.

'Mr. *Watson*, with whom I now lived in the closest Amity, had

unluckily the former Failing to a very great Excess; so that instead
of making a Fortune by his Profession, as some others did, he was
alternately rich and poor, and was often obliged to surrender to his
cooler Friends over a Bottle which they never tasted, that Plunder
that he had taken from Culls at the publick Table.

'However, we both made a Shift to pick up an uncomfortable
Livelihood, and for two Years I continued of the Calling, during
which Time I tasted all the Varieties of Fortune; sometimes flourishing in Affluence, and at others being obliged to struggle with almost
incredible Difficulties. To-day wallowing in Luxury, and To-morrow
reduced to the coarsest and most homely Fare. My fine Clothes
being often on my Back in the Evening, and at the Pawnshop the
next Morning.

'One Night as I was returning Pennyless from the Gaming-table,
I observed a very great Disturbance, and a large Mob gathered
together in the Street. As I was in no Danger from Pick-pockets, I
ventured into the Croud, where, upon Enquiry, I found that a Man
had been robbed and very ill used by some Ruffians. The wounded
Man appeared very bloody, and seemed scarce able to support himself on his Legs. As I had not therefore been deprived of my
Humanity by my present Life and Conversation, tho' they had left
me very little of either Honesty or Shame, I immediately offered my
Assistance to the unhappy Person, who thankfully accepted it, and
putting himself under my Conduct, begged me to convey him to
some Tavern, where he might send for a Surgeon, being, as he said,
faint with Loss of Blood. He seemed indeed highly pleased at
finding one who appeared in the Dress of a Gentleman. For as to
all the rest of the Company present their Outside was such that he
could not wisely place any Confidence in them.

'I took the poor Man by the Arm, and led him to the Tavern
where we kept our Rendezvous, as it happened to be the nearest at
Hand. A Surgeon happening luckily to be in the House, immediately attended, and applied himself to dressing his Wounds, which
I had the Pleasure to hear were not likely to be mortal.

'The Surgeon having very expeditiously and dextrously finished
his Business, began to enquire in what Part of the Town the
wounded Man lodged; who answered, "That he was come to Town
that very Morning; that his Horse was at an Inn in *Piccadilly*, and
that he had no other Lodging, and very little or no Acquaintance in
Town."

'This Surgeon, whose Name I have forgot, tho' I remember it
began with an R,[1] had the first Character in his Profession, and was
Serjeant-Surgeon to the King. He had moreover many good Quali-

1. Dr. John Ranby (1703–73), a highly   George II and Fielding's own doctor.
reputed physician, sergeant-surgeon to

ties, and was a very generous, good-natured Man, and ready to do any Service to his Fellow-Creatures. He offered his Patient the Use of his Chariot to carry him to his Inn, and at the same Time whispered in his Ear, "That if he wanted any Money, he would furnish him."

'The poor Man was not now capable of returning Thanks for this generous Offer: For having had his Eyes for some Time stedfastly on me, he threw himself back in his Chair, crying, O, my Son! my Son! and then fainted away.

'Many of the People present imagined this Accident had happened through his Loss of Blood; but I, who at the same Time began to recollect the Features of my Father, was now confirmed in my Suspicion, and satisfied that it was he himself who appeared before me. I presently ran to him, raised him in my Arms, and kissed his cold Lips with the utmost Eagerness. Here I must draw a Curtain over a Scene which I cannot describe: For though I did not lose my Being, as my Father for a while did, my Senses were however so overpowered with Affright and Surprize, that I am a Stranger to what past during some Minutes, and indeed till my Father had again recovered from his Swoon, and I found myself in his Arms, both tenderly embracing each other, while the Tears trickled a-pace down the Cheeks of each of us.

'Most of those present seemed affected by this Scene, which we, who might be considered as the Actors in it, were desirous of removing from the Eyes of all Spectators, as fast as we could; my Father therefore accepted the kind Offer of the Surgeon's Chariot, and I attended him in it to his Inn.

'When we were alone together, he gently upbraided me with having neglected to write to him during so long a Time, but entirely omitted the Mention of that Crime which had occasioned it. He then informed me of my Mother's Death, and insisted on my returning home with him, saying, "That he had long suffered the greatest Anxiety on my Account; that he knew not whether he had most feared my Death or wished it; since he had so many more dreadful Apprehensions for me. At last he said, a neighbouring Gentleman, who had just recovered a Son from the same Place, informed him where I was, and that to reclaim me from this Course of Life, was the sole Cause of his Journey to *London*." He thanked Heaven he had succeeded so far as to find me out by Means of an Accident which had like to have proved fatal to him; and had the Pleasure to think he partly owed his Preservation to my Humanity, with which he profest himself to be more delighted than he should have been with my filial Piety, if I had known that the Object of all my Care was my own Father.

'Vice had not so depraved my Heart, as to excite in it an Insensibility of so much paternal Affection, tho' so unworthily bestowed. I

presently promised to obey his Commands in my Return home with
him, as soon as he was able to travel, which indeed he was in a very
few Days, by the Assistance of that excellent Surgeon who had
undertaken his Cure.

'The Day preceding my Father's Journey (before which Time I
scarce ever left him) I went to take my Leave of some of my most
intimate Acquaintance, particularly of Mr. *Watson,* who dissuaded
me from burying myself, as he called it, out of a simple Compliance
with the fond Desires of a foolish old Fellow. Such Solicitations,
however, had no Effect, and I once more saw my own Home. My
Father now greatly solicited me to think of Marriage; but my Inclinations were utterly averse to any such Thoughts. I had tasted of
Love already, and perhaps you know the extravagant Excesses of
that most tender and most violent Passion.' Here the old Gentleman paused, and looked earnestly at *Jones*; whose Countenance
within a Minute's Space displayed the Extremities of both Red and
White. Upon which the old Man, without making any Observations, renewed his Narrative.

'Being now provided with all the Necessaries of Life, I betook
myself once again to Study, and that with a more inordinate Application than I had ever done formerly. The Books which now
employed my Time solely were those, as well ancient as modern,
which treat of true Philosophy, a Word which is by many thought
to be the Subject only of Farce and Ridicule. I now read over the
Works of *Aristotle* and *Plato,* with the rest of those inestimable
Treasures which ancient *Greece* had bequeathed to the World.

'These Authors, tho' they instructed me in no Science by which
Men may promise to themselves to acquire the least Riches, or
worldly Power, taught me, however, the Art of despising the highest
Acquisitions of both. They elevate the Mind, and steel and harden
it against the capricious Invasions of Fortune. They not only
instruct in the Knowledge of Wisdom, but confirm Men in her
Habits, and demonstrate plainly, that this must be our Guide, if we
propose ever to arrive at the greatest worldly Happiness; or to defend
ourselves with any tolerable Security against the Misery which every
where surrounds and invests us.

'To this I added another Study, compared to which all the Philosophy taught by the wisest Heathens is little better than a Dream,
and is indeed as full of Vanity as the silliest Jester ever pleased to
represent it. This is that divine Wisdom which is alone to be found
in the Holy Scriptures: For they impart to us the Knowledge and
Assurance of Things much more worthy our Attention, than all
which this World can offer to our Acceptance; of Things which
Heaven itself hath condescended to reveal to us, and to the smallest Knowledge of which the highest human Wit unassisted could
never ascend. I began now to think all the Time I had spent with

the best Heathen Writers, was little more than Labour lost: For ⌈ [2]however pleasant and delightful their Lessons may be, or however adequate to the right Regulation of our Conduct with Respect to this World only; yet when compared with the Glory revealed in Scripture, their highest Documents will appear as trifling, and of as little Consequence as the Rules by which Children regulate their childish little Games and Pastime. True it is, that Philosophy makes us wiser, but Christianity makes us better Men. Philosophy elevates and steels the Mind, Christianity softens and sweetens it. The Former makes us the Objects of human Admiration, the Latter of Divine Love. That insures us a temporal, but this an eternal Happiness.—But I am afraid I tire you with my Rhapsody.'

'Not at all,' cries *Partridge*; 'Lud forbid we should be tired with good Things.'

'I had spent,' continued the Stranger, 'about four Years in the most delightful Manner to myself, totally given up to Contemplation, and entirely unembarrassed[3] with the affairs of the World, when I lost the best of Fathers, and one whom I so entirely loved, that my Grief at his Loss exceeds all Description. I now abandoned my Books, and gave myself up for a whole Month to the Efforts of Melancholy and Despair. Time, however, the best Physician of the Mind, at length brought me Relief.' 'Ay, ay, *Tempus edax Rerum*,'[4] said *Partridge*. 'I then,' continued the Stranger, 'betook myself again to my former Studies, which I may say perfected my Cure: For Philosophy and Religion may be called the Exercises of the Mind, and when this is disordered they are as wholesome as Exercise can be to a distempered Body. They do indeed produce similar Effects with Exercise: For they strengthen and confirm the Mind; till Man becomes, in the noble Strain of *Horace*,

> *Fortis, & in seipso totus teres atque rotundus,*
> *Externi ne quid valeat per læve morari;*
> *In quem manca ruit semper Fortuna.*—'[5]

Here *Jones* smiled at some Conceit which intruded itself into his Imagination; but the Stranger, I believe, perceived it not, and proceeded thus.

2. This begins signature N, Volume II, of the third and fourth editions. See Textual Appendix, below, p. 765.
3. Typographical error, previously correct, but misspelled "unembarassed" in the fourth edition.
4. See above, p. 320.
5. *Satires* II.vii.86–88. See below, p. 583. Fielding alludes to Horace's metaphor of the bowling ball also in *Of the Remedy of Affliction* (Henley ed., *Complete Works of Henry Fielding, Esq.*, London, 1903, XVI.98), *A Proposal for Making an Effectual Provision for the Poor* (Henley, XIII.143), and *The Covent-Garden Journal*, no. 21 (Jensen ed., I.260). Jones may be smiling at the humorous argument of this *Satire*, in which Davus, Horace's slave, demonstrates that his master is himself a slave to his passions, or Tom may be smiling at the Old Man's Horatian claim of self-reliance so recently after relying on Tom's rescue. Fielding, in a footnote, gives the following translation: "Firm in himself, who on himself relies, / Polish'd and round, who runs his proper Course / And breaks Misfortunes with superior force. / MR. FRANCIS."

'My Circumstances were now greatly altered by the Death of that best of Men: For my Brother, who was now become Master of the House, differed so widely from me in his Inclinations, and our Pursuits in Life had been so very various, that we were the worst of Company to each other; but what made our living together still more disagreeable, was the little Harmony which could subsist between the few who resorted to me, and the numerous Train of Sportsmen who often attended my Brother from the Field to the Table: For such Fellows, besides the Noise and Nonsense with which they persecute the Ears of sober Men, endeavour always to attack them with Affronts[6] and Contempt. This was so much the Case, that neither I myself, nor my Friends, could ever sit down to a Meal with them, without being treated with Derision, because we were unacquainted with the Phrases of Sportsmen. For Men of true Learning, and almost universal Knowledge, always compassionate the Ignorance of others: but Fellows who excel in some little, low, contemptible Art, are always certain to despise those who are unacquainted with that Art.

'In short, we soon separated, and I went by the Advice of a Physician to drink the *Bath* Waters: For my violent Affliction, added to a sedentary Life, had thrown me into a kind of paralytic Disorder, for which those Waters are accounted an almost certain Cure. The second Day after my Arrival, as I was walking by the River, the Sun shone so intensely hot (tho' it was early in the Year) that I retired to the Shelter of some Willows, and sat down by the Riverside. Here I had not been seated long before I heard a Person on the other Side the Willows, sighing and bemoaning himself bitterly. On a sudden, having uttered a most impious Oath, he cried, "I am resolved to bear it no longer," and directly threw himself into the Water. I immediately started, and ran towards the Place, calling at the same Time as loudly as I could for Assistance. An Angler happened luckily to be a fishing a little below me, tho' some very high Sedge had hid him from my Sight. He immediately came up, and both of us together, not without some Hazard of our Lives, drew the Body to the Shore. At first we perceived no Sign of Life remaining; but having held the Body up by the Heels (for we soon had Assistance enough) it discharged a vast Quantity of Water at the Mouth, and at length began to discover some Symptoms of Breathing, and a little afterwards to move both its Hands and its Legs.

'An Apothecary, who happened to be present among others, advised that the Body, which seemed now to have pretty well emptied itself of Water, and which began to have many convulsive

6. Fielding's "Errata" sheet to the first edition corrected this from "Affront" to "Affronts," as it remains in the second and third editions. The fourth edition's "Affront," which seems both unauthor-ized and unidiomatic, is probably a fossil from the first edition, since copy for all of signature N was probably marked on first-edition pages.

Motions, should be directly taken up, and carried into a warm Bed. This was accordingly performed, the Apothecary and myself attending.

'As we were going towards an Inn, for we knew not the Man's Lodgings, luckily a Woman met us, who after some violent Screaming, told us, that the Gentleman lodged at her House.

'When I had seen the Man safely deposited there, I left him to the Care of the Apothecary, who, I suppose, used all the right Methods with him; for the next Morning I heard he had perfectly recovered his Senses.

'I then went to visit him, intending to search out, as well as I could, the Cause of his having attempted so desperate an Act, and to prevent, as far as I was able, his pursuing such wicked Intentions for the future. I was no sooner admitted into his Chamber, than we both instantly knew each other; for who should this Person be, but my good Friend Mr. *Watson!* Here I will not trouble you with what past at our first Interview: For I would avoid Prolixity as much as possible.' 'Pray let us hear all,' cries *Partridge*, 'I want mightily to know what brought him to *Bath.*'

'You shall hear every Thing material,' answered the Stranger; and then proceeded to relate what we shall proceed to write, after we have given a short breathing Time to both ourselves and the Reader.

Chapter XIV.

In which the Man of the Hill concludes his History.

'Mr. *Watson*,' continued the Stranger, 'very freely acquainted me, that the unhappy Situation of his Circumstances, occasioned by a Tide of Ill-luck, had in a Manner forced him to a Resolution of destroying himself.

'I now began to argue very seriously with him, in Opposition to this Heathenish, or indeed Diabolical Principle of the Lawfulness of Self-Murder; and said every Thing which occurred to me on the Subject; but to my great Concern, it seemed to have very little effect on him. He seemed not at all to repent of what he had done, and gave me Reason to fear, he would soon make a second Attempt of the like horrible Kind.

'When I had finished my Discourse, instead of endeavouring to answer my Arguments, he looked me stedfastly in the Face, and with a Smile said, "You are strangely altered, my good Friend, since I remember you. I question whether any of our Bishops could make a better Argument against Suicide than you have entertained me with; but unless you can find Somebody who will lend me a cool Hundred, I must either hang, or drown, or starve; and in my Opinion the last Death is the most terrible of the three."

'I answered him very gravely, that I was indeed altered since I had seen him last. That I had found Leisure to look into my Follies, and to repent of them. I then advised him to pursue the same Steps; and at last concluded with an Assurance, that I myself would lend him a hundred Pound, if it would be of any Service to his Affairs, and he would not put it into the Power of a Die to deprive him of it.

'Mr. *Watson*, who seemed almost composed in Slumber by the former Part of my Discourse, was roused by the latter. He seized my Hand eagerly, gave me a thousand Thanks, and declared I was a Friend indeed; adding, that he hoped I had a better Opinion of him, than to imagine he had profited so little by Experience, as to put any Confidence in those damned Dice, which had so often deceived him. "No, no," cries he, "let me but once handsomely be set up again, and if ever Fortune makes a broken Merchant of me afterwards, I will forgive her."

'I very well understood the Language of *setting up*, and *broken Merchant*. I therefore said to him with a very grave Face, Mr. *Watson*, you must endeavour to find out some Business, or Employment, by which you may procure yourself a Livelihood; and I promise you, could I see any Probability of being repaid hereafter, I would advance a much larger Sum than what you have mentioned, to equip you in any fair and honourable Calling; but as to Gaming, besides the Baseness and Wickedness of making it a Profession, you are really, to my own Knowledge, unfit for it, and it will end in your certain Ruin.

"Why now, that's strange," answered he, "neither you, nor any of my Friends, would ever allow me to know any thing of the Matter, and yet, I believe I am as good a Hand at every Game as any of you all; and I heartily wish I was to play with you only for your whole Fortune; I should desire no better Sport, and I would let you name your Game into the Bargain: But come, my dear Boy, have you the Hundred in your Pocket?"

'I answered, I had only a Bill for 50*l*. which I delivered him, and promised to bring him the rest next Morning; and after giving him a little more Advice, took my Leave.

'I was indeed better than my Word: For I returned to him that very Afternoon. When I entered the Room, I found him sitting up in his Bed at Cards with a notorious Gamester. This Sight, you will imagine, shocked me not a little; to which I may add the Mortification of seeing my Bill delivered by him to his Antagonist, and thirty Guineas only given in Exchange for it.

'The other Gamester presently quitted the Room, and then *Watson* declared he was ashamed to see me; "but, says he, I find Luck runs so damnably against me, that I will resolve to leave off Play for ever. I have thought of the kind Proposal you made me ever since, and I promise you there shall be no Fault in me, if I do not put it in Execution."

'Though I had no great Faith in his Promises, I produced him the Remainder of the Hundred in consequence of my own; for which he gave me a Note, which was all I ever expected to see in Return for my Money.

'We were prevented from any further Discourse at present, by the Arrival of the Apothecary; who with much Joy in his Countenance, and without even asking his Patient how he did, proclaimed there was great News arrived in a Letter to himself, which he said would shortly be publick, "That the Duke of *Monmouth*[1] was landed in the West with a vast Army of *Dutch*; and that another vast Fleet hovered over the Coast of *Norfolk*, and was to make a Descent there, in order to favour the Duke's Enterprize with a Diversion on that Side."

'This Apothecary was one of the greatest Politicians of his Time. He was more delighted with the most paultry Packet, than with the best Patient; and the highest Joy he was capable of, he received from having a Piece of News in his Possession an Hour or two sooner than any other Person in the Town. His Advices, however, were seldom authentic; for he would swallow almost any thing as a Truth, a Humour which many made use of to impose upon him.

'Thus it happened with what he at present communicated; for it was known within a short Time afterwards, thàt the Duke was really landed; but that his Army consisted only of a few Attendants; and as to the Diversion in *Norfolk*, it was entirely false.

'The Apothecary staid no longer in the Room than while he acquainted us with his News; and then, without saying a Syllable to his Patient on any other Subject, departed to spread his Advices all over the Town.

'Events of this Nature in the Public are generally apt to eclipse all private Concerns. Our Discourse, therefore, now became entirely political. For my own Part, I had been for some Time very seriously affected with the Danger to which the Protestant Religion was so visibly exposed,[2] under a popish Prince; and thought the Apprehension of it alone sufficient to justify that Insurrection: For no real Security can ever be found against the persecuting Spirit of Popery, when armed with Power, except the depriving it of that Power, as woeful Experience presently shewed. You know how King *James* behaved after getting the better of this Attempt; how little he

---

1. The acknowledged illegitimate son of Charles II, though his actual father was probably Robert Sidney, with whom Lucy Waters, his mother and the king's mistress, had previously lived. After Charles's death, Monmouth invaded England, from an unofficial exile in Holland, landing at Lyme Regis and marching eastward against his uncle, James II, on 11 June 1685, to be soon defeated, captured, and beheaded.

2. Fielding changed the following bracketed section in the third edition, but restored it in the fourth. See Textual Appendix, pp. 766–67.

valued either his Royal Word, or Coronation-Oath, or the Liberties and Rights of his People. But all had not the Sense to foresee this at first; and therefore the Duke of *Monmouth* was weakly supported; yet all could feel when the Evil came upon them; and therefore all united, at last, to drive out that King, against whose Exclusion a great Party among us had so warmly contended, during the Reign of his Brother, and for whom they now fought with such Zeal and Affection.'

'What you say,' interrupted *Jones,* 'is very true; and it has often struck me, as the most wonderful Thing I ever read of in History, that so soon after this convincing Experience, which brought our whole Nation to join so unanimously in expelling King *James,* for the Preservation of our Religion and Liberties, there should be a Party among us mad enough to desire the placing his Family again on the Throne.' 'You are not in Earnest!' answered the old Man; 'there can be no such Party. As bad an Opinion as I have of Mankind, I cannot believe them infatuated to such a Degree! There may, be some hot-headed Papists led by their Priests to engage in this desperate Cause, and think it a Holy War; but that Protestants, that are Members of the Church of *England,* should be such Apostates, such *Felos de se,*[3] I cannot believe it; no, no, young Man, unacquainted as I am with what has past in the World for these last thirty Years, I cannot be so imposed upon as to credit so foolish a Tale: But I see you have a Mind to sport with my Ignorance.' 'Can it be possible,' replied *Jones,* 'that you have lived so much out of the World as not to know, that during that Time there have been two Rebellions in favour of the Son of King *James,* one of which is now actually raging in the very Heart of the Kingdom?' At these Words the old Gentleman started up, and, in a most solemn Tone of Voice, conjured *Jones* by his Maker to tell him, if what he said was really true: Which the other as solemnly affirming, he walked several Turns about the Room, in a profound Silence, then cried, then laughed, and, at last, fell down on his Knees, and blessed God, in a loud Thanksgiving Prayer, for having delivered him from all Society with Human Nature, which could be capable of such monstrous Extravagances. After which, being reminded by *Jones* that he had broke off his Story, he resumed it again in this Manner.

'As Mankind, in the Days I was speaking of, was not yet arrived to that Pitch of Madness which I find they are capable of now, and which, to be sure, I have only escaped by living alone, and at a Distance from the Contagion, there was a considerable Rising in favour of *Monmouth*; and my Principles strongly inclining me to take the same Part, I determined to join him; and Mr. *Watson,* from different Motives concurring in the same Resolution (for the Spirit of a

3. A suicide—"a felon as to himself."

Gamester will carry a Man as far upon such an Occasion as the Spirit of Patriotism,) we soon provided ourselves with all Necessaries, and went to ⌐the Duke at *Bridgewater*.

'The unfortunate Event of this Enterprize you are, I conclude, as well acquainted with as myself. I escaped, together with Mr. *Watson*, from the Battle at *Sedgemore*, in which Action I received a slight Wound. We rode near forty Miles together on the *Exeter* Road, and then abandoning our Horses, scrambled as well as we could through the Fields and Bye-Roads, till we arrived at a little wild Hut on a Common, where a poor old Woman took all the Care of us she could, and dressed my Wound with Salve, which quickly healed it.'

'Pray, Sir, where was the Wound,' says *Partridge*. The Stranger satisfied him it was in his Arm, and then continued his Narrative. 'Here, Sir,' said he, 'Mr. *Watson* left me the next Morning, in order, as he pretended, to get us some Provision from the Town of *Cullumpton*; but—can I relate it? or can you believe it?—This Mr. *Watson*, this Friend, this base, barbarous, treacherous Villain, betrayed me to a Party of Horse belonging to King *James*, and, at his Return, delivered me into their Hands.

'The Soldiers, being six in Number, had now seized me, and were conducting me to *Taunton* Goal;[4] but neither my present Situation, nor the Apprehensions of what might happen to me, were half so irksome to my Mind, as the Company of my false Friend, who, having surrendered himself, was likewise considered as a Prisoner, tho' he was better treated, as being to make his Peace at My Expence. He at first endeavoured to excuse his Treachery; but when he received nothing but Scorn and Upbraiding from me, he soon changed his Note, abused me as the most atrocious and malicious Rebel, and laid all his own Guilt to my Charge, who, as he declared, had solicited, and even threatened him, to make him take up Arms against his gracious, as well as lawful Sovereign.

'This false Evidence, (for, in Reality, he had been much the forwarder of the two) stung me to the Quick, and raised an Indignation scarce conceivable by those who have not felt it. However, Fortune at length took Pity on me; for as we were got a little beyond *Wellington*, in a narrow Lane, my Guards received a false Alarm, that near fifty of the Enemy were at hand, upon which they shifted for themselves, and left me and my Betrayer to do the same. That Villain immediately ran from me, and I am glad he did, or I should have certainly endeavoured, though I had no Arms, to have executed Vengeance on his Baseness.

'I was now once more at Liberty, and immediately withdrawing

4. A misspelling of *Gaol* ("jail") so   variant. "Goal" stands unchanged in all
widespread in the eighteenth-century as   four editions.
to stand as an acceptable (and amusing)

from the Highway into the Fields, I travelled on, scarce knowing
which Way I went, and making it my chief Care to avoid all public
Roads, and all Towns, nay, even the most homely Houses; for I
imagined every human Creature whom I saw, desirous of betraying
me.

'At last, after rambling several Days about the Country, during
which the Fields afforded me the same Bed, and the same Food,
which Nature bestows on our Savage Brothers of the Creation, I at
length arrived at this Place, where the Solitude and Wildness of the
Country invited me to fix my Abode. The first Person with whom I
took up my Habitation was the Mother of this old Woman, with
whom I remained concealed, till the News of the glorious Revolution put an End to all my Apprehensions of Danger, and gave me
an Opportunity of once more visiting my own Home, and of enquiring a little into my Affairs, which I soon settled as agreeably to my
Brother as to myself; having resigned every Thing to him, for which
he paid me the Sum of a thousand Pounds, and settled on me an
Annuity for Life.

'His Behaviour in this last Instance, as in all others, was selfish
and ungenerous. I could not look on him as my Friend, nor indeed
did he desire that I should; so I presently took my Leave of him, as
well as of my other Acquaintance; and from that Day to this my
History is little better than a Blank.'

'And is it possible, Sir,' said *Jones*, 'That you can have resided
here, from that Day to this?' 'O no, Sir,' answered the Gentleman,
'I have been a great Traveller, and there are few Parts of *Europe*
with which I am not acquainted.' 'I have not, Sir,' cried *Jones*, 'the
Assurance to ask it of you now. Indeed it would be cruel, after so
much Breath as you have already spent. But you will give me Leave
to wish for some further Opportunity of hearing the excellent
Observations, which a Man of your Sense and Knowledge of the
World must have made in so long a Course of Travels.' 'Indeed,
young Gentleman,' answered the Stranger, 'I will endeavour to satisfy your Curiosity on this Head likewise, as far as I am able.' *Jones*
attempted fresh Apologies, but was prevented; and while he and
Partridge sat with greedy and impatient Ears. the Stranger proceeded as in the next Chapter.

Chapter XV.

A *brief History of* Europe. *And a curious Discourse between Mr.*
Jones *and the Man of the Hill.*

'In *Italy*, the Landlords are very silent. In France they are more
talkative, but yet civil. In *Germany* and *Holland* they are generally
very impertinent. And as for their Honesty, I believe it is pretty

equal in all those Countries. The *Laquais à Louage*[1] are sure to lose no Opportunity of cheating you: And as for the Postilions, I think they are pretty much alike all the World over.[2] These, Sir, are the Observations on Men which I made in my [Travels, for these were the only Men I ever conversed with.][3] My Design, when I went abroad, was to divert myself by seeing the [wondrous] Variety [of Prospects, Beasts, Birds, Fishes, Insects, and Vegetables,] with which God [has] been pleased to enrich the several Parts of this Globe. A Variety, which as it must give great Pleasure to a contemplative Beholder, so doth it [admirably] display the [Power and Wisdom and Goodness of the Creator.] Indeed, to say the Truth, there is but one Work in his whole Creation that doth him any Dishonour, and with that I have long since avoided holding any Conversation.'

'You will pardon me,' cries *Jones,* 'but I have always imagined, that there is in this very Work you mention, as great Variety as in all the rest; for besides the Difference of Inclination, Customs and Climates have, I am told, introduced the utmost Diversity into Human Nature.' 'Very little indeed,' answered the other; 'those who travel in order to acquaint themselves with the different Manners of Men, might spare themselves much Pains, by going to a Carnival at *Venice;* for there they will see at once all which they discover in the several Courts of *Europe.* The same Hypocrisy, the same Fraud; in short, the same Follies and Vices, dressed in different Habits. In *Spain* these are equipped with much Gravity; and in *Italy,* with vast Splendor. In *France,* a Knave is dressed like a Fop; and in the Northern Countries, like a Sloven. But Human Nature is every where the same, every where the Object of Detestation and [Scorn.]

['As for my own Part, I past through all these Nations, as you perhaps may have done through a Croud at a Shew, jostling to get by them, holding my Nose with one Hand, and defending my Pockets with the other, without speaking a Word to any of them, while I was pressing on to see what I wanted to see; which, however entertaining it might be in itself, scarce made me Amends for the Trouble the Company gave me.'

'Did not you find some of the Nations among which you trav-

---

1. Jensen points out this typographical error (p. 328, n. 1). The first edition reads "Laquais a Louange." Fielding's "Errata" changed "*Louange*" ("praise") to "*Louage*" ("hire"), making the phrase sensible: "footmen for hire," that is, manservants hired for short periods by tourists. Fielding emended this to "*Valets a Louage*" in the third edition. The fourth edition reads "*Laquais à Louange*," an evident misreading from first-edition pages here serving as copy.

Although "Louange" is clearly wrong, the new accent on the *a* indicates an intent to return to the full French phrase.
2. Postilions are boys who ride the near (left-hand) horse of the leading pair of coach-horses, with or without a coachman in the driver's seat. Sometimes used loosely for any boy in charge of horses for hire.
3. For these and subsequent bracketed passages, see Textual Appendix, pp. 767–68.

elled, less troublesome to you than others?' said *Jones*. 'O yes,'
replied the old Man; 'the *Turks* were much more tolerable to me
than the *Christians*. For they are Men of profound Taciturnity, and
never disturb a Stranger with Questions. Now and then indeed they
bestow a short Curse upon him, or spit in his Face as he walks the
Streets, but then they have done with him; and a Man may live an
Age in their Country without hearing a dozen Words from them.
But of all the People I ever saw, Heaven defend me from the
French. With their damned Prate and Civilities, and doing the
Honour of their Nation to Strangers, (as they are pleased to call it)
but indeed setting forth their own Vanity; they are so troublesome,
that I had infinitely rather pass my Life with the *Hottentots*, than
set my Foot in *Paris* again. They are a nasty People, but their Nastiness is mostly *without*; whereas in *France*, and some other Nations
that I won't name, it is all *within*, and makes them stink much
more to my Reason than that of *Hottentots* does to my Nose.]

'Thus, Sir, I have ended the History of my Life; for as to all that
Series of Years, during which I have lived retired here, [it affords]
no Variety to entertain you, and [may be almost] considered as one
Day. [The Retirement has been so compleat, that I could hardly
have enjoyed a more absolute Solitude in the Deserts of the *The-
bais*, than here in the midst of this populous Kingdom. As I have
no Estate, I am plagued with no Tenants or Stewards; my Annuity
is paid me pretty regularly, as indeed it ought to be; for it is much
less than what I might have expected, in Return for what I gave up.
Visits I admit none; and the old Woman who keeps my House
knows, that her Place entirely depends upon her saving me all the
Trouble of buying the Things that I want, keeping off all Sollicitation or Business from me, and holding her Tongue whenever I am
within hearing. As my Walks are all by Night, I am pretty secure in
this wild, unfrequented Place from meeting any Company. Some
few Persons I have met by Chance, and sent them home heartily
frighted, as from the Oddness of my Dress and Figure they took
me for a Ghost or a Hobgoblin. But what has happened To-night
shews, that even here I cannot be safe from the Villainy of Men;
for without your Assistance I had not only been robbed, but very
probably murdered.']

Jones thanked the Stranger for the Trouble he had taken in relating his Story, and then expressed some Wonder how he could possibly endure a Life of such Solitude; 'in which,' says he, 'you may
well complain of the Want of Variety. Indeed I am astonished how
you have filled up, or rather killed, so much of your Time.'

'I am not at all surprised,' answered the other, 'that to one whose
Affections and Thoughts are fixed on the World, my Hours should
appear to have wanted Employment in this Place; but there is one

single Act, for which the whole Life of Man is infinitely too short. What Time can suffice for the Contemplation and Worship of that glorious, immortal, and eternal Being, among the Works of whose stupendous Creation, not only this Globe, but even those number-less Luminaries which we may here behold spangling all the Sky, tho' they should many of them be Suns lighting different Systems of Worlds, may possibly appear but as a few Atoms, opposed to the whole Earth which we inhabit? Can a Man who, by Divine Medita-tions, is admitted, as it were, into the Conversation of this ineffable, incomprehensible Majesty, think Days, or Years, or Ages, too long for the Continuance of so ravishing an Honour? Shall the trifling Amusements, the palling Pleasures, the silly Business of the World, roll away our Hours too swiftly from us; and shall the Pace of Time seem sluggish to a Mind exercised in Studies so high, so important, and so glorious! As no Time is sufficient, so no Place is improper for this great Concern. On what Object can we cast our Eyes, which may not inspire us with Ideas of his Power, of his Wisdom, and of his Goodness? It is not necessary, that the rising Sun should dart his fiery Glories over the Eastern Horizon; nor that the boisterous Winds should rush from their Caverns and shake the lofty Forest; nor that the opening Clouds should pour their Deluges on the Plains: It is not necessary, I say, that any of these should proclaim his Majesty; there is not an Insect, not a Vegetable, of so low an Order in the Creation, as not to be honoured with bearing Marks of the Attributes of its great Creator; Marks not only of his Power, but of his Wisdom and Goodness. Man alone, the King of this Globe, the last and greatest Work of the Supreme Being, below the Sun; Man alone hath basely dishonoured his own Nature, and by Dis-honesty, Cruelty, Ingratitude, and Treachery, hath called his Mak-er's Goodness in Question, by puzzling us to account how a benevo-lent Being should form so foolish, and so vile an Animal. Yet this is the Being from whose Conversation you think, I suppose, that I have been unfortunately restrained; and without whose blessed Society, Life, in your Opinion, must be tedious and insipid.'

'In the former Part of what you said,' replied *Jones,* 'I most heart-ily and readily concur; but I believe, as well as hope, that the Abhor-rence which you express for Mankind, in the Conclusion, is much too general. Indeed you here fall into an Error, which, in my little Experience, I have observed to be a very common one, by taking the Character of Mankind from the worst and basest among them; whereas indeed, as an excellent Writer[4] observes, nothing should be esteemed as characteristical of a Species, but what is to be found among the best and most perfect Individuals of that Species. This

4. Shaftesbury, *Characteristics* (1727) III.213, 216–19, 221; II.92–93 (Bryant, p. 182).

Error, I believe, is generally committed by those who, from Want of proper Caution in the Choice of their Friends and Acquaintance, have suffered Injuries from bad and worthless Men; two or three Instances of which are very unjustly charged on all Human Nature.'

'I think I had Experience enough of it,' answered the other. 'My first Mistress, and my first Friend, betrayed me in the basest Manner, and in Matters which threatened to be of the worst of Consequences, even to bring me to a shameful Death.'

'But you will pardon me,' cries *Jones*, 'if I desire you to reflect who that Mistress, and who that Friend were. What better, my good Sir, could be expected in Love derived from the Stews, or in Friendship first produced and nourished at the Gaming-Table! To take the Characters of Women from the former Instance, or of Men from the latter, would be as unjust as to assert, that Air is a nauseous and unwholesome Element, because we find it so in a Jakes. I have lived but a short Time in the World, and yet have known Men worthy of the highest Friendship, and Women of the highest Love.'

'Alas! young Man,' answered the Stranger, 'you have lived, you confess, but a very short Time in the World; I was somewhat older than you when I was of the same Opinion.'

'You might have remained so still,' replies *Jones*, 'if you had not been unfortunate, I will venture to say incautious, in the placing your Affections. If there was indeed much more Wickedness in the World than there is, it would not prove such general Assertions against human Nature, since much of this arrives by mere Accident, and many a Man who commits Evil, is not totally bad and corrupt in his Heart. In Truth, none seems to have any Title to assert human Nature to be necessarily and universally evil, but those whose own Minds afford them one Instance of this natural Depravity; which is not, I am convinced, your Case.'

'And such,' said the Stranger, 'will be always the most backward to assert any such Thing. Knaves will no more endeavour to persuade us of the Baseness of Mankind, than a Highwayman will inform you that there are Thieves on the Road. This would indeed be a Method to put you on your Guard, and to defeat their own Purposes. For which Reason tho' Knaves, as I remember, are very apt to abuse particular Persons; yet they never cast any Reflection on Human Nature in general.' The old Gentleman spoke this so warmly, that as *Jones* despaired of making a Convert, and was unwilling to offend, he returned no Answer.

The Day now began to send forth its first Streams of Light, when *Jones* made an Apology to the Stranger for having staid so long, and perhaps detained him from his Rest. The Stranger answered, 'He never wanted Rest less than at present; for that Day and Night

were indifferent Seasons to him, and that he commonly made use of
the former for the Time of his Repose, and of the latter for his
Walks and Lucubrations. However,' said he, 'it is now a most
lovely Morning, and if you can bear any longer to be without your
own Rest or Food, I will gladly entertain you with the Sight of
some very fine Prospects, which I believe you have not yet seen.'

Jones very readily embraced this Offer, and they immediately set
forward together from the Cottage. As for *Partridge*, he had fallen
into a profound Repose, just as the Stranger had finished his Story;
for his Curiosity was satisfied, and the subsequent Discourse was
not forcible enough in its Operation to conjure down the Charms
of Sleep. *Jones* therefore left him to enjoy his Nap; and as the
Reader may perhaps be, at this Season, glad of the same Favour, we
will here put an End to the Eighth Book of our History.

BOOK IX.

Containing twelve Hours.

Chapter I.

*Of those who lawfully may, and of those who may not write such
Histories as this.*

Among other good Uses for which I have thought proper to insti-
tute these several introductory Chapters, I have considered them as
a Kind of Mark or Stamp, which may hereafter enable a very indifferent Reader to distinguish what is true and genuine in this historic Kind of Writing, from what is false and counterfeit. Indeed it
seems likely that some such Mark may shortly become necessary,
since the favourable Reception which two or three Authors have
lately procured for their Works of this Nature from the Public, will
probably serve as an Encouragement to many others to undertake
the like. Thus a Swarm of foolish Novels, and monstrous Romances
will be produced, either to the great impoverishing of Booksellers,
or to the great Loss of Time, and Depravation of Morals in the
Reader; nay, often to the spreading of Scandal and Calumny, and
to the Prejudice of the Characters of many worthy and honest
People.

I question not but the ingenious Author of the Spectator was
principally induced to prefix *Greek* and *Latin* Mottos to every Paper
from the same Consideration of guarding against the Pursuit of
those Scribblers, who, having no Talents of a Writer but what is
taught by the Writing-master, and yet nowise afraid nor ashamed to

assume the same Titles with the greatest Genius, than their good Brother in the Fable was of braying in the Lion's Skin.[1]

By the Device therefore of his Motto, it became impracticable for any man to presume to imitate the Spectators, without understanding at least one Sentence in the learned Languages. In the same Manner I have now secured myself from the Imitation of those who are utterly incapable of any Degree of Reflection, and whose Learning is not equal to an Essay.

I would not be here understood to insinuate, that the greatest Merit of such historical Productions can ever lie in these introductory Chapters; but, in Fact, those Parts which contain mere Narrative only, afford much more Encouragement to the Pen of an Imitator, than those which are composed of Observation and Reflection. Here I mean such Imitators as *Rowe*[2] was of *Shakespear*, or as *Horace*[3] hints some of the *Romans* were of *Cato*, by bare Feet and sour Faces.

To invent good Stories, and to tell them well, are possibly very rare Talents, and yet I have observed few Persons who have scrupled to aim at both; and if we examine the Romances and Novels with which the World abounds, I think we may fairly conclude, that most of the Authors would not have attempted to shew their Teeth (if the Expression may be allowed me) in any other Way of Writing; nor could indeed have strung together a dozen Sentences on any other Subject whatever. *Scribimus indocti doctique passim*,[4] may be more truly said of the Historian and Biographer, than of any other Species of Writing: For all the Arts and Sciences (even Criticism itself) require some little Degree of Learning and Knowledge. Poetry indeed may perhaps be thought an Exception; but then it demands Numbers, or something like Numbers; whereas to the Composition of Novels and Romances, nothing is necessary but Paper, Pens and Ink, with the manual Capacity of using them. This, I conceive, their Productions shew to be the Opinion of the Authors themselves; and this must be the Opinion of their Readers, if indeed there be any such.

Hence we are to derive that universal Contempt, which the World, who always denominate the Whole from the Majority, have cast on all historical Writers, who do not draw their Materials from Records. And it is the Apprehension of this Contempt, that hath

1. One of Aesop's fables, actually by Avianus (c. A.D. 400), printed in Sir Roger L'Estrange's collection (see below, p. 477) among the fables of "Anianus" (p. 204). An ass in a lion's skin intimidates other animals until his ears and his voice betray him. In later versions, a fox tempts him to speak, and his bray gives him away. See below, note 1, p. 373.
2. Nicholas Rowe (1674–1718), playwright and editor of Shakespeare, wrote his *Jane Shore* (1714) "in Imitation of Shakespeare's Style."
3. *Epistles* I.xix.12–14.
4. Horace, *Epistles* II.i.17. The complete line reads, "Scribimus indocti doctique poemata passim" ("Taught and untaught, we write poems far and wide"). Fielding's note gives this translation: "—— Each desperate Blockhead dares to write: / Verse is the trade of every living Wight. / FRANCIS."

made us so cautiously avoid the Term Romance, a Name with which we might otherwise have been well enough contented. Though as we have good Authority for all our Characters, no less indeed than the vast authentic Doomsday-Book of Nature,[5] as is elsewhere hinted, our Labours have sufficient Title to the Name of History. Certainly they deserve some Distinction from those Works, which one of the wittiest of Men[6] regarded only as proceeding from a Pruritus, or indeed rather from a Looseness of the Brain.

But besides the Dishonour which is thus cast on one of the most useful as well as entertaining of all Kinds of Writing, there is just Reason to apprehend, that by encouraging such Authors, we shall propagate much Dishonour of another Kind; I mean to the Characters of many good and valuable Members of Society: For the dullest Writers, no more than the dullest Companions, are always inoffensive. They have both enough of Language to be indecent and abusive. And surely, if the Opinion just above cited be true, we cannot wonder, that Works so nastily derived should be nasty themselves, or have a Tendency to make others so.

To prevent therefore for the future, such intemperate Abuses of Leisure, of Letters, and of the Liberty of the Press, especially as the World seems at present to be more than usually threatned with them, I shall here venture to mention some Qualifications, every one of which are in a pretty high Degree necessary to this Order of Historians.

The first is Genius, without a full Vein of which, no Study, says *Horace*,[7] can avail us. By Genius I would understand that Power, or rather those Powers of the Mind, which are capable of penetrating into all Things within our Reach and Knowledge, and of distinguishing their essential Differences. These are no other than Invention and Judgment; and they are both called by the collective Name of Genius, as they are of those Gifts of Nature which we bring with us into the World. Concerning each of which many seem to have fallen into very great Errors: For by Invention, I believe, is generally understood a creative Faculty; which would indeed prove most Romance-Writers to have the highest Pretentions to it; whereas by Invention is really meant no more, (and so the Word signifies) than Discovery, or finding out; or to explain it at large, a quick and sagacious Penetration into the true Essence of all the Objects of our Contemplation. This, I think, can rarely exist without the Concomitancy of Judgment: For how we can be said to have discovered the

<hr>

5. Fielding alludes humorously to the *Domesday Book* (the title itself being a humorous allusion to the Last Judgment), a census of the lands, owners, and inhabitants of England ordered by William the Conqueror in 1086.
6. Pope, *Peri Bathous*—"Therefore is the desire of writing properly termed *pruritus*, the 'titilation of the generative faculty of the brain,' and the person is said to conceive; now such as conceive must bring forth" (Elwin and Courthope ed., vol. X, ch. III, p. 352).
7. *Ars Poetica* 409–10.

true Essence of two Things, without discerning their Difference, seems to me hard to conceive. Now this last is the undisputed Province of Judgment, and yet some few Men of Wit[8] have agreed with all the dull Fellows in the World, in representing these two to have been seldom or never the Property of one and the same Person.

But tho' they should be so, they are not sufficient for our Purpose without a good Share of Learning; for which I could again cite the Authority of *Horace*,[9] and of many others, if any was necessary to prove that Tools are of no Service to a Workman, when they are not sharpened by Art, or when he wants Rules to direct him in his Work, or hath no Matter to work upon. All these Uses are supplied by Learning: For Nature can only furnish us with Capacity, or, as I have chose to illustrate it, with the Tools of our Profession; Learning must fit them for Use, must direct them in it; and lastly, must contribute, Part at least, of the Materials. A competent Knowledge of History and of the *Belles Lettres*, is here absolutely necessary; and without this Share of Knowledge at least, to affect the Character of an Historian, is as vain as to endeavour at building a House without Timber or Mortar, or Brick or Stone. *Homer* and *Milton*, who, though they added the Ornament of Numbers to their Works, were both Historians of our Order, and Masters of all the Learning of their Times.

Again, there is another Sort of Knowledge beyond the Power of Learning to bestow, and this is to be had by Conversation. So necessary is this to the understanding the Characters of Men, that none are more ignorant of them than those learned Pedants, whose Lives have been entirely consumed in Colleges, and among Books; For however exquisitely human Nature may have been described by Writers, the true practical System can be learnt only in the World. Indeed the like happens in every other Kind of Knowledge. Neither Physic, nor Law, are to be practically known from Books. Nay, the Farmer, the Planter, the Gardener, must perfect by Experience what he hath acquired the Rudiments of by Reading. How accurately soever the ingenious Mr. *Miller*[1] may have described the Plant, he himself would advise his Disciple to see it in the Garden. As we must perceive, that after the nicest Strokes of a *Shakespear*, or a *Johnson*, of a *Wycherly*, or an *Otway*, some Touches of Nature

8. Locke, *Essay Concerning Human Understanding* II.xi.2; Addison, *The Spectator*, no. 62; Pope, *Essay on Criticism* I.80–85.

9. *Ars Poetica* 304–22.

1. Philip Miller (1691–1771), "Gardener to the Worshipful Company of Apothacaries, at their Bottanick Garden in *Chelsea*," England's leading botanist, and author of *The Gardener's Dictionary* (1731–37), handsome illustrated folios (and octavos) in eight editions up to 1768. The closest statement to Fielding's, in Miller's continually revised prefaces, is: ". . . therefore I would advise every one to make Trial of such new Fruits, before they propagate them in Plenty, and not take their Characters upon Trust" (1st ed., 1731, and 2nd. ed., 1733, p. xii). On the preceding page of his Preface, Miller alludes to the ass in the lion's skin, which Fielding has just mentioned (p. 371): he seems to have been reading Miller recently.

will escape the Reader, which the judicious Action of a *Garrick*, of a *Cibber*, or a *Clive*,[2] can convey to him; so on the real Stage, the Character shews himself in a stronger and bolder Light, than he can be described. And if this be the Case in those fine and nervous Descriptions, which great Authors themselves have taken from Life, how much more strongly will it hold when the Writer himself takes his Lines not from Nature, but from Books! Such Characters are only the faint Copy of a Copy, and can have neither the Justness nor Spirit of an Original.

Now this Conversation in our Historian must be universal, that is, with all Ranks and Degrees of Men: For the Knowledge of what is called High-Life, will not instruct him in low, nor *e converso*, will his being acquainted with the inferior Part of Mankind, teach him the Manners of the superior. And though it may be thought that the Knowledge of either may sufficiently enable him to describe at least that in which he hath been conversant; yet he will even here fall greatly short of Perfection: for the Follies of either Rank do in reality illustrate each other. For instance, the Affectation of High-Life appears more glaring and ridiculous from the Simplicity of the Low; and again, the Rudeness and Barbarity of this latter, strikes with much stronger Ideas of Absurdity, when contrasted with, and opposed to the Politeness which controuls the former. Besides, to say the Truth, the Manners of our Historian will be improved by both these Conversations: For in the one he will easily find Examples of Plainness, Honesty, and Sincerity; in the other of Refinement, Elegance, and a Liberality of Spirit; which last Quality I myself have scarce ever seen in Men of low Birth and Education.[3]

Nor will all the Qualities I have hitherto given my Historian avail him, unless he have what is generally meant by a good Heart, and be capable of feeling. The Author who will make me weep, says *Horace*,[4] must first weep himself. In reality, no Man can paint a Distress well, which he doth not feel while he is painting it; nor do

2. David Garrick (1717–79); Susannah Cibber (1714–66), daughter of musician Thomas Arne, second wife of Colly Cibber's son, Theophilus; Catherine ("Kitty") Clive (1711–85). [There is a peculiar propriety in mentioning this great Actor, and these two most justly celebrated Actresses in this Place; as they have all formed themselves on the Study of Nature only; and not on the Imitation of their Predecessors. Hence they have been able to excel all who have gone before them; a degree of merit which the servile Herd of Imitators can never possibly arrive at.—*Fielding's note*.]
3. "Henry Fielding was fond of colouring his pictures of life with the glowing and variegated tints of Nature, by conversing with persons of every situation and calling, as I have frequently been informed by one of my great-aunts, the late Mrs. Hussey, who knew him intimately. I have heard her say, that Mr. Fielding never suffered his talent for sprightly conversation to mildew for a moment; and that his manners were so gentlemanly, that even the lower classes, with which he frequently condescended particularly to chat, such as Sir Roger De Coverly's old friends, the Vauxhall watermen, they seldom outstepped the limits of propriety." John Thomas Smith, *Nollekens and His Times* (London: Henry Colburn, 1828), I.124 n. See below, p. 409.
4. *Ars Poetica* 102–3.

I doubt, but that the most pathetic and affecting Scenes have been writ with Tears. In the same Manner it is with the Ridiculous. I am convinced I never make my Reader laugh heartily, but where I have laughed before him; unless it should happen at any Time, that instead of laughing with me, he should be inclined to laugh at me. Perhaps this may have been the Case at some passages in this Chapter, from which Apprehension I will here put an End to it.

Chapter II.

Containing a very surprizing Adventure indeed, which Mr. Jones met with in his Walk, with the Man of the Hill.

Aurora now first opened her Casement, *Anglicè*, the Day began to break, when *Jones* walked forth in Company with the Stranger, and mounted *Mazard* Hill; of which they had no sooner gained the Summit, than one of the most noble Prospects in the World presented itself to their View, and which we would likewise present to the Reader; but for two Reasons. *First*, We despair of making those who have seen this Prospect, admire our Description. *Secondly*, We very much doubt whether those, who have not seen it, would understand it.

Jones stood for some Minutes fixed in one Posture, and directing his Eyes towards the South; upon which the old Gentleman asked, What he was looking at with so much Attention? 'Alas, Sir,' answered he with a Sigh, 'I was endeavouring to trace out my own Journey hither. Good Heavens! what a Distance is *Gloucester* from us! What a vast Tract of Land must be between me and my own Home.' 'Ay, ay, young Gentleman,' cries the other, 'and, by your Sighing, from what you love better than your own Home, or I am mistaken. I perceive now the Object of your Contemplation is not within your Sight, and yet I fancy you have a Pleasure in looking that Way.' *Jones* answered with a Smile, 'I find, old Friend, you have not yet forgot the Sensations of your Youth.——I own my Thoughts were employed as you have guessed.'

They now walked to that Part of the Hill which looks to the North-West, and which hangs over a vast and extensive Wood. Here they were no sooner arrived, than they heard at a Distance the most violent Screams of a Woman, proceeding from the Wood below them. *Jones* listened a Moment, and then, without saying a Word to his Companion (for indeed the Occasion seemed sufficiently pressing) ran, or rather slid, down the Hill, and without the least Apprehension or Concern for his own Safety, made directly to the Thicket whence the Sound had issued.

He had not entered far into the Wood before he beheld a most shocking Sight indeed, a Woman stript half naked, under the Hands of a Ruffian, who had put his Garter round her Neck, and was endeavouring to draw her up to a Tree. *Jones* asked no Questions at this Interval; but fell instantly upon the Villain, and made such good Use of his trusty Oaken Stick, that he laid him sprawling on the Ground, before he could defend himself, indeed almost before he knew he was attacked; nor did he cease the Prosecution of his Blows, till the Woman herself begged him to forbear, saying, she believed he had sufficiently done his Business.

The poor Wretch then fell upon her Knees to *Jones*, and gave him a thousand Thanks for her Deliverance: He presently lifted her up, and told her he was highly pleased with the extraordinary Accident which had sent him thither for her Relief, where it was so improbable she should find any; adding, that Heaven seemed to have designed him as the happy Instrument of her Protection. 'Nay,' answered she, 'I could almost conceive you to be some good Angel; and to say the Truth, you look more like an Angel than a Man, in my Eye.' Indeed he was a charming Figure, and if a very fine Person, and a most comely Set of Features, adorned with Youth, Health, Strength, Freshness, Spirit and Good Nature, can make a Man resemble an Angel, he certainly had that Resemblance.

The redeemed Captive had not altogether so much of the human-angelic Species: She seemed to be, at least, of the middle Age, nor had her Face much Appearance of Beauty; but her Clothes being torn from all the upper Part of her Body, her Breasts, which were well formed, and extremely white, attracted the Eyes of her Deliverer, and for a few Moments they stood silent, and gazing at each other; till the Ruffian on the Ground beginning to move, *Jones* took the Garter which had been intended for another Purpose, and bound both his Hands behind him. And now, on contemplating his Face, he discovered, greatly to his Surprize, and perhaps not a little to his Satisfaction, this very Person to be no other than Ensign *Northerton*. Nor had the Ensign forgotten his former Antagonist, whom he knew the Moment he came to himself. His Surprize was equal to that of *Jones*; but I conceive his Pleasure was rather less on this Occasion.

Jones helped *Northerton* upon his Legs, and then looking him steadfastly in the Face, 'I fancy, Sir,' said he, 'you did not expect to meet me any more in this World, and I confess I had as little Expectation to find you here. However, Fortune, I see, hath brought us once more together, and hath given me Satisfaction for the Injury I have received, even without my own Knowledge.'

'It is very much like a Man of Honour indeed,' answered *Northerton*, 'to take Satisfaction by knocking a Man down behind his Back. Neither am I capable of giving you Satisfaction here, as I have no Sword; but if you dare behave like a Gentleman, let us go where I can furnish myself with one, and I will do by you as a Man of Honour ought.'

'Doth it become such a Villain as you are,' cries *Jones*, 'to contaminate the Name of Honour by assuming it? But I shall waste no Time in Discourse with you—Justice requires Satisfaction of you now, and shall have it.' Then turning to the Woman, he asked her, if she was near her Home; or if not, whether she was acquainted with any House in the Neighbourhood, where she might procure herself some decent Cloaths, in order to proceed to a Justice of the Peace.

She answered, she was an entire Stranger in that Part of the World. *Jones* then recollecting himself, said he had a Friend near, who would direct them; indeed he wondered at his not following; but, in Fact, the good Man of the Hill, when our Heroe departed, sat himself down on the Brow, where, though he had a Gun in his Hand, he with great Patience and Unconcern, had attended the Issue.

Jones then stepping without the Wood, perceived the old Man sitting as we have just described him: He presently exerted his utmost Agility, and with surprizing Expedition ascended the Hill.

The old Man advised him to carry the Woman to *Upton*, which, he said, was the nearest Town, and there he would be sure of furnishing her with all Manner of Conveniencies. *Jones* having received his Direction to the Place, took his Leave of the Man of the Hill, and desiring him to direct *Partridge* the same Way, returned hastily to the Wood.

Our Heroe, at his Departure to make this Enquiry of his Friend, had considered, that as the Ruffian's Hands were tied behind him, he was incapable of executing any wicked Purposes on the poor Woman. Besides, he knew he should not be beyond the Reach of her Voice, and could return soon enough to prevent any Mischief. He had moreover declared to the Villain, that if he attempted the least Insult, he would be himself immediately the Executioner of Vengeance on him. But *Jones* unluckily forgot that tho' the Hands of *Northerton* were tied, his Legs were at Liberty; nor did he lay the least Injunction on the Prisoner, that he should not make what Use of these he pleased. *Northerton* therefore having given no Parole of that Kind, thought he might, without any Breach of Honour, depart, not being obliged, as he imagined, by any Rules, to wait for a formal Discharge. He therefore took up his Legs, which were at Liberty, and walked off thro' the Wood, which favoured his Retreat; nor did the Woman, whose Eyes were perhaps rather turned towards her Deliverer, once think of his Escape, or give herself any Concern or Trouble to prevent it.

Jones therefore, at his Return, found the Woman alone. He
would have spent some Time in searching for *Northerton*; but she
would not permit him; earnestly entreating that he would accompany her to the Town whither they had been directed. 'As to the
Fellow's Escape,' said she, 'it gives me no Uneasiness: For Philosophy and Christianity both preach up Forgiveness of Injuries. But
for you, Sir, I am concerned at the Trouble I give you; nay indeed
my Nakedness may well make me ashamed to look you in the Face;
and if it was not for the Sake of your Protection, I should wish to
go alone.'

Jones offered her his Coat; but, I know not for what Reason, she
absolutely refused the most earnest Solicitations to accept it. He
then begged her to forget both the Causes of her Confusion. 'With
regard to the former,' says he, 'I have done no more than my Duty
in protecting you; and as for the latter, I will entirely remove it, by
walking before you all the Way; for I would not have my Eyes
offend you, and I could not answer for my Power of resisting the
attractive Charms of so much Beauty.'

Thus our Heroe and the redeemed Lady walked in the same
Manner as *Orpheus* and *Eurydice* marched heretofore: But tho' I
cannot believe that *Jones* was designedly tempted by his Fair One
to look behind him, yet as she frequently wanted his Assistance to
help her over Stiles, and had besides many Trips and other Accidents, he was often obliged to turn about. However, he had better
Fortune than what attended poor *Orpheus*; for his brought his
Companion, or rather Follower, safe into the famous Town of
Upton.

Chapter III.

The Arrival of Mr. Jones, *with his Lady, at the Inn; with a very full
Description of the Battle of* Upton.

Tho' the Reader, we doubt not, is very eager to know who this
Lady was, and how she fell into the Hands of Mr. *Northerton*; we
must beg him to suspend his Curiosity for a short Time, as we are
obliged, for some very good Reasons, which hereafter perhaps he
may guess, to delay his Satisfaction a little longer.

Mr. *Jones* and his fair Companion no sooner entered the Town,
than they went directly to that Inn which, in their Eyes, presented
the fairest Appearance to the Street. Here *Jones*, having ordered a
Servant to shew a Room above Stairs, was ascending, when the
dishevelled Fair hastily following, was laid hold on by the Master of
the House, who cried, 'Hey day, where is that Beggar Wench going? Stay below Stairs, I desire you;' but *Jones* at that Instant thundered from above, 'Let the Lady come up,' in so authoritative a

Voice, that the good man instantly withdrew his Hands, and the
Lady made the best of her Way to the Chamber.

Here *Jones* wished her Joy of her safe Arrival, and then departed,
in order, as he promised, to send the Landlady up with some
Cloaths. The poor Woman thanked him heartily for all his Kindness, and said, she hoped she would see him again soon, to thank
him a thousand Times more. During this short Conversation, she
covered her white Bosom as well as she could possibly with her
Arms: For *Jones* could not avoid stealing a sly Peep or two, tho' he
took all imaginable Care to avoid giving any Offence.

Our Travellers had happened to take up their Residence at a
House of exceeding good Repute, whither *Irish* Ladies of strict
Virtue, and many Northern Lasses of the same Predicament, were
accustomed to resort in their Way to *Bath*. The Landlady therefore
would by no Means have admitted any Conversation of a disreputable Kind to pass under her Roof. Indeed so foul and contagious are
all such Proceedings, that they contaminate the very innocent
Scenes where they are committed, and give the Name of a bad
House, or of a House of ill Repute, to all those where they are suffered to be carried on.

Not that I would intimate, that such strict Chastity as was preserved in the Temple of V*esta* can possibly be maintained at a
public Inn. My good Landlady did not hope for such a Blessing,
nor would any of the Ladies I have spoken of, or indeed any others
of the most rigid Note, have expected or insisted on any such
Thing. But to exclude all vulgar Concubinage, and to drive all
Whores in Rags from within the Walls, is within the Power of
every one. This my Landlady very strictly adhered to; and this her
virtuous Guests, who did not travel in Rags, would very reasonably
have expected of her.

Now it required no very blameable Degree of Suspicion, to imagine that Mr. *Jones* and his ragged Companion had certain Purposes
in their Intention, which, tho' tolerated in some Christian Countries, connived at in others, and practiced in all, are however, as
expressly forbidden as Murder, or any other horrid Vice, by that
Religion which is universally believed in those Countries. The
Landlady therefore had no sooner received an Intimation of the
Entrance of the abovesaid Persons, than she began to meditate the
most expeditious Means for their Expulsion. In order to this, she
had provided herself with a long and deadly Instrument, with
which, in Times of Peace, the Chambermaid was wont to demolish
the Labours of the industrious Spider. In vulgar Phrase, she had
taken up the Broomstick, and was just about to sally from the
Kitchin, when *Jones* accosted her with a Demand of a Gown, and
other Vestments, to cover the half-naked Woman above Stairs.

Nothing can be more provoking to the human Temper, nor more

dangerous to that Cardinal Virtue, Patience, than Solicitations of extraordinary Offices of Kindness, on Behalf of those very Persons with whom we are highly incensed. For this Reason *Shakespear* hath artfully introduced his *Desdemona* soliciting Favours for *Cassio* of her Husband, as the Means of enflaming not only his Jealousy, but his Rage, to the highest Pitch of Madness; and we find the unfortunate Moor less able to command his Passion on this Occasion, than even when he beheld his valued Present to his Wife in the Hands of his supposed Rival. In fact, we regard these Efforts as Insults on our Understanding; and to such the Pride of Man is very difficultly brought to submit.

My Landlady, though a very good-tempered Woman, had, I suppose, some of this Pride in her Composition; for *Jones* had scarce ended his Request, when she fell upon him with a certain Weapon, which, tho' it be neither long, nor sharp, nor hard, nor indeed threatens from its Appearance with either Death or Wound, hath been however held in great Dread and Abhorrence by many wise Men; nay, by many brave ones; insomuch that some who have dared to look into the Mouth of a loaded Cannon, have not dared to look into a Mouth where this Weapon was brandished; and rather than run the Hazard of its Execution, have contented themselves with making a most pitiful and sneaking Figure in the Eyes of all their Acquaintance.

To confess the Truth, I am afraid Mr. *Jones* was one of these; for tho' he was attacked and violently belaboured with the aforesaid Weapon, he could not be provoked to make any Resistance; but in a most cowardly Manner applied, with many Entreaties, to his Antagonist to desist from pursuing her Blows: In plain *English*, he only begged her with the utmost Earnestness to hear him; but before he could obtain his Request, my Landlord himself entered into the Fray, and embraced that Side of the Cause which seemed to stand very little in need of Assistance.

There are a Sort of Heroes who are supposed to be determined in their chusing or avoiding a Conflict, by the Character and Behaviour of the Person whom they are to engage. These are said to know their Men, and *Jones*, I believe, knew his Woman; for tho' he had been so submissive to her, he was no sooner attacked by her Husband, than he demonstrated an immediate Spirit of Resentment, and enjoined him Silence under a very severe Penalty; no less than that, I think, of being converted into Fuel for his own Fire.

The Husband, with great Indignation, but with a Mixture of Pity, answered, 'You must pray first to be made able; I believe I am a better Man than yourself; ay, every Way, that I am;' and presently proceeded to discharge half a dozen Whores at the Lady above Stairs, the last which had scarce issued from his Lips, when a swinging Blow from the Cudgel that *Jones* carried in his Hand, assaulted him over the Shoulders.

It is a Question whether the Landlord or the Landlady was the most expeditious in returning this Blow. My Landlord, whose Hands were empty, fell to with his Fist, and the good Wife, uplifting her Broom, and aiming at the Head of *Jones*, had probably put an immediate End to the Fray, and to *Jones* likewise, had not the Descent of this Broom been prevented,—not by the miraculous Intervention of any Heathen Deity, but by a very natural, tho' fortunate Accident; *viz.* by the arrival of *Partridge*; who entered the House at that Instant (for Fear had caused him to run every Step from the Hill) and who, seeing the Danger which threatned his Master, or Companion, (which you chuse to call him) prevented so sad a Catastrophe, by catching hold of the Landlady's Arm, as it was brandished aloft in the Air.

The Landlady soon perceived the Impediment which prevented her Blow; and being unable to rescue her Arm from the Hands of *Partridge*, she let fall the Broom; and then leaving *Jones* to the Discipline of her Husband, she fell with the utmost Fury on that poor Fellow, who had already given some Intimation of himself, by crying, 'Zounds! do you intend to kill my Friend?'

Partridge, though not much addicted to Battle, would not however stand still when his Friend was attacked; nor was he much displeased with that Part of the Combat which fell to his Share: He therefore returned my Landlady's Blows as soon as he received them; and now the Fight was obstinately maintained on all Parts, and it seemed doubtful to which Side Fortune would incline, when the naked Lady, who had listened at the Top of the Stairs to the Dialogue which preceded the Engagement, descended suddenly from above, and without weighing the unfair Inequality of two to one, fell upon the poor Woman who was boxing with *Partridge*; nor did that great Champion desist, but rather redoubled his Fury, when he found fresh Succours were arrived to his Assistance.

Victory must now have fallen to the Side of the Travellers (for the bravest Troops must yield to Numbers) had not *Susan* the Chambermaid come luckily to support her Mistress. This *Susan* was as two-handed a Wench (according to the Phrase) as any in the Country, and would, I believe, have beat the famed *Thalestris*[1] herself, or any of her subject *Amazons*; for her Form was robust and

---

1. Queen of the Amazons, who is reputed to have traveled from her country to see Alexander the Great. She is featured in La Calprenède's *Cassandra* (1642–45), soon translated into English from the French, which continued to be the most popular romance of the eighteenth century. It fictionalizes the wars of Alexander and his love for Statira, Queen of Persia, who masquerades as "Cassandra." But Oroöndates (see below, p. 671) is really the hero of the piece. Pope names one of his viragoes "Thalestris," from the same source, in *The Rape of the Lock* IV.89 ff. See also below, p. 651.

manlike, and every way made for such Encounters. As her Hands
and Arms were formed to give Blows with great Mischief to an
Enemy, so was her Face as well contrived to receive Blows without
any great Injury to herself: Her Nose being already flat to her Face;
her Lips were so large, that no Swelling could be perceived in them,
and moreover they were so hard that a Fist could hardly make any
Impression on them. Lastly, her Cheek-Bones stood out, as if Nature
had intended them for two Bastions to defend her Eyes in those
Encounters for which she seemed so well calculated, and to which
she was most wonderfully well inclined.

This fair Creature entering the Field of Battle, immediately filed
to that Wing where her Mistress maintained so unequal a Fight
with one of either Sex. Here she presently challenged *Partridge* to
single Combat. He accepted the Challenge, and a most desperate
Fight began between them.

Now the Dogs of War being let loose, began to lick their bloody
Lips; now Victory with Golden Wings hung hovering in the Air.
Now Fortune taking her Scales from her Shelf, began to weigh the
Fates of *Tom Jones,* his Female Companion, and *Partridge,* against
the Landlord, his Wife, and Maid; all which hung in exact Ballance
before her; when a good-natured Accident put suddenly an End to
the bloody Fray, with which half of the Combatants had already sufficiently feasted. This Accident was the Arrival of a Coach and four;
upon which my Landlord and Landlady immediately desisted from
fighting, and at their Entreaty obtained the same Favour of their
Antagonists; but *Susan* was not so kind to *Partridge*; for that *Amazonian* Fair having overthrown and bestrid her Enemy, was now
cuffing him lustily with both her Hands, without any Regard to his
Request of a Cessation of Arms, or to those loud Exclamations of
Murder which he roared forth.

No sooner, however, had *Jones* quitted the Landlord, than he
flew to the Rescue of his defeated Companion, from whom he with
much Difficulty drew off the enraged Chambermaid; but *Partridge*
was not immediately sensible of his Deliverance; for he still lay flat
on the Floor, guarding his Face with his Hands, nor did he cease
roaring till *Jones* had forced him to look up, and to perceive that
the Battle was at an End.

The Landlord who had no visible Hurt, and the Landlady hiding
her well scratched Face with her Handerkerchief, ran both hastily
to the Door to attend the Coach, from which a young Lady and her
Maid now alighted. These the Landlady presently ushered into that
Room where Mr. *Jones* had at first deposited his fair Prize, as it was
the best Apartment in the House. Hither they were obliged to pass
through the Field of Battle, which they did with the utmost Haste,
covering their Faces with their Handkerchiefs, as desirous to avoid

the Notice of any one. Indeed their Caution was quite unnecessary: For the poor unfortunate *Helen*, the fatal Cause of all the Bloodshed, was entirely taken up in endeavouring to conceal her own Face, and *Jones* was no less occupied in rescuing *Partridge* from the Fury of *Susan*; which being happily effected, the poor Fellow immediately departed to the Pump to wash his Face, and to stop that bloody Torrent which *Susan* had plentifully set a flowing from his Nostrils.

Chapter IV.

In which the Arrival of a Man of War puts a final End to Hostilities, and causes the Conclusion of a firm and lasting Peace between all Parties.

A Serjeant and a File of Musqueteers, with a Deserter in their Custody, arrived about this Time. The Serjeant presently enquired for the principal Magistrate of the Town, and was informed by my Landlord, that he himself was vested in that Office. He then demanded his Billets, together with a Mug of Beer, and complaining it was cold, spread himself before the Kitchin Fire.

Mr. *Jones* was at this Time comforting the poor distressed Lady, who sat down at a Table in the Kitchin, and leaning her Head upon her Arm, was bemoaning her Misfortunes; but lest my fair Readers should be in Pain concerning a particular Circumstance, I think proper here to acquaint them, that before she had quitted the Room above Stairs, she had so well covered herself with a Pillowbere[1] which she there found, that her Regard to Decency was not in the least violated by the Presence of so many Men as were now in the Room.

One of the Soldiers now went up to the Serjeant, and whispered something in his Ear; upon which he steadfastly fixed his Eyes on the Lady, and having looked at her for near a Minute, he came up to her saying, 'I ask Pardon, Madam, but I am certain I am not deceived, you can be no other Person than Captain *Waters*'s Lady.'

The poor Woman, who in her present Distress had very little regarded the Face of any Person present, no sooner looked at the Serjeant, than she presently recollected him, and calling him by his Name, answered, 'That she was indeed the unhappy Person he imagined her to be; but added, I wonder any one should know me in this Disguise.' To which the Serjeant replied, 'he was very much surprized to see her Ladyship in such a Dress, and was afraid some Accident had happened to her.' 'An Accident hath happened to me, indeed,' says she, 'and I am highly obliged to this Gentleman

---

1. A pillowcase, apparently for a bed-width bolster.

(pointing to *Jones*) that it was not a fatal one, or that I am now living to mention it.' 'Whatever the Gentleman hath done,' cries the Serjeant, 'I am sure the Captain will make him Amends for it; and if I can be of any Service, your Ladyship may command me, and I shall think myself very happy to have it in my Power to serve your Ladyship; and so indeed may any one, for I know the Captain will well reward them for it.'

The Landlady who heard from the Stairs all that past between the Serjeant and Mrs. *Waters*, came hastily down, and running directly up to her, began to ask Pardon for the Offences she had committed, begging that all might be imputed to Ignorance of her Quality: For, 'Lud! Madam,' says she, 'how should I have imagined that a Lady of your Fashion would appear in such a Dress? I am sure, Madam, if I had once suspected that your Ladyship was your Ladyship, I would sooner have burnt my Tongue out, than have said what I have said: And I hope your Ladyship will accept of a Gown, till you can get your own Cloaths.'

'Prithee Woman,' says Mrs. *Waters*, 'cease your Impertinence: How can you imagine I should concern myself about any thing which comes from the Lips of such low Creatures as yourself. But I am surprized at your Assurance in thinking, after what is past, that I will condescend to put on any of your dirty Things. I would have you know, Creature, I have a Spirit above that.'

Here *Jones* interfered, and begg'd Mrs. *Waters* to forgive the Landlady, and to accept her Gown: 'For I must confess,' cries he, 'our Appearance was a little suspicious when first we came in: and I am well assured, all this good Woman did, was, as she professed, out of Regard to the Reputation of her House.'

'Yes, upon my truly was it,' says she; 'the Gentleman speaks very much like a Gentleman, and I see very plainly is so; and to be certain the House is well known to be a House of as good Reputation as any on the Road, and tho' I say it, is frequented by Gentry of the best Quality, both *Irish* and *English*. I defy any Body to say black is my Eye, for that Matter. And, as I was saying, if I had known your Ladyship to be your Ladyship, I would as soon have burnt my Fingers as have affronted your Ladyship; but truly where Gentry come and spend their Money, I am not willing that they should be scandalized by a Set of poor shabby Vermin, that wherever they go, leave more Lice than Money behind them; such Folks never raise my Compassion: For to be certain, it is foolish to have any for them, and if our Justices did as they ought, they would be all whipt out of the Kingdom; for to be certain it is what is most fitting for them. But as for your Ladyship, I am heartily sorry your Ladyship hath had a Misfortune, and if your Ladyship will do me the Honour to wear my Cloaths till you can get some of your Lady-

ship's own, to be certain the best I have is at your Ladyship's Service.'

Whether Cold, Shame, or the Persuasions of Mr. *Jones* prevailed
most on Mrs. *Waters*, I will not determine; but she suffered herself
to be pacified by this Speech of my Landlady, and retired with that
good Woman, in order to apparel herself in a decent Manner.

My Landlord was likewise beginning his Oration to *Jones*, but
was presently interrupted by that generous Youth, who shook him
heartily by the Hand; and assured him of entire Forgiveness, saying,
'If you are satisfied, my worthy Friend, I promise you I am;' and
indeed in one Sense the Landlord had the better Reason to be satisfied; for he had received a Bellyful of Drubbing, whereas *Jones* had
scarce felt a single Blow.

Partridge, who had been all this Time washing his bloody Nose
at the Pump, returned into the Kitchin at the Instant when his
Master and the Landlord were shaking Hands with each other. As
he was of a peaceable Disposition, he was pleased with those Symptoms of Reconciliation; and tho' his Face bore some Marks of
Susan's Fist, and many more of her Nails, he rather chose to be
contented with his Fortune in the last Battle, than to endeavour at
bettering it in another.

The Heroic *Susan* was likewise well contented with her Victory,
tho' it had cost her a Black-Eye, which *Partridge* had given her at
the first Onset. Between these two, therefore, a League was struck,
and those Hands which had been the Instruments of War, became
now the Mediators of Peace.

Matters were thus restored to a perfect Calm, at which the Serjeant, tho' it may seem so contrary to the Principles of his Profession, testified his Approbation. 'Why now, that's friendly, said he;
D—n me, I hate to see two People bear Ill-will to one another,
after they have had a Tussel. The only Way when Friends quarrel,
is to see it out fairly in a friendly Manner, as a Man may call it,
either with a Fist, or Sword, or Pistol, according as they like, and
then let it be all over: For my own Part, d—n me if ever I love my
Friend better than when I am fighting with him. To bear Malice is
more like a *Frenchman* than an *Englishman*.'

He then proposed a Libation as a necessary Part of the Ceremony
at all Treaties of this Kind. Perhaps the Reader may here conclude
that he was well versed in Antient History; but this, tho' highly
probable, as he cited no Authority to support the Custom, I will
not affirm with any Confidence. Most likely indeed it is, that he
founded his Opinion on very good Authority, since he confirmed it
with many violent Oaths.

Jones no sooner heard the Proposal, than immediately agreeing
with the learned Serjeant, he ordered a Bowl, or rather a large Mug,

filled with the Liquor used on these Occasions to be brought in, and then began the Ceremony himself. He placed his Right Hand in that of the Landlord, and seizing the Bowl with his Left, uttered the usual Words, and then made his Libation. After which the same was observed by all present. Indeed there is very little Need of being particular in describing the whole Form, as it differed so little from those Libations of which so much is recorded in Ancient Authors, and their modern Transcribers. The principal Difference lay in two Instances: For first, the present Company poured the Liquor only down their Throats; and, 2dly, The Serjeant, who officiated as Priest, drank the last; but he preserved, I believe, the antient Form in swallowing much the largest Draught of the whole Company, and in being the only Person present who contributed nothing towards the Libation, besides his good Offices in assisting at the Performance.

The good People now ranged themselves round the Kitchin Fire, where good Humour seemed to maintain an absolute Dominion, and *Partridge* not only forgot his shameful Defeat, but converted Hunger into Thirst, and soon became extremely facetious. We must, however, quit this agreeable Assembly for a while, and attend Mr. *Jones* to Mrs. *Waters*'s Apartment, where the Dinner which he had now bespoke was on the Table. Indeed it took no long Time in preparing, having been all drest three Days before, and required nothing more from the Cook than to warm it over again.

Chapter V.

An Apology for all Heroes who have good Stomachs, with a Description of a Battle of the amorous Kind.

Heroes, notwithstanding the high Ideas, which by the Means of Flatterers they may entertain of themselves, or the World may conceive of them, have certainly more of Mortal than Divine about them. However elevated their Minds may be, their Bodies at least (which is much the major Part of most) are liable to the worst Infirmities, and subject to the vilest Offices of human Nature. Among these latter the Act of Eating, which hath by several wise Men been considered as extremely mean and derogatory from the Philosophic Dignity, must be in some Measure performed by the greatest Prince, Heroe, or Philosopher upon Earth; nay, sometimes Nature hath been so frolicksome as to exact of these dignified Characters, a much more exorbitant Share of this Office, than she hath obliged those of the lowest Order to perform.

To say the Truth, as no known Inhabitant of this Globe is really more than Man, so none need be ashamed of submitting to what the Necessities of Man demand; but when those great Personages I have just mentioned, condescend to aim at confining such low Offices to themselves; as when by hoarding or destroying, they seem desirous to prevent any others from eating, they then surely become very low and despicable.

Now after this short Preface, we think it no Disparagement to our Heroe to mention the immoderate Ardour with which he laid about him at this Season. Indeed it may be doubted, whether *Ulysses*, who by the Way seems to have had the best Stomach of all the Heroes in that eating Poem of the Odyssey,[1] ever made a better Meal. Three Pounds at least of that Flesh which formerly had contributed to the Composition of an Ox, was now honoured with becoming Part of the individual Mr. *Jones*.

This Particular we thought ourselves obliged to mention, as it may account for our Heroe's temporary Neglect of his fair Companion; who eat but very little, and was indeed employed in Considerations of a very different Nature, which passed unobserved by *Jones*, till he had entirely satisfied that Appetite which a Fast of twenty-four Hours had procured him; but his Dinner was no sooner ended, than his Attention to other Matters revived; with these Matters therefore we shall now proceed to acquaint the Reader.

Mr. *Jones*, of whose personal Accomplishments we have hitherto said very little, was in reality, one of the handsomest young Fellows in the World. His Face, besides being the Picture of Health, had in it the most apparent Marks of Sweetness and Good-Nature. These Qualities were indeed so characteristical in his Countenance, that while the Spirit and Sensibility in his Eyes, tho' they must have been perceived by an accurate Observer, might have escaped the Notice of the less discerning, so strongly was this Good-nature painted in his Look, that it was remarked by almost every one who saw him.

It was, perhaps, as much owing to this, as to a very fine Complexion, that his Face had a Delicacy in it almost inexpressible, and which might have given him an Air rather too effeminate, had it not been joined to a most masculine Person and Mein; which latter had as much in them of the *Hercules*, as the former had of the *Adonis*. He was besides active, genteel, gay and good-humoured, and had a Flow of Animal Spirits, which enlivened every Conversation where he was present.

When the Reader hath duly reflected on these many Charms which all centered in our Heroe, and considers at the same Time the fresh Obligations which Mrs. *Waters* had to him, it will be a Mark more of Prudery than Candour to entertain a bad Opinion of her, because she conceived a very good Opinion of him.

But whatever Censures may be passed upon her, it is my Business

---

1. The poem begins with the feasting suitors, and contains many feasts, including the monstrous ones of **Polyphemus**.

to relate Matters of Fact with Veracity. Mrs. *Waters* had, in Truth, not only a good Opinion of our Heroe, but a very great Affection for him. To speak out boldly at once, she was in Love, according to the present universally received Sense of that Phrase, by which Love is applied indiscriminately to the desirable Objects of all our Passions, Appetites, and Senses, and is understood to be that Preference which we give to one Kind of Food rather than to another.

But tho' the Love to these several Objects may possibly be one and the same in all Cases, its Operations however must be allowed to be different; for how much soever we may be in Love with an excellent Surloin of Beef, or Bottle of *Burgundy*; with a Damask Rose, or *Cremona* Fiddle; yet do we never smile, nor ogle, nor dress, nor flatter, nor endeavour by any other Arts or Tricks to gain the Affection of the said Beef, *&c.* Sigh indeed we sometimes may; but it is generally in the Absence, not in the Presence of the beloved Object. For otherwise we might possibly complain of their Ingratitude and Deafness, with the same Reason as *Pasiphae*[2] doth of her Bull, whom she endeavoured to engage by all the Coquetry practiced with good Success in the Drawing Room, on the much more sensible, as well as tender, Hearts of the fine Gentlemen there.

The contrary happens, in that Love which operates between Persons of the same Species, but of different Sexes. Here we are no sooner in Love, than it becomes our principal Care to engage the Affection of the Object beloved. For what other Purpose indeed are our Youth instructed in all the Arts of rendering themselves agreeable? If it was not with a View to this Love, I question whether any of those Trades which deal in setting off and adorning the human Person would procure a Livelihood. Nay, those great Polishers of our Manners, who are by some thought to teach what principally distinguishes us from the Brute Creation, even Dancing-Masters themselves, might possibly find no Place in Society. In short, all the Graces which young Ladies and young Gentlemen too learn from others; and the many Improvements which, by the Help of a Looking-glass, they add of their own, are in Reality those very *Spicula & Faces Amoris*,[3] so often mentioned by *Ovid*; or, as they are sometimes called in our own Language, *The whole Artillery of Love*.

Now Mrs. *Waters* and our Heroe had no sooner sat down together, than the former began to play this Artillery upon the

2. The Queen of King Minos of Crete, who fell passionately in love with a white bull given Minos by Poseidon, disguised herself as a cow, and became mother thereby of the Minotaur, half bull, half man.

3. "The arrows and flames of love." Ovid connects *amor* directly with these words in only two phrases, one with *spicula* (*Ars Amatoria* II.708), and one with *face* (*Metamorphoses* I.461), and never uses the two together. But he frequently uses one or the other separately as metaphors connected with love, eyes flaming, agony burning in the breast, etc.

latter. But here, as we are about to attempt a Description hitherto unessayed either in Prose or Verse, we think proper to invoke the Assistance of certain Aerial Beings, who will, we doubt not, come kindly to our Aid on this Occasion.

'Say then, ye Graces, you that inhabit the heavenly Mansions of *Seraphina*'s Countenance; for you are truly Divine, are always in her Presence, and well know all the Arts of charming; say, what were the Weapons now used to captivate the Heart of Mr. *Jones*.

'First, from two lovely blue Eyes, whose bright Orbs flashed Lightning at their Discharge, flew forth two pointed Ogles. But happily for our Heroe, hit only a vast Piece of Beef which he was then conveying into his Plate, and harmless spent their Force. The fair Warrior perceived their Miscarriage, and immediately from her fair Bosom drew forth a deadly Sigh. A Sigh, which none could have heard unmoved, and which was sufficient at once to have swept off a dozen Beaus; so soft, so sweet, so tender, that the insinuating Air must have found its subtle Way to the Heart of our Heroe, had it not luckily been driven from his Ears by the coarse Bubbling of some bottled Ale, which at that Time he was pouring forth. Many other Weapons did she assay; but the God of Eating (if there be any such Deity; for I do not confidently assert it) preserved his Votary; or perhaps it may not be *Dignus Vindice nodus*,[4] and the present Security of *Jones* may be accounted for by natural Means: For as Love frequently preserves from the Attacks of Hunger, so may Hunger possibly, in some Cases, defend us against Love.

'The Fair One, enraged at her frequent Disappointments, determined on a short Cessation of Arms. Which Interval she employed in making ready every Engine of amorous Warfare for the renewing of the Attack, when Dinner should be over.

'No sooner then was the Cloth removed, than she again began her Operations. First, having planted her Right Eye side-ways against Mr. *Jones*, she shot from its Corner a most penetrating Glance; which, tho' great Part of its Force was spent before it reached our Heroe, did not vent itself absolutely without Effect. This the Fair One perceiving, hastily withdrew her Eyes, and leveled them downwards as if she was concerned for what she had done: Tho' by this Means she designed only to draw him from his Guard, and indeed to open his Eyes, through which she intended to surprize his Heart. And now, gently lifting up those two bright Orbs which had already begun to make an Impression on poor *Jones*, she discharged a Volley of small Charms at once from her

4. A famous rule of Horace's (*Ars Poetica* 191–92)—"*Nec deus intersit, nisi dignus vindice nodus / Inciderit*" ("Nor should a god intervene, unless a knot worthy such a deliverer should turn up"). See also *Jonathan Wild* II.xii.

whole Countenance in a Smile. Not a Smile of Mirth, nor of Joy; but a Smile of Affection, which most Ladies have always ready at their Command, and which serves them to shew at once their Good-Humour, their pretty Dimples, and their white Teeth.

'This Smile our Heroe received full in his Eyes, and was immediately staggered with its Force. He then began to see the Designs of the Enemy, and indeed to feel their Success. A Parley now was set on Foot between the Parties; during which the artful Fair so slily and imperceptibly carried on her Attack, that she had almost subdued the Heart of our Heroe, before she again repaired to Acts of Hostility. To confess the Truth, I am afraid Mr. *Jones* maintained a Kind of *Dutch* Defense,[5] and treacherously delivered up the Garrison, without duly weighing his Allegiance to the fair *Sophia*. In short, no sooner had the amorous Parley ended, and the Lady had unmasked the Royal Battery, by carelessly letting her Handkerchief drop from her Neck, than the Heart of Mr. *Jones* was entirely taken, and the fair Conqueror enjoyed the usual Fruits of her Victory.'

Here the Graces think proper to end their Description, and here we think proper to end the Chapter.

Chapter VI.

A friendly Conversation in the Kitchin, which had a very common, tho' not very friendly Conclusion.

While our Lovers were entertaining themselves in the Manner which is partly described in the foregoing Chapter; they were likewise furnishing out an Entertainment for their good Friends in the Kitchin. And this in a double Sense, by affording them Matter for their Conversation, and, at the same time, Drink to enliven their Spirits.

There were now assembled round the Kitchin Fire, besides my Landlord and Landlady, who occasionally went backward and forward, Mr. *Partridge*, the Serjeant, and the Coachman who drove the young Lady and her Maid.

Partridge having acquainted the Company with what he had learnt from the Man of the Hill, concerning the Situation in which Mrs. *Waters* had been found by *Jones*, the Serjeant proceeded to that Part of her History which was known to him. He said, she was the Wife of Mr. *Waters*, who was a Captain in their Regiment, and had often been with him at Quarters. 'Some Folks,' says he,

---

5. William Platt (*Notes & Queries*, 6 ser., III, 4 June 1881) traces the origin of a similar British expression, "Dutch courage," to the fact that the Dutch fled the Battle of Fontenoy, 1745, even though their British allies attacked the French successfully from the first, but eventually lost (Bryant, p. 187).

'used indeed to doubt whether they were lawfully married in a
Church or no. But, for my Part, that's no Business of mine; I must
own, if I was put to my Corporal Oath, I believe she is little better
than one of us; and I fancy the Captain may go to Heaven when
the Sun shines upon a rainy Day. But if he does, that is neither
here nor there; for he won't want Company. And the Lady, to give
the Devil his Due, is a very good Sort of Lady, and loves the Cloth,
and is always desirous to do strict Justice to it; for she hath begged
off many a poor Soldier, and, by her Good-will, would never have
any of them punished. But yet, to be sure, Ensign *Northerton* and
she were very well acquainted together, at our last Quarters, that is
the very Right and Truth of the Matter. But the Captain he knows
nothing about it; and as long as there is enough for him too, what
does it signify? He loves her not a bit the worse, and I am certain
would run any Man through the Body that was to abuse her, therefore I won't abuse her, for my Part. I only repeat what other Folks
say; and to be certain, what every body says, there must be some
Truth in.' 'Ay, ay, a great deal of Truth, I warrant you,' cries *Partridge*; Veritas *odium parit.*[1] 'All a Parcel of scandalous Stuff,'
answered the Mistress of the House. 'I am sure, now she is drest, she
looks like a very good Sort of Lady, and she behaves herself like one;
for she gave me a Guinea for the Use of my Cloaths.' 'A very good
Lady indeed,' cries the Landlord; 'and if you had not been a little too
hasty, you would not have quarrelled with her as you did at first.'
'You need mention that with my truly,' answered she; 'if it had not
been for your Nonsense, nothing had happened. You must be meddling with what did not belong to you, and throw in your Fool's
Discourse.' 'Well, well,' answered he, 'what's past cannot be
mended, so there's an End of the Matter.' 'Yes,' cries she, 'for this
once; but will it be mended ever the more hereafter? This is not the
first Time I have suffered for your Numscull's Pate. I wish you
would always hold your Tongue in the House, and meddle only in
Matters without Doors which concern you. Don't you remember
what happened about seven Years ago?'—'Nay, my Dear,' returned
he, 'don't rip up old Stories. Come, come, all's well, and I am sorry
for what I have done.' The Landlady was going to reply, but was
prevented by the Peace-making Serjeant, sorely to the Displeasure
of *Partridge*, who was a great Lover of what is called Fun, and a
great Promoter of those harmless Quarrels which tend rather to the
Production of comical than tragical Incidents.

The Serjeant asked *Partridge* whither he and his Master were
travelling? 'None of your Magisters,' answered *Partridge*; 'I am no
Man's Servant, I assure you; for tho' I have had Misfortunes in the

---

1. "Truth brings forth hatred." Terence,   *Septem Sapientum,* "Bias," 3 (Bryant).
Andria I.i (Mutter); Ausonius, *Ludus*

World, I write Gentleman after my Name; and as poor and simple
as I may appear now, I have taught Grammar-School in my Time.
Sed hei mihi! non sum quod fui.[2] 'No Offence, I hope, Sir,' said
the Serjeant; 'where then, if I may venture to be so bold, may you
and your Friend be travelling?'——'You have now denominated us
right,' says *Partridge.* '*Amici sumus.*[3] And I promise you my Friend
is one of the greatest Gentlemen in the Kingdom,' (at which
Words both Landlord and Landlady pricked up their Ears.) 'He is
the Heir of Squire *Allworthy.*' 'What, the Squire who doth so
much Good all over the Country?' cries my Landlady. 'Even he,'
answered *Partridge.* 'Then I warrant,' says she, 'he'll have a swinging great Estate hereafter.' 'Most certainly,' answered *Partridge.*
'Well,' replied the Landlady, 'I thought the first Moment I saw
him he looked like a good Sort of Gentleman; but my Husband
here, to be sure, is wiser than any body.' 'I own, my Dear,' cries he,
'it was a Mistake.' 'A Mistake indeed!' answered she; 'but when did
you ever know me to make such Mistakes?'—'But how comes it,
Sir,' cries the Landlord, 'that such a great Gentleman walks about
the Country afoot?' 'I don't know,' returned *Partridge*; 'great Gentlemen have Humours sometimes. He hath now a dozen Horses and
Servants at *Gloucester*; and nothing would serve him, but last
Night, it being very hot Weather, he must cool himself with a Walk
to yon high Hill, whither I likewise walked with him to bear him
Company; but if ever you catch me there again: For I was never so
frightened in all my Life. We met with the strangest Man
there.' 'I'll be hanged,' cries the Landlord, 'if it was not the
Man of the Hill, as they call him; if indeed he be a Man; but I
know several People who believe it is the Devil that lives there.'
'Nay, nay, like enough,' says *Partridge*; 'and now you put me in the
Head of it, I verily and sincerely believe it was the Devil; tho' I
could not perceive his cloven Foot but perhaps he might have the
Power given him to hide that, since evil Spirits can appear in what
Shapes they please.' 'And pray, Sir,' says the Serjeant, 'no Offence I
hope; but pray what Sort of a Gentleman is the Devil? For I have
heard some of our Officers say, There is no such Person; and that it
is only a Trick of the Parsons, to prevent their being broke; for if it
was publickly known that there was no Devil, the Parsons would be
of no more Use than we are in Time of Peace.' 'Those Officers,'
says *Partridge*, 'are very great Scholars, I suppose.' 'Not much of
Schollards neither,' answered the Serjeant; 'they have not half your
Learning, Sir, I believe; and to be sure, I thought there must be a
Devil, notwithstanding what they said, tho' one of them was a Captain; for methought, thinks I to myself, if there be no Devil, how

2. "But alas for me! I am not what I   3. "We are friends."
was."

can wicked People be sent to him, and I have read all that upon a Book.' 'Some of your Officers,' quoth the Landlord, 'will find there is a Devil, to their Shame, I believe. I don't question but he'll pay off some old Scores, upon my Account. Here was one quartered upon me half a Year, who had the Conscience to take up one of my best Beds, tho' he hardly spent a Shilling a Day in the House, and suffered his Men to roast Cabbages at the Kitchin Fire, because I would not give them a Dinner on a *Sunday*. Every good Christian must desire there should be a Devil for the Punishment of such Wretches.' 'Harkee, Landlord,' said the Serjeant, 'don't abuse the Cloth; for I won't take it.' 'D—n the Cloth,' answered the Landlord, 'I have suffered enough by them.' 'Bear Witness, Gentlemen,' says the Serjeant, he curses the King, and that's High Treason.' 'I curse the King! you Villain,' said the Landlord. 'Yes you did,' cries the Serjeant, 'you cursed the Cloth, and that's cursing the King. It's all one and the same; for every Man who curses the Cloth, would curse the King if he durst; so for Matter o'that, it's all one and the same Thing.' 'Excuse me there, Mr. Serjeant,' quoth *Partridge*, 'that's a *Non Sequitur*.' 'None of your outlandish Linguo,' answered the Serjeant, leaping from his Seat; 'I will not sit still and hear the Cloth abused.'——'You mistake me, Friend,' cries *Partridge*, 'I did not mean to abuse the Cloth; I only said your Conclusion was a *Non Sequitur*.'[4] 'You are another,' cries the Serjeant, 'an you come to that. No more a *Sequitur* than yourself. You are a Pack of Rascals, and I'll prove it; for I will fight the best Man of you all for twenty Pound.' This Challenge effectually silenced *Partridge*, whose Stomach for drubbing did not so soon return after the hearty Meal which he had lately been treated with; but the Coachman, whose Bones were less sore, and whose Appetite for Fighting was somewhat sharper, did not so easily brook the Affront, of which he conceived some Part at least fell to his Share. He started therefore from his Seat, and advancing to the Serjeant, swore he looked on himself to be as good a Man as any in the Army, and offered to box for a Guinea. The military Man accepted the Combat, but refused the Wager; upon which both immediately stript and engaged until the Driver of Horses was so well mauled by the Leader of Men, that he was obliged to exhaust his small Remainder of Breath in begging for Quarter.

The young Lady was now desirous to depart, and had given Orders for her Coach to be prepared; but all in vain; for the Coachman was disabled from performing his Office for that Evening. An antient Heathen would perhaps have imputed this Disability to the

---

4. This Word, which the Serjeant unhappily mistook for an Affront, is a Term in Logic, and means that the Conclusion doth not follow from the Premises [*Fielding's note*].

God of Drink, no less than to the God of War; for, in Reality, both the Combatants had sacrificed as well to the former Deity as to the latter. To speak plainly, they were both dead drunk, nor was *Partridge* in a much better Situation. As for my Landlord, Drinking was his Trade; and the Liquor had no more Effect on him, than it had on any other Vessel in his House.

The Mistress of the Inn being summoned to attend Mr. *Jones* and his Companion, at their Tea, gave a full Relation of the latter Part of the foregoing Scene; and at the same time expressed great Concern for the young Lady, 'who,' she said, 'was under the utmost Uneasiness at being prevented from pursuing her Journey. She is a sweet pretty Creature,' added she, 'and I am certain I have seen her Face before. I fancy she is in Love, and running away from her Friends. Who knows but some young Gentleman or other may be expecting her, with a Heart as heavy as her own.'

Jones fetched a hearty Sigh at those Words; of which, tho' Mrs. *Waters* observed it, she took no Notice while the Landlady continued in the Room; but after the Departure of that good Woman, she could not forbear giving our Heroe certain Hints of her suspecting some very dangerous Rival in his Affections. The aukward Behaviour of Mr. *Jones* on this Occasion convinced her of the Truth, without his giving her a direct Answer to any of her Questions; but she was not nice enough in her Amours to be greatly concerned at the Discovery. The Beauty of *Jones* highly charmed her Eye; but, as she could not see his Heart, she gave herself no Concern about it. She could feast heartily at the Table of Love, without reflecting that some other already had been, or hereafter might be, feasted with the same Repast. A Sentiment which, if it deals but little in Refinement, deals however much in Substance; and is less capricious, and perhaps less ill-natured and selfish than the Desires of those Females who can be contented enough to abstain from the Possession of their Lovers, provided they are sufficiently satisfied that no one else possesses them.

Chapter VII.

Containing a fuller Account of Mrs. Waters, *and by what Means she came into that distressful Situation from which she was rescued by* Jones.

Though Nature hath by no Means mixed up an equal Share either of Curiosity or Vanity in every human Composition, there is perhaps no Individual to whom she hath not allotted such a Proportion of both, as requires much Arts and Pains too, to subdue and keep under. A conquest, however, absolutely necessary to every one who would in any Degree deserve the Characters of Wisdom or Good-Breeding.

As *Jones* therefore might very justly be called a well-bred Man, he had stifled all that Curiosity which the extraordinary Manner in which he had found Mrs. *Waters*, must be supposed to have occasioned. He had indeed at first thrown out some few Hints to the Lady; but when he perceived her industriously avoiding any Explanation, he was contented to remain in Ignorance, the rather as he was not without Suspicion, that there were some Circumstances which must have raised her Blushes, had she related the whole Truth.

Now, since it is possible that some of our Readers may not so easily acquiesce under the same Ignorance, and as we are very desirous to satisfy them all, we have taken uncommon Pains to inform ourselves of the real Fact, with the Relation of which we shall conclude this Book.

This Lady then had lived some Years with one Captain *Waters*, who was a Captain in the same Regiment to which Mr. *Northerton* belonged. She past for that Gentleman's Wife, and went by his Name; and yet, as the Serjeant said, there were some Doubts concerning the Reality of their Marriage, which we shall not at present take upon us to resolve.

Mrs. *Waters*, I am sorry to say it, had for some Time contracted an Intimacy with the above mentioned Ensign, which did no great Credit to her Reputation. That she had a remarkable Fondness for that young Fellow is most certain; but whether she indulged this to any very criminal Lengths, is not so extremely clear, unless we will suppose that Women never grant every Favour to a Man but one, without granting him that one also.

The Division of the Regiment to which Captain *Waters* belonged, had two Days preceded the March of that Company to which Mr. *Northerton* was the Ensign; so that the former had reached *Worcester*, the very Day after the unfortunate Rencounter between *Jones* and *Northerton*, which we have before recorded.

Now it had been agreed between Mrs. *Waters* and the Captain, that she would accompany him in his March as far as *Worcester*, where they were to take their Leave of each other, and she was thence to return to *Bath*, where she was to stay till the End of the Winter's Campaign against the Rebels.

With this Agreement Mr. *Northerton* was made acquainted. To say the Truth, the Lady had made him an Assignation at this very Place, and promised to stay at *Worcester* till his Division came thither; with what View, and for what Purpose must be left to the

Reader's Divination: For though we are obliged to relate Facts, we are not obliged to do a Violence to our Nature by any Comments to the Disadvantage of the loveliest Part of the Creation.

Northerton no sooner obtained a Release from his Captivity, as we have seen, than he hasted away to overtake Mrs. *Waters*; which, as he was a very active nimble Fellow, he did at the last mentioned City, some few Hours after Captain *Waters* had left her: At his first Arrival he made no Scruple of acquainting her with the unfortunate Accident, which he made appear very unfortunate indeed: For he totally extracted every Particle of what could be called Fault, at least in a Court of Honour, though he left some Circumstances which might be questionable in a Court of Law.

Women, to their Glory be it spoken, are more generally capable of that violent and apparently disinterested Passion of Love, which seeks only the Good of its Object, than Men. Mrs. *Waters*, therefore, was no sooner apprized of the Danger to which her Lover was exposed, than she lost every Consideration besides that of his Safety; and this being a Matter equally agreeable to the Gentleman, it became the immediate Subject of Debate between them.

After much Consultation on this Matter, it was at length agreed, that the Ensign should go a-cross the Country to *Hereford*, whence he might find some Conveyance to one of the Sea-Ports in *Wales*, and thence might make his Escape abroad. In all which Expedition Mrs. *Waters* declared she would bear him Company; and for which she was able to furnish him with Money, a very material Article to Mr. *Northerton*, she having then in her Pocket three Bank Notes to the Amount of 90*l.* besides some Cash, and a Diamond Ring of pretty considerable Value on her Finger. All which she, with the utmost Confidence, revealed to this wicked Man, little suspecting she should by these Means inspire him with a Design of robbing her. Now as they must, by taking Horses from *Worcester*, have furnished any Pursuers with the Means of hereafter discovering their Rout, the Ensign proposed, and the Lady presently agreed to make their first Stage on Foot; for which Purpose the Hardness of the Frost was very seasonable.

The main Part of the Lady's Baggage was already at *Bath*, and she had nothing with her at present besides a very small Quantity of Linen, which the Gallant undertook to carry in his own Pockets. All Things, therefore, being settled in the Evening, they arose early the next Morning, and at Five o'Clock departed from *Worcester*, it being then above two Hours before Day. But the Moon which was then at the full, gave them all the Light she was capable of affording.

Mrs. *Waters* was not of that delicate Race of Women who are obliged to the Invention of Vehicles for the Capacity of removing themselves from one Place to another, and with whom consequently a Coach is reckoned among the Necessaries of Life. Her Limbs were indeed full of Strength and Agility, and as her Mind was no less animated with Spirit, she was perfectly able to keep Pace with her nimble Lover.

Having travelled on for some Miles in a High Road, which *Northerton* said he was informed led to *Hereford*, they came at the Break of Day to the Side of a large Wood, where he suddenly stopped, and affecting to meditate a Moment with himself, expressed some Apprehensions from travelling any longer in so public a Way. Upon which he easily persuaded his fair Companion to strike with him into a Path which seemed to lead directly through the Wood, and which at length brought them both to the Bottom of *Mazard-Hill*.

Whether the execrable Scheme which he now attempted to execute, was the Effect of previous Deliberation, or whether it now first came into his Head, I cannot determine. But being arrived in this lonely Place, where it was very improbable he should meet with any Interruption; he suddenly slipped his Garter from his Leg, and laying violent Hands on the poor Woman, endeavoured to perpetrate that dreadful and detestable Fact, which we have before commemorated, and which the providential Appearance of *Jones* did so fortunately prevent.

Happy was it for Mrs. *Waters*, that she was not of the weakest Order of Females; for no sooner did she perceive by his tying a Knot in his Garter, and by his Declarations, what his hellish Intentions were, than she stood stoutly to her Defence, and so strongly struggled with her Enemy, screaming all the while for Assistance, that she delayed the Execution of the Villain's Purpose several Minutes, by which Means Mr. *Jones* came to her Relief, at that very Instant when her Strength failed, and she was totally overpowered, and delivered her from the Ruffian's Hands, with no other Loss than that of her Cloaths, which were torn from her Back, and of the Diamond Ring, which during the Contention either dropped from her Finger, or was wrenched from it by *Northerton*.

Thus, Reader, we have given thee the Fruits of a very painful Enquiry, which, for thy Satisfaction, we have made into this Matter. And here we have opened to thee a Scene of Folly, as well as Villainy, which we could scarce have believed a human Creature capable of being guilty of; had we not remembered that this Fellow was at that Time firmly persuaded, that he had already committed a Murder, and had forfeited his Life to the Law. As he concluded therefore that his only Safety lay in Flight, he thought the possessing himself of this poor Woman's Money and Ring, would make him Amends for the additional Burthen he was to lay on his Conscience.

And here, Reader, we must strictly caution thee, that thou dost

not take any Occasion from the Misbehaviour of such a Wretch as
this, to reflect on so worthy and honourable a Body of Men, as are
the Officers of our Army in general. Thou wilt be pleased to consider, that this Fellow, as we have already informed thee, had neither the Birth nor Education of a Gentleman, nor was a proper
Person to be enrolled among the Number of such. If therefore his
Baseness can justly reflect on any besides himself, it must be only
on those who gave him his Commission.

BOOK X.

In which the History goes forward about Twelve Hours.

Chapter I.

*Containing Instructions very necessary to be perused by modern
Critics.*

Reader, it is impossible we should know what Sort of Person thou
wilt be: For perhaps, thou may'st be as learned in Human Nature
as *Shakespear* himself was, and, perhaps, thou may'st be no wiser
than some of his Editors. Now lest this latter should be the Case,
we think proper, before we go any farther together, to give thee a
few wholesome Admonitions; that thou may'st not as grosly misunderstand and misrepresent us, as some of the said Editors have misunderstood and misrepresented their Author.

First, then, we warn thee not too hastily to condemn any of the
Incidents in this our History, as impertinent and foreign to our
main Design, because thou dost not immediately conceive in what
Manner such Incident may conduce to that Design. This Work
may, indeed, be considered as a great Creation of our own; and for
a little Reptile of a Critic to presume to find Fault with any of its
Parts, without knowing the Manner in which the Whole is connected, and before he comes to the final Catastrophe, is a most
presumptuous Absurdity. The Allusion and Metaphor we have here
made use of, we must acknowledge to be infinitely too great for our
Occasion; but there is, indeed, no other, which is at all adequate to
express the Difference between an Author of the first Rate, and a
Critic of the lowest.

Another Caution we would give thee, my good Reptile, is, that
thou dost not find out too near a Resemblance between certain
Characters here introduced; as for Instance, between the Landlady
who appears in the Seventh Book, and her in the Ninth. Thou art

to know, Friend, that there are certain Characteristics, in which most Individuals of every Profession and Occupation agree. To be able to preserve these Characteristics, and at the same Time to diversify their Operations, is one Talent of a good Writer. Again, to mark the nice Distinction between two Persons actuated by the same Vice or Folly is another; and as this last Talent is found in very few Writers, so is the true Discernment of it found in as few Readers; though, I believe, the Observation of this forms a very principal Pleasure in those who are capable of the Discovery: Every Person, for Instance, can distinguish between Sir *Epicure Mammon*,[1] and Sir *Fopling Flutter*; but to note the Difference between Sir *Fopling Flutter* and Sir *Courtly Nice*, requires a more exquisite Judgment: For want of which, vulgar Spectators of Plays very often do great Injustice in the Theatre; where I have sometimes known a Poet in Danger of being convicted as a Thief, upon much worse Evidence than the Resemblance of Hands hath been held to be in the Law. In Reality, I apprehend every amorous Widow on the Stage would run the Hazard of being condemned as a servile Imitation of *Dido*, but that happily very few of our Playhouse Critics understand enough of *Latin* to read *Virgil*.

In the next Place, we must admonish thee, my worthy Friend, (for, perhaps, thy Heart may be better than thy Head) not to condemn a Character as a bad one, because it is not perfectly a good one. If thou dost delight in these Models of Perfection, there are Books enow written to gratify thy Taste; but as we have not, in the course of our Conversation, ever happened to meet with any such Person, we have not chosen to introduce any such here. To say the Truth, I a little question whether mere Man ever arrived at this consummate Degree of Excellence, as well as whether there hath ever existed a Monster bad enough to verify that

$$——nulla\ virtute\ redemptum$$
$$A\ vitiis——^2$$

in *Juvenal*: Nor do I, indeed, conceive the good Purposes served by inserting Characters of such angelic Perfection, or such diabolical Depravity, in any Work of Invention: Since from contemplating either, the Mind of Man is more likely to be overwhelmed with Sorrow and Shame, than to draw any good Uses from such Patterns; for in the former Instance he may be both concerned and ashamed to see a Pattern of Excellence, in his Nature, which he may reasonably despair of ever arriving at; and in contemplating the latter, he may be no less affected with those uneasy Sensations, at seeing the

1. In Ben Jonson's *The Alchemist* (1610); Sir Fopling Flutter in Etherege's *The Man of Mode* (1676); Sir Courtly Nice in John Crowne's *Sir Courtly Nice* (1685).
2. Whose Vices are not allayed with a single Virtue [*Fielding's note*]. Juvenal, *Satires* IV.2–3.

Nature, of which he is a Partaker, degraded into so odious and detestable a Creature.

In Fact, if there be enough of Goodness in a Character to engage the Admiration and Affection of a well-disposed Mind, though there should appear some of those little Blemishes, *quas humana parum cavit natura*,[3] they will raise our Compassion rather than our Abhorrence. Indeed, nothing can be of more moral Use than the Imperfections which are seen in Examples of this Kind; since such form a Kind of Surprize, more apt to affect and dwell upon our Minds, than the Faults of very vicious and wicked Persons. The Foibles and Vices of Men in whom there is great Mixture of Good, become more glaring Objects, from the Virtues which contrast them, and shew their Deformity; and when we find such Vices attended with their evil Consequence to our favourite Characters, we are not only taught to shun them for our own Sake, but to hate them for the Mischiefs they have already brought on those we love.

And now, my Friend, having given you these few Admonitions, we will, if you please, once more set forward with our History.

Chapter II.

Containing the Arrival of an Irish Gentleman, with very extraordinary Adventures which ensued at the Inn.

Now the little trembling Hare, which the Dread of all her numerous Enemies, and chiefly of that cunning, cruel, carnivorous Animal Man, had confined all the Day to her Lurking-place, sports wantonly o'er the Lawns: Now on some hollow Tree the Owl, shrill Chorister of the Night, hoots forth Notes which might charm the Ears of some modern Connoisseurs in Music: Now in the Imagination of the half-drunk Clown, as he staggers through the Church-yard, or rather Charnel-yard, to his Home, Fear paints the bloody Hobgoblin: Now Thieves and Ruffians are awake, and honest Watchmen fast asleep: In plain *English*, it was now Midnight; and the Company at the Inn, as well those who have been already mentioned in this History, as some others who arrived in the Evening, were all in Bed. Only *Susan* Chambermaid was now stirring, she being obliged to wash the Kitchin, before she retired to the Arms of the fond, expecting Hostler.

In this Posture were Affairs at the Inn, when a Gentleman arrived there Post. He immediately alighted from his Horse, and coming up to *Susan*, enquired of her, in a very abrupt and confused Manner, being almost out of Breath with Eagerness, whether there

---

3. "Which human nature guards against too little." Fielding has adjusted Horace's "quas aut incuria fudit, / Aut humana . . ." (*Ars Poetica* 352-53) to fit into his sentence. See below, p. 434, for the full passage.

was any Lady in the House. The Hour of Night, and the Behaviour of the Man, who stared very wildly all the Time, a little surprized *Susan*, so that she hesitated before she made any Answer: Upon which the Gentleman, with redoubled Eagerness, begg'd her to give him a true Information, saying, he had lost his Wife, and was come in Pursuit of her. 'Upon my Shoul,' cries he, 'I have been near catching her already in two or three Places, if I had not found her gone just as I came up with her. If she be in the House, do carry me up in the Dark and shew her to me; and if she be gone away before me; do tell me which Way I shall go after her to meet her, and upon my Shoul, I will make you the richest poor Woman in the Nation.' He then pulled out a Handful of Guineas, a Sight which would have bribed Persons of much greater Consequence than this poor Wench, to much worse Purposes.

Susan, from the Account she had received of Mrs. *Waters*, made not the least Doubt but that she was the very identical Stray whom the right Owner pursued. As she concluded, therefore, with great Appearance of Reason, that she never could get Money in an honester Way than by restoring a Wife to her Husband, she made no Scruple of assuring the Gentleman, that the Lady he wanted was then in the House; and was presently afterwards prevailed upon (by very liberal Promises, and some Earnest paid into her Hands) to conduct him to the Bed-chamber of Mrs. *Waters*.

It hath been a Custom long established in the polite World, and that upon very solid and substantial Reasons, that a Husband shall never enter his Wife's Apartment without first knocking at the Door. The many excellent Uses of this Custom need scarce be hinted to a Reader who hath any Knowledge of the World: For by this Means the Lady hath Time to adjust herself, or to remove any disagreeable Object out of the Way; for there are some Situations, in which nice and delicate Women would not be discovered by their Husbands.

To say the Truth, there are several Ceremonies instituted among the polished Part of Mankind, which, tho' they may, to coarser Judgments, appear as Matters of mere Form, are found to have much of Substance in them, by the more discerning; and lucky would it have been, had the Custom abovementioned been observed by our Gentleman in the present Instance. Knock, indeed, he did at the Door, but not with one of those gentle Raps which is usual on such Occasions. On the contrary, when he found the Door locked, he flew at it with such Violence, that the Lock immediately gave Way, the Door burst open, and he fell headlong into the Room.

He had no sooner recovered his Legs, than forth from the Bed, upon his Legs likewise appeared——with Shame and Sorrow are we obliged to proceed——our Heroe himself, who, with a menacing

Voice, demanded of the Gentleman who he was, and what he meant by daring to burst open his Chamber in that outrageous Manner.

The Gentleman at first thought he had committed a Mistake, and was going to ask Pardon and retreat, when, on a sudden, as the Moon shone very bright, he cast his Eyes on Stays, Gowns, Petti-coats, Caps, Ribbons, Stockings, Garters, Shoes, Clogs, &c. all which lay in a disordered Manner on the Floor. All these operating on the natural Jealousy of his Temper, so enraged him, that he lost all Power of Speech; and without returning any Answer to *Jones*, he endeavoured to approach the Bed.

Jones immediately interposing, a fierce Contention arose, which soon proceeded to Blows on both Sides. And now Mrs. *Waters* (for we must confess she was in the same Bed) being, I suppose, awak-ened from her Sleep, and seeing two Men fighting in her Bedcham-ber, began to scream in the most violent Manner, crying out Murder! Robbery! and more frequently Rape! which last, some, per-haps, may wonder she should mention, who do not consider that these Words of Exclamation are used by Ladies in a Fright, as Fa, la, la, ra, da, &c. are in Music, only as the Vehicles of Sound, and without any fixed Ideas.

Next to the Lady's Chamber was deposited the Body of an *Irish* Gentleman, who arrived too late at the Inn to have been mentioned before. This Gentleman was one of those whom the *Irish* call a Cal-abalaro, or Cavalier. He was a younger Brother of a good Family, and having no Fortune at Home, was obliged to look abroad in order to get one: For which Purpose he was proceeding to the *Bath* to try his Luck with Cards and the Women.

This young Fellow lay in Bed reading one of Mrs. *Behn's*[1] Novels; for he had been instructed by a Friend, that he would find no more effectual Method of recommending himself to the Ladies than the improving his Understanding, and filling his Mind with good Literature. He no sooner, therefore, heard the violent Uproar in the next Room, than he leapt from his Bolster, and taking his Sword in one Hand, and the Candle which burnt by him in the other, he went directly to Mrs. *Waters's* Chamber.

If the Sight of another Man in his Shirt at first added some Shock to the Decency of the Lady, it made her presently Amends by con-siderably abating her Fears; for no sooner had the Calabalaro enter'd the Room, than he cry'd out: 'Mr. *Fitzpatrick*, what the Devil is the *Maning* of this?' Upon which the other immediately answered, 'O, Mr. *Macklachlan*, I am rejoiced you are here,—This Villain hath debauched my Wife, and is got into Bed with her.'—'What Wife?' cries *Macklachlan*, 'do not I know Mrs. *Fitzpatrick* very well, and

---

1. Aphra Behn (1640–89). Fielding re-fers to her spicy romantic tales, though her *Oroonoko* (1688), the first anti-slav-ery novel, has real merit.

don't I see that the Lady, whom the Gentleman who stands here in his Shirt is lying in Bed with, is none of her?'

Fitzpatrick now perceiving, as well by the Glimpse he had of the Lady, as by her Voice, which might have been distinguished at a greater Distance than he now stood from her, that he had made a very unfortunate Mistake, began to ask many Pardons of the Lady; and then turning to *Jones* he said, 'I would have you take Notice I do not ask your Pardon, for you have *bate* me; for which I am resolved to have your Blood in the Morning.'

Jones treated this Menace with much Contempt; and Mr. *Macklachlan* answered, 'Indeed, Mr. *Fitzpatrick*, you may be ashamed of your ownself, to disturb People at this Time of Night: If all the People in the Inn were not asleep, you would have awakened them as you have me. The Gentleman has served you very rightly. Upon my Conscience, tho' I have no Wife, if you had treated her so, I would have cut your Throat.'

Jones was so confounded with his Fears for his Lady's Reputation, that he knew neither what to say or do; but the Invention of Women is, as hath been observed, much readier than that of Men. She recollected that there was a Communication between her Chamber and that of Mr. *Jones*; relying, therefore, on his Honour and her own Assurance, she answered, 'I know not what you mean, Villains! I am Wife to none of you. Help! Rape! Murder! Rape!'— And now the Landlady coming into the Room, Mrs. W*aters* fell upon her with the utmost Virulence, saying, 'She thought herself in a sober Inn, and not in a Bawdy House; but that a Set of Villains had broke into her Room, with an Intent upon her Honour, if not upon her Life; and both, she said, were equally dear to her.'

The Landlady now began to roar as loudly as the poor Woman in Bed had done before. She cry'd, 'She was undone, and that the Reputation of her House, which was never blown upon before, was utterly destroyed.' Then turning to the Men, she cry'd, 'What, in the Devil's Name, is the Reason of all this Disturbance in the Lady's Room?' *Fitzpatrick*, hanging down his Head, repeated, 'that he had committed a Mistake, for which he heartily asked Pardon,' and then retired with his Countryman. *Jones*, who was too ingenious to have missed the Hint given him by his Fair One, boldly asserted, 'That he had run to her Assistance upon hearing the Door broke open; with what Design he could not conceive, unless of robbing the Lady; which if they intended, he said, he had the good Fortune to prevent.' 'I never had a Robbery committed in my House since I have kept it,' cries the Landlady: 'I wou'd have you to know, Sir, I harbour no Highwaymen here; I scorn the Word, thof I say it. None but honest, good Gentlefolks, are welcome to my House; and, I thank good Luck, I have always had enow of such Customers; indeed as many as I could entertain. Here hath been my

Lord——' and then she repeated over a Catalogue of Names and Titles, many of which we might, perhaps, be guilty of a Breach of Privilege by inserting.

Jones, after much Patience, at length interrupted her, by making an Apology to Mrs. *Waters*, for having appeared before her in his Shirt, assuring her, 'That nothing but a Concern for her Safety could have prevailed on him to do it.' The Reader may inform himself of her Answer, and, indeed, of her whole Behaviour to the End of the Scene, by considering the Situation which she affected, it being that of a modest Lady, who was awakened out of her Sleep by three strange Men in her Chamber. This was the Part which she undertook to perform; and, indeed, she executed it so well, that none of our Theatrical Actresses could exceed her, in any of their Performances, either on or off the Stage.

And hence, I think, we may very fairly draw an Argument, to prove how extremely natural Virtue is to the Fair Sex: For tho' there is not, perhaps, one in ten thousand who is capable of making a good Actress; and even among these we rarely see two who are equally able to personate the same Character; yet this of Virtue they can all admirably well put on; and as well those Individuals who have it not, as those who possess it, can all act it to the utmost Degree of Perfection.

When the Men were all departed, Mrs. *Waters* recovering from her Fear, recovered likewise from her Anger, and spoke in much gentler Accents to the Landlady, who did not so readily quit her Concern for the Reputation of the House, in Favour of which she began again to number the many great Persons who had slept under her Roof; but the Lady stopt her short, and having absolutely acquitted her of having had any Share in the past Disturbance, begged to be left to her Repose, which, she said, she hoped to enjoy unmolested during the Remainder of the Night. Upon which the Landlady, after much Civility, and many Courtisies, took her Leave.

Chapter III.

A Dialogue between the Landlady, and Susan *the Chambermaid, proper to be read by all Innkeepers and their Servants; with the Arrival, and affable Behaviour of a beautiful young Lady; which may teach Persons of Condition how they may acquire the Love of the whole World.*

The Landlady remembering that *Susan* had been the only Person out of Bed when the door was burst open, resorted presently to her, to enquire into the first Occasion of the Disturbance, as well as who the strange Gentleman was, and when and how he arrived.

Susan related the whole Story which the Reader knows already, varying the Truth only in some Circumstances, as she saw convenient, and totally concealing the Money which she had received. But whereas her Mistress had in the Preface to her Enquiry spoken much in Compassion for the Fright which the Lady had been in, concerning any intended Depredations on her Virtue, *Susan* could not help endeavouring to quiet the Concern which her Mistress seemed to be under on that Account, by swearing heartily she saw *Jones* leap out from her Bed.

The Landlady fell into a violent Rage at these Words. 'A likely Story truly,' cried she, 'that a Woman should cry out, and endeavour to expose herself, if that was the Case! I desire to know what better Proof any Lady can give of her Virtue than her crying out, which, I believe, twenty People can witness for her she did? I beg, Madam, you would spread no such Scandal of any of my Guests: For it will not only reflect on them, but upon the House; and I am sure no Vagabonds, nor wicked beggarly People come here.'

'Well,' says *Susan*, 'then I must not believe my own Eyes.' 'No, indeed must you not always,' answered her Mistress, 'I would not have believed my own Eyes against such good Gentlefolks. I have not had a better Supper ordered this half Year than they ordered last Night; and so easy and good-humoured were they, that they found no Fault with my *Worcestershire* Perry, which I sold them for *Champagne*; and to be sure it is as well tasted, and as wholesome as the best *Champagne* in the Kingdom, otherwise I would scorn to give it 'em, and they drank me two Bottles. No, no, I will never believe any Harm of such sober good Sort of People.'

Susan being thus silenced, her Mistress proceeded to other Matters. 'And so you tell me,' continued she, 'that the strange Gentleman came Post, and there is a Footman without with the Horses; why then, he is certainly some of your great Gentlefolks too. Why did not you ask him whether he'd have any Supper? I think he is in the other Gentleman's Room; go up and ask whether he called. Perhaps he'll order something when he finds any Body stirring in the House to dress it. Now don't commit any of your usual Blunders, by telling him the Fire's out, and the Fowls alive. And if he should order Mutton, don't blab out, that we have none. The Butcher, I know, killed a Sheep just before I went to Bed, and he never refuses to cut it up warm when I desire it. Go, remember there's all Sorts of Mutton and Fowls; go, open the Door, with, *Gentlemen d'ye call*; and if they say nothing, ask what his Honour will be pleased to have for Supper. Don't forget his Honour. Go; if you don't mind all these Matters better, you'll never come to any Thing.'

Susan departed, and soon returned with an Account, that the two Gentlemen were got both into the same Bed. 'Two Gentlemen,' says the Landlady, 'in the same Bed! that's impossible; they are two errant Scrubs, I warrant them; and, I believe young Squire *Allwor-thy* guessed right, that the Fellow intended to rob her Ladyship: For if he had broke open the Lady's Door with any of the wicked Designs of a Gentleman, he would never have sneaked away to another Room to save the Expence of a Supper and a Bed to himself. They are certainly Thieves, and their searching after a Wife is nothing but a Pretence.'

In these Censures, my Landlady did Mr. *Fitzpatrick* great Injustice; for he was really born a Gentleman, though not worth a Groat; and tho', perhaps, he had some few Blemishes in his Heart as well as in his Head, yet being a sneaking, or a niggardly Fellow, was not one of them. In reality, he was so generous a Man, that whereas he had received a very handsome Fortune with his Wife, he had now spent every Penny of it, except some little Pittance which was settled upon her; and in order to possess himself of this, he had used her with such Cruelty, that together with his Jealousy, which was of the bitterest Kind, it had forced the poor Woman to run away from him.

This Gentleman then being well tired with his long Journey from *Chester* in one Day, with which, and some good dry Blows he had received in the Scuffle, his Bones were so sore, that added to the Soreness of his Mind, it had quite deprived him of any Appetite for eating. And being now so violently disappointed in the Woman, whom at the Maid's Instance, he had mistaken for his Wife, it never once entered into his Head, that she might nevertheless be in the House, though he had erred in the first Person he had attacked. He therefore yielded to the Dissuasions of his Friend from searching any farther after her that Night, and accepted the kind Offer of Part of his Bed.

The Footman and Post-boy were in a different Disposition. They were more ready to order than the Landlady was to provide; however, after being pretty well satisfied by them of the real Truth of the Case, and that Mr. *Fitzpatrick* was no Thief, she was at length prevailed on to set some cold Meat before them, which they were devouring with great Greediness, when *Partridge* came into the Kitchin. He had been first awaked by the Hurry which we have before seen; and while he was endeavouring to compose himself again on his Pillow, a Screech-Owl had given him such a Serenade at his Window, that he leapt in a most horrible Affright from his Bed, and huddling on his Cloaths with great Expedition, ran down to the Protection of the Company, whom he heard talking below in the Kitchin.

His Arrival detained my Landlady from returning to her Rest: For she was just about to leave the other two Guests to the Care of *Susan*; but the Friend of young Squire *Allworthy* was not to be so neglected, especially as he called for a Pint of Wine to be mulled. She immediately obeyed; by putting the same Quantity of Perry to the Fire: For this readily answered to the Name of every Kind of Wine.

The *Irish* Footman was retired to Bed, and the Post-boy was going to follow; but *Partridge* invited him to stay, and partake of his Wine, which the Lad very thankfully accepted. The Schoolmaster was indeed afraid to return to Bed by himself; and as he did not know how soon he might lose the Company of my Landlady, he was resolved to secure that of the Boy, in whose Presence he apprehended no Danger from the Devil, or any of his Adherents.

And now arrived another Post-boy at the Gate; upon which *Susan* being ordered out, returned, introducing two young Women in Riding-habits, one of which was so very richly laced, that *Partridge* and the Post-boy instantly started from their Chairs, and my Landlady fell to her Court'sies, and her Ladyships, with great Eagerness.

The Lady in the rich Habit said, with a Smile of great Condescension, 'If you will give me Leave, Madam, I will warm myself a few Minutes at your Kitchin Fire; for it is really very cold; but I must insist on disturbing no one from his Seat.' This was spoken on Account of *Partridge*, who had retreated to the other End of the Room, struck with the utmost Awe and Astonishment at the Splendor of the Lady's Dress. Indeed she had a much better Title to Respect than this: For she was one of the most beautiful Creatures in the World.

The Lady earnestly desired *Partridge* to return to his Seat, but could not prevail. She then pulled off her Gloves, and displayed to the Fire two Hands, which had every Property of Snow in them, except that of melting. Her Companion, who was indeed her Maid, likewise pulled off her Gloves, and discovered what bore an exact Resemblance, in Cold and Colour, to a Piece of frozen Beef.

'I wish, Madam,' quoth the latter, 'your Ladyship would not think of going any farther To-night. I am terribly afraid your Ladyship will not be able to bear the Fatigue.'

'Why sure,' cries the Landlady, 'her Ladyship's Honour can never intend it. O bless me, farther To-night indeed! Let me beseech your Ladyship not to think on't.——But to be sure, your Ladyship can't. What will your Honour be pleased to have for Supper? I have Mutton of all Kinds, and some nice Chicken.'

'I think, Madam,' said the Lady, 'it would be rather Breakfast than Supper; but I can't eat any Thing; and if I stay, shall only lie down for an Hour or two. However, if you please, Madam, you may get me a little Sack-whey, made very small and thin.'

'Yes, Madam,' cries the Mistress of the House, 'I have some

excellent White-wine.' 'You have no Sack then,' says the Lady. 'Yes, an't please your Honour, I have; I may challenge the Country for that—But let me beg your Ladyship to eat something.'

'Upon my Word, I can't eat a Morsel,' answered the Lady; 'and I shall be much obliged to you, if you will please to get my Apartment ready as soon as possible: For I am resolved to be on Horseback again in three Hours.'

'Why *Susan,*' cries the Landlady, 'is there a Fire lit yet in the *Wild-goose?*——I am sorry, Madam, all my best Rooms are full. Several People of the first Quality are now in Bed. Here's a great young Squire, and many other great Gentlefolks of Quality.'

Susan answered, 'That the *Irish* Gentlemen were got into the *Wild-goose.*'

'Was ever any Thing like it!' says the Mistress; 'why the Devil would you not keep some of the best Rooms for the Quality, when you know scarce a Day passes without some calling here?—If they be Gentlemen, I am certain, when they know it is for her Ladyship, they will get up again.'

'Not upon my Account,' says the Lady; 'I will have no Person disturbed for me. If you have a Room that is commonly decent, it will serve me very well, though it be never so plain. I beg, Madam, you will not give yourself so much Trouble on my Account.' 'O, Madam,' cries the other, 'I have several very good Rooms for that Matter, but none good enough for your Honour's Ladyship. However, as you are so condescending to take up with the best I have, do, *Susan,* get a Fire in the *Rose* this Minute. Will your Ladyship be pleased to go up now, or stay till the Fire is lighted?' 'I think, I have sufficiently warmed myself,' answered the Lady; 'so if you please I will go now; I am afraid I have kept People, and particularly that Gentleman (meaning *Partridge*) too long in the Cold already. Indeed I cannot bear to think of keeping any Person from the Fire this dreadful Weather.' She then departed with her Maid, the Landlady marching with two lighted Candles before her.

When that good Woman returned, the Conversation in the Kitchin was all upon the Charms of the young Lady. There is indeed in perfect Beauty a Power which none almost can withstand: For my Landlady, though she was not pleased at the Negative given to the Supper, declared she had never seen so lovely a Creature. *Partridge* ran out into the most extravagant Encomiums on her Face, though he could not refrain from paying some Compliments to the Gold Lace on her Habit: The Post-boy sung forth the Praises of her Goodness, which were likewise echoed by the other Post-boy, who was now come in. 'She's a true good Lady, I warrant her,' says he: 'For she hath Mercy upon dumb Creatures; for she asked me every now and tan upon the Journey, if I did not

think she should hurt the Horses by riding too fast; and when she
came in, she charged me to give them as much Corn as ever they
would eat.'

Such Charms are there in Affability, and so sure is it to attract
the Praises of all Kinds of People. It may indeed be compared to
the celebrated Mrs. *Hussey*.[1] It is equally sure to set off every
Female Perfection to the highest Advantage, and to palliate and
conceal every Defect. A short Reflection which we could not forbear
making in this Place, where my Reader hath seen the Loveliness of
an affable Deportment; and Truth will now oblige us to contrast it,
by shewing the Reverse.

1. A celebrated Mantua-maker in the
Strand, famous for setting off the Shapes
of Women [*Fielding's note*]. (A "mantua" is a dress.)

"One day, Mr. Fielding observed to
Mrs. Hussey, that he was then engaged
in writing a novel, which he thought
would be his best production; and that
he intended to introduce in it the characters of all his friends. Mrs. Hussey,
with a smile, ventured to remark, that
he must have many niches, and that
surely they must already be filled. 'I assure you, my dear Madam,' replied he,
'there shall be a bracket for a bust of
you.' Sometime after this, he informed
Mrs. Hussey, that the work was in the
press; but, immediately recollecting that
he had forgotten his promise to her,
went to the printer, and was time
enough to insert, in vol. iii p. 17, where
he speaks of the shape of Sophia Western—" [here follow Fielding's text and
footnote]. John Thomas Smith, I.125 n.
See above, p. 374, note 3.

Chapter IV.

Containing infallible Nostrums for procuring universal Disesteem and Hatred.

The Lady had no sooner laid herself on her Pillow, than the
Waiting-woman returned to the Kitchin to regale with some of
those Dainties which her Mistress had refused.

The Company, at her Entrance, shewed her the same Respect
which they had before paid to her Mistress, by rising; but she forgot
to imitate her, by desiring them to sit down again. Indeed it was
scarce possible they should have done so: For she placed her Chair
in such a Posture, as to occupy almost the whole Fire. She then
ordered a Chicken to be broiled that Instant, declaring if it was
not ready in a Quarter of an Hour, she would not stay for it. Now
tho' the said Chicken was then at Roost in the Stable, and required
the several Ceremonies of catching, killing, and picking, before it
was brought to the Grid-iron, my Landlady would nevertheless have
undertaken to do all within the Time; but the Guest being unfortunately admitted behind the Scenes, must have been Witness to
the *Fourberie*;[1] the poor Woman was therefore obliged to confess
that she had none in the House; 'but, Madam,' said she, 'I can get
any kind of Mutton in an Instant from the Butcher's.'

1. A fraud.

'Do you think then,' answered the Waiting-Gentlewoman, 'that I have the Stomach of a Horse to eat Mutton at this Time of Night? Sure you People that keep Inns imagine your Betters are like yourselves. Indeed I expected to get nothing at this wretched Place. I wonder my Lady would stop at it. I suppose none but Tradesmen and Grasiers ever call here.' The Landlady fired at this Indignity offered to her House; however she suppressed her Temper, and contented herself with saying, 'Very good Quality frequented it, she thanked Heaven!' 'Don't tell me,' cries the other, 'of Quality! I believe I know more of People of Quality than such as you.—But, prithee, without troubling me with any of your Impertinence, do tell me what I can have for Supper; for tho' I cannot eat Horse-flesh, I am really hungry.' 'Why truly, Madam,' answered the Landlady, 'you could not take me again at such a Disadvantage: For I must confess, I have nothing in the House, unless a cold Piece of Beef, which indeed a Gentleman's Footman and the Post-boy have almost cleared to the Bone.' 'Woman,' said Mrs. *Abigail,* (so for Shortness we will call her) 'I intreat you not to make me sick. If I had fasted a Month, I could not eat what had been touched by the Fingers of such Fellows: Is there nothing neat or decent to be had in this horrid Place?' 'What think you of some Eggs and Bacon, Madam,' said the Landlady. 'Are your Eggs new laid? Are you certain they were laid To-day? and let me have the Bacon cut very nice and thin; for I can't endure any Thing that's gross.—Prithee try if you can do a little tolerably for once, and don't think you have a Farmer's Wife, or some of those Creatures in the House.'— The Landlady began then to handle her Knife; but the other stopt her, saying, 'Good Woman, I must insist upon your first washing your Hands; for I am extremely nice, and have been always used from my Cradle to have every thing in the most elegant Manner.'

The Landlady, who governed herself with much Difficulty, began now the necessary Preparations; for as to *Susan,* she was utterly rejected, and with such Disdain that the poor Wench was as hard put to it, to restrain her Hands from Violence, as her Mistress had been to hold her Tongue. This indeed *Susan* did not entirely: For tho' she literally kept it within her Teeth, yet there it muttered many 'marry-come-ups, as good Flesh and Blood as yourself,' with other such indignant Phrases.

While the Supper was preparing, Mrs. *Abigail* began to lament she had not ordered a Fire in the Parlour; but she said, that was now too late, 'However,' said she, 'I have Novelty to recommend a Kitchin; for I do not believe I ever eat in one before.' Then turning to the Post-boys, she asked them, 'Why they were not in the Stable with their Horses? If I must eat my hard Fare here, Madam,' cries she to the Landlady, 'I beg the Kitchin may be kept clear, that I may not be surrounded with all the Black-guards in Town: As for you, Sir,' says she to *Partridge*, 'you look somewhat like a Gentleman, and may sit still if you please; I don't desire to disturb any body but Mob.'

'Yes, yes, Madam,' cries *Partridge*, 'I am a Gentleman, I do assure you, and I am not so easily to be disturbed. *Non semper vox casualis est verbo nominativus.*[2] This *Latin* she took to be some Affront, and answered, 'You may be a Gentleman, Sir; but you don't shew yourself as one, to talk *Latin* to a Woman.' *Partridge* made a gentle Reply, and concluded with more *Latin*; upon which she tossed up her Nose, and contented herself by abusing him with the Name of a great Scholar.

The Supper being now on the Table, Mrs. *Abigail* eat very heartily, for so delicate a Person; and while a second Course of the same was by her Order preparing, she said, 'And so, Madam, you tell me your House is frequented by People of great Quality?'

The Landlady answered in the Affirmative, saying, 'There were a great many very good Quality and Gentlefolks in it now. There's young Squire *Allworthy*, as that Gentleman there knows.'

'And pray who is this young Gentleman of Quality, this young Squire *Allworthy*?' said *Abigail*.

'Who should he be,' answered *Partridge*, 'but the Son and Heir of the great Squire *Allworthy*, of *Somersetshire*.'

'Upon my Word,' said she, 'you tell me strange News: For I know Mr. *Allworthy* of *Somersetshire* very well, and I know he hath no Son alive.'

The Landlady pricked up her Ears at this, and *Partridge* looked a little confounded. However, after a short Hesitation, he answered, 'Indeed, Madam, it is true, every body doth not know him to be Squire *Allworthy*'s Son; for he was never married to his Mother; but his Son he certainly is, and will be his Heir too as certainly as his Name is *Jones*.' At that word, *Abigail* let drop the Bacon, which she was conveying to her Mouth, and cried out, 'You surprize me, Sir. Is it possible Mr. *Jones* should be now in the House?' '*Quare non?*'[3] answered *Partridge*, 'it is possible, and it is certain.'

Abigail now made Haste to finish the Remainder of her Meal, and then repaired back to her Mistress, when the Conversation passed, which may be read in the next Chapter.

---

2. "The nominative for the verb is not always a case-taking word [but sometimes an infinitive verbl." Lily, p. 137, part of the text concerning the "first concord" between subjects and verbs, at the beginning of the "Syntaxis," a section of the grammar that Partridge (and Fielding) knows particularly well. See above, p. 4 and note 2, p. 62, and below, note 2, p. 519.
3. "Why not?"

Chapter V.

Shewing who the amiable Lady, and her unamiable Maid, were.

As in the Month of *June*, the Damask Rose, which Chance hath planted among the Lilies, with their candid Hue mixes his Vermilion: Or, as some playsome Heifer in the pleasant Month of *May* diffuses her odoriferous Breath over the flowery Meadows: Or as, in the blooming Month of *April*, the gentle, constant Dove, perched on some fair Bough, sits meditating on her Mate; so looking a hundred Charms and breathing as many Sweets, her Thoughts being fixed on her *Tommy*, with a Heart as good and innocent, as her Face was beautiful: *Sophia* (for it was she herself) lay reclining her lovely Head on her Hand, when her Maid entered the Room, and running directly to the Bed, cried, 'Madam—Madam—who doth your Ladyship think is in the House?' *Sophia* starting up, cried, 'I hope my Father hath not overtaken us.' 'No, Madam, it is one worth a hundred Fathers; Mr. *Jones* himself is here at this very Instant.' 'Mr. *Jones!*' says *Sophia*, 'it is impossible; I cannot be so fortunate.' Her Maid averred the Fact, and was presently detached by her Mistress to order him to be called; for she said she was resolved to see him immediately.

Mrs. *Honour* had no sooner left the Kitchin in the manner we have before seen, than the Landlady fell severely upon her. The poor Woman had indeed been loading her Heart with foul Language for some Time, and now it scoured out of her Mouth, as Filth doth from a Mud-Cart, when the Board which confines it is removed. *Partridge* likewise shovelled in his Share of Calumny; and (what may surprize the Reader) not only bespattered the Maid, but attempted to sully the Lily-white Character of *Sophia* herself. 'Never a Barrel the better Herring,' cries he. '*Noscitur a socio*,[1] is a true Saying. It must be confessed indeed that the Lady in the fine Garments is the civiller of the two; but I warrant neither of them are a Bit better than they should be. A Couple of *Bath* Trulls, I'll answer for them; your Quality don't ride about at this Time o'Night without Servants.' 'Sbodlikins, and that's true,' cries the Landlady, 'you have certainly hit upon the very Matter; for Quality don't come into a House without bespeaking a Supper, whether they eat or no.'

While they were thus discoursing, Mrs. *Honour* returned, and discharged her Commission, by bidding the Landlady immediately wake Mr. *Jones*, and tell him a Lady wanted to speak with him. The Landlady referred her to *Partridge*, saying, 'he was the Squire's Friend; but, for her Part, she never called Men-folks, especially

1. "He is known by his company" (proverbial).

Gentlemen,' and then walked sullenly out of the Kitchin. *Honour*
applied herself to *Partridge*; but he refused; 'For my Friend,' cries
he, 'went to Bed very late, and he would be very angry to be disturbed so soon.' Mrs. *Honour* insisted still to have him called,
saying, 'she was sure, instead of being angry, that he would be to
the highest Degree delighted when he knew the Occasion.' 'Another
Time, perhaps, he might,' cries *Partridge*; 'but *non omnia possumus
omnes*.[2] One Woman is enough at once for a reasonable Man.'
'What do you mean by one Woman, Fellow?' cries *Honour*. 'None
of your Fellow,' answered *Partridge*. He then proceeded to inform
her plainly, that *Jones* was in Bed with a Wench, and made use of
an Expression too indelicate to be here inserted; which so enraged
Mrs. *Honour*, that she called him Jackanapes, and returned in a violent Hurry to her Mistress, whom she acquainted with the Success
of her Errand, and with the Account she had received; which, if
possible, she exaggerated, being as angry with *Jones* as if she had
pronounced all the Words that came from the Mouth of *Partridge*.
She discharged a Torrent of Abuse on the Master, and advised her
Mistress to quit all Thoughts of a Man who had never shewn himself deserving of her. She then ripped up the Story of *Molly Seagrim*, and gave the most malicious Turn to his formerly quitting
Sophia herself; which, I must confess, the present Incident not a
little countenanced.

The Spirits of *Sophia* were too much dissipated by Concern to
enable her to stop the Torrent of her Maid. At last, however, she
interrupted her, saying, 'I never can believe this; some Villain hath
belied him. You say you had it from his Friend; but surely it is not
the Office of a Friend to betray such Secrets.' 'I suppose,' cries
Honour, 'the Fellow is his Pimp; for I never saw so ill-looked a Villain. Besides, such profligate Rakes as Mr. *Jones* are never ashamed
of these Matters.'

To say the Truth, this Behaviour of *Partridge* was a little inexcusable; but he had not slept off the Effect of the Dose which he swallowed the Evening before; which had, in the Morning, received the
Addition of above a Pint of Wine, or indeed rather of Malt Spirits;
for the Perry was by no means pure. Now that Part of his Head
which Nature designed for the Reservoir of Drink, being very shallow, a small Quantity of Liquor overflowed it, and opened the
Sluices of his Heart; so that all the Secrets there deposited run out.
These Sluices were indeed naturally very ill secured. To give the
best natured Turn we can to his Disposition, he was a very honest
Man; for as he was the most inquisitive of Mortals, and eternally
prying into the Secrets of others; so he very faithfully paid them by
communicating, in Return, every thing within his Knowledge.

2. See above, note 3, p. 314.

While *Sophia,* tormented with Anxiety, knew not what to believe, nor what Resolution to take, *Susan* arrived with the Sack-whey. Mrs. *Honour* immediately advised her Mistress, in a Whisper, to pump this Wench, who probably could inform her of the Truth. *Sophia* approved it, and began as follows: 'Come hither, Child, now answer me truly what I am going to ask you, and I promise you I will very well reward you. Is there a young Gentleman in this House, a handsome young Gentleman that—' Here *Sophia* blushed and was confounded——'A young Gentleman,' cries *Honour,* 'that came hither in Company with that saucy Rascal who is now in the Kitchin?' *Susan* answered, 'There was.'—'Do you know any Thing of any Lady?' continues *Sophia,* 'any Lady? I don't ask you whether she is handsome or no; perhaps she is not, that's nothing to the Purpose; but do you know of any Lady?' 'La, Madam,' cries *Honour,* 'you will make a very bad Examiner. Harkee, Child,' says she, 'is not that very young Gentleman now in Bed with some nasty Trull or other?' Here *Susan* smiled, and was silent. 'Answer the Question, Child,' says *Sophia,* 'and here's a Guinea for you.' 'A Guinea! Madam,' cries *Susan;* 'La, what's a Guinea? If my Mistress should know it, I shall certainly lose my Place that very Instant.' 'Here's another for you,' says *Sophia,* 'and I promise you faithfully your Mistress shall never know it.' *Susan,* after a very short Hesitation, took the Money, and told the whole Story, concluding with saying, 'If you have any great Curiosity, Madam, I can steal softly into his Room, and see whether he be in his own Bed or no.' She accordingly did this by *Sophia's* Desire, and returned with an Answer in the Negative.

Sophia now trembled and turned pale. Mrs. *Honour* begged her to be comforted, and not to think any more of so worthless a Fellow. 'Why there,' says *Susan,* 'I hope, Madam, your Ladyship won't be offended; but pray, Madam, is not your Ladyship's Name Madam *Sophia Western?'* 'How is it possible you should know me?' answered *Sophia.* 'Why that Man that the Gentlewoman spoke of, who is in the Kitchin, told about you last Night. But I hope your Ladyship is not angry with me.' 'Indeed, Child,' said she, 'I am not; pray tell me all, and I promise you I'll reward you.' 'Why, Madam,' continued *Susan,* 'that Man told us all in the Kitchin, that Madam *Sophia Western*—Indeed I don't know how to bring it out.'—Here she stopt, till having received Encouragement from *Sophia,* and being vehemently pressed by Mrs. *Honour,* she proceeded thus:— 'He told us, Madam, tho' to be sure it is all a Lie, that your Ladyship was dying for Love of the young Squire, and that he was going to the Wars to get rid of you. I thought to myself then he was a false-hearted Wretch; but now to see such a fine, rich, beautiful Lady as you be, forsaken for such an ordinary Woman; for to be sure so she is, and another Man's Wife into the Bargain. It is such a strange unnatural Thing, in a Manner.'

Sophia gave her a third Guinea, and telling her she would certainly be her Friend, if she mentioned nothing of what had passed, nor informed any one who she was, dismissed the Girl with Orders to the Post-Boy to get the Horses ready immediately.

Being now left alone with her Maid, she told her trusty Waiting-Woman, 'That she never was more easy than at present. I am now convinced,' said she, 'he is not only a Villain, but a low despicable Wretch. I can forgive all rather than his exposing my Name in so barbarous a Manner. That renders him the Object of my Contempt. Yes, *Honour*, I am now easy. I am indeed. I am very easy;' and then she burst into a violent Flood of Tears.

After a short Interval, spent by *Sophia*, chiefly in crying, and assuring her Maid that she was perfectly easy, *Susan* arrived with an Account that the Horses were ready, when a very extraordinary Thought suggested itself to our young Heroine, by which Mr. *Jones* would be acquainted with her having been at the Inn, in a Way, which, if any Sparks of Affection for her remained in him, would be at least some Punishment for his Faults.

The Reader will be pleased to remember a little Muff, which hath had the Honour of being more than once remembered already in this History. This Muff, ever since the Departure of Mr. *Jones*, had been the constant Companion of *Sophia* by Day, and her Bed-fellow by Night; and this Muff she had at this very Instant upon her Arm; whence she took it off with great Indignation, and having writ her Name with her Pencil upon a Piece of Paper which she pinned to it, she bribed the Maid to convey it into the empty Bed of Mr. *Jones*, in which, if he did not find it, she charged her to take some Method of conveying it before his Eyes in the Morning.

Then having paid for what Mrs. *Honour* had eaten, in which Bill was included an Account for what she herself might have eaten, she mounted her Horse, and once more assuring her Companion that she was perfectly easy, continued her Journey.

Chapter VI.

Containing, among other Things, the Ingenuity of Partridge, *the Madness of* Jones, *and the Folly of* Fitzpatrick.

It was now past Five in the Morning, and other Company began to rise and come to the Kitchin, among whom were the Serjeant and the Coachman, who being thoroughly reconciled, made a Libation, or, in the *English* Phrase, drank a hearty Cup together.

In this drinking nothing more remarkable happened than the

Behaviour of *Partridge*, who, when the Serjeant drank a Health to King *George*, repeated only the Word King: Nor could he be brought to utter more; for tho' he was going to fight against his own Cause, yet he could not be prevailed upon to drink against it.

Mr. *Jones* being now returned to his own Bed, (but from whence he returned we must beg to be excused from relating) summoned *Partridge* from this agreeable Company, who, after, a ceremonious Preface, having obtained Leave to offer his Advice, delivered himself as follows:

'It is, Sir, an old Saying, and a true one, that a wise Man may sometimes learn Counsel from a Fool; I wish therefore I might be so bold as to offer you my Advice, which is to return home again, and leave these *Horrida Bella*,[1] these bloody Wars, to Fellows who are contented to swallow Gunpowder, because they have nothing else to eat. Now every body knows your Honour wants for nothing at home; when that's the Case, why should any Man travel abroad?'

'*Partridge*,' cries *Jones*, 'thou art certainly a Coward; I wish therefore thou would'st return home thyself, and trouble me no more.'

'I ask your Honour's Pardon,' cries *Partridge*, 'I spoke on your Account more than my own; for as to me, Heaven knows my Circumstances are bad enough, and I am so far from being afraid, that I value a Pistol, or a Blunderbuss, or any such Thing, no more than a Pop-gun. Every Man must die once, and what signifies the Manner how; besides, perhaps, I may come off with the Loss only of an Arm or a Leg. I assure you, Sir, I was never less afraid in my Life; and so if your Honour is resolved to go on, I am resolved to follow you. But, in that Case, I wish I might give my Opinion. To be sure it is a scandalous Way of travelling, for a great Gentleman like you to walk afoot. Now here are two or three good Horses in the Stable, which the Landlord will certainly make no Scruple of trusting you with; but if he should, I can easily contrive to take them; and let the worst come to the worst, the King would certainly pardon you, as you are going to fight in his Cause.'

Now as the Honesty of *Partridge* was equal to his Understanding, and both dealt only in small Matters, he would never have attempted a Roguery of this Kind, had he not imagined it altogether safe, for he was one of those who have more Consideration of the Gallows than of the Fitness of Things; but, in Reality, he thought he might have committed this Felony without any Danger: For, besides that he doubted not but the Name of Mr. *Allworthy* would sufficiently quiet the Landlord, he conceived they should be altogether safe, whatever Turn Affairs might take; as *Jones*, he imagined, would have Friends enough on one Side, and as his Friends would as well secure him on the other.

1. "Horrible wars." *Aeneid* VI.86.

When Mr. *Jones* found that *Partridge* was in earnest in this Proposal, he very severely rebuked him, and that in such bitter Terms, that the other attempted to laugh it off, and presently turned the Discourse to other Matters, saying, he believed they were then in a Bawdy-House, and that he had with much ado prevented two Wenches from disturbing his Honour in the Middle of the Night. 'Heyday!' says he, 'I believe they got into your Chamber whether I would or no; for here lies the Muff of one of them on the Ground.' Indeed, as *Jones* returned to his Bed in the Dark, he had never perceived the Muff on the Quilt, and in leaping into his Bed he had tumbled it on the Floor. This *Partridge* now took up, and was going to put into his Pocket, when *Jones* desired to see it. The Muff was so very remarkable, that our Heroe might possibly have recollected it without the Information annexed. But his Memory was not put to that hard Office; for at the same Instant he saw and read the Words *Sophia Western* upon the Paper which was pinned to it. His Looks now grew frantic in a Moment, and he eagerly cried out, 'Oh Heavens, how came this Muff here!' 'I know no more than your Honour,' cried *Partridge*; 'but I saw it upon the Arm of one of the Women who would have disturbed you, if I would have suffered them.' 'Where are they?' cries *Jones*, jumping out of Bed, and laying hold of his Clothes. 'Many Miles off, I believe, by this Time,' said *Partridge*. And now *Jones*, upon further Enquiry, was sufficiently assured that the Bearer of this Muff was no other than the lovely *Sophia* herself.

The Behaviour of *Jones* on this Occasion, his Thoughts, his Looks, his Words, his Actions, were such as *beggar all Description*.[2] After many bitter Execrations on *Partridge*, and not fewer on himself, he ordered the poor Fellow, who was frightened out of his Wits, to run down and hire him Horses at any Rate; and a very few Minutes afterwards, having shuffled on his Clothes, he hastened down Stairs to execute the Orders himself, which he had just before given.

But before we proceed to what passed on his Arrival in the Kitchin, it will be necessary to recur to what had there happened since *Partridge* had first left it on his Master's Summons.

The Serjeant was just marched off with his Party, when the two *Irish* Gentlemen arose, and came down Stairs; both complaining, that they had been so often waked by the Noises in the Inn, that they had never once been able to close their Eyes all Night.

The Coach, which had brought the young Lady and her Maid, and which perhaps, the Reader may have hitherto concluded was her own, was indeed a returned Coach belonging to Mr. *King* of *Bath*, one of the worthiest and honestest Men that ever dealt in

2. *Antony and Cleopatra* II.ii.203.

Horse-flesh, and whose Coaches we heartily recommend to all our
Readers who travel that Road. By which Means they may, perhaps,
have the Pleasure of riding in the very Coach, and being driven by
the very Coachman, that is recorded in this History.

The Coachman having but two Passengers, and hearing Mr.
Maclachlan was going to *Bath*, offered to carry him thither at a very
moderate Price. He was induced to this by the Report of the Hostler, who said, that the Horse which Mr. *Maclachlan* had hired
from *Worcester*, would be much more pleased with returning to his
Friends there, than to prosecute a long Journey; for that the said
Horse was rather a two-legged than a four-legged Animal.

Mr. *Maclachlan* immediately closed with the Proposal of the
Coachman, and, at the same Time, persuaded his Friend *Fitzpatrick* to accept of the fourth Place in the Coach. This conveyance
the Soreness of his Bones made more agreeable to him than a
Horse; and being well assured of meeting with his Wife at *Bath*, he
thought a little Delay would be of no Consequence.

Macklachlan, who was much the sharper Man of the two, no
sooner heard that this Lady came from *Chester*, with the other Circumstances which he learned from the Hostler, than it came into
his Head that she might possibly be his Friend's Wife; and presently acquainted him with this Suspicion, which had never once
occurred to *Fitzpatrick* himself. To say the Truth, he was one of
those Compositions which Nature makes up in too great a Hurry,
and forgets to put any Brains into their Head.

Now it happens to this Sort of Men, as to bad Hounds, who
never hit off a Fault themselves; but no sooner doth a Dog of
Sagacity open his Mouth, than they immediately do the same, and
without the Guidance of any Scent, run directly forwards as fast as
they are able. In the same Manner, the very Moment Mr. *Maclachlan* had mentioned his Apprehension, Mr. *Fitzpatrick* instantly concurred, and flew directly up Stairs to surprize his Wife before he
knew where she was; and unluckily (as Fortune loves to play Tricks
with those Gentlemen who put themselves entirely under her Conduct) ran his Head against several Doors and Posts to no Purpose.
Much kinder was she to me, when she suggested that Simile of the
Hounds, just before inserted; since the poor Wife may, on these
Occasions, be so justly compared to a hunted Hare. Like that little
wretched Animal she pricks up her Ears to listen after the Voice of
her Pursuer; like her, flies away trembling when she hears it; and
like her, is generally overtaken and destroyed in the End.

This was not however the Case at present; for after a long fruitless
Search, Mr. *Fitzpatrick* returned to the Kitchin, where, as if this
had been a real Chace, entered a Gentleman hallowing as Hunters

do when the Hounds are at a Fault. He was just alighted from his
Horse, and had many Attendants at his Heels.

Here, Reader, it may be necessary to acquaint thee with some
Matters, which, if thou dost know already, thou art wiser than I
take thee to be. And this Information thou shalt receive in the next
Chapter.

Chapter VII.

In which are concluded the Adventures that happened at the Inn at Upton.

In the first Place then, this Gentleman just arrived was no other
Person than Squire *Western* himself, who was come hither in Pursuit of his Daughter; and had he fortunately been two Hours earlier,
he had not only found her, but his Niece into the Bargain; for such
was the Wife of Mr. *Fitzpatrick*, who had run away with her five
Years before, out of the Custody of that sage Lady Madam *Western*.

Now this Lady had departed from the Inn much about at the
same Time with *Sophia*: For having been waked by the Voice of
her Husband, she had sent up for the Landlady, and being by her
apprized of the Matter, had bribed the good Woman, at an extravagant Price, to furnish her with Horses for her Escape. Such Preva-
lence had Money in this Family; and tho' the Mistress would have
turned away her Maid for a corrupt Hussy, if she had known as
much as the Reader, yet she was no more Proof against Corruption
herself than poor *Susan* had been.

Mr. *Western* and his Nephew were not known to one another;
nor indeed would the former have taken any Notice of the latter, if
he had known him; for this being a stolen Match, and consequently
an unnatural one in the Opinion of the good Squire, he had, from
the Time of her committing it, abandoned the poor young Creature, who was then no more than Eighteen, as a Monster, and had
never since suffered her to be named in his Presence.

The Kitchin was now a Scene of universal Confusion, *Western*
enquiring after his Daughter, and *Fitzpatrick* as eagerly after his
Wife, when *Jones* entered the Room, unfortunately having *Sophia*'s
Muff in his Hand.

As soon as *Western* saw *Jones*, he set up the same Holla as is
used by Sportsmen when their Game is in View. He then immediately run up and laid hold of *Jones*, crying, 'We have got the Dog
Fox, I warrant the Bitch is not far off.' The Jargon which followed
for some Minutes, where many spoke different Things at the same

Time, as it would be very difficult to describe, so would it be no less unpleasant to read.

Jones having, at length, shaken Mr. *Western* off, and some of the Company having interfered between then, our Heroe protested his Innocence as to knowing any thing of the Lady; when Parson *Supple* stepped up, and said, 'It is Folly to deny it; for why, the Marks of Guilt are in thy Hands. I will myself asseverate and bind it by an Oath, that the Muff thou bearest in thy Hand belongeth unto Madam *Sophia*; for I have frequently observed her, of later Days, to bear it about her.' 'My Daughter's Muff!' cries the Squire, in a Rage. 'Hath he got my Daughter's Muff! Bear Witness the Goods are found upon him. I'll have him before a Justice of Peace this Instant. Where is my Daughter, Villain?' 'Sir,' said *Jones*, 'I beg you would be pacified. The Muff, I acknowledge, is the young Lady's; but, upon my Honour, I have never seen her.' At these Words *Western* lost all Patience, and grew inarticulate with Rage.

Some of the Servants had acquainted *Fitzpatrick* who Mr. *Western* was. The good *Irishman* therefore thinking he had now an Opportunity to do an Act of Service to his Uncle, and by that Means might possibly obtain his Favour, stept up to *Jones*, and cried out, 'Upon my Conscience, Sir, you may be ashamed of denying your having seen the Gentleman's Daughter before my Face, when you know I found you there upon the Bed together.' Then turning to *Western*, he offered to conduct him immediately to the Room where his Daughter was; which Offer being accepted, he, the Squire, the Parson, and some others, ascended directly to Mrs. *Waters*'s Chamber, which they entered with no less Violence than Mr. *Fitzpatrick* had done before.

The poor Lady started from her Sleep with as much Amazement as Terror, and beheld at her Bed-side a Figure which might very well be supposed to have escaped out of *Bedlam*. Such Wildness and Confusion were in the Looks of Mr. *Western*: who no sooner saw the Lady, than he started back, shewing sufficiently by his Manner, before he spoke, that this was not the Person sought after.

So much more tenderly do Women value their Reputation than their Persons, that tho' the latter seemed now in more Danger than before; yet as the former was secure, the Lady screamed not with such Violence as she had done on the other Occasion. However, she no sooner found herself alone, than she abandoned all Thoughts of further Repose; and as she had sufficient Reason to be dissatisfied with her present Lodging, she dressed herself with all possible Expedition.

Mr. *Western* now proceeded to search the whole House, but to as little Purpose as he had disturbed poor Mrs. *Waters*. He then returned disconsolate into the Kitchin, where he found *Jones* in the Custody of his Servants.

This violent Uproar had raised all the People in the House, tho'
it was yet scarcely Day-light. Among these was a grave Gentleman,
who had the Honour to be in the Commission of the Peace for the
County of *Worcester*. Of which Mr. *Western* was no sooner
informed, than he offered to lay his Complaint before him. The
Justice declined executing his Office, as he said he had no Clerk
present, nor no Book about Justice Business; and that he could not
carry all the Law in his Head about stealing away Daughters, and
such sort of Things.

Here Mr. *Fitzpatrick* offered to lend him his Assistance; informing the Company that he had been himself bred to the Law. (And
indeed he had served three Years as Clerk to an Attorney in the
North of *Ireland*, when chusing a genteeler Walk in Life, he quitted his Master, came over to *England*, and set up that Business
which requires no Apprenticeship, namely, that of a Gentleman, in
which he had succeeded as hath been already partly mentioned.)

Mr. *Fitzpatrick* declared that the Law concerning Daughters was
out of the present Case; that stealing a Muff was undoubtedly
Felony, and the Goods being found upon the Person, were sufficient
Evidence of the Fact.

The Magistrate, upon the Encouragement of so learned a Coadjutor, and upon the violent Intercession of the Squire, was at length
prevailed upon to seat himself in the Chair of Justice, where being
placed, upon viewing the Muff which *Jones* still held in his Hand,
and upon the Parson's swearing it to be the Property of Mr. *Western*, he desired Mr. *Fitzpatrick* to draw up a Commitment, which
he said he would sign.

Jones now desired to be heard, which was at last, with Difficulty,
granted him. He then produced the Evidence of Mr. *Partridge*, as to
the finding it; but what was still more, *Susan* deposed that *Sophia*
herself had delivered the Muff to her, and had ordered her to
convey it into the Chamber where Mr. *Jones* had found it.

Whether a natural Love of Justice, or the extraordinary Comeliness of *Jones*, had wrought on *Susan* to make the Discovery, I will
not determine; but such were the Effects of her Evidence, that the
Magistrate, throwing himself back in his Chair, declared that the
Matter was now altogether as clear on the Side of the Prisoner, as it
had before been against him; with which the Parson concurred,
saying, The Lord forbid he should be instrumental in committing
an innocent Person to Durance. The Justice then arose, acquitted
the Prisoner, and broke up the Court.

Mr. *Western* now gave every one present a hearty Curse, and
immediately ordering his Horses, departed in Pursuit of his Daughter, without taking the least Notice of his Nephew *Fitzpatrick*, or
returning any Answer to his Claim of Kindred, notwithstanding all
the Obligations he had just received from that Gentleman. In the

Violence, moreover, of his Hurry, and of his Passion, he luckily forgot to demand the Muff of *Jones*: I say luckily; for he would have died on the Spot rather than have parted with it.

Jones likewise, with his Friend *Partridge*, set forward the Moment he had paid his Reckoning, in Quest of his lovely *Sophia*, whom he now resolved never more to abandon the Pursuit of. Nor could he bring himself even to take Leave of Mrs. *Waters*; of whom he detested the very Thoughts, as she had been, tho' not designedly, the Occasion of his missing the happiest Interview with *Sophia*, to whom he now vowed eternal Constancy.

As for Mrs. *Waters*, she took the Opportunity of the Coach which was going to *Bath*; for which Place she set out in Company with the two *Irish* Gentlemen, the Landlady kindly lending her her Clothes; in Return for which she was contented only to receive about double their Value, as a Recompence for the Loan. Upon the Road she was perfectly reconciled to Mr. *Fitzpatrick*, who was a very handsome Fellow, and indeed did all she could to console him in the Absence of his Wife.

Thus ended the many odd Adventures which Mr. *Jones* encountered at his Inn at *Upton*, where they talk, to this Day, of the Beauty and lovely Behaviour of the charming *Sophia*, by the Name of the *Somersetshire* Angel.

Chapter VIII.

In which the History goes backward.

Before we proceed any farther in our History, it may be proper to look a little back, in order to account for the extraordinary Appearance of *Sophia* and her Father at the Inn at *Upton*.

The Reader may be pleased to remember, that in the Ninth Chapter of the Seventh Book of our History, we left *Sophia*, after a long Debate between Love and Duty, deciding the Cause, as it usually, I believe, happens, in Favour of the former.

This Debate had arisen, as we have there shewn, from a Visit which her Father had just before made her, in order to force her Consent to a Marriage with *Blifil*; and which he had understood to be fully implied in her Acknowledgment, *that she neither must, nor could refuse any absolute Command of his.*

Now from this Visit the Squire retired to his Evening Potation, overjoyed at the Success he had gained with his Daughter; and as he was of a social Disposition, and willing to have Partakers in his Happiness, the Beer was ordered to flow very liberally into the Kitchin; so that before Eleven in the Evening, there was not a single

Person sober in the House, except only Mrs. *Western* herself, and the charming *Sophia*.

Early in the Morning a Messenger was dispatched to summon Mr. *Blifil*: For tho' the Squire imagined that young Gentleman had been much less acquainted than he really was, with the former Aversion of his Daughter; as he had not, however, yet received her Consent, he longed impatiently to communicate it to him, not doubting but that the intended Bride herself would confirm it with her Lips. As to the Wedding, it had the Evening before been fixed, by the Male Parties, to be celebrated on the next Morning save one.

Breakfast was now set forth in the Parlour, where Mr. *Blifil* attended, and where the Squire and his Sister likewise were assembled; and now *Sophia* was ordered to be called.

O, *Shakespear*, had I thy Pen! O, *Hogarth*, had I thy Pencil! then would I draw the Picture of the poor Serving-Man, who, with pale Countenance, staring Eyes, chattering Teeth, faultering Tongue, and trembling Limbs,

> (E'en such a Man, so faint, so spiritless,
> So dull, so dead in Look, so woe-be-gone,
> Drew *Priam*'s Curtains in the dead of Night,
> And would have told him, half his *Troy* was burn'd)[1]

enter'd the Room, and declared,—*That Madam* Sophia *was not to be found.*

'Not to be found!' cries the Squire, starting from his Chair; 'Zounds and D——nation! Blood and Fury! Where, when, how, what,—Not to be found! where?'

'La! Brother,' said Mrs. *Western*, with true political Coldness, 'you are always throwing yourself into such violent Passions for nothing. My Niece, I suppose, is only walked out into the Garden. I protest you are grown so unreasonable, that it is impossible to live in the House with you.'

'Nay, nay,' answered the Squire, returning as suddenly to himself, as he had gone from himself; 'if that be all the Matter, it signifies not much; but, upon my Soul, my Mind misgave me, when the Fellow said she was not to be found.' He then gave Orders for the Bell to be rung in the Garden, and sat himself contentedly down.

No two Things could be more the Reverse of each other than were the Brother and Sister, in most Instances; particularly in this, That as the Brother never foresaw any thing at a Distance, but was most sagacious in immediately seeing every Thing the Moment it had happened; so the Sister eternally foresaw at a Distance, but was not so quick-sighted to Objects before her Eyes. Of both these the

1. Shakespeare, *Henry the Fourth*, Part II, I.i.70–73.

Reader may have observed Examples: And, indeed, both their several Talents were excessive: For as the Sister often foresaw what
never came to pass, so the Brother often saw much more than was
actually the Truth.

This was not however the Case at present. The same Report was
brought from the Garden, as before had been brought from the
Chamber, that Madam *Sophia* was not to be found.

The Squire himself now sallied forth, and began to roar forth the
Name of *Sophia* as loudly, and in as hoarse a Voice, as whilome did
Hercules[2] that of *Hylas:* And as the Poet tells us, that the whole
Shore echoed back the Name of that beautiful Youth; so did the
House, the Garden, and all the Neighboring Fields, resound
nothing but the Name of *Sophia,* in the hoarse Voices of the Men,
and in the shrill Pipes of the Women; while Echo seemed so
pleased to repeat the beloved Sound, that if there is really such a
Person, I believe *Ovid* hath belied her Sex.

Nothing reigned for a long Time but Confusion; 'till at last the
Squire having sufficiently spent his Breath, returned to the Parlour,
where he found Mrs. *Western* and Mr. *Blifil,* and threw himself,
with the utmost Dejection in his Countenance, into a great Chair.

Here Mrs. *Western* began to apply the following Consolation:

'Brother, I am sorry for what hath happened; and that my Niece
should have behaved herself in a Manner so unbecoming her
Family; but it is all your own Doings, and you have nobody to
thank but yourself. You know she hath been educated always in a
Manner directly contrary to my Advice, and now you see the Consequence. Have I not a thousand Times argued with you about giving
my Niece her own Will? But you know I never could prevail upon
you: and when I had taken so much Pains to eradicate her headstrong Opinions, and to rectify your Errors in Policy, you know she
was taken out of my Hands; so that I have nothing to answer for.
Had I been trusted entirely with the Care of her Education, no
such Accident as this had ever befallen you: So that you must comfort yourself by thinking it was all your own Doing; and, indeed,
what else could be expected from such Indulgence?'——

'Zounds! Sister,' answered he, 'you are enough to make one mad.
Have I indulged her? have I given her her Will?—It was no longer
ago than last Night that I threatned, if she disobeyed me, to confine her to her Chamber, upon Bread and Water, as long as she
lived.—You would provoke the Patience of *Job.*"

'Did ever Mortal hear the like?' replied she. 'Brother, if I had not
the Patience of fifty *Jobs,* you would make me forget all Decency
and Decorum. Why would you interfere? Did I not beg you, did I

2. Virgil, *Eclogues* VI 43–44; Ovid, *Metamorphoses* III.356–401.

not entreat you to leave the whole Conduct to me? You have
defeated all the Operations of the Campaign by one false Step.
Would any Man in his Senses have provoked a Daughter by such
Threats as these? How often have I told you, that *English* Women
are not to be treated like *Ciracessian*[3] Slaves. We have the Protection of the World: We are to be won by gentle Means only, and
not to be hectored, and bullied, and beat into Compliance. I thank
Heaven, no *Salique* Law[4] governs here. Brother, you have a Roughness in your Manner which no Woman but myself would bear. I do
not wonder my Niece was frightned and terrified into taking this
Measure; and to speak honestly, I think my Niece will be justified
to the World for what she hath done. I repeat it to you again,
Brother, you must comfort yourself by remembring that it is all your
own Fault. How often have I advised—' Here *Western* rose hastily
from his Chair, and, venting two or three horrid Imprecations, ran
out of the Room.

When he was departed, his Sister expressed more Bitterness (if
possible) against him, than she had done while he was present; for
the Truth of which she appealed to Mr. *Blifil*, who, with great
Complacence, acquiesced entirely in all she said; but excused all the
Faults of Mr. *Western*, 'as they must be considered,' he said, 'to
have proceeded from the too inordinate Fondness of a Father,
which must be allowed the Name of an amiable Weakness.' 'So
much the more inexcusable,' answered the Lady; 'for whom doth he
ruin by his Fondness, but his own Child?' To which *Blifil* immediately agreed.

Mrs. *Western* then began to express great Confusion on the
Account of Mr. *Blifil*, and of the Usage which he had received from
a Family to which he intended so much Honour. On this Subject
she treated the Folly of her Niece with great Severity; but concluded with throwing the whole on her Brother, who, she said, was
inexcusable to have proceeded so far without better Assurances of
his Daughter's Consent: 'But he was (says she) always of a violent,
headstrong Temper; and I can scarce forgive myself for all the Advice
I have thrown away upon him.'

After much of this Kind of Conversation, which, perhaps, would
not greatly entertain the Reader, was it here particularly related,
Mr. *Blifil* took his Leave, and returned home, not highly pleased
with his Disappointment; which, however, the Philosophy which he
had acquired from *Square*, and the Religion infused into him by
Thwackum, together with somewhat else, taught him to bear rather
better than more passionate Lovers bear these Kinds of Evils.

Chapter IX.

The Escape of Sophia.

It is now Time to look after *Sophia;* whom the Reader, if he loves her half so well as I do, will rejoice to find escaped from the Clutches of her passionate Father, and from those of her dispassionate Lover.

Twelve Times did the iron Register of Time beat on the sonorous Bell-metal, summoning the Ghosts to rise, and walk their nightly Round.—In plainer Language, it was Twelve o'Clock, and all the Family, as we have said, lay buried in Drink and Sleep, except only Mrs. We'stern, who was deeply engaged in reading a political Pamphlet, and except our Heroine, who now softly stole down Stairs, and having unbarred and unlocked one of the House Doors, sallied forth, and hastened to the Place of Appointment.

Notwithstanding the many pretty Arts, which Ladies sometimes practice, to display their Fears on every little Occasion, (almost as many as the other Sex uses to conceal theirs) certainly there is a Degree of Courage, which not only becomes a Woman, but is often necessary to enable her to discharge her Duty. It is, indeed, the Idea of Fierceness, and not of Bravery, which destroys the Female Character: For who can read the Story of the justly celebrated *Arria,*[1] without conceiving as high an Opinion of her Gentleness and Tenderness, as of her Fortitude? At the same Time, perhaps, many a Woman who shrieks at a Mouse, or a Rat, may be capable of poisoning a Husband; or, what is worse, of driving him to poison himself.

Sophia, with all the Gentleness which a Woman can have, had all the Spirit which she ought to have. When, therefore, she came to the Place of Appointment, and, instead of meeting her Maid, as was agreed, saw a Man ride directly up to her, she neither screamed out, nor fainted away: Not that her Pulse then beat with its usual Regularity; for she was, at first, under some Surprize and Apprehension: But these were relieved almost as soon as raised, when the Man, pulling off his Hat, asked her, in a very submissive Manner, 'If her Ladyship did not expect to meet another Lady?' And then proceeded to inform her, 'that he was sent to conduct her to that Lady.'

Sophia could have no possible Suspicion of any Falshood in this Account: She therefore mounted resolutely behind the Fellow, who conveyed her safe to a Town about Five Miles distant, where she

---

1. The wife of Paetus, sentenced to kill himself for plotting against Claudius, A.D. 42. When he hesitated, Arria stabbed herself and handed him the dagger, saying, "Paetus, it does not hurt me" (Pliny, *Epistles* III.16).

had the Satisfaction of finding the good Mrs. *Honour:* For as the
Soul of the Waiting-woman was wrapt up in those very Habili-
ments which used to enwrap her Body, she could by no means bring
herself to trust them out of her Sight. Upon these, therefore, she
kept Guard in Person, while she detached the aforesaid Fellow after
her Mistress, having given him all proper Instructions.

They now debated what Course to take, in order to avoid the
Pursuit of Mr. *Western,* who, they knew, would send after them in
a few Hours. The *London* Road had such Charms for *Honour,* that
she was desirous of going on directly; alleging, that as *Sophia* could
not be missed till Eight or Nine the next Morning, her Pursuers
would not be able to overtake her, even though they knew which
Way she had gone. But *Sophia* had too much at Stake to venture
any Thing to Chance; nor did she dare trust too much to her
tender Limbs, in a Contest which was to be decided only by Swift-
ness. She resolved, therefore, to travel across the Country, for at
least twenty or thirty Miles, and then to take the direct Road to
London. So, having hired Horses to go twenty Miles one Way,
when she intended to go twenty Miles the other, she set forward
with the same Guide, behind whom she had ridden from her Father's House; the Guide having now taken up behind him, in the
Room of *Sophia,* a much heavier, as well as much less lovely Burthen; being, indeed, a huge Portmanteau, well stuffed with those
outside Ornaments, by means of which the fair *Honour* hoped to
gain many Conquests, and, finally, to make her Fortune in *London*
City.

When they had gone about Two hundred Paces from the Inn, on
the *London* Road, *Sophia* rode up to the Guide, and, with a Voice
much fuller of Honey than was ever that of *Plato,* though his
Mouth is supposed to have been a Bee-hive,[2] begged him to take
the first Turning which led toward *Bristol.*

Reader, I am not superstitious, nor any great Believer of modern
Miracles. I do not, therefore, deliver the following as a certain
Truth, for, indeed, I can scarce credit it myself: But the Fidelity
of an Historian obliges me to relate what hath been confidently
asserted. The Horse, then, on which the Guide rode, is reported to
have been so charmed by *Sophia*'s Voice, that he made a full Stop,
and exprest an Unwillingness to proceed any farther.

Perhaps, however, the Fact may be true, and less miraculous than
it hath been represented; since the natural Cause seems adequate
to the Effect: For as the Guide at that Moment desisted from a
constant Application of his armed Right Heel, (for, like *Hudibras,*
he wore but one Spur)[3] it is more than possible, that this Omission

2. Bees are supposed to have fed the infant Plato with honey (Cicero, *De Divi-*
natione. I.78—Mutter). Fielding had said
this of *Anacreon* in the first edition, correcting to *Plato* in the fourth.
3. *Hudibras* I.i.447.

alone might occasion the Beast to stop, especially as this was very frequent with him at other Times.

But if the Voice of *Sophia* had really an Effect on the Horse, it had very little on the Rider. He answered somewhat surlily, 'That Measter had ordered him to go a different Way, and that he should lose his Place, if he went any other than that he was ordered.'

Sophia finding all her Persuasions had no Effect, began now to add irresistible Charms to her Voice; Charms, which, according to the Proverb, makes the old Mare trot, instead of standing still; Charms! to which modern Ages have attributed all that irresistible Force, which the Antients imputed to perfect Oratory. In a Word, she promised she would reward him to his utmost Expectation.

The Lad was not totally deaf to these Promises; but he disliked their being indefinite: For tho' perhaps he had never heard that Word; yet that in Fact was his Objection. He said, 'Gentlevolks did not consider the Case of poor Volks; that he had like to have been turned away the other Day, for riding about the Country with a Gentleman from Squire *Allworthy*'s, who did not reward him as he should have done.'

'With whom?' says *Sophia* eagerly—'With a Gentleman from Squire *Allworthy*'s,' repeated the Lad; 'the Squire's Son, I think, they call 'un.'—'Whither? which Way did he go?' says *Sophia*. 'Why a little o' one Side o' *Bristol*, about twenty Miles off,' answered the Lad.—'Guide me,' says *Sophia*, 'to the same Place, and I'll give thee a Guinea, or two, if one is not sufficient.' 'To be certain,' said the Boy, 'it is honestly worth two, when your Ladyship considers what a Risk I run; but, however, if your Ladyship will promise me the two Guineas, I'll e'en venture: To be certain it is a sinful Thing to ride about my Master's Horses; but one Comfort is, I can only be turned away, and two Guineas will partly make me Amends.'

The Bargain being thus struck, the Lad turned aside into the *Bristol* Road, and *Sophia* set forward in Pursuit of *Jones*, highly contrary to the Remonstrances of Mrs. *Honour*, who had much more Desire to see *London*, than to see Mr. *Jones*: For indeed she was not his Friend with her Mistress, as he had been guilty of some Neglect in certain pecuniary Civilities, which are by Custom due to the Waiting-gentlewoman in all Love Affairs, and more especially in those of a clandestine Kind. This we impute rather to the Careless-ness of his Temper, than to any Want of Generosity; but perhaps she derived it from the latter Motive. Certain it is that she hated him very bitterly on that Account, and resolved to take every Oppor-tunity of injuring him with her Mistress. It was therefore highly unlucky for her, that she had gone to the very same Town and Inn whence *Jones* had started, and still more unlucky was she, in having stumbled on the same Guide, and on this accidental Discovery which *Sophia* had made.

Our Travellers arrived at *Hambrook*[4] at the Break of Day, where *Honour* was against her Will charged to enquire the Rout which Mr. *Jones* had taken. Of this, indeed, the Guide himself could have informed them; but *Sophia*, I know not for what Reason, never asked him the Question.

When Mrs. *Honour* had made her Report from the Landlord, *Sophia*, with much Difficulty, procured some indifferent Horses, which brought her to the Inn, where *Jones* had been confined rather by the Misfortune of meeting with a Surgeon, than by having met with a broken Head.

Here *Honour* being again charged with a Commission of Enquiry, had no sooner applied herself to the Landlady, and had described the Person of Mr. *Jones*, than that sagacious Woman began, in the vulgar Phrase, to smell a Rat. When *Sophia* therefore entered the Room, instead of answering the Maid, the Landlady addressing herself to the Mistress began the following Speech. 'Good-lack-a-day! why there now, who would have thought it! I protest the loveliest Couple that ever Eye beheld. I-fackins, Madam, it is no Wonder the Squire run on so about your Ladyship. He told me indeed you was the finest Lady in the World, and to be sure so you be. Mercy on him, poor Heart, I bepitied him, so I did, when he used to hug his Pillow, and call it his dear Madam *Sophia*.—I did all I could to dissuade him from going to the Wars: I told him there were Men enow that were good for nothing else but to be killed, that had not the Love of such fine Ladies.' 'Sure,' says *Sophia*, 'the good Woman is distracted.' 'No, no,' cries the Landlady, 'I am not distracted. What, doth your Ladyship think I don't know then? I assure you he told me all.' 'What saucy Fellow,' cries *Honour*, 'told you any thing of my Lady?' 'No saucy Fellow,' answered the Landlady, 'but the young Gentleman you enquired after, and a very pretty young Gentleman he is, and he loves Madam *Sophia Western* to the Bottom of his Soul.' 'He love my Lady! I'd have you to know, Woman, she is Meat for his Master.' —'Nay, *Honour*,' said *Sophia*, interrupting her, 'don't be angry with the good Woman; she intends no Harm.' 'No, marry don't I,' answered the Landlady, emboldened by the soft Accents of *Sophia*; and then launched into a long Narrative too tedious to be here set down, in which some Passages dropt, that gave a little Offence to *Sophia*, and much more to her Waiting-woman, who hence took Occasion to abuse poor *Jones* to her Mistress the Moment they were alone together, saying, 'that he must be a very pitiful Fellow,

4. This was the Village where Jones met the Quaker [*Fielding's note*].

and could have no Love for a Lady, whose Name he would thus prostitute in an Ale-house.'

Sophia did not see his Behaviour in so very disadvantageous a Light, and was perhaps more pleased with the violent Raptures of his Love (which the Landlady exaggerated as much as she had done every other Circumstance) than she was offended with the rest; and indeed she imputed the whole to the Extravagance, or rather Ebullience of his Passion, and to the Openness of his Heart.

This Incident, however, being afterwards revived in her Mind, and placed in the most odious Colours by *Honour*, served to heighten and give Credit to those unlucky Occurrences at *Upton*, and assisted the Waiting-woman in her Endeavours to make her Mistress depart from that Inn without seeing *Jones*.

The Landlady finding *Sophia* intended to stay no longer than till her Horses were ready, and that without either eating or drinking, soon withdrew; when *Honour* began to take her Mistress to Task, (for indeed she used great Freedom) and after a long Harangue, in which she reminded her of her Intention to go to *London*, and gave frequent Hints of the Impropriety of pursuing a young Fellow, she at last concluded with this serious Exhortation: 'For Heaven's Sake, Madam, consider what you are about, and whither you are going.'

This Advice to a Lady who had already rode near forty Miles, and in no very agreeable Season, may seem foolish enough. It may be supposed she had well considered and resolved this already; nay, Mrs. *Honour*, by the Hints she threw out, seemed to think so; and this I doubt not is the Opinion of many Readers, who have, I make no Doubt, been long since well convinced of the Purpose of our Heroine, and have heartily condemned her for it as a wanton Baggage.

But in Reality this was not the Case. *Sophia* had been lately so distracted between Hope and Fear, her Duty and Love to her Father, her Hatred to *Blifil*, her Compassion, and (why should we not confess the Truth?) her Love for *Jones*; which last the Behaviour of her Father, of her Aunt, of every one else, and more particularly of *Jones* himself, had blown into a Flame, that her Mind was in that confused State, which may be truly said to make us ignorant of what we do, or whither we go, or rather indeed indifferent as to the Consequence of either.

The prudent and sage Advice of her Maid, produced, however, some cool Reflection; and she at length determined to go to *Gloucester*, and thence to proceed directly to *London*.

But unluckily a few Miles before she entered that Town, she met the Hack-Attorney, who, as is before mentioned, had dined there with Mr. *Jones*. This Fellow being well known to Mrs. *Honour*, stopt and spoke to her; of which *Sophia* at that Time took little Notice, more than to enquire who he was.

But having had a more particular Account from *Honour* of this Man afterwards at *Gloucester*, and hearing of the great Expedition he usually made in travelling, for which (as hath been before observed) he was particularly famous; recollecting likewise, that she had overheard Mrs. *Honour* inform him, that they were going to *Gloucester*, she began to fear lest her Father might, by this Fellow's Means, be able to trace her to that City; wherefore if she should there strike into the *London* Road, she apprehended he would certainly be able to overtake her. She therefore altered her Resolution; and having hired Horses to go a Week's Journey, a Way which she did not intend to travel, she again set forward after a light Refreshment, contrary to the Desire and earnest Entreaties of her Maid, and to the no less vehement Remonstrances of Mrs. *Whitefield*, who from good Breeding, or perhaps from good Nature (for the poor young Lady appeared much fatigued) press'd her very heartily to stay that Evening at *Gloucester*.

Having refreshed herself only with some Tea, and with lying about two Hours on the Bed, while her Horses were getting ready, she resolutely left Mrs. *Whitefield*'s about Eleven at Night, and striking directly into the *Worcester* Road, within less than four Hours arrived at that very Inn where we last saw her.

Having thus traced our Heroine very particularly back from her Departure, till her Arrival at *Upton*, we shall in a very few Words bring her Father to the same Place; who having received the first Scent from the Post-boy, who conducted his Daughter to *Hambrook*, very easily traced her afterwards to *Gloucester*; whence he pursued her to *Upton*, as he had learned Mr. *Jones* had taken that Rout, (for *Partridge*, to use the Squire's Expression, left every where a strong Scent behind him) and he doubted not in the least but *Sophia* travelled, or, as he phrased it, ran the same Way. He used indeed a very coarse Expression, which need not be here inserted; as Fox-hunters, who alone would understand it, will easily suggest it to themselves.

BOOK XI.

Containing about three Days.

Chapter I.

A *Crust for the Critics.*

In our last initial Chapter, we may be supposed to have treated that formidable Set of Men, who are called Critics, with more Freedom than becomes us; since they exact, and indeed generally

receive, great Condescension from Authors. We shall in this, therefore, give the Reasons of our Conduct to this august Body; and here
we shall perhaps place them in a Light, in which they have not
hitherto been seen.

This Word Critic is of *Greek* Derivation, and signifies Judgment.
Hence I presume some Persons who have not understood the Original, and have seen the *English* Translation of the Primitive, have
concluded that it meant Judgment in the legal Sense, in which it is
frequently used as equivalent to Condemnation.

I am the rather inclined to be of that Opinion, as the greatest
Number of Critics hath of late Years been found amongst the Lawyers. Many of these Gentlemen, from Despair, perhaps, of ever
rising to the Bench in *Westminster-hall,* have placed themselves on
the Benches at the Playhouse, where they have exerted their judicial
Capacity, and have given Judgment, *i.e.* condemned without Mercy.

The Gentlemen would perhaps be well enough pleased, if we
were to leave them thus compared to one of the most important
and honourable Offices in the Commonwealth, and, if we intended
to apply to their Favour, we would do so; but as we design to deal
very sincerely and plainly too with them, we must remind them of
another Officer of Justice of a much lower Rank; to whom, as they
not only pronounce, but execute their own Judgment, they bear
likewise some remote Resemblance.

But in reality there is another Light, in which these modern Critics may with great Justice and Propriety be seen; and this is that of
a common Slanderer. If a person who prys into the Characters of
others, with no other Design but to discover their Faults, and to
publish them to the World, deserves the Title of a Slanderer of the
Reputations of Men; why should not a Critic, who reads with the
same malevolent View, be as properly stiled the Slanderer of the
Reputation of Books?

Vice hath not, I believe, a more abject Slave; Society produces
not a more odious Vermin; nor can the Devil receive a Guest more
worthy of him, nor possibly more welcome to him, than a Slanderer. The World, I am afraid, regards not this Monster with half
the Abhorrence which he deserves; and I am more afraid to assign
the Reason of this criminal Lenity shewn towards him; yet it is certain that the Thief looks innocent in the Comparison; nay, the
Murderer himself can seldom stand in Competition with his Guilt:
For Slander is a more cruel Weapon than a Sword, as the Wounds
which the former gives are always incurable. One Method, indeed,
there is of killing, and that the basest and most execrable of all,
which bears an exact Analogy to the Vice here disclaimed against,
and that is Poison. A Means of Revenge so base, and yet so horrible, that it was once wisely distinguished by our Laws from all other
Murders, in the peculiar Severity of the Punishment.

Besides the dreadful Mischiefs done by Slander, and the Baseness of the Means by which they are effected, there are other Circumstances that highly aggravate its atrocious Quality: For it often proceeds from no Provocation, and seldom promises itself any Reward, unless some black and infernal Mind may propose a Reward in the Thoughts of having procured the Ruin and Misery of another.

Shakespear hath nobly touched this Vice, when he says,

> *Who steals my Purse steals Trash, 'tis something, nothing;*
> *'Twas mine, 'tis his, and hath been Slave to Thousands:*
> *But he that filches from me my good Name,*
> *Robs me of that* WHICH NOT ENRICHES HIM,
> BUT MAKES ME POOR INDEED.[1]

With all this my good Reader will doubtless agree; but much of it will probably seem too severe, when applied to the Slanderer of Books. But let it here be considered, that both proceed from the same wicked Disposition of Mind, and are alike void of the Excuse of Temptation. Nor shall we conclude the Injury done this Way to be very slight, when we consider a Book as the Author's Offspring, and indeed as the Child of his Brain.

The Reader who hath suffered his Muse to continue hitherto in a Virgin State, can have but a very inadequate Idea of this Kind of paternal Fondness. To such we may parody the tender Exclamation of *Macduff*.[2] *Alas! Thou hast written no Book.* But the Author whose Muse hath brought forth, will feel the pathetic Strain, perhaps will accompany me with Tears (especially if his Darling be already no more) while I mention the Uneasiness with which the big Muse bears about her Burden, the painful Labour with which she produces it, and lastly, the Care, the Fondness, with which the tender Father nourishes his Favourite, till it be brought to Maturity, and produced into the World.

Nor is there any paternal Fondness which seems less to savour of absolute Instinct, and which may so well be reconciled to worldly Wisdom, as this. These Children may most truly be called the Riches of their Father; and many of them have with true filial Piety fed their Parent in his old Age: so that not only the Affection, but the Interest of the Author may be highly injured by these Slanderers, whose poisonous Breath brings his Book to an untimely End.

Lastly, the Slander of a Book is, in Truth, the Slander of the Author: For as no one can call another Bastard, without calling the Mother a Whore; so neither can any one give the Names of sad Stuff, horrid Nonsense, &c. to a Book, without calling the Author a Blockhead; which tho' in a moral Sense it is a preferable Appellation to that of Villain, is perhaps rather more injurious to his worldly Interest.

1. *Othello* III.iii.157–61.   2. *Macbeth* IV.iii.216.

Now however ludicrous all this may appear to some, others, I doubt not, will feel and acknowledge the Truth of it; nay, may, perhaps, think I have not treated the Subject with decent Solemnity; but surely a Man may speak Truth with a smiling Countenance. In reality, to depreciate a Book maliciously, or even wantonly, is at least a very ill-natured Office; and a morose snarling Critic may, I believe, be suspected to be a bad Man.

I will therefore endeavour in the remaining Part of this Chapter, to explain the Marks of this Character, and to shew what Criticism I here intend to obviate: For I can never be understood, unless by the very Persons here meant, to insinuate, that there are no proper Judges of Writing, or to endeavour to exclude from the Commonwealth of Literature any of those noble Critics, to whose Labours the learned World are so greatly indebted. Such were *Aristotle*, *Horace*, and *Longinus* among the Antients, *Dacier* and *Bossu* among the *French*, and some perhaps among us; who have certainly been duly authorised to execute at least a judicial Authority in *Foro Literario*.[3]

But without ascertaining all the proper Qualifications of a Critic, which I have touched on elsewhere, I think I may very boldly object to the Censures of any one past upon Works which he hath not himself read. Such Censurers as these, whether they speak from their own Guess or Suspicion, or from the Report and Opinion of others, may properly be said to slander the Reputation of the Book they condemn.

Such may likewise be suspected of deserving this Character, who without assigning any particular Faults, condemn the whole in general defamatory Terms; such as vile, dull, da——d Stuff, *&c.* and particularly by the Use of the Monosyllable Low ; a Word which becomes the Mouth of no Critic who is not Right Honourable.

Again, tho' there may be some Faults justly assigned in the Work; yet if those are not in the most essential Parts, or, if they are compensated by greater Beauties, it will favour rather of the Malice of a Slanderer, than of the Judgment of a true Critic, to pass a severe Sentence upon the whole, merely on account of some vicious Part. This is directly contrary to the Sentiments of *Horace*.[4]

> *Verum ubi plura nitent in carmine, non ego paucis*
> *Offendor maculis, quas aut incuria fudit,*
> *Aut humana parum cavit natura——*

> But where the Beauties, more in Number, shine,
> I am not angry, when a casual Line

---

3. "In the literary forum," the field of literary criticism.
4. *Ars Poetica* 351–53; in Philip Francis's translation, lines 477–80. Francis (1708–73), Gibbon's schoolmaster at Eshur, was a celebrated translator of Horace, Aeschines, and Demosthenes. See above, p. 400.

(That with some trivial Faults unequal flows)
A careless Hand, or human Frailty shows.

MR. FRANCIS.

For as *Martial* says, *Aliter non fit, Avite, Liber*.[5] *No Book can be otherwise composed*. All Beauty of Character, as well as of Countenance, and indeed of every Thing human, is to be tried in this Manner. Cruel indeed would it be, if such a Work as this History, which hath employed some Thousands of Hours in the composing, should be liable to be condemned, because some particular Chapter, or perhaps Chapters, may be obnoxious to very just and sensible Objections. And yet nothing is more common than the most rigourous Sentence upon Books supported by such Objections, which, if they were rightly taken (and that they are not always) do by no Means go to the Merit of the whole. In the Theatre especially, a single Expression which doth not coincide with the Taste of the Audience, or with any individual Critic of that Audience, is sure to be hissed; and one Scene which should be disapproved, would hazard the whole Piece. To write within such severe Rules as these, is as impossible as to live up to some splenetic Opinions; and if we judge according to the Sentiments of some Critics, and of some Christians, no Author will be saved in this World, and no Man in the next.

Chapter II.

The Adventures which Sophia *met with, after her leaving* Upton.

Our History, just before it was obliged to turn about, and travel backwards, had mentioned the Departure of *Sophia* and her Maid from the Inn; we shall now therefore pursue the Steps of that lovely Creature, and leave her unworthy Lover a little longer to bemoan his Ill-Luck, or rather his ill Conduct.

Sophia having directed her Guide to travel through Bye-Roads across the Country, they now passed the *Severn*, and had scarce got a Mile from the Inn, when the young Lady, looking behind her, saw several Horses coming after on full Speed. This greatly alarmed her Fears, and she called to the Guide to put on as fast as possible.

He immediately obeyed her, and away they rode a full Gallop. But the faster they went, the faster were they followed; and as the Horses behind were somewhat swifter than those before, so the former were at length overtaken. A happy Circumstance for poor *Sophia*; whose Fears, joined to her Fatigue, had almost overpowered her Spirits; but she was now instantly relieved by a female Voice,

---

5. "There's no other way to make a book, Grandpop" (than with "some things good, some mediocre, some bad"). Martial, *Epigrammata* I.xvi.

that greeted her in the softest Manner, and with the utmost Civility. This Greeting, *Sophia*, as soon as she could recover her Breath, with like Civility, and with the highest Satisfaction to herself, returned.

The Travellers who joined *Sophia*, and who had given her such Terror, consisted, like her own Company, of two Females and a Guide. The two Parties proceeded three full Miles together before any one offered again to open their Mouths; when our Heroine, having pretty well got the better of her Fear, (but yet being somewhat surprized that the other still continued to attend her, as she pursued no great Road, and had already passed through several Turnings) accosted the strange Lady in a most obliging Tone; and said, 'She was very happy to find they were both travelling the same Way.' The other, who, like a Ghost, only wanted to be spoke to, readily answered, 'That the Happiness was entirely hers; that she was a perfect Stranger in that Country, and was so overjoyed at meeting a Companion of her own Sex, that she had perhaps been guilty of an Impertinence which required great Apology, in keeping Pace with her.' More Civilities passed between these two Ladies; for Mrs. *Honour* had now given Place to the fine Habit of the Stranger, and had fallen into the Rear. But tho' *Sophia* had great Curiosity to know why the other Lady continued to travel on through the same Bye-roads with herself, nay, tho' this gave her some Uneasiness; yet Fear, or Modesty, or some other Consideration, restrained her from asking the Question.

The strange Lady now laboured under a Difficulty which appears almost below the Dignity of History to mention. Her Bonnet had been blown from her Head not less than five Times within the last Mile; nor could she come at any Ribbon or Handkerchief to tye it under her Chin. When *Sophia* was informed of this, she immediately supplied her with a Handkerchief for this Purpose; which while she was pulling from her Pocket, she perhaps too much neglected the Management of her Horse, for the Beast now unluckily making a false Step, fell upon his Fore-Legs, and threw his fair Rider from his Back.

Tho' *Sophia* came Head foremost to the Ground, she happily received not the least Damage; and the same Circumstances which had perhaps contributed to her Fall, now preserved her from Confusion; for the Lane which they were then passing, was narrow and very much over-grown with Trees, so that the Moon could here afford very little Light, and was moreover, at present, so obscured in a Cloud, that it was almost perfectly dark. By these Means the young Lady's Modesty, which was extremely delicate, escaped as free from Injury as her Limbs, and she was once more reinstated in her Saddle, having received no other Harm than a little Fright by her Fall.

Day-light at length appeared in its full Lustre; and now the two
Ladies, who were riding over a Common Side by Side, looking
steadfastly at each other, at the same Moment both their Eyes
became fixed; both their Horses stopt, and both speaking together,
with equal Joy pronounced, the one the Name of *Sophia*, the other
that of *Harriet*.

This unexpected Encounter surprized the Ladies much more
than I believe it will the sagacious Reader, who must have imagined
that the strange Lady could be no other than Mrs. *Fitzpatrick*, the
Cousin of Miss *Western*, whom we before-mentioned to have sallied from the Inn a few Minutes after her.

So great was the Surprise and Joy which these two Cousins con-
ceived at this Meeting (for they had formerly been most intimate
Acquaintance and Friends, and had long lived together with their
Aunt *Western*) that it is impossible to recount half the Congratula-
tions which passed between them, before either asked a very natural
Question of the other, namely, whither she was going.

This at last, however, came first from Mrs. *Fitzpatrick*; but easy
and natural as the Question may seem, *Sophia* found it difficult to
give it a very ready and certain Answer. She begged her Cousin
therefore to suspend all Curiosity till they arrived at some Inn,
'which I suppose,' says she, 'can hardly be far distant; and believe
me, *Harriet*, I suspend as much Curiosity on my Side; for indeed I
believe our Astonishment is pretty equal.'

The Conversation which passed between these Ladies on the
Road, was, I apprehend, little worth relating; and less certainly was
that between the two Waiting-women: For they likewise began to
pay their Compliments to each other. As for the Guides, they were
debarred from the Pleasure of Discourse, the one being placed in
the Van, and the other obliged to bring up the Rear.

In this Posture they travelled many Hours, till they came into a
wide and well-beaten Road, which, as they turned to the Right,
soon brought them to a very fair promising Inn; where they all
alighted: But so fatigued was *Sophia*, that, as she had sat her Horse
during the last five or six Miles with great Difficulty, so was she
now incapable of dismounting from him without Assistance. This
the Landlord, who had hold of her Horse, presently perceiving,
offered to lift her in his Arms from her Saddle; and she too readily
accepted the Tender of his Service. Indeed Fortune seems to have
resolved to put *Sophia* to the Blush that Day, and the second malicious Attempt succeeded better than the first; for my Landlord had
no sooner received the young Lady in his Arms, than his Feet,
which the Gout had lately very severely handled, gave way, and
down he tumbled; but at the same Time, with 'no less Dexterity
than Gallantry, contrived to throw himself under his charming Burthen, so that he alone received any Bruise from the Fall; for the

great Injury which happened to *Sophia*, was a violent Shock given to her Modesty, by an immoderate Grin, which, at her rising from the Ground, she observed in the Countenances of most of the Bye-Standers. This made her suspect what had really happened, and what we shall not here relate, for the Indulgence of those Readers who are capable of laughing at the Offence given to a young Lady's Delicacy. Accidents of this Kind we have never regarded in a comical Light; nor will we scruple to say, that he must have a very inadequate Idea of the Modesty of a beautiful young Woman, who would wish to sacrifice it to so paultry a Satisfaction as can arise from Laughter.

This Fright and Shock, joined to the violent Fatigue which both her Mind and Body had undergone, almost overcame the excellent Constitution of *Sophia*, and she had scarce Strength sufficient to totter into the Inn, leaning on the Arm of her Maid. Here she was no sooner seated than she called for a Glass of Water; but Mrs. *Honour*, very judiciously, in my Opinion, changed it into a Glass of Wine.

Mrs. *Fitzpatrick* hearing from Mrs. *Honour*, that *Sophia* had not been in Bed during the two last Nights, and observing her to look very pale and wan with her Fatigue, earnestly entreated her to refresh herself with some Sleep. She was yet a Stranger to her History, or her Apprehensions; but had she known both, she would have given the same Advice; for Rest was visibly necessary for her; and their long Journey through Bye-Roads so entirely removed all Danger of Pursuit, that she was herself perfectly easy on that Account.

Sophia was easily prevailed on to follow the Counsel of her Friend, which was heartily seconded by her Maid. Mrs. *Fitzpatrick* likewise offered to bear her Cousin Company, which *Sophia*, with much Complaisance, accepted.

The Mistress was no sooner in Bed, than the Maid prepared to follow her Example. She began to make Apologies to her Sister *Abigail* for leaving her alone in so horrid a Place as an Inn; but the other stopped her short, being as well inclined to a Nap as herself, and desired the Honour of being her Bedfellow. *Sophia*'s Maid agreed to give her a Share of her Bed, but put in her Claim to all the Honour. So after many Court'sies and Compliments, to Bed together went the Waiting-women, as their Mistresses had done before them.

It was usual with my Landlord (as indeed it is with the whole Fraternity) to enquire particularly of all Coachmen, Footmen, Postboys, and others, into the Names of all his Guests; what their Estate was, and where it lay. It cannot therefore be wondered at,

that the many particular Circumstances which attended our Travellers, and especially their retiring all to Sleep at so extraordinary and
unusual an Hour as ten in the Morning, should excite his Curiosity.
As soon therefore as the Guides entered the Kitchin, he began to
examine who the Ladies were, and whence they came; but the
Guides, tho' they faithfully related all they knew, gave him very
little Satisfaction. On the contrary, they rather enflamed his Curiosity than extinguished it.

This Landlord had the Character, among all his Neighbours, of
being a very sagacious Fellow. He was thought to see farther and
deeper into Things than any Man in the Parish, the Parson himself
not excepted. Perhaps his Look had contributed not a little to procure him this Reputation; for there was in this something wonderfully wise and significant, especially when he had a Pipe in his
Mouth; which, indeed, he seldom was without. His Behaviour, likewise, greatly assisted in promoting the Opinion of his Wisdom. In
his Deportment he was solemn, if not sullen; and when he spoke,
which was seldom, he always delivered himself in a slow Voice; and
though his Sentences were short, they were still interrupted with
many Hums and Ha's, Ay, Ays, and other Expletives: So that
though he accompanied his Words with certain explanatory Gestures, such as shaking, or nodding the Head, or pointing with his
Forefinger, he generally left his Hearers to understand more than he
expressed; nay, he commonly gave them a Hint, that he knew much
more than he thought proper to disclose. This last Circumstance
alone, may, indeed, very well account for his Character of Wisdom;
since Men are strangely inclined to worship what they do not
understand. A grand Secret, upon which several Imposers on Mankind have totally relied for the Success of their Frauds.

This polite Person now taking his Wife aside, asked her, 'What
she thought of the Ladies lately arrived?' 'Think of them?' said the
Wife, 'why what should I think of them?' 'I know,' answered he,
'what I think. The Guides tell strange Stories. One pretends to be
come from *Gloucester*, and the other from *Upton*; and neither of
them, for what I can find, can tell whither they are going. But what
People ever travel across the Country from *Upton* hither, especially
to *London?* And one of the Maid-Servants, before she alighted from
her Horse, asked, if this was not the *London* Road? Now I have put
all these Circumstances together, and whom do you think I have
found them out to be?' 'Nay,' answered she, 'you know I never pretend to guess at your Discoveries.'—'It is a good Girl,' replied he,
chucking her under the Chin; 'I must own you have always submitted to my Knowledge of these Matters. Why then, depend upon it;
mind what I say,—depend upon it, they are certainly some of the

Rebel Ladies,[1] who, they say, travel with the young Chevalier; and
have taken a round-about Way to escape the Duke's Army.'

'Husband,' quoth the Wife, 'you have certainly hit it; for one of
them is drest as fine as any Princess; and, to be sure, she looks for
all the World like one.—But yet, when I consider one Thing.'—
'When you consider,' cries the Landlord contemptuously——
'Come, pray let's hear what you consider.'——'Why it is,' answered
the Wife, 'that she is too humble to be any very great Lady; for
while our *Betty* was warming the Bed, she called her nothing but
Child, and my Dear, and Sweetheart; and when *Betty* offered to
pull off her Shoes and Stockings, she would not suffer her, saying,
she would not give her the Trouble.'

'Pugh!' answered the Husband, 'That is nothing. Dost think,
because you have seen some great Ladies rude and uncivil to Persons below them, that none of them know how to behave themselves when they come before their Inferiors? I think I know People
of Fashion when I see them. I think I do. Did not she call for a
Glass of Water when she came in? Another Sort of Women would
have called for a Dram; you know they would. If she be not a
Woman of very great Quality, sell me for a Fool; and, I believe,
those who buy me will have a bad Bargain. Now, would a Woman
of her Quality travel without a Footman, unless upon some such
extraordinary Occasion?' 'Nay, to be sure, Husband,' cries she, 'you
know these Matters better than I, or most Folk.' 'I think I do
know something,' said he. 'To be sure,' answered the Wife, 'the
poor little Heart looked so piteous, when she sat down in the Chair,
I protest I could not help having a Compassion for her, almost as
much as if she had been a poor Body. But what's to be done, Husband? If an she be a Rebel, I suppose you intend to betray her up
to the Court. Well, she's a sweet-tempered, good-humoured Lady,
be she what she will, and I shall hardly refrain from crying when I
hear she is hanged or beheaded.' 'Pooh,' answered the Husband!
——But as to what's to be done it is not so easy a Matter to deter-

1. Prince Charles Edward Louis Philip
Casimir Stuart—"Bonnie Prince Charlie," the Young Pretender and Young
Chevalier (his father, James Francis Edward, James II's son, was the Old Pretender and the Chevalier de St. George)
—tried to make good his and his father's
pretentions to the throne vacated by
James II. He landed on the island of
Eriskay, western Scotland, from France,
with seven men, on 23 July 1745, to
gather an army of Scotch clansmen and
others and to invade England in Nov.,
1745, launching the Jacobite Rebellion
that is the background for *Tom Jones.*
He started an affair with Miss Clementina
Walkinshaw while besieging Stirling,
Scotland, when on retreat toward the end
of his campaign. (They had a daughter,
his only child, who eventually nursed him
through his last illness.) Flora Macdon-
ald later obtained him a passport and
helped him escape the British disguised
as a woman. Jenny Cameron, a lady in
her late forties, was present among her
father's clansmen when Prince Charles
raised his flag at Glenfinnan, and later
was among the company when he held
court in Edinburgh, but had virtually no
personal acquaintance with him. Nevertheless, Whig pamphleteers pictured her
as his Amazonian mistress and companion
at arms.

mine. I hope, before she goes away, we shall have the News of a
Battle: For if the Chevalier should get the better, she may gain us
Interest at Court, and make our Fortunes without betraying her.'
'Why that's true,' replied the Wife; 'and I heartily hope she will
have it in her Power. Certainly she's a sweet good Lady; it would go
horribly against me to have her come to any Harm.' 'Pooh,' cries
the Landlord, 'Women are always so tender-hearted. Why you
would not harbour Rebels, would you?' 'No, certainly,' answered
the Wife; 'And as for betraying her, come what will on't, nobody
can blame us. It is what any body would do in our Case.'

While our politic Landlord, who had not, we see, undeservedly
the Reputation of great Wisdom among his Neighbours, was
engaged in debating this Matter with himself, (for he paid little
Attention to the Opinion of his Wife) News arrived that the
Rebels had given the Duke the Slip, and had got a Day's March
towards *London*; and soon after arrived a famous *Jacobite* Squire,
who, with great Joy in his Countenance, shook the Landlord by the
Hand, saying, 'All's our own, Boy, Ten thousand honest *Frenchmen*
are landed in *Suffolk*. Old *England* for ever! Ten thousand *French*,
my brave Lad! I am going to tap away directly.'

This News determined the Opinion of the wise Man, and he
resolved to make his Court to the young Lady, when she arose; for
he had now (he said) discovered that she was no other than
Madam *Jenny Cameron* herself.

Chapter III.

*A very short Chapter, in which however is a Sun, a Moon, a Star,
and an Angel.*

The Sun (for he keeps very good Hours at this Time of the
Year) had been some Time retired to Rest, when *Sophia* arose
greatly refreshed by her Sleep; which, short as it was, nothing but
her extreme Fatigue could have occasioned; for tho' she had told
her Maid, and perhaps herself too, that she was perfectly easy, when
she left *Upton*; yet it is certain her Mind was a little affected with
that Malady which is attended with all the restless Symptoms of a
Fever, and is perhaps the very Distemper which Physicians mean (if
they mean any thing) by the Fever on the Spirits.

Mrs. Fitzpatrick likewise left her Bed at the same Time; and
having summoned her Maid, immediately dressed herself. She was
really a very pretty Woman, and had she been in any other Company but that of *Sophia*, might have been thought beautiful; but
when Mrs. *Honour* of her own Accord attended, (for her Mistress
would not suffer her to be waked) and had equipped our Heroine,

the Charms of Mrs. *Fitzpatrick* who had performed the Office of
the Morning-Star, and had preceded greater Glories, shared the
Fate of that Star, and were totally eclipsed the Moment those Glories shone forth.

Perhaps *Sophia* never looked more beautiful than she did at this
Instant. We ought not therefore to condemn the Maid of the Inn
for her Hyperbole; who when she descended, after having lighted
the Fire, declared, and ratified it with an Oath, that if ever there
was an Angel upon Earth, she was now above Stairs.

Sophia had acquainted her Cousin with her Design to go to
London; and Mrs. *Fitzpatrick* had agreed to accompany her; for the
Arrival of her Husband at *Upton* had put an End to her Design of
going to *Bath*, or to her Aunt *Western*. They had therefore no
sooner finished their Tea, than *Sophia* proposed to set out, the
Moon then shining extremely bright, and as for the Frost she defied
it; nor had she any of those Apprehensions which many young
Ladies would have felt at travelling by Night; for she had, as we
have before observed, some little Degree of natural Courage; and
this her present Sensations, which bordered somewhat on Despair,
greatly encreased. Besides, as she had already travelled twice with
Safety, by the Light of the Moon, she was the better emboldened
to trust to it a third Time.

The Disposition of Mrs. *Fitzpatrick* was more timorous; for tho'
the greater Terrors had conquered the less, and the Presence of her
Husband had driven her away at so unseasonable an Hour from
Upton; yet being now arrived at a Place where she thought herself
safe from his Pursuit, these lesser Terrors of I know not what, operated so strongly, that she earnestly intreated her Cousin to stay till
the next Morning, and not expose herself to the Dangers of travelling by Night.

Sophia, who was yielding to an Excess, when she could neither
laugh nor reason her Cousin out of these Apprehensions, at last
gave way to them. Perhaps indeed, had she known of her Father's
Arrival at *Upton*, it might have been more difficult to have persuaded her; for as to *Jones*, she had, I am afraid, no great Horror at
the Thoughts of being overtaken by him; nay, to confess the Truth,
I believe she rather wished than feared it; though I might honestly
enough have concealed this Wish from the Reader, as it was one of
those secret spontaneous Emotions of the Soul, to which the
Reason is often a Stranger.

When our young Ladies had determined to remain all that Evening in their Inn, they were attended by the Landlady, who desired
to know what their Ladyships would be pleased to eat. Such
Charms were there in the Voice, in the Manner, and in the affable
Deportment of *Sophia*, that she ravished the Landlady to the high-

est Degree; and that good Woman, concluding that she had attended *Jenny Cameron*, became in a Moment a staunch *Jacobite*, and wished heartily well to the young Pretender's Cause, from the great Sweetness and Affability with which she had been treated by his supposed Mistress.

The two Cousins began now to impart to each other their reciprocal Curiosity, to know what extraordinary Accidents on both Sides occasioned this so strange and unexpected Meeting. At last Mrs. *Fitzpatrick*, having obtained of *Sophia* a Promise of communicating likewise in her Turn, began to relate what the Reader, if he is desirous to know her History, may read in the ensuing Chapter.

Chapter IV.

The History of Mrs. Fitzpatrick.

Mrs. *Fitzpatrick*, after a Silence of a few Moments, fetching a deep Sigh, thus began:

'It is natural to the Unhappy to feel a secret Concern in recollecting those Periods of their Lives which have been most delightful to them. The Remembrance of past Pleasures affects us with a kind of tender Grief, like what we suffer for departed Friends; and the Ideas of both may be said to haunt our Imaginations.

'For this Reason, I never reflect without Sorrow on those Days (the happiest far of my Life) which we spent together, when both were under the Care of my Aunt *Western*. Alas! why are Miss *Graveairs*, and Miss *Giddy* no more? You remember, I am sure, when we knew each other by no other Names. Indeed you gave the latter Appellation with too much Cause. I have since experienced how much I deserved it. You, my *Sophia*, was always my Superior in every thing, and I heartily hope you will be so in your Fortune. I shall never forget the wise and matronly Advice you once gave me, when I lamented being disappointed of a Ball, though you could not be then fourteen Years old.—O my *Sophy*, how blest must have been my Situation, when I could think such a Disappointment a Misfortune; and when indeed it was the greatest I had ever known!'

'And yet, my dear *Harriet*,' answered *Sophia*, 'it was then a serious Matter with you. Comfort yourself therefore with thinking, that whatever you now lament may hereafter appear as trifling and contemptible as a Ball would at this Time.'

'Alas, my *Sophia*,' replied the other Lady, 'you yourself will think otherwise of my present Situation; for greatly must that tender Heart be altered, if my Misfortunes do not draw many a Sigh, nay many a Tear, from you. The Knowledge of this should perhaps deter me from relating what I am convinced will so much affect you.'—Here Mrs. *Fitzpatrick* stopt, till at the repeated Entreaties of *Sophia*, she thus proceeded.

'Though you must have heard much of my Marriage; yet as Matters may probably have been misrepresented, I will set out from the very Commencement of my unfortunate Acquaintance with my present Husband; which was at *Bath*, soon after you left my Aunt, and returned home to your Father.

'Among the gay young Fellows, who were at this Season at *Bath*, Mr. *Fitzpatrick* was one. He was handsome, degagé, extremely gallant, and in his Dress exceeded most others. In short, my Dear, if you was unluckily to see him now, I could describe him no better than by telling you he was the very Reverse of every Thing which he is: For he hath rusticated himself so long, that he is become an absolute wild *Irishman*. But to proceed in my Story; the Qualifications which he then possessed so well recommended him, that though the People of Quality at that Time lived separate from the rest of the Company, and excluded them from all their Parties, Mr. *Fitzpatrick* found Means to gain Admittance. It was perhaps no easy Matter to avoid him; for he required very little or no Invitation; and as being handsome and genteel, he found it no very difficult Matter to ingratiate himself with the Ladies; so, he having frequently drawn his Sword, the Men did not care publickly to affront him. Had it not been for some such Reason, I believe he would have been soon expelled by his own Sex; for surely he had no strict Title to be preferred to the *English* Gentry; nor did they seem inclined to shew him any extraordinary Favour. They all abused him behind his Back, which might probably proceed from Envy; for by the Women he was well received, and very particularly distinguished by them.

'My Aunt, tho' no Person of Quality herself, as she had always lived about the Court, was enrolled in that Party: For by whatever Means you get into the Polite Circle, when you are once there, it is sufficient Merit for you that you are there. This Observation, young as you was, you could scarce avoid making from my Aunt, who was free, or reserved, with all People just as they had more or less of this Merit.

'And this Merit, I believe, it was, which principally recommended Mr. *Fitzpatrick* to her Favour. In which he so well succeeded, that he was always one of her private Parties. Nor was he backward in returning such Distinction; for he soon grew so very particular in his Behaviour to her, that the Scandal Club first began to take Notice of it, and the better disposed Persons made a Match between them. For my own Part, I confess, I made no Doubt but that his Designs were strictly honourable, as the Phrase is; that is, to rob a Lady of her Fortune by way of Marriage. My Aunt was, I conceived, neither young enough nor handsome enough, to attract much wicked Inclination; but she had matrimonial Charms in great Abundance.

'I was the more confirmed in this Opinion from the extraordinary Respect which he shewed to myself, from the first Moment of our Acquaintance. This I understood as an Attempt to lessen, if possible, that Disinclination which my Interest might be supposed to give me towards the Match; and I know not but in some Measure it had that Effect: For as I was well contented with my own Fortune, and of all People the least a Slave to interested Views; so I could not be violently the Enemy of a Man with whose Behaviour to me I was greatly pleased; and the more so, as I was the only Object of such Respect; for he behaved at the same Time to many Women of Quality without any Respect at all.

'Agreeable as this was to me, he soon changed it into another Kind of Behaviour, which was perhaps more so. He now put on much Softness and Tenderness, and languished and sighed abundantly. At Times indeed, whether from Art or Nature I will not determine, he gave his usual Loose to Gayety and Mirth; but this was always in general Company, and with other Women; for even in a Country-Dance, when he was not my Partner, he became grave; and put on the softest Look imaginable, the Moment he approached me. Indeed he was in all Things so very particular towards me, that I must have been blind not to have discovered it. And, and, and—' 'And you was more pleased still, my dear *Harriet*,' cries *Sophia*; 'you need not be ashamed,' added she sighing; 'for sure there are irresistible Charms in Tenderness, which too many Men are able to affect.' 'True,' answered her Cousin, 'Men, who in all other Instances want common Sense, are very *Machiavels* in the Art of Loving. I wish I did not know an Instance.—Well, Scandal now began to be as busy with me as it had before been with my Aunt; and some good Ladies did not scruple to affirm, that Mr. *Fitzpatrick* had an Intrigue with us both.

'But what may seem astonishing; my Aunt never saw, nor in the least seemed to suspect that which was visible enough, I believe, from both our Behaviours. One would indeed think, that Love quite puts out the Eyes of an old Woman. In Fact, they so greedily swallow the Addresses which are made to them, that like an outrageous Glutton, they are not at Leisure to observe what passes amongst others at the same Table. This I have observed in more Cases than my own; and this was so strongly verified by my Aunt, that, tho' she often found us together at her Return from the Pump, the least canting Word of his, pretending Impatience at her Absence, effectually smothered all Suspicion. One Artifice succeeded with her to Admiration. This was his treating me like a little Child, and never calling me by any other Name in her Presence, but that of pretty Miss. This indeed did him some Disservice with your humble Servant; but I soon saw through it, especially as in her Absence he behaved to me, as I have said, in a different Manner. However, if I was not greatly disobliged by a Conduct of which I had discovered the Design, I smarted very severely for it: For my Aunt really conceived me to be what her Lover (as she thought him) called me, and treated me, in all Respects, as a perfect Infant. To say the Truth, I wonder she had not insisted on my again wearing Leading-strings.

'At last, my Lover (for so he was) thought proper, in a most solemn Manner, to disclose a Secret which I had known long before. He now placed all the Love which he had pretended to my Aunt to my Account. He lamented, in very pathetic Terms, the Encouragement she had given him, and made a high Merit of the tedious Hours, in which he had undergone her Conversation.— What shall I tell you, my dear *Sophia?*—Then I will confess the Truth. I was pleased with my Man. I was pleased with my Conquest. To rival my Aunt delighted me; to rival so many other Women charmed me. In short, I am afraid, I did not behave as I should do, even upon the very first Declaration.—I wish I did not almost give him positive Encouragement before we parted.

'The *Bath* now talked loudly, I might almost say, roared against me. Several young Women affected to shun my Acquaintance, not so much, perhaps, from any real Suspicion, as from a Desire of banishing me from a Company, in which I too much engrossed their favourite Man. And here I cannot omit expressing my Gratitude to the Kindness intended me by Mr. *Nash;*[1] who took me one Day aside, and gave me Advice, which if I had followed, I had been a happy Woman. "Child," says he, "I am sorry to see the Familiarity which subsists between you and a Fellow who is altogether unworthy of you, and I am afraid will prove your Ruin. As for your old stinking Aunt, if it was to be no Injury to you, and pretty *Sophy Western*, (I assure you I repeat his Words) I should be heartily glad, that the Fellow was in Possession of all that belongs to her. I never advise old Women: For if they take it into their Heads to go to the Devil, it is no more possible, than worth while, to keep them from him. Innocence and Youth and Beauty are worthy a better Fate, and I would save them from his Clutches. Let me advise you therefore, dear Child, never suffer this Fellow to be particular with you again."—Many more Things he said to me, which I have now forgotten, and indeed I attended very little to them at that Time:

---

1. Richard "Beau" Nash (1674–1762), a gambler who in 1705 established the Assembly Rooms at Bath and drew up a code of dress and etiquette, becoming the acknowledged and absolute master of ceremonies for the resort.

For Inclination contradicted all he said; and besides I could not be persuaded, that Women of Quality would condescend to Familiarity with such a Person as he described.

'But I am afraid, my Dear, I shall tire you with a Detail of so many minute Circumstances. To be concise therefore, imagine me married; imagine me, with my Husband, at the Feet of my Aunt; and then imagine the maddest Woman in *Bedlam* in a raving Fit, and your Imagination will suggest to you no more than what really happened.

'The very next Day my Aunt left the Place, partly to avoid seeing Mr. *Fitzpatrick* or myself, and as much perhaps to avoid seeing any one else; for, tho' I am told she hath since denied every thing stoutly, I believe she was then a little confounded at her Disappointment. Since that Time I have written to her many Letters; but never could obtain an Answer, which I must own sits somewhat the heavier, as she herself was, tho' undesignedly, the Occasion of all my Sufferings: For had it not been under the Colour of paying his Addresses to her, Mr. *Fitzpatrick* would never have found sufficient Opportunities to have engaged my Heart, which, in other Circumstances, I still flatter myself would not have been an easy Conquest to such a Person. Indeed, I believe, I should not have erred so grosly in my Choice, if I had relied on my own Judgment; but I trusted totally to the Opinion of others, and very foolishly took the Merit of a Man for granted, whom I saw so universally well received by the Women. What is the Reason, my Dear, that we who have Understandings equal to the wisest and greatest of the other Sex, so often make Choice of the silliest Fellows for Companions and Favourites? It raises my Indignation to the highest Pitch, to reflect on the Numbers of Women of Sense who have been undone by Fools.' Here she paused a Moment; but *Sophia* making no Answer, she proceeded as in the next Chapter.

Chapter V.

In which the History of Mrs. Fitzpatrick *is continued.*

We remained at *Bath* no longer than a Fortnight after our Wedding: For as to any Reconciliation with my Aunt, there were no Hopes; and of my Fortune, not one Farthing could be touched till I was of Age, of which I now wanted more than two Years. My Husband therefore was resolved to set out for *Ireland*; against which I remonstrated very earnestly, and insisted on a Promise which he had made me before our Marriage, that I should never take this Journey against my Consent; and indeed I never intended to consent to it; nor will any Body, I believe, blame me for that Resolution; but this, however, I never mentioned to my Husband, and petitioned only for the Reprieve of a Month; but he had fixed the Day, and to that Day he obstinately adhered.

'The Evening before our Departure, as we were disputing this Point with great Eagerness on both Sides, he started suddenly from his Chair, and left me abruptly, saying, he was going to the Rooms. He was hardly out of the House, when I saw a Paper lying on the Floor, which, I suppose, he had carelessly pulled from his Pocket, together with his Handkerchief. This Paper I took up, and finding it to be a Letter, I made no Scruple to open and read it; and indeed I read it so often, that I can repeat it to you almost Word for Word. This then was the Letter.

To Mr. Brian Fitzpatrick.

Sir,

"Yours received, and am surprized you should use me in this Manner, as have never seen any of your Cash, unless for one Linsey-Woolsey Coat, and your Bill now is upwards of 150 *l.* Consider, Sir, how often you have fobbed me off with your being shortly to be married to this Lady, and t'other Lady; but I can neither live on Hopes or Promises, nor will my Woollen-draper take any such in Payment. You tell me you are secure of having either the Aunt or the Niece, and that you might have married the Aunt before this, whose Jointure you say is immense, but that you prefer the Niece on account of her ready Money. Pray, Sir, take a Fool's Advice for once, and marry the first you can get. You will pardon my offering my Advice, as you know I sincerely wish you well. Shall draw on you *per* next Post, in favour of Messieurs *John Drugget* and Company, at fourteen Days, which doubt not your honouring, and am,

Sir,
Your humble Servant,
SAM. COSGRAVE."

'This was the Letter Word for Word. Guess, my dear Girl, guess how this Letter affected me. *You prefer the Niece on account of her Ready Money!* If every one of these Words had been a Dagger, I could with Pleasure have stabbed them into his Heart; but I will not recount my frantic Behaviour on the Occasion. I had pretty well spent my Tears before his Return home; but sufficient Remains of them appeared in my swollen Eyes. He threw himself sullenly into his Chair, and for a long Time we were both silent. At length in a haughty Tone he said, "I hope, Madam, your Servants have packed up all your Things; for the Coach will be ready by Six in the Morning." My Patience was totally subdued by this Provocation, and

I answered, No, Sir, there is a Letter still remains unpacked; and then throwing it on the Table, I fell to upbraiding him with the most bitter Language I could invent.

'Whether Guilt, or Shame, or Prudence, restrained him, I cannot say; but tho' he is the most passionate of Men, he exerted no Rage on this Occasion. He endeavoured on the contrary to pacify me by the most gentle Means. He swore the Phrase in the Letter to which I principally objected was not his, nor had he ever written any such. He owned indeed the having mentioned his Marriage, and that Preference which he had given to myself, but denied with many Oaths the having assigned any such Reason. And he excused the having mentioned any such Matter at all, on account of the Straits he was in for Money, arising, he said, from his having too long neglected his Estate in *Ireland*. And this, he said, which he could not bear to discover to me, was the only Reason of his having so strenuously insisted on our Journey. He then used several very endearing Expressions, and concluded by a very fond Caress, and many violent Protestations of Love.

'There was one Circumstance, which, tho' he did not appeal to it, had much Weight with me in his Favour, and that was the Word Jointure in the Taylor's Letter, whereas my Aunt never had been married, and this Mr. *Fitzpatrick* well knew.——As I imagined therefore that the Fellow must have inserted this of his own Head, or from Hearsay, I persuaded myself he might have ventured likewise on that odious Line on no better Authority. What Reasoning was this, my Dear? Was I not an Advocate rather than a Judge? —But why do I mention such a Circumstance as this, or appeal to it for the Justification of my Forgiveness!—In short, had he been guilty of twenty times as much, half the Tenderness and Fondness which he used, would have prevailed on me to have forgiven him. I now made no farther Objections to our setting out, which we did the next Morning, and in a little more than a Week arrived at the Seat of Mr. *Fitzpatrick*.

'Your Curiosity will excuse me from relating any Occurrences which past during our Journey: For it would indeed be highly disagreeable to travel it over again, and no less so to you to travel it over with me.

'This Seat then, is an ancient Mansion-House: If I was in one of those merry Humours, in which you have so often seen me, I could describe it to you ridiculously enough. It looked as if it had been formerly inhabited by a Gentleman. Here was Room enough, and not the less Room on account of the Furniture: For indeed there was very little in it. An old Woman,[1] who seemed coeval with the

---

1. See above, note 1, p. 338. Chamont, brother of Monimia, describes at length "a wrinkled hag, with age grown dou-ble," who tells him to hasten to save his sister (II.i.246–56).

Building, and greatly resembled her whom *Chamont* mentions in the *Orphan*, received us at the Gate, and in a Howl scarce human, and to me unintelligible, welcomed her Master home. In short, the whole Scene was so gloomy and melancholy, that it threw my Spirits into the lowest Dejection; which my Husband discerning, instead of relieving, encreased by two or three malicious Observations. "There are good Houses, Madam," says he, "as you find, in other Places besides *England*; but perhaps you had rather be in a dirty Lodgings at *Bath*."

'Happy, my Dear, is the Woman, who in any State of Life, hath a cheerful good-natured Companion to support and comfort her; but why do I reflect on happy Situations only to aggravate my own Misery! My Companion, far from clearing up the Gloom of Solitude, soon convinced me, that I must have been wretched with him in any Place, and in any Condition. In a Word, he was a surly Fellow, a Character you have perhaps never seen: For indeed no Woman ever sees it exemplified, but in a Father, a Brother, or a Husband; and tho' you have a Father, he is not of that Character. This surly Fellow had formerly appeared to me the very Reverse, and so he did still to every other Person. Good Heaven! how is it possible for a Man to maintain a constant Lie in his Appearance abroad and in Company, and to content himself with shewing disagreeable Truth only at home? Here, my Dear, they make themselves Amends for the uneasy Restraint which they put on their Tempers in the World; for I have observed the more merry and gay and good-humoured my Husband hath at any Time been in Company, the more sullen and morose he was sure to become at our next private Meeting. How shall I describe his Barbarity? To my Fondness he was cold and insensible. My little comical Ways, which you, my *Sophy*, and which others have called so agreeable, he treated with Contempt. In my most serious Moments he sung and whistled; and whenever I was thoroughly dejected and miserable, he was angry, and abused me: For though he was never pleased with my good Humour, nor ascribed it to my Satisfaction in him; yet my low Spirits always offended him, and those he imputed to my Repentance of having (as he said) married an *Irishman*.

'You will easily conceive, my dear *Graveairs*; (I ask your Pardon, I really forgot myself) that when a Woman makes an imprudent Match in the Sense of the World; that is, when she is not an arrant Prostitute to pecuniary Interest, she must necessarily have some Inclination and Affection for her Man. You will as easily believe that this Affection may possibly be lessened; nay, I do assure you, Contempt will wholly eradicate it. This Contempt I now began to entertain for my Husband, whom I now discovered to be—I must use the Expression—an arrant Blockhead. Perhaps you will wonder I

did not make this Discovery long before; but Women will suggest a
thousand Excuses to themselves for the Folly of those they like:
Besides, give me Leave to tell you, it requires a most penetrating
Eye to discern a Fool through the Disguises of Gayety and Good-
breeding.

'It will be easily imagined, that when I once despised my Husband, as I confess to you I soon did, I must consequently dislike his
Company; and indeed I had the Happiness of being very little troubled with it; for our House was now most elegantly furnished, our
Cellars well stocked, and Dogs and Horses provided in great Abundance. As my Gentleman therefore entertained his Neighbours with
great Hospitality; so his Neighbours resorted to him with great
Alacrity; and Sports and Drinking consumed so much of his Time,
that a small Part of his Conversation, that is to say, of his Ill-hu-
mours, fell to my Share.

'Happy would it have been for me, if I could as easily have
avoided all other disagreeable Company; but alas! I was confined to
some which constantly tormented me; and the more, as I saw no
Prospect of being relieved from them. These Companions were my
own racking Thoughts, which plagued, and in a manner haunted me
Night and Day. In this Situation I past through a Scene, the Horrors
of which can neither be painted nor imagined. Think, my Dear, figure, if you can, to yourself what I must have undergone. I became a
Mother by the Man I scorned, hated, and detested. I went through
all the Agonies and Miseries of a Lying-in, (ten Times more painful
in such a Circumstance, than the worst Labour can be, when one
endures it for a Man one loves,) in a Desert, or rather indeed a
Scene of Riot and Revel, without a Friend, without a Companion,
or without any of those agreeable Circumstances which often alle-
viate, and perhaps sometimes more than compensate the Sufferings
of our Sex at that Season.'

Chapter VI.

In which the Mistake of the Landlord throws Sophia *into a dreadful
Consternation.*

Mrs. *Fitzpatrick* was proceeding in her Narrative, when she was
interrupted by the Entrance of Dinner, greatly to the Concern of
Sophia: For the Misfortunes of her Friend had raised her Anxiety,
and left her no Appetite, but what Mrs. *Fitzpatrick* was to satisfy
by her Relation.

The Landlord now attended with a Plate under his Arm, and
with the same Respect in his Countenance and Address, which he
would have put on, had the Ladies arrived in a Coach and Six.

The married Lady seemed less affected with her own Misfortunes than was her Cousin: For the former eat very heartily, whereas the latter could hardly swallow a Morsel. *Sophia* likewise shewed more Concern and Sorrow in her Countenance than appeared in the other Lady; who having observed these Symptoms in her Friend, begged her to be comforted, saying, 'Perhaps all may yet end better than either you or I expect.'

Our Landlord thought he had now an Opportunity to open his Mouth, and was resolved not to omit it. 'I am sorry, Madam,' cries he, 'that your Ladyship can't eat; for to be sure you must be hungry after so long fasting. I hope your Ladyship is not uneasy at any thing: For, as Madam there says, all may end better than any body expects. A Gentleman who was here just now, brought excellent News; and perhaps some Folks who have given other Folks the Slip, may get to *London* before they are overtaken; and if they do, I make no Doubt, but they will find People who will be very ready to receive them.'

All Persons under the Apprehension of Danger convert whatever they see and hear into the Objects of that Apprehension. *Sophia* therefore immediately concluded from the foregoing Speech, that she was known and pursued by her Father. She was now struck with the utmost Consternation, and for a few Minutes deprived of the Power of Speech; which she no sooner recovered, than she desired the Landlord to send his Servants out of the Room, and then addressing herself to him, said: 'I perceive, Sir, you know who we are; but I beseech you;—nay, I am convinced, if you have any Compassion or Goodness, you will not betray us.'

'I betray your Ladyship!' quoth the Landlord; 'No;' (and then he swore several very hearty Oaths) 'I would sooner be cut into ten thousand Pieces. I hate all Treachery. I! I never betrayed any one in my Life yet, and I am sure I shall not begin with so sweet a Lady as your Ladyship. All the World would very much blame me if I should, since it will be in your Ladyship's Power so shortly to reward me. My Wife can witness for me, I knew your Ladyship the Moment you came into the House: I said it was your Honour, before I lifted you from your Horse, and I shall carry the Bruises I got in your Ladyship's Service to the Grave; but what signified that, as long as I saved your Ladyship? To be sure some People this Morning would have thought of getting a Reward; but no such Thought ever entered into my Head. I would sooner starve than take any Reward for betraying your Ladyship.'

'I promise you, Sir,' says *Sophia*, 'if it be ever in my Power to reward you, you shall not lose by your Generosity.'

'Alack-a-day, Madam!' answered the Landlord, 'in your Ladyship's Power! Heaven put it as much into your Will. I am only afraid your Honour will forget such a poor Man as an Innkeeper; but if your Ladyship should not, I hope you will remember what Reward I refused—refused! that is, I would have refused, and to be sure it may be called refusing; for I might have had it certainly; and to be sure you might have been in some Houses;—but for my Part, would not methinks for the World have your Ladyship wrong me so much, as to imagine I ever thought of betraying you, even before I heard the good News.'

'What News pray?' says *Sophia*, something eagerly.

'Hath not your Ladyship heard it then?' cries the Landlord, 'nay, like enough: For I heard it only a few Minutes ago; and if I had never heard it, may the Devil fly away with me this Instant, if I would have betrayed your Honour; no, if I would, may I,—Here he subjoined several dreadful Imprecations, which *Sophia* at last interrupted, and begged to know what he meant by the News.—He was going to answer, when Mrs. *Honour* came running into the Room, all pale and breathless, and cried out, 'Madam, we are all undone, all ruined, they are come, they are come!' These Words almost froze up the Blood of *Sophia*; but Mrs. *Fitzpatrick* asked *Honour*, who were come?—'Who?' answered she, 'why the *French*; several hundred thousands of them are landed, and we shall be all murdered and ravished.'

As a Miser, who hath in some well-built City a Cottage value Twenty Shillings, when at a Distance he is alarmed with the News of a Fire, turns pale and trembles at his Loss; but when he finds the beautiful Palaces only are burnt, and his own Cottage remains safe, he comes instantly to himself and smiles at his good Fortunes: Or as (for we dislike something in the former Simile) the tender Mother, when terrified with the Apprehension that her darling Boy is drowned, is struck senseless and almost dead with Consternation; but when she is told that little Master is safe, and the *Victory*[2] only with Twelve hundred brave Men gone to the Bottom, Life and Sense again return, maternal Fondness enjoys the sudden Relief from all its Fears, and the general Benevolence which at another Time would have deeply felt the dreadful Catastrophe, lies fast asleep in her Mind.

So *Sophia*, than whom none was more capable of tenderly feeling the general Calamity of her Country, found such immediate Satisfaction from the Relief of those Terrors she had of being overtaken by her Father, that the Arrival of the *French* scarce made any

2. The flagship of Admiral Sir John Balchen, whose fleet of twenty-two ships, returning victorious from a sortie against France and Spain at Lisbon, was hit by a terrific storm in the English Channel. All the rest limped home, but the *Victory* went down with all hands off the coast of France on the night of 4–5 Oct. 1744. Some 975 men, plus 80 midshipmen in training, were aboard. Only a few pieces of wreckage were recovered. Nelson's famous flagship, launched in 1765, was named for her, after considerable debate about ill omens.

Impression on her. She gently chid her Maid for the Fright into which she had thrown her; and said, 'she was glad it was no worse; for that she had feared somebody else was come.'

'Ay, ay,' quoth the Landlord smiling, 'her Ladyship knows better Things; she knows the *French* are our very best Friends, and come over hither only for our Good. They are the People who are to make old *England* flourish again. I warrant her Honour thought the Duke was coming; and that was enough to put her into a Fright. I was going to tell your Ladyship the News.—His Honour's Majesty, Heaven bless him, hath given the Duke the Slip; and is marching as fast as he can to *London,* and Ten thousand *French* are landed to join him on the Road.'

Sophia was not greatly pleased with this News, nor with the Gentleman who related it; but as she still imagined he knew her (for she could not possibly have any Suspicion of the real Truth) she durst not shew any Dislike. And now the Landlord, having removed the Cloth from the Table, withdrew; but at his Departure frequently repeated his Hopes of being remembered hereafter.

The Mind of *Sophia* was not at all easy under the Supposition of being known at this House; for she still applied to herself many Things which the Landlord had addressed to *Jenny Cameron;* she therefore ordered her Maid to pump out of him by what Means he had become acquainted with her Person, and who had offered him the Reward for betraying her; she likewise ordered the Horses to be in Readiness by Four in the Morning, at which Hour Mrs. *Fitzpatrick* promised to bear her Company; and then composing herself as well as she could, she desired that Lady to continue her Story.

Chapter VII.

In which Mrs. Fitzpatrick *concludes her History.*

While Mrs. *Honour,* in Pursuance of the Commands of her Mistress, ordered a Bowl of Punch, and invited my Landlord and Landlady to partake of it, Mrs. *Fitzpatrick* thus went on with her Relation.

'Most of the Officers who were quartered at a Town in our Neighbourhood were of my Husband's Acquaintance. Among these was a Lieutenant, a very pretty Sort of Man, and who was married to a Woman so agreeable both in her Temper and Conversation, that from our first knowing each other, which was soon after my Lying-in, we were almost inseparable Companions; for I had the good Fortune to make myself equally agreeable to her.

'The Lieutenant, who was neither a Sot nor a Sportsman, was frequently of our Parties; indeed he was very little with my Husband,

and no more than good Breeding constrained him to be, as he lived almost constantly at our House. My Husband often expressed much Dissatisfaction at the Lieutenant's preferring my Company to his; he was very angry with me on that Account, and gave me many a hearty Curse for drawing away his Companions; saying, "I ought to be d—ned for having spoiled one of the prettiest Fellows in the World, by making a Milk-sop of him.

'You will be mistaken, my dear *Sophia*, if you imagine that the Anger of my Husband arose from my depriving him of a Companion; for the Lieutenant was not a Person with whose Society a Fool could be pleased; and if I should admit the Possibility of this, so little Right had my Husband to place the Loss of his Companion to me, that I am convinced it was my Conversation alone which induced him ever to come to the House. No, Child, it was Envy, the worst and most rancorous Kind of Envy, the Envy of Superiority of Understanding. The Wretch could not bear to see my Conversation preferred to his, by a Man of whom he could not entertain the least Jealousy. O my dear *Sophy*, you are a Woman of Sense; if you marry a Man, as is most probable you will, of less Capacity than yourself, make frequent Trials of his Temper before Marriage, and see whether he can bear to submit to such a Superiority.—Promise me, *Sophy*, you will take this Advice; for you will hereafter find its Importance.' 'It is very likely I shall never marry at all,' answered *Sophia*; 'I think, at least, I shall never marry a Man in whose Understanding I see any Defects before Marriage; and I promise you I would rather give up my own, than see any such afterwards.'—'Give up your Understanding!' replied Mrs. *Fitzpatrick*, 'Oh fie, Child, I will not believe so meanly of you. Every thing else I might myself be brought to give up: but never this. Nature would not have allotted this Superiority to the Wife in so many Instances, if she had intended we should all of us have surrendered it to the Husband. This indeed Men of Sense never expect of us; of which the Lieutenant I have just mentioned was one notable Example; for tho' he had a very good Understanding, he always acknowledged (as was really true) that his Wife had a better. And this, perhaps, was one Reason of the Hatred my Tyrant bore her.

'Before he would be so governed by a Wife, he said, especially such an ugly B——(for indeed she was not a regular Beauty, but very agreeable, and extremely genteel) he would see all the Women upon Earth at the Devil, which was a very usual Phrase with him. He said, he wondered what I could see in her to be so charmed with her Company; since this Woman, says he, hath come among us, there is an End of your beloved Reading, which you pretended to like so much, that you could not afford Time to return the Visits of the Ladies, in this Country;' and I must confess I had been

guilty of a little Rudeness this Way; for the Ladies there are at least
no better than the mere Country Ladies here; and I think I need
make no other Excuse to you for declining any Intimacy with them.

'This Correspondence however continued a whole Year, even all
the while the Lieutenant was quartered in that Town; for which I
was contented to pay the Tax of being constantly abused in the
Manner above-mentioned by my Husband; I mean when he was at
home; for he was frequently absent a Month at a Time at *Dublin*,
and once made a Journey of two Months to *London*; in all which
Journeys I thought it a very singular Happiness that he never once
desired my Company; nay, by his frequent Censures on Men who
could not travel, as he phrased it, without a Wife tied up to their
Tail, he sufficiently intimated that had I been never so desirous of
accompanying him, my Wishes would have been in vain; but,
Heaven knows, such Wishes were very far from my Thoughts.

'At length my Friend was removed from me, and I was again left
to my Solitude, to the tormenting Conversation with my own
Reflections, and to apply to Books for my only Comfort. I now read
almost all Day long.—How many Books do you think I read in
three Months?' 'I can't guess, indeed, Cousin,' answered *Sophia*.—
—'Perhaps half a Score!' 'Half a Score! half a Thousand, Child,'
answered the other. 'I read a good deal in *Daniel's English* History
of *France*; a great deal in *Plutarch's* Lives; the *Atalantis*, *Pope's*
Homer, *Dryden's* Plays, *Chillingworth*, the *Countess D'Anois*,[1]
and *Lock's* Human Understanding.

'During this Interval I wrote three very supplicating, and, I
thought, moving Letters to my Aunt; but as I received no Answer
to any of them, my Disdain would not suffer me to continue my
Application.'—Here she stopt, and looking earnestly at *Sophia*, said,
'Methinks, my Dear, I read something in your Eyes which
reproaches me of a Neglect in another Place, where I should have
met with a kinder Return.' 'Indeed, dear *Harriet*,' answered *Sophia*,
'your Story is an Apology for any Neglect; but indeed I feel that I
have been guilty of a Remissness, without so good an Excuse.—Yet
pray proceed; for I long, tho' I tremble, to hear the End.'

Thus then Mrs. *Fitzpatrick* resumed her Narrative, 'My Husband
now took a second Journey to *England*, where he continued
upwards of three Months. During the greater Part of this Time, I

---

1. Père Gabriel Daniel (1649–1728), a Jesuit, author of *Histoire de France depuis l'établissement de la monarchie Française* (1713, English trans., 1726); Mary Manley, *The New Atalantis* (1709), a spicy novel about amorous intrigues of prominent people presented as affairs on an imaginary Mediterranean island; William Chillingworth, *The Religion of Protestants, a Safe Way to Salvation* (1637), a controversial book arguing both for Biblical authority and for individual freedom to interpret it, commended by Locke and generally esteemed; Countess Marie-Catherine d'Aulnoy, *Histoire de Hypolite, Comte de Douglas* (1690; trans. as *Hypolitus, Earl of Douglas*, 1708), a thriller long popular; she was noted for her fairy tales.

led a Life which nothing but having led a worse, could make me think tolerable; for perfect Solitude can never be reconciled to a social Mind, like mine, but when it relieves you from the Company of those you hate. What added to my Wretchedness, was the Loss of my little Infant: Not that I pretend to have had for it that extravagant Tenderness of which I believe I might have been capable under other Circumstances; but I resolved, in every Instance, to discharge the Duty of the tenderest Mother; and this Care prevented me from feeling the Weight of that, heaviest of all Things, when it can be at all said to lie heavy on our Hands.

'I had spent full ten Weeks almost entirely by myself, having seen no body all that Time, except my Servants, and a very few Visiters, when a young Lady, a Relation to my Husband, came from a distant Part of *Ireland* to visit me. She had staid once before a Week at my House, and then I gave her a pressing Invitation to return; for she was a very agreeable Woman, and had improved good natural Parts by a proper Education. Indeed she was to me a most welcome Guest.

'A few Days after her Arrival, perceiving me in very low spirits, without enquiring the Cause, which indeed she very well knew, the young Lady fell to compassionating my Case. She said, "Tho' Politeness had prevented me from complaining to my Husband's Relations of his Behavior; yet they all were very sensible of it, and felt great Concern upon that Account; but none more than herself:" And after some more general Discourse on this Head, which I own I could not forbear countenancing; at last, after much previous Precaution, and enjoined Concealment, she communicated to me, as a profound Secret—that my Husband kept a Mistress.

'You will certainly imagine, I heard this News with the utmost Insensibility—Upon my Word, if you do, your Imagination will mislead you. Contempt had not so kept down my Anger to my Husband, but that Hatred rose again on this Occasion. What can be the Reason of this? Are we so abominably selfish, that we can be concerned at others having Possession even of what we despise? Or are we not rather abominably vain, and is not this the greatest Injury done to our Vanity? What think you, *Sophia*?'

'I don't know, indeed,' answered *Sophia*, 'I have never troubled myself with any of these deep Contemplations; but I think the Lady did very ill in communicating to you such a Secret.'

'And yet, my Dear, this Conduct is natural,' replied Mrs. *Fitzpatrick*; 'and when you have seen and read as much as myself, you will acknowledge it to be so.'

'I am sorry to hear it is natural,' returned *Sophia*; 'for I want neither Reading nor Experience to convince me, that it is very dishonourable and very ill-natured: Nay, it is surely as ill-bred to tell a

Husband or Wife of the Faults of each other, as to tell them of their own.'

'Well,' continued Mrs. *Fitzpatrick,* 'my Husband at last returned; and if I am thoroughly acquainted with my own Thoughts, I hated him now more than ever; but I despised him rather less: For certainly nothing so much weakens our Contempt, as an Injury done to our Pride or our Vanity.

'He now assumed a Carriage to me, so very different from what he had lately worn, and so nearly resembling his Behaviour the first Week of our Marriage, that had I now had any Spark of Love remaining, he might, possibly, have rekindled my Fondness for him. But though Hatred may succeed to Contempt, and may, perhaps, get the better of it, Love, I believe, cannot. The Truth is, the Passion of Love is too restless to remain contented, without the Gratification which it receives from its Object; and one can no more be inclined to love without loving, than we can have Eyes without seeing. When a Husband, therefore, ceases to be the Object of this Passion, it is most probable some other Man—I say, my Dear, if your Husband grows indifferent to you—if you once come to despise him—I say,—that is,—if you have the Passion of Love in you—Lud! I have bewildered myself so,—but one is apt, in these abstracted Considerations, to lose the Concatenation of Ideas, as Mr. *Locke* says.—In short, the Truth is—In short, I scarce know what it is; but, as I was saying, my Husband returned, and his Behaviour, at first, greatly surprized me; but he soon acquainted me with the Motive; and taught me to account for it. In a Word, then, he had spent and lost all the ready Money of my Fortune; and as he could mortgage his own Estate no deeper, he was now desirous to supply himself with Cash for his Extravagance, by selling a little Estate of mine, which he could not do without my Assistance; and to obtain this Favour was the whole and sole Motive of all the Fondness which he now put on.

'With this I peremptorily refused to comply. I told him, and I told him truly, that had I been possessed of the *Indies* at our first Marriage, he might have commanded it all: For it had been a constant Maxim with me, that where a Woman disposes of her Heart, she should always deposite her Fortune; but as he had been so kind, long ago, to restore the former into my Possession, I was resolved likewise to retain what little remained of the latter.

'I will not describe to you the Passion into which these Words, and the resolute Air in which they were spoken, threw him: Nor will I trouble you with the whole Scene which succeeded between us. Out came, you may be well assured, the Story of the Mistress; and out it did come, with all the Embellishments which Anger and Disdain could bestow upon it.

'Mr. *Fitzpatrick* seemed a little Thunder-struck with this, and more confused than I had seen him; tho' his Ideas are always confused enough, Heaven knows. He did not, however, endeavour to exculpate himself; but took a Method which almost equally confounded me. What was this but Recrimination! He affected to be jealous;—he may, for ought I know, be inclined enough to Jealousy in his natural Temper: Nay, he must have had it from Nature, or the Devil must have put it into his Head; for I defy all the World to cast a just Aspersion on my Character: Nay, the most scandalous Tongues have never dared censure my Reputation. My Fame, I thank Heaven, hath been always as spotless as my Life; and let Falshood itself accuse that, if it dare. No, my dear *Graveairs*, however provoked, however ill treated, however injured in my Love, I have firmly resolved never to give the least Room for Censure on this Account.—And yet, my Dear, there are some People so malicious, some Tongues so venomous, that no Innocence can escape them. The most undesigned Word, the most accidental Look, the least Familiarity, the most innocent Freedom, will be misconstrued, and magnified into I know not what, by some People. But I despise, my dear *Graveairs*, I despise all such Slander. No such Malice, I assure you, ever gave me an uneasy Moment. No, no, I promise you I am above all that.—But where was I? O let me see, I told you my Husband was jealous—And of whom, pray?—Why of whom but the Lieutenant I mentioned to you before? He was obliged to resort above a Year and more back, to find any Object for this unaccountable Passion, if indeed he really felt any such, and was not an arrant Counterfeit, in order to abuse me.

'But I have tired you already with too many Particulars. I will now bring my Story to a very speedy Conclusion. In short, then, after many Scenes very unworthy to be repeated, in which my Cousin engaged so heartily on my Side, that Mr. *Fitzpatrick* at last turned her out of Doors; when he found I was neither to be soothed nor bullied into Compliance, he took a very violent Method indeed. Perhaps you will conclude he beat me; but this, tho' he hath approached very near to it, he never actually did. He confined me to my Room, without suffering me to have either Pen, Ink, Paper, or Book; and a Servant every Day made my Bed, and brought me my Food.

'When I had remained a Week under this Imprisonment, he made me a Visit, and, with the Voice of a Schoolmaster, or, what is often much the same, of a Tyrant, asked me, "If I would yet comply?" I answered very stoutly, "That I would die first." "Then so you shall, and be d—n'd," cries he; "for you shall never go alive out of this Room."

'Here I remained a Fortnight longer; and, to say the Truth, my

Constancy was almost subdued, and I began to think of Submission; when one Day, in the Absence of my Husband, who was gone abroad for some short Time, by the greatest good Fortune in the World, an Accident happened.—I—at a Time when I began to give Way to the utmost Despair—every Thing would be excusable at such a Time—at that very Time I received—But it would take up an Hour to tell you all Particulars.—In one Word, then, (for I will not tire you with Circumstances) Gold, the common Key to all Padlocks, opened my Door, and set me at Liberty.

'I now made haste to *Dublin,* where I immediately procured a Passage to *England;* and was proceeding to *Bath,* in order to throw myself into the Protection of my Aunt, or of your Father, or of any Relation who would afford it me. My Husband overtook me last Night, at the Inn where I lay, and which you left a few Minutes before me; but I had the good Luck to escape him, and to follow you.

'And thus, my Dear, ends my History: A tragical one, I am sure, it is to myself; but, perhaps, I ought rather to apologize to you for its Dulness.'

Sophia heaved a deep Sigh, and answered, 'Indeed, *Harriet,* I pity you from my Soul!—But what could you expect? Why, why, would you marry an *Irishman?*'

'Upon my Word,' replied her Cousin, 'your Censure is unjust. There are, among the *Irish,* Men of as much Worth and Honour, as any among the *English:* Nay, to speak the Truth, Generosity of Spirit is rather more common among them. I have known some Examples there too of good Husbands; and, I believe, these are not very plenty in *England.* Ask me, rather, what I could expect when I married a Fool; and I will tell you a solemn Truth; I did not know him to be so.'—'Can no Man,' said *Sophia,* in a very low and alter'd Voice, 'do you think, make a bad Husband, who is not a Fool?' 'That,' answered the other, 'is too general a Negative; but none, I believe, is so likely as a Fool to prove so. Among my Acquaintance, the silliest Fellows are the worst Husbands; and I will venture to assert, as a Fact, that a Man of Sense rarely behaves very ill to a Wife, who deserves very well.'

Chapter VIII.

A dreadful Alarm in the Inn, with the Arrival of an unexpected Friend of Mrs. Fitzpatrick.

Sophia now, at the Desire of her Cousin, related—not what follows, but what hath gone before in this History: For which Reason the Reader will, I suppose, excuse me, for not repeating it over again.

One Remark, however, I cannot forbear making on her Narrative, namely, that she made no more mention of *Jones*, from the Beginning to the End, than if there had been no such Person alive. This I will neither endeavour to account for, nor to excuse. Indeed, if this may be called a Kind of Dishonesty, it seems the more inexcusable, from the apparent Openness and explicit Sincerity of the other Lady.—But so it was.

Just as *Sophia* arrived at the Conclusion of her Story, there arrived in the Room where the two Ladies were sitting, a Noise, not unlike, in Loudness, to that of a Pack of Hounds just let out from their Kennel; nor, in Shrillness, to Cats, when caterwauling; or, to Screech-Owls; or, indeed, more like (for what Animal can resemble a human Voice?) to those Sounds, which, in the pleasant Mansions of that Gate, which seems to derive its Name from a Duplicity of Tongues, issue from the Mouths, and sometimes from the Nostrils of those fair River Nymphs, ycleped of old the *Naïades*; in the vulgar Tongue translated Oyster-Wenches: For when, instead of the antient Libations of Milk and Honey and Oil, the rich Distillation from the Juniper-Berry, or perhaps, from Malt, hath, by the early Devotion of their Votaries, been poured forth in great Abundance, should any daring Tongue with unhallowed License prophane; *i. e.* depreciate the delicate fat *Milton* Oyster,[1] the Plaice sound and firm, the Flounder as much alive as when in the Water, the Shrimp as big as a Prawn, the fine Cod alive but a few Hours ago, or any other of the various Treasures, which those Water-Deities, who fish the Sea and Rivers, have committed to the Care of the Nymphs, the angry *Naïades* lift up their immortal Voices, and the prophane Wretch is struck deaf for his Impiety.

Such was the Noise, which now burst from one of the Rooms below; and soon the Thunder, which long had rattled at a Distance, began to approach nearer and nearer, 'till, having ascended by Degrees up Stairs, it at last entered the Apartment where the Ladies were. In short, to drop all Metaphor and Figure, Mrs. *Honour* having scolded violently below Stairs, and continued the same all the Way up, came in to her Mistress in a most outragious Passion, crying out, 'What doth your Ladyship think? Would you imagine, that this impudent Villain, the Master of this House, hath had the Impudence to tell me, nay, to stand it out to my Face, that your Ladyship is that nasty, stinking Wh—re, (*Jenny Cameron* they call her) that runs about the Country with the Pretender? Nay, the lying, saucy Villain, had the Assurance to tell me, that your Ladyship had owned yourself to be so: But I have clawed the Rascal; I have left the Marks of my Nails in his impudent Face. My Lady!' says I, 'you saucy Scoundrel: My Lady is Meat for no Pretenders.

---

1. Milton, a town famous for its oysters, is located at the head of the Swale, an estuary in Kent, just south of the mouth of the Thames.

She is a young Lady of as good Fashion, and Family, and Fortune, as any in *Somersetshire*. Did you never hear of the great Squire *Western*, Sirrah? She is his only Daughter; she is,——and Heiress to all his great Estate. My Lady to be called a nasty *Scotch* Wh——re by such a Varlet—To be sure, I wish I had knocked his Brains out with the Punch-bowl.'

The principal Uneasiness with which *Sophia* was affected on this Occasion, *Honour* had herself caused, by having in her Passion discovered who she was. However, as this Mistake of the Landlord sufficiently accounted for those Passages which *Sophia* had before mistaken, she acquired some Ease on that Account; nor could she, upon the whole, forbear smiling. This enraged *Honour*, and she cried, 'Indeed, Madam, I did not think your Ladyship would have made a laughing Matter of it. To be called Whore by such an impudent low Rascal. Your Ladyship may be angry with me, for ought I know, for taking your Part, since proffered Service, they say, stinks; but to be sure I could never bear to hear a Lady of mine called Whore.—Nor will I bear it. I am sure your Ladyship is as virtuous a Lady as ever sat Foot on *English* Ground, and I will claw any Villain's Eyes out who dares for to offer to presume for to say the least Word to the contrary. No body ever could say the least ill of the Character of any Lady that ever I waited upon.'

Hinc illæ Lachrymæ;[2] in plain Truth, *Honour* had as much Love for her Mistress as most Servants have, that is to say—But besides this, her Pride obliged her to support the Character of the Lady she waited on; for she thought her own was in a very close Manner connected with it. In Proportion as the Character of her Mistress was raised, hers likewise, as she conceived, was raised with it; and, on the contrary, she thought the one could not be lowered without the other.

On this Subject, Reader, I must stop a Moment to tell thee a Story. 'The famous *Nell Gwynn*,[3] stepping one Day from a House where she had made a short Visit into her Coach, saw a great Mob assembled, and her Footman all bloody and dirty; the Fellow being asked by his Mistress, the Reason of his being in that Condition, answered, "I have been fighting, Madam, with an impudent Rascal who called your Ladyship a Wh——re." "You Blockhead," replied Mrs. *Gwynn*, "at this Rate you must fight every Day of your Life; why, you Fool, all the World knows it." "Do they?" cries the Fellow, in a muttering Voice, after he had shut the Coach Door, "they shan't call me a Whore's Footman for all that." '

Thus the Passion of Mrs. *Honour* appears natural enough, even if it were to be no otherwise accounted for; but, in reality, there was

2. See above, note 6, p. 315.
3. Eleanor Gwyn (1650–87), notable   comic actress, though illiterate, and mistress of Charles II.

another Cause of her Anger; for which we must beg Leave to remind our Reader of a Circumstance mentioned in the above Simile. There are indeed certain Liquors, which being applied to our Passions, or to Fire, produce Effects the very Reverse of those produced by Water, as they serve to kindle and inflame, rather than to extinguish. Among these, the generous Liquor called Punch is one. It was not therefore without Reason, that the learned Dr. *Cheney*[4] used to call drinking Punch, pouring liquid Fire down your Throat.

Now Mrs. *Honour* had unluckily poured so much of this liquid Fire down her Throat, that the Smoke of it began to ascend into her Pericranium, and blinded the Eyes of Reason which is there supposed to keep her Residence, while the Fire itself from the Stomach easily reached the Heart, and there inflamed the noble Passion of Pride. So that upon the whole, we shall cease to wonder at the violent Rage of the Waiting-woman; tho' at first sight we must confess the Cause seems inadequate to the Effect.

Sophia, and her Cousin both, did all in their Power to extinguish these Flames which had roared so loudly all over the House. They at length prevailed; or, to carry the Metaphor one Step farther, the Fire having consumed all the Fuel which the Language affords, to wit, every reproachful Term in it, at last went out of its own Accord.

But tho' Tranquillity was restored above Stairs, it was not so below; where my Landlady highly resenting the Injury done to the Beauty of her Husband, by the Flesh-Spades of Mrs. *Honour*, called aloud for Revenge and Justice. As to the poor Man who had principally suffered in the Engagement, he was perfectly quiet. Perhaps the Blood which he lost, might have cooled his Anger: For the Enemy had not only applied her Nails to his Cheeks, but likewise her Fist to his Nostrils, which lamented the Blow with Tears of Blood in great Abundance. To this we may add Reflections on his Mistake; but indeed nothing so effectually silenced his Resentment, as the Manner in which he now discovered his Error; for as to the Behaviour of Mrs. *Honour*, it had the more confirmed him in his Opinion: but he was now assured by a Person of great Figure, and who was attended by a great Equipage, that one of the Ladies was a Woman of Fashion and his intimate Acquaintance.

By the Orders of this Person, the Landlord now ascended, and acquainted our fair Travellers, that a great Gentleman below desired to do them the Honour of waiting on them. *Sophia* turned pale, and trembled at this Message, tho' the Reader will conclude it was too civil, notwithstanding the Landlord's Blunder, to have

---

4. Dr. George Cheyne (1671–1743), vegetarian, author of—among other works —*The English Malady, or A Treatise of Nervous Diseases of All Kinds* (1733), which Samuel Johnson twice urged Boswell to read. Fielding mentions him as a murderer of the language in *The Champion*, 17 May 1740 and 12 June 1740.

come from her Father; but Fear hath the common Fault of a Justice of Peace, and is apt to conclude hastily from every slight Circumstance, without examining the Evidence on both Sides.

To ease the Reader's Curiosity, therefore, rather than his Apprehensions, we proceed to inform him, that an *Irish* Peer had arrived very late that Evening at the Inn in his Way to *London*. This Nobleman having sallied from his Supper at the Hurricane before commemorated, had seen the Attendant of Mrs. *Fitzpatrick*, and upon a short Enquiry, was informed, that her Lady, with whom he was very particularly acquainted, was above. This Information he had no sooner received, than he addressed himself to the Landlord, pacified him, and sent him up Stairs with Compliments rather civiller than those which were delivered.

It may perhaps be wondered at, that the Waiting-woman herself was not the Messenger employed on this Occasion; but we are sorry to say, she was not at present qualified for that, or indeed for any other Office. The Rum (for so the Landlord chose to call the Distillation from Malt) had basely taken the Advantage of the Fatigue which the poor Woman had undergone, and had made terrible Depredations on her noble Faculties, at a Time when they were very unable to resist the Attack.

We shall not describe this tragical Scene too fully; but we thought ourselves obliged by that historic Integrity which we profess, shortly to hint a Matter which we would otherwise have been glad to have spared. Many Historians indeed, for want of this Integrity, or of Diligence, to say no worse, often leave the Reader to find out these little Circumstances in the Dark, and sometimes to his great Confusion and Perplexity.

Sophia was very soon eased of her causeless Fright by the Entry of the noble Peer, who was not only an intimate Acquaintance of Mrs. *Fitzpatrick*, but in Reality a very particular Friend of that Lady. To say Truth, it was by his Assistance, that she had been enabled to escape from her Husband; for this Nobleman had the same gallant Disposition with those renowned Knights, of whom we read in heroic Story, and had delivered many an imprisoned Nymph from Durance. He was indeed as bitter an Enemy to the savage Authority too often exercised by Husbands and Fathers, over the Young and Lovely of the other Sex, as ever Knight-Errant was to the barbarous Power of Enchanters: Nay, to say Truth, I have often suspected that those very Enchanters with which Romance every where abounds, were in Reality no other than the Husbands of those Days; and Matrimony itself was perhaps the enchanted Castle in which the Nymphs were said to be confined.

This Nobleman had an Estate in the Neighbourhood of *Fitzpa-*

trick, and had been for some Time acquainted with the Lady. No sooner therefore did he hear of her Confinement, than he earnestly applied himself to procure her Liberty; which he presently effected, not by storming the Castle, according to the Example of antient Heroes; but by corrupting the Governor, in Conformity with the modern Art of War; in which Craft is held to be preferable to Valour, and Gold is found to be more irresistible than either Lead or Steel.

This Circumstance, however, as the Lady did not think it material enough to relate to her Friend, we would not at that Time impart it to the Reader. We rather chose to leave him a while under a Supposition, that she had found, or coined, or by some very extraordinary, perhaps supernatural Means, had possessed herself of the Money with which she had bribed her Keeper, than to interrupt her Narrative by giving a Hint of what seemed to her of too little Importance to be mentioned.

The Peer, after a short Conversation, could not forbear expressing some Surprize at meeting the Lady in that Place; nor could he refrain from telling her, he imagined she had been gone to *Bath.* Mrs. *Fitzpatrick* very freely answered, 'That she had been prevented in her Purpose by the Arrival of a Person she need not mention. In short,' says she, 'I was overtaken by my Husband (for I need not affect to conceal what the World knows too well already.) I had the good Fortune to escape in a most surprizing Manner, and am now going to *London* with this young Lady, who is a near Relation of mine, and who hath escaped from as great a Tyrant as my own.'

His Lordship concluding that this Tyrant was likewise a Husband, made a Speech full of Compliments to both the Ladies, and as full of Invectives against his own Sex; nor indeed did he avoid some oblique Glances at the matrimonial Institution itself, and at the unjust Powers given by it to Man over the more sensible, and more meritorious Part of the Species. He ended his Oration with an Offer of his Protection, and of his Coach and Six, which was instantly accepted by Mrs. *Fitzpatrick*, and at last, upon her Persuasions, by *Sophia.*

Matters being thus adjusted, his Lordship took his Leave, and the Ladies retired to Rest, where Mrs. *Fitzpatrick* entertained her Cousin with many high Encomiums on the Character of the noble Peer, and enlarged very particularly on his great Fondness for his Wife; saying, she believed he was almost the only Person of high Rank, who was entirely constant to the Marriage Bed. 'Indeed,' added she, 'my dear *Sophy*, that is a very rare Virtue amongst Men of Condition. Never expect it when you marry; for, believe me, if you do, you will certainly be deceived.'

A gentle Sigh stole from *Sophia* at these Words, which perhaps contributed to form a Dream of no very pleasant Kind; but as she never revealed this Dream to any one, so the Reader cannot expect to see it related here.

Chapter IX.

The Morning introduced in some pretty Writing. A Stage Coach. The Civility of Chambermaids. The heroic Temper of Sophia. *Her Generosity. The Return to it. The Departure of the Company, and their Arrival at* London; *with some Remarks for the Use of Travellers.*

Those Members of the Society, who are born to furnish the Blessings of Life, now began to light their Candles, in order to pursue their daily Labours, for the Use of those who are born to enjoy these Blessings. The sturdy Hind now attends the Levee of his Fellow Labourer the Ox; the cunning Artificer, the diligent Mechanic spring from their hard Mattress; and now the bonny House-maid begins to repair the disordered Drum-Room, while the riotous Authors of that Disorder, in broken interrupted Slumbers tumble and toss, as if the Hardness of Down disquieted their Repose.

In simple Phrase, the Clock had no sooner struck Seven, than the Ladies were ready for their Journey; and at their Desire, his Lordship and his Equipage were prepared to attend them.

And now a Matter of some Difficulty arose; and this was how his Lordship himself should be conveyed: For tho' in Stage-Coaches, where Passengers are properly considered as so much Luggage, the ingenious Coachman stows half a Dozen with perfect Ease into the Place of four: for well he contrives that the fat Hostess, or well-fed Alderman, may take up no more Room than the slim Miss, or taper Master; it being the Nature of Guts, when well squeezed, to give Way, and to lie in a narrow Compass; yet in these Vehicles which are called, for Distinction-sake, Gentlemens Coaches, tho' they are often larger than the others, this Method of packing is never attempted.

His Lordship would have put a short End to the Difficulty, by very gallantly desiring to mount his Horse; but Mrs. *Fitzpatrick* would by no means consent to it. It was therefore concluded that the *Abigails* should by Turns relieve each other on one of his Lordship's Horses, which was presently equipped with a Side-Saddle for that Purpose.

Every Thing being settled at the Inn, the Ladies discharged their former Guides, and *Sophia* made a Present to the Landlord, partly to repair the Bruise which he had received under herself, and partly on Account of what he had suffered under the Hands of her enraged Waiting-woman. And now *Sophia* first discovered a Loss which gave her some Uneasiness; and this was of the hundred Pound Bank-Bill which her Father had given her at their last Meeting; and which, within a very inconsiderable Trifle, was all the Treasure she was at present worth. She searched every where, and shook and tumbled all her Things to no Purpose, the Bill was not to be found: And she was at last fully persuaded that she had lost it from her Pocket, when she had the Misfortune of tumbling from her Horse in the dark Lane, as before recorded. A Fact that seemed the more probable, as she now recollected some Discomposure in her Pockets which had happened at that Time, and the great Difficulty with which she had drawn forth her Handkerchief the very Instant before her Fall, in order to relieve the Distress of Mrs. *Fitzpatrick*.

Misfortunes of this Kind, whatever Inconveniences they may be attended with, are incapable of subduing a Mind in which there is any Strength, without the Assistance of Avarice. *Sophia* therefore, tho' nothing could be worse timed than this Accident, at such a Season, immediately got the better of her Concern, and with her wonted Serenity and Cheerfulness of Countenance, returned to her Company. His Lordship conducted the Ladies into the Vehicle, as he did likewise Mrs. *Honour*, who, after many Civilities, and more Dear Madams, at last yielded to the well-bred Importunities of her Sister *Abigail*, and submitted to be complimented with the first Ride in the Coach; in which indeed she would afterwards have been contented to have pursued her whole Journey, had not her Mistress, after several fruitless Intimations, at length forced her to take her Turn on Horseback.

The Coach now having received its Company, began to move forwards, attended by many Servants, and by two led Captains, who had before rode with his Lordship, and who would have been dismissed from the Vehicle upon a much less worthy Occasion, than was this of accommodating two Ladies. In this they acted only as Gentlemen; but they were ready at any Time to have performed the Office of a Footman, or indeed would have condescended lower, for the Honour of his Lordship's Company, and for the Convenience of his Table.

My Landlord was so pleased with the Present he had received from *Sophia*, that he rather rejoiced in than regretted his Bruise, or his Scratches. The Reader will perhaps be curious to know the *Quantum* of this Present; but we cannot satisfy his Curiosity. Whatever it was, it satisfied the Landlord for his bodily Hurt; but he lamented he had not known before how little the Lady valued her Money; 'for to be sure,' says he, 'one might have charged every Article double, and she would have made no Cavil at the Reckoning.'

His Wife however was far from drawing this Conclusion; whether she really felt any Injury done to her Husband more than he did himself, I will not say; certain it is, she was much less satisfied with the Generosity of *Sophia*. 'Indeed,' cries she, 'My Dear, the Lady knows better how to dispose of her Money than you imagine. She might very well think we should not put up such a Business without some Satisfaction, and the Law would have cost her an infinite deal more than this poor little Matter, which I wonder you would take.' 'You are always so bloodily wise,' quoth the Husband: 'It would have cost her more, would it? Dost fancy I don't know that as well as thee? But would any of that more, or so much, have come into our Pockets? Indeed, if Son *Tom* the Lawyer had been alive, I could have been glad to have put such a pretty Business into his Hands. He would have got a good Picking out of it; but I have no Relation now who is a Lawyer, and why should I go to Law for the Benefit of Strangers?' 'Nay, to be sure,' answered she, 'you must know best.' 'I believe I do,' replied he. 'I fancy when Money is to be got, I can smell it out as well as another. Every body, let me tell you, would not have talked People out of this. Mind that, I say; every body would not have cajoled this out of her, mind that.' The Wife then joined in the Applause of her Husband's Sagacity; and thus ended the short Dialogue between them on this Occasion.

We will therefore take our Leave of these good People, and attend his Lordship and his fair Companions, who made such good Expedition, that they performed a Journey of ninety Miles in two Days, and on the second Evening arrived in *London*, without having encountered any one Adventure on the Road worthy the Dignity of this History to relate. Our Pen, therefore, shall imitate the Expedition which it describes, and our History shall keep Pace with the Travellers who are its Subject. Good Writers will indeed do well to imitate the ingenious Traveller in this Instance, who always proportions his Stay at any Place, to the Beauties, Elegancies, and Curiosities which it affords. At *Eshur*, at *Stowe*, at *Wilton*, at *Eastbury*, and at *Prior's Park*,[1] Days are too short for the ravished Imagination; while we admire the wondrous Power of Art in improving Nature. In some of these, Art chiefly engages our Admiration; in

---

1. Great country estates, noted for their grounds and gardens: "Eshur" is Claremont House, near Esher, Sussex, about 10 miles southwest of London, built in 1708 by Sir John Vanbrugh, with grounds by Capability Brown; Stowe House, Buckinghamshire, about 60 miles northwest of London, in 200 acres of grounds by Capability Brown and William Kent; Wilton House, at Wilton, Wiltshire, 86 miles west-southwest of London, seat of the earls of Pembroke (Sidney started the *Arcadia* there); Eastbury, Dorsetshire, the estate of Baron Motcombe, George Bubb Dodington, to whom Fielding had dedicated his poem *Of True Greatness* (1741); Prior's Park, the Palladian mansion at Bath of Fielding's friend and patron Ralph Allen.

others, Nature and Art contend for our Applause; but in the last, the former seems to triumph. Here Nature appears in her richest Attire, and Art dressed with the modestest Simplicity, attends her benignant Mistress. Here Nature indeed pours forth the choicest Treasures which she hath lavished on this World; and here human Nature presents you with an Object which can be exceeded only in the other.

The same Taste, the same Imagination, which luxuriously riots in these elegant Scenes, can be amused with Objects of far inferior Note. The Woods, the Rivers, the Lawns of *Devon* and of *Dorset*, attract the Eye of the ingenious Traveller, and retard his Pace, which Delay he afterwards compensates by swiftly scouring over the gloomy Heath of *Bagshot*, or that pleasant Plain which extends itself Westward from *Stockbridge*, where no other object than one single Tree only in sixteen Miles presents itself to the View, unless the Clouds, in Compassion to our tired Spirits, kindly open their variegated Mansions to our Prospect.

Not so travels the Money-meditating Tradesman, the sagacious Justice, the dignified Doctor, the warm-clad Grazier, with all the numerous Offspring of Wealth and Dulness. On they jogg, with equal Pace, through the verdant Meadows, or over the barren Heath, their Horses measuring four Miles and a half *per* Hour with the utmost Exactness; the Eyes of the Beast and of his Master being alike directed forwards, and employed in contemplating the same Objects in the same manner. With equal Rapture the good Rider surveys the proudest Boasts of the Architect, and those fair Buildings, with which some unknown Name hath adorned the rich Cloathing-Town; where Heaps of Bricks are piled up as a kind of Monument, to shew that Heaps of Money have been piled there before.

And now, Reader, as we are in haste to attend our Heroine, we will leave to thy Sagacity to apply all this to the *Bœotian*[2] Writers, and to those Authors who are their Opposites. This thou wilt be abundantly able to perform without our Aid. Bestir thyself therefore on this Occasion; for tho' we will always lend thee proper Assistance in difficult Places, as we do not, like some others, expect thee to use the Arts of Divination to discover our Meaning; yet we shall not indulge thy Laziness where nothing but thy own Attention is required; for thou art highly mistaken if thou dost imagine that we intended, when we began this great Work, to leave thy Sagacity nothing to do; or that, without sometimes exercising this Talent, thou wilt be able to travel through our Pages with any Pleasure or Profit to thyself.

2. Pronounced "Bee-ócean." Boeotia, in central Greece, of which Thebes was the capital, was proverbial for stupidity (Horace, *Epistles* II.i.244).

Chapter X.

Containing a Hint or two concerning Virtue, and a few more concerning Suspicion.

Our Company being arrived at *London*, were set down at his Lordship's House, where, while they refreshed themselves after the Fatigue of their Journey, Servants were dispatched to provide a Lodging for the two Ladies; for as her Ladyship was not then in Town, Mrs. *Fitzpatrick* would by no means consent to accept a Bed in the Mansion of the Peer.

Some Readers will perhaps condemn this extraordinary Delicacy, as I may call it, of Virtue, as too nice and scrupulous; but we must make Allowances for her Situation, which must be owned to have been very ticklish; and when we consider the Malice of censorious Tongues, we must allow, if it was a Fault, the Fault was an Excess on the right Side, and which every Woman who is in the self-same Situation will do well to imitate. The most formal Appearance of Virtue, when it is only an Appearance, may perhaps, in very abstracted Considerations, seem to be rather less commendable than Virtue itself without this Formality; but it will however be always more commended; and this, I believe, will be granted by all, that it is necessary, unless in some very particular Cases, for every Woman to support either the one or the other.

A Lodging being prepared, *Sophia* accompanied her Cousin for that Evening; but resolved early in the Morning to enquire after the Lady, into whose Protection, as we have formerly mentioned, she had determined to throw herself, when she quitted her Father's House. And this she was the more eager in doing, from some Observations she had made during her Journey in the Coach.

Now as we would by no means fix the odious Character of Suspicion on *Sophia*, we are almost afraid to open to our Reader the Conceits which filled her Mind concerning Mrs. *Fitzpatrick*; of whom she certainly entertained at present some Doubts; which, as they are very apt to enter into the Bosoms of the worst of People, we think proper not to mention more plainly, till we have first suggested a Word or two to our Reader touching Suspicion in general.

Of this there have always appeared to me to be two Degrees. The first of these I chuse to derive from the Heart, as the extreme Velocity of its Discernment seems to denote some previous inward Impulse, and the rather, as this superlative Degree often forms its own Objects; sees what is not, and always more than really exists. This is that quick-sighted Penetration, whose Hawk's Eyes no Symptom of Evil can escape; which observes not only upon the Actions, but upon the Words and Looks of Men; and as it proceeds

from the Heart of the Observer, so it dives into the Heart of the
Observed, and there espies Evil, as it were, in the first Embryo; nay
sometimes before it can be said to be conceived. An admirable Faculty, if it were infallible; but as this Degree of Perfection is not
even claimed by more than one mortal Being; so from the Fallibility of such acute Discernment have arisen many sad Mischiefs and
most grievous Heart-akes to Innocence and Virtue. I cannot help
therefore regarding this vast Quicksightedness into Evil, as a vicious
Excess, and as a very pernicious Evil in itself. And I am the more
inclined to this Opinion, as I am afraid it always proceeds from a
bad Heart, for the Reasons I have above mentioned, and for one
more, namely, because I never knew it the Property of a good one.
Now from this Degree of Suspicion I entirely and absolutely acquit
Sophia.

A second Degree of this Quality seems to arise from the Head.
This is indeed no other than the Faculty of seeing what is before
your Eyes, and of drawing Conclusions from what you see. The
former of these is unavoidable by those who have any Eyes, and the
latter is perhaps no less certain and necessary a Consequence of our
having any Brains. This is altogether as bitter an Enemy to Guilt,
as the former is to Innocence; nor can I see it in an unamiable
Light, even though, through human Fallibility, it should be sometimes mistaken. For Instance, if a Husband should accidentally surprize his Wife in the Lap or in the Embraces of some of those
pretty young Gentlemen who profess the Art of Cuckold-making, I
should not highly, I think, blame him for concluding something
more than what he saw, from the Familiarities which he really had
seen, and which we are at least favourable enough to, when we call
them innocent Freedoms. The Reader will easily suggest great
Plenty of Instances to himself: I shall add but one more, which
however unchristian it may be thought by some, I cannot help
esteeming to be strictly justifiable; and this is a Suspicion that a
Man is capable of doing what he hath done already, and that it is
possible for one who hath been a Villain once, to act the same Part
again. And to confess the Truth, of this Degree of Suspicion I
believe *Sophia* was guilty. From this Degree of Suspicion she had,
in Fact, conceived an Opinion, that her Cousin was really not better
than she should be.

The Case, it seems, was this: Mrs. *Fitzpatrick* wisely considered,
that the Virtue of a young Lady is, in the World, in the same Situation with a poor Hare, which is certain, whenever it ventures
abroad, to meet its Enemies: For it can hardly meet any other. No
sooner therefore was she determined to take the first Opportunity of
quitting the Protection of her Husband, than she resolved to cast
herself under the Protection of some other Man; and whom could

she so properly chuse to be her Guardian as a Person of Quality, of
Fortune, of Honour; and who, besides a gallant Disposition which
inclines Men to Knight-Errantry, that is, to be the Champions of
Ladies in Distress, had often declared a violent Attachment to herself, and had already given her all the Instances of it in his Power?

But as the Law hath foolishly omitted this Office of Vice-Hus-
band, or Guardian to an eloped Lady; and as Malice is apt to
denominate him by a more disagreeable Appelation; it was concluded that his Lordship should perform all such kind Offices to the
Lady in secret, and without publickly assuming the Character of her
Protector. Nay, to prevent any other Person from seeing him in this
Light, it was agreed that the Lady should proceed directly to *Bath,*
and that his Lordship should first go to *London,* and thence should
go down to that Place by the Advice of his Physicians.

Now all this *Sophia* very plainly understood, not from the Lips or
Behaviour of Mrs. *Fitzpatrick,* but from the Peer, who was infinitely
less expert at retaining a Secret, than was the good Lady; and perhaps the exact Secrecy which Mrs. *Fitzpatrick* had observed on this
Head in her Narrative, served not a little to heighten those Suspicions which were now risen in the Mind of her Cousin.

Sophia very easily found out the Lady she sought; for indeed
there was not a Chairman in Town to whom her House was not
perfectly well known; and as she received, in Return of her first
Message, a most pressing Invitation, she immediately accepted it.
Mrs. *Fitzpatrick* indeed did not desire her Cousin to stay with her
with more Earnestness than Civility required. Whether she had discerned and resented the Suspicion above-mentioned, or from what
other Motive it arose, I cannot say; but certain it is, she was full as
desirous of parting with *Sophia,* as *Sophia* herself could be of
going.

The young Lady, when she came to take Leave of her Cousin,
could not avoid giving her a short Hint of Advice. She begged her,
for Heaven's Sake, to take care of herself, and to consider in how
dangerous a Situation she stood; adding, she hoped some Method
would be found of reconciling her to her Husband. 'You must
remember, my Dear,' says she, 'the Maxim which my Aunt *Western* hath so often repeated to us both; *That whenever the matrimonial Alliance is broke, and War declared between Husband and
Wife, she can hardly make a disadvantageous Peace for herself on
any Conditions.* These are my Aunt's very Words, and she hath had
a great deal of Experience in the World.' Mrs. *Fitzpatrick*
answered, with a contemptuous Smile, 'Never fear me, Child, take
care of yourself; for you are younger than I. I will come and visit
you in a few Days; but, dear *Sophy,* let me give you one Piece of
Advice: Leave the Character of *Graveairs* in the Country; for,
believe me, it will sit very aukwardly upon you in this Town.'

Thus the two Cousins parted, and *Sophia* repaired directly' to Lady *Bellaston*, where she found a most hearty, as well as a most polite Welcome. The Lady had taken a great Fancy to her when she had seen her formerly with her Aunt *Western*. She was indeed extremely glad to see her, and was no sooner acquainted with the Reasons which induced her to leave the Squire and fly to *London*, than she highly applauded her Sense and Resolution; and after expressing the highest Satisfaction in the Opinion which *Sophia* had declared she entertained of her Ladyship, by chusing her House for an Asylum, she promised her all the Protection which it was in her Power to give.

As we have now brought *Sophia* into safe Hands, the Reader will, I apprehend, be contented to deposite her there a while, and to look a little after other Personages, and particularly poor *Jones*, whom we have left long enough to do Penance for his past Offences, which, as is the Nature of Vice, brought sufficient Punishment upon him themselves.

BOOK XII.

Containing the same individual Time with the former.

Chapter I.

Shewing what is to be deemed Plagiarism in a modern Author, and what is to be considered as lawful Prize.

The learned Reader must have observed, that in the Course of this mighty Work, I have often translated Passages out of the best antient Authors, without quoting the Original or without taking the least Notice of the Book from whence they were borrowed.

This Conduct in Writing is placed in a very proper Light by the ingenious Abbé *Bannier*,[1] in his Preface to his Mythology, a Work of great Erudition, and of equal Judgment. "It will be easy," says he, "for the Reader to observe, that I have frequently had greater Regard to him, than to my own Reputation: For an Author certainly pays him a considerable Compliment, when, for his Sake, he suppresses learned Quotations that come in his Way, and which would have cost him but the bare Trouble of transcribing."

1. Fielding's misspelling of *Banier*. Author of *La Mythologie et les Fables Expliquées par L'Histoire* (1739–40). Andrew Millar, Fielding's publisher, published the English translation, *Mythology and Fables of the Ancients* (1739–41), reissued 9 Jan. 1748, about the time Fielding may have been writing this part of *Tom Jones*. Cross (II.106–7) believes that Fielding wrote the advertisement for Millar's reissue; Fielding praises Banier again on 30 Jan. in *The Jacobite's Journal* and says nothing more of him before or since.

To fill up a Work with these Scraps may indeed be considered as a downright Cheat on the learned World, who are by such Means imposed upon to buy a second time in Fragments and by Retail what they have already in Gross, if not in their Memories, upon their Shelves; and it is still more cruel upon the Illiterate, who are drawn in to pay for what is of no manner of Use to them. A Writer who intermixes great Quantity of *Greek* and *Latin* with his Works, deals by the Ladies and fine Gentlemen in the same paultry Manner with which they are treated by the Auctioneers, who often endeavour so to confound and mix up their Lots, that, in order to purchase the Commodity you want, you are obliged at the same Time to purchase that which will do you no Service.

And yet as there is no Conduct so fair and disinterested, but that it may be misunderstood by Ignorance, and misrepresented by Malice, I have been sometimes tempted to preserve my own Reputation, at the Expence of my Reader, and to transcribe the Original, or at least to quote Chapter and Verse, whenever I have made Use either of the Thought or Expression of another. I am indeed in some Doubt that I have often suffered by the contrary Method; and that by suppressing the original Author's Name, I have been rather suspected of Plagiarism, than reputed to act from the amiable Motive above assigned by that justly celebrated *Frenchman*.

Now to obviate all such Imputations for the future, I do here confess and justify the Fact. The Antients may be considered as a rich Common, where every Person who hath the smallest Tenement in *Parnassus*, hath a free Right to fatten his Muse. Or, to place it in a clearer Light, we Moderns are to the Antients what the Poor are to the Rich. By the Poor here I mean, that large and venerable Body which, in *English*, we call The Mob. Now, whoever hath had the Honour to be admitted to any Degree of Intimacy with this Mob, must well know that it is one of their established Maxims, to plunder and pillage their rich Neighbours without any Reluctance; and that this is held to be neither Sin nor Shame among them. And so constantly do they abide and act by this Maxim, that in every Parish almost in the Kingdom, there is a Kind of Confederacy ever carrying on against a certain Person of Opulence called the Squire, whose Property is considered as Free-Booty by all his poor Neighbours; who, as they conclude that there is no manner of Guilt in such Depredations, look upon it as a Point of Honour and moral Obligation to conceal, and to preserve each other from Punishment on all such Occasions.

In like Manner are the Antients, such as *Homer, Virgil, Horace, Cicero,* and the rest, to be esteemed among us Writers, as so many wealthy Squires, from whom we, the Poor of *Parnassus,* claim an immemorial Custom of taking whatever we can come at. This Liberty I demand, and this I am as ready to allow again to my poor

Neighbours in their Turn. All I profess, and all I require of my Brethren, is to maintain the same strict Honesty among ourselves, which the Mob shew to one another. To steal from one another, is indeed highly criminal and indecent; for this may be strictly stiled defrauding the Poor (sometimes perhaps those who are poorer than ourselves) or, to see it under the most opprobrious Colours, robbing the Spital.

Since therefore upon the strictest Examination, my own Conscience cannot lay any such pitiful Theft to my Charge, I am contented to plead guilty to the former Accusation; nor shall I ever scruple to take to myself any Passage which I shall find in an antient Author to my Purpose, without setting down the Name of the Author from whence it was taken. Nay, I absolutely claim a Property in all such Sentiments the Moment they are transcribed into my Writings, and I expect all Readers henceforwards to regard them as purely and entirely my own. This Claim however I desire to be allowed me only on Condition, that I preserve strict Honesty towards my poor Brethren, from whom if ever I borrow any of that little of which they are possessed, I shall never fail to put their Mark upon it, that it may be at all Times ready to be restored to the right Owner.

The Omission of this was highly blameable in one Mr. *Moore,*[2] who having formerly borrowed some Lines of *Pope* and Company, took the Liberty to transcribe six of them into his Play of the *Rival Modes.* Mr. *Pope* however very luckily found them in the said Play, and laying violent Hands on his own Property, transferred it back again into his own Works; and for a further Punishment, imprisoned the said *Moore* in the loathsome Dungeon of the *Dunciad,* where his unhappy Memory now remains, and eternally will remain, as a proper Punishment for such his unjust Dealings in the poetical Trade.

Chapter II.

In which, tho' the Squire doth not find his Daughter, something is found which puts an End to his Pursuit.

The History now returns to the Inn at *Upton,* whence we shall first trace the Footsteps of Squire *Western;* for as he will soon arrive at an End of his Journey, we shall have then full Leisure to attend our Heroe.

The Reader may be pleased to remember, that the said Squire

2. James Moore Smythe. For his play *The Rival Modes* (1727), he borrowed five lines from Pope's *Miscellanies,* with Pope's permission, on the understanding that they would be acknowledged as Pope's. Smythe apparently failed to acknowledge them. Pope consequently describes him as a phantom made by the Goddess of Dulness, fat, with "brain of feathers, and a heart of lead" (*Dunciad* II.30–46).

departed from the Inn in great Fury, and in that Fury he pursued his Daughter. The Hostler having informed him that she had crossed the *Severn,* he likewise past that River with his Equipage, and rode full Speed, vowing the utmost Vengeance against poor *Sophia,* if he should but overtake her.

He had not gone far, before he arrived at a Cross-way. Here he called a short Council of War, in which, after hearing different Opinions, he at last gave the Direction of his Pursuit to Fortune, and struck directly into the *Worcester* Road.

In this Road he proceeded about two Miles when he began to bemoan himself most bitterly, frequently crying out, 'What Pity is it! Sure never was so unlucky a Dog as myself?' and then burst forth a Volley of Oaths and Execrations.

The Parson attempted to administer Comfort to him on this Occasion. 'Sorrow not, Sir,' says he, 'like those without Hope. Howbeit we have not yet been able to overtake young Madam, we may account it some good Fortune, that we have hitherto traced her Course aright. Peradventure she will soon be fatigated with her Journey, and will tarry in some Inn, in order to renovate her corporeal Functions; and in that Case, in all moral Certainty, you will very briefly be *compos voti.*[1]

'Pogh! D—n the Slut,' answered the Squire, 'I am lamenting the Loss of so fine a Morning for Hunting. It is confounded hard to lose one of the best Scenting Days, in all Appearance, which hath been this Season, and especially after so long a Frost.'

Whether Fortune, who now and then shews some Compassion in her wantonest Tricks, might not take Pity of the Squire; and as she had determined not to let him overtake his Daughter, might not resolve to make him Amends some other Way, I will not assert; but he had hardly uttered the Words just before commemorated, and two or three Oaths at their Heels, when a Pack of Hounds began to open their melodious Throats at a small Distance from them, which the Squire's Horse and his Rider both perceiving, both immediately pricked up their Ears, and the Squire crying, 'She's gone, she's gone! Damn me if she is not gone!' instantly clapped Spurs to the Beast, who little needed it, having indeed the same Inclination with his Master; and now the whole Company crossing into a Corn-field, rode directly towards the Hounds, with much Hallowing and Hooping, while the poor Parson, blessing himself, brought up the Rear.

Thus Fable reports, that the fair *Grimalkin,* whom *Venus,* at the Desire of a passionate Lover, converted from a Cat into a fine Woman, no sooner perceived a Mouse, than mindful of her former Sport, and still retaining her pristine Nature, she leapt from the Bed of her Husband to pursue the little Animal.

1. "Having what you want"—a common   *Ars Amatoria* I.486).
phrase (Horace, *Ars Poetica* 76; Ovid,

What are we to understand by this? Not that the Bride was displeased with the Embraces of her amorous Bridegroom: For tho' some have remarked that Cats are subject to Ingratitude; yet Women and Cats too will be pleased and purr on certain Occasions. The Truth is, as the sagacious Sir *Roger L'Estrange*[2] observes, in his deep Reflections, that 'if we shut Nature out at the Door, she will come in at the Window; and that Puss, tho' a Madam, will be a Mouser still.' In the same Manner we are not to arraign the Squire of any Want of Love for his Daughter: For in reality he had a great deal; we are only to consider that he was a Squire and a Sportsman, and then we may apply the Fable to him, and the judicious Reflections likewise.

The Hounds ran very hard, as it is called, and the Squire pursued over Hedge and Ditch, with all his usual Vociferation and Alacrity, and with all his usual Pleasure; nor did the Thoughts of *Sophia* ever once intrude themselves to allay the Satisfaction he enjoyed in the Chace, which he said, was one of the finest he ever saw, and which he swore was very well worth going fifty Miles for. As the Squire forgot his Daughter, the Servants, we may easily believe, forgot their Mistress; and the Parson, after having express'd much Astonishment in *Latin* to himself, at length likewise abandoned all farther Thoughts of the young Lady, and jogging on at a Distance behind, began to meditate a Portion of Doctrine for the ensuing *Sunday*.

The Squire who owned the Hounds, was highly pleased with the Arrival of his Brother Squire and Sportsman: For all Men approve Merit in their own Way, and no Man was more expert in the Field than Mr. *Western*, nor did any other better know how to encourage the Dogs with his Voice, and to animate the Hunt with his Holla.

Sportsmen, in the Warmth of a Chace, are too much engaged to attend to any Manner of Ceremony; nay, even to the Offices of Humanity: For if any of them meet with an Accident by tumbling into a Ditch, or into a River, the rest pass on regardless, and generally leave him to his Fate; during this Time, therefore, the two Squires, tho' often close to each other, interchanged not a single Word. The Master of the Hunt, however, often saw and approved the great Judgment of the Stranger in drawing the Dogs when they were at a Fault, and hence conceived a very high Opinion of his Understanding, as the Number of his Attendants inspired no small Reverence to his Quality. As soon thereafter as the Sport was ended by the Death of the little Animal which had occasioned it, the two Squires met, and in all Squire-like Greeting, saluted each other.

2. *The Fables of Aesop and Other Eminent Mythologists with Moral Reflections* (1692), "A Cat and Venus," Fable LXI (4th ed., 1704), p. 61: "The *Woman's* Leaping at the *Mouse*, tells us also how Impossible it is to make Nature change her Bias, and that *if we Shut her out at the Door, She'll come in at the Window*," and several lines later, ". . . for *Puss*, even when she's a *Madam*, will be a *Mouser* still."

The Conversation was entertaining enough, and what we may perhaps relate in an Appendix, or on some other Occasion; but as it nowise concerns this History, we cannot prevail on ourselves to give it a Place here. It concluded with a second Chace, and that with an Invitation to Dinner. This being accepted was followed by a hearty Bout of Drinking, which ended in as hearty a Nap on the Part of Squire *Western.*

Our Squire was by no means a Match either for his Host, or for Parson *Supple,* at his Cups that Evening; for which the violent Fatigue of Mind as well as Body that he had undergone, may very well account, without the least Derogation from his Honour. He was indeed, according to the vulgar Phrase, whistle-drunk; for before he had swallowed the third Bottle, he became so entirely overpowered, that tho' he was not carried off to Bed till long after, the Parson considered him as absent, and having acquainted the other Squire with all relating to *Sophia,* he obtained his Promise of seconding those Arguments which he intended to urge the next Morning for Mr. *Western's* Return.

No sooner therefore had the good Squire shaken off his Evening, and began to call for his Morning Draught, and to summon his Horses in order to renew his Pursuit, than Mr. *Supple* began his Dissuasives, which the Host so strongly seconded, that they at length prevailed, and Mr. *Western* agreed to return home; being principally moved by one Argument, *viz.* That he knew not which Way to go, and might probably be riding farther from his Daughter instead of towards her. He then took Leave of his Brother Sportsman, and expressing great Joy that the Frost was broken (which might perhaps be no small Motive to his hastening home) set forwards, or rather backwards, for *Somersetshire;* but not before he had first dispatched Part of his Retinue in quest of his Daughter, after whom he likewise sent a Volley of the most bitter Execrations which he could invent.

Chapter III.

The Departure of Jones *from* Upton, *with what past between him and* Partridge *on the Road.*

At length we are once more come to our Heroe; and to say Truth, we have been obliged to part with him so long, that considering the Condition in which we left him, I apprehend many of our Readers have concluded we intended to abandon him for ever; he being at present in that Situation in which prudent People usually desist from enquiring any farther after their Friends, lest they should be shocked by hearing such Friends had hanged themselves.

But, in reality, if we have not all the Virtues, I will boldly say, neither have we all the Vices of a prudent Character; and tho' it is not easy to conceive Circumstances much more miserable than those of poor *Jones* at present, we shall return to him, and attend upon him with the same Diligence as if he was wantoning in the brightest Beams of Fortune.

Mr. *Jones* then, and his Companion *Partridge*, left the Inn a few Minutes after the Departure of Squire *Western*, and pursued the same Road on Foot; for the Hostler told them, that no Horses were by any Means to be at that Time procured at *Upton*. On they marched with heavy Hearts; for tho' their Disquiet proceeded from very different Reasons, yet displeased they were both; and if *Jones* sighed bitterly, *Partridge* grunted altogether as sadly at every Step.

When they came to the Cross-roads where the Squire had stopt to take Counsel, *Jones* stopt likewise, and turning to *Partridge*, asked his Opinion which Track they should pursue. 'Ah, Sir!' answered *Partridge*, 'I wish your Honour would follow my Advice.' 'Why should I not?' replied *Jones*; 'for it is now indifferent to me whither I go, or what becomes of me?' 'My Advice then,' said *Partridge*, 'is that you immediately face about and return home: For who that hath such a Home to return to, as your Honour, would travel thus about the Country like a Vagabond? I ask Pardon, *sed vox ea sola reperta est*.'[1]

'Alas!' cries *Jones*, 'I have no Home to return to;—but if my Friend, my Father would receive me, could I bear the Country from which *Sophia* is flown—Cruel *Sophia*! Cruel! No. Let me blame myself—No, let me blame thee. D—nation seize thee, Fool, Blockhead! thou hast undone me, and I will tear thy Soul from thy Body.'—At which Words he laid violent Hands on the Collar of poor *Partridge*, and shook him more heartily than an Ague Fit, or his own Fears had ever done before.

Partridge fell trembling on his Knees, and begged for Mercy, vowing he had meant no Harm—when *Jones*, after staring wildly on him for a Moment, quitted his Hold; and discharged a Rage on himself, that had it fallen on the other, would certainly have put an End to his Being, which indeed the very Apprehension of it had almost effected.

We would bestow some Pains here in minutely describing all the mad Pranks which *Jones* played on this Occasion, could we be well assured that the Reader would take the same Pains in perusing them; but as we are apprehensive that after all the Labour which

---

1. "But only this form is found." This is the ending of the last line of four verses in Lily (p. 93) for memorizing rules concerning certain nouns. Partridge is applying this mnemonic tag from the school grammar to say, with accidental wit: "Vagabond!—sorry, but there's no other word for it." See above, p. 4.

we should employ in painting this Scene, the said Reader would be very apt to skip it entirely over, we have saved ourself that Trouble. To say the Truth, we have, from this Reason alone, often done great Violence to the Luxuriance of our Genius, and have left many excellent Descriptions out of our Work, which would otherwise have been in it. And this Suspicion, to be honest, arises, as is generally the Case, from our own wicked Heart; for we have, ourselves, been very often most horridly given to jumping, as we have run through the Pages of voluminous Historians.

Suffice it then simply to say, that *Jones,* after having played the Part of a Madman for many Minutes, came, by Degrees, to himself; which no sooner happened, than turning to *Partridge,* he very earnestly begged his Pardon for the Attack he had made on him in the Violence of his Passion; but concluded, by desiring him never to mention his Return again; for he was resolved never to see that Country any more.

Partridge easily forgave, and faithfully promised to obey the Injunction now laid upon him. And then *Jones* very briskly cried out: 'Since it is absolutely impossible for me to pursue any farther the Steps of my Angel—I will pursue those of Glory. Come on, my brave Lad, now for the Army:—It is a glorious Cause, and I would willingly sacrifice my Life in it, even tho' it was worth my preserving.' And so saying, he immediately struck into the different Road from that which the Squire had taken, and, by mere Chance, pursued the very same thro' which *Sophia* had before passed.

Our Travellers now marched a full Mile, without speaking a Syllable to each other, tho' *Jones,* indeed, muttered many Things to himself. As to *Partridge,* he was profoundly silent: For he was not, perhaps, perfectly recovered from his former Fright; besides, he had Apprehensions of provoking his Friend to a second Fit of Wrath; especially as he now began to entertain a Conceit, which may not, perhaps, create any great Wonder in the Reader. In short, he began now to suspect that *Jones* was absolutely out of his Senses.

At length, *Jones* being weary of Soliloquy, addressed himself to his Companion, and blamed him for his Taciturnity: For which the poor Man very honestly accounted, from his Fear of giving Offence. And now this Fear being pretty well removed, by the most absolute Promises of Indemnity, *Partridge* again took the Bridle from his Tongue; which, perhaps, rejoiced no less at regaining its Liberty, than a young Colt, when the Bridle is slipt from his Neck, and he is turned loose into the Pastures.

As *Partridge* was inhibited from that Topic which would have first suggested itself, he fell upon that which was next uppermost in his Mind, namely, the Man of the Hill. 'Certainly, Sir,' says he, 'that could never be a Man, who dresses himself, and lives after such a strange Manner, and so unlike other Folks. Besides, his Diet, as the old Woman told me, is chiefly upon Herbs, which is a fitter Food for a Horse than a Christian: Nay, Landlord at *Upton* says, that the Neighbours thereabouts have very fearful Notions about him. It runs strangely in my Head, that it must have been some Spirit, who, perhaps, might be sent to forewarn us: And who knows, but all that Matter which he told us, of his going to Fight, and of his being taken Prisoner, and of the great Danger he was in of being hanged, might be intended as a Warning to us, considering what we are going about: Besides, I dreamt of nothing all last Night, but of Fighting; and methought the Blood ran out of my Nose, as Liquor out of a Tap. Indeed, Sir, *infandum, Regina, jubes renovare Dolorem.*'[2]

'Thy Story, *Partridge,*' answered *Jones,* 'is almost as ill applied as thy *Latin.* Nothing can be more likely to happen than Death to Men who go into Battle. Perhaps we shall both fall in it,—and what then?' 'What then!' replied *Partridge*; 'Why then there is an End of us, is there not? When I am gone, all is over with me. What matters the Cause to me, or who gets the Victory, if I am killed? I shall never enjoy any Advantage from it. What are all the ringing of Bells, and Bonfires, to one that is six Foot under Ground? There will be an End of poor *Partridge.*' 'And an End of poor *Partridge,*' cries *Jones,* 'there must be one Time or other. If you love *Latin,* I will repeat you some fine Lines out of *Horace,* which would inspire Courage into a Coward.

> *Dulce & decorum est pro patria mori.*
> *Mors & fugacem persequitur virum*
> *Nec parcit imbellis juventæ*
> *Poplitibus, timidoque tergo.*[3]

'I wish you would construe them,' cries *Partridge*; 'for *Horace* is a hard Author, and I cannot understand as you repeat them.'

'I will repeat you a bad Imitation, or rather Paraphrase of my own,' said *Jones*; 'for I am but an indifferent Poet.

> 'Who would not die in his dear Country's Cause?
> Since, if base Fear his dastard Step withdraws,
> From Death he cannot fly:—One common Grave
> Receives, at last, the Coward and the Brave.'

'That's very certain,' cries *Partridge.* 'Ay, sure, *Mors omnibus communis:*[4] But there is a great Difference between dying in one's

2. See above, p. 322.
3. Horace, *Odes* III.ii.13–16; *timidoque* should be *timidove.*
4. "Death is common to all." Lily, p. 143 (from Cicero), in a passage illustrat- ing the dative, which also contains Partridge's *immunes,* soon to follow, and his *Scaevolae* on p. 519, below. He has already used this phrase by substituting *Ars* for *Mors* (above, p. 321).

Bed a great many Years hence, like a good Christian, with all our
Friends crying about us, and being shot To-day or To-morrow, like
a mad Dog; or, perhaps, hacked in twenty Pieces with a Sword, and
that too before we have repented of all our Sins. O Lord have
Mercy upon us! To be sure, the Soldiers are a wicked Kind of
People. I never loved to have any Thing to do with them. I could
hardly bring myself ever to look upon them as Christians. There is
nothing but Cursing and Swearing among them. I wish your
Honour would repent: I heartily wish you would repent, before it is
too late; and not think of going among them.—Evil Communication corrupts good Manners.[5] That is my principal Reason. For as
for that Matter, I am no more afraid than another Man, not I; as to
Matter of that. I know all human Flesh must die; but yet a Man
may live many Years for all that. Why I am a middle-aged Man
now, and yet I may live a great Number of Years. I have read of
several who have lived to be above a hundred, and some a great deal
above a hundred. Not that I hope, I mean that I promise myself, to
live to any such Age as that neither.—But if it be only to Eighty or
Ninety: Heaven be praised, that is a great Ways off yet; and I am
not afraid of dying then, no more than another Man: But, surely,
to tempt Death before a Man's Time is come, seems to me downright Wickedness and Presumption. Besides, if it was to do any
Good indeed; but let the Cause be what it will, what mighty
Matter of Good can two People do? And, for my Part, I understand
nothing of it. I never fired off a Gun above ten Times in my Life;
and then it was not charged with Bullets. And for the Sword, I
never learned to fence, and know nothing of the Matter. And then
there are those Cannons, which certainly it must be thought the
highest Presumption to go in the Way of; and no-body but a Madman—I ask Pardon; upon my Soul, I meant no Harm: I beg I may
not throw your Honour into another Passion.'

'Be under no Apprehension, *Partridge*,' cries *Jones*; 'I am now so
well convinced of thy Cowardice, that thou couldst not provoke me
on any Account.' 'Your Honour,' answered he, 'may call me
Coward, or any thing else you please. If loving to sleep in a whole
Skin makes a Man a Coward, *non immunes ab illis malis sumus.*[6] I
never read in my Grammar, that a Man can't be a good Man without fighting. *Vir bonus est quis? Qui consulta Patrum, qui leges
juraque servat.*[7] Not a Word of Fighting; and I am sure the Scripture is so much against it, that a Man shall never persuade me he is
a good Christian, while he sheds Christian-blood.'

5. See above, p. 164.
6. "We are not immune to those evils."
Partridge reverses the example from
Pliny quoted in Lily, p. 143, by adding
non ("not") to the stoic statement.
7. "Who is a good man? He who keeps

the decisions of his fathers, who keeps
the laws and the civil rights" (Horace,
Epistles I.xvi.40–41), quoted in Lily, p.
138, the same page containing Fielding's
rara avis (above, pp. 141 and 307).

Chapter IV.

The Adventure of a Beggar-man.

Just as *Partridge* had uttered that good and pious Doctrine, with which the last Chapter concluded, they arrived at another Crossway, when a lame Fellow in Rags asked them for Alms; upon which *Partridge* gave him a severe Rebuke, saying, 'Every Parish ought to keep their own Poor.' *Jones* then fell a laughing, and asked *Partridge*, if he was not ashamed, with so much Charity in his Mouth, to have no Charity in his Heart. 'Your Religion,' says he, 'serves you only for an Excuse for your Faults, but is no Incentive to your Virtue. Can any Man who is really a Christian abstain from relieving one of his Brethren in such a miserable Condition?' And at the same time putting his Hand in his Pocket, he gave the poor Object a Shilling.

'Master,' cries the Fellow, after thanking him, 'I have a curious Thing here in my Pocket, which I found about two miles off, if your Worship will please to buy it. I should not venture to pull it out to every one; but as you are so good a Gentleman, and so kind to the Poor, you won't suspect a Man of being a Thief only because he is poor.' He then pulled out a little gilt Pocket-Book, and delivered it into the Hands of *Jones*.

Jones presently opened it, and (guess, Reader, what he felt,) saw in the first Page the Words *Sophia Western*, written by her own fair Hand. He no sooner read the Name, than he prest it close to his Lips; nor could he avoid falling into some very frantic Raptures, notwithstanding his Company; but, perhaps, these very Raptures made him forget he was not alone.

While *Jones* was kissing and mumbling the Book, as if he had an excellent brown butter'd Crust in his Mouth, or as if he had really been a Bookworm, or an Author, who had nothing to eat but his own Works, a Piece of Paper fell from its Leaves to the Ground, which *Partridge* took up, and delivered to *Jones*, who presently perceived it to be a Bank-Bill. It was, indeed, the very Bill which *Western* had given his Daughter, the Night before her Departure; and a *Jew* would have jumped to purchase it at five Shillings less than 100*l*.

The Eyes of *Partridge* sparkled at this News, which *Jones* now proclaimed aloud; and so did (tho' with somewhat a different Aspect) those of the poor Fellow who had found the Book; and who (I hope from a Principle of Honesty) had never opened it: But we should not deal honestly by the Reader, if we omitted to inform him of a Circumstance, which may be here a little material, *viz*. That the Fellow could not read.

Jones, who had felt nothing but pure Joy and Transport from the finding the Book, was affected with a Mixture of Concern at this new Discovery: For his Imagination instantly suggested to him, that the Owner of the Bill might possibly want it, before he should be able to convey it to her. He then acquainted the Finder, that he knew the Lady to whom the Book belonged, and would endeavour to find her out as soon as possible, and return it her.

The Pocket-Book was a late Present from Mrs. *Western* to her Niece: It had cost five and twenty Shillings, having been bought of a celebrated Toyman; but the real Value of the Silver, which it contained in its Clasp, was about 18*d*. and that Price the said Toyman, as it was altogether as good as when it first issued from his Shop, would now have given for it. A prudent Person would, however, have taken proper Advantage of the Ignorance of this Fellow, and would not have offered more than a Shilling, or perhaps Six-pence for it; nay, some perhaps would have given nothing, and left the Fellow to his Action of Trover, which some learned Serjeants may doubt whether he could, under these Circumstances, have maintained.

Jones, on the contrary, whose Character was on the Outside of Generosity, and may perhaps not very unjustly have been suspected of Extravagance, without any Hesitation, gave a Guinea in Exchange for the Book. The poor Man, who had not for a long Time before been possessed of so much Treasure, gave Mr. *Jones* a thousand Thanks, and discovered little less of Transport in his Mus-cles, than *Jones* had before shewn, when he had first read the Name of *Sophia Western.*

The Fellow very readily agreed to attend our Travellers to the Place where he had found the Pocket-Book. Together, therefore, they proceeded directly thither; but not so fast as Mr. *Jones* desired; for his Guide unfortunately happened to be lame, and could not possibly travel faster than a Mile an Hour. As this Place, therefore, was at above three Miles Distance, though the Fellow had said otherwise, the Reader need not be acquainted how long they were in walking it.

Jones opened the Book a hundred Times during their Walk, kissed it as often, talked much to himself, and very little to his Companions. At all which the Guide exprest some Signs of Aston-ishment to *Partridge*; who more than once shook his Head, and cry'd, 'poor Gentleman! *orandum est ut sit mens sana in corpore sano.*'[1]

At length they arrived at the very Spot where *Sophia* unhappily dropt the Pocket-Book, and where the Fellow had as happily found

1. "One should pray for a sound mind　*Satires* X.356). See also below, p. 487.
in a sound body"—Lily, p. 157 (Juvenal,

it. Here *Jones* offered to take Leave of his Guide, and to improve
his Pace; but the Fellow, in whom that violent Surprize and Joy
which the first Receipt of the Guinea had occasioned, was now considerably abated, and who had now had sufficient Time to recollect
himself, put on a discontented Look, and, scratching his Head, said,
'He hoped his Worship would give him something more. Your
Worship,' said he, 'will, I hope, take it into your Consideration,
that if I had not been honest I might have kept the Whole.' And,
indeed, this the Reader must confess to have been true. 'If the
Paper there,' said he, 'be worth 100*l*. I am sure the finding it
deserves more than a Guinea. Besides, suppose your Worship
should never see the Lady, nor give it her—and though your Worship looks and talks very much like a Gentleman, yet I have only
your Worship's bare Word: And, certainly, if the right Owner ben't
to be found, it all belongs to the first Finder. I hope your Worship
will consider all these Matters. I am but a poor Man, and therefore
don't desire to have all; but it is but reasonable I should have my
Share. Your Worship looks like a good Man, and, I hope, will consider my Honesty: For I might have kept every Farthing, and nobody ever the wiser.' 'I promise thee, upon my Honour,' cries
Jones, 'that I know the right Owner, and will restore it her.' 'Nay,
your Worship,' answered the Fellow, 'may do as you please as to
that: if you will but give me my Share, that is one Half of the
Money; your Honour may keep the rest yourself if you please;' and
concluded with swearing by a very vehement Oath, 'that he would
never mention a Syllable of it to any Man living.'

'Lookee, Friend,' cries *Jones*, 'the right Owner shall certainly
have again all that she lost; and as for any further Gratuity, I really
cannot give it you at present; but let me know your Name, and
where you live, and it is more than possible, you may hereafter have
further Reason to rejoice at this Morning's Adventure.'

'I don't know what you mean by Venture,' cries the Fellow; 'it
seems, I must venture whether you will return the Lady her Money
or no: But I hope your Worship will consider—' 'Come, come,'
said *Partridge*, 'tell his Honour your Name, and where you may be
found; I warrant you will never repent having put the Money into
his Hands.' The Fellow seeing no Hopes of recovering the Possession of the Pocket-Book, at last complied in giving in his Name and
Place of Abode, which *Jones* writ upon a Piece of Paper with the
Pencil of *Sophia*; and then placing the Paper in the same Page
where she had writ her Name, he cried out, 'There, Friend, you are
the happiest Man alive; I have joined your name to that of an
Angel.' 'I don't know any thing about Angels,' answered the Fellow;
'but I wish you would give me a little more Money, or else return
me the Pocket-Book.' *Partridge* now waxed wroth: He called the

poor Cripple by several vile and opprobrious Names, and was absolutely proceeding to beat him, but *Jones* would not suffer any such
Thing: And now telling the Fellow he would certainly find some
Opportunity of serving him, Mr. *Jones* departed as fast as his Heels
would carry him; and *Partridge*, into whom the Thoughts of the
hundred Pound had infused new Spirits, followed his Leader; while
the Man who was obliged to stay behind, fell to cursing them both,
as well as his Parents; 'For had they,' says he, 'sent me to Charity-
School to learn to write and read and cast Account, I should have
known the Value of these Matters as well as other People.'

Chapter V.

Containing more Adventures which Mr. *Jones and his Companion met on the Road.*

Our Travellers now walked so fast, that they had very little Time
or Breath for Conversation; *Jones* meditating all the Way on
Sophia, and *Partridge* on the Bank-Bill, which, though it gave him
some Pleasure, caused him at the same Time to repine at Fortune,
which, in all his Walks, had never given him such an Opportunity
of shewing his Honesty. They had proceeded above three Miles,
when *Partridge,* being unable any longer to keep up with *Jones,*
called to him, and begged him a little to slacken his Pace: With
this he was the more ready to comply, as he had for some Time lost
the Footsteps of the Horses, which the Thaw had enabled him to
trace for several Miles, and he was now upon a wide Common
where were several Roads.

He here therefore stopt to consider which of these Roads he
should pursue, when on a sudden they heard the Noise of a Drum
that seemed at no great Distance. This Sound presently alarmed the
Fears of *Partridge,* and he cried out, 'Lord have Mercy upon us all;
they are certainly a coming!' 'Who is coming?' cried *Jones*; for Fear
had long since given Place to softer Ideas in his Mind; and since his
Adventure with the lame Man, he had been totally intent on pursuing *Sophia,* without entertaining one Thought of an Enemy.
'Who!' cries *Partridge,* 'why the Rebels: But why should I call
them Rebels? they may be very honest Gentlemen, for any thing I
know to the contrary. The Devil take him that affronts them, I say.
I am sure, if they have nothing to say to me, I will have nothing to
say to them, but in a civil Way. For Heaven's Sake, Sir, don't
affront them if they should come, and perhaps they may do us no
Harm; but would it not be the wiser Way to creep into some of
yonder Bushes till they are gone by? What can two unarmed Men
do perhaps against Fifty thousand? Certainly nobody but a

Madman; I hope your Honour is not offended; but certainly no
Man who hath *Mens sana in Corpore sano'*——Here *Jones* interrupted this Torrent of Eloquence, which Fear had inspired, saying,
'That by the Drum he perceived they were near some Town.' He
then made directly towards the Place whence the Noise proceeded,
bidding *Partridge* 'take Courage, for that he would lead him into no
Danger;' and adding, 'it was impossible the Rebels should be so
near.'

Partridge was a little comforted with this last Assurance; and tho'
he would more gladly have gone the contrary Way, he followèd his
Leader, his Heart beating Time, but not after the Manner of
Heroes, to the Music of the Drum, which ceased not till they had
traversed the Common, and were come into a narrow Lane.

And now *Partridge*, who kept even Pace with *Jones*, discovered
something painted flying in the Air, a very few Yards before him,
which fancying to be the Colours of the Enemy, he fell a bellowing,
'O Lord, Sir, here they are; there is the Crown and Coffin.[1] Oh
Lord! I never saw any thing so terrible; and we are within Gun-
shot of them already.'

Jones no sooner looked up than he plainly perceived what it was
which *Partridge* had thus mistaken. '*Partridge*,' says he, 'I fancy you
will be able to engage this whole Army yourself; for by the Colours
I guess what the Drum was which we heard before, and which beats
up for Recruits to a Puppet-show.'

'A Puppet-show!' answered *Partridge*, with most eager Transport.
'And is it really no more than that? I love a Puppet-show of all the
Pastimes upon Earth. Do, good Sir, let us tarry and see it. Besides I
am quite famish'd to Death; for it is now almost dark, and I have
not eat a Morsel since Three o'Clock in the Morning.'

They now arrived at an Inn, or indeed an Alehouse, where *Jones*
was prevailed upon to stop, the rather as he had no longer any
Assurance of being in the Road he desired. They walked both
directly into the Kitchin, where *Jones* began to enquire if no Ladies
had passed that Way in the Morning, and *Partridge* as eagerly examined into the State of their Provisions; and indeed his Enquiry met

1. Partridge mistakes a puppeteer's
painted showcloth for Bonnie Prince
Charlie's standard, which he had raised
in Glenfinnan, Scotland, 19 August 1745,
to proclaim his father (James, the "Old
Chevalier" or "Old Pretender," son of
James II) King of Great Britain and
Ireland, with Charles as Prince of Wales
and sole Regent of the kingdom. But the
flag was red silk, with a square white
center and, some say, a blue border. Captured at Culloden (16 April 1746) was "a
plain white colours said to be the Standard" (Jean Munroe and Iain Cameron
Taylor, *Glenfinnan and the '45* [Edin-
burgh: The National Trust for Scotland,
n.d.], p. 15). Mutter notes that political
cartoonists added a coffin with crown
(presumably Stuart) above. "The Rebellion Displayed" (1 November 1745)
shows an ass bearing the banner, with
three crowns above the coffin (the three
Stuarts). Why this puppeteer should display a crown and coffin to advertise *The
Provoked Husband*, as his play soon
proves to be, is a mystery, unless Partridge's imagination is painting the cloth.

with the better Success; for *Jones* could not hear News of *Sophia*; but *Partridge*, to his great Satisfaction, found good Reason to expect very shortly the agreeable Sight of an excellent smoking Dish of Eggs and Bacon.

In strong and healthy Constitutions Love hath a very different Effect from what it causes in the puny Part of the Species. In the latter it generally destroys all that Appetite which tends towards the Conservation of the Individual; but in the former, tho' it often induces Forgetfulness, and a Neglect of Food, as well as of every thing else; yet place a good Piece of well-powdered Buttock before a hungry Lover, and he seldom fails very handsomely to play his Part. Thus it happened in the present Case; for tho' *Jones* perhaps wanted a Prompter, and might have travelled much farther, had he been alone, with an empty Stomach; yet no sooner did he sit down to the Bacon and Eggs, then he fell to as heartily and voraciously as *Partridge* himself.

Before our Travellers had finished their Dinner, Night came on, and as the Moon was now past the Full, it was extremely dark. *Partridge* therefore prevailed on *Jones* to stay and see the Puppet-show, which was just going to begin, and to which they were very eagerly invited by the Master of the said Show, who declared that his Figures were the finest which the World had ever produced, and that they had given great Satisfaction to all the Quality in every Town in *England*.

The Puppet-show was performed with great Regularity and Decency. It was called the fine and serious Part of the *Provoked Husband*;[2] and it was indeed a very grave and solemn Entertainment, without any low Wit or Humour, or Jests; or, to do it no more than Justice, without any thing which could provoke a Laugh. The Audience were all highly pleased. A grave Matron told the Master she would bring her two Daughters the next Night, as he did not shew any Stuff; and an Attorney's Clerk, and an Exciseman, both declared, that the Characters of Lord and Lady *Townley* were well preserved, and highly in Nature. *Partridge* likewise concurred with this Opinion.

The Master was so highly elated with these Encomiums, that he could not refrain from adding some more of his own. He said, 'The present Age was not improved in any Thing so much as in their Puppet-shows; which, by throwing out *Punch* and his Wife *Joan*,

2. A play by Colley Cibber (1728), completed from Sir John Vanbrugh's *Journey to London*, left unfinished at his death in 1726. Vanbrugh's scenes were the "low" ones, about the country rustic who comes to London; Cibber's were "the fine and serious part." The play was hissed for political reasons (Cibber's association with the government of Sir Robert Walpole), but the hissers made the mistake of damning Vanbrugh's scenes and letting Cibber's "serious" ones escape (thinking they were Vanbrugh's), much to Cibber's delight.

and such idle Trumpery, were at last brought to be a rational Entertainment. I remember,' said he, 'when I first took to the Business, there was a great deal of low Stuff that did very well to make Folks laugh; but was never calculated to improve the Morals of young People, which certainly ought to be principally aimed at in every Puppet-show: For why may not good and instructive Lessons be conveyed this Way, as well as any other? My Figures are as big as the Life, and they represent the Life in every Particular; and I question not but People rise from my little *Drama* as much improved as they do from the great.' 'I would by no means degrade the Ingenuity of your Profession,' answered *Jones*; 'but I should have been glad to have seen my old Acquaintance Master *Punch*, for all that; and so far from improving, I think, by leaving out him and his merry Wife *Joan*, you have spoiled your Puppet-show.'

The Dancer of Wires conceived an immediate and high Contempt for *Jones*, from these Words. And with much Disdain in his Countenance, he replied, 'Very probably, Sir, that may be your Opinion; but I have the Satisfaction to know the best Judges differ from you, and it is impossible to please every Taste. I confess, indeed, some of the Quality at *Bath*, two or three Years ago, wanted mightily to bring Punch again upon the Stage. I believe I lost some Money for not agreeing to it; but let others do as they will; a little Matter shall never bribe me to degrade my own Profession, nor will I ever willingly consent to the spoiling the Decency and Regularity of my Stage, by introducing any such low Stuff upon it.'

'Right, Friend,' cries the Clerk, 'you are very right. Always avoid what is low. There are several of my Acquaintance in *London*, who are resolved to drive every thing which is low from the Stage.' 'Nothing can be more proper,' cries the Exciseman, pulling his Pipe from his Mouth. 'I remember,' added he, '(for I then lived with my Lord) I was in the Footman's Gallery, the Night when this Play of the *Provoked Husband* was acted first. There was a great deal of low Stuff in it about a Country Gentleman come up to Town to stand for Parliament-man; and there they brought a Parcel of his Servants upon the Stage, his Coachman I remember particularly; but the Gentlemen in our Gallery could not bear any thing so low, and they damned it. I observe, Friend, you have left all that Matter out, and you are to be commended for it.'

'Nay, Gentlemen,' cries *Jones*, 'I can never maintain my Opinion against so many; indeed if the Generality of his Audience dislike him, the learned Gentleman who conducts the Show, may have done very right in dismissing Punch from his Service.'

The Master of the Show then began a second Harangue, and

said much of the great Force of Example, and how much the inferior Part of Mankind would be deterred from Vice, by observing
how odious it was in their Superiors; when he was unluckily interrupted by an Incident, which, though perhaps we might have omitted it at another Time, we cannot help relating at present, but not
in this Chapter.

Chapter VI.

*From which it may be inferred, that the best Things are liable to be
misunderstood and misinterpreted.*

A Violent Uproar now arose in the Entry, where my Landlady
was well cuffing her Maid both with her Fist and Tongue. She had
indeed missed the Wench from her Employment, and, after a little
Search, had found her on the Puppet-show Stage in Company with
the *Merry Andrew*, and in a Situation not very proper to be
described.[1]

Tho' *Grace* (for that was her Name) had forfeited all Title to
Modesty; yet had she not Impudence enough to deny a Fact in
which she was actually surprized; she therefore took another Turn,
and attempted to mitigate the Offence. 'Why do you beat me in
this manner, Mistress?' cries the Wench. 'If you don't like my
Doings, you may turn me away. If I am a W—e (for the other had
liberally bestowed that Appellation on her) my Betters are so as
well as I? What was the fine Lady in the Puppet-show just now. I
suppose she did not lie all Night out from her Husband for
nothing.'

The Landlady now burst into the Kitchin, and fell foul on both
her Husband and the poor Puppet-mover. 'Here, Husband,' says
she, 'you see the Consequence of harbouring these People in your
House. If one doth draw a little Drink the more for them, one is
hardly made Amends for the Litter they make; and then to have
one's House made a Bawdyhouse of by such lousy Vermin. In short,
I desire you would be gone To-morrow Morning; for I will tolerate

1. Fielding is recasting an actual uproar in London "about 1745," when a puppeteer named Griffin decided to take a share in the fifteen-year-old mistress his
Merry Andrew had acquired, at fourteen, while drumming up the show—one
Nancy Dawson, soon to develop, under Griffin's initial tutelage, into London's
most noted dancer. One day, as his wife was busy taking tickets, Griffin put down
his fiddle and took up Miss Dawson on the stage, behind the curtain. The jealous Merry Andrew told the wife, who marched backstage with Griffin's fiddle
and broke it over his head as the An-drew beat the scratching and screaming
Nancy and a sly customer drew back the curtain for the gathering audience (*Authentic Memoirs of the Celebrated Miss Nancy D*WS*N* [London: Tom Dawson, 1765?], summarized by George Speight, *The History of the English Puppet Theatre* [London: George G. Har-rap, 1955], pp. 152–53).

no more such Doings. It is only the Way to teach our Servants Idleness and Nonsense; for to be sure nothing better can be learned by such idle Shows as these. I remember when Puppet shows were made of good Scripture Stories, as *Jephthah*'s Rash Vow,[2] and such good Things, and when wicked People were carried away by the Devil. There was some Sense in those Matters; but as the Parson told us last *Sunday*, nobody believes in the Devil now-a-days; and here you bring about a Parcel of Puppets drest up like Lords and Ladies, only to turn the Heads of poor Country Wenches; and when their Heads are once turned topsy-turvy, no wonder every thing else is so.'

Virgil,[3] I think, tells us, that when the Mob are assembled in a riotous and tumultuous Manner, and all Sorts of missile Weapons fly about, if a Man of Gravity and Authority appears amongst them, the Tumult is presently appeased, and the Mob, which when collected into one Body, may be well compared to an Ass, erect their long Ears at the grave Man's Discourse.

On the contrary, when a Set of grave Men and Philosophers are disputing; when Wisdom herself may in a Manner be considered as present, and administring Arguments to the Disputants; should a Tumult arise among the Mob, or should one Scold, who is herself equal in Noise to a mighty Mob, appear among the said Philosophers; their Disputes cease in a Moment, Wisdom no longer performs her ministerial Office, and the Attention of every one is immediately attracted by the Scold alone.

Thus the Uproar aforesaid, and the Arrival of the Landlady, silenced the Master of the Puppet-show, and put a speedy and final End to that grave and solemn Harangue, of which we have given the Reader a sufficient Taste already. Nothing indeed could have happened so very inopportune as this Accident; the most wanton Malice of Fortune could not have contrived such another Stratagem to confound the poor Fellow, while he was so triumphantly descanting on the good Morals inculcated by his Exhibitions. His Mouth was now as effectually stopt, as that of a Quack must be, if in the Midst of a Declamation on the great Virtues of his Pills and Powders, the Corpse of one of his Martyrs should be brought forth, and deposited before the Stage, as a Testimony of his Skill.

2. Judges xi.30–40. Jephthah vowed to sacrifice the first living thing that came from his house to meet him if he returned victorious over the Ammonites. His beloved daughter became his victim. A painted crown and coffin might appropriately advertise this puppet show, a crown for King Jephthah, a coffin for his daughter. *Jephthah's Rash Vow*, originating at least as early as 1600, remained one of the three most popular shows on Biblical themes well into the eighteenth century, ranking with *Solomon and the Queen of Sheba* after *The Creation of the World* (Speight, p. 165).

3. *Aeneid* I.148–52—". . . silent arrectisque auribus adstant" ("they grow quiet and stand by with ears erect"). Fielding's imagination has supplied the donkey to fill in Virgil's picture.

Instead, therefore, of answering my Landlady, the Puppet-show Man ran out to punish his *Merry-Andrew*; and now the Moon beginning to put forth her Silver Light, as the Poets call it (tho' she looked at that Time more like a Piece of Copper) *Jones* called for his Reckoning, and ordered *Partridge*, whom my Landlady had just awaked from a profound Nap, to prepare for his Journey; but *Partridge* having lately carried two Points, as my Reader hath seen before, was emboldened to attempt a third, which was to prevail with *Jones* to take up a Lodging that Evening in the House where he then was. He introduced this with an affected Surprize at the Intention which Mr. *Jones* declared of removing; and after urging many excellent Arguments against it, he at last insisted strongly, that it could be to no manner of Purpose whatever: For that unless *Jones* knew which Way the Lady was gone, every Step he took might very possibly lead him the farther from her; 'for you find, Sir,' said he, 'by all the People in the House, that she is not gone this Way. How much better therefore, would it be to stay till the Morning, when we may expect to meet with Some-body to enquire of?'

This last Argument had indeed some Effect on *Jones*, and while he was weighing it, the Landlord threw all the Rhetoric of which he was Master, into the same Scale. 'Sure, Sir,' said he, 'your Servant gives you most excellent Advice: For who would travel by Night at this Time of the Year?' He then began in the usual Stile to trumpet forth the excellent Accommodation which his House afforded; and my Landlady likewise opened on the Occasion—But not to detain the Reader with what is common to every Host and Hostess, it is sufficient to tell him, *Jones* was at last prevailed on to stay and refresh himself with a few Hours Rest, which indeed he very much wanted; for he had hardly shut his Eyes since he had left the Inn where the Accident of the broken Head had happened.

As soon as *Jones* had taken a Resolution to proceed no farther that Night, he presently retired to Rest, with his two Bed-fellows the Pocket-Book, and the Muff; but *Partridge*, who at several Times had refreshed himself with several Naps, was more inclined to Eating than to Sleeping, and more to Drinking than to either.

And now the Storm which *Grace* had raised being at an End, and my Landlady being again reconciled to the Puppet-man, who on his Side forgave the indecent Reflections which the good Woman in her Passion had cast on his Performances, a Face of perfect Peace and Tranquillity reigned in the Kitchin; where sat assembled round the Fire, the Landlord and Landlady of the House, the Master of the Puppet-show, the Attorney's Clerk, the Exciseman, and the ingenious Mr. *Partridge*; in which Company past the agreeable Conversation which will be found in the next Chapter.

Chapter VII.

*Containing a Remark or two of our own, and many more of the
good Company assembled in the Kitchin.*

Though the Pride of *Partridge* did not submit to acknowledge
himself a Servant; yet he condescended in most Particulars to imitate the Manners of that Rank. One Instance of this was his greatly
magnifying the Fortune of his Companion, as he called *Jones*: such
is a general Custom with all Servants among Strangers, as none of
them would willingly be thought the Attendant on a Beggar: For
the higher the Situation of the Master is, the higher consequently is
that of the Man in his own Opinion; the Truth of which Observation appears from the Behaviour of all the Footmen of the Nobility.

But tho' Title and Fortune communicate a Splendor all around
them, and the Footmen of Men of Quality and of Estate think
themselves entitled to a Part of that Respect which is paid to the
Quality and Estates of their Masters; it is clearly otherwise with
Regard to Virtue and Understanding. These Advantages are strictly
personal, and swallow themselves all the Respect which is paid to
them. To say the Truth, this is so very little, that they cannot well
afford to let any others partake with them. As these therefore reflect
no Honour on the Domestick, so neither is he at all dishonoured by
the most deplorable Want of both in his Master. Indeed it is otherwise in the Want of what is called Virtue in a Mistress, the Consequence of which we have before seen: For in this Dishonour there
is a Kind of Contagion, which, like that of Poverty, communicates
itself to all who approach it.

Now for these Reasons we are not to wonder that Servants (I
mean among the Men only) should have so great Regard for the
Reputation of the Wealth of their Masters, and little or none at all
for their Character in other Points, and that tho' they would be
ashamed to be the Footman of a Beggar, they are not so to attend
upon a Rogue, or a Blockhead; and do consequently make no Scruple to spread the Fame of the Iniquities and Follies of their said
Masters as far as possible, and this often with great Humour and
Merriment. In reality, a Footman is often a Wit, as well as a Beau,
at the Expence of the Gentleman whose Livery he wears.

After *Partridge*, therefore, had enlarged greatly on the vast Fortune to which Mr. *Jones* was Heir, he very freely communicated an
Apprehension which he had begun to conceive the Day before, and
for which, as we hinted at that very Time, the Behaviour of *Jones*
seemed to have furnished a sufficient Foundation. In short, he was
now pretty well confirmed in an Opinion, that his Master was out

of his Wits, with which Opinion he very bluntly acquainted the good Company round the Fire.

With this Sentiment the Puppet-show Man immediately coincided. 'I own,' said he, 'the Gentleman surprized me very much, when he talked so absurdly about Puppet-shows. It is indeed hardly to be conceived that any Man in his Senses should be so much mistaken; what you say now, accounts very well for all his monstrous Notions. Poor Gentleman! I am heartily concerned for him; indeed he hath a strange Wildness about his Eyes, which I took notice of before, tho' I did not mention it.'

The Landlord agreed with this last Assertion, and likewise claimed the Sagacity of having observed it. 'And certainly,' added he, 'it must be so: For no one but a Madman would have thought of leaving so good a House, to ramble about the Country at that Time of Night.'

The Exciseman pulling his Pipe from his Mouth, said, 'He thought the Gentleman looked and talked a little wildly;' and then turning to *Partridge*, 'If he be a Madman,' says he, 'he should not be suffered to travel thus about the Country; for possibly he may do some Mischief. It is pity he was not secured and sent home to his Relations.'

Now some Conceits of this Kind were likewise lurking in the Mind of *Partridge*: For as he was now persuaded that *Jones* had run away from Mr. *Allworthy*, he promised himself the highest Rewards, if he could by any Means convey him back. But Fear of *Jones*, of whose Fierceness and Strength he had seen, and indeed felt some Instances, had however represented any such Scheme as impossible to be executed, and had discouraged him from applying himself to form any regular Plan for the Purpose. But no sooner did he hear the Sentiments of the Exciseman, than he embraced that Opportunity of declaring his own, and expressed a hearty Wish that such a Matter could be brought about.

'Could be brought about?' says the Exciseman; 'why there is nothing easier.'

'Ah! Sir,' answered *Partridge*; 'you don't know what a Devil of a Fellow he is. He can take me up with one Hand, and throw me out at Window; and he would too, if he did but imagine—'

'Pogh!' says the Exciseman. 'I believe I am as good a Man as he. Besides here are five of us.'

'I don't know what five,' cries the Landlady, 'My Husband shall have nothing to do in it. Nor shall any violent Hands be laid upon any Body in my House. The young Gentleman is as pretty a young Gentleman as ever I saw in my Life, and I believe he is no more mad than any of us. What do you tell of his having a wild Look with his Eyes? They are the prettiest Eyes I ever saw, and he hath

the prettiest Look with them; and a very modest civil young Man
he is. I am sure I have bepitied him heartily ever since the Gentleman there in the Corner told us he was crost in Love. Certainly
that is enough to make any Man, especially such a sweet young
Gentleman as he is, to look a little otherwise than he did before.
Lady, indeed! What the Devil would the Lady have better than
such a handsome Man with a great Estate? I suppose she is one of
your Quality folks, one of your Townly Ladies that we saw last
Night in the Puppet-show, who don't know what they would be at.'

The Attorney's Clerk likewise declared he would have no Concern in the Business, without the Advice of Council. 'Suppose,' says
he, 'an Action of false Imprisonment should be brought against us,
what Defence could we make? Who knows what may be sufficient
Evidence of Madness to a Jury? But I only speak upon my own
Account; for it don't look well for a Lawyer to be concerned in
these Matters, unless it be as a Lawyer. Juries are always less favourable to us than to other People. I don't therefore dissuade you, Mr.
Thomson (to the Exciseman) nor the Gentleman, nor any Body
else.'

The Exciseman shook his Head at this Speech, and the Puppet-
show-Man said, 'Madness was sometimes a difficult Matter for a
Jury to decide: For I remember,' says he, 'I was once present at a
Trial of Madness, where twenty Witnesses swore that the Person
was as mad as a *March* Hare; and twenty others, that he was as
much in his Senses as any Man in *England.*—And indeed it was
the Opinion of most People, that it was only a Trick of his Relations to rob the poor Man of his Right.'

'Very likely!' cries the Landlady, 'I myself knew a poor Gentleman who was kept in a Mad-house all his Life by his Family, and
they enjoyed his Estate, but it did them no Good: For tho' the
Law gave it them, it was the Right of another.'

'Pogh!' cries the Clerk, with great Contempt, 'Who hath any
Right but what the Law gives them? If the Law gave me the best
Estate in the Country, I should never trouble myself much who had
the Right.'

'If it be so,' says *Partridge,* '*Felix quem faciunt aliena pericula
cautum.*'[1]

My Landlord, who had been called out by the Arrival of a Horse-
man at the Gate, now returned into the Kitchin, and with an
affrighted Countenance cried out, 'What do you think, Gentlemen?
The Rebels have given the Duke the Slip, and are got almost to

1. Lily's Third Concord, the rule for relative pronouns: "But when there com-
eth a Nominative Case between the Relative and the Verb, the Relative shall
be such Case as the Verb will have after
him; as, *Felix quem faciunt aliena pericula cautum,* Happy is he whom other
Mens Harms do make beware" (p. 43).
Mutter cites Cyllenus's *Tibullus* (1493).

London—It is certainly true, for a Man on Horseback just now told me so.'

'I am glad of it with all my Heart,' cries *Partridge*, 'then there will be no fighting in these Parts.'

'I am glad,' cries the Clerk, 'for a better Reason; for I would always have Right take Place.'

'Ay but,' answered the Landlord, 'I have heard some People say this Man hath no Right.'

'I will prove the contrary in a Moment,' cries the Clerk; 'if my Father dies seized of a Right; do you mind me, seized of a Right, I say; Doth not that Right descend to his Son? And doth not one Right descend as well as another?'

'But how can he have any Right to make us Papishes?' says the Landlord.

'Never fear that,' cries *Partridge*. 'As to the Matter of Right, the Gentleman there hath proved it as clear as the Sun; and as to the Matter of Religion, it is quite out of the Case. The Papists themselves don't expect any such Thing. A Popish Priest, whom I know very well, and who is a very honest Man, told me upon his Word and Honour they had no such Design.'

'And another Priest of my Acquaintance,' said the Landlady, 'hath told me the same Thing—But my Husband is always so afraid of Papishes. I know a great many Papishes that are very honest Sort of People, and spend their Money very freely; and it is always a Maxim with me, that one Man's Money is as good as another's.'

'Very true, Mistress,' said the Puppet-show-Man, 'I don't care what Religion comes, provided the Presbyterians are not uppermost; for they are Enemies to Puppet-shows.'

'And so you would sacrifice your Religion to your Interest;' cries the Exciseman; 'and are desirous to see Popery brought in, are you?'

'Not I truly,' answered the other, 'I hate Popery as much as any Man; but yet it is a Comfort to one, that one should be able to live under it, which I could not do among Presbyterians. To be sure every Man values his Livelihood first; that must be granted; and I warrant if you would confess the Truth, you are more afraid of losing your Place than any Thing else; but never fear, Friend, there will be an Excise under another Government as well as under this.'

'Why certainly,' replied the Exciseman, 'I should be a very ill Man, if I did not honour the King, whose Bread I eat. That is no more than natural, as a Man may say: For what signifies it to me that there would be an Excise-office under another Government, since my Friends would be out, and I could expect no better than to follow them? No, no, Friend, I shall never be bubbled out of my Religion in Hopes only of keeping my Place under another Government; for I should certainly be no better, and very probably might be worse.'

'Why, that is what I say,' cries the Landlord, 'whenever Folks say who knows what may happen? Odsooks! should not I be a Block-head to lend my Money to I know not who, because mayhap he may return it again? I am sure it is safe in my own Bureau, and there I will keep it.'

The Attorney's Clerk had taken a great Fancy to the Sagacity of *Partridge*. Whether this proceeded from the great Discernment which the former had into Men, as well as Things, or whether it arose from the Sympathy between their Minds; for they were both truly *Jacobites* in Principle; they now shook Hands heartily, and drank Bumpers of Strong Beer to Healths which we think proper to bury in Oblivion.

These Healths were afterwards pledged by all present, and even by my Landlord himself, tho' reluctantly; but he could not with-stand the Menaces of the Clerk, who swore he would never set his Foot within his House again, if he refused. The Bumpers which were swallowed on this Occasion soon put an End to the Conversa-tion. Here, therefore, we will put an End to the Chapter.

Chapter VIII.

In which Fortune seems to have been in a better Humour with Jones *than we have hitherto seen her.*

As there is no wholesomer, so perhaps there are few stronger Sleeping Potions than Fatigue. Of this *Jones* might be said to have taken a very large Dose, and it operated very forcibly upon him. He had already slept nine Hours, and might perhaps have slept longer, had he not been awakened by a most violent Noise at his Cham-ber-Door, where the Sound of many heavy Blows was accompanied with many Exclamations of Murder. *Jones* presently leapt from his Bed, where he found the Master of the Puppet-show belabouring the Back and Ribs of his poor Merry Andrew, without either Mercy or Moderation.

Jones instantly interposed on Behalf of the Suffering Party, and pinned the insulting Conqueror up to the Wall: For the Puppet-show-man was no more able to contend with *Jones*, than the poor Party-coloured Jester had been to contend with this Puppet-man.

But tho' the Merry Andrew was a little Fellow, and not very strong, he had nevertheless some Choler about him. He therefore no sooner found himself delivered from the Enemy, than he began to attack him with the only Weapon at which he was his Equal. From this he first discharged a Volley of general abusive Words, and thence proceeded to some particular Accusations—'D—n your Bl—d, you Rascal,' says he, 'I have not only supported you, (for to me you owe all the Money you get) but I have saved you from the

Gallows. Did you not want to rob the Lady of her fine Riding-Habit, no longer ago than Yesterday, in the Back-Lane here? Can you deny that you wished to have her alone in a Wood to strip her, to strip one of the prettiest Ladies that ever was seen in the World? and here you have fallen upon me, and have almost murdered me for doing no Harm to a Girl as willing as myself, only because she likes me better than you.'

Jones no sooner heard this, than he quitted the Master, laying on him at the same time the most violent Injunctions of Forbearance from any further Insult on the Merry Andrew; and then taking the poor Wretch with him into his own Apartment, he soon learnt Tidings of his *Sophia*, whom the Fellow, as he was attending his Master with his Drum the Day before, had seen pass by. He easily prevailed with the Lad to shew him the exact Place, and then having summoned *Partridge*, he departed with the utmost Expedition.

It was almost Eight of the Clock before all Matters could be got ready for his Departure: For *Partridge* was not in any Haste; nor could the Reckoning be presently adjusted; and when both these were settled and over, *Jones* would not quit the Place, before he had perfectly reconciled all Differences between the Master and the Man.

When this was happily accomplished, he set forwards, and was by the trusty Merry Andrew conducted to the Spot by which *Sophia* had past; and then having handsomely rewarded his Conductor, he again pushed on with the utmost Eagerness, being highly delighted with the extraordinary Manner in which he received his Intelligence. Of this *Partridge* was no sooner acquainted, than he, with great Earnestness, began to prophesy, and assured *Jones*, that he would certainly have good Success in the End: For, he said, 'two such Accidents could never have happened to direct him after his Mistress, if Providence had not designed to bring them together at last.' And this was the first Time that *Jones* lent any Attention to the superstitious Doctrines of his Companion.

They had not gone above two Miles, when a violent Storm of Rain overtook them; and as they happened to be at the same Time in Sight of an Alehouse, *Partridge*, with much earnest Entreaty, prevailed with *Jones* to enter, and weather the Storm. Hunger is an Enemy (if indeed it may be called one) which partakes more of the *English* than of the *French* Disposition; for tho' you subdue this never so often, it will always rally again in Time; and so it did with *Partridge*, who was no sooner arrived within the Kitchin, than he began to ask the same Questions which he had asked the Night before. The Consequence of this was an excellent cold Chine being produced upon the Table, upon which not only *Partridge*, but *Jones*

himself, made a very hearty Breakfast, tho' the latter began to
grow again uneasy, as the People of the House could give him no
fresh Information concering *Sophia*.

Their Meal being over, *Jones* was again preparing to sally,
notwithstanding the Violence of the Storm still continued; but *Partridge* begged heartily for another Mugg; and at last casting his
Eyes on a Lad at the Fire, who had entered into the Kitchin, and
who at that Instant was looking as earnestly at him, he turned suddenly to *Jones*, and cried, 'Master, give me your Hand, a single
Mugg shan't serve the Turn this Bout. Why here's more News of
Madam *Sophia* come to Town. The Boy there standing by the Fire
is the very Lad that rode before her. I can swear to my own Plaister
on his Face.' 'Heavens bless you, Sir,' cries the Boy, 'it is your own
Plaister sure enough; I shall have always Reason to remember your
Goodness; for it hath almost cured me.'

At these Words *Jones* started from his Chair, and bidding the
Boy follow him immediately, departed from the Kitchin into a private Apartment; for so delicate was he with regard to *Sophia*, that
he never willingly mentioned her Name in the Presence of many
People; and tho' he had, as it were, from the Overflowings of his
Heart, given *Sophia* as a Toast among the Officers, where he
thought it was impossible she should be known; yet even there the
Reader may remember how difficultly he was prevailed upon to
mention her Sir-name.

Hard therefore was it, and perhaps, in the Opinion of many sagacious Readers, very absurd and monstrous, that he should principally owe his present Misfortune to the supposed Want of that Delicacy with which he so abounded; for, in Reality, *Sophia* was much
more offended at the Freedoms which she thought (and not without good Reason) he had taken with her Name and Character,
than at any Freedoms, in which, under his present Circumstances,
he had indulged himself with the Person of another Woman; and
to say Truth, I believe *Honour* could never have prevailed on her to
leave *Upton* without seeing her *Jones*, had it not been for those two
strong Instances of a Levity in his Behaviour, so void of Respect,
and indeed so highly inconsistent with any Degree of Love and
Tenderness in great and delicate Minds.

But so Matters fell out, and so I must relate them; and if any
Reader is shocked at their appearing unnatural, I cannot help it. I
must remind such Persons, that I am not writing a System, but a
History, and I am not obliged to reconcile every Matter to the
received Notions concerning Truth and Nature. But if this was
never so easy to do, perhaps it might be more prudent in me to
avoid it. For Instance, as the Fact at present before us now stands,
without any Comment of mine upon it, tho' it may at first Sight

offend some Readers, yet upon more mature Consideration, it must please all; for wise and good Men may consider what happened to *Jones* at *Upton* as a just Punishment for his Wickedness, with regard to Women, of which it was indeed the immediate Consequence; and silly and bad Persons may comfort themselves in their Vices, by flattering their own Hearts that the Characters of Men are rather owing to Accident than to Virtue. Now perhaps the Reflections which we should be here inclined to draw, would alike contradict both these Conclusions, and would shew that these Incidents contribute only to confirm the great, useful and uncommon Doctrine, which it is the Purpose of this whole Work to inculcate, and which we must not fill up our Pages by frequently repeating, as an ordinary Parson fills his Sermon by repeating his Text at the End of every Paragraph.

We are contented that it must appear, however unhappily *Sophia* had erred in her Opinion of *Jones*, she had sufficient Reason for her Opinion; since, I believe, every other young Lady would, in her Situation, have erred in the same Manner. Nay, had she followed her Lover at this very Time, and had entered this very Alehouse the Moment he was departed from it, she would have found the Landlord as well acquainted with her Name and Person as the Wench at *Upton* had appeared to be. For while *Jones* was examining his Boy in Whispers in an inner Room, *Partridge*, who had no such Delicacy in his Disposition, was in the Kitchin very openly catechising the other Guide who had attended Mrs. *Fitzpatrick*; by which Means the Landlord, whose Ears were open on all such Occasions, became perfectly well acquainted with the Tumble of *Sophia* from her Horse, *&c.* with the Mistake concerning *Jenny Cameron*, with the many Consequences of the Punch, and, in short, with almost every Thing which had happened at the Inn, whence we dispatched our Ladies in a Coach and Six, when we last took our Leaves of them.

Chapter IX.

Containing little more than a few odd Observations.

Jones had been absent a full half Hour, when he returned into the Kitchin in a Hurry, desiring the Landlord to let him know that Instant what was to pay. And now the Concern which *Partridge* felt at being obliged to quit the warm Chimney-corner, and a Cup of excellent Liquor, was somewhat compensated by hearing that he was to proceed no farther on Foot; for *Jones*, by Golden Arguments, had prevailed with the Boy to attend him back to the Inn whither he had before conducted *Sophia*; but to this however the

Lad consented, upon Condition that the other Guide would wait
for him at the Alehouse; because, as the Landlord at *Upton* was an
intimate Acquaintance of the Landlord at *Gloucester*, it might
some Time or other come to the Ears of the latter, that his Horses
had been let to more than one Person; and so the Boy might be
brought to Account for Money which he wisely intended to put in
his own Pocket.

We were obliged to mention this Circumstance, trifling as it may
seem, since it retarded Mr. *Jones* a considerable Time in his setting
out; for the Honesty of this latter Boy was somewhat high—that is,
somewhat high priced, and would indeed have cost *Jones* very dear,
had not *Partridge*, who, as we have said, was a very cunning Fellow,
artfully thrown in half a Crown to be spent at that very Alehouse,
while the Boy was waiting for his Companion. This half Crown the
Landlord no sooner got Scent of, than he opened after it with such
vehement and persuasive Out-cry, that the Boy was soon overcome,
and consented to take half a Crown more for his Stay. Here we
cannot help observing, that as there is so much of Policy in the
lowest Life, great Men often overvalue themselves on those Refine-
ments in Imposture, in which they are frequently excelled by some
of the lowest of the Human Species.

The Horses being now produced, *Jones* directly leapt into the
Side-Saddle, on which his dear *Sophia* had rid. The Lad indeed very
civilly offered him the Use of his; but he chose the Side-Saddle,
probably because it was softer. *Partridge*, however, tho' full as
effeminate as *Jones*, could not bear the Thoughts of degrading his
Manhood; he therefore accepted the Boy's Offer; and now *Jones*,
being mounted on the Side-Saddle of his *Sophia*, the Boy on that of
Mrs. *Honour*, and *Partridge* bestriding the third Horse, they set forwards on their Journey, and within four Hours arrived at the Inn
where the Reader hath already spent so much Time. *Partridge* was
in very high Spirits during the whole Way, and often mentioned to
Jones the many good Omens of his future Success, which had
lately befriended him; and which the Reader, without being the
least superstitious, must allow to have been peculiarly fortunate.
Partridge was moreover better pleased with the present Pursuit of
his Companion, than he had been with his Pursuit of Glory; and
from these very Omens, which assured the Pedagogue of Success, he
likewise first acquired a clear Idea of the Amour between *Jones* and
Sophia; to which he had before given very little Attention, as he
had originally taken a wrong Scent concerning the Reasons of
Jones's Departure; and as to what happened at *Upton*, he was too
much frightened just before and after his leaving that Place, to
draw any other Conclusions from thence, than that poor *Jones* was
a downright Madman: A Conceit which was not at all disagreeable

to the Opinion he before had of his extraordinary Wildness, of which, he thought, his Behaviour on their quitting *Gloucester* so well justified all the Accounts he had formerly received. He was now however pretty well satisfied with his present Expedition, and henceforth began to conceive much worthier Sentiments of his Friend's Understanding.

The Clock had just struck Three when they arrived, and *Jones* immediately bespoke Post-Horses; but unluckily there was not a Horse to be procured in the whole Place; which the Reader will not wonder at, when he considers the Hurry in which the whole Nation, and especially this Part of it, was at this Time engaged, when Expresses were passing and repassing every Hour of the Day and Night.

Jones endeavoured all he could to prevail with his former Guide to escorte him to *Coventry*; but he was inexorable. While he was arguing with the Boy in the Inn-yard, a Person came up to him, and saluting him by his Name, enquired how all the good Family did in *Somersetshire*; and now *Jones* casting his Eyes upon this Person, presently discovered him to be Mr. *Dowling* the Lawyer, with whom he had dined at *Gloucester*, and with much Courtesy returned his Salutation.

Dowling very earnestly pressed Mr. *Jones* to go no further that Night; and backed his Solicitations with many unanswerable Arguments, such as, that it was almost dark, that the Roads were very dirty, and that he would be able to travel much better by Day-light, with many others equally good, some of which *Jones* had probably suggested to himself before; but as they were then ineffectual, so they were still; and he continued resolute in his Design, even tho' he should be obliged to set out on Foot.

When the good Attorney found he could not prevail on *Jones* to stay, he as strenuously applied himself to persuade the Guide to accompany him. He urged many Motives to induce him to undertake this short Journey, and at last concluded with saying, 'Do you think the Gentleman won't very well reward you for your Trouble?'

Two to one are odds at every other thing, as well as Foot-ball. But the Advantage which this united Force hath in Persuasion or Entreaty, must have been visible to a curious Observer; for he must have often seen, that when a Father, a Master, a Wife, or any other Person in Authority, have stoutly adhered to a Denial against all the Reasons which a single Man could produce, they have afterwards yielded to the Repetition of the same Sentiments by a second or third Person, who hath undertaken the Cause without attempting to advance any thing new in its Behalf. And hence perhaps proceeds the Phrase of seconding an Argument or a Motion, and the great Consequence this is of in all Assemblies of public

Debate. Hence likewise probably it is, that in our Courts of Law we often hear a learned Gentleman (generally a Serjeant) repeating for an Hour together what another learned Gentleman who spoke just before him, had been saying.

Instead of accounting for this, we shall proceed in our usual Manner to exemplify it in the Conduct of the Lad above-mentioned, who submitted to the Persuasions of Mr. *Dowling*, and promised once more to admit *Jones* into his Side-Saddle; but insisted on first giving the poor Creatures a good Bait, saying, they had travelled a great way, and been rid very hard. Indeed this Caution of the Boy was needless; for *Jones*, notwithstanding his Hurry and Impatience, would have ordered this of himself; for he by no means agreed with the Opinion of those who consider Animals as mere Machines, and when they bury their Spurs in the Belly of their Horse, imagine the Spur and the Horse to have an equal Capacity of feeling Pain.

While the Beasts were eating their Corn, or rather were supposed to eat it; (for as the Boy was taking Care of himself in the Kitchin, the Hostler took great Care that his Corn should not be consumed in the Stable) Mr. *Jones*, at the earnest Desire of Mr. *Dowling*, accompanied that Gentleman into his Room, where they sat down together over a Bottle of Wine.

Chapter X.

In which Mr. Jones *and Mr.* Dowling *drink a Bottle together.*

Mr. *Dowling*, pouring out a Glass of Wine, named the Health of the good Squire *Allworthy*; adding, 'If you please, Sir, we will likewise remember his Nephew and Heir, the young Squire: Come, Sir, here's Mr. *Blifil* to you, a very pretty young Gentleman; and who, I dare swear, will hereafter make a very considerable Figure in his Country. I have a Borough for him myself in my Eye.'

'Sir,' answered *Jones*, 'I am convinced you don't intend to affront me, so I shall not resent it; but, I promise you, you have joined two Persons very improperly together; for one is the Glory of the Human Species, and the other is a Rascal who dishonours the Name of Man.'

Dowling stared at this. He said, 'He thought both the Gentlemen had a very unexceptionable Character. As for Squire *Allworthy* himself,' says he, 'I never had the Happiness to see him; but all the World talks of his Goodness. And, indeed, as to the young Gentleman, I never saw him but once, when I carried him the News of the Loss of his Mother; and then I was so hurried, and drove, and tore with the Multiplicity of Business, that I had hardly Time to converse with him; but he looked so like a very honest Gentleman, and behaved himself so prettily, that I protest I never was more delighted with any Gentleman since I was born.'

'I don't wonder,' answered *Jones*, 'that he should impose upon you in so short an Acquaintance; for he hath the Cunning of the Devil himself, and you may live with him many Years without discovering him. I was bred up with him from my Infancy, and we were hardly ever asunder; but it is very lately only, that I have discovered half the Villainy which is in him. I own I never greatly liked him. I thought he wanted that Generosity of Spirit, which is the sure Foundation of all that is great and noble in Human Nature. I saw a Selfishness in him long ago which I despised; but it is lately, very lately, that I have found him capable of the basest and blackest Designs; for, indeed, I have at last found out, that he hath taken an Advantage of the Openness of my own Temper, and hath concerted the deepest Project, by a long Train of wicked Artifice, to work my Ruin, which at last he hath effected.'

'Ay! Ay!' cries *Dowling*, 'I protest then, it is a Pity such a Person should inherit the great Estate of your Uncle *Allworthy*.'

'Alas, Sir,' cries *Jones*, 'you do me an Honour to which I have no Title. It is true, indeed, his Goodness once allowed me the Liberty of calling him by a much nearer Name; but as this was only a voluntary Act of Goodness, I can complain of no Injustice when he thinks proper to deprive me of this Honour; since the Loss cannot be more unmerited than the Gift originally was. I assure you, Sir, I am no Relation of Mr. *Allworthy*; and if the World, who are incapable of setting a true Value on his Virtue, should think, in his Behaviour by me, he hath dealt hardly by a Relation, they do an Injustice to the best of Men: For I——but I ask your Pardon, I shall trouble you with no Particulars relating to myself; only as you seemed to think me a Relation of Mr. *Allworthy*, I thought proper to set you right in a Matter that might draw some Censures upon him, which I promise you I would rather lose my Life, than give Occasion to.'

'I protest, Sir,' cried *Dowling*, 'you talk very much like a Man of Honour; but instead of giving me any Trouble, I protest it would give me great Pleasure to know how you came to be thought a Relation of Mr. *Allworthy*'s, if you are not. Your Horses won't be ready this half Hour, and as you have sufficient Opportunity, I wish you would tell me how all that happened; for I protest it seems very surprizing that you should pass for a Relation of a Gentleman, without being so.'

Jones, who in the Compliance of his Disposition (tho' not in his Prudence) a little resembled his lovely *Sophia*, was easily prevailed

on to satisfy Mr. *Dowling*'s Curiosity, by relating the History of his
Birth and Education, which he did, like *Othello*,[1]

> ————even from his boyish Years,
> To th' very Moment he was bad to tell;

the which to hear, *Dowling*, like *Desdemona*, did *seriously incline*;

> He swore 'twas strange, 'twas passing strange;
> 'Twas pitiful, 'twas wonderous pitiful.

Mr. *Dowling* was indeed very greatly affected with this Relation;
for he had not divested himself of Humanity by being an Attorney.
Indeed nothing is more unjust than to carry our Prejudices against a
Profession into private Life, and to borrow our Idea of a Man from
our Opinion of his Calling. Habit, it is true, lessens the Horror of
those Actions which the Profession makes necessary, and consequently habitual; but in all other Instances, Nature works in Men
of all Professions alike; nay, perhaps, even more strongly with those
who give her, as it were, a Holiday, when they are following their
ordinary Business. A Butcher, I make no doubt, would feel Compunction at the Slaughter of a fine Horse; and though a Surgeon
can conceive no Pain in cutting off a Limb, I have known him compassionate a Man in a Fit of the Gout. The common Hangman,
who hath stretched the Necks of Hundreds, is known to have trembled at his first Operation on a Head: And the very Professors of
Human Blood-shedding, who in their Trade of War butcher Thousands, not only of their Fellow Professors, but often of Women and
Children, without Remorse; even these, I say, in Times of Peace,
when Drums and Trumpets are laid aside, often lay aside all their
Ferocity, and become very gentle Members of civil Society. In the
same Manner an Attorney may feel all the Miseries and Distresses
of his Fellow Creatures, provided he happens not to be concerned
against them.

Jones, as the Reader knows, was yet unacquainted with the very
black Colours in which he had been represented to Mr. *Allworthy*;
and as to other Matters he did not shew them in the most disadvantageous Light: For though he was unwilling to cast any Blame
on his former Friend and Patron; yet he was not very desirous of
heaping too much upon himself. *Dowling* therefore observed, and
not without Reason, that very ill Offices must have been done him
by some Body: 'For certainly,' cries he, 'the Squire would never
have disinherited you only for a few Faults, which any young Gen-

---

1. Fielding quotes (with some adjust-
ment) from I.iii.132–61: "... even from
my boyish days / To th'very moment
that he bade me tell it. / ... Would
Desdemona seriously incline; / ... She
swore, in faith, 'twas strange, 'twas passing strange; / 'Twas pitiful, 'twas wondrous pitiful."

tleman might have committed. Indeed, I cannot properly say disinherited; for to be sure by Law you cannot claim as Heir. That's certain; that no Body need go to Counsel for. Yet when a Gentleman had in a Manner adopted you thus as his own Son, you might reasonably have expected some very considerable Part, if not the Whole; nay, if you had expected the Whole, I should not have blamed you: For certainly all Men are for getting as much as they can, and they are not to be blamed on that Account.'

'Indeed you wrong me,' said *Jones*, 'I should have been contented with very little: I never had any View upon Mr. *Allworthy*'s Fortune; nay, I believe, I may truly say, I never once considered what he could or might give me. This I solemnly declare, if he had done a Prejudice to his Nephew in my Favour, I would have undone it again. I had rather enjoy my own Mind than the Fortune of another Man. What is the poor Pride arising from a magnificent House, a numerous Equipage, a splendid Table, and from all the other Advantages or Appearances of Fortune, compared to the warm, solid Content, the swelling Satisfaction, the thrilling Transports, and the exulting Triumphs, which a good Mind enjoys, in the Contemplation of a generous, virtuous, noble, benevolent Action? I envy not *Blifil* in the Prospect of his Wealth; nor shall I envy him in the Possession of it. I would not think myself a Rascal half an Hour, to exchange Situations. I believe, indeed, Mr. *Blifil* suspected me of the Views you mention; and I suppose these Suspicions, as they arose from the Baseness of his own Heart, so they occasioned his Baseness to me. But, I thank Heaven, I know, I feel, ——I feel my Innocence, my Friend; and I would not part with that Feeling for the World.——For as long as I know I have never done, nor even designed an Injury to any Being whatever,

> *Pone me pigris ubi nulla campis*
> *Arbor æstiva recreatur aura,*
> *Quod latus mundi nebulae, malusque*
> *Jupiter urget.*

> *Pone, sub curru nimium propinqui*
> *Solis in Terra dominibus negata;*
> *Dulce ridentem Lalagen amabo,*
> *Dulce loquentem.*[2]

He then filled a Bumper of Wine, and drank it off to the Health of his dear *Lalage*; and filling *Dowling*'s Glass likewise up to the

2. Horace, *Odes* I.xxii. 17–24. Fielding's note gives this translation: "Place me where never Summer Breeze / Unbinds the Glebe, or warms the Trees; / Where ever lowering Clouds appear, / And angry *Jove* deforms th' inclement Year. / Place me beneath the burning Ray, / Where rolls the rapid Carr of Day; / Love and the Nymph shall charm my Toils, / The Nymph who sweetly speaks, and sweetly smiles. / MR. *Francis*." On Dr. Philip Francis, see above, note 4, p. 434.

Brim, insisted on his pledging him. 'Why then here's Miss *Lalage*'s Health, with all my Heart,' cries *Dowling*. 'I have heard her toasted often, I protest, though I never saw her; but they say she's extremely handsome.'

Though the *Latin* was not the only part of this Speech which *Dowling* did not perfectly understand; yet there was somewhat in it, that made a very strong Impression upon him. And though he endeavoured by winking, nodding, sneering, and grinning, to hide the Impression from *Jones*, (for we are as often ashamed of thinking right as of thinking wrong) it is certain he secretly approved as much of his Sentiments as he understood, and really felt a very strong Impulse of Compassion for him. But we may possibly take some other Opportunity of commenting upon this, especially if we should happen to meet Mr. *Dowling* any more in the Course of our History. At present we are obliged to take our Leave of that Gentleman a little abruptly, in Imitation of Mr. *Jones*; who was no sooner informed, by *Partridge*, that his Horses were ready, than he deposited his Reckoning, wished his Companion a good Night, mounted, and set forward towards *Coventry*, tho' the Night was dark, and it just then began to rain very hard.

Chapter XI.

The Disasters which befel Jones *on his Departure for* Coventry; *with the sage Remarks of* Partridge.

No Road can be plainer than that from the place where they now were to *Coventry*; and though neither *Jones* nor *Partridge*, nor the Guide had ever travelled it before, it would have been almost impossible to have missed their Way, had it not been for the two Reasons mentioned in the Conclusion of the last Chapter.

These two Circumstances, however, happening both unfortunately to intervene, our Travellers deviated into a much less frequented Track; and after riding full Six Miles, instead of arriving at the stately Spires of *Coventry*, they found themselves still in a very dirty Lane, where they saw no Symptoms of approaching the Suburbs of a large City.

Jones now declared that they must certainly have lost their Way; but this the Guide insisted upon was impossible; a Word which, in common Conversation, is often used to signify not only improbable, but often what is really very likely, and, sometimes, what hath certainly happened: An hyperbolical Violence like that which is so frequently offered to the Words Infinite and Eternal; by the former of which it is usual to express a Distance of half a Yard, and by the latter, a Duration of five Minutes. And thus it is as usual to assert the Impossibility of losing what is already actually lost. This was, in fact, the Case at present: For notwithstanding all the confident Assertions of the Lad to the contrary, it is certain they were no more in the right Road to *Coventry*, than the fraudulent, griping, cruel, canting Miser is in the right Road to Heaven.

It is not, perhaps, easy for a Reader who hath never been in those Circumstances, to imagine the Horror with which Darkness, Rain, and Wind fill Persons who have lost their Way in the Night; and who, consequently, have not the pleasant Prospect of warm Fires, dry Cloaths, and other Refreshments, to support their Minds in struggling with the Inclemencies of the Weather. A very imperfect Idea of this Horror will, however, serve sufficiently to account for the Conceits which now filled the Head of *Partridge*, and which we shall presently be obliged to open.

Jones grew more and more positive that they were out of their Road; and the Boy himself, at last, acknowledged he believed they were not in the right Road to *Coventry*; tho' he affirmed, at the same Time, it was impossible they should have mist the Way. But *Partridge* was of a different Opinion. He said, 'When they first set out he imagined some Mischief or other would happen.—Did not you observe, Sir,' said he to *Jones*, 'that old Woman who stood at the Door just as you was taking Horse? I wish you had given her a small Matter, with all my Heart; for she said then you might repent it; and at that very Instant it began to rain, and the Wind hath continued rising ever since. Whatever some People may think, I am very certain it is in the Power of Witches to raise the Wind whenever they please. I have seen it happen very often in my Time: And if ever I saw a Witch in all my Life, that old Woman was certainly one. I thought so to myself at that very Time; and if I had any Halfpence in my Pocket, I would have given her some: For to be sure it is always good to be charitable to those Sort of People, for Fear what may happen; and many a Person hath lost his Cattle by saving a Halfpenny.'

Jones, tho' he was horridly vexed at the Delay which this Mistake was likely to occasion in his Journey, could not help smiling at the Superstition of his Friend, whom an Accident now greatly confirmed in his Opinion. This was a Tumble from his Horse; by which, however, he received no other Injury than what the Dirt conferred on his Cloaths.

Partridge had no sooner recovered his Legs, than he appealed to his Fall, as conclusive Evidence of all he had asserted; but *Jones*, finding he was unhurt, answered with a Smile: 'This Witch of yours, *Partridge*, is a most ungrateful Jade, and doth not, I find, distinguish her Friends from others in her Resentment. If the old Lady had been angry with me for neglecting her, I don't see why she should tumble you from your Horse, after all the Respect you have expressed for her.'

'It is ill jesting,' cries *Partridge*, 'with People who have Power to do these Things; for they are often very malicious. I remember a Farrier, who provoked one of them, by asking her when the Time she had bargained with the Devil for, would be out; and within three Months from that very Day one of his best Cows was drowned. Nor was she satisfied with that: for a little Time afterwards he lost a Barrel of Best-Drink: For the old Witch pulled out the Spigot, and let it run all over the Cellar, the very first Evening he had tapped it, to make merry with some of his Neighbours. In short, nothing ever thrived with him afterwards; for she worried the poor Man so, that he took to Drinking; and in a Year or two his Stock was seized, and he and his Family are now come to the Parish.'

The Guide, and perhaps his Horse too, were both so attentive to this Discourse, that, either thro' Want of Care, or by the Malice of the Witch, they were now both sprawling in the Dirt.

Partridge entirely imputed this Fall, as he had done his own, to the same Cause. He told Mr. *Jones*, 'it would certainly be his Turn next;' and earnestly intreated him 'to return back, and find out the old Woman, and pacify her. We shall very soon,' added he, 'reach the Inn; For tho' we have seemed to go forward, I am very certain we are in the identical Place in which we were an Hour ago; and I dare swear if it was Day-light, we might now see the Inn we set out from.'

Instead of returning any Answer to this sage Advice, *Jones* was entirely attentive to what had happened to the Boy, who received no other Hurt than what had before befallen *Partridge*, and which his Cloaths very easily bore, as they had been for many Years inured to the like. He soon regained his Side-Saddle, and, by the hearty Curses and Blows which he bestowed on his Horse, quickly satisfied Mr. *Jones* that no Harm was done.

Chapter XII.

Relates that Mr. Jones *continued his Journey contrary to the Advice of* Partridge, *with what happened on that Occasion.*

They now discovered a Light at some Distance, to the great Pleasure of *Jones*, and to the no small Terror of *Partridge*, who firmly believed himself to be bewitched, and that this Light was a *Jack with a Lantern*, or somewhat more mischievous.

But how were these Fears increased, when, as they approached nearer to this Light, (or Lights as they now appeared) they heard a confused Sound of Human Voices; of singing, laughing, and hallow-ing, together with a strange Noise that seemed to proceed from some Instruments; but could hardly be allowed the Name of Music! Indeed, to favour a little the Opinion of *Partridge*, it might very well be called Music bewitched.

It is impossible to conceive a much greater Degree of Horror than what now seized on *Partridge*; the Contagion of which had reached the Post-Boy, who had been very attentive to many Things that the other had uttered. He now therefore joined in petitioning *Jones* to return; saying he firmly believed what *Partridge* had just before said, that tho' the Horses seemed to go on, they had not moved a Step forwards during at least the last half Hour.

Jones could not help smiling in the midst of his Vexation, at the Fears of these poor Fellows. 'Either we advance,' says he, 'towards the Lights, or the Lights have advanced towards us; for we are now at a very little Distance from them; but how can either of you be afraid of a Set of People who appear only to be merry-making?'

'Merry-making, Sir!' cries *Partridge*; 'who could be merry-making at this Time of Night, and in such a Place, and such Weather? They can be nothing but Ghosts or Witches, or some Evil Spirits or other, that's certain.'

'Let them be what they will,' cries *Jones*, 'I am resolved to go up to them, and enquire the Way to *Coventry*. All Witches, *Partridge*, are not such ill-natured Hags as that we had the Misfortune to meet with last.'

'Oh Lord, Sir!' cries *Partridge*, 'there is no knowing what Humour they will be in; to be sure it is always best to be civil to them; but what if we should meet with something worse than Witches, with Evil Spirits themselves?—Pray, Sir, be advised; pray, Sir, do. If you had read so many terrible Accounts as I have of these Matters, you would not be so Fool-hardy.—The Lord knows whither we have got already, or whither we are going: For sure such Darkness was never seen upon Earth, and I question whether it can be darker in the other World.'

Jones put forwards as fast as he could, notwithstanding all these Hints and Cautions, and poor *Partridge* was obliged to follow: For tho' he hardly dared to advance, he dared still less to stay behind by himself.

At length they arrived at the Place whence the Lights and differ-ent Noises had issued. This *Jones* perceived to be no other than a Barn where a great Number of Men and Women were assembled, and diverting themselves with much apparent Jollity.

Jones no sooner appeared before the great Doors of the Barn, which were open, than a masculine and very rough Voice from within demanded who was there?—To which *Jones* gently answered, A Friend; and immediately asked the Road to *Coventry*.

'If you are a Friend,' cries another of the Men in the Barn, 'you had better alight till the Storm is over;' (for indeed it was now more violent than ever) 'you are very welcome to put up your Horse; for there is sufficient Room for him at one End of the Barn.'

'You are very obliging,' returned *Jones*; 'and I will accept your Offer for a few Minutes, whilst the Rain continues; and here are two more who will be glad of the same Favour.' This was accorded with more Good-will than it was accepted: For *Partridge* would rather have submitted to the utmost Inclemency of the Weather, than have trusted to the Clemency of those whom he took for Hobgoblins; and the poor Post-Boy was now infected with the same Apprehensions; but they were both obliged to follow the Example of *Jones*; the one because he durst not leave his Horse, and the other because he feared nothing so much as being left by himself.

Had this History been writ in the Days of Superstition, I should have had too much Compassion for the Reader to have left him so long in Suspence, whether *Beelzebub* or *Satan* was about actually to appear in Person, with all his Hellish Retinue; but as these Doctrines are at present very unfortunate, and have but few if any Believers, I have not been much aware of conveying any such Terrors. To say Truth, the whole Furniture of the infernal Regions hath long been appropriated by the Managers of Playhouses, who seem lately to have lain them by as Rubbish, capable only of affecting the Upper Gallery; a Place in which few of our Readers ever sit.

However, tho' we do not suspect raising any great Terror on this Occasion, we have reason to fear some other Apprehensions may here arise in our Reader, into which we would not willingly betray him; I mean, that we are going to take a Voyage into Fairy Land, and to introduce a Set of Beings into our History, which scarce any one was ever childish enough to believe, though many have been foolish enough to spend their Time in writing and reading their Adventures.

To prevent therefore any such Suspicions, so prejudicial to the Credit of an Historian, who professes to draw his Materials from Nature only, we shall now proceed to acquaint the Reader who these People were, whose sudden Appearance had struck such Terrors into *Partridge*, had more than half frightened the Post-Boy, and had a little surprized even Mr. *Jones* himself.

The People then assembled in this Barn were no other than a Company of *Egyptians*, or as they are vulgarly called *Gypsies*, and they were now celebrating the Wedding of one of their Society.

It is impossible to conceive a happier Set of People than appeared here to be met together. The utmost Mirth indeed shewed itself in every Countenance; nor was their Ball totally void of all Order and Decorum. Perhaps it had more than a Country Assembly is sometimes conducted with: For these People are subject to a

formal Government and Laws of their own, and all pay Obedience
to one great Magistrate, whom they call their King.

Greater Plenty likewise was no where to be seen, than what flourished in this Barn. Here was indeed no Nicety nor Elegance, nor
did the keen Appetite of the Guests require any. Here was good
Store of Bacon, Fowls, and Mutton, to which every one present
provided better Sauce himself, than the best and dearest *French*
Cook can prepare.

Æneas is not described under more Consternation in the Temple of *Juno,*

> *Dum stupet obtutuque hæret defixus in uno,*[1]

than was our Hero at what he saw in this Barn. While he was looking every where round him with Astonishment, a venerable Person
approach'd him with many friendly Salutations, rather of too hearty
a Kind to be called courtly. This was no other than the King of the
Gypsies himself. He was very little distinguished in Dress from his
Subjects, nor had he any *Regalia* of Majesty to support his Dignity;
and yet there seemed (as Mr. *Jones* said)to be somewhat in his Air
which denoted Authority, and inspired the Beholders with an Idea
of Awe and Respect; tho' all this was perhaps imaginary in *Jones*;
and the Truth may be, that such Ideas are incident to Power, and
almost inseparable from it.

There was somewhat in the open Countenance and courteous
Behaviour of *Jones*, which being accompanied with much Comeliness of Person, greatly recommended him at first Sight to every
Beholder. These were perhaps a little heighten'd in the present
Instance, by that profound Respect which he paid to the King of
the *Gypsies*, the Moment he was acquainted with his Dignity, and
which was the sweeter to his *Gypseian* Majesty, as he was not used
to receive such Homage from any but his own Subjects.

The King ordered a Table to be spread with the choicest of their
Provisions for his Accommodation; and having placed himself at his
Right Hand, his Majesty began to discourse our Hero in the follow-
ing Manner:

'Me doubt not, Sir, but you have often seen some of my People,
who are what you call de Parties detache: For dey go about every
where; but me fancy you imagine not we be so considrable Body as
we be; and may be you will surprise more, when you hear de *Gypsy*
be as orderly and well govern People as any upon Face of de Earth.

'Me have Honour, as me say, to be deir King, and no Monarch
can do boast of more dutiful Subject, ne no more affectionate. How

---

1. "While he is astounded, and standing
glued in a single gaze" (*Aeneid* I.495).
While Aeneas is looking at a series of
pictures about the Trojan war, Dido enters.

'Me vil tell you,' said the King, 'how the Difference is between you and us. My People rob your People, and your People rob one anoder.'

Jones afterwards proceeded very gravely to sing forth the Happiness of those Subjects who live under such a Magistrate.

Indeed their Happiness appears to have been so compleat, that we are aware lest some Advocate for arbitrary Power should hereafter quote the Case of those People, as an Instance of the great Advantages which attend that Government above all others.

And here we will make a Concession, which would not perhaps have been expected from us. That no limited Form of Government is capable of rising to the same Degree of Perfection, or of producing the same Benefits to Society with this. Mankind have never been so happy, as when the greatest Part of the then known World was under the Dominion of a single Master; and this State of their Felicity continued during the Reigns of five successive Princes.[2] This was the true Æra of the Golden Age, and the only Golden Age, which ever had any Existence, unless in the warm Imaginations of the Poets, from the Expulsion from *Eden* down to this Day.

In reality, I know but of one solid Objection to absolute Monarchy. The only Defect in which excellent Constitution seems to be the Difficulty of finding any Man adequate to the Office of an absolute Monarch: For this indispensably requires three Qualities very difficult, as it appears from History, to be found in princely Natures: First, a sufficient Quantity of Moderation in the Prince, to be contented with all the Power which is possible for him to have. 2dly, Enough of Wisdom to know his own Happiness. And, 3dly, Goodness sufficient to support the Happiness of others, when not only compatible with, but instrumental to his own.

Now if an absolute Monarch, with all these great and rare Qualifications, should be allowed capable of conferring the greatest Good on Society; it must be surely granted, on the contrary, that absolute Power vested in the Hands of one who is deficient in them all, is likely to be attended with no less a Degree of Evil.

In short, our own Religion furnishes us with adequate Ideas of the Blessing, as well as Curse which may attend absolute Power. The Pictures of Heaven and of Hell will place a very lively Image of both before our Eyes: For though the Prince of the latter can have no Power, but what he originally derives from the omnipotent Sovereign in the former; yet it plainly appears from Scripture, that absolute Power in his infernal Dominions is granted to their Diabolical Ruler. This is indeed the only absolute Power which can by Scripture be derived from Heaven. If therefore the several Tyrannies

2. *Nerva, Trajan, Adrian*, and the two *Antonini* [*Fielding's note*].

upon Earth can prove any Title to a divine Authority, it must be
derived from this original Grant to the Prince of Darkness, and
these subordinate Deputations must consequently come immediately from him whose Stamp they so expresly bear.

To conclude, as the Examples of all Ages shew us that Mankind
in general desire Power only to do Harm, and when they obtain it,
use it for no other Purpose; it is not consonant with even the least
Degree of Prudence to hazard an Alteration, where our Hopes are
poorly kept in Countenance by only two or three Exceptions out of
a thousand Instances to alarm our Fears. In this case it will be
much wiser to submit to a few Inconveniencies arising from the
dispassionate Deafness of Laws, than to remedy them by applying
to the passionate open Ears of a Tyrant.

Nor can the Example of the *Gypsies,* tho' possibly they may have
long been happy under this Form of Government, be here urged;
since we must remember the very material Respect in which they
differ from all other People, and to which perhaps this their Happiness is entirely owing, namely, that they have no false Honours
among them; and that they look on Shame as the most grievous
Punishment in the World.

Chapter XIII.

A *Dialogue between* Jones *and* Partridge.

The honest Lovers of Liberty will, we doubt not, pardon that
long Digression into which we were led at the Close of the last
Chapter, to prevent our History from being applied to the Use of
the most pernicious Doctrine which Priestcraft had ever the Wickedness or the Impudence to preach.

We will now proceed with Mr. *Jones,* who, when the Storm was
over, took Leave of his *Egyptian* Majesty, after many Thanks for
his courteous Behaviour and kind Entertainment, and set out for
Coventry; to which Place (for it was still dark) a *Gypsy* was ordered
to conduct him.

Jones having, by reason of his Deviation, travelled eleven Miles
instead of six, and most of those through very execrable Roads,
where no Expedition could have been made in Quest of a Midwife,
did not arrive at *Coventry* till near Twelve. Nor could he possibly
get again into the Saddle till past Two; for Post-Horses were now
not easy to get; nor were the Hostler or Post-Boy in half so great a
Hurry as himself, but chose rather to imitate the tranquil Disposition of *Partridge;* who being denied the Nourishment of Sleep, took
all Opportunities to supply its Place with every other Kind of Nourishment, and was never better pleased than when he arrived at an

Inn, nor ever more dissatisfied than when he was again forced to leave it.

Jones now travelled Post; we will follow him therefore, according to our Custom, and to the Rules of *Longinus*,[1] in the same Manner. From *Coventry* he arrived at *Daventry*, from *Daventry* at *Stratford*, and from *Stratford* at *Dunstable*, whither he came the next Day a little after Noon, and within a few Hours after *Sophia* had left it; and though he was obliged to stay here longer than he wished, while a Smith, with great Deliberation, shoed the Post-Horse he was to ride, he doubted not but to overtake his *Sophia* before she should set out from *St. Albans*; at which Place he concluded, and very reasonably, that his Lordship would stop and dine.

And had he been right in this Conjecture, he most probably would have overtaken his Angel at the aforesaid Place; but unluckily my Lord had appointed a Dinner to be prepared for him at his own House in *London*, and in order to enable him to reach that Place in proper Time, he had ordered a Relay of Horses to meet him at *St. Albans*. When *Jones* therefore arrived there, he was informed that the Coach and Six had set out two Hours before.

If fresh Post-Horses had been now ready, as they were not, it seemed so apparently impossible to overtake the Coach before it reached *London*, that *Partridge* thought he had now a proper Opportunity to remind his Friend of a Matter which he seemed entirely to have forgotten; what this was the Reader will guess, when we inform him that *Jones* had eat nothing more than one poached Egg since he had left the Alehouse where he had first met the Guide returning from *Sophia*; for with the Gypsies, he had feasted only his Understanding.

The Landlord so entirely agreed with the Opinion of Mr. *Partridge*, that he no sooner heard the latter desire his friend to stay and dine, than he very readily put in his Word, and retracting his Promise before given of furnishing the Horses immediately, he assured Mr. *Jones* he would lose no Time in bespeaking a Dinner, which, he said, could be got ready sooner than it was possible to get the Horses up from Grass, and to prepare them for their Journey by a Feed of Corn.

1. Dionysius Cassius Longinus, a Greek of the third century A.D., presumed author of *On the Sublime* (probably of an earlier date and by some earlier author called Longinus). *On the Sublime* contains no rule very close to Fielding's idea of speeding up the style to catch a speeding subject. Longinus's Chapter X praises omitting unnecessary bombast, and XIX–XXI commend asyndeton, the omitting of connectives to gain emotive speed and power. But Fielding may have in mind Longinus's praise of a description of Phaeton's precipitous ride, where "the author mounts the chariot along with the charioteer, runs the peril with him, and has been furnished with wings like the horses" (trans. Thomas R. R. Stebbing, London, 1867, ch. XV, pp. 59–60). Fielding's own dramatic burlesque, *Tumble-Down Dick, or, Phaeton in the Suds* (1736), indicates an interest in *Phaeton* that may have called his attention to this passage—and, of course, Jones is now "travelling post," with fresh horses at every stage.

Jones was at length prevailed on, chiefly by the latter Argument of the Landlord; and now a Joint of Mutton was put down to the Fire. While this was preparing, *Partridge* being admitted into the same Apartment with his Friend or Master, began to harangue in the following Manner.

'Certainly, Sir, if ever Man deserved a young Lady, you deserve young Madam *Western*; for what a vast Quantity of Love must a Man have, to be able to live upon it without any other Food, as you do? I am positive I have eat thirty times as much within these last twenty four Hours as your Honour, and yet I am almost famished; for nothing makes a Man so hungry as travelling, especially in this cold raw Weather. And yet I can't tell how it is, but your Honour is seemingly in perfect good Health, and you never looked better nor fresher in your Life. It must be certainly Love that you live upon.'

'And a very rich Diet too, *Partridge*,' answered *Jones*. 'But did not Fortune send me an excellent Dainty Yesterday? Dost thou imagine I cannot live more than twenty-four Hours on this dear Pocket-Book?'

'Undoubtedly,' cries *Partridge*, 'there is enough in that Pocket-Book to purchase many a good Meal. Fortune sent it to your Honour very opportunely for present Use, as your Honour's Money must be almost out by this Time.'

'What do you mean?' answered *Jones*; 'I hope you don't imagine that I should be dishonest enough, even if it belonged to any other Person, besides Miss *Western*——

'Dishonest!' replied *Partridge*, 'Heaven forbid I should wrong your Honour so much; but where's the Dishonesty in borrowing a little for present spending, since you will be so well able to pay the Lady hereafter? No, indeed, I would have your Honour pay it again, as soon as it is convenient, by all Means; but where can be the Harm in making Use of it now you want it. Indeed if it belonged to a poor Body, it would be another thing; but so great a Lady to be sure can never want it, especially now as she is along with a Lord, who it can't be doubted will let her have whatever she hath Need of. Besides, if she should want a little, she can't want the whole, therefore I would give her a little; but I would be hanged before I mentioned the having found it at first, and before I got some Money of my own; for *London*, I have heard, is the very worst of Places to be in without Money. Indeed, if I had not known to whom it belonged, I might have thought it was the Devil's Money, and have been afraid to use it; but as you know otherwise, and came honestly by it, it would be an Affront to Fortune to part with it all again, at the very Time when you want it most; you can hardly expect she should ever do you such another good Turn; for

Fortuna nunquam perpetuo est bona.[2] You will do as you please, nothwithstanding all I say; but for my Part, I would be hanged before I mentioned a Word of the Matter.'

'By what I can see, *Partridge*,' cries *Jones*, 'hanging is a Matter *non longe alienum à Scævolæ studiis.*[3] 'You should say *alienus*,' says *Partridge*—'I remember the Passage; it is an Example under *Communis, Alienus, immunis, variis casibus serviunt.*' 'If you do remember it,' cries *Jones*, 'I find you don't understand it; but I tell thee, Friend, in plain *English*, that he who finds another's Property, and wilfully detains it from the known Owner, deserves *in Foro Conscientiæ,*[4] to be hanged no less than if he had stolen it. And as for this very identical Bill which is the Property of my Angel, and was once in her dear Possession, I will not deliver it into any Hands but her own, upon any Consideration whatever; no, tho' I was as hungry as thou art, and had no other Means to satisfy my craving Appetite; this I hope to do before I sleep; but if it should happen otherwise, I charge thee, if thou wouldst not incur my Displeasure for ever, not to shock me any more by the bare Mention of such detestable Baseness.'

'I should not have mentioned it now,' cries *Partridge*, 'if it had appeared so to me; for I'm sure I scorn any Wickedness as much as another; but perhaps you know better; and yet I might have imagined that I should not have lived so many Years, and have taught school so long, without being able to distinguish between *Fas & Nefas;*[5] but it seems we are all to live and learn. I remember my old Schoolmaster, who was a prodigious great Scholar, used often to say, *Polly Matete cry Town is my Daskalon.*[6] The *English* of which, he told us, was, That a Child may sometimes teach his Grandmother

2. "Fortune is never perpetually good." Lily, p. 136, an example of the first "concord," on the first page of the "Syntaxis." See above, pp. 62 and 411. Mutter identifies Terence, *Hecyra* III.iii.46, "slightly altered."

3. "Not far different from the studies of Scaevola." Quintus Musius Scaevola founded Roman legal studies; Cicero, the source of this quotation (*Ad Atticum* IV.xvi.3—Mutter), studied under Scaevola's uncle. But Partridge is right. The line appears as an illustration under "*Communis, alienus, immunis, variis casibus serviunt*" ("*Communis, alienus,* and *immunis* are governed by various cases") in Lily, p. 143, the same passage containing Partridge's *mors omnibus communis* and *non immunes* (above, p. 481). Fielding himself, beginning with the first edition, erroneously capitalizes *Alienus* in Partridge's quotation following, apparently taking it as the noun ("another's property, a stranger") rather than the

adjective under discussion ("another's").

4. "In the forum of conscience."

5. "Lawful and unlawful."

6. Partridge's garble of Πολλοὶ μαθηταὶ κρεῖττονες διδασκάλων ("Polloi mathetai kreittones didaskalon"). "Many pupils are better than their teachers"—a saying, source unknown, quoted by Cicero (Mutter). It appears in an unimportant letter to Varro (*Epistolae ad Familiares* IX.7). Cicero is referring humorously to his former pupil Dolabella, who, returning to Italy ahead of Caesar from the defeat of Pompey, will know better than Cicero by which road Caesar will be coming: "I suppose he will act as my schoolmaster," writes Cicero, then quotes the Greek line. In *Amelia* VIII.v, Fielding refers to "the common Greek proverb—that the scholar is often superior to the master." Professor Ralph Loomis has called my attention both to Mutter's note and to *Amelia*.

to suck Eggs. I have lived to a fine Purpose truly, if I am to be taught my Grammar at this Time of Day. Perhaps, young Gentleman, you may change your Opinion, if you live to my Years: For I remember I thought myself as wise when I was a Stripling of one or two and twenty as I am now. I am sure I always taught *alienus,* and my Master read it so before me.'

There were not many Instances in which *Partridge* could provoke *Jones,* nor were there many in which *Partridge* himself could have been hurried out of his Respect. Unluckily however they had both hit on one of these. We have already seen *Partridge* could not bear to have his Learning attacked, nor could *Jones* bear some Passage or other in the foregoing Speech. And now looking upon his Companion with a contemptuous and disdainful Air (a thing not usual with him) he cried, '*Partridge,* I see thou art a conceited old Fool, and I wish thou art not likewise an old Rogue. Indeed if I was as well convinced of the latter as I am of the former, thou shouldst travel no farther in my Company.'

The sage Pedagogue was contented with the Vent which he had already given to his Indignation; and, as the vulgar Phrase is, immediately drew in his Horns. He said, he was sorry he had uttered any thing which might give Offence, for that he had never intended it; but *Nemo omnibus horis sapit.*[7]

As *Jones* had the Vices of a warm Disposition, he was entirely free from those of a cold one; and if his Friends must have confest his Temper to have been a little too easily ruffled, his Enemies must at the same time have confest, that it as soon subsided; nor did it at all resemble the Sea, whose Swelling is more violent and dangerous after a Storm is over, than while the Storm itself subsists. He instantly accepted the Submission of *Partridge,* shook him by the Hand, and with the most benign Aspect imaginable, said twenty kind Things, and at the same Time very severely condemned himself, tho' not half so severely as he will most probably be condemned by many of our good Readers.

Partridge was now highly comforted, as his Fears of having offended were at once abolished, and his Pride completely satisfied by *Jones* having owned himself in the Wrong, which Submission he instantly applied to what had principally nettled him, and repeated, in a muttering Voice, 'To be sure, Sir, your Knowledge may be superior to mine in some Things; but as to the Grammar, I think I may challenge any Man living. I think, at least, I have that at my Finger's End.'

If any thing could add to the Satisfaction which the poor Man

7. "No man is wise at all hours." Lily, p. 158, a slightly abbreviated version of Pliny the Younger, *Historiae Naturalis*

VII.xli.2. See above, p. 97, and below, p. 659.

now enjoyed, he received this Addition by the Arrival of an excellent Shoulder of Mutton, that at this Instant came smoaking to the Table. On which, having both plentifully feasted, they again mounted their Horses, and set forward for *London*.

Chapter XIV.

What happened to Mr. Jones *in his Journey from St.* Albans.

They were got about two Miles beyond *Barnet*, and it was now the Dusk of the Evening, when a genteel looking Man, but upon a very shabby Horse, rode up to *Jones*, and asked him whether he was going to *London*, to which *Jones* answered in the Affirmative. The Gentleman replied, 'I should be obliged to you, Sir, if you will accept of my Company; for it is very late, and I am a Stranger to the Road.' *Jones* readily complied with the Request; and on they travelled together, holding that Sort of Discourse which is usual on such Occasions.

Of this, indeed, Robbery was the principal Topic; upon which Subject the Stranger expressed great Apprehensions; but *Jones* declared he had very little to lose, and consequently as little to fear. Here *Partridge* could not forbear putting in his Word. 'Your Honour,' said he, 'may think it a little, but I am sure, if I had a hundred Pound Bank Note in my Pocket, as you have, I should be very sorry to lose it; but, for my Part, I never was less afraid in my Life; for we are four of us, and if we all stand by one another, the best Man in *England* can't rob us. Suppose he should have a Pistol, he can kill but one of us, and a Man can die but once—That's my Comfort, a Man can die but once.'

Besides the Reliance on superior Numbers, a kind of Valour which hath raised a certain Nation among the Moderns to a high Pitch of Glory, there was another Reason for the extraordinary Courage which *Partridge* now discovered; for he had at present as much of that Quality as was in the Power of Liquor to bestow.

Our Company were now arrived within a Mile of *Highgate*, when the Stranger turned short upon *Jones*, and pulling out a Pistol, demanded that little Bank Note which *Partridge* had mentioned.

Jones was at first somewhat shocked at this unexpected Demand; however, he presently recollected himself, and told the Highwayman, all the Money he had in his Pocket was entirely at his Service; and so saying, he pulled out upwards of three Guineas, and offered to deliver it; but the other answered with an Oath, That would not do. *Jones* answered coolly, He was very sorry for it, and returned the Money into his Pocket.

The Highwayman then threatned, if he did not deliver the Bank

Note that Moment, he must shoot him; holding his Pistol at the same Time very near to his Breast. *Jones* instantly caught hold of the Fellow's Hand, which trembled so that he could scarce hold the Pistol in it, and turned the Muzzle from him. A Struggle then ensued, in which the former wrested the Pistol from the Hand of his Antagonist, and both came from their Horses on the Ground together, the Highwayman upon his Back, and the victorious *Jones* upon him.

The poor Fellow now began to implore Mercy of the Conqueror; for, to say the Truth, he was in Strength by no Means a Match for *Jones.* 'Indeed, Sir,' says he, 'I could have had no Intention to shoot you; for you will find the Pistol was not loaded. This is the first Robbery I ever attempted, and I have been driven by Distress to this.'

At this Instant, at about an hundred and fifty Yards Distance, lay another Person on the Ground, roaring for Mercy in a much louder Voice than the Highwayman. This was no other than *Partridge* himself, who endeavouring to make his Escape from the Engagement, had been thrown from his Horse, and lay flat on his Face, not daring to look up, and expecting every Minute to be shot.

In this Posture he lay, till the Guide, who was no otherwise concerned than for his Horses, having secured the stumbling Beast, came up to him and told him, his Master had got the better of the Highwayman.

Partridge leapt up at his News, and ran back to the Place, where *Jones* stood with his Sword drawn in his Hand to guard the poor Fellow; which *Partridge* no sooner saw, than he cried out, 'Kill the Villain, Sir, run him through the Body, kill him this Instant.'

Luckily however for the poor Wretch he had fallen into more merciful Hands; for *Jones* having examined the Pistol, and found it to be really unloaded, began to believe all the Man had told him before *Partridge* came up; namely, that he was a Novice in the Trade, and that he had been driven to it by the Distress he mentioned, the greatest indeed imaginable, that of five hungry Children, and a Wife lying in of a sixth, in the utmost Want and Misery. The Truth of all which the Highwayman most vehemently asserted, and offered to convince Mr. *Jones* of it, if he would take the Trouble to go to his House, which was not above two Miles off; saying, 'That he desired no Favour, but upon Condition of proving all he had alledged.'

Jones at first pretended that he would take the Fellow at his Word, and go with him, declaring that his Fate should depend entirely on the Truth of his Story. Upon this the poor Fellow immediately expressed so much Alacrity, that *Jones* was perfectly

satisfied with his Veracity, and began now to entertain Sentiments
of Compassion for him. He returned the Fellow his empty Pistol,
advised him to think of honester Means of relieving his Distress,
and gave him a couple of Guineas for the immediate Support of his
Wife and his Family; adding, 'he wished he had more for his Sake,
for the hundred Pound that had been mentioned, was not his own.'

Our Readers will probably be divided in their Opinions concerning this Action; some may applaud it perhaps as an Act of extraordinary Humanity, while those of a more saturnine Temper will consider it as a Want of Regard to that Justice which every Man owes
his Country. *Partridge* certainly saw it in that Light; for he testified
much Dissatisfaction on the Occasion, quoted an old Proverb, and
said, He should not wonder if the Rogue attacked them again
before they reached *London*.

The Highwayman was full of Expressions of Thankfulness and
Gratitude. He actually dropt Tears, or pretended so to do. He
vowed he would immediately return home, and would never afterwards commit such a Transgression; whether he kept his Word or
no, perhaps may appear hereafter.

Our Travellers having remounted their Horses, arrived in Town
without encountering any new Mishap. On the Road much pleasant Discourse passed between *Jones* and *Partridge*, on the Subject
of their last Adventure. In which *Jones* exprest a great Compassion
for those Highwaymen who are, by unavoidable Distress, driven as
it were, to such illegal Courses, as generally bring them to a shameful Death. 'I mean,' said he, 'those only whose highest Guilt
extends no farther than to Robbery, and who are never guilty of
Cruelty nor Insult to any Person, which is a Circumstance that, I
must say, to the Honour of our Country, distinguishes the Robbers
of *England* from those of all other Nations; for Murder is, amongst
those, almost inseparably incident to Robbery.'

'No doubt,' answered *Partridge*, 'it is better to take away one's
Money than one's Life; and yet it is very hard upon honest Men,
that they can't travel about their Business without being in Danger
of these Villains. And to be sure it would be better that all Rogues
were hanged out of the Way, than that one honest Man should
suffer. For my own Part, indeed, I should not care to have the
Blood of any of them on my own Hands; but it is very proper for
the Law to hang them all. What Right hath any Man to take Sixpence from me, unless I give it him? Is there any Honesty in such a
Man?'

'No surely,' cries *Jones*, 'no more than there is in him who takes
the Horses out of another Man's Stable, or who applies to his own
Use the Money which he finds, when he knows the right Owner.'

These Hints stopt the Mouth of *Partridge*, nor did he open it again till *Jones* having thrown some sarcastical Jokes on his Cowardice, he offered to excuse himself on the Inequality of Fire-Arms, saying, 'A thousand naked Men are nothing to one Pistol; for though, it is true, it will kill but one at a single Discharge, yet who can tell but that one may be himself.'

BOOK XIII.

Containing the Space of Twelve Days.

Chapter I.

An Invocation.

Come, bright Love of Fame, inspire my glowing Breast: Not thee I call, who over swelling Tides of Blood and Tears, dost bear the Heroe on to Glory, while Sighs of Millions waft his spreading Sails; but thee, fair, gentle Maid, whom *Mnesis*,[1] happy Nymph, first on the Banks of *Hebrus*, did produce. Thee, whom *Mæonia* educated, whom *Mantua* charm'd, and who, on that fair Hill which overlooks the proud Metropolis of *Britain*, sat'st, with thy *Milton*, sweetly tuning the Heroic Lyre; fill my ravished Fancy with the Hopes of charming Ages yet to come. Foretel me that some tender Maid, whose Grandmother is yet unborn, hereafter, when, under the fictitious Name of *Sophia*, she reads the real Worth which once existed in my *Charlotte*, shall from her sympathetic Breast, send forth the heaving Sigh. Do thou teach me not only to foresee, but to enjoy, nay, even to feed on future Praise. Comfort me by a solemn Assurance, that when the little Parlour in which I sit at this Instant, shall be reduced to a worse furnished Box, I shall be read, with Honour, by those who never knew nor saw me, and whom I shall neither know nor see.

And thou, much plumper Dame,[2] whom no airy Forms nor

1. Fielding is inventing a Muse, whom he calls "Love of Fame," from traditional classic lore. All the muses were daughters of Mnemosyne (Memory), so Fielding makes up his own name, Mnesis ("memory," in Greek) for Love of Fame's mother. Hebrus is the river on whose shores Orpheus sang and into whose waters the Bacchantes threw his head and harp, after he had rejected all women and had sung of divine pederasty and the unnatural lusts of maidens

(Ovid, *Metamorphoses* X.152 ff. and XI). Orpheus, the son of Caliope, the muse of heroic-epic poetry, obviously found fame. Maeonia is Homer's (supposed) home; Mantua, Virgil's. Milton points out that even Caliope, the muse herself, couldn't save Orpheus, then writes: "Fame is the spur that the clear spirit doth raise / (That last infirmity of Noble mind)"—*Lycidas* 58–71.
2. Evidently Fortune.

Phantoms of Imagination cloathe: Whom the well-seasoned Beef, and Pudding richly stained with Plumbs delight. Thee, I call; of whom in a *Treckschuyte*[3] in some *Dutch* Canal the fat Ufrow Gelt,[4] impregnated by a jolly Merchant of *Amsterdam*, was delivered: In *Grubstreet* School didst thou suck in the Elements of thy Erudition. Here hast thou, in thy maturer Age, taught Poetry to tickle not the Fancy, but the Pride of the Patron. Comedy from thee learns a grave and solemn Air; while Tragedy storms loud, and rends th' affrighted Theatres with its Thunder. To sooth thy wearied Limbs in Slumber, Alderman History tells his tedious Tale; and again to awaken thee, Monsieur Romance performs his surprizing Tricks of Dexterity. Nor less thy well-fed Bookseller obeys thy Influence. By thy Advice the heavy, unread, Folio Lump, which long had dozed on the dusty Shelf, piece-mealed into Numbers, runs nimbly through the Nation. Instructed by thee some Books, like Quacks, impose on the World by promising Wonders; while others turn Beaus, and trust all their Merits to a gilded Outside. Come, thou jolly Substance, with thy shining Face, keep back thy Inspiration, but hold forth thy tempting Rewards; thy shining, chinking Heap; thy quickly-convertible Bank-Bill, big with unseen Riches; thy often-varying Stock; the warm, the comfortable House; and, lastly, a fair Portion of that bounteous Mother, whose flowing Breasts yield redundant Sustenance for all her numerous Offspring, did not some too greedily and wantonly drive their Brethren from the Teat. Come thou, and if I am too tasteless of thy valuable Treasures, warm my Heart with the transporting Thought of conveying them to others. Tell me, that through thy Bounty, the prattling Babes, whose innocent Play hath often been interrupted by my Labours, may one Time be amply rewarded for them.

And now this ill-yoked Pair, this lean Shadow and this fat Substance, have prompted me to write, whose Assistance shall I invoke to direct my Pen?

First, Genius; thou Gift of Heaven; without whose Aid, in vain we struggle against the Stream of Nature. Thou, who dost sow the generous Seeds which Art nourishes, and brings to Perfection. Do thou kindly take me by the Hand, and lead me through all the Mazes, the winding Labyrinths of Nature. Initiate me into all those Mysteries which profane Eyes never beheld. Teach me, which to thee is no difficult Task, to know Mankind better than they know themselves. Remove that Mist which dims the Intellects of Mortals, and causes them to adore Men for their Art, or to detest them for their Cunning in deceiving others, when they are, in Reality, the Objects only of Ridicule, for deceiving themselves. Strip off the thin

3. Barge.   4. Mrs. Gold.

Disguise of Wisdom from Self-Conceit, of Plenty from Avarice, and of Glory from Ambition. Come thou, that hast inspired thy *Aristophanes*, thy *Lucian*, thy *Cervantes*, thy *Rabelais*, thy *Moliere*, thy *Shakespear*, thy *Swift*, thy *Marivaux*, fill my Pages with Humour; 'till Mankind learn the Good-Nature to laugh only at the Follies of others, and the Humility to grieve at their own.

And thou, almost the constant Attendant on true Genius, Humanity, bring all thy tender Sensations. If thou hast already disposed of them all between thy *Allen* and thy *Lyttleton*,[5] steal them a little while from their Bosoms. Not without these the tender Scene is painted. From these alone proceed the noble disinterested Friendship, the melting Love, the generous Sentiment, the ardent Gratitude, the soft Compassion, the candid Opinion; and all those strong Energies of a good Mind, which fill the moistened Eyes with Tears, the glowing Cheeks with Blood, and swell the Heart with Tides of Grief, Joy and Benevolence.

And thou, O Learning, (for without thy Assistance nothing pure, nothing correct, can Genius produce) do thou guide my Pen. Thee, in thy Favourite Fields, where the limpid, gently-rolling *Thames* washes thy *Etonian* Banks, in early Youth I have worshipped. To thee, at thy birchen Altar, with true *Spartan* Devotion, I have sacrificed my Blood. Come, then, and from thy vast, luxuriant Stores, in long Antiquity piled up, pour forth the rich Profusion. Open thy *Mæonian* and thy *Mantuan* Coffers, with whatever else includes thy Philosophic, thy Poetic, and thy Historical Treasures, whether with *Greek* or *Roman* Characters thou hast chosen to inscribe the ponderous Chests: Give me a-while that Key to all thy Treasures, which to thy *Warburton*[6] thou hast entrusted.

Lastly, come, Experience, long conversant with the Wise, the Good, the Learned, and the Polite. Nor with them only, but with every Kind of Character, from the Minister at his Levee, to the Bailiff in his Spunging-House; from the Dutchess at her Drum, to the Landlady behind her Bar. From thee only can the Manners of Mankind be known; to which the recluse Pedant, however great his Parts, or extensive his Learning may be, hath ever been a Stranger.

Come all these, and more, if possible; for arduous is the Task I have undertaken: And without all your Assistance, will, I find, be too heavy for me to support. But if you all smile on my Labours, I hope still to bring them to a happy Conclusion.

5. See above, notes 1 and 2, p. 5.
6. William Warburton (1698–1779), a vigorous theological controversialist, editor of Shakespeare (1747) and, later, of Pope. Fielding refers to him playfully in his notes to *Tom Thumb* (1731) but compliments him in *A Journey from This World to the Next* (1743). Warburton's friendship with Ralph Allen probably led to Fielding's acquaintance with him (Cross, I, 376–77).

Chapter II.

What befel Mr. Jones on his Arrival in London.

The learned Dr. *Misaubin*[1] used to say, that the proper Direction to him was, *To Dr.* Misaubin, *in the World*; intimating, that there were few People in it to whom his great Reputation was not known. And, perhaps, upon a very nice Examination into the Matter, we shall find that this Circumstance bears no inconsiderable Part among the many Blessings of Grandeur.

The great Happiness of being known to Posterity, with the Hopes of which we so delighted ourselves in the preceding Chapter, is the Portion of few. To have the several Elements which compose our Names, as *Sydenham*[2] expresses it, repeated a thousand Years hence, is a Gift beyond the Power of Title and Wealth: and is scarce to be purchased, unless by the Sword and the Pen. But to avoid the scandalous Imputation, while we yet live, of being *one whom Nobody knows*, (a Scandal, by the By, as old as the Days of *Homer*[3]) will always be the envied Portion of those, who have a legal Title either to Honour or Estate.

From that Figure, therefore, which the *Irish* Peer, who brought *Sophia* to Town, hath already made in this History, the Reader will conclude, doubtless, it must have been an easy Matter to have discovered his House in *London*, without knowing the particular Street or Square which he inhabited, since he must have been one *whom every body knows*. To say the Truth, so it would have been to any of those Tradesmen who are accustomed to attend the Regions of the Great: For the Doors of the Great are generally no less easy to find, than it is difficult to get Entrance into them. But *Jones*, as well as *Partridge*, was an entire Stranger in *London*; and as he happened to arrive first in a Quarter of the Town, the Inhabitants of which have very little Intercourse with the Housholders of *Hanover* or *Grosvenor* Square, (for he entered through *Gray's-Inn Lane*) so he rambled about some Time, before he could even find his Way to those happy Mansions, where Fortune segregates from the Vulgar, those magnanimous Heroes, the Descendants of ancient *Britons*, *Saxons*, or *Danes*, whose Ancestors being born in better

1. See above, p. 182.
2. Thomas Sydenham, *Tractatus de Podagra et Hydrope* ("A Treatise on Gout and Dropsy," 1683). Fielding suffered from both diseases. In his foreword, Sydenham asks what it will avail him to have the eight letters composing *Sydenham* pass from mouth to mouth among men who can have no more idea of what he was than he of them. Fielding translates the same passage in *The Champion*, 3 May 1740.
3. A prophet had predicted that Odysseus would return to Ithaça after twenty years, alone and unknown to all. Fielding annotates this: "See the 2d Odyssey ver. 175."

Days, by sundry Kinds of Merit, have entailed Riches and Honour on their Posterity.

Jones being at length arrived at those terrestrial *Elysian* Fields, would now soon have discovered his Lordship's Mansion; but the Peer unluckily quitted his former House when he went for *Ireland*; and as he was just entered into a new one, the Fame of his Equipage had not yet sufficiently blazed in the Neighbourhood: So that after a successless Enquiry 'till the Clock had struck Eleven, *Jones*, at least, yielded to the Advice of *Partridge*, and retreated to the *Bull* and *Gate* in *Holborn*, that being the Inn where he had first alighted, and where he retired to enjoy that kind of Repose, which usually attends Persons in his Circumstances.

Early in the Morning he again set forth in Pursuit of *Sophia*; and many a weary Step he took to no better Purpose than before. At last, whether it was that Fortune relented, or whether it was no longer in her Power to disappoint him, he came into the very Street which was honoured by his Lordship's Residence; and being directed to the House, he gave one gentle Rap at the Door.

The Porter, who, from the Modesty of the Knock, had conceived no high Idea of the Person approaching, conceived but little better from the Appearance of Mr. *Jones*, who was drest in a Suit of Fustian, and had by his Side the Weapon formerly purchased of the Serjeant; of which, tho' the Blade might be composed of well-tempered Steel, the Handle was composed only of Brass, and that none of the brightest. When *Jones*, therefore, enquired after the young Lady, who had come to Town with his Lordship, this Fellow answered surlily, 'That there were no Ladies there.' *Jones* then desired to see the Master of the House; but was informed that his Lordship would see no-body that Morning. And upon growing more pressing, the Porter said, 'He had positive Orders to let no Person in; but if you think proper,' said he, 'to leave your Name, I will acquaint his Lordship; and if you call another Time, you shall know when he will see you.'

Jones now declared, 'that he had very particular Business with the young Lady, and could not depart without seeing her.' Upon which the Porter, with no very agreeable Voice or Aspect, affirmed, 'That there was no young Lady in that House, and consequently none could he see;' adding, 'Sure you are the strangest Man I ever met with; for you will not take an Answer.'

I have often thought, that by the particular Description of *Cerberus* the Porter of Hell, in the 6th *Æneid*, *Virgil* might possibly intend to satirize the Porters of the Great Men in his Time; the Picture, at least, resembles those who have the Honour to attend at the Doors of our Great Men. The Porter in his Lodge, answers exactly to *Cerberus* in his Den, and, like him, must be appeased by a Sop, before Access can be gained to his Master. Perhaps *Jones* might have seen him in that Light, and have recollected the Passage, where the Sibyl, in order to procure an Entrance for *Æneas*, presents the Keeper of the *Stygian* Avenue with such a Sop. *Jones*, in like Manner, now began to offer a Bribe to the human *Cerberus*, which a Footman overhearing, instantly advanced, and declared 'if Mr. *Jones* would give him the Sum proposed, he would conduct him to the Lady.' *Jones* instantly agreed, and was forthwith conducted to the Lodging of Mrs. *Fitzpatrick*, by the very Fellow who had attended the Ladies thither the Day before.

Nothing more aggravates ill Success than the near Approach to Good. The Gamester, who loses his Party at Piquet by a single Point, laments his bad Luck ten Times as much as he who never came within a Prospect of the Game. So in a Lottery, the Proprietors of the next Numbers to that which wins the great Prize, are apt to account themselves much more unfortunate than their Fellow-Sufferers. In short, these kind of hair-breadth Missings of Happiness, look like the Insults of Fortune, who may be considered as thus playing Tricks with us, and wantonly diverting herself at our Expence.

Jones, who more than once already had experienced this frolicksome Disposition of the Heathen Goddess, was now again doomed to be tantalized in the like Manner: For he arrived at the Door of Mrs. *Fitzpatrick*, about ten Minutes after the Departure of *Sophia*. He now addressed himself to the Waiting-woman belonging to Mrs. *Fitzpatrick*; who told him the disagreeable News, that the Lady was gone, but could not tell him whither; and the same Answer he afterwards received from Mrs. *Fitzpatrick* herself. For as that Lady made no doubt but that Mr. *Jones* was a Person detached from her Uncle *Western*, in Pursuit of his Daughter, so she was too generous to betray her.

Though *Jones* had never seen Mrs. *Fitzpatrick*, yet he had heard that a Cousin of *Sophia* was married to a Gentleman of that Name. This, however, in the present Tumult of his Mind, never once recurred to his Memory: But when the Footman, who had conducted him from his Lordship's, acquainted him with the great Intimacy between the Ladies, and with their calling each other Cousin, he then recollected the Story of the Marriage which he had formerly heard; and as he was presently convinced that this was the same Woman, he became more surprized at the Answer which he had received, and very earnestly desired Leave to wait on the Lady herself; but she as positively refused him that Honour.

Jones, who, though he had never seen a Court, was better bred than most who frequent it, was incapable of any rude or abrupt Behaviour to a Lady. When he had received, therefore, a peremptory Denial, he retired for the present, saying to the Waiting woman, 'That if this was an improper Hour to wait on her Lady, he would return in the Afternoon; and that he then hoped to have the Honour of seeing her.' The Civility with which he uttered this, added to the great Comeliness of his Person, made an Impression on the Waiting-woman, and she could not help answering; 'Perhaps, Sir, you may:' And, indeed, she afterwards said every Thing to her Mistress, which she thought most likely to prevail on her to admit a Visit from the handsome young Gentleman; for so she called him.

Jones very shrewdly suspected, that *Sophia* herself was now with her Cousin, and was denied to him; which he imputed to her Resentment of what had happened at *Upton*. Having, therefore, dispatched *Partridge* to procure him Lodgings, he remained all Day in the Street; watching the Door where he thought his Angel lay concealed; but no Person did he see issue forth, except a Servant of the House, and in the Evening he returned to pay his Visit to Mrs. *Fitzpatrick*, which that good Lady at last condescended to admit.

There is a certain Air of natural Gentility, which it is neither in the Power of Dress to give, nor to conceal. Mr. *Jones*, as hath been before hinted, was possessed of this in a very eminent Degree. He met, therefore, with a Reception from the Lady, somewhat different from what his Apparel seemed to demand; and after he had paid her his proper Respects, was desired to sit down.

The Reader will not, I believe, be desirous of knowing all the Particulars of this Conversation, which ended very little to the Satisfaction of poor *Jones*. For though Mrs. *Fitzpatrick* soon discovered the Lover, (as all Women have the Eyes of Hawks in those Matters) yet she still thought it was such a Lover, as a generous Friend of the Lady should not betray her to. In short, she suspected this was the very Mr. *Blifil*, from whom *Sophia* had flown; and all the Answers which she artfully drew from *Jones*, concerning Mr. *All-worthy*'s Family, confirmed her in this Opinion. She therefore strictly denied any Knowledge concerning the Place whither *Sophia* was gone; nor could *Jones* obtain more than a Permission to wait on her again the next Evening.

When *Jones* was departed, Mrs. *Fitzpatrick* communicated her Suspicion concerning Mr. *Blifil*, to her Maid; who answered, 'Sure, Madam, he is too pretty a Man, in my Opinion, for any Woman in the World to run away from. I had rather fancy it is Mr. *Jones*.'— 'Mr. *Jones*,' said the Lady, 'what *Jones*?' For *Sophia* had not given the least Hint of any such Person in all their Conversation: But Mrs. *Honour* had been much more communicative, and had acquainted her Sister *Abigail* with the whole History of *Jones*, which this now again related to her Mistress.

Mrs. *Fitzpatrick* no sooner received this Information, than she immediately agreed with the Opinion of her Maid; and, what is very unaccountable, saw Charms in the gallant, happy Lover, which she had over-looked in the slighted Squire. 'Betty,' says she, 'you are certainly in the right: He is a very pretty Fellow, and I don't wonder that my Cousin's Maid should tell you so many Women are fond of him. I am sorry now I did not inform him where my Cousin was: And yet if he be so terrible a Rake as you tell me, it is a Pity she should ever see him any more; for what but her Ruin can happen from marrying a Rake and a Beggar against her Father's Consent. I protest, if he be such a Man as the Wench described him to you, it is but an Office of Charity to keep her from him; and, I am sure, it would be unpardonable in me to do otherwise, who have tasted so bitterly of the Misfortunes attending such Marriages.'

Here she was interrupted by the Arrival of a Visitor, which was no other than his Lordship; and as nothing passed at this Visit either new or extraordinary, or any ways material to this History, we shall here put an End to this Chapter.

Chapter III.

A Project of Mrs. Fitzpatrick, and her Visit to Lady Bellaston.

When Mrs. *Fitzpatrick* retired to Rest, her Thoughts were entirely taken up by her Cousin *Sophia* and Mr. *Jones*. She was, indeed, a little offended with the former, for the Disingenuity which she now discovered. In which Meditation she had not long exercised her Imagination, before the following Conceit suggested itself: That could she possibly become the Means of preserving *Sophia* from this Man, and of restoring her to her Father, she should, in all human Probability, by so great a Service to the Family, reconcile to herself both her Uncle and her Aunt *Western*.

As this was one of her most favourite Wishes, so the Hope of Success seemed so reasonable, that nothing remained but to consider of proper Methods to accomplish her Scheme. To attempt to reason the Case with *Sophia*, did not appear to her one of those Methods: For as *Betty* had reported from Mrs. *Honour*, that *Sophia* had a violent Inclination to *Jones*, she conceived, that to dissuade her from the Match, was an Endeavour of the same Kind as it would be, very heartily and earnestly to entreat a Moth not to fly into a Candle.

If the Reader will please to remember, that the Acquaintance which *Sophia* had with Lady *Bellaston*, was contracted at the House of Mrs. *Western*, and must have grown at the very Time

when Mrs. *Fitzpatrick* lived with this latter Lady, he will want no
Information, that Mrs. *Fitzpatrick* must have been acquainted with
her likewise. They were, besides, both equally her distant Relations.

After much Consideration, therefore, she resolved to go early in
the Morning to that Lady, and endeavour to see her, unknown to
Sophia, and to acquaint her with the whole Affair. For she did not
in the least doubt, but that the prudent Lady, who had often ridiculed romantic Love, and indiscreet Marriages, in her Conversation,
would very readily concur in her Sentiments concerning this Match,
and would lend her utmost Assistance to prevent it.

This Resolution she accordingly executed; and the next Morning
before the Sun, she huddled on her Cloaths, and at a very unfash-
ionable, unseasonable, unvisitable Hour went to Lady *Bellaston*, to
whom she got Access, without the least Knowledge or Suspicion of
Sophia, who though not asleep, lay at that Time awake in her Bed,
with *Honour* snoring by her Side.

Mrs. *Fitzpatrick* made many Apologies for an early, abrupt Visit,
at an Hour when she said 'she should not have thought of disturbing her Ladyship, but upon Business of the utmost Consequence.'
She then opened the whole Affair, told all she had heard from
Betty; and did not forget the Visit which *Jones* had paid to herself
the preceding Evening.

Lady *Bellaston* answered with a Smile, 'Then you have seen this
terrible Man, Madam; pray is he so very fine a Figure as he is represented? For *Etoff* entertained me last Night almost two Hours with
him. The Wench I believe is in Love with him by Reputation.'
Here the Reader will be apt to wonder; but the Truth is that Mrs.
Etoff, who had the Honour to pin and unpin the Lady *Bellaston*,
had received complete Information concerning the said Mr. *Jones*,
and had faithfully conveyed the same to her Lady last Night (or
rather that Morning) while she was undressing; on which Accounts
she had been detained in her Office above the Space of an Hour
and half.

The Lady indeed, tho' generally well enough pleased with the
Narratives of Mrs. *Etoff* at those Seasons, gave an extraordinary
Attention to her Account of *Jones*; for *Honour* had described him
as a very handsome Fellow, and Mrs. *Etoff* in her Hurry added so
much to the Beauty of his Person to her Report, that Lady *Bellaston* began to conceive him to be a kind of Miracle in Nature.

The Curiosity which her Woman had inspired, was now greatly
increased by Mrs. *Fitzpatrick*, who spoke as much in Favour of the
Person of *Jones*, as she had before spoken in Dispraise of his Birth,
Character and Fortune.

When Lady *Bellaston* had heard the whole, she answered gravely,
'Indeed, Madam, this is a matter of great Consequence. Nothing

can certainly be more commendable than the Part you act; and I shall be very glad to have my Share in the Preservation of a young Lady of so much Merit, and for whom I have so much Esteem.'

'Doth not your Ladyship think,' says Mrs. *Fitzpatrick* eagerly, 'that it would be the best Way to write immediately to my Uncle, and acquaint him where my Cousin is?'

The Lady pondered a little upon this, and thus answered—'Why, no, Madam, I think not. *Di Western*[1] hath described her Brother to me to be such a Brute, that I cannot consent to put any Woman under his Power who hath escaped from it. I have heard he behaved like a Monster to his own Wife; for he is one of those Wretches who think they have a Right to tyrannize over us, and from such I shall ever esteem it the Cause of my Sex to rescue any Woman who is so unfortunate to be under their Power.—The Business, dear Cousin, will be only to keep Miss *Western* from seeing this young Fellow, till the good Company, which she will have an Opportunity of meeting here, give her a properer Turn.'

'If he should find her out, Madam,' answered the other, 'your Ladyship may be assured he will leave nothing unattempted to come at her.'

'But, Madam,' replied the Lady, 'it is impossible he should come here—tho' indeed it is possible he may get some Intelligence where she is, and then may lurk about the House—I wish therefore I knew his Person.

'Is there no Way, Madam, by which I could have a Sight of him? For otherwise you know, Cousin, she may contrive to see him here without my Knowledge.' Mrs. *Fitzpatrick* answered, 'That he had threatened her with another Visit that Afternoon, and that if her Ladyship pleased to do her the Honour of calling upon her then, she would hardly fail of seeing him between Six and Seven; and if he came earlier she would, by some Means or other, detain him till her Ladyship's Arrival.—Lady *Bellaston* replied, 'she would come the Moment she could get from Dinner, which she supposed would be by Seven at farthest; for that it was absolutely necessary she should be acquainted with his Person. Upon my Word, Madam,' says she, 'it was very good to take this Care of Miss *Western;* but common Humanity, as well as Regard to our Family, requires it of us both; for it would be a dreadful Match indeed.'

Mrs. *Fitzpatrick* failed not to make a proper Return to the Compliment which Lady *Bellaston* had bestowed on her Cousin, and after some little immaterial Conversation withdrew; and getting as fast as she could into her Chair, unseen by *Sophia* or *Honour*, returned home.

---

1. Fielding later calls her "Bell" (p. 667).

Chapter IV.

Which consists of Visiting.

Mr. *Jones* had walked within Sight of a certain Door during the whole Day, which, though one of the shortest, appeared to him to be one of the longest in the whole Year. At length the Clock having struck Five, he returned to Mrs. *Fitzpatrick*, who, though it was a full Hour earlier than the decent Time of visiting, received him very civilly; but still persisted in her Ignorance concerning *Sophia*.

Jones, in asking for his Angel, had drop'd the Word Cousin; upon which Mrs. *Fitzpatrick* said, 'Then, Sir, you know we are related; and as we are, you will permit me the Right of enquiring into the Particulars of your Business with my Cousin.' Here *Jones* hesitated a good while, and at last answered, He had a considerable Sum of Money of hers in his Hands, which he desired to deliver to her. He then produced the Pocket-book, and acquainted Mrs. *Fitzpatrick* with the Contents, and with the Method in which they came into his Hands. He had scarce finished his Story when a most violent Noise shook the whole House. To attempt to describe this Noise to those who have heard it, would be in vain; and to aim at giving any Idea of it to those who have never heard the like, would be still more vain: For it may be truly said,

> ——————*Non acuta*
> *Sic geminant Corybantes Æra.*[1]

The Priests of Cybele *do not so rattle their sounding Brass.*

In short a Footman knocked, or rather thundered at the Door. *Jones* was a little surprised at the Sound, having never heard it before; but Mrs. *Fitzpatrick* very calmly said, that as some Company were coming, she could not make him any Answer now; but if he pleased to stay till they were gone, she intimated she had something to say to him.

The Door of the Room now flew open, and, after pushing in her Hoop sideways before her, entered Lady *Bellaston*, who having first made a very low Curtesy to Mrs. *Fitzpatrick*, and as low a one to Mr. *Jones*, was ushered to the upper End of the Room.

We mention these minute Matters for the Sake of some Country Ladies of our Acquaintance, who think it contrary to the Rules of Modesty to bend their Knees to a Man.

The Company were hardly well settled, before the Arrival of the Peer lately mentioned caused a fresh Disturbance and a Repetition of Ceremonials.

These being over, the Conversation began to be (as the Phrase

1. Horace, *Odes* I.xvi.7–8.

is) extremely brilliant. However, as nothing past in it which can be thought material to this History, or, indeed, very material in itself, I shall omit the Relation; the rather as I have known some very fine polite Conversation grow extremely dull, when transcribed into Books, or repeated on the Stage. Indeed this mental Repast is a Dainty, of which those who are excluded from polite Assemblies, must be contented to remain as ignorant as they must of the several Dainties of *French* Cookery, which are served only at the Tables of the Great. To say the Truth, as neither of these are adapted to every Taste, they might both be often thrown away on the Vulgar.

Poor *Jones* was rather a Spectator of this elegant Scene, than an Actor in it; for though in the short Interval before the Peer's Arrival, Lady *Bellaston* first, and afterwards Mrs. *Fitzpatrick*, had addressed some of their Discourse to him; yet no sooner was the noble Lord entered, than he engrossed the whole Attention of the two Ladies to himself; and as he took no more Notice of *Jones* than if no such Person had been present, unless by now and then staring at him, the Ladies followed his Example.

The Company had now staid so long, that Mrs. *Fitzpatrick* plainly perceived they all designed to stay out each other. She therefore resolved to rid herself of *Jones*, he being the Visitant to whom she thought the least Ceremony was due. Taking therefore an Opportunity of a Cessation of Chat, she addressed herself gravely to him, and said, 'Sir, I shall not possibly be able to give you an Answer To-night, as to that Business; but if you please to leave Word where I may send to you To-morrow'——

Jones had natural, but not artificial good Breeding. Instead therefore of communicating the Secret of his Lodgings to a Servant, he acquainted the Lady herself with it particularly, and soon after very ceremoniously withdrew.

He was no sooner gone than the great Personages who had taken no Notice of him present, began to take much Notice of him in his Absence; but if the Reader hath already excused us from relating the more brilliant Part of this Conversation, he will surely be very ready to excuse the Repetition of what may be called vulgar Abuse: Though, perhaps, it may be material to our History to mention an Observation of Lady *Bellaston*, who took her Leave in a few Minutes after him, and then said to Mrs. *Fitzpatrick*, at her Departure, 'I am satisfied on the Account of my Cousin; she can be in no Danger from this Fellow.'

Our History shall follow the Example of Lady *Bellaston*, and take Leave of the present Company, which was now reduced to two Persons; between whom, as nothing passed, which in the least concerns us or our Reader, we shall not suffer ourselves to be diverted by it from Matters which must seem of more Consequence to all those who are at all interested in the Affairs of our Heroe.

Chapter V.

An Adventure which happened to Mr. Jones, *at his Lodgings, with some Account of a young Gentleman who lodged there, and of the Mistress of the House, and her two Daughters.*

The next Morning as early as it was decent, *Jones* attended at Mrs. *Fitzpatrick*'s Door, where he was answered that the Lady was not at Home; an Answer which surprized him the more, as he had walked backwards and forwards in the Street from Break of Day; and if she had gone out, he must have seen her. This Answer, however, he was obliged to receive, and not only now, but to five several Visits which he made her that Day.

To be plain with the Reader, the noble Peer had from some Reason or other, perhaps from a Regard for the Lady's Honour, insisted that she should not see Mr. *Jones*, whom he looked on as a Scrub, any more; and the Lady had complied in making that Promise to which we now see her so strictly adhere.

But as our gentle Reader may possibly have a better Opinion of the young Gentleman than her Ladyship, and may even have some Concern, should it be apprehended, that during this unhappy Separation from *Sophia*, he took up his Residence either at an Inn, or in the Street; we shall now give an Account of his Lodging, which was indeed in a very reputable House, and in a very good Part of the Town.

Mr. *Jones* then had often heard Mr. *Allworthy* mention the Gentlewoman at whose House he used to lodge when he was in Town. This Person, who, as *Jones* likewise knew, lived in *Bond-street*, was the Widow of a Clergyman, and was left by him at his Decease, in Possession of two Daughters, and of a compleat Set of Manuscript Sermons.

Of these two Daughters, *Nancy*, the elder, was now arrived at the Age of Seventeen, and *Betty*, the younger, at that of Ten.

Hither *Jones* had dispatched *Partridge*, and in this House he was provided with a Room for himself in the second Floor, and with one for *Partridge* in the fourth.

The first Floor was inhabited by one of those young Gentlemen, who, in the last Age, were called Men of Wit and Pleasure about Town, and properly enough: For as Men are usually denominated from their Business or Profession, so Pleasure may be said to have been the only Business or Profession of those Gentlemen to whom Fortune had made all useful Occupations unnecessary. Play-Houses, Coffee-Houses, and Taverns were the Scenes of their Rendezvous. Wit and Humour were the Entertainment of their looser Hours, and Love was the Business of their more serious

Moments. Wine and the Muses conspired to kindle the brightest
Flames in their Breasts; nor did they only admire, but some were
able to celebrate the Beauty they admired, and all to judge of the
Merit of such Compositions.

Such therefore were properly called the Men of Wit and Pleas-
sure; but I question whether the same Appelation may, with the
same Propriety, be given to those young Gentlemen of our Times,
who have the same Ambition to be distinguished for Parts. Wit certainly they have nothing to do with. To give them their Due, they
soar a Step higher than their Predecessors, and may be called Men
of Wisdom and Vertù (take heed you do not read Virtue). Thus at
an Age when the Gentlemen abovementioned employed their Time
in toasting the Charms of a Woman, or in making Sonnets in her
Praise; in giving their Opinion of a Play at the Theatre, or of
a Poem at *Will*'s or *Button*'s;[1] these Gentlemen are considering of
Methods to bribe a Corporation, or meditating Speeches for the
House of Commons, or rather for the Magazines. But the Science
of Gaming is that which above all others employs their Thoughts.
These are the Studies of their graver Hours, while for their Amuse-
ments they have the vast Circle of Connoisseurship, Painting,
Music, Statuary, and natural Philosophy, or rather *unnatural*, which
deals in the Wonderful, and knows nothing of Nature, except her
Monsters and Imperfections.

When *Jones* had spent the whole Day in vain Enquiries after
Mrs. *Fitzpatrick*, he returned at last disconsolate to his Apartment.
Here while he was venting his Grief in private, he heard a violent
Uproar below Stairs; and soon after a female Voice begged him for
Heaven's Sake to come and prevent Murder. *Jones*, who was never
backward on any Occasion to help the Distressed, immediately ran
down Stairs; when stepping into the Dining-room, whence all the
Noise issued, he beheld the young Gentleman of Wisdom and
Vertú just before mentioned, pinned close to the Wall by his Footman, and a young Woman standing by, wringing her Hands, and
crying out, 'He will be murdered, he will be murdered;' And indeed
the poor Gentleman seemed in some Danger of being choaked,
when *Jones* flew hastily to his Assistance, and rescued him just as he
was breathing his last, from the unmerciful Clutches of the Enemy.

Though the Fellow had received several Kicks and Cuffs from the

1. Famous coffee houses. Will's, established by William Urwin sometime in
the 1650's at No. 1 Bow Street, at the
corner of Russell, was flourishing as a
center for the wits surrounding John
Dryden when Samuel Pepys first dropped
by in Dec., 1663. Young Alexander
Pope, at eleven years, was taken to see
and hear Dryden expatiate there. Wycherly, Congreve, and Addison were habit-
ués. The first number of Steele's *Tatler*
(Apr., 1709) says that all its poetry will
be datelined from Will's.

About 1712, Addison set up his former
servant Daniel Button in a coffee house
in Russell Street, directly opposite from
Will's, which had begun to lose its glam-
our after Dryden's death in 1700. The
success of Addison's *Cato* (1713) established Button's as a Whig center.

little Gentleman, who had more Spirit than Strength, he had made
it a kind of Scruple of Conscience to strike his Master, and would
have contented himself with only choaking him; but towards *Jones*
he bore no such Respect: He no sooner therefore found himself a
little roughly handled by his new Antagonist, than he gave him one
of those Punches in the Guts, which, tho' the Spectators at *Broughton's* Amphitheatre[2] have such exquisite Delight in seeing them,
convey but very little Pleasure in the Feeling.

The lusty Youth had no sooner received this Blow, than he meditated a most grateful Return; and now ensued a Combat between
Jones and the Footman, which was very fierce, but short; for this
Fellow was no more able to contend with *Jones*, than his Master
had before been to contend with him.

And now Fortune, according to her usual Custom, reversed the
Face of Affairs. The former Victor lay breathless on the Ground, and
the vanquished Gentleman had recovered Breath enough to thank
Mr. *Jones* for his seasonable Assistance: He received likewise the
hearty Thanks of the young Woman present, who was indeed no
other than Miss *Nancy*, the eldest Daughter of the House.

The Footman having now recovered his Legs, shook his Head at
Jones, and with a sagacious Look, cry'd,—'O d—n me, I'll have
nothing more to do with you; you have been upon the Stage, or I
am d—nably mistaken:' And indeed we may forgive this his Suspicion; for such was the Agility and Strength of our Heroe, that he
was perhaps a Match for one of the First-Rate Boxers, and could,
with great Ease, have beaten all the muffled[3] Graduates of Mr.
Broughton's School.

The Master foaming with Wrath, ordered his Man immediately
to strip, to which the latter very readily agreed, on Condition of
receiving his Wages. This Condition was presently complied with,
and the Fellow was discharged.

And now the young Gentleman, whose Name was *Nightingale*,
very strenuously insisted, that his Deliverer should take Part of a
Bottle of Wine with him; to which *Jones*, after much Entreaty,
consented; tho' more out of Complaisance than Inclination; for the
Uneasiness of his Mind fitted him very little for Conversation at

2. John Broughton (1705–89), "the
father of British pugilism," patronized
by the élite and backed by the Duke of
Cumberland. On his next page, Fielding
gives a footnote quoting his advertisement of 1 Feb. 1747.
3. Lest Posterity should be puzzled by
this Epithet, I think proper to explain it
by an Advertisement which was published *Feb.* 1, 1747.

N.B. Mr. *Broughton* proposes, with
proper Assistance, to open an Academy
at his House in the *Hay-Market*, for the
Instruction of those who are willing to
be initiated in the Mystery of Boxing;

where the whole Theory and Practice of
that truly British art, with all the various
Stops, Blows, Cross-Buttocks, &c. incident to Combatants, will be fully taught
and explain'd; and that Persons of Quality and Distinction may not be deterred
from entering into *a Course of those
Lectures*, they will be given with the utmost Tenderness and Regard to the Delicacy of the Frame and Constitution of
the Pupil, for which Reason Muffles are
provided, that will effectually secure
them from the Inconveniency of black
Eyes, broken Jaws, and bloody Noses
[*Fielding's note*].

this Time. Miss *Nancy* likewise, who was the only Female then in the House, her Mamma and Sister being both gone to the Play, condescended to favour them with her Company.

When the Bottle and Glasses were on the Table, the Gentleman began to relate the Occasion of the preceding Disturbance.

'I hope, Sir,' said he to *Jones*, 'you will not, from this Accident, conclude, that I make a Custom of striking my Servants; for I assure you this is the first Time I have been guilty of it in my Remembrance, and I have passed by many provoking Faults in this very Fellow, before he could provoke me to it; but when you hear what hath happened this Evening, you will, I believe, think me excusable. I happened to come home several Hours before my usual Time, when I found four Gentlemen of the Cloth at Whisk by my Fire;—and my *Hoyle*,⁴ Sir,—my best *Hoyle*, which cost me a Guinea, lying open on the Table, with a Quantity of Porter spilt on one of the most material Leaves of the whole Book. This, you will allow, was provoking; but I said nothing till the rest of the honest Company were gone, and then gave the Fellow a gentle Rebuke, who, instead of expressing any Concern, made me a pert Answer, "That Servants must have their Diversions as well as other People; that he was sorry for the Accident which had happened to the Book; but that several of his Acquaintance had bought the same for a Shilling; and that I might stop as much in his Wages if I pleased:" I now gave him a severer Reprimand than before, when the Rascal had the Insolence to——In short, he imputed my early coming home to—In short, he cast a Reflection—He mentioned the Name of a young Lady, in a Manner—in such a Manner that incensed me beyond all Patience, and, in my Passion, I struck him.'

Jones answered, 'That he believed no Person living would blame him; for my Part,' said he, 'I confess I should, on the last mentioned Provocation, have done the same Thing.'

Our Company had not sat long before they were joined by the Mother and Daughter, at their Return from the Play. And now they all spent a very chearful Evening together; for all but *Jones* were heartily merry, and even he put on as much constrained Mirth as possible. Indeed half his natural Flow of animal Spirits, joined to the Sweetness of his Temper, was sufficient to make a most amiable Companion; and notwithstanding the Heaviness of his Heart, so agreeable did he make himself on the present Occasion, that, at their breaking up, the young Gentleman earnestly desired his further Acquaintance. Miss *Nancy* was well pleased with him; and the Widow, quite charmed with her new Lodger, invited him with the other, next Morning to Breakfast.

4. Edmond Hoyle's *Short Treatise on Whist* (1742, and many successive editions) established the rules of the game for well over a century. He later published a book on other games, "according to Hoyle."

Jones, on his Part, was no less satisfied. As for Miss *Nancy*, tho' a very little Creature, she was extremely pretty, and the Widow had all the Charms which can adorn a Woman near fifty. As she was one of the most innocent Creatures in the World, so she was one of the most chearful. She never thought, nor spoke, nor wished any ill, and had constantly that Desire of pleasing, which may be called the happiest of all Desires in this, that it scarce ever fails of attaining its Ends, when not disgraced by Affectation. In short, though her Power was very small, she was in her Heart one of the warmest Friends. She had been a most affectionate Wife, and was a most fond and tender Mother.

As our History doth not, like a News-Paper, give great Characters to People who never were heard of before, nor will ever be heard of again; the Reader may hence conclude, that this excellent Woman will hereafter appear to be of some Importance in our History.

Nor was *Jones* a little pleased with the young Gentleman himself, whose Wine he had been drinking. He thought he discerned in him much good Sense, though a little too much tainted with Town Foppery; but what recommended him most to *Jones* were some Sentiments of great Generosity and Humanity, which occasionally dropt from him; and particularly many Expressions of the highest Disinterestedness in the Affair of Love. On which Subject the young Gentleman delivered himself in a Language which might have very well become an *Arcadian* Shepherd of Old, and which appeared very extraordinary when proceeding from the Lips of a modern fine Gentleman; but he was only one by Imitation, and meant by Nature for a much better Character.

Chapter VI.

What *arrived while the Company were at Breakfast, with some Hints concerning the Government of Daughters.*

Our Company brought together in the Morning the same good Inclinations towards each other, with which they had separated the Evening before; but poor *Jones* was extreme disconsolate; for he had just received Information from *Partridge*, that Mrs. *Fitzpatrick* had left her Lodging, and that he could not learn whither she was gone. This News highly afflicted him, and his Countenance, as well as his Behaviour, in Defiance of all his Endeavours to the contrary, betrayed manifest Indications of a disordered Mind.

The Discourse turned at present, as before, on Love; and Mr. *Nightingale* again expressed many of those warm, generous, and disinterested Sentiments upon this Subject, which wise and sober Men call romantic, but which wise and sober Women generally regard in a better Light. Mrs. *Miller*, (for so the Mistress of the House was called) greatly approved these Sentiments; but when the young

Gentleman appealed to Miss *Nancy*, she answered only, 'That she believed the Gentleman who had spoke the least, was capable of feeling the most.'

This Compliment was so apparently directed to *Jones*, that we should have been sorry had he passed it by unregarded. He made her indeed a very polite Answer, and concluded with an oblique Hint, that her own Silence subjected her to a Suspicion of the same Kind: For indeed she had scarce opened her Lips either now or the last Evening.

'I am glad, *Nanny*,' says Mrs. *Miller*, 'the Gentleman hath made the Observation; I protest I am almost of his Opinion. What can be the Matter with you, Child? I never saw such an Alteration. What is become of all your Gayety? Would you think, Sir, I used to call her my little Prattler. She hath not spoke twenty Words this Week.'

Here their Conversation was interrupted by the Entrance of a Maid-Servant, who brought a Bundle in her Hands, which, she said, 'was delivered by a Porter for Mr. *Jones*.' She added, 'that the Man immediately went away, saying, it required no Answer.'

Jones expressed some Surprize on this Occasion, and declared it must be some Mistake: But the Maid persisting that she was certain of the Name, all the Women were desirous of having the Bundle immediately opened; which Operation was at length performed by little *Betsey*, with the Consent of Mr. *Jones*; and the Contents were found to be a Domino, a Mask, and a Masquerade Ticket.

Jones was now more positive than ever, in asserting that these Things must have been delivered by Mistake; and Mrs. *Miller* herself expressed some Doubt, and said, 'she knew not what to think.' But when Mr. *Nightingale* was asked, he delivered a very different Opinion. 'All I can conclude from it, Sir,' said he, 'is that you are a very happy Man: For I make no Doubt but these were sent you by some Lady whom you will have the Happiness of meeting at the Masquerade.'

Jones had not a sufficient Degree of Vanity to entertain any such flattering Imagination; nor did Mrs. *Miller* herself give much Assent to what Mr. *Nightingale* had said, 'till Miss *Nancy* having lifted up the Domino, a Card dropt from the Sleeve, in which was written as follows:

To *Mr.* Jones.

The Queen of the Fairies sends you this;
Use her Favours not amiss.

Mrs. *Miller* and Miss *Nancy* now both agreed with Mr. *Nightingale*; nay, *Jones* himself was almost persuaded to be of the same Opinion. And as no other Lady but Mrs. *Fitzpatrick*, he thought, knew his Lodging, he began to flatter himself with some Hopes, that it came from her, and that he might possibly see his *Sophia*. These Hopes had surely very little Foundation; but as the Conduct of Mrs. *Fitzpatrick*, in not seeing him according to her Promise, and in quitting her Lodgings, had been very odd and unaccountable, he conceived some faint Hopes, that she (of whom he had formerly heard a very whimsical Character) might possibly intend to do him that Service, in a strange Manner, which she declined doing by more ordinary Methods. To say the Truth, as nothing certain could be concluded from so odd and uncommon an Incident, he had the greater Latitude to draw what imaginary Conclusions from it he pleased. As his Temper therefore was naturally sanguine, he indulged it on this Occasion, and his Imagination worked up a thousand Conceits, to favour and support his Expectations of meeting his dear *Sophia* in the Evening.

Reader, if thou hast any good Wishes towards me, I will fully repay them, by wishing thee to be possessed of this sanguine Disposition of Mind: Since, after having read much, and considered long on that Subject of Happiness which hath employed so many great Pens, I am almost inclined to fix it in the Possession of this Temper; which puts us, in a Manner, out of the Reach of Fortune, and makes us happy without her Assistance. Indeed the Sensations of Pleasure it gives are much more constant, as well as much keener than those which that blind Lady bestows; Nature having wisely contrived, that some Satiety and Languor should be annexed to all our real Enjoyments, lest we should be so taken up by them, as to be stopt from further Pursuits. I make no manner of Doubt but that, in this Light, we may see the imaginary future Chancellor just called to the Bar, the Archbishop in Crape, and the Prime Minister at the Tail of an Opposition, more truly happy than those who are invested with all the Power and Profit of these respective Offices.

Mr. *Jones* having now determined to go to the Masquerade that Evening, Mr. *Nightingale* offered to conduct him thither. The young Gentleman, at the same Time, offered Tickets to Miss *Nancy* and her Mother; but the good Woman would not accept them. She said, 'she did not conceive the Harm which some People imagined in a Masquerade; but that such extravagant Diversions were proper only for Persons of Quality and Fortune, and not for young Women who were to get their Living, and could, at best, hope to be married to a good Tradesman.'——'A Tradesman!' cries *Nightingale*, 'you shan't undervalue my *Nancy*. There is not a Nobleman upon Earth above her Merit.' 'O fie! Mr. *Nightingale*,' answered Mrs. *Miller*, 'you must not fill the Girl's Head with such Fancies: But if it was her good Luck (says the Mother with a Simper) to find a Gentleman of your generous Way of Thinking, I hope she would make a better Return to his Generosity, than to give her Mind up to extravagant Pleasures. Indeed where young Ladies bring great Fortunes themselves, they have some Right to insist on spending what is their own; and on that Account, I have heard the Gentlemen say, a Man has sometimes a better Bargain with a poor Wife, than with a rich one.—But let my Daughters marry whom they will, I shall endeavour to make them Blessings to their Husbands:—I beg, therefore, I may hear of no more Masquerades. *Nancy* is, I am certain, too good a Girl to desire to go; for she must remember when you carried her thither last Year, it almost turned her Head; and she did not return to herself, or to her Needle, in a Month afterwards.'

Though a gentle Sigh, which stole from the Bosom of *Nancy*, seemed to argue some secret Disapprobation of these Sentiments, she did not dare openly to oppose them. For as this good Woman had all the Tenderness, so she had preserved all the Authority of a Parent; and as her Indulgence to the Desires of her Children, was restrained only by her Fears for their Safety and future Welfare, so she never suffered those Commands, which proceeded from such Fears, to be either disobeyed or disputed. And this the young Gentleman who had lodged two Years in the House, knew so well, that he presently acquiesced in the Refusal.

Mr. *Nightingale*, who grew every Minute fonder of *Jones*, was very desirous of his Company that Day to Dinner at the Tavern, where he offered to introduce him to some of his Acquaintance; but *Jones* begged to be excused, 'as his Cloaths,' he said, 'were not yet come to Town.'

To confess the Truth, Mr. *Jones* was now in a Situation, which sometimes happens to be the Case of young Gentlemen of much better Figure than himself. In short, he had not one Penny in his Pocket; a Situation in much greater Credit among the ancient Philosophers, than among the modern wise Men who live in *Lombard Street*, or those who frequent *White*'s Chocolate-House. And, perhaps, the great Honours which those Philosophers have ascribed to an empty Pocket, may be one of the Reasons of that high Contempt in which they are held in the aforesaid Street and Chocolate-House.

Now if the antient Opinion, that Men might live very comfortably on Virtue only, be, as the modern wise Men just above-mentioned pretend to have discovered, a notorious Error; no less false is, I apprehend, that Position of some Writers of Romance, that a Man can live altogether on Love: For however delicious Repasts this may afford to some of our Senses or Appetites, it is most certain it can afford none to others. Those, therefore, who have placed too great a Confidence in such Writers, have experienced their

Error when it was too late; and have found that Love was no more capable of allaying hunger, than a Rose is capable of delighting the Ear, or a Violin of gratifying the Smell.

Notwithstanding, therefore, all the Delicacies which Love had set before him, namely, the Hopes of seeing *Sophia* at the Masquerade; on which, however ill-founded his Imagination might be, he had voluptuously feasted during the whole Day, the Evening no sooner came, than Mr. *Jones* began to languish for some Food of a grosser Kind. *Partridge* discovered this by Intuition, and took the Occasion to give some oblique Hints concerning the Bank-Bill, and when these were rejected with Disdain, he collected Courage enough once more to mention a Return to Mr. *Allworthy*.

'*Partridge*,' cries *Jones*, 'you cannot see my Fortune in a more desperate Light than I see it myself; and I begin heartily to repent, that I suffered you to leave a Place, where you was settled, and to follow me. However, I insist now on your returning home; and for the Expence and Trouble which you have so kindly put yourself to on my Account, all the Cloaths I left behind in your Care, I desire you would take as your own. I am sorry I can make you no other Acknowledgment.'

He spoke these Words with so pathetic an Accent, that *Partridge*, among whose Vices Ill-nature or Hardness of Heart were not numbered, burst into Tears; and after swearing he would not quit him in his Distress, he began with the most earnest Intreaties to urge his Return home. 'For Heaven's Sake, Sir,' says he, 'do but consider: What can your Honour do? How is it possible you can live in this Town without Money? Do what you will, Sir, or go wherever you please, I am resolved not to desert you.—But pray, Sir, consider,—Do pray, Sir, for your own Sake, take it into your Consideration; and I'm sure,' says he, 'that your own Good-Sense will bid you return home.'

'How often shall I tell thee,' answered *Jones*, 'that I have no Home to return to? Had I any Hopes that Mr. *Allworthy*'s Doors would be open to receive me, I want no Distress to urge me:—Nay, there is no other Cause upon Earth, which could detain me a Moment from flying to his Presence; but, alas! that I am for ever banished from. His last Words were,—O *Partridge*, they still ring in my Ears——His last Words were, when he gave me a Sum of Money, what it was I know not, but considerable I'm sure it was. —His last Words were—"I am resolved from this Day forward, on no Account, to converse with you any more."'

Here Passion stopt the Mouth of *Jones*, as Surprize, for a Moment, did that of *Partridge*: But he soon recovered the Use of Speech, and after a short Preface, in which he declared he had no Inquisitiveness in his Temper, enquired, what *Jones* meant by a considerable Sum; he knew not how much; and what was become of the Money.

In both these Points he now received full Satisfaction; on which he was proceeding to comment, when he was interrupted by a Message from Mr. *Nightingale*, who desired his Master's Company in his Apartment.

When the two Gentlemen were both attired for the Masquerade, and Mr. *Nightingale* had given Orders for Chairs to be sent for, a Circumstance of Distress occurred to *Jones*, which will appear very ridiculous to many of my Readers. This was how to procure a Shilling; but if such Readers will reflect a little on what they have themselves felt from the Want of a Thousand Pound, or, perhaps, of Ten or Twenty, to execute a favourite Scheme, they will have a perfect Idea of what Mr. *Jones* felt on this Occasion. For this Sum, therefore, he applied to *Partridge*, which was the first he had permitted him to advance, and was the last he intended that poor Fellow should advance in his Service. To say the Truth, *Partridge* had lately made no Offer of this Kind; whether it was that he desired to see the Bank-Bill broke in upon, or that Distress should prevail on *Jones* to return home, or from what other Motive it proceeded, I will not determine.

Chapter VII.

Containing the Whole Humours of a Masquerade.

Our Cavaliers now arrived at that Temple, where *Heydegger*,[1] the great *Arbiter Deliciarum*, the great High Priest of Pleasure presides; and, like other Heathen Priests, imposes on his Votaries by the pretended Presence of the Deity, when in Reality no such Deity is there.

Mr. *Nightingale* having taken a Turn or two with his Companion, soon left him, and walked off with a Female, saying, 'Now you are here, Sir, you must beat about for your own Game.'

Jones began to entertain strong Hopes that his *Sophia* was present; and these Hopes gave him more Spirits than the Lights, the Music, and the Company; though these are pretty strong Antidotes against the Spleen. He now accosted every Woman he saw, whose Stature, Shape, or Air, bore any Resemblance to his Angel. To all of whom he endeavoured to say something smart, in order to engage

1. John James Heidegger (1659?–1749), of Swiss extraction, an associate of Handel's in establishing Italian opera in London, reputed to be the ugliest man in town. He was widely popular, was called "Count," and conducted masquerades at the Opera House as Master of the Revels to the Court of George II. Fielding's first published work, *The Masquerade* (1728), a playfully satiric poem, is dedicated to "C———T H——D——G—— R," and contains a passage about Heidegger's horribly ugly mask, which turns out to be his natural face.

an Answer, by which he might discover that Voice which he thought it impossible he should mistake. Some of these answered by a Question, in a squeaking Voice, *Do you know me?* Much the greater Numbers said, *I don't know you, Sir*; and nothing more. Some called him an impertinent Fellow; some made him no Answer at all; some said, *Indeed I don't know your Voice, and I shall have nothing to say to you*; and many gave him as kind Answers as he could wish, but not in the Voice he desired to hear.

Whilst he was talking with one of these last, (who was in the Habit of a Shepherdess) a Lady in a Domino came up to him, and slapping him on the Shoulder, whispered him, at the same Time, in the Ear, 'If you talk any longer with that Trollop, I will acquaint Miss *Western.*'

Jones no sooner heard that Name, than, immediately quitting his former Companion, he applied to the Domino, begging and entreating her to shew him the Lady she had mentioned, if she was then in the Room.

The Mask walked hastily to the upper End of the innermost Apartment before she spoke; and then, instead of answering him, sat down, and declared she was tired. *Jones* sat down by her, and still persisted in his Entreaties; at last the Lady coldly answered, 'I imagined Mr. *Jones* had been a more discerning Lover; than to suffer any Disguise to conceal his Mistress from him.' 'Is she here then, Madam?' replied *Jones*, with some Vehemence. Upon which the Lady cry'd.—'Hush, Sir, you will be observed.—I promise you, upon my Honour, Miss *Western* is not here.'

Jones now taking the Mask by the Hand, fell to entreating her in the most earnest Manner, to acquaint him where he might find *Sophia:* And when he could obtain no direct Answer, he began to upbraid her gently for having disappointed him the Day before; and concluded, saying, 'Indeed, my good Fairy Queen, I know your Majesty very well, notwithstanding the affected Disguise of your Voice. Indeed, Mrs. *Fitzpatrick*, it is a little cruel to divert yourself at the Expence of my Torments.'

The Mask answered, 'Though you have so ingeniously discovered me, I must still speak in the same Voice, lest I should be known by others. And do you think, good Sir, that I have no greater Regard for my Cousin, than to assist in carrying on an Affair between you two, which must end in her Ruin, as well as your own? Besides, I promise you, my Cousin is not mad enough to consent to her own Destruction, if you are so much her Enemy as to tempt her to it.'

'Alas, Madam,' said *Jones*, 'you little know my Heart, when you call me an Enemy of *Sophia.*'

'And yet to ruin any one,' cries the other, 'you will allow, is the Act of an Enemy; and when by the same Act you must knowingly and certainly bring Ruin on yourself, is it not Folly or Madness, as

well as Guilt? Now, Sir, my Cousin hath very little more than her
Father will please to give her; very little for one of her Fashion,—
you know him, and you know your own Situation.'

Jones vowed he had no such Design on *Sophia*, 'That he would
rather suffer the most violent of Deaths than sacrifice her Interest
to his Desires. He said, he knew how unworthy he was of her every
Way; that he had long ago resolved to quit all such aspiring
Thoughts, but that some strange Accidents had made him desirous
to see her once more, when he promised he would take Leave of her
for ever. No, Madam,' concluded he, 'my Love is not of that base
Kind, which seeks its own Satisfaction, at the Expense of what is
most dear to its Object. I would sacrifice every Thing to the Possession of my *Sophia*, but *Sophia* herself.'

Though the Reader may have already conceived no very sublime
Idea of the Virtue of the Lady in the Mask; and tho' possibly she
may hereafter appear not to deserve one of the first Characters of
her Sex; yet, it is certain, these generous Sentiments made a strong
Impression upon her, and greatly added to the Affection she had
before conceived for our young Heroe.

The Lady now, after a Silence of a few Moments, said, 'She did
not see his Pretensions to *Sophia* so much in the Light of Presumption, as of Imprudence. Young Fellows,' says she, 'can never have
too aspiring Thoughts. I love Ambition in a young Man, and I
would have you cultivate it as much as possible. Perhaps you may
succeed with those who are infinitely superior in Fortune; nay, I am
convinced there are Women,—but don't you think me a strange
Creature, Mr. *Jones*, to be thus giving Advice to a Man, with whom
I am so little acquainted, and one with whose Behaviour to me I
have so little Reason to be pleased?'

Here *Jones* began to apologize, and to hope he had not offended
in any thing he had said of her Cousin.—To which the Mask
answered, 'And are you so little versed in the Sex, to imagine you
can well affront a Lady more, than by entertaining her with your
Passion for another Woman? If the Fairy Queen had conceived no
better Opinion of your Gallantry, she would scarce have appointed
you to meet her at a Masquerade.'

Jones had never less Inclination to an Amour than at present; but
Gallantry to the Ladies was among his Principles of Honour; and he
held it as much incumbent on him to accept a Challenge to Love,
as if it had been a Challenge to Fight. Nay, his very Love to *Sophia*
made it necessary for him to keep well with the Lady, as he made
no doubt but she was capable of bringing him into the Presence of
the other.

He began therefore to make a very warm Answer to her last
Speech, when a Mask, in the Character of an old Woman, joined
them. This Mask was one of those Ladies who go to a Masquerade

only to vent Ill-nature, by telling People rude Truths, and by endeavouring, as the Phrase is, to spoil as much Sport as they are able. This good Lady therefore, having observed *Jones*, and his Friend, whom she well knew, in close Consultation together in a Corner of the Room, concluded she could no where satisfy her Spleen better than by interrupting them. She attacked them therefore, and soon drove them from their Retirement; nor was she contented with this, but pursued them to every Place which they shifted to avoid her; till Mr. *Nightingale* seeing the Distress of his Friend, at last relieved him, and engaged the old Woman in another Pursuit.

While *Jones* and his Mask were walking together about the Room, to rid themselves of the Teazer, he observed his Lady speak to several Masks, with the same Freedom of Acquaintance as if they had been barefaced. He could not help expressing his Surprize at this, saying, 'Sure, Madam, you must have infinite Discernment to know People in all Disguises.' To which the Lady answered, 'You cannot conceive any Thing more insipid and childish than a Masquerade to the People of Fashion, who in general know one another as well here, as when they meet in an Assembly or a Drawing-room; nor will any Woman of Condition converse with a Person with whom she is not acquainted. In short, the Generality of Persons whom you see here, may more properly be said to kill Time in this Place, than in any other; and generally retire from hence more tired than from the longest Sermon. To say the Truth, I begin to be in that Situation myself; and if I have any Faculty at guessing, you are not much better pleased. I protest it would be almost Charity in me to go home for your Sake.' 'I know but one Charity equal to it,' cries *Jones*, 'and that is to suffer me to wait on you home.' 'Sure,' answered the Lady, 'you have a strange Opinion of me, to imagine, that upon such an Acquaintance, I would let you into my Doors at this Time o' Night. I fancy you impute the Friendship I have shewn my Cousin, to some other Motive. Confess honestly; don't you consider this contrived Interview as little better than a downright Assignation? Are you used, Mr. *Jones*, to make these sudden Conquests?' 'I am not used, Madam,' said *Jones*, 'to submit to such sudden Conquests; but as you have taken my Heart by Surprize, the rest of my Body hath a Right to follow; so you must pardon me if I resolve to attend you wherever you go.' He accompanied these Words with some proper Actions; upon which the Lady, after a gentle Rebuke, and saying their Familiarity would be observed, told him, 'She was going to sup with an Acquaintance, whither she hoped he would not follow her; for if you should,' said she, 'I shall be thought an unaccountable Creature, though my Friend indeed is not censorious, yet I hope you won't follow me; I protest I shall not know what to say, if you do.'

The Lady presently after quitted the Masquerade, and *Jones*, notwithstanding the severe Prohibition he had received, presumed to attend her. He was now reduced to the same Dilemma we have mentioned before, namely, the Want of a Shilling, and could not relieve it by borrowing as before. He therefore walked boldly on after the Chair in which his Lady rode, pursued by a grand Huzza, from all the Chairmen present, who wisely take the best Care they can to discountenance all walking afoot by their Betters. Luckily however the Gentry who attend at the Opera-House were too busy to quit their Stations, and as the Lateness of the Hour prevented him from meeting many of their Brethren in the Street, he proceeded without Molestation, in a Dress, which, at another Season, would have certainly raised a Mob at his Heels.

The Lady was set down in a Street, not far from *Hanover-Square*, where the Door being presently opened, she was carried in, and the Gentleman, without any Ceremony, walked in after her.

Jones and his Companion were now together in a very well-furnished and well-warm'd Room, when the Female still speaking in her Masquerade Voice, said, she was surprized at her Friend, who must absolutely have forgot her Appointment; at which after venting much Resentment, she suddenly exprest some Apprehension from *Jones*, and asked him what the World would think of their having been alone together in a House at that Time of Night? But instead of a direct Answer to so important a Question, *Jones* began to be very importunate with the Lady to unmask, and at length having prevailed, there appeared not Mrs. *Fitzpatrick*, but the Lady *Bellaston* herself.

It would be tedious to give the particular Conversation, which consisted of very common and ordinary Occurrences, and which lasted from two till six o'Clock in the Morning. It is sufficient to mention all of it that is any wise material to this History. And this was a Promise that the Lady would endeavour to find out *Sophia*, and in a few Days bring him to an Interview with her, on Condition that he would then take his Leave of her. When this was thoroughly settled, and a second Meeting in the Evening appointed at the same Place, they separated; the Lady returned to her House, and *Jones* to his Lodgings.

Chapter VIII.

Containing a Scene of Distress, which will appear very extraordinary to most of our Readers.

Jones having refreshed himself with a few Hours Sleep, summoned *Partridge* to his Presence; and delivering him a Bank Note of fifty Pounds, ordered him to go and change it. *Partridge* received this with sparkling Eyes, though when he came to reflect farther, it raised in him some Suspicions not very advantageous to the Honour of his Master; to these the dreadful Idea he had of the Masquerade, the Disguise in which his Master had gone out and returned, and his having been abroad all Night, contributed. In plain Language, the only Way he could possibly find to account for the Possession of this Note, was by Robbery; and, to confess the Truth, the Reader, unless he should suspect it was owing to the Generosity of Lady *Bellaston*, can hardly imagine any other.

To clear therefore the Honour of Mr. *Jones*, and to do Justice to the Liberality of the Lady, he had really received this Present from her, who, though she did not give much into the Hackney Charities of the Age, such as building Hospitals, *&c.* was not, however, entirely void of that Christian Virtue; and conceived (very rightly I think) that a young Fellow of Merit, without a Shilling in the World, was no improper Object of this Virtue.

Mr. *Jones* and Mr. *Nightingale* had been invited to dine this Day with Mrs. *Miller*. At the appointed Hour therefore the two young Gentlemen, with the two Girls, attended in the Parlour, where they waited from Three till almost Five before the good Woman appeared. She had been out of Town to visit a Relation, of whom, at her Return, she gave the following Account.

'I hope, Gentlemen, you will pardon my making you wait; I am sure if you knew the Occasion.—I have been to see a Cousin of mine, about six Miles off, who now lies in.—It should be a Warning to all Persons (says she, looking at her Daughters) how they marry indiscreetly. There is no Happiness in this World without a Competency. O *Nancy!* how shall I describe the wretched Condition in which I found your poor Cousin; she hath scarce lain in a Week, and there was she, this dreadful Weather, in a cold Room, without any Curtains to her Bed, and not a Bushel of Coals in her House to supply her with Fire: Her second Son, that sweet little Fellow, lies ill of a Quinzy in the same Bed with his Mother; for there is no other Bed in the House. Poor little *Tommy!* I believe, *Nancy*, you will never see your Favourite any more; for he is really very ill. The rest of the Children are in pretty good Health; but *Molly*, I am afraid, will do herself an Injury: She is but thirteen Years old, Mr. *Nightingale*, and yet, in my Life, I never saw a better Nurse: She tends both her Mother and her Brother; and what is wonderful in a Creature so young, she shows all the Chearfulness in the World to her Mother; and yet I saw her—I saw the poor Child, Mr. *Nightingale*, turn about, and privately wipe the Tears from her Eyes.' Here Mrs. *Miller* was prevented, by her own Tears, from going on, and there was not, I believe, a Person present, who did not accompany her in them; at length she had a little recovered herself, and proceeded thus: 'In all this Distress the Mother supports her Spirits in a surprizing Manner. The Danger of her Son sits heaviest upon her, and yet she endeavours as much as possible to conceal even this Concern, on her Husband's Account. Her Grief, however, sometimes gets the better of all her Endeavours; for she was always extravagantly fond of this Boy, and a most sensible, sweet-tempered Creature it is. I protest I was never more affected in my Life, than when I heard the little Wretch, who is hardly yet seven Years old, while his Mother was wetting him with her Tears, beg her to be comforted.——Indeed, Mamma, cry'd the Child, I shan't die; God Almighty, I'm sure, won't take *Tommy* away; let Heaven be ever so fine a Place, I had rather stay here and starve with you and my Papa, than go to it.—— Pardon me, Gentlemen, I can't help it,' (says she, wiping her Eyes) 'such Sensibility and Affection in a Child——And yet, perhaps, he is least the Object of Pity; for a Day or two will, most probably, place him beyond the Reach of all human Evils. The Father is indeed most worthy of Compassion. Poor Man, his Countenance is the very Picture of Horror, and he looks rather like one dead than alive. Oh Heavens! what a Scene did I behold at my first coming into the Room! The good Creature was lying behind the Bolster, supporting at once both his Child and his Wife. He had nothing on but a thin Waistcoat; for his Coat was spread over the Bed, to supply the Want of Blankets.——When he rose up, at my Entrance, I scarce knew him. As comely a Man, Mr. *Jones*, within this Fortnight, as you ever beheld; Mr. *Nightingale* hath seen him. His Eyes sunk, his Face pale, with a long Beard. His Body shivering with Cold, and worn with Hunger too; for my Cousin says, she can hardly prevail upon him to eat.—He told me himself in a Whisper —he told me—I can't repeat it—he said, he could not bear to eat the Bread his Children wanted. And yet, can you believe it, Gentlemen? In all this Misery, his Wife has as good Cawdle as if she lay in, in the midst of the greatest Affluence; I tasted it, and I scarce ever tasted better—The Means of procuring her this,' he said, 'he believed was sent him by an Angel from Heaven; I know not what he meant; for I had not Spirits enough to ask a single Question.

'This was a Love-Match, as they call it, on both Sides; that is, a Match between two Beggars. I must indeed say I never saw a fonder Couple; but what is their Fondness good for, but to torment each other?' 'Indeed, Mamma,' cries *Nancy*, 'I have always looked on my Cousin *Anderson* (for that was her Name) as one of the happiest of Women.' 'I am sure,' says Mrs. *Miller*, 'the Case at present is much otherwise; for any one might have discerned that the tender Consideration of each others Sufferings, makes the most intolerable Part of their Calamity, both to the Husband and the Wife. Compared to which, Hunger and Cold, as they affect their own Persons only, are scarce Evils. Nay, the very Children, the youngest, which is not two Years old, excepted, feel in the same Manner; for they are a most loving Family; and if they had but a bare Competency, would be the happiest People in the World.' 'I never saw the least Sign of Misery at her House,' replied *Nancy*; 'I am sure my Heart bleeds for what you now tell me.'—'O Child,' answered the Mother, 'she hath always endeavoured to make the best of every Thing. They have always been in great Distress; but, indeed, this absolute Ruin hath been brought upon them by others. The poor Man was Bail for the Villain his Brother; and about a Week ago, the very Day before her Lying-in, their Goods were all carried away, and sold by an Execution. He sent a Letter to me of it by óne of the Bailiffs, which the Villain never delivered.——What must he think of my suffering a Week to pass before he heard of me?'

It was not with dry Eyes that *Jones* heard this Narrative; when it was ended, he took Mrs. *Miller* apart with him into another Room, and delivering her his Purse, in which was the Sum of 5*ol.* desired her to send as much of it as she thought proper to these poor People. The Look which Mrs. *Miller* gave *Jones*, on this Occasion, is not easy to be described. She burst into a Kind of Agony of Transport, and cry'd out,——'Good Heavens! Is there such a Man in the World?'—But recollecting herself, she said, 'Indeed I know one such; but can there be another?' 'I hope, Madam,' cries *Jones*, 'there are many who have common Humanity: For to relieve such Distresses in our Fellow-Creatures, can hardly be called more.' Mrs. *Miller* then took ten Guineas, which were the utmost he could prevail with her to accept, and said, 'She would find some Means of conveying them early the next Morning;' adding, that she had herself done some little Matter for the poor People, and had not left them in quite so much Misery as she found them.

They then returned to the Parlour, where *Nightingale* express'd much Concern at the dreadful Situation of these Wretches, whom indeed he knew; for he had seen them more than once at Mrs. *Miller's.* He inveighed against the Folly of making oneself liable for the Debts of others; vented many bitter Execrations against the Brother; and concluded with wishing something could be done for the unfortunate Family. 'Suppose, Madam,' said he, 'you should recommend them to Mr. *Allworthy?* Or what think you of a Collection? I will give them a Guinea with all my Heart.'

Mrs. *Miller* made no Answer; and *Nancy*, to whom her Mother had whispered the Generosity of *Jones*, turned pale upon the Occasion; though if either of them was angry with *Nightingale*, it was surely without Reason. For the Liberality of *Jones*, if he had known it, was not an Example which he had any Obligation to follow; and there are Thousands who would not have contributed a single Halfpenny, as indeed he did not in Effect, for he made no Tender of any thing; and therefore as the others thought proper to make no Demand, he kept his Money in his Pocket.

I have in Truth observed, and shall never have a better Opportunity than at present to communicate my Observation, that the World are in general divided into two Opinions concerning Charity, which are the very reverse of each other. One Party seems to hold, that all Acts of this Kind are to be esteemed as voluntary Gifts, and however little you give (if indeed no more than your good Wishes) you acquire a great Degree of Merit in so doing.— Others, on the contrary, appear to be as firmly persuaded, that Beneficence is a positive Duty, and that whenever the Rich fall greatly short of their Ability in relieving the Distresses of the Poor, their pitiful Largesses are so far from being meritorious, that they have only Performed their Duty by Halves, and are in some Sense more contemptible than those who have entirely neglected it.

To reconcile these different Opinions is not in my Power. I shall only add, that the Givers are generally of the former Sentiment, and the Receivers are almost universally inclined to the latter.

Chapter IX.

Which treats of Matters of a very different Kind from those in the preceding Chapter.

In the Evening *Jones* met his Lady again, and a long Conversation again ensued between them; but as it consisted only of the same ordinary Occurrences as before, we shall avoid mentioning Particulars, which we despair of rendring agreeable to the Reader; unless he is one whose Devotion to the fair Sex, like that of the Papists to their Saints, wants to be raised by the Help of Pictures. But I am so far from desiring to exhibit such Pictures to the Public, that I would wish to draw a Curtain over those that have been lately set forth in certain *French* Novels; very bungling Copies of which have been presented us here, under the Name of Translations.

Jones grew still more and more impatient to see *Sophia*; and finding, after repeated Interviews with Lady *Bellaston*, no Likelihood of obtaining this by her Means; (for, on the contrary, the Lady began to treat even the Mention of the Name of *Sophia* with Resentment;) he resolved to try some other Method. He made no

Doubt but that Lady *Bellaston* knew where his Angel was, so he thought it most likely, that some of her Servants should be acquainted with the same Secret. *Partridge* therefore was employed to get acquainted with those Servants, in order to fish this Secret out of them.

Few Situations can be imagined more uneasy than that to which his poor Master was at present reduced; for besides the Difficulties he met with in discovering *Sophia*, besides the Fears he had of having disobliged her, and the Assurances he had received from Lady *Bellaston* of the Resolution which *Sophia* had taken against him, and of her having purposely concealed herself from him, which he had sufficient Reason to believe might be true; he had still a Difficulty to combat, which it was not in the Power of his Mistress to remove, however kind her Inclination might have been. This was the exposing of her to be disinherited of all her Father's Estate, the almost inevitable Consequence of their coming together without a Consent, which he had no Hopes of ever obtaining.

Add to all these the many Obligations which Lady *Bellaston*, whose violent Fondness we can no longer conceal, had heaped upon him; so that by her Means he was now become one of the best dress'd Men about Town; and was not only relieved from those ridiculous Distresses we have before-mentioned, but was actually raised to a State of Affluence, beyond what he had ever known.

Now though there are many Gentlemen who very well reconcile it to their Consciences to possess themselves of the whole Fortune of a Woman, without making her any Kind of Return; yet to a Mind the Proprietor of which doth not deserve to be hang'd, nothing is, I believe, more irksome than to support Love with Gratitude only; especially where Inclination pulls the Heart a contrary Way. Such was the unhappy Case of *Jones*; for tho' the virtuous Love he bore to *Sophia*, and which left very little Affection for any other Woman, had been entirely out of the Question, he could never have been able to have made an adequate Return to the generous Passion of this Lady, who had indeed been once an Object of Desire; but was now entered at least into the Autumn of Life; though she wore all the Gayety of Youth both in her Dress and Manner; nay, she contrived still to maintain the Roses in her Cheeks; but these, like Flowers forced out of Season by Art, had none of that lively blooming Freshness with which Nature, at the proper Time, bedecks her own Productions. She had, besides, a certain Imperfection, which renders some Flowers, tho' very beautiful to the Eye, very improper to be placed in a Wilderness of Sweets, and what above all others is most disagreeable to the Breath of Love.

Though *Jones* saw all these Discouragements on the one Side, he felt his Obligations full as strongly on the other; nor did he less plainly discern the ardent Passion whence those Obligations proceeded, the extreme Violence of which if he failed to equal, he well knew the Lady would think him ungrateful; and, what is worse, he would have thought himself so. He knew the tacit Consideration upon which all her Favours were conferred; and as his Necessity obliged him to accept them, so his Honour, he concluded, forced him to pay the Price. This therefore he resolved to do, whatever Misery it cost him, and to devote himself to her, from that great Principle of Justice, by which the Laws of some Countries oblige a Debtor who is no otherwise capable of discharging his Debt, to become the Slave of his Creditor.

While he was meditating on these Matters, he received the following Note from the Lady.

'A very foolish, but a very perverse Accident hath happened since our last Meeting, which makes it improper I should see you any more at the usual Place. I will, if possible, contrive some other Place by To-morrow. In the mean Time, Adieu.'

This Disappointment, perhaps, the Reader may conclude was not very great; but if it was, he was quickly relieved; for in less than an Hour afterwards another Note was brought him from the same Hand, which contained as follows.

'I have altered my Mind since I wrote, a Change, which if you are no Stranger to the tenderest of all Passions, you will not wonder at. I am now resolved to see you this Evening, at my own House, whatever may be the Consequence. Come to me exactly at seven; I dine abroad, but will be at Home by that Time. A Day, I find, to those that sincerely love seems longer than I imagined.

'If you should accidentally be a few Moments before me, bid them shew you into the Drawing-Room.'

To confess the Truth, *Jones* was less pleased with this last Epistle, than he had been with the former, as he was prevented by it from complying with the earnest Entreaties of Mr. *Nightingale*, with whom he had now contracted much Intimacy and Friendship. These Entreaties were to go with that young Gentleman and his Company to a new Play, which was to be acted that Evening, and which a very large Party had agreed to damn, from some Dislike they had taken to the Author, who was a Friend to one of Mr. *Nightingale*'s Acquaintance. And this Sort of Funn, our Heroe, we are ashamed to confess, would willingly have preferred to the above kind Appointment; but his Honour got the better of his Inclination.

Before we attend him to this intended Interview with the Lady, we think proper to account for both the preceding Notes, as the Reader may possibly be not a little surprized at the Imprudence of Lady *Bellaston* in bringing her Lover to the very House where her Rival was lodged.

First then, the Mistress of the House where these Lovers had hitherto met, and who had been for some Years a Pensioner to that Lady, was now become a Methodist, and had that very Morning waited upon her Ladyship, and after rebuking her very severely for her past Life, had positively declared, that she would, on no account, be instrumental in carrying on any of her Affairs for the future.

The Hurry of Spirits into which this Accident threw the Lady, made her despair of possibly finding any other Convenience to meet *Jones* that Evening; but as she began a little to recover from her Uneasiness at the Disappointment, she set her Thoughts to work, when luckily it came into her Head to propose to *Sophia* to go to the Play, which was immediately consented to, and a proper Lady provided for her Companion. Mrs. *Honour* was likewise dispatched with Mrs. *Etoff* on the same Errand of Pleasure; and thus her own House was left free for the safe Reception of Mr. *Jones*, with whom she promised herself two or three Hours of uninterrupted Conversation, after her Return from the Place where she dined, which was at a Friend's House in a pretty distant Part of the Town, near her old Place of Assignation, where she had engaged herself before she was well apprized of the Revolution that had happened in the Mind and Morals of her late Confidante.

Chapter X.

A *Chapter which, tho' short, may draw Tears from some Eyes.*

Mr. *Jones* was just dress'd to wait on Lady *Bellaston*, when Mrs. *Miller* rapp'd at his Door; and being admitted, very earnestly desired his Company below Stairs to drink Tea in the Parlour.

Upon his Entrance into the Room, she presently introduced a Person to him, saying, 'This Sir, is my Cousin, who hath been so greatly beholden to your Goodness, for which he begs to return you his sincerest Thanks.'

The Man had scarce entered upon that Speech, which Mrs. *Miller* had so kindly prefaced, when both *Jones* and he looking steadfastly at each other, showed at once the utmost Tokens of Surprize. The Voice of the latter began instantly to faulter; and, instead of finishing his Speech, he sunk down into a Chair, crying, 'It is so, I am convinced it is so!'

'Bless me, what's the Meaning of this?' cries Mrs. *Miller*, 'you are not ill, I hope, Cousin? Some Water, a Dram this Instant.'

'Be not frighted, Madam,' cries *Jones*, 'I have almost as much Need of a Dram as your Cousin. We are equally surprized at this unexpected Meeting. Your Cousin is an Acquaintance of mine, Mrs. *Miller*.'

'An Acquaintance!' cries the Man.——'Oh Heaven!'

'Ay, an Acquaintance,' repeated *Jones*, 'and an honoured acquaintance too. When I do not love and honour the Man who dares venture every thing to preserve his Wife and Children from instant Destruction, may I have a Friend capable of disowning me in Adversity.'

'O you are an excellent young Man,' cries Mrs. *Miller*,—'yes, indeed, poor Creature! he hath ventured every thing—If he had not had one of the best of Constitutions, it must have killed him.'

'Cousin,' cries the Man, who had now pretty well recovered himself; 'this is the Angel from Heaven whom I meant. This is he to whom before I saw you, I owed the Preservation of my *Peggy*. He it was to whose Generosity every Comfort, every Support which I have procured for her, was owing. He is indeed the worthiest, bravest, noblest of all human Beings. O Cousin, I have Obligations to this Gentleman of such a Nature!'

'Mention nothing of Obligations,' cries *Jones* eagerly, 'not a Word, I insist upon it, not a Word.' (Meaning, I suppose, that he would not have him betray the Affair of the Robbery to any Person)—'If by the Trifle you have received from me, I have preserved a whole Family, sure Pleasure was never bought so cheap.'

'O, Sir,' cries the Man, 'I wish you could this Instant see my House. If any Person had ever a Right to the Pleasure you mention, I am convinced it is yourself. My Cousin tells me, she acquainted you with the Distress in which she found us. That, Sir, is all greatly removed, and chiefly by your Goodness.—My Children have now a Bed to lie on,———and they have———they have———eternal Blessings reward you for it—they have Bread to eat. My little Boy is recovered; My Wife is out of Danger, and I am happy. All, all owing to you, Sir, and to my Cousin here, one of the best of Women. Indeed, Sir, I must see you at my House.—Indeed my Wife must see you, and thank you.—My Children too must express their Gratitude.——Indeed, Sir, they are not without a Sense of their Obligation; but what is my Feeling when I reflect to whom I owe, that they are now capable of expressing their Gratitude.———Oh, Sir! the little Hearts which you have warmed had now been cold as Ice without your Assistance.'——

Here *Jones* attempted to prevent the poor Man from proceeding;

but indeed the Overflowing of his own Heart would of itself have stopped his Words. And now Mrs. *Miller* likewise began to pour forth Thanksgivings, as well in her own Name, as in that of her Cousin, and concluded with saying, she doubted not but such Goodness would meet a glorious Reward.

Jones answered, 'He had been sufficiently rewarded already. Your Cousin's Account, Madam,' said he, 'hath given me a Sensation more pleasing than I have ever known. He must be a Wretch who is unmoved at hearing such a Story; how transporting then must be the Thought of having happily acted a Part in this Scene! If there are Men who cannot feel the Delight of giving Happiness to others, I sincerely pity them, as they are incapable of tasting what is, in my Opinion, a great Honour, a higher Interest, and a sweeter Pleasure, than the ambitious, the avaritious, or the voluptuous Man can ever obtain.'

The Hour of Appointment being now come, *Jones* was forced to take a hasty Leave, but not before he had heartily shaken his Friend by the Hand, and desired to see him again as soon as possible; promising, that he would himself take the first Opportunity of visiting him at his own House. He then stept into his Chair, and proceeded to *Lady Bellaston's*, greatly exulting in the Happiness which he had procured to this poor Family; nor could he forbear reflecting without Horror on the dreadful Consequences which must have attended them, had he listened rather to the Voice of strict Justice than to that of Mercy, when he was attacked on the high Road.

Mrs. *Miller* sung forth the Praises of *Jones* during the whole Evening, in which Mr. *Anderson*,[1] while he stayed, so passionately accompanied her, that he was often on the very Point of mentioning the Circumstances of the Robbery. However, he luckily recollected himself, and avoided an Indiscretion which would have been so much the greater, as he knew Mrs. *Miller* to be extremely strict and nice in her Principles. He was likewise well apprized of the Loquacity of this Lady; and yet such was his Gratitude, that it had almost got the better both of Discretion and Shame, and made him publish that which would have defamed his own Character, rather than omit any Circumstances which might do the fullest Honour to his Benefactor.

Chapter XI.

In which the Reader will be surprized.

Mr. *Jones* was rather earlier than the Time appointed, and earlier than the Lady, whose Arrival was hindered not only by the Distance of the Place where she dined, but by some other cross Acci-

1. *"Enderson"* in the first edition, corrected to *"Anderson"* in the second (to match first mention, p. 551), reverts to *"Enderson"* in the third and fourth: the third was set from the first; the fourth from the third. See below, p. 692.

dents, very vexatious to one in her Situation of Mind. He was accordingly shewn into the Drawing-Room, where he had not been many Minutes before the Door opened, and in came——— no other than *Sophia* herself, who had left the Play before the End of the first Act; for this, as we have already said, being a new Play, at which two large Parties met, the one to damn, and the other to applaud, a violent Uproar, and an Engagement between the two Parties had so terrified our Heroine, that she was glad to put herself under the Protection of a young Gentleman, who safely conveyed her to her Chair.

As Lady *Bellaston* had acquainted her that she should not be at Home till late, *Sophia* expecting to find no one in the Room, came hastily in, and went directly to a Glass which almost fronted her, without once looking towards the upper End of the Room, where the Statue of *Jones* now stood motionless.———In this Glass it was, after contemplating her own lovely Face, that she first discovered the said Statue; when instantly turning about, she perceived the Reality of the Vision: Upon which she gave a violent Scream, and scarce preserved herself from fainting, till *Jones* was able to move to her and support her in his Arms.

To paint the Looks or Thoughts of either of these Lovers is beyond my Power. As their Sensations, from their mutual Silence, may be judged to have been too big for their own Utterance, it cannot be supposed, that I should be able to express them: And the Misfortune is, that few of my Readers have been enough in Love, to feel by their own Hearts what past at this Time in theirs.

After a Short Pause, *Jones*, with faultering Accents, said,———'I see, Madam, you are surprized.'———'Surprized!' answered she; 'Oh Heavens! Indeed, I am surprized. I almost doubt whether you are the Person you seem.' 'Indeed,' cries he, 'my *Sophia*, pardon me, Madam, for this once calling you so, I am that very wretched *Jones*, whom Fortune after so many Disappointments, hath, at last, kindly conducted to you. Oh! my *Sophia*, did you know the Thousand Torments I have suffered in this long, fruitless Pursuit'—'Pursuit of whom?' said *Sophia*, a little recollecting herself, and assuming a reserved Air.———'Can you be so cruel to ask that Question?' cries *Jones*. 'Need I say of you?' 'Of me?' answered *Sophia*: 'Hath Mr. *Jones* then any such important Business with me?' 'To some, Madam,' cries *Jones*, 'this might seem an important Business,' (giving her the Pocket-Book). 'I hope, Madam, you will find it of the same Value, as when it was lost.' *Sophia* took the Pocket-Book, and was going to speak, when he interrupted her, thus;——— 'Let us not, I beseech you, lose one of these precious Moments which Fortune hath so kindly sent us.—O my *Sophia*, I have Business of a much superior Kind.——Thus, on my Knees, let me ask your Pardon.'———'My Pardon?' cries she;———'Sure, Sir, after what is past, you cannot expect, after what I have heard'——'I scarce know what I say,' answered *Jones*. 'By Heavens! I scarce wish you should pardon me. O my *Sophia*, henceforth never cast away a Thought on such a Wretch as I am. If any Remembrance of me should ever intrude to give a Moment's Uneasiness to that tender Bosom, think of my Unworthiness; and let the Remembrance of what past at *Upton* blot me for ever from your Mind'——

Sophia stood trembling all this while. Her Face was whiter than Snow, and her Heart was throbbing through her Stays. But at the mention of *Upton*, a Blush arose in her Cheeks, and her Eyes, which before she had scarce lifted up were turned upon *Jones* with a Glance of Disdain. He understood this silent Reproach, and replied to it thus: 'O my *Sophia*, my only Love, you cannot hate or despise me more for what happened there, than I do myself: But yet do me the Justice to think, that my *Heart* was never unfaithful to you. *That* had no Share in the Folly I was guilty of; it was even then unalterably yours. Though I despaired of possessing you, nay, almost of ever seeing you more, I doated still on your charming Idea, and could *seriously* love no other Woman. But if my Heart had not been engaged, she, into whose Company I accidentally fell at that cursed Place, was not an Object of serious Love. Believe me, my Angel, I never have seen her from that Day to this; and never intend, or desire, to see her again.' *Sophia*, in her Heart, was very glad to hear this; but forcing into her Face an Air of more Coldness than she had yet assumed; 'Why,' said she, 'Mr. *Jones*, do you take the Trouble to make a Defence, where you are not accused? If I thought it worth while to accuse you, I have a Charge of unpardonable Nature indeed.' 'What is it, for Heaven's Sake?' answered *Jones*, trembling and pale, expecting to hear of his Amour with Lady *Bellaston*. 'Oh,' said she, 'How is it possible! Can every Thing noble, and every Thing base, be lodged together in the same Bosom?' Lady *Bellaston*, and the ignominious Circumstance of having been *kept*, rose again in his Mind, and stopt his Mouth from any Reply. 'Could I have expected,' proceeded *Sophia*, 'such Treatment from you? Nay from any Gentleman, from any Man of Honour? To have my Name traduced in Public; in Inns, among the meanest Vulgar! To have any little Favours that my unguarded Heart may have too lightly betrayed me to grant, boasted of there! Nay, even to hear that you had been forced to fly from my Love!'

Nothing could equal *Jones*'s Surprize at these Words of *Sophia*; but yet, not being guilty, he was much less embarrassed how to defend himself, than if she had touched that tender String, at which his Conscience had been alarmed. By some Examination he presently found, that her supposing him guilty of so shocking an

Outrage against his Love, and her Reputation, was entirely owing to *Partridge*'s Talk at the Inns, before Landlords and Servants; for *Sophia* confessed to him, it was from them that she received her Intelligence. He had no very great Difficulty to make her believe that he was entirely innocent of an Offence so foreign to his Character; but she had a great deal to hinder him from going instantly home, and putting *Partridge* to Death, which he more than once swore he would do. This Point being cleared up, they soon found themselves so well pleased with each other, that *Jones* quite forgot he had begun the Conversation with conjuring her to give up all Thoughts of him; and she was in a Temper to have given Ear to a Petition of a very different Nature: For before they were aware, they had both gone so far, that he let fall some Words that sounded like a Proposal of Marriage. To which she replied, 'That, did not her Duty to her Father forbid her to follow her own Inclinations, Ruin with him would be more welcome to her, than the most affluent Fortune with another Man.' At the mention of the Word Ruin he started, let drop her Hand, which he had held for some Time, and striking his Breast with his own, cried out, 'Oh, *Sophia*, can I then ruin thee? No; by Heavens, no! I never will act so base a Part. Dearest *Sophia*, whatever it costs me, I will renounce you; I will give you up: I will tear all such Hopes from my Heart, as are inconsistent with your real Good. My Love I will ever retain, but it shall be in Silence; it shall be at a Distance from you; it shall be in some foreign Land; from whence no Voice, no Sigh of my Despair, shall ever reach and disturb your Ears. And when I am dead'—He would have gone on, but was stopt by a Flood of Tears which *Sophia* let fall in his Bosom, upon which she leaned, without being able to speak one Word. He kissed them off, which, for some Moments, she allowed him to do without any Resistance; but then recollecting herself, gently withdrew out of his Arms; and, to turn the Discourse from a Subject too tender, and which she found she could not support, bethought herself to ask him a Question she never had Time to put to him before, 'How he came into that Room?' He begun to stammer, and would, in all Probability, have raised her Suspicions by the Answer he was going to give, when, at once, the Door opened, and in came Lady *Bellaston*.

Having advanced a few Steps, and seeing *Jones* and *Sophia* together, she suddenly stopt; when after a Pause of a few Moments, recollecting herself with admirable Presence of Mind, she said,— tho' with sufficient Indications of Surprize both in Voice and Countenance—'I thought, Miss *Western*, you had been at the Play?'

Though *Sophia* had no Opportunity of learning of *Jones* by what Means he had discovered her, yet as she had not the least Suspicion of the real Truth, or that *Jones* and Lady *Bellaston* were acquainted, so she was very little confounded: And the less, as the Lady had, in all their Conversations on the Subject, entirely taken her Side against her Father. With very little Hesitation, therefore, she went through the whole Story of what had happened at the Playhouse, and the Cause of her hasty Return.

The length of this Narrative gave Lady *Bellaston* an Opportunity of rallying her Spirits, and of considering in what manner to act. And as the Behaviour of *Sophia* gave her Hopes that *Jones* had not betrayed her, she put on an Air of Good-Humour, and said, 'I should not have broke in so abruptly upon you, Miss *Western,* if I had known you had Company.'

Lady *Bellaston* fixed her eyes on *Sophia* whilst she spoke these Words. To which that poor young Lady, having her Face over-spread with Blushes and Confusion, answered, in a stammering Voice, 'I am sure, Madam, I shall always think the Honour of your Ladyship's Company——' 'I hope, at least,' cries Lady *Bellaston,* 'I interrupt no Business.'—'No, Madam,' answered *Sophia,* 'our Business was at an End. Your Ladyship may be pleased to remember, I have often mentioned the Loss of my Pocket-book, which this Gentleman having very luckily found, was so kind to return it to me with the Bill in it.'

Jones, ever since the Arrival of Lady *Bellaston,* had been ready to sink with Fear. He sat kicking his Heels, playing with his Fingers, and looking more like a Fool, if it be possible, than a young booby Squire, when he is first introduced into a polite Assembly. He began, however, now to recover himself; and taking a Hint from the Behaviour of Lady *Bellaston,* who, he saw, did not intend to claim any Acquaintance with him, he resolved as entirely to affect the Stranger on his Part. He said, 'Ever since he had the Pocket-Book in his Possession, he had used great Dilligence in enquiring out the Lady whose Name was writ in it; but never till that Day could be so fortunate to discover her.'

Sophia had, indeed, mentioned the Loss of her Pocket-Book to Lady *Bellaston;* but as *Jones,* for some Reason or other, had never once hinted to her that it was in his Possession, she believed not one Syllable of what *Sophia* now said, and wonderfully admired the extreme Quickness of the young Lady, in inventing such an Excuse. The Reason of *Sophia*'s leaving the Playhouse met with no better Credit; and though she could not account for the Meeting between these two Lovers, she was firmly persuaded it was not accidental.

With an affected Smile, therefore, she said—'Indeed, Miss *Western,* you have had very good Luck in recovering your Money. Not only as it fell into the Hands of a Gentleman of Honour, but as he happened to discover to whom it belonged. I think you would not consent to have it advertised.—It was great good Fortune, Sir, that you found out to whom the Note belonged.'

'O Madam,' cries *Jones*, 'it was inclosed in a Pocket-Book, in which the young Lady's Name was written.'

'That was very fortunate indeed,' cries the Lady;—'And it was no less so, that you heard Miss *Western* was at my House; for she is very little known.'

Jones had at length perfectly recovered his Spirits; and as he conceived he had now an Opportunity of satisfying *Sophia*, as to the Question she had asked him just before Lady *Bellaston* came in, he proceeded thus: 'Why, Madam,' answered he, 'it was by the luckiest Chance imaginable I made this Discovery. I was mentioning what I had found, and the Name of the Owner, the other Night, to a Lady at the Masquerade, who told me, she believed she knew where I might see Miss *Western*; and if I would come to her House the next Morning, she would inform me. I went according to her Appointment, but she was not at home; nor could I ever meet with her till this Morning, when she directed me to your Ladyship's House. I came accordingly, and did myself the Honour to ask for your Ladyship; and upon my saying that I had very particular Business, a Servant shewed me into this Room; where I had not been long before the young Lady returned from the Play.'

Upon his mentioning the Masquerade, he look'd very slyly at Lady *Bellaston*, without any Fear of being remarked by *Sophia*; for she was visibly too much confounded to make any Observations. This Hint a little alarmed the Lady, and she was silent; when *Jones*, who saw the Agitations of *Sophia's* Mind, resolved to take the only Method of relieving her, which was by retiring: But before he did this, he said, 'I believe, Madam, it is customary to give some Reward on these Occasions;—I must insist on a very high one for my Honesty;—It is, Madam, no less than the Honour of being permitted to pay another Visit here.'

'Sir,' replied the Lady, 'I make no Doubt that you are a Gentleman, and my Doors are never shut to People of Fashion.'

Jones then, after proper Ceremonials, departed, highly to his own Satisfaction, and no less to that of *Sophia*; who was terribly alarmed lest Lady *Bellaston* should discover what she knew already but too well.

Upon the Stairs *Jones* met his old Acquaintance Mrs. *Honour*, who, notwithstanding all she had said against him, was now so well-bred to behave with great Civility. This Meeting proved indeed a lucky Circumstance, as he communicated to her the House where he lodged, with which *Sophia* was unacquainted.

Chapter XII.

In which the Thirteenth Book is concluded.

The elegant Lord *Shaftsbury*[1] somewhere objects to telling too much Truth: By which it may be fairly inferred, that, in some Cases, to lie, is not only excusable but commendable.

And surely there are no Persons who may so properly challenge a Right to this commendable Deviation from Truth, as young Women in the Affair of Love; for which they may plead Precept, Education, and above all, the Sanction, nay, I may say, the Necessity of Custom, by which they are restrained, not from submitting to the honest Impulses of Nature (for that would be a foolish Prohibition) but from owning them.

We are not, therefore, ashamed to say, that our Heroine now pursued the Dictates of the abovementioned Right Honourable Philosopher. As she was perfectly satisfied then, that Lady *Bellaston* was ignorant of the Person of *Jones*, so she determined to keep her in that Ignorance, though at the Expence of a little Fibbing.

Jones had not been long gone, before Lady Bellaston cry'd, 'Upon my Word, a good pretty young Fellow; I wonder who he is: For I don't remember ever to have seen his Face before.'

'Nor I neither, Madam,' cries *Sophia*, 'I must say he behaved very handsomely in relation to my Note.'

'Yes; and he is a very handsome Fellow,' said the Lady; 'don't you think so?'

'I did not take much Notice of him,' answered *Sophia*; but I thought he seemed rather aukward and ungenteel than otherwise.'

'You are extremely right,' cries Lady *Bellaston*: 'You may see, by his Manner, that he hath not kept good Company. Nay, notwithstanding his returning your Note, and refusing the Reward, I almost question whether he is a Gentleman.——I have always observed there is a Something in Persons well-born, which others can never acquire.——I think I will give Orders not to be at Home to him.'

'Nay sure, Madam,' answered *Sophia*, 'one can't suspect after what he hath done:——Besides, if your Ladyship observed him, there was an Elegance in his Discourse, a Delicacy, a Prettiness of Expression that, that—

'I confess,' said Lady *Bellaston*, 'the Fellow hath Words——And indeed, *Sophia*, you must forgive me, indeed you must.'

'I forgive your Ladyship!' said *Sophia*.

1. "An Essay on the Freedom of Wit," sec. II, par. 2 (*Characteristics*, 1727, I,62)—"For we can never do more Injury to Truth, than by discovering [i.e., revealing] too much of it, on some occasions" [to people of limited understanding]. See above, p. 303.

'Yes indeed you must,' answered she laughing; 'for I had a horrible Suspicion when I first came into the Room——I vow you must forgive it; but I suspected it was Mr. *Jones* himself.'

'Did your Ladyship indeed?' cries *Sophia*, blushing, and affecting a Laugh.

'Yes, I vow I did,' answered she, 'I can't imagine what put it into my Head: For, give the Fellow his due, he was genteely drest; which, I think, dear *Sophy*, is not commonly the Case with your Friend.'

'This Raillery,' cries *Sophia*, 'is a little cruel, Lady *Bellaston*, after my Promise to your Ladyship.'

'Not at all, Child,' said the Lady;—'It would have been cruel before; but after you have promised me never to marry without your Father's Consent, in which you know is implied your giving up *Jones*, sure you can bear a little Raillery on a Passion which was pardonable enough in a young Girl in the Country, and of which you tell me you have so entirely got the better. What must I think, my dear *Sophy*, if you cannot bear a little Ridicule even on his Dress? I shall begin to fear you are very far gone indeed; and almost question whether you have dealt ingenuously with me.'

'Indeed, Madam,' cries *Sophia*, 'your Ladyship mistakes me, if you imagine I had any Concern on his Account.'

'On his Account?' answered the Lady: 'You must have mistaken me; I went no farther than his Dress;——for I would not injure your Taste by any other Comparison—I don't imagine, my dear *Sophy*, if your Mr. *Jones* had been such a Fellow as this——'

'I thought,' says *Sophia*, 'your Ladyship had allowed him to be handsome.'—

'Whom, pray?' cried the Lady, hastily.

'Mr. *Jones*,' answered *Sophia*;—and immediately recollecting herself, 'Mr. *Jones*!——no, no; I ask your Pardon;—I mean the Gentleman who was just now here.'

'O *Sophy*! *Sophy*!' cries the Lady; 'this Mr. *Jones*, I am afraid, still runs in your Head.'

'Then upon my Honour, Madam,' said *Sophia*, 'Mr. *Jones* is as entirely indifferent to me, as the Gentleman who just now left us.'

'Upon my Honour,' said Lady *Bellaston*, 'I believe it. Forgive me, therefore, a little innocent Raillery; but I promise you I will never mention his Name any more.'

And now the two Ladies separated, infinitely more to the Delight of *Sophia* than of Lady *Bellaston*, who would willingly have tormented her Rival a little longer, had not Business of more Importance called her away. As for *Sophia*, her Mind was not perfectly easy under this first Practice of Deceit: upon which, when she retired to her Chamber, she reflected with the highest Uneasiness and conscious Shame. Nor could the peculiar Hardship of her Situation, and the Necessity of the Case, at all reconcile her Mind to her Conduct; for the Frame of her Mind was too delicate to bear the Thought of having been guilty of a Falshood, however qualified by Circumstances. Nor did this Thought once suffer her to close her Eyes during the whole succeeding Night.

BOOK XIV.

Containing two Days.

Chapter I.

An Essay to prove that an Author will write the better, for having some Knowledge of the Subject on which he writes.

As several Gentlemen in these Times, by the wonderful Force of Genius only, without the least Assistance of Learning, perhaps, without being well able to read, have made a considerable Figure in the Republic of Letters; the modern Critics, I am told, have lately begun to assert, that all kind of Learning is entirely useless to a Writer; and, indeed, no other than a kind of Fetters on the natural Spriteliness and Activity of the Imagination, which is thus weighed down, and prevented from soaring to those high Flights which otherwise it would be able to reach.

This Doctrine, I am afraid, is, at present, carried much too far: For why should Writing differ so much from all other Arts? the Nimbleness of a Dancing Master is not at all prejudiced by being taught to move; nor doth any Mechanic, I believe, exercise his Tools the worse by having learnt to use them. For my own Part, I cannot conceive that *Homer* or *Virgil* would have writ with more Fire, if, instead of being Masters of all the Learning of their Times, they had been as ignorant as most of the Authors of the present Age. Nor do I believe that all the Imagination, Fire, and Judgment of *Pitt*[1] could have produced those Orations that have made the Senate of *England* in these our Times a Rival in Eloquence to *Greece* and *Rome,* if he had not been so well read in the Writings of *Demosthenes* and *Cicero,* as to have transferred their whole Spirit into his Speeches, and with their Spirit, their Knowledge too.

I would not here be understood to insist on the same Fund of

1. William Pitt (1708–78), schoolmaster of Fielding's at Eton, famed for his oratory and statesmanship. He was created First Earl of Chatham in 1766, and was the father of the even more famous William Pitt (his second and favorite son), who became Prime Minister from 1783 to 1801, and again from 1804 until his death in 1806.

Learning in any of my Bretheren, as *Cicero*[2] persuades us is necessary to the Composition of an Orator. On the contrary, very little
Reading is, I conceive, necessary to the Poet, less to the Critic, and
the least of all to the Politician. For the first, perhaps, *Byshe's*[3] Art
of Poetry, and a few of our modern Poets, may suffice; for the
second, a moderate Heap of Plays; and for the last, an indifferent
Collection of political Journals.

To say the Truth, I require no more than that a Man should have
some little Knowledge of the Subject on which he treats, according
to the old Maxim of Law, *Quam quisque norit artem in eâ se
exerceat.*[4] With this alone a Writer may sometimes do tolerably
well; and indeed without this, all the other Learning in the World
will stand him in little Stead.

For Instance let us suppose that *Homer* and *Virgil, Aristotle* and
Cicero, Thucydides and *Livy* could have met all together, and have
clubbed their several Talents to have composed a Treatise on the
Art of Dancing; I believe it will be readily agreed they could not
have equalled the excellent Treatise which Mr. *Essex*[5] hath given
us on that Subject, entitled, *The Rudiments of genteel Education.*
And, indeed, should the excellent Mr. *Broughton*[6] be prevailed on
to set *Fist* to Paper, and to complete the abovesaid Rudiments, by
delivering down the true Principles of Athletics, I question whether
the World will have any Cause to lament, that none of the great
Writers, either antient or modern, have ever treated about that
noble and useful Art.

To avoid a Multiplicity of Examples in so plain a Case, and to
come at once to my Point, I am apt to conceive, that one Reason
why many *English* Writers have totally failed in describing the
Manners of upper Life, may possibly be, that in Reality they know
nothing of it.

This is a Knowledge unhappily not in the Power of many
Authors to arrive at. Books will give us a very imperfect Idea of it;
nor will the Stage a much better: The fine Gentleman formed upon
reading the former will almost always turn out a Pedant, and he
who forms himself upon the latter, a Coxcomb.

Nor are the Characters drawn from these Models better supported. *Vanbrugh* and *Congreve* copied Nature; but they who copy
them draw as unlike the present Age, as *Hogarth* would do if he was

2. *De Oratore,* Bk. I.
3. Edward Bysshe, *The Art of Poetry*
(1702), mainly a book of quotations arranged by subject (Shakes. Head).
4. "Let anyone who has learned an art
practice it." Cicero, *Tusculan Disputations* I.18, referring to this as a familiar
Greek aphorism (Mutter).
5. John Essex wrote no book by this
title, but Fielding gives the subject of

Essex's first book (*For the Further Improvement of Dancing . . . ,* trans. from
the French, 1710) a title garbled from
his second: *The Young Ladies' Conduct;
or, Rules for Education under Several
Heads, with Instruction upon Dress both
before and after Marriage, and Advice
to Young Wives* (1722).
6. See above, p. 538.

to paint a Rout or a Drum in the Dresses of *Titian* and of *Vandyke*. In short, Imitation here will not do the Business. The Picture must be after Nature herself. A true Knowledge of the World is gained only by Conversation, and the Manners of every Rank must be seen in order to be known.

Now it happens that this higher Order of Mortals is not to be seen, like all the rest of the Human Species, for nothing, in the Streets, Shops, and Coffee-houses: Nor are they shewn like the upper Rank of Animals, for so much a Piece. In short, this is a Sight to which no Persons are admitted, without one or other of these Qualifications, *viz.* either Birth or Fortune, or what is equivalent to both, the honourable Profession of a Gamester. And, very unluckily for the World, Persons so qualified very seldom care to take upon themselves the bad Trade of Writing; which is generally entered upon by the lower and poorer Sort, as it is a Trade which many think requires no Kind of Stock to set up with.

Hence those strange Monsters in Lace and Embroidery, in Silks and Brocades, with vast Wigs and Hoops; which, under the Name of Lords and Ladies, strut the Stage, to the great Delight of Attornies and their Clerks in the Pit, and of the Citizens and their Apprentices in the Galleries; and which are no more to be found in real Life, than the Centaur, the Chimera, or any other Creature of mere Fiction. But to let my Reader into a Secret, this Knowledge of upper Life, though very necessary for preventing Mistakes, is no very great Resource to a Writer whose Province is Comedy, or that Kind of Novels, which, like this I am writing, is of the comic Class.

What Mr. *Pope*[7] says of Women is very applicable to most in this Station, who are indeed so entirely made up of Form and Affectation, that they have no Character at all, at least, none which appears. I will venture to say the highest Life is much the dullest, and affords very little Humour or Entertainment. The various Callings in lower Spheres produce the great Variety of humorous Characters; whereas here, except among the few who are engaged in the Pursuit of Ambition, and the fewer still who have a Relish for Pleasure, all is Vanity and servile Imitation. Dressing and Cards, eating and drinking, bowing and courtesying, make up the Business of their Lives.

Some there are however of this Rank, upon whom Passion exercises its Tyranny, and hurries them far beyond the Bounds which Decorum prescribes; of these, the Ladies are as much distinguished by their noble Intrepidity, and a certain superior Contempt of Reputation, from the frail ones of meaner Degree, as a virtuous Woman of Quality is by the Elegance and Delicacy of her Sentiments from the honest Wife of a Yeoman or Shopkeeper. Lady *Bel-*

7. *Of the Characters of Women: An Epistle to a Lady,* opening lines—"Nothing so true as what you once let fall,   /'Most Women have no Characters at all.' "

laston was of this intrepid Character; but let not my Country Readers conclude from her, that this is the general Conduct of Women of Fashion, or that we mean to represent them as such. They might as well suppose, that every Clergyman was represented by *Thwackum*, or every Soldier by Ensign *Northerton*.

There is not indeed a greater Error than that which universally prevails among the Vulgar, who borrowing their Opinion from some ignorant Satirists, have affixed the Character of Lewdness to these Times. On the contrary, I am convinced there never was less of Love Intrigue carried on among Persons of Condition, than now. Our present Women have been taught by their Mothers to fix their Thoughts only on Ambition and Vanity, and to despise the Pleasures of Love as unworthy their Regard; and being afterwards, by the Care of such Mothers, married without having Husbands, they seem pretty well confirmed in the Justness of those Sentiments; whence they content themselves, for the dull Remainder of Life, with the Pursuit of more innocent, but I am afraid more childish Amusements, the bare Mention of which would ill suit with the Dignity of this History. In my humble Opinion, the true Characteristic of the present *Beau Monde,* is rather Folly than Vice, and the only Epithet which it deserves is that of *Frivolous.*

Chapter II.

Containing Letters and other Matters which attend Amours.

Jones had not long been at Home, before he received the following Letter.

'I was never more surprized than when I found you was gone. When you left the Room, I little imagined you intended to have left the House without seeing me again. Your Behaviour is all of a Piece, and convinces me how much I ought to despise a Heart which can doat upon an Idiot; though I know not whether I should not admire her Cunning more than her Simplicity: Wonderful both! For though she understood not a Word of what passed between us, she yet had the Skill, the Assurance, the——what shall I call it? to deny to my Face, that she knows you, or ever saw you before.——Was this a Scheme laid between you, and have you been base enough to betray me?——O how I despise her, you, and all the World, but chiefly myself! for—I dare not write what I should afterwards run mad to read; but remember, I can detest as violently as I have loved.'

Jones had but little Time given him to reflect on this Letter, before a second was brought him from the same Hand; and this, likewise, we shall set down in the precise Words.

'When you consider the Hurry of Spirits in which I must have writ, you cannot be surprized at any Expressions in my former Note.——Yet, perhaps, on Reflection, they were rather too warm. At least I would, if possible, think all owing to the odious Play-house, and to the Impertinence of a Fool, which detained me beyond my Appointment.—How easy is it to think well of those we love?——Perhaps you desire I should think so. I have resolved to see you To-Night; so come to me immediately.

'P. S. I have ordered to be at Home to none but yourself.

'P. S. Mr. *Jones* will imagine I shall assist him in his Defence; for I believe he cannot desire to impose on me more than I desire to impose on myself.

'P.S. Come immediately.'

To the Men of Intrigue I refer the Determination, whether the angry or the tender Letter gave the greatest Uneasiness to *Jones*. Certain it is, he had no violent Inclination to pay any more Visits that Evening, unless to one single Person. However he thought his Honour engaged, and had not this been Motive sufficient, he would not have ventured to blow the Temper of Lady *Bellaston* into that Flame of which he had Reason to think it susceptible, and of which he feared the Consequence might be a Discovery to *Sophia*, which he dreaded. After some discontented Walks therefore about the Room, he was preparing to depart, when the Lady kindly prevented him, not by another Letter, but by her own Presence. She entered the Room very disordered in her Dress, and very discomposed in her Looks, and threw herself into a Chair, where having recovered her Breath, she said,——'You see, Sir, when Women have gone one Length too far, they will stop at none. If any Person would have sworn this to me a Week ago, I would not have believed it of myself.' 'I hope, Madam, said *Jones*, my charming Lady *Bellaston* will be as difficult to believe any thing against one who is so sensi-ble of the many Obligations she hath conferred upon him.' 'Indeed! says she, sensible of Obligations! Did I expect to hear such cold Language from Mr. *Jones*?' 'Pardon me, my dear Angel, said he, if after the Letters I have received, the Terrors of your Anger, though I know not how I have deserved it'——'And have I then, says she with a Smile, so angry a Countenance?—Have I really brought a chiding Face with me?'——'If there be Honour in Man, said he, I have done nothing to merit your Anger.——You remem-ber the Appointment you sent me——I went in Pursuance——'I beseech you, cry'd she, do not run through the odious Recital—— Answer me but one Question, and I shall be easy—Have you not betrayed my Honour to her?—*Jones* fell upon his Knees, and began

to utter the most violent Protestations, when *Partridge* came dancing and capering into the Room, like one drunk with Joy, crying
out, 'She's found! she's found!—Here, Sir, here, she's here,—Mrs.
Honour is upon the Stairs.' 'Stop her a Moment, cries *Jones*,—
Here, Madam, step behind the Bed, I have no other Room nor
Closet, nor Place on Earth to hide you in; sure never was so damn'd
an Accident.'——'D—n'd indeed! said the Lady, as she went to her
Place of Concealment; and, presently afterwards in came Mrs. *Honour*. 'Hey day! says she, Mr. *Jones*, what's the Matter?—That impudent Rascal your Servant, would scarce let me come up Stairs. I hope
he hath not the same Reason to keep me from you as he had at
Upton.—I suppose you hardly expected to see me; but you have certainly bewitched my Lady. Poor dear young Lady! To be sure, I
loves her as tenderly as if she was my own Sister. Lord have Mercy
upon you, if you don't make her a good Husband; and to be sure if
you do not, nothing can be bad enough for you.' *Jones* begged her
only to whisper, for that there was a Lady dying in the next Room.
'A Lady! cries she; ay, I suppose one of your Ladies.—O Mr. *Jones*,
there are too many of them in the World; I believe we are got into
the House of one, for my Lady *Bellaston* I darst to say is no better
than she should be.'—'Hush! hush! cries *Jones*, every Word is overheard in the next Room.' 'I don't care a Farthing, cries *Honour*, I
speaks no Scandal of any one; but to be sure the Servants make no
Scruple of saying as how her Ladyship meets Men at another Place
—where the House goes under the Name of a poor Gentlewoman,
but her Ladyship pays the Rent, and many's the good Thing
besides, they say, she hath of her.'—Here *Jones*, after expressing the
utmost Uneasiness, offered to stop her Mouth,—'Hey day! why
sure Mr. *Jones* you will let me speak, I speaks no Scandal, for I only
says what I heard from others,—and thinks I to myself much good
may it do the Gentlewoman with her Riches, if she comes by it in
such a wicked Manner. To be sure it is better to be poor and
honest.' 'The Servants are Villains, cries *Jones*, and abuse their
Lady unjustly.—'Ay to be sure Servants are always Villains, and so
my Lady says, and won't hear a Word of it.'—'No, I am convinced,
says *Jones*, my *Sophia* is above listening to such base Scandal.' 'Nay,
I believe it is no Scandal neither, cries *Honour*, for why should she
meet Men at another House?—It can never be for any Good: For if
she had a lawful Design of being courted, as to be sure any Lady
may lawfully give her Company to Men upon that Account; why
where can be the Sense'—'I protest, cries *Jones*, I can't hear all this
of a Lady of such Honour, and a Relation of *Sophia*; Besides you
will distract the poor Lady in the next Room.——Let me intreat
you to walk with me down Stairs.'—'Nay, Sir, if you won't let me
speak, I have done—Here, Sir, is a Letter from my young Lady,—
what would some Men give to have this? But, Mr. *Jones*, I think

you are not over and above generous, and yet I have heard some Servants say—but I am sure you will do me the Justice to own I never saw the Colour of your Money.' Here *Jones* hastily took the Letter, and presently after slip'd five Pieces into her Hand. He then returned a thousand Thanks to his dear *Sophia* in a Whisper, and begged her to leave him to read her Letter; she presently departed, not without expressing much grateful Sense of his Generosity.

Lady *Bellaston* now came from behind the Curtain. How shall I describe her Rage? Her Tongue was at first incapable of Utterance; but Streams of Fire darted from her Eyes, and well indeed they might, for her Heart was all in a Flame. And now as soon as her Voice found Way, instead of expressing any Indignation against *Honour*, or her own Servants, she began to attack poor *Jones*. 'You see, said she, what I have sacrificed to you, my Reputation, my Honour,—gone for ever! And what Return have I found? Neglected, slighted for a Country Girl, for an Idiot.'—'What Neglect, Madam, or what Slight, cries *Jones*, have I been guilty of? —'Mr. *Jones*, said she, it is in vain to dissemble, if you will make me easy, you must entirely give her up; and as a Proof of your Intention, shew me the Letter.'————'What Letter, Madam? said *Jones*. 'Nay, surely, said she, you cannot have the Confidence to deny your having received a Letter by the Hands of that Trollop.' 'And can your Ladyship, cries he, ask of me what I must part with my Honour before I grant? Have I acted in such a Manner by your Ladyship? Could I be guilty of betraying this poor innocent Girl to you, what Security could you have, that I should not act the same Part by yourself? A Moment's Reflection will, I am sure, convince you, that a Man with whom the Secrets of a Lady are not safe, must be the most contemptible of Wretches.' 'Very well, said she —I need not insist on your becoming this contemptible Wretch in your own Opinion; for the Inside of the Letter could inform me of nothing more than I know already. I see the Footing you are upon.' —Here ensued a long Conversation, which the Reader, who is not too curious, will thank me for not inserting at length. It shall suffice therefore to inform him, that Lady *Bellaston* grew more and more pacified, and at length believed, or affected to believe, his Protestations, that his meeting with *Sophia* that Evening was merely accidental, and every other Matter which the Reader already knows, and which as *Jones* set before her in the strongest Light, it is plain that she had in Reality no Reason to be angry with him.

She was not however in her Heart perfectly satisfied with his Refusal to shew her the Letter; so deaf are we to the clearest Reason, when it argues against our Prevailing Passions. She was indeed well convinced that *Sophia* possessed the first Place in *Jones*'s Affections; and yet, haughty and amorous as this Lady was, she submitted at last to bear the second Place; or to express it more properly in a legal Phrase, was contented with the Possession of that of which another Woman had the Reversion.

It was at length agreed, that *Jones* should for the future visit at the House: For that *Sophia*, her Maid, and all the Servants would place these Visits to the Account of *Sophia*; and that she herself would be considered as the Person imposed upon.

This Scheme was contrived by the Lady, and highly relished by *Jones*, who was indeed glad to have a Prospect of seeing his *Sophia* at any Rate; and the Lady herself was not a little pleased with the Imposition on *Sophia*, which *Jones*, she thought, could not possibly discover to her for his own Sake.

The next Day was appointed for the first Visit, and then, after proper Ceremonials, the Lady *Bellaston* returned Home.

Chapter III.

Containing various Matters.

Jones was no sooner alone, than he eagerly broke open his Letter, and read as follows.

'Sir, it is impossible to express what I have suffered since you left this House; and as I have Reason to think you intend coming here again, I have sent *Honour*, though so late at Night, as she tells me she knows your Lodgings, to prevent you. I charge you, by all the Regard you have for me, not to think of visiting here; for it will certainly be discovered; nay, I almost doubt from some Things which have dropt from her Ladyship, that she is not already without some Suspicion. Something favourable perhaps may happen; we must wait with Patience; but I once more entreat you, if you have any Concern for my Ease, do not think of returning hither.'

This Letter administred the same Kind of Consolation to poor *Jones*, which *Job*[1] formerly received from his Friends. Besides disappointing all the Hopes which he promised to himself from seeing *Sophia*, he was reduced to an unhappy Dilemma, with Regard to Lady *Bellaston*; for there are some certain Engagements, which, as he well knew, do very difficultly admit of any Excuse for the Failure; and to go, after the strict Prohibition from *Sophia*, he was not to be forced by any human Power. At length, after much Deliberation, which during that Night supply'd the Place of Sleep, he determined to feign himself sick: For this suggested itself as the only means of failing the appointed Visit, without incensing Lady *Bellaston*, which he had more than one Reason of desiring to avoid.

The first Thing however which he did in the Morning was to

1. Probably the advice that God would eventually turn up something good for him (viii.20–21), which, along with his friends' other arguments and scoldings, consoles Job not at all.

write an Answer to *Sophia*, which he enclosed in one to *Honour*. He then dispatched another to Lady *Bellaston*, containing the abovementioned Excuse; and to this he soon received the following Answer.

'I am vexed that I cannot see you here this Afternoon, but more concerned for the Occasion; take great Care of yourself, and have the best Advice, and I hope there will be no Danger.—I am so tormented all this Morning with Fools, that I have scarce a Moment's Time to write to you. Adieu.'

'*P. S.* I will endeavour to call on you this Evening at nine.—Be sure to be alone.'

Mr. *Jones* now received a Visit from Mrs. *Miller*, who, after some formal Introduction, began the following Speech. 'I am very sorry, Sir, to wait upon you on such an Occasion; but I hope you will consider the ill Consequence which it must be to the Reputation of my poor Girls, if my House should once be talked of as a House of ill Fame. I hope you won't think me therefore guilty of Impertinence, if I beg you not to bring any more Ladies in at that Time of Night. The Clock had struck two before one of them went away.' 'I do assure you, Madam, said *Jones*, the Lady who was here last Night, and who staid the latest (for the other only brought me a Letter) is a Woman of very great Fashion, and my near Relation.' 'I don't know what Fashion she is of, answered Mrs. *Miller*, but I am sure no Woman of Virtue, unless a very near Relation indeed would visit a young Gentleman at ten at Night, and stay four Hours in his Room with him alone; besides, Sir, the Behaviour of her Chairmen shews what she was; for they did nothing but make Jests all the Evening in the Entry, and asked Mr. *Partridge* in the hearing of my own Maid, if Madam intended to stay with his Master all Night; with a great deal of Stuff not proper to be repeated. I have really a great Respect for you, Mr. *Jones*, upon your own Account, nay I have a very high Obligation to you for your Generosity to my Cousin. Indeed I did not know how very good you had been till lately. Little did I imagine to what dreadful Courses the poor Man's Distress had driven him. Little did I think when you gave me the ten Guineas, that you had given them to a Highwayman! O Heavens! What Goodness have you shewn? How have you preserved this Family.—The Character which Mr. *Allworthy* hath formerly given me of you, was, I find, strictly true.—And indeed if I had no Obligation to you, my Obligations to him are such, that, on his Account, I should shew you the utmost Respect in my Power.— Nay, believe me, dear Mr. *Jones*, if my Daughters and my own Reputation were out of the Case, I should, for your own Sake, be sorry that so pretty a young Gentleman should converse with these Women; but if you are resolved to do it, I must beg you to take another Lodging; for I do not myself like to have such Things carried on under my Roof; but more especially upon the Account of my Girls, who have little, Heaven knows, besides their Characters to recommend them.' *Jones* started and changed Colour at the Name of *Allworthy*. 'Indeed, Mrs. *Miller*, answered he a little warmly, I do not take this at all kind. I will never bring any Slander on your House; but I must insist on seeing what Company I please in my own Room; and if that gives you any Offence, I shall, as soon as I am able, look for another Lodging.' 'I am sorry we must part then, Sir, said she, but I am convinced Mr. *Allworthy* himself would never come within my Doors, if he had the least Suspicion of my keeping an ill House.'—'Very well, Madam,' said *Jones*.—'I hope, Sir, said she, 'you are not angry; for I would not for the World offend any of Mr. *Allworthy*'s Family. I have not slept a wink all Night about this Matter.'—'I am sorry, I have disturbed your Rest, Madam,' said *Jones*, 'but I beg you will send *Partridge* up to me immediately;' which she promised to do, and then with a very low Courtesy retired.

As soon as *Partridge* arrived, *Jones* fell upon him in the most outrageous manner.—'How often,' said he, 'am I to suffer for your Folly, or rather for my own in keeping you? Is that Tongue of yours resolved upon my Destruction?' '—What have I done, Sir?' answered affrighted *Partridge*. 'Who was it gave you Authority to mention the Story of the Robbery, or that the Man you saw here was the Person?'—'I Sir?' cries *Partridge*. 'Now don't be guilty of a Falshood in denying it,' said *Jones*.—'If I did mention such a Matter,' answers *Partridge*, 'I am sure, I thought no Harm: For I should not have opened my Lips, if it had not been to his own Friends and Relations, who, I imagined, would have let it go no farther.' 'But I have a much heavier Charge against you,' cries *Jones*, 'than this. How durst you, after all the Precautions I gave you, mention the Name of Mr. *Allworthy* in this House?' *Partridge* denied that he ever had, with many Oaths. 'How else,' said *Jones*, 'should Mrs. *Miller* be acquainted that there was any Connection between him and me? And it is but this Moment she told me, she respected me on his Account.'—'O Lord, Sir,' said *Partridge*, 'I desire only to be heard out; and to be sure, never was any thing so unfortunate; hear me but out, and you will own how wrongfully you have accused me. When Mrs. *Honour* came down Stairs last Night, she met me in the Entry, and asked me when my Master had heard from Mr. *Allworthy*; and to be sure Mrs. *Miller* heard the very Words; and the Moment Madam *Honour* was gone, she called me into the Parlour to her.' 'Mr. *Partridge*,' says she, 'What Mr. *Allworthy* is that the Gentlewoman mentioned? Is it the great Mr. *Allworthy* of *Somersetshire?*' Upon my Word, Madam,' says I, I know nothing of the Matter.'—'Sure, says she, 'Your Master is not the Mr. *Jones* I have heard Mr. *Allworthy* talk of?' Upon my Word, Madam,' says I, I know nothing of the Matter.'—'Then,' says she, turning to her Daughter *Nancy*, says she, 'as sure as ten Pence this is the very young Gentleman, and he agrees exactly with the Squire's Description.' 'The Lord above knows who it was told her; for I am the arrantest Villain that ever walked upon two Legs if ever it came out of my Mouth.—I promise you, Sir, I can keep a Secret when I am desired.—Nay, Sir, so far was I from telling her any thing about Mr. *Allworthy*, that I told her the very direct contrary: For though I did not contradict it at that Moment, yet, as second Thoughts, they say, are best; so when I came to consider that some Body must have informed her, thinks I to myself, I will put an End to the Story; and so I went back again into the Parlour some Time afterwards, and says I, Upon my Word, says I, whoever, says I, told you that this Gentleman was Mr. *Jones*; that is, says I, that this Mr. *Jones* was that Mr. *Jones*, told you a confounded Lie: And I beg, says I, you will never mention any such Matter, says I; for my Master, says I, will think I must have told you so; and I defy any Body in the House, ever to say, I mentioned any such Word. To be certain, Sir, it is a wonderful Thing, and I have been thinking with myself ever since, how it was she came to know it; not but I saw an old Woman here t'other Day a begging at the Door, who looked as like her we saw in *Warwickshire*, that caused all that Mischief to us. To be sure it is never good to pass by an old Woman without giving her something, especially if she looks at you; for all the World shall never persuade me but that they have a great Power to do Mischief, and to be sure I shall never see an old Woman again, but I shall think to myself, *Infandum, Regina, jubes renovare Dolorem.*[2]

The Simplicity of *Partridge* set *Jones* a laughing, and put a final End to his Anger, which had indeed seldom any long Duration in his Mind; and instead of commenting on his Defence, he told him he intended presently to leave those Lodgings, and ordered him to go and endeavour to get him others.

Chapter IV.

Which we hope will be very attentively perused by young People of both Sexes.

Partridge had no sooner left Mr. *Jones*, than Mr. *Nightingale*, with whom he had now contracted a great Intimacy, came to him, and after a short Salutation, said, 'So, *Tom*, I hear you had Company very late last Night. Upon my Soul, you are a happy Fellow,

2. See above, p. 322.

who have not been in Town above a Fortnight, and can keep
Chairs waiting at your Door till two in the Morning.' He then ran
on with much common-place Raillery of the same Kind, till *Jones*
at last interrupted him, saying, 'I suppose you have received all this
Information from Mrs. *Miller*, who hath been up here a little while
ago to give me Warning. The good Woman is afraid, it seems, of
the Reputation of her Daughters.' 'O she is wonderfully nice,' says
Nightingale, 'upon that Account; if you remember, she would not
let *Nancy* go with us to the Masquerade.' 'Nay, upon my Honour, I
think she's in the Right of it,' says *Jones*; 'however I have taken her
at her Word, and have sent *Partridge* to look for another Lodging.'
'If you will,' says *Nightingale*, 'we may, I believe, be again together;
for to tell you a Secret, which I desire you won't mention in the
Family, I intend to quit the House to-day.'—'What, hath Mrs.
Miller given you Warning too, my Friend?' cries *Jones*. 'No,'
answered the other; 'but the Rooms are not convenient enough.—
Besides, I am grown weary of this Part of the Town. I want to be
nearer the Places of Diversion; so I am going to *Pall-mall*.'—'And
do you intend to make a Secret of your going away?' said *Jones*. 'I
promise you,' answered *Nightingale*, 'I don't intend to bilk my
Lodgings; but I have a private Reason for not taking a formal
Leave.' 'Not so private,' answered *Jones*; 'I promise you, I have seen
it ever since the second Day of my coming to the House.—Here
will be some wet Eyes on your Departure.—Poor *Nancy*, I pity her,
faith!—Indeed, *Jack*, you have play'd the Fool with that Girl.—You
have given her a Longing, which, I am afraid, Nothing will ever
cure her of.'—*Nightingale* answered, 'What the Devil would you
have me do? Would you have me marry her to cure her?'—'No,'
answered *Jones*, 'I would not have had you make Love to her, as
you have often done in my Presence. I have been astonished at the
Blindness of her Mother in never seeing it.' 'Pugh, see it!' cries
Nightingale, 'What the Devil should she see?' 'Why see,' said
Jones, 'that you have made her Daughter distractedly in Love with
you. The poor Girl cannot conceal it a Moment, her Eyes are never
off from you, and she always colours every Time you come into the
Room. Indeed, I pity her heartily; for she seems to be one of the
best natured, and honestest of human Creatures.' 'And so,'
answered *Nightingale*, 'according to your Doctrine, one must not
amuse one's self by any common Gallantries with Women, for fear
they should fall in Love with us.' 'Indeed, *Jack*,' said *Jones*, 'you
wilfully misunderstand me; I do not fancy Women are so apt to fall
in Love; but you have gone far beyond common Gallantries.'—
'What, do you suppose,' says *Nightingale*, 'that we have been a-bed
together?' 'No, upon my Honour,' answered *Jones*, very seriously, 'I
do not suppose so ill of you; nay, I will go farther, I do not imagine
you have laid a regular premeditated Scheme for the Destruction of

the Quiet of a poor little Creature, or have even foreseen the Consequence: For I am sure thou art a very good natured Fellow; and such a one can never be guilty of a Cruelty of that Kind; But at the same Time you have pleased your own Vanity, without considering that this poor Girl was made a Sacrifice to it; and while you have had no Design but of amusing an idle Hour, you have actually given her Reason to flatter herself, that you had the most serious Designs in her Favour. Prithee, *Jack*, answer me honestly: To what have tended all those elegant and luscious Descriptions of Happiness arising from violent and mutual Fondness; all those warm Professions of Tenderness, and generous, disinterested Love? Did you imagine she would not apply them? Or, speak ingenuously, did not you intend she should?' 'Upon my Soul, *Tom*,' cries *Nightingale*, 'I did not think this was in thee. Thou wilt make an admirable Parson —So, I suppose, you would not go to Bed to *Nancy* now, if she would let you?'—'No,' cries *Jones*, 'may I be d—n'd if I would.' '*Tom*, *Tom*,' answered *Nightingale*, 'last Night; remember last Night.

—When ev'ry Eye was clos'd, and the pale Moon,
And silent Stars shone conscious of the Theft.'[1]

'Lookee, Mr. *Nightingale*,' said *Jones*, 'I am no canting Hypocrite, nor do I pretend to the Gift of Chastity, more than my Neighbours. I have been guilty with Women, I own it; but am not conscious that I have ever injured any—Nor would I, to procure Pleasure to myself, be knowingly the Cause of Misery to any human Being.'

'Well, well,' said *Nightingale*, 'I believe you, and I am convinced you acquit me of any such Thing.'

'I do, from my Heart,' answered *Jones*, 'of having debauched the Girl, but not from having gained her Affections.'

'If I have,' said *Nightingale*, 'I am sorry for it; but Time and Absence will soon wear off such Impressions. It is a Receipt I must take myself: For to confess the Truth to you,—I never liked any Girl half so much in my whole Life; but I must let you into the whole Secret, *Tom*. My Father hath provided a Match for me, with a Woman I never saw; and she is now coming to Town, in order for me to make my Addresses to her.'

At these Words *Jones* burst into a loud Fit of Laughter; when *Nightingale* cried,—'Nay, prithee don't turn me into Ridicule. The Devil take me if I am not half mad about this Matter! my poor *Nancy*! Oh *Jones*, *Jones*, I wish I had a Fortune in my own Possession.'

---

1. Nicholas Rowe, *The Fair Penitent* (1703) I.i—"When ev'ry Eye was clos'd, and the pale Moon / And Stars alone, shone conscious of the Theft, / ..." Lothario is telling of his theft of Calista's chastity by climbing into her room, and bed.

'I heartily wish you had,' cries *Jones*; 'for if this be the Case, I sincerely pity you both: But surely you don't intend to go away without taking your Leave of her?'

'I would not,' answered *Nightingale*, 'undergo the Pain of taking Leave for ten thousand Pound; besides, I am convinced, instead of answering any good Purpose, it would only serve to inflame my poor *Nancy* the more. I beg therefore, you would not mention a Word of it To-day, and in the Evening, or To-morrow Morning, I intend to depart.'

Jones promised he would not; and said, upon Reflection he thought, as he had determined and was obliged to leave her, he took the most prudent Method. He then told *Nightingale*, he should be very glad to lodge in the same House with him; and it was accordingly agreed between them, that *Nightingale* should procure him either the Ground Floor, or the two Pair of Stairs; for the young Gentleman himself was to occupy that which was between them.

This *Nightingale*, of whom we shall be presently obliged to say a little more, was in the ordinary Transactions of Life a Man of strict Honour, and what is more rare among young Gentlemen of the Town, one of strict Honesty too; yet in Affairs of Love he was somewhat loose in his Morals; not that he was even here as void of Principle as Gentlemen sometimes are, and oftener affect to be; but it is certain he had been guilty of some indefensible Treachery to Women, and had in a certain Mystery, called *Making Love*, practised many Deceits, which, if he had used in Trade he would have been counted the greatest Villain upon Earth.

But as the World, I know not well for what Reason, agree to see this Treachery in a better Light, he was so far from being ashamed of his Iniquities of this Kind, that he gloried in them, and would often boast of his Skill in gaining of Women, and his Triumphs over their Hearts, for which he had before this Time received some Rebukes from *Jones*, who always exprest great Bitterness against any Misbehaviour to the fair Part of the Species, who, if considered, he said, as they ought to be, in the Light of the dearest Friends, were to be cultivated, honoured, and caressed with the utmost Love and Tenderness; but, if regarded as Enemies, were a Conquest of which a Man ought rather to be ashamed than to value himself upon it.

Chapter V.

A *short Account of the History of* Mrs. Miller.

Jones this Day eat a pretty good Dinner for a sick Man, that is to say, the larger Half of a Shoulder of Mutton. In the Afternoon he received an Invitation from Mrs. *Miller* to drink Tea: For that good Woman having learnt, either by Means of *Partridge*, or by some other Means natural or supernatural, that he had a Connection with Mr. *Allworthy*, could not endure the Thoughts of parting with him in an angry Manner.

Jones accepted the Invitation; and no sooner was the Tea-kettle removed, and the Girls sent out of the Room, than the Widow, without much Preface, began as follows: 'Well, there are very surprizing Things happen in this World; but certainly it is a wonderful Business, that I should have a Relation of Mr. *Allworthy* in my House, and never know any Thing of the Matter. Alas! Sir, you little imagine what a Friend that best of Gentlemen hath been to me and mine. Yes, Sir, I am not ashamed to own it; it is owing to his Goodness, that I did not long since perish for Want, and leave my poor little Wretches, two destitute, helpless, friendless Orphans, to the Care, or rather to the Cruelty of the World.

'You must know, Sir, though I am now reduced to get my Living by letting Lodgings, I was born and bred a Gentlewoman. My Father was an Officer of the Army, and died in a considerable Rank: But he lived up to his Pay; and as that expired with him, his Family, at his Death, became Beggars. We were three Sisters. One of us had the good Luck to die soon after of the Small-pox: A Lady was so kind as to take the second out of Charity, as she said, to wait upon her. The Mother of this Lady had been a Servant to my Grandmother; and having inherited a vast Fortune from her Father, which he had got by Pawnbroking, was married to a Gentleman of great Estate and Fashion. She used my Sister so barbarously, often upbraiding her with her Birth and Poverty, calling her in Derision a Gentlewoman, that I believe she at length broke the Heart of the poor Girl. In short, she likewise died within a Twelvemonth after my Father. Fortune thought proper to provide better for me, and within a Month from his Decease I was married to a Clergyman, who had been my Lover a long Time before, and who had been very ill-used by my Father on that Account: For though my poor Father could not give any of us a Shilling, yet he bred us up as delicately, considered us, and would have had us consider ourselves as highly, as if we had been the richest Heiresses. But my dear Husband forgot all this Usage, and the Moment we were become fatherless, he immediately renewed his Addresses to me so warmly, that I, who always liked, and now more than ever esteemed him, soon comply'd. Five Years did I live in a State of perfect Happiness with that best of Men, 'till at last—Oh! cruel, cruel Fortune that ever separated us, that deprived me of the kindest of Husbands, and my poor Girls of the tenderest Parent.—O my poor Girls! you never knew the Blessing which ye lost.—I am ashamed, Mr. *Jones*, of this womanish Weakness; but I shall never mention him without Tears.'—'I ought rather, Madam,' said *Jones*, 'to be ashamed that I do not accompany you.'—'Well, Sir,' continued she, 'I was now left a second Time in a much worse Condition than before; besides the terrible Affliction I was to encounter, I had now two Children to provide for; and was, if possible, more pennyless than ever, when that great, that good, that glorious Man, Mr. *Allworthy*, who had some little Acquaintance with my Husband, accidentally heard of my Distress, and immediately writ this Letter to me. Here, Sir,—here it is; I put it into my Pocket to show it you. This is the Letter, Sir; I must and will read it to you.

"Madam,

I Heartily condole with you on your late grievous Loss, which your own good Sense, and the excellent Lessons you must have learnt from the worthiest of Men, will better enable you to bear, than any Advice which I am capable of giving. Nor have I any Doubt that you, whom I have heard to be the tenderest of Mothers, will suffer any immoderate Indulgence of Grief to prevent you from discharging your Duty to those poor Infants, who now alone stand in Need of your Tenderness.

"However, as you must be supposed at present to be incapable of much worldly Consideration, you will pardon my having ordered a Person to wait on you, and to pay you Twenty Guineas, which I beg you will accept 'till I have the Pleasure of seeing you, and believe me to be, Madam, *&c.*"

'This Letter, Sir, I received within a Fortnight after the irreparable Loss I have mentioned, and within a Fortnight afterwards, Mr. *Allworthy*,—the blessed Mr. *Allworthy*, came to pay me a Visit, when he placed me in the House where you now see me, gave me a large Sum of Money to furnish it, and settled an Annuity of 50*l.* a Year upon me, which I have constantly received ever since. Judge then, Mr. *Jones*, in what Regard I must hold a Benefactor, to whom I owe the Preservation of my Life, and of those dear Children, for whose Sake alone my Life is valuable.—Do not, therefore, think me impertinent, Mr. *Jones*, (since I must esteem one for whom I know Mr. *Allworthy* hath so much Value) if I beg you not to converse with these wicked Women. You are a young Gentleman, and do not know half their artful Wiles. Do not be angry with me, Sir, for what I said upon account of my House; you must be sensible it would be the Ruin of my poor dear Girls. Besides, Sir, you cannot but be acquainted, that Mr. *Allworthy* himself would never forgive my conniving at such Matters, and particularly with you.'

'Upon my Word, Madam,' said *Jones*, 'you need make no farther

Apology; nor do I in the least take any Thing ill you have said: But give me Leave, as no one can have more Value than myself for Mr. *Allworthy*, to deliver you from one Mistake, which, perhaps, would not be altogether for his Honour: I do assure you, I am no Relation of his.'

'Alas! Sir,' answered she, 'I know you are not. I know very well who you are; for Mr. *Allworthy* hath told me all: But I do assure you, had you been twenty Times his Son, he could not have expressed more Regard for you, than he hath often expressed in my Presence. You need not be ashamed, Sir, of what you are; I promise you no good Person will esteem you the less on that Account. No, Mr. *Jones*; the Words 'dishonourable Birth' are Nonsense, as my dear dear Husband used to say, unless the Word 'Dishonourable' be applied to the Parents; for the Children can derive no real Dishonour from an Act of which they are intirely innocent.'

Here *Jones* heaved a deep Sigh, and then said, 'Since I perceive, Madam, you really do know me, and Mr. *Allworthy* hath thought proper to mention my Name to you; and since you have been so explicit with me as to your own Affairs, I will acquaint you with some more Circumstances concerning myself.' And these Mrs. *Miller* having expressed great Desire and Curiosity to hear, he began and related to her his whole History, without once mentioning the Name of *Sophia*.

There is a Kind of Sympathy in honest Minds, by Means of which they give an easy Credit to each other. Mrs. *Miller* believed all which *Jones* told her to be true, and exprest much Pity and Concern for him. She was beginning to comment on the Story, but *Jones* interrupted her: For as the Hour of Assignation now drew nigh, he began to stipulate for a second Interview with the Lady that Evening, which he promised should be the last at her House; swearing, at the same Time, that she was one of great Distinction, and that nothing but what was intirely innocent was to pass between them; and I do firmly believe he intended to keep his Word.

Mrs. *Miller* was at length prevailed on, and *Jones* departed to his Chamber, where he sat alone till Twelve o'Clock, but no Lady *Bellaston* appeared.

As we have said that this Lady had a great Affection for *Jones*, and as it must have appeared that she really had so, the Reader may perhaps wonder at the first Failure of her Appointment, as she apprehended him to be confined by Sickness, a Season when Friendship seems most to require such Visits. This Behaviour, therefore, in the Lady, may, by some, be condemned as unnatural; but that is not our Fault; for our Business is only to record Truth.

Chapter VI.

Containing a Scene which we doubt not will affect all our Readers.

Mr. *Jones* closed not his Eyes during all the former Part of the Night; not owing it to any Uneasiness which he conceived at being disappointed by Lady *Bellaston*; nor was *Sophia* herself, though most of his waking Hours were justly to be charged to her Account, the present Cause of dispelling his Slumbers. In Fact, poor *Jones* was one of the best-natured Fellows alive, and had all that Weakness which is called Compassion, and which distinguishes this imperfect Character from that noble Firmness of Mind, which rolls a Man, as it were, within himself, and, like a polished Bowl,[1] enables him to run through the World, without being once stopped by the Calamities which happen to others. He could not help, therefore, compassionating the Situation of poor *Nancy*, whose Love for Mr. *Nightingale* seemed to him so apparent, that he was astonished at the Blindness of her Mother, who had more than once, the preceding Evening, remarked to him the great Change in the Temper of her Daughter, 'who from being,' she said, 'one of the liveliest, merriest Girls in the World, was, on a sudden, become all Gloom and Melancholy.'

Sleep, however, at length got the better of all Resistance; and now, as if he had really[2] been a Deity, as the Antients imagined, and an offended one too, he seemed to enjoy his dear-bought Conquest. To speak simply, and without any Metaphor, Mr. *Jones* slept 'till Eleven the next Morning, and would, perhaps, have continued in the same quiet Situation much longer, had not a violent Uproar awakened him.

Partridge was now summoned, who, being asked what was the Matter, answered, 'That there was a dreadful Hurricane below Stairs; that Miss *Nancy* was in Fits; and that the other Sister, and the Mother, were both crying and lamenting over her.' *Jones* expressed much Concern at this News, which *Partridge* endeavoured to relieve, by saying, with a Smile, 'He fancied the young Lady was in no Danger of Death; for that *Susan* (which was the Name of the Maid) had given him to understand, it was nothing more than a common Affair. In short,' said he, 'Miss *Nancy* hath had a Mind to be as wise as her Mother; that's all. She was a little hungry, it seems, and so sat down to Dinner before Grace was said; and so there is a Child coming for the *Foundling-Hospital*.'—'Pri-

1. See above, p. 358.
2. The fourth edition reads "already" here and "dressed" below (p. 584, line 5), obviously the type-setter's misreadings of the "really" and "dressing" in the first three editions.

thee leave thy stupid jesting,' cries *Jones*, 'Is the Misery of these poor Wretches a Subject of Mirth? Go immediately to Mrs. *Miller*, and tell her, I beg Leave—Stay, you will make some Blunder; I will go myself; for she desired me to breakfast with her.' He then rose, and dressed himself as fast as he could: And while he was dressing,[3] *Partridge*, notwithstanding many severe Rebukes, could not avoid throwing forth certain Pieces of Brutality, commonly called Jests, on this Occasion. *Jones* was no sooner dressed than he walked down Stairs, and knocking at the Door was presently admitted, by the Maid, into the outward Parlour, which was as empty of Company as it was of any Apparatus for eating. Mrs. *Miller* was in the inner Room with her Daughter, whence the Maid presently brought a Message to Mr. *Jones*, 'that her Mistress hoped he would excuse the Disappointment, but an Accident had happened, which made it impossible for her to have the pleasure of his Company at Breakfast that Day; and begged his Pardon for not sending him up Notice sooner.' *Jones* 'desired she would give herself no Trouble about any Thing so trifling as his Disappointment; that he was heartily sorry for the Occasion; and that if he could be of any Service to her, she might command him.'

He had scarce spoke these Words, when Mrs. *Miller*, who heard them all, suddenly threw open the Door, and coming out to him, in a Flood of Tears, said, 'O Mr. *Jones*, you are certainly one of the best young Men alive. I give you a thousand Thanks for your kind Offer of your Service; but, alas! Sir, it is out of your Power to preserve my poor Girl.—O my Child, my Child! She is undone, she is ruined for ever!' 'I hope, Madam,' said *Jones*, 'no Villain'—'O Mr. *Jones*,' said she, 'that Villain who Yesterday left my Lodgings, hath betrayed my poor Girl; hath destroyed her,—I know you are a Man of Honour. You have a good—a noble Heart, Mr. *Jones*. The Actions to which I have been myself a Witness, could proceed from no other. I will tell you all: Nay, indeed, it is impossible, after what hath happened, to keep it a Secret. That *Nightingale*, that barbarous Villain, hath undone my Daughter. She is—she is—oh! Mr. *Jones*, my Girl is with Child by him; and in that Condition he hath deserted her. Here! here, Sir, is his cruel Letter; read it Mr. *Jones*, and tell me if such another Monster lives.'

The Letter was as follows.

'*Dear* Nancy,

'As I found it impossible to mention to you what, I am afraid, will be no less shocking to you, than it is to me, I have taken this Method to inform you, that my Father insists upon my immediately paying my Addresses to a young Lady of Fortune, whom he

3. See note 2, p. 583.

hath provided for my—I need not write the detested Word. Your own good Understanding will make you sensible, how entirely I am obliged to an Obedience, by which I shall be for ever excluded from your dear Arms. The Fondness of your Mother may encourage you to trust her with the unhappy Consequence of our Love, which may be easily kept a Secret from the World, and for which I will take Care to provide, as I will for you. I wish you may feel less on this Account than I have suffered: But summon all your Fortitude to your Assistance, and forgive and forget the Man, whom Nothing but the Prospect of certain Ruin could have forced to write this Letter. I bid you forget me, I mean only as a Lover; but the best of Friends you shall ever find in

'Your *faithful, though unhappy*

'J. N.'

When *Jones* had read this Letter, they both stood silent during a Minute, looking at each other; at last he began thus. 'I cannot express, Madam, how much I am shocked at what I have read; yet let me beg you, in one Particular, to take the Writer's Advice. Consider the Reputation of your Daughter,'——'It is gone, it is lost, Mr. *Jones*, cry'd she, as well as her Innocence. She received the Letter in a Room-full of Company, and immediately swooning away upon opening it, the Contents were known to every one present. But the Loss of her Reputation, bad as it is, is not the worst; I shall lose my Child; she hath attempted twice to destroy herself already: and though she hath been hitherto prevented, vows she will not out-live it; nor could I myself out-live any Accident of that Nature. —What then will become of my little *Betsy*, a helpless infant Orphan? And the poor little Wretch will, I believe, break her Heart at the Miseries with which she sees her Sister and myself distracted, while she is ignorant of the Cause.—O 'tis the most sensible, and best-natured little Thing. The barbarous cruel——hath destroyed us all. O my poor Children! Is this the Reward of all my Cares? Is this the Fruit of all my Prospects? Have I so chearfully undergone all the Labours and Duties of a Mother? Have I been so tender of their Infancy, so careful of their Education? Have I been toiling so many Years, denying myself even the Conveniencies of Life to provide some little Sustenance for them, to lose one or both in such a manner?' 'Indeed, Madam,' said *Jones*, with Tears in his Eyes, 'I pity you from my Soul.'——'O Mr. *Jones*,' answered she, 'even you, though I know the Goodness of your Heart, can have no Idea of what I feel. The best, the kindest, the most dutiful of Children! O my poor *Nancy*, the Darling of my Soul! the Delight of my Eyes; the Pride of my Heart: Too much, indeed, my Pride; for to those foolish, ambitious Hopes, arising from her Beauty, I owe her Ruin. Alas! I saw with Pleasure the Liking which this young Man had for her. I thought it an honourable Affection; and flattered my foolish Vanity with the Thoughts of seeing her married to one so much her Superior. And a thousand Times in my Presence, nay, often in yours, he hath endeavoured to sooth and encourage these Hopes by the most generous Expressions of disinterested Love, which he hath always directed to my poor Girl, and which I, as well as she, believed to be real. Could I have believed that these were only Snares laid to betray the Innocence of my Child, and for the Ruin of us all?'—At these Words little *Betsy* came running into the Room, crying, 'Dear Mamma, for Heaven's sake come to my Sister; for she is in another Fit, and my Cousin can't hold her.' Mrs. *Miller* immediately obeyed the Summons; but first ordered *Betsy* to stay with Mr. *Jones*, and begged him to entertain her a few Minutes, saying, in the most pathetic Voice, 'Good Heaven! let me preserve one of my Children at least.'

Jones, in Compliance with this Request, did all he could to comfort the little Girl, though he was, in Reality, himself very highly affected with Mrs. *Miller's* Story. He told her, 'her Sister would be soon very well again: That by taking on in that Manner, she would not only make her Sister worse, but make her Mother ill too.' 'Indeed, Sir,' says she, 'I would not do any Thing to hurt them for the World. I would burst my Heart rather than they should see me cry.—But my poor Sister can't see me cry.—I am afraid she will never be able to see me cry any more. Indeed, I can't part with her; indeed I can't.—And then poor Mamma too, what will become of her?—She says she will die too, and leave me: But I am resolved I won't be left behind.' 'And are you not afraid to die, my little *Betsy?*' said *Jones*. 'Yes,' answered she, 'I was always afraid to die; because I must have left my Mamma, and my Sister; but I am not afraid of going any where with those I love.'

Jones was so pleased with this Answer, that he eagerly kissed the Child; and soon after Mrs. *Miller* returned, saying, 'She thanked Heaven, *Nancy* was now come to herself. And now, *Betsy*,' says she, 'you may go in; for your Sister is better, and longs to see you.' She then turned to *Jones*, and began to renew her Apologies for having disappointed him of his Breakfast.

'I hope, Madam,' said *Jones*, 'I shall have a more exquisite Repast than any you could have provided for me. This, I assure you, will be the Case, if I can do any Service to this little Family of Love. But whatever Success may attend my Endeavours, I am resolved to attempt it. I am very much deceived in Mr. *Nightingale*, if, notwithstanding what hath happened, he hath not much Goodness of Heart at the Bottom, as well as a very violent Affection for your Daughter. If this be the Case, I think the Picture which I shall lay before him, will affect him. Endeavour, Madam, to comfort yourself, and Miss *Nancy*, as well as you can. I will go instantly in quest of Mr. *Nightingale*; and I hope to bring you good News.'

Mrs. *Miller* fell upon her Knees, and invoked all the Blessings of Heaven upon Mr. *Jones*; to which she afterwards added the most passionate Expressions of Gratitude. He then departed to find Mr. *Nightingale*, and the good Woman returned to comfort her Daughter, who was somewhat cheared at what her Mother told her; and both joined in resounding the Praises of Mr. *Jones*.

Chapter VII.

The Interview between Mr. Jones and Mr. Nightingale.

The Good or Evil we confer on others, very often, I believe, recoils on ourselves. For as Men of a benign Disposition enjoy their own Acts of Beneficence, equally with those to whom they are done, so there are scarce any Natures so entirely diabolical, as to be capable of doing Injuries, without paying themselves some Pangs, for the Ruin which they bring on their fellow Creatures.

Mr. *Nightingale*, at least, was not such a Person. On the contrary, *Jones* found him in his new Lodgings, sitting melancholy by the Fire, and silently lamenting the unhappy Situation in which he had placed poor *Nancy*. He no sooner saw his Friend appear, than he rose hastily to meet him; and after much Congratulation said, 'Nothing could have been more opportune than this kind Visit; for I was never more in the Spleen in my Life.'

'I am sorry,' answered *Jones*, 'that I bring News very unlikely to relieve you; nay, what I am convinced must, of all other, shock you the most. However, it is necessary you should know it. Without further Preface then, I come to you, Mr. *Nightingale*, from a worthy Family, which you have involved in Misery and Ruin.' Mr. *Nightingale* changed Colour at these Words; but *Jones*, without regarding it, proceeded, in the liveliest Manner, to paint the tragical Story, with which the Reader was acquainted in the last Chapter.

Nightingale never once interrupted the Narration, though he discovered violent Emotions at many Parts of it. But when it was concluded, after fetching a deep Sigh, he said, 'What you tell me, my Friend, affects me in the tenderest Manner. Sure there never was so cursed an Accident as the poor Girl's betraying my Letter. Her Reputation might otherwise have been safe, and the Affair might have remained a profound Secret; and then the Girl might have gone off never the worse; for many such Things happen in this Town: And if the Husband should suspect a little, when it is too late, it will be his wiser Conduct to conceal his Suspicion both from his Wife and the World.'

'Indeed, my Friend,' answered *Jones*, 'this could not have been the Case with your poor *Nancy*. You have so entirely gained her Affections, that it is the Loss of you, and not of her Reputation, which afflicts her, and will end in the Destruction of her and her Family.' 'Nay, for that Matter, I promise you,' cries *Nightingale*, 'she hath my Affections so absolutely, that my Wife, whoever she is to be, will have very little Share in them.' 'And is it possible then,' said *Jones*, 'you can think of deserting her?' 'Why what can I do?' answered the other. 'Ask Miss *Nancy*,' replied *Jones* warmly. 'In the Condition to which you have reduced her, I sincerely think she ought to determine what Reparation you shall make her. Her Interest alone, and not yours, ought to be your sole Consideration. But if you ask me what you shall do? What can you do less,' cries *Jones*, 'than fulfil the Expectations of her Family, and her own. Nay, I sincerely tell you, they were mine too, ever since I first saw you together. You will pardon me, if I presume on the Friendship you have favoured me with, moved as I am with Compassion for those poor Creatures. But your own Heart will best suggest to you, whether you have never intended, by your Conduct, to persuade the Mother, as well as the Daughter, into an Opinion, that you designed honourably: And if so, though there may have been no direct Promise of Marriage in the Case, I will leave to your own good Understanding, how far you are bound to proceed.'

'Nay, I must not only confess what you have hinted,' said *Nightingale*; 'but, I am afraid, even that very Promise you mention I have given.' 'And can you, after owning that,' said *Jones*, 'hesitate a Moment?' 'Consider, my Friend,' answered the other; 'I know you are a Man of Honour, and would advise no one to act contrary to its Rules; if there were no other Objection, can I, after this Publication of her Disgrace, think of such an Alliance with Honour?' 'Undoubtedly,' replied *Jones*, 'and the very best and truest Honour, which is Goodness, requires it of you. As you mention a Scruple of this Kind, you will give me Leave to examine it. Can you, with Honour, be guilty of having, under false Pretences, deceived a young Woman and her Family, and of having, by these Means, treacherously robbed her of her Innocence? Can you, with Honour, be the knowing, the wilful Occasion, nay, the artful Contriver of the Ruin of a human Being? Can you, with Honour, destroy the Fame, the Peace, nay, probably, both the Life and Soul too of this Creature? Can Honour bear the Thought, that this Creature is a tender, helpless, defenceless, young Woman? A young Woman who loves, who doats on you, who dies for you; who hath placed the utmost Confidence in your Promises; and to that Confidence hath sacrificed every Thing which is dear to her? Can Honour support such Contemplations as these a Moment?'

'Common Sense, indeed,' said *Nightingale*, 'warrants all you say; but yet you well know the Opinion of the World is so contrary to it, that was I to marry a Whore, though my own, I should be ashamed of ever showing my Face again.'

'Fie upon it, Mr. *Nightingale*,' said *Jones*, 'do not call her by so ungenerous a Name: When you promised to marry her, she became your Wife; and she hath sinned more against Prudence than Virtue. And what is this World, which you would be ashamed to face, but the Vile, the Foolish, and the Profligate? Forgive me, if I say such a Shame must proceed from false Modesty, which always attends false Honour as its Shadow.—But I am well assured there is not a Man of real Sense and Goodness in the World, who would not honour and applaud the Action. But admit no other would, would not your own Heart, my Friend, applaud it? And do not the warm, rapturous Sensations, which we feel from the Consciousness of an honest, noble, generous, benevolent Action, convey more Delight to the Mind, than the undeserved Praise of Millions? Set the Alternative fairly before your Eyes. On the one Side, see this poor, unhappy, tender, believing Girl, in the Arms of her wretched Mother, breathing her last. Hear her breaking Heart in Agonies, sighing out your Name; and lamenting, rather than accusing, the Cruelty which weighs her down to Destruction. Paint to your Imagination the Circumstances of her fond, despairing Parent, driven to Madness, or, perhaps, to Death, by the Loss of her lovely Daughter. View the poor, helpless, Orphan-Infant: And when your Mind hath dwelt a Moment only on such Ideas, consider yourself as the Cause of all the Ruin of this poor, little, worthy, defenceless Family. On the other Side, consider yourself as relieving them from their temporary Sufferings. Think with what Joy, with what Transports, that lovely Creature will fly to your Arms. See her Blood returning to her pale Cheeks, her Fire to her languid Eyes, and Raptures to her tortured Breast. Consider the Exultations of her Mother, the Happiness of all. Think of this little Family made, by one Act of yours, completely happy. Think of this Alternative, and sure I am mistaken in my Friend, if it requires any long Deliberation, whether he will sink these Wretches down for ever, or, by one generous, noble Resolution, raise them all from the Brink of Misery and Despair, to the highest Pitch of human Happiness. Add to this but one Consideration more; the Consideration that it is your Duty so to do—That the Misery from which you will relieve these poor People, is the Misery which you yourself have wilfully brought upon them.'

'O my dear Friend,' cries *Nightingale*, 'I wanted not your Eloquence to rouse me. I pity poor *Nancy* from my Soul, and would willingly give any Thing in my Power, that no Familiarities had ever passed between us. Nay, believe me, I had many Struggles with my Passion before I could prevail with myself to write that cruel Letter, which hath caused all the Misery in that unhappy Family. If I had no Inclinations to consult but my own, I would marry her To-morrow Morning: I would, by Heaven; but you will easily imagine how impossible it would be to prevail on my Father to consent to such a Match; besides, he hath provided another for me; and To-morrow, by his express Command, I am to wait on the Lady.'

'I have not the Honour to know your Father,' said *Jones*; 'but suppose he could be persuaded, would you yourself consent to the only Means of preserving these poor People?' 'As eagerly as I would pursue my Happiness,' answered *Nightingale*; 'for I never shall find it in any other Woman.—O my dear Friend, could you imagine what I have felt within these twelve Hours for my poor Girl, I am convinced she would not engross all your Pity. Passion leads me only to her; and if I had any foolish Scruples of Honour, you have fully satisfied them: Could my Father be induced to comply with my Desires, nothing would be wanting to compleat my own Happiness, or that of my *Nancy*.'

'Then I am resolved to undertake it,' said *Jones*. 'You must not be angry with me, in whatever Light it may be necessary to set this Affair, which, you may depend on it, could not otherwise be long hid from him: For Things of this Nature make a quick Progress, when once they get abroad, as this unhappily hath already. Besides, should any fatal Accident follow, as upon my Soul I am afraid will, unless immediately prevented, the Publick would ring of your Name in a Manner which, if your Father hath common Humanity, must offend him. If you will therefore tell me where I may find the old Gentleman, I will not lose a Moment in the Business; which while I pursue, you cannot do a more generous Action than by paying a Visit to the poor Girl. You will find I have not exaggerated in the Account I have given of the Wretchedness of the Family.'

Nightingale immediately consented to the Proposal; and now having acquainted *Jones* with his Father's Lodging, and the Coffee-house where he would most probably find him, he hesitated a Moment, and then said, 'My dear *Tom*, you are going to undertake an Impossibility. If you knew my Father, you would never think of obtaining his Consent.—Stay, there is one Way—Suppose you told him I was already married, it might be easier to reconcile him to the Fact after it was done; and, upon my Honour, I am so affected with what you have said, and I love my *Nancy* so passionately, I almost wish it was done, whatever might be the Consequence.'

Jones greatly approved the Hint, and promised to pursue it. They then separated, *Nightingale* to visit his *Nancy*, and *Jones* in quest of the old Gentleman.

Chapter VIII.

What passed between Jones *and old Mr.* Nightingale; *with the Arrival of a Person not yet mentioned in this History.*

Notwithstanding the Sentiment of the *Roman* Satirist, which denies the Divinity of *Fortune*,[1] and the Opinion of *Seneca* to the same Purpose; *Cicero*, who was, I believe, a wiser Man than either of them, expresly holds the contrary; and certain it is, there are some Incidents in Life so very strange and unaccountable, that it seems to require more than human Skill and Foresight in producing them.

Of this Kind was what now happened to *Jones*, who found Mr. *Nightingale* the elder in so critical a Minute, that *Fortune*, if she was really worthy all the Worship she received at *Rome*, could not have contrived such another. In short, the old Gentleman and the Father of the young Lady whom he intended for his Son, had been hard at it for many Hours; and the latter was just now gone, and had left the former delighted with the Thoughts that he had succeeded in a long Contention, which had been between the two Fathers of the future Bride and Bridegroom; in which both endeavoured to over-reach the other, and, as it not rarely happens in such Cases, both had retreated fully satisfied of having obtained the Victory.

This Gentleman whom Mr. *Jones* now visited, was what they call a Man of the World; that is to say, a Man who directs his Conduct in this World, as one who being fully persuaded there is no other, is resolved to make the most of this. In his early Years he had been bred to Trade; but having acquired a very good Fortune, he had lately declined his Business; or, to speak more properly, had changed it from dealing in Goods, to dealing only in Money, of which he had always a plentiful Fund at Command, and of which he knew very well how to make a very plentiful Advantage, sometimes of the Necessities of private Men, and sometimes of those of the Public. He had indeed conversed so entirely with Money, that it may be almost doubted, whether he imagined there was any other Thing really existing in the World: This at least may be certainly averred, that he firmly believed nothing else to have any real Value.

The Reader will, I fancy, allow, that Fortune could not have

---

1. Bryant (pp. 216–17) identifies Juvenal, *Satires* X.365–66, who says Fortune would have no divinity if men had wisdom, and didn't themselves put her in the skies (the same idea is found in *Satires* XIV.315–16), but Bryant cannot find it in Seneca. She also points out that Cicero (*De Natura Deorum* III.61) seems to agree that Fortune is not divine: "I cannot understand, without further illumination, why [Fate and Fortune] should be thought divine."

culled out a more improper Person for Mr. *Jones* to attack with any Probability of Success; nor could the whimsical Lady have directed this Attack at a more unseasonable Time.

As Money then was always uppermost in this Gentleman's Thoughts; so the Moment he saw a Stranger within his Doors, it immediately occurred to his Imagination, that such Stranger was either come to bring him Money, or to fetch it from him. And according as one or other of these Thoughts prevailed, he conceived a favourable or unfavourable Idea of the Person who approached him.

Unluckily for *Jones*, the latter of these was the Ascendant at present; for as a young Gentleman had visited him the Day before, with a Bill from his Son for a Play Debt, he apprehended, at the first Sight of *Jones*, that he was come on such another Errand. *Jones* therefore had no sooner told him, that he was come on his Son's Account, than the old Gentleman, being confirmed in his Suspicion, burst forth into an Exclamation, 'That he would lose his Labour.' 'Is it then possible, Sir, answered *Jones*, that you can guess my Business?' 'If I do guess it,' replied the other, 'I repeat again to you, you will lose your Labour. What, I suppose you are one of those Sparks who lead my Son into all those Scenes of Riot and Debauchery, which will be his Destruction; but I shall pay no more of his Bills I promise you. I expect he will quit all such Company for the future. If I had imagined otherwise, I should not have provided a Wife for him; for I would be instrumental in the Ruin of no Body.' 'How, Sir,' said *Jones*, 'and was this Lady of your providing?' 'Pray, Sir,' answered the old Gentleman, 'how comes it to be any Concern of yours?'—'Nay, dear Sir,' replied *Jones*, 'be not offended that I interest myself in what regards your Son's Happiness, for whom I have so great an Honour and Value. It was upon that very Account I came to wait upon you. I can't express the Satisfaction you have given me by what you say; for I do assure you your Son is a Person for whom I have the highest Honour.—Nay, Sir, it is not easy to express the Esteem I have for you, who could be so generous, so good, so kind, so indulgent to provide such a Match for your Son; a Woman who, I dare swear, will make him one of the happiest Men upon Earth.'

There is scarce any thing which so happily introduces Men to our good Liking, as having conceived some Alarm at their first Appearance; when once those Apprehensions begin to vanish, we soon forget the Fears which they occasioned, and look on ourselves as indebted for our present Ease, to those very Persons who at first rais'd our Fears.

Thus it happened to *Nightingale*, who no sooner found that *Jones* had no Demand on him, as he suspected, than he began to be pleased with his Presence. 'Pray, good Sir, said he, be pleased to sit

down. I do not remember to have ever had the Pleasure of seeing
you before; but if you are a Friend of my Son, and have any thing
to say concerning this young Lady, I shall be glad to hear you. As to
her making him happy, it will be his own Fault if she doth not. I
have discharged my Duty, in taking Care of the main Article. She
will bring him a Fortune capable of making any reasonable, prudent,
sober man happy.' 'Undoubtedly, cries *Jones*, for she is in herself a
Fortune; so beautiful, so genteel, so sweet-tempered, and so well
educated; she is indeed a most accomplished young Lady; sings
admirably well, and hath a most delicate Hand at the Harpsichord.'
'I did not know any of these Matters, answered the old Gentleman,
for I never saw the Lady; but I do not like her the worse for what
you tell me; and I am the better pleased with her Father for not
laying any Stress on these Qualifications in our Bargain. I shall
always think it a Proof of his Understanding. A silly Fellow would
have brought in these Articles as an Addition to her Fortune; but to
give him his due, he never mentioned any such Matter; though to
be sure they are no Disparagements to a Woman.' 'I do assure you,
Sir, cries *Jones*, she hath them all in the most eminent Degree: For
my Part I own I was afraid you might have been a little backward, a
little less inclined to the Match: For your Son told me you had
never seen the Lady; therefore I came, Sir, in that Case, to entreat
you, to conjure you, as you value the Happiness of your Son, not to
be averse to his Match with a Woman who hath not only all the
good Qualities I have mentioned, but many more.'—'If that was
your Business, Sir,' said the old Gentleman, 'we are both obliged to
you; and you may be perfectly easy; for I give you my Word I was
very well satisfied with her Fortune.' 'Sir, answered *Jones*, I honour
you every Moment more and more. To be so easily satisfied, so very
moderate on that Account, is a Proof of the Soundness of your
Understanding, as well as the Nobleness of your Mind.'—'Not so
very moderate, young Gentleman, not so very moderate,' answered
the Father.—'Still more and more noble, replied *Jones*, and give me
Leave to add, sensible: For sure it is little less than Madness to consider Money as the sole Foundation of Happiness. Such a Woman
as this with her little, her nothing of a Fortune.'—'I find, cries
the old Gentleman, you have a pretty just Opinion of Money, my
Friend, or else you are better acquainted with the Person of the
Lady than with her Circumstances. Why pray, what Fortune do
you imagine this Lady to have?—'What Fortune? cries *Jones*, why
too contemptible a one to be named for your Son.' 'Well, well, well,
said the other, perhaps he might have done better.'—'That I deny,
said *Jones*, for she is one of the best of Women.' 'Ay, ay, but in
Point of Fortune I mean—answered the other.—And yet as to that
now, how much do you imagine your Friend is to have?'—'How
much, cries *Jones*, how much!—Why at the utmost, perhaps 200*l.*'

'Do you mean to banter me, young Gentleman? said the Father a little angry.'—'No, upon my Soul, answered *Jones*, I am in Earnest; nay I believe I have gone to the utmost Farthing. If I do the Lady an Injury, I ask her Pardon.' 'Indeed you do, cries the Father. I am certain she hath fifty Times that Sum, and she shall produce fifty to that, before I consent that she shall marry my Son.' 'Nay, said *Jones*, it is too late to talk of Consent now—If she had not fifty Farthings your Son is married.'—'My Son married! answered the old Gentleman with Surprize.' 'Nay, said *Jones*, I thought you was unacquainted with it.'—'My Son married to Miss *Harris!* answered he again—'To Miss *Harris!* said *Jones*; No, Sir, to Miss *Nancy Miller*, the Daughter of Mrs. *Miller*, at whose House he lodged; a young Lady, who, though her Mother is reduced to let Lodgings'—'Are you bantering, or are you in Earnest?' cries the Father with a most solemn Voice. 'Indeed, Sir, answered *Jones*, I scorn the Character of a Banterer. I came to you in most serious Earnest, imagining, as I find true, that your Son had never dared acquaint you with a Match so much inferior to him in Point of Fortune, tho' the Reputation of the Lady will suffer it no longer to remain a Secret.'

While the Father stood like one struck suddenly dumb at this News, a Gentleman came into the Room, and saluted him by the Name of Brother.

But though these two were in Consanguinity so nearly related, they were in their Dispositions almost the Opposites to each other. The Brother who now arrived had likewise been bred to Trade, in which he no sooner saw himself worth 6000*l.* than he purchased a small Estate with the greatest Part of it, and retired into the Country; where he married the Daughter of an unbeneficed Clergyman; a young Lady who, though she had neither Beauty nor Fortune, had recommended herself to his Choice, entirely by her good Humour, of which she possessed a very large Share.

With this Woman he had, during twenty-five Years, lived a Life more resembling the Model which certain Poets ascribe to the Golden Age, than any of those Patterns which are furnished by the present Times. By her he had four Children, but none of them arrived at Maturity except only one Daughter, whom in vulgar Language he and his Wife had spoiled; that is, had educated with the utmost Tenderness and Fondness; which she returned to such a Degree, that she had actually refused a very extraordinary Match with a Gentleman a little turned of forty, because she could not bring herself to part with her Parents.

The young Lady whom Mr. *Nightingale* had intended for his Son was a near Neighbour of his Brother, and an Acquaintance of his Niece; and in reality it was upon the Account of his projected Match, that he was now come to Town; not indeed to forward, but to dissuade his Brother from a Purpose which he conceived would inevitably ruin his Nephew; for he foresaw no other Event from a Union with Miss *Harris,* notwithstanding the Largeness of her Fortune, as neither her Person nor Mind seemed to him to promise any Kind of matrimonial Felicity; for she was very tall, very thin, very ugly, very affected, very silly, and very ill-natured.

His Brother therefore no sooner mentioned the Marriage of his Nephew with Miss *Miller,* than he exprest the utmost Satisfaction; and when the Father had very bitterly reviled his Son, and pronounced Sentence of Beggary upon him, the Uncle began in the following Manner.

'If you was a little cooler, Brother, I would ask you whether you love your Son for his Sake, or for your own. You would answer, I suppose, and so I suppose you think, for his Sake; and doubtless it is his Happiness which you intended in the Marriage you proposed for him.

'Now, Brother, to prescribe Rules of Happiness to others, hath always appeared to me very absurd, and to insist on doing this very tyrannical. It is a vulgar Error I know; but it is nevertheless an Error. And if this be absurd in other Things, it is mostly so in the Affair of Marriage, the Happiness of which depends entirely on the Affection which subsists between the Parties.

'I have therefore always thought it unreasonable in Parents to desire to chuse for their Children on this Occasion; since to force Affection is an impossible Attempt; nay, so much doth Love abhor Force, that I know not whether through an unfortunate but uncurable Perverseness in our Natures, it may not be even impatient of Persuasion.

'It is, however, true, that though a Parent will not, I think, wisely prescribe, he ought to be consulted on this Occasion; and in Strictness perhaps should at least have a negative Voice. My Nephew therefore, I own, in marrying without asking your Advice, hath been guilty of a Fault. But honestly speaking, Brother, have you not a little promoted this Fault? Have not your frequent Declarations on this Subject, given him a moral Certainty of your Refusal, where there was any Deficiency in Point of Fortune? nay, doth not your present Anger arise solely from that Deficiency? And if he hath failed in his Duty here, did you not as much exceed that Authority, when you absolutely bargained with him for a Woman without his Knowledge, whom you yourself never saw, and whom if you had seen and known as well as I, it must have been Madness in you, to have ever thought of bringing her into your Family.

'Still I own my Nephew in a Fault; but surely it is not an unpardonable Fault. He hath acted indeed without your Consent, in a Matter in which he ought to have asked it; but it is in a Matter in which his Interest is principally concerned; you yourself must and will acknowledge, that you consulted his Interest only, and if he unfortunately differed from you, and hath been mistaken in his Notion of Happiness, will you, Brother, if you love your Son, carry him still wider from the Point? Will you increase the ill Consequences of his simple Choice? Will you endeavour to make an Event certain Misery to him, which may accidentally prove so? In a Word, Brother, because he hath put it out of your Power to make his Circumstances as affluent as you would, will you distress them as much as you can?'

By the Force of the true Catholick Faith, St. *Antony*[1] won upon the Fishes. *Orpheus* and *Amphion* went a little farther, and by the Charms of Music enchanted Things merely inanimate. Wonderful both! But neither History nor Fable have ever yet ventured to record an Instance of any one, who by Force of Argument and Reason hath triumphed over habitual Avarice.

Mr. *Nightingale*, the Father, instead of attempting to answer his Brother, contented himself with only observing, that they had always differed in their Sentiments concerning the Education of their Children. 'I wish, said he, Brother, you would have confined your Care to your own Daughter, and never have troubled yourself with my Son, who hath, I believe, as little profited by your Precepts, as by your Example:' For young *Nightingale* was his Uncle's Godson, and had lived more with him than with his Father. So that the Uncle had often declared, he loved his Nephew almost equally with his own Child.

Jones fell into Raptures with this good Gentleman; and when after much Persuasion, they found the Father grew still more and more irritated, instead of appeased, *Jones* conducted the Uncle to his Nephew at the House of Mrs. *Miller*.

Chapter IX.

Containing strange Matters.

At his Return to his Lodgings, *Jones* found the Situation of Affairs greatly altered from what they had been in at his Departure. The Mother, the two Daughters, and young Mr. *Nightingale*, were now sat down to Supper together, when the Uncle was, at his own Desire, introduced without any Ceremony into the Company, to all of whom he was well known; for he had several Times visited his Nephew [2] at that House.

The old Gentleman immediately walked up to Miss *Nancy*,

1. St. Anthony of Padua (1195–1231)— not to be confused with the Egyptian St. Anthony (c. 250–350), the first Christian monk—was famed for eloquence; medieval pictures show fish jumping out of the water to hear him. Orpheus played the lyre and sang so beautifully that beasts, trees, and rocks gathered around. When Amphion and his brother were walling Thebes, Amphion charmed the stones into place with his lyre.
2. Fourth edition erroneously reads "Mother" here and "Nephew" in the next sentence, indicated by brackets.

saluted and wished her joy, as he did afterwards the [Mother] and the other Sister; and lastly, he paid the proper Compliments to his Nephew, with the same good Humour and Courtesy, as if his Nephew had married his equal or superior in Fortune, with all the previous Requisites first performed.

Miss *Nancy* and her supposed Husband both turned pale, and looked rather foolish than otherwise upon the Occasion; but Mrs. *Miller* took the first Opportunity of withdrawing; and having sent for *Jones* into the Dining Room, she threw herself at his Feet, and in a most passionate Flood of Tears, called him her good Angel, the Preserver of her poor little Family, with many other respectful and endearing Appellations, and made him every Acknowledgment which the highest Benefit can extract from the most grateful Heart.

After the first Gust of her Passion was a little over, which she declared, if she had not vented, would have burst her, she proceeded to inform Mr. *Jones*, that all Matters were settled between Mr. *Nightingale* and her Daughter, and that they were to be married the next Morning: At which Mr. *Jones* having expressed much Pleasure, the poor Woman fell again into a Fit of Joy and Thanksgiving, which he at length with Difficulty silenced, and prevailed on her to return with him back to the Company, whom they found in the same good Humour in which they had left them.

This little Society now past two or three very agreeable Hours together, in which the Uncle, who was a very great Lover of his Bottle, had so well ply'd his Nephew, that this latter, though not drunk, began to be somewhat flustered; and now Mr. *Nightingale* taking the old Gentleman with him up Stairs into the Apartment he had lately occupied, unbosomed himself as follows:

'As you have been always the best and kindest of Uncles to me, and as you have shewn such unparallelled Goodness in forgiving this Match, which to be sure may be thought a little improvident; I should never forgive myself if I attempted to deceive you in any thing.' He then confessed the Truth, and opened the whole Affair.

'How, *Jack!* said the old Gentleman, and are you really then not married to this young Woman?' 'No, upon my Honour, answered *Nightingale*, I have told you the simple Truth.' 'My dear Boy, cries the Uncle kissing him, I am heartily glad to hear it. I never was better pleased in my Life. If you had been married I should have assisted you as much as was in my Power, to have made the best of a bad Matter; but there is a great Difference between considering a Thing which is already done and irrecoverable, and that which is yet to do. Let your Reason have fair Play, *Jack*, and you will see this Match in so foolish and preposterous a Light, that there will be no Need of any dissuasive Arguments.' 'How, Sir! replies young *Nightingale*, is there this Difference between having already done an Act, and being in Honour engaged to do it?' 'Pugh, said the Uncle,

Honour is a Creature of the World's making, and the World hath
the Power of a Creator over it, and may govern and direct it as they
please. Now you well know how trivial these Breaches of Contract
are thought; even the grossest make but the Wonder and Conversation of a Day. Is there a Man who afterwards will be more backward in giving you his Sister or Daughter? Or is there any Sister or
Daughter who would be more backward to receive you? Honour is
not concerned in these Engagements.' 'Pardon me, dear Sir, cries
Nightingale, I can never think so; and not only Honour, but Conscience and Humanity are concerned. I am well satisfied, that was I
now to disappoint the young Creature, her Death would be the
Consequence, and I should look upon myself as her Murderer; nay,
as her Murderer by the cruelest of all Methods, by breaking her
Heart.' 'Break her Heart, indeed! no, no, *Jack*, cries the Uncle, the
Hearts of Women are not so soon broke; they are tough, Boy, they
are tough.' 'But, Sir,' answered *Nightingale*, 'my own Affections are
engaged, and I never could be happy with any other Woman. How
often have I heard you say, that Children should be always suffered
to chuse for themselves, and that you would let my Cousin *Harriet*
do so!' 'Why ay,' replied the old Gentleman, 'so I would have
them; but then I would have them chuse wisely.—Indeed, *Jack*, you
must and shall leave this Girl.'—'Indeed, Uncle,' cries the other, 'I
must and will have her.' 'You will, young Gentleman?' said the
Uncle; 'I did not expect such a Word from you. I should not
wonder if you had used such Language to your Father, who hath
always treated you like a Dog, and kept you at the Distance which a
Tyrant preserves over his Subjects; but I, who have lived with you
upon an equal Footing, might surely expect better Usage: But I
know how to account for it all! it is all owing to your preposterous
Education, in which I have had too little Share. There is my
Daughter now, whom I have brought up as my Friend, never doth
any Thing without my Advice, nor ever refuses to take it when I
give it her.' 'You have never yet given her Advice in an Affair of
this Kind,' said *Nightingale*, 'for I am greatly mistaken in my
Cousin, if she would be very ready to obey even your most positive
Commands in abandoning her Inclinations.' 'Don't abuse my Girl,'
answered the old Gentleman with some Emotion; 'don't abuse my
Harriet. I have brought her up to have no Inclinations contrary to
my own. By suffering her to do whatever she pleases, I have enured
her to a Habit of being pleased to do whatever I like.' 'Pardon me,
Sir,' said *Nightingale*, 'I have not the least Design to reflect on my
Cousin, for whom I have the greatest Esteem; and indeed I am con-
vinced you will never put her to so severe a Trial, or lay such hard
Commands on her as you would do on me.—But, dear Sir, let us
return to the Company; for they will begin to be uneasy at our long
Absence. I must beg one Favour of my dear Uncle, which is that he

would not say any Thing to shock the poor Girl or her Mother.' 'O
you need not fear me,' answered he, 'I understand myself too well
to affront Women; so I will readily grant you that Favour; and in
Return I must expect another of you.' 'There are but few of your
Commands, Sir,' said *Nightingale*, 'which I shall not very chearfully
obey.' 'Nay, Sir, I ask nothing,' said the Uncle, 'but the Honour of
your Company home to my Lodging, that I may reason the Case a
little more fully with you: For I would, if possible, have the Satisfaction of preserving my Family, notwithstanding the headstrong
Folly of my Brother, who, in his own Opinion, is the wisest Man
in the World.'

Nightingale, who well knew his Uncle to be as headstrong as
his Father, submitted to attend him Home, and then they both
returned back into the Room, where the old Gentleman promised
to carry himself with the same Decorum which he had before maintained.

Chapter X.

A *short Chapter, which concludes the Book.*

The long Absence of the Uncle and Nephew had occasioned
some Disquiet in the Minds of all whom they had left behind
them; and the more, as during the preceding Dialogue, the Uncle
had more than once elevated his Voice, so as to be heard down
Stairs; which, tho' they could not distinguish what he said, had
caused some evil foreboding in *Nancy* and her Mother, and indeed
even in *Jones* himself.

When the good Company therefore again assembled, there was a
visible Alteration in all their Faces; and the good Humour which, at
their last Meeting, universally shone forth in every Countenance,
was now changed into a much less agreeable Aspect. It was a
Change indeed common enough to the Weather in this Climate,
from Sunshine to Clouds, from *June* to *December*.

This Alteration was not however greatly remarked by any present;
for as they were all now endeavouring to conceal their own
Thoughts, and to act a Part, they became all too busily engaged in
the Scene to be Spectators of it. Thus neither the Uncle nor
Nephew saw any Symptoms of Suspicion in the Mother or Daughter; nor did the Mother or Daughter remark the over-acted Complaisance of the old Man, nor the counterfeit Satisfaction which
grinned in the Features of the young one.

Something like this, I believe, frequently happens, where the
whole Attention of two Friends being engaged in the Part which
each is to act, in order to impose on the other, neither sees nor suspects the Art practiced against himself; and thus the Thrust of both

(to borrow no improper Metaphor on the Occasion) alike takes Place.

From the same Reason it is no unusual Thing for both Parties to be over-reached in a Bargain, though the one must be always the greater Loser; as was he who sold a blind Horse, and received a bad Note in Payment.

Our Company in about half an Hour broke up, and the Uncle carried off his Nephew; but not before the latter had assured Miss *Nancy*, in a Whisper, that he would attend her early in the Morning, and fulfil all his Engagements.

Jones, who was the least concerned in this Scene, saw the most. He did indeed suspect the very Fact; for besides observing the great Alteration in the Behaviour of the Uncle, the Distance he assumed, and his overstrained Civility to Miss *Nancy*; the carrying off a Bridegroom from his Bride at that Time of Night, was so extraordinary a Proceeding, that it could be accounted for, only by imagining that young *Nightingale* had revealed the whole Truth, which the apparent Openness of his Temper, and his being flustered with Liquor, made too probable.

While he was reasoning with himself, whether he should acquaint these poor People with his Suspicion, the Maid of the House informed him, that a Gentlewoman desired to speak with him. ————He went immediately out, and taking the Candle from the Maid, ushered his Visitant up Stairs, who, in the Person of Mrs. *Honour*, acquainted him with such dreadful News concerning his *Sophia*, that he immediately lost all Consideration for every other Person; and his whole Stock of Compassion was entirely swallowed up in Reflections on his own Misery, and on that of his unfortunate Angel.

What this dreadful Matter was, the Reader will be informed, after we have first related the many preceding Steps which produced it, and those will be the Subject of the following Book.

BOOK XV.

In which the History advances about two Days.

Chapter I.

Too short to need a Preface.

There are a Set of Religious, or rather Moral Writers, who teach that Virtue is the certain Road to Happiness, and Vice to Misery, in this World. A very wholesome and comfortable Doctrine, and to which we have but one Objection, namely, That it is not true.

Indeed, if by Virtue these Writers mean the Exercise of those Cardinal Virtues, which like good House-wives stay at home, and mind only the Business of their own Family, I shall very readily concede the Point; For so surely do all these contribute and lead to Happiness, that I could almost wish, in Violation of all the antient and modern Sages, to call them rather by the Name of Wisdom, than by that of Virtue: For with Regard to this Life, no System, I conceive, was ever wiser than that of the antient *Epicureans*, who held this Wisdom to constitute the chief Good;[1] nor foolisher than that of their Opposites, those modern *Epicures*, who place all Felicity in the abundant Gratification of every sensual Appetite.

But if by Virtue is meant (as I almost think it ought) a certain relative Quality, which is always busying itself without Doors, and seems as much interested in pursuing the Good of others as its own; I cannot so easily agree that this is the surest Way to human Happiness; because I am afraid we must then include Poverty and Contempt, with all the Mischiefs which Backbiting, Envy, and Ingratitude can bring on Mankind, in our Idea of Happiness; nay, sometimes perhaps we shall be obliged to wait upon the said Happiness to a Goal; since many by the above Virtue have brought themselves thither.

I have not now Leisure to enter upon so large a Field of Speculation, as here seems opening upon me; my Design was to wipe off a Doctrine that lay in my Way; since while Mr. *Jones* was acting the most virtuous Part imaginable in labouring to preserve his Fellow-creatures from Destruction, the Devil, or some other evil Spirit, one perhaps cloathed in human Flesh, was hard at Work to make him completely miserable in the Ruin of his *Sophia*.

This therefore would seem an Exception to the above Rule, if indeed it was a Rule; but as we have in our Voyage through Life seen so many other Exceptions to it, we chuse to dispute the Doctrine on which it is founded, which we don't apprehend to be Christian, which we are convinced is not true, and which is indeed destructive of one of the noblest Arguments that Reason alone can furnish for the belief of Immortality.

But as the Reader's Curiosity (if he hath any) must be now awake, and hungry, we shall provide to feed it as fast as we can.

Chapter II.

In which is opened a very black Design against Sophia.

I remember a wise old Gentleman, who used to say, 'When Children are doing Nothing, they are doing Mischief.' I will not enlarge this quaint Saying to the most beautiful Part of the Creation

1. See note 5, p. 7.

in general; but so far I may be allowed, that when the Effects of female Jealousy do not appear openly in their proper Colours of Rage and Fury, we may suspect that mischievous Passion to be at work privately, and attempting to undermine, what it doth not attack above ground.

This was exemplified in the Conduct of Lady *Bellaston*, who, under all the Smiles which she wore in her Countenance, concealed much Indignation against *Sophia*; and as she plainly saw, that this young Lady stood between her and the full Indulgence of her Desires, she resolved to get rid of her by some Means or other; nor was it long before a very favourable Opportunity of accomplishing this presented itself to her.

The Reader may be pleased to remember, that when *Sophia* was thrown into that Consternation at the Play-house, by the Wit and Humour of a Set of young Gentlemen who call themselves the Town, we informed him, that she had put herself under the Protection of a young Nobleman, who had very safely conducted her to her Chair.

This Nobleman, who frequently visited Lady *Bellaston*, had more than once seen *Sophia* there, since her Arrival in Town, and had conceived a very great Liking to her; which Liking, as Beauty never looks more amiable than in Distress, *Sophia* had in this Fright so encreased, that he might now, without any great Impropriety, be said to be actually in Love with her.

It may easily be believed, that he would not suffer so handsome an Occasion of improving his Acquaintance with the beloved Object as now offered itself, to elapse, when even Good-breeding alone might have prompted him to pay her a Visit.

The next Morning therefore, after this Accident, he waited on *Sophia*, with the usual Compliments, and Hopes that she had received no Harm from her last Night's Adventure.

As Love, like Fire, when once thoroughly kindled, is soon blown into a Flame; *Sophia* in a very short Time completed her Conquest. Time now flew away unperceived, and the noble Lord had been two Hours in Company with the Lady, before it entered into his Head that he had made too long a Visit. Though this Circumstance alone would have alarmed *Sophia*, who was somewhat more a Mistress of Computation at present; she had indeed much more pregnant Evidence from the Eyes of her Lover of what past within his Bosom; nay, though he did not make any open Declaration of his Passion, yet many of his Expressions were rather too warm, and too tender, to have been imputed to Complaisance, even in the Age when such Complaisance was in Fashion; the very Reverse of which is well known to be the reigning Mode at present.

Lady *Bellaston* had been apprised of his Lordship's Visit at his first Arrival; and the Length of it very well satisfied her, that Things went as she wished, and as indeed she had suspected the second Time she saw this young Couple together. This Business she rightly, I think, concluded, that she should by no Means forward by mixing in the Company while they were together; she therefore ordered her Servants, that when my Lord was going, they should tell him, she desired to speak with him; and employed the intermediate Time in meditating how best to accomplish a Scheme which she made no doubt but his Lordship would very readily embrace the Execution of.

Lord *Fellamar* (for that was the Title of this young Nobleman) was no sooner introduced to her Ladyship, than she attacked him in the following Strain: 'Bless me, my Lord, are you here yet? I thought my Servants had made a Mistake, and let you go away; and I wanted to see you about an Affair of some Importance.' ——'Indeed, Lady *Bellaston*,' said he, 'I don't wonder you are astonished at the Length of my Visit: For I have staid above two Hours, and I did not think I had staid above half a one.' —'What am I to conclude from thence, my Lord?' said she, 'The Company must be very agreeable which can make Time slide away so very deceitfully.'—'Upon my Honour,' said he, 'the most agreeable I ever saw. Pray tell me, Lady *Bellaston*, who is this blazing Star which you have produced among us all of a sudden?'—'What blazing Star, my Lord?' said she, affecting a Surprize. 'I mean,' said he, 'the Lady I saw here the other Day, whom I had last Night in my Arms at the Play-house, and to whom I have been making that unreasonable Visit.'—'O my Cousin *Western!*' said she, 'why that blazing Star, my Lord, is the Daughter of a Country Booby Squire, and hath been in Town about a Fortnight, for the first Time.'—'Upon my Soul,' said he, 'I should swear she had been bred in a Court; for besides her Beauty, I never saw any Thing so genteel, so sensible, so polite.'—'O brave!' cries the Lady, 'my Cousin hath you, I find.'—'Upon my Honour,' answered he, 'I wish she had: For I am in Love with her to Distraction.'—'Nay, my Lord,' said she, 'it is not wishing yourself very ill neither, for she is a very great Fortune: I assure you she is an only Child, and her Father's Estate is a good 3000*l.* a Year.' 'Then I can assure you, Madam,' answered the Lord, 'I think her the best Match in *England.*' 'Indeed, my Lord,' replied she, 'if you like her, I heartily wish you had her.' 'If you think so kindly of me, Madam,' said he, 'as she is a Relation of yours, will you do me the Honour to propose it to her Father?' 'And are you really then in earnest?' cries the Lady, with an affected Gravity. 'I hope, Madam,' answered he, 'you have

a better Opinion of me, than to imagine I would jest with your
Ladyship in an Affair of this Kind.' 'Indeed then,' said the Lady, 'I
will most readily propose your Lordship to her Father; and I can, I
believe, assure you of his joyful Acceptance of the Proposal; but
there is a Bar, which I am almost ashamed to mention; and yet it is
one you will never be able to conquer. You have a Rival, my Lord,
and a Rival who, though I blush to name him, neither you, nor all
the World will ever be able to conquer.' 'Upon my Word, Lady
Bellaston,' cries he, 'you have struck a Damp to my Heart, which
hath almost deprived me of Being.' 'Fie! my Lord,' said she, 'I
should rather hope I had struck Fire into you. A Lover, and talk of
Damps in your Heart! I rather imagined you would have asked your
Rival's Name, that you might have immediately entered the Lists
with him.' 'I promise you, Madam,' answered he, 'there are very few
Things I would not undertake for your charming Cousin: But pray
who is this happy Man?'—'Why he is,' said she, 'what I am sorry to
say most happy Men with us are, one of the lowest Fellows in the
World. He is a Beggar, a Bastard, a Foundling, a Fellow in meaner
Circumstances than one of your Lordship's Footmen.' 'And is it possible,' cried he, 'that a young Creature with such Perfections should
think of bestowing herself so unworthily?' 'Alas! my Lord,'
answered she, 'consider the Country—the Bane of all young
Women is the Country. There they learn a Set of romantic Notions
of Love, and I know not what Folly, which this Town and good
Company can scarce eradicate in a whole Winter.' 'Indeed,
Madam,' replied my Lord, 'your Cousin is of too immense a Value
to be thrown away: Such Ruin as this must be prevented.' 'Alas!'
cries she, 'my Lord, how can it be prevented? The Family have
already done all in their Power; but the Girl is, I think, intoxicated,
and nothing less than Ruin will content her. And to deal more
openly with you, I expect every Day to hear she is run away with
him.' 'What you tell me, Lady *Bellaston*,' answered his Lordship,
'affects me most tenderly, and only raises my Compassion instead of
lessening my Adoration of your Cousin. Some Means must be found
to preserve so inestimable a Jewel. Hath your Ladyship endeavoured
to reason with her?' Here the Lady affected a Laugh, and cried, 'My
dear Lord, sure you know us better than to talk of reasoning a
young Woman out of her Inclinations? These inestimable Jewels
are as deaf as the Jewels they wear: Time, my Lord, Time is the
only Medicine to cure their Folly; but this is a Medicine, which I
am certain she will not take; nay, I live in hourly Horrors on her
Account. In short, nothing but violent Methods will do.' 'What is
to be done?' cries my Lord, 'What Methods are to be taken?—Is
there any Method upon Earth?—Oh! Lady *Bellaston!* there is

nothing which I would not undertake for such a Reward.'—'I really know not,' answered the Lady, after a Pause; and then pausing again, she cried out,—'Upon my Soul, I am at my Wit's End on this Girl's Account.—If she can be preserved, something must be done immediately; and as I say, nothing but violent Methods will do.—If your Lordship hath really this Attachment to my Cousin, (and to do her Justice, except in this silly Inclination, of which she will soon see her Folly, she is every Way deserving) I think there may be one Way, indeed it is a very disagreeable one, and what I am almost afraid to think of.——It requires a great Spirit, I promise you.' 'I am not conscious, Madam,' said he, 'of any Defect there; nor am I, I hope, suspected of any such. It must be an egregious Defect indeed, which could make me backward on this Occasion.' 'Nay, my Lord,' answered she, 'I am far from doubting you. I am much more inclined to doubt my own Courage; for I must run a monstrous Risque. In short, I must place such a Confidence in your Honour as a wise Woman will scarce ever place in a Man on any Consideration.' In this Point likewise my Lord very well satisfied her; for his Reputation was extremely clear, and common Fame did him no more than Justice, in speaking well of him. 'Well then,' said she, 'my Lord,—I—I vow, I can't bear the Apprehension of it.—No, it must not be.—At least every other Method shall be tried. Can you get rid of your Engagements, and dine here to-day? Your Lordship will have an Opportunity of seeing a little more of Miss *Western.*—I promise you we have no Time to lose. Here will be no Body but Lady *Betty,* and Miss *Eagle,* and Colonel *Hampsted,* and *Tom Edwards;* they will all go soon,—and I shall be at Home to no Body. Then your Lordship may be a little more explicit. Nay, I will contrive some Method to convince you of her Attachment to this Fellow.' My Lord made proper Compliments, accepted the Invitation, and then they parted to dress, it being now past three in the Morning, or to reckon by the old Style in the Afternoon.

Chapter III.

A *further Explanation of the foregoing Design.*

Tho' the Reader may have long since concluded Lady *Bellaston* to be a Member (and no inconsiderable one) of the Great World, she was in reality a very considerable Member of the *Little World;* by which Appellation was distinguished a very worthy and honourable Society which not long since flourished in this Kingdom.

Among other good Principles upon which this Society was founded, there was one very remarkable: For as it was a Rule of an honourable Club of Heroes, who assembled at the Close of the late War, that all the Members should every Day fight once at least; so 'twas in this, that every Member should, within the twenty-four Hours, tell at least one merry Fib, which was to be propagated by all the Brethren and Sisterhood.

Many idle Stories were told about this Society, which from a certain Quality may be, perhaps not unjustly, supposed to have come from the Society themselves. As, that the Devil was the President; and that he sat in Person in an Elbow-Chair at the upper End of the Table: But upon very strict Enquiry, I find there is not the least Truth in any of those Tales, and that the Assembly consisted in reality of a Set of very good Sort of People, and the Fibs which they propagated were of a harmless Kind, and tended only to produce Mirth and good Humour.

Edwards was likewise a Member of this comical Society. To him therefore Lady *Bellaston* applied as a proper Instrument for her Purpose, and furnished him with a Fib, which he was to vent whenever the Lady gave him her Cue; and this was not to be till the Evening, when all the Company but Lord *Fellamar* and himself were gone, and while they were engaged in a Rubbers at Whist.

To this Time then, which was between Seven and Eight in the Evening, we will convey our Reader; when Lady *Bellaston*, Lord *Fellamar*, Miss *Western*, and *Tom* being engaged at Whist, and in the last Game of their Rubbers, *Tom* received his Cue from Lady *Bellaston*, which was, 'I protest, *Tom*, you are grown intolerable lately; you used to tell us all the News of the Town, and now you know no more of the World than if you lived out of it.'

Mr. *Edwards* then began as follows: 'The Fault is not mine, Madam; it lies in the Dulness of the Age, that doth nothing worth talking of.—O la! though now I think on't, there hath a terrible Accident befallen poor Colonel *Wilcox*.—Poor *Ned*.—You know him, my Lord, every Body knows him; faith! I am very much concerned for him.'

'What is it, pray?' says Lady *Bellaston*.

'Why, he hath killed a Man this Morning in a Duel, that's all.'

His Lordship, who was not in the Secret, asked gravely, whom he had killed? To which *Edwards* answered, 'A young Fellow we none of us know; a *Somersetshire* Lad just come to Town, one *Jones* his Name is; a near Relation of one Mr. *Allworthy*, of whom your Lordship I believe hath heard. I saw the Lad lie dead in a Coffeehouse.—Upon my Soul he is one of the finest Corpses I ever saw in my Life.'

Sophia, who just began to deal as *Tom* had mentioned that a Man was killed, stopt her Hand, and listened with Attention, (for all Stories of that Kind affected her) but no sooner had he arrived at the latter Part of the Story, than she began to deal again; and having dealt three Cards to one, and seven to another, and ten to a third, at last dropt the rest from her Hand, and fell back in her chair.

The Company behaved as usually on these Occasions. The usual Disturbance ensued, the usual Assistance was summoned, and *Sophia* at last, as it is usual, returned again to Life, and was soon after, at her earnest Desire, led to her own Apartment; where, at my Lord's Request, Lady *Bellaston* acquainted her with the Truth, attempted to carry it off as a Jest of her own, and comforted her with repeated Assurances, that neither his Lordship, nor *Tom*, though she had taught him the Story, were in the true Secret of the Affair.

There was no farther Evidence necessary to convince Lord *Fellamar* how justly the Case had been represented to him by Lady *Bellaston*; and now at her Return into the Room, a Scheme was laid between these two noble Persons, which, though it appeared in no very heinous Light to his Lordship, (as he faithfully promised, and faithfully resolved too, to make the Lady all the subsequent Amends in his Power by Marriage;) yet many of our Readers, we doubt not, will see with just Detestation.

The next Evening at Seven was appointed for the fatal Purpose, when Lady *Bellaston* undertook that *Sophia* should be alone, and his Lordship should be introduced to her. The whole Family were to be regulated for the Purpose, most of the Servants dispatched out of the House; and for Mrs. *Honour*, who, to prevent Suspicion, was to be left with her Mistress till his Lordship's Arrival, Lady *Bellaston* herself was to engage her in an Apartment as distant as possible from the Scene of the intended Mischief, and out of the Hearing of *Sophia*.

Matters being thus agreed on, his Lordship took his Leave, and her Ladyship retired to Rest, highly pleased with a Project, of which she had no Reason to doubt the Success, and which promised so effectually to remove *Sophia* from being any future Obstruction to her Amour with *Jones*, by a Means of which she should never appear to be guilty, even if the Fact appeared to the World; but this she made no doubt of preventing by huddling up a marriage, to which she thought the ravished *Sophia* would easily be brought to consent, and at which all the rest of her Family would rejoice.

But Affairs were not in so quiet a Situation in the Bosom of the other Conspirator: His Mind was tost in all the distracting Anxiety so nobly described by *Shakespear*.

> *Between the Acting of a dreadful Thing,*
> *And the first Motion, all the Interim is*
> *Like a Phantasma, or a hideous Dream:*
> *The Genius and the mortal Instruments*
> *Are then in Council; and the State of Man,*
> *Like to a little Kingdom, suffers then*
> *The Nature of an Insurrection.*—[1]

Though the Violence of his Passion had made him eagerly embrace the first Hint of this Design, especially as it came from a Relation of the Lady, yet when that Friend to Reflection, a Pillow, had placed the Action itself in all its natural black Colours before his Eyes, with all the Consequences which must, and those which might probably attend it; his Resolution began to abate, or rather indeed go over to the other Side; and after a long Conflict which lasted a whole Night between Honour and Appetite, the former at length prevailed, and he determined to wait on Lady *Bellaston*, and to relinquish the Design.

Lady *Bellaston* was in Bed, though very late in the Morning, and *Sophia* sitting by her Bedside, when the Servant acquainted her that Lord *Fellamar* was below in the Parlour; upon which her Ladyship desired him to stay, and that she would see him presently; but the Servant was no sooner departed than poor *Sophia* began to intreat her Cousin not to encourage the Visits of that odious Lord (so she called him, though a little unjustly) upon her Account. 'I see his Design,' said she; 'for he made downright Love to me Yesterday Morning; but as I am resolved never to admit it, I beg your Ladyship not to leave us alone together any more, and to order the Servants that, if he enquires for me, I may be always denied to him.'

'La! Child,' says Lady *Bellaston*, 'you Country Girls have nothing but Sweet-hearts in your Head; you fancy every Man who is civil to you is making Love. He is one of the most gallant young Fellows about Town, and I am convinced means no more than a little Gallantry. Make Love to you indeed! I wish with all my Heart he would, and you must be an arrant mad Woman to refuse him.'

'But as I shall certainly be that mad Woman,' cries *Sophia*, 'I hope his Visits shall not be intruded upon me.'

'O Child,' said Lady *Bellaston*, 'you need not be so fearful; if you resolve to run away with that *Jones*, I know no Person who can hinder you.'

'Upon my Honour, Madam,' cries *Sophia*, 'your Ladyship injures me. I will never run away with any Man; nor will I ever marry contrary to my Father's Inclinations.'

'Well, Miss *Western*,' said the Lady, 'if you are not in a Humour

1. *Julius Caesar* II.i.63–69.

to see Company this Morning, you may retire to your own Apartment; for I am not frightned at his Lordship, and must send for him up into my Dressing-Room.'

Sophia thanked her Ladyship, and withdrew; and presently afterwards *Fellamar* was admitted up Stairs.

Chapter IV.

By which it will appear how dangerous an Advocate a Lady is, when she applies her Eloquence to an ill Purpose.

When Lady *Bellaston* heard the young Lord's Scruples, she treated them with the same Disdain with which one of those Sages of the Law, called *Newgate* Solicitors, treats the Qualms of Conscience in a young Witness. 'My dear Lord,' said she, 'you certainly want a Cordial. I must send to Lady *Edgely* for one of her best Drams. Fie upon it! have more Resolution. Are you frightned by the Word *Rape?* Or are you apprehensive—? Well! if the Story of *Helen* was modern, I should think it unnatural. I mean the Behaviour of *Paris*, not the Fondness of the Lady; for all Women love a Man of Spirit. There is another Story of the *Sabine* Ladies,—and that too, I thank Heaven, is very ancient. Your Lordship, perhaps, will admire my Reading; but I think Mr. *Hook*[1] tells us, they made tolerable good Wives afterwards. I fancy few of my married Acquaintance were ravished by their Husbands.' 'Nay, dear Lady *Bellaston*,' cried he, 'don't ridicule me in this Manner.' 'Why, my good Lord,' answered she, 'do you think any Woman in *England* would not laugh at you in her Heart, whatever Prudery she might wear in her Countenance?—You force me to use a strange Kind of Language, and to betray my Sex most abominably: But I am contented with knowing my Intentions are good, and that I am endeavouring to serve my Cousin; for I think you will make her a Husband notwithstanding this; or, upon my Soul, I would not even persuade her to fling herself away upon an empty Title. She should not upbraid me hereafter with having lost a Man of Spirit; for that his Enemies allow this poor young Fellow to be.'

Let those who have had the Satisfaction of hearing Reflections of this Kind from a Wife or a Mistress, declare whether they are at all sweetened by coming from a female Tongue. Certain it is, they sunk deeper into his Lordship than any Thing which *Demosthenes* or *Cicero* could have said on the Occasion.

Lady *Bellaston* perceiving she had fired the young Lord's Pride, began now, like a true Orator, to rouse other Passions to its Assist-

1. Nathaniel Hook, *Roman History, from the Building of Rome to the Ruin of the Commonwealth* (1738) I.ii.14–15. Hook was amanuensis to the Dowager Duchess of Marlborough, whom Fielding had defended in *A Full Vindication of the Dutchess Dowager of Marlborough* (1742).

ance. 'My Lord,' says she, in a graver Voice, 'you will be pleased to remember, you mentioned this Matter to me first; for I would not appear to you in the Light of one who is endeavouring to put off my Cousin upon you. Fourscore thousand Pounds do not stand in Need of an Advocate to recommend them.' 'Nor doth Miss West-ern,' said he, 'require any Recommendation from her Fortune; for in my Opinion, no Woman ever had half her Charms.' 'Yes, yes, my Lord;' replied the Lady, looking in the Glass, 'there have been Women with more than half her Charms, I assure you; not that I need lessen her on that Account: She is a most delicious Girl, that's certain; and within these few Hours she will be in the Arms of one, who surely doth not deserve her, though I will give him his Due, I believe he is truly a Man of Spirit.'

'I hope so, Madam,' said my Lord; 'tho' I must own he doth not deserve her; for unless Heaven, or your Ladyship disappoint me, she shall within that Time be in mine.'

'Well spoken, my Lord,' answered the Lady, 'I promise you no Disappointment shall happen from my Side; and within this Week I am convinced I shall call your Lordship my Cousin in Public.'

The Remainder of this Scene consisted entirely of Raptures, Excuses, and Compliments, very pleasant to have heard from the Parties; but rather dull when related at second Hand. Here, there-fore, we shall put an End to this Dialogue, and hasten to the fatal Hour, when every Thing was prepared for the Destruction of poor *Sophia*.

But this being the most tragical Matter in our whole History, we shall treat it in a Chapter by itself.

Chapter V.

Containing some Matters which may affect, and others which may surprize the Reader.

The Clock had now struck Seven, and poor *Sophia*, alone and melancholy, sat reading a Tragedy. It was *The Fatal Marriage*;[1] and she was now come to that Part where the poor distrest *Isabella* dis-poses of her Wedding-Ring.

Here the Book dropt from her Hand, and a Shower of Tears ran down into her Bosom. In this Situation she had continued a Minute, when the Door opened, and in came Lord *Fellamar*. *Sophia* started from her Chair at his Entrance; and his Lordship advancing forwards, and making a low Bow, said, 'I am afraid, Miss *Western*, I break in upon you abruptly.' 'Indeed, my Lord,' says

---

1. By Thomas Southerne (1694), II.ii. Isabella, widowed (as she mistakenly be-lieves) and destitute, sends a servant out to pawn her last treasure, her cherished wedding ring, to feed her children.

she, 'I must own myself a little surprized at this unexpected Visit.'
'If this Visit be unexpected, Madam,' answered Lord *Fellamar*, 'my
Eyes must have been very faithless Interpreters of my Heart, when
last I had the Honour of seeing you: For surely you could not otherwise have hoped to detain my Heart in your Possession, without
receiving a Visit from its Owner.' *Sophia*, confused as she was,
answered this Bombast (and very properly, I think) with a Look of
inconceivable Disdain. My Lord than made another and a longer
Speech of the same Sort. Upon which *Sophia*, trembling, said, 'Am
I really to conceive your Lordship to be out of your Senses? Sure,
my Lord, there is no other Excuse for such Behaviour.'—'I am,
indeed, Madam, in the Situation you suppose,' cries his Lordship;
'and sure you will pardon the Effects of a Frenzy which you yourself
have occasioned: For Love hath so totally deprived me of Reason,
that I am scarce accountable for any of my Actions.' 'Upon my
Word, my Lord,' said *Sophia*, 'I neither understand your Words
nor your Behaviour.'——'Suffer me then, Madam,' cries he, 'at your
Feet to explain both, by laying open my Soul to you, and declaring
that I doat on you to the highest Degree of Distraction. O most
adorable, most divine Creature! what Language can express the Sentiments of my Heart?' 'I do assure you, my Lord,' said *Sophia*, 'I
shall not stay to hear any more of this.' 'Do not,' cries he, 'think of
leaving me thus cruelly: Could you know half the Torments which
I feel, that tender Bosom must pity what those Eyes have caused.'
Then fetching a deep Sigh, and laying hold of her Hand, he ran on
for some Minutes in a Strain which would be little more pleasing to
the Reader than it was to the Lady; and at last concluded with a
Declaration, 'That if he was Master of the World, he would lay it
at her Feet.' *Sophia* then forcibly pulling away her Hand from his,
answered with much Spirit, 'I promise you, Sir, your World and its
Master, I should spurn from me with equal Contempt.' She then
offered to go, and Lord *Fellamar* again laying hold of her Hand,
said, 'Pardon me, my beloved Angel, Freedoms which nothing but
Despair could have tempted me to take.—Believe me, could I have
had any Hope that my Title and Fortune, neither of them inconsiderable, unless when compared with your Worth, would have been
accepted, I had, in the humblest Manner, presented them to your
Acceptance.—But I cannot lose you.—By Heaven, I will sooner
part with my Soul.—You are, you must, you shall be only mine.'
'My Lord,' says she, 'I intreat you to desist from a vain Pursuit; for,
upon my Honour, I will never hear you on this Subject. Let go my
Hand, my Lord; for I am resolved to go from you this Moment; nor
will I ever see you more.' 'Then, Madam,' cries his Lordship, 'I must
make the Best Use of this Moment; for I cannot live, nor will I live
without you.'—'What do you mean, my Lord?' said *Sophia*; 'I will
raise the Family.' 'I have no Fear, Madam,' answered he, 'but of

losing you, and that I am resolved to prevent, the only Way which Despair points to me.'—He then caught her in his Arms: Upon which she screamed so loud, that she must have alarmed some one to her Assistance, had not Lady *Bellaston* taken Care to remove all Ears.

But a more lucky Circumstance happened for poor *Sophia*: Another Noise now broke forth, which almost drowned her Cries; for now the whole House rang with, 'Where is she? D——n me, I'll unkennel her this Instant. Shew me her Chamber, I say. Where is my Daughter? I know she's in the House, and I'll see her if she's above Ground. Shew me where she is.'—At which last Words the Door flew open, and in came Squire *Western*, with his Parson, and a Set of Myrmidons[2] at his Heels.

How miserable must have been the Condition of poor *Sophia*, when the enraged Voice of her Father was welcome to her Ears? Welcome indeed it was, and luckily did he come; for it was the only Accident upon Earth which could have preserved the Peace of her Mind from being for ever destroyed.

Sophia, notwithstanding her Fright, presently knew her Father's Voice; and his Lordship, notwithstanding his Passion, knew the Voice of Reason, which peremptorily assured him, it was not now a Time for the Perpetration of his Villainy. Hearing, therefore, the Voice approach, and hearing likewise whose it was; (for as the Squire more than once roared forth the Word Daughter, so *Sophia*, in the midst of her Struggling, cried out upon her Father;) he thought proper to relinquish his Prey, having only disordered her Handkerchief, and with his rude Lips committed Violence on her lovely Neck.

If the Reader's Imagination doth not assist me, I shall never be able to describe the Situation of these two Persons when *Western* came into the Room. *Sophia* tottered into a Chair, where she sat disordered, pale, breathless, bursting with Indignation at Lord *Fella-mar*; affrighted, and yet more rejoiced at the Arrival of her Father.

His Lordship sat down near her, with the Bag of his Wig hanging over one of his Shoulders, the rest of his Dress being somewhat disordered, and rather a greater Proportion of Linnen than is usual appearing at his Bosom. As to the rest, he was amazed, affrighted, vexed, and ashamed.

As to Squire *Western*, he happened, at this Time, to be overtaken by an Enemy, which very frequently pursues, and seldom fails to overtake, most of the Country Gentlemen in this Kingdom. He was, literally speaking, drunk; which Circumstance, together with his natural Impetuosity, could produce no other Effect, than his running immediately up to his Daughter, upon whom he fell foul with his Tongue in the most inveterate Manner; nay, he had proba-

2. Achilles's warriors (*Iliad*) were Myrmidons—people from Thessaly.

bly committed Violence with his Hands, had not the Parson interposed, saying, 'For Heaven's Sake, Sir, animadvert that you are in
the House of a great Lady. Let me beg you to mitigate your Wrath;
it should minister a Fullness of Satisfaction that you have found
your Daughter; for as to Revenge, it belongeth not unto us. I discern great Contrition in the Countenance of the young Lady. I
stand assured, if you will forgive her, she will repent her of all past
Offences, and return unto her Duty.'

The Strength of the Parson's Arms had at first been of more
Service than the Strength of his Rhetoric. However, his last Words
wrought some Effect, and the Squire answered, 'I'll forgee her if she
wull ha un. If wot ha un, *Sophy*, I'll forgee thee all. Why dost unt
speak? Shat ha un? D—n me, shat ha un? Why dost unt answer?
Was ever such a stubborn Tuoad?'

'Let me intreat you, Sir, to be a little more moderate,' said the
Parson; 'you frighten the young Lady so, that you deprive her of all
Power of Utterance.'

'Power of mine A—,' answered the Squire. 'You take her Part
then, you do? A pretty Parson truly, to side with an undutiful
Child. Yes, yes, I will gee you a Living with a Pox. I'll gee un to
the Devil sooner.'

'I humbly crave your Pardon,' said the Parson; 'I assure your
Worship, I meant no such Matter.'

My Lady *Bellaston* now entered the Room, and came up to the
Squire, who no sooner saw her, than resolving to follow the Instruc-
tions of his Sister, he made her a very civil Bow, in the rural
Manner, and paid her some of his best Compliments. He then
immediately proceeded to his Complaints, and said, 'There, my
Lady Cousin; there stands the most undutiful Child in the World:
She hankers after a beggarly Rascal, and won't marry one of the
greatest Matches in all *England*, that we have provided for her.'

'Indeed, Cousin *Western*,' answered the Lady, 'I am persuaded
you wrong my Cousin. I am sure she hath a better Understanding. I
am convinced she will not refuse what she must be sensible is so
much to her Advantage.'

This was a wilful Mistake in Lady *Bellaston*; for she well knew
whom Mr. *Western* meant; though perhaps she thought he would
easily be reconciled to his Lordship's Proposals.

'Do you hear there,' quoth the Squire, 'what her Ladyship says?
All your Family are for the Match. Come, *Sophy*, be a good Girl,
and be dutiful, and make your Father happy.'

'If my Death will make you happy, Sir,' answered *Sophia*, 'you
will shortly be so.'

'It's a Lie, *Sophy*; it's a d—n'd Lie, and you know it,' said the
Squire.

'Indeed, Miss *Western*,' said Lady *Bellaston*, 'you injure your

Father; he hath nothing in View but your Interest in this Match; and I and all your Friends must acknowledge the highest Honour done to your Family in the Proposal.'

'Ay, all of us,' quoth the Squire: 'Nay, it was no Proposal of mine. She knows it was her Aunt proposed it to me first.—Come, *Sophy*, once more let me beg you to be a good Girl, and gee me your Consent before your Cousin.'

'Let me give him your Hand, Cousin,' said the Lady. 'It is the Fashion now-a-days to dispense with Time and long Courtships.'

'Pugh,' said the Squire, 'what signifies Time; won't they have Time enough to court afterwards? People may court very well after they have been a bed together.'

As Lord *Fellamar* was very well assured, that he was meant by Lady *Bellaston*, so never having heard nor suspected a Word of *Blifil*, he made no Doubt of his being meant by the Father. Coming up therefore to the Squire, he said, 'Though I have not the Honour, Sir, of being personally known to you; yet, as I find I have the Happiness to have my Proposals accepted, let me intercede, Sir, in Behalf of the young Lady, that she may not be more solicited at this Time.'

'You intercede, Sir!' said the Squire, 'why, who the Devil are you?'

'Sir, I am Lord *Fellamar*,' answered he, 'and am the happy Man, whom I hope you have done the Honour of accepting for a Son-in-law.'

'You are a Son of a B—,' replied the Squire, 'for all your laced Coat. You my Son-in-law, and be d—n'd to you!'

'I shall take more from you, Sir, than from any Man,' answered the Lord; 'but I must inform you, that I am not used to hear such Language without Resentment.'

'Resent my A—,' quoth the Squire. 'Don't think I am afraid of such a Fellow as thee art! Because hast a got a Spit there dangling at thy Side. Lay by your Spit, and I'll give thee enough of meddling with what doth not belong to thee.—I'll teach you to Father-in-law me, I'll lick thy Jacket.'

'It's very well, Sir,' said my Lord, 'I shall make no Disturbance before the Ladies. I am very well satisfied. Your humble Servant, Sir; Lady *Bellaston*, your most obedient.'

His Lordship was no sooner gone, than Lady *Bellaston* coming up to Mr. *Western*, said, 'Bless me, Sir, what have you done? You know not whom you have affronted; he is a Nobleman of the first Rank and Fortune, and Yesterday made Proposals to your Daughter; and such as I am sure you must accept with the highest Pleasure.'

'Answer for yourself, Lady Cousin,' said the Squire, 'I will have nothing to do with any of your Lords. My Daughter shall have an honest Country Gentleman; I have pitched upon one for her,—and she shall ha' un. I am sorry for the Trouble she hath given your Ladyship with all my Heart.' Lady *Bellaston* made a civil Speech upon the Word Trouble, to which the Squire answered, 'Why that's kind,—and I would do as much for your Ladyship. To be sure Relations should do for one another. So I wish your Ladyship a good Night.—Come, Madam, you must go along with me by fair Means, or I'll have you carried down to the Coach.'

Sophia said she would attend him without Force; but begged to go in a Chair, for she said she should not be able to ride any other Way.

'Prithee,' cries the Squire, 'wout unt persuade me canst not ride in a Coach, wouldst? That's a pretty Thing surely. No, no, I'll never let thee out of my Sight any more till art married, that I promise thee.' *Sophia* told him she saw he was resolved to break her Heart. 'O break thy Heart and be d—n'd,' quoth he, 'if a good Husband will break it. I don't value a Brass Varden, not a Hapenny of any undutiful B— upon Earth.' He then took violently hold of her hand; upon which the Parson once more interfered, begging him to use gentle Methods. At that the Squire thundered out a Curse, and bid the Parson hold his Tongue, saying, 'At'n't in Pulpit now? when art a got up there I never mind what dost say; but I won't be Priest-ridden, nor taught how to behave myself by thee. I wish your Ladyship a good Night. Come along, *Sophy*; be a good Girl, and all shall be well. Shat ha un, d—n me, shat ha un.'

Mrs. *Honour* appeared below Stairs, and with a low Curtesy to the Squire, offered to attend her Mistress; but he pushed her away, saying, 'Hold, Madam, hold, you come no more near my House.' 'And will you take my Maid away from me?' said *Sophia*. 'Yes, indeed, Madam, will I,' cries the Squire: 'You need not fear being without a Servant; I will get you another Maid, and a better Maid than this, who, I'd lay five Pound to a Crown, is no more a Maid than my Grannum. No, no, *Sophy*, she shall contrive no more Escapes I promise you.' He then packed up his Daughter and the Parson into the Hackney Coach, after which he mounted himself, and ordered it to drive to his Lodgings. In the Way thither he suffered *Sophia* to be quiet, and entertained himself with reading a Lecture to the Parson on good Manners, and a proper Behaviour to his Betters.

It is possible he might not so easily have carried off his Daughter from Lady *Bellaston*, had that good Lady desired to have detained her; but in reality, she was not a little pleased with the Confinement into which *Sophia* was going: And as her Project with Lord *Fellamar* had failed of Success, she was well contented that other violent Methods were now going to be used in Favour of another Man.

Chapter VI.

By what Means the Squire came to discover his Daughter.

Though the Reader in many Histories is obliged to digest much more unaccountable Appearances than this of Mr. *Western*, without any Satisfaction at all; yet, as we dearly love to oblige him whenever it is in our Power, we shall now proceed to shew by what Method the Squire discovered where his Daughter was.

In the third Chapter then of the preceding Book, we gave a Hint (for it is not our Custom to unfold at any Time more than is necessary for the Occasion) that Mrs. *Fitzpatrick*, who was very desirous of reconciling her Uncle and Aunt *Western*, thought she had a probable opportunity, by the Service of preserving *Sophia* from committing the same Crime which had drawn on herself the Anger of her Family. After much Deliberation therefore she resolved to inform her Aunt *Western* where her Cousin was, and accordingly she writ the following Letter, which we shall give the Reader at length, for more Reasons than one.

'Honoured Madam,

'The Occasion of my writing this will perhaps make a Letter of mine agreeable to my dear Aunt, for the. Sake of one of her Nieces, tho' I have little Reason to hope it will be so on the Account of another.

'Without more Apology, as I was coming to throw my unhappy Self at your Feet, I met, by the strangest Accident in the World, my Cousin *Sophy*, whose History you are better acquainted with than myself, though, alas! I know infinitely too much; enough indeed to satisfy me, that unless she is immediately prevented, she is in Danger of running into the same fatal Mischief, which, by foolishly and ignorantly refusing your most wise and prudent Advice, I have unfortunately brought on myself.

'In short, I have seen the Man, nay, I was most part of Yesterday in his Company, and a charming young Fellow I promise you he is. By what Accident he came acquainted with me is too tedious to tell you now; but I have this Morning changed my Lodgings to avoid him, lest he should by my Means discover my Cousin; for he doth not yet know where she is, and it is adviseable he should not, till my Uncle hath secured her.—No Time therefore is to be lost; and I need only inform you, that she is now with Lady *Bellaston*, whom I have seen, and who hath, I find, a Design of concealing her from her Family. You know, Madam, she is a strange Woman; but nothing could misbecome me more, than to presume to give any

Hint to one of your great Understanding, and great Knowledge of the World, besides barely informing you of the Matter of Fact.

'I hope, Madam, the Care which I have shewn on this Occasion for the Good of my Family, will recommend me again to the Favour of a Lady who hath always exerted so much Zeal for the Honour and true Interest of us all; and that it may be a Means of restoring me to your Friendship, which hath made so great a Part of my former, and is so necessary to my future Happiness. I am,

> 'With the utmost Respect,
> 'Honoured Madam,
> 'Your most dutiful obliged Niece,
> 'And most Obedient,
> 'Humble Servant,
>   '*Harriet Fitzpatrick.*'

Mrs. *Western* was now at her Brother's House, where she had resided ever since the Flight of *Sophia*, in order to administer Comfort to the poor Squire in his Affliction. Of this Comfort which she doled out to him in daily Portions, we have formerly given a Specimen.

She was now standing with her Back to the Fire, and, with a Pinch of Snuff in her Hand, was dealing forth this daily Allowance of Comfort to the Squire, while he smoaked his Afternoon Pipe, when she received the above Letter; which she had no sooner read than she delivered it to him, saying, 'There, Sir, there is an Account of your lost Sheep. Fortune hath again restored her to you, and if you will be governed by my Advice, it is possible you may yet preserve her.'

The Squire had no sooner read the Letter than he leaped from his Chair, threw his Pipe into the Fire, and gave a loud Huzza for Joy. He then summoned his Servants, called for his Boots, and ordered the *Chevalier* and several other Horses to be saddled, and that Parson *Supple* should be immediately sent for. Having done this, he turned to his Sister, caught her in his Arms, and gave her a close Embrace, saying, 'Zounds! you don't seem pleased; one would imagine you was sorry I have found the Girl.'

'Brother,' answered she, 'the deepest Politicians, who see to the Bottom, discover often a very different Aspect of Affairs, from what swims on the Surface. It is true indeed, Things do look rather less desperate than they did formerly in *Holland*, when *Lewis* the fourteenth[1] was at the Gates of *Amsterdam*; but there is a Delicacy required in this Matter, which you will pardon me, Brother, if I suspect you want. There is a Decorum to be used with a Woman of

---

1. Louis XIV suddenly invaded Holland in 1672, but William of Orange checked him before Amsterdam by opening the sluices in the dikes and flooding vast areas.

Figure, such as Lady *Bellaston*, Brother, which requires a Knowledge of the World superior, I am afraid, to yours.'

'Sister,' cries the Squire, 'I know you have no Opinion of my Parts; but I'll shew you on this Occasion who is a Fool. Knowledge quotha! I have not been in the Country so long without having some Knowledge of Warrants and the Law of the Land. I know I may take my own wherever I can find it. Shew me my own Daughter, and if I don't know how to come at her, I'll suffer you to call me Fool as long as I live. There be Justices of Peace in *London*, as well as in other Places.'

'I protest,' cries she, 'you make me tremble for the Event of this Matter, which if you will proceed by my Advice, you may bring to so good an Issue. Do you really imagine, Brother, that the House of a Woman of Figure is to be attacked by Warrants and brutal Justices of the Peace? I will inform you how to proceed. As soon as you arrive in Town, and have got yourself into a decent Dress (for indeed, Brother, you have none at present fit to appear in) you must send your Compliments to Lady *Bellaston*, and desire Leave to wait on her. When you are admitted to her Presence, as you certainly will be, and have told her your Story, and have made proper Use of my Name, (for I think you just know one another only by Sight, though you are Relations,) I am confident she will withdraw her Protection from my Niece, who hath certainly imposed upon her. This is the only Method.—Justices of Peace indeed! do you imagine any such Event can arrive to a Woman of Figure in a civilized Nation?'

'D——n their Figures,' cries the Squire; 'a pretty civilized Nation truly, where Women are above the Law. And what must I stand sending a Parcel of Compliments to a confounded Whore, that keeps away a Daughter from her own natural Father? I tell you, Sister, I am not so ignorant as you think me.—I know you would have Women above the Law, but it is all a Lie; I heard his Lordship say at Size, that no one is above the Law. But this of yours is *Hannover* Law,[2] I suppose.'

'Mr. *Western*,' said she, 'I think you daily improve in Ignorance ——I protest you are grown an arrant Bear.'

'No more a Bear than yourself, Sister *Western*,' said the Squire. —'Pox! you may talk of your Civility an you will, I am sure you never shew any to me. I am no Bear, no, nor no Dog neither, though I know Somebody, that is something that begins with a

2. When Queen Anne (the last Stuart, daughter of James II) died childless in 1714 (she had had ten miscarriages, two children who died shortly after birth, and one son who died at eleven), England invited the Elector of Hanover, great-grandson of James I through his daughter Elizabeth, and second cousin to Queen Mary and Queen Anne, to become George I (1714–27). Now, in 1745, George II (1727–60) is on the throne, and Western, typical of country squires, supports the Stuarts as the native and rightful line and despises all things Hanoverian, even though the Hanoverians are Stuarts too.

B—; but Pox! I will shew you I have a got more good Manners than some Folks.'

'Mr. *Western*,' answered the Lady, 'you may say what you please, *Je vous mesprise de tout mon Cœur*.[3] I shall not therefore be angry.—Besides, as my Cousin with that odious *Irish* Name justly says, I have that Regard for the Honour and true Interest of my Family, and that Concern for my Niece, who is a Part of it, that I have resolved to go to Town myself upon this Occasion; for indeed, indeed, Brother, you are not a fit Minister to be employed at a polite Court.——*Greenland—Greenland* should always be the Scene of the Tramontane Negotiation.'

'I thank Heaven,' cries the Squire, 'I don't understand you now. You are got to your *Hannoverian* Linguo. However, I'll shew you I scorn to be behind-hand in Civility with you; and as you are not angry for what I have said, so I am not angry for what you have said. Indeed I have always thought it a Folly for Relations to quarrel; and if they do now and then give a hasty Word, why People should give and take; for my Part I never bear Malice; and I take it very kind of you to go up to *London*; for I never was there but twice in my Life, and then I did not stay above a Fortnight at a Time; and to be sure I can't be expected to know much of the Streets and the Folks in that Time. I never denied that you know'd all these Matters better than I. For me to dispute that would be all as one, as for you to dispute the Management of a Pack of Dogs, or the finding a Hare sitting, with me.'—'Which I promise you,' says she, 'I never will.' '—Well, and I promise you,' returned he, 'that I never will dispute the t'other.'

Here then a League was struck (to borrow a Phrase from the Lady) between the contending Parties; and now the Parson arriving, and the Horses being ready, the Squire departed, having promised his Sister to follow her Advice, and she prepared to follow him the next Day.

But having communicated these Matters to the Parson on the Road, they both agreed that the prescribed Formalities might very well be dispensed with; and the Squire having changed his Mind, proceeded in the Manner we have already seen.

Chapter VII.

In which various Misfortunes befel poor Jones.

Affairs were in the aforesaid Situation, when Mrs. *Honour* arrived at Mrs. *Miller's*, and called *Jones* out from the Company, as we have before seen, with whom, when she found herself alone, she began as follows.

---

3. "I scorn you with all my heart."

'O my dear Sir, how shall I get Spirits to tell you; you are undone, Sir, and my poor Lady's undone, and I am undone.' 'Hath any thing happened to *Sophia?*' cries *Jones,* staring like a Mad-man. 'All that is bad,' cries *Honour;* 'O I shall never get such another Lady! O that I should ever live to see this Day!' At these Words *Jones* turned pale as Ashes, trembled and stammered; but *Honour* went on. 'O, Mr. *Jones,* I have lost my Lady for ever.' 'How! What! for Heaven's Sake tell me.—O my dear *Sophia!*'—'You may well call her so,' said *Honour;* 'she was the dearest Lady to me.—I shall never have such another Place.'—'D—n your Place,' cries *Jones;* 'where is? what! what is become of my *Sophia?*' 'Ay, to be sure,' cries she, 'Servants may be d—n'd. It signifies nothing what becomes of them, tho' they are turned away, and ruined ever so much. To be sure they are not Flesh and Blood like other People. No to be sure, it signifies nothing what becomes of them.'—'If you have any Pity, any Compassion,' cries *Jones,* 'I beg you will instantly tell me what hath happened to *Sophia?*' 'To be sure I have more Pity for you than you have for me, answered *Honour;* I don't d—n you because you have lost the sweetest Lady in the World. To be sure you are worthy to be pitied, and I am worthy to be pitied too: For to be sure if ever there was a good Mistress'—'What hath happened, cries *Jones,* in almost a raving Fit.——'What?——What? said *Honour;* why the worst that could have happened both for you and for me.——Her Father is come to Town, and hath carried her away from us both.' Here *Jones* fell on his Knees in Thanksgiving that it was no worse.—'No worse! repeated *Honour,* what could be worse for either of us? He carried her off, swearing she should marry Mr. *Blifil;* that's for your Comfort; and for poor me, I am turned out of Doors.' 'Indeed Mrs. *Honour,* answered *Jones,* you frightned me out of my Wits. I imagined some most dreadful sudden Accident had happened to *Sophia;* something, compared to which, even the seeing her married to *Blifil* would be a Trifle; but while there is Life, there are Hopes, my dear *Honour.* Women in this Land of Liberty cannot be married by actual brutal Force.' 'To be sure, Sir, said she, that's true. There may be some Hopes for you; but alack-a-day! what Hopes are there for poor me? And to be sure, Sir, you must be sensible I suffer all this upon your Account. All the Quarrel the Squire hath to me is for taking your Part, as I have done, against Mr. *Blifil.*' 'Indeed Mrs. *Honour,* answered he, I am sensible of my Obligations to you, and will leave nothing in my Power undone to make you amends.' 'Alas, Sir, said she, what can make a Servant amends for the Loss of one Place, but the getting another altogether as good!'—'Do not despair, Mrs. *Honour,* said *Jones,* I hope to reinstate you again in the same.' 'Alack-a-day, Sir, said she, how can I flatter myself with such Hopes, when I know it is a Thing impossible; for the Squire is so set against me: And yet if you should ever have my Lady, as to be sure I now hopes heartily you will; for you are a generous good-natured Gentleman, and I am sure you loves her, and to be sure she loves you as dearly as her own Soul; it is a Matter in vain to deny it; because as why, every Body that is in the least acquainted with my Lady, must see it; for, poor dear Lady, she can't dissemble; and if two People who loves one another a'n't happy, why who should be so? Happiness don't always depend upon what People has; besides, my Lady has enough for both. To be sure therefore as one may say, it would be all the Pity in the World to keep two such Loviers asunder; nay, I am convinced for my Part, you will meet together at last; for if it is to be, there is no preventing it. If a Marriage is made in Heaven, all the Justices of Peace upon Earth can't break it off. To be sure I wishes that Parson *Supple* had but a little more Spirit to tell the Squire of his Wickedness in endeavouring to force his Daughter contrary to her Liking; but then his whole Dependance is on the Squire, and so the poor Gentleman, though he is a very religious good sort of Man, and talks of the Badness of such Doings behind the Squire's Back, yet he dares not say his Soul is his own to his Face. To be sure I never saw him make so bold as just now, I was afeared the Squire would have struck him.—I would not have your Honour be melancholy, Sir, nor despair; Things may go better, as long as you are sure of my Lady, and that I am certain you may be; for she never will be brought to consent to marry any other Man. Indeed, I am terribly afeard the Squire will do her a Mischief in his Passion: For he is a prodigious passionate Gentleman, and I am afeard too the poor Lady will be brought to break her Heart; for she is as tender-hearted as a Chicken; it is pity methinks, she had not a little of my Courage. If I was in Love with a young Man, and my Father offered to lock me up, I'd tear his Eyes out, but I'd come at him; but then there's a great Fortune in the Case, which it is in her Father's Power either to give her or not; that, to be sure, may make some Difference.'

Whether *Jones* gave strict Attention to all the foregoing Harangue, or whether it was for want of any Vacancy in the Discourse, I cannot determine; but he never once attempted to answer, nor did she once stop, till *Partridge* came running into the Room, and informed him that the great Lady was upon the Stairs.

Nothing could equal the Dilemma to which *Jones* was now reduced. *Honour* knew nothing of any Acquaintance that subsisted between him and Lady *Bellaston*, and she was almost the last Person in the World to whom he would have communicated it. In this Hurry and Distress, he took (as is common enough) the worst Course, and instead of exposing her to the Lady, which would have been of little Consequence, he chose to expose the Lady to her; he therefore resolved to hide *Honour*, whom he had but just time to convey behind the Bed, and to draw the Curtains.

The Hurry in which *Jones* had been all Day engaged on Account of his poor Landlady and her Family, the Terrors occasioned by Mrs. *Honour*, and the Confusion into which he was thrown by the sudden Arrival of Lady *Bellaston*, had altogether driven former Thoughts out of his Head; so that it never once occur'd to his Memory to act the Part of a sick Man; which indeed, neither the Gaiety of his Dress, nor the Freshness of his Countenance would have at all supported.

He received her Ladyship therefore rather agreeably to her Desires than to her Expectations, with all the good Humour he could muster in his Countenance, and without any real or affected Appearance of the least Disorder.

Lady *Bellaston* no sooner entered the Room, than she squatted herself down on the Bed: 'So, my dear *Jones*,' said she, 'you find nothing can detain me long from you. Perhaps I ought to be angry with you, that I have neither seen nor heard from you all Day; for I perceive your Distemper would have suffered you to come abroad: Nay, I suppose you have not sat in your Chamber all Day drest up like a fine Lady to see Company after a Lying in; but however, don't think I intend to scold you: For I never will give you an Excuse for the cold Behaviour of a Husband, by putting on the ill Humour of a Wife.'

'Nay, Lady *Bellaston*,' said *Jones*, 'I am sure your Ladyship will not upbraid me with Neglect of Duty, when I only waited for Orders. Who, my dear Creature, hath Reason to complain? Who missed an Appointment last Night, and left an unhappy Man to expect, and wish, and sigh, and languish?'

'Do not mention it, my dear Mr. *Jones*,' cried she. 'If you knew the Occasion, you would pity me. In short, it is impossible to conceive what Women of Condition are obliged to suffer from the Impertinence of Fools, in order to keep up the Farce of the World. I am glad, however, all your languishing and wishing have done you no harm: For you never looked better in your Life. Upon my Faith! *Jones*, you might at this Instant sit for the Picture of *Adonis*.'

There are certain Words of Provocation which Men of Honour hold can properly be answered only by a Blow. Among Lovers possibly there may be some Expressions which can be answered only by a Kiss. Now the Compliment which Lady *Bellaston* now made *Jones* seems to be of this Kind, especially as it was attended with a Look in which the Lady conveyed more soft Ideas than it was possible to express with her Tongue.

Jones was certainly at this Instant in one of the most disagreeable and distress'd Situations imaginable; for to carry on the Comparison we made use of before, tho' the Provocation was given by the Lady, *Jones* could not receive Satisfaction, nor so much as offer to ask it, in the Presence of a third Person; Seconds in this kind of Duels not being according to the Law of Arms. As this Objection did not occur to Lady *Bellaston*, who was ignorant of any other Woman being there but herself, she waited some time in great Astonishment for an Answer from *Jones*, who conscious of the ridiculous Figure he made, stood at a Distance, and not daring to give the proper Answer, gave none at all. Nothing can be imagined more comic, nor yet more tragical than this Scene would have been, if it had lasted much longer. The Lady had already changed Colour two or three times; had got up from the Bed and sat down again, while *Jones* was wishing the Ground to sink under him, or the House to fall on his Head, when an odd Accident freed him from an Embarrassment out of which neither the Eloquence of a *Cicero*, nor the Politics of a *Machiavel* could have delivered him, without utter Disgrace.

This was no other than the Arrival of young *Nightingale* dead drunk; or rather in that State of Drunkenness which deprives Men of the Use of their Reason, without depriving them of the Use of their Limbs.

Mrs. *Miller* and her Daughters were in Bed, and *Partridge* was smoaking his Pipe by the Kitchin Fire; so that he arrived at Mr. *Jones*'s Chamber Door without any Interruption. This he burst open, and was entering without any Ceremony, when *Jones* started from his Seat, and ran to oppose him; which he did so effectually, that *Nightingale* never came far enough within the Door to see who was sitting on the Bed.

Nightingale had in Reality mistaken *Jones*'s Apartment for that in which himself had lodged; he therefore strongly insisted on coming in, often swearing that he would not be kept from his own Bed. *Jones*, however, prevailed over him, and delivered him into the Hands of *Partridge*, whom the Noise on the Stairs soon summoned to his Master's Assistance.

And now *Jones* was unwillingly obliged to return to his own Apartment, where at the very Instant of his Entrance he heard Lady *Bellaston* venting an Exclamation, though not a very loud one; and at the same Time, saw her flinging herself into a Chair in a vast Agitation, which in a Lady of a tender Constitution would have been an Hysteric Fit.

In reality the Lady, frightened with the Struggle between the two Men, of which she did not know what would be the Issue, as she heard *Nightingale* swear many Oaths he would come to his own Bed, attempted to retire to her known Place of Hiding, which to her great Confusion she found already occupied by another.

'Is this Usage to be borne, Mr. *Jones?*' cries the Lady, '—basest of Men?——What Wretch is this to whom you have exposed me?' 'Wretch!' cries *Honour*, bursting in a violent Rage from her Place of Concealment——'marry come up?—Wretch forsooth!—As poor a Wretch as I am, I am honest; that is more than some Folks who are richer can say.'

Jones, instead of applying himself directly to take off the Edge of Mrs. *Honour*'s Resentment, as a more experienced Gallant would have done, fell to cursing his Stars, and lamenting himself as the most unfortunate Man in the World; and presently after, addressing himself to Lady *Bellaston*, he fell to some very absurd Protestations of Innocence. By this time the Lady having recovered the Use of her Reason, which she had as ready as any Woman in the World, especially on such Occasions, calmly replied; 'Sir, you need make no Apologies, I see now who the Person is; I did not at first know Mrs. *Honour*; but now I do, I can suspect nothing wrong between her and you; and I am sure she is a Woman of too good Sense to put any wrong Constructions upon my Visit to you; I have been always her Friend, and it may be in my Power to be much more hereafter.'

Mrs. *Honour* was altogether as placable, as she was passionate. Hearing therefore Lady *Bellaston* assume the soft Tone, she likewise softened her's.——'I'm sure, Madam,' says she, 'I have been always ready to acknowledge your Ladyship's Friendships to me; sure I never had so good a Friend as your Ladyship——and to be sure now I see it is your Ladyship that I spoke to, I could almost bite my Tongue off for very mad.——I Constructions upon your Ladyship——to be sure it doth not become a Servant as I am to think about such a great Lady—I mean I was a Servant: For indeed I am no Body's Servant now, the more miserable Wretch is me.——I have lost the best Mistress.'——Here *Honour* thought fit to produce a Shower of Tears.—'Don't cry, Child,' says the good Lady, 'Ways perhaps may be found to make you amends. Come to me to-morrow Morning.' She then took up her Fan which lay on the Ground, and without even looking at *Jones*, walked very majestically out of the Room; there being a kind of Dignity in the Impudence of Women of Quality, which their Inferiors vainly aspire to attain to in Circumstances of this Nature.

Jones followed her down Stairs, often offering her his Hand, which she absolutely refused him, and got into her Chair without taking any Notice of him as he stood bowing before her.

At his Return up Stairs, a long Dialogue past between him and Mrs. *Honour*, while she was adjusting herself after the Discomposure she had undergone. The Subject of this was his Infidelity to her young Lady; on which she enlarged with great Bitterness; but *Jones* at last found means to reconcile her, and not only so, but to obtain a Promise of most inviolable Secrecy, and that she would the next Morning endeavour to find out *Sophia*, and bring him a further Account of the Proceedings of the Squire.

Thus ended this unfortunate Adventure to the Satisfaction only of Mrs. *Honour*; for a Secret (as some of my Readers will perhaps acknowledge from Experience) is often a very valuable Possession; and that not only to those who faithfully keep it, but sometimes to such as whisper it about till it come to the Ears of every one, except the ignorant Person, who pays for the supposed concealing of what is publickly known.

Chapter VIII.

Short and sweet.

Notwithstanding all the Obligations she had received from *Jones*, Mrs. *Miller* could not forbear in the Morning some gentle Remonstrances for the Hurricane which had happened the preceding Night in his Chamber. These were however so gentle and so friendly; professing, and indeed truly, to aim at nothing more than the real Good of Mr. *Jones* himself, that he, far from being offended, thankfully received the Admonition of the good Woman, expressed much Concern for what had past, excused it as well as he could, and promised never more to bring the same disturbances into the House.

But though Mrs. *Miller* did not refrain from a short Expostulation in private at their first meeting; yet the Occasion of his being summoned down Stairs that Morning was of a much more agreeable Kind; being indeed to perform the Office of a Father to Miss *Nancy*, and to give her in Wedlock to Mr. *Nightingale*, who was now ready drest, and full as sober as many of my Readers will think a Man ought to be who receives a Wife in so imprudent a Manner.

And here perhaps it may be proper to account for the Escape which this young Gentleman had made from his Uncle, and for his Appearance in the Condition in which we have seen him the Night before.

Now when the Uncle had arrived at his Lodgings with his Nephew, partly to indulge his own Inclinations (for he dearly loved his Bottle) and partly to disqualify his Nephew from the immediate Execution of his Purpose, he ordered Wine to be set on the Table; with which he so briskly ply'd the young Gentleman, that this latter, who, though not much used to Drinking, did not detest it so as to be guilty of Disobedience, or of Want of Complaisance by refusing, was soon completely finished.

Just as the Uncle had obtained this Victory, and was preparing a Bed for his Nephew, a Messenger arrived with a Piece of News, which so entirely disconcerted and shocked him, that he in a Moment lost all Consideration for his Nephew, and his whole Mind became entirely taken up with his own Concerns.

This sudden and afflicting News was no less than that his Daughter had taken the Opportunity of almost the first Moment of his Absence, and had gone off with a neighbouring young Clergyman; against whom, tho' her Father could have had but one Objection, namely, that he was worth nothing, yet she had never thought proper to communicate her Amour even to that Father; and so artfully had she managed, that it had never been once suspected by any, till now that it was consummated.

Old Mr. *Nightingale* no sooner received this Account, than in the utmost Confusion he ordered a Post-chaise to be instantly got ready, and having recommended his Nephew to the Care of a Servant, he directly left the House, scarce knowing what he did, nor whither he went.

The Uncle thus departed, when the Servant came to attend the Nephew to Bed, had waked him for that Purpose, and had at last made him sensible that his Uncle was gone, he, instead of accepting the kind Offices tendered him, insisted on a Chair being called; with this the Servant, who had received no strict Orders to the contrary, readily complied; and thus being conducted back to the House of Mrs. *Miller*, he had staggered up to Mr. *Jones's* Chamber, as hath been before recounted.

This Bar of the Uncle being now removed (though young *Nightingale* knew not as yet in what Manner) and all Parties being quickly ready, the Mother, Mr. *Jones*, Mr. *Nightingale*, and his Love stept into a Hackney-Coach, which conveyed him to Doctor's Commons; where Miss *Nancy* was, in vulgar Language, soon made an honest Woman, and the poor Mother became in the purest Sense of the Word, one of the happiest of all human Beings.

And now Mr. *Jones* having seen his good Offices to that poor Woman and her Family brought to a happy Conclusion, began to apply himself to his own Concerns; but here lest many of my Readers should censure his Folly for thus troubling himself with the Affairs of others, and lest some few should think he acted more disinterestedly than indeed he did, we think proper to assure our Reader, that he was so far from being unconcerned in this Matter, that he had indeed a very considerable Interest in bringing it to that final Consummation.

To explain this seeming Paradox at once, he was one who could truly say with him in *Terence, Homo sum: Humani nihil a me alienum puto.*[1] He was never an indifferent Spectator of the Misery or Happiness of any one; and he felt either the one or the other in

1. From *Heautontimorumenos* ("The Self-Torturer") I.i.25—"I am a man: I consider nothing human foreign to me." This speech became immediately famous. St. Augustine reports that Terence's audience burst into applause over it. See also Steele's *Spectator*, no. 502 (Shakespeare Head ed.).

greater Proportion as he himself contributed to either. He could not therefore be the Instrument of raising a whole Family from the lowest State of Wretchedness to the highest Pitch of Joy without conveying great Felicity to himself; more perhaps than worldly Men often purchase to themselves by undergoing the most severe Labour, and often by wading through the deepest Iniquity.

Those Readers who are of the same Complexion with him, will perhaps think this short Chapter contains abundance of Matter; while others may probably wish, short as it is, that it had been totally spared as impertinent to the main Design, which I suppose they conclude is to bring Mr. *Jones* to the Gallows, or if possible, to a more deplorable Catastrophe.

Chapter IX.

Containing Love-Letters of several sorts.

Mr. *Jones*, at his Return Home, found the following Letters lying on his Table, which he luckily opened in the Order they were sent.

LETTER I.

'Surely I am under some strange Infatuation; I cannot keep my Resolutions a Moment, however strongly made or justly founded. Last Night I resolved never to see you more; this Morning I am willing to hear if you can, as you say, clear up this Affair. And yet I know that to be impossible. I have said every Thing to myself which you can invent.——Perhaps not. Perhaps your Invention is stronger. Come to me therefore the Moment you receive this. If you can forge an Excuse I almost promise you to believe it. Betrayed to——I will think no more.—Come to me directly.—This is the third Letter I have writ, the two former are burnt——I am almost inclined to burn this too—I wish I may preserve my Senses.—Come to me presently.'

LETTER II.

'If you ever expect to be forgiven, or even suffered within my Doors, come to me this Instant.'

LETTER III.

'I now find you was not at Home when my Notes came to your Lodgings. The Moment you receive this let me see you;—I shall not stir out; nor shall any Body be let in but yourself. Sure nothing can detain you long.'

Jones had just read over these three Billets, when Mr. *Nightingale* came into the Room. 'Well *Tom*,' said he, 'any News from

Lady *Bellaston* after last Night's Adventure?' (for it was now no
Secret to any one in that House who the Lady was.) 'The Lady *Bellaston?*' answered *Jones* very gravely.—'Nay, dear *Tom*,' cries *Nightingale*, 'don't be so reserved to your Friends. Though I was too
drunk to see last Night, I saw her at the Masquerade. Do you
think I am ignorant who the Queen of the Fairies is?' 'And did you
really then know the Lady at the Masquerade?' said *Jones*. 'Yes,
upon my Soul, did I,' said *Nightingale*; 'and have given you twenty
Hints of it since, though you seemed always so tender on that Point,
that I would not speak plainly. I fancy, my Friend, by your extreme
Nicety in this Matter, you are not so well acquainted with the
Character of the Lady, as with her Person. Don't be angry, *Tom*,
but, upon my Honour, you are not the first young Fellow she hath
debauched. Her Reputation is in no Danger, believe me.'

Though *Jones* had no Reason to imagine the Lady to have been
of the vestal Kind when his Amour began; yet as he was thoroughly
ignorant of the Town, and had very little Acquaintance in it, he
had no Knowledge of that Character which is vulgarly called a
Demirep; that is to say, a Woman who intrigues with every Man
she likes, under the Name and Appearance of Virtue; and who,
though some over-nice Ladies will not be seen with her, is visited
(as they term it) by the whole Town; in short, whom every Body
knows to be what no Body calls her.

When he found, therefore, that *Nightingale* was perfectly
acquainted with his Intrigue, and began to suspect, that so scrupulous a Delicacy as he had hitherto observed, was not quite necessary
on the Occasion, he gave a latitude to his Friend's Tongue, and
desired him to speak plainly what he knew, or had ever heard of the
Lady.

Nightingale, who in many other Instances, was rather too effeminate in his Disposition, had a pretty strong Inclination to Tittle-
Tattle. He had no sooner, therefore, received a full Liberty of speaking from *Jones*, than he entered upon a long Narrative concerning
the Lady; which as it contained many Particulars highly to her Dishonour, we have too great a Tenderness for all Women of Condition
to repeat. We would cautiously avoid giving an Opportunity to the
future Commentators on our Works, of making any malicious Application; and of forcing us to be against our Will, the Author of
Scandal, which never entered into our Head.

Jones having very attentively heard all that *Nightingale* had to
say, fetched a deep Sigh, which the other observing, cried, 'Heyday!
Why thou art not in Love. I hope! Had I imagined my Stories
would have affected you, I promise you should never have heard
them.' 'O my dear Friend,' cries *Jones*, 'I am so entangled with this
Woman, that I know not how to extricate myself. In Love indeed?

No, my Friend, but I am under Obligations to her, and very great ones. Since you know so much, I will be very explicit with you. It is owing perhaps solely to her, that I have not before this, wanted a Bit of Bread. How can I possibly desert such a Woman? and yet I must desert her, or be guilty of the blackest Treachery to one, who deserves infinitely better of me than she can: A Woman, my *Nightingale*, for whom I have a Passion which few can have an Idea of. I am half distracted with Doubts how to Act.' 'And is this other, pray, an honourable Mistress?' cries *Nightingale*. 'Honourable?' answered *Jones*; 'No Breath ever yet durst sully her Reputation. The sweetest Air is not purer, the limpid Stream not clearer than her Honour. She is all over, both in Mind and Body, consummate Perfection. She is the most beautiful Creature in the Universe; and yet she is Mistress of such noble, elevated Qualities, that though she is never from my Thoughts, I scarce ever think of her Beauty; but when I see it.'—'And can you, my good Friend,' cries *Nightingale*, 'with such an Engagement as this upon your Hands, hesitate a Moment about quitting such a——' 'Hold,' said *Jones*, 'no more Abuse of her; I detest the Thought of Ingratitude.' 'Pooh!' answered the other, 'you are not the first upon whom she hath conferred Obligations of this Kind. She is remarkably liberal where she likes; though, let me tell you, her Favours are so prudently bestowed, that they should rather raise a Man's Vanity, than his Gratitude.' In short, *Nightingale* proceeded so far on this Head, and told his Friend so many Stories of the Lady, which he swore to the Truth of, that he entirely removed all Esteem for her from the Breast of *Jones*; and his Gratitude was lessened in Proportion. Indeed he began to look on all the Favours he had received, rather as Wages than Benefits, which depreciated not only her, but himself too in his own Conceit, and put him quite out of Humour with both. From this Disgust, his Mind, by a natural Transition turned towards *Sophia:* Her Virtue, her Purity, her Love to him, her Sufferings on his Account, filled all his Thoughts, and made his Commerce with Lady *Bellaston* appear still more odious. The Result of all was, that though his turning himself out of her *Service*, in which Light he now saw his Affair with her, would be the Loss of his Bread; yet he determined to quit her, if he could but find a handsome Pretence; which being communicated to his Friend, *Nightingale* considered a little, and then said, 'I have it, my Boy! I have found out a sure Method: Propose Marriage to her, and I would venture hanging upon the Success.' 'Marriage!' cries *Jones*. 'Ay, propose Marriage,' answered *Nightingale*, 'and she will declare off in a Moment. I knew a young Fellow whom she kept formerly, who made the Offer to her in earnest, and was presently turned off for his Pains.'

Jones declared he could not venture the Experiment. 'Perhaps,' said he, 'she may be less shocked at this Proposal from one Man than from another. And if she should take me at my Word, where am I then? Caught in my own Trap, and undone for ever.' 'No;' answered *Nightingale*, 'not if I can give you an Expedient, by which you may, at any Time, get out of the Trap.'——'What Expedient can that be?' replied Jones. 'This,' answered *Nightingale*. 'The young Fellow I mentioned, who is one of the most intimate Acquaintances I have in the World, is so angry with her for some ill Offices she hath since done him, that I am sure he would, without any Difficulty, give you a Sight of her Letters; upon which you may decently break with her; and declare off before the Knot is ty'd, if she should really be willing to tie it, which I am convinced she will not.'

After some Hesitation, *Jones*, upon the Strength of this Assurance, consented; but as he swore he wanted the Confidence to propose the Matter to her Face, he wrote the following Letter, which *Nightingale* dictated.

'*Madam*,

'I am extremely concerned, that, by an unfortunate Engagement abroad, I should have missed receiving the Honour of your Ladyships Commands the Moment they came; and the Delay which I must now suffer of vindicating myself to your Ladyship, greatly adds to this Misfortune. O Lady *Bellaston*, what a Terror have I been in, for Fear your Reputation should be exposed by these perverse Accidents. There is one only Way to secure it. I need not name what that is. Only permit me to say, that as your Honour is as dear to me as my own; so my sole Ambition is to have the Glory of laying my Liberty at your Feet; and believe me when I assure you, I can never be made completely happy, without you generously bestow on me a legal Right of calling you mine for ever. I am,

'*Madam*,
'*With most profound Respect,*
'*Your Ladyship's most Obliged,*
Obedient humble Servant,
'*Thomas Jones.*'

To this she presently returned the following Answer.

'Sir,

'When I read over your serious Epistle, I could from its Coldness and Formality, have sworn that you already had the legal Right you mention; nay, that we had, for many Years, composed that monstrous Animal a Husband and Wife. Do you really then imagine me a Fool? Or do you fancy yourself capable of so entirely persuading me out of my Senses, that I should deliver my whole Fortune into your Power, in order to enable you to support your Pleasures at my Expence. Are these the Proofs of Love which I expected? Is this the Return for——but I scorn to upbraid you, and am in great Admiration of your profound Respect.

'P. S. I am prevented from Revising:—Perhaps I have said more than I meant.——Come to me at Eight this Evening.'

Jones, by the Advice of his Privy-council, replied.

'Madam,

'It is impossible to express how much I am shocked at the Suspicion you entertain of me. Can Lady *Bellaston* have conferred Favours on a Man whom she could believe capable of so base a Design? Or can she treat the most solemn Tie of Love with Contempt? Can you imagine, Madam, that if the Violence of my Passion, in an unguarded Moment, overcame the Tenderness which I have for your Honour, I would think of indulging myself in the Continuance of an Intercourse which could not possibly escape long the Notice of the World; and which when discovered, must prove so fatal to your Reputation? If such be your Opinion of me, I must pray for a sudden Opportunity of returning those pecuniary Obligations, which I have been so unfortunate to receive at your Hands; and for those of a more tender Kind, I shall ever remain, *&c.*' And so concluded in the very Words with which he had concluded the former Letter.

The Lady answered as follows:

'I see you are a Villain; and I despise you from my Soul. If you come here I shall not be at Home.'

Though *Jones* was well satisfied with his Deliverance from a Thraldom which those who have ever experienced it, will, I apprehend, allow to be none of the lightest, he was not, however, perfectly easy in his Mind. There was, in this Scheme, too much of Fallacy to satisfy one who utterly detested every Species of Falshood or Dishonesty: nor would he, indeed, have submitted to put it in Practice, had he not been involved in a distressful Situation, where he was obliged to be guilty of some Dishonour, either to the one Lady or the other; and surely the Reader will allow, that every good Principle, as well as Love, pleaded strongly in Favour of *Sophia*.

Nightingale, highly exulted in the Success of his Stratagem, upon which he received many Thanks, and much Applause from his Friend. He answered, 'Dear *Tom*, we have conferred very different Obligations on each other. To me you owe the regaining your Liberty; to you I owe the Loss of mine. But if you are as happy in the one Instance as I am in the other, I promise you, we are the two happiest Fellows in *England.*'

The two Gentlemen were now summoned down to Dinner, where Mrs. *Miller,* who performed herself the Office of Cook, had exerted her best Talents, to celebrate the Wedding of her Daughter. This joyful Circumstance she ascribed principally to the friendly Behaviour of *Jones,* her whole Soul was fired with Gratitude towards him, and all her Looks, Words, and Actions were so busied in expressing it, that her Daughter, and even her new Son-in-law, were very little the Objects of her Consideration.

Dinner was just ended when Mrs. *Miller* received a Letter; but as we have had Letters enough in this Chapter, we shall communicate the Contents in our next.

Chapter X.

Consisting partly of Facts, and partly of Observations upon them.

The Letter then which arrived at the End of the preceding Chapter was from Mr. *Allworthy,* and the Purport of it was his Intention to come immediately to Town, with his Nephew *Blifil,* and a Desire to be accommodated with his usual Lodgings, which were the first Floor for himself, and the second for his Nephew.

The Chearfulness which had before displayed itself in the Countenance of the poor Woman, was a little clouded on this Occasion. This News did indeed a good deal disconcert her. To requite so disinterested a Match with her Daughter, by presently turning her new Son-in-law out of Doors, appeared to her very unjustifiable on the one Hand; and on the other, she could scarce bear the Thoughts of making any Excuse to Mr. *Allworthy,* after all the Obligations received from him, for depriving him of Lodgings which were indeed strictly his Due: For that Gentleman, in conferring all his numberless Benefits on others, acted by a Rule diametrically opposite to what is practised by most generous People. He contrived, on all Occasions, to hide his Beneficence not only from the World, but even from the Object of it. He constantly used the Words *Lend* and *Pay,* instead of *Give;* and by every other Method he could invent, always lessened with his Tongue the Favours he conferred while he was heaping them with both his Hands. When he settled the Annuity of 50 *l.* a Year, therefore, on Mrs. *Miller,* he told her, 'it was in Consideration of always having her First-Floor when he was in Town,' (which he scarce ever intended to be) but that she might let it at any other Time, for that he would always send her a Month's Warning.' He was now, however, hurried to

Town so suddenly that he had no Opportunity of giving such
Notice; and this Hurry probably prevented him, when he wrote for
his Lodgings, adding, *if they were then empty:* For he would most
certainly have been well satisfied to have relinquished them on a
less sufficient Excuse, than what Mrs. *Miller* could now have made.

But there are a Sort of Persons, who, as *Prior*[1] excellently well
remarks, direct their Conduct by something

> *Beyond the fix'd and settled Rules*)
> *Of Vice and Virtue in the Schools,* }
> *Beyond the Letter of the Law.*)

To these it is so far from being sufficient that their Defence
would acquit them at the *Old-Bailey*, that they are not even contented, though Conscience, the severest of all Judges, should discharge them. Nothing short of the Fair and Honourable will satisfy
the Delicacy of their Minds; and if any of their Actions fall short of
this Mark, they mope and pine, are as uneasy and restless as a Murderer, who is afraid of a Ghost, or of the Hangman.

Mrs. *Miller* was one of these. She could not conceal her Uneasiness at this Letter; with the Contents of which she had no sooner
acquainted the Company, and given some Hints of her Distress,
than *Jones*, her good Angel, presently relieved her Anxiety. 'As for
myself, Madam,' said he, 'my Lodging is at your Service at a
Moment's Warning: And Mr. *Nightingale*, I am sure, as he cannot
yet prepare a House fit to receive his Lady, will consent to return to
his new Lodging, whither Mrs. *Nightingale* will certainly consent to
go.' With which Proposal both Husband and Wife instantly agreed.

The Reader will easily believe, that the Cheeks of Mrs. *Miller*
began again to glow with additional Gratitude to *Jones*; but, perhaps, it may be more difficult to persuade him, that Mr. *Jones*
having, in his last Speech, called her Daughter Mrs. *Nightingale*, (it
being the first Time that agreeable Sound had ever reached her
Ears) gave the fond Mother more Satisfaction, and warmed her
Heart more towards *Jones*, than his having dissipated her present
Anxiety.

The next Day was then appointed for the Removal of the new-
married Couple, and of Mr. *Jones*, who was likewise to be provided
for in the same House with his Friend. And now the Serenity of the
Company was again restored, and they past the Day in the utmost
Chearfulness, all except *Jones*, who, though he outwardly accompa-
nied the rest in their Mirth, felt many a bitter Pang on the
Account of his *Sophia*; which were not a little heightened by the
News of Mr. *Blifil*'s coming to Town, (for he clearly saw the Inten-

1. Matthew Prior (1664–1721). Fielding
quotes the opening lines of "Paulo Pur-
gante and His Wife." He quotes other
lines from this poem, and alludes to
them again, in *Amelia* IV.ii and XII.ii.

tion of his Journey:) And what greatly aggravated his Concern was, that Mrs. *Honour*, who had promised to enquire after *Sophia*, and to make her Report to him early the next Evening, had disappointed him.

In the Situation that he and his Mistress were in at this Time, there were scarce any Grounds for him to hope, that he should hear any good News; yet he was as impatient to see Mrs. *Honour*, as if he had expected she would bring him a Letter with an Assignation in it from *Sophia*, and bore the Disappointment as ill. Whether this Impatience arose from that natural Weakness of the human Mind, which makes it desirous to know the worst, and renders Uncertainty the most intolerable of Pains; or whether he still flattered himself with some secret Hopes, we will not determine. But that it might be the last, whoever has loved cannot but know. For of all the Powers exercised by this Passion over our Minds, one of the most wonderful is that of supporting Hope in the midst of Despair. Difficulties, Improbabilities, nay Impossibilities are quite overlooked by it; so that to any Man extremely in Love, may be applied what *Addison* says of *Cæsar*,[2]

The Alps, *and* Pyrenæans, *sink before him!*

Yet it is equally true, that the same Passion will sometimes make Mountains of Molehills, and produce Despair in the midst of Hope; but these cold Fits last not long in good Constitutions. Which Temper *Jones* was now in, we leave the Reader to guess, having no exact Information about it; but this is certain, that he had spent two Hours in Expectation, when being unable any longer to conceal his Uneasiness, he retired to his Room; where his Anxiety had almost made him frantick, when the following Letter was brought him from Mrs. *Honour*, with which we shall present the Reader *verbatim & literatim.*

'S I R,
'I shud sartenly haf kaled on you a cordin too mi Prommiss haddunt itt bin that hur Lashipp prevent mee; for too bee sur, Sir, you nose very well that evere Persun must luk furst at ome, and sartenly such anuther offar mite not ave ever hapned, so as I shud ave bin justly to blam, had I not excepted of it when her Laship was so veri kind as to offar to mak mee hur one Uman without mi ever askin any such thing, to bee sur shee is won of thee best Ladis in thee Wurld, and Pepil who sase to the Kontrari must bee veri wiket Pepil in thare Harts. To be sur if ever I ave sad any thing of that Kine it as bin thru Ignorens and I am hartili sorri for it. I nose your Onur to be a Genteelman of more Onur and Onesty, if I ever said ani such thing, to repete it to hurt a pore Servant that as alwais ad

thee gratest Respect in thee World for ure Onur. To bee sur won shud kepe wons Tung within one's Teeth, for no Boddi nose what may hapen; and too bee sur if ani Boddi ad tolde mee Yesterday, that I shud haf bin in so gud a Plase to Day, I shud not haf beleeved it; for too bee sur I never was a dremd of any such Thing, nor shud I ever have soft after ani other Bodi's Plase; but as her Lashipp wass so kine of her one a cord too give it mee without askin, to be sure Mrs. *Etoff* herself, nor no other Boddi can blam mee for exceptin such a Thing when it fals in mi Waye. I beg ure Onur not too menshion ani thing of what I haf sad, for I wish ure Onur all thee gud Luk in thee Wurld; and I don't cuestion butt thatt u wil haf Madam *Sophia* in the End; butt ass to miself ure Onur nose I kant bee of ani farder Sarvis to u in that Matar, nou bein under thee Cumand off anuthar Parson, and nott mi one Mistres. I begg ure Onur to say nothing of what past, and belive me to be, Sir,

> 'Ure Onur's umble Sarvant
> 'To Cumand till Deth,
> *'Honour Blackmore.'*

Various were the Conjectures which *Jones* entertained on this Step of Lady *Bellaston*; who in reality had little farther Design than to secure within her own House the Repository of a Secret, which she chose should make no farther Progress than it had made already; but mostly she desired to keep it from the Ears of *Sophia*; for though that young Lady was almost the only one who would never have repeated it again, her Ladyship could not persuade herself of this; since as she now hated poor *Sophia* with most implacable Hatred, she conceived a reciprocal Hatred to herself to be lodged in the tender Breast of our Heroine, where no such Passion had ever yet found an Entrance.

While *Jones* was terrifying himself with the Apprehension of a thousand dreadful Machinations, and deep political Designs, which he imagined to be at the Bottom of the Promotion of *Honour*, Fortune, who hitherto seems to have been an utter Enemy to his Match with *Sophia*, tried a new Method to put a final End to it, by throwing a Temptation in his Way, which in his present desperate Situation it seemed unlikely he should be able to resist.

Chapter XI.

Containing curious, but not unprecedented Matter.

There was a Lady, one Mrs. *Hunt*, who had often seen *Jones* at the House where he lodged, being intimately acquainted with the Women there, and indeed a very great Friend to Mrs. *Miller*. Her Age was about Thirty; for she owned Six and Twenty; her Face and

Person very good, only inclining a little too much to be fat. She had been married young by her Relations to an old *Turkey* merchant, who having got a great Fortune, had left off Trade. With him she lived without Reproach, but not without Pain, in a State of great Self-denial, for about twelve Years; and her Virtue was rewarded by his dying, and leaving her very rich. The first Year of her Widowhood was just at an End, and she had past it in a good deal of Retirement, seeing only a few particular Friends, and dividing her Time between her Devotions and Novels, of which she was always extremely fond. Very good Health, a very warm Constitution, and a good deal of Religion, made it absolutely necessary for her to marry again; and she resolved to please herself in her second Husband, as she had done her Friends in the first. From her the following Billet was brought to *Jones*.

'Sir,

'From the first Day I saw you I doubt my Eyes have told you too plainly, that you were not indifferent to me; but neither my Tongue nor my Hand should have ever avowed it, had not the Ladies of the Family where you are lodged given me such a Character of you, and told me such Proofs of your Virtue and Goodness, as convince me you are not only the most agreeable, but the most worthy of Men. I have also the Satisfaction to hear from them, that neither my Person, Understanding, or Character are disagreeable to you. I have a Fortune sufficient to make us both happy, but which cannot make me so without you. In thus disposing of myself I know I shall incur the Censure of the World; but if I did not love you more than I fear the World, I should not be worthy of you. One only Difficulty stops me: I am informed you are engaged in a Commerce of Gallantry with a Woman of Fashion. If you think it worth while to sacrifice that to the Possession of me, I am yours; if not, forget my Weakness, and let this remain an eternal Secret between you and

'*Arabella Hunt.*'

At the reading of this *Jones* was put into a violent Flutter. His Fortune was then at a very low Ebb, the Source being stopt from which hitherto he had been supplied. Of all he had received from Lady *Bellaston* not above five Guineas remained, and that very Morning he had been dunned by a Tradesman for twice that Sum. His honourable Mistress was in the Hands of her Father, and he had scarce any Hopes ever to get her out of them again. To be subsisted at her Expence from that little Fortune she had independent of her Father, went much against the Delicacy both of his Pride and his Love. This Lady's Fortune would have been exceeding convenient to him, and he could have no Objection to her in any Respect. On the contrary, he liked her as well as he did any Woman except Sophia. But to abandon *Sophia*, and marry another, that was impossible; he could not think of it upon any Account. Yet why should he not, since it was plain she could not be his? Would it not be kinder to her, than to continue her longer engaged in a hopeless Passion for him? Ought he not to do so in Friendship to her? This Notion prevailed some Moments, and he had almost determined to be false to her from a high Point of Honour; but that Refinement was not able to stand very long against the Voice of Nature, which cried in his Heart, that such Friendship was Treason to Love. At last he called for Pen, Ink, and Paper, and writ as follows to Mrs. *Hunt*.

'Madam,

'It would be but a poor Return to the Favour you have done me, to sacrifice any Gallantry to the Possession of you, and I would certainly do it, though I were not disengaged, as at present I am, from any Affair of that Kind. But I should not be the honest Man you think me, if I did not tell you, that my Affections are engaged to another, who is a Woman of Virtue, and one that I never can leave, though it is probable I shall never possess her. God forbid that in Return of your Kindness to me, I should do you such an Injury, as to give you my Hand, when I cannot give you my Heart. No, I had much rather starve than be guilty of that. Even though my Mistress were married to another, I would not marry you unless my Heart had entirely effaced all Impressions of her. Be assured that your Secret was not more safe in your own Breast, than in that of

'Your most Obliged, and

'Grateful Humble Servant,

'*T. Jones*.'

When our Heroe had finished and sent this Letter, he went to his Scrutore, took out Miss *Western*'s Muff, kiss'd it several Times, and then strutted some Turns about his Room, with more Satisfaction of Mind than ever any *Irishman* felt in carrying off a Fortune of fifty thousand Pounds.

Chapter XII.

A *Discovery* made by Partridge.

While *Jones* was exulting in the Consciousness of his Integrity, *Partridge* came capering into the Room, as was his Custom when he brought, or fancied he brought, any good Tidings. He had been dispatched that Morning, by his Master, with Orders to endeavour, by the Servants of Lady *Bellaston*, or by any other Means, to discover whither *Sophia* had been conveyed; and he now returned, and with a joyful Countenance told our Heroe, that he had found the lost Bird. 'I have seen, Sir,' says he, 'black *George*, the Gamekeeper, who is one of the Servants whom the Squire hath brought with him to Town. I knew him presently, though I have not seen him these several Years; but you know, Sir, he is a very remarkable Man, or to use a purer Phrase, he hath a most remarkable Beard, the largest and blackest I ever saw. It was some Time however before black *George* could recollect me.'—'Well, but what is your good News?' cries *Jones*, 'What do you know of my *Sophia*?'—'You shall know presently, Sir,' answered *Partridge*, 'I am coming to it as fast as I can.—You are so impatient, Sir, you would come at the Infinitive Mood, before you can get to the Imperative.[1] As I was saying, Sir, it was some Time before he recollected my Face.'——'Confound your Face,' cries *Jones*, 'what of my *Sophia*?'—'Nay, Sir,' answered *Partridge*, 'I know nothing more of Madam *Sophia*, than what I am going to tell you; and I should have told you all before this if you had not interrupted me; but if you look so angry at me, you will frighten all of it out of my Head, or to use a purer Phrase, out of my Memory. I never saw you look so angry since the Day we left *Upton*, which I shall remember if I was to live a thousand Years.' —'Well, pray go on in your own Way,' said *Jones*, 'you are resolved to make me mad I find.' 'Not for the World,' answered *Partridge*, 'I have suffered enough for that already; which, as I said, I shall bear in my Remembrance the longest Day I have to live.'—'Well, but black *George*?' cries *Jones*,—'Well, Sir, as I was saying, it was a long Time before he could recollect me; for indeed I am very much altered since I saw him. *Non sum qualis eram*.[2] I have had Troubles in the World, and nothing alters a Man so much as Grief. I have heard it will change the Colour of a Man's Hair in a Night. However, at last, know me he did, that's sure enough; for we are both of an Age, and were at the same Charity School. *George* was a great Dunce, but no Matter for that; all Men do not thrive in the World according to their Learning. I am sure I have Reason to say so; but it will be all one a thousand Years hence. Well, Sir,—where was I?—O—well, we no sooner knew each other, than after many hearty Shakes by the Hand, we agreed to go to an Alehouse and take a Pot, and by good luck the Beer was some of the best I have met with since I have been in Town.—Now, Sir, I am coming to the Point; for no sooner did I name you, and told him, that you and I came to Town together, and had lived together ever since, than he called for another Pot, and swore he would drink to your Health; and

---

1. Lily's *Grammar* arranges the moods as Indicative, Imperative, Optative, Potential, Subjunctive, and Infinitive.

2. "I am not what I was." Horace, *Odes* IV.i.3. See below, p. 722.

indeed he drank your Health so heartily, that I was overjoyed to see there was so much Gratitude left in the World: And after we had emptied that Pot, I said I would be my Pot too, and so we drank another to your Health; and then I made haste Home to tell you the News.'

'What News?' cries *Jones*, 'you have not mentioned a Word of my *Sophia!*'—'Bless me! I had like to have forgot that. Indeed we mentioned a great deal about young Madam *Western*, and *George* told me all; that Mr. *Blifil* is coming to Town in order to be married to her. He had best make Haste then, says I, or some Body will have her before he comes; and indeed, says I, Mr. *Seagrim*, it is a thousand Pities some Body should not have her; for he certainly loves her above all the Women in the World. I would have both you and she know that it is not for her Fortune he follows her; for I can assure you as to Matter of that, there is another Lady, one of much greater Quality and Fortune than she can pretend to, who is so fond of some Body, that she comes after him Day and Night.'

Here *Jones* fell into a Passion with *Partridge*, for having, as he said, betrayed him; but the poor Fellow answered, he had mentioned no Name: 'Besides, Sir,' said he, 'I can assure you, *George* is sincerely your Friend, and wished Mr. *Blifil* at the Devil more than once; nay, he said he would do any Thing in his Power upon Earth to serve you; and so I am convinced he will.—Betray you indeed! why I question whether you have a better Friend than *George* upon Earth, except myself, or one that would go farther to serve you.'

'Well,' says *Jones*, a little pacified, 'you say this Fellow, who I believe indeed is enough inclined to be my Friend, lives in the same House with *Sophia?*'

'In the same House!' answered *Partridge*; 'why, Sir, he is one of the Servants of the Family, and very well drest I promise you he is; if it was not for his black Beard, you would hardly know him.'

'One Service then at least he may do me,' says *Jones*; 'sure he can certainly convey a Letter to my *Sophia*.'

'You have hit the Nail *ad unguem*,'[3] cries *Partridge*; 'How came I not to think of it? I will engage he shall do it upon the very first mentioning.'

'Well then,' said *Jones*, 'do you leave me at present, and I will write a Letter which you shall deliver to him To-morrow Morning; for I suppose you know where to find him.'

'O yes, Sir,' answered *Partridge*, 'I shall certainly find him again;

---

3. Fielding puts Partridge into an unconscious and wonderfully nonsensical pun— *ad unguem* means loosely, "to perfection," but it means literally, "to a fingernail," derived from the sculptor's testing his work for smoothness by running his fingernail over its surface. Instead of saying, "You have hit the nail on the head," Partridge, trying to show off his Latin, says inadvertently, "You have hit the nail on the fingernail."

there is no Fear of that. The Liquor is too good for him to stay away long. I make no Doubt but he will be there every Day he stays in Town.'

'So you don't know the Street then where my *Sophia* is lodged?' cries *Jones*.

'Indeed, Sir, I do,' says *Partridge*.

'What is the Name of the Street?' cries *Jones*.

'The Name, Sir, why here, Sir, just by,' answered *Partridge*, 'not above a Street or two off. I don't indeed know the very Name; for as he never told me, if I had asked, you know it might have put some Suspicion into his Head. No, no, Sir, let me alone for that. I am too cunning for that, I promise you.'

'Thou art most wonderfully cunning indeed,' replied *Jones*; 'however I will write to my Charmer, since I believe you will be cunning enough to find him To-morrow at the Alehouse.'

And now having dismissed the sagacious *Partridge*, Mr. *Jones* sat himself down to write, in which Employment we shall leave him for a Time. And here we put an End to the fifteenth Book.

BOOK XVI.

Containing the Space of Five Days

Chapter I.

Of Prologues.

I have heard of a Dramatic Writer[1] who used to say, he would rather write a Play than a Prologue; in like manner, I think, I can with less Pains write one of the Books of this History, than the Prefatory Chapter to each of them.

To say the Truth, I believe many a hearty Curse hath been devoted on the Head of that Author, who first instituted the Method of prefixing to his Play that Portion of Matter which is called the Prologue; and which at first was Part of the Piece itself, but of latter Years hath had usually so little Connexion with the Drama before which it stands, that the Prologue to one Play might as well serve for any other. Those indeed of more modern Date, seem all to be written on the same three Topics, *viz.* an abuse of the Taste of the Town, a Condemnation of all contemporary Authors, and, an Elogium on the Performance just about to be rep-

---

1. Probably Fielding himself.

resented. The Sentiments in all these are very little varied, nor is it possible they should; and indeed I have often wondered at the great Invention of Authors, who have been capable of finding such various Phrases to express the same thing.

In like manner I apprehend, some future Historian (if any one shall do me the Honour of imitating my Manner) will, after much scratching his Pate, bestow some good Wishes on my Memory, for having first established these several initial Chapters; most of which, like Modern Prologues, may as properly be prefixed to any other Book in this History as to that which they introduce, or indeed to any other History as to this.

But however Authors may suffer by either of these Inventions, the Reader will find sufficient Emolument in the one, as the Spectator hath long found in the other.

First, it is well known, that the Prologue serves the Critic for an Opportunity to try his Faculty of Hissing, and to tune his Cat-call to the best Advantage; by which means, I have known those Musical Instruments so well prepared, that they have been able to play in full Concert at the first rising of the Curtain.

The same Advantages may be drawn from these Chapters, in which the Critic will be always sure of meeting with something that may serve as a Whetstone to his noble Spirit; so that he may fall with a more hungry Appetite for Censure on the History itself. And here his Sagacity must make it needless to observe how artfully these Chapters are calculated for that excellent Purpose; for in these we have always taken Care to intersperse somewhat of the sour or acid Kind, in order to sharpen and stimulate the said Spirit of Criticism.

Again, the indolent Reader, as well as Spectator, finds great Advantage from both these; for as they are not obliged either to see the one or read the others, and both the Play and the Book are thus protracted, by the former they have a Quarter of an Hour longer allowed them to sit at Dinner, and by the latter they have the Advantage of beginning to read at the fourth or fifth Page instead of the first; a Matter by no means of trivial Consequence to Persons who read Books with no other View than to say they have read them, a more general Motive to reading than is commonly imagined; and from which not only Law Books, and Good Books, but the Pages of *Homer* and *Virgil*, of *Swift* and *Cervantes* have been often turned over.

Many other are the Emoluments which arise from both these, but they are for the most part so obvious that we shall not at present stay to enumerate them; especially since it occurs to us that the principal Merit of both the Prologue and the Preface is that they be short.

Chapter II.

A whimsical Adventure which befel the Squire, with the distressed
Situation of Sophia.

We must now convey the Reader to Mr. *Western*'s Lodgings
which were in *Piccadilly*, where he was placed by the Recommendation of the Landlord at the *Hercules Pillars* at *Hide-Park Corner*;
for at the Inn, which was the first he saw on his Arrival in Town,
he placed his Horses, and in those Lodgings, which were the first he
heard of, he deposited himself.

Here when *Sophia* alighted from the Hackney-Coach, which
brought her from the House of Lady *Bellaston*, she desired to retire
to the Apartment provided for her, to which her Father very readily
agreed, and whither he attended her himself. A short Dialogue, neither very material nor pleasant to relate minutely, then passed
between them, in which he pressed her vehemently to give her Consent to the Marriage with *Blifil*, who, as he acquainted her, was to
be in Town in a few Days; but instead of complying, she gave a
more peremptory and resolute Refusal than she had ever done
before. This so incensed her Father, that after many bitter Vows
that he would force her to have him whether she would or no, he
departed from her with many hard Words and Curses, locked the
Door and put the Key into his Pocket.

While *Sophia* was left with no other Company than what attend
the closest State Prisoner, namely, Fire and Candle, the Squire sat
down to regale himself over a Bottle of Wine, with his Parson and
the Landlord of the *Hercules Pillars*, who, as the Squire said, would
make an excellent third Man, and could inform them of the News
of the Town, and how Affairs went; for to be sure, says he, he
knows a great deal since the Horses of many of the Quality stand at
his House.

In this agreeable Society, Mr. *Western* past that Evening and
great part of the succeeding Day, during which Period nothing happened of sufficient Consequence to find a Place in this History. All
this Time *Sophia* past by herself; for her Father swore she should
never come out of her Chamber alive, unless she first consented to
marry *Blifil*; nor did he ever suffer the Door to be unlocked unless
to convey her Food, on which Occasions he always attended himself.

The second Morning after his Arrival, while he and the Parson
were at Breakfast together on a Toast and Tankard, he was informed
that a Gentleman was below to wait on him.

'A Gentleman!' quoth the Squire, 'who the Devil can he be? Do, Doctor, go down and see who 'tis. Mr. *Blifil* can hardly be come to Town yet.——Go down, do, and know what his Business is.'

The Doctor returned with an Account that it was a very well drest Man, and by the Ribbon in his Hat, he took him for an Officer of the Army; that he said he had some particular Business, which he could deliver to none but Mr. *Western* himself.

'An Officer!' cries the Squire, 'what can any such Fellow have to do with me? If he wants an Order for Baggage-Waggons, I am no Justice of Peace here, nor can I grant a Warrant——Let un come up then, if he must speak to me.'

A very genteel Man now entered the Room; who having made his Compliments to the Squire, and desired the Favour of being alone with him, delivered himself as follows.

'Sir, I come to wait upon you by the Command of my Lord *Fellamar*; but with a very different Message from what I suppose you expect, after what past the other Night.'

'My Lord who?' cries the Squire, 'I never heard the Name o'un.'

'His Lordship,' said the Gentleman, 'is willing to impute every thing to the Effect of Liquor, and the most trifling Acknowledgement of that Kind will set every thing right; for as he hath the most violent Attachment to your Daughter, you, Sir, are the last Person upon Earth, from whom he would resent an Affront; and happy is it for you both that he hath given such publick Demonstrations of his Courage, as to be able to put up an Affair of this Kind, without Danger of any Imputation on his Honour. All he desires therefore, is, that you will before me make some Acknowledgment; the slightest in the World will be sufficient; and he intends this Afternoon to pay his Respects to you, in order to obtain your Leave of visiting the young Lady on the Footing of a Lover.'

'I don't understand much of what you say, Sir,' said the Squire; 'but I suppose, by what you talk about my Daughter, that this is the Lord which my Cousin Lady *Bellaston* mentioned to me, and said something about his courting my Daughter. If so be, that how, that be the Case—you may give my Service to his Lordship, and tell un the Girl is disposed of already.'

'Perhaps, Sir,' said the Gentleman, 'you are not sufficiently apprized of the Greatness of this Offer. I believe such a Person, Title, and Fortune would be no where refused.

'Lookee, Sir,' answered the Squire, 'to be very plain, my Daughter is bespoke already; but if she was not, I would not marry her to a Lord upon any Account; I hate all Lords; they are a Parcel of Courtiers and *Hannoverians*, and I will have nothing to do with them.'——

'Well, Sir,' said the Gentleman, 'if that is your Resolution, the Message I am to deliver to you, is, that my Lord desires the Favour of your Company this Morning in *Hide-Park*.'

'You may tell my Lord,' answered the Squire, 'that I am busy and cannot come. I have enough to look after at home, and can't stir abroad on any Account.'

'I am sure, Sir,' quoth the other, 'you are too much a Gentleman to send such a Message; you will not, I am convinced, have it said of you, that after having affronted a noble Peer, you refuse him Satisfaction. His Lordship would have been willing, from his great Regard to the young Lady, to have made up Matters in another Way; but unless he is to look on you as a Father, his Honour will not suffer his putting up such an Indignity as you must be sensible you offered him.'

'I offered him!' cries the Squire; 'it is a d—n'd Lie, I never offered him any Thing.'

Upon these Words the Gentleman returned a very short verbal Rebuke, and this he accompanied at the same time with some manual Remonstrances, which no sooner reached the Ears of Mr. *Western*, than that worthy Squire began to caper very briskly about the Room, bellowing at the same time with all his Might, as if desirous to summon a greater Number of Spectators to behold his Agility.

The Parson, who had left great part of the Tankard unfinished, was not retired far; he immediately attended therefore on the Squire's Vociferation, crying, 'Bless me! Sir, what's the Matter?'—'Matter?' quoth the Squire, 'here's a Highway-man, I believe, who wants to rob and murder me—for he hath fallen upon me with that Stick there in his Hand, when I wish I may be d—n'd if I gid un the least Provocation.'

'How, Sir,' said the Captain, 'did you not tell me I ly'd?'

'No, as I hope to be saved,' answered the Squire.—'I believe I might say, " 'Twas a Lie that I had offered any Affront to my Lord,"—'but I never said the Word *you lie*.—I understand myself better, and you might have understood yourself better than to fall upon a naked Man. If I had a Stick in my Hand, you would not have dared strike me. I'd have knocked thy Lantern Jaws about thy Ears. Come down into Yard this Minute, and I'll take a Bout with thee at single Stick for a broken Head, that I will; or I will go into naked Room and box thee for a Belly-full. At unt half a Man, at unt I'm sure.'

The Captain, with some Indignation, replied, 'I see, Sir, you are below my Notice, and I shall inform his Lordship you are below his.—I am sorry I have dirtied my Fingers with you.'—At which Words he withdrew, the Parson interposing to prevent the Squire from stopping him, in which he easily prevailed, as the other, though he made some Efforts for the Purpose, did not seem very violently bent on Success. However, when the Captain was departed, the Squire sent many Curses and some Menaces after him; but as these did not set out from his Lips till the Officer was at the Bottom of the Stairs, and grew louder and louder as he was more and more remote, they did not reach his Ears, or at least did not retard his Departure.

Poor *Sophia* however, who, in her Prison, heard all her Father's Outcries from first to last, began now first to thunder with her Foot, and afterwards to scream as loudly as the old Gentleman himself had done before, though in a much sweeter Voice. These Screams soon silenced the Squire, and turned all his Consideration towards his Daughter, whom he loved so tenderly, that the least Apprehension of any Harm happening to her, threw him presently into Agonies: For except in that single Instance in which the whole future Happiness of her Life was concerned, she was sovereign Mistress of his Inclinations.

Having ended his Rage against the Captain, with swearing he would take the Law of him, the Squire now mounted up Stairs to *Sophia*, whom, as soon as he had unlocked and opened the Door, he found all pale and breathless. The Moment however that she saw her Father, she collected all her Spirits, and catching him hold by the Hand, she cry'd passionately, 'O my dear Sir, I am almost frightned to Death; I hope to Heaven no Harm hath happened to you.'—'No, no,' cries the Squire, 'no great Harm. The Rascal hath not hurt me much, but rat me if I don't ha the La o'un.' 'Pray, dear Sir,' says she, 'tell me what's the Matter, who is it that hath insulted you?' 'I don't know the Name o'un,' answered *Western*, 'some Officer Fellow I suppose that we are to pay for beating us, but I'll make him pay this Bout, if the Rascal hath got any thing, which I suppose he hath not. For thof he was drest out so vine, I question whether he had got a Voot of Land in the World.' 'But, dear Sir,' cries she, 'what was the Occasion of your Quarrel?' 'What should it be, *Sophy?*' answered the Squire, 'but about you, *Sophy*. All my Misfortunes are about you; you will be the Death of your poor Father at last. Here's a Varlet of a Lord, the Lord knows who forsooth! who hath a taan a Liking to you, and because I would not gi un my Consent, he sent me a Kallenge. Come, do be a good Girl, *Sophy*, and put an End to all your Father's Troubles; come do, consent to ha un; he will be in Town within this Day or two; do but promise me to marry un as soon as he comes, and you will make me the happiest Man in the World, and I will make you the happiest Woman; you shall have the finest Cloaths in *London*, and the finest Jewels, and a Coach and Six at your Command. I promised *Allworthy* already to give up half my Estate,—Odrabbet it! I should hardly stick at giving up the whole.' 'Will my Papa be so kind,' says she, 'as to hear me speak!'—'Why wout ask, *Sophy?'* cries he, 'when dost know I had rather hear thy Voice, than the Musick of the best Pack of Dogs in *England.*—Hear thee, my dear little Girl! I hope I shall hear thee as long as I live: for if I was ever to lose that Pleasure, I would not gee a Brass Varden to live a Moment longer. Indeed, *Sophy,* you do not know how I love you, indeed you don't, or you never could have run away and left your poor Father, who hath no other Joy, no other Comfort upon Earth but his little *Sophy.'* At these Words the Tears stood in his Eyes; and *Sophia,* (with the Tears streaming from hers) answered, 'Indeed, my dear Papa, I know you have loved me tenderly, and Heaven is my Witness how sincerely I have returned your affection; nor could any thing but an Apprehension of being forced into the Arms of this Man, have driven me to run from a Father whom I love so passionately, that I would, with Pleasure, sacrifice my Life to his Happiness; nay, I have endeavoured to reason myself into doing more, and had almost worked up a Resolution, to endure the most miserable of all Lives, to comply with your Inclination. It was that Resolution alone to which I could not force my Mind; nor can I ever.' Here the Squire began to look wild, and the Foam appeared at his Lips, which *Sophia* observing, begged to be heard out, and then proceeded, 'If my Father's Life, his Health, or any real Happiness of his was at Stake, here stands your resolved Daughter, may Heaven blast me, if there is a Misery I would not suffer to preserve you.—No, that most detested, most loathsome of all Lots would I embrace, I would give my Hand to *Blifil* for your Sake.'—'I tell thee, it will preserve me,' answers the Father; 'it will gee me Health, Happiness, Life, every thing.—Upon my Soul I shall die if dost refuse me; I shall break my Heart, I shall upon my Soul.'—'Is it possible,' says she, 'you can have such a Desire to make me miserable?' 'I tell thee noa,' answered he loudly, 'd—n me if there is a Thing upon Earth I would not do to see thee happy.'—'And will not my dear Papa allow me to have the least Knowledge of what will make me so? If it be true that Happiness consists in Opinion; what must be my Condition, when I shall think myself the most miserable of all the Wretches upon Earth?' 'Better think yourself so,' said he, 'than know it by being married to a poor bastardly Vagabond.' 'If it will content you, Sir,' said *Sophia,* 'I will give you the most solemn Promise never to marry him nor any other while my Papa lives, without his Consent. Let me dedicate my whole Life to your Service; let me be again your poor *Sophy,* and my whole Business and Pleasure be, as it hath been, to please and divert you.' 'Lookee, *Sophy,'* answered the Squire, 'I am not to be choused in this

Manner. Your Aunt *Western* would then have Reason to think me the Fool she doth. No, no, *Sophy*, I'd have you to know I have a got more Wisdom, and know more of the World than to take the Word of a Woman in a Matter where a Man is concerned.' 'How, Sir, have I deserved this Want of Confidence?' said she, 'Have I ever broke a single Promise to you? Or have I ever been found guilty of a Falshood from my Cradle?' 'Lookee, *Sophy*,' cries he, 'that's neither here nor there. I am determin'd upon this Match, and have him you shall, d—n me if shat unt. D—n me if shat unt, though dost hang thyself the next Morning.' At repeating which Words he clinched his Fist, knit his Brows, bit his Lips, and thundered so loud, that the poor afflicted, terrified *Sophia* sunk trembling into her Chair, and had not a Flood of Tears come immediately to her Relief, perhaps worse had followed.

Western beheld the deplorable Condition of his Daughter with no more Contrition or Remorse, than the Turnkey of *Newgate* feels at viewing the Agonies of a tender Wife, when taking her last Farewell of her condemned Husband; or rather he looked down on her with the same Emotions which arise in an honest fair Tradesman, who sees his Debtor dragged to Prison for 1*ol.* which, though a just Debt, the Wretch is wickedly unable to pay. Or, to hit the Case still more nearly, he felt the same Compunction with a Bawd when some poor Innocent whom she hath ensnared into her Hands, falls into Fits at the first Proposal of what is called seeing Company. Indeed this Resemblance would be exact, was it not that the Bawd hath an Interest in what she doth, and the Father, though perhaps he may blindly think otherwise, can in Reality have none in urging his Daughter to almost an equal Prostitution.

In this Condition he left his poor *Sophia*, and departing with a very vulgar Observation on the Effect of Tears, he locked the Room, and returned to the Parson, who said every Thing he durst in Behalf of the young Lady, which though perhaps it was not quite so much as his duty required, yet was it sufficient to throw the Squire into a violent Rage, and into many indecent Reflections on the whole Body of the Clergy, which we have too great an Honour for that sacred Function to commit to Paper.

Chapter III.

What happened to Sophia *during her Confinement.*

The Landlady of the House where the Squire lodged had begun very early to entertain a strange Opinion of her Guests. However, as she was informed that the Squire was a Man of a vast Fortune, and as she had taken Care to exact a very extraordinary Price for her

Rooms, she did not think proper to give any Offence; for though she was not without some Concern for the Confinement of poor *Sophia*, of whose great Sweetness of Temper and Affability, the Maid of the House had made so favourable a Report, which was confirmed by all the Squire's Servants, yet she had much more Concern for her own Interest, than to provoke one, whom, as she said, she perceived to be a very hastish Kind of a Gentleman.

Though *Sophia* eat but little, yet she was regularly served with her Meals; indeed I believe if she had liked any one Rarity, that the Squire, however angry, would have spared neither Pains nor Cost to have procured it for her; since, however strange it may appear to some of my Readers, he really doated on his Daughter, and to give her any Kind of Pleasure was the highest Satisfaction of his Life.

The Dinner Hour being arrived, black *George* carried her up a Pullet, the Squire himself (for he had sworn not to part with the Key) attending the Door. As *George* deposited the Dish, some Compliments passed between him and *Sophia* (for he had not seen her since she left the Country, and she treated every Servant with more Respect than some Persons shew to those who are in a very slight Degree their Inferiors) *Sophia* would have had him take the Pullet back, saying, she could not eat; but *George* begged her to try, and particularly recommended to her the Eggs, of which he said it was full.

All this Time the Squire was waiting at the Door; but *George* was a great Favourite with his Master, as his Employment was in Concerns of the highest Nature, namely, about the Game, and was accustomed to take many Liberties. He had officiously carried up the Dinner, being, as he said, very desirous to see his young Lady; he made therefore no Scruple of keeping his Master standing above ten Minutes, while Civilities were passing between him and *Sophia*, for which he received only a good-humoured Rebuke at the Door when he returned.

The Eggs of Pullets, Partridges, Pheasants, *&c.* were, as *George* well knew, the most favourite Dainties of *Sophia*. It was therefore no Wonder, that he who was a very good-natured Fellow, should take Care to supply her with this Kind of Delicacy, at a Time when all the Servants in the House were afraid she would be starved; for she had scarce swallowed a single Morsel in the last forty Hours.

Though Vexation hath not the same Effect on all Persons, as it usually hath on a Widow, whose Appetite it often renders sharper than it can be rendered by the Air on *Bansted* Downs, or *Salisbury* Plain; yet the sublimest Grief, notwithstanding what some People may say to the contrary, will eat at last. And *Sophia* herself, after some little Consideration, began to dissect the Fowl, which she found to be as full of Eggs as *George* had reported it.

But if she was pleased with these, it contained something which would have delighted the Royal Society much more; for if a Fowl with three Legs be so invaluable a Curiosity, when perhaps Time hath produced a Thousand such, at what Price shall we esteem a Bird which so totally contradicts all the Laws of Animal Œconomy, as to contain a Letter in its Belly? *Ovid* tells us of a Flower into which *Hyacinthus* was metamorphosed, that bears Letters on its Leaves, which *Virgil*[1] recommended as a Miracle to the Royal Society of his Day; but no Age nor Nation hath ever recorded a Bird with a Letter in its Maw.

But though a Miracle of this Kind might have engaged all the *Academies des Sciences* in *Europe*, and perhaps in a fruitless Enquiry; yet the Reader by barely recollecting the last Dialogue which passed between Messieurs *Jones* and *Partridge*, will be very easily satisfied from whence this Letter came, and how it found its Passage into the Fowl.

Sophia, notwithstanding her long Fast, and notwithstanding her favourite Dish was there before her, no sooner saw the Letter than she immediately snatched it up, tore it open, and read as follows.

'Madam,

'Was I not sensible to whom I have the Honour of writing, I should endeavour, however difficult, to paint the Horrors of my Mind, at the Account brought me by Mrs. *Honour*: But as Tenderness alone can have any true Idea of the Pangs which Tenderness is capable of feeling; so can this most amiable Quality which my *Sophia* possesses in the most eminent Degree, sufficiently inform her what her *Jones* must have suffered on this melancholy Occasion. Is there a Circumstance in the World which can heighten my Agonies, when I hear of any Misfortune which hath befallen you? Surely there is one only, and with that I am accursed. It is, my *Sophia*, the dreadful Consideration that I am myself the wretched Cause. Perhaps I here do myself too much Honour, but none will envy me an Honour which costs me so extremely dear. Pardon me this Presumption, and pardon me a greater still, if I ask you whether my Advice, my Assistance, my Presence, my Absence, my Death, or my Tortures can bring you any Relief? Can the most perfect Admiration, the most watchful Observance, the most ardent Love, the most melting Tenderness, the most resigned Submission to your Will, make you Amends for what you are to sacrifice to my Happiness? If they can, fly, my lovely Angel, to those Arms which are ever open to receive and protect you; and to which, whether you

1. *Metamorphoses* X.209–16. The letters are *Ai Ai*, the Greek cry of grief. Virgil (*Eclogues* III.106–7) alludes cryptically to the phenomenon ("Tell me in what country flowers are born inscribed with the names of kings, and you can have Phyllis all to yourself"), but Virgil does not call it a miracle, nor recommend it to the attention of any scientific society.

bring yourself alone, or the Riches of the World with you, is, in my Opinion, an Alternative not worth regarding. If, on the contrary, Wisdom shall predominate, and, on the most mature Reflection, inform you, that the Sacrifice is too great; and if there be no Way left to reconcile your Father, and restore the Peace of your dear Mind, but by abandoning me, I conjure you drive me for ever from your Thoughts, exert your Resolution, and let no Compassion for my Sufferings bear the least Weight in that tender Bosom. Believe me, Madam, I so sincerely love you better than myself, that my great and principal End is your Happiness. My first Wish (why would not Fortune indulge me in it?) was, and pardon me if I say, still is to see you every Moment the happiest of Women; my second Wish is to hear you are so; but no Misery on Earth can equal mine, while I think you owe an uneasy Moment to him who is,

> 'Madam,
> 'In every Sense, and to every Purpose,
> 'Your devoted
> '*Thomas Jones.*'

What *Sophia* said, or did, or thought upon this Letter, how often she read it, or whether more than once, shall all be left to our Reader's Imagination. The Answer to it he may perhaps see hereafter; but not at present; for this Reason, among others, that she did not now write any, and that for several good Causes, one of which was this, she had no Paper, Pen, nor Ink.

In the Evening while *Sophia* was meditating on the Letter she had received, or on something else, a violent Noise from below disturbed her Meditations. This Noise was no other than a round Bout at Altercation between two Persons. One of the Combatants, by his Voice, she immediately distinguished to be her Father; but she did not so soon discover the shriller Pipes to belong to the Organ of her Aunt *Western*, who was just arrived in Town, where having, by means of one of her Servants, who stopt at the *Hercules Pillars*, learnt where her Brother lodged, she drove directly to his Lodgings.

We shall therefore take our Leave at present of *Sophia*, and with our usual Good-Breeding, attend her Ladyship.

Chapter IV.

In which Sophia is delivered from her Confinement.

The Squire and the Parson (for the Landlord was now otherwise engaged) were smoaking their Pipes together, when the Arrival of the Lady was first signified. The Squire no sooner heard her Name, than he immediately ran down to usher her up Stairs; for he was a great Observer of such Ceremonials, especially to his Sister, of whom he stood more in Awe than of any other human Creature, though he never would own this, nor did he perhaps know it himself.

Mrs. *Western*, on her Arrival in the Dining-Room, having flung herself into a Chair, began thus to harangue. 'Well, surely no one ever had such an intolerable Journey. I think the Roads, since so many Turnpike Acts, are grown worse than ever. La, Brother, how could you get into this odious Place? No Person of Condition, I dare swear, ever set Foot here before.' 'I don't know,' cries the Squire, 'I think they do well enough; it was Landlord recommended them. I thought as he knew most of the Quality, he could best shew me where to get among um.' 'Well, and where's my Niece?' says the Lady, 'have you been to wait upon Lady *Bellaston* yet?' 'Ay, ay,' cries the Squire, 'your Niece is safe enough; she is up Stairs in Chamber.' 'How,' answered the Lady, 'is my Niece in this House, and doth she not know of my being here?' 'No, no Body can well get to her,' says the Squire, 'for she is under Lock and Key. I have her safe; I vetched her from my Lady Cousin the first Night I came to Town, and I have taken Care o' her ever since; she is as secure as a Fox in a Bag, I promise you.' 'Good Heaven!' returned Mrs. *Western*, 'what do I hear! I thought what a fine Piece of Work would be the Consequence of my Consent to your coming to Town yourself; nay, it was indeed your own headstrong Will, nor can I charge myself with having ever consented to it. Did not you promise me, Brother, that you would take none of these headstrong Measures? Was it not by these headstrong Measures that you forced my Niece to run away from you in the Country? Have you a Mind to oblige her to take such another Step?' 'Z—ds and the Devil,' cries the Squire, dashing his Pipe on the Ground, 'did ever Mortal hear the like? when I expected you would have commended me for all I have done, to be fallen upon in this Manner!' 'How! Brother,' said the Lady, 'have I ever given you the least Reason to imagine I should commend you for locking up your Daughter? Have I not often told you, that Women in a free Country are not to be treated with such arbitrary Power? We are as free as the Men, and I heartily wish I could not say we deserve that Freedom better. If you expect I should stay a Moment longer in this wretched House, or that I should ever own you again as my Relation, or that I should ever trouble myself again with the Affairs of your Family, I insist upon it that my Niece be set at Liberty this Instant.' This she spoke with so commanding an Air, standing with her Back to the Fire, with one Hand behind her, and a Pinch of Snuff in the other, that I question whether *Thalestris*[1] at the Head of her Amazons ever made a more tremendous Figure. It is no Wonder therefore

1. See above, p. 381.

that the poor Squire was not Proof against the Awe which she inspired. 'There,' he cried, throwing down the Key, 'There it is, do whatever you please. I intended only to have kept her up till *Blifil* came to Town; which can't be long; and now if any Harm happens in the mean Time, remember who is to be blamed for it.'

'I will answer it with my Life,' cried Mrs. *Western,* 'but I shall not intermeddle at all, unless upon one Condition, and that is, that you will commit the whole entirely to my Care, without taking any one Measure yourself, unless I shall eventually appoint you to act. If you ratify these Preliminaries, Brother, I yet will endeavour to preserve the Honour of your Family; if not, I shall continue in a neutral State.'

'I pray you, good Sir,' said the Parson, 'permit yourself this once to be admonished by her Ladyship; peradventure by communing with young Madam *Sophia,* she will effect more than you have been able to perpetrate by more rigorous Measures.'

'What dost thee open upon me?' cries the Squire. 'If thee dost begin to babble, I shall whip thee in presently.'

'Fie, Brother,' answered the Lady, 'is this Language to a Clergyman? Mr. *Supple* is a Man of Sense, and gives you the best Advice; and the whole World, I believe, will concur in his Opinion; but I must tell you, I expect an immediate Answer to my categorical Proposals. Either cede your Daughter to my Disposal, or take her wholly to your own surprizing Discretion, and then I here, before Mr. *Supple,* evacuate the Garrison, and renounce you and your Family for ever.'

'I pray you let me be a Mediator,' cries the Parson; 'let me supplicate you.'

'Why there lies the Key on the Table,' cries the Squire. 'She may take un up, if she pleases; who hinders her?'

'No, Brother,' answered the Lady, 'I insist on the Formality of its being delivered me, with a full Ratification of all the Concessions stipulated.'

'Why then I will deliver it to you.—There 'tis,' cries the Squire. 'I am sure, Sister, you can't accuse me of ever denying to trust my Daughter to you. She hath a lived wi' you a whole Year and muore to a Time, without my ever zeeing her.'

'And it would have been happy for her,' answered the Lady, 'if she had always lived with me. Nothing of this Kind would have happened under my Eye.'

'Ay, certainly,' cries he, 'I only am to blame.'

'Why, you are to blame, Brother,' answered she, 'I have been often obliged to tell you so, and shall always be obliged to tell you so. However, I hope you will now amend, and gather so much Experience from past Errors, as not to defeat my wisest Machinations by your Blunders. Indeed, Brother, you are not qualified for these Negotiations. All your whole Scheme of Politics is wrong. I once more, therefore, insist, that you do not intermeddle. Remember only what is past.'——

'Z—ds and Bl—d, Sister,' cries the Squire, 'What would you have me say? You are enough to provoke the Devil.'

'There now,' said she, 'just according to the old Custom. I see, Brother, there is no talking to you. I will appeal to Mr. *Supple*, who is a Man of Sense, if I said any Thing which could put any human Creature into a Passion; but you are so wrong-headed every Way.'

'Let me beg you, Madam,' said the Parson, 'not to irritate his Worship.'

'Irritate him?' said the Lady;—'Sure you are as great a Fool as himself. Well, Brother, since you have promised not to interfere, I will once more undertake the Management of my Niece. Lord have Mercy upon all Affairs which are under the Directions of Men. The Head of one Woman is worth a thousand of yours.' And now having summoned a Servant to shew her to *Sophia*, she departed, bearing the Key with her.

She was no sooner gone, than the Squire (having first shut the Door) ejaculated twenty Bitches, and as many hearty Curses against her, not sparing himself for having ever thought of her Estate; but added, 'Now one hath been a Slave so long, it would be pity to lose it at last, for want of holding out a little longer. The Bitch can't live for ever, and I know I am down for it upon the Will.'

The Parson greatly commended this Resolution; and now the Squire having ordered in another Bottle, which was his usual Method when any Thing either pleased or vexed him, did, by drinking plentifully of this medicinal Julap, so totally wash away his Choler, that his Temper was become perfectly placid and serene, when Mrs. *Western* returned with *Sophia* into the Room. The young Lady had on her Hat and Capuchin, and the Aunt acquainted Mr. *Western*, 'that she intended to take her Niece with her to her own Lodgings; for, indeed, Brother,' says she, 'these Rooms are not fit to receive a Christian Soul in.'

'Very well, Madam,' quoth *Western*, 'whatever you please. The Girl can never be in better Hands than yours; and the Parson here can do me the Justice to say, that I have said fifty Times behind your Back, that you was one of the most sensible Women in the World.'

'To this,' cries the Parson, 'I am ready to bear Testimony.'

'Nay, Brother,' says Mrs. *Western*, 'I have always, I'm sure, given you as favourable a Character. You must own you have a little too much Hastiness in your Temper; but when you will allow yourself Time to reflect, I never knew a Man more reasonable.'

'Why then, Sister, if you think so,' said the Squire, 'here's your good Health with all my Heart. I am a little passionate sometimes, but I scorn to bear any Malice. *Sophy*, do you be a good Girl, and do every Thing your Aunt orders you.'

'I have not the least Doubt of her,' answered Mrs. *Western*. 'She hath had already an Example before her Eyes, in the Behaviour of that Wretch her Cousin *Harriet*, who ruined herself by neglecting my Advice.—O Brother, what think you? You was hardly gone out of Hearing, when you set out for *London*, when who should arrive but that impudent Fellow with the odious *Irish* Name—that *Fitzpatrick*. He broke in abruptly upon me without Notice, or I would not have seen him. He ran on a long, unintelligible Story about his Wife, to which he forced me to give him a Hearing; but I made him very little Answer, and delivered him the Letter from his Wife, which I bid him answer himself. I suppose the Wretch will endeavour to find us out; but I beg you will not see her, for I am determined I will not.'

'I zee her?' answered the Squire; 'you need not fear me. I'll ge no Encouragement to such undutiful Wenches. It is well for the Fellow her Husband, I was not at Huome. Od rabbit it, he should have taken a Dance thru the Horse-pond, I promise un. You zee, *Sophy*, what Undutifulness brings Volks to. You have an Example in your own Family.'

'Brother,' cries the Aunt, 'you need not shock my Niece by such odious Repetitions. Why will you not leave every Thing entirely to me?' 'Well, well; I wull, I wull,' said the Squire.

And now Mrs. *Western*, luckily for *Sophia*, put an End to the Conversation, by ordering Chairs to be called. I say luckily; for had it continued much longer, fresh Matter of Dissension would, most probably, have arisen between the Brother and Sister; between whom Education and Sex made the only Difference; for both were equally violent, and equally positive; they had both a vast Affection for *Sophia*, and both a sovereign Contempt for each other.

Chapter V.

In which Jones *receives a Letter from* Sophia, *and goes to a Play with Mrs.* Miller *and* Partridge.

The Arrival of *Black George* in Town, and the good Offices which that grateful Fellow had promised to do for his old Benefactor, greatly comforted *Jones* in the midst of all the Anxiety and Uneasiness which he had suffered on the Account of *Sophia*; from whom, by the Means of the said *George*, he received the following Answer to his Letter, which *Sophia*, to whom the Use of Pen, Ink, and Paper was restored with her Liberty, wrote the very Evening when she departed from her Confinement.

'Sir,

'As I do not doubt your Sincerity in what you write, you will be pleased to hear that some of my Afflictions are at an End, by the Arrival of my Aunt *Western*, with whom I am at present, and with whom I enjoy all the Liberty I can desire. One Promise my Aunt hath insisted on my making, which is, that I will not see or converse with any Person without her Knowledge and Consent. This Promise I have most solemnly given, and shall most inviolably keep: And tho' she had not expresly forbidden me Writing, yet that must be an Omission from Forgetfulness; or this, perhaps, is included in the Word conversing. However, as I cannot but consider this as a Breach of her generous Confidence in my Honour, you cannot expect that I shall, after this, continue to write myself, or to receive Letters, without her Knowledge. A Promise is with me a very sacred Thing, and to be extended to every Thing understood from it, as well as to what is expressed by it; and this Consideration may perhaps, on Reflection, afford you some Comfort. But why should I mention a Comfort to you of this Kind? For though there is one Thing in which I can never comply with the best of Fathers, yet am I firmly resolved never to act in Defiance of him, or to take any Step of Consequence without his Consent. A firm Persuasion of this, must teach you to divert your Thoughts from what Fortune hath (perhaps) made impossible. This your own Interest persuades you. This may reconcile, I hope, Mr. *Allworthy* to you; and if it will, you have my Injunctions to pursue it. Accidents have laid some Obligations on me, and your good Intentions probably more. Fortune may, perhaps, be sometimes kinder to us both than at present. Believe this, that I shall always think of you as I think you deserve, and am,

'Sir,
'Your *Obliged Humble Servant*,
'Sophia Western.

'I charge you write to me no more—at present at least; and accept this, which is now of no Service to me, which I know you must want, and think you owe the Trifle only to that Fortune by which you found it.'[1]

A Child who hath just learnt his Letters, would have spelt this Letter out in less Time than *Jones* took in reading it. The Sensations it occasioned were a Mixture of Joy and Grief; somewhat like what divide the Mind of a good Man, when he peruses the Will of his deceased Friend, in which a large Legacy, which his Distresses

1. Meaning, perhaps, the Bank-bill for 100*l* [*Fielding's note*].

make the more welcome, is bequeathed to him. Upon the whole, however, he was more pleased than displeased; and indeed the Reader may probably wonder that he was displeased at all; but the Reader is not quite so much in Love as was poor *Jones*: And Love is a Disease, which, though it may in some Instances resemble a Consumption, (which it sometimes causes) in others proceeds in direct Opposition to it, and particularly in this, that it never flatters itself, or sees any one Symptom in a favourable Light.

One Thing gave him complete Satisfaction, which was, that his Mistress had regained her Liberty, and was now with a Lady where she might at least assure herself of a decent Treatment. Another comfortable Circumstance, was the Reference which she made to her Promise of never marrying any other Man: For however disinterested he might imagine his Passion, and notwithstanding all the generous Overtures made in his Letter, I very much question whether he could have heard a more afflicting Piece of News, than that *Sophia* was married to another, though the Match had been never so great, and never so likely to end in making her completely happy. That refined Degree of *Platonic* Affection which is absolutely detached from the Flesh, and is indeed entirely and purely spiritual, is a Gift confined to the female Part of the Creation; many of whom I have heard declare, (and doubtless with great Truth) that they would, with the utmost Readiness, resign a Lover to a Rival, when such Resignation was proved to be necessary for the temporal Interest of such Lover. Hence, therefore, I conclude, that this Affection is in Nature, though I cannot pretend to say, I have ever seen an Instance of it.

Mr. *Jones* having spent three Hours in reading and kissing the aforesaid Letter, and being, at last, in a State of good Spirits, from the last mentioned Considerations, he agreed to carry an Appointment, which he had before made, into Execution. This was to attend Mrs. *Miller*, and her younger Daughter, into the Gallery at the Playhouse, and to admit Mr. *Partridge* as one of the Company. For as *Jones* had really that Taste for Humour which many affect, he expected to enjoy much Entertainment in the Criticisms of *Partridge*; from whom he expected the simple Dictates of Nature, unimproved indeed, but likewise unadulterated by Art.

In the first Row then of the first Gallery did Mr. *Jones*, Mrs. *Miller*, her youngest Daughter, and *Partridge*, take their Places. *Partridge* immediately declared, it was the finest Place he had ever been in. When the first Music was played, he said, 'It was a Wonder how so many Fidlers could play at one Time, without putting one another out.' While the Fellow was lighting the upper Candles, he cried out to Mrs. *Miller*. 'Look, look, Madam, the very Picture of the Man in the End of the common-Prayer Book, before the Gunpowder-Treason Service.'[2] Nor could he help observing, with a Sigh, when all the Candles were lighted, 'That here were Candles enough burnt in one Night, to keep an honest poor Family for a whole Twelve-month.'

As soon as the Play, which was *Hamlet* Prince of *Denmark*, began, *Partridge* was all Attention, nor did he break Silence till the Entrance of the Ghost; upon which he asked *Jones*, 'What Man that was in the strange Dress; something,' said he, 'like what I have seen in a Picture. Sure it is not Armour, is it?' *Jones* answered, 'That is the Ghost.' To which *Partridge* replied with a Smile, 'Persuade me to that, Sir, if you can. Though I can't say I ever actually saw a Ghost in my Life, yet I am certain I should know one, if I saw him, better than that comes to. No, no, Sir, Ghosts don't appear in such Dresses as that, neither.' In this Mistake, which caused much Laughter in the Neighbourhood of *Partridge*, he was suffered to continue, 'till the Scene between the Ghost and *Hamlet*, when *Partridge* gave that Credit to Mr. *Garrick*,[3] which he had denied to *Jones*, and fell into so violent a Trembling, that his Knees knocked against each other. *Jones* asked him what was the Matter, and whether he was afraid of the Warrior upon the Stage? 'O la! Sir,' said he, 'I perceive now it is what you told me. I am not afraid of any Thing; for I know it is but a Play. And if it was really a Ghost, it could do one no Harm at such a Distance, and in so much Company; and yet if I was frightened, I am not the only Person.' 'Why, who,' cries *Jones*, 'dost thou take to be such a Coward here besides thyself!' 'Nay, you may call me Coward if you will; but if that little Man there upon the Stage is not frightned, I never saw any Man frightned in my Life. Ay, ay; *go along with you!* Ay, to be sure! Who's Fool then? Will you? Lud have Mercy upon such Fool-hardiness!—Whatever happens it is good enough for you.—*Follow you?* I'd follow the devil as soon. Nay, perhaps, it is the Devil—for they say he can put on what Likeness he pleases.—Oh! here he is again.—*No farther!* No, you have gone far enough already; farther than I'd have gone for all the King's Dominions.' *Jones* offered to speak, but *Partridge* cried, 'Hush, hush, dear Sir, don't you hear

2. The Gunpowder Plot, of which Guy Fawkes was the instigator, was an unsuccessful attempt by some Roman Catholics to blow up the Houses of Parliament on 5 Nov. 1605. An act of Parliament then instituted a service of thanksgiving for the Church of England; the form of which was issued by royal proclamation in 1606. In 1622, this service was revised and adopted by the Convocation of the Church of England, and added at the end of the Book of Common Prayer. When William III acceded to the throne in 1688, two bishops made several changes and additions to cele-brate the symbolic deliverance of England by William, who had landed in England on Nov. 5, the very date of Parliament's salvation from gunpowder. This new service, the one that Partridge knew (preceded by an etching of Guy Fawkes, with dark lantern in hand) was made official by proclamation in 1690. In recent years, the text of 1662 has been reinstituted (Bryant, pp. 225–26).

3. David Garrick (1717–79), the greatest actor of the age, played *Hamlet* several times in May, 1746, at Covent Garden (Cross II.192).

him!' And during the whole Speech of the Ghost, he sat with his Eyes fixed partly on the Ghost, and partly on *Hamlet*, and with his Mouth open; the same Passions which succeeded each other in *Hamlet*, succeeding likewise in him.

When the Scene was over, *Jones* said. 'Why, *Partridge*, you exceed my Expectations. You enjoy the Play more than I conceived possible.' 'Nay, Sir,' answered *Partridge*, 'if you are not afraid of the Devil, I can't help it; but to be sure it is natural to be surprized at such Things, though I know there is nothing in them: Not that it was the Ghost that surprized me neither; for I should have known that to have been only a Man in a strange Dress: But when I saw the little Man so frightned himself, it was that which took hold of me.' 'And dost thou imagine then, *Partridge*,' cries *Jones*, 'that he was really frightened?' 'Nay, Sir,' said *Partridge*, 'did not you your-self observe afterwards, when he found it was his own Father's Spirit, and how he was murdered in the Garden, how his Fear for-sook him by Degrees, and he was struck dumb with Sorrow, as it were, just as I should have been, had it been my own Case.—But hush! O la! What Noise is that? There he is again.—Well, to be cer-tain, though I know there is nothing at all in it, I am glad I am not down yonder, where those Men are.' Then turning his Eyes again upon *Hamlet*, 'Ay, you may draw your Sword; what signifies a Sword against the Power of the Devil?'

During the second Act, *Partridge* made very few Remarks. He greatly admired the Fineness of the Dresses; nor could he help observing upon the King's Countenance. 'Well,' said he, 'how People may be deceived by Faces? *Nulla fides fronti*[4] is, I find, a true Saying. Who would think, by looking in the King's Face, that he had ever committed a Murder?' He then enquired after the Ghost; but *Jones*, who intended he should be surprised, gave him no other Satisfaction, than 'that he might possibly see him again soon, and in a Flash of Fire.'

Partridge sat in fearful Expectation of this; and now, when the Ghost made his next Appearance, *Partridge* cried out, 'There, Sir, now; what say you now? Is he frightened now or no? As much frightened as you think me, and, to be sure, no Body can help some Fears, I would not be in so bad a Condition as what's his Name, Squire *Hamlet*, is there, for all the World. Bless me! What's become of the Spirit? As I am a living Soul, I thought I saw him sink into the Earth.' 'Indeed, you saw right,' answered *Jones*. 'Well, well,' cries *Partridge*, 'I know it is only a Play; and besides, if there was any Thing in all this, Madam *Miller* would not laugh so: For as to you, Sir, you would not be afraid, I believe, if the Devil was here in person.—There, there—Ay, no Wonder you are in

4. "No trust in faces" (Juvenal, *Satires* II.8).

such a Passion; shake the vile wicked Wretch to Pieces. If she was my own Mother I should serve her so. To be sure, all Duty to a Mother is forfeited by such wicked Doings.—Ay, go about your Business; I hate the Sight of you.'

Our Critic was now pretty silent till the Play, which *Hamlet* introduces before the King. This he did not at first understand, 'till *Jones* explained it to him; but he no sooner entered into the Spirit of it, then he began to bless himself that he had never committed Murder. Then turning to Mrs. *Miller*, he asked her, 'If she did not imagine the King looked as if he was touched; though he is,' said he, 'a good Actor, and doth all he can to hide it. Well, I would not have so much to answer for, as that wicked Man there hath, to sit upon a much higher Chair than he sits upon.—No wonder he run away; for your Sake I'll never trust an innocent Face again.'

The Grave-digging Scene next engaged the Attention of *Partridge*, who expressed much Surprize at the Number of Skulls thrown upon the Stage. To which *Jones* answered, 'That it was one of the most famous Burial-places about Town.' 'No wonder then,' cries *Partridge*, 'that the Place is haunted. But I never saw in my Life a worse Grave-digger. I had a Sexton when I was Clerk, that should have dug three Graves while he is digging one. The Fellow handles a Spade as if it was the first Time he had ever had one in his Hand. Ay, ay, you may sing. You had rather sing than work, I believe.'—Upon *Hamlet's* taking up the Skull, he cried out, 'Well it is strange to see how fearless some Men are: I never could bring myself to touch any Thing belonging to a dead Man on any Account.——He seemed frightened enough too at the Ghost I thought. *Nemo omnibus horis sapit.*'[5]

Little more worth remembring occurred during the Play; at the End of which *Jones* asked him, which of the Players he had liked best?' To this he answered, with some Appearance of Indignation at the Question, 'The King without Doubt.' 'Indeed, Mr. *Partridge*,' says Mrs. *Miller*, 'you are not of the same Opinion with the Town; for they are all agreed, that *Hamlet* is acted by the best Player who ever was on the Stage.' 'He the best Player!' cries *Partridge*, with a contemptuous Sneer, 'Why I could act as well as he myself. I am sure if I had seen a Ghost, I should have looked in the very same Manner, and done just as he did. And then, to be sure, in that Scene, as you called it, between him and his Mother, where you told me he acted so fine, why, Lord help me, any Man, that is, any good Man, that had such a Mother, would have done exactly the same. I know you are only joking with me; but, indeed, Madam, though I was never at a Play in *London*, yet I have seen acting

---

5. "No man is wise at all hours." Lily, p. 158, after Pliny the Younger, *Histo-* *riae Naturalis* VII.xli, par. 2. See above, pp. 97 and 520.

before in the Country; and the King for my Money; he speaks all
his Words distinctly, half as loud again as the other.—Any Body
may see he is an Actor.'

While Mrs. *Miller* was thus engaged in Conversation with *Partridge*, a Lady came up to Mr. *Jones*, whom he immediately knew
to be Mrs. *Fitzpatrick*. She said, she had seen him from the other
Part of the Gallery, and had taken that Opportunity of speaking to
him, as she had something to say, which might be of great Service
to himself. She then acquainted him with her Lodgings, and made
him an Appointment the next Day in the Morning; which, upon
Recollection, she presently changed to the Afternoon; at which
Time *Jones* promised to attend her.

Thus ended the Adventure at the Play-house; where *Partridge*
had afforded great Mirth, not only to *Jones* and Mrs. *Miller*, but to
all who sat within Hearing, who were more attentive to what he
said than to any Thing that passed on the Stage.

He durst not go to Bed all that Night, for Fear of the Ghost; and
for many Nights after, sweated two or three Hours before he went
to sleep, with the same Apprehensions, and waked several Times in
great Horrors, crying out, 'Lord have Mercy upon us! there it is.'

Chapter VI.

In which the History is obliged to look back.

It is almost impossible for the best Parent to observe an exact
Impartiality to his Children, even though no superior Merit should
biass his Affection; but sure a Parent can hardly be blamed, when
that Superiority determines his Preference.

As I regard all the Personages of this History in the Light of my
Children; so I must confess the same inclination of Partiality to
Sophia; and for that I hope the Reader will allow me the same
Excuse, from the Superiority of her Character.

This extraordinary Tenderness, which I have for my Heroine,
never suffers me to quit her any long Time without the utmost
Reluctance. I could now, therefore, return impatiently to enquire,
what hath happened to this lovely Creature since her Departure
from her Father's, but that I am obliged first to pay a short Visit to
Mr. *Blifil*.

Mr. *Western*, in the first Confusion into which his Mind was
cast, upon the sudden News he received of his Daughter, and in the
first Hurry to go after her, had not once thought of sending any
Account of the Discovery to *Blifil*. He had not gone far, however,
before he recollected himself, and accordingly stopt at the very first

Inn he came to, and dispatched away a Messenger to acquaint *Blifil* with his having found *Sophia*, and with his firm Resolution to marry her to him immediately, if he would come up after him to Town.

As the Love which *Blifil* had for *Sophia* was of that violent Kind, which nothing but the Loss of her Fortune, or some such Accident, could lessen, his Inclination to the Match was not at all altered by her having run away, though he was obliged to lay this to his own Account. He very readily, therefore, embraced this Offer. Indeed, he now proposed the Gratification of a very strong Passion besides Avarice, by marrying this young Lady, and this was Hatred: For he concluded that Matrimony afforded an equal Opportunity of satisfying either Hatred or Love; and this Opinion is very probably verified by much Experience. To say the Truth, if we are to judge by the ordinary Behaviour of married Persons to each other, we shall perhaps be apt to conclude, that the Generality seek the Indulgence of the former Passion only in their Union of every Thing but of Hearts.

There was one Difficulty, however, in his Way, and this arose from Mr. *Allworthy*. That good Man, when he found by the Departure of *Sophia*, (for neither that, nor the Cause of it, could be concealed from him) the great Aversion which she had for his Nephew, began to be seriously concerned that he had been deceived into carrying Matters so far. He by no Means concurred with the Opinion of those Parents, who think it as immaterial to consult the Inclinations of their Children in the Affair of Marriage, as to sollicit the good Pleasure of their Servants when they intend to take a Journey; and who are, by Law or Decency at least, with-held often from using absolute Force. On the contrary, as he esteemed the Institution to be of the most sacred Kind, he thought every preparatory Caution necessary to preserve it holy and inviolate; and very wisely concluded, that the surest Way to effect this, was by laying the Foundation in previous Affection.

Blifil indeed soon cured his Uncle of all Anger on the Score of Deceit, by many Vows and Protestations that he had been deceived himself, with which the many Declarations of *Western* very well tallied; but now to persuade *Allworthy* to consent to the renewing his Addresses, was a Matter of such apparent Difficulty, that the very Appearance was sufficient to have deterred a less enterprizing Genius; but this young Gentleman so well knew his own Talents, that nothing within the Province of Cunning seemed to him hard to be atchieved.

Here then he represented the Violence of his own Affection, and the Hopes of subduing Aversion in the Lady by Perseverance. He begged that in an Affair on which depended all his future Repose, he might at least be at Liberty to try all fair Means for Success. Heaven forbid, he said, that he should ever think of prevailing by any other than the most gentle Methods! 'Besides, Sir, said he, if they fail, you may then (which will be surely Time enough) deny your Consent.' He urged the great and eager Desire which Mr. *Western* had for the Match, and lastly, he made great Use of the Name of *Jones*, to whom he imputed all that had happened; and from whom, he said, to preserve so valuable a young Lady was even an Act of Charity.

All these Arguments were well seconded by *Thwackum*, who dwelt a little stronger on the Authority of Parents than Mr. *Blifil* himself had done. He ascribed the Measures which Mr. *Blifil* was desirous to take, to Christian Motives; 'and though,' says he, 'the good young Gentleman hath mentioned Charity last, I am almost convinced, it is his first and principal Consideration.'

Square, possibly, had he been present, would have sung to the same Tune, though in a different Key, and would have discovered much moral Fitness in the Proceeding; but he was now gone to *Bath* for the Recovery of his Health.

Allworthy, though not without Reluctance, at last yielded to the Desires of his Nephew. He said, he would accompany him to *London*, where he might be at Liberty to use every honest Endeavour to gain the Lady: 'But I declare,' said he, 'I will never give my Consent to any absolute Force being put on her Inclinations, nor shall you ever have her, unless she can be brought freely to Compliance.'

Thus did the Affection of *Allworthy* for his Nephew betray the superior Understanding to be triumphed over by the inferior; and thus is the Prudence of the best of Heads often defeated, by the Tenderness of the best of Hearts.

Blifil having obtained this unhoped for Acquiescence in his Uncle, rested not till he carried his Purpose into Execution. And as no immediate Business required Mr. *Allworthy*'s Presence in the Country, and little Preparation is necessary to Men for a Journey, they set out the very next Day, and arrived in Town that Evening, when Mr. *Jones*, as we have seen, was diverting himself with *Partridge*, at the Play.

The Morning after his Arrival, Mr. *Blifil* waited on Mr. *Western*, by whom he was most kindly and graciously received, and from whom he had every possible Assurance (perhaps more than was possible) that he should very shortly be as happy as *Sophia* could make him; nor would the Squire suffer the young Gentleman to return to his Uncle, till he had, almost against his Will, carried him to his Sister.

Chapter VII.

In which Mr. Western *pays a Visit to his Sister, in Company with Mr.* Blifil.

Mrs. *Western* was reading a Lecture on Prudence, and Matrimonial Politics to her Niece, when her Brother and *Blifil* broke in with less Ceremony than the Laws of Visiting require. *Sophia* no sooner saw *Blifil*, than she turned pale, and almost lost the Use of all her Faculties; but her Aunt on the contrary waxed red, and having all her Faculties at Command began to exert her Tongue on the Squire.

'Brother,' said she, 'I am astonished at your Behaviour, will you never learn any Regard to Decorum? Will you still look upon every Apartment as your own, or as belonging to one of your Country Tenants? Do you think yourself at Liberty to invade the Privacies of Women of Condition, without the least Decency or Notice?'——'Why, what a Pox! is the Matter now? quoth the Squire, one would think, I had caught you at——'None of your Brutality, Sir, I beseech you,' answered she. '——You have surprized my poor Niece so, that she can hardly, I see, support herself.——Go, my Dear, retire and endeavour to recruit your Spirits; for I see you have Occasion.' At which Words, *Sophia*, who never received a more welcome Command, hastily withdrew.

'To be sure, Sister,' cries the Squire, 'you are mad, when I have brought Mr. *Blifil* here to court her, to force her away.'

'Sure, Brother,' says she, 'you are worse than mad, when you know in what Situation Affairs are, to——I am sure, I ask Mr. *Blifil* Pardon, but he knows very well to whom to impute so disagreeable a Reception. For my own Part, I am sure, I shall always be very glad to see Mr. *Blifil*; but his own good Sense would not have suffered him to proceed so abruptly, had you not compelled him to it.'

Blifil bowed and stammered and looked like a Fool; but *Western*, without giving him Time to form a Speech for the Purpose, answered, 'Well, well, I am to blame if you will, I always am, certainly; but come, let the Girl be fetched back again, or let Mr. *Blifil* go to her——He's come up on Purpose, and there is no Time to be lost.'

'Brother,' cries Mrs. *Western*, 'Mr. *Blifil*, I am confident, understands himself better than to think of seeing my Niece any more this Morning after what hath happened. Women are of a nice Contexture; and our Spirits when disordered, are not to be recomposed in a Moment. Had you suffered Mr. *Blifil* to have sent his Compliments to my Niece, and to have desired the Favour of waiting on her in the Afternoon, I should possibly have prevailed on her to have seen him; but now I despair of bringing about any such Matter.'

'I am very sorry, Madam,' cried *Blifil*, 'that Mr. *Western's* extraordinary Kindness to me, which I can never enough acknowledge, should have occasioned——' 'Indeed, Sir,' said she, interrupting him, 'you need make no Apologies, we all know my Brother so well.'

'I don't care what any Body knows of me,' answered the Squire, —'but when must he come to see her? for consider, I tell you, he is come up on Purpose, and so is *Allworthy*.' 'Brother,' said she, 'whatever Message Mr. *Blifil* thinks proper to send to my Niece, shall be delivered to her; and I suppose, she will want no Instructions to make a proper Answer. I am convinced she will not refuse to see Mr. *Blifil* at a proper Time.'——'The Devil she won't,' answered the Squire.—'Odsbud!—Don't we know,——I say nothing, but some Volk are wiser than all the World.——If I might have had my Will, she had not run away before: And now I expect to hear every Moment she is guone again. For as great a Fool as some Volk think me, I know very well she hates'——'No Matter, Brother,' replied Mrs. *Western*, 'I will not hear my Niece abused. It is a Reflection on my Family. She is an Honour to it; and she will be an Honour to it, I promise you. I will pawn my whole Reputation in the World on her Conduct.—I shall be glad to see you, Brother, in the Afternoon; for I have somewhat of Importance to mention to you.——At present Mr. *Blifil*, as well as you, must excuse me; for I am in haste to dress.'——'Well but,' said the Squire, 'do appoint a Time.'—'Indeed,' said she, 'I can appoint no Time.—I tell you, I will see you in the Afternoon.'—'What the Devil would you have me do?' cries the Squire, turning to *Blifil*, 'I can no more turn her, than a Beagle can turn an old Hare. Perhaps, she will be in a better Humour in the Afternoon.'—'I am condemned, I see, Sir, to Misfortune,' answered *Blifil*, 'but I shall always own my Obligations to you.'——He then took a ceremonious Leave of Mrs. *Western*, who was altogether as ceremonious on her Part; and then they departed, the Squire muttering to himself with an Oath, that *Blifil* should see his Daughter in the Afternoon.

If Mr. *Western* was little pleased with this Interview, *Blifil* was less. As to the former, he imputed the whole Behaviour of his Sister to her Humour only, and to her Dissatisfaction at the Omission of Ceremony in the Visit; but *Blifil* saw a little deeper into Things. He suspected somewhat of more Consequence, from two or three Words which dropt from the Lady; and, to say the Truth, he suspected right, as will appear when I have unfolded the several Matters which will be contained in the following Chapter.

Chapter VIII.

Schemes of Lady Bellaston for the Ruin of Jones.

Love had taken too deep a Root in the Mind of Lord *Fellamar* to be plucked up by the rude Hands of Mr. *Western*. In the Heat of Resentment he had indeed given a Commission to Captain *Egglane*, which the Captain had far exceeded in the Execution; nor had it been executed at all, had his Lordship been able to find the Captain after he had seen Lady *Bellaston*, which was in the Afternoon of the Day after he had received the Affront; but so industrious was the Captain in the Discharge of his Duty, that having after long Enquiry found out the Squire's Lodgings very late in the Evening, he sat up all Night at a Tavern, that he might not miss the Squire in the Morning, and by that Means missed the Revocation which my Lord had sent to his Lodgings.

In the Afternoon then next after the intended Rape of *Sophia*, his Lordship, as we have said, made a visit to Lady *Bellaston*, who laid open so much of the Character of the Squire, that his Lordship plainly saw the Absurdity he had been guilty of in taking any Offence at his Words, especially as he had those honourable Designs on his Daughter. He then unbosomed the Violence of his Passion to Lady *Bellaston*, who readily undertook the Cause, and encouraged him with certain Assurance of a most favourable Reception, from all the Elders of the Family, and from the Father himself when he should be sober, and should be made acquainted with the Nature of the Offer made to his Daughter. The only Danger, she said, lay in the Fellow she had formerly mentioned, who, though a Beggar and a Vagabond, had by some Means or other, she knew not what, procured himself tolerable Cloaths, and past for a Gentleman. 'Now,' says she, 'as I have, for the Sake of my Cousin, made it my Business to enquire after this Fellow, I have luckily found out his Lodgings'; with which she then acquainted his Lordship. 'I am thinking, my Lord,' added she, '(for this Fellow is too mean for your personal Resentment) whether it would not be possible for your Lordship to contrive some Method of having him pressed and sent on board a Ship. Neither Law nor Conscience forbid this Project: for the Fellow, I promise you, however well drest, is but a Vagabond, and as proper as any Fellow in the Streets to be pressed into the Service; and as for the conscientious Part, surely the Preservation of a young Lady from such Ruin is a most meritorious Act; nay, with Regard to the Fellow himself, unless he could succeed (which Heaven forbid) with my Cousin, it may probably be the Means of preserving him from the Gallows, and perhaps may make his Fortune in an honest Way.'

Lord *Fellamar* very heartily thanked her Ladyship, for the Part which she was pleased to take in the Affair, upon the Success of which his whole future Happiness entirely depended. He said, he saw at present no Objection to the pressing Scheme, and would consider of putting it in Execution. He then most earnestly recommended to her Ladyship, to do him the Honour of immediately mentioning his Proposals to the Family; to whom, he said, he offered a *Carte Blanche*, and would settle his Fortune in almost any Manner they should require. And after uttering many Ecstasies and Raptures concerning *Sophia*, he took his Leave and departed, but not before he had received the strongest Charge to beware of *Jones*, and to lose no Time in securing his Person where he should no longer be in a Capacity of making any Attempts to the Ruin of the young Lady.

The Moment Mrs. *Western* was arrived at her Lodgings, a Card was dispatched with her Compliments to Lady *Bellaston*; who no sooner received it, than with the Impatience of a Lover, she flew to her Cousin, rejoiced at this fair Opportunity, which beyond her Hopes offered itself: for she was much better pleased with the Prospect of making the Proposals to a Woman of Sense, and who knew the World, than to a Gentleman whom she honoured with the Appellation of *Hottentot*; though indeed from him she apprehended no Danger of a Refusal.

The two Ladies being met, after very short previous Ceremonials, fell to Business, which was indeed almost as soon concluded as begun; for Mrs. *Western* no sooner heard the Name of Lord *Fellamar* than her Cheeks glowed with Pleasure; but when she was acquainted with the Eagerness of his Passion, the Earnestness of his Proposals, and the Generosity of his Offer, she declared her full Satisfaction in the most explicit Terms.

In the Progress of their Conversation, their Discourse turned to *Jones*, and both Cousins very pathetically lamented the unfortunate Attachment which both agreed *Sophia* had to that young Fellow; and Mrs. *Western* entirely attributed it to the Folly of her Brother's Management. She concluded however at last, with declaring her Confidence in the good Understanding of her Niece, who though she would not give up her Affection in Favour of *Blifil*, will, I doubt not, says she, soon be prevailed upon to sacrifice a simple Inclination to the Addresses of a fine Gentleman, who brings her both a Title and a large Estate: 'For indeed,' added she, 'I must do *Sophy* the Justice to confess, this *Blifil* is but a hideous kind of Fellow, as you know, *Bellaston*, all Country Gentlemen are, and hath nothing but his Fortune to recommend him.'

'Nay,' said Lady *Bellaston*, 'I don't then so much wonder at my Cousin; for I promise you, this *Jones* is a very agreeable Fellow, and hath one Virtue which the Men say is a great Recommendation to us. What do you think, *Bell*—I shall certainly make you laugh; nay, I can hardly tell you myself for laughing—Will you believe that the Fellow hath had the Assurance to make Love to me? But if you should be inclined to disbelieve it, here is Evidence enough, his own Hand-writing, I assure you.' She then delivered her Cousin the Letter with the Proposals of Marriage, which if the Reader hath a Desire to see, he will find already on Record in the XVth Book of this History.

'Upon my Word, I am astonished,' said Mrs. *Western*, 'this is indeed a Master-piece of Assurance. With your Leave, I may possibly make some Use of this Letter.' 'You have my full Liberty,' cries Lady *Bellaston*, 'to apply it to what Purpose you please. However, I would not have it shewn to any but Miss *Western*, nor to her unless you find Occasion.' 'Well, and how did you use the Fellow?' returned Mrs. *Western*. 'Not as a Husband,' said the Lady. 'I am not married, I promise you, my Dear. You know, *Bell*,[1] I have try'd the Comforts once already; and once I think is enough for any reasonable Woman.'

This Letter, Lady *Bellaston* thought would certainly turn the Balance against *Jones* in the Mind of *Sophia*, and she was emboldened to give it up, partly by her Hopes of having him instantly dispatched out of the Way, and partly by having secured the Evidence of *Honour*, who, upon sounding her, she saw sufficient Reason to imagine, was prepared to testify whatever she pleased.

But perhaps the Reader may wonder why Lady *Bellaston*, who in her Heart hated *Sophia*, should be so desirous of promoting a Match, which was so much to the Interest of the young Lady. Now, I would desire such Readers to look carefully into human Nature, Page almost the last, and there he will find in scarce legible Characters, that Women, notwithstanding the preposterous Behaviour of Mothers, Aunts, &c. in matrimonial Matters, do in Reality think it so great a Misfortune to have their Inclinations in Love thwarted, that they imagine, they ought never to carry Enmity higher than upon these Disappointments; again, he will find it written much about the same Place, that a Woman who hath once been pleased

1. The first three editions read "Bel." Fielding earlier calls Mistress Western "Di" (p. 533). On this error, "the most corrupt passage to be found anywhere in the novel," together with the "error" of changing "Black Jack" to "Black George" in the fourth edition (see above, note 2, p. 98), Cross rests his case that Fielding made no corrections after those for the second edition (II.124), a case rather thoroughly disproved by the evidence in editions three and four.

with the Possession of a Man, will go above half way to the Devil, to prevent any other Woman from enjoying the same.

If he will not be contented with these Reasons, I freely confess I see no other Motive to the Actions of that Lady, unless we will conceive she was bribed by Lord *Fellamar,* which for my own Part I see no Cause to suspect.

Now this was the Affair which Mrs. *Western* was preparing to introduce to *Sophia,* by some prefatory Discourse on the Folly of Love, and on the Wisdom of legal Prostitution for Hire, when her Brother and *Blifil* broke abruptly in upon her; and hence arose all that Coldness in her Behaviour to *Blifil,* which tho' the Squire, as was usual with him, imputed to a wrong Cause, infused into *Blifil* himself (he being a much more cunning Man) a Suspicion of the real Truth.

Chapter IX.

In which Jones pays a Visit to Mrs. Fitzpatrick.

The Reader may now perhaps be pleased to return with us to Mr. *Jones,* who at the appointed Hour attended on Mrs. *Fitzpatrick;* but before we relate the Conversation which now past, it may be proper, according to our Method, to return a little back, and to account for so great an Alteration of Behaviour in this Lady, that from changing her Lodging principally to avoid Mr. *Jones,* she had now industriously, as hath been seen, sought this Interview.

And here we shall need only to resort to what happened the preceding Day, when hearing from Lady *Bellaston,* that Mr. *Western* was arrived in Town, she went to pay her Duty to him, at his Lodgings at *Piccadilly,* where she was received with many scurvy Compellations too coarse to be repeated, and was even threatned to be kicked out of Doors. From hence an old Servant of her Aunt *Western,* with whom she was well acquainted, conducted her to the Lodgings of that Lady, who treated her not more kindly, but more politely; or, to say the Truth, with Rudeness in another Way. In short, she returned from both, plainly convinced not only that her Scheme of Reconciliation had proved abortive, but that she must for ever give over all Thoughts of bringing it about by any Means whatever. From this Moment Desire of Revenge only filled her Mind; and in this Temper meeting *Jones* at the Play, an Opportunity seemed to her to occur of effecting this Purpose.

The Reader must remember, that he was acquainted by Mrs. *Fitzpatrick,* in the Account she gave of her own Story, with the Fondness Mrs. *Western* had formerly shewn for Mr. *Fitzpatrick* at *Bath,* from the Disappointment of which, Mrs. *Fitzpatrick* derived the great Bitterness her Aunt had expressed toward her. She had therefore no Doubt but that the good Lady would as easily listen to the Addresses of Mr. *Jones*, as she had before done to the other; for the Superiority of Charms was clearly on the Side of Mr. *Jones*; and the Advance which her Aunt had since made in Age, she concluded, (how justly I will not say) was an Argument rather in Favour of her Project than against it.

Therefore, when *Jones* attended after a previous Declaration of her Desire of serving him, arising, as she said, from a firm Assurance how much she should by so doing oblige *Sophia*; and after some Excuses for her former Disappointment, and after acquainting Mr. *Jones* in whose Custody his Mistress was, of which she thought him ignorant; she very explicitly mentioned her Scheme to him, and advised him to make sham Addresses to the older Lady, in order to procure an easy Access to the younger, informing him at the same Time of the Success which Mr. *Fitzpatrick* had formerly owed to the very same Stratagem.

Mr. *Jones* expressed great Gratitude to the Lady for the kind Intentions towards him which she had expressed, and indeed testified, by this Proposal; but besides intimating some Diffidence of Success from the Lady's Knowledge of his Love to her Niece, which had not been her Case in Regard to Mr. *Fitzpatrick*, he said, he was afraid Miss *Western* would never agree to an Imposition of this Kind, as well from her utter Detestation of all Fallacy, as from her avowed Duty to her Aunt.

Mrs. *Fitzpatrick* was a little nettled at this; and indeed, if it may not be called a Lapse of the Tongue, it was a small Deviation from Politeness in *Jones*, and into which he scarce would have fallen, had not the Delight he felt in praising *Sophia*, hurried him out of all Reflection; for this Commendation of one Cousin was more than a tacit Rebuke on the other.

'Indeed, Sir,' answered the Lady, with some Warmth, 'I cannot think there is any thing easier than to cheat an old Woman with a Profession of Love, when her Complexion is amorous; and tho' she is my Aunt, I must say there never was a more liquorish one than her Ladyship. Can't you pretend that the Despair of possessing her Niece, from her being promised to *Blifil*, has made you turn your Thoughts towards her? As to my Cousin *Sophia*, I can't imagine her to be such a Simpleton as to have the least Scruple on such an Account, or to conceive any harm in punishing one of these Haggs for the many Mischiefs they bring upon Families, by their tragicomic Passions; for which I think it is pity they are not punishable by Law. I had no such Scruple myself; and yet I hope my Cousin *Sophia* will not think it an Affront when I say she cannot detest every real Species of Falshood more than her Cousin *Fitzpatrick*.

To my Aunt indeed I pretend no Duty, nor doth she deserve any. However, Sir, I have given you my Advice, and if you decline pursuing it, I shall have the less Opinion of your Understanding,—that's all.'

Jones now clearly saw the Error he had committed, and exerted his utmost Power to rectify it; but he only faultered and stuttered into Nonsense and Contradiction. To say the Truth, it is often safer to abide by the Consequences of the first Blunder, than to endeavour to rectify it; for by such Endeavours, we generally plunge deeper instead of extricating ourselves; and few Persons will on such Occasions have the good Nature, which Mrs. *Fitzpatrick* displayed to *Jones*, by saying, with a Smile, 'You need attempt no more Excuses; for I can easily forgive a real Lover, whatever is the Effect of Fondness for his Mistress.'

She then renewed her Proposal, and very fervently recommended it, omitting no Argument which her Invention could suggest on the Subject; for she was so violently incensed against her Aunt, that scarce any Thing was capable of affording her equal Pleasure with exposing her; and like a true Woman, she would see no difficulties in the Execution of a favourite Scheme.

Jones however persisted in declining the Undertaking, which had not indeed the least Probability of Success. He easily perceived the Motives which induced Mrs. *Fitzpatrick* to be so eager in pressing her Advice. He said, he would not deny the tender and passionate Regard he had for *Sophia*; but was so conscious of the Inequality of their Situations, that he could never flatter himself so far as to hope that so divine a young Lady would condescend to think on so unworthy a Man; nay he protested, he could scarce bring himself to wish she should. He concluded with a Profession of generous Sentiments, which we have not at present Leisure to insert.

There are some fine Women (for I dare not here speak in too general Terms) with whom Self is so predominant, that they never detach it from any Subject; and as Vanity is with them a ruling Principle, they are apt to lay hold of whatever Praise they meet with; and, though the Property of others, convey it to their own Use. In the Company of these Ladies it is impossible to say any Thing handsome of another Woman, which they will not apply to themselves; nay, they often improve the Praise they seize; as for Instance, if her Beauty, her Wit, her Gentility, her good Humour deserve so much Commendation, what do I deserve who possess those Qualities in so much more eminent a Degree?

To these Ladies a Man often recommends himself while he is commending another Woman; and while he is expressing Ardour and generous Sentiments for his Mistress, they are considering what

a charming Lover this Man would make to them, who can feel all
this Tenderness for an inferior Degree of Merit. Of this, strange as
it may seem, I have seen many Instances besides Mrs. *Fitzpatrick*,
to whom all this really happened, and who now began to feel a
Somewhat for Mr. *Jones*, the Symptoms of which she much sooner
understood than poor *Sophia* had formerly done.

To say the Truth, perfect Beauty in both Sexes is a more irresistible Object than it is generally thought; for notwithstanding some of
us are contented with more homely Lots, and learn by Rote (as
Children are to repeat what gives them no Idea) to despise Outside, and to value more solid Charms; yet I have always observed at
the Approach of consummate Beauty, that these more solid Charms
only shine with that Kind of Lustre which the Stars have after the
Rising of the Sun.

When *Jones* had finished his Exclamations, many of which would
have become the Mouth of *Oroondates*[1] himself, Mrs. *Fitzpatrick*
heaved a deep Sigh, and taking her Eyes off from *Jones*, on
whom they had been some Time fixed, and dropping them on
the Ground, she cried, 'Indeed, Mr. *Jones*, I pity you; but it is the
Curse of such Tenderness to be thrown away on those who are
insensible of it. I know my Cousin better than you, Mr. *Jones*, and
I must say, any Woman who makes no Return to such a Passion,
and such a Person, is unworthy of both.'

'Sure, Madam,' said *Jones*, 'you can't mean'—'Mean?' cries Mrs.
Fitzpatrick, 'I know not what I mean; there is something, I think,
in true Tenderness bewitching; few Women ever meet with it in
Men, and fewer still know how to value it when they do. I never
heard such truly noble Sentiments, and I can't tell how it is, but
you force one to believe you. Sure she must be the most contemptible of Women who can overlook such Merit.'

The Manner and Look with which all this was spoke, infused a
Suspicion into *Jones*, which we don't care to convey in direct
Words to the Reader. Instead of making any Answer, he said, 'I am
afraid, Madam, I have made too tiresome a Visit,' and offered to
take his Leave.

'Not at all, Sir,' answered Mrs. *Fitzpatrick*, 'Indeed I pity you,
Mr. *Jones*; indeed I do: But if you are going, consider of the
Scheme I have mentioned. I am convinced you will approve it, and
let me see you again as soon as you can.—To-morrow Morning if
you will, or at least some time To-morrow. I shall be at Home all
Day.'

Jones then, after many Expressions of Thanks very respectfully
retired; nor could Mrs. *Fitzpatrick* forbear making him a Present of

1. See above, p. 381.

a Look at Parting, by which if he had understood Nothing, he must have had no Understanding in the Language of the Eyes. In reality it confirmed his Resolution of returning to her no more; for faulty as he hath hitherto appeared in this History, his whole Thoughts were now so confined to his *Sophia*, that I believe no Woman upon Earth could have now drawn him into an Act of Inconstancy.

Fortune however, who was not his Friend, resolved, as he intended to give her no second Opportunity, to make the best of this; and accordingly produced the tragical Incident which we are now in sorrowful Notes to record.

Chapter X.

The Consequence of the preceding Visit.

Mr. *Fitzpatrick* having received the Letter before-mentioned, from Mrs. *Western*, and being by that Means acquainted with the Place to which his Wife was retired, returned directly to *Bath*, and thence the Day after set forward to *London*.

The Reader hath been already often informed of the jealous Temper of this Gentleman. He may likewise be pleased to remember the Suspicion which he had conceived of *Jones* at *Upton*, upon his finding him in the Room with Mrs. *Waters*; and though sufficient Reasons had afterwards appeared entirely to clear up that Suspicion, yet now the reading so handsome a Character of Mr. *Jones* from his Wife, caused him to reflect, that she likewise was in the Inn at the same Time, and jumbled together such a Confusion of Circumstances in a Head which was naturally none of the clearest, that the whole produced that green-eyed Monster mentioned by *Shakespear* in his Tragedy of *Othello*.[1]

And now as he was enquiring in the Street after his Wife, and had just received Directions to the Door, unfortunately Mr. *Jones* was issuing from it.

Fitzpatrick did not yet recollect the Face of *Jones*; however, seeing a young well-dressed Fellow coming from his Wife, he made directly up to him, and asked him what he had been doing in that House: 'For I am sure,' said he, 'you must have been in it, as I saw you come out of it.'

Jones answered very modestly, 'That he had been visiting a Lady there.' To which *Fitzpatrick* replied, 'what Business have you with the Lady?' Upon which *Jones*, who now perfectly remembered the Voice, Features, and indeed Coat, of the Gentleman, cried out,——'Ha, my good Friend! give me your Hand; I hope there is no ill

---

1. Iago says, "O beware, my lord, of jealousy! / It is the green-eyed monster, which doth mock / The meat it feeds on" (III.iii.165–67).

Blood remaining between us, upon a small Mistake which happened so long ago.'

'Upon my Soul, Sir,' said *Fitzpatrick*, 'I don't know your Name, nor your Face.' 'Indeed, Sir,' said *Jones*, 'Neither have I the Pleasure of knowing your Name, but your Face I very well remember to have seen before, at *Upton*, where a foolish Quarrel happened between us, which, if it is not made up yet, we will now make up over a Bottle.'

'At *Upton!*' cried the other.—'Ha! upon my Soul, I believe your Name is *Jones*.' 'Indeed,' answered he, 'It is.'—'O, upon my Soul,' cries *Fitzpatrick*, 'you are the very Man I wanted to meet.—Upon my Soul I will drink a Bottle with you presently; but first I will give you a great Knock over the Pate. There is for you, you Rascal. Upon my Soul, if you do not give me Satisfaction for that Blow, I will give you another.' And then drawing his Sword put himself in a Posture of Defence, which was the only Science he understood.

Jones was a little staggered by the Blow which came somewhat unexpectedly; but presently recovering himself he also drew, and though he understood nothing of Fencing, prest on so boldly upon *Fitzpatrick*, that he beat down his Guard, and sheathed one half of his Sword in the Body of the said Gentleman, who had no sooner received it, than he stept backwards, dropt the Point of his Sword, and leaning upon it, cried, 'I have Satisfaction enough: I am a dead Man.'

'I hope not,' cries *Jones*, 'but whatever be the Consequence, you must be sensible you have drawn it upon yourself.' At this Instant a Number of Fellows rushed in and seized *Jones*, who told them, he should make no Resistance, and begged some of them at least would take care of the wounded Gentleman.

'Ay,' cries one of the Fellows, 'the wounded Gentleman will be taken Care enough of; for I suppose he hath not many Hours to live. As for you, Sir, you have a Month at least good yet.' 'D—n me, *Jack*,' said another, 'he hath prevented his Voyage; he's bound to another Port now;' and many other such Jests was our poor *Jones* made the Subject of, by these Fellows, who were indeed the Gang employed by Lord *Fellamar*, and had dogged him into the House of Mrs. *Fitzpatrick*, waiting for him at the Corner of the Street when this unfortunate Accident happened.

The Officer who commanded this Gang very wisely concluded, that his Business was now to deliver his Prisoner into the Hands of the Civil Magistrate. He ordered him therefore to be carried to a public House, where having sent for a Constable, he delivered him to his Custody.

The Constable seeing Mr. *Jones* very well drest, and hearing that the Accident had happened in a Duel, treated his Prisoner with great Civility, and, at his Request, dispatched a Messenger to enquire after the wounded Gentleman, who was now at a Tavern under the Surgeon's Hands. The Report brought back was, that the Wound was certainly mortal, and there were no Hopes of Life. Upon which the Constable informed *Jones*, that he must go before a Justice. He answered, 'Wherever you please: I am indifferent as to what happens to me; for though I am convinced I am not guilty of Murder in the Eye of the Law, yet the Weight of Blood I find intolerable upon my Mind.'

Jones was now conducted before the Justice, where the Surgeon who dressed Mr. *Fitzpatrick* appeared, and deposed, that he believed the Wound to be mortal; upon which the Prisoner was committed to the *Gate-house*. It was very late at Night, so that *Jones* would not send for *Partridge* till the next Morning; and as he never shut his Eyes till seven, so it was near twelve before the poor Fellow, who was greatly frightened at not hearing from his Master so long, received a Message which almost deprived him of his Being, when he heard it.

He went to the *Gate-house* with trembling Knees and a beating Heart, and was no sooner arrived in the Presence of *Jones*, than he lamented the Misfortune that had befallen him, with many Tears, looking all the while frequently about him in great Terror; for as the News now arrived that Mr. *Fitzpatrick* was dead, the poor Fellow apprehended every Minute that his Ghost would enter the Room. At last he delivered him a Letter, which he had like to have forgot, and which came from *Sophia* by the Hands of black *George*.

Jones presently dispatched every one out of the Room, and having eagerly broke open the Letter, read as follows.

'You owe the hearing from me again to an Accident which I own surprizes me. My Aunt hath just now shewn me a Letter from you to Lady *Bellaston*, which contains a Proposal of Marriage. I am convinced it is your own Hand; and what more surprizes me, is, that it is dated at the very Time when you would have me imagine you was under such Concern on my Account.—I leave you to comment on this Fact. All I desire is, that your Name may never more be mentioned to

'S.W.'

Of the present Situation of Mr. *Jones*'s Mind, and of the Pangs with which he was now tormented, we cannot give the Reader a better Idea, than by saying, his Misery was such, that even *Thwackum* would almost have pitied him. But bad as it is, we shall at present leave him in it, as his good Genius (if he really had any) seems to have done. And here we put an End to the sixteenth Book of our History.

BOOK XVII.

Containing Three Days.

Chapter I.

Containing a Portion of introductory Writing.

When a Comic Writer hath made his principal Characters as happy as he can; or when a Tragic Writer hath brought them to the highest Pitch of human Misery, they both conclude their Business to be done, and that their Work is come to a Period.

Had we been of the Tragic Complexion, the Reader must now allow we were very nearly arrived at this Period, since it would be difficult for the Devil, or any of his Representatives on Earth, to have contrived much greater Torments for poor *Jones*, than those in which we left him in the last Chapter; and as for *Sophia*, a good-natured Woman would hardly wish more Uneasiness to a Rival, than what she must at present be supposed to feel. What then remains to complete the Tragedy but a Murder or two, and a few moral Sentences.

But to bring our Favourites out of their present Anguish and Distress, and to land them at last on the Shore of Happiness, seems a much harder Task; a Task indeed so hard that we do not undertake to execute it. In Regard to *Sophia*, it is more than probable, that we shall somewhere or other provide a good Husband for her in the End, either *Blifil*, or my Lord, or Somebody else; but as to poor *Jones*, such are the Calamities in which he is at present involved, owing to his Imprudence, by which if a Man doth not become Felon to the World, he is at least a *Felo de se*;[1] so destitute is he now of Friends, and so persecuted by Enemies, that we almost despair of bringing him to any Good; and if our Reader delights in seeing Executions, I think he ought not to lose any Time in taking a first Row at *Tyburn*.

This I faithfully promise, that notwithstanding any Affection, which we may be supposed to have for this Rogue, whom we have unfortunately made our Heroe, we will lend him none of that supernatural Assistance with which we are entrusted, upon Condition that we use it only on very important Occasions. If he doth not therefore find some natural Means of fairly extricating himself from all his Distresses, we will do no Violence to the Truth and Dignity

---

1. "A felon as to himself," a suicide. See above, p. 363.

of History for his Sake; for we had rather relate that he was hanged at *Tyburn* (which may very probably be the Case) than forfeit our Integrity, or shock the Faith of our Reader.

In this the Antients had a great Advantage over the Moderns. Their Mythology, which was at that Time more firmly believed by the Vulgar than any Religion is at present, gave them always an Opportunity of delivering a favourite Heroe. Their Deities were always ready at the Writer's Elbow, to execute any of his Purposes; and the more extraordinary the Invention was, the greater was the Surprize and Delight of the credulous Reader. Those Writers could with greater Ease have conveyed a Heroe from one Country to another, nay from one World to another, and have brought him back again, than a poor circumscribed Modern can deliver him from a Goal.

The *Arabians* and *Persians* had an equal Advantage in writing their Tales from the *Genii* and *Fairies*, which they believe in as an Article of their Faith, upon the Authority of the *Koran* itself. But we have none of these Helps. To natural Means alone are we confined; let us try therefore what by these Means may be done for poor *Jones*; though, to confess the Truth, something whispers me in the Ear, that he doth not yet know the worst of his Fortune; and that a more shocking Piece of News than any he hath yet heard, remains for him in the unopened Leaves of Fate.

Chapter II.

The generous and grateful Behaviour of Mrs. Miller.

Mr. *Allworthy* and Mrs. *Miller* were just sat down to Breakfast, when *Blifil*, who had gone out very early that Morning, returned to make one of the Company.

He had not been long seated before he began as follows, 'Good Lord! my dear Uncle, what do you think hath happened? I vow I am afraid of telling it you, for fear of shocking you with the Remembrance of ever having shewn any Kindness to such a Villain.' 'What is the Matter, Child,' said the Uncle, 'I fear I have shewn Kindness in my Life to the Unworthy more than once. But Charity doth not adopt the Vices of its Objects.' 'O, Sir,' returned *Blifil*, 'it is not without the secret Direction of Providence that you mention the Word Adoption. Your adopted Son, Sir, that *Jones*, that Wretch whom you nourished in your Bosom, hath proved one of the greatest Villains upon Earth.' 'By all that's sacred 'tis false,' cries Mrs. *Miller*. 'Mr. *Jones* is no Villain. He is one of the worthiest Creatures breathing; and if any other Person had called him Villain, I would have thrown all this boiling Water in his Face.' Mr.

Allworthy looked very much amazed at this Behaviour. But she did not give him Leave to speak, before turning to him, she cry'd, 'I hope you will not be angry with me; I would not offend you, Sir, for the World; but indeed I could not bear to hear him called so.' 'I must own, Madam,' said *Allworthy* very gravely, 'I am a little surprized to hear you so warmly defend a Fellow you do not know.' 'O I do know him, Mr. *Allworthy*,' said she, 'indeed I do; I should be the most ungrateful of all Wretches if I denied it. O he hath preserved me and my little Family; we have all Reason to bless him while we live.—And I pray Heaven to bless him, and turn the Hearts of his malicious Enemies. I know, I find, I see he hath such.' 'You surprize me, Madam, still more,' said *Allworthy*, 'sure you must mean some other. It is impossible you should have any such Obligations to the Man my Nephew mentions.' 'Too surely,' answered she, 'I have Obligations to him of the greatest and tenderest Kind. He hath been the Preserver of me and mine.—Believe me, Sir, he hath been abused, grossly abused to you; I know he hath, or you, whom I know to be all Goodness and Honour, would not, after the many kind and tender Things I have heard you say of this poor helpless Child, have so disdainfully called him Fellow. Indeed, my best of Friends, he deserves a kinder Appellation from you, had you heard the good, the kind, the grateful Things which I have heard him utter of you. He never mentions your Name but with a sort of Adoration. In this very Room I have seen him on his Knees, imploring all the Blessings of Heaven upon your Head. I do not love that Child there better than he loves you.'

'I see, Sir, now,' said *Blifil*, with one of those grinning Sneers with which the Devil marks his best Beloved, 'Mrs. *Miller* really doth know him. I suppose you will find she is not the only one of your Acquaintance to whom he hath exposed you. As for my Character, I perceive by some Hints she hath thrown out, he hath been very free with it, but I forgive him.' 'And the Lord forgive you, Sir,' says Mrs. *Miller*, 'we have all Sins enough to stand in Need of his Forgiveness.'

'Upon my Word, Mrs. *Miller*,' said *Allworthy*, 'I do not take this Behaviour of yours to my Nephew, kindly; and I do assure you as any Reflections which you cast upon him must come only from that wickedest of Men, they would only serve, if that were possible, to heighten my Resentment against him: For I must tell you, Mrs. *Miller*, the young Man who now stands before you, hath ever been the warmest Advocate for the ungrateful Wretch whose Cause you espouse. This, I think, when you hear it from my own Mouth, will make you wonder at so much Baseness and Ingratitude.'

'You are deceived, Sir,' answered Mrs. *Miller*, 'if they were the last Words which were to issue from my Lips, I would say you were

deceived; and I once more repeat it, the Lord forgive those who
have deceived you. I do not pretend to say the young Man is without Faults; but they are all the Faults of Wildness and of Youth;
Faults which he may, nay which I am certain he will relinquish,
and if he should not, they are vastly over-balanced by one of the
most humane tender honest Hearts that ever Man was blest with.'

'Indeed, Mrs. *Miller*,' said *Allworthy*, 'had this been related of
you, I should not have believed it.' 'Indeed, Sir,' answered she, 'you
will believe every Thing I have said, I am sure you will; and when
you have heard the Story which I shall tell you, (for I will tell you
all) you will be so far from being offended, that you will own (I
know your Justice so well) that I must have been the most despicable and most ungrateful of Wretches, if I had acted any other Part
than I have.'

'Well, Madam,' said *Allworthy*, 'I shall be very glad to hear any
good Excuse for a Behaviour which I must confess, I think wants an
Excuse. And now, Madam, will you be pleased to let my Nephew
proceed in his Story without Interruption. He would not have introduced a Matter of slight Consequence with such a Preface. Perhaps
even this Story will cure you of your Mistake.'

Mrs. *Miller* gave Tokens of Submission, and then Mr. *Blifil*
began thus. 'I am sure, Sir, if you don't think proper to resent the
ill Usage of Mrs. *Miller*, I shall easily forgive what affects me only. I
think your Goodness hath not deserved this Indignity at her
Hands.' 'Well, Child,' said *Allworthy*, 'But what is this new Instance? What hath he done of late?' 'What?' cries *Blifil*, 'notwithstanding all Mrs. *Miller* hath said, I am very sorry to relate, and
what you should never have heard from me, had it not been a Matter impossible to conceal from the whole World. In short, he hath
killed a Man; I will not say murdered,——for perhaps it may not
be so construed in Law, and I hope the best for his Sake.'

Allworthy looked shocked, and blessed himself; and then turning
to Mrs. *Miller*, he cried, 'Well, Madam, what say you now?'

'Why, I say, Sir,' answered she, 'that I never was more concerned
at any Thing in my Life; but, if the Fact be true, I am convinced
the Man, whoever he is, was in Fault. Heaven knows there are
many Villains in this Town, who make it their Business to provoke
young Gentlemen. Nothing but the greatest Provocation could have
tempted him; for of all the Gentlemen I ever had in my House, I
never saw one so gentle, or so sweet-tempered. He was beloved by
every one in the House, and every one who came near it.'

While she was thus running on, a violent Knocking at the
Door interrupted their Conversation, and prevented her from proceeding further or from receiving any Answer; for as she concluded
this was a Visiter to Mr. *Allworthy*, she hastily retired, taking with

her her little Girl, whose Eyes were all over blubbered at the melancholy News she heard of *Jones*, who used to call her his little Wife, and not only gave her many Play-things, but spent whole Hours in playing with her himself.

Some Readers may perhaps be pleased with these minute Circumstances, in relating of which we follow the Example of *Plutarch*, one of the best of our Brother Historians; and others to whom they may appear trivial, will, we hope, at least pardon them, as we are never prolix on such Occasions.

Chapter III.

The Arrival of Mr. Western, *with some Matters concerning the Paternal Authority.*

Mrs. *Miller* had not long left the Room, when Mr. *Western* entered; but not before a small wrangling Bout had pass'd between him and his Chairmen; for the Fellows who had taken up their Burden at the *Hercules Pillars*, had conceived no Hopes of having any future good Customer in the Squire; and they were moreover farther encouraged by his Generosity, (for he had given them of his own Accord Sixpence more than their Fare;) they therefore very boldly demanded another Shilling, which so provoked the Squire, that he not only bestowed many hearty Curses on them at the Door, but retained his Anger after he came into the Room; swearing that all the *Londoners* were like the Court, and thought of nothing but plundering Country Gentlemen. 'D——n me, says he, if I won't walk in the Rain rather than get into one of their Handbarrows again. They have jolted me more in a Mile than Brown Bess would in a long Fox Chace.'

When his Wrath on this Occasion was a little appeased, he resumed the same passionate Tone on another. 'There,' says he, 'there is fine Business forwards now. The Hounds have changed at last, and when we imagined we had a Fox to deal with, Od rat-it, it turns out to be a Badger at last.'

'Pray, my good Neighbour,' said *Allworthy*, 'drop your Metaphors, and speak a little plainer.' 'Why then,' says the Squire, 'to tell you plainly, we have been all this Time afraid of a Son of a Whore of a Bastard of Somebody's, I don't know who's, not I—— And now here is a confounded Son of a Whore of a Lord, who may be a Bastard too for what I know or care, for he shall never have a Daughter of mine by my Consent. They have beggared the Nation, but they shall never beggar me. My Land shall never be sent over to *Hannover*.'

'You surprize me much, my good Friend,' said *Allworthy*. 'Why, zounds! I am surprized myself,' answered the Squire, 'I went to zee Sister *Western* last Night, according to her own Appointment, and there I was a had into a whole Room-full of Women.—There was my Lady Cousin *Bellaston*, and my Lady *Betty*, and my Lady *Catharine*, and my Lady I don't know who; d—n me if ever you catch me among such a Kennel of Hoop-petticoat B—s. D—n me, I'd rather be run by my own Dogs, as one *Acton*[1] was, that the Story Book says was turned into a Hare; and his own Dogs kill'd un, and eat un. Od-rabbet-it, no Mortal was ever run in such a manner; if I dodged one Way, one had me, if I offered to clap back, another snap'd me. O! certainly one of the greatest Matches in *England*, says one Cousin (here he attempted to mimic them); 'A very advantageous Offer indeed,' cries another Cousin, (for you must know they be all my Cousins, thof I never zeed half oum before.) "Surely," says that fat a—se B—, my Lady *Bellaston*, "Cousin, you must be out of your Wits to think of refusing such an Offer."

'Now I begin to understand,' says *Allworthy*, 'some Person hath made Proposals to Miss *Western*, which the Ladies of the Family approve, but is not to your Liking.'

'My Liking!' said *Western*, 'how the Devil should it? I tell you it is a Lord, and those are always Volks whom you know I always resolved to have nothing to do with. Did unt I refuse a matter of vorty Years Purchase now for a Bit of Land, which one oum had a Mind to put into a Park, only because I would have no Dealings with Lords, and dost think I would marry my Daughter zu? Besides, ben't I engaged to you, and did I ever go off any Bargain when I had promised?'

'As to that Point, Neighbour,' said *Allworthy*, 'I entirely release you from any Engagement. No Contract can be binding between Parties who have not a full Power to make it at the Time, nor ever afterwards acquire the Power of fulfilling it.'

'Slud! then,' answered *Western*, 'I tell you I have Power, and I will fulfil it. Come along with me directly to *Doctors Commons*, I will get a Licence; and I will go to Sister and take away the Wench by Force, and she shall ha un, or I will lock her up and keep her upon Bread and Water as long as she lives.'

'Mr. *Western*,' said *Allworthy*, 'shall I beg you will hear my full Sentiments on this Matter?' 'Hear thee! ay to be sure, I will,' answered he. 'Why then, Sir,' cries *Allworthy*, 'I can truly say, without a Compliment either to you or the young Lady, that when this

1. Western means Actaeon, a mighty hunter, who saw Diana and her maidens bathing, for which she turned him into a stag, to be chased and eaten by his own dogs (Ovid, *Metamorphoses* III.155 ff.). Mutter remarks that Acton was a suburban district of London where Fielding himself had once lived, but Fielding did not lease Fordhook, a farm at the edge of Ealing village, a mile northwest of Acton village, until the summer of 1752, at least four years after he wrote this passage.

Match was proposed, I embraced it very readily and heartily, from my Regard to you both. An Alliance between two Families so nearly Neighbours, and between whom there had always existed so mutual an Intercourse and good Harmony, I thought a most desirable Event; and with Regard to the young Lady, not only the concurrent Opinion of all who knew her, but my own Observation assured me that she would be an inestimable Treasure to a good Husband. I shall say nothing of her personal Qualifications, which certainly are admirable; her Good-nature, her charitable Disposition, her Modesty are too well known to need any Panegyric: But she hath one Quality which existed in a high Degree in that best of Women, who is now one of the first of Angels, which as it is not of a glaring Kind, more commonly escapes Observation; so little indeed is it remarked, that I want a Word to express it. I must use Negatives on this Occasion. I never heard any thing of Pertness, or what is called Repartee out of her Mouth; no Pretence to Wit, much less to that Kind of Wisdom, which is the Result only of great Learning and Experience; the Affectation of which, in a young Woman, is as absurd as any of the Affectations of an Ape. No dictatorial Sentiments, no judicial Opinions, no profound Criticisms. Whenever I have seen her in the Company of Men, she hath been all Attention, with the Modesty of a Learner, not the Forwardness of a Teacher. You'll pardon me for it, but I once, to try her only, desired her Opinion on a Point which was controverted between Mr. *Thwackum* and Mr. *Square.* To which she answered with much Sweetness, "You will pardon me, good Mr. *Allworthy,* I am sure you cannot in Earnest think me capable of deciding any Point in which two such Gentlemen disagree." *Thwackum* and *Square,* who both alike thought themselves sure of a favourable Decision, seconded my Request. She answered with the same good Humour, "I must absolutely be excused; for I will affront neither so much, as to give my Judgment on his Side." Indeed, she always shewed the highest Deference to the Understandings of Men; a Quality absolutely essential to the making a good Wife. I shall only add, that as she is most apparently void of all Affectation, this Deference must be certainly real.'

Here *Blifil* sighed bitterly; upon which *Western,* whose Eyes were full of Tears at the Praise of *Sophia,* blubbered out, 'Don't be Chicken-hearted, for shat ha her, d——n me, shat ha her, if she was twenty Times as good.'

'Remember your Promise, Sir,' cried *Allworthy,* 'I was not to be interrupted.' 'Well, shat unt,' answered the Squire, 'I won't speak another Word.'

'Now, my good Friend,' continued *Allworthy,* 'I have dwelt so long on the Merit of this young Lady, partly as I really am in Love with her Character, and partly that Fortune (for the Match in that Light is really advantageous on my Nephew's Side) might not be imagined to be my principal View in having so eagerly embraced the Proposal. Indeed I heartily wished to receive so great a jewel into my Family; but tho' I may wish for many good Things, I would not therefore steal them, or be guilty of any Violence or Injustice to possess myself of them. Now to force a Woman into a Marriage contrary to her Consent or Approbation, is an Act of such Injustice and Oppression, that I wish the Laws of our Country could restrain it; but a good Conscience is never lawless in the worst-regulated State, and will provide those Laws for itself, which the Neglect of Legislators hath forgotten to supply. This is surely a Case of that Kind; for is it not cruel, nay impious, to force a Woman into that State against her Will; for her Behaviour in which she is to be accountable to the highest and most dreadful Court of Judicature, and to answer at the Peril of her Soul? To discharge the Matrimonial Duties in an adequate Manner is no easy Task, and shall we lay this Burthen upon a Woman, while we at the same Time deprive her of all that Assistance which may enable her to undergo it? Shall we tear her very Heart from her, while we enjoin her Duties to which a whole Heart is scarce equal. I must speak very plainly here, I think Parents who act in this Manner are Accessaries to all the Guilt which their Children afterwards incur, and of Course must, before a just Judge, expect to partake of their Punishment; but if they could avoid this, good Heaven! is there a Soul who can bear the Thought of having contributed to the Damnation of his Child?

'For these Reasons, my best Neighbour, as I see the Inclinations of this young Lady are most unhappily averse to my Nephew, I must decline any further Thoughts of the Honour you intended him, tho' I assure you I shall always retain the most grateful Sense of it.'

'Well, Sir,' said *Western*, (the Froth bursting forth from his Lips the Moment they were uncorked) 'you cannot say but I have heard you out, and now I expect you'll hear me; and if I don't answer every Word on't, why then I'll consent to gee the Matter up. First then I desire you to answer me one Question, Did not I beget her? Did not I beget her? answer me that. They say indeed it is a wise Father that knows his own Child; but I am sure I have the best Title to her, for I bred her up. But I believe you will allow me to be her Father, and if I be, am I not to govern my own Child? I ask you that, am I not to govern my own Child? And if I am to govern her in other Matters, surely I am to govern her in this which concerns her most. And what am I desiring all this while? Am I desiring her to do any Thing for me? To give me any Thing?—Zu

much on t'other Side, that I am only desiring her to take away half
my Estate now, and t'other half when I die. Well, and what is it all
vor? Why is unt it to make her happy? It's enough to make one
mad to hear Volks talk; if I was going to marry myself, then she
would ha Reason to cry and to blubber; but, on the contrary, han't
I offered to bind down my Land in such a Manner, that I could not
marry if I wou'd, seeing as narro' Woman upon Earth would ha
me. What the Devil in Hell can I do more? I contribute to her
Damnation!—Zounds! I'd zee all the World d—d bevore her little
Vinger should be hurt. Indeed, Mr. *Allworthy*, you must excuse me,
but I am surprized to hear you talk in zuch a Manner, and I must
say, take it how you will, that I thought you had more Sense.'

Allworthy resented this Reflection only with a Smile; nor could
he, if he would have endeavoured it, have conveyed into that Smile
any Mixture of Malice or Contempt. His Smiles at Folly were
indeed such as we may suppose the Angels bestow on the Absurdities of Mankind.

Blifil now desired to be permitted to speak a few Words. 'As to
using any Violence on the young Lady, I am sure I shall never consent to it. My Conscience will not permit me to use Violence on
any one, much less on a Lady for whom, however cruel she is to me,
I shall always preserve the purest and sincerest Affection; but yet I
have read, that Women are seldom proof against Perseverance.
Why may I not hope then by such Perseverance at last to gain
those Inclinations, in which for the future I shall, perhaps, have no
Rival; for as for this Lord, Mr. *Western* is so kind to prefer me to
him; and sure, Sir, you will not deny but that a Parent hath at least
a negative Voice in these Matters; nay, I have heard this very young
Lady herself say so more than once, and declare, that she thought
Children inexcuseable who married in direct Opposition to the Will
of their Parents. Besides, though the other Ladies of the Family
seem to favour the Pretentions of my Lord, I do not find the Lady
herself is inclined to give him any Countenance; alas! I am too well
assured she is not; I am too sensible that wickedest of Men remains
uppermost in her Heart.'

'Ay, ay, so he does,' cries *Western*.

'But surely,' says *Bilfil*, 'when she hears of this Murder which he
hath committed, if the Law should spare his Life'—

'What's that?' cries *Western*, 'Murder! hath he committed a
Murder, and is there any Hopes of seeing him hanged?——Tol de
rol, tol lol de rol.' Here he fell a singing and capering about the
Room.

'Child,' says *Allworthy*, 'this unhappy Passion of yours distresses
me beyond Measure. I heartily pity you, and would do every fair
Thing to promote your Success.'

'I desire no more,' cries *Blifil,* 'I am convinced my dear Uncle hath a better Opinion of me than to think that I myself wou'd accept of more.'

'Lookee,' says *Allworthy,* 'you have my Leave to write, to visit, if she will permit it,—but I insist on no Thoughts of Violence. I will have no Confinement, nothing of that Kind attempted.'

'Well, well,' cries the Squire, 'nothing of that Kind shall be attempted; we will try a little longer what fair Means will effect; and if this Fellow be but hanged out of the Way—Tol lol de rol. I never heard better News in my Life; I warrant every Thing goes to my Mind.—Do, prithee, dear *Allworthy,* come and dine with me at the *Hercules Pillars:* I have bespoke a Shoulder of Mutton roasted, and a Spare-rib of Pork, and a Fowl and Egg-Sauce. There will be Nobody but ourselves, unless we have a Mind to have the Landlord; for I have sent Parson *Supple* down to *Basingstoke* after my Tobacco Box, which I left at an Inn there, and I would not lose it for the World; for it is an old Acquaintance of above Twenty Years standing. I can tell you Landlord is a vast comical Bitch, you will like un hugely.'

Mr. *Allworthy* at last agreed to this Invitation, and soon after the Squire went off, singing and capering at the Hopes of seeing the speedy tragical End of poor *Jones.*

When he was gone, Mr. *Allworthy* resumed the aforesaid Subject with much Gravity. He told his Nephew, 'he wished with all his heart he would endeavour to conquer a Passion, in which I cannot,' says he, 'flatter you with any Hopes of succeeding. It is certainly a vulgar Error, that Aversion in a Woman may be conquered by Perseverance. Indifference may, perhaps, sometimes yield to it; but the usual Triumphs gained by Perseverance in a Lover, are over Caprice, Prudence, Affectation, and often an exorbitant Degree of Levity, which excites Women not over-warm in their Constitutions, to indulge their Vanity by prolonging the Time of Courtship, even when they are well-enough pleased with the Object, and resolve (if they ever resolve at all) to make him a very pitiful Amends in the End. But a fixed Dislike, as I am afraid this is, will rather gather Strength, than be conquered by Time. Besides, my Dear, I have another Apprehension which you must excuse. I am afraid this Passion which you have for this fine young Creature, hath her beautiful Person too much for its Object, and is unworthy of the Name of that Love, which is the only Foundation of matrimonial Felicity. To admire, to like, and to long for the Possession of a beautiful Woman, without any Regard to her Sentiments towards us, is, I am afraid, too natural: But Love, I believe, is the Child of Love only; at least, I am pretty confident, that to love the Creature who we are assured hates us, is not in human Nature. Examine your Heart, therefore, thoroughly, my good Boy, and if, upon Examination, you have but the least Suspicion of this Kind, I am sure your own Virtue and Religion will impel you to drive so vicious a Passion from your Heart, and your good Sense will soon enable you to do it without Pain.'

The Reader may pretty well guess *Blifil's* Answer; but if he should be at a Loss, we are not, at present, at Leisure to satisfy him, as our History now hastens on to Matters of higher Importance, and we can no longer bear to be absent from *Sophia.*

Chapter IV.

An extraordinary Scene between Sophia *and her Aunt.*

The lowing Heifer, and the bleating Ewe in Herds and Flocks, may ramble safe and unregarded through the Pastures. These are, indeed, hereafter doomed to be the Prey of Man; yet many Years are they suffered to enjoy their Liberty undisturbed. But if a plump Doe be discovered to have escaped from the Forest, and to repose herself in some Field or Grove, the whole Parish is presently alarmed, every Man is ready to set his Dogs after her; and if she is preserved from the rest by the good Squire, it is only that he may secure her for his own eating.

I have often considered a very fine young Woman of Fortune and Fashion, when first found strayed from the Pale of her Nursery, to be in pretty much the same Situation with this Doe. The Town is immediately in an Uproar, she is hunted from Park to Play, from Court to Assembly, from Assembly to her own Chamber, and rarely escapes a single Season from the Jaws of some Devourer or other: For if her Friends protect her from some, it is only to deliver her over to one of their own chusing, often more disagreeable to her than any of the rest: While whole Herds or Flocks of other Women securely, and scarce regarded, traverse the Park, the Play, the Opera, and the Assembly; and though, for the most Part at least, they are at last devoured, yet for a long Time do they wanton in Liberty, without Disturbance or Controul.

Of all these Paragons, none ever tasted more of this Persecution than poor *Sophia.* Her ill Stars were not contented with all that she had suffered on Account of *Blifil,* they now raised her another Pursuer, who seemed likely to torment her no less than the other had done. For though her Aunt was less violent, she was no less assiduous in teazing her, than her Father had been before.

The Servants were no sooner departed after Dinner, than Mrs. *Western,* who had opened the Matter to *Sophia,* informed her, 'That she expected his Lordship that very Afternoon, and intended to take the first Opportunity of leaving her alone with him.' 'If you do, Madam,' answered *Sophia*, with some Spirit, 'I shall take the first Opportunity of leaving him by himself.' 'How! Madam!' cries the Aunt; 'is this the Return you make me for my Kindness, in relieving you from your Confinement at your Father's?' 'You know, Madam,' said *Sophia*, 'the Cause of that Confinement was a Refusal to comply with my Father, in accepting a Man I detested; and will my dear Aunt, who hath relieved me from that Distress, involve me in another equally bad?' 'And do you think then, Madam,' answered Mrs. *Western*, 'that there is no Difference between my Lord *Fellamar*, and Mr. *Blifil?*' 'Very little, in my Opinion,' cries *Sophia*; 'and if I must be condemned to one, I would certainly have the Merit of sacrificing myself to my Father's Pleasure.' 'Then my Pleasure, I find,' said the Aunt, 'hath very little Weight with you; but that Consideration shall not move me. I act from nobler Motives. The View of aggrandizing my Family, of ennobling yourself, is what I proceed upon. Have you no Sense of Ambition? Are there no Charms in the Thoughts of having a Coronet on your Coach!' 'None, upon my Honour,' said *Sophia*. 'A Pincushion upon my Coach would please me just as well.' 'Never mention Honour,' cries the Aunt. 'It becomes not the Mouth of such a Wretch. I am sorry, Niece, you force me to use these Words; but I cannot bear your groveling Temper; you have none of the Blood of the *Westerns* in you. But however mean and base your own Ideas are, you shall bring no Imputation on mine. I will never suffer the World to say of me, that I encouraged you in refusing one of the best Matches in England; a Match which, besides its Advantage in Fortune, would do Honour to almost any Family, and hath indeed, in Title, the Advantage of ours.' 'Surely,' says *Sophia*, 'I am born deficient, and have not the Senses with which other People are blessed: There must be certainly some Sense which can relish the Delights of Sound and Show, which I have not: For surely Mankind would not labour so much, nor sacrifice so much for the obtaining, nor would they be so elate and proud with possessing, what appeared to them, as it doth to me, the most insignificant of all Trifles.'

'No, no, Miss;' cries the Aunt; 'you are born with as many Senses as other People; but I assure you, you are not born with a sufficient Understanding to make a Fool of me, or to expose my Conduct to the World. So I declare this to you upon my Word, and you know, I believe, how fixed my Resolutions are, unless you agree to see his Lordship this Afternoon, I will, with my own Hands, deliver you To-morrow Morning to my Brother, and will never henceforth interfere with you nor see your Face again.' *Sophia* stood a few Moments silent after this Speech, which was uttered in a most angry and peremptory Tone; and then bursting into Tears, she cry'd, 'Do with me, Madam, whatever you please; I am the most misera- ble, undone Wretch upon Earth; if my dear Aunt forsakes me, where shall I look for a Protector?'—'My dear Niece,' cries she, 'you will have a very good Protector in his Lordship; a Protector, whom nothing but a Hankering after that vile Fellow *Jones* can make you decline.' 'Indeed, Madam,' said *Sophia*, 'you wrong me. How can you imagine, after what you have shewn me, if I had ever any such Thoughts, that I should not banish them for ever. If it will satisfy you, I will receive the Sacrament upon it, never to see his Face again.'—'But Child, dear Child,' said the Aunt, 'be reasonable: Can you invent a single Objection?'——'I have already, I think, told you a sufficient Objection,' answered *Sophia*.——'What,' cries the Aunt; 'I remember none.' 'Sure, Madam,' said *Sophia*, 'I told you he had used me in the rudest and vilest Manner.' 'Indeed, Child,' answered she, 'I never heard you, or did not understand you:—But what do you mean by this rude vile Manner?' 'Indeed, Madam,' said *Sophia*, 'I am almost ashamed to tell you. He caught me in his Arms, pulled me down upon the Settee, and thrust his Hand into my Bosom, and kissed it with such Violence, that I have the Mark upon my left Breast at this Moment.'——'Indeed!' said Mrs. *West- ern*. 'Yes indeed, Madam,' answered *Sophia*; 'my Father luckily came in at that Instant, or Heaven knows what Rudeness he intended to have proceeded to.' 'I am astonished and confounded,' cries the Aunt. 'No Woman of the Name of *Western* hath been ever treated so, since we were a Family. I would have torn the Eyes of a Prince out, if he had attempted such Freedoms with me. It is impossible: Sure, *Sophia*, you must invent this to raise my Indigna- tion against him.' 'I hope, Madam,' said *Sophia*, 'you have too good an Opinion of me, to imagine me capable of telling an Untruth. Upon my Soul it is true.' 'I should have stabbed him to the Heart had I been present,' returned the Aunt. 'Yet surely he could have no dishonourable Design: It is impossible; he durst not: Besides, his Proposals shew he had not; for they are not only honourable but generous. I don't know; the Age allows too great Freedoms. A dis- tant Salute is all I would have allowed before the Ceremony. I have had Lovers formerly, not so long ago neither; several Lovers, tho' I never would consent to Marriage, and I never encouraged the least Freedom. It is a foolish Custom, and what I never would agree to. No Man kissed more of me than my Cheek. It is as much as one can bring oneself to give Lips up to a Husband; and, indeed, could I ever have been persuaded to marry, I believe I should not have soon been brought to endure so much.' 'You will pardon me, dear Madam,' said *Sophia*, 'if I make one Observation: You own you have had many Lovers, and the World knows it, even if you should deny it. You refused them all, and I am convinced one Coronet at least among them.' 'You say true, dear *Sophy*,' answered she; 'I had once the Offer of a Title.' 'Why then,' said *Sophia*, 'will you not suffer me to refuse this once?' 'It is true, Child,' said she, 'I have refused the Offer of a Title; but it was not so good an Offer; that is, not so very, very good an Offer.'——'Yes, Madam,' said *Sophia*; 'but you have had very great Proposals from Men of vast Fortunes. It was not the first, nor the second, nor the third advantageous Match that offered itself.' 'I own it was not,' said she. 'Well, Madam,' continued *Sophia*, 'and why may not I expect to have a second perhaps better than this? You are now but a young Woman, and I am convinced would not promise to yield to the first Lover of Fortune, nay, or of Title too. I am a very young Woman, and sure I need not despair.' 'Well, my dear, dear *Sophy*,' cries the Aunt, 'what would you have me say?' 'Why I only beg that I may not be left alone, at least this Evening: Grant me that, and I will submit, if you think, after what is past, I ought to see him in your Company.' 'Well, I will grant it,' cries the Aunt. '*Sophy*, you know I love you, and can deny you nothing. You know the Easiness of my Nature; I have not always been so easy. I have been formerly thought cruel; by the Men I mean. I was called the cruel *Parthenissa*. I have broke many a Window that has had Verses to the cruel *Parthenissa*[1] in it. *Sophy*, I was never so handsome as you, and yet I had something of you formerly. I am a little altered. Kingdoms and States, as *Tully Cicero* says in his Epistles,[2] undergo Altera- tions, and so must the human Form.' Thus run she on for near half an Hour upon herself, and her Conquests and her Cruelty, 'till the Arrival of my Lord, who, after a most tedious Visit, during which Mrs. *Western* never once offered to leave the Room, retired, not much more satisfied with the Aunt than with the Niece. For *Sophia* had brought her Aunt into so excellent a Temper, that she con- sented to almost every Thing her Niece said; and agreed, that a little distant Behaviour might not be improper to so forward a Lover.

Thus *Sophia* by a little well directed Flattery, for which surely none will blame her, obtained a little Ease for herself, and, at least, put off the evil Day. And now we have seen our Heroine in a better Situation than she hath been for a long Time before, we will look a little after Mr. *Jones*, whom we left in the most deplorable Situa- tion that can well be imagined.

1. Heroine of Roger Boyle's romance of that name (1654–55), for whose love a Median and an Arabian prince perform endless feats of arms. Young lovers af- fected the names and language of such seventeenth-century romances well into the eighteenth century.

2. Fielding again pokes a classicist's fun at Mrs. Western: no such statement ap- pears in Cicero's letters (*Epistolae ad Familiares*), or anywhere else in his works. See above, pp. 245, 252, and 425.

Chapter V.

Mrs. Miller *and Mr.* Nightingale *visit* Jones *in the Prison.*

When Mr. *Allworthy* and his Nephew went to meet Mr. *West-ern*, Mrs. *Miller* set forwards to her Son-in-law's Lodgings, in order to acquaint him with the Accident which had befallen his Friend *Jones*; but he had known it long before from *Partridge*, (for *Jones*, when he left Mrs. *Miller*, had been furnished with a Room in the same House with Mr. *Nightingale*.) The good Woman found her Daughter under great Affliction on Account of Mr. *Jones*, whom having comforted as well as she could, she set forwards to the *Gate-house*, where she heard he was, and where Mr. *Nightingale* was arrived before her.

The Firmness and Constancy of a true Friend is a Circumstance so extremely delightful to Persons in any Kind of Distress, that the Distress itself, if it be only temporary, and admits of Relief, is more than compensated by bringing this Comfort with it. Nor are Instances of this Kind so rare, as some superficial and inaccurate Observers have reported. To say the Truth, Want of Compassion is not to be numbered among our general Faults. The black Ingredi-ent which fouls our Disposition is Envy. Hence our Eye is seldom, I am afraid, turned upward to those who are manifestly greater, better, wiser, or happier than ourselves, without some Degree of Malignity; while we commonly look downwards on the Mean and Miserable, with sufficient Benevolence and Pity. In Fact, I have remarked, that most of the Defects which have discovered them-selves in the Friendships within my Observation, have arisen from Envy only; a hellish Vice; and yet one from which I have known very few absolutely exempt. But enough of a Subject which, if pur-sued, would lead me too far.

Whether it was that Fortune was apprehensive lest *Jones* should sink under the Weight of his Adversity, and that she might thus lose any future Opportunity of tormenting him; or whether she really abated somewhat of her Severity towards him, she seemed a little to relax her Persecution, by sending him the Company of two such faithful Friends, and what is perhaps more rare, a faithful Servant. For *Partridge*, though he had many Imperfections, wanted not Fidelity; and though Fear would not suffer him to be hanged for his Master, yet the World, I believe, could not have bribed him to desert his Cause.

While *Jones* was expressing great Satisfaction in the Presence of his Friends, *Partridge* brought an Account, that Mr. *Fitzpatrick* was still alive, though the Surgeon declared that he had very little

Hopes. Upon which Jones fetching a deep Sigh, *Nightingale* said to him; 'My dear *Tom*, why should you afflict yourself so upon an Accident, which, whatever be the Consequence, can be attended with no Danger to you, and in which your Conscience cannot accuse you of having been in the least to blame. If the Fellow should die, what have you done more than taken away the Life of a Ruffian in your own Defence? So will the Coroner's Inquest certainly find it; and then you will be easily admitted to Bail: And though you must undergo the Form of a Trial, yet it is a Trial which many Men would stand for you for a Shilling.' 'Come, come, Mr. *Jones*,' says Mrs. *Miller*, 'cheer yourself up. I knew you could not be the Aggressor, and so I told Mr. *Allworthy*, and so he shall acknowledge too before I have done with him.'

Jones gravely answered, 'That whatever might be his Fate, he should always lament the having shed the Blood of one of his Fellow-creatures, as one of the highest Misfortunes which could have befallen him. But I have another Misfortune of the tenderest Kind. — O! Mrs. *Miller*, I have lost what I held most dear upon Earth.' 'That must be a Mistress,' said Mrs. *Miller*, 'But come, come; I know more than you imagine;' (for indeed *Partridge* had blabbed all) 'and I have heard more than you know. Matters go better, I promise you, than you think; and I would not give *Blifil* Sixpence for all the Chance which he hath of the Lady.'

'Indeed, my dear Friend, indeed,' answered *Jones*, 'you are an entire Stranger to the Cause of my Grief. If you was acquainted with the Story, you would allow my Case admitted of no Comfort. I apprehend no Danger from *Blifil*. I have undone myself.' 'Don't despair,' replied Mrs. *Miller*; 'you know not what a Woman can do, and if any Thing be in my Power, I promise you I will do it to serve you. It is my Duty. My Son, my dear Mr. *Nightingale*, who is so kind to tell me he hath Obligations to you on the same Account, knows it is my Duty. Shall I go to the Lady myself? I will say any Thing to her you would have me say.'

'Thou best of Women,' cries *Jones*, taking her by the Hand, 'talk not of Obligations to me;—but, as you have been so kind to mention it, there is a Favour which, perhaps, may be in your Power. I see you are acquainted with the Lady (how you came by your Information I know not) who sits indeed very near my Heart. If you could contrive to deliver this, (giving her a Paper from his Pocket) I shall for ever acknowledge your Goodness.'

'Give it me,' said Mrs. *Miller*. 'If I see it not in her own Possession before I sleep, may my next Sleep be my last. Comfort yourself, my good young Man; be wise enough to take Warning from past Follies, and I warrant all shall be well, and I shall yet see you happy with the most charming young Lady in the World; for so I hear from every one she is.'

'Believe me, Madam,' said he, 'I do not speak the common Cant of one in my unhappy Situation. Before this dreadful Accident happened, I had resolved to quit a Life of which I was become sensible of the Wickedness as well as Folly. I do assure you notwithstanding the Disturbances I have unfortunately occasioned in your House, for which I heartily ask your Pardon, I am not an abandoned Profligate. Though I have been hurried into Vices, I do not approve a vicious Character; nor will I ever, from this Moment, deserve it.'

Mrs. *Miller* expressed great Satisfaction in these Declarations, in the Sincerity of which she averred she had an entire Faith: And now, the Remainder of the Conversation past in the joint Attempts of that good Woman and Mr. *Nightingale*, to cheer the dejected Spirits of Mr. *Jones*, in which they so far succeeded, as to leave him much better comforted and satisfied than they found him; to which happy Alteration nothing so much contributed as the kind Undertaking of Mrs. *Miller*, to deliver his Letter to *Sophia*, which he despaired of finding any Means to accomplish: For when *Black George* produced the last from *Sophia*, he informed *Partridge*, that she had strictly charged him, on Pain of having it communicated to her Father, not to bring her any Answer. He was moreover not a little pleased, to find he had so warm an Advocate to Mr. *Allworthy* himself in this good Woman, who was in Reality, one of the worthiest Creatures in the World.

After about an Hour's Visit from the Lady, (for *Nightingale* had been with him much longer) they both took their Leave, promising to return to him soon; during which Mrs. *Miller* said, she hoped to bring him some good News from his Mistress, and Mr. *Nightingale* promised to enquire into the State of Mr. *Fitzpatrick*'s Wound, and likewise to find out some of the Persons who were present at the Rencounter.

The former of these went directly in Quest of *Sophia*, whither we likewise shall now attend her.

Chapter VI.

In which Mrs. Miller *pays a Visit to* Sophia.

Access to the young Lady was by no Means difficult; for as she lived now on a perfect friendly Footing with her Aunt, she was at full Liberty to receive what Visitants she pleased.

Sophia was dressing, when she was acquainted that there was a Gentlewoman below to wait on her: As she was neither afraid, nor ashamed, to see any of her own Sex, Mrs. *Miller* was immediately admitted.

Curt'sies, and the usual Ceremonials between Women who are Strangers to each other, being past, *Sophia* said, 'I have not the Pleasure to know you, Madam.' 'No, Madam,' answered Mrs. *Miller*, 'and I must beg Pardon for intruding upon you. But when you know what has induced me to give you this Trouble, I hope'— 'Pray, what is your Business, Madam?' said *Sophia*, with a little Emotion. 'Madam, we are not alone,' replied Mrs. *Miller*, in a low Voice. 'Go out, *Betty*,' said *Sophia*.

When *Betty* was departed, Mrs. *Miller* said, 'I was desired, Madam, by a very unhappy young Gentleman, to deliver you this Letter.' *Sophia* changed Colour when she saw the Direction, well knowing the Hand, and after some Hesitation, said,—'I could not conceive, Madam, from your Appearance, that your Business had been of such a Nature.—Whomever you brought this Letter from I shall not open it. I should be sorry to entertain an unjust Suspicion of any one; but you are an utter Stranger to me.'

'If you will have Patience, Madam,' answered Mrs. *Miller*, 'I will acquaint you who I am, and how I came by that Letter.' 'I have no Curiosity, Madam, to know any Thing,' cries *Sophia*, 'but I must insist on your delivering that Letter back to the Person who gave it you.'

Mrs. *Miller* then fell upon her Knees, and in the most passionate Terms, implored her Compassion; to which *Sophia* answered: 'Sure, Madam, it is surprizing you should be so very strongly interested in the Behalf of this Person. I would not think, Madam,'—'No, Madam,' says Mrs. *Miller*, 'you shall not think any thing but the Truth. I will tell you all, and you will not wonder that I am interested. He is the best natured Creature that ever was born.'—She then began and related the Story of Mr. *Anderson*[1]—After this she cried, 'This, Madam, this is his Goodness; but I have much more tender Obligations to him. He hath preserved my Child.'—Here, after shedding some Tears, she related every Thing concerning that Fact, suppressing only those Circumstances which would have most reflected on her Daughter, and concluded with saying, 'Now, Madam, you shall judge whether I can ever do enough for so kind, so good, so generous a young Man; and sure he is the best and worthiest of all human Beings.'

The Alterations in the Countenance of *Sophia*, had hitherto been chiefly to her Disadvantage, and had inclined her Complexion to too great Paleness; but she now waxed redder, if possible, than Vermilion, and cried, 'I know not what to say; certainly what arises

1. All four editions read "*Henderson*," but all four also read "*Anderson*" on first mention (p. 551), and the second edition, though uniquely, corrects "*Ender-* son" to "*Anderson*" on second mention (p. 558), giving "*Anderson*" a slight statistical and probable preference.

from Gratitude cannot be blamed.——But what Service can my reading this Letter do your Friend, since I am resolved never'—Mrs. *Miller* fell again to her Entreaties, and begged to be forgiven, but she could not, she said, carry it back. 'Well, Madam,' says *Sophia*, 'I cannot help it, if you will force it upon me.—Certainly you may leave it whether I will or no.' What *Sophia* meant, or whether she meant any Thing, I will not presume to determine; but Mrs. *Miller* actually understood this as a Hint, and presently laying the Letter down on the Table, took her Leave, having first begged Permission to wait again on *Sophia*; which Request had neither Assent nor Denial.

The Letter lay upon the Table no longer than till Mrs. *Miller* was out of Sight; for then *Sophia* opened and read it.

This Letter did very little Service to his Cause; for it consisted of little more than Confessions of his own Unworthiness, and bitter Lamentations of Despair, together with the most solemn Protestations of his unalterable Fidelity to *Sophia*, of which, he said, he hoped to convince her, if he had ever more the Honour of being admitted to her Presence; and that he could account for the Letter to Lady *Bellaston*, in such a Manner, that though it would not entitle him to her Forgiveness, he hoped at least to obtain it from her Mercy. And concluded with vowing, that nothing was ever less in his Thoughts than to marry Lady *Bellaston*.

Though *Sophia* read the Letter twice over with great Attention, his Meaning still remained a Riddle to her; nor could her Invention suggest to her any Means to excuse *Jones*. She certainly remained very angry with him, though indeed Lady *Bellaston* took up so much of her Resentment, that her gentle Mind had but little left to bestow on any other Person.

That Lady was most unluckily to dine this very Day with her Aunt *Western*, and in the Afternoon, they were all three by Appointment, to go together to the Opera, and thence to Lady *Thomas Hatchet*'s Drum. *Sophia* would have gladly been excused from all, but she would not disoblige her Aunt; and as to the Arts of counterfeiting Illness, she was so entirely a Stranger to them, that it never once entered into her Head. When she was drest, therefore, down she went, resolved to encounter all the Horrors of the Day, and a most disagreeable one it proved; for Lady *Bellaston* took every Opportunity very civilly and slily to insult her; to all which her Dejection of Spirits disabled her from making any Return; and indeed, to confess the Truth, she was at the very best but an indifferent Mistress of Repartee.

Another Misfortune which befel poor *Sophia*, was the Company of Lord *Fellamar*, whom she met at the Opera, and who attended her to the Drum. And though both Places were too publick to admit of any Particularities, and she was farther relieved by the Musick at the one Place, and by the Cards at the other, she could not however enjoy herself in his Company: For there is something of Delicacy in Women, which will not suffer them to be even easy in the Presence of a Man whom they know to have Pretensions to them, which they are disinclined to favour.

Having in this Chapter twice mentioned a Drum, a Word which our Posterity, it is hoped, will not understand in the Sense it is here applied, we shall, notwithstanding our present Haste, stop a Moment to describe the Entertainment here meant, and the rather as we can in a Moment describe it.

A Drum then, is an Assembly of well dressed Persons of both Sexes, most of whom play at Cards, and the rest do nothing at all; while the Mistress of the House performs the Part of the Landlady at an Inn, and like the Landlady of an Inn prides herself in the Number of her Guests, though she doth not always, like her, get any Thing by it.

No wonder then as so much Spirits must be required to support any Vivacity in these Scenes of Dulness, that we hear Persons of Fashion eternally complaining of the Want of them; a Complaint confined entirely to upper Life. How insupportable must we imagine this Round of Impertinence to have been to *Sophia*, at this Time; how difficult must she have found it to force the Appearance of Gaiety into her Looks, when her Mind dictated nothing but the tenderest Sorrow, and when every Thought was charged with tormenting Ideas.

Night however, at last, restored her to her Pillow, where we will leave her to soothe her Melancholy at least, though incapable we fear of Rest, and shall pursue our History, which something whispers us, is now arrived at the Eve of some great Event.

Chapter VII.

A *pathetic* Scene *between* Mr. Allworthy *and* Mrs. Miller.

Mrs. *Miller* had a long Discourse with Mr. *Allworthy*, at his Return from Dinner, in which she acquainted him with *Jones*'s having unfortunately lost all which he was pleased to bestow on him at their Separation; and with the Distresses to which that Loss had subjected him; of all which she had received a full Account from the faithful Retailer *Partridge*. She then explained the Obligations she had to *Jones*; not that she was entirely explicit with Regard to her Daughter: For though she had the utmost Confidence in Mr. *Allworthy*, and though there could be no Hopes of keeping an Affair secret, which was unhappily known to more than half a Dozen; yet she could not prevail with herself to mention those Circumstances which reflected most on the Chastity of poor *Nancy*; but smothered that Part of her Evidence as cautiously as if she had been before a Judge, and the Girl was now on her Trial for the Murder of a Bastard.

Allworthy said, there were few Characters so absolutely vicious as not to have the least Mixture of Good in them. 'However,' says he, 'I cannot deny but that you had some Obligations to the Fellow, bad as he is, and I shall therefore excuse what hath past already, but must insist you never mention his Name to me more; for I promise you, it was upon the fullest and plainest Evidence that I resolved to take the Measures I have taken.' 'Well, Sir,' says she, 'I make not the least Doubt, but Time will shew all Matters in their true and natural Colours, and that you will be convinced this poor young Man deserves better of you than some other Folks that shall be nameless.'

'Madam,' cries *Allworthy*, a little ruffled, 'I will not hear any Reflections on my Nephew; and if you ever say a Word more of that Kind, I will depart from your House that Instant. He is the worthiest and best of Men; and I once more repeat it to you, he hath carried his Friendship to this Man to a blameable Length, by too long concealing Facts of the blackest Die. The Ingratitude of the Wretch to this good young Man is what I most resent: for, Madam, I have the greatest Reason to imagine he had laid a Plot to supplant my Nephew in my Favour, and to have disinherited him.'

'I am sure, Sir,' answered Mrs. *Miller*, a little frightned, (for though Mr. *Allworthy* had the utmost Sweetness and Benevolence in his Smiles, he had great Terror in his Frowns) 'I shall never speak against any Gentleman you are pleased to think well of. I am sure, Sir, such Behaviour would very little become me, especially when the Gentleman is your nearest Relation; but, Sir, you must not be angry with me, you must not indeed, for my good Wishes to this poor Wretch. Sure I may call him so now, though once you would have been angry with me, if I had spoke of him with the least Disrespect. How often have I heard you call him your Son? How often have you prattled to me of him, with all the Fondness of a Parent? Nay, Sir, I cannot forget the many tender Expressions, the many good Things you have told me of his Beauty, and his Parts, and his Virtues; of his Good-nature and Generosity.—I am sure, Sir, I cannot forget them: For I find them all true. I have experienced them in my own Cause. They have preserved my Family. You must pardon my Tears, Sir, indeed you must, when I consider the cruel Reverse of Fortune which this poor Youth, to whom I am so much obliged, hath suffered: When I consider the Loss of your Favour, which I know he valued more than his Life, I must, I must lament him. If you had a Dagger in your Hand, ready to plunge into my Heart, I must lament the Misery of one whom you have loved, and I shall ever love.'

Allworthy was pretty much moved with this Speech, but it seemed not to be with Anger: For after a short Silence, taking Mrs. *Miller* by the Hand, he said very affectionately to her: 'Come, Madam, let us consider a little about your Daughter. I cannot blame you, for rejoicing in a Match which promises to be advantageous to her; but you know this Advantage, in a great Measure, depends on the Father's Reconciliation. I know Mr. *Nightingale* very well, and have formerly had Concerns with him; I will make him a Visit, and endeavour to serve you in this Matter. I believe he is a worldly Man; but as this is an only Son, and the Thing is now irretrievable, perhaps he may in Time be brought to Reason. I promise you I will do all I can for you.'

Many were the Acknowledgements which the poor Woman made to *Allworthy*, for this kind and generous Offer, nor could she refrain from taking this Occasion again to express her Gratitude towards *Jones*, 'to whom,' said she, 'I owe the Opportunity of giving you, Sir, this present Trouble.' *Allworthy* gently stopped her; but he was too good a Man to be really offended with the Effects of so noble a Principle as now actuated Mrs. *Miller*; and indeed had not this new Affair inflamed his former Anger against *Jones*, it is possible he might have been a little softened towards him, by the Report of an Action which Malice itself could not have derived from an evil Motive.

Mr. *Allworthy* and Mrs. *Miller* had been above an Hour together, when their Conversation was put an End to, by the Arrival of *Blifil*, and another Person, which other Person was no less than Mr. *Dowling*, the Attorney, who was now become a great Favourite with Mr. *Blifil*, and whom Mr. *Allworthy*, at the Desire of his Nephew, had made his Steward; and had likewise recommended him to Mr. *Western*, from whom the Attorney received a Promise of being promoted to the same Office upon the first Vacancy; and in the mean Time, was employed in transacting some Affairs which the Squire then had in *London*, in Relation to a Mortgage.

This was the principal Affair which then brought Mr. *Dowling* to Town; therefore he took the same Opportunity to charge himself with some Money for Mr. *Allworthy*, and to make a Report to him of some other Business; in all which as it was of much too dull a Nature to find any Place in this History, we will leave the Uncle, Nephew, and their Lawyer concerned, and resort to other Matters.

Chapter VIII.

Containing various Matters.

Before we return to Mr. *Jones*, we will take one more View of *Sophia*.

Though that young Lady had brought her Aunt into great good Humour by those soothing Methods, which we have before related, she had not brought her in the least to abate of her Zeal for the Match with Lord *Fellamar*. This Zeal was now inflamed by Lady *Bellaston*, who had told her the preceding Evening, that she was well satisfied from the Conduct of *Sophia*, and from her Carriage to his Lordship, that all Delays would be dangerous, and that the only Way to succeed, was to press the Match forward with such Rapidity, that the young Lady should have no Time to reflect, and be obliged to consent, while she scarce knew what she did. In which Manner, she said, one half of the Marriages among People of Condition were brought about. A Fact very probably true, and to which I suppose is owing the mutual Tenderness which afterwards exists among so many happy Couples.

A Hint of the same Kind was given by the same Lady to Lord *Fellamar*; and both these so readily embraced the Advice, that the very next Day was, at his Lordship's Request, appointed by Mrs. *Western* for a private Interview between the young Parties. This was communicated to *Sophia* by her Aunt, and insisted upon in such high Terms, that, after having urged every Thing she possibly could invent against it, without the least Effect, she at last agreed to give the highest Instance of Complaisance which any young Lady can give, and consented to see his Lordship.

As Conversations of this Kind afford no great Entertainment, we shall be excused from reciting the whole that past at this Interview; in which, after his Lordship had made many Declarations of the most pure and ardent Passion, to the silent, blushing *Sophia*; she at last collected all the Spirits she could raise, and with a trembling low Voice, said, 'My Lord, you must be yourself conscious whether your former Behaviour to me hath been consistent with the Professions you now make.' 'Is there,' answered he, 'no Way by which I can attone for Madness? What I did, I am afraid, must have too plainly convinced you, that the Violence of Love had deprived me of my Senses.' 'Indeed, my Lord,' said she, 'it is in your Power to give me a Proof of an Affection which I much rather wish to encourage, and to which I should think myself more beholden.' 'Name it, Madam,' said my Lord, very warmly.—'My Lord,' says she, looking down upon her Fan, 'I know you must be sensible how uneasy this pretended Passion of yours hath made me.'—'Can you be so cruel to call it pretended?' says he. 'Yes, my Lord,' answered *Sophia*, 'all Professions of Love to those whom we persecute, are most insulting Pretences. This Pursuit of yours is to me a most cruel Persecution; nay, it is taking a most ungenerous Advantage of my unhappy Situation.' 'Most lovely, most adorable Charmer, do not accuse me,' cries he, 'of taking an ungenerous Advantage, while I have no Thoughts but what are directed to your Honour and Interest, and while I have no View, no Hope, no Ambition but to throw myself, Honour, Fortune, every Thing at your Feet.' 'My Lord,' says she, 'it is that Fortune, and those Honours, which give you the Advantage of which I complain. These are the Charms which have seduced my Relations, but to me they are Things indifferent. If your Lordship will merit my Gratitude, there is but one Way.'—'Pardon me, divine Creature,' said he, 'there can be none. All I can do for you is so much your Due, and will give me so much Pleasure, that there is no Room for your Gratitude.'—'Indeed, my Lord,' answered she, 'you may obtain my Gratitude, my good Opinion, every kind Thought and Wish which it is in my Power to bestow; nay, you may obtain them with Ease; for sure to a generous Mind it must be easy to grant my Request. Let me beseech you then, to cease a Pursuit, in which you can never have any Success. For your own Sake as well as mine, I intreat this Favour: For sure you are too noble to have any Pleasure in tormenting an unhappy Creature. What can your Lordship propose but Uneasiness to yourself, by a Perseverance, which, upon my Honour, upon my Soul, cannot, shall not prevail with me, whatever Distresses you may drive me to.' Here my Lord fetched a deep Sigh, and then said—'Is it then, Madam, that I am so unhappy to be the Object of your Dislike and Scorn; or will you pardon me if I suspect there is some other?'—Here he hesitated, and *Sophia* answered with some Spirit, 'My Lord, I shall not be accountable to you for the Reasons of my Conduct. I am obliged to your Lordship for the generous Offer you have made; I own it is beyond either my Deserts or Expectations; yet I hope, my Lord, you will not insist on my Reasons, when I declare I cannot accept it.' Lord *Fellamar* returned much to this, which we do not perfectly understand, and perhaps it could not all be strictly reconciled either to Sense or Grammar; but he concluded his ranting Speech with saying, 'That if she had pre-engaged herself to any Gentleman, however unhappy it would make him, he should think himself bound in Honour to desist.' Perhaps my Lord laid too much Emphasis on the Word Gentleman; for we cannot else well account for the Indignation with which he inspired

Sophia, who, in her Answer, seemed greatly to resent some Affront he had given her.

While she was speaking, with her Voice more raised than usual, Mrs. *Western* came into the Room, the Fire glaring in her Cheeks, and the Flames bursting from her Eyes. 'I am ashamed,' says she, 'my Lord, of the Reception which you have met with. I assure your Lordship we are all sensible of the Honour done us; and I must tell you, Miss *Western*, the Family expect a different Behaviour from you.' Here my Lord interfered on behalf of the young Lady, but to no Purpose; the Aunt proceeded till *Sophia* pulled out her Handkerchief, threw herself into a Chair, and burst into a violent Fit of Tears.

The Remainder of the Conversation between Mrs. *Western* and his Lordship, till the latter withdrew, consisted of bitter Lamentations on his Side, and on hers of the strongest Assurances that her Niece should and would consent to all he wished. 'Indeed, my Lord,' says she, 'the Girl hath had a foolish Education, neither adapted to her Fortune nor her Family. Her Father, I am sorry to say it, is to blame for every Thing. The Girl hath silly Country Notions of Bashfulness. Nothing else, my Lord, upon my Honour; I am convinced she hath a good Understanding at the Bottom, and will be brought to Reason.'

This last Speech was made in the Absence of *Sophia*; for she had sometime before left the Room, with more Appearance of Passion than she had ever shewn on any Occasion; and now his Lordship, after many Expressions of Thanks to Mrs. *Western*, many ardent Professions of Passion which nothing could conquer, and many Assurances of Perseverance, which Mrs. *Western* highly encouraged, took his Leave for this Time.

Before we relate what now passed between Mrs. *Western* and *Sophia*, it may be proper to mention an unfortunate Accident which had happened, and which had occasioned the Return of Mrs. *Western* with so much Fury, as we have seen.

The Reader then must know, that the Maid who at present attended on *Sophia*, was recommended by Lady *Bellaston*, with whom she had lived for some Time in the Capacity of a Combbrush; she was a very sensible Girl, and had received the strictest Instructions to watch her young Lady very carefully. These Instructions, we are sorry to say, were communicated to her by Mrs. *Honour*, into whose Favour Lady *Bellaston* had now so ingratiated herself, that the violent Affection which the good Waiting-woman had formerly borne to *Sophia*, was entirely obliterated by that great Attachment which she had to her new Mistress.

Now when Mrs. *Miller* was departed, *Betty*, (for that was the

Name of the Girl) returning to her young Lady, found her very
attentively engaged in reading a long Letter, and the visible Emotions which she betrayed on that Occasion, might have well
accounted for some Suspicions which the Girl entertained; but
indeed they had yet a stronger Foundation, for she had overheard
the whole Scene which passed between *Sophia* and Mrs. *Miller.*

Mrs. *Western* was acquainted with all this Matter by Betty, who,
after receiving many Commendations, and some Rewards for her
Fidelity, was ordered, that if the Woman who brought the Letter,
came again, she should introduce her to Mrs. *Western* herself.

Unluckily Mrs. *Miller* returned at the very Time when *Sophia*
was engaged with his Lordship. *Betty*, according to Order, sent her
directly to the Aunt; who being Mistress of so many Circumstances
relating to what had past the Day before, easily imposed upon the
poor Woman to believe that *Sophia* had communicated the whole
Affair; and so pumped every Thing out of her which she knew,
relating to the Letter, and relating to *Jones.*

This poor Creature might indeed be called Simplicity itself. She
was one of that Order of Mortals, who are apt to believe every
Thing which is said to them: to whom Nature hath neither
indulged the offensive nor defensive Weapons of Deceit, and who
are consequently liable to be imposed upon by any one, who will
only be at the Expense of a little Falshood for that Purpose. Mrs.
Western having drained Mrs. *Miller* of all she knew, which indeed
was but little, but which was sufficient to make the Aunt suspect a
great deal, dismissed her with Assurances that *Sophia* would not see
her, that she would send no Answer to the Letter, nor ever receive
another; nor did she suffer her to depart, without a handsome Lecture on the Merits of an Office, to which she could afford no better
Name than that of Procuress.——This Discovery had greatly discomposed her Temper, when coming into the Apartment next to
that in which the Lovers were, she overheard *Sophia* very warmly
protesting against his Lordship's Addresses. At which the Rage
already kindled, burst forth, and she rushed in upon her Niece in a
most furious Manner, as we have already described together with
what past at that Time till his Lordship's Departure.

No sooner was Lord *Fellamar* gone, than Mrs. *Western* returned
to *Sophia*, whom she upbraided in the most bitter Terms, for the ill
Use she had made of the Confidence reposed in her; and for her
Treachery in conversing with a Man with whom she had offered
but the Day before to bind herself in the most solemn Oath, never
more to have any Conversation. *Sophia* protested she had maintained no such Conversation. 'How! How! Miss *Western*,' said the
Aunt, 'will you deny your receiving a Letter from him Yesterday?'
'A Letter, Madam!' answered *Sophia*, somewhat surprized. 'It is not
very well bred, Miss,' replies the Aunt, 'to repeat my Words. I say a

Letter, and I insist upon your shewing it me immediately.' 'I scorn a Lie, Madam,' said *Sophia*, 'I did receive a Letter, but it was without my Desire, and indeed I may say against my Consent.' 'Indeed, indeed, Miss,' cries the Aunt, 'you ought to be ashamed of owning you had received it at all; but where is the Letter? for I will see it.'

To this peremptory Demand *Sophia* paused some Time before she returned an Answer; and at last only excused herself by declaring she had not the Letter in her Pocket, which was indeed true; upon which her Aunt losing all manner of Patience, asked her Niece this short Question, whether she would resolve to marry Lord *Fellamar* or no? to which she received the strongest Negative. Mrs. *Western* then replied with an Oath, or something very like one, that she would early the next Morning deliver her back into her Father's Hand.

Sophia then began to reason with her Aunt in the following Manner; 'Why, Madam, must I of Necessity be forced to marry at all? Consider how cruel you would have thought it in your own Case, and how much kinder your Parents were in leaving you to your Liberty. What have I done to forfeit this Liberty? I will never marry contrary to my Father's Consent, nor without asking yours. —And when I ask the Consent of either improperly, it will be then Time enough to force some other Marriage upon me.' 'Can I bear to hear this,' cries Mrs. *Western*, 'from a Girl who hath now a Letter from a Murderer in her Pocket?' 'I have no such Letter, I promise you,' answered *Sophia*; 'and if he be a *Murderer*, he will soon be in no Condition to give you any further Disturbance.' 'How, Miss *Western*,' said the Aunt, 'have you the Assurance to speak of him in this Manner, to own your Affection for such a Villain to my Face!' 'Sure, Madam,' said *Sophia*, 'you put a very strange Construction on my Words.' 'Indeed, Miss *Western*,' cries the Lady, 'I shall not bear this Usage; you have learnt of your Father this manner of treating me; he hath taught you to give me the Lie. He hath totally ruined you by his false System of Education; and please Heaven he shall have the Comfort of its Fruits: For once more I declare to you, that to-morrow Morning I will carry you back. I will withdraw all my Forces from the Field, and remain henceforth, like the wise King of *Prussia*,[1] in a State of perfect Neutrality. You are both too wise to be regulated by my Measures; so prepare yourself; for To-morrow Morning you shall evacuate this House.'

Sophia remonstrated all she could; but her Aunt was deaf to all she said. In this Resolution therefore we must at present leave her, as there seems to be no Hopes of bringing her to change it.

---

1. In 1745 (the year of the events in *Tom Jones*), Frederick the Great left his allies in the War of the Austrian Succession (France, Spain, and Bavaria)—after he had gained most of Silesia for himself —and signed a separate peace with Austria, England, Holland, and Sardinia.

Chapter IX.

What happened to Mr. Jones *in the Prison.*

Mr. *Jones* past above twenty-four melancholy Hours by himself, unless when relieved by the Company of *Partridge*, before Mr. *Nightingale* returned; not that this worthy young Man had deserted or forgot his Friend; for indeed, he had been much the greatest Part of the Time employed in his Service.

He had heard upon Enquiry that the only Persons who had seen the Beginning of the unfortunate Rencounter, were a Crew belonging to a Man of War, which then lay at *Deptford*. To *Deptford* therefore he went, in search of this Crew, where he was informed that the Men he sought after, were all gone ashore. He then traced them from Place to Place, till at last he found two of them drinking together, with a third Person, at a Hedge-Tavern, near *Aldersgate*.

Nightingale desired to speak with *Jones* by himself (for *Partridge* was in the Room when he came in.) As soon as they were alone, *Nightingale* taking *Jones* by the Hand, cried, 'Come, my brave Friend, be not too much dejected at what I am going to tell you—I am sorry I am the Messenger of bad News; but I think it my Duty to tell you.' 'I guess already what that bad News is,' cries *Jones*. 'The poor Gentleman then is dead.'——'I hope not,' answered *Nightingale*. 'He was alive this Morning; though I will not flatter you; I fear from the Accounts I could get, that his Wound is mortal. But if the Affair be exactly as you told it, your own Remorse would be all you would have Reason to apprehend, let what would happen; but forgive me, my dear *Tom*, if I entreat you to make the worst of your Story to your Friends. If you disguise any Thing to us, you will only be an Enemy to yourself.'

'What Reason, my dear *Jack*, have I ever given you,' said *Jones*, 'to stab me with so cruel a Suspicion?' 'Have Patience,' cries *Nightingale*, 'and I will tell you all. After the most diligent Enquiry I could make, I at last met with two of the Fellows who were present at this unhappy Accident, and I am sorry to say, they do not relate the Story so much in your Favour as you yourself have told it.' 'Why, what do they say?' cries *Jones*. 'Indeed what I am sorry to repeat, as I am afraid of the Consequence of it to you. They say that they were at too great a Distance to overhear any Words that passed between you; but they both agree that the first Blow was given by you.' 'Then upon my Soul,' answered *Jones*, 'they injure me. He not only struck me first, but struck me without the least Provocation. What should induce those Villains to accuse me falsely?' 'Nay, that I cannot guess,' said *Nightingale*, 'and if you yourself, and I who am so heartily your Friend, cannot conceive a Reason why they should belie you, what Reason will an indifferent Court of Justice be able to assign, why they should not believe them? I repeated the Question to them several Times, and so did another Gentleman who was present, who, I believe, is a Sea-fareing Man, and who really acted a very friendly Part by you; for he begged them often to consider, that there was the Life of a Man in the Case; and asked them over and over if they were certain; to which they both answered, that they were, and would abide by their Evidence upon Oath. For Heaven's Sake, my dear Friend, recollect yourself; for if this should appear to be the Fact, it will be your Business to think in Time of making the best of your Interest. I would not shock you; but you know, I believe, the Severity of the Law, whatever verbal Provocations may have been given you.' 'Alas! my Friend,' cries *Jones*, 'what Interest hath such a Wretch as I? Besides, do you think I would even wish to live with the Reputation of a Murderer? If I had any Friends, (as alas! I have none) could I have the Confidence to solicit them to speak in the Behalf of a Man condemned for the blackest Crime in Human Nature? Believe me I have no such Hope; but I have some Reliance on a Throne still greatly superior; which will, I am certain, afford me all the Protection I merit.'

He then concluded with many solemn and vehement Protestations of the Truth of what he had at first asserted.

The Faith of *Nightingale* was now again staggered, and began to incline to credit his Friend, when Mrs. *Miller* appeared, and made a sorrowful Report of the Success of her Embassy; which when *Jones* had heard, he cried out most heroically, 'Well, my Friend, I am now indifferent as to what shall happen, at least with Regard to my Life; and if it be the Will of Heaven that I shall make an Atonement with that for the Blood I have spilt, I hope the Divine Goodness will one Day suffer my Honour to be cleared, and that the Words of a dying Man at least, will be believed, so far as to justify his Character.'

A very mournful Scene now past between the Prisoner and his Friends, at which, as few Readers would have been pleased to be present, so few, I believe, will desire to hear it particularly related. We will, therefore, pass on to the Entrance of the Turnkey, who acquainted *Jones*, that there was a Lady without who desired to speak with him, when he was at Leisure.

Jones declared his Surprize at this Message. He said, 'He knew no Lady in the World whom he could possibly expect to see there.' However, as he saw no Reason to decline seeing any Person, Mrs. *Miller* and Mr. *Nightingale* presently took their Leave, and he gave Orders to have the Lady admitted.

If *Jones* was surprized at the News of a Visit from a Lady, how greatly was he astonished when he discovered this Lady to be no other than Mrs. *Waters!* In his Astonishment then we shall leave him a-while, in order to cure the Surprize of the Reader, who will likewise, probably, not a little wonder at the Arrival of this Lady.

Who this Mrs. *Waters* was, the Reader pretty well knows; what she was, he must be perfectly satisfied. He will therefore be pleased to remember, that this Lady departed from *Upton* in the same Coach with Mr. *Fitzpatrick* and the other *Irish* Gentleman, and in their Company travelled to the *Bath*.

Now there was a certain Office in the Gift of Mr. *Fitzpatrick* at that Time vacant, namely, that of a Wife; for the Lady who had lately filled that Office had resigned, or at least deserted her Duty. Mr. *Fitzpatrick* therefore having thoroughly examined Mrs. *Waters* on the Road, found her extremely fit for the Place, which, on their Arrival at *Bath*, he presently conferred upon her, and she, without any Scruple, accepted. As Husband and Wife this Gentleman and Lady continued together all the Time they stayed at *Bath*, and as Husband and Wife they arrived together in Town.

Whether Mr. *Fitzpatrick* was so wise a Man as not to part with one good Thing till he had secured another, which he had at present only a Prospect of regaining; or whether Mrs. *Waters* had so well discharged her Office, that he intended still to retain her as Principal, and to make his Wife (as is often the Case) only her Deputy, I will not say; but certain it is he never mentioned his Wife to her, never communicated to her the Letter given him by Mrs. *Western*, nor ever once hinted his Purpose of repossessing his Wife; much less did he ever mention the Name of *Jones*. For though he intended to fight with him wherever he met him, he did not imitate those prudent Persons who think a Wife, a Mother, a Sister, or sometimes a whole Family, the safest Seconds on these Occasions. The first Account therefore which she had of all this, was delivered to her from his Lips, after he was brought home from the Tavern where his Wound had been drest.

As Mr. *Fitzpatrick* however had not the clearest Way of telling a Story at any Time, and was now, perhaps, a little more confused than usual, it was some Time before she discovered, that the Gentleman who had given him this Wound was the very same Person from whom her Heart had received a Wound, which, though not of a mortal Kind, was yet so deep that it had left a considerable Scar behind it. But no sooner was she acquainted that Mr. *Jones* himself was the Man who had been committed to the Gatehouse for this supposed Murder, than she took the first Opportunity of committing Mr. *Fitzpatrick* to the Care of his Nurse, and hastened away to visit the Conqueror.

She now entered the Room with an Air of Gaiety, which received an immediate Check from the melancholy Aspect of poor *Jones*, who started and blessed himself when he saw her. Upon which she said, 'Nay, I do not wonder at your Surprize; I believe you did not expect to see me; for few Gentlemen are troubled here with Visits from any Lady, unless a Wife. You see the Power you have over me, Mr. *Jones*. Indeed I little thought when we parted at *Upton*, that our next Meeting would have been in such a Place.' 'Indeed, Madam,' says *Jones*, 'I must look upon this Visit as kind; few will follow the Miserable, especially to such dismal Habitations.' 'I protest, Mr. *Jones*,' says she, 'I can hardly persuade myself you are the same agreeable Fellow I saw at *Upton*. Why, your Face is more miserable than any Dungeon in the Universe. What can be the Matter with you?' 'I thought, Madam,' said *Jones*, 'as you knew of my being here, you knew the unhappy Reason.' 'Pugh,' says she, 'you have pinked a Man in a Duel, that's all.' *Jones* exprest some Indignation at this Levity, and spoke with the utmost Contrition for what had happened. To which she answered, 'Well then, Sir, if you take it so much to Heart, I will relieve you; the Gentleman is not dead; and, I am pretty confident, is in no Danger of dying. The Surgeon indeed who first dressed him was a young Fellow, and seemed desirous of representing his Case to be as bad as possible, that he might have the more Honour from curing him; but the King's Surgeon[1] hath seen him since, and says, unless from a Fever, of which there are at present no Symptoms, he apprehends not the least Danger of Life.' *Jones* shewed great Satisfaction in his Countenance at this Report; upon which she affirmed the Truth of it, adding, 'By the most extraordinary Accident in the World I lodge at the same House, and have seen the Gentleman; and I promise you he doth you Justice, and says, Whatever be the Consequence, that he was entirely the Aggressor, and that you was not in the least to blame.'

Jones expressed the utmost Satisfaction at the Account which Mrs. *Waters* brought him. He then informed her of many Things which she well knew before, as who Mr. *Fitzpatrick* was, the Occasion of his Resentment, *&c.* He likewise told her several Facts of which she was ignorant, as the Adventure of the Muff, and other Particulars, concealing only the Name of *Sophia*. He then lamented the Follies and Vices of which he had been guilty; every one of which, he said, had been attended with such ill Consequences, that he should be unpardonable if he did not take Warning, and quit those vicious Courses for the future. He lastly concluded with assuring her of his Resolution to sin no more, lest a worse Thing should happen to him.

---

1. See above, p. 355.

Mrs. *Waters* with great Pleasantry ridiculed all this, as the Effects of low Spirits and Confinement. She repeated some Witticisms about *the Devil when he was sick,*[2] and told him, 'She doubted not but shortly to see him at Liberty, and as lively a Fellow as ever; and then,' says she, 'I don't question but your Conscience will be safely delivered of all these Qualms that it is now so sick in breeding.'

Many more Things of this Kind she uttered, some of which it would do her no great Honour, in the Opinion of some Readers, to remember; nor are we quite certain but that the Answers made by *Jones* would be treated with Ridicule by others. We shall therefore suppress the rest of this Conversation, and only observe, that it ended at last with perfect Innocence, and much more to the Satisfaction of *Jones* than of the Lady: For the former was greatly transported with the News she had brought him; but the latter was not altogether so pleased with the penitential Behaviour of a Man whom she had at her first Interview conceived a very different Opinion of from what she now entertained of him.

Thus the Melancholy occasioned by the Report of Mr. *Nightingale* was pretty well effaced; but the Dejection into which Mrs. *Miller* had thrown him still continued. The Account she gave, so well tallied with the Words of *Sophia* herself in her Letter, that he made not the least Doubt but that she had disclosed his Letter to her Aunt, and had taken a fixed Resolution to abandon him. The Torments this Thought gave him, were to be equalled only by a Piece of News which Fortune yet had in Store for him, and which we shall communicate in the second Chapter of the ensuing Book.

BOOK XVIII.

Containing about Six Days.

Chapter I.

A Farewel to the Reader.

We are now, Reader, arrived at the last Stage of our long Journey. As we have therefore travelled together through so many Pages, let us behave to one another like Fellow-Travellers in a Stage-Coach, who have passed several Days in the Company of each

2. A medieval Latin proverb, "When the wolf was sick he would be a monk, but when he recovered he was a wolf again"; some anonymous wit revised this to "When the devil was sick he would be a monk; when the devil was well he was a monk" (Bryant, p. 230).

other; and who, notwithstanding any Bickerings or little Animosities which may have occurred on the Road, generally make all up at last, and mount, for the last Time, into their Vehicle with Chearfulness and Good-Humour; since after this one Stage, it may possibly happen to us, as it commonly happens to them, never to meet more.

As I have here taken up this Simile, give me Leave to carry it a little farther. I intend then in this last Book to imitate the good Company I have mentioned in their last Journey. Now it is well known, that all Jokes and Raillery are at this Time laid aside; whatever Characters any of the Passengers have for the Jest-sake personated on the Road, are now thrown off, and the Conversation is usually plain and serious.

In the same Manner, if I have now and then, in the Course of this Work, indulged any Pleasantry for thy Entertainment, I shall here lay it down. The Variety of Matter, indeed, which I shall be obliged to cram into this Book, will afford no Room for any of those ludicrous Observations which I have elsewhere made, and which may sometimes, perhaps, have prevented thee from taking a Nap when it was beginning to steal upon thee. In this last Book thou wilt find nothing (or at most very little) of that Nature. All will be plain Narrative only; and, indeed, when thou hast perused the many great Events which this Book will produce, thou wilt think the Number of Pages contained in it, scarce sufficient to tell the Story.

And now, my Friend, I take this Opportunity (as I shall have no other) of heartily wishing thee well. If I have been an entertaining Companion to thee, I promise thee it is what I have desired. If in any Thing I have offended, it was really without any Intention. Some Things perhaps here said may have hit thee or thy Friends; but I do most solemnly declare they were not pointed at thee or them. I question not but thou hast been told, among other Stories of me, that thou wast to travel with a very scurrilous Fellow: But whoever told Thee so, did me an Injury. No Man detests and despises Scurrility more than myself; nor hath any Man more Reason; for none hath ever been treated with more: And what is a very severe Fate, I have had some of the abusive Writings of those very Men fathered upon me, who in other of their Works have abused me themselves with the utmost Virulence.

All these Works, however, I am well convinced, will be dead long before this Page shall offer itself to thy Perusal: For however short the Period may be of my own Performances, they will most probably outlive their own infirm Author, and the weakly Productions of his abusive Cotemporaries.[1]

1. "Cotemporaries" is good eighteenth-century usage for modern "contemporaries."

Chapter II.

Containing a very tragical Incident.

While *Jones* was employed in those unpleasant Meditations, with which we left him tormenting himself, *Partridge* came stumbling into the Room with his Face paler than Ashes, his Eyes fixed in his Head, his Hair standing an End,[1] and every Limb trembling. In short, he looked as he would have done had he seen a Spectre, or had he indeed been a Spectre himself.

Jones, who was little subject to Fear, could not avoid being somewhat shocked at this sudden Appearance. He did indeed himself change Colour, and his Voice a little faultered, while he asked him what was the Matter.

'I hope, Sir,' said *Partridge*, 'you will not be angry with me. Indeed I did not listen, but I was obliged to stay in the outward Room. I am sure I wish I had been a hundred Miles off, rather than have heard what I have heard.' 'Why what is the Matter?' said *Jones*. 'The Matter, Sir? O good Heaven!' answered *Partridge*, 'was that Woman who is just gone out, the Woman who was with you at *Upton*?' 'She was, *Partridge*,' cries *Jones*. 'And did you really, Sir, go to Bed with that Woman?' said he trembling——'I am afraid what past between us, is no Secret,' said *Jones*.—'Nay, but pray, Sir, for Heaven's Sake, Sir, answer me,' cries *Partridge*. 'You know I did,' cries *Jones*.—'Why then the Lord have Mercy upon your Soul, and forgive you,' cries *Partridge*; 'but as sure as I stand here alive, you have been a Bed with your own Mother.'

Upon these Words, *Jones* became in a Moment a greater Picture of Horror than *Partridge* himself. He was indeed, for some Time, struck dumb with Amazement, and both stood staring wildly at each other. At last his Words found Way, and in an interrupted Voice he said.—'How! how! What's this you tell me?' 'Nay, Sir,' cries *Partridge*, 'I have not Breath enough left to tell you now—but what I have said is most certainly true—That Woman who now went out is your own Mother. How unlucky was it for you, Sir, that I did not happen to see her at that Time, to have prevented it? Sure the Devil himself must have contrived to bring about this Wickedness.'

'Sure,' cries *Jones*, 'Fortune will never have done with me, 'till she hath driven me to Distraction. But why do I blame Fortune? I am myself the Cause of all my Misery. All the dreadful Mischiefs which have befallen me, are the Consequences only of my own Folly and Vice. What thou hast told me, *Partridge*, hath almost deprived me of my Senses. And was Mrs. *Waters* then——But why

1. Idiomatic for "on end." See p. 151.

do I ask? for thou must certainly know her.——If thou hast any Affection for me; nay, if thou hast any Pity, let me beseech thee to fetch this miserable Woman back again to me. O good Heavens! Incest—with a Mother! To what am I reserved?' He then fell into the most violent and frantic Agonies of Grief and Despair, in which *Partridge* declared he would not leave him: But at last having vented the first Torrent of Passion, he came a little to himself; and then having acquainted *Partridge* that he would find this wretched Woman in the same House where the wounded Gentleman was lodged, he dispatched him in quest of her.

If the Reader will please to refresh his Memory, by turning to the Scene at *Upton* in the Ninth Book, he will be apt to admire the many strange Accidents which unfortunately prevented any Interview between *Partridge* and Mrs. *Waters*, when she spent a whole Day there with Mr. *Jones*. Instances of this Kind we may frequently observe in Life, where the greatest Events are produced by a nice Train of little Circumstances; and more than one Example of this may be discovered by the accurate Eye, in this our History.

After a fruitless Search of two or three Hours, *Partridge* returned back to his Master, without having seen Mrs. *Waters*. *Jones*, who was in a State of Desperation at his Delay, was almost raving mad when he brought him this Account. He was not long however in this Condition, before he received the following Letter.

 'Sir,

 'Since I left you, I have seen a Gentleman, from whom I have learnt something concerning you which greatly surprizes and affects me; but as I have not at present Leisure to communicate a Matter of such high Importance, you must suspend your Curiosity till our next Meeting, which shall be the first Moment I am able to see you. O Mr. *Jones*, little did I think, when I past that happy Day at *Upton*, the Reflection upon which is like to embitter all my future Life, who it was to whom I owed such perfect Happiness. Believe me to be ever sincerely your unfortunate

          '*J. Waters.*

'*P.S.* I would have you comfort yourself as much as possible; for Mr. *Fitzpatrick* is in no Manner of Danger; so that whatever other grievous Crimes you may have to repent of, the Guilt of Blood is not among the Number.'

Jones having received the Letter, let it drop (for he was unable to hold it, and indeed had scarce the Use of any one of his Faculties). *Partridge* took it up, and having received Consent by Silence, read it likewise; nor had it upon him a less sensible Effect. The Pencil, and not the Pen, should describe the Horrors which appeared in both their Countenances. While they both remained speechless, the Turnkey entered the Room, and without taking any Notice of what sufficiently discovered itself in the Faces of them both, acquainted *Jones* that a Man without desired to speak with him. This Person was presently introduced, and was no other than Black *George*.

As Sights of Horror were not so usual to *George* as they were to the Turnkey, he instantly saw the great Disorder which appeared in the Face of *Jones*. This he imputed to the Accident that had happened, which was reported in the very worst Light in Mr. *Western's* Family; he concluded therefore that the Gentleman was dead, and that Mr. *Jones* was in a fair Way of coming to a shameful End. A Thought which gave him much Uneasiness; for *George* was of a compassionate Disposition, and notwithstanding a small Breach of Friendship which he had been over-tempted to commit, was, in the main, not insensible of the Obligations he had formerly received from Mr. *Jones*.

The poor Fellow therefore scarce refrained from a Tear at the present Sight. He told *Jones* he was heartily sorry for his Misfortunes, and begged him to consider, if he could be of any Manner of Service. 'Perhaps, Sir,' said he, 'you may want a little Matter of Money upon this Occasion; if you do, Sir, what little I have is heartily at your Service.'

Jones shook him very heartily by the Hand, and gave him many Thanks for the kind Offer he had made; but answered, 'He had not the least Want of that Kind.' Upon which *George* began to press his Services more eagerly than before. *Jones* again thanked him, with Assurances that he wanted nothing which was in the Power of any Man living to give. 'Come, come, my good Master, answered *George*, do not take the Matter so much to Heart. Things may end better than you imagine; to be sure you ant the first Gentleman who hath killed a Man, and yet come off.' 'You are wide of the Matter, *George*,' said *Partridge*, 'the Gentleman is not dead, nor like to die. Don't disturb my Master, at present, for he is troubled about a Matter in which it is not in your Power to do him any good.' 'You don't know what I may be able to do, Mr. *Partridge*,' answered *George*, 'if his Concern is about my young Lady, I have some News to tell my Master.——'What do you say, Mr. *George*?' cry'd *Jones*, 'Hath any thing lately happened in which my *Sophia* is concerned? My *Sophia*! How dares such a Wretch as I mention her so prophanely.'—'I hope she will be yours yet,' answered *George*.——'Why, yes, Sir, I have something to tell you about her. Madam *Western* hath just brought Madam *Sophia* home, and there hath been a terrible to do. I could not possibly learn the very Right of it; but my Master he hath been in a vast big Passion, and so was Madam *Western*, and I heard her say as she went out of Doors into her Chair, that she would never set her Foot in Master's House again. I don't know what's the Matter, not I, but every thing was very quiet when I came out; but *Robin*, who waited at Supper, said he had never seen the Squire for a long while in such good Humour with young Madam; that he kiss'd her several Times, and swore she should be her own Mistress, and he never would think of confining her any more. I thought this News would please you, and so I slipp'd out, though it was so late, to inform you of it.' Mr. *Jones* assured *George* that it did greatly please him; for though he should never more presume to lift his Eyes towards that incomparable Creature, nothing could so much relieve his Misery as the Satisfaction he should always have, in hearing of her Welfare.

The rest of the Conversation which passed at the Visit, is not important enough to be here related. The Reader will therefore forgive us this abrupt breaking off, and be pleased to hear how this great good Will of the Squire towards his Daughter was brought about.

Mrs. *Western*, on her first Arrival at her Brother's Lodging, began to set forth the great Honours and Advantages which would accrue to the Family by the Match with Lord *Fellamar*, which her Niece had absolutely refused; in which Refusal, when the Squire took the Part of his Daughter, she fell immediately into the most violent Passion, and so irritated and provoked the Squire, that neither his Patience nor his Prudence could bear it any longer; upon which there ensued between them both so warm a Bout at Altercation, that perhaps the Regions of *Billingsgate* never equalled it. In the Heat of this Scolding Mrs. *Western* departed, and had consequently no Leisure to acquaint her Brother with the Letter which *Sophia* received, which might have possibly produced ill Effects; but to say Truth I believe it never once occurred to her Memory at this Time.

When Mrs. *Western* was gone, *Sophia*, who had been hitherto silent, as well indeed from Necessity as Inclination, began to return the Compliment which her Father had made her, in taking her Part against her Aunt, by taking his likewise against the Lady. This was the first Time of her so doing, and it was in the highest Degree acceptable to the Squire. Again he remembered that Mr. *Allworthy* had insisted on an entire Relinquishment of all violent Means; and indeed as he made no doubt but that *Jones* would be hanged, he did not in the least question succeeding with his Daughter by fair Means; he now therefore once more gave a Loose to his natural Fondness for her, which had such an Effect on the dutiful, grateful, tender and affectionate Heart of *Sophia*, that had her Honour given to *Jones*, and something else perhaps in which he was concerned, been removed, I much doubt whether she would not have sacrificed herself to a Man she did not like, to have obliged her Father. She promised him she would make it the whole Business of her Life to oblige him, and would never marry any Man against his Consent; which brought the old Man so near to his highest Happiness, that he was resolved to take the other Step, and went to Bed completely drunk.

Chapter III.

Allworthy *visits old* Nightingale; *with a strange Discovery that he made on that Occasion.*

The Morning after these Things had happened, Mr. *Allworthy* went according to his Promise to visit old *Nightingale*, with whom his Authority was so great, that after having sat with him three Hours, he at last prevailed with him to consent to see his Son.

Here an Accident happened of a very extraordinary Kind; one indeed of those strange Chances, whence very good and grave Men have concluded that Providence often interposes in the Discovery of the most secret Villainy, in order to caution Men from quitting the Paths of Honesty, however warily they tread in those of Vice.

Mr. *Allworthy*, at his Entrance into Mr. *Nightingale's*, saw Black *George*; he took no Notice of him, nor did Black *George* imagine he had perceived him. However, when their Conversation on the principal Point was over, *Allworthy* asked *Nightingale* whether he knew one *George Seagrim*, and upon what Business he came to his House. 'Yes,' answered *Nightingale*, 'I know him very well, and a most extraordinary Fellow he is, who, in these Days, hath been able to hoard up 500 *l.* from renting a very small Estate of 30 *l.* a Year.' 'And is this the Story which he hath told you?' cries *Allworthy*. 'Nay, it is true, I promise you,' said *Nightingale*, 'for I have the Money now in my own Hands, in five Bank Bills, which I am to lay out either in a Mortgage, or in some Purchase in the North of *England*.' The Bank Bills were no sooner produced at *Allworthy's* Desire, than he blessed himself at the Strangeness of the Discovery. He presently told *Nightingale*, that these Bank Bills were formerly his, and then acquainted him with the whole Affair. As there are no Men who complain more of the Frauds of Business than Highwaymen, Gamesters, and other Thieves of that Kind; so there are none who so bitterly exclaim against the Frauds of Gamesters, &c. as Usurers, Brokers, and other Thieves of this Kind; whether it be that the one Way of cheating is a Discountenance or Reflection upon the other, or that Money, which is the common Mistress of all Cheats, makes them regard each other in the Light of Rivals; but *Nightingale* no sooner heard the Story, than he exclaimed against the Fellow in Terms much severer than the Justice and Honesty of *Allwor-thy* had bestowed on him.

Allworthy desired *Nightingale* to retain both the Money and the Secret till he should hear farther from him; and if he should in the mean Time see the Fellow, that he would not take the least Notice to him of the Discovery which he had made. He then returned to his Lodgings, where he found Mrs. *Miller* in a very dejected Condition, on Account of the Information she had received from her Son-in-law. Mr. *Allworthy*, with great Chearfulness, told her that he had much good News to communicate; and with little further Preface, acquainted her, that he had brought Mr. *Nightingale* to consent to see his Son, and did not in the least doubt to effect a perfect Reconciliation between them; though he found the Father more sowered by another Accident of the same Kind, which had happened in his Family. He then mentioned the running away of the Uncle's Daughter, which he had been told by the old Gentleman, and which Mrs. *Miller*, and her Son-in-law, did not yet know.

The Reader may suppose Mrs. *Miller* received this Account with great Thankfulness and no less Pleasure; but so uncommon was her Friendship to *Jones*, that I am not certain whether the Uneasiness she suffered for his Sake, did not overbalance her Satisfaction at hearing a Piece of News tending so much to the Happiness of her own Family; nor whether even this very News, as it reminded her of the Obligations she had to *Jones*, did not hurt as well as please her; when her grateful Heart said to her, 'While my own Family is happy, how miserable is the poor Creature, to whose Generosity we owe the Beginning of all this Happiness!'

Allworthy having left her a little while to chew the Cud (if I may use that Expression) on these first Tidings, told her, he had still something more to impart, which he believed would give her Pleasure. 'I think,' said he, 'I have discovered a pretty considerable Treasure belonging to the young Gentleman, your Friend; but perhaps indeed, his present Situation may be such, that it will be of no Service to him.' The latter Part of the Speech gave Mrs. *Miller* to understand who was meant, and she answered with a Sigh, 'I hope not, Sir.' 'I hope so too,' cries *Allworthy*, 'with all my Heart; but my Nephew told me this Morning, he had heard a very bad Account of the Affair.'—'Good Heaven! Sir, said she — Well, I must not speak, and yet it is certainly very hard to be obliged to hold one's Tongue when one hears'——'Madam,' said *Allworthy*, 'you may say whatever you please, you know me too well to think I have a Prejudice against any one; and as for that young Man, I assure you I should be heartily pleased to find he could acquit himself of every thing, and particularly of this sad Affair. You can testify the Affection I have formerly borne him. The World, I know, censured me for loving him so much. I did not withdraw that Affection from him without thinking I had the justest Cause. Believe me, Mrs. *Miller*, I should be glad to find I have been mistaken.' Mrs. *Miller* was going eagerly to reply, when a Servant acquainted her, that a Gentleman without desired to speak with her immediately. *Allworthy* then enquired for his Nephew, and was told, that he had been for some Time in his Room with the Gentleman who used to come to him, and whom Mr. *Allworthy* guessing rightly to be Mr. *Dowling*, he desired presently to speak with him.

When *Dowling* attended, *Allworthy* put the Case of the Bank Notes to him, without mentioning any Name, and asked in what manner such a Person might be punished. To which *Dowling* answered, he thought he might be indicted on the Black Act;[1] but said, as it was a Matter of some Nicety, it would be proper to go to Council. He said he was to attend Council presently upon an Affair of Mr. *Western's*, and if Mr. *Allworthy* pleased he would lay the Case before them. This was agreed to; and then Mrs. *Miller* opening the Door, cry'd, 'I ask Pardon, I did not know you had Company;' but *Allworthy* desired her to come in, saying, he had finished his Business. Upon which Mr. *Dowling* withdrew, and Mrs. *Miller* introduced Mr. *Nightingale* the younger, to return Thanks for the great Kindness done him by *Allworthy*; but she had scarce Patience to let the young Gentleman finish his Speech before she interrupted him, saying, 'O Sir, Mr. *Nightingale*, brings great News about poor Mr. *Jones*; he hath been to see the wounded Gentleman, who is out of all Danger of Death, and, what is more, declares he fell upon poor Mr. *Jones* himself, and beat him. I am sure, Sir, you would not have Mr. *Jones* be a Coward. If I was a Man myself, I am sure if any Man was to strike me, I should draw my Sword. Do pray, my Dear, tell Mr. *Allworthy*, tell him all yourself.' *Nightingale* then confirmed what Mrs. *Miller* had said; and concluded with many handsome Things of *Jones*, who was, he said, one of the best-natured Fellows in the World, and not in the least inclined to be quarrelsome. Here *Nightingale* was going to cease, when Mrs. *Miller* again begged him to relate all the many dutiful Expressions he had heard him make use of towards Mr. *Allworthy*. 'To say the utmost Good of Mr. *Allworthy*,' cries *Nightingale*, 'is doing no more than strict Justice, and can have no Merit in it; but indeed I must say, no Man can be more sensible of the Obligations he hath to so good a Man, than is poor *Jones*. Indeed, Sir, I am convinced the Weight of your Displeasure is the heaviest Burthen he lies under. He hath often lamented it to me, and hath as often protested in the most solemn Manner he hath never been intentionally guilty of any Offence towards you; nay, he hath sworn he would

1. A statute (9 George I, cap. 22, 1723) to punish people committing outrages at night, especially poaching, with faces blackened for camouflage.

rather die a Thousand Deaths than he would have his Conscience upbraid him with one disrespectful, ungrateful, or undutiful Thought towards you. But I ask Pardon, Sir, I am afraid I presume to intermeddle too far in so tender a Point.' 'You have spoke no more than what a Christian ought,' cries Mrs. *Miller*. 'Indeed, Mr. *Nightingale*,' answered *Allworthy*, 'I applaud your generous Friendship, and I wish he may merit it of you. I confess, I am glad to hear the Report you bring from this unfortunate Gentleman; and if that Matter should turn out to be as you represent it (and indeed I doubt nothing of what you say) I may perhaps, in Time, be brought to think better than lately I have of this young Man: For this good Gentlewoman here, nay all who know me, can witness that I loved him as dearly as if he had been my own Son. Indeed I have considered him as a Child sent by Fortune to my Care. I still remember the innocent, the helpless Situation in which I found him. I feel the tender Pressure of his little Hands at this Moment. —He was my Darling, indeed he was.' At which Words he ceased, and the Tears stood in his Eyes.

As the Answer which Mrs. *Miller* made may lead us into fresh Matters, we will here stop to account for the visible Alteration in Mr. *Allworthy*'s Mind, and the Abatement of his Anger to *Jones*. Revolutions of this Kind, it is true, do frequently occur in Histories and dramatic Writers, for no other Reason than because the History or Play draws to a Conclusion, and are justified by Authority of Authors; yet though we insist upon as much Authority as any Author whatever, we shall use this Power very sparingly, and never but when we are driven to it by Necessity, which we do not at present foresee will happen in this Work.

This Alteration then in the Mind of Mr. *Allworthy*, was occasioned by a Letter he had just received from Mr. *Square*, and which we shall give the Reader in the Beginning of the next Chapter.

Chapter IV.

Containing two Letters in very different Stiles.

'*My worthy Friend*,

'I informed you in my last, that I was forbidden the Use of the Waters, as they were found by Experience rather to encrease than lessen the Symptoms of my Distemper. I must now acquaint you with a Piece of News, which, I believe, will afflict my Friends more than it hath afflicted me. Dr. *Harrington* and Dr. *Brewster*[1] have informed me, that there is no Hopes of my Recovery.

'I have somewhere read, that the great Use of Philosophy is to

---

1. Drs. Edward Harrington and Thomas Brewster of Bath had both subscribed to   Fielding's *Miscellanies* (1743).

learn to die.[2] I will not therefore so far disgrace mine, as to shew any Surprize at receiving a Lesson which I must be thought to have so long studied. Yet, to say the Truth, one Page of the Gospel teaches this Lesson better than all the Volumes of antient or modern Philosophers. The Assurance it gives us of another Life is a much stronger Support to a good Mind, than all the Consolations that are drawn from the Necessity of Nature, the Emptiness or Satiety of our Enjoyments here, or any other Topic of those Declamations which are sometimes capable of arming our Minds with a stubborn Patience in bearing the Thoughts of Death; but never of raising them to a real Contempt of it, and much less of making us think it is a real Good. I would not here be understood to throw the horrid Censure of Atheism, or even the absolute Denial of Immortality, on all who are called Philosophers. Many of that Sect, as well antient as modern, have, from the Light of Reason, discovered some Hopes of a future State; but, in Reality, that Light was so faint and glimmering, and the Hopes were so incertain and precarious, that it may be justly doubted on which Side their Belief turned. *Plato* himself concludes his *Phædon* with declaring, that his best Arguments amount only to raise a Probability; and *Cicero*[3] himself seems rather to profess an Inclination to believe, than any actual Belief in the Doctrines of Immortality. As to myself, to be very sincere with you, I never was much in earnest in this Faith, till I was in earnest a Christian.

'You will perhaps wonder at the latter Expression; but I assure you it hath not been till very lately, that I could, with Truth, call myself so. The Pride of Philosophy had intoxicated my Reason, and the sublimest of all Wisdom appeared to me, as it did to the *Greeks* of old, to be Foolishness. God hath however been so gracious to shew me my Error in Time, and to bring me into the Way of Truth, before I sunk into utter Darkness for ever.

'I find myself beginning to grow weak, I shall therefore hasten to the main Purpose of this Letter.

'When I reflect on the Actions of my past Life, I know of nothing which sits heavier upon my Conscience, than the Injustice I have been guilty of to that poor Wretch, your adopted Son. I have indeed not only connived at the Villainy of others, but been myself active in Injustice towards him. Believe me, my dear Friend, when I tell you on the Word of a dying Man, he hath been basely injured. As to the principal Fact, upon the Misrepresentation of which you discarded him, I solemnly assure you he is innocent. When you lay upon your supposed Death-bed, he was the only Person in the House who testified any real Concern; and what hap-

2. Plato, *Phaedo* 64, 81, and Cicero, discussing Plato's concept, *Tusculan Disputations* I.xxx.74,75.

3. Same *Tusculan Disputation* as in the preceding note (I.xxx).

pened afterwards arose from the Wildness of his Joy on your Recovery; and, I am sorry to say it, from the Baseness of another Person (but it is my Desire to justify the Innocent, and to accuse none.) Believe me, my Friend, this young Man hath the noblest Generosity of Heart, the most perfect Capacity for Friendship, the highest Integrity, and indeed every Virtue which can enoble a Man. He hath some Faults, but among them is not to be numbred the least Want of Duty or Gratitude towards you. On the contrary, I am satisfied when you dismissed him from your House, his Heart bled for you more than for himself.

'Worldly Motives were the wicked and base Reasons of my concealing this from you so long; to reveal it now I can have no Inducement but the Desire of serving the Cause of Truth, of doing Right to the Innocent, and of making all the Amends in my Power for a past Offence. I hope this Declaration therefore will have the Effect desired, and will restore this deserving young Man to your Favour; the hearing of which, while I am yet alive, will afford the utmost Consolation to,

'*Sir*,

'*Your most obliged*,

'*Obedient humble Servant*,

'Thomas Square.'

The Reader will, after this, scarce wonder at the Revolution so visably appearing in Mr. *Allworthy*, notwithstanding he received from *Thwackum*, by the same Post, another Letter of a very different Kind, which we shall here add, as it may possibly be the last Time we shall have Occasion to mention the Name of that Gentleman.

'*Sir*,

'I am not at all surprized at hearing from your worthy Nephew a fresh Instance of the Villainy of Mr. *Jones*[4] the Atheist's young Pupil. I shall not wonder at any Murders he may commit; and I heartily pray that your own Blood may not seal up his final Commitment to the Place of Wailing and Gnashing of Teeth.

'Though you cannot want sufficient Calls to Repentance for the many unwarrantable Weaknesses exemplified in your Behaviour to this Wretch, so much to the Prejudice of your own lawful Family, and of your Character. I say, tho' these may sufficiently be supposed to prick and goad your Conscience at this Season; I should yet be wanting to my Duty, if I spared to give you some Admonition, in order to bring you to a due Sense of your Errors. I therefore pray you seriously to consider the Judgment which is likely to overtake this wicked Villain; and let it serve at least as a Warning to you,

4. A third-edition emendation for one correcting an obvious ambiguity.
"*Square*," in editions one, two, and four,

that you may not for the future despise the Advice of one who is so indefatigable in his Prayers for your Welfare.

'Had not my Hand been with-held from due Correction, I had scourged much of this diabolical Spirit out of a Boy, of whom from his Infancy I discovered the Devil had taken such entire Possession; but Reflections of this Kind now come too late.

'I am sorry you have given away the Living of *Westerton* so hastily. I should have applied on that Occasion earlier, had I thought you would not have acquainted me previous to the Disposition.——Your Objection to Pluralities is being righteous over-much. If there were any Crime in the Practice, so many godly Men would not agree to it. If the Vicar of *Aldergrove* should die (as we hear he is in a declining Way) I hope you will think of me, since I am certain you must be convinced of my most sincere Attachment to your highest Welfare. A Welfare to which all worldly Considerations are as trifling as the small Tithes mentioned in Scripture are, when compared to the weighty Matters of the Law.

'I am, Sir,

'Your faithful humble Servant,

'Roger Thwackum.'

This was the first Time *Thwackum* ever wrote in this authoritative Stile to *Allworthy*, and of this he had afterward sufficient Reason to repent, as in the Case of those who mistake the highest Degree of Goodness for the lowest Degree of Weakness. *Allworthy* had indeed never liked this Man. He knew him to be proud and ill-natured; he also knew that his Divinity itself was tinctured with his Temper, and such as in many Respects he himself did by no means approve: But he was at the same Time an excellent Scholar, and most indefatigable in teaching the two Lads. Add to this the strict Severity of his Life and Manners, an unimpeached Honesty, and a most devout Attachment to Religion. So that upon the whole, though *Allworthy* did not esteem nor love the Man, yet he could never bring himself to part with a Tutor to the Boys, who was, both by Learning and Industry, extremely well qualified for his Office; and he hoped, that as they were bred up in his own House, and under his own Eye, he should be able to correct whatever was wrong in *Thwackum's* Instructions.

Chapter V.

In which the History is continued.

Mr. *Allworthy*, in his last Speech, had recollected some tender Ideas concerning *Jones*, which had brought Tears into the good Man's Eyes. This Mrs. *Miller* observing, said, 'Yes, yes, Sir, your

Goodness to this poor young Man is known, notwithstanding all your Care to conceal it; but there is not a single Syllable of Truth in what those Villains said. Mr. *Nightingale* hath now discovered the whole Matter. It seems these Fellows were employed by a Lord, who is a Rival of poor Mr. *Jones*, to have pressed him on board a Ship.——I assure them I don't know who they will press next. Mr. *Nightingale* here hath seen the Officer himself, who is a very pretty Gentleman, and hath told him all, and is very sorry for what he undertook, which he would never have done, had he known Mr. *Jones* to have been a Gentleman; but he was told that he was a common strolling Vagabond.'

Allworthy stared at all this, and declared he was a Stranger to every Word she said. 'Yes, Sir,' answered she, 'I believe you are.——It is a very different Story, I believe, from what those Fellows told the Lawyer.'

'What Lawyer, Madam? what is it you mean?' said *Allworthy*. 'Nay, nay,' said she, 'this is so like you to deny your own Goodness; but Mr. *Nightingale* here saw him.' 'Saw whom, Madam?' answered he. 'Why your Lawyer, Sir,' said she, 'that you so kindly sent to enquire into the Affair.' 'I am still in the Dark, upon my Honour,' said *Allworthy*. 'Why then do you tell him, my dear Sir,' cries she. 'Indeed, Sir,' said *Nightingale*, 'I did see that very Lawyer who went from you when I came into the Room, at an Alehouse in *Aldersgate*, in Company with two of the Fellows who were employed by Lord *Fellamar* to press Mr. *Jones*, and who were by that means present at the unhappy Rencounter between him and Mr. *Fitzpatrick*.' 'I own, Sir,' said Mrs. *Miller*, 'When I saw this Gentleman come into the Room to you, I told Mr. *Nightingale* that I apprehended you had sent him thither to enquire into the Affair.' *Allworthy* shewed Marks of Astonishment in his Countenance at this News, and was indeed for two or three Minutes struck dumb by it. At last, addressing himself to Mr. *Nightingale*, he said, 'I must confess myself, Sir, more surprized at what you tell me, than I have ever been before at any Thing in my whole Life. Are you certain this was the Gentleman?' 'I am most certain,' answered *Nightingale*. 'At *Aldersgate*?' cries *Allworthy*. 'And was you in Company with this Lawyer and the two Fellows?'——'I was, Sir,' said the other, 'very near half an Hour.'——'Well, Sir,' said *Allworthy*, 'and in what Manner did the Lawyer behave? Did you hear all that past between him and the Fellows?' 'No, Sir,' answered *Nightingale*, 'they had been together before I came.——In my Presence the Lawyer said little; but after I had several Times examined the Fellows, who persisted in a Story directly contrary to what I had heard from Mr. *Jones*, and which I find by Mr. *Fitzpatrick* was a rank Falshood; the Lawyer then desired the Fellows to say nothing but

what was the Truth, and seemed to speak so much in Favour of
Mr. *Jones*, that when I saw the same Person with you, I concluded
your Goodness had prompted you to send him thither.'—'And did
you not send him thither?' says Mrs. *Miller*.——'Indeed I did not,'
answered *Allworthy*; 'nor did I know he had gone on such an
Errand 'till this Moment.'——'I see it all!' said Mrs. *Miller*:
'Upon my Soul, I see it all! No Wonder they have been closetted so
close lately. Son *Nightingale*, let me beg you run for these Fellows
immediately—find them out if they are above Ground. I will go
myself.'——'Dear Madam,' said *Allworthy*, 'be patient, and do me
the Favour to send a Servant up Stairs to call Mr. *Dowling* hither,
if he be in the House, or if not, Mr. *Blifil*.' Mrs. *Miller* went out
muttering something to herself, and presently returned with an
Answer. 'That Mr. *Dowling* was gone; but that the t'other, as she
called him, was coming.'

Allworthy was of a cooler Disposition than the good Woman,
whose Spirits were all up in Arms in the Cause of her Friend. He
was not however without some Suspicions which were near a-kin to
hers. When *Blifil* came into the Room, he asked him with a very
serious Countenance, and with a less friendly Look than he had
ever before given him, 'Whether he knew any Thing of Mr. *Dowling*'s having seen any of the Persons who were present at the Duel
between *Jones* and another Gentleman?'

There is nothing so dangerous as a Question which comes by Surprize on a Man, whose Business it is to conceal Truth, or to defend
Falsehood. For which Reason those worthy Personages, whose noble
Office it is to save the Lives of their Fellow Creatures at the *Old-
Bailey*, take the utmost Care, by frequent previous Examination, to
divine every Question, which may be asked their Clients on the Day
of Trial, that they may be supply'd with proper and ready Answers,
which the most fertile Invention cannot supply in an Instant.
Besides, the sudden and violent Impulse on the Blood, occasioned
by these Surprizes, causes frequently such an Alteration in the
Countenance, that the Man is obliged to give Evidence against
himself. And such indeed were the Alterations which the Countenance of *Blifil* underwent from this sudden Question, that we can
scarce blame the Eagerness of Mrs. *Miller*, who immediately cry'd
out, 'Guilty, upon my Honour! Guilty, upon my Soul!'

Mr. *Allworthy* sharply rebuked her for this Impetuosity; and then
turning to *Blifil*, who seemed sinking into the Earth, he said, 'Why
do you hesitate, Sir, at giving me an Answer? You certainly must
have employed him; for he would not, of his own Accord, I believe,
have undertaken such an Errand, and especially without acquainting me.'

Blifil then answered, 'I own, Sir, I have been guilty of an

Offence, yet may I hope your Pardon?'——'My Pardon?' said *All-worthy* very angrily.—'Nay, Sir,' answered *Blifil*, 'I knew you would be offended; yet surely my dear Uncle will forgive the Effects of the most amiable of human Weaknesses. Compassion for those who do not deserve it, I own, is a Crime; and yet it is a Crime from which you yourself are not entirely free. I know I have been guilty of it in more than one Instance to this very Person; and I will own I did send Mr. *Dowling*, not on a vain and fruitless Enquiry, but to dis-cover the Witnesses, and to endeavour to soften their Evidence. This, Sir, is the Truth; which though I intended to conceal from you, I will not deny.'

'I confess,' said *Nightingale*, 'this is the Light in which it ap-peared to me from the Gentleman's Behaviour.'

'Now, Madam,' said *Allworthy*, 'I believe you will once in your Life own you have entertained a wrong Suspicion, and are not so angry with my Nephew as you was.'

Mrs. *Miller* was silent; for though she could not so hastily be pleased with *Blifil*, whom she looked upon to have been the Ruin of *Jones*, yet in this particular Instance he had imposed upon her as well as upon the rest; so entirely had the Devil stood his Friend. And indeed, I look upon the vulgar Observation, *That the Devil often deserts his Friends, and leaves them in the Lurch*, to be a great Abuse on that Gentleman's Character. Perhaps he may some-times desert those who are only his Cup Acquaintance; or who, at most, are but half his; but he generally stands by those who are thoroughly his Servants, and helps them off in all Extremities, 'till their Bargain expires.

As a conquered Rebellion strengthens a Government, or as Health is more perfectly established by Recovery from some Dis-eases; so Anger, when removed, often gives new Life to Affec-tion. This was the Case of Mr. *Allworthy*; for *Blifil* having wiped off the greater Suspicion, the lesser, which had been raised by *Square*'s Letter, sunk of Course, and was forgotten; and *Thwackum*, with whom he was greatly offended, bore alone all the Reflections which *Square* had cast on the Enemies of *Jones*.

As for that young Man, the Resentment of Mr. *Allworthy* began more and more to abate towards him. He told *Blifil*, 'he did not only forgive the extraordinary Efforts of his Good-Nature, but would give him the Pleasure of following his Example.' Then turn-ing to Mrs. *Miller*, with a Smile which would have become an Angel, he cry'd, 'What say you, Madam; shall we take a Hackney-Coach, and all of us together pay a Visit to your Friend? I promise you it is not the first Visit I have made in a Prison.'

Every Reader, I believe, will be able to answer for the worthy Woman; but they must have a great deal of Good-Nature, and be well acquainted with Friendship, who can feel what she felt on this Occasion. Few, I hope, are capable of feeling what now past in the Mind of *Blifil*; but those who are, will acknowledge, that it was impossible for him to raise any Objection to this Visit. Fortune, however, or the Gentleman lately mentioned above, stood his Friend, and prevented his undergoing so great a Shock: For at the very Instant when the Coach was sent for, *Partridge* arrived, and having called Mrs. *Miller* from the Company acquainted her with the dreadful Accident lately come to Light; and hearing Mr. *Allworthy*'s Intention, begged her to find some Means of stopping him; 'for,' says he, 'the Matter must at all Hazards be kept a Secret from him; and if he should now go, he will find Mr. *Jones* and his Mother, who arrived just as I left him, lamenting over one another the horrid Crime they have ignorantly committed.'

The poor Woman, who was almost deprived of her Senses at his dreadful News, was never less capable of Invention than at present. However, as Women are much readier at this than Men, she bethought herself of an Excuse, and returning to *Allworthy* said, 'I am sure, Sir, you will be surprized at hearing any Objection from me to the kind Proposal you just now made; and yet I am afraid of the Consequence of it, if carried immediately into Execution. You must imagine, Sir, that all the Calamities which have lately befallen this poor young Fellow, must have thrown him into the lowest Dejection of Spirits: And now, Sir, should we all on a sudden fling him into such a violent Fit of Joy, as I know your Presence will occasion, it may, I am afraid, produce some fatal Mischief, especially as his Servant who is without, tells me he is very far from being well.'

'Is his Servant without?' cries *Allworthy*; 'Pray call him hither. I will ask him some Questions concerning his Master.'

Partridge was at first afraid to appear before Mr. *Allworthy*; but was at length persuaded, after Mrs. *Miller*, who had often heard his whole Story from his own Mouth, had promised to introduce him.

Allworthy recollected *Partridge* the Moment he came into the Room, though many Years had passed since he had seen him. Mrs. *Miller* therefore might have spared here a formal Oration, in which indeed she was something prolix: For the Reader, I believe, may have observed already that the good Woman, among other Things, had a Tongue always ready for the Service of her Friends.

'And are you,' said *Allworthy* to *Partridge*, 'the Servant of Mr. *Jones*?' 'I can't say, Sir, answered he, that I am regularly a Servant, but I live with him, an't please your Honour, at present. *Non sum qualis eram*,[1] as your Honour very well knows.'

Mr. *Allworthy* then asked him many Questions concerning *Jones*,

1. See above, p. 638.

as to his Health, and other Matters; to all which *Partridge*
answered, without having the least Regard to what was, but considered only what he would have Things appear; for a strict Adherence
to Truth was not among the Articles of this honest Fellow's Morality, or his Religion.

During this Dialogue Mr. *Nightingale* took his Leave, and presently after Mrs. *Miller* left the Room, when *Allworthy* likewise dispatched *Blifil*; for he imagined that *Partridge*, when alone with
him, would be more explicit than before Company. They were no
sooner left in private together, than *Allworthy* began as in the following Chapter.

Chapter VI.

In which the History is farther continued.

'Sure, Friend,' said the good Man, 'you are the strangest of all
human Beings. Not only to have suffered as you have formerly, for
obstinately persisting in a Falshood; but to persist in it thus to the
last, and to pass thus upon the World for a Servant of your own
Son? What Interest can you have in all this? What can be your
Motive?'

'I see, Sir,' said *Partridge*, falling down upon his Knees, 'that your
Honour is prepossessed against me, and resolved not to believe any
Thing I say, and therefore what signifies my Protestations? but yet
there is one above who knows that I am not the Father of this
young Man.'

'How!' said *Allworthy*, 'Will you yet deny what you was formerly
convicted of upon such unanswerable, such manifest Evidence?
Nay, what a Confirmation is your being now found with this very
Man, of all which twenty Years ago appeared against you. I thought
you had left the Country; nay, I thought you had been long since
dead.—In what Manner did you know any Thing of this young
Man? Where did you meet with him, unless you had kept some
Correspondence together? Do not deny this; for I promise you it
will greatly raise your Son in my Opinion, to find that he hath such
a Sense of filial Duty, as privately to support his Father for so many
Years.'

'If your Honour will have Patience, to hear me,' said *Partridge*, 'I
will tell you all.'——Being bid go on, he proceeded thus: 'When
your Honour conceived that Displeasure against me, it ended in my
Ruin soon after; for I lost my little School; and the Minister, thinking I suppose it would be agreeable to your Honour, turned me out
from the Office of Clerk; so that I had nothing to trust to but the
Barber's Shop, which in a Country Place like that, is a poor Liveli-

hood; and when my Wife died (for 'till that Time I received a Pension of 12*l.* a Year from an unknown Hand, which indeed I believe was your Honour's own, for no Body that ever I heard of doth these Things besides) but as I was saying, when she died, this Pension forsook me; so that now as I owed two or three small Debts, which began to be troublesome to me, (particularly one[1] which an Attorney brought up by Law-charges from 15 *s.* to near 30 *l.*) and as I found all my usual Means of living had forsook me, I packed up my little All as well as I could, and went off.

'The first Place I came to was *Salisbury*, where I got into the Service of a Gentleman belonging to the Law, and one of the best Gentlemen that ever I knew; for he was not only good to me, but I know a Thousand good and charitable Acts which he did while I staid with him; and I have known him often refuse Business, because it was paultry and oppressive.'——'You need not be so particular,' said *Allworthy*; 'I know this Gentleman, and a very worthy Man he is, and an Honour to his Profession.'——'Well, Sir,' continued *Partridge*, 'from hence I removed to *Lymington*, where I was above three Years in the Service of another Lawyer, who was likewise a very good Sort of a Man, and to be sure one of the merriest Gentlemen in *England*. Well, Sir, at the End of the three Years I set up a little School, and was likely to do well again, had it not been for a most unlucky Accident. Here I kept a Pig; and one Day, as ill Fortune would have it, this Pig broke out, and did a Trespass I think they call it, in a Garden belonging to one of my Neighbours, who was a proud, revengeful Man, and employed a Lawyer, one—one—I can't think of his Name; but he sent for a Writ against me, and had me to *Size*.[2] When I came there, Lord have Mercy upon me—to hear what the Counsellors said. There was one that told my Lord a Parcel of the confoundedst Lies about me; he said, that I used to drive my Hogs into other Folks Gardens, and a great deal more; and at last he said, He hoped I had at last brought my Hogs to a fair Market. To be sure, one would have thought, that instead of being Owner only of one poor little Pig, I had been the greatest Hog-merchant in *England*. Well'—'Pray,' said *Allworthy*, 'do not be so particular. I have heard nothing of your Son yet.' 'O it was a great many Years,' answered *Partridge*, 'before I saw my Son, as you are pleased to call him.—I went over to *Ireland* after this, and taught School at *Cork*, (for that one Suit ruined me again, and I lay seven Years in *Winchester* Goal.)'—'Well,' said *Allwor-*

---

1. This is a Fact which I knew happen to a poor Clergyman in *Dorsetshire*, by the Villainy of an Attorney, who not contented with the exorbitant Costs to which the poor Man was put by a single Action, brought afterwards another Action on the Judgment, as it was called. A Method frequently used to oppress the Poor, and bring money into the Pockets of Attorneys, to the great Scandal of the Law, of the Nation, of Christianity, and even of Human Nature itself [*Fielding's note*].

2. "And had me summoned to appear at the Assizes"—called him into court.

thy, 'pass that over till your Return to *England.*'—'Then, Sir,' said he, 'it was about half a Year ago that I landed at *Bristol,* where I stayed some Time, and not finding it do there, and hearing of a Place between that and *Gloucester,* where the Barber was just dead, I went thither, and there I had been about two Months when Mr. *Jones* came thither.' He then gave *Allworthy* a very particular Account of their first Meeting, and of every Thing as well as he could remember, which had happened from that Day to this; frequently interlarding his Story with Panegyrics on *Jones,* and not forgetting to insinuate the great Love and Respect which he had for *Allworthy.* He concluded with saying, 'Now, Sir, I have told your Honour the whole Truth.' And then repeated a most solemn Protestation, 'That he was no more the Father of *Jones* than of the Pope of *Rome;*' and imprecated the most bitter Curses on his Head, if he did not speak Truth.

'What am I to think of this Matter?' cries *Allworthy.* 'For what Purpose should you so strongly deny a Fact, which I think it would be rather your Interest to own?'—'Nay, Sir,' answered *Partridge,* (for he could hold no longer) 'if your Honour will not believe me, you are like soon to have Satisfaction enough. I wish you had mistaken the Mother of this young Man, as well as you have his Father.'—And now being asked what he meant, with all the Symptoms of Horror, both in his Voice and Countenance, he told *Allworthy* the whole Story, which he had a little before expressed such Desire to Mrs. *Miller* to conceal from him.

Allworthy was almost as much shocked at this Discovery as *Partridge* himself had been while he related it. 'Good Heavens!' says he, 'in what miserable Distresses do Vice and Imprudence involve Men! How much beyond our Designs are the Effects of Wickedness sometimes carried!' He had scarce uttered these Words, when Mrs. *Waters* came hastily and abruptly into the Room. *Partridge* no sooner saw her, than he cried, 'Here, Sir, here is the very Woman herself. This is the unfortunate Mother of Mr. *Jones;* I am sure she will acquit me before your Honour.'—'Pray, Madam'—

Mrs. *Waters,* without paying any Regard to what *Partridge* said, and almost without taking any Notice of him, advanced to Mr. *Allworthy.* 'I believe, Sir, it is so long since I had the Honour of seeing you, that you do not recollect me.'—'Indeed,' answered *Allworthy,* 'you are so very much altered, on many Accounts, that had not this Man already acquainted me who you are, I should not have immediately called you to my Remembrance. Have you, Madam, any particular Business which brings you to me?'—*Allworthy* spoke this with great Reserve; for the Reader may easily believe he was not well pleased with the Conduct of this Lady; neither with what he had formerly heard, nor with what *Partridge* had now delivered.

Mrs. *Waters* answered,——'Indeed, Sir, I have very particular Business with you; and it is such as I can impart only to yourself.— I must desire therefore the Favour of a Word with you alone; for I assure you, what I have to tell you is of the utmost Importance.'

Partridge was then ordered to withdraw, but before he went, he begged the Lady to satisfy Mr. *Allworthy* that he was perfectly innocent. To which she answered,—'You need be under no Apprehension, Sir, I shall satisfy Mr. *Allworthy* very perfectly of that Matter.'

Then *Partridge* withdrew, and that past between Mr. *Allworthy* and Mrs. *Waters* which is written in the next Chapter.

Chapter VII.

Continuation of the History.

Mrs. *Waters* remaining a few Moments silent, Mr. *Allworthy* could not refrain from saying, 'I am sorry, Madam, to perceive by what I have since heard, that you have made so very ill a Use— 'Mr. *Allworthy*,' says she, interrupting him, 'I know I have Faults, but Ingratitude to you is not one of them. I never can nor shall forget your Goodness, which I own I have very little deserved; but be pleased to wave all upbraiding me at present, as I have so important an Affair to communicate to you concerning this young Man, to whom you have given my Maiden Name of *Jones*.'

'Have I then,' said *Allworthy*, 'ignorantly punished an innocent Man, in the Person of him who hath just left us? Was he not the Father of the Child?'—'Indeed he was not,' said Mrs. *Waters*. 'You may be pleased to remember, Sir, I formerly told you, you should one Day know; and I acknowledge myself to have been guilty of a cruel Neglect, in not having discovered it to you before. Indeed I little knew how necessary it was.'—'Well, Madam,' said *Allworthy*, 'be pleased to proceed.' 'You must remember, Sir,' said she, 'a young Fellow, whose Name was *Summer*.' 'Very well,' cries *Allworthy*, 'he was the Son of a Clergyman of great Learning and Virtue, for whom I had the highest Friendship.' 'So it appeared, Sir,' answered she; 'for I believe you bred the young Man up, and maintained him at the University; where, I think, he had finished his Studies, when he came to reside at your House; a finer Man, I must say, the Sun never shone upon; for, besides the handsomest Person I ever saw, he was so genteel, and had so much Wit and good Breeding.' 'Poor Gentleman,' said *Allworthy*, 'he was indeed untimely snatched away; and little did I think he had any Sins of this Kind to answer for; for I plainly perceive, you are going to tell me he was the Father of your Child.'

'Indeed, Sir,' answered she, 'he was not.' 'How?' said *Allworthy*, 'to what then tends all this Preface?' 'To a Story, Sir,' said she, 'which I am concerned falls to my Lot to unfold to you.—O, Sir, prepare to hear something which will surprize you, will grieve you.' 'Speak,' said *Allworthy*, 'I am conscious of no Crime, and cannot be afraid to hear.'—'Sir,' said she, 'that Mr. *Summer*, the Son of your Friend, educated at your Expence, who, after living a Year in the House as if he had been your own Son, died there of the Small-pox, was tenderly lamented by you, and buried as if he had been your own; that *Summer*, Sir, was the Father of this Child.'—'How!' said *Allworthy*, 'you contradict yourself.'—'That I do not,' answered she, 'he was indeed the Father of this Child, but not by me.' 'Take Care, Madam,' said *Allworthy*, 'do not, to shun the Imputation of any Crime, be guilty of Falshood. Remember there is one from whom you can conceal nothing, and before whose Tribunal Falshood will only aggravate your Guilt.' 'Indeed, Sir,' says she, 'I am not his Mother; nor would I now think myself so for the World.' 'I know your Reason,' said *Allworthy*, 'and shall rejoice as much as you to find it otherwise; yet you must remember, you yourself confest it before me.'—'So far what I confest,' said she, 'was true, that these Hands conveyed the Infant to your Bed; conveyed it thither at the Command of its Mother; at her Commands I afterwards owned it, and thought myself, by her Generosity, nobly rewarded, both for my Secrecy and my Shame.' 'Who could this Woman be?' said *Allworthy*. 'Indeed I tremble to name her,' answered Mrs. *Waters*. 'By all this Preparation I am to guess that she was a Relation of mine,' cried he. 'Indeed she was a near one.' At which Words *Allworthy* started, and she continued—'You had a Sister, Sir.'—'A Sister!' repeated he, looking aghast.—'As there is Truth in Heaven,' cries she, 'your Sister was the Mother of that Child you found between your Sheets.' 'Can it be possible?' cries he, 'good Heavens!' 'Have Patience, Sir,' said Mrs. *Waters*, 'and I will unfold to you the whole Story. Just after your Departure for *London*, Miss *Bridget* came one Day to the House of my Mother. She was pleased to say she had heard an extraordinary Character of me, for my Learning and superior Understanding to all the young Women there, so she was pleased to say. She then bid me come to her to the great House; where when I attended, she employed me to read to her. She expressed great Satisfaction in my Reading, shewed great Kindness to me, and made me many Presents. At last she began to catechise me on the Subject of Secrecy, to which I gave her such satisfactory Answers, that, at last, having locked the Door of her Room, she took me into her Closet, and then locking that Door likewise, she said, she should convince me of the vast Reliance she had on my Integrity, by communicating a Secret in which her

Honour, and consequently her Life was concerned. She then stopt, and after a Silence of a few Minutes, during which she often wiped her Eyes, she enquired of me, if I thought my Mother might safely be confided in. I answered, I would stake my Life on her Fidelity. She then imparted to me the great Secret which laboured in her Breast, and which, I believe, was delivered with more Pains than she afterwards suffered in Child-birth. It was then contrived, that my Mother and myself only should attend at the Time, and that Mrs. *Wilkins* should be sent out of the Way, as she accordingly was, to the very furthest Part of *Dorsetshire*, to enquire the Character of a Servant; for the Lady had turned away her own Maid near three Months before; during all which Time I officiated about her Person upon Trial, as she said, tho', as she afterwards declared, I was not sufficiently handy for the Place. This, and many other such Things which she used to say of me, were all thrown out to prevent any Suspicion which *Wilkins* might hereafter have, when I was to own the Child; for she thought it could never be believed she would venture to hurt a young Woman with whom she had intrusted such a Secret. You may be assured, Sir, I was well paid for all these Affronts, which, together with being informed with the Occasion of them, very well contented me. Indeed the Lady had a greater Suspicion of Mrs. *Wilkins* than of any other Person; not that she had the least Aversion to the Gentlewoman, but she thought her incapable of keeping a Secret, especially from you, Sir: For I have often heard Miss *Bridget* say, that if Mrs. *Wilkins* had committed a Murder, she believed she would acquaint you with it. At last the expected Day came, and Mrs. *Wilkins*, who had been kept a Week in Readiness, and put off from Time to Time, upon some Pretence or other, that she might not return too soon, was dispatched. Then the Child was born, in the Presence only of myself and my Mother, and was by my Mother conveyed to her own House, where it was privately kept by her till the Evening of your Return, when I, by the Command of Miss *Bridget*, conveyed it into the Bed where you found it. And all Suspicions were afterwards laid asleep by the artful Conduct of your Sister, in pretending Ill-will to the Boy, and that any Regard she shewed him was out of meer Complaisance to you.'

Mrs. *Waters* than made many Protestations of the Truth of this Story, and concluded by saying, 'Thus, Sir, you have at last discovered your Nephew; for so I am sure you will hereafter think him, and I question not but he will be both an Honour and a Comfort to you under that Appellation.'

'I need not, Madam,' said *Allworthy*, 'express my Astonishment at what you have told me; and yet surely you would not, and could not, have put together so many Circumstances to evidence an

Untruth. I confess, I recollect some Passages relating to that *Summer,* which formerly gave me a Conceit, that my Sister had some Liking to him. I mentioned it to her: For I had such a Regard to the young Man, as well on his own Account, as on his Father's, that I should willingly have consented to a Match between them; but she exprest the highest Disdain of my unkind Suspicion, as she called it; so that I never spoke more on the Subject. Good Heavens! Well! the Lord disposeth all Things.—Yet sure it was a most unjustifiable Conduct in my Sister to carry this Secret with her out of the World.' 'I promise you, Sir,' said Mrs. *Waters,* 'she always profest a contrary Intention, and frequently told me, she intended one Day to communicate it to you. She said indeed, she was highly rejoiced that her Plot had succeeded so well, and that you had of your own Accord taken such a Fancy to the Child, that it was yet unnecessary to make any express Declaration. Oh! Sir, had that Lady lived to have seen this poor young Man turned like a Vagabond from your House; nay, Sir, could she have lived to hear that you had yourself employed a Lawyer to prosecute him for a Murder of which he was not guilty.—Forgive me, Mr. *Allworthy,* I must say it was unkind.—Indeed you have been abused, he never deserved it of you.' 'Indeed, Madam,' said *Allworthy,* 'I have been abused by the Person, whoever he was, that told you so.' 'Nay, Sir,' said she, 'I would not be mistaken, I did not presume to say you were guilty of any Wrong. The Gentleman who came to me, proposed no such Matter: He only said, taking me for Mr. *Fitzpatrick's* Wife, that if Mr. *Jones* had murdered my Husband, I should be assisted with any Money I wanted to carry on the Prosecution, by a very worthy Gentleman, who, he said, was well apprized what a Villain I had to deal with. It was by this Man I found out who Mr. *Jones* was; and this Man, whose Name is *Dowling,* Mr. *Jones* tells me, is your Steward. I discovered his Name by a very odd Accident; for he himself refused to tell it me; but *Partridge,* who met him at my Lodgings the second Time he came, knew him formerly at *Salisbury.*'

'And did this Mr. *Dowling,*' says *Allworthy,* with great Astonishment in his Countenance, 'tell you that I would assist in the Prosecution?'—'No, Sir,' answered she, 'I will not charge him wrongfully. He said I should be assisted, but he mentioned no Name.—Yet you must pardon me, Sir, if from Circumstances I thought it could be no other.'——'Indeed, Madam,' says *Allworthy,* 'from Circumstances I am too well convinced it was another.——Good Heaven! by what wonderful Means is the blackest and deepest Villainy sometimes discovered!—Shall I beg you, Madam, to stay till the Person you have mentioned comes; for I expect him every Minute; nay he may be, perhaps, already in the House.'

Allworthy then stept to the Door, in order to call a Servant, when in came, not Mr. *Dowling*, but the Gentleman who will be seen in the next Chapter.

Chapter VIII.

Further Continuation.

The Gentleman who now arrived was no other than Mr. *Western*. He no sooner saw *Allworthy*, than, without considering in the least the Presence of Mrs. *Waters*, he began to vociferate in the following Manner. 'Fine Doings at my House! A rare Kettle of Fish I have discovered at last; who the Devil would be plagued with a Daughter?' 'What's the Matter, Neighbour?' said *Allworthy*. 'Matter enough,' answered *Western*, 'when I thought she was a just coming to; nay, when she had in a Manner promised me to do as I would ha her, and when I was a hoped to have had nothing more to do than to have sent for the Lawyer, and finished all. What do you think I have found out? that the little B— hath bin playing Tricks with me all the while, and carrying on a Correspondence with that Bastard of yours. Sister *Western*, whom I have quarrelled with upon her Account, sent me Word o't, and I ordered her Pockets to be searched when she was asleep, and here I have got un signed with the Son of a Whore's own Name. I have not had Patience to read half o't, for 'tis longer than one of Parson *Supple*'s Sermons; but I find plainly it is all about Love; and indeed what should it be else? I have packed her up in Chamber again, and To-morrow Morning down she goes into the Country, unless she consents to be married directly, and there she shall live in a Garret upon Bread and Water all her Days; and the sooner such a B— breaks her Heart the better, though d—n her, that I believe is too tough. She will live long enough to plague me.' 'Mr. *Western*,' answered *Allworthy*, 'you know I have always protested against Force, and you yourself consented that none should be used.' 'Ay,' cries he, 'that was only upon Condition that she would consent without. What the Devil and Doctor *Faustus*! shan't I do what I will with my own Daughter, especially when I desire nothing but her own Good?' 'Well, Neighbour,' answered *Allworthy*, 'if you will give me Leave, I will undertake once to argue with the young Lady.' 'Will you,' said *Western*, 'why that is kind now and neighbourly, and mayhap you will do more than I have been able to do with her; for I promise you she hath a very good Opinion of you.' 'Well, Sir,' said *Allworthy*, 'if you will go Home, and release the young Lady from her Captivity, I will wait upon her within this half Hour.'—'But suppose,' said *Western*, 'she should run away with un in the mean Time? for

Lawyer *Dowling* tells me, there is no Hopes of hanging the Fellow
at last; for that the Man is alive, and like to do well, and that he
thinks *Jones* will be out of Prison again presently.'——'How,' said
Allworthy, 'what did you employ him then to enquire, or to do any
Thing in that Matter?' 'Not I,' answered *Western*, 'he mentioned it
to me just now of his own Accord.'—'Just now!' cries *Allworthy*,
'why where did you see him then? I want much to see Mr. *Dowling*.'—'Why you may see un an you will presently at my Lodgings;
for there is to be a Meeting of Lawyers there this Morning, about a
Mortgage.—Icod! I shall lose two or dree thousand Pounds, I
believe, by that honest Gentleman, Mr. *Nightingale*.'—'Well, Sir,'
said *Allworthy*, 'I will be with you within the half Hour.' 'And do
for once,' cries the Squire, 'take a Fool's Advice; never think of
dealing with her by gentle Methods, take my Word for it, those
will never do. I have tried um long enough. She must be frightened
into it, there is no other Way. Tell her I'm her Father; and of the
horrid Sin of Disobedience, and of the dreadful Punishment of it in
t'other World, and then tell her about being locked up all her Life
in a Garret in this, and being kept only on Bread and Water.' 'I
will do all I can,' said *Allworthy*; 'for I promise you, there is
nothing I wish for more than an Alliance with this amiable Creature.' 'Nay, the Girl is well enough for Matter o'that,' cries the
Squire, 'a Man may go farther and meet with worse Meat; that I
may declare o' her, thof she be my own Daughter. And if she will
but be obedient to me, there is n'arrow a Father within a hundred
Miles o' the Place, that loves a Daughter better than I do: But I see
you are busy with the Lady here, so I will go Huome and expect
you, and so your humble Servant.'

As soon as Mr. *Western* was gone. Mrs. *Waters* said, 'I see, Sir,
the Squire hath not the least Remembrance of my Face. I believe,
Mr. *Allworthy*, you would not have known me neither. I am very
considerably altered since that Day when you so kindly gave me
that Advice, which I had been happy had I followed.'—'Indeed,
Madam,' cries *Allworthy*, 'it gave me great Concern when I first
heard the contrary.' 'Indeed, Sir,' says she, 'I was ruined by a very
deep Scheme of Villainy, which if you knew, though I pretend not
to think it would justify me in your Opinion, it would at least mitigate my Offence, and induce you to pity me; you are not now at
Leisure to hear my whole Story; but this I assure you, I was
betrayed by the most solemn Promises of Marriage; nay, in the Eye
of Heaven I was married to him: For after much reading on the
Subject, I am convinced that particular Ceremonies are only requisite to give a legal Sanction to Marriage, and have only a worldly Use
in giving a Woman the Privileges of a Wife; but that she who lives
constant to one Man, after a solemn private Affiance, whatever

the World may call her, hath little to charge on her own Conscience.' 'I am sorry, Madam,' said *Allworthy*, 'you made so ill an
Use of your Learning. Indeed it would have been well that you had
been possessed of much more, or had remained in a State of Ignorance. And yet, Madam, I am afraid you have more than this Sin to
answer for.' 'During his Life,' answered she, 'which was above a
Dozen Years, I most solemnly assure you, I had not. And consider,
Sir, on my Behalf, what is in the Power of a Woman stript of her
Reputation, and left destitute; whether the good-natured World
will suffer such a stray Sheep to return to the Road of Virtue, even
if she was never so desirous. I protest then I would have chose it
had it been in my Power; but Necessity drove me into the Arms of
Capt. *Waters*, with whom, though still unmarried, I lived as a Wife
for many Years, and went by his Name. I parted with this Gentleman at *Worcester*, on his March against the Rebels, and it was
then I accidentally met with Mr. *Jones*, who rescued me from the
Hands of a Villain. Indeed he is the worthiest of Men. No young
Gentleman of his Age is, I believe, freer from Vice, and few have
the twentieth Part of his Virtues; nay, whatever Vices he hath had,
I am firmly persuaded he hath now taken a Resolution to abandon
them.' 'I hope he hath,' cries *Allworthy*, 'and I hope he will preserve that Resolution. I must say I have still the same Hopes with
Regard to yourself. The World, I do agree, are apt to be too unmerciful on these Occasions; yet Time and Perseverance will get the
better of this their Disinclination, as I may call it, to Pity; for
though they are not, like Heaven, ready to receive a penitent
Sinner; yet a continued Repentance will at length obtain Mercy
even with the World. This you may be assured of, Mrs. *Waters*,
that whenever I find you are sincere in such good Intentions, you
shall want no Assistance in my Power to make them effectual.'

Mrs. *Waters* fell now upon her Knees before him, and, in a
Flood of Tears, made him many most passionate Acknowledgments
of his Goodness, which, as she truly said, savoured more of the
divine than human Nature.

Allworthy raised her up, and spoke in the most tender Manner,
making Use of every Expression which his Invention could suggest
to comfort her, when he was interrupted by the Arrival of Mr.
Dowling, who, upon his first Entrance, seeing Mrs. *Waters*, started,
and appeared in some Confusion; from which he soon recovered
himself as well as he could, and then said, he was in the utmost
Haste to attend Council at Mr. *Western's* Lodgings; but however,
thought it his Duty to call and acquaint him with the Opinion of
Council, upon the Case which he had before told him, which was,
that the Conversion of the Moneys in that Case could not be questioned in a Criminal Cause, but that an Action of Trover might be

brought, and if it appeared to the Jury to be the Moneys of Plaintiff, that Plaintiff would recover a Verdict for the Value.

Allworthy, without making any Answer to this, bolted the Door, and then advancing with a stern Look to *Dowling*, he said, 'Whatever be your Haste, Sir, I must first receive an Answer to some Questions. Do you know this Lady?'—'That Lady, Sir?' answered *Dowling*, with great Hesitation. *Allworthy* then, with the most solemn Voice, said, 'Look you, Mr. *Dowling*, as you value my Favour, or your Continuance a Moment longer in my Service, do not hesitate nor prevaricate; but answer faithfully and truly to every Question I ask.—Do you know this Lady?'—'Yes, Sir,' said *Dowling*, 'I have seen the Lady.' 'Where, Sir?' 'At her own Lodgings.'——'Upon what Business did you go thither, Sir; and who sent you?' 'I went, Sir, to enquire, Sir, about Mr. *Jones*.' 'And who sent you to enquire about him?' 'Who, Sir; why, Sir, Mr. *Blifil* sent me.' 'And what did you say to the Lady concerning that Matter?' 'Nay, Sir, it is impossible to recollect every Word.' 'Will you please, Madam, to assist the Gentleman's Memory?' 'He told me, Sir,' said Mrs. *Waters*, "that if Mr. *Jones* had murdered my Husband, I should be assisted by any Money I wanted to carry on the Prosecution, by a very worthy Gentleman, who was well apprized what a Villain I had to deal with." These, I can safely swear, were the very Words he spoke.'—'Were these the Words, Sir?' said *Allworthy*. 'I cannot charge my Memory exactly,' cries *Dowling*, 'but I believe I did speak to that Purpose.'——'And did Mr. *Blifil* order you to say so?' 'I am sure, Sir, I should not have gone on my own Accord, nor have willingly exceeded my Authority in Matters of this Kind. If I said so, I must have so understood Mr. *Blifil's* Instructions.' 'Look you, Mr. *Dowling*,' said *Allworthy*, 'I promise you before this Lady, that whatever you have done in this Affair by Mr. *Blifil's* Order, I will forgive; provided you now tell me strictly the Truth: For I believe what you say, that you would not have acted of your own Accord, and without Authority, in this Matter.—Mr. *Blifil* then likewise sent you to examine the two Fellows at *Aldersgate*?'—'He did, Sir.' 'Well, and what Instructions did he then give you? Recollect as well as you can, and tell me, as near as possible, the very Words he used.'——'Why, Sir, Mr. *Blifil* sent me to find out the Persons who were Eye-Witnesses of this Fight. He said, he feared they might be tampered with by Mr. *Jones*, or some of his Friends. He said, Blood required Blood; and that not only all who concealed a Murderer, but those who omitted any Thing in their Power to bring him to Justice, were Sharers in his Guilt. He said, he found you was very desirous of having the Villain brought to Justice, though it was not proper you should appear in it.'—'He did so?' says *Allworthy*.—'Yes, Sir,' cries *Dowling*, 'I should not, I am sure, have proceeded such Lengths for the Sake of any other Person living but your Worship.'—'What Lengths, Sir?' said *Allworthy*.—'Nay, Sir,' cries *Dowling*, 'I would not have your Worship think I would, on any Account, be guilty of Subordination of Perjury; but there are two Ways of delivering Evidence. I told them therefore, that if any Offers should be made them on the other Side, they should refuse them, and that they might be assured they should lose nothing by being honest Men, and telling the Truth. I said, we were told, that Mr. *Jones* had assaulted the Gentleman first, and that if that was the Truth, they should declare it; and I did give them some Hints that they should be no Losers.'—'I think you went Lengths indeed,' cries *Allworthy*.—'Nay, Sir,' answered *Dowling*, 'I am sure I did not desire them to tell an Untruth;—nor should I have said what I did, unless it had been to oblige you.'——'You would not have thought, I believe,' says *Allworthy*, 'to have obliged me, had you known that this Mr. *Jones* was my own Nephew.'—'I am sure, Sir,' answered he, 'it did not become me to take any Notice of what I thought you desired to conceal.'—'How!' cries *Allworthy*, 'and did you know it then?'—'Nay, Sir,' answered *Dowling*, 'if your Worship bids me speak the Truth, I am sure I shall do it.—Indeed, Sir, I did know it; for they were almost the last Words which Madam *Blifil* ever spoke, which she mentioned to me as I stood alone by her Bedside, when she delivered me the Letter I brought your Worship from her.'—'What Letter?' cries *Allworthy*.—'The Letter, Sir,' answered *Dowling*, 'which I brought from *Salisbury*, and which I delivered into the Hands of Mr. *Blifil*.—'O Heavens!' cries *Allworthy*, 'Well, and what were the Words? What did my Sister say to you?'—'She took me by the Hand,' answered he, 'and as she delivered me the Letter, said, "I scarce know what I have written. Tell my Brother, Mr. *Jones* is his Nephew—He is my Son.——Bless him," says she, and then fell backward, as if dying away. I presently called in the People, and she never spoke more to me, and died within a few Minutes afterwards.'—*Allworthy* stood a Minute silent, lifting up his Eyes, and then turning to *Dowling*, said,— 'How came you, Sir, not to deliver me this Message?' 'Your Worship,' answered he, 'must remember that you was at that Time ill in Bed; and being in a violent Hurry, as indeed I always am, I delivered the Letter and Message to Mr. *Blifil*, who told me he would carry them both to you, which he hath since told me he did, and that your Worship, partly out of Friendship to Mr. *Jones*, and partly out of Regard to your Sister, would never have it mentioned; and did intend to conceal it from the World; and therefore, Sir, if you had not mentioned it to me first, I am certain I should never have thought it belonged to me to say any Thing of the Matter, either to your Worship, or any other Person.'

We have remarked somewhere already, that it is possible for a Man to convey a Lie in the Words of Truth; this was the Case at present: For *Blifil* had, in Fact, told *Dowling* what he now related; but had not imposed upon him, nor indeed had imagined he was able so to do. In Reality, the Promises which *Blifil* had made to *Dowling*, were the Motives which had induced him to Secrecy; and as he now very plainly saw *Blifil* would not be able to keep them, he thought proper now to make his Confession, which the Promises of Forgiveness, joined to the Threats, the Voice, the Looks of *Allworthy*, and the Discoveries he had made before, extorted from him, who was besides taken unawares, and had no Time to consider of Evasions.

Allworthy appeared well satisfied with this Relation, and having enjoined on *Dowling* strict Silence as to what had past, conducted that Gentleman himself to the Door, lest he should see *Blifil*, who was returned to his Chamber, where he exulted in the Thoughts of his last Deceit on his Uncle, and little suspected what had since passed below Stairs.

As *Allworthy* was returning to his Room, he met Mrs. *Miller* in the Entry, who, with a Face all pale and full of Terror, said to him, 'O! Sir, I find this wicked Woman hath been with you, and you know all; yet do not on this Account abandon the poor young Man. Consider, Sir, he was ignorant it was his own·Mother; and the Discovery itself will most probably break his Heart, without your Unkindness.'

'Madam,' says *Allworthy*, 'I am under such an Astonishment at what I have heard, that I am really unable to satisfy you; but come with me into my Room. Indeed, Mrs. *Miller*, I have made surprizing Discoveries, and you shall soon know them.'

The poor Woman followed him trembling; and now *Allworthy* going up to Mrs. *Waters*, took her by the Hand, and then turning to Mrs. *Miller* said, 'What Reward shall I bestow upon this Gentlewoman for the Services she hath done me?—O! Mrs. *Miller*, you have a thousand Times heard me call the young Man to whom you are so faithful a Friend, my Son. Little did I then think he was indeed related to me at all.—Your Friend, Madam, is my Nephew; he is the Brother of that wicked Viper which I have so long nourished in my Bosom.—She will herself tell you the whole Story, and how the Youth came to pass for her Son. Indeed, Mrs. *Miller*, I am convinced that he hath been wronged, and that I have been abused; abused by one whom you too justly suspected of being a Villain. He is, in Truth, the worst of Villains.'

The Joy which Mrs. *Miller* now felt, bereft her of the Power of Speech, and might perhaps have deprived her of her Senses, if not of Life, had not a friendly Shower of Tears come seasonably to her

Relief. At length recovering so far from her Transport as to be able
to speak, she cried: 'And is my dear Mr. *Jones* then your Nephew,
Sir? and not the Son of this Lady? and are your Eyes opened to
him at last? and shall I live to see him as happy as he deserves?' 'He
certainly is my Nephew,' says *Allworthy*, 'and I hope all the rest.'
—'And is this the dear good Woman, the Person,' cries she, 'to
whom all this Discovery is owing!'—'She is indeed,' says *Allworthy*.
—'Why then,' cried Mrs. *Miller*, upon her Knees, 'may Heaven
shower down its choicest Blessings upon her Head, and for this one
good Action forgive her all her Sins, be they never so many.'

Mrs. *Waters* then informed them, that she believed *Jones* would
very shortly be released; for that the Surgeon was gone, in Company
with a Nobleman, to the Justice who committed him, in order to
certify that Mr. *Fitzpatrick* was out of all Manner of Danger, and
to procure his Prisoner his Liberty.

Allworthy said, he should be glad to find his Nephew there at his
Return home; but that he was then obliged to go on some Business
of Consequence. He then called to a Servant to fetch him a Chair,
and presently left the two Ladies together.

Mr. *Blifil* hearing the Chair ordered, came down Stairs to attend
upon his Uncle; for he never was deficient in such Acts of Duty. He
asked his Uncle if he was going out? which is a civil Way of asking
a Man whither he is going: To which the other making no Answer,
he again desired to know, when he would be pleased to return?—
Allworthy made no Answer to this neither, till he was just going
into his Chair, and then turning about, he said.—'Harkee, Sir, do
you find out, before my Return, the Letter which your Mother sent
me on her Death-bed.' *Allworthy* then departed, and left *Blifil* in a
Situation to be envied only by a Man who is just going to be
hanged.

Chapter IX.

A further Continuation.

Allworthy took an Opportunity whilst he was in the Chair, of
reading the Letter from *Jones* to *Sophia*, which *Western* delivered
him; and there were some Expressions in it concerning himself,
which drew Tears from his Eyes. At length he arrived at Mr. *Western's*, and was introduced to *Sophia*.

When the first Ceremonies were past, and the Gentleman and
Lady had taken their Chairs, a Silence of some Minutes ensued;
during which, the latter, who had been prepared for the Visit by
her Father, sat playing with her Fan, and had every Mark of Confusion both in her Countenance and Behaviour. At length *Allworthy*,

who was himself a little disconcerted, began thus; 'I am afraid, Miss *Western*, my Family hath been the Occasion of giving you some Uneasiness! to which, I fear I have innocently become more instrumental than I intended. Be assured, Madam, had I at first known how disagreeable the Proposals had been, I should not have suffered you to have been so long persecuted. I hope therefore you will not think the Design of this Visit is to trouble you with any further Solicitations of that kind, but entirely to relieve you from them.'

'Sir,' said *Sophia*, with a little modest Hesitation, 'this Behaviour is most kind and generous, and such as I could expect only from Mr. *Allworthy*: But as you have been so kind to mention this Matter, you will pardon me for saying it hath indeed given me great Uneasiness, and hath been the Occasion of my suffering much cruel Treatment from a Father, who was, 'till that unhappy Affair, the tenderest and fondest of all Parents. I am convinced, Sir, you are too good and generous to resent my Refusal of your Nephew. Our Inclinations are not in our own Power; and whatever may be his Merit, I cannot force them in his Favour.' 'I assure you, most amiable young Lady,' said *Allworthy*, 'I am capable of no such Resentment, had the Person been my own Son, and had I entertained the highest Esteem for him. For you say truly, Madam, we cannot force our Inclinations, much less can they be directed by another.' 'Oh! Sir,' answered *Sophia*, 'every Word you speak proves you to deserve that good, that great, that benevolent Character the whole World allows you. I assure you, Sir, nothing less than the certain Prospect of future Misery could have made me resist the Commands of my Father.' 'I sincerely believe you, Madam,' replied *Allworthy*, 'and I heartily congratulate you on your prudent Foresight, since by so justifiable a Resistance you have avoided Misery indeed.' 'You speak now, Mr. *Allworthy*,' cries she, 'with a Delicacy which few Men are capable of feeling; but surely in my Opinion, to lead our Lives with one to whom we are indifferent, must be a State of Wretchedness —Perhaps that Wretchedness would be even increased by a Sense of the Merits of an Object to whom we cannot give our Affections. If I had married Mr. *Blifil*.—'Pardon my interrupting you, Madam,' answered *Allworthy*, 'but I cannot bear the Supposition.—Believe me, Miss *Western*, I rejoice from my Heart, I rejoice in your Escape.—I have discovered the Wretch, for whom you have suffered all this cruel Violence from your Father, to be a Villain.' 'How, Sir!' cries *Sophia*,—'you must believe this surprizes me.'—'It hath surprized me, Madam,' answered *Allworthy*, 'and so it will the World.—But I have acquainted you with the real Truth.' 'Nothing but Truth,' says *Sophia*, 'can, I am convinced, come from the Lips of Mr. *Allworthy*.—Yet, Sir, such sudden, such unexpected News —Discovered, you say—may Villainy be ever so.'—'You will soon enough hear the Story,' cries *Allworthy*,—'at present let us not mention so detested a Name—I have another Matter of a very serious Nature to propose.—O! Miss *Western*, I know your vast Worth, nor can I so easily part with the Ambition of being allied to it.—I have a near Relation, Madam, a young Man whose Character is, I am convinced, the very opposite to that of this Wretch, and whose Fortune I will make equal to what his was to have been.— Could I, Madam, hope you would admit a Visit from him?' *Sophia*, after a Minutes Silence, answered, 'I will deal with the utmost Sincerity with Mr. *Allworthy*. His Character and the Obligation I have just received from him, demand it. I have determined at present to listen to no such Proposals from any Person. My only Desire is to be restored to the Affection of my Father, and to be again the Mistress of his Family. This, Sir, I hope to owe to your good Offices. Let me beseech you, let me conjure you by all the Goodness which I, and all who know you, have experienced; do not the very Moment when you have released me from one Persecution, do not engage me in another, as miserable and as fruitless.' 'Indeed, Miss *Western*,' replied *Allworthy*, 'I am capable of no such Conduct; and if this be your Resolution, he must submit to the Disappointment, whatever Torments he may suffer under it.' 'I must smile now, Mr. *Allworthy*,' answered *Sophia*, 'when you mention the Torments of a Man whom I do not know, and who can consequently have so little Acquaintance with me.' 'Pardon me, dear young Lady,' cries *Allworthy*, 'I begin now to be afraid he hath had too much Acquaintance for the Repose of his future Days; since, if ever Man was capable of a sincere, violent and noble Passion, such, I am convinced, is my unhappy Nephew's for Miss *Western*.' 'A Nephew of yours! Mr. *Allworthy*,' answered *Sophia*. 'It is surely strange, I never heard of him before.' 'Indeed! Madam,' cries *Allworthy*, 'it is only the Circumstance of his being my Nephew to which you are a Stranger, and which, 'till this Day, was a Secret to me.—Mr. *Jones*, who has long loved you, he! he is my Nephew.' 'Mr. *Jones* your Nephew, Sir?' cries *Sophia*, 'Can it be possible?'—'He is indeed, Madam,' answered *Allworthy*: 'He is my own Sister's Son—— as such I shall always own him; nor am I ashamed of owning him. I am much more ashamed of my past Behaviour to him; but I was as ignorant of his Merit as of his Birth. Indeed, Miss *Western*, I have used him cruelly—Indeed I have.—Here the good Man wiped his Eyes, and after a short Pause proceeded—'I never shall be able to reward him for his Sufferings without your Assistance.— Believe me, most amiable young Lady, I must have a great Esteem of that Offering which I make to your Worth. I know he hath been guilty of Faults; but there is great Goodness of Heart at the Bottom. Believe me, Madam, there is.'—Here he stopped, seeming to expect an Answer, which he presently received from Sophia, after she had a little recovered herself from the Hurry of Spirits into which so strange and sudden Information had thrown her: 'I sincerely wish you Joy, Sir, of a Discovery in which you seem to have such Satisfaction. I doubt not but you will have all the Comfort you can promise yourself from it. The young Gentleman hath certainly a thousand good Qualities, which makes it impossible he should not behave well to such an Uncle.'—'I hope, Madam,' said *Allworthy*, ' he hath those good Qualities which must make him a good Husband.—He must, I am sure, be of all Men the most abandoned, if a Lady of your Merit should condescend'—'You must pardon me, Mr. *Allworthy*,' answered *Sophia*, 'I cannot listen to a Proposal of this Kind. Mr. *Jones*, I am convinced, hath much Merit; but I shall never receive Mr. *Jones* as one who is to be my Husband——Upon my Honour I never will.—'Pardon me, Madam,' cries *Allworthy*, 'if I am a little surprized, after what I have heard from Mr. *Western*——I hope the unhappy young Man hath done nothing to forfeit your good Opinion, if he had ever the Honour to enjoy it.—Perhaps he may have been misrepresented to you, as he was to me. The same Villainy may have injured him every where.—He is no Murderer, I assure you, as he hath been called.'—'Mr. *Allworthy*,' answered *Sophia*, 'I have told you my Resolution. I wonder not at what my Father hath told you; but whatever his Apprehensions or Fears have been, if I know my Heart, I have given no Occasion for them; since it hath always been a fixed Principle with me, never to have marry'd without his Consent. This is, I think, the Duty of a Child to a Parent; and this, I hope, nothing could ever have prevailed with me to swerve from. I do not indeed conceive, that the Authority of any Parent can oblige us to marry, in direct Opposition to our Inclinations. To avoid a Force of this Kind, which I had reason to suspect, I left my Father's House, and sought Protection elsewhere. This is the Truth of my Story; and if the World, or my Father, carry my Intentions any farther, my own Conscience will acquit me.' 'I hear you, Miss *Western*,' cries *Allworthy*, with Admiration. 'I admire the Justness of your Sentiments; but surely there is more in this. I am cautious of offending you, young Lady; but am I to look on all which I have hitherto heard or seen, as a Dream only? And have you suffered so much Cruelty from your Father on the Account of a Man to whom you have been always absolutely indifferent?' 'I beg, Mr. *Allworthy*,' answered *Sophia*, 'you will not insist on my Reasons;—Yes, I have suffered indeed: I will not, Mr. *Allworthy*, conceal—I will be very sincere with you—I own I had a great Opinion of Mr. *Jones*—I believe—I know I have suffered for my Opinion—I have been treated cruelly by my Aunt, as well as by my Father; but that is now past—I beg I may not be farther press'd; for whatever hath been, my Resolution is now fixed. Your Nephew, Sir, hath many Virtues—he hath great Virtues, Mr. *Allworthy*. I question not but he will do you Honour in the World, and make you happy.'—'I wish I could make him so, Madam,' replied *Allworthy*; 'but that I am convinced is only in your Power. It is that Conviction which hath made me so earnest a Solicitor in his Favour.' 'You are deceived; indeed, Sir, you are deceived,' said *Sophia*—'I hope not by him—It is sufficient to have deceived me. Mr. *Allworthy*, I must insist on being prest no farther on this Subject.—I should be sorry —Nay, I will not injure him in your Favour. I wish Mr. *Jones* very well. I sincerely wish him well; and I repeat it again to you, whatever Demerit he may have to me, I am certain he hath many good Qualities. I do not disown my former Thoughts; but nothing can ever recall them. At present there is not a Man upon Earth whom I would more resolutely reject than Mr. *Jones*; nor would the Addresses of Mr. *Blifil* himself be less agreeable to me.'

Western had been long impatient for the Event of this Conference, and was just now arrived at the Door to listen; when having heard the last Sentiments of his Daughter's Heart, he lost all Temper, and bursting open the Door in a Rage, cried out.—'It is a Lie. It is a d—n'd Lie. It is all owing to that d—d'd Rascal *Juones*; and if she could get at un, she'd ha un any Hour of the Day.' Here *Allworthy* interposed, and addressing himself to the Squire with some Anger in his Look, he said, 'Mr. *Western*, you have not kept your Word with me. You promised to abstain from all Violence.' —'Why so I did,' cries *Western*, 'as long as it was possible; but to hear a Wench telling such confounded Lies.—Zounds! Doth she think if she can make Vools of other Volk, she can make one of me?—No, no, I know her better than thee dost.' 'I am sorry to tell you, Sir,' answered *Allworthy*, 'it doth not appear by your Behaviour to this young Lady, that you know her at all. I ask Pardon for what I say; but I think our Intimacy, your own Desires, and the Occasion justify me. She is your Daughter, Mr. *Western*, and I think she doth Honour to your Name. If I was capable of Envy, I should sooner envy you on this Account, than any other Man whatever.'— 'Odrabbit it,' cries the Squire, 'I wish she was thine with all my Heart—wouldst soon be glad to be rid of the Trouble o' her.'—'Indeed, my good Friend,' answered *Allworthy*, 'you yourself are the Cause of all the Trouble you complain of. Place that Confidence in the young Lady which she so well deserves, and I am certain you will be the happiest Father on Earth.'—'I Confidence in her!' cries the Squire.—' 'Sblood! what Confidence can I place in her, when she won't do as I wou'd ha her? Let her gi but her Consent to marry as I would ha her, and I'll place as much Confidence in her as wouldst ha me.'—'You have[1] no Right, Neighbour,' answered *All-worthy*, 'to insist on any such Consent. A negative Voice your Daughter allows you, and God and Nature have thought proper to allow you no more.' 'A negative Voice?' cries the Squire—Ay! ay! I'll shew you what a negative Voice I ha.——Go along, go into your Chamber, go, you Stubborn.'—'Indeed, Mr. *Western*,' said *Allworthy*,—'Indeed, you use her cruelly—I cannot bear to see this —You shall, you must behave to her in a kinder Manner. She deserves the best of Treatment.' 'Yes, yes,' said the Squire, 'I know what she deserves: Now she's gone, I'll shew you what she deserves ——See here, Sir, here is a Letter from my Cousin, my Lady *Bellaston*, in which she is so kind to gi me to understand, that the Fellow is got out of Prison again; and here she advises me to take all the Care I can o' the Wench. Odzookers! Neighbour *Allworthy*, you don't know what it is to govern a Daughter.'

The Squire ended his Speech with some Compliments to his own Sagacity; and then *Allworthy*, after a formal Preface, acquainted him with the whole Discovery which he had made concerning *Jones*, with his Anger to *Blifil*, and with every Particular which hath been disclosed to the Reader in the preceding Chapters.

Men over-violent in their Dispositions, are, for the most Part, as changeable in them. No sooner then was *Western* informed of Mr. *Allworthy*'s Intention to make *Jones* his Heir, than he joined heartily with the Uncle in every Commendation of the Nephew, and became as eager for her Marriage with *Jones*, as he had before been to couple her to *Blifil*.

Here Mr. *Allworthy* was again forced to interpose, and to relate what had passed between him and *Sophia*, at which he testified great Surprize.

The Squire was silent a Moment, and looked wild with Astonishment at this Account——At last he cried out, 'Why what can be the Meaning of this, Neighbour *Allworthy*? Vond o un she was, that I'll be sworn to.—Odzookers! I have hit o't. As sure as a Gun I have hit o the very right o't. It's all along o Zister. The Girl hath got a Hankering after this Son of a Whore of a Lord. I vound 'em together at my Cousin, my Lady *Bellaston*'s. He hath turned the Head o' her that's certain—but d—n me if he shall ha her—I'll ha no Lords nor Courtiers in my Vamily.'

Allworthy now made a long Speech, in which he repeated his Resolution to avoid all violent Measures, and very earnestly recommended gentle Methods to Mr. *Western*, as those by which he might be assured of succeeding best with his Daughter. He then took his Leave, and returned back to Mrs. *Miller*, but was forced to

---

1. The fourth edition reads "ha," in a typographical transfer from Western's preceding speech.

comply with the earnest Entreaties of the Squire, in promising to bring Mr. *Jones* to visit him that Afternoon, that he might, as he said, 'make all Matters up with the young Gentleman.' At Mr. *Allworthy*'s Departure, *Western* promised to follow his Advice in his Behaviour to *Sophia*, saying, 'I don't know how 'tis, but d—n me, *Allworthy*, if you don't make me always do just as you please; and yet I have as good an Esteate as you, and am in the Commission of the Peace as well as yourself.'

Chapter X.

Wherein the History begins to draw towards a Conclusion.

When *Allworthy* returned to his Lodgings, he heard Mr. *Jones* was just arrived before him. He hurried therefore instantly into an empty Chamber, whither he ordered Mr. *Jones* to be brought to him alone.

It is impossible to conceive a more tender or moving Scene, than the Meeting between the Uncle and Nephew, (for Mrs. *Waters*, as the Reader may well suppose, had at her last Visit discovered to him the Secret of his Birth.) The first Agonies of Joy which were felt on both Sides, are indeed beyond my Power to describe: I shall not therefore attempt it. After *Allworthy* had raised *Jones* from his Feet, where he had prostrated himself, and received him into his Arms, 'O my Child,' he cried, 'how have I been to blame! How have I injured you! What Amends can I ever make you for those unkind, those unjust Suspicions which I have entertained; and for all the Sufferings they have occasioned to you?' 'Am I not now made Amends?' cries *Jones*, 'Would not my Sufferings, if they had been ten Times greater, have been now richly repaid? O my dear Uncle! this Goodness, this Tenderness overpowers, unmans, destroys me. I cannot bear the Transports which flow so fast upon me. To be again restored to your Presence, to your Favour; to be once more thus kindly received by my great, my noble, my generous Benefactor'——'Indeed, Child,' cries *Allworthy*, 'I have used you cruelly.'——He then explained to him all the Treachery of *Blifil*, and again repeated Expressions of the utmost Concern, for having been induced by that Treachery to use him so ill. 'O talk not so,' answered *Jones*; 'Indeed, Sir, you have used me nobly. The wisest Man might be deceived as you were, and, under such a Deception, the best must have acted just as you did. Your Goodness displayed itself in the Midst of your Anger, just as it then seemed. I owe every Thing to that Goodness of which I have been most unworthy. Do not put me on Self-accusation, by carrying your generous Sentiments too far. Alas, Sir, I have not been punished more than I have deserved; and it shall be the whole Business of my future Life to deserve that Happiness you now bestow on me; for believe me, my dear Uncle, my Punishment hath not been thrown away upon me: Though I have been a great, I am not a hardened Sinner; I thank Heaven I have had Time to reflect on my past Life, where, though I cannot charge myself with any gross Villainy, yet I can discern Follies and Vices more than enough to repent and to be ashamed of; Follies which have been attended with dreadful Consequences to myself, and have brought me to the Brink of Destruction.' 'I am rejoiced, my dear Child,' answered *Allworthy*, 'to hear you talk thus sensibly; for as I am convinced Hypocrisy (good Heaven how have I been imposed on by it in others!) was never among your Faults; so I can readily believe all you say. You now see, *Tom*, to what Dangers Imprudence alone may subject Virtue (for Virtue, I am now convinced, you love in a great Degree.) Prudence is indeed the Duty which we owe to ourselves; and if we will be so much our own Enemies as to neglect it, we are not to wonder if the World is deficient in discharging their Duty to us; for when a Man lays the Foundation of his own Ruin, others will, I am afraid, be too apt to build upon it. You say, however, you have seen your Errors; and will reform them. I firmly believe you, my dear Child; and therefore, from this Moment you shall never be reminded of them by me. Remember them only yourself so far, as for the future to teach you the better to avoid them; but still remember, for your Comfort, that there is this great Difference between those Faults which Candor may construe into Imprudence, and those which can be deduced from Villainy only. The former, perhaps, are even more apt to subject a Man to Ruin; but if he reform, his Character will, at length, be totally retrieved; the World, though not immediately, will, in Time, be reconciled to him; and he may reflect, not without some Mixture of Pleasure, on the Dangers he hath escaped: But Villainy, my Boy, when once discovered, is irretrievable; the Stains which this leaves behind, no Time will wash away. The Censures of Mankind will pursue the Wretch, their Scorn will abash him in Publick; and if Shame drives him into Retirement, he will go to it with all those Terrors with which a weary Child, who is afraid of Hobgoblins, retreats from Company to go to Bed alone. Here his murdered Conscience will haunt him. Repose, like a false Friend, will fly from him. Where-ever he turns his Eyes, Horror presents itself; if he looks backward, unavailable Repentance treads on his Heels; if forward, incurable Despair stares him in the Face; till, like a condemned Prisoner confined in a Dungeon, he detests his present Condition, and yet dreads the Consequence of that Hour which is to relieve him from it. Comfort yourself, I say, my Child, that this is not your Case; and rejoice, with Thankfulness to him

who hath suffered you to see your Errors, before they have brought
on you that Destruction, to which a Persistance in even those Errors
must have led you. You have deserted them; and the Prospect now
before you is such, that Happiness seems in your own Power.'—At
these words *Jones* fetched a deep Sigh; upon which, when *Allworthy* remonstrated, he said, 'Sir, I will conceal nothing from you: I
fear there is one Consequence of my Vices I shall never be able to
retrieve. O my dear Uncle, I have lost a Treasure'—'You need say
no more,' answered *Allworthy*; 'I will be explicit with you; I know
what you lament; I have seen the young Lady, and have discoursed
with her concerning you. This I must insist on, as an Earnest of
your Sincerity in all you have said, and of the Stedfastness of your
Resolution, that you obey me in one Instance. To abide intirely by
the Determination of the young Lady, whether it shall be in your
Favour, or no. She hath already suffered enough from Sollicitations
which I hate to think of; she shall owe no further Constraint to my
Family: I know her Father will be as ready to torment her now on
your Account, as he hath formerly been on another's; but I am
determined she shall suffer no more Confinement, no more Violence, no more uneasy Hours.'—'O my dear Uncle,' answered *Jones*,
'lay, I beseech you, some Command on me, in which I shall have
some Merit in Obedience. Believe me, Sir, the only Instance in
which I could disobey you, would be to give an uneasy Moment to
my *Sophia*.[1] No, Sir, if I am so miserable to have incurred her Displeasure beyond all Hope of Forgiveness, that alone, with the
dreadful Reflection of causing her Misery, will be sufficient to over-
power me. To call *Sophia* mine is the greatest, and now the only
additional Blessing which Heaven can bestow; but it is a Blessing
which I must owe to her alone.' 'I will not flatter you, Child,' cries
Allworthy; 'I fear your Case is desperate: I never saw stronger
Marks of an unalterable Resolution in any Person, than appeared in
her vehement Declarations against receiving your Addresses; for
which, perhaps, you can account better than myself.'—'Oh, Sir! I
can account too well,' answered *Jones*; 'I have sinned against her
beyond all Hope of Pardon; and guilty as I am, my Guilt unfortunately appears to her in ten Times blacker than the real Colours. O
my dear Uncle, I find my Follies are irretrievable; and all your
Goodness cannot save me from Perdition.'

A Servant now acquainted them, that Mr. *Western* was below
Stairs; for his Eagerness to see *Jones* could not wait till the After-
noon. Upon which *Jones*, whose Eyes were full of Tears, begged his
Uncle to entertain *Western* a few Minutes, till he a little recovered
himself: To which the good Man consented, and having ordered
Mr. *Western* to be shewn into a Parlour, went down to him.

1. I am grateful to Eleanor Hutchens for
pointing out, among several other helpful
points, that *Instance* here means "command," not "case," as I had thought.

Mrs. *Miller* no sooner heard that *Jones* was alone, (for she had not seen him since his Release from Prison,) than she came eagerly into the Room, and advancing towards *Jones*, wished him heartily Joy of his new-found Uncle, and his happy Reconciliation; adding, 'I wish I could give you Joy on another Account, my dear Child; but any thing so inexorable I never saw.' *Jones*, with some Appearance of Surprize, asked her what she meant. 'Why then,' says she, 'I have been with your young Lady, and have explained all Matters to her, as they were told me by my Son *Nightingale*. She can have no longer any Doubt about the Letter; of that I am certain; for I told her my Son *Nightingale* was ready to take his Oath, if she pleased, that it was all his own Invention, and the Letter of his inditing. I told her the very Reason of sending the Letter ought to recommend you to her the more, as it was all upon her Account, and a plain Proof, that you was resolved to quit all your Profligacy for the future; that you had never been guilty of a single Instance of Infidelity to her since your seeing her in Town. I am afraid I went too far there; but Heaven forgive me: I hope your future Behaviour will be my Justification. I am sure I have said all I can; but all to no Purpose. She remains inflexible. She says, she had forgiven many Faults on account of Youth; but expressed such Detestation of the Character of a Libertine, that she absolutely silenced me. I often attempted to excuse you; but the Justness of her Accusation flew in my Face. Upon my Honour, she is a lovely Woman, and one of the sweetest and most sensible Creatures I ever saw. I could have almost kissed her for one Expression she made use of. It was a Sentiment worthy of *Seneca*, or of a Bishop.' "I once fancied, Madam," said she, "I had discovered great Goodness of Heart in Mr. *Jones*; and for that I own I had a sincere Esteem: but an entire Profligacy of Manners will corrupt the best Heart in the World; and all which a good natured Libertine can expect, is, that we should mix some Grains of Pity with our Contempt and Abhorrence." She is an angelic Creature, that is the Truth on't.'—'O Mrs. *Miller*,' answered *Jones*, 'can I bear to think I have lost such an Angel!' 'Lost! No,' cries Mrs. *Miller*; 'I hope you have not lost her yet. Resolve to leave such vicious Courses, and you may yet have Hopes: Nay, if she should remain inexorable, there is another young Lady, a sweet pretty young Lady, and a swinging Fortune, who is absolutely dying for Love of you. I heard of it this very Morning, and I told it to Miss *Western*; nay, I went a little beyond the Truth again; for I told her you had refused her; but indeed I knew you would refuse her.——And here I must give you a little Comfort: When I mentioned the young Lady's Name, who is no other than the pretty Widow *Hunt*, I thought she turned pale; but when I said you had refused her, I will be sworn her Face was all over Scarlet in an Instant; and these were her very Words, "I will not deny but that I believe he has some Affection for me."

Here the Conversation was interrupted by the Arrival of *Western*, who could no longer be kept out of the Room even by the Authority of *Allworthy* himself; though this, as we have often seen, had a wonderful Power over him.

Western immediately went up to *Jones*, crying out, 'My old Friend *Tom*, I am glad to see thee with all my Heart. All past must be forgotten. I could not intend any Affront to thee, because, as *Allworthy* here knows, nay, dost know it thyself, I took thee for another Person; and where a Body means no Harm, what signifies a hasty Word or two? one Christian must forget and forgive another.' 'I hope, Sir,' said *Jones*, 'I shall never forget the many Obligations I have had to you; but as for any Offence towards me, I declare I am an utter Stranger.'——'A't,' says *Western*, 'then give me thy Fist, a't as hearty an honest Cock as any in the Kingdom. Come along with me; I'll carry thee to thy Mistress this Moment.' Here *Allworthy* interposed; and the Squire being unable to prevail either with the Uncle or Nephew, was, after some Litigation, obliged to consent to delay introducing *Jones* to *Sophia* till the Afternoon; at which Time *Allworthy*, as well in Compassion to *Jones*, as in Compliance with the eager Desires of *Western*, was prevailed upon to promise to attend at the Tea-table.

The Conversation which now ensued was pleasant enough; and with which, had it happened earlier in our History, we would have entertained our Reader; but as we have now Leisure only to attend to what is very material, it shall suffice to say, that Matters being entirely adjusted as to the Afternoon-visit, Mr. *Western* again returned home.

Chapter XI.

The History draws nearer to a Conclusion.

When Mr. *Western* was departed, *Jones* began to inform Mr. *Allworthy* and Mrs. *Miller*, that his Liberty had been procured by two noble Lords, who, together with two Surgeons, and a Friend of Mr. *Nightingale*'s had attended the Magistrate by whom he had been committed, and by whom, on the Surgeons Oaths, that the wounded Person was out of all Manner of Danger from his Wound, he was discharged.

One only of these Lords, he said, he had ever seen before, and that no more than once; but the other had greatly surprized him, by asking his Pardon for an Offence he had been guilty of towards him, occasioned, he said, entirely by his Ignorance who he was.

Now the Reality of the Case with which *Jones* was not acquainted till afterwards, was this. The Lieutenant whom Lord *Fellamar* had employed, according to the Advice of Lady *Bellaston*, to press *Jones*, as a Vagabond, into the Sea Service, when he came to report to his Lordship the Event which we have before seen, spoke very favourably of the Behaviour of Mr. *Jones* on all Accounts, and strongly assured that Lord, that he must have mistaken the Person; for that *Jones* was certainly a Gentleman: insomuch that his Lordship, who was strictly a Man of Honour, and would by no Means have been guilty of an Action which the World in general would have condemned, began to be much concerned for the Advice which he had taken.

Within a Day or two after this, Lord *Fellamar* happened to dine with the *Irish* Peer, who, in a Conversation upon the Duel, acquainted his Company with the Character of *Fitzpatrick*; to which indeed he did not do strict Justice, especially in what related to his Lady. He said, she was the most innocent, the most injured Woman alive, and that from Compassion alone he had undertaken her Cause. He then declared an Intention of going the next Morning to *Fitzpatrick*'s Lodgings, in order to prevail with him, if possible, to consent to a Separation from his Wife, who, the Peer said, was in Apprehensions for her Life, if she should ever return to be under the Power of her Husband. Lord *Fellamar* agreed to go with him, that he might satisfy himself more concerning *Jones*, and the Circumstances of the Duel; for he was by no Means easy concerning the Part he had acted. The Moment his Lordship gave a Hint of his Readiness to assist in the Delivery of the Lady, it was eagerly embraced by the other Nobleman, who depended much on the Authority of Lord *Fellamar*, as he thought it would greatly contribute to awe *Fitzpatrick* into a Compliance; and perhaps he was in the right; for the poor *Irishman* no sooner saw these noble Peers had undertaken the Cause of his Wife, than he submitted, and Articles of Separation were soon drawn up, and signed between the Parties.

Fitzpatrick had been so well satisfied by Mrs. *Waters* concerning the Innocence of his Wife with *Jones* at *Upton*, or perhaps from some other Reasons, was now become so indifferent to that Matter, that he spoke highly in Favour of *Jones*, to Lord *Fellamar*, took all the Blame upon himself, and said the other had behaved very much like a Gentleman, and a Man of Honour; and upon that Lord's further Enquiry concerning Mr. *Jones*, *Fitzpatrick* told him he was Nephew to a Gentleman of very great Fashion and Fortune, which was the Account he had just received from Mrs. *Waters*, after her Interview with *Dowling*.

Lord *Fellamar* now thought it behoved him to do every Thing in his Power to make Satisfaction to a Gentleman whom he had so grosly injured, and without any Consideration of Rivalship, (for he had now given over all Thoughts of *Sophia*) determined to procure Mr. *Jones*'s Liberty, being satisfied as well from *Fitzpatrick* as his Surgeon, that the Wound was not mortal. He therefore prevailed with the *Irish* Peer to accompany him to the Place where *Jones* was confined, to whom he behaved as we have already related.

When *Allworthy* returned to his Lodgings, he immediately carried *Jones* into his Room, and then acquainted him with the whole Matter, as well what he had heard from Mrs. *Waters*, as what he had discovered from Mr. *Dowling*.

Jones expressed great Astonishment, and no less Concern at this Account; but without making any Comment or Observation upon it. And now a Message was brought from Mr. *Blifil*, desiring to know if his Uncle was at Leisure, that he might wait upon him. *Allworthy* started and turned pale, and then in a more passionate Tone than I believe he had ever used before, bid the Servant tell *Blifil*, he knew him not. 'Consider, dear Sir,'—cries *Jones*, in a trembling Voice.——'I have considered,' answered *Allworthy*, 'and you yourself shall carry my Message to the Villain.—No one can carry him the Sentence of his own Ruin so properly, as the Man whose Ruin he hath so villainously contrived.'——'Pardon me, dear Sir,' said *Jones*; 'a Moment's Reflection will, I am sure, convince you of the contrary. What might perhaps be but Justice from another Tongue would from mine be Insult? and to whom?—My own Brother, and your Nephew.—Nor did he use me so barbarously.—Indeed that would have been more inexcusable than any Thing he hath done. Fortune may tempt Men of no very bad Dispositions to Injustice; but Insults proceed only from black and rancorous Minds, and have no Temptations to excuse them.—Let me beseech you, Sir, to do nothing by him in the present Height of your Anger. Consider, my dear Uncle, I was not myself condemned unheard.' *Allworthy* stood silent a Moment, and then embracing *Jones*, he said with Tears gushing from his Eyes, 'O my Child! to what Goodness have I been so long blind!'

Mrs. *Miller* entring the Room at that Moment, after a gentle Rap, which was not perceived, and seeing *Jones* in the Arms of his Uncle, the poor Woman, in an Agony of Joy, fell upon her Knees, and burst forth into the most ecstatic Thanksgivings to Heaven, for what had happened.—Then running to *Jones*, she embraced him eagerly, crying, 'My dearest Friend, I wish you Joy a thousand and a thousand Times of this blest Day;' and next Mr. *Allworthy* himself received the same Congratulations. To which he answered, 'Indeed, indeed, Mrs. *Miller*, I am beyond Expression happy.' Some few more Raptures having passed on all Sides, Mrs. *Miller* desired them both to walk down to Dinner in the Parlour, where she said there were a very happy Set of People assembled; being indeed no other than Mr. *Nightingale* and his Bride, and his Cousin *Harris* with her Bridegroom.

Allworthy excused himself from dining with the Company, saying he had ordered some little Thing for him and his Nephew in his own Apartment; for that they had much private Business to discourse of, but would not resist promising the good Woman, that both he and *Jones* would make Part of her Society at Supper.

Mrs. Miller then asked what was to be done with *Blifil*, 'for indeed, says she, I cannot be easy while such a Villain is in my House.'—*Allworthy* answered, 'He was as uneasy as herself on the same Account.' 'O!' cries she, 'if that be the Case, leave the Matter to me; I'll soon shew him the Outside of my Doors, I warrant you. Here are two or three lusty Fellows below Stairs.' 'There will be no Need of any Violence, cries *Allworthy*; if you will carry him a Message from me, he will, I am convinced, depart of his own Accord.' 'Will I?' said Mrs. *Miller*, 'I never did any Thing in my Life with a better Will.' Here *Jones* interfered, and said, 'He had considered the Matter better, and would, if Mr. *Allworthy* pleased, be himself the Messenger.' 'I know, says he, already enough of your Pleasure, Sir, and I beg Leave to acquaint him with it by my own Words. Let me beseech you, Sir, added he, to reflect on the dreadful Consequences of driving him to violent and sudden Despair. How unfit, alas! is this poor Man to die in his present Situation.' This Suggestion had not the least Effect on Mrs. *Miller*. She left the Room crying, 'You are too good, Mr. *Jones*, infinitely too good to live in this World.' But it made a deeper Impression on *Allworthy*. 'My good Child, said he, I am equally astonished at the Goodness of your Heart and the Quickness of your Understanding. Heaven indeed forbid that this Wretch should be deprived of any Means or Time for Repentance. That would be a shocking Consideration indeed. Go to him therefore and use your own Discretion; yet do not flatter him with any Hopes of my Forgiveness; for I shall never forgive Villainy farther than my Religion obliges me, and that extends not either to our Bounty or our Conversation.'

Jones went up to *Blifil's* Room, whom he found in a Situation which moved his Pity, though it would have raised a less amiable Passion in many Beholders. He cast himself on his Bed, where he lay abandoning himself to Despair, and drowned in Tears; not in such Tears as flow from Contrition, and wash away Guilt from Minds which have been seduced or surprized into it unawares, against the Bent of their natural Dispositions, as will sometimes happen from human Frailty, even to the Good: No, these Tears were such as the frighted Thief sheds in his Cart, and are indeed the Effects of that Concern which the most savage Natures are seldom deficient in feeling for themselves.

It would be unpleasant and tedious to paint this Scene in full Length. Let it suffice to say, that the Behaviour of *Jones* was kind to Excess. He omitted nothing which his Invention could supply, to raise and comfort the drooping Spirits of *Blifil*, before he communicated to him the Resolution of his Uncle, that he must quit the House that Evening. He offered to furnish him with any Money he wanted, assured him of his hearty Forgiveness of all he had done against him, that he would endeavour to live with him hereafter as a Brother, and would leave nothing unattempted to effectuate a Reconciliation with his Uncle.

Blifil was at first sullen and silent, balancing in his Mind whether he should yet deny all: But finding at last the Evidence too strong against him, he betook himself at last to Confession. He then asked Pardon of his Brother in the most vehement Manner, prostrated himself on the Ground, and kissed his Feet: In short, he was now as remarkably mean, as he had been before remarkably wicked.

Jones could not so far check his Disdain, but that it a little discovered itself in his Countenance at this extreme Servility. He raised his Brother the Moment he could from the Ground, and advised him to bear his Afflictions more like a Man; repeating, at the same Time, his Promises, that he would do all in his Power to lessen them: For which *Blifil* making many Professions of his Unworthiness, poured forth a Profusion of Thanks: And then he having declared he would immediately depart to another Lodging, *Jones* returned to his Uncle.

Among other Matters, *Allworthy* now acquainted *Jones* with the Discovery which he made concerning the 500 *l.* Bank-Notes. 'I have,' said he, 'already consulted a Lawyer, who tells me, to my great Astonishment, that there is no Punishment for a Fraud of this Kind. Indeed, when I consider the black Ingratitude of this Fellow toward you, I think a Highwayman, compared to him, is an innocent Person.'

'Good Heaven!' says *Jones*, 'is it possible?——I am shocked beyond Measure at this News. I thought there was not an honester Fellow in the World.—The Temptation of such a Sum was too great for him to withstand; for smaller Matters have come safe to me through his Hand. Indeed, my dear Uncle, you must suffer me to call it Weakness rather than Ingratitude; for I am convinced the poor Fellow loves me, and hath done me some Kindnesses, which I can never forget; nay, I believe he hath repented of this very Act: For it is not above a Day or two ago, when my Affairs seemed in the most desperate Situation, that he visited me in my Confinement, and offered me any Money I wanted. Consider, Sir, what a Temptation to a Man who hath tasted such bitter Distress, it must be to have a Sum in his Possession, which must put him and his Family beyond any future Possibility of suffering the like.'

'Child,' cries *Allworthy*, 'you carry this forgiving Temper too far.

Such mistaken Mercy is not only Weakness but borders on Injustice, and is very pernicious to Society, as it encourages Vice. The Dishonesty of this Fellow I might perhaps have pardoned, but never his Ingratitude. And give me Leave to say, when we suffer any Temptation to attone for Dishonesty itself, we are as candid and merciful as we ought to be; and so far I confess I have gone; for I have often pitied the Fate of a Highwayman, when I have been on the Grand Jury; and have more than once applied to the Judge on the Behalf of such as have had any mitigating Circumstances in their Case; but when Dishonesty is attended with any blacker Crime, such as Cruelty, Murder, Ingratitude, or the like, Compassion and Forgiveness then become Faults. I am convinced the Fellow is a Villain, and he shall be punished; at least as far as I can punish him.'

This was spoke with so stern a Voice, that *Jones* did not think proper to make any Reply: Besides, the Hour appointed by Mr. *Western* now drew so near, that he had barely Time left to dress himself. Here therefore ended the present Dialogue, and *Jones* retired to another Room, where *Partridge* attended, according to Order, with his Cloaths.

Partridge had scarce seen his Master since the happy Discovery. The poor Fellow was unable either to contain or express his Transports. He behaved like one frantic, and made almost as many Mistakes while he was dressing *Jones*, as I have seen made by Harlequin[1] in dressing himself on the Stage.

His Memory, however, was not in the least deficient. He recollected now many Omens and Presages of this happy Event, some of which he had remarked at the Time, but many more he now remembered; nor did he omit the Dreams he had dreamt the Evening before his meeting with *Jones*; and concluded with saying, 'I always told your Honour something boded in my Mind, that you would one Time or other have it in your Power to make my Fortune.' *Jones* assured him, that this Boding should as certainly be verified with regard to him, as all the other Omens had been to himself; which did not a little add to all the Raptures which the poor Fellow had already conceived on account of his Master.

Chapter XII.

Approaching still nearer to the End.

Jones being now completely dressed, attended his Uncle to Mr. *Western's*. He was indeed one of the finest Figures ever beheld, and his Person alone would have charmed the greater Part of Womankind; but we hope it hath already appeared in this History, that

1. The role made famous by John Rich. See above, p. 160.

Nature, when she formed him, did not totally rely, as she some-times doth, on this Merit only, to recommend her Work.

Sophia, who, angry as she was, was likewise set forth to the best Advantage, for which I leave my female Readers to account, appeared so extremely beautiful that even *Allworthy,* when he saw her, could not forbear whispering *Western,* that he believed she was the finest Creature in the World. To which *Western* answered, in a Whisper overheard by all present, 'So much the better for *Tom;*—for d—n me if he shan't ha the tousling her.' *Sophia* was all over Scarlet at these Words, while *Tom's* Countenance was altogether as pale, and he was almost ready to sink from his Chair.

The Tea-table was scarce removed, before *Western* lugged *All-worthy* out of the Room, telling him, He had Business of Conse-quence to impart, and must speak to him that Instant in private before he forgot it.

The Lovers were now alone, and it will, I question not, appear strange to many Readers, that those who had so much to say to one another, when Danger and Difficulty attended their Conversation; and who seemed so eager to rush into each others Arms, when so many Bars lay in their Way, now that with Safety they were at Lib-erty to say or do whatever they pleased, should both remain for some Time silent and motionless; insomuch that a Stranger of mod-erate Sagacity might have well concluded, they were mutually indif-ferent: But so it was, however strange it may seem; both sat with their Eyes cast downwards on the Ground, and for some Minutes continued in perfect Silence.

Mr. *Jones,* during this Interval, attempted once or twice to speak, but was absolutely incapable, muttering only, or rather sighing out, some broken Words; when *Sophia* at length, partly out of Pity to him, and partly to turn the Discourse from the Subject which she knew well enough he was endeavouring to open, said;—

'Sure, Sir, you are the most fortunate Man in the World in this Discovery.' 'And can you really, Madam, think me so fortunate,' said *Jones,* sighing, 'while I have incurred your Displeasure?'—'Nay, Sir,' says she, 'as to that, you best know whether you have deserved it.' 'Indeed, Madam,' answered he, 'you yourself are as well apprized of all my Demerits. Mrs. *Miller* hath acquainted you with the whole Truth. O! my *Sophia,* am I never to hope for Forgive-ness?'—'I think, Mr. *Jones,*' said she, 'I may almost depend on your own Justice, and leave it to yourself to pass Sentence on your own Conduct.'——'Alas! Madam,' answered he, 'it is Mercy, and not Justice, which I implore at your Hands. Justice I know must con-demn me—Yet not for the Letter I sent to Lady *Bellaston.* Of that I most solemnly declare, you have had a true Account.' He then insisted much on the Security given him by *Nightingale,* of a fair

Pretence for breaking off, if, contrary to their Expectations, her Ladyship should have accepted his Offer; but confest, that he had been guilty of a great Indiscretion, to put such a Letter as that into her Power, 'which,' said he, 'I have dearly paid for, in the Effect it has upon you.' 'I do not, I cannot,' says she, 'believe otherwise of that Letter than you would have me. My Conduct, I think, shews you clearly I do not believe there is much in that. And yet, Mr. *Jones*, have I not enough to resent? After what past at *Upton*, so soon to engage in a new Amour with another Woman, while I fancied, and you pretended, your Heart was bleeding for me!——Indeed you have acted strangely. Can I believe the Passion you have profest to me to be sincere? Or if I can, what Happiness can I assure myself of with a Man capable of so much Inconstancy?' 'O! my *Sophia*,' cries he, 'do not doubt the Sincerity of the purest Passion that ever inflamed a human Breast. Think, most adorable Creature, of my unhappy Situation, of my Despair.—Could I, my *Sophia*, have flattered myself with the most distant Hopes of being ever permitted to throw myself at your Feet, in the Manner I do now, it would not have been in the Power of any other Woman to have inspired a Thought which the severest Chastity could have condemned. Inconstancy to you! O *Sophia!* if you can have Goodness enough to pardon what is past, do not let any cruel future Apprehensions shut your Mercy against me.—No Repentance was ever more sincere. O! let it reconcile me to my Heaven in this dear Bosom.' 'Sincere Repentance, Mr. *Jones*,' answered she, 'will obtain the Pardon of a Sinner, but it is from one who is a perfect Judge of that Sincerity. A human Mind may be imposed on; nor is there any infallible Method to prevent it. You must expect however, that if I can be prevailed on by your Repentance to pardon you, I will at least insist on the strongest Proof of its Sincerity.'—'O! name any Proof in my Power,' answered *Jones* eagerly. 'Time,' replied she; 'Time, alone Mr. *Jones*, can convince me that you are a true Penitent, and have resolved to abandon these vicious Courses, which I should detest you for, if I imagined you capable of persevering in them.' 'Do not imagine it,' cries *Jones*. 'On my Knees I intreat, I implore your Confidence, a Confidence which it shall be the Business of my Life to deserve.' 'Let it then,' said she, 'be the Business of some Part of your Life to shew me you deserve it. I think I have been explicit enough in assuring you, that when I see you merit my Confidence, you will obtain it. After what is past, Sir, can you expect I should take you upon your Word?'

He replied, 'Don't believe me upon my Word; I have a better Security, a Pledge for my Constancy, which it is impossible to see and to doubt.' 'What is that?' said *Sophia*, a little surprized. 'I will show you, my charming Angel,' cried *Jones*, seizing her Hand, and

carrying her to the Glass. 'There, behold it there in that lovely
Figure, in that Face, that Shape, those Eyes, that Mind which
shines through [those][1] Eyes: Can the Man who shall be in Possession of these be inconstant? Impossible! my *Sophia*: They would fix a
Dorimant, a Lord *Rochester*.[2] You could not doubt it, if you could
see yourself with any Eyes but your own.' *Sophia* blushed, and half
smiled; but forcing again her Brow into a Frown, 'If I am to judge,'
said she, 'of the future by the past, my Image will no more remain
in your Heart when I am out of your Sight, than it will in this
Glass when I am out of the Room.' 'By Heaven, by all that is
sacred,' said *Jones*, 'it never was out of my Heart. The Delicacy of
your Sex cannot conceive the Grossness of ours, nor how little one
Sort of Amour has to do with the Heart.' 'I will never marry a
Man,' replied *Sophia*, very gravely, 'who shall not learn Refinement
enough to be as incapable as I am myself of making such a Distinction.' 'I will learn it,' said *Jones*. 'I have learnt it already. The first
Moment of Hope that my *Sophia* might be my Wife, taught it me
at once; and all the rest of her Sex from that Moment became as
little the Objects of Desire to my Sense, as of Passion to my Heart.'
'Well,' said *Sophia*, 'the Proof of this must be from Time. Your Situation, Mr. *Jones*, is now altered, and I assure you I have great Satisfaction in the Alteration. You will now want no Opportunity of
being near me, and convincing me that your Mind is altered too.'
'O! my Angel,' cries *Jones*, 'how shall I thank thy Goodness? And
are you so good to own, that you have a Satisfaction in my Prosperity?—Believe me, believe me, Madam, it is you alone have given a
Relish to that Prosperity, since I owe to it the dear Hope—O! my
Sophia, let it not be a distant one.—I will be all Obedience to your
Commands. I will not dare to press any Thing further than you
permit me. Yet let me intreat you to appoint a short Trial. O! tell
me, when I may expect you will be convinced of what is most solemnly true.' 'When I have gone voluntarily thus far, Mr. *Jones*,' said
she, 'I expect not to be pressed. Nay, I will not.'—'O don't look
unkindly thus, my *Sophia*,' cries he. 'I do not, I dare not press you.
—Yet permit me at least once more to beg you would fix the
Period. O! consider the Impatience of Love.'—'A Twelve-month,
perhaps,' said she.—'O! my *Sophia*,' cries he, 'you have named an
Eternity.'—'Perhaps it may be something sooner,' says she, 'I will
not be teazed. If your Passion for me be what I would have it, I
think you may now be easy.'—'Easy, *Sophia*, call not such an exult-

---

1. The first three editions read "those";
the fourth reads "these," an odd rhetorical slip: the typesetter may have
erroneously picked up the "these" in the
phrase following.

2. Dorimant, in George Etherege's *The
Man of Mode, or Sir Fopling Flutter*
(1676), is a fictive picture of the real
rake of rakes, the Earl of Rochester
(1648–80).

ing Happiness as mine by so cold a Name.—O! transporting
Thought! am I not assured that the blessed Day will come, when I
shall call you mine; when Fears shall be no more; when I shall have
that dear, that vast, that exquisite, ecstatic Delight of making my
Sophia happy?'—'Indeed, Sir,' said she, 'that Day is in your own
Power.'—'O! my dear, my divine Angel,' cried he, 'these Words
have made me mad with Joy.—But I must, I will thank those dear
Lips which have so sweetly pronounced my Bliss.' He then caught
her in his Arms, and kissed her with an Ardour he had never ventured before.

At this Instant, *Western*, who had stood some Time listening,
burst into the Room, and with his hunting Voice and Phrase, cried
out, 'To her Boy, to her, go to her.—That's it, little Honeys, O
that's it. Well, what is it all over? Hath she appointed the Day,
Boy? What shall it be To-morrow or next Day? It shan't be put off
a Minute longer than next Day I am resolved.' 'Let me beseech
you, Sir,' says *Jones*, 'don't let me be the Occasion'—'Beseech mine
A—,' cries *Western*, 'I thought thou had'st been a Lad of higher
Mettle, than to give Way to a Parcel of Maidenish Tricks.—I tell
thee 'tis all Flimflam. Zoodikers! she'd have the Wedding to Night
with all her Heart. Would'st not *Sophy*? Come confess, and be an
honest Girl for once. What, art dumb? Why dost not speak?' 'Why
should I confess, Sir?' says *Sophia*, 'since it seems you are so well
acquainted with my Thoughts.'—'That's a good Girl,' cries he, 'and
dost consent then?' 'No indeed, Sir,' says *Sophia*, 'I have given no
such Consent.'—'And wunt nut ha un then To-morrow, nor next
Day?' says *Western*——'Indeed, Sir,' says she, 'I have no such
Intention.' 'But I can tell thee,' replied he, 'why hast nut, only
because thou dost love to be disobedient, and to plague and vex thy
Father.'—'Pray, sir,' said *Jones* interfering.—'I tell thee thou at a
Puppy,' cries he. 'When I forbid her, then it was all nothing but
Sighing and Whining, and Languishing and Writing; now I am vor
thee, she is against thee. All the Spirit of contrary, that's all. She is
above being guided and governed by her Father, that is the whole
Truth on't. It is only to disblige and contradict me.' 'What would
my Papa have me do?' cries *Sophia*. 'What would I ha thee do?'
says he, 'why gi un thy Hand this Moment.'——'Well, Sir,' said
Sophia, 'I will obey you.—There is my Hand, Mr. *Jones*.' 'Well,
and will you consent to ha un to-morrow Morning?' says *Western*.
——'I will be obedient to you, Sir,' cries she.—'Why then to-morrow Morning be the Day,' cries he.—'Why then to-morrow Morning shall be the Day, Papa, since you will have it so,' says *Sophia*.
Jones then fell upon his Knees, and kissed her Hand in an Agony of
Joy, while *Western* began to caper and dance about the Room,

presently crying out,—'Where the Devil is *Allworthy*? He is without now, a talking with that d—d Lawyer *Dowling*, when he should
be minding other Matters.' He then sallied out in Quest of him,
and very opportunely left the Lovers to enjoy a few tender Minutes
alone.

But he soon returned with *Allworthy*, saying, 'If you won't believe
me, you may ask her yourself. Hast nut gin thy Consent, *Sophy*, to
be married To-morrow?' 'Such are your Commands, Sir,' cries
Sophia, 'and I dare not be guilty of Disobedience.' 'I hope Madam,'
cries *Allworthy*, 'my Nephew will merit so much Goodness, and will
be always as sensible as myself, of the great Honour you have done
my Family. An Alliance with so charming and so excellent a young
Lady would indeed be an Honour to the greatest in *England*.'
'Yes,' cries *Western*, 'but if I had suffered her to stand shill I shall
I, dilly dally, you might not have had that Honour yet awhile; I
was forced to use a little fatherly Authority to bring her to.' 'I hope
not, Sir,' cries *Allworthy*. 'I hope there is not the least Constraint.'
'Why there,' cries *Western*, 'you may bid her unsay all again, if you
will. Do'st repent heartily of thy Promise, do'st not, *Sophy*?'
'Indeed, Papa,' cries she, 'I do not repent, nor do I believe I ever
shall, of any Promise in Favour of Mr. *Jones*.' 'Then, Nephew,'
cries *Allworthy*, 'I felicitate you most heartily; for I think you are
the happiest of Men. And, Madam, you will give me Leave to congratulate you on this joyful Occasion: Indeed I am convinced you
have bestowed yourself on one who will be sensible of your great
Merit, and who will at least use his best Endeavours to deserve it.'
'His best Endeavours!' cries *Western*, 'that he will I warrant un.—
Harkee, *Allworthy*, I'll bet thee five Pound to a Crown we have a
Boy to-morrow nine Months: But prithee tell me what wut ha!
Wut ha *Burgundy*, *Champaigne*, or what? for please *Jupiter*, we'll
make a Night on't.' 'Indeed, Sir,' said Allworthy, 'you must excuse
me; both my Nephew and I were engaged, before I suspected this
near Approach of his Happiness.'—'Engaged!' quoth the Squire,
'never tell me.—I won't part with thee to Night upon any Occasion.
Shalt sup here, please the Lord *Harry*.' 'You must pardon me, my
dear Neighbour,' answered *Allworthy*; 'I have given a solemn Promise, and that you know I never break.' 'Why, prithee, who art
engaged to?' cries the Squire.—*Allworthy* then informed him, as
likewise of the Company.—'Odzookers!' answered the Squire, 'I will
go with thee, and so shall *Sophy*; for I won't part with thee to
Night; and it would be barbarous to part *Tom* and the Girl.' This
Offer was presently embraced by *Allworthy*; and *Sophia* consented,
having first obtained a private Promise from her Father, that he
would not mention a Syllable concerning her Marriage.

Chapter the last.

In which the History is concluded.

Young *Nightingale* had been that Afternoon, by Appointment, to wait on his Father, who received him much more kindly than he expected. There likewise he met his Uncle, who was returned to Town in Quest of his new-married Daughter.

This Marriage was the luckiest Incident which could have happened to the young Gentleman; for these Brothers lived in a constant State of Contention about the Government of their Children, both heartily despising the Method which each other took. Each of them therefore now endeavoured as much as he could to palliate the Offence which his own Child had committed, and to aggravate the Match of the other. This Desire of triumphing over his Brother, added to the many Arguments which *Allworthy* had used, so strongly operated on the old Gentleman, that he met his Son with a smiling Countenance, and actually agreed to sup with him that Evening at Mrs. *Miller's.*

As for the other, who really loved his Daughter with the most immoderate Affection, there was little Difficulty in inclining him to a Reconciliation. He was no sooner informed by his Nephew, where his Daughter and her Husband were, than he declared he would instantly go to her. And when he arrived there, he scarce suffered her to fall upon her Knees, before he took her up, and embraced her with a Tenderness which affected all who saw him; and in less than a Quarter of an Hour was as well reconciled to both her and her Husband, as if he had himself joined their Hands.

In this Situation were Affairs when Mr. *Allworthy* and his Company arrived to complete the Happiness of Mrs. *Miller,* who no sooner saw *Sophia,* than she guessed every Thing that had happened; and so great was her Friendship to *Jones,* that it added not a few Transports to those she felt on the Happiness of her own Daughter.

There have not, I believe, been many Instances of a Number of People met together, where every one was so perfectly happy, as in this Company. Amongst whom the Father of young *Nightingale* enjoyed the least perfect Content; for notwithstanding his Affection for his Son; notwithstanding the Authority and the Arguments of *Allworthy,* together with the other Motive mentioned before, he could not so entirely be satisfied with his Son's Choice; and perhaps the Presence of *Sophia* herself tended a little to aggravate and heighten his Concern, as a Thought now and then suggested itself, that his Son might have had that Lady, or some such other. Not that any of the Charms which adorned either the Person or Mind of *Sophia*, created the Uneasiness: It was the Contents of her Father's Coffers which set his Heart a longing. These were the Charms which he could not bear to think his Son had sacrificed to the Daughter of Mrs. *Miller*.

The Brides were both very pretty Women; but so totally were they eclipsed by the Beauty of *Sophia*, that had they not been two of the best-tempered Girls in the World, it would have raised some Envy in their Breasts; for neither of their Husbands could long keep his Eyes from *Sophia*, who sat at the Table like a Queen receiving Homage, or rather like a superiour Being receiving Adoration from all around her. But it was an Adoration which they gave, not which she exacted: For she was as much distinguished by her Modesty and Affability, as by all her other Perfections.

The Evening was spent in much true Mirth. All were happy, but those the most, who had been most unhappy before. Their former Sufferings and Fears gave such a Relish to their Felicity, as even Love and Fortune in their fullest Flow could not have given without the Advantage of such a Comparison. Yet as great Joy, especially after a sudden Change and Revolution of Circumstances, is apt to be silent, and dwells rather in the Heart than on the Tongue, *Jones* and *Sophia* appeared the least merry of the whole Company. Which *Western* observed with great Impatience, often crying out to them, 'Why do'st not talk, Boy! Why do'st look so grave! Hast lost thy Tongue, Girl! Drink another Glass of Wine, sha't drink another Glass.' And the more to enliven her, he would sometimes sing a merry Song, which bore some Relation to Matrimony, and the Loss of a Maidenhead. Nay, he would have proceeded so far on that Topic, as to have driven her out of the Room, if Mr. *Allworthy* had not checkt him sometimes by Looks, and once or twice by a *Fie!* Mr. *Western*. He began indeed once to debate the Matter, and assert his Right to talk to his own Daughter as he thought fit; but as no Body seconded him, he was soon reduced to Order.

Notwithstanding this little Restraint, he was so pleased with the Chearfulness and Good-Humour of the Company, that he insisted on their meeting the next Day at his Lodgings. They all did so; and the lovely *Sophia*, who was now in private become a Bride too, officiated as the Mistress of the Ceremonies, or, in the polite Phrase, did the Honours of the Table. She had that Morning given her Hand to *Jones*, in the Chapel at *Doctors Commons*, where Mr. *Allworthy*, Mr. *Western*, and Mrs. *Miller* were the only Persons present.

Sophia had earnestly desired her Father, that no others of the Company, who were that Day to dine with him, should be acquainted with her Marriage. The same Secrecy was enjoined to Mrs. *Miller*, and *Jones* undertook for *Allworthy*: This somewhat reconciled the Delicacy of *Sophia* to the publick Entertainment, which, in Compliance with her Father's Will, she was obliged to go to, greatly against her own Inclinations. In Confidence of this Secrecy, she went through the Day pretty well, till the Squire, who was now advanced into the second Bottle, could contain his Joy no longer, but, filling out a Bumper, drank a Health to the Bride. The Health was immediately pledged by all present, to the great Confusion of our poor blushing *Sophia*, and the great Concern of *Jones* upon her Account. To say Truth, there was not a Person present made wiser by this Discovery; for Mrs. *Miller* had whispered it to her Daughter, her Daughter to her Husband, her Husband to his Sister, and she to all the rest.

Sophia now took the first Opportunity of withdrawing with the Ladies, and the Squire sat in to his Cups, in which he was, by Degrees, deserted by all the Company, except the Uncle of young *Nightingale*, who loved his Bottle as well as *Western* himself. These two therefore sat stoutly to it, during the whole Evening, and long after that happy Hour which had surrendered the charming *Sophia* to the eager Arms of her enraptured *Jones*.

Thus, Reader, we have at length brought our History to a Conclusion, in which, to our great Pleasure, tho' contrary perhaps to thy Expectation, Mr. *Jones* appears to be the happiest of all human Kind: For what Happiness this World affords equal to the Possession of such a Woman as *Sophia*, I sincerely own I have never yet discovered.

As to the other Persons who have made any considerable Figure in this History, as some may desire to know a little more concerning them, we will proceed in as few Words as possible, to satisfy their Curiosity.

Allworthy hath never yet been prevailed upon to see *Blifil*, but he hath yielded to the Importunity of *Jones*, backed by *Sophia*, to settle 200*l.* a Year upon him; to which *Jones* hath privately added a third. Upon this Income he lives in one of the northern Counties, about 200 Miles distant from *London*, and lays up 200*l.* a Year out of it, in order to purchase a Seat in the next Parliament from a neighboring Borough, which he has bargained for with an Attorney there. He is also lately turned Methodist, in hopes of marrying a very rich Widow of that Sect, whose Estate lies in that Part of the Kingdom.

Square died soon after he writ the before-mentioned Letter; and as to *Thwackum*, he continues at his Vicarage. He hath made many fruitless Attempts to regain the Confidence of *Allworthy*, or to ingratiate himself with *Jones*, both of whom he flatters to their

Faces, and abuses behind their Backs. But in his stead, Mr. *Allwor-thy* hath lately taken Mr. *Abraham Adams*[1] into his House, of whom *Sophia* is grown immoderately fond, and declares he shall have the Tuition of her Children.

Mrs. *Fitzpatrick* is separated from her Husband, and retains the little Remains of her Fortune. She lives in Reputation at the polite End of the Town, and is so good an Œconomist, that she spends three Times the Income of her Fortune, without running in Debt. She maintains a perfect Intimacy with the Lady of the *Irish* Peer; and in Acts of Friendship to her repays all the Obligations she owes to her Husband.

Mrs. *Western* was soon reconciled to her Niece *Sophia*, and hath spent two Months together with her in the Country. Lady *Bellaston* made the latter a formal Visit at her Return to Town, where she behaved to *Jones*, as to a perfect Stranger, and with great Civility, wished him Joy on his Marriage.

Mr. *Nightingale* hath purchased an Estate for his Son in the Neighbourhood of *Jones*, where the young Gentleman, his Lady, Mrs. *Miller*, and her little Daughter reside, and the most agreeable Intercourse subsists between the two Families.

As to those of lower Account, Mrs. *Waters* returned into the Country, had a Pension of 60 *l.* a Year settled upon her by Mr. *All-worthy*, and is married to Parson *Supple*, on whom, at the Instance of *Sophia*, *Western* hath bestowed a considerable Living.

Black George hearing the Discovery that had been made, run away, and was never since heard of; and *Jones* bestowed the Money on his Family, but not in equal Proportions, for *Molly* had much the greatest Share.

As for *Partridge*, *Jones* hath settled 50 *l.* a Year on him; and he hath again set up a School, in which he meets with much better Encouragement than formerly; and there is now a Treaty of Marriage on Foot, between him and Miss *Molly Seagrim*, which, through the Mediation of *Sophia*, is likely to take Effect.

We now return to take Leave of Mr. *Jones* and *Sophia*, who, within two Days after their Marriage, attended Mr. *Western* and Mr. *Allworthy* into the Country. *Western* hath resigned his Family Seat, and the greater Part of his Estate to his Son-in-law, and hath retired to a lesser House of his, in another Part of the Country, which is better for Hunting. Indeed he is often as a Visitant with Mr. *Jones*, who as well as his Daughter, hath an infinite Delight in doing every Thing in their Power to please him. And this Desire of theirs is attended with such Success, that the old Gentleman

1. The famous Parson Adams of Field-ing's first novel, *Joseph Andrews* (1742), who demonstrates himself to be a very   poor teacher, though he thinks himself the best in the world.

declares he was never happy in his Life till now. He hath here a
Parlour and Anti-chamber to himself, where he gets drunk with
whom he pleases; and his Daughter is still as ready as formerly to
play to him whenever he desires it; for *Jones* hath assured her, that
as next to pleasing her, one of his highest Satisfactions is to contribute to the Happiness of the old Man; so the great Duty which she
expresses and performs to her Father renders her almost equally
dear to him, with the Love which she bestows on himself.

Sophia hath already produced him two fine Children, a Boy and
a Girl, of whom the old Gentleman is so fond, that he spends
much of his Time in the Nursery, where he declares the tattling of
his little Grand-Daughter, who is above a Year and half old, is
sweeter music than the finest Cry of Dogs in *England.*

Allworthy was likewise greatly liberal to *Jones* on the Marriage,
and hath omitted no Instance of shewing his Affection to him
and his Lady, who love him as a Father. Whatever in the Nature of
Jones had a Tendency to Vice, has been corrected by continual
Conversation with this good Man, and by his Union with the lovely
and virtuous *Sophia.* He hath also, by Reflexion on his past Follies,
acquired a Discretion and Prudence very uncommon in one of his
lively Parts.

To conclude, as there are not to be found a worthier Man and
Woman, than this fond Couple, so neither can any be imagined
more happy. They preserve the purest and tenderest Affection for
each other, an Affection daily encreased and confirmed by mutual
Endearments, and mutual Esteem. Nor is their Conduct towards
their Relations and Friends less amiable, than towards one another.
And such is their Condescension, their Indulgence, and their
Beneficence to those below them, that there is not a Neighbour, a
Tenant or a Servant who doth not most gratefully bless the Day
when Mr. *Jones* was married to his *Sophia.*

F I N I S.

Textual Appendix

Andrew Millar published Fielding's *Tom Jones* in six small volumes (duodecimo) on Friday, 10 February 1749, by which date privileged sales had already exhausted his stock. He rushed another six-volume edition into publication on Tuesday, 28 February. Though none of the title-pages announces an edition's number, both William Strahan's printing ledger and modern scholarship designate this the second edition. Nevertheless, it does little more than pick up errors and reset the first edition, since Millar, underestimating sales, had evidently broken up the type. On Wednesday, 12 April 1749, Millar published the third edition, in four volumes, containing more than two thousand changes to the basic text of the two six-volume editions, including the only extended revision Fielding was to give any part of *Tom Jones*: a thorough rewriting of three paragraphs in the Man of the Hill's story (VIII.xiv.362–64), and a cutting of three more (VIII.xv.366–67). The fourth edition, also in four volumes—dated 1750, published Monday, 11 December 1749, the last during Fielding's life—follows the third, line for line, except as it tidies up a number of remaining anomalies, making some typographical slips of its own, and adds about twelve hundred changes more.[1]

1. Gerard E. Jensen, who collated all four editions, supplies these statistics, and tentatively re-dates the first two editions as 10 and 28 February 1749 ("Proposals for a Definitive Edition of Fielding's *Tom Jones*," *The Library*, 18 [1937], 319–20). Cross had dated edition one 28 February, editions two and three 13 April, and edition four 12 December (II.117–18, 121, 123; III.317). Cross knew that in January Millar had announced publication for 10 February, but, finding no subsequent advertisements until 28 February, Cross assumed a delay in plans. In 1935, P. D. Munday published part of a letter by Joseph Spence (dated 15 April 1749) that explains the difficulty: "Tom Jones is my old acquaintance, now; for I read him before it was published. . . . A set of 2,500 Copies [actually 2,000, by Strahan's ledger] was sold before it was published; which is perhaps an unheard-of case. That I may not seem to write in riddles, you must know that the way here generally is, to send in the number of books to each of the Booksellers they deal with, four or five days before the publication, that they may oblige people who are eager for a new thing. In ys Case, the 10th of Febrʸ ws fixt for ye publication, & by the 10th, all the books were disposed of" ("Fielding's 'Tom Jones,'" *Notes & Queries*, 169 [1935], 456). Naturally, Millar, with no books left to advertise on 10 February, placed no "*This Day is publish'd*" in the newspapers for his first edition. His advertisements on 28 February, which speak of "It being impossible to get Sets bound fast enough," obviously refer to the second edition, rushed out to meet the demand. The April advertisements, in which Cross reads a simultaneous second and third edition, actually announce "*A New Edition, in Four Volumes*" (the third), and then go on to list some other books by Fielding and his sister Sarah, headed by "1. The same Work in 6 vol. 8vo. on a larger Letter" (i.e., the remaining copies of the second edition). Cross, using the Tuesday-Thursday-Saturday *St. James's Evening Post*, misses by one day the third and fourth editions, announced in *The General Advertiser*, a daily, as Wednesday, 12 April, and Monday, 11 December. Jensen (pp. 316–17) quotes the entries from Strahan's ledger, first published by J. Paul de Castro in "The Printing of Fielding's Works," *The Library*, 4th ser., 1 (March 1921), 263–64.

But the fourth edition also veers off suddenly from the third to restore the Man of the Hill to its original form, and this unexpected turn threw Aurélien Digeon and a number of successors quite off the track. Wilbur L. Cross, assuming from scanty evidence that Fielding forsook *Tom Jones* after correcting for the second edition, had declared "Millar and his men" (II.125) responsible for all subsequent changes. But then Digeon discovered the many changes in the third edition, as well as the Man-of-the-Hill restoration in the fourth. He thought the third edition's revision of the Man of the Hill an improvement and the fourth edition's restoration an astonishment.[2]

In the revision, Fielding had emphatically strengthened the old man's statements against the Catholics and the Stuarts, and had then cut some of his subsequent travelogue. Digeon found the revision consistent with the deepened religious feeling soon to emerge in Fielding's *Amelia* (1751); and excising some travelogue seemed a mercy, as indeed it does still. To return to the original version was unthinkable. (The excision, incidentally, contained some severe strictures against the French, which could hardly have pleased M. Digeon.) Therefore, to Cross's "Millar and his men" Digeon added a hypothetical Catholic compositor, or at least a Jacobite, who, unable to bear the new religious and political outburst, substituted the calmer original version on his own. The third edition, said Digeon, was Fielding's final word.

Digeon's engaging, intelligent, and significant scholarship is hard to resist, wrong though it is in this one important instance. Consequently, we find Gerard E. Jensen, in 1937, making an extensive case for the third edition, even in the face of his own evidence. Millar had announced the fourth as "A *new Edition. . . . / . . . * Carefully revis'd and corrected / By HENRY FIELDING, *Esq*;" [3] —but this "should not mislead us," says Jensen (p. 322). On 25 March 1749, Fielding had sold Millar all rights in *Tom Jones*, "with all Improvements, Additions or Alterations whatsoever which now are or hereafter shall at any time be made by me the s.d Henry Fielding, or any one else by my authority . . ." (Cross, II.118–19). Jensen thence posits two assisting hands: (1) a classicist, perhaps the Rev. William Young, authorized to check out the quotations,

2. *Le texte des romans de Fielding* (Paris: Librairie Hachette, 1923, pp. 72–77.
3. *The London Evening-Post*, no. 3450, Tuesday, 12 December 1749. The same wording had already appeared in its advertisements on 28 and 30 November announcing that the new edition *"Next Week will be publish'd."* The same advertisements in *The Whitehall Evening-Post: or, London Intelligencer* put a period after "Corrected," which would strengthen Jensen's case by separating Fielding to some extent from the correcting, but most of the advertisements do not put a period between "corrected" and *"By* HENRY FIELDING. . . ." *The General Advertiser* of 11 December omits "revised and corrected" altogether. Millar's advertisements do not distinguish the second edition from the first (which confused Cross); they distinguish the third merely as *"A New Edition,* in *Four Volumes,"* saying nothing about revisions and corrections.

who was also a "pedantic busybody," perhaps assigned to the grammar but overreaching his assignment; (2) a Digeonian compositor who reverted to the first edition without Fielding's knowledge, although "it is difficult to discover any adequate reason for the substitution" (pp. 322–24). And indeed it is, unless Fielding wanted it. No compositor would insert it cheerfully. For he must now sweat blood to fit the longer version back into the twenty-four pages of signature N, Volume II, which hold the controversial passages in both third and fourth editions. Jensen's compositorial case will not stand inspection,[4] nor will his arguments against other fourth-edition revisions.

Nonetheless, on the strength of Digeon and Jensen, the third edition has prospered. To abet the confusion, as Jensen points out (p. 314, n. 1), A. W. Pollard had, in 1900, called the fourth edition the third, rightly declaring it authoritative, but apparently counting the two six-volume editions as one.[5] Then the Shakespeare Head edition (1926) chose the actual third, with its errors intact. And two popular paperbacks and several scholars have recently compounded the mistake.

However much we may wish that Fielding had not restored the unimportant bit of travel and the old man's comments on his solitude, we must concede, I think, that Fielding had patched over his third-edition cuts a little awkwardly. Moreover, the restored first-edition political passage is surely more valid dramatically, and it is certainly more temperate. Fielding seems to have had second thoughts, in the leisure after the rush for the third edition, deciding to leave the Man of the Hill as he originally was.

Whatever one thinks of the third-edition passages below, as against the restored text, one cannot argue away the presence of Fielding's hand throughout the fourth edition. The first change we encounter, for instance (I.i.26), from "all polite Lovers of eating" to "all Lovers of polite eating," which Pollard first pointed out in 1900, certainly suggests an author sharpening a phrase. Where

4. Both editions set a thirty-six-line page, not counting the catch-line. Beginning on p. 265 (which begins signature N in both editions, marked with a light ⌈ on p. 358, present edition), the compositor starts setting more tightly to gain space, but can gain only five lines by the bottom of p. 272. Now, on p. 273, fourth edition, where the restoration begins, he must not only squeeze his type but also set each page two lines long (going to three lines long on p. 280) to come out even with the end of the chapter, and Book, on p. 284, a thirty-five-line page that, in edition three, held only five lines and an ornament. From p. 284, line 14, the fourth edition returns to following the third, line for line, to the end of the volume, except for one phrasal emenda-tion on p. 288 (see this Appendix, below, p. 766). Jensen states that "extensive rewriting" begins on p. 265 (the last four pages of VIII.xiii) and that Fielding revised three chapters (Jensen, pp. 321, 325, 330). Actually, only *resetting* begins on p. 265, and these last four pages of chapter xiii contain only one small change: "where we were not treated" (third edition) reverts to the first-edition reading "without being treated" (p. 359, present edition). Chapters xiv and xv contain the only extended revisions, three paragraphs in each.

5. "Bibliographical Note," *The History of Tom Jones, a Foundling* (London: Macmillan, 1900), p. v.

Jensen sees only a pedantic meddler, we can also see an author rescuing a blurred meaning, changing "I was obliged to declare myself" to "I myself was obliged to declare," as he ends an important authorial comment, and closes his chapter with a flourish (III.vii.107). Here is a change just four pages beyond the Man-of-the-Hill restoration, where Fielding is supposed not to be (successive editions in parentheses):

(1) no less indeed than Doomsday Book, or the vast authentic Book of Nature. . . .

(2 and 3) no less indeed than the vast authentic Book of Nature. . . .

(4) no less indeed than the vast authentic Doomsday-Book of Nature. . . . (IX.i.372).

A number of such small adjustments show beyond doubt that Millar advertised truly: the fourth edition is indeed "Carefully revis'd and corrected" by Henry Fielding. Moreover, not one of the small corrections of detail is sufficiently un-Fieldinglike to force aside the basic bibliographical principle that alterations appearing in an author's book during his lifetime are his, unless proved otherwise.

Revisions in the Man of the Hill's Story (VIII.xiv,xv)

The first of Fielding's two third-edition revisions replaced the section bracketed in this volume on pages 362–64, starting with the third sentence of the paragraph that begins "Events of this nature. . . ." The third edition (12 April 1749) contained the revision below—which Fielding rejected in turn for the fourth edition (11 December 1749, dated 1750), restoring the original reading. Fielding spliced his revision into sentences already there, as the brackets below indicate.

'[Events of this Nature . . . the Danger to which the Protestant Religion was so visibly exposed,] that nothing but the immediate Interposition of Providence seemed capable of preserving it: For King *James* had indeed declared War against the Protestant Cause. He had brought known Papists into the Army, and attempted to bring them into the Church, and into the University. Popish Priests swarmed thro' the Nation, appeared publickly in their Habits, and boasted that they should shortly walk in Procession through the Streets. Our own Clergy were forbid to preach against Popery, and Bishops were ordered to suspend those who did; and to do the Business at once, an illegal ecclesiastical Commission was erected, little inferior to an Inquisition, of which, probably, it was intended to be the Ringleader. Thus, as our Duty to the King can never be called more than our second Duty, he had discharged us from this, by making it incompatible with our preserving the first, which is surely to Heaven. Besides this, he had dissolved his Subjects from their Allegiance by breaking his Coronation Oath, to which their Allegiance is annexed; for he had imprisoned Bishops, because they would not give up their Religion; and turned out Judges, because they would not absolutely surrender the Law into his Hands; nay, he seized this himself; and when he claimed a dispensing Power, he declared himself, in fact, as absolute as any Tyrant ever was or can be. I have recapitulated these Matters in full, lest some of them should have been omitted in History; and I think nothing less than such Provocations as I have here mentioned, nothing less than certain and imminent Danger to their Religion and Liberties, can justify, or even mitigate, the dreadful Sin of Rebellion in any People.'

'I promise you, Sir,' says *Jones*, 'all these Facts, and more, I have read in History; but I will tell you a Fact which is not yet recorded, and of which I suppose you are ignorant. There is actually now a Rebellion on Foot in this Kingdom, in Favour of the Son of that very King *James*, a profest Papist, more bigoted, if possible, than his Father, and this carried on by Protestants, against a King who hath never, in *one Single Instance*, made the least Invasion on our Liberties.'

'Prodigious indeed!' answered the Stranger, 'you tell me what would be incredible of a Nation which did not deserve the Character that Virgil gives of a Woman, V*arium & Mutabile Semper*. Surely this is to be unworthy of the Care which Providence seems to have taken of us, in the Preservation of our Religion against the powerful Designs and constant Machinations of Popery. A Preservation so strange and unaccountable, that I almost think we may appeal to it, as to a Miracle for the Proof of its Holiness. Prodigious indeed! a Protestant Rebellion in favour of a Popish Prince! The Folly of Mankind is as wonderful as their Knavery——
——But to conclude my Story; I resolved to take Arms in Defence of my Country, of my Religion, and my Liberty; and Mr. *Watson* joined in the same Resolution. We soon provided ourselves with all Necessaries, and joined the Duke at *Bridgewater*.

'The unfortunate Event of this Enterprize you are [perhaps better] acquainted with [than] myself. . . .'

The second of Fielding's two major revisions in the third edition deletes paragraphs four and five, and most of paragraph six, in the next chapter (VIII.xv), beginning in the present text at the first bracket on p. 366. But Fielding also makes some unusually extensive changes in the chapter's first paragraph. Brackets in the present text (fourth edition) on p. 366 and in the third-edition version below indicate where the two versions vary:

. . . in my [Travels.] My Design, when I went abroad was to divert myself by seeing the [great] Variety [ ] with which God [hath] been pleased to enrich the several Parts of this Globe. A Variety, which as it must give great Pleasure to a contemplative Beholder, so doth it [greatly] display the [vast Powers of its omnipotent Author]. Indeed, . . .

Then Fielding proceeds to the major cuts of paragraphs four, five, and six, with three minor changes at the transitions, none of which he kept when restoring the original reading in the fourth edition: (1) "Avoidance" for "Scorn," which seems much the more accurate word, since "Avoidance" hardly makes sense, even from the Man of the Hill's viewpoint; (2) "they" for "it," thus erroneously throwing the reference to "Years" rather than to "Series"; (3) "may almost be" for "may be almost," which seems the more naturally colloquial. The text of the third edition thus reads (variations again bracketed):

. . . of Detestation and [Avoidance]. 'Thus, Sir, I have ended the History of my Life; for as to all that Series of Years [in which] I have [retired] here, [they afford] no Variety to entertain you, and [may almost be] considered as one Day.'
    Jones thanked the Stranger. . . .

Again Fielding reverted to his original reading for the fourth edition.

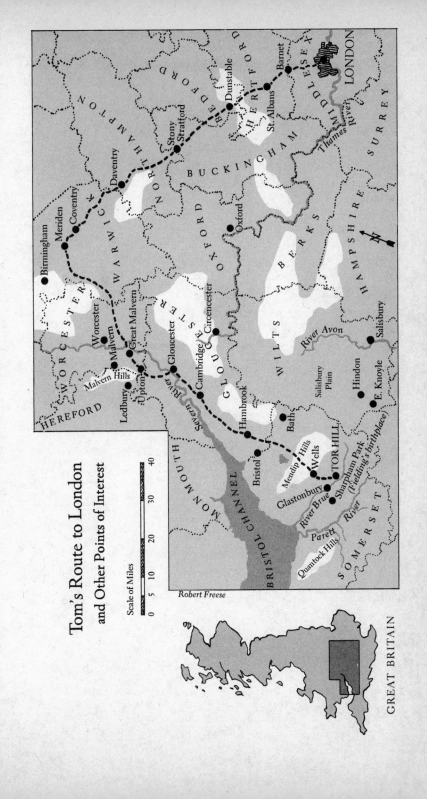

Tom's Route to London
and Other Points of Interest

Scale of Miles

0   5   10   20   30   40

Robert Freese

GREAT BRITAIN

Contemporary Reactions

CAPTAIN LEWIS THOMAS

[A Very Amazing Entertainment]†

* * * I am just got up from a very Amazing entertainment; to use a Metaphor in the Foundling, I have been these four or five days last past a fellow traveller of Harry Fieldings, & a very agreeable Journey I have had. Character, Painting, Reflection, Humour, excellent each in its Kind, in short I found every thing there, You said I should find, when you gave me an Account of the Writing. If my design had been to propagate virtue by appearing publickly in its defence, I should rather have been ye Author of Tom Jones than of five Folio Volumes of sermons.—so much for my opinion of the Book, on which, I could write a great deal of Common Place, if I was not writing to You, & had not indeed myself some better employment.

I read it in company with a Brother officer who came to Carlisle on purpose to live with me, & is a sort of eleve of mine. When we came to ye conversation piece of the officers, he was reading to me, & stopt suddenly when he came to my Name, to ask if I was acquainted with Fielding, "for here is your Picture with yr Name Under it, & the Greek Book in yr. Pocket." It was really Whimsical he should have Pitch'd on my name when he mention'd a circumstance that agreed with the character I bore in the Regiment. My Army Friends, (such of 'em as can read,) will think I was the Person design'd; but I assur'd him I had not the honour to be in the least known to Mr. Fielding. And tho' there were as many Figures in it as an old Gothick Cathedral, I was not considerable enough to have ye least Nich there. He has drawn a Portrait of my Friend Mrs. Whitfield at ye Bell in Gloucester such as Painters commonly draw; (I remember I was once at Ramsay's & saw a Picture that pleased me extreamly, it was a Young Lady that would have justified a mans falling in Love at ye first sight; upon my praising it, Ramsay told me if I would walk into ye Next Room I might see ye Original; I saw her indeed, but tho' there was some resemblance in the features, hardly a grace appear'd that had so much charm'd me in the Copy—) I breakfasted two or three times with Mrs. Whitfield, we talk'd of nothing but gayety & Assemblies; she let me into a Short History of her Lovers, & told me ye conquests she had made when Younger, & if I might put any faith in

†From a letter dated 3 April 1749. In J. P. Feil, "Fielding's Character of Mrs. Whitefield," *Philological Quarterly*, 39 (1960), 509–10. Thomas refers to *Tom Jones* VII.xii.284, where Ensign Northerton says, "There's Thomas of our Regiment, always carries a *Homo* [i.e., Homer] in his Pocket. . . ."

her own Commentaries, she had had as many occasions of triumph as Julius Caesar; in short I went away extremely disgusted with the Folly & behaviour of my Coquet Landlady. How ye Devil came it into Fielding's head to praise this Woman so exuberantly? If I was Master of the Bell Inn, I vow I should be absolutely Jealous.

ASTRAEA AND MINERVA HILL

[A Double Merit]†

* * * Having with much ado got over some Reluctance, that was bred by a familiar coarseness in the *Title*, we went through the whole six volumes; and found much (masqu'd) merit, in 'em All: a double merit, both of Head, and *Heart*. Had there been only That of the last sort, you love it I am sure, too much, to leave a Doubt of your resolving to examine it—However, if you do, it shoud be when you can best spare it your attention—Else, the Author introduces all his Sections, (and too often interweaves the *serious* Body of his meanings) with long Runs of bantering Levity, which his good sense may suffer the Effect of. It is true, he seems to wear this Lightness, as a grave Head sometimes wears a Feather; which tho' He and Fashion may consider as an ornament, Reflection will condemn, as a Disguise, and *covering*.

* * *

Meanwhile, it is an honest pleasure, which we take in adding, that (exclusive of one wild, detach'd and independent Story of a *Man of the Hill*, that neither brings on Anything, nor rose from Anything that went before it) All the changefull windings of the Author's Fancy carry on a course of regular Design; and end in an extremely moving Close, where Lines that seem'd to wander and run different ways, meet, All, in an instructive Center.

The whole Piece consists of an inventive race of Disappointments and Recoveries. It excites Curiosity, and holds it watchful. It has just and pointed Satire; but it is a partial Satire, and confin'd too narrowly: It sacrifices to Authority, and Interest.——Its *Events* reward Sincerity, and punish and expose Hypocrisy; shew Pity and Benevolence in amiable Lights, and Avarice and Brutality in very

†From a letter to Samuel Richardson, 27 July 1749. Forster MSS., XV.ii folios 74–77; Dorothy Brewster, *Aaron Hill* (New York: Columbia University Press, 1913), pp. 270–71; Ronald Paulson and Thomas Lockwood, *Henry Fielding, The Critical Heritage* (London: Routledge and Kegan Paul, 1969; New York: Barnes & Noble, 1969), pp. 172–74. Richardson had playfully commissioned Astraea and Minerva, the daughters of his friend Aaron Hill, to give him their opinion of *Tom Jones*.

despicable ones. In every Part it has Humanity for its Intention; in too many, it *seems* wantoner than It was meant to be: It has bold shocking Pictures; and (I fear) not unresembling ones, in high Life and in low.——And (to conclude this too adventurous guess-work from a Pair of forward Baggages) woud, everywhere, (we think) *deserve* to please.——if stript of what the Author thought himself most sure to *please by*.

SAMUEL RICHARDSON

[A Very Bad Tendency]†

* * * I must confess, that I have been prejudiced by the Opinion of Several judicious Friends against the truly coarse-titled Tom Jones; and so have been discouraged from reading it.—I was told, that it was a rambling Collection of Waking Dreams, in which Probability was not observed: And that it had a very bad Tendency. And I had Reason to think that the Author intended for his Second View (His *first*, to fill his Pocket, by accommodating it to the reigning Taste) in writing it, to whiten a vicious Character, and to make Morality bend to his Practices. What Reason has he to make his Tom illegitimate, in an Age where Keeping is become a Fashion? Why did he make him a common—What shall I call it?—And a Kept Fellow, the Lowest of all Fellows, yet in Love with a Young Creature who was trapsing after him, a Fugitive from her Father's House?—Why did he draw his Heroine so fond, so foolish, and so insipid?—Indeed he has one Excuse—He knows not how to draw a delicate Woman—He has not been accustomed to such Company —And is too prescribing, too impetuous, too immoral, I will venture to say, to take any other Byass than that a perverse and crooked Nature has given him; or Evil Habits, at least, have confirm'd in him. Do Men expect Grapes of Thorns, or Figs of Thistles? But, perhaps, I think the worse of the Piece because I know the Writer, and dislike his Principles, both Public and Private, tho' I wish well to the *Man*, and Love Four worthy Sisters of his, with whom I am well acquainted. And indeed should admire him, did he make the Use of his Talents which I wish him to make; For the Vein of Humour, and Ridicule, which he is Master of, might, if properly turned, do great Service to ye Cause of Virtue.

†From a letter to Astraea and Minerva Hill, 4 August 1749. Forster MSS., XV.ii. 78–79; Austin Dobson, *Fielding* (London: Macmillan, 1883), pp. 139–40; John Carroll, *Selected Letters of Samuel Richardson* (Oxford: Clarendon Press, 1964), pp. 127–28; Paulson and Lockwood, pp. 174–75.

"ORBILIUS"

An Examen of *The History of Tom Jones, A Foundling*†

To the Man-Mountain

Most Sublime SIR,

AMONG all the personages I have been so long acquainted with, I could not think of any one so proper for a Patron of the following laborious *Examen*, as yourself: For are you not the worthy Progenitor of *the Man of the Hill?* And can you be supposed to be interested in the Event of the Story of an insignificant *Foundling*, any more than your Son, who has been so impertinently made to interrupt the Thread of it? It is true, Mr. *F*. has *murdered* you, as he has done the rest of his Characters. But, this notwithstanding, all the World knows you are still alive, and will live as long as the immortal *Gulliver*. Let this therefore be added, by way of Appendix to the rest of Mr. *F*.'s Incredibilities; and believe me to be the common Friend of you, and of *the Man in the Moon*, where the modern Philosophy has discovered an *illustrious* Group of your Brethren, as far surpassing our sublunary ones, as you surpass them all in Size, and equal them in Duration. I am, Sir, in *profound* Admiration of your *extensive* Abilities,

Your most HUMBLE *Servant,*

(*and never was the diminutive Epithet*

more properly applied)

ORBILIUS

Letter I

The Task of examining Mr. *F*.'s late celebrated Performance, called *The History of a Foundling*, chiefly with a View to Morals, at your Request, I willingly undertake. But as, in attending my Author in every Stage, and through every Inn he drives to (where I shall at least be sure of good Chear), I foresee that I shall be obliged to run to some Length, I will not take up your Time by a longer Introduction.

---

†London: W. Owen, 1750. But *The Gentleman's Magazine* (p. 576) and *London Magazine* (p. 580) list the *Examen* as published in December, 1749 (Frederick T. Blanchard, *Fielding the Novelist* [New Haven: Yale University Press, 1927], p. 39); *Old England* advertised it as published on December 9 (Paulson and Lockwood, p. 187). These selections are only a small portion of the *Examen* by Orbilius (a pseudonym), who comments on the whole of *Tom Jones*, chapter by chapter. Orbilius's identity is unknown.

In prosecuting my Design, I shall not be deterred by any thing that looks like (or is) Prolixity in my Author; but give to every Chapter its full Weight of Censure (if Censure it deserves); agreeably to the Practice of the great *Bentleius*,[1] of formidable Memory to all bad Writers, whether on Subjects of Religion, Learning, or Humour.

And first we alight at the Portal, which will give us a specious Plan of the whole Fabric.

The Dedication

Does Mr. *F.* really owe the *Existence* he mentions to the worthy Gentleman, to whom he dedicates this Monument of his Labours? This seems not to be so agreeable as might be wished to his Patron's *Dislike of public Praise,* of which Mr. *F.* thinks it convenient to assure us, especially as the Author declares at the End of this Epistle (as he calls it), that what he hath said in it, *is not only without, but absolutely against* his Patron's *Consent.* If this were true, with regard to the *First Edition,* methinks it was very disobliging in Mr. *F.* to continue this excessive and disgustful Incense throughout the future Editions: For it cannot be doubted, but that Mr. *L.* made use of all his Interest with Mr. *F.* to get him to omit what was so offensive to his Modesty, after he had seen it in Print.

There are other Persons praised, as well as Mr. *L.* in this Dedication; who, no doubt, will take very great Pride in the Merit they have with the Public, in contributing to the Existence of this renowned Author.

The present Work, it seems, is the *Labour of some Years.* Can that be? *Some Years* about such a Performance as *Tom Jones!*— We all took Mr. *F.* to be endowed with quicker Parts than this *Labour of his Brain* warrants our ascribing to him; since, instead of a *Minerva,* he has only been delivered of her Owl. If a Man presents his Readers with his *Dreams,* need he take up *Years* in telling them? *John Bunyan* perform'd, as it seems, a Work infinitely superior and more useful, with much greater Ease. And *John Bunyan's* Performance was a Work of Genius: But *John Bunyan was a* Genius, though a grave one. Mr. *F.* on the contrary, is so volatile, that I dare say he never pursued any one thing for a Year together; much less such a *skipping* Work as this before us; which, though it comprehends an unmeasurable Length of Time, need not have cost much in writing, if we may guess by the Correctness of the Style. *John Dryden,* otherwise an incomparable Writer, boasted of his having produced a bad Play in a Fortnight: Mr. *F.* more inconsistently, of having spent *some Years* (which others may interpret

1. Richard Bentley (1662–1742), a brilliant but prickly classical scholar, theologian, and critic. [*Editor*]

many) in corrupting Youth, *i.e.*, in writing *Tom Jones*. Yet *the Reader*, Mr. F. tells us, will find *nothing in the whole Course* of his Performance, *prejudicial to the Cause of* RELIGION *and* VIRTUE: Nothing *inconsistent with the* STRICTEST RULES *of* DECENCY; that is, according to Mr. *F.*'s Notions of Decency, we may presume; *nor which can offend even the* CHASTEST *Eye in the Persual.*—TO RECOMMEND GOODNESS AND INNOCENCE, HATH BEEN the Author's SINCERE ENDEAVOUR IN THIS HISTORY. How unhappy, if he should fail in an Endeavour *so sincere!* Could one imagine, that after this solemn Declaration, the Author cannot, in the same Paragraph, forbear giving a loose Picture of VIRTUE itself, by *his Idea of that Loveliness which* Plato *asserts there is in her* NAKED *Charms?* Whether this Gentleman hath not wronged *Plato* by this Epithet, which was only inserted for the sake of the Pleasure he takes in such Images, will be seen by the Passage itself referred to, as it stands in *Cic. de Fin.* Lib. II. *Oculorum, inquit* Plato, *est in nobis sensus acerrimus*: *quibus* SAPIENTIAM *non cernimus. Quam illa ardentes amores excitaret sui, si videretur!*[2] I have put on my Spectacles; but cannot see here any Word answering to the Adjective NAKED;—not to take Notice, that what *Plato* says of Philosophy, Mr. *F.* makes him say of Virtue: But this comes of citing without Book; or producing AUTHORITIES without AUTHORS, in a Work too that took up so much Time, and cost him so much Labour. But more of this, when we come to Book XVIII. Chap. III. Our Author *hath* (for I shall use his own elegant Termination of *th* instead of *s* in the third Person Singular, as often as the auxiliary Verbs *do* and *have* shall occur) been very fair, in presenting so early to the Eye of the Reader a Criterion, by which to judge of his whole Work: And I will not anticipate, but proceed to try him by this Criterion, through all his following Scenes. A worthy Design he *hath* had: Pray Heaven it be found as well executed as formed! He *hath shewn*, he says, *that no Acquisition of Guilt can compensate the Loss of that solid inward Comfort of Mind, which is the sure Companion of Innocence and Virtue.* More he says to prove the Goodness of his Moral. And as ALL HIS WIT AND HUMOUR (*p.* 14.) have been employed in the Piece before us, this will furnish us with a further Criterion how far this W*it and* Humour of his really extend: Which, by the Majority of Readers, have been thought inexhaustible.

But before we proceed, it may be proper (in order to elucidate several Points which I shall but just touch upon, and to save you the Trouble of referring to the Book for any Matters that may be

---

2. "The eyes, says Plato, are our keenest sense, but we cannot see Wisdom with them. What burning love of her would she have stirred, if she could be seen!" Cicero, *De Finibus Bonorum et Malorum* II.xvi.52. See note 5, p. 7, above [*Editor*].

doubtful) briefly to give you a Sketch of this *delectable* History, so far as the Hero and Heroine are concerned.

Tom Jones, then, the spurious or misbegotten Issue of *Miss Bridget Allworthy*, and dropt by that Lady in her Brother Mr. *Allworthy's* Bed, is by this Gentleman, in order, I suppose, to illustrate his Prudence, as well as Morality, educated in so *genteel*, or rather loose a Manner, between the contrary Disciplines of the rigid Churchman Mr. *Thwackum*, and the Moral Philosopher Mr. *Square*, as gives an unhappy Prognostic of his future Follies and Vices; since a Man, who in his Youth has not had the Advantage of some settled Principles of Religion, rarely settles himself afterwards in right Principles or Practices (who better than our Author should have known that?) This being the Case, it is no Wonder that *Tom* scarce finds himself released from the too slack Government under which he had been educated, but he plunges into every Debauchery. Add to this, That *Allworthy*, though a Man of Virtue himself, had not the Prudence to instil into his vicious Foster-Son a Remembrance of his disadvantageous Birth, which might have restrained him from many Enormities; nor even to give him any Employment, which might teach him, that he was not born merely to gratify his natural Propensity, which led him headlong into an early Commerce with Women. The first whom he attempted, and successfully, was *Moll Seagrim*, the (*fair*, shall I say? or) sooty Daughter of *Black*-guard *George* (Two exemplary Characters of our Author; whose *sincere Endeavour hath been to recommend* GOODNESS *and* INNOCENCE). The Effects of this Commerce discovering itself, and some of *Tom's* other Actions being *misrepresented*, as Mr. *F.* will have it, to *Allworthy*, he is, with as much Improbability, as there was Folly and Weakness in his first Adoption by that Gentlemen, dismissed with Money, and a Bill for 500l. in his Pocket; the latter (he being a *near Relation* of our Author's *Parson Adams*, it may be presumed) he soon carelesly lost: And, as I before hinted, had no Talents to recommend himself to any reputable Livelihood: The too natural Consequence of which was, his returning to his former evil Courses; which he did as soon as they offered themselves; first, by the Means of Mrs. *Waters* (the Paramour of Captain *Waters*, who is only introduced as one of Mr. *Bayes's* Lumber-Troop,[3] to *fill up*, not to *further*, our Author's wonderful Plot); who inveigles the Hero on the Road, after he had rescued her from being robbed and murdered; and, next, by his Amours with Lady *Bellaston*, to whom he goes to inquire News of *Sophia*, under the *plausible* Pretence of restoring to the latter the 100l. Bill, which, as an Instance of the Author's Invention, she had as heedlessly dropped as the Hero had his 500l. To Lady *Bellaston*, suitably to his infamous Birth, he per-

---

3. The comic army in Buckingham, et al., *The Rehearsal* (1671). [*Editor*]

formed the Offices of a *Maskwell*,[4] for which she becomes his Trib-
utary. In this scandalous and despicable manner does he live with
that Quality-Strumpet, till, having dangerously wounded one *Fitz-
Patrick*, who had married a Cousin of *Sophia*, he is thrown into
Prison, and is in imminent Peril of his Neck: Whence at last he is
rescued by the *seasonable* Recovery of *Fitz-Patrick*, and as *seasonable* Arrival of *Allworthy*; to whom the whole History of his *honourable* Birth is revealed by that very Mrs. *Waters*, who had personated his Mother, and debauched (if we may use the Word of one
before debauched) her supposed Son. This Discovery restores her
Credit with *Allworthy*, who had banished her the Country on her
false Confession, that she was the Mother of *Tom*; and at the same
time ingratiates the latter with his Uncle *Allworthy*. Nothing therefore remains but the rewarding Mr. *Jones* for his former Rogueries,
with as fine and as virtuous a Woman as our Author and his honourable Coadjutor are capable of painting: Which leads me to say
something of

Sophia: Who was the Daughter of 'Squire *Western*, an ignorant,
clownish, obstinate, Jacobite Country Justice. A Whig, or ministerial Justice, no doubt, he had been, with a small Change in his
Qualities, had our Author been so *many Years* about this Work, as
to have drawn this Character, when he thought himself a [5] *Champion*, and capable of wielding the Club of *Hercules*; which was
indeed *Herculis cothurnos optare infanti*.[6] *Sophia* herself is with
great Pomp introduced to the Veneration of the Reader for her
Modesty, and other good Qualities; but as it is certain, that Mr. *F.*
is utterly unable (as we see in all his Pieces, but most flagrantly in
this) to draw a Woman of true Virtue and Modesty; so in nothing
is she so illustrious as in her Partiality to the well-known Debauch-
eries of *Jones*, and in her Elopement from her Father's House, on
Pretence of avoiding a disgustful Match with *Blifil*, the legitimate
Son of *Allworthy's* Sister, which nevertheless she had no just
Ground to fear, as we shall hereafter shew: However, out she sets,
partly padding it, partly riding; arrives at her Relation's, the worthy
Lady *Bellaston*; who, being acquainted with her strong Attachment
to *Jones*, baffles her for some time, in order to keep the Hero to her-
self: At last, forms a Plot to have her ravished by Lord *Fellamar*: A
strangely unnecessary Scheme! (but not the less likely to be Mr.
F.'s for *that*) since that Nobleman was afterwards to patch up a
Marriage with her for her Fortune's sake, as well as for the real
Affection he seems to have borne her, when he would have courted

4. The villain in Congreve's *The Double
Dealer* (1694). [*Editor*]
5. The Author of the *Champion* takes
the Name of *Hercules Vinegar*: A *Vinegar*
no doubt! he knew his own Excellence;
and rightly assumed the Character of a

Bear-garden Hero. [*Orbilius's note*]
6. "To choose Hercules's boots for a
baby." Quintilian, *Institutio Oratoria*
VI.i.36 (Paulson and Lockwood, p. 192).
[*Editor*]

her honourably: But Lady *Bellaston*, being disappointed in her admirable Project, lays a Scheme to have *Jones* pressed; in which also failing by his being arrested, an open Way seems to be made for *Sophia* to run into his Arms, after a few sham Reluctances on her Part, and some few Sparks of Displeasure at *Jones's* supposed publishing her Story in Inns, *&c.* not in the least reproaching him with his repeated Failures in Point of Fidelity.

And now arrives the Time, when our Author, being at a Loss to contrive Ways and Means to raise the Character of his Hero, since he could not in Merit, and would not at *Tyburn*, reconciles him to *Allworthy* by the Means before mentioned; *Allworthy* reconciles him to *Sophia*; and the Fiddles strike up (not without the Melody of Marrow-bones and Cleavers, we presume) to the Joy of every Fortune-hunter and rathe-ripe Virgin in the Kingdom.

* * *

Book XIII. Chap. VIII

Fifty Pounds given to *Jones* for his Gallantry is a most excellent Instance of *Christian Charity! Jones's* indeed to *Anderson* is praiseworthy. But this impudent Quality-Whore's is beneath Censure. Can any thing be more odious, than for a Woman of Figure to divest herself of her Dignity for a vile Satisfaction, and heap on her Partner in Guilt so ample a Reward of his Baseness?' Where is Female Decency, that seeks to be courted, even when its own Inclination forwards the Courtship? Can any *English* Lady of Quality be so gross a Sensualist?—Perhaps she may: But is this corrupted Scene to be called Nature? And shall an Author glory in describing the Jakes of an human Mind, and say that he drew his Character from the *original Book of Nature*, as he expresses himself Book VII. Chap. XII? Ought he not rather to conclude with *Thwackum*, Book III. Chap. III. *that the human Mind, since the Fall, is nothing but a Sink of Iniquity?* Now then is the Time that the worthy Mr. *Jones* is *Right Honourably* taken into Keeping: In which he well makes as illustrious a Figure as any-where else in this Work.

* * *

Chap. X

That so great a Voluptuary as Mr. *Jones* should be alternately committing Acts of Debauchery, and tasting, by conferring, the Pleasures of Beneficence (which he does in this Chapter by leaving his Beneficiary, to attend the Call of the infamous Lady *Bellaston*), is an Inconsistency in Character never before heard of. To *earn the Wages of Iniquity*, in order with those Wages to merit Heaven by Acts of disinterested Beneficence, may qualify him indeed for a Place in the *Roman* Calendar of Saints, but in no other Chair of Beatification, I doubt. And Mr. *F.* must certainly have searched the Breviary to find so mixt a Character, where Instances of Oddity are easily to be met with, which, in any less grave Book, might perhaps pass for Instances of Humour also.

* * *

ANONYMOUS

[Review of Pierre Antoine de la Place, *Histoire de Tom Jones, ou L'Enfant Trouvé* (1750)]†

* * * In *France* the ladies would be shock'd at the repeated breaches of faith in *Tom Jones* to his mistress, and fathers and mothers would exclaim against that resolute boldness with which Miss *Western* abandons her father's house to preserve herself inviolate to her lover. In *England* they are not so rigorous; every father and mother indeed, in *London* as well as *Paris*, would be glad to have their children perfectly obedient to their will; but the love of liberty in the *English*, renders them generally more disposed to forgive the disobedience of a daughter, when her obedience might make her miserable. Inconstancy in a lover, will no more be pardon'd by an *English* than a *French* woman, but the first will sooner pass by a slight neglect; in general, the *English* ladies are more jealous of a man's sentiments, the *French* of his actions. M. *de la Place*, the translator of this piece, would have done well perhaps to have inserted these remarks, which we have ventur'd to make, in his *preliminary discourse*, in order to prevent those objections which some cavillers might make against M. *Fielding*.

"* * * if Mr. *Fielding* had written for the *French*, he would probably have suppressed a multitude of passages, excellent indeed in themselves, but which would appear to a *Frenchman*, unseasonable or misplaced. When he has once warmed his imagination with the interesting result of an intrigue highly pathetic, and artfully laid, he becomes impatient under all sorts of digressions, dissertations, or moral touches, and regards all such ornaments, however fine, as obstacles to the pleasure which he is in haste to enjoy. I have done no more than what the author himself would have done."

†*The Gentleman's Magazine*, 20 (March, 1750), 117–118. De la Place addresses a complimentary preface to Fielding. The reviewer translates and quotes de la Place's explanation for his omitting Fielding's authorial commentary in his translation.

ANONYMOUS

An Essay on the New Species of Writing Founded by Mr. Fielding†

Mr. *Fielding* therefore, who sees all the little Movements by which human Nature is actuated, found it necessary to open a new Vein of Humour. * * * For chrystal Palaces and winged Horses, we find homely Cots and ambling Nags; and instead of Impossibility, what we experience every Day.

* * *

We will here * * * briefly observe what deserves Reproof in Mr. *Fielding*'s last Piece, *viz.* Tom Jones; a Performance which on the whole perhaps is the most lively Book ever publish'd, but our Author has here and there put his Claim to that Privilege of being dull, which the Critics have indulg'd to the Writers of Books of any Length.

> —*Opere in longo fas est obrepere sommnum.*
> HOR.

> ———Sleep
> O'er Works of Length allowably may creep.
> FRANCIS.

The most glaring Instance of this kind in all this Author's Works is the long unenliven'd Story of *the Man of the Hill*; which makes up so great a Part of a Volume. A Narration which neither interests or entertains the Reader, and is of no more Service than in filling up so many Pages. The Substance of the Story is such as (to make use of Mr. *Shirley*'s Phrase)

> '*almost staggers Credibility.*'[1]

For though I have heard it affirm'd, that there is such a Character as the *Man of the Hill*; yet I believe the Generality of Readers concurr'd with me in thinking it chimerical and unnaturally singular. I am very sorry Mr. *Fielding* should have introduc'd so improbable a Story. * * *

†London: W. Owen, 1751; reprint edition, ed. Alan D. McKillop (Los Angeles: Augustan Reprint Society, publication no. 95, 1962), pp. 6, 15–16, 43–45.
1. William Shirley, *Edward the Black Prince* (1750), p. 1.

[Samuel Johnson on Fielding]

From *The Rambler*†

This Kind of Writing may be termed not improperly the Comedy of Romance, and is to be conducted nearly by the Rules of Comic Poetry. Its Province is to bring about natural Events by easy Means, and to keep up Curiosity without the Help of Wonder; it is therefore precluded from the Machines and Expedients of the Heroic Romance, and can neither employ Giants to snatch away a Lady from the nuptial Rites, nor Knights to bring her back from Captivity; it can neither bewilder its Personages in Desarts, nor lodge them in imaginary Castles.

* * *

The Task of our present Writers is very different; it requires, together with that Learning which is to be gained from Books, that Experience which can never be attained by solitary Diligence, but must arise from general Converse, and accurate Observation of the living World. Their Performances have, as *Horace* expresses it, *plus oneris quantum veniae minus*,[1] little Indulgence, and therefore more Difficulty. They are engaged in Portraits of which every one knows the Original, and can therefore detect any Deviation from Exactness of Resemblance. Other Writings are safe, except from the Malice of Learning; but these are in danger from every common Reader; as the Slipper ill executed was censured by a Shoemaker who happened to stop in his Way at the *Venus* of *Apelles*.

But the Danger of not being approved as just Copyers of human Manners, is not the most important Apprehension that an Author of this Sort ought to have before him. These Books are written chiefly to the Young, the Ignorant, and the Idle, to whom they serve as Lectures of Conduct, and Introductions into Life. They are the Entertainment of Minds unfurnished with Ideas, and therefore easily susceptible of Impressions; not fixed by Principles, and therefore easily following the Current of Fancy; not informed by Experience, and consequently open to every false Suggestion and partial Account.

* * * when an Adventurer is levelled with the rest of the World, and acts in such Scenes of the universal Drama, as may be the Lot of any other Man, young Spectators fix their Eyes upon him with

†No. 4 (31 March 1750). Johnson does not mention Fielding, but his remarks about "this kind of writing," "the comedy of romance," suggest that he knows something of Fielding's preface to *Joseph Andrews* (though he claimed never to have read the book), and his remarks about making men rather "cunning than good" and about prudence suggest that he is addressing himself principally to the morality of *Tom Jones*.

1. *Epistles* II.i.170. [*Editor*]

closer Attention, and hope by observing his Behaviour and Success to regulate their own Practices, when they shall be engaged in the like Part.

For this Reason these familiar Histories may perhaps be made of greater Use than the Solemnities of professed Morality, and convey the Knowledge of Vice and Virtue with more Efficacy than Axioms and Definitions. But if the Power of Example is so great, as to take Possession of the Memory by a kind of Violence, and produce Effects almost without the Intervention of the Will, Care ought to be taken that, when the Choice is unrestrained, the best Examples only should be exhibited; and that which is likely to operate so strongly, should not be mischievous or uncertain in its Effects.

The chief Advantages which these Fictions have over real Life is, that their Authors are at liberty, tho' not to invent, yet to select Objects, and to cull from the Mass of Mankind, those Individuals upon which the Attention ought most to be employ'd; as a Diamond, though it cannot be made, may be polished by Art, and placed in such a Situation, as to display that Lustre which before was buried among common Stones.

It is justly considered as the greatest Excellency of Art, to imitate Nature; but it is necessary to distinguish those Parts of Nature, which are most proper for Imitation: Greater Care is still required in representing Life, which is so often discoloured by Passion, or deformed by Wickedness. If the World be promiscuously described, I cannot see of what Use it can be to read the Account; or why it may not be as safe to turn the Eye immediately upon Mankind, as upon a Mirrour which shows all that presents itself without Discrimination.

It is therefore not a sufficient Vindication of a Character, that it is drawn as it appears; for many Characters ought never to be drawn; nor of a Narrative, that the Train of Events is agreeable to Observation and Experience; for that Observation which is called Knowledge of the World, will be found much more frequently to make Men cunning than good. The Purpose of these Writings is surely not only to show Mankind, but to provide that they may be seen hereafter with less Hazard; to teach the Means of Avoiding the Snares which are laid by TREACHERY for INNOCENCE, without infusing any Wish for that Superiority with which the Betrayer flatters his Vanity; to give the Power of counteracting Fraud without the Temptation to practice it; to initiate Youth by mock Encounters in the Art of necessary Defence, and to increase Prudence without impairing Virtue.

Many Writers for the sake of following Nature, so mingle good and bad Qualities in their principal Personages, that they are both equally conspicuous; and as we accompany them through their

Adventures with Delight, and are led by Degrees to interest ourselves in their Favour, we lose the Abhorrence of their Faults, because they do not hinder our Pleasure, or, perhaps, regard them with some Kindness for being united with so much Merit.

* * *

* * * while Men consider Good and Evil as springing from the same Root, they will spare the one for the sake of the other, and in judging, if not of others at least of themselves, will be apt to estimate their Virtues by their Vices. To this fatal Error all those will contribute, who confound the Colours of Right and Wrong, and instead of helping to settle their Boundaries, mix them with so much Art, that no common Mind is able to disunite them.

In Narratives, where historical Veracity has no Place, I cannot discover why there should not be exhibited the most perfect Idea of Virtue; of Virtue not angelical, nor above Probability; for what we cannot credit we shall never imitate; but the highest and purest Kind that Humanity can reach, which, when exercised in such Trials as the various Revolutions of Things shall bring upon it, may, by conquering some Calamities, and enduring others, teach us what we may hope, and what we can perform. Vice, for Vice is necessary to be shewn, should always disgust; nor should the Graces of Gaiety, or the Dignity of Courage, be so united with it, as to reconcile it to the Mind. Wherever it appears, it should raise Hatred by the Malignity of its Practices; and Contempt, by the Meanness of its Stratagems; for while it is supported by either Parts or Spirit, it will be seldom heartily abhorred. The *Roman* Tyrant was content to be hated, if he was but feared; and there are Thousands of the Readers of Romances willing to be thought wicked, if they may be allowed to be Wits. It is therefore to be always inculcated, that Virtue is the highest Proof of a superior Understanding, and the only solid Basis of Greatness; and that Vice is the natural Consequence of narrow Thoughts, that begins in Mistake, and ends in Ignominy.

From *Boswell's Life of Johnson*†

'Sir, (continued he,) there is all the difference in the world between characters of nature and characters of manners; and *there* the difference between the characters of Fielding and those of ?hardson. Characters of manners are very entertaining; but they ?o be understood, by a more superficial observer, than characters ?ture, where a man must dive into the recesses of the human

swell, *The Life of Dr. Samuel* ?. George Birkbeck Hill, rev. ?l, 6 vols. (Oxford: Claren- don Press, 1934–65), II, 48–49 (spring, 1768), II, 173–75 (6 April 1772).

It always appeared to me that he estimated the compositions of Richardson too highly, and that he had an unreasonable prejudice against Fielding. In comparing those two writers, he used this expression; 'that there was as great a difference between them as between a man who knew how a watch was made, and a man who could tell the hour by looking on the dial-plate.' This was a short and figurative state of his distinction between drawing characters of nature and characters only of manners. But I cannot help being of opinion, that the neat watches of Fielding are as well constructed as the large clocks of Richardson, and that his dial-plates are brighter. Fielding's characters, though they do not expand themselves so widely in dissertation, are as just pictures of human nature, and I will venture to say, have more striking features, and nicer touches of the pencil; and though Johnson used to quote with approbation a saying of Richardson's, 'that the virtues of Fielding's heroes were the vices of a truly good man', I will venture to add, that the moral tendency of Fielding's writings, though it does not encourage a strained and rarely possible virtue, is ever favourable to honour and honesty, and cherishes the benevolent and generous affections. He who is as good as Fielding would make him, is an amiable member of society, and may be led on by more regulated instructors, to a higher state of ethical perfection.

* * *

Fielding being mentioned, Johnson exclaimed, 'he was a blockhead'; and upon my expressing my astonishment at so strange an assertion, he said, 'What I mean by his being a blockhead is that he was a barren rascal.' BOSWELL. 'Will you not allow, Sir, that he draws very natural pictures of human life?' JOHNSON. 'Why, Sir, it is of very low life. Richardson used to say, that had he not known who Fielding was, he should have believed he was an ostler. Sir, there is more knowledge of the heart in one letter of Richardson's, than in all "Tom Jones". I, indeed, never read "Joseph Andrews".' ERSKINE. 'Surely, Sir, Richardson is very tedious.' JOHNSON. 'Why, Sir, if you were to read Richardson for the story, your impatience would be so much fretted that you would hang yourself. But you must read him for the sentiment, and consider the story as only giving occasion to the sentiment.'—I have already given my opinion of Fielding; but I cannot refrain from repeating here my wonder at Johnson's excessive and unaccountable depreciation of one of the best writers that England has produced. 'Tom Jones' has stood the test of publick opinion with such success, as to have established its great merit, both for the story, the sentiments, and the manners, and also the varieties of diction, so as to leave no doubt of its having an animated truth of execution throughout.

From Hannah More, *Correspondence*†

I never saw Johnson really angry with me but once; and his displeasure did him so much honour that I loved him the better for it. I alluded rather flippantly, I fear, to some witty passage in Tom Jones: he replied, 'I am shocked to hear you quote from so vicious a book. I am sorry to hear you have read it: a confession which no modest lady should ever make. I scarcely know a more corrupt work.' I thanked him for his correction; assured him I thought full as ill of it now as he did, and had only read it at an age when I was more subject to be caught by the wit, than able to descern the mischief. Of Joseph Andrews I declared my decided abhorrence. He went so far as to refuse to Fielding the great talents which are ascribed to him, and broke into a noble panegyric on his competitor, Richardson; who, he said, was as superior to him in talents as in virtue; and whom he pronounced to be the greatest genius that had shed its lustre on this path of literature.

†From a letter to her sister, 1780, in *Memoirs of the Life and Correspondence of Mrs. Hannah More* (London, 1834), I.168.

Criticism

SAMUEL TAYLOR COLERIDGE

Notes on *Tom Jones*†

Manners change from generation to generation, and with manners morals appear to change,—actually change with some, but appear to change with all but the abandoned. A young man of the present day who should act as Tom Jones is supposed to act at Upton, with Lady Bellaston, &c. would not be a Tom Jones; and a Tom Jones of the present day, without perhaps being in the ground a better man, would have perished rather than submit to be kept by a harridan of fortune. Therefore this novel is, and, indeed, pretends to be, no exemplar of conduct. But, notwithstanding all this, I do loathe the cant which can recommend Pamela and Clarissa Harlowe as strictly moral, though they poison the imagination of the young with continued doses of *tinct. lyttæ*,[1] while Tom Jones is prohibited as loose. I do not speak of young women;—but a young man whose heart or feelings can be injured, or even his passions excited, by aught in this novel, is already thoroughly corrupt. There is a cheerful, sunshiny, breezy spirit that prevails everywhere, strongly contrasted with the close, hot, day-dreamy continuity of Richardson. Every indiscretion, every immoral act, of Tom Jones (and it must be remembered that he is in every one taken by surprise—his inward principles remaining firm—) is so instantly punished by embarrassment and unanticipated evil consequences of his folly, that the reader's mind is not left for a moment to dwell or run riot on the criminal indulgence itself. In short, let the requisite allowance be made for the increased refinement of our manners,—and then I dare believe that no young man who consulted his heart and conscience only, without adverting to what the world would say— could rise from the perusal of Fielding's Tom Jones, Joseph Andrews, or Amelia, without feeling himself a better man;—at least, without an intense conviction that he could not be guilty of a base act.

If I want a servant or mechanic, I wish to know what he does:— but of a friend, I must know what he is. And in no writer is this momentous distinction so finely brought forward as by Fielding. We do not care what Blifil does;—the deed, as separate from the agent, may be good or ill; but Blifil is a villain;—and we feel him to be so from the very moment he, the boy Blifil, restores Sophia's poor captive bird to its native and rightful liberty.

* * *

†From *The Complete Works*, ed. W. G. T. Shedd (London, 1856), IV.379–81. The essay from which this excerpt is taken was written around 1826. 1. "Tincture of madness." [*Editor*]

Even in the most questionable part of Tom Jones, I can not but think, after frequent reflection, that an additional paragraph, more fully and forcibly unfolding Tom Jones's sense of self-degradation on the discovery of the true character of the relation in which he had stood to Lady Bellaston, and his awakened feeling of the dignity of manly chastity, would have removed in great measure any just objections,—at all events relatively to Fielding himself, and with regard to the state of manners in his time.

* * *

SAMUEL TAYLOR COLERIDGE
[A Master of Composition]†

What a master of composition Fielding was! Upon my word, I think the Œdipus Tyrannus, the Alchemist, and Tom Jones, the three most perfect plots ever planned. And how charming, how wholesome, Fielding always is! To take him up after Richardson is like emerging from a sick-room heated by stoves into an open lawn on a breezy day in May.

DAVID GOLDKNOPF
The Failure of Plot in *Tom Jones*‡

The structural design of *Tom Jones* admirably expresses the neo-classical faith in balance, proportion, reciprocity—one might almost say—in *design*. Why then, one may wonder, did Fielding impose upon this meticulously organized work an elaborate superstructure of authorial interpretation, supplied mainly, but by no means entirely, by the famous introductory chapters? The answer, I believe, lies in the inadequacy of the novel's inner structure—that is to say, its plot—to its sense-supporting task: a disproportion which impelled Fielding to supplement the basic morphology of the work with embellishments of great charm but dubious esthetic relevance, making, as it were, a grace of necessity. Since *Tom Jones* appears to be the most strongly and scrupulously plotted novel of its time, this view is likely to provoke disagreement. But a more sophisticated examination of the structure of *Tom Jones* than it may seem, in its innocence, to require will, I think, bear out my premise.

†From "Table Talk" (5 July 1834— three weeks before Coleridge's death), in *The Complete Works*, ed. W. G. T. Shedd (London, 1856), VI.521.

‡From *Criticism*, 11 (1969), 262–74. Copyright 1969 by the Wayne State University Press. Reprinted by permission of the Wayne State University Press.

By way of preliminary ground-clearing let us first dispose of certain of Fielding's own critical prejudgements on his novels. In the preface to *Joseph Andrews*, it will be recalled, he justified the picaro high-jinks by asserting that the work at hand was a variant form of an established genre—established by Homer no less—the comic epic. But like his claim to the inspiration of the *Aeneid* for *Amelia*, the reference to the apocryphal Homeric work was wishful. The comic-epic strain in *Joseph Andrews* and *Tom Jones* had its source not in the noble works of the past but in Fielding's embarrassment in coping with outrageous situations. That is to say, he slid into the mock-epic mode to reconcile his appetite for vulgarity with his respect for the neo-classical concept of decorum. Consequently, his theory, if it may be dignified as such, of the comic-epic at best solves a problem of diction on the few occasions to which it applies, not of style in any fundamental sense, and certainly not of form.

In *Tom Jones*, Fielding attacked the genre-issue much more contentiously: by impugning the motives, questioning the competence, and belittling the intelligence of the critics (Ch. I of Book V) and by frankly glorifying the value of "marvellous" or "surprising" narrative action, provided only that it lie within the natural capability, and be consonant with the normal propensities, of the characters involved (Ch. I of Book VIII). There is a mood of bluster in these passages, which, I believe, symptomizes the strain set up in Fielding's imagination by the difficulty of his task. Playing peek-a-boo behind Homer was all well and good when it was a question of legitimizing a larky entertainment which began as a pointed satire on another novel, debouched into a general survey of affectation, and ended as pure romance. In *Tom Jones*, however, Fielding was trying to bring both the picaresque exuberance which was his natural bent and the new, aggressive empiricism of his age under a discipline fundamentally unsympathetic to both, the neo-classical canon. It is true that *all* structure bears a slight odor of hypocrisy in the realistic novel, since it presents life under false colors: as a work of art. But in the case of *Tom Jones* the plot falls so far short of doing justice to the author's comprehensive vision that he must repeatedly choose between his narrative and intellectual commitments. I propose now to examine the structure of this novel, in such detail as will perhaps help us to understand his dilemma and its influence on the evolution of the novel.

The overall architectonics of the novel—its tripodal division into six books devoted to country life, six to city life, and six intervening books to the passage of the principals from one to the other—has often been commented on. Apparently the country is the proper sphere for uncomplicated, naturally good characters, such as Tom and Sophia, but only after they have been tested and tempered by the stresses of city life. This, however, does not explain the length and importance of the middle section, the effect of which is to attenuate the rural-urban polarity. Fielding himself, in his some-what disingenuous remarks on "the bill of fare to the feast" in the first chapter of Tom Jones, ignores this middle section entirely. The fact remains, however, that we have not two but three environ-ments to deal with, country, city, and on-the-road, and the last, as we shall see, is much more than a transition between the other two: it has a quite independent character and meaning.

How does each environment condition the action taking place within it? The distinctive structural principle in the first section is socio-political, in the second, symbolic, and in the third, reticula-tive. This is not to say that each mode is confined to one section of the novel: only that each operates most decisively in one section. But the point is perhaps best clarified by illustration.

When I speak of the socio-political structuring of the first part of the novel I am thinking of how two secondary characters, Allworthy and Western, dominate the first six books, how a court life is orga-nized about each and how their style in exercising power sets the course of the novel. I doubt whether any novel before Tom Jones used the social order in this way: that is, as an armature for the nar-rative.

We should here consider not only what Fielding is doing but what he might have done had he so chosen. Novels have often been structured by means of family configuration. This is to some extent true of Clarissa. There is hardly one full-fledged family in Tom Jones: father, mother, and children. (The family of Black George may, I think, be passed over in this connection.) Certainly Allwor-thy and Western aren't family men, since the most important member of a family, Mother, is missing; the fact that both have shadow-wives, in the form of sisters, merely emphasizes their non-uxorial condition. In addition, Western has only one child, and the bachelor Allworthy of course none. Fielding's neo-classical taste for parallelism is much in evidence in Tom Jones. Here the redundancy is almost unnatural. Fielding wants it, I think, for two reasons. The more obvious one is that the extrinsic similarities between Western and Allworthy underscore their intrinsic dissimilarities; against an almost identical background the differences between the physical and the moral man stand out in sharpest relief. The less obvious but no less important reason is that, by excluding the distracting claim to our attention which family-life would introduce, Fielding brings the squirarchical social structure into additional prominence. Fielding is consistent in this strategy. For example, after Partridge's wife dies, Fielding might have married Partridge to Jenny Jones and turned Tom Jones over to his putative parents under Allworthy's avuncular supervision. This wouldn't have botched up the action as much as one might think; the major obstacle to the marriage of Tom and Sophia, their difference in fortune, would still have existed. But as a new focus of interest the family would then have competed with the squirarchical organization.

That is why, it seems to me, the early part of the novel is taken up with creating an ancestry rather than a family for Tom. The bastard, and especially the foundling, is a threat to the social order. He may be anybody's child (as the end of the novel surely demonstrates). But by the same token, once his parents are designated, he need not, and for Fielding's purposes should not, become part of a family. And, as if to make sure that he does not, both "parents" are quickly gotten out of the way.

Another element in the squirarchical operation that Fielding ignores is the economic one. Both Allworthy and Western have large estates. A convenient way to develop and differentiate their characters would be to show them at their work, yet we hardly glimpse that facet of their lives. By excluding precisely the central interest in Defoe's novels, how people keep body and soul together, Fielding again avoids a competing focus of attention.

In short, Fielding seems to be making an effort, consciously or otherwise, to purify Allworthy's and Western's socio-political function. This in turn is exemplified by the administration of justice. The fact that Allworthy and Western are justices-of-the-peace (as men in their position normally would be) is useful to Fielding in that it permits them to serve as nodal points in certain plot-reticulations. But the justice-of-the-peace role was of course much more than apparatus for Fielding. Consider the various aspects of justice which the novel examines. Tom's mother deprived him of the legal right to a mother, and when she tries to make amends, Blifil continues the injustice. In defiance of her legal rights, Sophia is imprisoned and mentally tortured. By reason of Allworthy's *de facto* adoption of Tom, Tom's banishment is also a serious injustice, compounded of course by his innocence. Nor is that Allworthy's first offense of the kind; the near-sainted man almost destroyed Partridge's life. (When Partridge tells him, near the close of the novel that he spent seven years in Winchester Prison, Allworthy quickly passes over that.)

What Fielding has done then is to make the metaphorical pillars of rural society, Allworthy and Western, the main structural members of the first six books, arching this part of the novel between them. It now becomes highly significant that characters so different in personality and philosophy should cooperate, partly by design and partly through chance, to commit serious injustices against blameless individuals, notably Tom and Sophia. Whether or not

Fielding intended a moral critique of the squirarchical order, that nevertheless *is* the effect of the first section of *Tom Jones*; and it is achieved, as I have noted, by giving widely contrastive personalities a similar position, power, and function—and by ignoring powers and functions not unique to that position.

I have already referred to the length and importance of the on-the-road section of *Tom Jones*; in fact it carries almost as much narrative freight as either of the other sections. But travel favors a picaresque looseness of structure, contrary, as we have seen, to Fielding's aim in this novel, and the central section therefore presents difficult problems in narrative organization.

Again a constructive comparison may be drawn with *Joseph Andrews*. The main current of action in *Joseph Andrews* is from the city to the country, while the reverse is true of *Tom Jones*; and there is of course a corresponding thematic contrast too (between, let us say, the Edenic tropism and the going-out-into-the-world impulse in man). But with respect to our present subject, structure, the most striking difference is the far greater prominence of the on-the-road section in *Joseph Andrews*. This, in turn, is indicative of Fielding's relative indifference to problems of form in that novel. He lingers on the road because it gives him greater opportunities for picaresque capers. In *Tom Jones*, on the other hand, Fielding's problem is how to bring itinerant action under the discipline of neo-classical balance and reciprocation. His basic solution is to energize the action by means of a much-used stratagem, the chase, then to structure the chase around Upton Inn. It is there, for example, that Sophia's pursuit of Tom is reversed, and the subordinate chases, Fitzpatrick's pursuit of his wife and Squire Western's of his daughter, are dovetailed into the main pursuit.

Yet the conveniences of plot no more exhaust the role of the inns in this part of the novel than they do the justice-of-the-peace role in the first part. For the inns in *Tom Jones* are much more than busy buildings with doors that can be opened at the wrong time; their power to stir the imagination lies far beyond that of mere mad-cap contrivance. Inns in general have rich symbolic overtones, as anyone who has listened to the discourses of naive travellers is likely to have noted. In strange surroundings our basic needs recover their primitive supremacy, and the ordinary *gasthaus* assumes the aura of the dubious castle where the wayfarer seeks his nervous night's shelter. Can we not, each of us, recall with unusual vividness nondescript places where we once stayed overnight? This effect would not have escaped Fielding, who earned his living for many years as a circuit lawyer. Ample literary precedence for his interest also existed: conspicuously *The Canterbury Tales* and a work which we know had a strong influence on Fielding, *Don Quixote*. Nor would it be stretching a point too far to call attention to the nativity of Jesus.

Though my concern is with the structure of *Tom Jones* rather than with symbolic explication, a few perhaps self-evident remarks on the ambiguity of the inn-symbol may help to explain its richness and dynamism in this section of the novel. The inn is a settlement on the bank of the road, intermediate in its sociological openness between a rural and urban environment. The permanence of the inn derives from the needs of its transient patrons. At the same time the inn offers those transients a facsimile of home: shelter and rest, food, companionship. Offers at a price, that is. But the commingling of hospitality and remuneration is also [in] keeping with the ambivalence of the inn-symbol.

But whatever the inns "mean," they do radiate a significance which transcends the actions taking place within them: which is another way of saying they *are* symbols. How that significance inspirits and supports the narrative may become clearer after we have considered an element in this part of the novel which, unlike the inns, has attracted a good deal of critical attention: namely, the old-man-of-the-hill episode.

What puzzles the reader of course is the irrelevance of this episode to the plot-structure of the novel. But more puzzling, it seems to me, is the trouble Fielding takes to emphasize the irrelevance. Jones and Partridge are vaguely—very vaguely—headed for the fields of war. How meaningless this adventure is Fielding has made clear in a typical stroke: Jones and his companion are in opposite camps in this conflict, don't know it, and don't care when they find out about it! We have, then, a narrative ebb; nothing lies before our hero—except "life." At this point, as they walk uneventfully along a dark country road, they see a hill.

> Here Jones stopped short, and directing his eyes upward, stood for a while silent. At length he called to his companion and said, 'Partridge, I wish I was at the top of this hill; it must certainly afford a charming prospect, especially by this light; for the solemn gloom which the moon casts on all objects is beyond expression beautiful, especially to an imagination which is desirous of cultivating melancholy ideas.'

So we appear to be in for some hill-climbing and the cultivation of melancholy ideas. Having no taste for either, Partridge objects and a debate ensues. *Then* Partridge sees a nearby light and prevails upon his companion to abandon the hill-climbing project.

Well then, why was it mentioned at all? Partridge might have seen the light at once, which would have eliminated all reference to the hill, or the attempt on the old man's life could even have been brought forward as a narrative introduction to the episode. For this contextual reason, and without regard as yet for the content of the old-man-of-the-hill episode, it seems to me that this is a case where technique makes a point. Let us now look into the episode itself to see whether we can find out what the point is. Is the episode part of Tom's "education"? That is hard to believe since Tom spontaneously rejects the old man's misanthropic philosophy both before and after hearing his story, and in the same way: by brave altruistic action. Is the story meant then to prefigure the perils awaiting Tom: extravagance, gambling, wenching, and stealing? But only one of these has ever been a temptation to Tom and that he yields to soon after his arrival at Upton Inn. Well, one may say, Tom failed to get the message and the novel points out the consequences. But the fact is that the novel does not at all support the notion of Tom as a skirt-chaser. He is the one who is pursued and, as a result, has three affairs (one per section of the novel), which, in the distribution of the ages and classes of women involved, is about the minimum necessary for Tom's sexual education.

It is obvious that the old-man episode is not only isolated from the main narrative-line but is irrelevant to the development and even the representation of any of the characters (except of course the old man himself). It is obvious because Fielding has made it so. He brings the narrative to a dead halt, calls our attention to the fact that he *has* arrested it, parenthesizes the episode in question by one of those parallelisms so dear to him—for properly speaking it begins with Jones' preventing one murder and ends with his preventing another: all to signal a general moral comment *on* the narrative from a platform above it. Nor is this conspicuous elevation of attention through narrative interruption and discontinuity unique. The most familiar examples are of course the introductory chapters of each book.

However, Fielding's technique here will be less mystifying, if we realize that the resonating effect of the old-man episode takes place on a symbolic, rather than a substantive level; and that, I believe, is where we must look for the main unifying process in the second part of *Tom Jones*. (For example, the old man's house serves as a kind of inn, too, sheltering Jones and Partridge for the night, but the experience it offers is of course quite different from the life of the inn; the openness and human interaction of inn-life is set off against the motif of alienation and misanthropy which the old-man's life illustrates.) If, on the other hand, we concentrate purely on the plot-aspect of the narrative, the pattern of the chase, we will be unable to account for the sustained and residual effects of the on-the-road episodes upon us. And we may even fail to realize how coarsely monotonous the movement of the narrative from lodging to lodging would be, were it not for the profounder currents on which it is carried.

In both the first and second parts of *Tom Jones*, the organizational means are appropriate to the environment portrayed: the squirarchical social order to the life of the country, the symbolism of the inn to the life of the road. Proceeding now to the third, or city-life section, we shall hope to find organizational means appropriate to the new milieu. This is not the case, however, and for this reason, among others, the final section is the least satisfactory in the novel.

The failure here is in a sense one of default. Few of the characters are urban, for example; instead the "country" and "road" characters pour in to create an enclave within the city. This is part of the reason why the life of the city is unsensed, except as a tenuous atmosphere of intrigue and menace. I say "part of the reason" because even Lady Bellaston and Lord Fellamar, who presumably represent distinctively urban moral values, are inadequately connected with the London organism. Nightingale is of course the city parallel of Sophia; he too is being coerced into marrying someone other than his choice. But there is nothing particularly urban about his character or condition, or his efforts to reconcile the two. The political and financial fever of the city is seldom evident, its frantically energetic middle class is hardly to be seen, and the low-life of the city, such as the work of the press-gang, is reported indirectly, if at all. (For that matter a good deal of the action is reported indirectly.) It is curious that Fielding, who spent most of his adult life in or near London, was unable to recreate that milieu with vividness or conviction. Instead, he uses it as a stage with many entrances, in the manner of the farceur, which he was early in his literary career, hectically complicating the lives of his characters in the twenty-minutes before the final curtain.

That indeed is how the third part of the novel is organized—in a word, by *plot*. Coincidence is used with abandon. Parallelisms are forced. (Lady Bellaston hides when Honour visits Tom; Honour hides when Lady Bellaston visits Tom.) Information is gratuitously withheld. (Mrs. Waters could have relieved Tom's despair in prison, without revealing his mother's identity.) When we think of *Tom Jones* as over-contrived, and even its kindest critics are likely to make that concession, we are probably thinking of the "city" part of the novel, forgetting how engagingly, and for the most part naturally, incidents flow into each other before then. And though it is true, as E. M. Forster pointed out in *Aspects of The Novel*, that plot tends to become particularly prominent in the final, or clean-up stage of a novel, we cannot ignore the extent or effect of this domination in *Tom Jones*. Especially damaging in the third part is the fact that it offers very little *except* plot. The sociological and ethical insights of the first part and the symbolic penetration of the second are both absent, so that the bare apparatus of plot comes into full view.

And yet the plot which is elaborated and resolved in the third part of the novel is the one that was introduced and developed in the earlier parts. Let us then consider this inner structure of the novel in relation to its overall organization. Ian Watt, in *The Rise of the Novel,* calls attention to Coleridge's opinion that *Tom Jones, The Alchemist,* and *Oedipus Rex* had the three most perfect plots in existence. This may be so if we consider only the *internal* mechanism of the plots. Plot, however, isn't simply an abstract exercise in ingenuity. Its degree of perfection can be estimated finally only by how much and how well it contributes to the overall sense of the work, and in this light a very great difference may be seen between the plot of *Tom Jones* and of the other works cited. For the pattern of action in *Oedipus Rex* or *The Alchemist* is a perfect vehicle for the meaning at large, while in *Tom Jones* the vehicle repeatedly stops and starts, the author's lighthearted discourses on the intellectual landscape alternating with rollicking horn-tooting rides for the sake of the ride. Comparing such widely different works is of course very difficult—almost whimsical, for apparent similarities are seen on closer analysis to be shallow or technical. Thus the chorus in *Oedipus Rex* and the authorial intrusions in *Tom Jones* might seem to have analogous functions. But the chorus participates in or comments directly on the action, while Fielding's personal interventions are designed to add intellectual dignity to the action of his work. The chorus complements the plot; Fielding's voice supplements it.

We are now, I should think, in a better position to analyze the inadequacy of plot in *Tom Jones.* Plot, as I have noted, cannot be regarded for long as an abstract exercise in ingenuity. It "means" something. But "meaning" does not here refer to a particular message, such as, in *Tom Jones,* that "the facts will out," or "true love will always triumph," which may at most be considered the story's moral; it comprises, fundamentally, the structuring principles embodied in the action. For example, the high degree of *formalism* in the plot of *Tom Jones*—balance, dichotomy, reciprocity—is part of the plot's meaning. It embodies the kind of sense which the author is trying to read into human existence, just as the resolution of the Allworthy-Western and the Thwackum-Square antitheses in the action-errors of both elements is also an expression of the author's philosophy. And it is a quite different philosophy than the one embodied in the causally sequenced, forward-driving dynamism of the plot in many Victorian novels, or in the double-visioned plots of Greek drama, divided as they are between the described action of the past and the presented action of a single day, so that we are always aware of the traction exercised by destiny on past events.

Let us then consider in further detail the Fielding-philosophy which seeks expression in the plot of *Tom Jones*. To begin with, it was severely conditioned by the intellectual polarization of the author's age: a polarization which created an unusually flat cognitive landscape, as if the mind of man, in passing from the religious depths of the past to the psychological complexities of the future, was enjoying a respite from confusion and enigma. This flatness applied particularly to Fielding's view of human nature. Each man's nature was fixed—by what it is hard to say. But this premise seriously restricted the novelist's freedom of movement because it meant that his characters had no place to come from and no place to go to: that is, a man's basic nature was not formed or modified by past experience, nor could his present experience be expected to change his character in any fundamental way. What then could be *done* with human nature in the novel? It could be exposed. Thus it could be shown that Blifil's apparent nature was different from his "real" nature. But as to why he was frigidly selfish—well, he *was* (though I suppose something can be made of the fact that Jones was a love-child while Blifil was the offspring of an opportunistic union).

Fielding's problem as a novelist therefore was to get out of the hole which the "fixed-nature" premise had dug for him. His procedure was something as follows. He assumed, first, that many people were basically "good"; second, that the troubles of good people originated in errors of judgment; third, that judgment could be refined by the astute observation of human conduct (the moral function of the novelist); and fourth, that it was in the natural order of things for goodness, disciplined by sound judgment, to be rewarded.

How tenable this vision is need not concern us here, for we are interested in how well it was formulated and sustained by the plot of *Tom Jones*. To answer that question we should try to imagine the novel without the introductory chapters, the numerous editorial embellishments and enlightenments, the old-man-of-the-hill episode, the visit with the gypsies, etc., all of which are only tenuously or arbitrarily referenced to the main story, and most of which would probably have been sacrificed in a plot-oriented age. The result would certainly have been a drastically diminished work, a banal, romantic comedy.

This in turn raises the question of how these interpolations operate. First, their bulk and placement is such as to slow down the pace of the story considerably. This in itself gives it a more reflective tone. Second, the author compensates for the disengagement of our interest in the narrative by setting up a comrader[y] between himself and us. But the palship is founded on the shared attitude of condescension toward the narrative! The digressions, distractions and interruptions are Fielding's way of telling us not to get too wrapped up in his silly story.

This denigration of plot in *Tom Jones*, evident though it is, may be easily overlooked in our admiration of the plot's technical ingenuities. V. S. Pritchett, for example, appears to have done so in *The Living Novel & Later Appreciations*. His chapter on Fielding, "The Ancestor," has shrewd things to say on the indebtedness of the English novel to Fielding, but he misses the point, it seems to me, in observing that "The English novel started in *Tom Jones*, because the stage taught Fielding to break the monotony of flat, continuous narrative"; for this, and the quite accurate and sensible description of Fielding's story-telling techniques which follows, fail to address the question: what does the plot-structure *do* for *Tom Jones*—do, as compared for example to what the plot-structure does for *Hard Times*, or *Jane Eyre?* Not very much. It is therefore misleading to intimate that *Tom Jones* contributed plot-structure to the development of the English novel, in the substantive sense that Defoe's novels contributed social realism, or Richardson's psychological sensibility. The plot of *Tom Jones* does not at all anticipate the forward-raked, dynamic type of plotting which was to carry a significant weight of the total sense in Victorian and post-Victorian novels. It looked back rather on an already decaying neo-classical set of values. Composition rather than dynamism was its chief goal and virtue; the overall division of the novel into three balanced sections, clearly circumscribed with respect to locale and organizing techniques itself makes this point. Again and again balance, reciprocation, and intermediate closures are used to drain plot-tension, or intellectual or narrative digressions to dissipate propulsive energy. Dorothy Van Ghent was obliquely taking note of this feature, it seems to me, when she found the dominant metaphor for the functional form of *Tom Jones* in architecture. This form may be effective, it may be attractive; but it did not point the way to the novel of the future. To assume that it does is to take into account only the expert mortise-and-tenon work and ignore its weakness as vehicle. Fielding himself may have been aware of this. Perhaps that is why the man who began his career as a novelist with raw spoofs of *Pamela* became near the end of it an admirer of Richardson, whose *Clarissa* was avant garde (though in many ways repulsive).

Let me state the case as baldly as I can. Fundamentally, the narrative base of *Tom Jones* is trivial: boy meets—loses—gets girl. In other words, it is a serious novel told in callow terms. Therefore Fielding must come to its assistance in his own person. Undoubtedly the novel owes much of its charm and memorability to the author's interventions. Yet, as a *systematic procedure* for upgrading the applicability and stature of the work, they signalize his failure to integrate intelligence and imagination.

This is not the proper place to speculate on the reasons for this failure, beyond perhaps recalling a few suggestions already made. It is possible that Fielding began to sense the fundamental discordancy between the neo-classical canon and the budding romanticism of the novel. Also, a poverty of symbolism denies depth and resonance to large portions of the novel. The incidents, however animated, have no afterlife, and it is this afterlife which creates the polyphonic effect we call organic form. The defect is particularly serious, as I have pointed out, in the third part of the novel, where the action occurs in a sociological vacuum so that there is no resonating medium for the episodes at all.

It may seem strange that I do not here refer to a defect more often mentioned than those above: the fact that the emotional life of Fielding's characters is as stereotyped as their behavior is, at times, exceptional. However, this criticism, by implication, sets up a generic ideal for the novel which I am not prepared to defend. Fielding's characters *are* generalized, almost allegorized, but that of itself does not make his novels inferior to those of psychological sensibility. At any rate there is not much point in criticizing an author for being what he constitutionally is. What interests us is his achievement within his limitations. Few readers would place *Tom Jones* among the greatest novels; fewer still would deny that it is a civilized and ingratiating work, aglow with the benevolent intelligence which was in the author's eyes the supreme human and perhaps divine virtue.

But that much granted, it appears that I too have judged *Tom Jones* against a synthetic ideal, the "integrated" work of art—and worse, judged it unfairly. For may it not be said that the novelistic and the essayistic (*cum* exemplary) elements of the novel do complement each other, under color of the author's personality? Yes—if we think of *Tom Jones* as *sui generis*. But if we consider its contributions to the novel-form, our opinion, as I have already suggested, becomes much less favorable. First, we must attribute to Fielding, at least in part, the convention of chumminess between author and reader, so damaging to the realism of many Victorian novels. Second, we perceive in *Tom Jones* what a frail reed is plot when it is not inspirited by symbolism or fortified by sociological insight. For the critic, *Tom Jones* has the advantage of being *imaginable* without these assets, while a similarly impoverished *Bleak House*, let us say, would be an unspeakable gothic mess. So we see that the perfect plot is not enough. When the plot-net has been tightened and hauled out of the sea of human experience, very little significance is found therein. It is Fielding's charming explanations of the meanings that got away which we remember. And perhaps that is not only the kindest but the fairest critical judgment which may be passed on *Tom Jones*: it is a triumph of one of the most delightful personalities ever to grace the pages of English literature—Fielding's.

JOHN PRESTON

Plot as Irony: The Reader's Role in *Tom Jones*†

I

Those who admire the plot of *Tom Jones* often find themselves in some embarrassment. To become engrossed in what Professor Kermode calls 'the Swiss precision of the plotting'[1] seems only to increase the difficulty of gauging the novel's imaginative scope. In this sense we must agree with Arnold Kettle 'that in *Tom Jones* there is too much plot.'[2] Fielding's smooth stage-managing of the action may well be thought to trivialise the book. This, indeed, is what Andrew Wright in effect concedes when he maintains that Fielding's art is serious because it is play, 'a special kind of entertainment.'[3] His reading of the plot supports the view that we should 'take *Tom Jones* on an ornamental level,' that Fielding provides 'a kind of ideal delight.'[4] But, granted that comedy depends on our feeling able to reshape life, and that the delight we take in this is properly a function of art's 'seriousness,' yet it may seem that this reading of *Tom Jones* gives away too much. After all, any achieved work of art takes on the status of play. That is what art is, in relation to life. And it may be that the works we recognize as 'playful' (the Savoy operas for instance) are just those in which play forfeits its seriousness. So, whilst appreciating the ease with which Fielding turns everything into delight, we have still to explain how he can, as James thought, 'somehow really enlarge, make everyone and everything important.'[5] We know that Fielding's presence as narrator contributes to this impression. Can we say that the plot of the novel confirms it?

It may be thought that to do so we should need to be more convinced that the plot was sensitive to the inner experience of the characters. We are not usually satisfied with plot which does not emanate from some 'inwardness,' some subtlety in attending to the growth of consciousness. Forster's distinction between plot and story will help to show why this is so. Story is to be considered 'a

†From *ELH*, 35 (1968), 365–80. Copyright 1968 by the Johns Hopkins Press. Reprinted in *The Created Self* (London: Heinemann Educational Books Ltd., 1970). Reprinted by permission of the Johns Hopkins Press.

1. *Tom Jones* (Signet Classics, 1963), p. 859.
2. *An Introduction to the English Novel* (London, 1951), I.77.
3. *Henry Fielding, Mask and Feast* (London, 1965), p. 22.
4. *Ibid.*, pp. 72, 30.
5. *The Art of the Novel* (New York, 1934), p. 68.

very low form' of art because it offers a sequence which has no meaning apart from that given by the sense of time. The significance of a train of events, the sense that it is 'caused,' arises when we discover in it the signs of personal will, of motives and desires and of the adjustments they call for. This is the kind of causality Forster illustrates: 'The king died, and then the queen died of grief.' [6] Causality without these signs may be as trivial and meaningless as story. Consider 'The king died, and then the queen dyed all the curtains black.' This too is a plot: it answers the question 'why?'. But it does not take that question seriously. And it looks as if the plot of *Tom Jones* is unserious in this way. That is why there is something self-defeating about the attempts to analyse it: Fielding has answered the questions of the plot facetiously. Yet I do not think we are justified in deducing from this, as Ian Watt does, 'a principle of considerable significance for the novel form in general: namely, that the importance of the plot is in inverse proportion to that of character.'[7] In fact Fielding makes it quite clear that he has been deliberately unserious about the plot. It is not typical; it has been designed specifically to serve his own special and rather subtle purpose.

There is no doubt that he means to draw attention to the artificiality of the plot. Why else, towards the close of the novel, recommend us to turn back 'to the scene at Upton in the ninth book' and 'to admire the many strange accidents which unfortunately prevented any interview between Partridge and Mrs. Waters' (XVIII, ii)? 'Fielding,' says Frank Kermode, 'cannot forbear to draw attention to his cleverness.' [8] But is this likely? Fielding expected his readers to know what sort of writer would do this. He had already presented several such on the stage in his 'rehearsal' plays. Trapwit is a good example. He is the vain author of an incoherent and unfunny comedy ('It is written, Sir, in the exact and true spirit of Moliere,' *Pasquin*, I, i); and he too is particularly proud of the plot.

> Now, Mr. Fustian, the plot, which has hitherto been only carried on by hints, and open'd itself like the infant spring by small and imperceptible degrees to the audience, will display itself, like a ripe matron, in its full summer's bloom; and cannot, I think, fail with its attractive charms, like a loadstone, to catch the admiration of every one like a trap, and raise an applause like thunder, till it makes the whole house like a hurricane. (*Pasquin*, III, i)

Fielding means us to see that in *Tom Jones* the sequences are those of farce and that the real skill consists in using them in a certain way, to get at some truth about human nature. The plot not only

---

6. *Aspects of the Novel* (London, 1927),   p. 279.
Ch. 5.
7. *The Rise of the Novel* (London, 1957)   8. *Op. cit.*, p. 857.

does not develop character, it actually subdues character to the demands of comic action. It will have to be in the shape of this action that we discern the shape of human behaviour. And Fielding wants to make sure that we get the right impression of that shape.

We would do well, then, not to take Fielding's self-congratulation at face value. In reminding us of Book IX he intends us to be more subtle about it than he himself claims to be. We find there, of course, 'a plot-node of extraordinary complexity'; [9] but may too easily assume, as Kermode does, that this is exactly what robs this and subsequent actions of 'the full sense of actual life—real, unpredictable, not subject to mechanical patterning.' [1] Actually the succeeding events *are* unpredictable. We could not possibly foresee from Book IX that Fitzpatrick and Mrs. Waters would go off together as 'husband and wife,' that Tom would be attacked by Fitzpatrick (though for his supposed affair with Mrs. Fitzpatrick, not his actual one with Mrs. Waters), or that this would involve him again with Mrs. Waters, or in what ways. When we look back on the completed sequence, it is true, we see it differently: the unpredictable suddenly appears to have hardened into the arbitrary. After all, we think, it *was* only a trick of the plotting. But, really, the plot faces two ways. From one side it looks like a forced solution, from the other an open question. In one way it looks arbitrary and contrived, in another it not only makes the reader guess but *keeps* him guessing at what has happened. The latter aspect of the plot is sustained by what Eleanor Hutchens calls 'substantial irony': 'a curious and subtle means used by Fielding to add irony to a given detail of plotting is to leave the reader to plot a sequence for himself.' [2] The reader has not, in fact, been told everything and is sometimes as much in the dark as the characters themselves. But irony of this kind is only contributory to the ironic shift by means of which the whole direction of the novel is reversed, and the plot has to sustain two contradictory conclusions simultaneously.

It is left to the reader to make this irony work. Fielding suggests as much by placing the reader in a dilemma. He draws him into the middle of the action, which then looks free-ranging, unpredictable, open-ended. If the plot is to behave like life, the reader must be unable to see his way before him. But he can only play this game once. On re-reading the novel he knows in advance the answer to all riddles, the outcome of all confusions. The plot thus poses questions about the way it should be read. Is it impossible to read the book more than once? Or is it necessary to read the book at least twice in order to understand it? On second reading do we reject the first, or are we in some way expected to keep them both in mind at

9. *Ibid.*, p. 857.
1. *Ibid.*, p. 859.
2. *Irony in* Tom Jones (University, Ala., 1965), p. 41.

once? This last is, I think, the only possibility Fielding leaves open for us, and it is this dual response which secures the ironic structure of the plot.

II

I think we can see why this must be so if we examine more closely the two 'faces' of the plot, and consider first what the book looks like when we can take the action as a diagram, or 'architecturally,' as Dorothy van Ghent does. She writes of it as a 'Palladian palace perhaps; . . . simply, spaciously, generously, firmly grounded in Nature, . . . The structure is all out in the light of intelligibility.' This, she considers, diminishes its scope: 'Since Fielding's time, the world has found itself not quite so intelligible . . . there was much —in the way of doubt and darkness—to which Fielding was insensitive.' [3] Ian Watt offers a similar reading: 'it reflects the general literary strategy of neo-classicism . . . [it makes] visible in the human scene the operations of universal order.' Its function, he claims, is to reveal the important fact 'that all human particles are subject to an invisible force which exists in the universe whether they are there to show it or not.' The plot must act like a magnet 'that pulls every individual particle out of the random order brought about by temporal accident and human imperfection.' [4] Read in this way it will appear as a paradigm of the Deistic world picture:

> All Nature is but Art, unknown to thee;
> All Chance, Direction, which thou canst not see.
> (*An Essay on Man*, i, 289–290)

Is this likely to be Fielding's meaning? It is true that in *The Champion* he asserts (against the Deists in fact) his belief in 'this vast regular frame of the universe, and all the artful and cunning machines therein,' and denies that they could be 'the effects of chance, of an irregular dance of atoms.' But he is still more concerned to deny that the Deity is 'a lazy, unactive being, regardless of the affairs of this world, that the soul of man, when his body dieth, lives no more, but returns to common matter with that of the brute creation' (Jan. 22, 1739–40). As James A. Work has shown,[5] the concept of universal order was nothing for Fielding if it was not the evidence of God's providence and a support for personal faith. In fact the essay on Bolingbroke brings out specifically the moral and intellectual impropriety of reducing the Divine order to the status of a work of art. Bolingbroke, Fielding reasons, must

3. *The English Novel: Form and Function* (New York, 1961), pp. 80–81.
4. *Op. cit.*, p. 271.
5. 'Henry Fielding, Christian Censor,' in *The Age of Johnson*, ed. F. W. Hilles (New Haven and London, 1949), pp. 140–142.

be making game of eternal verities in considering 'the Supreme Being in the light of a dramatic poet, and that part of his works which we inhabit as a drama.' It is the impiety that is offensive of course, the 'ludicrous treatment of the Being so universally . . . acknowledged to be the cause of all things.' But involved in this is the mistrust of those artists who 'aggrandise their profession with such kind of similes.' Fielding's own procedure, if Ian Watt were right, would be uncomfortably close to this, and it may be that, once more, we should not take him literally when he claims to be in this position.

The beginning of Book X is an occasion when he does so:

> First, then, we warn thee not too hastily to condemn any of the incidents in this our history, as impertinent and foreign to our main design, because thou dost not immediately conceive in what manner such incident may conduce to that design. This work may, indeed, be considered as a great creation of our own; and for a little reptile of a critic to presume to find fault with any of its parts, without knowing the manner in which the whole is connected, and before he comes to the final catastrophe, is a most presumptuous absurdity. (X, i)

This is equivocal. It may be taken to indicate that this is the structural centre of the novel, the peripeteia. It occurs at the height of the book's confusion and may be necessary to reassure the reader that the author is still in control. Yet it would be naive of Fielding to think that this was the way to do so, especially as he adopts a tone that suggests otherwise. He sounds touchy and self-defensive and tries to browbeat the reader. To claim that the work is 'a great creation of our own' is arrogant in the way that the essay on Bolingbroke indicated, and the arrogance is blatant in 'a little reptile of a critic.' Fielding clearly wants to discredit the narrator and, in the process, to make fun again of the pretensions of the plot. He makes a similar point in a different way in the introduction to Book XVII. Now he is asserting that affairs have got beyond his control.

> . . . to bring our favourites out of their present anguish and distress, and to land them at last on the shore of happiness, seems a much harder task; a task, indeed, so hard, that we do not undertake to execute it. In regard to Sophia, it is more than probable, that we shall somewhere or other provide a good husband for her in the end, either Blifil, or my lord, or somebody else; but as to poor Jones, . . . we almost despair of bringing him to any good. (XVII, i)

He cannot invoke supernatural assistance: 'to natural means alone we are confined. Let us see, therefore, what by these means may be done for poor Jones' (XVII, i). But this again is a kind of boast. At any rate it draws attention to the hard work and (paradoxically) the artifice necessary to reach a 'natural' outcome. It is another way of claiming that the design is intact. His pride in his own skill is obtrusive here as elsewhere. But this can hardly mean that Fielding had the kind of vanity which is the mark of the bad writer, unsure of his own powers.

We must conclude, I think, that to pose as a bad writer will help Fielding to avoid slipping into shallow rationalism. If he poses as the invisible Divine presence behind events, it is with a full sense of the kind of error this would be. What in one sense is an ironic parody of a form is, in a more profound way, an ironic repudiation of spiritual arrogance. In the same way the plot is less an assertion of Augustan rationality than a recognition of the confusion the rationalist can hardly tolerate. It is in fact a vehicle for what is self-contradictory, what is emotionally as well as intellectually confusing in human experience.

III

This is an aspect of the plot that Eleanor Hutchens admirably describes:

> Substantial irony is an integral part of the fabric of *Tom Jones*. Just as the straightforward plot moves from misfortune to prosperity along a tightly linked causal chain but brings the hero full circle back to the place of beginning, so the concomitant irony of plot turns things back upon themselves transformed. This larger structure is repeated in multitudinous smaller ironies of plot, character, and logic. . . . The reversal of truth and expectation accompanies plot and theme as a sort of ironic *doppelgänger*.[6]

Her main concern is to identify the specific episodes ('ironies of the plot . . . so numerous as to defy complete cataloguing'[7]) which add an ironic dimension to the whole narrative. But what she calls the 'concomitant irony of plot' can be taken to refer to a reversal of meaning in the plot as a whole, and it is in this way that it produces the effect we noted, of seeming to face two ways at once. The 'causal chain' that 'Fielding-as-narrator' boasts about seems to strengthen the possibility of a comprehensible order in human experience. But the plot also moves through a causal sequence of a different kind, a sequence of coincidence, chance meetings and meetings missed, good luck and bad, unplanned and unforeseen events. From this point of view it is easier to see that Fielding is dealing with the unpredictable, not in character or motive—his theory of 'conservation of character' leads in quite a different direction—but, to use his own term, in the 'history,' the shape of events. The

6. *Op. cit.*, p. 67.   7. *Ibid.*, p. 39.

meaning of history, as Philip Stevick has shown,[8] interested Fielding profoundly and the plot of *Tom Jones*, set against actual historical events, helps to define that meaning.

The episode of Sophia's little bird (IV, iii), which Eleanor Hutchens cites as an example of irony of substance,[9] is even more interesting as a model of this ironic meaning in the action as a whole. The causal links are firm: the bird is a present from Tom, therefore Sophia cherishes it, therefore Blifil lets it escape, therefore Tom tries to catch it and falls, therefore Sophia raises the alarm, therefore Allworthy and the rest come and eventually pass judgment on the two boys. The sequence does, it is true, depend on character and motive; but, like the plot as a whole, it finds these less interesting than their consequences in the actions and opinions of others. The episode is trimmed to the requirements of parable: it moves from personal predicament to moral judgment. In this way the episode suggests how the whole plot will be designed to exercise and refine the faculty of judgment, an aspect of the book I examined in a previous article.[1] At this stage, however, it is more to the point to note that the action in this episode can be traced through another kind of sequence. It springs from a paradoxical situation: the affection of Tom and Sophia is expressed in the captivity, Blifil's malicious envy in the releasing of the bird. There is truth to feeling in that situation; it is carefully staged, no doubt, but does not seem forced. Yet the subsequent action is quite fortuitous. Tom's actions could not have been predicted, for we had not even been told that he was near at hand; the branch need not have broken; there was no reason to expect that the bird would be caught and carried away by 'a nasty hawk.' The events no longer seem to explain each other. What seemed to have an almost mathematical logic now defies rationalisation. Actions cannot be foreseen, nor can their consequences be calculated: Blifil's malice, for instance, is better served by chance than by design. And intention, will, desire, all are overruled by Fortune.

This is one essential meaning of the plot. It is designed to tolerate the random decisions of Fortune. If Fielding has an arbitrary way with the plot this is not in order to square it with some concept of Reason or Nature, the 'one clear, unchang'd and universal light,' but to reflect our actual experience. 'I am not writing a system, but a history,' he reminds his readers, 'and I am not obliged to reconcile every matter to the received notions concerning truth and nature' (XII, viii). And in *The Champion* he argues that the historian especially should be prepared to allow for the effects of chance. 'I have often thought it a blemish in the works of Tacitus,

---

8. 'Fielding and the Meaning of History,' *PMLA*, Vol. LXXIX, p. 561.
9. *Op. cit.*, p. 61.

1. '*Tom Jones* and the "Pursuit of True Judgment,"' *ELH*, Vol. 33, No. 3, Sept., 1966, p. 315.

that he ascribes so little to the interposition of this invincible being; but, on the contrary, makes the event of almost every scheme to depend on a wise design, and proper measure taken to accomplish it' (Dec. 6, 1739). He goes so far as to assert that wisdom is 'of very little consequence in the affairs of this world: human life appears to me to resemble the game of hazard, much more than that of chess; in which latter, among good players, one false step must infallibly lose the game; whereas, in the former, the worst that can happen is to have the odds against you, which are never more than two to one' (Ib.). No doubt this extreme position is offered with due irony. Fielding briskly corrects it in the opening chapter of *Amelia*: men accuse Fortune 'with no less absurdity in life, than a bad player complains of ill luck at the game of chess.' Also, as Irvin Ehrenpreis observes, Fielding can see a way to resist Fortune: he 'opposes Christian providence to pagan Fortune. Since it operates by chance, fortune may indeed advance vice and obstruct virtue. . . . But steady prudent goodness will attract the blessing of the Lord, and wisdom is justified of her children.' [2] Yet this is not to argue that Fielding rejects the role of Fortune, or does not feel its force. On the contrary, he implies that Fortune is the term we must use to describe the human condition, the element in which human qualities are formed and human virtues and vices operate. This is in fact the source of his moral confidence. *Amelia*, as George Sherburn points out, is intended to cure the hero of 'psychological flaccidity' and of thinking that in an often irrational world 'moral energy is futile.' [3] And *Tom Jones* celebrates 'that solid inward comfort of mind which is the sure companion of innocence and virtue' (Dedication), and which will not be at the mercy of Fortune. A 'sanguine' temper, says Fielding, 'puts us, in a manner, out of the reach of Fortune, and makes us happy without her assistance' (XIII, vi).

There are, then, qualities of mind which rise above Fortune; but Fortune is the medium in which they operate. And, above all, Fortune is the medium of comedy. This, certainly, is what more than anything makes it tolerable. But, particularly because it is the source for comic complication, we shall want to see how it opposes the idea of a benevolently ordered world. Since comedy does in the end fulfil our expectations, it may after all persuade us that Fielding is tampering with events and trying to make the plot act 'as a kind of magnet.' But in fact Fielding creates his comedy out of the way his characters try to dominate Fortune and fail. They try to make things turn out as they want them to, but neither the narrator nor the reader can be persuaded that the desired conclusion has been

2. *Fielding*: Tom Jones (London, 1964), p. 51.
3. 'Fielding's Social Outlook,' *Eight-* *eenth-Century English Literature*, ed. J. L. Clifford (New York and Oxford, 1959), p. 263.

812 · *John Preston*

reached by trying. It is itself the gift of Fortune. The beauty of the comedy is not that it establishes a coherent universe, but that for the time being it allows the reader to believe in *good* Fortune.

The basis of the comic action is the 'pursuit motif' which Dorothy van Ghent has identified with such clarity.[4] It is implicit in the story of Sophia's little bird, and later comes to dominate events. Sophia follows Tom, Squire Western chases Sophia, Tom later pursues Sophia, Fitzpatrick pursues his wife, Allworthy and Blifil follow the Westerns to town, where Blifil will pursue Sophia. In the Upton scenes the theme comes to a climax in an intricate comic entanglement. And Fielding turns to 'epic' simile to underline what is happening. 'Now the little trembling hare, which the dread of all her numerous enemies, and chiefly of that cunning, cruel, carnivorous animal, man, had confined all the day to her lurking place, sports wantonly o'er the lawns; . . .' (X, ii). The simile of the hunt is used again in Book X, Chapter vi to describe Fitzpatrick's pursuit of his wife: 'Now it happens to this sort of men, as to bad hounds, who never hit off a fault themselves, . . .' And Fielding makes sure that we notice what he is doing: 'Much kinder was she [Fortune] to me, when she suggested that simile of the hounds, just before inserted; since the poor wife may, on these occasions, be so justly compared to a hunted hare.' Immediately afterwards, 'as if this had been a real chase,' Squire Western arrives 'hallooing as hunters do when the hounds are at fault.' Later, Mrs. Fitzpatrick uses the image to describe her own situation: she 'wisely considered that the virtue of a young lady is, in the world, in the same situation with a poor hare, which is certain, whenever it ventures abroad, to meet its enemies; for it can hardly meet any other' (XI, x). These images bring out an element of crudity in the motif: 'we have got the dog-fox, I warrant the bitch is not far off' (X, vii). The chases are anything but rational; they are headlong, indiscreet, urged on by primitive instinct. Thus, when Western is easily diverted from one pursuit to another, from the chase of his daughter to the chase of a hare, Fielding quotes the story of the cat who was changed into a woman yet 'leaped from the bed of her husband' to chase a mouse. 'What are we to understand by this?', he asks. 'The truth is, as the sagacious Sir Roger l' Estrange observes, in his deep reflections, that "if we shut nature out at the door, she will come in at the window; and that puss, though a madam, will be a mouser still" ' (XII, ii). Dorothy van Ghent, who notes that 'instinctive drives must . . . be emphasized as an important constituent of "human nature," ' does not in fact observe that Fielding explicitly links them in this way with the theme of pursuit. Her idea is that the book is based on 'a conflict between natural, instinctive feeling, and those appearances

4. *Op. cit.*, p. 72.

with which people disguise, deny, or inhibit natural feeling.'[5] This is not convincing. It seems better to follow Fielding's hints that the action, a series of rash pursuits, shows human behaviour to be irrational, governed chiefly by instinct not reflection, and therefore particularly exposed to Fortune.

These factors in human behaviour are above all what bring about the loosening of the causal chain and frustrate the intentions of the characters. In Book XII, Chapter viii, Fielding acknowledges that it must seem 'hard,' indeed 'very absurd and monstrous' that Tom should offend Sophia, not by his actual unfaithfulness but by his supposed 'indelicacy' in cheapening her name. Some, he thinks, will regard 'what happened to him at Upton as a just punishment for his wickedness with regard to women of which indeed it was the immediate consequence'; and others, 'silly and bad persons,' will argue from it that 'the characters of men are rather owing to accident than to virtue'; but the author himself admits no more than that it confirms the book's 'great, useful and uncommon doctrine,' which, however, 'we must not fill up our pages with frequently repeating.' He proceeds to show the absurdity of trying to adjust our behaviour to a system of cause and effect. Tom becomes totally unlike himself, no longer a creature of appetite but a romantic lover, as Partridge tells him: 'Certainly, sir, if ever man deserved a young lady, you deserve young Madam Western; for what a vast quantity of love must a man have, to be able to live upon it without any other food, as you do?' (XII, xiii). Yet this does not make Tom immune from Fortune; when he reaches Mrs. Fitzpatrick's house in London he misses Sophia by ten minutes. 'In short, this kind of hair-breadth missings of happiness look like the insults of fortune, who may be considered as thus playing tricks with us, and wantonly diverting herself at our expense' (XIII, ii). In the end his romantic persistence leads him to the most discreditable episode of the book: after hanging round Mrs. Fitzpatrick's door all day he finally enters her drawing room to meet Lady Bellaston.

Similarly, the dénouement, the solving of all the riddles, is brought about by chance, indeed by mistake. Tom can do nothing to help himself. In the end it is Mrs. Waters who is able to explain matters. But she herself is at first ignorant who Tom is. She only discovers that Jones is Bridget Allworthy's child when she is visited by the lawyer Dowling. He in turn has been sent by Blifil to say that she 'should be assisted with any money [she] wanted to carry on the prosecution' against Jones. It is his malice, apparently so obstructive, which, in spite of his intentions, leads to the ending we desire. Our expectations are realised only by being twice contradicted.

5. *Op. cit.*, p. 68.

IV

It is now possible to see why the reading of the plot should be able to sustain a large irony. We shall be tempted into a choice of readings. But, if we think ourselves objective, surveying a complete design which has been distanced by its past tense and assimilated into 'history,' we may well find in it a degree of order that Fielding hardly intended. If, on the other hand, Fielding is trying in many ways to undermine our sense of objectivity and privilege, we must find ourselves drawn into the confusion and hazard of the action, aware now of 'history' as a process in which we are involved, moving toward effects we cannot predict: we are not allowed to understand more of the course of events than the characters do. Yet, as we have seen, this kind of involvement is only possible on the first reading. Fielding has written into the narrative an assumption that must be contradicted by subsequent readings. Indeed, one cannot read even once through the book without finding that many passages have come to take on an altered meaning.

Irvin Ehrenpreis sees this as confirming that, like *Oedipus Rex*, the book is essentially a sustained dramatic irony. Behind the many moments of 'discovery,' of 'sudden understanding' which he regards as really the action of the book there is, he says, 'the supreme recognition scene disclosing the true parentage of Tom Jones. The opening books of the novel are permeated with ironies that depend on his being Bridget Allworthy's firstborn child, or young Blifil's elder brother, or Mr. Allworthy's proper heir.' What we admire, what Coleridge must have been praising, is 'the cheerful ease with which Fielding suspends his highest revelation till the end, the outrageous clues with which he dares assault our blindness in the meantime.'[6] This seems to me an important truth about the novel. But it seems also to imply other more complex truths which Mr. Ehrenpreis does not consider. Apparently Fielding can, even on a second reading, be supposed to be 'suspending' the final revelation; we can be held to retain our 'blindness' in spite of what we have discovered. That is, we have a sense of duality not only in the book itself but in our own response to it. We recognize our 'blindness' just because we no longer suffer from it. We know and do not know simultaneously: we are both outside and inside the pattern of events. Like Eliot's Tiresias we 'have foresuffered all,' yet are still capable of being surprised. If the book has a core of dramatic irony, it is one in which the reader knows himself to be caught, or of which he knows himself to be the source. He is the observer of his own ironic mistakes. Our responses to the book are, we may say, part of the reason for

6. *Op. cit.*, pp. 23–24.

Fielding's laughter, a laughter in which we share. We are, in short, never quite ignorant nor yet entirely omniscient. In this way the book leads us to one of the most rewarding experiences of comedy: it simultaneously confuses and enlightens, it produces both question and answer, doubt and reassurance.[7] This is a far cry from the imitation of Universal Reason; yet it offers a way out of the confusion of human experience. The book suggests the power of control in the very act of undermining that power; or, from another point of view, can play with the possibilities of confusion because the sense of control is never lost. It can accept the reality of fortune because it has achieved the wisdom that an acceptance of fortune gives.

Chapters vii, viii and ix of Book V are a notable example of this procedure. Allworthy is ill and is not expected to live. This is the situation as the other characters understand it, and Fielding says nothing that would allow us to understand more of it. Our only advantage over them is in our emotional detachment, as for instance, when we see them betray their dissatisfaction at Allworthy's legacies. When the attorney from Salisbury arrives we know no more than they do who he is or what news he brings. In fact we know less than Blifil; like the other characters we are his dupes. Fielding gives no sign that there is anything more in the situation; indeed by depicting at some length the disappointed greed of Allworthy's dependants he implies that the scene can only carry this limited and obvious irony. Yet our experience of the rest of the novel persuades us that there is much more to be seen. On a second reading, we know already that Allworthy's illness will not be fatal; this, in fact, is what keeps the scene within the limits of comic decorum. This is what enables R. S. Crane to say that as the novel progresses things become both more and more, and less and less serious, that it offers a 'comic analogue of fear.'[8] Also we know, what Fielding appeared to think we should not know, that the attorney is the lawyer Dowling and that he brings Bridget Allworthy's own dying words, 'Tell my brother, Mr. Jones is his nephew—He is my son—Bless him!', words that are not recorded in the novel until Book XVIII, Chapter viii. Now the scene at Allworthy's death-bed is superimposed on the silent, unacknowledged presence of that other death-bed. Fielding chose deliberately *not* to present this as a dramatic irony. The scene as he renders it takes all its significance from information he has denied us, from knowledge we import into the scene, as it were without his consent. The words that are not spoken reverberate thus throughout the novel. But, as they have *not* been spoken, their sound is produced in one part of

7. Cf. Ehrenpreis, *op. cit.*, p. 66: 'such surprises combine puzzlement with relief'; and p. 65: 'The same agent seems repeatedly to save us from perils to which he alone has exposed us; we are continually being lost and found by the same guide.'

8. 'The Concept of Plot and the Plot of *Tom Jones,' Critics and Criticism* (Chicago, 1952), pp. 635–636.

the reader's mind whilst he is deaf to it with the other. In fact, as Ehrenpreis shows, what is at the centre of his attention is the *fact* of their not being spoken, the audacity with which Fielding so nearly gives away the riddle of the book. We admire his skill in keeping it dark, but could not do so if we did not at the same time know what it was.

In another way, however, our dual vision of things actually seems to undermine our confidence in the narrator. Since we are left to supply information necessary to the full understanding of a scene, we fancy ourselves better informed than the narrator himself. Often enough, indeed, the narrator professes his inadequacy: 'the fact is true; and perhaps may be sufficiently accounted for by suggesting . . .' (V, x). But this, as Eleanor Hutchens shows,[9] is an ironic trick designed to make us attend in exactly the way the author desires. There is, however, a much more pervasive sense that the narrator cannot (or does not) reveal many things that the reader nevertheless is aware of. Of course the reader is aware of them only because he at last appreciates the design the author has had in mind from the beginning. But since the author does not actually write such things into the text of the novel, since he leaves the reader to supply them silently, he gives the impression that in some important ways the novel has written itself.

In the scenes we have been discussing, Fielding observes that Blifil is offended at Tom's riotous behaviour so soon after Allworthy's illness and Bridget's death. There is apparently no doubt as to Blifil's feelings and motives; '. . . Mr. Blifil was highly offended at a behaviour which was so inconsistent with the sober and prudent reserve of his own temper.' Yet, however little sympathy we feel for Blifil, we sense that there is some justice in his attitude: 'He bore it too with the greater impatience, as it appeared to him very indecent at this season: "When," as he said, "the house was a house of mourning, on the account of his dear mother." Jones's ready sympathy and remorse reflect our own response: 'he offered to shake Mr. Blifil by the hand, and begged his pardon, saying, his excessive joy for Mr. Allworthy's recovery had driven every other thought out of his mind.' Yet, after all, this does not shake our conviction that Blifil is hateful: he soon reverts to the behaviour we expect of him: 'Blifil scornfully rejected his hand; and, with much indignation, answered, it was little to be wondered at, if tragical spectacles made no impression on the blind; but, for his part, he had the misfortune to know who his parents were, and consequently must be affected with their loss' (V, ix). These are the terms in which the narrator has constructed the episode. This must be our reading of it as it stands. Yet that is not the way in which we do read it. When Blifil speaks of his mother's death we know that he knows that she is also Tom's mother. Tom's generous sympathy, then, far from helping to justify Blifil, actually heightens our sense of outrage. And Blifil's response, no longer just a gratuitous and insulting sneer at Tom's illegitimacy, becomes a piercing revelation of his own utter inhumanity. Not only can he allow Tom to remain ignorant that his mother has just died, he can actually, with staggering impudence, make his words a concealed taunt. He finds it possible to use his knowledge for a cruel secret game: 'he had the misfortune to know who his parents were, and consequently must be affected with their loss.'

There are, then, areas of meaning which the narrator does not even mention. But his reticence does not prevent us becoming conscious of them. Thus the book begins to escape from the narrow designs imposed on it, from the conscious intention of the narrator. After all it does seem to acquire something of the 'full sense of actual life.' Fielding is not always obtrusive; in fact, it is at this deep level, where the authenticity of the book is most in question, that he is least in evidence. We noted that in those instances where he pushed himself forward he was wanting the reader to look elsewhere for the real intention. But though the text is centred on the unpredictable, on the random behaviour of Fortune, the full scope of the novel is to be measured in the dual meaning of the plot. The author leaves the book to itself, or rather, to the reader. In other words, Fielding has been able by means of the plot, to create a reader wise enough to create the book he reads.

MARTIN C. BATTESTIN

Fielding's Definition of Wisdom: Some Functions of Ambiguity and Emblem in *Tom Jones*†

To alter the terms of his own simile for the ancient authors, Fielding's novels may be considered as a rich common, where every critic has a free right to fatten his bibliography. As the number of commentaries in recent years attests, *Tom Jones* offers an ample field for critical investigation, with many aspects requiring a variety of approaches. At present I wish to explore only two of these: the substance and the form of the novel's most important theme, the definition of Wisdom.

In dedicating the book to Lyttelton, Fielding himself provides

†From *ELH*, 35 (1968), 188–217. Copyright by the Johns Hopkins Press. Reprinted by permission of the author and the publisher.

the clue both to his moral purpose in *Tom Jones* and (in part at least) to his method of implementing that purpose. He declares

> that to recommend Goodness and Innocence hath been my sincere Endeavour in this History. This honest Purpose you have been pleased to think I have attained: And to say the Truth, it is likeliest to be attained in Books of this Kind; for an Example is a Kind of Picture, in which Virtue becomes as it were an Object of Sight, and strikes us with an Idea of that Loveliness, which *Plato* asserts there is in her naked Charms.
>
> Besides displaying that Beauty of Virtue which may attract the Admiration of Mankind, I have attempted to engage a stronger Motive to Human Action in her Favour, by convincing Men, that their true Interest directs them to a Pursuit of her.[1]

The dominant ethical theme of *Tom Jones* turns upon the meaning of "Virtue" and of the phrase, our "true Interest"—what Squire Allworthy calls "the Duty which we owe to ourselves" (XVIII.x). One method Fielding chooses to present this theme is implicit in the Platonic figure of Virtue's irresistible "Charms" and in the metaphor of the "Pursuit of her." Fielding's statement, then, is schematic, pointing both to the doctrine of the novel and to the means, which may be described as iconomatic, by which the novelist transforms the abstraction of his theme into "an Object of Sight."

Tom Jones, in a sense, is an exercise in the fictive definition of Virtue, or moral Wisdom—just as Fielding's earlier novels, *Joseph Andrews* and *Jonathan Wild*, may be regarded as attempts to represent through word and action the true meaning of such concepts as Charity, Chastity, and Greatness. To achieve this purpose, Fielding employs many devices—characterization, for one, by which certain figures in the novel become "Walking Concepts," as Sheldon Sacks has observed,[2] acting out the meaning of various virtues and vices. At present, however, I am concerned with only two of these techniques: Fielding's exploitation of verbal ambiguity—the power of the word, as it were, to define the moral vision or blindness of character and reader alike—and his attempt to delineate emblematically the meaning of true Wisdom. The problem for the critic, fundamentally, is to ascertain the nature of that Wisdom which Fielding, together with the philosophers and divines of the Christian humanist tradition, wished to recommend. For this we may conveniently recall Cicero's distinction in *De Officiis* (I.xliii) between the two kinds of wisdom, the speculative and the practical, *sophia* and *prudentia*:

> And then, the foremost of all virtues is wisdom—what the Greeks call σοφία; for by prudence, which they call φρόνησις, we

---

1. Quotations from *Tom Jones* are from the 4th edition (1750).

2. See *Fiction and the Shape of Belief* (Berkeley and Los Angeles, 1964).

understand something else, namely, the practical knowledge of things to be sought for and of things to be avoided.[3]

The apprehension of *sophia* was the goal of Plato's philosopher; the acquisition of *prudentia*—which begins with the intimation that the Good, the True, and the Beautiful are one—is the quest of the *vir honestus*. Fielding's intention in *Tom Jones* is to demonstrate the nature, function, and relationship of these correlative ethical concepts.

I. Prudence: The Function of Ambiguity

Prudence (together with the more or less synonymous word *discretion*) is the central ethical concept of *Tom Jones*.[4] The term recurs and reverberates throughout the novel, acquiring something of the quality and function of a musical motif. Yet its meanings are curiously ambivalent: according to the context, which Fielding carefully controls, prudence is either the fundamental vice, subsuming all others, or the essential virtue of the completely moral man. It exists, as the exegetical tradition might express it, *in malo et in bono*. At the very start of the narrative Bridget Allworthy, the prude of easy virtue, is said to be remarkable for "her Prudence" and "discreet . . . in her Conduct" (I.ii); but on the last page of the novel Tom Jones himself is represented as a fit partner for Sophia only because he has "by Reflexion on his past Follies, acquired a Discretion and Prudence very uncommon in one of his lively Parts." In one sense, prudence is the summarizing attribute of Blifil, the villain of the piece, and it is the distinguishing trait of a crowded gallery of meretricious and self-interested characters from every rank of society—of Deborah Wilkins (I.v, vi), Jenny Jones (I.ix), Mrs. Seagrim (IV.viii), Mrs. Western (VI.xiv), Partridge (VIII.ix), Mrs. Honour (X.ix), Lady Bellaston (XIII.iii, XV.ix). Antithetically, however, the acquisition of prudence is recognized by the good characters of the novel—by Allworthy, Sophia, and ultimately by Jones—as the indispensable requisite of the moral man. "Prudence," Allworthy maintains, "is indeed the Duty which we owe to ourselves" (XVIII.x). Sophia alone, of all the characters in the novel, is possessed of prudence in this positive sense (XII.x). And the lack of it in Jones is the source of all his "Calamities" (XVII.i), all his "miserable Distresses" (XVIII.vi).

References to prudence, understood in either the positive or pejorative sense, may be found elsewhere in Fielding's writings; but

3. Walter Miller, trans. (Loeb Classical Library, 1913).

4. Only recently have critics begun to direct serious attention to this theme in the novel: see Eleanor N. Hutchens, " 'Prudence' in *Tom Jones*: A Study of Connotative Irony," *PQ*, XXXIX (1960), 496–507, and the excellent discussion by Glenn W. Hatfield in Chapter V of his forthcoming book, *Henry Fielding and the Language of Irony* (University of Chicago Press).

only in *Tom Jones* does the word recur with such frequency and insistence. Indeed, as I wish to suggest, Fielding's intention to recommend this virtue affected the very shape and character of *Tom Jones*: the choice and representation of the principal characters, the organization of the general movement of the narrative, and the content of particular scenes were determined in significant ways in accordance with a broadly allegorical system designed both to define the virtue of prudence and to demonstrate its essential relevance to the moral life. Unfortunately for modern readers, the passage of time has obscured the meaning of this concept in the novel. To repair that disadvantage, it will be necessary to recover the classical, Christian, and contemporary contexts which Fielding drew upon.

Prudentia in the Christian humanist tradition is practical wisdom —the chief of the four cardinal virtues: prudence, justice, temperance, and fortitude. According to Cicero, who was principally responsible for its meaning during the period in question, prudence is essentially the ability to distinguish between good and evil. It is a rational faculty, therefore, which depends on the proper functioning of memory, intelligence, and foresight: memory enabling us to recall what has happened, so that we may learn from experience; intelligence enabling us to discern the truth of circumstances as they really are; and foresight enabling us, on the basis of past knowledge and with the aid of a penetrating judgment, to estimate the future consequences of present actions and events.[5] Prudence is, in other words, that perspicacity of moral *vision* which alone permits us to perceive the truth behind appearances and to proceed from the known to the obscure; it implies, furthermore, the power to *choose* between good and evil and to determine the proper and effective means of achieving the one and avoiding the other.[6] As such it is the *ars vivendi*—the "Art of Life," as Fielding calls it in *Amelia* (I.i)—the supreme rational virtue and the most hard won, the possession only of the *vir honestus*.

Although by the seventeenth century a curious process of redefinition had begun which resulted eventually in our present perverse understanding of the term—a process by which the noblest virtue of antiquity has come to signify nothing more than a mean-spirited and cautious expediency—prudence in its orginal sense continued to find advocates among poets, moralists, and divines who cherished the humanist values. Following the examples of George Turberville and Alexander Barclay, John Denham in 1668 published a poem on

---

5. See Cicero, *De Inventione*, II.liii.160: "Prudentia est rerum bonarum et malarum neutrarumque scientia. Partes eius: memoria, intelligentia, providentia. Memoria est per quam animus repetit illa quae fuerunt; intelligentia, per quam ea perspicit quae sunt; providentia, per quam futurum aliquid videtur ante quam factum est."
6. Cf. Cicero, *De Natura Deorum*, III.xv.38, and *De Finibus*, V.vi.16.

the subject based on the Latin of Mancinus.[7] As Denham represents it, the primary function of prudence is to distinguish the essential characters of things, to determine "What's decent or undecent, false or true" (l. 2) :[8]

> Hee's truly Prudent, who can separate
> Honest from Vile, and still adhere to that;
> Their difference to measure, and to reach,
> Reason well rectify'd must Nature teach.
>
> (ll. 3–6)

Since the prudent man has given over the government of himself to "Clear-sighted Reason" (l. 13), he recognizes that the passions, the irrational impulses of the natural man, are his enemies. Reminiscent of Aristotle's characterization of youth in the "Three Ages of Man," the imprudent are rash and incontinent, "To their Wills Wedded, to their Errours slaves" (l. 39). Accordingly, Denham exhorts his readers: "Let not low Pleasures thy high Reason blind" (l. 147). For Denham and Mancinus, as for Cicero, prudence is identical with clarity of moral vision and with the pragmatic ability to act upon this knowledge. The prudent man carefully weighs "Things past, and future with the present" (l. 175), and he understands "the means, the manner, and the end" (l. 186) of any course of action:

> Some secrets deep in abstruse Darkness lye;
> To search them, thou wilt need a piercing Eye.
> Not rashly therefore to such things assent,
> Which undeceiv'd, thou after may'st repent; . . .
>
> (ll. 21–24)

> Look forward what's to come, and back what's past,
> Thy life will be with Praise and Prudence grac'd:
> What loss, or gain may follow thou may'st guess,
> Thou then wilt be secure of the success; . . .
>
> (ll. 207–10)

Prudence thus instructs us in true values and desirable ends, and she discloses the most expedient and efficacious means of attaining them. She is Fortune's foe and champion of "the Golden Mean" (ll. 249–50).

---

7. Dominicus Mancinus' influential work on the cardinal virtues, *Libellus de quattuor virtutibus et omnibus officiis ad bene beateque vivendum*, was originally published at Paris in 1488. In the sixteenth century at least three English translations appeared: an anonymous prose version, c. 1520; Barclay's *The Myrrour of good manners*, c. 1523; and Tuberville's *A plaine Path to perfect Vertue*, 1568.

8. Quotations from Denham's "Of Prudence" are from Theodore Howard Banks, ed., *Poetical Works* (New Haven, 1928).

For "the Classical Reader" of the next century, as Fielding called his more literate contemporaries in the Preface to *Joseph Andrews,* this exalted understanding of prudence still obtained. For Fielding's friends Christopher Smart and James Harris, prudence was "the Queen and Directress of all the other Moral Virtues,"[9] the faculty "instructing us how to discern the *real Difference of all Particulars,* and suggesting the proper Means, by which we may either *avoid* or *obtain* them."[1] In *Polymetis* (1747) Joseph Spence noticed, with special reference to Cicero, that "PRUDENCE, (or Good Sense) stands in the front of all the virtues," being the faculty by which emperors keep "the whole world in order" and by which in "lower life . . . all the affairs of human life are regulated and disposed, as they ought to be" (p. 138).

One of the fullest contemporary expositions of this virtue occurs in an article "On Prudence" appearing in Sir John Hill's *British Magazine* for March 1749, one month after the publication of *Tom Jones.* This essay, Number XLI in the series called "The Moralist," begins by celebrating the dignity and antiquity of the concept.

> PRUDENCE is at once the noblest and the most valuable of all the qualifications we have to boast of: It at the same time gives testimony of our having exerted the faculties of our souls in the wisest manner, and conducts us through life with that ease and tranquillity, that all the boasted offices of other accomplishments can never give us. The ancient Moralists with great reason placed it in the first rank of human endowments, and called it the parent and guide of all the other virtues. Without prudence, nothing in our lives is good, nothing decent, nothing truly agreeable or permanent: It is the rule and ornament of all our actions; and is to our conduct in this motly world of chances, what physick is to the body, the surest means of preventing disorders, and the only means of curing them.[2]

To further define the nature and function of this virtue, "the Moralist" invokes the traditional metaphor of sight, opposing the unerring perspicacity of the rational, to the blindness and brutishness of the passionate man: "Prudence is the just estimation and trial of all things; it is the eye that sees all, and that ought to direct all, and ordain all: and when any favourite passion hoodwinks it for the time, man ceases to be man, levels himself with the brutes, and gives up that sacred prerogative his reason, to be actuated by meanest [*sic*] of all principles."[3] The special provinces of prudence are the judgment and the will: seeing what is right and how to attain it, the prudent man translates this knowledge into action—deeds

9. Smart, *The Student's Companion* (1748), s. v. "Prudence."
1. Harris, "Concerning Happiness, A Dialogue," in *Three Treatises* (1744), p. 171.
2. *The British Magazine,* IV (March 1749), 77.
3. *Ibid.,* IV, 78.

"which will make ourselves and our fellow-creatures most happy,
and do the greatest honour in our power to our nature, and to the
great creator of it."[4] Again, the prudent man looks to the past
(memory), the present (judgment), and the future (foresight); his
own and others' past experiences inform his perception of present
exigencies and enable him to predict the probable consequences of
actions and events.[5] The prudent man alone is equipped to survive
in a world of deceitful appearances and hostile circumstances, for
only he "sees things in their proper colours, and consequently
expects those things from them which ruin others by the surprize of
their coming on"; only he "is guarded against what are called the
changes and chances that undo all things."[6] Although, as Tillotson
and William Sherlock observed,[7] not even prudence can always
foresee the improbable casualties which occur under the direction of
Providence, yet she is, however fallible, our only proper guide.

Prudence in this positive sense is indeed, as Allworthy insists,
"the Duty which we owe to ourselves," that self-discipline and practical sagacity which Fielding's open-hearted and impetuous hero
must acquire. But as Tom Jones has his half-brother Blifil, or
Amelia her sister Betty, so every virtue has its counterfeit, its
kindred vice which mimics it. The result is a kind of sinister parody
of excellence. Thus Cicero warns against confusing false prudence
and true, a vulgar error by which the clever hypocrite, bent only on
pursuing his own worldly interest, passes for a wise and upright
man. Such are the scoundrels of this world who—practised in what
Fielding liked to call "the *Art of Thriving*"[8]—wear the mask of
prudence, separating moral rectitude from expediency.[9] It is
"wisdom [*prudentia*]," Cicero writes, "which cunning [*malitia*]
seeks to counterfeit,"[1] so as the better to dupe and use us. The distinction between the two prudences, true and false, is clearly drawn
in this passage from Isaac Barrow's sermon, "Of the Virtue and
Reasonableness of Faith":

> With faith also must concur the virtue of prudence; in all
> its parts and instances: therein is exerted a sagacity, discerning
> things as they really are in themselves, not as they appear through
> the masks and disguises of fallacious semblance, whereby they
> would delude us; not suffering us to be abused by the gaudy
> shews, the false glosses, the tempting allurements of things;
> therein we must use discretion in prizing things rightly, according
> to their true nature and intrinsick worth; in chusing things really

4. *Loc. cit.*
5. *Ibid.*, IV, 78–79.
6. *Ibid.*, IV, 79.
7. See John Tillotson, Sermon XXXVI,
"Success not always Answerable to the
Probability of Second Causes," *Works*
(1757), III, 28–29; and William Sherlock, *A Discourse Concerning the Divine*

Providence, 9th ed. (1747), p. 43.
8. "An Essay on the Knowledge of the
Characters of Men," in *Miscellanies*
(1743), I, 183.
9. Cicero, *De Officiis*, II.iii, III.xvii.
1. *Ibid.*, III.xxv; trans. W. Miller (Loeb
Classical Library, 1913).

good, and rejecting things truly evil, however each kind may seem to our erroneous sense; therein we must have a good prospect extending itself to the final consequences of things; so that looking over present contingencies we descry what certainly will befal us through the course of eternal ages.

In faith is exercised that prudence, which guideth and prompteth us to walk by the best rules, to act in the best manner, to apply the best means, towards attainment of the best ends.

The prudence of faith is indeed the only prudence considerable; all other prudence regarding objects very low and ignoble, tending to designs very mean, or base, having fruits very poor or vain; to be wise about affairs of this life (these fleeting, these empty, these deceitful shadows) is a sorry wisdom; to be wise in *purveying for the flesh*, is the wisdom of a beast, which is wise enough to prog for its sustenance; to be wise in gratifying fancy, is the wisdom of a child, who can easily entertain and please himself with trifles; to be wise in contriving mischief, or embroiling things, is the wisdom of a fiend; in which the old serpent, or grand politician of hell, doth exceed all the *Machiavels* in the world; this (as St. *James* saith) is earthly, sensual, *devilish wisdom*; but the wisdom of faith, or that *wisdom, which is from above, is first pure, then peaceable; gentle, easy to be entreated, full of mercy and good works*.[2]

This passage from Fielding's "favourite" divine [3] provides an admirable gloss on the antithetical meanings of prudence in *Tom Jones* though we need not consider Barrow's sermon a "source" for Fielding's ideas on the subject. As we have seen, the concept of true prudence was a commonplace among those well read in the classics or their modern commentators. So, too, was the notion of its shadow and opposite, false prudence, the "mock Wisdom" of this world.[4] This is the characteristic of the whole "tribe" of hypocrites and politicians, of whom, as Robert South declared, Machiavelli was "the great patron and *coryphœus*."[5] Thus, in language anticipating Fielding's anatomy of hypocrisy in "An Essay on the Knowledge of the Characters of Men," Tillotson warned that "The politicians of the world" pretend to wisdom; "but theirs is rather a craftiness than a wisdom. Men call it prudence; but they are glad to use many arts to set it off, and make it look like wisdom; by silence, and secrecy, and formality, and affected gravity, and nods, and gestures. The scripture calls it 'the wisdom of this world,' I Cor. ii. 6. and a 'fleshly wisdom,' 2 Cor. i. 12. It is wisdom misapplied, it is the pursuit of a wrong end."[6] Similarly, Bishop Hoadly cited "the *Instance* of *Wisdom* and *Cunning*" to illustrate his observation that

2. Barrow, Sermon II, *Works*, 5th ed. (1741), II, 26.
3. *The Covent-Garden Journal*, No. 29 (11 April 1752).
4. *Ibid.*, No. 69 (4 November 1752).
5. South, Sermon IX, "The Wisdom of This World," *Sermons Preached upon Several Occasions* (1843), I, 140.
6. Tillotson, Sermon CXXXVI, "The wisdom, glory, and sovereignty of God," *op. cit.*, VIII, 109.

"THERE is hardly any one Vertue, or Excellence, in the *Best* Part of Mankind, but what is attempted to be imitated, or mimicked, by Something in the *Worst*; designed to make the same Appearance, but in reality as distant in Nature from it, as a *Shadow* from a *Substance*; nay, as contradictory to it, as *Evil* is to *Good*, or as a monstrous *Defect* is to *Perfection* itself." [7] And to adduce one other of many possible examples, only a few months before *Tom Jones* went to press an essay by "the Moralist" in Hill's *British Magazine* defined "that species of wit, which we, to distinguish it from real prudence, whose form it affects to appear in, call *Cunning*," the author regretting that the "many often miss the distinction between this shadow of wisdom and wisdom itself; and the vile successful villain is too often said to have rais'd himself to all his happiness and honours by his wisdom." [8]

This, then, is the point of Fielding's deliberately ambiguous use of the term in *Tom Jones*: the difficulty of distinguishing true prudence from false, wisdom from cunning. Even an Allworthy can mistake the characters of men, can fail to penetrate the pious disguises of the Blifils of this world. True prudence, Fielding would assert in *Amelia*, was "the Art of Life"; false prudence, he had declared in "An Essay on the Knowledge of the Characters of Men," was "the *Art of Thriving*," the signal talent and virtue of Blifil and Jonathan Wild, of Shamela and Stephen Grub, [9] indeed of a host of self-seeking hypocrites and worldly politicians who threaten to defeat the good-natured children of his comedies, to confound his cheerful vision of charity and order. These are the Enemy, whom he made it his business, as ironist and as magistrate, to expose and punish.

As we have seen, these meanings of prudence, true and false, were commonplaces of the Christian humanist tradition. By the eighteenth century, however, this noblest of the cardinal virtues of the Ancients had suffered from reinterpretation by writers of bromidic conduct books addressed chiefly to a middle-class audience of shopkeepers and schoolboys. Debased and vulgarized, *prudentia*, the hard-earned wisdom of the *vir honestus*, had become—if in name only—the property of the *vir œconomicus*. In the process, ironically, its counterfeit and shadow came, in effect, to be taken for the thing itself: self-discipline, discretion, foresight, expediency came to be valued for mercenary reasons—not as the way to self-knowledge and a virtuous conduct, but as the surest means of prospering in the world. This modern definition of prudence deepens the ambiguities

7. Benjamin Hoadly, Letter XXX, *The London Journal* (20 April 1723), in John Hoadly, ed., *Works* (1773), III, 105. See also Letter XC, *The London Journal* (25 July 1724), where Hoadly further analyzes "this *Cunning*" as being "but the Ape of Wisdom," a "Bastard Species" (ibid., III, 328–329).
8. "The Moralist," No. XXXII ("Some Thoughts on Cunning") *op. cit.*, III (July 1748), 281.
9. See *The True Patriot*, 14 January 1746.

of the term in *Tom Jones*. In this new context, the prudent person is coolly self-interested—even, in fact, hypocritical: he prizes the reputation of virtue more than virtue itself, since a good name can be profitable to him, will enable him more easily to use others to his own advantage; he is seldom open or candid (and then only by design), since he must conceal his true motives from those he hopes to gain by; he is never passionate, since only the man who is in control of himself can hope to manipulate others.

Though the difference is great between the grasping malevolence of Blifil, let us say, and the desire of his mother to conceal her indiscretions, both characters are "prudent" in this new sense. Consider, for example, the worldly counsel of Balthazar Gracian in *The Art of Prudence: or, A Companion for a Man of Sense*.[1] In a series of three hundred maxims Gracian provides a sort of *vade mecum* for the aspiring hypocrite, a layman's guide to "the *Art of Thriving*": thus, to adduce a random sample of his wisdom, he advises his readers, variously, "*Not to be too free, nor open*" (Maxim III), "*To find out a Mans* Foible, *or weak side*" (XXVI), "*Never to be disorder'd with Passion*" (LII), "*Under the Veil of another Man's Interest, to find one's Own*" (CXLIV [misnumbered CLXIV]), "*To be able to Cast the Blame and Misfortunes upon Others*" (CXLIX), "*To know how to use Friends*" (CLVIII), "*never* [to] *lose the Favour of him that is Happy, to take Compassion on a Wretch*" (CLXIII), "*To Act all that is agreeable by one's Self, and all that's Odious by others*" (CLXXXVII), "*To take Advantage of another Man's Wants*" (CLXXXIX), "*Not to make one's Self too Intelligible*" (CCLIII). The Blifils, indeed the Iagos, of this world have clearly heeded Gracian's exhortation to proceed in all things with "Pious Craft" (CXLIV). We may recognize each of Fielding's villains in the master's delineation of the "expert Person," who "uses for Weapons the stratagems of Intention": "He never does, what he seems to have a mind to do. He takes aim, 'tis true, but that only to deceive the Eyes of those that look upon him. He blurts out a word, and afterwards does what no body dreamt of" (XIII). Another maxim, explaining the necessity for the prudent man "*To Dissemble*" (XCVIII), makes clear why Fielding's hearty and good-natured heroes—a Tom Jones or a Parson Adams, let us say—are so ill-equipped for the business of life, so vulnerable to the designs of their predatory neighbors:

PASSIONS are the Breaches of the Mind. The most useful Knowledge is the Art of Disguising one's Thoughts. He that shews his Game, runs the risque of losing it. . . .

---

1. First translated into English in 1685 under the title, *The Courtiers Manual Oracle: or, The Art of Prudence*. My references are to *The Art of Prudence* (1702).

. . . he that disguises [his passions], preserves his Credit, at least in appearance. Our Passions are the Infirmities of our Reputation.

Gracian's work is only one of several handbooks on prudence addressed to a public apparently eager to penetrate the mysteries of worldly prosperity and *"Pollitricks,"* to use Fielding's fine coinage in *Jonathan Wild* (II.v). Among the most popular of these was William de Britaine's *Humane Prudence: or, The Art by which a Man may Raise Himself and His Fortune to Grandeur* (1680), which reached a twelfth edition by 1729. In a piece of typical advice De Britaine admonishes the reader "to try in the first Place to subdue your Passions, or at least so artificially to disguise them, that no Spy may be able to unmask your Thoughts; here to dissemble, is a great Point of Prudence; for by this means you so cunningly hide all your Imperfections, that no Eye shall be able to discover them." [2] Applying the general precept to the particular case of his most promising disciples, De Britaine concludes with a section entitled, "*Sententiæ Stellares:* or, Maxims of Prudence to be observed by Artisans of State." A similar work was Thomas Fuller's *Introductio ad Prudentiam: or, Directions, Counsels, and Cautions, tending to prudent Management of Affairs in Common Life,* which had gone through three editions by 1731. Fuller, a physician of Queen's College, Cambridge, designed this collection of 1,761 apothegms to direct his son (as Mentor had directed Telemachus!) in the ways of flourishing in the world.

Fuller's motive was shared by several other writers who attempted to anatomize the modern art of prudence for the benefit of schoolboys[3]—most of them appealing to the selfish interests of their readers in pious language formerly reserved for nobler themes. The terms prudence, wisdom, and virtue were, in effect, emptied of their original significance and euphemistically made to refer to the practice of duplicity and the pursuit of personal gain. By such means the middle-class mind achieved a comfortable reconciliation between morality and Mammon. Though published five years after *Tom Jones,* James Burgh's discussion of prudence in Book I of *The Dignity of Human Nature* (1754) not only serves to clarify Fielding's use of the term, but also illustrates some of the subtler ways by which the *prudentia* of the Christian humanist tradition became transmuted into the cardinal virtue in the pantheon of middle-class values. Burgh, a school-master by profession, represents prudence as

2. De Britaine, *Humane Prudence,* 12th ed. (1729), p. 61.
3. See, for example, Nathaniel Lardner, *Counsels of Prudence for the Use of Young People* (1735). Another work, which I have been unable to locate, is *The Young Gentleman and Lady Instructed in Principles of Politeness, Prudence, and Virtue,* 2 vols.; it was advertised as printed for Edward Wicksteed and published in October 1747.

a turn of mind, which puts a person upon looking forward, and enables him to judge rightly of the consequences of his behaviour, so as to avoid the misfortunes into which rashness precipitates many, and to gain the ends which a wise and virtuous man ought to pursue.

It is evident to the meanest understanding, that there is a fitness or unfitness, a suitableness or unsuitableness of things to one another, which is not to be changed, without some change presupposed in the things, or their circumstances. Prudence is the knowledge and observance of this propriety of behaviour to times and cirmumstances, and probable consequences, according to their several varieties.[4]

In itself this definition is close enough to Cicero's or Barrow's and could well serve as a description of that rational temper which Tom Jones requires. In context, however, Burgh differs from Fielding in identifying the function of prudence with the attainment of selfish ends: the language the philosophers had used to define the *ars vivendi* now comfortably justifies the modern art of prospering in the world. Prudence is "indispensably necessary," Burgh advises, not so much for the health of the private soul, but to frustrate the designs of the envious and to enable us to move profitably through life.[5] Here, as in other works on the subject, the great enemies of prudence are inexperience and rashness: the lack of "a due knowledge" of mankind, together with that "natural vivacity and warmth of youth" which lead us, with Tom Jones, to behave in a "forward and precipitate manner . . . [to] the disappointment of our designs." [6] Through the colors and devices of such rhetoric, Right Reason is transmogrified into shrewdness, a politic circumspection; and the ideal of self-discipline becomes the rationale for thriving. Prudence in this sense is that virtue which a Robinson Crusoe or a Pamela so well understands.

The concept of prudence in *Tom Jones* is deliberately complex, as significant yet as elusive as the meaning of wisdom itself. The single term carries with it at least three distinct meanings derivative from the ethical and historical contexts we have been exploring: (1) it may signify *prudentia*, the supreme rational virtue of the Christian humanist tradition, that practical wisdom which Tom Jones, like the *vir honestus*, must acquire; (2) it may signify the shadow and antithesis of this virtue—reason in the service of villainy —that malevolent cunning which characterizes the hypocrite Blifil; or (3) it may signify that prostitute and self-protective expediency, that worldy wisdom, which, owing to the influence of Gracian, De Britaine, Fuller, and the other pious-sounding perpetrators of a middle-class morality, replaced the humanist concept of *prudentia* in the

4. Burgh, *The Dignity of Human Nature* (1754), p. 3. 5. *Loc. cit.* 6. *Ibid.*, p. 4.

popular mind. These are the basic variations on the theme. According to the context in *Tom Jones*, one of these meanings will be dominant, but the others echo in the reader's memory effecting a kind of ironic counterpoint and ultimately, as it were, testing his own sense of values, his own ability to make necessary ethical distinctions between goods real or merely apparent.

In Book XII, Chapter iii, Fielding protests: "if we have not all the Virtues, I will boldly say, neither have we all the Vices of a prudent Character." The vices of the prudent characters in *Tom Jones* —of Blifil, Bridget Allworthy, Lady Bellaston, and their kind— should not be sufficiently evident. The positive meaning of prudence in the novel, however, is perhaps less obvious, for the virtue which Fielding recommends is essentially synthetic, combining the *prudentia* of the philosophers with certain less ignoble features of the modern version. What Tom Jones fundamentally lacks, of course, is *prudentia*: moral vision and self-discipline. Although he intuitively perceives the difference between Sophia and the daughters of Eve, he is too much the creature of his passions to be able to act upon that knowledge. He moves through life committing one good-natured indiscretion after another, unable to learn from past experiences or to foresee the future consequences of his rash behavior. Only in prison, at the nadir of his misfortunes, does the full meaning of his imprudence appear to him. To Mrs. Waters, Jones "lamented the Follies and Vices of which he had been guilty; every one of which, he said, had been attended with such ill Consequences, that he should be unpardonable if he did not take Warning, and quit those vicious Courses for the future," and he concludes with a "Resolution to sin no more, lest a worse Thing should happen to him" (XVII.ix). When, moments later, he is informed that Mrs. Waters, the woman he had slept with at Upton, is his own mother, Jones arrives at last at the crucial moment of self-awareness toward which the novel has been moving. Rejecting Partridge's suggestion that ill luck or the devil himself had contrived this ultimate horror, Fielding's hero accepts his own responsibility for his fate: "Sure . . . Fortune will never have done with me, 'till she hath driven me to Distraction. But why do I blame Fortune? I am myself the Cause of all my Misery. All the dreadful Mischiefs which have befallen me, are the Consequences only of my own Folly and Vice" (XVIII.ii). Here is at once the climax and the resolution of the theme of *prudentia* in the novel—a theme to which Fielding would return in *Amelia*, where, in the introductory chapter, he propounded at length the lesson Tom Jones learned: "I question much, whether we may not by natural means account for the Success of Knaves, the Calamities of Fools, with all the Miseries in which Men of Sense sometimes involve themselves by quitting the Directions of Prudence, and following the blind Guidance of a predominant Passion; in short, for all the ordinary Phenomena which are imputed to Fortune; whom, perhaps, Men accuse with no less Absurdity in Life, then a bad Player complains of ill Luck at the Game of Chess." [7] Prudence in this sense is the supreme virtue of the Christian humanist tradition, entailing knowledge and discipline of the self and the awareness that our lives, ultimately, are shaped not by circumstances, but by reason and the will. This, Fielding concludes, echoing Cicero, is "the Art of Life."

Although this is the fundamental positive meaning of prudence in *Tom Jones*, Fielding extends the concept to accommodate a nobler, purified version of that worldly wisdom so assiduously inculcated by the moderns. Since the business of life was a matter not simply of preserving the moral health of one's soul, but also of surviving in a world too quick to judge by appearances, it was necessary to have a proper regard to one's reputation. In Maxim XCIX Gracian warned that "THINGS are not taken for what they really are, but for what they appear to be. . . . It is not enough to have a good Intention, if the Action look ill" (see also CXXX), and Fuller's apothegms (for example, Nos. 1425 and 1590) similarly emphasize that "a fair Reputation" is necessary to all men. Fielding, however, is careful to distinguish his own version of prudence from that of the cynical proponents of a self-interested dissimulation—those who cared not at all for virtue, but only for the appearance of virtue. Good-nature and charity are the indispensable qualifications of Fielding's heroes—of Parson Adams, Heartfree, Tom Jones, Captain Booth—who demand our affection despite their naïveté, their foibles and indiscretions. But Fielding was concerned that the good man preserve his good name; otherwise he became vulnerable to the malicious designs of his enemies and subject to the disdain of his friends. The difficulty of distinguishing truth from appearances is Fielding's constant theme: the classical *prudentia* enables us to make these crucial discriminations; prudence in the modern sense, on the other hand, is in part the awareness that such distinctions are rarely made by the generality of men, that we are judged by appearances and must therefore conduct ourselves with discretion. As early as *The Champion* (22 November 1739) Fielding had insisted on this point: "I would . . . by no Means recommend to Mankind to cultivate Deceit, or endeavour to appear what they are not; on the contrary, I wish it were possible to induce the World to make a diligent Enquiry into Things themselves, to withold them from giving too hasty a Credit to the outward Shew and first Impression; I would only convince my Readers, *That it is not enough to have Virtue, without we also take Care to preserve, by a certain Decency and Dignity of Behaviour, the outward Appearance of it also."* [8] This, too, is the "very useful Lesson" Fielding sets forth in *Tom Jones* for the benefit of his youthful readers, who will find

> . . . that Goodness of Heart, and Openness of Temper, tho' these may give them great Comfort within, and administer to an honest Pride in their own Minds, will by no Means, alas! do their Business in the World. Prudence and Circumspection are necessary even to the best of Men. They are indeed as it were a Guard to Virtue, without which she can never be safe. It is not enough that your Designs, nay that your Actions, are intrinsically good, you must take Care they shall appear so. If your Inside be never so beautiful, you must preserve a fair Outside also. This must be constantly looked to, or Malice and Envy will take Care to blacken it so, that the Sagacity and Goodness of an *Allworthy* will not be able to see thro' it, and to discern the Beauties within. Let this, my young Readers, be your constant Maxim, That no Man can be good enough to enable him to neglect the Rules of Prudence; nor will Virtue herself look beautiful, unless she be bedecked with the outward Ornaments of Decency and Decorum. (III.vii)

Like Virtue herself, Sophia is concerned to preserve her good name, the outward sign of her true character (XIII.xi). And Allworthy more than once echoes his author's sentiments in advising Jones that prudence is "the Duty which we owe to ourselves" (XVIII.x), that it is, together with religion, the sole means of putting the good-natured man in possession of the happiness he deserves (V.vii).

As the recommendation of Charity and Chastity is the underlying purpose of Fielding's first novel, *Joseph Andrews*, the dominant ethical concern of *Tom Jones* is the anatomy of Prudence. It is a process as essential as the discrimination of vice from virtue, of selfishness from self-discipline, and as significant to life as the pursuit of wisdom. Lacking prudence, Tom Jones is a prey to hypocrites and knaves and too often the victim of his own spontaneities, his own generous impulses and extravagancies. For Fielding in this his greatest novel, virtue was as much a matter of the understanding and the will as of the heart. Prudence, he implies, is the name each man gives to that wisdom, worldly or moral, which he prizes. This is the fundamental paradox of the novel as of life. Fielding's rhetorical strategy—his ironic use of the same word to convey antithetical meanings—forces the reader to assess his own sense of values, to distinguish the true from the false. We, too, are implicated, as it were, in Tom Jones' awkward progress toward that most distant and elusive of goals—the marriage with Wisdom herself.

8. Quoted from the 1741 reprint, I, 23.

II. Sophia and the Functions of Emblem

Since it is a *practical* virtue, Fielding may thus define prudence, negatively and positively, by associating the word with various examples of moral behavior chosen to illustrate those disparate meanings of the concept which he meant either to ridicule or recommend. In action the "prudence" of Blifil or Mrs. Western may be distinguished from the "prudence" of Sophia; the deed to which the word is applied controls our sense of Fielding's intention, whether ironic or sincere. The nature of *speculative* wisdom, on the other hand, is less easily and effectively conveyed by means of the counterpoint of word and action: *sophia* was a mystery even Socrates could describe only figuratively—a method to which Fielding alludes in the Dedication to *Tom Jones* when he invokes the Platonic metaphor of the "naked Charms" of Virtue imaged as a beautiful woman.[9] In *Tom Jones* the meaning of *sophia* is presented to the reader as "an Object of Sight" in the character of Fielding's heroine.

Although it has apparently escaped the attention of his critics, the emblemizing technique Fielding here employs—which it is our present purpose to consider in its various manifestations in *Tom Jones*—is one of the most distinctive resources of his art as a novelist. More than any other writer of his day—unless, perhaps, one accepts J. Paul Hunter's provocative interpretation of Defoe's method in *Robinson Crusoe*[1]—Fielding organized his novels schematically, choosing his characters and shaping his plots so as to objectify an abstract moral theme which is the germ of his fiction. There is what may be called an iconomatic impulse behind much of Fielding's art: many of his most memorable episodes and characters, and the general design and movement of such books as *Joseph Andrews* and *Tom Jones*, may be seen to function figuratively as emblem or allegory, as the embodiment in scene or character or action of Fielding's themes. *Tom Jones* is not of course an allegory in the same sense or in the same way that *The Faerie Queene*, let us say, is an allegory; nevertheless, both these works have certain

---

9. Cf. *Phaedrus*, 250D: "wisdom would arouse terrible love, if such a clear image of it were granted as would come through sight" (trans. H. N. Fowler, Loeb Classical Library, 1914). See also Cicero, *De Finibus*, II.xvi, and *De Officiis*, I.v; and Seneca, *Epistulae Morales*, CXV.6. The specific notion of the naked charms of Virtue, imaged as a beautiful woman, is only implicit in Plato. Fielding was especially fond of this commonplace: see, for example, *The Champion* (24, 26 January 1739/40),

and "An Essay on Conversation" and "An Essay on the Knowledge of the Characters of Men"—both published in the *Miscellanies* (1743), I, 159, 217. For a discussion of this image and its relation to the moral theme of Fielding's last novel, see Alan Wendt, "The Naked Virtue of Amelia," *ELH*, XXVII (1960), 131–148.

1. See Hunter, *The Reluctant Pilgrim: Defoe's Emblematic Method and Quest for Form in 'Robinson Crusoe'* (Baltimore, 1966).

schematic intentions and certain narrative and scenic techniques in common. *Tom Jones* differs from the conventional allegory in that Fielding's *story* is primary and autonomous: characters, events, setting have an integrity of their own and compel our interest in and for themselves; they do not require, at every point in the narrative, to be read off as signs and symbols in some controlling ideational system. Whereas Una is "the One," Sophia Western is the girl whom Tom Jones loves and her family bullies. Spenser's heroine engages our intellect; Fielding's our affection and sympathy. Yet at the same time Fielding shares with the allegorist the desire to *render* the abstractions of his theme—in this instance, to find the particular shape and image for the complementary concepts of Providence and Prudence, of divine Order and human Virtue, which were the bases for his comic vision of life. What Charles Woods observed of Fielding's plays, invoking a favorite term of the critic Sneerwell in *Pasquin*, pertains as well to the novels, where Fielding deserts the "realistic" mode for the "Emblematical."[2]

The general figurative strategy in *Tom Jones* is implicit in the passage from Fielding's Dedication comparing "Virtue" (i.e., *sophia*) to a beautiful woman and our "true Interest" (i.e., *prudentia*) to the "Pursuit of her." Although Sophia Western is first of all a character in Fielding's novel, she is also the emblematic redaction of the Platonic metaphor. After his expulsion from Paradise Hall, Tom Jones' journey is at first aimless and uncertain: "*The World,* as *Milton* phrases it, *lay all before him*; and *Jones*, no more than *Adam*, had any Man to whom he might resort for Comfort or Assistance" (VII.ii). After the crisis at Upton, however, his pursuit of Sophia will symbolize his gradual and painful attainment of *prudentia*, of self-knowledge and clarity of moral vision. The marriage of Tom and Sophia is thus the necessary and inevitable culmination of Fielding's theme: it is a symbolic union signifying the individual's attainment of true wisdom.

To illustrate this quasi-allegorical dimension of *Tom Jones*, we may consider, first of all, the ways in which Fielding renders the Platonic metaphor of Virtue—in which the idea of *sophia* becomes associated with the girl Sophy Western. Without forgetting his heroine's role and function in the story itself, from time to time in the course of the narrative Fielding makes the reader aware that Sophia's beauty is ultimately the physical manifestation of a spiritual perfection almost divine, that she is for him as for Tom Jones, the Idea of Virtue incarnate. Like much of his comedy Fielding's introduction of Sophia "*in the Sublime*" style (IV.ii) is both playful and serious, mocking the extravagancies of romance while at the

---

2. Fielding, *The Author's Farce*, ed. Charles B. Woods (Lincoln, Neb., 1966), p. xvi.

same time invoking the old values of honor and virtue which romance celebrates. By a process of allusion—to mythology, art, poetry, and his own more immediate experience—Fielding presents his heroine as the ideal woman, the representative of a beauty of form and harmony of spirit so absolute as to be a sort of divine vitalizing force in man and nature alike. She is like "the lovely *Flora*," goddess of springtime, whom every flower rises to honor and who is the cause of the perfect harmony of the birds that celebrate her appearance: "From Love proceeds your Music, and to Love it returns." Her beauty excels that of the Venus de Medici, the statue considered by Fielding's contemporaries to be "the standard of all female beauty and softness." [3] She is the idealization in art of his dead wife Charlotte, "whose Image never can depart from my Breast." But what is clear above all is that her beauty is only the reflection of her spiritual nature: "the Outside of *Sophia* . . . this beautiful Frame," is but the emblem of her "Mind," which diffuses "that Glory over her Countenance, which no Regularity of Features can give." Like Elizabeth Drury, Donne's ideal woman in *The Anniversaries*, to whom Fielding here expressly compares her, Sophy Western is also the image and embodiment of "*Sophia* or the *Divine Wisdom*." [4]

For Jones, of course, Sophia *is* the perfection of beauty and virtue that her name implies: she is "my Goddess," he declares to Mrs. Honour; "as such I will always worship and adore her while I have Breath" (IV.xiv). And he can scarcely think of her except in terms of divinity itself: he stands in awe of her "heavenly Temper" and "divine Goodness" (V.vi); she is his "dear . . . divine Angel" (XVIII.xii). Such sentiments are, to be sure, the usual effusions and hyperbole of the adolescent lover, but they work together none the less to reinforce the reader's sense of Sophy's perfections. In answer to the landlady's insipid description of his mistress as "a sweet young Creature," Jones supplies a truer definition, applying to Sophia alone Jaffeir's apostrophe to Woman in *Venice Preserved* (I.i):

'A sweet Creature!' cries *Jones*, 'O Heavens!

> *Angels are painted fair to look like her.*
> *There's in her all that we believe of Heaven,*
> *Amazing Brightness, Purity and Truth,*
> *Eternal Joy, and everlasting Love.'* (VIII.ii)

Like his author, Jones insists that Sophia's physical beauty is only the imperfect manifestation of her essential spiritual nature. It is

3. Joseph Spence, *Polymetis* (1747), p. 66.
4. The quotation is from Jacob Boehme, *The Way to Christ* (Bath, 1775), p. 56, as given in Frank Manley, ed., *John Donne: The Anniversaries* (Baltimore, 1963), p. 38. On the identification of "the noble Virgin Sophia" with the biblical figure of Wisdom, see Manley's Introduction, pp. 37–38.

her "charming Idea" that he doats on (XIII.xi). Thus, when his friend Nightingale inquires if she is "honourable," Jones protests that her virtues are so dazzling as to drive all meaner considerations from his thoughts; it is not her body but the spiritual reality it expresses which demands his love:

> 'Honourable?' answered *Jones* . . . 'The sweetest Air is not purer, the limpid Stream not clearer than her Honour. She is all over, both in Mind and Body, consummate Perfection. She is the most beautiful Creature in the Universe; and yet she is Mistress of such noble, elevated Qualities, that though she is never from my Thoughts, I scarce ever think of her Beauty; but when I see it.' (XV.ix)

Twice during the novel Fielding symbolically dramatizes the distinction he wishes his readers to make between the girl Sophy Western and her "Idea"—that is, in a Platonic sense, the mental image or form of that essential spiritual Beauty of which his heroine's lovely face is but an imperfect manifestation.[5] As Socrates had regretted that mortal eyes were able to behold only the shadow of *sophia,* reflected as in a glass darkly,[6] so Fielding uses the conventional emblem of the mirror to dramatize the nature of his allegory, to demonstrate that what is ultimately important about Sophia is not her physical charms, but her spiritual reality. The use of the mirror as an emblem of the mind's powers to conceptualize and abstract was common among iconographers. "The Glass," writes a commentator upon Ripa's emblems, "wherein we see no real Images, is a Resemblance of our *Intellect*; wherein we phancy many Ideas of Things that are not seen"; or it "denotes *Abstraction,* that is to say, by Accidents, which the Sense comprehends; the Understanding comes to know their Nature, as we, by seeing the accidental Forms of Things in a Glass, consider their Essence." [7] Fielding introduces this emblem at the moment when his hero, having pursued Sophia from Upton, is reunited with her in Lady Bellaston's town house (XIII.xi). The first sight the lovers have of each other is of their images reflected in a mirror:

> . . . *Sophia* expecting to find no one in the Room, came hastily in, and went directly to a Glass which almost fronted her, without once looking towards the upper End of the Room, where the Statue of *Jones* now stood motionless.—In this Glass it was, after contemplating her own lovely Face, that she first discovered the

---

5. The definition of *idea* given in George Richardson's *Iconology: or, A Collection of Emblematical Figures, Moral and Instructive* (1778–79), is as follows: "In general, [Idea] is the image of any thing, which, though not seen, is conceived in the mind. Plato defines it, the essence sent forth by the divine spirit, which is entirely separated from the matter of created things" (I,82).

6. *Phaedo,* 99D–E.

7. See Isaac Fuller and Peirce Tempest, *Iconologia: or, Moral Emblems, by Caesar Ripa* (1709), Figures 229 and 269, folios 57 and 67.

said Statue; when instantly turning about, she perceived the Reality of the Vision. . . .

The vision in the mirror that has momentarily turned Jones to a statue is the visible projection of the ideal image of Sophia he has carried in his mind. Whatever his indiscretions, he assures her that his "*Heart* was never unfaithful": "Though I despaired of possessing you, nay, almost of ever seeing you more, I doated still on your charming Idea, and could *seriously* love no other Woman."

Still clearer, perhaps, is Fielding's use of the mirror emblem toward the close of the novel (XVIII.xii), in a scene designed both to stress the allegorical identity of Sophia and to dramatize Socrates' declaration in the *Phaedrus* (250D) that "wisdom would arouse terrible love, if such a clear image of it were granted as would come through the sight." But, as Fielding observed in *The Champion* (5 July 1740), few there are "whose Eyes are able to behold Truth without a Glass." Protesting that "No Repentance was ever more sincere," and pleading that his contrition "reconcile" him to his "Heaven in this dear Bosom," Jones attempts to overcome Sophia's doubts as to his sincerity by making her confront the vision of her own beauty and virtue reflected in a mirror. To behold and possess not the image merely, but the reality itself, would, as Socrates had said, convert even the most inveterate reprobate to the love of virtue:

> [Jones] replied, 'Don't believe me upon my Word; I have a better Security, a Pledge for my Constancy, which it is impossible to see and to doubt.' 'What is that?' said *Sophia*, a little surprized. 'I will show you, my charming Angel,' cried *Jones*, seizing her Hand, and carrying her to the Glass. 'There, behold it there in that lovely Figure, in that Face, that Shape, those Eyes, that Mind which shines through these Eyes: Can the Man who shall be in Possession of these be inconstant? Impossible! my *Sophia*: They would fix a *Dorimant*, a Lord *Rochester*. You could not doubt it, if you could see yourself with any Eyes but your own.' *Sophia* blushed, and half smiled; but forcing again her Brow into a Frown, 'If I am to judge,' said she, 'of the future by the past, my Image will no more remain in your Heart when I am out of your Sight, than it will in this Glass when I am out of the Room.' 'By Heaven, by all that is sacred,' said *Jones*, 'it never was out of my Heart.'

Such passages demand to be read on more than one level: Sophy Western's image in the glass is the literalizing of the Platonic metaphor, the dramatization of Fielding's meaning in the broadly allegorical scheme of the novel. Ultimately, her true identity is ideal, an abstraction.

Within the paradigmatic universe of *Tom Jones*—in which the values of Fielding's Christian humanism are systematically rendered and enacted—Sophy Western is both cynosure and avatar, the controlling center of the theme of Virtue and its incarnation. Though she is, above all, the woman that Tom loves, she is also, as Fielding's Dedication implies, the emblem and embodiment of that ideal Wisdom her name signifies. Without her Paradise Hall and the country from which Tom has been driven are unbearable, meaningless (XII.iii)—an Eden empty of grace. To win her in marriage is the supreme redemptive act, a divine dispensation which for Jones, as for every man, restores joy and order to a troubled world: "To call *Sophia* mine is the greatest . . . Blessing which Heaven can bestow" (XVIII.x). But for one of Jones' passionate nature the conditions upon which she may be won are exacting, nothing less, indeed, than the acquisition of *prudentia*: Tom must perfect his "Understanding," as Sophia herself insists (XI.vii), must learn not only to distinguish between the values of the spirit and those of the flesh, between the true and the false, but to discipline his will so that this knowledge may govern his life. Having learned this lesson at last, Jones is able to withstand the blandishments of such sirens as Mrs. Fitzpatrick, for, as the narrator observes, "his whole Thoughts were now so confined to his *Sophia*, that I believe no Woman upon Earth could have now drawn him into an Act of Inconstancy" (XVI.ix). On the eve of their wedding, as the company of brides and grooms convenes, Sophia is revealed presiding over the feast of virtuous love, eclipsing the beauty of the women, adored by every man: she "sat at the Table like a Queen receiving Homage, or rather like a superiour Being receiving Adoration from all around her. But it was an Adoration which they gave, not which she exacted: For she was as much distinguished by her Modesty and Affability, as by all her other Perfections" (XVIII.xiii). In its way not unlike the banquet of Socrates, the wedding dinner of Tom and Sophia celebrates the power of Beauty and Virtue. In the light of such passages, Jones' "Quest" for "his lovely *Sophia*" (X.vii) takes on a symbolic dimension: it is the dramatization of Fielding's expressed concern in the novel to convince "Men, that their true Interest directs them to a Pursuit of [Virtue]."

Fielding's method of projecting the abstractions of his theme in image and action is comparable, in a way, to the poet's device of personification. It is also the correlative in fiction of the graphic artist's use of emblem and allegorical design. Following Horace, Fielding recognized the sisterhood of the two art forms.[8] In this respect, as in others, he may be compared with Pope, many of whose

8. For an excellent discussion of the relationship between poetry and painting in the eighteenth century, see Jean H. Hagstrum, *The Sister Arts: The Tradition of Literary Pictorialism and English Poetry from Dryden to Gray* (Chicago, 1958).

descriptions—that of the triumph of Vice in the *Epilogue to the Satires. Dialogue I* (ll.151 ff.), for example, or of Dulness holding court in *The Dunciad* (IV. 17 ff.)—have the effect of allegorical *tableaux*, pictorially conceived and composed in order to carry the poet's meaning before the visual imagination. Fielding himself more than once observed the relationship between his own satiric art and that of his friend Hogarth, the "comic History Painter," who well understood the use of symbolic detail to render and characterize abstractions.[9] Particularly "Hogarthian" in conception and effect, for instance, is the image Fielding presents of the philosopher Square after his hilarious exposure in Molly Seagrim's bedroom (V.v). At the critical moment the rug behind which he has concealed himself falls away, and the august metaphysician—who has made a career of denouncing the body—is revealed in the closet, clad only in a blush and Molly's nightcap and fixed "in a Posture (for the Place would not near admit his standing upright) as ridiculous as can possibly be conceived":

> The Posture, indeed, in which he stood, was not greatly unlike that of a Soldier who is tyed Neck and Heels; or rather resembling the Attitude in which we often see Fellows in the public Streets of *London*, who are not suffering but deserving Punishment by so standing. He had a Night-cap belonging to *Molly* on his Head, and his two large Eyes, the Moment the Rug fell, stared directly at *Jones*; so that when the Idea of Philosophy was added to the Figure now discovered, it would have been very difficult for any Spectator to have refrained from immoderate Laughter.

The distinctive quality of this passage is graphic. It is as close to the pictorial as the artist in words can bring it: the sense of composition, of attitude is there; the subject has been frozen at the critical moment in time, his chagrin economically defined by the two features, the night cap and the astonished stare, which explain and characterize it. What is more, the scene has an emblematic effect: it serves as the pictorial projection of an *idea*—namely, of the theory of "the true Ridiculous," which, as the Preface to *Joseph Andrews* makes clear, Fielding thought to consist principally in the comic disparity between what we are and what we profess to be. As the literal revelation of the naked truth behind the drapery of pretension, the exposure of Square is the quintessential scene in Fielding's fiction.

Other scenes in the novel are pictorially conceived, and for a variety of effects. Most obvious of these is Fielding's ironic imitation of

9. For Fielding's compliments to Hogarth, see, among many other references, the Preface to *Joseph Andrews* and *Tom Jones* (I.xi, II.iii, III.vi, VI.viii, X.viii), where Fielding refers the reader to particular Hogarth prints to clarify the description of Bridget Allworthy, Mrs. Partridge, and Thwackum.

one of the most celebrated historical *tableaux* of the period: Plate VI of Charles Le Brun's magnificent series depicting the victories of Alexander.[1] As Le Brun had represented the vanquished King Porus being carried before the magnanimous conqueror, so Fielding, with due regard to the arrangement and attitudes of his figures, describes the scene after Jones' and Western's bloody victory over the forces of Blifil and Thwackum (V.xii):

> At this time, the following was the Aspect of the bloody Field. In one Place, lay on the Ground, all pale and almost breathless, the vanquished *Blifil*. Near him stood the Conqueror *Jones*, almost covered with Blood, part of which was naturally his own, and Part had been lately the Property of the Reverend Mr. *Thwackum*. In a third Place stood the said *Thwackum*, like King *Porus*, sullenly submitting to the Conqueror. The last Figure in the Piece was *Western the Great*, most gloriously forbearing the vanquished Foe.

Analysis of Fielding's mock-heroicism must clearly extend beyond his burlesque allusions to Homer and Virgil to such skillful imitations of specific masterpieces of historical art.

Certain other scenes in *Tom Jones* recall the art of the painter of "prospect" pieces, wherein, however, Fielding has chosen and arranged the features of the landscape for their allegorical or emblematic suggestiveness. Such are the descriptions, almost iconological in effect, of Allworthy's estate and of the view from Mazard Hill. The prospect at Paradise Hall (I.iv), while apparently a static landscape, is carefully organized so as to carry the reader's eye, and hence his imagination, from the immediate and local outward to the distant and infinite, thereby implicitly presenting the characteristic quality and intention of Fielding's art in the novel, which is a continual translation of particulars into universals: the spring, gushing from its source at the summit of the hill, flows downward to a lake in the middle distance, from whence issues a river which the eye follows as it meanders for several miles before it empties itself in the sea beyond. The scene takes on yet another significant dimension once we are aware that it is composed of elements associating Paradise Hall, the place of Tom Jones' birth and the home of his spiritual father, both with the estates of Fielding's patrons, George Lyttelton and Ralph Allen, and with Glastonbury Tor, which rises fully visible from the threshold of Sharpham Park,

---

1. Done at the command of Louis XIV, Le Brun's series depicting the victories of Alexander now hangs in the Louvre. Copies of the official engravings by the Audrans were commissioned in England and published by Carington Bowles. The series was much admired: see, for example, Farquhar's *Beaux' Stratagem* (1707), IV, and Charles Gildon, *The Complete Art of Poetry* (1718), I, 230. When Louis Laguerre was commissioned to commemorate Marlborough's victories over the French, he looked to Le Brun's *tableaux* for a model (see Margaret Whinney and Oliver Millar, *English Art, 1625–1744* [Oxford, 1957], pp. 305–306).

Fielding's own birthplace and the seat of his maternal grandfather.[2] Paradise Hall is very much the product of Fielding's symbolic imagination; it is his own, as well as his hero's, spiritual home. Equally suggestive, and more obviously emblematic, is the subsequent description of Allworthy walking forth to survey his estate as dawn breaks, bathing the creation in light. The glory of this good man— who is, more than any other character except Sophia herself, the center of the novel's moral universe—is rendered in terms of the sun, traditional symbol of the deity:[3]

It was now the Middle of *May*, and the Morning was remarkably serene, when Mr. *Allworthy* walked forth on the Terrace, where the Dawn opened every Minute that lovely Prospect we have before described to his Eye. And now having sent forth Streams of Light, which ascended the Blue Firmament before him, as Harbingers preceding his Pomp, in the full Blaze of his Majesty up rose the Sun; than which one Object alone in this lower Creation could be more glorious, and that Mr. *Allworthy* himself presented; a human Being replete with Benevolence, meditating in what Manner he might render himself most acceptable to his Creator, by doing most Good to his Creatures.

A final illustration of Fielding's emblematic art in *Tom Jones* will serve to return us to the theme of Wisdom. As in presenting the "Idea" of *sophia*, Fielding, at one significant moment in the novel, also drew upon conventional iconological techniques in order vis-

2. In describing Allworthy's seat, Fielding's intentions are as much allusive and symbolic as they are chorographical. The description is based upon elements associated primarily with Sharpham Park and secondarily with Hagley Park and Prior Park, the estates of Lyttelton and Allen respectively. From the doorway at Sharpham Park Fielding would have looked daily across the moors at Glastonbury and Tor Hill. The prospect from Allworthy's Paradise Hall corresponds in general with the view westward from Tor Hill (see Wilbur L. Cross, *The History of Henry Fielding* [New Haven, 1918], II, 165). The "Style" of Paradise Hall itself is doubtless in honor of a mutual friend of Fielding's and Lyttelton's, Sanderson Miller (1717–80), amateur architect and pioneer of the Gothic revival. In 1747–48 and 1749–50 Lyttelton erected a ruined castle and a rotunda of Miller's design at Hagley Park; indeed, until his second wife disapproved, he had wanted Miller to build him a Gothic house. Like Allworthy's mansion, furthermore, Hagley Hall is situated on the south side of a hill, nearer the bottom than the top, yet high enough to command a pleasant view of the valley. And many of the details in Fielding's description echo Thomson's celebration of Hagley Park in "Spring," ll. 900-958 (*Seasons*, 1744 ed.). At the same time, in the third paragraph of the chapter, Fielding does not forget Ralph Allen, whose house, an example of "the best *Grecian* Architecture," he had praised earlier in *Joseph Andrews* (III.i, vi) and *A Journey from This World to the Next* (I.v): Allen's Palladian mansion stands on the summit of a hill down which a stream falls into a lake which is visible "from every Room in the Front."

3. For an elaborate gloss on the sun as "*A fit Emblem, or rather Adumbration of God*," see William Turner's *Compleat History of the Most Remarkable Providences* (1697), pp. 14–19. The sun, according to Turner (and many others), is "the *Eye of Heaven*" (p. 14) and a symbol of God's "Benignity and Beneficence" (p. 18). It is with this latter attribute of the Deity that both Barrow and Fielding particularly associated the sun. Wrote Barrow: "Such is a charitable man; the sun is not more liberal of his light and warmth, than he is of beneficial influence" (Sermon XXVII, "The Nature, Properties and Acts of Charity," *op. cit.*, I, 261). In the verse epistle "Of Good-Nature," Fielding, recalling Matthew V:45, exclaims: "Oh! great Humanity, whose beams benign,/ Like the sun's rays, on just and unjust shine."

ually to project the meaning of *prudentia*. The scene occurs at the opening of Book IX, Chapter ii, as Tom Jones contemplates the prospect from atop Mazard Hill. Structurally, the scene holds a crucial position between the narrative of the Old Man of the Hill and the pivotal events at Upton; thematically, it is the emblematic statement of the nature of true prudence and of Tom's progress along the way to acquiring that virtue. Fielding's basic device was entirely familiar. We will recall that it was conventional for poets and philosophers alike to translate the notion of the prudent man's intellectual apprehension of past, present, and future into physical and spatial terms: to look in the direction from whence one has come is to contemplate the meaning of the past; to look in the direction one is going is to consider what the future holds in store. The iconology of Prudence traditionally represented this virtue in the likeness of a figure with two (or three) faces—one, often the face of an old man, looking to the left or behind; the other, that of a young man or woman, looking to the right or ahead. Titian's *Allegory of Prudence*—the symbolism of which Professor Panofsky has brilliantly explicated [4]—depicts a head with three faces and bears a Latin inscription reading: "The prudent man of today profits from past experience in order not to imperil the future." [5] Following the design by Caesar Ripa, whose *Iconologia* (1593) was the standard work well into the eighteenth century, most emblematists represented Prudence with two faces, while retaining the sense of Titian's symbolism. George Richardson explains the significance of the design as follows: "The ancients have represented this virtue with two faces, the one young, and the other old, to indicate that prudence is acquired by consideration of things past, and a foresight of those to come." [6] The persistence of this metaphor, associating Prudence with the vision of distant things, is further suggested by Pope's personification of this virtue in *The Dunciad* (I.49), where the image of Prudence with her perspective glass was drawn from a different, but obviously related, iconological tradition.

As we have already remarked, what Tom Jones must acquire before he is ready to marry Sophia and return to the country of his birth is prudence—the ability to learn from past experience, both his own and others', so as to distinguish the true from the false and to estimate the future consequences of his present behavior. To invoke the Aristotelian notion of the "Three Ages of Man," [7] at

4. Erwin Panofsky, *Meaning in the Visual Arts,* Doubleday Anchor Books (Garden City, N.Y., 1955), pp. 146–168.
5. Because she regards past, present, and future, Prudence is represented in Dante's *Purgatorio,* XXIX, as a figure with three eyes. See also Francisco degli Allegri, *Tractato Nobilissimo della Prudentia et Iustitia* (Venice, 1508): British Museum, Prints and Drawings. 163*.a.23.
6. Richardson, *op. cit.,* II, 23–24. For earlier emblems of Prudence, based on Ripa and representing a figure with two faces, see the following: Jacques de Bie and J. Baudoin, *Iconologie* (Paris, 1644), pp. 160, 164, and Fuller and Tempest, *op. cit.,* Figure 251 and folio 63.
7. See Aristotle, *Rhetoric,* II.xii–xiv.

this juncture in Tom's progress toward maturity he is presented
with the extreme alternatives of youth and age—the rashness and
passion which characterize his own adolescence, and which define
all that is most and least admirable about him, as opposed to the
cowardly cynicism of the Old Man of the Hill. Having heard the
wretched history of the Old Man and rejected his misanthropy,
Tom has profited from one lesson that experience has to teach him;
but, as events in Upton will soon prove, he has not yet mastered
the more difficult test of his own past follies. As Upton represents
the apex of the rising action of the novel and the turning point in
Tom's progress, so at this stage in the narrative Fielding's hero
stands literally at the summit of a high hill, from which he can
survey the vast terrain that separates him from his home and mistress, and, by facing in the opposite direction, regard the obscure
and tangled wood which, it will appear, contains the woman who
will abruptly dislodge Sophia from his thoughts and involve him in
the near fatal consequences of his own imprudence. The prospect
Fielding describes, with a warning that we may not fully "understand" it, allegorizes the theme of prudence in the novel, rendering
spiritual and temporal matters in terms of physical and spatial ana-
logues: the view southward toward "Home" representing the meaning of the past, the view northward toward the dark wood imaging
the problem of the future. As the Old Man shrewdly remarks to his
young companion: "I perceive now the Object of your Contemplation is not within your Sight":

> *Aurora* now first opened her Casement, *Anglicè*, the Day began
> to break, when *Jones* walked forth in Company with the Stranger,
> and mounted *Mazard* Hill; of which they had no sooner gained
> the Summit, than one of the most noble Prospects in the World
> presented itself to their View, and which we would likewise present
> to the Reader; but for two Reasons. *First*, We despair of making
> those who have seen this Prospect, admire our Description. *Sec-
> ondly*, We very much doubt whether those, who have not seen it,
> would understand it.
>
> *Jones* stood for some Minutes fixed in one Posture, and direct-
> ing his Eyes towards the South; upon which the old Gentleman
> asked, What he was looking at with so much Attention? 'Alas,
> Sir,' answered he with a Sigh, 'I was endeavouring to trace out
> my own Journey hither. Good Heavens! what a Distance is
> *Gloucester* from us! What a vast Tract of Land must be between
> me and my own Home.' 'Ay, ay, young Gentleman,' cries the
> other, 'and, by your Sighing, from what you love better than your
> own Home, or I am mistaken. I perceive now the Object of your
> Contemplation is not within your Sight, and yet I fancy you have
> a Pleasure in looking that Way.' *Jones* answered with a Smile, 'I
> find, old Friend, you have not yet forgot the Sensations of your

youth.—I own my Thoughts were employed as you have guessed.'

They now walked to that Part of the Hill which looks to the North-West, and which hangs over a vast and extensive Wood.

Here they were no sooner arrived, than they heard at a Distance the most violent Screams of a Woman, proceeding from the Wood below them. *Jones* listened a Moment, and then, without saying a Word to his Companion (for indeed the Occasion seemed sufficiently pressing) ran, or rather slid, down the Hill, and without the least Apprehension or Concern for his own Safety, made directly to the Thicket whence the Sound had issued.

Occurring midway through Jones' journey—and through his progress toward maturity, toward the acquisition of prudence—the scene atop Mazard Hill is the emblematic projection of Fielding's theme. The past and its meaning are plain and clear to Jones, but not plain and clear enough; the future is obscure and tangled, fraught with sudden and unforeseen dangers. Sophia is abruptly supplanted in his thoughts by the more immediate appeal of another woman, in whose arms at Upton Tom will forget, for the moment at least, the lesson of his past follies and the claims of his true mistress. It is his affair with Jenny Jones at Upton that will result in his estrangement from Sophia and, eventually, in the anxious knowledge that his behavior, however generous and gallant, has apparently involved him in the sin of incest. What Tom sees looking south from Mazard Hill reassures us about his essential health of spirit, about those values he ultimately cherishes. His precipitous descent, however, reflects those qualities of character which are both his greatest strength and his weakness: on the one hand, courage and self-lessness, prompting him to the assistance of injured frailty; on the other, that rashness which is the source of his vulnerability as a moral agent.

Despite the number of illuminating studies in recent years, the technical resources of Fielding's art as a novelist have not yet been fully disclosed, nor have we as yet adequately appreciated the degree to which Fielding applied the devices of his craft to the communication of his serious concerns as a moralist. If the structure of *Tom Jones* is organic in an Aristotelian sense—as Professor Crane has shown it to be—it is also schematic, the expression through emblem, parable, and significant design of Fielding's controlling themes. If *Tom Jones* is the playful celebration of the feast of life —as Andrew Wright has insisted—it is also the expression in art of Fielding's Christian vision. The ways in which such devices as ambiguity, allegory, and emblem function together to define the theme of Wisdom in the novel may be taken as one more measure of Fielding's intention and his achievement.

R. S. CRANE

The Plot of Tom Jones†

I

Of all the plots constructed by English novelists that of *Tom Jones* has probably elicited the most unqualified praise. There is "no fable whatever," according to Fielding's first biographer, that "affords, in its solution, such artful states of suspence, such beautiful turns of surprise, such unexpected incidents, and such sudden discoveries, sometimes apparently embarrassing, but always promising the catastrophe, and eventually promoting the completion of the whole." [1] Not since the days of Homer, it seemed to James Beattie, had the world seen "a more artful epick fable." "The characters and adventures are wonderfully diversified: yet the circumstances are all so natural, and rise so easily from one another, and co-operate with so much regularity in bringing on, even while they seem to retard, the catastrophe, that the curiosity of the reader . . . grows more and more impatient as the story advances, till at last it becomes downright anxiety. And when we get to the end . . . we are amazed to find, that of so many incidents there should be so few superfluous; that in such variety of fiction there should be so great probability; and that so complex a tale should be perspicuously conducted, and with perfect unity of design." [2] These are typical of the eulogies that preceded and were summed up in Coleridge's famous verdict in 1834: "What a master of composition Fielding was! Upon my word, I think the Œdipus Tyrannus, The Alchemist, and *Tom Jones*, the three most perfect plots ever planned." [3] More recent writers have tended to speak less hyperbolically and, like Scott, to insist that "even the high praise due to the construction and arrangement of the story is inferior to that claimed by the truth, force, and spirit of the characters," [4] but it is hard to think of any important modern discussion of the novel that does not contain at least a few sentences on Fielding's "ever-to-be-praised skill as an architect of plot." [5]

†From *The Journal of General Education*, 4 (1950), 112–30. Copyright 1950 by the Pennsylvania State University Press. Reprinted by permission of the publisher.

1. Arthur Murphy (1762), quoted in Frederic T. Blanchard, *Fielding the Novelist: A Study in Historical Criticism* (New Haven, 1926), p. 161.
2. *Dissertations Moral and Critical* (1783), quoted in Blanchard, *op. cit.*, pp. 222–23.
3. *Ibid.*, pp. 320–21. ["Table Talk," 5 July 1834—*Editor*.]
4. *Ibid.*, p. 327 [*Fielding*, Ballantyne "Lives," 1821—*Editor*].
5. The phrase is Oliver Elton's in *A Survey of English Literature, 1730–1780* (New York, 1928), I, 195. Cf. also Wilbur L. Cross, *The History of Henry Fielding* (New Haven, 1918), II, 160–61; Aurélien Digeon, *Les Romans de Fielding* (Paris, 1923), pp. 210–16; Elizabeth Jenkins, *Henry Fielding* (London, 1947), pp. 57–58; and George Sherburn, in *A Literary History of England*, ed. Albert C. Baugh (New York and London, 1948), pp. 957–58.

The question I wish to raise concerns not the justice of any of these estimates but rather the nature and critical adequacy of the conception of plot in general and of the plot of *Tom Jones* in particular that underlies most if not all of them. Now it is a striking fact that in all the more extended discussions of Fielding's masterpiece since 1749 the consideration of the plot has constituted merely one topic among several others, and a topic, moreover, so detached from the rest that once it is disposed of the consideration of the remaining elements of character, thought, diction, and narrative technique invariably proceeds without further reference to it. The characters are indeed agents of the story, but their values are assessed apart from this, in terms sometimes of their degrees of conformity to standards of characterization in literature generally, sometimes of the conceptions of morality they embody, sometimes of their relation to Fielding's experiences or prejudices, sometimes of their reflection, taken collectively, of the England of their time. The other elements are isolated similarly, both from the plot and from one another: what is found important in the thought, whether of the characters or of the narrator, is normally not its function as an artistic device but its doctrinal content as a sign of the "philosophy" of Fielding; the style and the ironical tone of the narrative are frequently praised, but in relation solely to what they contribute to the general literary satisfaction of the reader; and what is perhaps more significant, the wonderful comic force of the novel, which all have delighted to commend, is assumed to be independent of the plot and a matter exclusively of particular incidents, of the characters of some, but not all, of the persons, and of occasional passages of burlesque or witty writing.

All this points to a strictly limited definition of plot as something that can be abstracted, for critical purposes, from the moral qualities of the characters and the operations of their thought. This something is merely the material continuity of the story considered in relation to the general pleasure we take in any fiction when our curiosity about the impending events is aroused, sustained, and then satisfied to a degree or in a manner we could not anticipate. A plot in this sense—the sense in which modern novelists pride themselves on having got rid of plot—can be pronounced good in terms simply of the variety of incidents it contains, the amount of suspense and surprise it evokes, and the ingenuity with which all the happenings in the beginning and middle are made to contribute to the resolution at the end. Given the definition, indeed, no other criteria are possible, and no others have been used by any of the critics of *Tom Jones* since the eighteenth century who have declared its plot to be one of the most perfect ever planned. They have uniformly judged it as interesting story merely—and this whether, as by most of the earlier writers, "the felicitous contrivance and happy extrication of the story" is taken to be the chief "beauty" of the novel or whether, as generally nowadays, preference is given to its qualities of character and thought. It is clearly of plot in no completer sense than this that Oliver Elton is thinking when he remarks that, although some "have cared little for this particular excellence, and think only of Partridge, timorous, credulous, garrulous, faithful, and an injured man; of Squire Western, and of the night at Upton, and of wit and humour everywhere," still "the common reader, for whom Fielding wrote, cares a great deal, and cares rightly, for plot; and so did Sophocles." [6]

Now it is evident that when plot is conceived thus narrowly, in abstraction from the peculiar characters and mental processes of the agents, it must necessarily have, for the critic, only a relatively external and nonfunctional relation to the other parts of the work. That is why, in most discussions of *Tom Jones* the literary treatment of the plot (as distinguished from mere summary of the happenings) is restricted to the kind of enthusiastic general appreciation of which I have given some examples, supplemented by more particular remarks on various episodes, notably those of the Man of the Hill and of Mrs. Fitzpatrick, which appear to do little to advance the action. The plot, in these discussions, is simply one of many sources of interest and pleasure afforded by a novel peculiarly rich in pleasurable and interesting things, and the problem of its function with respect to the other ingredients is evaded altogether. Occasionally, it is true, the question has been faced; but even in those critics, like W. L. Cross and Oliver Elton, who have made it most explicit, the formulas suggested never give to the plot of *Tom Jones* the status of more than an external and enveloping form in relation to which the rest of the novel is content. It is not, as they see it, an end but a means, and they describe it variously, having no language but metaphor for the purpose, as a "framework" in which character (which is Fielding's "real 'bill of fare'") is "set"; as a device, essentially "artificial," for bringing on the stage "real men and women"; as a "mere mechanism," which, except now and then in the last two books, "does not obtrude," for keeping readers alert through six volumes.[7]

I do not believe, however, that it is necessary to remain content with this very limited and abstract definition of plot or with the miscellaneous and fragmentized criticism of *Tom Jones* that has always followed from it. I shall assume that any novel or drama is a composite of three elements, which unite to determine its character and effect—the things that are imitated (or "rendered") in it, the linguistic medium in which they are imitated, and the manner or

6. *Op. cit.*, I, 195.   *cit.*, I, 195–96.
7. Cross, *op cit.*, II, 159–61; Elton, *op.*

technique of imitation; and I shall assume further that the things imitated necessarily involve human beings interacting with one another in ways determined by, and in turn affecting, their moral characters and their states of mind (i.e., their reasonings, emotions, and attitudes). If this is granted, we may say that the plot of any novel or drama is the particular temporal synthesis effected by the writer among the elements of action, character, and thought that constitute the matter of his invention. It is impossible, therefore, to state adequately what any plot is unless we include in our formula all three of the elements or causes of which the plot is the synthesis; and it follows also that plots may differ in structure according as one or another of the three causal ingredients is taken as the synthesizing principle. There are, thus, plots of action, plots of character, and plots of thought. In the first, the synthesizing principle is a completed change, gradual or sudden, in the fortunes of the protagonist, determined and effected by character and thought (as in *Œdipus* and James's *The Ambassadors*); in the second, the principle is a completed process of change in the moral character of the protagonist, precipitated or molded by action and made manifest both in it and in thought and feeling (as in Thackeray's *Pendennis*); in the third, the principle is a completed process of change in the thought of the protagonist and consequently in his feelings, conditioned and directed by character and action (as in Pater's *Marius the Epicurean*). All these types of construction, and not merely the first, are plots in the meaning of our definition; and it is mainly, perhaps, because most of the familiar classic plots, including that of *Tom Jones*, have been of the first kind that so many critics have tended to reduce plot to action alone.[8]

If this is granted, we may go further. For a plot, in the enlarged sense here given to the term, is not merely a particular synthesis of particular materials of character, thought, and action, but such a synthesis endowed necessarily, because it imitates in words a sequence of human activities, with a certain power to affect our opinions and emotions. We are bound, as we read or listen, to form expectations about what is coming and to feel more or less determinate desires relatively to our expectations. At the very least, if we are interested at all, we desire to know what is going to happen or how the problems faced by the characters are going to be solved. This is a necessary condition of our pleasure in all plots, and there are many good ones—in the classics of pure detective fiction, for example—the power of which depends almost exclusively on the pleasure we take in inferring progressively, from complex or ambiguous signs, the true state of affairs. For some readers and even some

8. This accounts in large part, I think, for the depreciation of "plot" in E. M. Forster's *Aspects of the Novel*, and for his notion of a rivalry between "plot" and "character," in which one or the other may "triumph."

critics this would seem to be the chief source of delight in many plots that have obviously been constructed on more specific principles: not only *Tom Jones*, as we have seen, but Œdipus has been praised as a mystery story, and it is likely that much of Henry James's popularity is due to his remarkable capacity for provoking a superior kind of inferential activity. What distinguishes all the more developed forms of imaginative literature, however, is that, though they presuppose this instinctive pleasure in learning, they go beyond it and give us plots of which the effects derive in a much more immediate way from the particular ethical qualities perceptible in their agents' characters and mental activities and in the human situations in which they are engaged. When this is the case, we cannot help becoming, in a greater or less degree, emotionally involved; for some of the characters we wish good, for others ill, and, depending on our inferences as to the events, we feel hope or fear, pity or satisfaction, or some modification of these or similar emotions. The peculiar power of any plot of this kind, as it unfolds, is a result of our state of knowledge at any point in complex interaction with our desires for the characters as morally differentiated beings; and we may be said to have grasped the plot in the full artistic sense only when we have analyzed this interplay of desires and expectations sequentially in relation to the incidents by which it is produced.

It is, of course, an essential condition of such an effect that the writer should so have combined his elements of action, character, and thought as to have achieved a complete and ordered whole, with all the parts needed to carry the protagonist, by probable or necessary stages, from the beginning to the end of his change: we should not have, otherwise, any connected series of expectations wherewith to guide our desires. In itself, however, this structure is only the matter or content of the plot and not its form; the form of the plot—in the sense of that which makes its matter into a definite artistic thing—is rather its distinctive "working or power," as the form of the plot in a tragedy, for example, is the capacity of its unified sequence of actions to effect through pity and fear a cartharsis of such emotions.

But if this is granted, then certain consequences follow for the criticism of dramas and novels. It is evident, in the first place, that no artistically developed plot can be called excellent merely in terms of its unity, the number and variety of its incidents, or the extent to which it produces suspense and surprise. These are but properties of its matter, and their achievement, even to a high degree, in any particular plot does not inevitably mean that the emotional effect of the whole will not still be diffused or weak. They are, therefore, only necessary and not sufficient conditions of a good plot, the positive excellence of which depends upon the capacity of its peculiar synthesis of character, action, and thought to move our feelings powerfully and pleasurably in a certain definite way.

But this capacity, which constitutes the form of the plot, is obviously, from an artistic point of view, the most important virtue any drama or novel can have; it is that, indeed, which most sharply distinguishes works of imitation from all other kinds of literary productions. It follows, consequently, that the plot, considered formally, of any artistic work is, in relation to the work as a whole, not simply a means—a "framework" or "mere mechanism"—but rather the final end which everything in the work, if that is to be felt as a whole, must be made, directly or indirectly, to serve. For the critic, therefore, the form of the plot is a first principle, which he must grasp as clearly as possible for any work he proposes to examine before he can deal adequately with the questions raised by its parts. This does not mean that we cannot derive other relevant principles of judgment from the general causes of pleasure operative in all artistic imitations, irrespective of the particular effect, serious or comic, that is aimed at in a given kind of work. The most important of these unquestionably, is the imitative principle itself, the principle that we are in general more convinced and moved when things are "rendered" for us through probable signs than when they are given merely in "statement," without illusion, after the fashion of a scenario.[9] Critical judgments, valid enough if they are not taken absolutely, may also be drawn from considerations of the general possibilities of language as a literary medium, of the known potentialities of a given manner of representation (e.g., dramatic or narrative), and of the various conditions of suspense and surprise. We are not likely to feel keenly the emotional effect of a work in which the worse rather than the better alternatives among these different expedients are consistently chosen or chosen in crucial scenes. And the same thing can be said of works in which the thought, however clearly serving an artistic use, is generally uninteresting or stale, or in which the characters of the agents, though right enough in conception for the intended effect, are less than adequately "done," or in which we perceive that the most has not been made of the possibilities implicit in the incidents. Such criticism of parts in terms of general principles is indispensable, but it is no substitute for—and its conclusions, affirmative as well as negative, have constantly to be checked by—the more specific kind of criticism of a work that takes the form of the plot as its starting point and then inquires how far and in what ways its peculiar power is maximized

9. The meaning and force of this will be clear to anyone who has compared in detail the text of *The Ambassadors* with James's preliminary synopsis of the novel (*The Notebooks of Henry James* [New York, 1947], pp. 372–415). See also the excellent remarks of Allen Tate, apropos of *Madame Bovary,* in his "Techniques of Fiction" (*Forms of Modern Fiction,* ed. William Van O'Connor [Minneapolis, 1948], esp. pp. 37–45).

by the writer's invention and development of particular episodes, his step-by-step rendering of the characters of his people, his use and elaboration of thought, his handling of diction and imagery, and his decisions as to the order, method, scale, and point of view of his representation.

All this is implied, I think, in the general hypothesis about plot which I have been outlining here and which I now propose to illustrate further in a re-examination of the "ever-to-be-praised" plot of *Tom Jones*.

II

It is necessary to look first at its matter and to begin by asking what is the unifying idea by which this is held together. Elementary as the question is, I have not read any answers to it that do not, in one way or another, mistake one of the parts of Fielding's novel for the whole. Doubtless the most common formula is that which locates the essence of the story in the sustained concealment and final disclosure of Tom's parentage. "It is pleasant," writes Oliver Elton, "to consider *Tom Jones* as a puzzle and to see how well the plan works out." For others the most important unifying factor is the love affair of Tom and Sophia; for still others, the conflict between Tom and Blifil; for others again, the quasi-picaresque sequence of Tom's adventures with women and on the road. The novel, it is true, would be quite different in its total effect if any of these four lines of action had been left out, but it is obvious that no one of them so subsumes all the others as to justify us in considering it, even on the level of material action, as the principle of the whole. A distinctive whole there is, however, and I venture to say that it consists, not in any mere combination of these parts, but rather in the dynamic system of actions, extending throughout the novel, by which the divergent intentions and beliefs of a large number of persons of different characters and states of knowledge belonging to or somehow related to the neighboring families of the Allworthys and the Westerns are made to co-operate, with the assistance of Fortune, first to bring Tom into an incomplete and precarious union, founded on an affinity of nature in spite of a disparity of status, with Allworthy and Sophia; then to separate him as completely as possible from them through actions that impel both of them, one after the other, to reverse their opinions of his character; and then, just as he seems about to fulfill the old prophecy that "he was certainly born to be hanged," to restore them unexpectedly to him in a more entire and stable union of both affection and fortune than he has known before.

The unity of *Tom Jones* is contained in this formula, but only potentially; and before we can properly discuss the plot as an artistic principle we must examine, in some detail, the intricate scheme of probabilities, involving moral choices, mistaken judgments, and accidents of Fortune, which bind its many parts together from the time we first see Tom in Allworthy's bed until we leave him, calmly enjoying his double good luck, at the end of Book XVIII.

There are three major stages in the action, the first of which, constituting in relation to the other two stages a "beginning," is complete by chapter vii of Book V. The starting point of everything is Bridget's scheme to provide security for both herself and her illegitimate son by palming off Tom on Allworthy as a foundling, with the intention, however, of ultimately informing her brother of the truth. The first part of the plan works beautifully: the affection which "the good man" at once conceives for the child assures Tom of a proper home and upbringing, and suspicion is diverted from his mother by Allworthy's discovery of parents for him, first in Jenny Jones (who, as Bridget's agent, is in the secret) and then in Partridge (who is not), and by the consequent departure of both of these from the neighborhood. In the end, too, Bridget's second purpose is fulfilled; but meanwhile she has put both parts of her scheme for Tom in jeopardy by her marriage (facilitated, again, by Allworthy's "penetration") with Captain Blifil. As a result, no early disclosure of Tom's true parentage is possible, and in addition the boy acquires a potential rival, in the younger Blifil, for both the affection and the fortune of Allworthy. On the other hand, although the intrigue against him begins immediately after the marriage, its only result at this stage, thanks to the goodness of Allworthy and the obvious innocence of Tom, is to make him thought of henceforth as the son of Partridge. This damages him in the eyes of the "world," but his status as a protégé and heir, along with young Blifil, of the benevolent Allworthy is still secure and will remain secure so long as his protector has no reason to think him unworthy of his favor.

A second phase of the "beginning" opens in Book III, with the emergence of moral character in the two half-brothers. There are now, so far as Tom is concerned, two main problems. The first has to do with his relation to Allworthy, for whom by this time he has come to feel as strong an affection as Allworthy has felt, and continues to feel, for him. There can be no change on his part no matter what Allworthy does, since his feelings are based not on any opinion of interest but on the instinctive love of one good nature for another; and there can equally be no change on Allworthy's part that will lead to a separation between them unless something happens to convince him that Tom's nature is after all bad. That under certain circumstances Allworthy should be capable of such a verdict on Tom is made probable, generally, by the excessive confidence in his ability to judge of character which has led him long before to condemn Partridge, and, particularly, by his implicit and, in the face of Bridget's favoritism for Tom, even aggressive belief in the good intentions of young Blifil, as well as in the integrity of the learned men he has chosen, in his wisdom, as tutors for the two boys.

Occasions for passing judgment on Tom present themselves increasingly from his fourteenth year; and Blifil, seconded by Thwackum and Square, misses no chance of using them to blacken his character in his guardian's eyes. The occasions are given by Tom's well-intentioned but quixotic and imprudently managed actions toward Black George and his family, before and after his seduction by Molly. In the first series of these, no harm, in spite of Blifil, is done; on the contrary, as we are told, Tom by his generosity has "rather improved than injured the affection which Mr. Allworthy was inclined to entertain for him." And it is the same at first with the actions that culminate in Tom's mistaken confession that he is the father of Molly's child; angry as Allworthy is at Tom's incontinence, he is "no less pleased with the honour and honesty of his self-accusation" and he begins "to form in his mind the same opinion of this young fellow, which, we hope, our reader may have conceived"; it is only later, after having pardoned him, that he is induced by the sophistry of Square to entertain his "first bad impression concerning Jones." But even this is not fatal to Tom: he is assured again after his injury, though with a warning for the future, that what has happened is "all forgiven and forgotten"; he remains a beneficiary, in proportion to his supposed status, in Allworthy's will; and he is thought of by Allworthy, as we learn from the latter's speech in Book V, chapter vii, as one who has "much goodness, generosity, and honour" in his temper and needs only "prudence and religion" to make him actually happy. Fortune, it is clear, is still, however hesitatingly, on the side of Tom.

The other problem concerns the attachment that has been developing meanwhile between Tom and Sophia. The basis of the attachment is again one of likeness of nature, and the function of the incidents in Books IV and V in which the two are thrown together (Tom's intervention on behalf of Black George, his rescue of Sophia and his convalescence at her house, the affair of the muff, etc.) is simply to make credible its rapid progress, in spite of Tom's initial indifference and his entanglement with Molly, to the stage of mutual recognition reached in Book V, chapter vi. From this point on, we need not expect any change in Tom's feelings toward Sophia, no matter what he may do in his character as gallant; and there is an equally strong probability, in terms of her character, that

Sophia will never cease to love Tom. She is, for one thing, a better judge of persons than Allworthy and is in no danger of being deceived, as he is, by the formal appearances of virtue in Blifil and of vice in Tom. "To say the truth, Sophia, when very young, discerned that Tom, though an idle, thoughtless, rattling rascal, was nobody's enemy but his own; and that Master Blifil, though a prudent, discreet, sober young gentleman, was at the same time strongly attached to the interest only of one single person . . ." (IV, v). She has, moreover, been even more completely aware than Allworthy of Tom's affair with Molly, and yet, for all her hurt pride, she has not altered her opinion of his worth; Tom, it is evident, will have to behave, or appear to behave, much worse than this before she will decide to cast him off. In the meantime, however, their union is apparently condemned by circumstances to be one of affection only. Her father, though very fond of Tom, will not approve a marriage which offers, because of Tom's low status, so little prospect of fortune for his beloved daughter; she will not act counter to her father's wishes, even though she will not agree to marry against her own feelings; and as for Tom, though his life is now "a constant struggle between honour and inclination," he can do nothing that will injure Sophia, show ingratitude to Western, or violate his more than filial piety toward Allworthy. The only possible resolution of their problem, it is plain, must be some event that will alter fundamentally Tom's position as a foundling.

Such an event is indeed impending at precisely this point in the action. For Bridget, dying, has just confided her secret to her attorney Dowling and has commanded him to carry the all-important message to Allworthy in fulfilment of the second part of her original design.

Blifil, however, aided by Fortune (which now turns temporarily against Tom), here intervenes, with two important results: immediately, that a chain of happenings is set in motion, constituting the "middle" of the plot, which leads to the complete separation of Tom from both Allworthy and Sophia; and remotely, that, when Bridget's message is at last delivered in Book XVIII, the position to which Tom is then restored is made, by reason of the delay, one of even greater security and happiness than would have been possible had his relationship to Allworthy become known at the time Bridget intended to reveal it.

The action from the moment when Bridget gives Dowling her message to the moment, many weeks later, when Allworthy receives it falls into three main parts. The first part begins with Allworthy's illness and ends with Tom's expulsion and Sophia's flight. The events in this stage form a single complex sequence, in which Fortune conspires with the malice and ambition of Blifil, the pride and family tyranny of the Westerns, and the easily imposed-on sense of justice of Allworthy, first to thwart the purpose of Bridget and then to turn the indiscreet manifestations of Tom's love for Allworthy and joy at his recovery and of Sophia's love for Tom into occasions for the condemnation and banishment of Tom as "an abandoned reprobate" and for the persecution of Sophia as a recalcitrant daughter. The separating action of the novel thus comes to its first major climax, with Tom now resolved, for the sake of Sophia, to renounce her and leave the country, and with Sophia, unable to endure the prospect of a marriage with Blifil, determined to seek refuge in London with her cousin Lady Bellaston, not without hopes of again seeing Tom. Blifil, now dearer than ever to Allworthy because of Tom's "ill-treatment of that good young man," has apparently triumphed, though not completely, since Sophia is still out of his grasp. In reality, he has already made his fatal mistake, the mistake that will inevitably ruin him and restore Tom if and when Allworthy discovers it; and in addition, by driving Tom out, he has made it more rather than less probable that the truth he has concealed will eventually come to light, since, besides himself, it is also known, in part or in whole, to three other persons—Partridge, Jenny Jones, and Dowling—any or all of whom it is more likely now than before that Tom will meet.

This is, in fact, what happens during the next stage of the action, all the incidents of which converge on bringing Tom into contact, first with Partridge, then with Dowling, and finally with Jenny (now Mrs. Waters). The first meeting leads to a kind of negative resolution: Tom now knows that he is not Partridge's son. From the meetings with the others, who alone, save Blifil, know the whole truth, no resolution immediately follows, being prevented in both cases by the same causes that have determined Tom's fate hitherto: in the case of Jenny by Fortune, which sees to it that there is no encounter between her and Partridge at Upton; in the case of Dowling, who is ready to sell his knowledge for a price, by Tom's quixotic disinterestedness. The crucial discovery is thus postponed, but when we consider that Tom is now known to Dowling and to Jenny (though to the latter not as Bridget's son) and that both of these now become attached to persons in the Allworthy-Western circle—Jenny to Sophia's cousin-in-law Fitzpatrick and Dowling to Blifil—it is clear that the probability of its eventually taking place, and possibly in more auspicious circumstances, is increased rather than diminished by what has occurred.

In the meantime, with the happenings at Upton, the complication has entered its last and longest and, for Tom, most distressing phase, the climax of which, at the end of Book XVI, is his receipt in prison of Sophia's letter of condemnation and dismissal. The principal villain is again Fortune, which as we have been told (V,x), "seldom doth things by halves," and which, having already robbed Tom of the good will of Allworthy, now seems bent on completing his unhappiness by using his too complaisant good nature and his capacity for indiscretion to deprive him of Sophia and perhaps even of his life. It all begins with the chapter of accidents at the inn, where, because of his gallantry to Jenny, Tom first has an angry encounter with Fitzpatrick (who is seeking his runaway wife) and then misses Sophia, who departs at once on learning of his infidelity and makes her way, in the company of Mrs. Fitzpatrick, to London and Lady Bellaston. Some harm has now been done, but not much, as Tom learns when, having pursued her to London, he finally meets her again at Lady Bellaston's and is told, in a tender scene, that what has really disturbed her has not been so much his misconduct with Jenny, which she can forgive, as Partridge's free use of her name in public.

This happy resolution, however, comes too late; for already, although with the best intentions—namely, of finding his way to Sophia—Tom has been seduced into the affair with Lady Bellaston which is his closest approach, in the novel, to a base act. The affair does indeed lead him to Sophia, but only by chance, and then under circumstances which, while they do not betray him to Sophia, turn the wrath of his new mistress against her and lead to a fresh series of efforts to separate her from Tom. The first of these, the attempted rape by Lord Fellamar, is thwarted when Western, having learned of his daughter's whereabouts, rescues her in the nick of time and carries her away to his lodgings to face another course of family persecution and threats of imminent marriage to Blifil. It is on hearing of this that Tom, his thoughts now centered wholly on Sophia in spite of his despair of ever winning her, decides to break with Lady Bellaston, and adopts the expedient for doing so without dishonor which nearly leads to his ruin. For the effect of his proposal of marriage is to draw the Lady's vengeful feelings upon himself and Sophia at once, with the result that she arranges for his kidnapping by a press gang at the same time that she makes sure that Sophia will never marry him by sending her the letter of proposal as proof of his villainy. With Sophia her scheme succeeds, so incapable of any other interpretation does the evidence seem. She is foiled, however, in her design against Tom, and once more by a delayed effect of the events at Upton. But the meeting which Fortune brings about with the still angry Fitzpatrick, though it saves Tom from being pressed into the navy, spares him only for what promises to be a worse fate.

The separating action has now come to its second major climax —much the more serious of the two for Tom, since he has not only lost Sophia as well as Allworthy but lost her, he thinks, as a direct result of his own vice and folly. He can still, if Fitzpatrick dies, be separated from his life, but otherwise all the possibilities of harm to him contained in his original situation have been exhausted. Not, however, all the possibilities of good; for the very same incidents proceeding from the affair at Upton which have so far been turned by Fortune against Tom have also had consequences which Fortune, bent upon doing nothing by halves, may yet exploit in his favor.

The most important of these in the long run is the moral change that has been produced by his recent experiences in Tom himself, as manifested by his break with Lady Bellaston and by his rejection of the honorable advances of Mrs. Hunt and the dishonorable advances of Mrs. Fitzpatrick. It is not so much what he is, however, as what he is thought to be by Allworthy and Sophia that immediately counts; and he has had the good luck, by virtue of coming to London, of acquiring in Mrs. Miller a character witness who knows the best as well as the worst of him and who will at least be listened to by her old friend and benefactor Allworthy and perhaps by Sophia. There is, moreover, as a result of what has happened, rather less danger than before that Sophia, who, in spite of her reason, still loves Tom, will be forced to marry Blifil; for, though she is again in the power of her family, the machinations of Lady Bellaston have led to a conflict between the two Westerns over the rival merits of Blifil and Lord Fellamar. Time has thus been gained for Tom; and meanwhile Allworthy and Blifil have come up to town in response to Western's summons and have taken lodgings with Mrs. Miller. Dowling has come too, and so also has Jenny, now living with Fitzpatrick in lieu of the wife he has been seeking since Upton and whose whereabouts he has just learned. All those, in short, who know Bridget's secret—and Blifil's villainy in suppressing it at the time of her death—are now assembled, for the first time, in close proximity to Allworthy. And then Blifil, made overconfident by his success and believing Fitzpatrick about to die of his wound, decides to use the opportunity afforded by the presence of Lord Fellamar's press gang at the duel to strike one last blow at Tom.

But this time all the acts of Fortune work to the advantage of our hero, and the resolution moves rapidly to its end, first by the reunion of Tom with Allworthy and then by his reunion with Sophia. The first requires a reversal of Allworthy's judgment of Tom's character and actions at the time of his banishment. This is prepared by Mrs. Miller's insistence upon his present goodness and the services he has rendered her family, but the decisive event is the letter from the dying and repentant Square, which sets in a new light Tom's acts during Allworthy's illness, although without clearly implicating Blifil. The result is to restore Tom to his foster-father's affections more or less on the footing which he had at the beginning of Book V, but with the added circumstance that he has since suffered unjust persecution. The new Tom is not yet fully known, or the entire extent and cause of the injuries that have been done to him. Mrs. Miller indeed suspects, but the blindness of Allworthy prevents a discovery; and it requires a second intervention of Fortune, aided by the rashness of Blifil, to bring the revelation about. For not only does Blifil think Fitzpatrick's wound more serious than it is, but in his zeal to gather all possible evidence damaging to Tom he has made it inevitable that Jenny will come to know who Tom is, that she will at once go to Allworthy with her story, that Dowling will then be questioned, and that he, seeing where his profit now lies, will tell the whole truth about the suppression of Bridget's dying message. Thus here again Fortune has done nothing by halves, with the result that the exclusive place which Blifil has all along sought for himself in Allworthy's fortune and favor is now, with his unmasking and subsequent banishment, properly accorded to Tom. In relation to the original conditions of the action, moreover, the reversal is equally complete: Bridget's intended disclosure of her secret has at last been made, and with it both of her mistakes —of concealing Tom's parentage and then of marrying the elder Blifil—are finally canceled out.

The reunion with Sophia is likewise prepared by Mrs. Miller, who is able to convince her that Tom's letter proposing marriage to Lady Bellaston was at worst an indiscretion. But though Allworthy also intervenes on his nephew's behalf and though Western is now as violent an advocate for Tom as he has earlier been for Blifil, the resolution comes only when Sophia, faced with the repentant young man, finds once more (as after his previous affairs with Molly and Jenny) that her love for him is stronger than her injured pride and that it is now a pleasure to be able to obey her father's commands.

It is in nothing short of this total system of actions, moving by probable or necessary connections from beginning, through middle, to end, that the unity of the plot of *Tom Jones* is to be found. It is the unity, clearly, of a complex plot, built on two continuous but contrary lines of probability, both stemming from the double scheme of Bridget respecting Tom and from her marriage with Captain Blifil, and both reinforced, from Book III onward, by the combination in Tom's character of goodness and indiscretion: the one producing immediately, throughout the complication, ever more bad fortune and distress for Tom, the other at the same time preparing for him the good luck he finally comes to enjoy after the discovery and reversal in Book XVIII. It is no wonder that this "plot," in which so many incidents, involving so many surprising turns, are all subsumed so brilliantly under one principle of action, should have been praised by all those critics from the eighteenth century to the present who have had a taste for intricate and ingenious constructions of this kind.

If the plot of *Tom Jones* is still to be praised, however, it ought to be for reasons more relevant than these to the special artistic quality of the novel we continue to read. For what we have discussed so far as the "plot" is merely the abstract action of the novel as unified and made probable by its basic elements of character and thought. It is not the plot proper but only its necessary substrate, and if we are to say what the plot proper is and be able to use our account for critical purposes, we must go beyond the material system of actions—which Fielding might have had fully developed in his mind before writing a word of *Tom Jones*—and look for the formal principle which, in the novel as finally composed for readers in an ordered arrangement of paragraphs, chapters, and books, actually operates to determine our emotionalized expectations for Tom and our subsequent reactions when the hoped-for or feared events occur.

III

In stating this principle for any plot, we must consider three things: (1) the general estimate we are induced to form, by signs in the work, of the moral character and deserts of the hero, as a result of which we tend, more or less ardently, to wish for him either good or bad fortune in the end; (2) the judgments we are led similarly to make about the nature of the events that actually befall the hero or seem likely to befall him, as having either painful or pleasurable consequences for him, and this in greater or less degree and permanently or temporarily; and (3) the opinions we are made to entertain concerning the degree and kind of his responsibility for what happens to him, as being either little or great and, if the latter, the result either of his acting in full knowledge of what he is doing or of some sort of mistake. The form of a given plot is a function of the particular correlation among these three variables which the completed work is calculated to establish, consistently and progressively, in our minds; and in these terms we may say that the plot of *Tom Jones* has a pervasively comic form. The precise sense, however, in which its form is comic is a rather special one, which needs to be carefully defined.

To begin with, it is obviously a plot in which the complication generates much pain and inner suffering for the hero, as a result of misfortunes which would seem genuinely serious to any good person. He is schemed against by a villain who will not stop even at judicial murder to secure his ends, and, what is worse in his eyes, he loses the good will of the two people whom he most loves, and loses it as a consequence not simply of the machinations of his enemies but of his own mistaken acts. From near the beginning until close to the end, moreover, he is made to undergo an almost continuous series of distressing indignities: to be insulted on the score of his birth, to be forbidden the sight of Sophia, to see her being pushed into a hated marriage with Blifil and persecuted when she refuses, to be banished abruptly from home, to be reduced to poverty and forced to take money from Lady Bellaston, to be laid in wait for by a press gang, to be compelled to run a man through in self-defense, and finally, in prison, to be faced with the prospect of a disgraceful death.

The hero, furthermore, to whom all this happens is a naturally good man—not notably virtuous, but, for all his faults, at least the equal of ourselves and of any other character in the novel in disinterestedness, generosity, and tender benevolent feeling. These traits are impressed upon us in the third book and are never obscured even in the worst of Tom's troubles in London; they are, in fact, revivified for us, just at the point when we might be most tempted to forget them, by the episodes of Anderson and of Mrs. Miller's daughter. We like Tom, therefore, even if we do not admire him, and we wish for him the good fortune with Allworthy and Sophia which he properly wishes for himself and which, in terms of his basic moral character, he deserves to get. We follow him through his troubles and distresses, consequently, with a desire that he will eventually be delivered from them and reunited to his friend and mistress, and this all the more when, at the climax of his difficulties, we see him acting, for the first time, in a way we can entirely approve; in the end, when our wishes for him are unexpectedly realized, and to a fuller degree than we had anticipated, we feel some of the joy which Fielding says (XVIII, xiii) was then felt by the principal characters themselves. "All were happy, but those the most who had been most unhappy before. Their former sufferings and fears gave such a relish to their felicity as even love and fortune, in their fullest flow, could not have given without the advantage of such a comparison."

Having conceived a plot in which so sympathetic a character is subjected in the complication to experiences so painful, it would have been relatively easy for Fielding to write a novel similar in form to his *Amelia*, that is to say, a tragi-comedy of common life designed to arouse and then to dissipate, by a sudden happy resolution, emotions of fear and pity for his hero and of indignation toward his enemies. There is, indeed, an even greater material basis for such an effect in *Tom Jones* than in the later novel: the evils that threaten Tom and the indignities he undergoes are, in the abstract, more serious than anything Booth has to fear, and the same thing is true of the persecutions endured by Sophia as compared with those which Amelia is made to suffer. And yet nothing is more evident than that, whereas the emotions awakened in us by the distresses of Booth and Amelia are the graver emotions of anxiety and compassion that yield what Fielding calls "the pleasure of tenderness," [1] our feelings for Tom and Sophia, as we anticipate or view in actuality the greater evils that befall them prior to the final discovery, partake only in the mildest degree of this painful quality. We do not actively fear for or pity either of them, and our indignation at the actions of their enemies—even the actions of Blifil—never develops into a sustained punitive response.

Nor is the reason for this hard to find. It is generally the case that whatever tends to minimize our fear in a plot that involves threats of undeserved misfortune for the sympathetic characters tends also to minimize our pity when the misfortune occurs and likewise our indignation against the doers of the evil; and fear for Tom and Sophia as they move toward the successive climaxes of their troubles is prevented from becoming a predominant emotion in the complication of *Tom Jones* chiefly by two things.

The first is our perception, which in each case grows stronger as the novel proceeds, that the persons whose actions threaten serious consequences for the hero and heroine are all persons for whom, though in varying degrees, we are bound to feel a certain contempt. The most formidable of them all is of course Blifil. As a villain, however, he is no Iago but merely a clever opportunist who is likely to overreach himself (as the failure of his first schemes shows) and whose power of harm depends entirely on the blindness of Allworthy; he deceives Tom only temporarily and Sophia and Mrs. Miller not at all; and after we have seen the display of his personal ineptitude in the proposal scene with Sophia, we are prepared to wait, without too much active suspense, for his final showing-up. Blifil is too coldly selfish, perhaps, to strike us as positively ridiculous, but in the characters of the other agents of misfortune the comic strain is clear. It is most obvious, needless to say, in Squire Western and his sister: who can really fear that the persecutions directed against the determined and resourceful Sophia by such a blundering pair of tyrants can ever issue in serious harm? For Allworthy, too, in spite of his excellent principles, it is hard for us to maintain entire respect; we should certainly take more seriously his condemnation of Tom in Book VI had we not become accustomed, as a result of earlier incidents in the novel, to smile at a man who could believe in the goodness of the two Blifils and whose pride in his own judg-

1. *Amelia*, III, i.

ment could make him dispose so precipitously of Jenny and Partridge. There are evident comic traits also in all the persons who cause trouble for Tom and Sophia in the later part of the action: in Dowling, the man always in a hurry; in Lady Bellaston, the great dame who pursues a plebeian with frenzied letters and nocturnal visits to his lodgings; in Lord Fellamar, the half-hearted rake; in Fitzpatrick, the unfaithful but jealous husband who will not believe the evidence of his own eyes. In respect of her relations with Tom, though not otherwise, Sophia, too, must be added to the list, as a virtuous girl with a proper amount of spirit (not to say vanity) whose good resolutions against Tom never survive for long in the presence of her lover. These are all manifestations of the ineffectual or ridiculous in a plot in which the impending events are materially painful, and they contribute, on the principle that we fear less or not at all when the agents of harm to a hero are more or less laughable persons, to induce in us a general feeling of confidence that matters are not really as serious as they appear.

A second ground of security lies in the nature of the probabilities for future action that are made evident progressively as the novel unfolds. From the beginning until the final capitulation of Sophia, the successive incidents constantly bring forth new and unexpected complications, each seemingly fraught with more suffering for Tom than the last; but as we read we instinctively infer from past occurrences to what will probably happen next or in the end, and what steadily cumulates in this way, in spite of the gradual worsening of Tom's situation, is an opinion that, since nothing irreparable has so far happened to him, nothing ever will. In one sense—that which relates to its material events—the action becomes more and more serious as it moves to its climax, in another sense—that which relates to our expectations—less and less serious; and I think that any close reader who keeps in mind the earlier parts of the novel as he attends to the later is inevitably made aware of this, with the result that, though his interest mounts, his fear increasingly declines. We come thus to the first climax in Book VI recalling such things as Jenny's assurance to Allworthy that she will someday make known the whole truth, the sudden reversal of the elder Blifil's sinister plans, the collapse, after initial success, of young Blifil's first schemes against Tom, and Tom's return to favor with Allworthy after the incident of Molly's arrest; and all these memories inevitably operate to check the rise of any long-range apprehensions. And it is the same, too, with the second and apparently much more serious climax at the end of Book XVI, when Tom, dismissed by Sophia, lies in prison awaiting the death of Fitzpatrick, who has been given up by his surgeon: we cannot but remember how, in the affairs of Molly and then of Mrs. Waters, Sophia has more than once demonstrated her inability to inflict any great or prolonged punishment on Tom for his sins with other women and how, on the occasion of Allworthy's illness in Book V, the outcome had completely disappointed the gloomy predictions of the doctor.

The attenuation, in these ways, of fear, pity, and indignation is a necessary condition of the peculiar comic pleasure which is the form of the plot in *Tom Jones*, but it is only a negative and hence not a sufficient condition. A comic effect of any kind would be impossible if we took Tom's increasingly bad prospects with the same seriousness as he himself takes them, but what in a positive sense makes Fielding's plot comic is the combination of this feeling of security with our perception of the decisive role which Tom's own blunders are made to play, consistently, in the genesis of all the major difficulties into which he is successively brought—always, of course, with the eager assistance of Fortune and of the malice or misunderstanding of others. The importance of this becomes clear at once when we consider how much trouble he would have spared himself had he not mistaken his seduction by Molly for a seduction of her by him; had he not got drunk when he learned of Allworthy's recovery or fought with Blifil and Thwackum; had he not suggested to Western that he be allowed to plead Blifil's case with Sophia; had he not allowed himself to be seduced by Jenny at Upton; had he not thought that his very love for Sophia, to say nothing of his gallantry, required him "to keep well" with the lady at the masquerade; and, lastly, had he not accepted so uncritically Nightingale's scheme for compelling her to break off the affair.

The truth is that each successive stage of the plot up to the beginning of the denouement in Book XVII is precipitated by a fresh act of imprudence or indiscretion on the part of Tom, for which he is sooner or later made to suffer not only in his fortune but his feelings, until, in the resolution of each sequence, he discovers that the consequences of his folly are after all not so serious as he has feared. This characteristic pattern emerges, even before the start of the complication proper, in the episode of Tom's relations with Molly and Sophia in Book IV and the first part of Book V; it dominates the prolonged suspense of his relations with Allworthy from the time of the latter's illness to the final discovery; and it determines the course of his troubles with Sophia from Upton to the meeting in London and from the ill-conceived proposal scheme to her sudden surrender at the end.

The comic pleasure all this gives us is certainly not of the same kind as that produced by such classic comic plots as (say) Ben Jonson's *The Silent Woman* or, to take a more extreme instance of the type, his *Volpone*, in which a morally despicable person is made, by reason of his own folly or lapse from cleverness, to suffer a humiliating and, to him, though not to others, painful reversal of fortune.

The comedy of Blifil is indeed of this simple punitive kind,[2] but our suspense concerning Bilfil is only in a secondary way determinative of the effect of Fielding's novel, and the comedy of Tom and hence of the plot as a whole is of a different sort. It is not simple comedy but mixed, the peculiar power of which depends upon the fact that the mistaken acts of the hero which principally excite our amusement are the acts of a man for whom throughout the plot we entertain sympathetic feelings because of the general goodness of his character: we do not want, therefore, to see him suffer any permanent indignity or humiliation, and we never cease to wish good fortune for him in the end. This favorable attitude, moreover, is not contradicted by anything in the acts themselves from which his troubles spring. We perceive that in successive situations involving threats to his fortune or peace of mind, he invariably does some imprudent or foolish thing, which cannot fail, the circumstances being what, in our superior knowledge, we see them to be, to result for him in painful embarrassment and regret; but we realize that his blunders arise from no permanent weakness of character but are merely the natural errors of judgment, easily corrigible in the future, of an inexperienced and too impulsively generous and gallant young man. We look forward to the probable consequences of his indiscretions, therefore, with a certain anticipatory reluctance and apprehension—a kind of faint alarm which is the comic analogue of fear; it is some such feeling, I think, that we experience, if only momentarily, when Tom gets drunk and goes into the wood with Molly and when, much later, he sends his proposal letter to Lady Bellaston. We know that trouble, more trouble than the young man either foresees or deserves, is in store for him as a result of what he has done, and since, foolish as he is, we favor him against his enemies, the expectation of his inevitable suffering cannot be purely and simply pleasant.

And yet the expectation is never really painful in any positive degree, and it is kept from becoming so by our counter-expectation, established by the devices I have mentioned, that, however acute may be Tom's consequent sufferings, his mistakes will not issue in any permanent frustration of our wishes for his good. In this security that no genuine harm has been done, we can view his present distresses—as when he anguishes over the wrong he thinks he has done to Molly, or finds Sophia's muff in his bed at Upton or receives her letter—as the deserved consequences of erroneous actions for which any good man would naturally feel embarrassment or shame. We do not therefore pity him in these moments, for all his self-accusations and cries of despair, but rather, in a quiet way, laugh at him as a man who has behaved ridiculously or beneath

2. I borrow this term from Elder Olson's "An Outline of Poetic Theory," in *Critiques and Essays in Criticism, 1920–* *1948*, ed. Robert W. Stallman (New York, 1949), p. 273.

himself and is now being properly punished. And our comic pleasure continues into the subsequent resolving scenes—the discovery of Molly in bed with Square, the meeting with Sophia in London, and the final anticlimax of her agreement to marry him the next morning—when it appears that Tom has after all worried himself overmuch; for we now see that he has been doubly ridiculous, at first in not taking his situation seriously enough and then in taking it more seriously than he should. But Tom is a good man, and we expect him to get better, and so our amused reaction to his sufferings lacks entirely the punitive quality that characterizes comedy of the Jonsonian type. If the anticipatory emotion is a mild shudder of apprehension, the climactic emotion—the comic analogue of pity—is a kind of friendly mirth at his expense ("poor Tom," we say to ourselves), which easily modulates, in the happy denouement, into unsentimental rejoicing at his not entirely deserved good fortune.

This, however, is not quite all; for not only does Tom's final good fortune seem to us at least partly undeserved in terms of his own behavior, but we realize, when we look back from the end upon the long course of the action, that he has, in truth, needed all the luck that has been his. Again and again he has been on the verge of genuinely serious disaster; and, though we expect him to survive and hence do not fear for him in prospect, we perceive, at the resolution of each of his major predicaments, that there has been something of a hairbreadth quality in his escape. The cards have indeed been stacked against him; from the beginning to the ultimate discovery, he has been a young man whose lack of security and imprudence more than offset his natural goodness, living in a world in which the majority of people are ill-natured and selfish, and some of them actively malicious, and in which the few good persons are easily imposed upon by appearances. It is against this background of the potentially serious—more than ever prominent in the London scenes—that the story of Tom's repeated indiscretions is made to unfold, with the result that though, as I have argued, the pleasure remains consistently comic, its quality is never quite that of the merely amiable comedy, based likewise upon the blunders of sympathetic protagonists, of such works as *She Stoops To Conquer* or *The Rivals*. We are not disposed to feel, when we are done laughing at Tom, that all is right with the world or that we can count on Fortune always intervening, in the same gratifying way, on behalf of the good.

IV

This or something very close to this, I think, is the intended "working or power" of *Tom Jones*, and the primary question for the critic concerns the extent to which Fielding's handling of the constituent parts of the novel is calculated to sustain and maximize this special pleasure which is its form.

It must be said that he sometimes fails. There are no perfect works of art, and, though many of the faults that have been found in *Tom Jones* are faults only on the supposition that it should have been another kind of novel, still enough real shortcomings remain to keep one's enthusiasm for Fielding's achievement within reasonable bounds. There are not infrequent *longueurs*, notably in the Man of the Hill's story (whatever positive values this may have), in Mrs. Fitzpatrick's narrative to Sophia (useful as this is in itself), in the episode of Tom's encounter with the gypsies, and in the final complications of the Nightingale affair. With the best will in the world, too, it is impossible not to be shocked by Tom's acceptance of fifty pounds from Lady Bellaston on the night of his first meeting with her at the masquerade and his subsequent emergence as "one of the best-dressed men about town"; it is necessary, no doubt, that he should now fall lower than ever before, but surely not so low as to make it hard for us to infer his act from our previous knowledge of his character and of the rather modest limits hitherto of his financial need; for the moment at least, a different Tom is before our eyes. And there are also more general faults. The narrator, for one thing, though it is well that he should intrude, perhaps intrudes too much in a purely ornamental way; the introductory essays, thus, while we should not like to lose them from the canon of Fielding's writings, serve only occasionally the function of chorus, and the returns from them, even as embellishment, begin to diminish before the end. What chiefly strikes the modern reader, however, is the extent of Fielding's reliance, in the novel as a whole, on techniques of narrative now largely abandoned by novelists who have learned their art since the middle of the nineteenth century. It could be shown, I think, that as compared with most of his predecessors, the author of *Tom Jones* had moved a long way in the direction of the imitative and dramatic. Yet it cannot be denied that in many chapters where he might better have "rendered" he merely "states" and that even in the most successful of the scenes in which action and dialogue predominate he leaves far less to inference than we are disposed to like.[3]

Despite all this, however, there are not many novels of comparable length in which the various parts are conceived and developed with a shrewder eye to what is required for a maximum realization of the form.[4] A few examples of this will have to serve, and it is natural to start with the manner in which Fielding handles the incidents that follow directly from Tom's mistakes. The pattern of all

---

3. Perhaps the chief exception to this, in its relatively large use of "intimation," is the scene of Tom's conversation with Dowling in Book XII, chap. x.

4. I am indebted for several points in what follows to an unpublished essay by one of my students, Mr. Melvin Seiden.

of these is much the same: Tom first commits an indiscretion, which is then discovered, and the discovery results in his immediate or eventual embarrassment. Now it is clear that the comic pleasure will be enhanced in proportion as, in each incident, the discovery is made unexpectedly and by precisely those persons whose knowledge of what Tom has done will be most damaging to him, and by as many of these as possible so that the consequences for him are not simple but compounded. Fielding understood this well, and the effects of his understanding are repeatedly evident in *Tom Jones*, from Book IV to the end of the complication. Consider, for example, how he manages the discovery of Tom's original entanglement with Molly. It is necessary, of course, when Molly is arrested after the fight in the churchyard, that Tom should at once rush to All-worthy with his mistaken confession; but it is not necessary—only highly desirable—that he should intervene in the fight himself as Molly's champion, that Blifil and Square should be with him at the time, that the news of the arrest should reach him while he is dining with Western and Sophia, whose charm he is just beginning to perceive, and that, when he leaves in a hurry, the Squire should joke with his daughter about what he suspects. Or, again, there is the even more complicated and comically disastrous sequence that begins with Tom's drunkenness after Allworth's recovery. This in itself is ridiculous, since we know the illness has never been serious; but observe how satisfyingly the succeeding embarrassments are made to pile up: Tom's hilarious joy leading to his fight with Blifil; this to his retirement to the grove, his romantic meditation on Sophia, and his surrender to Molly; this to the discovery of his new folly by Blifil and Thwackum; this to the second fight, much blood-ier than the first; and this in turn, when the Westerns unexpectedly appear on the scene, to Sophia's fresh discovery of Tom's wildness and, what is much more serious, to the misconstruction of her faint-ing fit by her aunt, with results that lead presently to the proposal of a match with Blifil, the foolish intervention of Tom, the discov-ery by Western of the true state of affairs, his angry appeal to All-worthy, Blifil's distorted version of what has happened, Tom's expulsion from home, and Sophia's imprisonment. All this is proba-ble enough, but there is something of the comically wonderful in the educing of so many appropriately extreme consequences from a cause in itself so apparently innocent and trivial. And the same art of making the most out of incidents for the sake of the comic sus-pense of the plot can be seen at work through the rest of the novel: in the great episode at Upton, for example, where all the happen-ings are contrived to produce, immediately or remotely, a maximum of pseudo-serious suffering for Tom, and also in the various later scenes in which the discovery to Sophia of Tom's intrigue with her cousin is first narrowly averted, with much embarrassment to him, and then finally made under circumstances that could hardly be worse for the young man. A less accomplished artist seeking to achieve the same general effect through his plot would certainly have missed many of these opportunities.

A less accomplished artist, again, would never have been able to invent or sustain characters so good for the form, as well as so interesting in themselves, as the two Westerns and Partridge. We need not dwell on the multiple uses to which these great humorists are put; it is more important, since the point has been less often discussed, or discussed in part to Fielding's disadvantage, to consider what merits can be found in his handling of the other characters, such as Tom himself, Allworthy, Sophia, and Blifil, who are intended to seem morally sympathetic or antipathetic to us and comically inferior only by virtue of their erroneous acts. With the exception of Sophia, who is made charming and lively enough to constitute in herself good fortune for Tom, they are not endowed with any notably particularized traits, and the question for criticism is whether, given the comic form of the novel as a whole, any more lifelike "doing" would not have entailed a departure from the mean which this imposed. I think the answer is clear for Blifil: he must be made to seem sufficiently formidable in the short run to arouse comic apprehension for Tom but not so formidable as to excite in us active or prolonged feelings of indignation; and any further individualizing of him than we get would almost certainly have upset this balance to the detriment of the whole. The answer is clear also, I think, for Tom. We must consistently favor him against his enemies and think it probable that he should suffer acute embarrassment and remorse when he discovers the consequences of his mistakes; but, on the other hand, any appreciably greater particularizing of his sympathetic traits than is attempted would inevitably have made it difficult for us not to feel his predicaments as seriously as he does himself, and that would have been an error; it is not the least happy of Fielding's inventions, for example, that he repeatedly depicts Tom, especially when he is talking to Sophia or thinking about her, in terms of the clichés of heroic romance. There remains Allworthy, and concerning him the chief doubt arises from a consideration of the important part he is given, along with Sophia, in the definition of Tom's final good fortune. For the purposes of the comic complication it is sufficient that we should see him acting in the character of a severely just magistrate who constantly administers injustice through too great trust in his knowledge of men; it is not for this, however, but for his "amiability" that Tom loves him and cherishes his company in the end; yet of Allworthy's actual possession of that quality we are given few clear signs.

A whole essay, finally, could be written on the masterly way in which Fielding exploited the various devices implicit in his third-person "historical" mode of narration in the service of his comic form. Broadly speaking, his problem was twofold: first, to establish and maintain in the reader a general frame of mind appropriate to the emotional quality of the story as a whole and, second, to make sure that the feelings aroused by his characters at particular moments or stages of the action were kept in proper alignment with the intended over-all effect.

That the first problem is adequately solved there can be little doubt; long before we come to the incidents in which Tom's happiness is put in jeopardy by his own blunders and the malice of Blifil, we have been prepared to expect much unmerited calamity and distress for him, and at the same time to view the prospect without alarm. Our security would doubtless have been less had not Fielding chosen to represent at length the events contained in Books I and II, with the vivid impressions they give of the fallibility of Allworthy on the one hand and of the impotence for permanent harm of the elder Blifil on the other: we cannot but look forward to a repetition of this pattern in the later parts of the novel. This is less important, however, as a determinant of our frame of mind than the guidance given us by the clearly evident attitude of Fielding's narrator. He is, we perceive, a man we can trust, who knows the whole story and still is not deeply concerned; one who understands the difference between good men and bad and who can yet speak with amused indulgence of the first, knowing how prone they are to weakness of intellect, and with urbane scorn, rather than indignation, of the second, knowing that most of them, too, are fools. This combination of sympathetic moral feeling with ironical detachment is bound to influence our expectations from the first, and to the extent that it does so, we tend to anticipate the coming troubles with no more than comic fear.

It is when the troubles come, in Book V and later, that Fielding's second problem emerges; for, given the kinds of things that then happen to Tom and especially the seriousness with which, as a good man, he necessarily takes them, there is always a danger that our original comic detachment may give way, temporarily, to tragicomic feelings of fear, pity, and indignation. That this seldom happens is another sign of how successfully, in *Tom Jones*, the handling of the parts is kept consonant with the formal demands of the whole. It is a question primarily of maximizing the general comic expectations of the reader by minimizing the possible noncomic elements in his inferences about particular situations; and the devices which Fielding uses for the purpose are of several kinds. Sometimes the result is achieved by preventing our attention from concentrating long or closely on potential causes of distress for Tom; it is notable, for example, that we are given no representation of Blifil scheming Tom's ruin before his speech to Allworthy in Book VI, chapter xi, and that from this point until Book XVI Blifil and his intentions are not again brought to the fore. Sometimes the device consists in slurring over a painful scene by generalized narration and then quickly diverting us to an obviously comic sequence in another line of action: this is what Fielding does, to excellent effect, with the incident of Tom's condemnation and banishment; we should feel much more keenly for him if, in the first place, we were allowed to hear more of his talk with Allworthy and, in the second place, were not plunged so soon after into the ridiculous quarrels of the Westerns. Or, again, the expedient may take the simple form of a refusal by the narrator to describe feelings of Tom which, if they were represented directly and at length, might easily excite a noncomic response; as in the accounts of his "madness" at Upton after he finds Sophia's muff and of the torments he endures ("such that even Thwackum would almost have pitied him") when her message of dismissal comes to him in prison. And the same general minimizing function is also served by the two episodes in the middle part of the novel which have occasioned so much discussion among Fielding's critics. Both the story told to Tom by the Man of the Hill and that recounted to Sophia by Mrs. Fitzpatrick have plainly the character of elaborate negative analogies to the moral states of the listeners, from which it is possible for the reader to infer, on the eve of the most distressing part of the complication for the hero and heroine, that nothing that may happen to them will be really bad.

These are but a few of the things that can be said, in the light of our general hypothesis about plot, concerning the plot of *Tom Jones* and its relation to the other parts of the novel. They will perhaps suffice to call attention to some aspects of Fielding's constructive art that have commonly been left out of account, from 1749 to the present, even by those who have praised it most highly.

WILLIAM EMPSON

Tom Jones†

I had been meaning to write about *Tom Jones* before, but this essay bears the marks of shock at what I found said about the book by recent literary critics, and my students at Sheffield; I had to consider why I find the book so much better than they do. Middleton

†From *The Kenyon Review*, 20 (1958), 217–49. Copyright 1958 by *The Kenyon*   *Review*. Reprinted by permission of the author and the publisher.

Murry was working from the same impulse of defense in the chief of the *Unprofessional Essays* (1956) written shortly before he died; I agree with him so much that we chose a lot of the same quotations, but he was still thinking of Fielding as just "essentially healthy" or something like that, and I think the defense should be larger. Of American critics, I remember a detailed treatment of the plot by a Chicago Aristotelian,[1] who praised what may be called the calculations behind the structure; I thought this was just and sensible, but assumed the basic impulse behind the book to be pretty trivial. English critics tend to bother about *Tom Jones* more than American ones and also to wince away from it more, because it is supposed to be so frightfully English, and they are rightly uneasy about national self-praise; besides, he is hearty and they tend to be anti-hearty. What nobody will recognize, I feel, is that Fielding set out to preach a doctrine in *Tom Jones* (1749), and said so, a high-minded though perhaps abstruse one. As he said after the attacks on *Joseph Andrews* (1742) that he would not write another novel, we may suppose that he wouldn't have written *Tom Jones* without at least finding for himself the excuse that he had this important further thing to say. Modern critics tend to assume both (a) that it isn't artistic to preach any doctrine and (b) that the only high-minded doctrine to preach is despair and contempt for the world; I think the combination produces a critical blind spot, so I hope there is some general interest in this attempt to defend *Tom Jones*, even for those who would not mark the book high anyhow.

Fielding, then, is regarded with a mixture of acceptance and contempt, as a worthy old boy who did the basic engineering for the novel because he invented the clockwork plot, but tiresomely boisterous, "broad" to the point of being insensitive to fine shades, lacking in any of the higher aspirations, and hampered by a style which keeps his prosy commonsense temperament always to the fore. Looking for a way out of this clump of prejudices, I think the style is the best place to start. If you take an interest in Fielding's opinions, which he seems to be expressing with bluff directness, you can get to the point of reading *Tom Jones* with fascinated curiosity, baffled to make out what he really does think about the filial duties of a daughter, or the inherent virtues of a gentleman, or the Christian command of chastity. To leap to ambiguity for a solution may seem Empson's routine paradox, particularly absurd in the case of Fielding; but in a way, which means for a special kind of ambiguity, it has always been recognized about him. His readers have always felt sure that he is somehow recommending the behavior of Tom Jones, whether they called the result healthy or immoral; whereas the book makes plenty of firm assertions that Tom is doing wrong. The

1. R. S. Crane. [*Editor*]

reason why this situation can arise is that the style of Fielding is a habitual double irony; or rather, he moves the gears of his car up to that as soon as the road lets it use its strength. This form, though logically rather complicated, needs a show of lightness and careless-ness whether it is being used to cheat or not; for that matter, some speakers convey it all the time by a curl of the tongue in their tone of voice. Indeed, I understand that some Americans regard every upper-class English voice as doing that, however unintentionally; to divide the national honors, I should think the reason for the suspi-cion is that every tough American voice is doing it too. Single irony presumes a censor; the ironist (A) is fooling a tyrant (B) while appealing to the judgment of a person addressed (C). For double irony A shows both B and C that he understands both their posi-tions; B can no longer forbid direct utterance, but I think can always be picked out as holding the more official or straight-faced belief. In real life this is easier than single irony (because people aren't such fools as you think), so that we do not always notice its logical structure. Presumably A hopes that each of B and C will think "He is secretly on my side, and only pretends to sympathize with the other"; but A may hold some wise balanced position between them, or contrariwise may be feeling "a plague on both your houses." The trick is liable to be unpopular, and perhaps liter-ary critics despise its evasiveness, so that when they talk about irony they generally seem to mean something else; but a moderate amount of it is felt to be balanced and unfussy. The definition may seem too narrow, but if you generalize the term to cover almost any complex state of mind it ceases to be useful. I do not want to make large claims for "double irony," but rather to narrow it down enough to show why it is peculiarly fitted for *Tom Jones*.

There it serves a purpose so fundamental that it can come to seem as massive as the style of Gibbon, who seems to have realized this in his sentence of praise. He had already, in Chapter xxxii of the *Decline and Fall*, describing a Byzantine palace intrigue, com-pared it in a footnote to a passage of *Tom Jones*, "the romance of a great master, which may be considered the history of human nature." This would be about 1780; in 1789, discussing ancestors at the beginning of his *Autobiography*, for example the claim of Field-ing's family to be related to the Hapsburgs, he said, "But the romance of *Tom Jones*, that exquisite picture of human manners, will outlive the palace of the Escurial and the imperial eagle of the House of Austria." This has more to do with Fielding than one might think, especially with his repeated claim, admitted to be rather comic but a major source of his nerve, that he was capable of making a broad survey because he was an aristocrat and had known high life from within. I take it that Gibbon meant his own irony not merely to attack the Christians (in that use it is "single") but to rise to a grand survey of the strangeness of human affairs. Of course both use it for protection against rival moralists, but its major use is to express the balance of their judgment. Fielding is already doing this in *Joseph Andrews*, but there the process seems genuinely casual. In *Tom Jones* he is expressing a theory about ethics, and the ironies are made to interlock with the progress of the demonstration. The titanic plot, which has been praised or found tiresome taken alone, was devised to illustrate the theory, and the screws of the engine of his style are engaging the sea. That is, the feeling that he is proving a case is what gives *Tom Jones* its radiance, making it immensely better, I think, than the other two novels (though perhaps there is merely less discovery about proving the sad truths of *Amelia*); it builds up like Euclid. Modern critics seem unable to feel this, apparently because it is forbidden by their aesthetic principles, even when Fielding tells them he is doing it; whereas Dr. Johnson and Sir John Hawkins, for example, took it seriously at once, and complained bitterly that the book had an immoral purpose. It certainly becomes much more interesting if you attend to its thesis; even if the thesis retains the shimmering mystery of a mirage.

Consider for example what Fielding says (XII.8) when he is reflecting over what happened when Sophia caught Tom in bed with Mrs. Waters at the Upton Inn, and incidentally telling us that that wasn't the decisive reason why Sophia rode away in anger, never likely to meet him again:

> I am not obliged to reconcile every matter to the received notions concerning truth and nature. But if this was never so easy to do, perhaps it might be more prudent in me to avoid it. For instance, as the fact before us now stands, without any comment of mine upon it, though it may at first sight offend some readers, yet, upon more mature consideration, it must please all; for wise and good men may consider what happened to Jones at Upton as a just punishment for his wickedness in regard to women, of which it was indeed the immediate consequence; and silly and bad persons may comfort themselves in their vices by flattering their own hearts that the characters of men are owing rather to accident than to virtue. Now, perhaps the reflections which we should be here inclined to draw would alike contradict both these conclusions, and would show that these incidents contribute only to confirm the great, useful, and uncommon doctrine which it is the whole purpose of this work to inculcate, and which we must not fill up our pages by frequently repeating, as an ordinary parson fills up his sermon by repeating his text at the end of every paragraph.

He does, as I understand, partly tell us the doctrine elsewhere, but never defines it as his central thesis; perhaps he chooses to put the claim here because XII is a rather desultory book, fitting in various incidents which the plot or the thesis will require later, and conveying the slowness of travel before the rush of London begins in XIII. To say "the fact before us" makes Fielding the judge, and his readers the jury. He rather frequently warns them that they may not be able to understand him, and I think this leaves the modern critic, who assumes he meant nothing, looking rather comical. Perhaps this critic would say it is Empson who fails to see the joke of Fielding's self-deprecating irony; I answer that the irony of the book is double, here as elsewhere. Fielding realizes that any man who puts forward a general ethical theory implies a claim to have very wide ethical experience, therefore should be ready to laugh at his own pretensions; but also he isn't likely to mean nothing when he jeers at you for failing to see his point. Actually, the modern critic does know what kind of thing the secret is; but he has been badgered by neo-classicism and neo-Christianity and what not, whereas the secret is humanist, liberal, materialist, recommending happiness on earth and so forth; so he assumes it is dull, or the worldly advice of a flippant libertine.

Nobody would want to argue such points who had felt the tone of the book; it is glowing with the noble beauty of its gospel, which Fielding indeed would be prepared to claim as the original Gospel. The prose of generalized moral argument may strike us as formal, but it was also used by Shelley, who would also appeal to the Gospels to defend a moral novelty, as would Blake; an idea that the Romantics were original there seems to confuse people nowadays very much. When Fielding goes really high in *Tom Jones* his prose is like an archangel brooding over mankind, and I suppose is actually imitating similar effects in Handel; one might think it was like Bach, and that Handel would be too earthbound, but we know Fielding admired Handel. I admit that the effect is sometimes forced, and strikes us as the theatrical rhetoric of the Age of Sentiment; but you do not assume he is insincere there if you recognize that at other times the effect is very real.

A moderate case of this high language comes early in the book when Squire Allworthy is discussing charity with Captain Blifil (II.5). The captain is trying to ruin young Tom so as to get all the estate for himself, and has just remarked that Christian charity is an ideal, so ought not to be held to mean giving anything material; Allworthy falls into a glow at this, and readily agrees that there can be no merit in merely discharging a duty, especially such a pleasant one; but goes on:

> To confess the truth, there is one degree of generosity (of charity I would have called it), which seems to have some show of merit, and that is where, from a principle of benevolence and Christian love, we bestow on another what we really want ourselves; where,

in order to lessen the distresses of another, we condescend to share some part of them, by giving what even our necessities cannot well spare. This is, I think, meritorious; but to relieve our brethren only with our superfluities—

—to do one thing and another, go the balanced clauses, "this seems to be only being rational creatures." Another theme then crosses his mind for the same grand treatment:

As to the apprehension of bestowing bounty on such as may here-after prove unworthy objects, merely because many have proved such, surely it can never deter a good man from generosity.

This too is argued with noble rhetoric, and then the captain inserts his poisoned barb. Now, the passage cannot be single irony, meant to show Allworthy as a pompous fool; he is viewed with wonder as a kind of saint (e.g. he is twice said to smile like an angel, and he is introduced as the most glorious creature under the sun), also he stood for the real benefactor Allen whom Fielding would be ashamed to laugh at. Fielding shows a Proust-like delicacy in regu-larly marking a reservation about Allworthy without ever letting us laugh at him (whereas critics usually complain he is an all-white character). Allworthy is something less than all-wise; the plot itself requires him to believe the villains and throw Tom out of Paradise Hall, and the plot is designed to carry larger meanings. The reason why he agrees so eagerly with the captain here, I take it, apart from his evidently not having experienced what he is talking about, is a point of spiritual delicacy or gentlemanly politeness—he cannot appear to claim credit for looking after his own cottagers, in talking to a guest who is poor; that was hardly more than looking after his own property, and the reflection distracts him from gauging the captain's motives. What is more important, he speaks as usual of doing good on principle, and here the central mystery is being touched upon.

One might think the answer is: "Good actions come only from good impulses, that is, those of a good heart, not from good princi-ples"; the two bad tutors of Jones make this idea obvious at the beginning (especially III.5). Dr. Johnson and Sir John Hawkins denounced the book as meaning this, and hence implying that morality is no use (by the way, in my *Complex Words*, p. 173, I ascribed a sentence of Hawkins to Johnson, but they make the same points). Fielding might well protest that he deserved to escape this reproach; he had twice stepped out of his frame in the novel to explain that he was not recommending Tom's imprudence, and that he did not mean to imply that religion and philosophy are bad because bad men can interpret them wrongly. But he seems to have started from this idea in his first revolt against the ethos of Richard-

son which made him write *Shamela* and *Joseph Andrews*; I think it
was mixed with a class belief, that well-brought-up persons (with
the natural ease of gentlemen) do not need to keep prying into
their own motives as these hypocritical Nonconformist types do. As
a novelist he never actually asserts this idea, which one can see is
open to misuse, and in *Tom Jones* (1749) he has made it only part
of a more interesting idea; but, after he had been attacked for using
it there, he arranged an ingenious reply in the self-defensive *Amelia*
(1751). He gave the opinion outright to the silly Booth, a freethinker who disbelieves in free will (III.5); you are rather encouraged
to regard Booth as a confession of the errors of the author when
young. When he is converted at the end of the novel (XII.5) the
good parson laughs at him for having thought this a heresy, saying
it is why Christianity provides the motives of heaven and hell. This
was all right as an escape into the recesses of theology; but it was
the Calvinists who had really given up free will, and Fielding could
hardly want to agree with them; at any rate Parson Adams, in
Joseph Andrews, had passionately disapproved of salvation by faith.
Fielding was a rather special kind of Christian, but evidently sincere
in protesting that he was one. Adams is now usually regarded as
sweetly Anglican, but his brother parson (in I.17) suspects he is the
devil, after he has sternly rejected a series of such doctrines as give a
magical importance to the clergy. I take it Fielding set himself up
as a moral theorist, later than *Joseph Andrews*, because he decided
he could refute the view of Hobbes, and of various thinkers prominent at the time who derived from Hobbes, that incessant egotism
is logically inevitable or a condition of our being. We lack the
moral treatise in the form of answers to Bolingbroke which he set
out to write when dying, but can gather an answer from *Tom Jones*,
perhaps from the firm treatment of the reader in VI.1, which introduces the troubles of the lovers and tells him that no author can
tell him what love means unless he is capable of experiencing it.
The doctrine is thus: "If good by nature, you can imagine other
people's feelings so directly that you have an impulse to act on
them as if they were your own; and this is the source of your greatest pleasures as well as of your only genuinely unselfish actions." A
modern philosopher might answer that this makes no logical difference, but it clearly brings a large practical difference into the suasive
effect of the argument of Hobbes, which was what people had
thought worth discussing in the first place. The most striking illustration is in the sexual behavior of Jones, where he is most scandalous; one might, instead, find him holy, because he never makes love
to a woman unless she first makes love to him. Later on (XIII.7)
we find he thinks it a point of honor to accept such a challenge
from a woman, no less than a challenge to fight from a man (and

that is the absolute of honor, the duel itself); but in his first two cases, Molly Seagrim and Sophia, he is unconscious that their advances have aroused him, and very grateful when they respond. Fielding reveres the moral beauty of this, but is quite hardheaded enough to see that such a man is too easily fooled by women; he regards Tom as dreadfully in need of good luck, and feels like a family lawyer when he makes the plot give it to him. He is thus entirely sincere in repeating that Tom needed to learn prudence; but how this relates to the chastity enjoined by religion he does not explain. We may however observe that nobody in the novel takes this prohibition quite seriously all the time; even Allworthy, when he is friends again, speaks only of the imprudence of Tom's relations with Lady Bellaston (XVIII.10). In any case, the sexual affairs are only one of the many applications of the doctrine about mutuality of impulse; I think this was evidently the secret message which Fielding boasts of in *Tom Jones*, a book which at the time was believed to be so wicked that it had caused earthquakes.

We need not suppose he was well up in the long history of the question, but I would like to know more about his relations to Calvin; Professor C. S. Lewis, in his *Survey of Sixteenth-Century Literature*, brings out what unexpected connections Calvin can have. He maintained that no action could deserve heaven which was done in order to get to heaven; hence we can only attain good, that is non-egotist, motives by the sheer grace of God. In its early years the doctrine was by no means always regarded as grim; and it has an eerie likeness to the basic position of Fielding, that the well born soul has good impulses of its own accord, which only need directing. At least, a humble adherent of either doctrine may feel baffled to know how to get into the condition recommended. However, I take it this likeness arises merely because both men had seriously puzzled their heads over the Gospel, and tried to give its paradoxes their full weight. Fielding never made a stronger direct copy of a gospel parable than in *Joseph Andrews*, when Joseph is dying naked in the snow and an entire coachload finds worldly reasons for letting him die except for the postboy freezing on the outside, who gives Joseph his overcoat and is soon after transported for robbing a henroost. But I think he felt the paradoxes of Jesus more as a direct challenge after he had trained and practiced as a lawyer, and had come into line for a job as magistrate; that is, when he decided to write *Tom Jones*. He first wrote in favor of the Government on the 1745 Rebellion, in a stream of indignant pamphlets, and this was what made him possible as a magistrate; he was horrified at the public indifference at the prospect of a Catholic conquest, from which he expected rack and fire. He must then also be shocked at the indifference, or the moon-eyed preference for the invader, shown by all the characters in *Tom Jones*; nor can he approve the reaction of the Old Man of the Hill, who thanks God he has renounced so lunatic a world. To realize that Fielding himself is not indifferent here, I think, gives a further range to the vistas of the book, because all the characters are being as imprudent about it as Tom Jones about his own affairs; and this at least encourages one to suppose that there was a fair amount going on in Fielding's mind.

Tom Jones is a hero because he is born with good impulses; indeed, as the boy had no friend but the thieving gamekeeper Black George, among the lethal hatreds of Paradise Hall, he emerges as a kind of noble savage. This is first shown when, keen to shoot a bird, he follows it across the boundary and is caught on Squire Western's land; two guns were heard, but he insists he was alone. The keeper had yielded to his request and come too; if Tom says so, the keeper will be sacked, and his wife and children will starve, but Tom as a little gentleman at the great house can only be beaten. "Tom passed a very melancholy night" because he was afraid the beating might make him lose his honor by confessing, says Fielding, who adds that it was as severe as the tortures used in some foreign countries to induce confessions. The reader first learns to suspect the wisdom of Allworthy by hearing him say (III.2) that Tom acted here on a mistaken point of honor; though he only says it to defend Tom from further assaults by the bad tutors, who discuss the point with splendid absurdity. Whether it was "true," one would think, depended on whether the child thought Allworthy himself could be trusted not to behave unjustly. I have no respect for the critics who find the moralizing of the book too obvious; the child's honor really is all right after that; he is a fit judge of other ideas of honor elsewhere. Modern readers would perhaps like him better if they realized his basic likeness to Huck Finn; Mark Twain and Fielding were making much the same protest, even to the details about dueling. But Mark Twain somehow could not bear to have Huck grow up, whereas the chief idea about Tom Jones, though for various reasons it has not been recognized, is that he is planned to become awestrikingly better during his brief experience of the world. You are first meant to realize this is happening halfway through the book, when the Old Man of the Hill is recounting his life, and Tom is found smiling quietly to himself at a slight error in the ethical position of that mystical recluse (VIII.13). Old Man is a saint, and Fielding can provide him with some grand devotional prose, but he is too much of a stoic to be a real gospel Christian, which is what Tom is turning into as we watch him.

All critics call the recital of Old Man irrelevant, though Saintsbury labors to excuse it; but Fielding meant to give a survey of all human experience (that is what he meant by calling the book an epic) and Old Man provides the extremes of degradation and divine ecstasy which Tom has no time for; as part of the structure of ethical thought he is essential to the book, the keystone at the middle of the arch. The critics could not have missed understanding this if they hadn't imagined themselves forbidden to have intellectual interests, as Fielding had. For that matter, the whole setting of the book in the 1745 Rebellion gets its point when it interlocks with the theory and practice of Old Man. So far from being "episodic," the incident is meant to be such an obvious pulling together of the threads that it warns us to keep an eye on the subsequent moral development of Tom. As he approaches London unarmed, he is challenged by a highwayman; removing the man's pistol, and inquiring about the motives, he gives half of all he has to the starving family—rather more than half, to avoid calculation. Fielding of course knew very well that this was making him carry out one of the paradoxes of Jesus, though neither Fielding nor Tom must ever say so. The first time he earns money by selling his body to Lady Bellaston, a physically unpleasant duty which he enters upon believing at each step that his honor requires it (and without which, as the plot goes, he could probably not have won through to marrying Sophia), he tosses the whole fifty to his landlady, Mrs. Miller, for a hard luck case who turns out to be the same highwayman, though she will only take ten; when the man turns up to thank him, with mutual recognition, Tom congratulates him for having enough honor to fight for the lives of his children, and proceeds to Lady Bellaston "greatly exulting in the happiness he has procured," also reflecting on the evils that "strict justice" would have caused here (XIII.10). His next heroic action is to secure marriage for his land-lady's daughter, pregnant by his fellow lodger Nightingale, thus "saving the whole family from destruction"; it required a certain moral depth, because the basic difficulty was to convince Nightingale that this marriage, which he greatly desired, was not forbidden to him by his honor. We tend now to feel that Tom makes a grossly obvious moral harangue, but Nightingale feels it has pooh-poohed what he regards as the moral side of the matter, removing his "foolish scruples of honor" so that he can do what he prefers (XIV.7). Indeed the whole interest of the survey of ideas of honor is that different characters hold such different ones; no wonder critics who do not realize this find the repetition of the word tedious. These chapters in which the harangues of Tom are found obvious are interwoven with others in which his peculiar duty as regards Lady Bellaston has to be explained, and we pass on to the crimes which poor Lord Fellamar could be made to think his honor required. Critics would not grumble in the same way at Euclid, for being didactic in the propositions they have been taught already and immoral in the ones they refuse to learn. The threats of rape for Sophia and enslavement for Tom, as the plot works out, are simply further specimens of the code of honor; that danger for Tom is settled when Lord Fellamar gathers, still from hearsay, that the bastard is really a gentleman and therefore ought not to be treated as a kind of stray animal—he is "much concerned" at having been misled (XVIII.11). There is a less familiar point about codes of honor (indeed it struck the Tory critic Saintsbury as a libel on squires) when we find that Squire Western regards dueling as a Whig townee corruption, and proposes wrestling or singlestick with Lord Fellamar's second (XVI.2); but Fielding means Western to be right for once, not to prove that the old brute is a coward, and had said so in his picture of country life (V.12). When you consider what a tyrant Western is on his estate, it really does seem rather impressive that he carries no weapon.

Fielding meant all this as part of something much larger than a picture of the ruling-class code of honor; having taken into his head that he is a moral theorist, he has enough intelligence to be interested by the variety of moral codes in the society around him. A tribe, unlike a man, can exist by itself, and when found has always a code of honor (though not police, prisons and so forth) without which it could not have survived till found; such is the basis upon which any further moral ideas must be built. That is why Fielding makes Tom meet the King of the Gypsies, who can rule with no other force but shame because his people have no false honors among them (XII.12)—the incident is rather forced, because he is obviously not a gypsy but a Red Indian, just as Old Man, with his annuity and his housekeeper, has obviously no need to be dressed in skins like Robinson Crusoe; but they make you generalize the question. By contrast to this, the society which Fielding describes is one in which many different codes of honor, indeed almost different tribes, exist concurrently. The central governing class acts by only one of these codes and is too proud to look at the others (even Western's); but they would be better magistrates, and also happier and more sensible in their private lives, if they would recognize that these other codes surround them. It is to make this central point that Fielding needs the technique of double irony, without which one cannot express imaginative sympathy for two codes at once.

It strikes me that modern critics, whether as a result of the neo-Christian movement or not, have become oddly resistant to admitting that there is more than one code of morals in the world, whereas the central purpose of reading imaginative literature is to accustom yourself to this basic fact. I do not at all mean that a literary critic ought to avoid making moral judgments; that is useless as well as tiresome, because the reader has enough sense to start guessing round it at once. A critic had better say what his own opinions are, which can be done quite briefly, while recognizing that the person in view held different ones. (As for myself here, I agree with Fielding and wish I were as good.) The reason why Fielding could put a relativistic idea across on his first readers (though apparently not on modern critics) was that to them the word *honor* chiefly suggested the problem whether a gentleman had to duel whenever he was huffed; one can presume they were already bothered by it, because it was stopped a generation or two later—in England, though not in the America of Huckleberry Finn. But Fielding used this, as he used the Nightingale marriage, merely as firm ground from which he could be allowed to generalize; and he does not find relativism alarming, because he feels that to understand codes other than your own is likely to make your judgments better. Surely a "plot" of this magnitude is bound to seem tiresome unless it is frankly used as a means by which, while machining the happy ending, the author can present all sides of the question under consideration and show that his attitude to it is consistent. The professional Victorian novelists understood very well that Fielding had set a grand example there, and Dickens sometimes came near it, but it is a hard thing to plan for.

All the actions of Tom Jones are reported to Allworthy and Sophia, and that is why they reinstate him; they are his judges, like the reader. Some readers at the time said it was willfull nastiness of Fielding to make Tom a bastard, instead of discovering a secret marriage at the end; and indeed he does not explain (XVIII.7) why Tom's mother indignantly refused to marry his father when her brother suggested it (Fielding probably knew a reason, liking to leave us problems which we can answer if we try, as Dr. Dudden's book shows, but I cannot guess it). But there is a moral point in leaving him a bastard; he is to inherit Paradise Hall because he is held to deserve it, not because the plot has been dragged round to make him the legal heir. Lady Mary Wortley Montagu, a grand second cousin of Fielding who thought him low, said that *Amelia* seemed to her just as immoral as his previous books, and she could not understand why Dr. Johnson forgave it, because it too encouraged young people to marry for love and expect a happy ending. She had enjoyed the books, and thought that Richardson's were just as immoral. I take it that, after a rather uncomfortable marriage for money, she found herself expected to give a lot of it away to her poor relations, so she thought they all ought to have married for money. Wrong though she may have been, the 18th century assumption that a novel has a moral seems to me sensible; *Tom Jones* really was likely to make young people marry for love, not only because that is presented as almost a point of honor but because the plot does not make the gamble seem hopeless. The machinery of the happy ending derives from the fairy tale, as Fielding perhaps recognized, as well as wanting to sound like Bunyan, when he called the house Paradise Hall. The third son seeking his fortune gives his crust to the withered crone and thus becomes a prince because she is Queen of the Fairies; the moral is that this was the right thing to do, even if she hadn't been, but the tale also suggests to the child that maybe this isn't such a bad bet as you might think, either. The mind of Fielding, as he gets near in the actual writing to the end of a plot which he is clearly following from a complete dated skeleton, begins to play round what it means when an author, as it were, tosses up to see whether to give his characters joy or sorrow; he is the creator here, he remarks, but he will promise not to work miracles, and so forth. Rather earlier, he positively asserts that generous behavior like Tom's is not rewarded with happiness on earth, indeed that it would probably be unchristian to suppose so. This is in one of the introductory chapters of literary prattle (XV.1); it is answered in XV.8, after a joke about whether Tom has selfish motives for a good action (and the reader who remembers IV.11 may well brace himself to hear a new scandal about Tom), by a firm assertion that the immediate results of such behavior are among the greatest happinesses that earth can provide. However, this play of mind does not arrive at telling us what the happy ending means, and indeed could not, as its chief function is to make the suspense real even for a thoughtful reader. I take it that the childish magic of the fairy tale, and its elder brother, the belief that good actions ought to be done because they will be rewarded in heaven, are reinforced in this novel by a practical idea which would not always apply; the outstanding moral of *Tom Jones*, if you look at it as Lady Mary did but less sourly, is that when a young man leaves home he is much more in a goldfish bowl than he thinks. The reader is to be influenced in favor of Tom's behavior by seeing it through the eyes of Allworthy and Sophia, whom one might think sufficiently high-class and severe. But the end conveys something much more impressive than that these examiners give him a pass degree; he has become so much of a gospel Christian that he cannot help but cast a shadow even on them. Against all reason and principle, and therefore to the consternation of Allworthy, he forgives Black George.

George robbed him, just after he was cast out, of the money Allworthy had given him to save him from degradation, for example, being pressed to sea as a vagabond, which nearly occurred. The gamekeeper was an old friend rather than a remote peasant, had become comfortable solely through the efforts of Tom to get him a job, and one would also think, as Tom's supposed natural-father-in-law, must have had an interest in letting him even now have a sporting chance. Fielding rated friendship specially highly, and always speaks of this betrayal in the tone of sad wonder he keeps for desperate cases. He says nothing himself about Tom forgiving George, but makes Allworthy give a harangue calling it wicked because harmful to society. We are accustomed in Fielding to hear characters wriggle out of the absolute command by Jesus to forgive, comically bad ones as a rule, and now the ideal landlord is saddled with it. The time must clearly come, if a man carries through a consistent program about double irony, when he himself does not know the answer; and here, as it should do, it comes at the end of the novel. The practical lawyer and prospective magistrate would have to find the Gospel puzzling on this point; it is quite fair for Fielding still to refuse to admit that Allworthy is in the wrong, because he may well suspect that the command of Jesus would bring anarchy. To be sure, this is not one of the impressive tests of Tom; he is merely behaving nicely, just when everything is falling into his hands, and would lose our sympathy if he didn't; it comes to him naturally, which not all the previous cases did. But still, we have been moving through a landscape of the ethic of human impulses, and when Tom rises above Allworthy he is like a mountain.

There is already a mystery or weird pathos about George when he is first worked back into the plot (XV.12). Partridge is overjoyed, after all their troubles in London, to meet someone who loves Tom so much:

> Betray you indeed! why I question whether you have a better friend than George upon earth, except myself, or one that would go further to serve you.

The reader is bound to take this as single irony at first, but Fielding is soon cheerfully explaining that George really did wish Tom well, as much as a man could who loved money more than anything else; and then we get him offering money to Tom in prison. Though not allowed to be decisive for the plot, he is useful in smuggling a letter to Sophia and trustworthy in hiding it from his employer. As to his love of money, we should remember that we have seen his family starving (III.9) after a bad bit of 18th century administration by Allworthy. I think Fielding means to play a trick, just after the theft, when he claims to put us fully inside the mind of George; acting as go-between, George wonders whether to steal also the bit of money sent by Sophia to the exile, and decides that would be unsafe (VI.13). No doubt we are to believe the details, but Fielding still feels free, in his Proust-like way, to give a different picture of the man's character at the other end of the novel; I take it he refused to believe that the "inside" of a person's mind (as given by

Richardson in a letter, perhaps) is much use for telling you the real source of his motives. George of course has not reformed at the end; he has arranged to come to London with his new employer, Western, the more safely to cash the bill he stole, though, as he chooses the lawyer who is the father of Nightingale, the precaution happens to be fatal. I think the mind of Fielding held in reserve a partial justification for George, though he was careful with it and would only express it in the introductory prattle to Book XII, where both the case of George and its country setting are particularly far from our minds; indeed, I had to read the book again to find where this comment is put. While pretending to discuss literary plagiarism, Fielding lets drop that the villagers on these great estates consider it neither sin nor shame to rob their great neighbors, and a point of honor to protect any other villagers who have done so. George might assume, one can well imagine, that Tom was going to remain a grandee somehow whatever quarrels he had; in fact, Tom at the time is so much wrapped up in his unhappy love affair that he seems hardly to realize himself how much he will need money. On this view, it would be shameful for George to miss a chance of robbing Tom; for one thing, it would be robbing his own family, as the soldier reflects in VII.14. I agree that, so far from advancing this argument, Fielding never weakens the tone of moral shock with which he regards the behavior of George (who was right to be so ashamed that he ran away); but I think he means you to gather that the confusion between different moral codes made it intelligible. This background I think adds to the rather thrilling coolness with which Tom does not reply to the harangue of Allworthy denouncing his forgiveness; it is in any case time for him to go and dress to meet Sophia.

Sophia has the same kind of briefing as a modern Appointments Board; thus she does not waste time over his offer of marriage to Lady Bellaston; Sophia holds the document, but understands that this was merely the way to get rid of Lady Bellaston; so it joins the list of points already cleared. The decisive question in her mind is whether he has become a libertine, that is, whether his impulses have become corrupted; if they have, she is quite prepared again to refuse to unite by marriage the two largest estates in Somersetshire. Fielding has been blamed for making the forgiveness of Tom too easy, but I think his training as a bad playwright served him well here, by teaching him what he could throw away. A reader does not need to hear the case again, and Fielding disapproved of women who argue, indeed makes Allworthy praise Sophia for never doing it; and he himself has a certain shyness about expressing his doctrine, or perhaps thought it dangerous to express clearly. Beastly old Western comes yelling in to say for the average reader that we can't be bothered with further discussion of the matter, and Sophia decides that she can allow it to have settled itself. The fit reader, interested in the doctrine, is perhaps meant to feel rather disappointed that it is not preached, but also that this is good taste in a way, because after all the man's impulses have evidently not been corrupted. Even so, it is nothing like the view of Flaubert, Conrad and so forth, that a novelist is positively not allowed to discuss the point of his novel.

I want now, though there is so much else to choose from in this rich book, to say something about the thought of incest which terrifies Jones in prison; both because it affects the judgment of Sophia and because it has been a major bone of contention among other critics. Dr. F. H. Dudden, in his treatise *Henry Fielding* (1952), though concerned to do justice to an author whose morals have been maligned, admits that he had a rather nasty habit of dragging fear of incest into his plots (it also comes into *Joseph Andrews*); but decides that he means no harm by it, and that it was probably just an effect of having to write bad plays when he was young. On the other hand a *Times Lit. Supp.* reviewer, quoted with indignation by Middleton Murry in *Unprofessional Essays*, had thought this frightening of Jones a specially moral part of the plot. When he goes to bed with Mrs. Waters at Upton, says the reviewer, Fielding

> seems to be making light of it, or even conniving at it. Yet it is the first step in a moral progress downhill. . . . And then, much later in the book, evidence comes to light which suggests [that she was his mother]. . . . Fielding's connivance was a pretence. He has sprung a trap on Tom and us; he has made us realize—as a serious novelist always makes us realize, and a frivolous novelist often makes us forget—that actions have their consequences. . . . It is this sense of the moral structure of life that makes Fielding important.

I could have quoted more sanctimonious bits, but this was the part which Middleton Murry found perverse:

> What to a more normal sensibility constitutes the one doubtful moment in the book—the one moment at which we feel that Fielding *may* have sounded a wrong note, by suggesting an awful possibility outside the range of the experience he invites us to partake—becomes in this vision the one thing which makes the book considerable.

The reviewer of course was trying to speak up for Fielding, and make him something better than a flippant libertine; and it is in favor of his view that the Upton incident is the one place where Fielding says in person that casual sex is forbidden by Christianity as expressly as murder (IX.3). Dr. Dudden might be expected to agree with the reviewer; he maintains you have only to attend to the text to find that Fielding always not only denounces sin but arranges to have it punished "inexorably and terribly." This indeed is one half of what Fielding intended, though the adverbs hardly describe the purring tone of the eventual forgiveness of Tom, as when we are told that he has, "by reflection on his past follies, acquired a discretion and prudence very uncommon in one of his lively parts." Instead, we find that Dr. Dudden agrees with Middleton Murry; they are more in sympathy with Fielding than the reviewer, but feel they have to confess that the incest trick is rather bad; chiefly, I think, because they like him for being healthy, and that seems clearly not.

I think the basic reason why Fielding twice uses this fear is that he had a philosophical cast of mind, and found it curious that those who laugh at ordinary illicit sex take incest very seriously. As to *Joseph Andrews*, the starting point is that Fielding is to parody Richardson's Pamela, a servant who made her master marry her by refusing to be seduced. He had already done this briefly and fiercely in *Shamela*, where an ex-prostitute acts like Pamela out of conscious calculation—the moral is that Pamela is *un*consciously calculating, and that girls ought not to be encouraged to imitate this minx. He is now to do it by swapping the sexes; a footman would be cowardly, or have some other low motive, if he refused a lady, and a lady would be lacking in the delicacy of her caste if she even wanted a footman. Thus the snobbish Fielding, in opposition to the democratic Richardson, can prove that the class structure ought not to be disturbed. Or rather, he did not actually have to write this stuff, because he could rely on his readers to imagine he had, as they still do. It is false to say, as is regularly said, that Fielding started on his parody and then wrote something else because he found he was a novelist; he did not start on it at all. From the first words, he treats his story with an almost overrefined, a breathless delicacy; and by the time Lady Booby has offered marriage, and Joseph, though attracted by her, still refuses her because he wants to marry his humble sweetheart, most of the laughing readers should be pretty well outfaced. No doubt Fielding himself, if the story had been outlined at his club, would have laughed as heartily as the others; but he is concerned in this novel, where he is rather oddly safe from being thought a hypocrite, to show that his sympathy is so broad that he can see the question all round, like a judge. I think he did discover something in writing it, but not what is usually said; he discovered how much work he could leave the public to do for him. One type of reader would be jeering at Joesph, and another admiring him, and feeling indignant with the first type; and both of them would hardly notice what the author was writing down. You can understand that he might want to take some rather firm step, towards the end, to recover their attention. What he is really describing is the chastity of the innocent Joseph, adding of course the piercing simplicity of his criticisms of the great world; Parson Adams, whom Fielding certainly does not intend us to think contemptible, preaches to him a rather overstrained doctrine of chastity all along. Just as all seems ready for the happy ending with his humble sweetheart, a twist of the plot makes them apparently brother and sister; they decide to live together chastely, as Parson Adams had always said they should be able to do. Here the clubmen who form Type A of the intended readers no longer dare to jeer at Joseph for believing he has a duty of chastity; the opposed groups are forced to combine. I thus think that this turn of the plot is entirely justified; for that matter, I think that modern critics are rather too fond of the strategic device of claiming to be embarrassed.

In *Tom Jones*, I can't deny, the trick is chiefly used to heighten the excitement at the end of the plot—Tom must go either right up or right down. I agree with the *Times Lit. Supp.* reviewer that it marks a change in the attitude of hero, but it comes only as an extra at the end of a gradual development, Saintsbury defended Tom's relations with Lady Bellaston by saying that the rule against a gentleman taking money from a mistress had not yet been formulated; certainly it doesn't seem to have hampered the first Duke of Marlborough, but Tom comes to suspect of his own accord that some such rule has been formulated. He felt it when he first met Sophia in London (XIII.11); "the ignominious circumstance of his having been kept" rose in his mind when she began to scold him, and stopped his mouth; the effect of this was good, because her actual accusations came as a relief and were the more easy to argue off convincingly. It is not till XV.9 that Nightingale, as a fair return for the teaching of basic morals, warns him that he is liable to become despised by the world, and explains that the way to break with Lady Bellaston is to offer her marriage. Learning that he is one of a series makes Tom feel free to break with her, which he thought before would be ungrateful. By the way, I take it Fielding admired her firmness about marriage, as a protest against unjust laws on women's property; her criminal plot against the lovers is chiefly meant as a satire against the worldly code—she can be taken as sincere in telling Lord Fellamar that the intention is to save her ward Sophia from ruin, and Fielding only means to describe her unconsciousness when he adds in XVI.8 that women support this code out of jealousy. Tom refuses to marry a rich widow immediately afterwards (XV.11); this is the sternest of his tests, and he is "put into a violent flutter," because he suspects it is a duty of honor to accept this fortune so as to release Sophia from misery. He seems like Galahad when he rejects the point of honor for love, and it does prove that in learning "prudence," which is how Fielding and Allworthy describe his moral reform, he is not falling into the opposite error of becoming a calculating type. We next have him refusing to make love to Mrs. Fitzpatrick, while easily rejecting her spiteful advice to make love to Sophia's aunt (XVI.9). Both she and Lady Bellaston are affronted by his frank preference for Sophia and yet find their passions excited by its generosity—"strange as it may seem, I have seen many instances." The last of the series is his refusal to go to bed with Mrs. Waters when she visits him in jail with the news that her supposed husband is not dying, so that he is safe from execution (XVII.9); this might seem ungenerous rather than reformed, but he has just heard from Mrs. Miller that Sophia has become determined to refuse him because of his incontinency. The next and final book opens with the supposed discovery that Mrs. Waters is his mother, so that he committed incest with her at Upton. This throws him into a state of shaking horror which serves to illustrate his courage; we realize how undisturbed he was before at the prospect of being hanged for an act of self-defense. It is thus not the case that Tom was shocked into disapproving of his previous looseness by the thought that it might cause accidental incest, because this fear came after he had become prudent; still less that the fear of death and the horror of incest were needed together to crack such a hard nut as the conscience of Tom, because he has been freed from the fear of death just before the other alarm arrives. (I understand he was technically in danger under ecclesiastical law, but prosecution was very unlikely; in any case the question never occurs to him.) Fielding as a magistrate, surely, would think it contemptible to cheat a prisoner into reform by this trick, whereas the *Times Lit. Supp.* reviewer seems to assume it would be moral. What one can say is that the shock puts Tom into a grave frame of mind, suitable for meeting Sophia; and Sophia really does need winning over, with some extra moral solemnity however acquired, because she is quite pigheaded enough to fly in the face of the world all over again, and start refusing Tom just because he has become the heir.

My own objection to this bit about incest has long been something quite different, which I should think occurs oftener to a modern reader; and I think the book feels much better when it is cleared up. I thought the author was cheating in a way that whodunit authors often do, that is, he put in a twist to make the end more exciting though the characters would not really have acted so. Those who dislike Fielding generally say that he makes his characters so obvious, especially from making them so selfish, that they become tiresome like performing toys; but the reason why Mrs. Waters gets misunderstood here is that here as always she is unusually generous-minded. A penniless but clever girl, she learned Latin under Partridge when he was a village schoolmaster and did so well that he kept her on as an assistant, but she learned too much Latin; a fatal day came (II.3) when he jovially used Latin to ask her to pass a dish at dinner, and "the poor girl smiled, perhaps at the badness of the Latin, and, when her mistress cast eyes upon her, blushed, possibly with a consciousness of having laughed at her master." This at once made Mrs. Partridge certain not only that they were lovers but that they were jeering at her by using this code in her presence; and such is the way most of us fail to understand her final letter. A ruinous amount of fuss goes on, and it becomes convenient for her to work with Allworthy's sister in the secret birth of Jones, acting as her personal servant at the great house and paid extra to take the scandal of being his mother before leaving the district. The story is improbable, but as Fielding arranges it you can call it credible. Allworthy gives her a grand sermon against illicit love when she confesses to the bastard, but is impressed by the honor and generosity of her replies; he sends her an allowance, but stops it when he hears she has run off with a sergeant. We next see her when Jones saves her life (IX.2); the villain Northerton is trying to murder her for what money she carries, and it is startling for the reader to be told, what Jones is too delicate to ask her (IX.7), that she was only wandering about with this man to save him from being hanged, and only carrying the money to give it to him. She had expected to rejoin Captain Waters after his winter campaign against the rebels, but meanwhile Lieutenant Northerton was afraid of being hanged for murdering Jones (whereas it has been very lucky for Jones that the drunken assault removed him from the army), and needed to be led across hill country to a Welsh port. Fielding always admires women who can walk, instead of being tight-laced and townee, and though he tends to grumble at learned women he had evidently met a variety of them; he can forgive Mrs. Waters her Latin. She need not be more than thirty-six when she meets Tom, and the struggle has exposed her breasts, which it appears have lasted better than her face. She stops Tom from hunting for Northerton,

> earnestly entreating that he would accompany her to the town whither they had been directed. "As to the fellow's escape," said she, "it gives me no uneasiness; for philosophy and Christianity both preach up forgiveness of injuries. But for you, sir, I am concerned at the trouble I give you; nay, indeed, my nakedness may well make you ashamed to look me in the face; and if it were not for the sake of your protection, I would wish to go alone."

Jones offered her his coat; but, I know not for what reason, she absolutely refused the most earnest solicitation to accept it. He then begged her to forget both the causes of her confusion.

He walks before her all the way so as not to see her breasts, but she frequently asks him to turn and help her. The seduction is entirely free from any further designs on him; she is as foot-loose as a character in the *Faerie Queene*, though perhaps her happening to fall in with Fitzpatrick next morning at the Upton Inn is what saves Jones from finding her even a momentary responsibility. Even so, her capacity to handle Fitzpatrick is rather impressive; the only occupation of this gentleman is to hunt for the woman he cheated into marriage in the hope of bullying her out of what little of her money is secured from him by the law, after wasting the rest; one would hardly think he was worth milking, let alone the unpleasantness of his company, so that she had better have gone back to her officer. Perhaps she wanted to get to London; the only story about her is that she is independent. We are told at the end that she eventually married Parson Supple.

When Fielding says he doesn't know the reason he always means it is too complicated to explain. Walking with her lifesaver Jones she liked to appear pathetic, and she wanted to show her breasts, but also she really could not bear to let him take his coat off, not on such a cold night. The decision becomes a nuisance when they get to the inn because it makes her almost unacceptable, but this is got over; and she gathers from the landlady that Jones is in love with a younger woman.

The awkward behavior of Mr. Jones on this occasion convinced her of the truth, without his giving a direct answer to any of her questions; but she was not nice enough in her amours to be particularly concerned at the discovery. The beauty of Jones highly charmed her eye; but as she could not see his heart she gave herself no concern about it. She could feast heartily at the table of love, without reflecting that some other had been, or hereafter might be, feasted with the same repast. A sentiment which, if it deals but little in refinement, deals, however, much in substance; and is less capricious, and perhaps less ill-natured and selfish, than the desires of those females who can be contented enough to abstain from the possession of their lovers, provided that they are sufficiently satisfied that nobody else possesses them.

This seems to me a particularly massive bit of double irony, worthy to outlast the imperial eagles of the House of Austria, though I take it Fielding just believed what he said, and only knew at the back of his mind that the kind of man who would otherwise complain about it would presume it was irony.

Such is our main background information about Mrs. Waters when she visits him in prison, assures him that her supposed husband is recovering fast so that there is no question of murder, and is rather cross with him for refusing to make love to her. Then her entirely unexpected letter arrives, which I must give in full (XVIII.2):

> Sir—Since I left you I have seen a gentleman, from whom I have learned something concerning you which greatly surprises and affects me; but as I have not at present leisure to communicate a matter of such high importance, you must suspend your curiosity till our next meeting, which shall be the first moment I am able to see you. Oh, Mr. Jones, little did I think, when I passed that happy day at Upton, the reflection upon which is like to embitter all my future life, who it was to whom I owed such perfect happiness.—Believe me to be ever sincerely your unfortunate
>
> J. Waters.
>
> P.S.—I would have you comfort yourself as much as possible, for Mr. Fitzpatrick is in no manner of danger; so that, whatever other grievous crimes you may have to repent of, the guilt of blood is not among the number.

Partridge, who happened not to see Mrs. Waters at Upton, has seen her visit the prison and eavesdropped on her talk with Jones; so he has just horrified Jones by telling him she is his mother; they think this letter confirms the belief, and certainly it is hard to invent any other meaning. We are not told who the gentleman was till XVIII.8, when she tells Allworthy that the lawyer Dowling had visited her, and told her that

> if Mr. Jones had murdered my husband, I should be assisted with any money I wanted to carry on the prosecution, by a very worthy gentleman, who, he said, was well apprised what a villain I had to deal with. It was by this man I discovered who Mr. Jones was. . . . I discovered his name by a very odd accident; for he himself refused to tell it to me; but Partridge, who met him at my lodgings the second time he came, knew him formerly at Salisbury.

She assumed it was Allworthy who was persecuting Jones in this relentless manner, whereas Allworthy knows it must be Blifil, whom Dowling hopes to blackmail; and since she greatly revered Allworthy, though herself some kind of freethinker, she assumed that Jones had done something to deserve it—this explains the postscript "whatever other grievous crimes," "The second time" is an important detail; the second time Dowling came must have been after she wrote the letter, and was the first time Partridge came. As soon as Partridge saw her he would tell her Jones's fear of incest and she would dispel it; but Partridge has to come, to meet Dowling and

tell her his name (otherwise the plot of Blifil could not be exposed). We have next to consider how she knew, when she wrote
the letter, about the anger of Sophia; but Jones would tell her this
himself, when she visited him in prison, because he would feel he
had to offer a decent reason for refusing to go to bed with her. A
deep generosity, when she has thought things over after the
unpleasant talk with Dowling, is what makes her write down that if
Sophia refuses to marry Tom it will embitter all the rest of her life.
The delusion about incest is the kind of mistake which is always
likely if you interpret in selfish terms the remarks of a very unselfish
character. Certainly, the coincidences of the plot are rigged almost to
the point where we reject them unless we take them as ordained by
God; Fielding would be accustomed to hearing pious characters call
any bit of luck a wonderful proof of providence, and might hope
they would feel so about his plot—as Partridge encourages them to
do (e.g. XII.8). But the reaction of the character to the plot is not
rigged; she behaves as she always does.

I ought finally to say something about his attitude to the English
class system, because opinions about what he meant there seem
often to be decisive for the modern reader. What people found so
entertaining at the time, when Fielding attacked Richardson in a
rather explosive class situation (the eager readers of Richardson in
French were presumably heading toward the French Revolution)
was that the classes seemed to have swapped over. The printer's
apprentice was the gentlemanly expert on manners, indeed the first
English writer to be accepted as one by the polite French; whereas
if you went to see Fielding, they liked to say at the time, you would
find him drunk in bed with his cook and still boasting he was
related to the Hapsburgs. His answer to Richardson was thus: "But
I know what a gentleman is; I am one." The real difference was
about the meaning of the term; Fielding thought it should mean a
man fit to belong to the class which actually rules in his society,
especially by being a just judge. His behavior eventually made a lot
of people feel he had won the argument, though not till some time
after his death. To die poor and despised while attempting to
build up the obviously needed London Police Force, with obvious
courage and humanity, creating astonishment by his refusal to
accept the usual bribes for such dirty work, and leaving the job in
hands which continued it—this became too hard to laugh off; he
had done in the heart of London what empire-builders were being
revered for doing far away. He provided a new idea of the aristocrat,
with the added claim that it was an older tradition; and he did
seem to clear the subject up rather—you could hardly deny that he
was a better idea than Lord Chesterfield. An impression continued
that, if you are very rude and rough, that may mean you are particularly aristocratic, and good in an emergency; I doubt whether, with-

out Fielding, the Victorian novelists (however much they forbade their daughters to read his books) would have retained their trust in the rather hidden virtues of the aristocracy.

Much of this was wished onto Fielding later, but we have a series of jokes against the current idea of a gentleman during Tom's journey to London. The remarks in favor of the status are perhaps what need picking out. Tom leaves Old Man because he hears cries for help; he thus saves the life of Mrs. Waters from the villain Northerton, who might seem to justify the contempt for mankind of Old Man. This is at the beginning of Book IX; at the very end of it, after the reader has learned how bad the case is, Fielding urges him not to think he means to blame army officers in general:

> Thou wilt be pleased to consider that this fellow, as we have already informed thee, had neither the birth nor the education of a gentleman, nor was a proper person to be enrolled among the number of such. If, therefore, his baseness can justly reflect on any besides himself, it must be only on those who gave him his commission.

We learn incidentally, from this typical rounding on an administrator, that Fielding presumed men ought to be promoted to the ruling class, as a regular thing; the point is merely that the system of promotion should be adequate to save it from contempt. The exalted cynicism of Old Man (who by the way did not try to help Mrs. Waters, though he and not Tom had a gun) might make one suspect that adequate members of such a class cannot be found, and Fielding has kept in mind the social question of how you should do it. I have known readers think Fielding wanted to abolish gentlemen, and indeed the jokes against them are pretty fierce; but he had planted another remark at the beginning of Book IX, in the chapter of introductory prattle, which is clearly meant to fit the last words of that Book. An author needs to have experienced both low life and high life, he is saying; low life for honesty and sincerity; high life, dull and absurd though it is, for

> elegance, and a liberality of spirit; which last quality I have myself scarce ever seen in men of low birth and education.

The assertion seems moderate, perhaps hardly more than that most men don't feel free to look all round a question, unless their position is comfortable enough; but "liberality of spirit" feels rather near to the basic virtue of having good impulses. Of course, he does not mean that all gentlemen have it; the total egotism of young Blifil, a theoretically interesting case, with a breakdown into sadism, which critics have chosen to call unlifelike, is chiefly meant to make clear that they do not. But it seems mere fact that Fielding's society needed a governing class, however things may work out under universal education; so it is reasonable of him to take a reformist view, as the Communists would say, and merely recommend a better selection.

Indeed, it is perhaps flat to end this essay with an example which yields so placid a solution to a build-up of "double irony"; nor is it a prominent example, because after we get to London the ironies are about honor rather than gentility. But I suspect that today both halves of the puzzle about gentlemen are liable to work against him; he gets regarded as a coarse snob, whose jovial humor is intended to relax the laws only in favor of the privileged. This at least is unjust; no one attacked the injustices of privilege more fiercely. His position was not found placid at the time, and there is one class paradox which he repeatedly labored to drive home; though to judge from a survey of opinions on him (*Fielding the Novelist*, F. H. Blanchard, 1926) this line of defense never gave him any protection in his lifetime. "Only low people are afraid of having the low described to them, because only they are afraid of being exposed as themselves low." The paradox gives him a lot of powerful jokes, but so far from being farfetched it follows directly from his conception of a gentleman, which was if anything a literal-minded one. He means by it a person fit to sit on the bench as a magistrate, and naturally such a man needs to know all about the people he is to judge; indeed, the unusual thing about Fielding as a novelist is that he is always ready to consider what he would do if one of his characters came before him when he was on the bench. He is quite ready to hang a man, but also to reject the technical reasons for doing so if he decides that the man's impulses are not hopelessly corrupted. As to the reader of a novel, Fielding cannot be bothered with him unless he too is fit to sit on a magistrate's bench, prepared, in literature as in life, to handle and judge any situation. That is why the reader gets teased so frankly. The same kind of firmness, I think, is what makes the forgiveness by Tom at the end feel startling and yet sensible enough to be able to stand up to Allworthy. I think the chief reason why recent critics have belittled Fielding is that they find him intimidating.

WAYNE C. BOOTH

"Fielding" in Tom Jones†

It is frustrating to try to deal critically with [the effects of an author's intrusive comments], because they can in no way be demonstrated to the reader who has not experienced them. No amount of quotation, no amount of plot summary, can possibly show how

†From "Telling as Showing: Dramatized Narrators, Reliable and Unreliable," Chapter VIII of *The Rhetoric of Fiction* (Chicago: University of Chicago Press, 1961), pp. 94–96. Copyright 1961 by the University of Chicago Press. Reprinted by permission of the publisher.

fully the implied author's character dominates our reactions to the whole. About all we can do is to look closely at one work, *Tom Jones*, analyzing in static terms what in any successful reading is as sequential and dynamic as the action itself.[1]

Though the dramatized Fielding does serve to pull together many parts of *Tom Jones* that might otherwise seem disconnected, and though he serves dozens of other functions, from the standpoint of strict function he goes too far: much of his commentary relates to nothing but the reader and himself. If we really want to defend the book as art, we must somehow account for these "extraneous" elements. It is not difficult to do so, however, once we think of the effect of our intimacy on our attitude toward the book as a whole. If we read straight through all of the seemingly gratuitous appearances by the narrator, leaving out the story of Tom, we discover a running account of growing intimacy between the narrator and the reader, an account with a kind of plot of its own and a separate denouement. In the prefatory chapter to his final volume, the narrator makes this denouement explicit, suggesting a distinct interest in the "story" of his relationship with the reader. This interest certainly requires some explanation if we wish to claim that *Tom Jones* is a unified work of art and not half-novel, half-essay.

> We are now, reader, arrived at the last stage of our long journey. As we have, therefore, travelled together through so many pages, let us behave to one another like fellow-travellers in a stage-coach, who have passed several days in the company of each other; and who, notwithstanding any bickerings or little animosities which may have occurred on the road, generally make all up at last, and mount, for the last time, into their vehicle with cheerfulness and good-humour.

The farewell goes on for several paragraphs, and at times the bantering tone of much of the work is entirely abandoned. "And now, my friend, I take this opportunity (as I shall have no other) of heartily wishing thee well. If I have been an entertaining companion to thee, I promise thee it is what I have desired. If in anything I have offended, it was really without any intention."

It may be extravagant to use the term "subplot" for the story of our relationship with this narrator. Certainly the narrator's "life" and Tom Jones's life are much less closely parallel than we expect in most plots and subplots. In *Lear*, Gloucester's fate parallels and reinforces Lear's. In *Tom Jones*, the "plot" of our relationship with Fielding-as-narrator has no similarity to the story of Tom. There is no complication, not even any sequence except for the gradually increasing familiarity and intimacy leading to farewell. And much of

1. Perhaps the best defense of Fielding's commentary is that of A. D. McKillop, in *Early Masters of English Fiction* (Lawrence, Kan., 1956), esp. p. 123.

what we admire or enjoy in the narrator is in most respects quite different from what we like or enjoy in his hero.

Yet somehow a genuine harmony of the two dramatized elements is produced. It is from the narrator's norms that Tom departs when he gets himself into trouble, yet Tom is always in harmony with his most important norms. Not only does he reassure us constantly that Tom's heart is always in the right place, his presence reassures us of both the moral and the literary rightness of Tom's existence. As we move through the novel under his guidance, watching Tom sink to the depths, losing, as it appears, Allworthy's protection, Sophia's love, and his own shaky hold on decency, we experience for him what R. S. Crane has called the "comic analogue of fear." [2] And our growing intimacy with Fielding's dramatic version of himself produces a kind of comic analogue of the true believer's reliance on a benign providence in real life. It is not just that he promises a happy ending. In a fictional world that offers no single character who is both wise and good—even Allworthy, though all worthy, is no model of perspicacity—the author is always there on his platform to remind us, through his wisdom and benevolence, of what human life ought to be and might be. What is more, his self-portrait is of a life enriched by a vast knowledge of literary culture and of a mind of great creative power—qualities which could never be so fully conveyed through simply exercising them without comment on the dramatic materials of Tom's story.

For the reader who becomes too much aware of the author's claim to superlative virtues, the effect may fail. He may seem merely to be posing. For the reader with his mind on the main business, however, the narrator becomes a rich and provocative chorus. It is his wisdom and learning and benevolence that permeate the world of the book, set its comic tone between the extremes of sentimental indulgence and scornful indignation, and in a sense redeem Tom's world of hypocrites and fools.

One can imagine, perhaps, a higher standard of virtue, wisdom, or learning than the narrator's. But for most of us he succeeds in being the highest possible in his world—and, at least for the nonce, in ours. He is not trying to write for any other world, but for *this* one he strikes the precise medium between too much and too little piety, benevolence, learning, and worldly wisdom.[3] When he draws to the end of his farewell, then, at a time when we know we are to

2. *Critics and Criticism*, ed. R. S. Crane (Chicago, 1952), p. 637. [See p. 863, above—*Editor*.]

3. *Ibid.*, p. 652. William Empson gives a lively and convincing defense of Fielding's code and of the moral stature of *Tom Jones* in "*Tom Jones*," *Kenyon Review*, XX (Spring, 1958), 217–49. [See pp. 869–93, above—*Editor*.] Though Empson mars his case a bit by arriving "circuitously at what Fielding tells us plainly enough" (C. J. Rawson, "Professor Empson's *Tom Jones*," *Notes and Queries*, N.S., VI [November, 1959], 400), his statement is a valuable antidote to the oversimplifications which have been used in dismissing Fielding and his commentary.

lose him, and uses terms which inevitably move us across the barrier to death itself, we find, lying beneath our amusement at his playful mode of farewell, something of the same feeling we have when we lose a close friend, a friend who has given us a gift which we can never repay. The gift he leaves—his book—is himself, precisely himself. The author has created this self as he has written the book. The book and the friend are one. "For however short the period may be of my own performances, they will most probably outlive their own infirm author, and the weakly productions of his abusive contemporaries." Was Fielding literally infirm as he wrote that sentence? It matters not in the least. It is not Fielding we care about, but the narrator created to speak in his name.

LYALL H. POWERS

Tom Jones and Jacob de la Vallée†

The role of Marivaux in Anglo-French literary relations has been generally recognized: his connection with Richardson has received some close attention, but the influence of his novels on those of Fielding has been comparatively neglected.[1] The similarity between *Le Paysan parvenu* (1735) and *Joseph Andrews* has indeed been noted—after Fielding's encouragement in the opening chapter of Book III of that novel, where he mentions "the History of Marianne and le Paisan Parvenu." But the influence of Marivaux's novel on *Tom Jones* has barely been noticed. G.-E. Parfitt has observed that "Dans *Tom Jones* et *Joseph Andrews* on trouve les traits qui peuvent bien venir du *Paysan Parvenu*, car, des deux romans de Marivaux, celui-ci est évidemment le plus rapproché de l'esprit et du sujet des romans de Fielding."[2] And he adds a brief general comparison of Tom and Jacob de la Vallée. The striking similarity between these two heroes, which Parfitt merely touches on, encourages closer examination and invites us to consider Fielding's use of Marivaux's novel. We recall the passage in the introductory chapter of Book XIII of *Tom Jones*: "Come, thou that hast inspired thy Aristophanes, thy Lucian, thy Cervantes, thy Rabelais,

†From *Papers of the Michigan Academy of Science, Arts, and Letters*, 47 (1962), 659–67. Copyright 1962. Reprinted by permission of the Michigan Academy of Science, Arts, and Letters.

1. See, for example, Joseph Texte, *Jean-Jacques Rousseau et les origines du cosmopolitisme littéraire* (Paris, 1895), chap. III; and the unpublished dissertation of Sidney E. Glenn, "Some French Influences on Henry Fielding," Urbana, Illinois, 1932. See also F. C. Green, *Minuet*, London, 1935, and Alan D. McKillop, *Samuel Richardson*, Chapel Hill, 1936.

2. *L'Influence française dans les oeuvres de Fielding et dans le théâtre contemporain de ses comédies* (Paris, 1928), p. 120.

thy Molière, thy Shakespeare, thy Swift, thy Marivaux, fill my page with humour; till mankind learn the good-nature to laugh only at the folly of others, and the humility to grieve at their own."[3]

There are first, of course, certain obvious differences between these two novels of the picaresque tradition: *Le Paysan parvenu* is first-person narration, *Tom Jones* is third-person—and the narrative is regularly interrupted by generous comments in the author's own person; Jacob is nearly twenty when his career begins, while we know Tom almost before he is born, and it takes Fielding one-sixth of his novel to bring Tom to the age of Jacob. One important reason for Fielding's slowness in this is that he must set out all the various strands of his intricate plot before he can well start Tom on his way. The plot itself is another obvious difference between the novels: that of *Le Paysan* is rather severely simple, while that of *Tom Jones* is ingeniously complex.[4]

Perhaps the initial similarity to be noted is the generally humanistic attitude of Marivaux and Fielding in their handling of the question of good and evil as it affects their respective heroes. Fielding's benevolist treatment of Tom Jones is much like Marivaux's conception of Jacob as an *honnête homme*. In both cases the basis of judgment seems to be a humanistic ethic rather than religion. Indeed, as Oscar Haac has recently pointed out, Marivaux's "conception of *honnêteté* is like a religion which advocates the ideals of humility, kindness, and human understanding"—"a lay substitute for the Christian ideal of the gentleman."[5] In refusing the place offered him by his benefactor, M. de Fécour, in favor of the ailing Dorville, Jacob de la Vallée says, virtually, I am doing unto another as I would he do unto me.[6] Both heroes are guided through their adventures by a sort of instinctive goodness. Jacob regularly insists that his actions are motivated by natural promptings. In speaking of the mistress of his first conquest, Geneviève, Jacob explains his interested reaction in this way (I quote from the 1735 English translation):

> The *Doeux Yeux* of a Man of the *Beau Monde*, have nothing of Novelty for a polite Woman; ...
> But this was not my Case; for my Looks had nothing of Gallantry in them, nor had they any Notion of a Compliment. I was a Peasant, young and Handsome withall, and the Homage I paid her Charms, proceeded from nothing but the pure Pleasure I

3. *Tom Jones*, Modern Library; all quotations are from this edition, and subsequent references to book and chapter are given in the text.
4. See R. S. Crane, "The Plot of *Tom Jones*," *Journal of General Education*,

IV (1949–50), 112–130. [See pp. 844–69, above—*Editor*.]
5. "Marivaux and the *Honnete Homme*," *Romanic Review*, L (Dec. 1959), 266.
6. See *Le Paysan parvenu*, Classiques Garniers, p. 220.

took in seeing them. My Rusticity was void of dissimulation, and was only the greatest Flatterer by its not knowing how to flatter at all.[7]

Fielding describes what is essentially the same characteristic in his Tom Jones this way: "Mr. Jones had somewhat about him, which, though I think writers are not thoroughly agreed in its name, doth certainly inhabit some human breasts; whose use is not so properly to distinguish right from wrong, as to prompt and incite them to the former, and to restrain and withhold them from the latter" (IV, vi). Indeed, both Jacob and Tom participate to some extent in the ideal of the noble savage: that is to say, they are both young men of the natural countryside who are initially uncorrupted by the taints of modern civilization, and particularly free of hypocrisy. Marivaux insists more often on this characteristic of his hero than does Fielding, but the characteristic is not the less apparent in Jones for all that.

The instinctive tendency to do good guides the respective heroes through the list of adventures that comprise their respective novels, and this benevolent tendency is rewarded (suitably, as the reader is made to feel) at the conclusion of each novel. Both novels are, of course, success stories: in both, the hero passes through a series of adventures that brings him gradually nearer to his goal. In both instances the reader feels all along that the hero deserves a fair reward, but he is likewise pleased to see that as the hero progresses through the chain of experiences he is gradually rendered more fit to enjoy that reward. And it is in the style of presentation of that series of improving experiences that the novel of Fielding seems to indicate most clearly its debt to *Le Paysan parvenu*.

The method of development employed by Marivaux is summed up well enough for our purposes by an early editor of *Le Paysan parvenu*, Duviquet:

> En nous montrant un paysan marchant à la fortune, grâce à la bonne opinion que sa tournure inspire aux femmes, Marivaux a voulu faire passer son héros par toutes les modifications de ce qu'on appelle *amour*.[8]

The history of Jacob is a series of encounters with women who are attracted by his masculinity, and who contribute to his final success. Tom Jones is equally a favorite with the ladies, and his history is likewise punctuated by the intervention of various women who are attracted to him. If he does not pass through precisely the same graduated scale of amorous adventures that Jacob does, Tom Jones does experience three social levels of his world through their respec-

7. *Le Paysan Parvenu: or, the Fortunate Peasant. Being Memoirs of the Life of Mr. ——*. Translated from the French of M. de Marivaux (London, 1735), p. 16.

8. *Le Paysan parvenu, Oeuvres Complètes de Marivaux* (Paris, 1825–27), VIII, 45, note 1.

tive representatives, Molly Seagrim, Mrs. Waters, and Lady Bellaston, a series which is similar to Jacob's correspondents—Geneviève, Mme de Fécour, Mme de Ferval. Tom's career is, of course, something more than an *éducation sentimentale*, yet this aspect of his development is interestingly similar to Jacob's; and in any case, the heroes' stages of development are in both novels marked off by these amatory affairs. In comparing this aspect of the two novels we shall see most clearly the probable echoes of the French one in the English.

As the heroes pass along the series of "affairs" there is the constant question of their fidelity: as Jacob generously shares his favors with the various women he encounters, there is the shadow of Mlle Habert always in the background; and as Jones entertains the women he meets, there is at his back the shadow of Sophia. There is an important difference here, of course, which we shall consider more fully in a moment: Jacob de la Vallée is actually married to la Habert, while Tom Jones is not even engaged to Sophia —this is a difference which cannot but mitigate our condemnation of Tom's "infidelity." Nevertheless, in both novels it is the female figure at the heroes' back that makes them suffer pangs of conscience as they pursue their various escapades.

The initial liaison in both novels is entered before the hero is quite aware of the woman to whom he is to owe responsibility. Jacob's first real conquest is the unfortunate Geneviève, who wants to help him make his fortune in a way he cannot accept. Tom's first love is the earthy Molly Seagrim. These two girls are of about the same social standing, a good step beneath their successors in the life of the respective heroes. For both heroes the next woman encountered is she to whom they are to feel responsible during their subsequent careers with the obliging ladies. Beyond this, Mlle Habert and Sophia Western have little of importance in common. Their situations, however, are similar enough, as we see in comparing the roles of Mlle Habert *aînée* and Mrs. Western: these two furies, in their stout opposition to the respective heroes, contribute considerably to the discomfort of Mlle Habert *cadette* and of Sophia.

Both heroes, then, have been supplied with similar goads for their conscience as they set out on their other conquests. Jacob immediately wins the hearts of Mme d'Alain and her daughter, Agathe. Nothing of a serious nature can develop in that situation, for Mlle Habert is too near at hand. But these two serve to emphasize the idea of Jacob's attractiveness. As Mlle Habert *aînée* attempts to make trouble for Jacob by having him summoned before M. le Président, Jacob again gives evidence of his attractiveness for the fair sex as he at once wins to his side both la Présidente and Mme de Ferval. The latter plays an important role in the novel as she is the woman with whom Jacob is to become most deeply involved, and who comes closest to causing him serious trouble: while he is keeping a rendezvous with her, Jacob is interrupted by the Chevalier, who remembers him from the country and who might possibly expose him to society. Mme de Ferval appears in the least favorable light of any of the women who figure in Jacob's illicit affairs: she is actually a friend of the woman whom she is helping Jacob to deceive. Her value to Jacob is that she gives him money. Through la Ferval Jacob is enabled to meet and impress the lusty Mme de Fécour. This appealing creature— *à la gorge furieuse*—is perhaps the most likable of the women in Jacob's series of affairs. She is in many ways his female counterpart. Mme de Fécour is, with Jacob himself, the character who most clearly points ahead to the style of Fielding. She is a sort of embodiment of the attitude to love which is characteristic of the best of Fielding. Here is Jacob's sketch of her:

> Directly I saw a pretty fat Woman enter the Room, of a moderate Stature, but with one of the most furious Bosoms I had ever beheld; she seem'd otherwise a Woman without Ceremony, and at first sight a lover of Pleasure. . . .
> Mrs. Fecour was about three or four Years younger than Mrs. Ferval, I believe she had been handsome in her Youth; but what was now most observable in her Countenance, was a frank Cordial Air, which made it very agreeable to look at.
> . . . to which you may add a hale robust Look, a certain amiable Freshness of Complexion. . . .
> . . . it was one of her peculiar Qualities not so much as to know what Affectation meant.
> For example, if she lik'd you, this Bosom which I spoke of, was display'd to you a thousand different Ways, not so much with an Intention to tempt your Heart, as so to let you know that you had touch'd her's [*sic*]; it was her manner of declaring Love.
> (pp. 233–234)

Her association with Jacob consists rather in the promise of amorous joy than in the actual realization of it, but she takes her place in the series just the same.

The two women Jones first encounters after he has set out on his career are Mrs. Waters and Lady Bellaston. The resemblance of these two to Mme de Fécour is perhaps not obvious, yet Mrs. Waters' attitude to Tom is much like la Fécour's to Jacob: her amorous dalliance with Tom for the pure natural joy of it is quite what we should expect from *la dame à la gorge furieuse* (and it is to be remembered that the *gorge assez furieuse* of Mrs. Waters has its own rather important little role in the opening pages of the ninth book of *Tom Jones*). And Lady Bellaston shares many traits with her French predecessor, Mme de Ferval. Like la Ferval she is a woman of a certain age, perhaps just past her prime but still very attractive and a widow—or at least a woman who no longer has a husband. Lady Bellaston's relationship to the woman to whom the hero feels he is being untrue is even closer than the corresponding relationship of Mme de Ferval to Mlle Habert. And as la Ferval had supplied Jacob with gifts of money, so does Lady Bellaston supply Tom Jones. It is with her that Tom's dalliance leads him the farthest—he is reduced to proposing marriage in order to free himself, and this proposal almost proves to be his ultimate undoing, later on—and it is his affair with Lady Bellaston that comes closest to preventing him from gaining his ultimate reward, Sophia Western.

Tom Jones's relationship with Mrs. Miller, his landlady in London, and with her daughter Nancy recalls Jacob's situation with Mme d'Alain and her daughter. The attitude of Mrs. Miller is rather more sober than that of Mme d'Alain, but the initial attitude of Nancy is not much different from that of Agathe. But as far as functional value is concerned, the role of the Miller family in Fielding's novel more nearly follows that of the Dorvilles in Marivaux's. Jacob's generous *honnêteté* in his behavior to the Dorvilles gains their favor, but, furthermore, his association with them leads to his meeting the highly placed Comte de Dorsan and, apparently, to his ultimate success. Fielding's development is similar: Tom Jones's generosity to the Millers—and especially to Nancy—wins him their admiration, and they are instrumental in effecting his reconciliation with Squire Allworthy and gaining his ultimate reward, Sophia.

There are other, incidental similarities, such as the lengthy digressions in both novels: in *Le Paysan parvenu* the story of *le plaideur* told en route to Versailles, and Mme de Dorville's story of her encounter with the wolf; in *Tom Jones* we have the story of the Quaker, the long episode of the Man of the Hill, and the history of Mrs. Fitzpatrick. In both novels, all of these digressions serve as oblique commentary on the main fable: all have to do with unfortunate or loveless unions. There is, too, a reminiscence of the friendship of Jacob and Dorsan in Tom's friendship with Nightingale (the former associated with the Dorvilles, the latter associated with the Millers).

But we cannot pursue the parallels beyond Jacob's taking up with Dorsan, for this is as far as Marivaux leads his hero on the road to success. At the end of the fifth part Jacob seems comfortably set with his new friend and protector, yet he has not achieved that conclusive success the reader had hoped for and, indeed, been led to expect. Yet Fielding might well have perceived, as any sensitive reader can perceive, the direction in which the motives of the first five parts of Marivaux's novel were directing Jacob. His amorous education in manners has led Jacob a good distance, and in his reaction to the delightful Mme de Dorville we see a nobler refinement of sensibility. By the middle of the fifth part we are warned that Mme de la Vallée is not to live much longer; and, as scholars have pointed out, the continuation of Marivaux's novel through three additional parts seems to have followed with some faithfulness the expectations created in the first five: it seems logical that Jacob, safely widowed, should ultimately gain the hand of someone like the charming Mme de Vambures.

Whether, as it would appear, Marivaux's intention was precisely of that sort or not, the main lines of Jacob's career are established, and upon them Fielding seems to have relied to some considerable extent in fashioning the history of Tom Jones. Furthermore, the dramatic situations, the characters themselves, and the general attitude of Fielding's novel are strongly reminiscent of Marivaux's. In the treatment of the series of amatory adventures, both authors have attempted to excuse somewhat their respective heroes: not only do both distinguish nicely between the sentiment or passion that attracts the hero to the various "other" women, and the sentiment of true love; they both make it clear that in every case it is the "other" woman who is the aggressor and the hero the passive (though not unwilling) partner, so to speak. It is precisely here, however, in the handling of the question of infidelity, that the marked difference between the two novels is most noticeable—here that the originality and power of Henry Fielding most clearly emerge. The important differences in treatment are these: (1) that Jacob is a married man while Tom is a bachelor; (2) that Jacob's extramarital affairs are, in the narrow sense of the term, virtually chaste while Tom's affairs are manifestly not; and (3) that the figure to whom Jacob owes responsibility and who is therefore his prick of conscience (Mlle Habert) and the figure who would represent his ultimate reward (not yet created in the first five books) are combined by Fielding into the single character Sophia Western.

Now it would seem, at first glance, that Marivaux's arrangement gives him the advantage: Jacob's comparative chastity in his affairs makes the reader less liable to condemn him for libertinage; and furthermore, the satisfaction of Jacob's and the reader's expectations is but slightly postponed, for Jacob dutifully returns after his adventures to be engulfed by the eager limbs of the uxorious Habert. And for his dutiful attention to la Habert during his *éducation sentimentale*, we would agree that Jacob at last deserves to be rewarded with some true-love. But at second glance it becomes apparent that the advantage is really Fielding's: by keeping his hero a bachelor Fielding has to some considerable extent removed the stain of infidelity from Tom Jones; Tom of course feels guilty about his affairs, feels he is being unfaithful to his Sophie, but his infidelity (as he feels it) is in part a result of his despair, and at least Tom is legally free. In any case, Tom has a rather acceptable quasi-chivalric explanation for his behavior. Fielding writes (XIII, vii): "Jones had never less inclination to an amour than at present [the masquerade at which he hoped for a last interview with his Sophie]; but gallantry to the ladies was among his principles of honour, and he held it as much incumbent on him to accept a challenge to love as if it had been a challenge to fight." (This point is well argued in an essay by William Empson, who feels that in Tom's love affairs we have a good example of what he calls Fielding's doctrine of mutuality of impulse —"evidently the secret message which Fielding boasts of in *Tom Jones*." [9]) It is true that Jacob, like Tom, is regularly the passive partner; yet we feel strongly that Jacob is "on the make"—ready to take advantage of amorous ladies for the joy of it, yes, but principally for the advancement they may afford him.

But most important of all, surely, is Fielding's decision to unite in Sophia Western the functions of Marivaux's Mlle Habert and whoever would have been Jacob's final reward. As William Blake would certainly object to Jacob's *dutiful* attention to his wife, so to some extent must we. Jacob's regular return to Mlle Habert, his dutifulness, is unmistakably tinged with reluctance: [1] his fidelity is not inspired by true love, and it is quite apparent that his ultimate goal consistently lies beyond. The arrangement of Tom's situation is much more effective: his conscience is pricked by the figure of his Sophie, his duty to her is self-imposed and inspired by the sincerest love. How much better that the figure to whom he feels his duty is owing and the figure who is his ultimate goal and reward are one and the same!

I should conclude, then, that Fielding apparently saw in Marivaux's *Le Paysan parvenu* a reasonable and useful basic pattern for the instructive story of a young man's learning wisdom or prudence —much as he later found in the *Aeneid* a useful pattern for his *Amelia*. The main lines of Tom Jones's career follow rather closely those of Jacob de la Vallée's, but Fielding was interested, finally, in something more than a sort of *éducation sentimentale*: Tom indeed has his reward in the lovely Sophia, but he has gained something

9. "*Tom Jones*," *Kenyon Review*, XX (Spring, 1958), 217–249, esp. 224–226; quotation is from p. 226. [See pp. 869–93, above, especially p. 876—*Editor*.]
1. See for example Jacob's own expression of his attitude:
  "Revenons. Je m'en retourne enfin chez moi; je vais retrouver madame de La Vallée qui m'aimait tant. . . .
  "Je crois pourtant que je l'aurais aimée davantage si je n'avais été que

son amant (j'appelle aimer d'amour); mais quand on a d'aussi grandes obligations à une femme, en vérité, ce n'est pas avec de l'amour qu'un bon coeur les acquitte; il se pénètre de sentiments plus sérieux; il sent de l'amitié et *de la reconnaissance*; aussi en étais-je plein, et je pense que *l'amour en souffrait un peu*" (p. 259; my italics).

more even than this exceedingly well-named lady—he has gained
that necessary *sophia* we all wished him to have, that wise prudence
that makes him a full man. He has not, perhaps, gained that *hagia
sophia* won by the good Captain Booth of the later *Amelia*; but
Tom's wisdom, his prudence, is of an eminently practical sort and
his education has achieved a kind of perfection.

KENNETH REXROTH

Tom Jones†

Tom Jones has been compared to Ulysses and Huck Finn. Huck
he somewhat resembles; Ulysses not at all. He is more like a compound of Don Quixote and Sancho Panza, not a mixture but a
chemical compound of antagonistic qualities and virtues which has
produced a new being. You do not read far in the novel before you
become aware that Henry Fielding is constructing a character to
demonstrate a thesis. He is not preaching; Tom is not a dummy or
a stereotype on which proofs are hung like clothes. On the contrary,
the thesis is precisely his humanity, but Fielding's is a special vision
of man, common enough now, especially in America, but strange to
English fiction in his day.

If the novel were simply the portrayal of an ideal human type it
would have soon become unreadable. It is, of course, an immense
panorama of mid-eighteenth-century England, as populous as any
novel of Tolstoy's or Dostoevsky's. Comparison, however, with a
work like *War and Peace* immediately reveals a profound difference.
The plot of *Tom Jones* is not a "real life" story but a fairy tale, a
Märchen, disguised with realism. Nor are the subsidiary characters
fleshed out like the minor characters of the major Russian novelists.
Fielding carefully subordinates all other characters to Tom and
Sophie in a graded series of realizations. The nearer and more
important they are to the principals, the more complex they are,
but they are never very complex.

Blifil and Squire Allworthy are scarcely more rounded than the
characters of Ben Jonson's Theater of Humours. The minor figures
are reduced to bare essentials, quickly drawn stereotypes. The fairy-
tale plot is spun out and complicated endlessly, but it never becomes complex. Its situations are simple. They are pervaded with
a mocking double irony by the ambiguous comments of the omniscient author; the relations between the characters constantly lapse

†From *The Saturday Review*, 1 July
1967, p. 13. Copyright 1967 by Kenneth
Rexroth. Reprinted by permission of the
author.

—the double point of his double irony—is that it is precisely such personal historians who should make such admissions. Ultimately, the decorum of Brechtian alienation is a judgment on real, undecorous life.

The blubbery self-revelations of Richardson's novels, says Fielding, are lies. He would doubtless consider those of Proust or James lifelong evasions on the part of their authors. What he thought of the novel of objective revelation of character, of Defoe and his descendants, I do not know. The evidence is that Tom himself is patterned on Defoe—but the other characters not. Defoe, however, wrote false documents—novels presented as actual memoirs. Fielding did the opposite. As the novel approaches the conviction of reality Fielding always pulls the reader back—"this is not real." What is not real? Our judgments of "real life"? This is the essence of his irony. The omniscient author hoaxes the reader into believing *he* is omniscient and then pulls the throne from under him. Richardson, James, and Proust, on the other hand, really believed they had revealed the essences of human behavior.

Tom Jones is Fielding's conception of optimum man—but seen entirely from the outside. You feel, reflecting on the novel after long familiarity, that his imperviousness to probing and disinterestedness in self-probing was, to Fielding, an essential part of the optimum. Behind Rousseau's new and revolutionary concept of man at his best lies the inward-turning eye of Descartes's *cogito ergo sum.* Behind Fielding's Tom lies the clear and definite external sense data of John Locke, but he is an equally revolutionary type of person. Out of one came the endless self-questioning, Continental, radical, intellectual. Out of the other came the active, pragmatic man of whom Jefferson is probably the best exemplar—if the truth be told, a man who probably resembled Tom in more ways than one.

SHERIDAN BAKER

Bridget Allworthy: The Creative Pressures of Fielding's Plot†

R. S. Crane's essay will probably stand as the most comprehensive analysis of the famous plot of *Tom Jones.* Yet Eleanor Hutchens's recent book may remind us that Crane has slighted something: the pervasive irony of Fielding's storytelling. Indeed, Crane's

†From *Papers of the Michigan Academy of Science, Arts, and Letters,* 52 (1967), 345–56. Copyright 1967. Reprinted by permission of the Michigan Academy of Science, Arts, and Letters.

into farce. All this gives the book an air of quiet madness—
seen in an imperceptibly warped mirror or through a telescop
an abnormally sharp definition, the clarity and distortion of m

The plot and the thesis are one: Tom is that universal he
folk tale and myth—the foundling prince, the king's son raise
wolves, Moses in the bullrushes, whose princely qualities shine
in all his acts and eventually determine events so that his true h
tage is revealed. Fielding is defining a gentleman. The fact tl
many of the characters are as well or better born than Tom do
not disturb the logic. They are the bad aristocrats. He is a natur;
gentleman—but not a noble savage, rather a noble fallen among sav
ages; a savage noble, actually not a noble but a gentleman, quite
a different concept from Rousseau's.

There is hardly an episode that does not demonstrate Tom's gentlemanliness. Fielding defines gentlemanliness as generosity of soul.
Sin he may, but always for others' good. His relations with women
are always motivated by the desire to please or help. When he is
seduced by an old rip like Mrs. Waters, he responds with gratitude
—the reaction of a generous man to generosity. This response over-
whelms Mrs. Waters, and she responds at the crucial moment with
a generosity that literally saves Tom's life.

Tom is the Good-Natured Man, but by this Fielding means more
than his contemporaries meant by the eighteenth-century catch
phrase—something very like the "human-heartedness" of Confu-
cius. Several times Fielding interpolates little lectures on good
nature that sound exactly like translations from the Chinese. Tom
is very much the typical Chinese hero, and the novel could easily be
restated in Chinese terms and setting. Not least of its Chinese characteristics is its decorum. Fielding wrote *Tom Jones* against the
lachrymose soul-probing of Richardson's heroines, as a protest
against bad manners.

Fielding has been criticized again and again by a psychologistic
age for his characters' total lack of interiority. Whenever they so
much as reflect, the omniscient author makes fun of them and
always points out that they are deluding themselves. This is part of
the thesis—actions speak louder than words, and words than
thoughts, especially about oneself.

When his characters become unruly—when they violate his special concept of the etiquette of human-heartedness—Fielding
intrudes and admits that they are creations of his imagination and
he can make them do as he wishes (and then usually comments
that they have taken on a certain autonomy that escapes his control). This horrified Henry James, who considered it artistic treason
and said he would be no more shocked to find such admissions in
the histories of Gibbon and Macaulay. Of course Fielding's point

whole definition of plot, broadened from Aristotle as it is, now
appears both too broad and too narrow, confusing our two loosely
overlapped and undifferentiated notions of plot: (1) plot as everything that happens, (2) plot as the story's limited evidence for everything that happens.[1] The first is the story's life, fully understood
as to motives, causes, and effects; the second is disclosure, selection,
arrangement, concealment, and revelation. The first is story; the
second, storytelling. The first, I would call plot; the second, plotting.

And somewhere between these two contrary commitments—to
the facts of life and to their slow suggestion and partial disclosure
—the author produces character: the *human* interest, as it were.
Indeed, W. J. Harvey has recently challenged as inapplicable to the
novel the whole Aristotelian emphasis on plot, arguing that the primarily mythical force of plot has given ground to an interest in individuals, in non-mythic and even eccentric human personality.[2]
Whether the author starts with a person or a predicament, his plotting inevitably bestirs a meditation on the way people are and how
they act. Every stroke of his evidence is a stroke on some portrait
we must finally judge believable or factitious, as he shows us happenings, guides or misguides our interpretations of them, and guides
or misguides our attitudes toward the actor.[3]

Both plot and the author's plotting, then, add strokes to the final
portrait, and frequently from opposite directions, a process admirably illustrated by Fielding's Bridget Allworthy. Bridget has been
treated as little more than a cipher in Fielding's total, or, at best, as
a quaint type, hardly part of the action though the origin of it. She
seems almost a pure necessity of the plot and the plotting, but she
also stands as a supreme example of how plot generates character, as
the nearly fabulous story strains against the necessities of plotting a
realistic mystery and a moral education. The conflicting demands
produce in her something like the authentic conflicts and ambigui-

1. "The Plot of *Tom Jones*," *The Jour-nal of General Education*, IV (1950), 112–130 [see pp. 844–869, above—*Editor*]; *Irony in Tom Jones* (University of Alabama Press, 1965). Crane expands Aristotle's "plot" to include "character" and "thought," the next two of Aristo-tle's six ingredients of tragedy (*Poetics*, VI). To this, Crane then adds another kind of plot: a network of the reader's desires for and against the fortunes of the characters. Crane is speaking, in other words, of plot as happenings and plot as narration of happenings. But he does not pursue the distinction, and he soon so broadens "plot" as to equal vir-tually everything about the work and its effects—a surprising monism in so doughty an Aristotelian (see his "Cleanth Brooks; or, the Bankruptcy of

Critical Monism," *MP*, XLV [1947–48], 226–245). His term "form" is equally nonspecific, nonliteral, nonspatial, and fuzzy: form is a "capacity" to move us (not *has* a capacity, but *is*); form is a "working or power," a "final end" that everything must serve if the work is to be felt as a whole, a "first principle," and, finally, little more than a synonym for *kind*: "... a novel similar in form to ... *Amelia*, that is to say, a tragi-comedy of common life ..." (pp. 115, 116). All this is very like saying "the form of this jello is strawberry."
2. *Character and the Novel* (Cornell University Press, 1965), pp. 23–24.
3. I am happy to acknowledge my share in our general debt to Wayne C. Booth's *The Rhetoric of Fiction* (University of Chicago Press, 1961).

ties of human personality. Indeed, something of Fielding's pleasure in surmounting tactical difficulties accrues as living energy to Bridget's personality. In her, we can see the remarkable depth of character to be glimpsed throughout Fielding's great book in what has sometimes seemed only a brilliant art of surfaces.[4]

Bridget is a remarkable creation. She does not strike us immediately as thoroughly lifelike or even perhaps as a completely consistent characterization, as do such equivalent minor characters as Jane Austen's Mrs. Bennet, let us say. She seems at first a mere type, moved around as occasion variously demands. But on closer inspection, she proves breathtakingly lifelike, with surprising Freudian authenticities, and with enough vigor among seeming inconsistencies to suggest that if we knew her thoroughly she would seem thoroughly authentic, a unique individual yet thoroughly representative of the several typical roles life has put upon her. Necessity has produced this remarkable invention of a mother—the necessities of both plot and plotting. Bridget perhaps stands as the supreme example of characterization as a product of what Miss Hutchens calls Fielding's ironic and "lawyerlike delight in making facts add up to the unexpected." Fielding's external presentation is, as Miss Hutchens suggests, a network of the ironies of evidence, in which, as in court, people report the same facts differently, and the facts that seem to mean one thing may actually mean its opposite (p. 30). And the personality of Bridget Allworthy emerges from the conflicting evidence.

Fielding's plot and his telling of it require of Bridget two opposite kinds of character. The plot demands a passionate, lonely woman, *tendre-herted, slydynge of corage*. The telling—that is, the concealment of the plot—requires a comic old maid, above suspicion. The ancient formula of romance—which Fielding's readers would immediately recognize and anticipate, from the moment of the foundling's discovery—requires that the mysterious infant be of high birth. He must somehow prove to be the offspring of the most noble man in the book, but that man is too noble to produce incidental offspring, as Fielding immediately tells us. The squire's sister, the second character we meet, must be the actual mother, so that Jones's natural nobility of character may in the end prove, though illegitimate, authentically Allworthian after all. The noble scullion must prove to be the king's son, or the genetic mystery remains unsolved, in spite of the 18th century's admiration of natural noble savages, and unfulfilled the deep psychic need to discover as noble the parents of one's dreams.

But the telling of this story requires that the reader be immedi-

4. Miss Hutchens has already pointed out how Fielding silently lets the evidence indicate inescapable conclusions as to actions and motives in Captain Blifil's betrayal of his brother and Dowling's blackmailing of young Blifil (pp. 41–42).

ately and completely put off, or he will read the later evidence aright, see through the mystery too soon, and spoil the story. Hence the comic old maid. And the personality of Bridget Allworthy emerges as Fielding accumulates his evidence, moving from facts appropriate to the old maid toward those appropriate to the amorous lady she is indeed, beneath the surface. In this double game of deception and characterization, Fielding appropriates with literally dazzling effect type-characterizations he had acquired from standard theatrical stock for his own plays, ones he had already tried out in *Joseph Andrews* as Mrs. Slipslop and Lady Booby. To the Old Maid, he adds the Learned Lady and the Amorous Matron.[5] The Old Maid—unattractive, sour, hostile to beauty as an enemy of virginity—soon reveals herself as a Learned Lady too: her theological discussions lead first to marriage with Captain Blifil then to intellectual contempt for him, both attitudes demanded by the plot. Soon she shows all the symptoms of the Amorous Matron—of whom Congreve's Lady Wishfort is perhaps the archetype—a lady, in Fielding's books, usually married or widowed (as Bridget in natural fact is), moved to sexual indiscretion with younger men by the weight of about 40 winters.

These types in themselves work powerfully to conceal Fielding's plot, even for the modern reader. Their added strength for Fielding's well-acquainted audience probably about equals his audience's stronger assumptions of nobility in the mysterious foundling. All readers take these phases of Bridget's disclosure as mere portraits of types, comic pictures of human foibles for our amusement, which we think we understand thoroughly as we turn away in laughter without further inquiry. But the laugh is on us, and we eventually take pleasure at our own expense because we have agreed to be fooled by sitting down before our storyteller. These mere glimpses of types that have shut off further vision are really signs of a deeper consistency of personality.

After Bridget's bargain with Jenny Jones has successfully excluded suspicion, Fielding can safely give us the evidence, in increasingly audacious doses, that we are observing without fully knowing it a passionate woman whom plainness and social station have made play the prude, and whom desperate necessity has made duplicitous. From the first, what we take as amusing evidence of the Old Maid actually points to a subtler personality, one that is concealing both a past illegitimacy and further erotic longings. She is extremely discreet; she protests loudly against beauty as a sure road to ruin; she listens to juicy details at the keyhole to her brother's courtroom.

In summary, then, the plot demands an illegitimate child; illegiti-

5. See my unpublished dissertation, "Setting, Character, and Situation in the Plays and Novels by Henry Fielding" (University of California, Berkeley, 1950), pp. 255–261.

macy requires a certain waywardness; and, on the other hand, the plotting requires a prudish old maid. Fielding consistently reconciles these two opposites even in the earliest of the actions we are ever to learn of Bridget: those concerning her affair with Summer. But first we must face the question of why Fielding did not have Jones turn out legitimate in the end, which would have made many readers more comfortable—and would have made Bridget's character incidentally more conventional, and a good deal less subtle, less interesting, and even, oddly, less authentic. The answer, I think, is simple. Fielding could not have had Bridget marry Summer in secret because, on his sudden death, she would have revealed the marriage under pressure of her pregnancy, and the story would have been over before it had begun. Latterly, Jones must be illegitimate also to give Dowling an excuse for keeping quiet—namely, that Allworthy wants his sister's shame kept quiet. So the initial plot demands of Bridget a personality both wayward and deceptive.

Fielding must now devise a situation that will prevent Bridget's marriage, and a personality to match both this initial situation and what we are to see of her actions later. Allworthy's generosity, his willingness to go along with her later secret marriage to Captain Blifil, complicates the initial probabilities. Looking back, Allworthy remembers thinking that his sister "had some liking to" Mr. Summer:

> I mentioned it to her; for I had such a regard to the young man, as well on his own account as on his father's, that I should willingly have consented to a match between them; but she expressed the highest disdain of my unkind suspicion, as she called it; so that I never spoke more on the subject. (XVIII.vii)

Here we can see Fielding, at the end of his book, marvelously rationalizing from the typical Old Maid, whom his initial deception demanded, and deriving from the situation some curious depths of personality. Is Bridget's high disdain habitual, or a deliberate deception, or an embarrassed reaction? We do not know, but it could well and plausibly spring partially from all three, and the range of plausibilities expands and authenticates her personality.

She has reason to be uneasy about her love for Summer. First, he is about 20 years her junior, as we infer from Bridget's fortyish age at Tom's birth and from what we learn of Summer. He was just out of the university, with no fortune nor position of his own. Second, he has been raised in her brother's (and her) house almost "as if he had been your own [Allworthy's] son." Bridget, then, is virtually his aunt, and the comically echoed incest at the climax of the book echoes here with a certain Freudian impact, and is to echo again with Summer's son Tom (as Miss Hutchens has pointed out,

p. 40). Bridget has reason to be touchy about her affection for Summer, however early or late in its progress; and her touchy answer to Allworthy effectively shuts off what chances she had, before Summer's death loses them forever. Thus Bridget's standard Old-Maidish answer becomes the sign for an inner agony; she has answered "in character," and (we infer) hastily, to protect herself; her answer immediately plunges her more deeply into trouble, as she herself would have realized as soon as the words were out.[6]

We can understand Bridget's falling in love with Summer. Mrs. Waters, an experienced eye with young men, describes him as exactly the irresistible paragon the father of Tom Jones must be: "A finer man, I must say, the sun never shone upon; for, besides the handsomest person I ever saw, he was so genteel, and had so much wit and good breeding" (XVIII.vii).

I pass over the interestingly incestuous enthusiasm in Mrs. Waters's description of her young lover's father, to answer the question of how Summer could see anything in such an old stick as Bridget. Here, too, Fielding's hints suggest certain depths to Bridget's personality. In spite of her sour exterior, she is attractive to men. Of course, as Fielding points out, a good deal of her attraction lies in her brother's fortune, as he comments on the wonder that three of the four men he has mentioned at Allworthy's house "should fix their inclinations on a lady who was never greatly celebrated for her beauty, and who was, moreover, now a little descended into the vale of years" (III.vi).

Actually, *all* of the eligible males in the book seem to detect a certain amatory capacity in Bridget, forming a comic procession to be sure, but one that fits her personality to the plot and to the plotting from first to last, and deepens her personality in the process. She has five suitors in all: Summer, one Blifil then the other, then Thwackum and Square. Furthermore, at the outset young Summer, a clergyman's son with a fund of wit and gentility, must certainly have come to his opportunity by the same road as the rest: through the earnest discussion of theological matters, Bridget's crowning interest under her aspect as Learned Lady. And here Fielding simply adds a half-comic popular theory of his, already employed in *Shamela* and *The Female Husband*, a theory that seems to have a certain psychological validity: that religious intercourse, especially

6. Mrs. Waters describes her perturbation, and her maidenly concern for "honour," on another occasion—when she finally must tell her solitary secret for the first time: ". . . at last, having locked the door of her room, she took me into her closet, and then locking that door likewise, she said she would convince me of the vast reliance she had on my integrity, by communicating a secret in which her honour, and consequently her life, was concerned. She then stopped, and after a silence of a few minutes, during which she often wiped her eyes, she inquired of me if I thought my mother might safely be confided in. I answered, I would stake my life on her fidelity. She then imparted to me the great secret which laboured in her breast, and which, I believe, was delivered with more pains than she afterwards suffered in childbirth" (XVIII.vii).

the Methodistical, is wonderfully and deceptively conducive to the sexual.

The sexual comedy in Bridget's expectations with Captain Blifil, built like a plowman, bearded blackly to the eyes, is there for all to see and enjoy, along with Fielding's euphemistic irony. We smile to learn that in her honeymoon Bridget is "passionately fond of her new husband" (I.xiii). We do not see that with her *new* husband she is acting out for our unseeing eyes what had happened with the man who might have been her old—even when we learn that young Blifil is born, perfectly formed, a month before his time. For Bridget was such "a strict observer of all rules of decorum" that the courtship "filled the space of near a month," and that, after Bridget had "secured her lover," "in less than a month" they were man and wife (I.xi–xii). As Crane points out, she has indeed thwarted her own plans to have Allworthy recognize Jones as her son. But Jones is doing well enough. She wants her man, and seems to have deliberately "slipped," marrying secretly and in haste, to secure him.

As time goes on, Bridget grows more open and careless, as the growing audacity of Fielding's evidence authenticates her character, and assists both the plot and its concealment. After the welcome death of her husband, to whose memory Fielding erects the ironic and literal "monument of her affection," THIS STONE, she accepts the attentions of Thwackum and especially of Square, "a jolly fellow, or widow's man," "a comely man" (III.vi). And although "the only fruits she designed for herself were, flattery and courtship," Fielding intimates an actual affair with Square. Under Fielding's guidance the reader reads the evidence as a comic illustration of malicious gossiping: "However, she at last conversed with Square with such a degree of intimacy that malicious tongues began to whisper things of her, to which, as well for the sake of the lady, as that they were highly disagreeable to the rule of right and the fitness of things, we will give no credit, and therefore shall not blot our paper with them" (III.vi). But from what we already know of the double entendre in Bridget's kind of "conversation" (Hutchens, p. 115) and from what we already know and will learn about how Bridget conducts a "courtship," we may conclude that she is actively engaged with Square, and that her growing freedoms are akin to those of Mrs. Slipslop, whom age has freed from fear of pregnancy. The evidence is there, but on first reading we are likely to acquit Bridget, as Fielding and she doubtless intend us to, as a proper though foolish old maid of a widow, maliciously slandered.

Bridget's amatory propensity is now clearly before us, but we will not fully believe it, and, because of Jenny's and Partridge's false confessions, we will not conjecture from it to suspect Bridget's unwed motherhood, the great secret of the story. But, just in case we should here guess the truth, and almost for the sheer audacious fun of deception, Fielding now uses Bridget's amorousness anew for both his plot and plotting, and produces a sudden Freudian glimpse into Bridget's personality—one we can enjoy only when the game is over. Jones has now so become Mrs. Blifil's favorite "that it was impossible to mistake her any longer":

> She was so desirous of often seeing him, and discovered such satisfaction and delight in his company, that before he was eighteen years old he was become a rival to both Square and Thwackum; and what is worse, the whole country began to talk as loudly of her inclination to Tom as they had before done of that which she had shown to Square: on which account the philosopher conceived the most implacable hatred for our poor hero. (III.vi)

We do achieve the "impossible," mistaking her exactly as Fielding intends. We take her maternal love for its erotic analogue, and then pass it off as ridiculous. But we later learn that much more is here than meets the eye. The plot requires Square's hostility, since his false testimony about Tom's drunkenness will seal Tom's doom. Moreover, Fielding could hardly have found a motive stronger than sexual jealousy toward a younger man. Fielding's plotting requires deception, and Fielding could hardly have deceived us better than by his hinting at sexual interests to conceal the maternal. And yet Freud himself could hardly have devised a better case, as young Tom becomes the kind of young man Bridget could indeed love in every way, were he not her son, since he is indeed his father, young Summer, all over again. Tom is showing signs "of that gallantry of temper which greatly recommends men to women," and Bridget simply cannot resist the delights of his company, and what must be his playful courtliness with the old but flirtatious woman, whom he does not know as his mother. Here is indeed the hint of incest (Hutchens, p. 40) that plays comically and devilishly throughout Jones's affairs. And Square, driven off from his mistress by some quarrel over Tom, seeks out Molly Seagrim, only to be caught and laughed at by Tom, and confirmed in his hatred, especially as Tom seems to outshine him with the ladies wherever he turns. Fielding has sealed Tom's doom and our eyes, and deepened Bridget's characterization, all at one stroke.

But even this is not all, for here also is Bridget's slyness in retrieving the amorous slips she cannot resist. Her apparent carelessness with Tom is actually achieving, in the countryside's whispers, the surest protection she could devise for her secret. First, Fielding tells us, the countryside took her affection for Tom as a deceit under which she is laying plans for Tom's ruin and her son's triumph; and then, as Tom grows older and her affection more open, the country-

side takes him as her lover. But, characteristically, she also outma-
neuvers herself, for her true inclinations, which make such a convenient deceit, actually bring Tom dire consequences, through
Square, and by the time they arrive she is dead.

The slyness the plot demands of Bridget traces a necessary and
authentic connection in her personality between the Old Maid and
the Amorous Matron. Although Bridget slips, she is an excellent
planner, and yet, true to life, her plans work only partially. Neither
she nor Fortune can carry them out completely—except in the
triumphant end, where her mismanagements have ironically
achieved greater success for Tom than if she had actually revealed
her secret early, as she had planned (Crane, p. 119). Bridget has
looked carefully into the character of Jenny Jones and her mother,
but she has not seen (or has she?) that side of Jenny's character
that will get Jenny into trouble with Partridge and cause her to run
off with a recruiting officer carrying her secret away from Bridget's
supervision. Bridget has dismissed her maid, has kept Mrs. Wilkins
packed and ready to leave at the right time, to look into the character of a servant, Mrs. Wilkins's mission in life. Bridget has apparently even managed to get her brother off to London for three
months on some business, of which Fielding says: "though I know
not what it was; but judge of its importance by its having detained
him so long from home, whence he had not been absent a month at
a time during the space of many years" (I.iii). The baby is born,
kept out of the way at the Joneses, and placed in Allworthy's bed
on the night of his return. Here is Bridget's plan for the future, as
Mrs. Waters later tells Allworthy:

> And all suspicions were afterwards laid asleep by the artful con-
> duct of your sister, in pretending ill-will to the boy, and that any
> regard she showed him was out of mere complaisance to you.
> (XVIII.vii)

But Bridget is human, in thorough control of neither her plan nor
herself. When the baby is brought in the next morning, she is
silent. This is her crucial moment, and she cannot speak. But Fielding prevents our suspecting the real cause by making facetious spec-
ulations of his own. Contrary to Wilkins's expectations, Bridget
"intimated some compassion for the helpless little creature, and
commended her brother's charity" (I.iv). Soon she has recovered
sufficiently to ring out an adequate string of "sluts" and "jades"
against the unknown mother. When Allworthy leaves, and her plan
has succeeded, "having looked some time earnestly at the child
[whom she has not seen since birth, apparently], as it lay asleep in
the lap of Mrs. Deborah, the good lady could not forbear giving it a
hearty kiss, at the same time declaring herself wonderfully pleased

with its beauty and innocence" (I.v). Lest her plan fail, and her real emotion not pass with us as "mere complaisance" to her brother, Fielding diverts our attention by the comic trimming of Mrs. Wilkins to her mistress's moods. Bridget's orders for the child's welfare "were indeed so liberal, that, had it been a child of her own, she could not have exceeded them," but, "lest the virtuous reader . . . condemn her," Fielding reports appropriate mutterings about her "brother's whim" (I.v).

She is all too human. She marries Blifil, thwarts her plan for Tom, and endangers his position (Crane, p. 117). But she tries to maintain her plan to protect Tom by pretending "mere complaisance" in public and talking against him in private—to keep her brother on Tom's side. To her husband, who hates Tom as a rival to his son, she "frequently recommended . . . her own example, of conniving at the folly of her brother" (II.v). Soon she begins to hate Deborah Wilkins, actually for misreading the direction of the wind and favoring Bridget's legitimate but detested son over her illegitimate but loved one, but apparently, as Fielding ironically conjectures, because Wilkins has played up to Allworthy by favoring Tom too much in public. The strainings and turnings of her duplicity, along with Fielding's ironic conjectures about her motives, become a kind of paradigm for the subtlety and ambivalence of Bridget's feelings as she attempts to play her double role. She has a softer heart than one would think, beneath an adequate store of spite. She intercedes for Partridge—to spite her husband, Fielding implies—but clearly to make amends for injustice because she is, "as the reader must have perceived, a much better-tempered woman" than Deborah Wilkins (II.vi). To spite her husband, as Fielding suggests with considerable truth—which we first take at face value, then discount as deceptive irony, then accept again as psychological validity—she now begins "to caress [the foundling] almost equally with her own child" (II.vii).

But Bridget's initial plan of passing off real affection as "mere complaisance"—and thus managing public opinion and her brother by playing the resentful mother of Blifil in her private backbiting—gets out of hand. She cannot perfectly manage the feelings she tries to manipulate and to conceal. As she tries to manage her plan—and Thwackum and Square—we get a strange glimpse of psychic compensation for the strain: she "had more than once slyly caused [Thwackum] to whip Tom Jones, when Mr. Allworthy, who was an enemy to this exercise, was abroad; whereas she had never given any such orders concerning young Blifil" (III.vi). There it stands, uninterpreted, seeming at first only a natural show of resentment against an interloper, though a slyly vindictive one, and seeming in retrospect only a part of her plan. But it gives her a strangely authentic streak of sadism against the boy she cannot let alone, a sly pleasure in punishing her beloved love-child for the psychic strain he has caused her. Her plan would have worked as well without the whip. She seems to be defending herself against herself, under the excuse of her plan, especially since the next paragraph tells us of the growing "gallantry of temper" in Tom that soon makes him irresistible to his slyly passionate mother.

Fielding's art is indeed a lawyerlike designing from the ironic delights of evidence and its meanings and misinterpretations, as Eleanor Hutchens has suggested. And Bridget Allworthy is the supreme example of those details of motive, personality, and act that Fielding leaves for the reader to add up for himself (Hutchens, pp. 30, 41). She is the center of his mystery, and his problems of plot and plotting are never more difficult than with her. Likewise, the ironic joy he takes in our deception is never higher. And the pressures produce a strange and authentic case history, something of a wonder, something of an Aristotelian probable impossibility, which somehow stands strongly for the truth about human female and maternal personality without seeming more than a remarkable character in a remarkable book. A great deal of Fielding's power is in the brilliance of his ironic artistry and the joy we share with him in the storytelling. In Bridget, we can see something of what it is we had so long admired in Fielding's plot, in addition to the grand strategy Crane has described for us. Fielding's plot concerns the ironic fact that all people are types, and all types people. His plot is really also a comic plotting of the perverse ways of human fate and personality, and of human imperceptions of the evidence before our eyes.

FREDERICK W. HILLES

Art and Artifice in Tom Jones†

Standing before Fielding's tomb in Lisbon, a character in Kingsley Amis's I Like It Here thinks to himself:

Perhaps it was worth dying in your forties if two hundred years later you were the only non-contemporary novelist who could be read with unaffected interest, the only one who never had to be apologised for or excused on the grounds of changing taste.[1]

†From Imagined Worlds: Essays on Some English Novels and Novelists in Honour of John Butt, ed. Maynard Mack and Ian Gregor (London: Methuen & Company, 1968), pp. 91–110.

1. Kingsley Amis, I Like It Here (New York, 1958), p. 185.

So positive a vote of confidence is heart-warming, but the vote is by no means unanimous, the statement by no means unchallenged. The fact is that many twentieth-century readers have found even the best of Fielding's work disappointing, if not at times embarrassing. And surely Mr. Empson cannot be taken seriously when he suggests that the moderns who have belittled Fielding have done so because they have found him intimidating.[2] Intellectuals like Dr. Leavis are not easily intimidated. A different type of reader will be found among those students at a large state university in America who a few years ago voted that *Tom Jones* is the most overrated of English classics. Possibly like the "alert young people" for whom Ortega is spokesman[3] they were merely expressing their hostility to traditional art. Or their opinions might be more simply accounted for by the assumption that they had read the book with post-Jamesian spectacles. As John Butt remarked in his commentary on Fielding,[4] there are those who are inclined to impose certain demands upon earlier novelists without reflecting whether such demands can be justified.

An aspect of *Tom Jones* that seems to disturb some moderns is a matter that Fielding took pride in and for which he received high praise from his contemporaries. Arnold Kettle, noting the "carefully contrived but entirely non-symbolic plot", believes Fielding "is constantly finding that the contrivance of his plot does violence to the characters he has created".[5] Edwin Muir, who asserts that a "plot should not appear to be a plot", admires Fielding's brilliance but complains that the "plot of *Tom Jones* is an adroitly constructed framework for a picture of life, rather than an unfolding action".[6] Ian Watt, admitting that the book has "a very neat and entertaining formal structure", feels that this neatness suggests "the manipulated sequences of literature rather than the ordinary processes of life".[7] Even Digeon, one of the most devoted of latter-day Fieldingites, finds in this famous plot "a perfection which is almost too severe".[8]

Educated readers of the eighteenth century were well aware that the story had been "carefully contrived", "adroitly constructed". Note that two of the early commentators quoted at the beginning of Professor Crane's thoughtful essay make use of the word *artful* when expressing their admiration of the plot:[9] "No fable what-

2. Fielding ("Twentieth-Century Views"), ed. R. Paulson (New York, 1962), p. 145.
3. As quoted by W. C. Booth in *The Rhetoric of Fiction* (Chicago, 1961), p. 120. My indebtedness to this fine book will be obvious.
4. *Fielding* ("Writers and their Works") (London, 1959), p. 27.
5. *An Introduction to the English Novel* (London, 1951), p. 77.

6. *The Structure of the Novel* (London, 1954), pp. 39, 31.
7. *The Rise of the Novel* (London, 1957), p. 253.
8. Aurélien Digeon, *The Novels of Fielding* (London, 1953), p. 233.
9. "The Concept of Plot and the Plot of *Tom Jones*" in *Critics and Criticism*, ed. R. S. Crane (abridged ed., Chicago, 1957), p. 62.

ever", wrote Arthur Murphy, "affords, in its solution, such artful states of suspense". "Since the days of Homer", wrote James Beattie, "the world has not seen a more artful epick fable". Such remarks are forerunners of Coleridge's too frequently quoted praise of the plot. And Coleridge, it may be remembered, is one of the chief English authorities invoked by E. E. Stoll to support his thesis in *Art and Artifice in Shakespeare*. Neither Murphy nor Beattie nor Coleridge seem to have been dismayed because the neatness of this artful plot suggested "the manipulated sequences of literature". On the contrary this delighted them. What they admired was Fielding's superb control over the materials of his book.

To strengthen his argument Stoll brought in as collateral evidence "the placid and ample pages" of the early novel, with its "'heavy' fathers, tyrannical guardians, or amorous and barbarous aunts and duennas". What he particularly stressed when discussing *Tom Jones* was the unlikely behaviour of Squire Allworthy, who casts Tom out into the cold world and then, some five or six weeks later, welcomes him back while expelling Blifil.

> So lightly one cannot pass from belief and affection to disbelief and hatred, and back again. The human mind is not so immediately receptive and responsive. .... And this no one knows better than Fielding himself, when the plot or a situation is not at stake.[1]

Stoll, then, agrees that the plot at times "does violence to the characters", but the point he makes is that *Tom Jones* is not a factual account of the life of a young man; it is a work of literature. And Fielding's fame, he says, is at least partly owing to his skill in handling those arbitrary and artificial devices that one finds in most literary masterpieces. How Fielding handled such devices is a complex subject that has been discussed, sometimes in great detail, by a number of writers. What follows is an attempt not to develop Stoll's thesis but to re-examine and hopefully to reappraise some of these frankly artificial elements. And, in the light of what is said above, the carefully worked out formal structure is an obvious point of departure.

"The form of a novel", wrote Percy Lubbock long ago, "is something that none of us, perhaps, has ever really contemplated". We cannot, he regrets, "keep a book steady and motionless before us, so that we may have time to examine its shape and design". "Nobody", he continues, "would venture to criticize a building, a statue, a picture, with nothing before him but the memory of a single glimpse caught in passing".[2] Precisely what Lubbock had in

1. *Art and Artifice in Shakespeare* (Cambridge, 1938), pp. 65, 67f.

2. *The Craft of Fiction* (New York, 1921), pp. 3, 1.

mind by form he nowhere makes clear. But if for *Tom Jones* we are willing to accept, in Mark Schorer's words, "some external neoclassic notion of form",[3] most of the difficulties that bother Lubbock will vanish. The architectural critic, when examining the shape and design of a building, cannot limit himself to the façade as, in a sense, the critic of a painting may do. He must consider its appearance from all points of the compass and must bear in mind the arrangement of the interior as well as exterior. Presumably he will study carefully a set of blueprints. Somewhat analogous is the task of the critic of the novel. Necessarily he must take into consideration its shape and design, and to do so he must schematize it as best he can.

What I have in mind when speaking of shape and design is what E. M. Forster has called pattern—something different from the story or plot. In his words, "whereas the story appeals to our curiosity and the plot to our intelligence, the pattern appeals to our aesthetic sense, it causes us to see the book as a whole".[4] He discovers in *The Ambassadors* the shape of an hourglass, the same figure that some have seen in *Tom Jones*. More useful, it has seemed to me, when trying to see that book "as a whole", is an architectural figure. With Mrs. Van Ghent I conceive of *Tom Jones* as shaped like a Palladian mansion. Admitting with her that there is "a certain distortion involved in the attempt to represent a book by a visual figure",[5] I here rashly present a ground plan of *Tom Jones* because such a plan, however crude, does enable us to keep the book "steady and motionless before us". My plan is based on what John Wood originally designed for Prior Park, the stately home of Fielding's patron Ralph Allen. According to Wood, the extent of the whole, from the extreme left (the stables) to the extreme right (a picture gallery and bedrooms), "was proposed to answer that of three Sides of a Duodecagon, inscribed within a Circle of a Quarter of a Mile Diameter".[6]

The pattern of *Tom Jones* reflects the same mathematical exactitude. The novel is divided into eighteen books. As has often been pointed out, the first six of these deal with events in Somerset, at the homes of Allworthy and Western, and the last six with events in London. Tom and Sophia are separated in Book VI and do not see one another again until Book XIII. The central six books deal with events on the road while hero and heroine make their way from what had been home to London. Professor Crane's treatment of the plot, which as might be expected is along Aristotelian lines, results in valuable analysis but completely disguises this basic pat-

3. *Forms of Modern Fiction*, ed. W. V. O'Connor (Minneapolis, 1948), p. 26.
4. *Aspects of the Novel* (New York, 1927), p. 215.
5. Dorothy Van Ghent, *The English Novel* (New York, 1953), p. 80.
6. John Wood, *A Description of Bath* (2d ed., London, 1769), p. 96.

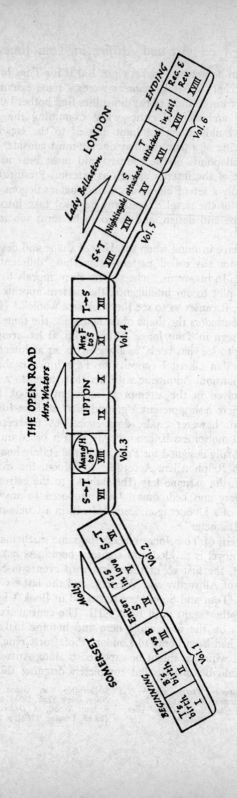

tern, thus making it difficult for the reader to see the book as a whole. Fielding had done what he could to make his pattern obvious. As originally published the novel appeared in six volumes, three books to a volume. Nor can the reader pass from one book to another unawares. The much discussed opening chapters to each book, in which the narrator talks about his craft, emphasize the formal structure. Where the symmetry is most obvious is in the middle. Books IX and X, at the very center, contain the hilarious episodes that occur in the inn at Upton. Just before them Tom learns something about the great world as he listens to the life history of the Man of the Hill; just after them Sophia learns something about life when Mrs. Fitzpatrick talks about her unhappy experiences as a married woman. The central section begins (Book VII) with Tom on his travels and Sophia preparing to leave home. She catches up with him at Upton, hears how he is occupying himself, and departs for London without seeing him. When Tom learns what she has done he forgets his military commitments and at once sets out in an attempt to overtake her. The pursuer has become the pursued.

Just how to sum up in shorthand a particular book, or just where to end "the beginning" or begin "the ending", can easily provoke argument, and such argument is fruitless. I am happy to agree with Professor Crane in considering Books XVII and XVIII as comprising the ending. In the opening chapter of XVII the narrator talks about bringing his work "to a period", promises Sophia a good husband (Lord Fellamar or Blifil or someone else), and drops dark hints about what will happen to poor Tom. All of the chief characters are now in London ready to play their parts in that final book which in good Aristotelian fashion provides us with Recognition and a Reversal of the Situation. Crane's "beginning" takes us through Allworthy's illness and Bridget's death (midway in Book V). To me it is more logical to consider the first two books the beginning, "after which", according to Aristotle, "something naturally is or comes to be".[7] Those books give us the setting and the origins of Tom and Blifil—at least as much of that "as is necessary or proper to acquaint the reader with in the beginning of this history". The story gets under way in III where Tom and Blifil are compared. Sophia makes her debut in IV, she and Tom realize in V that they are in love, and they are separated in VI when he is expelled from home. They meet once more in XIII, but are then kept apart until the finale. Tom is involved in young Nightingale's affairs, after which both heroine and hero are plotted against and under attack, XV beginning with Sophia's near rape and XVI ending with the duel between Tom and Fitzpatrick.

7. *Poetics* (tr. S. H. Butcher) VII, 3.

When Honour unexpectedly arrives in Tom's room (XIV.ii), thus forcing Lady Bellaston to hide, the embarrassed young man begs her to whisper, "for that there was a lady dying in the next room. 'A lady!' cries [Honour]; 'ay, I suppose one of your ladies. Oh, Mr. Jones, there are too many of them in the world' ". That seems to be the popular idea, that Tom is constantly surrounded by luscious damsels. Capitalizing upon the deserved success of the John Osborne–Tony Richardson adaptation, a new film has recently appeared that introduces "a 20th Century Tom Jones" and that, according to the advertisements, "gives a lesson in the art of pursuing the opposite sex". Presumably both producer and audience would be surprised to learn that Fielding's Tom is no gay Lothario. With the exception of Sophia there are only three women in his life, and in each case it is the lady who does the pursuing. "To confess the truth, he had rather too much diffidence in himself, and was not forward enough in seeing the advances of a young lady" (V.ii). Just how carefully Fielding has spaced these three affairs the diagram makes obvious. Molly, the young country trollop, is introduced in IV. Tom's relations with her are at their blackest in V when he once more succumbs to her although he now knows that he is in love with Sophia. In VI one of the charges leading to his expulsion is that he "yet converses" with "that wench". Thereafter she takes no part in his life. Now note that exactly balancing Tom's carryings-on with Molly is the last of his infidelities. He meets Lady Bellaston in XIII, the liaison is most offensive in XIV (he has now discovered Sophia), and it is forever ended near the conclusion of XV. The only other "lady" in his life (we readers see her as Jenny in the first and last books of the novel) is Mrs. Waters, who in regard to sophistication is somewhere between Molly and Lady Bellaston. Tom rescues her at the beginning of IX, is (with shame I write it, and with sorrow will it be read) actually in bed with her at the half-way point (the end of that book), and concludes the affair once and for all in X.

So symmetrical an arrangement calls attention to itself. Life is just not like this. Such neatness does in truth suggest the manipulated sequences of literature; the plot is indeed carefully contrived. As used by modern critics words like *manipulate* and *contrive* are pejoratives. They have not always been so and would not, I think, have been used in that way by Fielding and his contemporaries. Among definitions still authorized by the *Oxford English Dictionary* are for *manipulate*: to handle something with dexterity, to operate upon something with the mind and intelligence, to treat artistic matter, etc., with skill; and for *contrive*: to invent, devise, excogitate with ingenuity and cleverness a plan, to devise, invent, design a literary composition, etc. One meaning of *contrivance* is "the action of inventing or making with thought and skill". Now one of the silliest of Richardson's ill-tempered remarks about his rival was that he had "little or no invention".[8] Amusingly enough in the publisher's contract *Tom Jones* is said to have been invented as well as written by Henry Fielding. Certainly Fielding went out of his way to call attention, again and again, to his ingenuity. One of the best of the many commentators on *Tom Jones* momentarily slipped when, describing what happens in Book IX, he wrote: "Tom Jones and his servant Partridge arrive at the Upton inn escorting a certain Mrs. Waters . . ."[9] Of course Partridge did not escort Mrs. Waters to the inn. Near the end of the novel (XVIII.ii) Fielding asks us to

> admire the many strange accidents which unfortunately prevented any interview between Partridge and Mrs. Waters, when she spent a whole day [at Upton] with Mr. Jones. Instances of this kind we may frequently observe in life, where the greatest events are produced by a nice train of little circumstances; and more than one example of this may be discovered by the accurate eye, in this our history.

Fielding the narrator is constantly talking to us in this fashion. He is anything but "invisible, refined out of existence, indifferent, paring his fingernails". It may seem odd, then, to suggest that he was an eighteenth-century Joyce, that *Tom Jones* is an eighteenth-century *Ulysses*.[1] Fielding, of course, had Homer in mind as he wrote his epic and even refers directly to Ulysses in the epigraph on the title-page. But his relationship to Joyce is, I believe, something far more fundamental. Both were innovators; both superb literary craftsmen who enjoyed playing with words. Making allowances for the difference in idiom between the eighteenth and twentieth centuries, examine the following passage (XI.viii) where Sophia and her cousin hear

> a noise, not unlike, in loudness, to that of a pack of hounds just let out from their kennel; nor, in shrillness, to cats, when caterwauling; or, to screech-owls; or, indeed, more like (for what animal can resemble a human voice) to those sounds, which, in the pleasant mansions of that gate, which seems to derive its name from a duplicity of tongues, issue from the mouths, and sometimes from the nostrils of those fair river nymphs, ycleped of old the Napæa, or the Naïades; in the vulgar tongue translated oyster-wenches: for when, instead of the antient libations of milk and honey and oil, the rich distillation from the juniper-berry, or

8. *Selected Letters of Samuel Richardson*, ed. J. Carroll (Oxford, 1964), p. 197.

9. Digeon, *op. cit.*, p. 173.

1. In his introduction to the Mod. Lib. ed. of *Joseph Andrews* (1939), Howard Mumford Jones suggests that when writing *Ulysses* Joyce may have had Fielding's Preface to *Joseph Andrews* in mind. Bernard Benstock (*Joyce-again's Wake*, Seattle, 1965, p. 164) believes that Fielding's formula "was probably close to Joyce's interests during the construction of *Finnegan's Wake*".

perhaps, from malt, hath, by the early devotion of their votaries, been poured forth in great abundance, should any daring tongue with unhallowed license prophane; i.e. depreciate the delicate fat Milton oyster, the plaice sound and firm, the flounder as much alive as when in the water, the shrimp as big as a prawn, the fine cod alive but a few hours ago, or any other of the various treasures, which those water-deities, who fish the sea and rivers, have committed to the care of the nymphs, the angry Naïades lift up their immortal voices, and the prophane wretch is struck deaf for his impiety.

Overlooking what is immediately obvious in this excerpt, we can see that Fielding is here greatly widening his horizon, is enriching and deepening his narrative. Sophia and Harriet may be cooped up in a country inn on the Watling Street, some ninety miles from London; we the readers are not only there but in London itself as well as near the groves and by the streams of ancient Greece. Somewhat Joycean, I think, are the street-cries of the fishwives; Joycean too is the far-fetched pun on Billingsgate.

In the opening chapter of Book IV our attention is called to "sundry similes, descriptions, and other kind of poetical embellishments" that have been interspersed throughout the story. Presumably Henry Fielding the author here agrees with the narrator of *Tom Jones* in asserting that these "ornamental parts" are inserted merely to hold the reader's attention, that they have no other function. In fact, however, these embellishments are an integral part of the novel, and this, thanks to Joyce (among others), the modern reader can appreciate as, perhaps, the original reader did not. Here is the highly functional opening of a section of *Ulysses*:

The summer evening had begun to fold the world in its mysterious embrace. Far away in the west the sun was setting and the last glow of all too fleeting day lingered lovingly on sea and strand, on the proud promontory of dear old Howth guarding as ever the waters of the bay, on the weedgrown rocks along Sandymount shore and, last but not least, on the quiet church whence there streamed forth at times upon the stillness the voice of prayer to her who is in her pure radiance a beacon ever to the stormtossed heart of man, Mary, star of the sea.[2]

With that compare the following, (V.x) less subtle to our ears, no doubt, but performing much the same function:

It was now a pleasant evening in the latter end of June, when our hero was walking in a most delicious grove, where the gentle breezes fanning the leaves, together with the sweet trilling of a murmuring stream, and the melodious notes of nightingales, formed altogether the most enchanting harmony. In this scene,

2. P. 340 in Mod. Lib. ed.

so sweetly accommodated to love, he meditated on his dear Sophia. While his wanton fancy roved unbounded over all her beauties, and his lively imagination painted the charming maid in various ravishing forms, his warm heart melted with tenderness; and at length, throwing himself on the ground, by the side of a gently murmuring brook, he broke forth into the following ejaculation . . .

Fielding erred in dating this event in June, as an early reader noticed.[3] Tom had only recently broken his arm while hunting and within a month of this time was walking with shivering Partridge on a cold winter's night. I suggest that the author was so intent on his parody that he momentarily forgot his time-scheme. What one expects when reading a romance is that such an evening as this should occur in the merry month of June.

Our hero, speaking as a romantic hero should, declares that if only Sophia were his he would envy no one.

How contemptible would the brightest Circassian beauty, dressed in all the jewels of the Indies, appear to my eyes! But why do I mention another woman? Could I think my eyes capable of looking at any other with tenderness, these hands should tear them from my head.

One thinks of young Romeo, who—madly in love, he thinks, with the fair Rosaline—when told that others are more beautiful bursts out:

When the devout religion of mine eye
Maintains such falsehood, then turn tears to fires,
And those who, often drown'd, could never die,
Transparent heretics, be burnt for liars.

And then, knowing that the brightest beauties could no longer have charms for him, nor would a hermit be colder in their embraces,

he started up, and beheld—not his Sophia—no, nor a Circassian maid richly and elegantly attired for the grand Signior's seraglio. No; without a gown, in a shift that was somewhat of the coarsest, and none of the cleanest, bedewed likewise with some odoriferous effluvia, the produce of the day's labour, with a pitchfork in her hand, Molly Seagrim approached.

Here the echo is not of "vulgar" romances nor of Shakespeare, but (compare self-parody in Joyce) of this particular novel. The exaggerated periodic sentence recalls to us our first glimpse of the fair heroine:

for lo! adorned with all the charms in which nature can array her; bedecked with beauty, youth, sprightliness, innocence, modesty,

3. W. L. Cross, *History of Henry Fielding* (New Haven, 1918), II.193.

and tenderness, breathing sweetness from her rosy lips, and darting brightness from her sparkling eyes, the lovely Sophia comes!

Molly and Tom converse awhile and then—the sequel is not elevating. Funny it is—and this because Fielding's rhetoric has prepared us for it, but the simple fact is that our hero is drunk and behaving in a fashion unbecoming to heroes—at least to pre-twentieth-century heroes. Fielding looks facts in the face, as he makes plain at this very point in the novel. But a description of what was now going on in the thickest part of the grove would obviously be out of place in this particular story. *Tom Jones* differs in tone from, say, *Sanctuary* or *Lie Down in Darkness*. It is important for Fielding to soft-pedal the entire affair, and this he does skilfully. Tom's sexual misdemeanor is, we are reminded, the result of too much drinking, and the idea of drunkenness is made to seem less reprehensible by two classical allusions, the witty remark of "one Cleostratus", and the charitable opinion of Aristotle. Instead of being shocked at Tom's animalistic behavior we can still look upon him with affection. Immediately after this the hiding place occupied by Tom and Molly is equated with a cave that was described by a goddess as the shelter for a famous queen and a great epic hero. Of course it is the essence of the mock heroic to juxtapose the great and the little, and Molly's masquerading here as Dido prepares us for the tone of what immediately follows.

The battle is introduced by "a simile in Mr. Pope's period of a mile"—that is, by a rhetorical passage extended, as John Nichols put it, "to a disagreeable length".[4] It may be worth noting that the magnificent simile contains another pun, this one on the New Forest, and neatly links together the purely animalistic and what the author terms sacred. The bloody battle follows, at the end of which we are given this tableau:

> In one place lay on the ground, all pale, and almost breathless, the vanquished Blifil. Near him stood the conqueror Jones, almost covered with blood, part of which was naturally his own, and part had been lately the property of the Reverend Mr. Thwackum. In a third place stood the said Thwackum, like King Porus, sullenly submitting to the conqueror. The last figure in the piece was Western the Great, most gloriously forbearing the vanquished foe.

Sophia swoons, and the author then introduces a paragraph that has irritated some critics:

> The reader may remember, that in our description of this grove we mentioned a murmuring brook, which brook did not come there, as such gentle streams flow through vulgar romances, with

4. Pope's *Imitations of Horace*, ed. J. Butt (Vol. IV of Twickenham ed., Lon- don, 1939), p. 31n.

no other purpose than to murmur. No! Fortune had decreed to ennoble this little brook with a higher honour than any of those which wash the plains of Arcadia ever deserved.

Our hero, oblivious to what he had undergone that afternoon, flies to Sophia, picks her up and runs with her to the brook, and there revives her by besprinkling her face, head, and neck very plentifully. Moments later the author puts an end to the incident and to the book.

This whole episode, from the time Tom throws himself down by the brook until he has revived Sophia, nicely illustrates the function performed by those "poetical embellishments" that are especially prominent in this part of the novel. What would the book be without them? Somerset Maugham has supplied the answer. In his deplorable abridgement of *Tom Jones* the whole character of the book has been altered. It has become (I quote from the blurb) a "lively and romantic adventure story of a young man . . . handsome, high-spirited, and gallant with the ladies, [though] somewhat of a rogue".

There have been many readers who have thought the book would be improved if altered along the lines Maugham followed. Some two hundred years ago Lord Monboddo, who admired *Tom Jones* extravagantly, thought the work perfect except for two blemishes, the author's bringing himself into the book so frequently and the introduction of the mock-heroic, that "destroys the probability of the narrative, which ought to be carefully studied in all works, that, like Mr. Fielding's, are imitations of real life and manners".[5] The same criticism is heard today. A highly gifted modern author in an introduction to a school-text of *Tom Jones* praises the book for its lifelike hero but objects to the author's intrusions that "decompose a state of mind which has been adjusted to accepting as true and inevitable all that occurred from the day when Squire Allworthy" etc. etc. etc.[6] We are back to where we started. If characters and actions are really lifelike the author blunders when, for example, he talks about his murmuring brook.

But Fielding was writing a *comic* epic. He revelled in the exaggerations that one expects to find in comedy. The years he had spent as a dramatist, a writer of farce, influenced all his later writing.[7] There are sensitive readers of today who have declared that for them Sophia never recovers from the highly artificial way she is introduced to us. Fielding, it should be pointed out, compounded that artificiality. His introduction of Sophia is in turn introduced by the anecdote of the actor who enjoys his shoulder of mutton by having

5. F. T. Blanchard, *Fielding the Novelist* (New Haven, 1927), p. 227.
6. Collins Classics ed. (London, 1955), p. 29.
7. In his admirable *Fielding: Tom Jones* (Studies in Eng. Lit. 23, Arnold [London, 1964], pp. 40ff.), Irvin Ehrenpreis discusses at some length the theatrical elements in the novel.

disposed of the carpenters who had to precede him on to the stage. The unnamed actor, it happens, was Barton Booth; the play Ambrose Philips' *Distress Mother*, which Fielding had burlesqued in *The Covent-Garden Tragedy*. One of the most popular plays of the day, it owed its success in large part to the impressive bearing of this actor. "Whoever has seen Booth in the Character of *Pyrrhus* march to his Throne to receive *Orestes*", wrote Steele in *Spectator* 334, "is convinced that majestick and great Conceptions are expressed in the very Step". In the following paper (Fielding's model for Partridge's seeing Garrick play *Hamlet*) Sir Roger tells Mr. Spectator as he watches Pyrrhus make his grand entry "that he did not believe the King of France himself had a better Strut". Steele had also written the prologue to the play, and in it declared that Pyrrhus did not need attendants to prove himself royal. Fielding gives that statement another twist. Pyrrhus is fully and happily aware of the fact that he cannot make his grand entry unless preceded by his attendants. And we notice that the tragic hero is in reality a hungry actor, his courtiers mere stage hands. Ostensibly Fielding is gravely saying that people deserving of respect are naturally surrounded by attendants, but he is saying this in such a way as to make us aware of the world of make-believe. There is a considerable difference between that world and the one in which we live.

A king with a similar name may just possibly be playing a similar part at the end of that bloody battle we have just observed. One of the four figures in the quoted tableau was Thwackum looking like King Porus. No doubt the reader is expected to call up a mental picture of the historical Porus, a warrior almost seven feet tall, whose defeat was one of Alexander's proudest victories. Perhaps the original reader would think of LeBrun's heroic painting of Porus, familiar through engravings or the tapestry brought to England while Fielding was a boy. But Porus was a name with operatic connotations. Addison and Steele have fun with him in *Spectators* 31 and 36, and after the middle twenties his was a famous part in a great number of operas based on Metastasio's libretto, *Alessandro nelle Indie*. In 1746, just when Fielding is thought to have begun writing *Tom Jones*, "a new opera" was put on in London, *Alexander in India*, with music by Lampugnani. The part of Porus was taken by the famous castrato Monticelli. Operatic conventions being what they were, the audience would not be surprised to see the part of the gigantic fighter taken by a slightly built Italian who had often taken female parts. Burney remembered Monticelli as "having a beautiful face and figure".[8] The finale of the opera shows

8. Charles Burney, *A General History of Music*, ed. F. Mercer (New York, 1957), II.839. Burney is wrong and has led others astray in thinking that Lampugnani's *Allesandro nell'Indie* (1746) is the same opera as Lampugnani's *Roxana* (1743).

In the Yale Library in Italian and English is a new edition of Metastasio's *Alessandro nelle Indie*, published in London in 1746 with the cast that took part in Lampugnani's version that year.

the defeated Porus making his heroic reply to Alexander. In a high clear voice Monticelli sang, presumably in the original Italian:

> E la mia pena attendo.
> Sia qual tu vuoi, ma sia
> Sempre degna d'un Re la sorte mia.

—words that were translated (by Samuel Humphries?):

> Death I expect,
> And wait, thus, undismay'd.—My only boon
> Is, let my fall be worthy of the monarch.

Whether Fielding here had in mind the intrinsic artificiality of an operatic finale or not, he definitely alludes to *The Rehearsal* a few paragraphs later. Saying what he obviously meant to be serious ("surely", he remarked elsewhere [XI.i], "a man may speak truth with a smiling countenance"), he wishes that all quarrels could be decided by fisticuffs.

> Then would war, the pastime of monarchs, be almost inoffensive, and battles between great armies might be fought at the particular desire of several ladies of quality. . . . Then might the field be this moment well strewed with human carcasses, and the next, the dead men, or infinitely the greatest part of them, might get up, like Mr. Bayes's troops, and march off.

A page or two later brings this particular book to an end.

With the idea of artificiality in mind an examination of Book V as a whole may prove fruitful. The opening chapter contains its share of theatrical allusions: the validity of the unities is questioned, the hoots and hisses of a hostile audience are indirectly mentioned, and a good deal of fun is made of the English Pantomime. Then in order to illustrate what he solemnly calls his "new vein of knowledge" ("no other than that of contrast, which runs through all the works of creation, and may probably have a large share in constituting in us the idea of all beauty, as well natural as artificial") he refers to the powers of cosmetics which "at Bath particularly" enable ladies that are "as ugly as possible in the morning" to appear as beauties in the evening.

Not counting this introduction the book consists of eleven chapters, the central pivotal one describing Allworthy on his "death-bed". This chapter, perfectly comic in that throughout it contrasts what is true with what seems to be true, has been misread by some critics. The chapter heading seems innocent enough: "In which Mr. Allworthy appears on a sick-bed". The man in the bed and all who surround it assume he is dying. If one is tempted to read death-bed for sick-bed all is still well. Conditioned as we are by our author's choice of words, we note the verb. One meaning of "to appear" is "to seem, as distinguished from *to be*". Even on the first reading one should not be deceived by Allworthy's illness. It is introduced in a paragraph that talks about the medical profession, ending with what "the great" Dr. Misaubin is said to have said: "Bygar, me believe my pation take me for de undertaker, for dey never send for me till de physician have kill dem". We do not need to know that Fielding had dedicated his *Mock Doctor* (out of Molière) to Misaubin in one of his most delightful ironic pieces. We do not need to know that Fielding's friend Hogarth more than once went out of his way to introduce Misaubin into his satirical pictures. The tone of this particular passage speaks for itself, and we have already witnessed a number of mock doctors, beginning with young Blifil's uncle, who "had in his youth been obliged to study physic, or rather to say he studied it". By the time Allworthy takes to his bed we have learned what to think of "that learned Faculty, for whom we have so profound a respect". If we were still tempted to take Allworthy's illness seriously, we should be shocked at the way our author phrases the reactions of some of the company: "even the philosopher Square wiped his eyes, albeit unused to the melting mood. As to Mrs. Wilkins, she dropped her pearls as fast as the Arabian trees their medicinal gums". For those who know the story (and no one has read *Tom Jones* who has not read it more than once) there is grim humour in the knowledge that although Allworthy thinks he is dying, his sister has actually died; and the humour is grimmer when we contrast Blifil's behaviour just before and just after he learns of his mother's death—and of his actual relationship to Tom.

That chapter I have called pivotal. The five chapters preceding it perfectly exemplify that new vein of knowledge we have just read about. In the first two we move from sour to sweet, from sweet to sour. Though Tom is attracted to Sophia he is honour-bound to be faithful to Molly. Then the "little incident of the muff" drives away all defences as the God of Love marches in. The problem of how to break with Molly is pleasantly solved when "the wicked rug" falls, revealing Square among other female utensils. (The wicked rug echoes the Shakespearean wicked wall of I.viii, and prepares for the reverse twist given by the bed curtains in XV.vii.) Tom is thus free to tell Sophia of his love, just before hearing that Allworthy is dying. His great happiness when with Sophia is balanced in the second half of the book by his great joy at Allworthy's recovery. This leads him to drink too much, and we have already traced what happened to him after that. Suffice it to say that the book as a whole is, like the novel as a whole, symmetrically constructed, the action in the first half occurring for the most part at Squire Western's, in the second half in or near Squire Allworthy's. Square's humiliation in the first half of the book is balanced by Thwackum's in the second. At the beginning of the book Tom is an injured hero, having saved Sophia when her horse threw her; at the end of the book Tom is an injured hero, having brought Sophia back to life after her death-resembling swoon. And central to the whole book, as it is central to the whole novel, is the basic contrast between Tom and Blifil.

Dante's Inferno is divided into an upper and a lower Hell, the one reserved for those whose sins are of the flesh, the other for those whose sins are of the spirit. In Book V Tom shows himself to be lustful and gluttonous; there is a hint too of the prodigal in him. But Blifil perfectly qualifies himself for a permanent home in the City of Dis—in the Malebolge, that eighth circle of lower Hell where the deceitful are forever punished. This, the most basic of the many contrasts in *Tom Jones*, underlies almost everything Fielding produced. Before he became a novelist he angrily wrote in the person of Job Vinegar about a Swiftian people, the Ptfghsi-umgski:

> All great Vices as Drinking, Gaming, injuring their Neighbour by walking over his Land, or taking away a Cock or Hen from him, &c. are very severely punished, but for little Foibles, and which may rather be called Weaknesses than Crimes, such as Avarice, Ingratitude, Cruelty, Envy, Malice, Falsehood, and the rest of this kind, they are entirely overlooked.[9]

Beneath Fielding's fine control in *Tom Jones* is a passionate hatred of deceit, a burning desire to make men open their eyes to the way of the world. *Tom Jones* is spoken of as an optimistic novel. This, I suppose, is because it has a happy ending. But the author of a tragedy is not necessarily a pessimist, and a comic epic demands a gay conclusion. The author of *Tom Jones* is certainly aware of man's weaknesses and can hardly be called naive. That "virtue is the certain road to happiness, and vice to misery, in this world", he writes (XI.i), is a "very wholesome and comfortable doctrine, to which we have but one objection, namely, that it is not true". Like other eminent writers of his time Fielding is in his own fashion bidding us to clear our minds of cant.

In his own fashion. That ever present narrator who tells us about his own likes and dislikes is forcing us to read the book the way the author wishes it read. We may want to identify with the healthy, handsome, fundamentally decent hero and believe that what he is doing is really happening, but if so we are refusing to follow the direction posts erected by the author. He is not jesting when he says (I.ii) of his hostile critics: "Till they produce the authority by

9. *The Voyages of Mr. Job Vinegar from the Champion,* ed. S. J. Sackett, Augustan Reprint Society, No. 67, (1958), as quoted by Andrew Wright in *Henry Fielding: Mask and Feast* (Berkeley, Calif., 1965), p. 196.

which they are constituted judges, I shall not plead to their jurisdiction". In a comic epic in prose the narrator is a creator who sits above the world he has created and tells his readers what to look at and how to look at it. Allan Ramsay, one more of Fielding's contemporaries who applied the word *artful* to this story, said the reader believes it to be true "and is with difficulty recall'd from that belief by the author's confession from time to time of its being all a fiction".[1] This is not a complaint but a statement of fact. We are not allowed to identify with characters, as we are, for example, in *Clarissa*. The author insists upon our remaining detached so that we can see clearly. If we were to become involved we should no longer have that balanced view of mankind which the highly symmetrical, and in this sense symbolic, plot presents to us. The world of *Tom Jones* is not the real world; it is a reflection of a reflection of real life and thus has a form and structure denied to real life. The narrator speaks (XVII.i) of the surprise and delight the credulous reader found in the fictions of early writers. He assumes that we are more mature. He too wishes to surprise and delight, but his appeal is to the literate who will enjoy his artistry and while enjoying the story will be aware of the seriousness that underlies his comic creations.

Eliot is on record as having read *Ulysses* with surprise, delight, and terror.[2] Fielding's sagacious reader will be surprised and delighted but hardly terrified. Shocked as Dr. Johnson would be at the very idea, Fielding is that laughing philosopher who is called upon in *The Vanity of Human Wishes* to look at motley life with philosophic eye. Johnson's poem was published only a few weeks before *Tom Jones* made its bow, and it is to *Tom Jones* that we turn when seeking cheerful wisdom and instructive mirth.

1. F. T. Blanchard, *op. cit.*, p. 107. O'Connor (Minneapolis, 1948), p. 120.
2. *Forms of Modern Fiction*, ed. W. V.

Bibliography

I

Wilbur L. Cross's *The History of Henry Fielding*, 3 vols. (New Haven: Yale University Press, 1918) remains the definitive critical biography. F. Homes Dudden's *Henry Fielding: His Life, Works, and Times*, 2 vols. (New York: Oxford University Press, 1952) adds some historical background but no new facts, and its commentary, frequently a paraphrased and unacknowledged composite of previous criticism, is to be used with caution. Aurélien Digeon's *Le texte des romans de Fielding* (Paris: Librarie Hachette, 1923) is the pioneering textual study.

II

The best general studies of Fielding are: Aurélien Digeon, *The Novels of Fielding* (London: Routledge & Kegan Paul, 1925; reprinted New York: Russell & Russell, 1962); Frederick T. Blanchard, *Fielding the Novelist: A Study of the Novelist's Fame and Influence* (New Haven: Yale University Press, 1926); John Butt, *Fielding* (London: Longmans, Green, "Writers and Their Work," no. 57, 1954); and A. D. McKillop, "Henry Fielding," in *The Early Masters of English Fiction* (Lawrence: University of Kansas Press, 1956).

III

The following theoretical books are useful: Ethel Margaret Thornbury, *Henry Fielding's Theory of the Comic Prose Epic* (Madison: University of Wisconsin Press, 1931), which contains the sales-catalogue of Fielding's library; Maurice Johnson, *Fielding's Art of Fiction* (Philadelphia: University of Pennsylvania Press, 1961); Sheldon Sacks, *Fiction and the Shape of Belief* (Berkeley and Los Angeles: University of California Press, 1964); Andrew Wright, *Henry Fielding: Mask and Feast* (Berkeley and Los Angeles: University of California Press, 1965); Morris Golden, *Fielding's Moral Psychology* (Boston: University of Massachusetts Press, 1966); Michael Irwin, *Henry Fielding: The Tentative Realist* (New York: Oxford University Press, 1967); George R. Levine, *The Dry Mock: A Study of the Technique of Irony in Fielding's Early Work* (The Hague: Mouton, 1967); Robert Alter, *Fielding and the Nature of the Novel* (Cambridge: Harvard University Press, 1968); Glenn W. Hatfield, *Henry Fielding and the Language of Irony* (Chicago: University of Chicago Press, 1968).

Significant chapters on Fielding appear in V. S. Pritchett, *The Living Novel* (London: Chatto & Windus, 1946); Ian Watt, *The Rise of the Novel* (Berkeley and Los Angeles: University of California Press, 1957); E. M. W. Tillyard, *The Epic Strain in the English Novel* (London: Chatto & Windus, 1958); Martin Price, *To the Palace of Wisdom* (Carbondale: Southern Illinois University Press, 1964); Ronald Paulson, *Satire and the Novel in Eighteenth-Century England* (New Haven: Yale University Press, 1967); Arthur Sherbo, *Studies in the Eighteenth-Century English Novel* (East Lansing: Michigan State University Press, 1969); Leo Braudy, *Narrative Form in History and Fiction* (Princeton: Princeton University Press, 1970); and John Preston, *The Reader's Role in Eighteenth-Century Fiction* (London: William Heinemann, 1970). Claude J. Rawson's *Henry Fielding*, Profiles in Literature series (London: Routledge & Kegan Paul; New York: ·Humanities Press, 1968) is a useful reference, as is Ronald Paulson and Thomas Lockwood, eds., *Henry Fielding: The Critical Heritage* (London: Routledge & Kegan Paul, 1969).

IV

Some useful essays on various aspects of Fielding are: Sheridan Baker, "Henry Fielding and the Cliché," *Criticism*, 1 (1959), 354–61; "Henry Fielding's Comic Romances," *Papers of the Michigan Academy of Science, Arts, and Letters*, 45 (1960), 411–19; and "Fielding and the Irony of Form," *Eighteenth-Century Studies*, 2 (1968), 138–54; William B. Coley, "The Background of Fielding's Laughter," *ELH*, 26 (1959), 229–52; Arthur L. Cooke, "Henry Fielding and the Writers of Heroic Romance," *PMLA*, 62 (1947), 984–99; John S. Coolidge, "Fielding's 'Conservation of Character,' " *Modern Philology*, 57 (1960), 245–59: A. E. Dyson, "Satiric and Comic Theory in Relation to Fielding," *Modern Language Quarterly*, 18 (1957), 225–37; Frank Kermode, "Richardson and Fielding," *Cambridge Journal*, 4 (1950), 106–14; Marston La France, "Fielding's Use of the 'Humors' Tradition," *Bucknell Review*, 17 (1969), 53–63; William Park, "Fielding and Richardson," *PMLA*, 81 (1967), 381–88; George Sherburn, "Fielding's Social Outlook," *Philological Quarterly*, 35 (1956), 1–23; George R. Swann, "Fielding and Empirical Realism," in *Philosophical Parallelisms in Six English Novelists* (Philadelphia: University of Pennsylvania Press, 1929), pp. 251–73; James A. Work, "Henry Fielding, Christian Censor," in *The Age of Johnson: Essays Presented to Chauncey Brewster Tinker*, ed. Frederick W. Hilles (New Haven: Yale University Press, 1949), pp. 139–48.

V

In addition to the articles reprinted here, the following studies of *Tom Jones* are significant: Robert Alter, "The Picaroon Domesticated," in *Rogue's Progress: Studies in the Picaresque Novel* (Cambridge: Harvard University Press, 1964), pp. 80–105; Martin Battestin, "Tom Jones and 'His Egyptian Majesty': Fielding's Parable of Government," *PMLA*, 82 (1967), 68–77; and *"Tom Jones:* The Argument of Design," in H. K. Miller, ed., *The Augustan Milieu: Essays Presented to Louis A. Landa* (New York: Oxford University Press, 1970), pp. 289–319; Martin C. Battestin, "Osborne's *Tom Jones;* Adapting a Classic," *Virginia Quarterly Review*, 42 (1966), 378–93; Michael Bliss, "Fielding's Bill of Fare in *Tom Jones,*" *ELH*, 30 (1963), 236–43; William B. Coley, "Gide and Fielding," *Comparative Literature*, 11 (1959), 1–15; Irvin Ehrenpreis, *Fielding: Tom Jones* (New York: Barron's Educational Service, 1964); Eleanor Newman Hutchens, *Irony in Tom Jones* (University: University of Alabama Press, 1965); Alan D. McKillop, "Some Recent Views of *Tom Jones.*" *College English*, 21 (1959), 17–22; Jerome Mandel, "The Man of the Hill and Mrs. Fitzpatrick: Character and Narrative Technique in *Tom Jones,*" *Papers on Language and Literature*, 5 (1969), 26–38; Henry Knight Miller, "Some Functions of Rhetoric in *Tom Jones,*" *Philological Quarterly*, 45 (1966), 209–35; and "The Voices of Henry Fielding: Style in *Tom Jones,*" in *The Augustan Milieu: Essays Presented to Louis A. Landa*, ed. H. K. Miller (New York: Oxford University Press, 1970), pp. 262–88; John Preston, *"Tom Jones* and the 'Pursuit of True Judgment,' " *ELH*, 33 (1966), 315–26; Dorothy Van Ghent, "On *Tom Jones,*" in *The English Novel: Form and Function* (New York: Holt, Rinehart and Winston, 1953), pp. 65–81; Robert V. Wess, "The Probable and the Marvelous in *Tom Jones,*" *Modern Philology*, 68 (1970), 32–45.

NORTON CRITICAL EDITIONS